THE UNDEAD GYPSY

Also by Kit Fielding

Thursday Nights at the Bluebell Inn

THE UNDEAD GYPSY

KIT FIELDING

CORONET

First published in Great Britain in 2022 by Coronet
An Imprint of Hodder & Stoughton
An Hachette UK company

1

A CIP catalogue record for this title is available from the British Library

Hardback ISBN 9781529378597
eBook ISBN 9781529378603

Typeset in Sabon MT by Hewer Text UK Ltd, Edinburgh
Printed and bound in Great Britain by Clays Ltd, Elcograf S.p.A.

Hodder & Stoughton policy is to use papers that are natural, renewable
and recyclable products and made from wood grown in sustainable
forests. The logging and manufacturing processes are expected to
conform to the environmental regulations of the country of origin.

Hodder & Stoughton Ltd
Carmelite House
50 Victoria Embankment
London EC4Y 0DZ

www.hodder.co.uk

Thinking of you in heaven, lovely Sis. Wish you could have shared in this day.

To the memory of a dear friend – *a kushti mush* – who had barely started his journey on a different path.

The Ghost Road

What of those days that have travelled down a secret road,
to lie in adjacent wait,
to ambush in drowsy night,
to come alive by the conjuring words 'if only'?
The other life I could have seen,
the other self I could have been,
if at the cross I'd stepped into the unknown boldly,
and trodden unafraid and coldly,
without the whys and wherefores that open up
and grow like sores, and pulsate in the deep night
before dawn's tepid glow draws down my empty dreams.

Or did my unsure feet tread a spectre's road?
Does someone peep from behind moon-lashed cloud
at the person I am now?
And do they wish they had turned another way,
where a different, distant future lay,
waiting to be unfurled and in an alien wind flutter free?
And is that someone who took the other road
wishing they were me?

PROLOGUE
WINTER 1913

She's been to the town for bread and milk and she's walked back through the winter lanes to their atchen-tan while the light is still strong. From the gateway she stops and watches her rom; he's sitting by the fire, teasing it with wood shavings from his whittling of a figurine. He's young and thin but he has a hunch to his shoulders that adds years to his frame. Occasionally a shudder of a cough will rise up from his lungs and rattle in his throat. But it's not caused by the smoke of the fire or the chill of the December air. The cause is breeding in his lungs, wheezing in his chest and staining the white of his handkerchief with spots of crimson blood.

For now, until the blossom of spring whitens the hedgerows, they're staying in the shadow of a hill crowned with ancient elms. Here they've sited the waggon, tethered their Welsh cob and loosed their jukal, a tall grey lurcher who's nosing out his new territory. They're settling in for the cold season and it's here the romni will weave red-berried holly around hoops of hazel for the wreaths of the Christmas time and they'll hawk these wreaths and his whittlings of Jesus, Mary and Joseph, from door to door, from public house to public house. And, because she's little more than a girl and strikingly pretty – gypsy pretty, raven-haired and magpie-eyed – she'll be offered a palm for the reading. Or she'll be dealing out the tarot cards on the bar in the kitchema. She has an aura

I

about her that can easily draw an audience, and she has such a gift for the dukkerin, you'd have to see it to believe it.

On this winter's afternoon, she wants to creep up to him as he sits at the fire, surprise him with her presence, but the whippet at his feet lifts its head and points its nose to her. And he turns his head, smiles his welcome.

'Come and warm yerself,' he says, and there is a pleasure at the seeing of her in his voice. He raises his arm to draw her in, lets her rest herself against him. But there's more to this embrace, there's a contrivance that keeps his eyes straying to the waggon, to make her look where he's looking. She follows his gaze, sees what he's worked on while she was in town. It's a carving. The carving of the letters of her name over the door of their bow-topped vardo. Later he will pick these letters out in a soft rose-red paint in the spelling out of Lavinia.

They sit for an hour, warm and comfortable, disturbed only by the clearing of his lungs in his racking cough and his husky apologies for its intrusion until the afternoon begins to pull in and the temperature starts to fall. She calls the lurcher for company and thinks she'll take a walk up the hill. He says that he'll stay by the fire and tells the jukal to catch him a shoshi for the pot. And she laughs as the dog watches his mouth, excited in the understanding of his order.

Up here in the closing of this day, a bitter breeze shuffles the bare branches of the high elms, whispers into this ancient woodland. For Lavinia, there's an offer of a thick tree trunk for shelter as she looks down onto the burn of the fire and her man's hunched form. Over her coat her hands trace the firming, not-yet-noticeable sign of life inside her. She talks to the forming child as she strokes her stomach. She tells her daughter of a life lived and a life to come. And she tells of a life that won't reach into the next winter. Then she wonders who else in the future, even in a hundred years' time, will take this path to the higher ground and stand on this silent hill and feel what she feels.

1

All of this begins on a hot afternoon when a dusty white Transit van winds down a green-hedged lane and drives into a rather tatty gypsies' site known as Elm Hill Caravan Park. In this park there's a mixture of several static homes and an assortment of travelling caravans. Of these perhaps only two would make the cut onto *Big Fat Gypsy Weddings*. There's a rake of vehicles – a couple of trucks, a very shiny motorhome, a lorry with a tarmac roller in the back – that are parked outside their respective home-steads. In the middle of this acre site there's a shower block and toilets and two mountains of mixed metals; bits of cars, fridges, washing machines, tumble dryers, copper pipes, drums of cables from BT and several solar panels. Around the perimeter of this atchen-tan there's a crumbling chain-linked fence supported by concrete posts, where a tethered pony – Harry Potter embla-zoned and named – is flicking its tail at the nuisance of flies, and casting envy towards two free-running Exmoors. There's a couple of other things to notice about Elm Hill Caravan Park. One is that it's not on a hill, and the other is that Dutch elm disease annihilated the trees a generation ago.

But for now it's three o'clock on an over-warm summer's day and a couple of stringy dogs are scavenging around the rubbish bins, and a couple of stringy boys, kitted out in red Man U shirts, are kicking a football to each other. The Transit van, driven on site a little too fast, scuffs up a wave of dust as it skids to a halt. This intrusion brings football play to a halt and draws the boys' attention as they watch the van's side door slide open, the cab doors swing open and half-a-dozen men climb out and stretch their legs and pass around the fags. All of them look a little unkempt, on the edge of scruffiness; it's obvious that they're bona fide paid-up members of the travelling community.

After a couple of minutes of waiting, the driver, a bit on the impatient side and looking at his watch, gives a beep on his horn. This brings to life the sauntering approach of two more men and upsets a few more dogs who enter into a mad barking competition.

Of the two approaching we'll start with Danny Delaney. He's of middling height but compact with long arms, a bald head and a fighter's face. Which is what he is. He's a warrior of the ring with the flattened features to match and he's fighting at the venue that these men of the road are subscribing to. His companion and cousin is Silas Penfold and he's the opposite of Danny. Tall and lanky with spiky dark hair and a voice like a rasping of iron and he's using it to call loudly, 'Hurry up, Jimmy, we're running late.'

This Jimmy he's calling to is his brother, the last of the pick-ups, and if anyone's going to have a leading role in events you can see it would be this Jimmy. He's your typical Jack-the-lad, a lovable rogue; all the clichés that fit a six-foot-plus, dark-haired David Essex lookalike. He's in the doorway of his static home saying goodbye to his missus. It's a long goodbye, a bit more than a kiss and cuddle. Mind he can't be blamed for this because Jimmy's woman, Zilla, is a hell of a looker. She's got a good figure, dyed-blonde hair, tight-fitting jeans. (It's almost impossible to believe that she's mother to a fifteen-year-old; a boy who's taller than herself, and just under half her age, and who is, at this moment with his cousin Carter, hiding on the edge of a cornfield, sighting a gun barrel onto a descending pigeon.) But anyway, it's still a goodbye but she's loath to let him go.

'There's always drama, Jimmy. You know there's always trouble.'

Jimmy promises, 'Not this time Zilla.'

Then he slowly detaches himself from his woman as Silas delivers a more impatient, more grating, 'For God's sake get yer arse in gear, my pralla.'

His voice may sound a little on the harsh side but Silas can be excused because he's been chasing up Jimmy for more years than he cares to remember. A decade of age gives him a rank he never asked for and a responsibility he didn't want. But it's all done with the thick blood of brotherly love.

And now Jimmy, getting that arse in gear, joins the bus of men on their journey to an illegal dust-up where Danny's fighting third man on in a six-rounder.

Jimmy says to Danny, 'I hope you're good for it, 'cos I've put my social on you.'

There's nods all around because there's assorted lots of Jobseeker's Allowance, Housing Benefits and even a successful – although much rarer – Universal Credit beneficiary included in the punters. That's a fair amount of social security monies resting on Danny's battered nose, and Danny Delaney, thinking himself the local hero and thumping his chest like Tarzan does in those old black-and-white films, roars: 'Yer vonga's safe on me, boys.'

He takes a mighty pull on his cigarette, suppresses a cough in his throat and finishes with a husky, 'Best condition I ever been in. Best condition ever.'

The driver does a quick poll count, fires up the engine, whacks his toe down and the van leaves like it came in – a squealing of tyres and a cloud of dust. (This journey's started, a journey that leads to a long farm track in the middle of nowhere, to a huge old barn where there's a canvas square, roped into a ring for the dubious practising of the Noble Art of Self Defence.) The second the vehicle has left the site, the would-be football stars resume their interrupted practise of precision passing and their dreamings of Old Trafford.

Zilla has watched the van leave and she's praying to God there'll be no trouble but she also knows that this mob is not exactly a UN peacekeeping corps. She's still making her wishes when an older woman – old, really – joins Zilla in company and says:

'Don't worry, my Zilla.'

Now this woman is Meg and she uses the 'my' because one way or another she seems to be related to everyone on the site. It's like she's the elder of these people. The authority. The one they come to for advice or more. But if you thought Silas had a rasp for a voice, this woman's speech is a couple more notes down the scale. And it fits the way she looks. And her name fits as well because she's the gypsy crone of the storybook.

She's dark, she's thin, she's of an indeterminate age. She wears a pale-red shawl around her shoulders and a scarf around her head. She's of the type that could stop you in the street, bony fingers clutching your arm and fixing you with a glittering eye. Like she really knows something about you. Like she could really offer some insight into your life if you crossed her palm with silver. So when Meg says, 'Don't worry, my Zilla', it should offer Zilla some crumbs of comfort, but Zilla says, 'You know what they're like, Meg.' Meg nods because it's true and she's thinking that perhaps there are some worries in the offing.

From across the site there's growls and barks and curses and the rattle of a dustbin as two dogs have a bit of a set-to. One of these scrappers belongs to Meg, and her voice cracks like a whip as she shouts 'Wilma' three times before her dog comes slinking to her in resentful obedience, with its tail between its legs. This black-and-white dog's a cross between a Jack Russell – always up for some aggro – and a collie, and she's inherited the best, or worst, of both breeds. She's not exactly small but she's clean and pretty and long-legged, with a turn of speed that would rival a lurchers. Also this jukal is so close to Meg that in the days of witch-finding someone would have called her out as a familiar.

There's not much else goes on at Elm Hill Park, except that this hot day slides into warm evening as the site settles down for the night. Windows light up, televisions go on, mothers holler for their chavees to come in. Mikey clumps in the door with three pigeons and the shotgun. Meg calls home the errant Wilma who's been causing drama at the bins again. There's also a few shouts and a fair bit of screeching from a caravan where a newly married couple are living. It's one of those volatile relationships where the honeymoon period is short-lived. The marriage hasn't even made the change of the moon before they're either fighting or loving. Tonight it's fighting and it ends when there's a mighty slamming of the caravan door and hubby streaks to his van like a long dog. He's bent over the steering wheel and tearing away as the wife, adjusting her lower dress and following him out, screams at his getaway:

'You bastard.'

Then to everyone within hearing distance she laments very loudly. 'Waited till I was on the loo. The bastard.'

But he's gone and she won't see him until after the pubs have shut and that's when they'll probably continue their battle, this unlikely Romeo and Juliet.

From Silas's homestead there's a flash of a torch as Carter – dead spit of his father, and Mikey's pigeon partner – walks his whippet out. And there's also the flare of a match as Carter takes his chance for a few crafty drags as he's on the rounds for an absent Silas. He checks the sheds are locked, checks out the building on their patch. One of which is Danny's gym, a rough and ready room, concrete floor, rubber mats, couple of benches, several pairs of boxing gloves and a heavy bag suspended from a roof beam.

Carter can't resist this temptation. He pinches out his cigarette and does a whirlwind round on the bag. Then catching his breath, he relights his dog-end and locks the door. Now the securities are done he thinks he might have an hour on Fortnite in his bedroom. Or at least until his mother calls for lights out.

That's just a quick glimpse around Elm Hill and it's more interesting, for tonight at least, to spend some time with Meg, and she's sitting in her shiny motorhome, the one we got a glimpse of earlier. It's still warm and the door is open to the night and Meg's at a small table – a bottle of Bell's whisky and a tumbler at her elbow – lit by a single lamp. She's cupping her hands around a clouded crystal ball, set upon a square of green baize, and Meg's tutting from her mouth and shaking her head as she stares into it. 'Nothing,' she says to Wilma, who's curled up on the seat beside her. 'There's nothing.'

She strokes the crystal, taps the crystal and then leans back into her chair and takes a swig from her tumbler. She looks really pissed off.

She's about to become more so because outside in the dark and shadows there's an evil black cat on the prowl for a killing. It's a huge slinking animal, a feral pirate with yellow eyes and teeth like a tiger's. This cat's afraid of nothing and no one and its curiosity draws it into the doorway. And then its great head is peering through the opening and its ears flatten and its great pink mouth gapes open to hiss at Wilma.

Wilma's instantly onto this and even before her first shrill bark reaches Meg, the jukal has taken the shortest route. She's scrabbled over the table, toppled whisky bottle and glass and started the crystal ball rolling. Meg's eyes are between the dog and cat and she doesn't see the milky, cloudy sphere rolling into free fall until it's too late. Meg curses out a blast of indelicate language directed to an almighty bust-up of snarls and growls that's taking place on her doorstep.

She leaves them to it as she stoops to recover her glass orb of fortune. But as she rescues it, cradling it in her skinny fingers, the crystal shivers and clears into bright pictures. It seems the thump onto the floor has knocked some life into it. A blasphemy of 'Christ' joins 'Jesus' from Meg's mouth at what she sees is forming inside the crystal. There's a hundred images, a thousand images. There's images that will sneak into her mind during the day and images that will take her dreams in the night.

Meg draws her hands over the glass, wipes them away, sighs deeply and pours herself a hefty replenishment of the Bell's. And then she sits, with a sulking Wilma now confined under the table, and concentrates on what she's searching for. Five minutes go by. Ten minutes go by, and then a scene shimmers into her sight, settles into a view of an illegal prize-fight in a big old barn down a rough farm track. Meg watches for a while longer and then slowly shakes her head and thinks that Zilla was more than right.

2

At this venue, standing in the ring above a jostling noisy crowd, the referee is calling Danny – fighting as Dangerous Dan Delaney – and a very aptly named Skinny Boy Mitchel to the centre of the ring to touch gloves. He is a skinny boy and he is tall, perhaps topping Danny by six inches. He's like a line prop. Danny tries to stare him down, or rather up, but Skinny Boy is looking to the roof of the barn, like he's spotted something interesting up there. Maybe an owl in the rafters. Then it's a touch of gloves, a whack of leather on leather and the fight starts. Danny goes straight into top gear and launches himself flat out at Skinny Boy Mitchel.

But he's slippery, this skinny mush; he's tall and he's on his toes all the time.

Silas yells, 'Whack him in the ribs Danny.' That's the ribs that are so pronounced on this starved-looking lad you could play a tune on them. But not for Danny. He lunges forwards and punches thin air yet again. He can't raise a note, let alone a tune, on those bones.

Now anyone who's done a bit of scrapping will know that if you keep missing with your shots it gradually takes the strength out of you. You try too hard, hold your fists too tight. The sweep of your punches becomes so slow your opponent can see them coming a mile away. And then your guard begins to droop and your hands are not protecting your chin.

In the last minute of the third round that's what Skinny Boy Mitchel sees and, instead of backing away as he has all of the fight, this time he slips inside of Danny's long slow jab and cracks him soundly on the right side of his chin. He's so fast, this boy, that he's three skips back before Danny starts to wobble, starts to fall. That's all it takes; the only real punch that Skinny Boy has thrown and Danny ends up on his arse. Finished. Danny isn't dangerous anymore.

To say it went against expectations is an understatement and after a stunned silence the booing starts. There was a lot of vonga riding on Danny and people are not happy. It's one of those moods that's balancing on a knife-edge and there's plenty of hard men here looking cheated. So what the organisers do is to hurry the next bout up – one of the fighters has only a single glove on when he's pushed into the ring. Then with the MC shouting the introductions at the top of his voice, attention starts to switch to this bout. There's still a bubbling of tension but the focus is shifting back to the ring.

There may have been enough of that shift if Jimmy had kept his big mouth shut but when Danny, camouflaged in an over-sized overcoat and with a titfer hiding his bald head, joins Jimmy and Silas at the ringside and, in trying to salvage some honour, mutters to his cousins: 'I had him worried.'

Jimmy just had to say, 'You had him worried all right; he was worried he'd fuckin' killed you.' Which was meant to be a joke but probably wasn't the right thing to say to someone who'd been humiliated by a human beanpole. So it's bad enough that Skinny Boy Mitchel did what he did and it's bad enough that a lot of pockets are a lot lighter than expected. So how could it get worse?

It gets worse because Danny, frustrated with his performance and taking considerable umbrage at Jimmy's comment, lets fly a right-hander at Jimmy. It's almost like a play-fighting swing of a punch but the problem is that Danny expects Jimmy to duck and Jimmy expects Danny to recall the blow an inch from his jaw. So the punch is relaxed and deadly because neither of them do what's expected and the only meaningful dig that Danny has thrown all night lands smack on Jimmy's button. Jimmy folds up like a deck chair and, fighting to stay conscious, he sinks slowly to the floor of the old barn. Silas, caught in disbelief, takes his own swing at Danny, who does manage to duck, but has his hat swiped off in the process.

That's all it takes to light the fuse and that's all it takes to start a wildfire rippling through the crowd. In seconds it seems every man here is throwing punches or wrestling on the floor. There's pushing and shoving and grappling and a mighty chance to settle some old scores. All action's curtailed in the ring as the boxers, gloves resting on the top rope, become the audience. The ref's shouting forlornly, 'Break it up. Break it up down there.' But there's no possibility of him taking his duties seriously enough to enforce any rules on the melee below him.

There's two important things happen now and one of them has been a bit of a secret. This meeting, this illegal prize-fighting, has been monitored by the boys in blue. They knew a week ago what the set-up was and they've been trying to tug the beard of Hairy Dave, one of the promoters of the venue, for months. So an inside undercover plant gives the password on his mobile phone and half-a-dozen paddy waggons and police cars come roaring down the farm track. It follows then that more than a score of police-men in full riot gear – shields, crash helmets and batons – smash their way into the barn.

That's the first important thing.

The second is that a dazed Jimmy, couple of chipped teeth and blood in his mouth, is recovering from Danny's clout and getting himself upright. And because it takes him a long time to straighten out, the police are well inside. They're knocking all and sundry and trying to quell resistance with shield and baton. There are battles raging all over the barn floor and Police Constable Goldman, who's on his first raid, is excited and trying to impress his sergeant. He's pushed his way through to Danny and Silas and he's yelling, screaming almost, 'Give it up you two. Give it up.'

PC Goldman has lost his crash helmet – it must have been when Maltese Mike briefly held him in a headlock. So if he'd still had that helmet on, Jimmy's punch would not have put him on the sick for a month or two.

You see Jimmy's really groggy and as he's coming to, he aims the longest, slowest uppercut-cum-hook ever thrown in anger. His fist travels from his knees in a rising arc to the still blurry profile of his beloved cousin Danny. But this is the moment PC Goldman decides to thrust his head into the line of fire. And it's at this moment that Jimmy stumbles, falls forward and increases the power of that punch tenfold. The copper cops a perfect one right on the temple that should have been protected by the aforementioned helmet and PC Goldman drops like a stone. But this has been noted and a PC, following up, a really horrible bastard, decides poor Jimmy deserves a crack on the back of his head with the latest model of constabulary weaponry.

Things are a bit hazy for Jimmy after that; he's aware of a jolting journey to the local nick and being dumped into a cell containing the drunkest man in the whole world who has an unbelievable wind problem. What with that and a blinding headache, it's not a comfortable night for Jimmy. The following morning Jimmy is charged with resisting arrest, assaulting a policeman in the course of his duty, breach of the peace and God knows what else.

At the desk, the sergeant reckons that Jimmy'll be looking at six months minimum.

'Serves you fuckin' right, whacking one of us,' he says, and then mutters, 'still, it was only that creep Goldman.' As he passes over the plastic bag of Jimmy's belongings he laughs out the side of his mouth. Then it's a quick phone call from the errant gypsy and Silas, a black eye and a split lip, comes round to pick Jimmy up and take him home to his everloving. Which she certainly isn't this morning.

'You promised. You said no more trouble.'

Zilla's really fired up because she's been in this situation more times than she cares to recall.

Jimmy says, 'Look it was an accident. What happened was—' is as far as he gets. 'Accident? Accident? You del the gavver in the mooee and you say it's an accident?' She's shaking her blonde head and flashing her green eyes, and Jimmy, whose throat is dry and his head throbbing, says, 'Jesus, give it a rest, Zilla.'

'Rest? It's you that needs to give it a rest. You promised . . .'

Let's leave them there because nothing much is going to change for an hour or two, and Zilla hasn't yet realised that Jimmy has done all their money on a win for Danny Delaney that never materialised. It's going to be adding insult to injury when Zilla finds that out, and Mikey, catching the drift of the way things are going to be today, has already decided that school might be the best bet and he's sauntered down the road with Carter to catch the bus.

It'll be a better atmosphere in a couple of hours when Jimmy's done his bit of sweet-talking and Zilla's wilted just a little. But there'll still be a bit of tension around because Jimmy's due an appearance at the Magistrates' Court in the near future. Also at Elm Hill Park this morning there's not a sound from Romeo and Juliet's trailer. Romeo had sneaked home in the early hours, sneaked into their bed, sneaked alongside Juliet, sneaked into her, while she pretended to be asleep, then to wake up like a wildcat, which certainly spiced things up. Now they're having a long slow recovery loving and there should be a sign on the door saying, 'If this caravan's a-rocking, don't come a-knocking.'

And talking of caravans, it might be interesting to take a look at the back of Meg's property because here, facing the Elm-less Hill, is a piece of Travellers' history. In stark contrast to Meg's modern and shiny motorhome, this is a traditional vardo; a bow-top waggon with ash-spoked wheels, bright paintwork and a sparkle of brass fittings. The name Lavinia is carved into the woodwork above the door and if this old waggon could talk, it would have more than a century of stories to tell. It's a retreat for Meg, somewhere she can come to when the world becomes too loud.

But for now everything else, everyone here, is much the same as yesterday except that the motorhome has pulled out and Meg and Wilma are off on their travels. They've been on the road for three hours with Wilma on the passenger seat, cocking her head and watching the world go by. Their only break has been for a piddle in a lay-by – both of them that is – and now they're driving into another park-home site. But this isn't like the rather neglected one they left earlier; this is an upmarket, properly laid-out, clean, spacious, gardened, patioed, tarmacked park. The bungalow units here reek of retired money, of downsizing for income, and the cars parked in the driveways are the latest conscious-salving environmentally friendly models.

So what's Meg doing here and why does she cruise slowly through this estate, giving it a thorough once-over likes she owns it? Because she owns it, that's why. Meg owns the site and she pulls a ground rent from every property here. She gains a percentage of every drink poured in the recreation club and every loaf of bread sold in the grocery stores. She drives slowly through this estate and no one takes any notice of her and her respectable motorhome. And that's the way she likes it.

Two weeks later at the Elm Hill site it's the date of Jimmy's court appearance. On this morning there's a heavy, drifting rain blowing over the guilty party as he sips from a mug of tea outside his static home. He's smoking a soggy roll-up and wishing it was all over and Zilla is wondering how they're going to manage 'if it's a big fine, Jimmy?'

Jimmy wonders too because he hasn't got a ha'penny to scratch his arse with.

'But they shouldn't do me for much, Zilla. It was a fuckin' accident.'

He's still pleading the defence of hitting the wrong person. 'Could have happened to anybody.' But even Jimmy's solicitor – services purchased by the selling of Zilla's gold bracelet – shakes his head at this defence. Jimmy's optimism of turning mountains into molehills isn't gaining much traction in this situation.

Zilla's ready to go. She's all dolled up, blonde hair brushed out, bit o' slap on her face, tight skirt and three-quarter length coat. She looks like she's going for a night out, not an eleven o'clock meeting with the beak. Also going to the court, to add to family appeal, is young Mikey; this still-growing boy who's spoilt by his mother and treated like a man by Jimmy. A lot of the time now he cuts off school to help Jimmy with work picked up on the knocker. It might be clearing out a bit of rubbish, roof repairs, painting, collecting scrap or anything to add a few bob to their benefits. Jimmy and co. are at the sharp end of life and there's not much cash to spare in these hard times. There's only just enough over for Jimmy to spend a couple of nights in the kitchema swilling down beer. At the Magistrates' Court, Zilla and Meg – she's back on the scene today, keeping an eye on the proceedings – and some more of the tribe are in the public gallery, listening to PC Goldman giving his evidence from the stand. 'Come at me like a madman, he did. Like a wild animal.'

This is backed up by the second PC who says, 'I had to stop him, sir. Had to use my baton on him. It was the only way.'

He sounds as though he regretted it, and he must be a good actor because regret doesn't fit the blow struck with such extreme relish. Still no one's going to contradict him, and the magistrates – two dodderers and a sourpuss blue-rinse – nod along to the copper's words. These magistrates have already made up their minds about Jimmy, about unlicensed fights, about violent behaviour and they need to set an example.

'There's too much of this sort of thing and it will not be tolerated.'

This means that, despite a listless appeal for clemency – a pointing-out of Mikey and saying, 'A son needs his father' rather unconvincingly from Jimmy's solicitor – the sorry-looking Traveller is sentenced to the maximum six-month stretch at the renowned Godstone jail.

At the passing of this sentence, Zilla bursts into tears and, of course, Silas has a view on the magistrates' parentage. His actual words are much more colourful and it's only Danny hissing at him to 'shut the fuck up' that saves him from spending a night in the cells. But also in Silas's head is another voice and that belongs to a hot, dry afternoon in a darkened room. It's saying,

'You got to look out for our Jimmy, my Silas. You promise me.'

17

This is the voice of Liberty Penfold and it's weak and faltering and Silas has to lean in close to hear the words, words that are tinged with the scent of the Reaper.

'You promise me, my Silas.'

Silas makes his promise to Liberty Penfold, elderly father to himself and ancient father to Jimmy. He's tried to keep it, God knows he's tried, but Jimmy is Jimmy.

There's still a five-minute compassionate meeting under the courtroom for Zilla and Jimmy – more tears and a bit of sorrow and anger stirred together – and then Jimmy's escorted to the prison van by two officers.

And this part is over for Jimmy Penfold.

And the next part is beginning for Jimmy Penfold.

3

Jimmy's in his new home of a prison cell in Godstone jail with two bunks and a loo without a seat. He's unrolling his blankets on the bottom bunk and on the top bunk a large, muscular, Black man in a tight T-shirt is swinging his legs. He's smoking a fat roll-up and he drops to the floor and offers Jimmy a hand-shake and a laugh. 'I get to share with a pikey and you get to share with a nigger.' (There's not much political correctness in prison life.)

This is Jimmy's introduction to the guy the other inmates have nicknamed Tarzan because he's ideally built for the role and much more suited than Dangerous Danny Delaney's impres-sion of the character. This man, Rubin, towers over Jimmy and his handshake mangles Jimmy's fingers in the welcome of intro-duction. There's just time for Jimmy to wince and for Rubin to ask, 'What you in for then?' and get a start of an answer, before the meal bell goes and Rubin says, 'Better stick close to me, Jimmy Boy,' as he leads across the landing, down a metal stair-case and into a noise-smothered dining hall where watchful screws patrol up and down the aisles.

In the canteen it's obvious that Rubin collects respect from all the lags. Other prisoners make way for Rubin; a space appears in the queue, he gets doled extra spuds, an extra slice of meat, a healthy splash of gravy. And because of association, and being Rubin's shadow, Jimmy gets the same respectful treatment and he thinks that perhaps this stint at Her Majesty's Pleasure won't be too bad after all. And it most definitely is because Rubin's the Man at this correction centre. He's the one you go to when you want phone cards, tobacco, soft and not-so-soft drugs; the currency of prison life. He's the one who gets a 'Good morning' from the men in uniform and respect from the shaven heads and the bodybuilders. Jammy Jimmy, now rechristened Jane, in the Tarzan and Jane relationship, has struck lucky under this protectorate – he even risks the showers on his own but there is a niggling doubt in his head. It's the thought that you never really get something for nothing.

A couple of nights later it's the light of the moon that wakes Jimmy. It drifts in through the cell window on the three o'clock hour and breathes on his face as he lays in the bed he made for himself. Above him, Rubin is purring like a cat in his own land of nod. And beyond the ten-by-ten room, scores of other men are sleeping their sleep, dreaming their dreams, missing their families, missing their women and, in some cases, missing their men. And drifting further along the softly lit passages, and through the double-locked doors into P wing, the dreams are not for viewing because there's blood and death and such violence you could not imagine. And into this seeps the terrible sadness of children, of lives that ended while they were still growing.

In Rubin's cell, he's dreaming of a party that's reached full swing and where the music is loud and pulsating. There's a table with a bowl and a minute silver spoon and fine white powder chopped into orderly lines that Rubin's hoovering up. Around him there's drinking and laughter and dancing. And the dancing is the swaying suggestive moves that only some girls can do and, in his dream, Rubin's thinking that it's been a long time since he tasted dark skin. And then who should appear but Freedom, his beautiful princess, and she's sashaying towards him. Freedom, the girl he left at the prison gates four months ago 'Man,' he's thinking, 'this is my lucky night.' But it's not. He only has an instant to slip his arms around her, pull her sweet heat to him, breathe the scent of her, hear her whisper his name, before she dissolves in his hands and the party room darkens, fades into the ceiling of his cell, leaving him clutching at nothing. Not exactly nothing because Rubin's hand is on his corey and it's swollen like a marrow.

'Fuckin' raasclaat,' Rubin shouts in thwarted desire at the suddenness of the removal. There's a 'Jesus Christ' from a startled Jimmy who's nearly shot out of his bunk and then,

'Are you all right, Rubin?'

Rubin's sitting up, and now it's his head he's holding in his hands. 'Man,' he groans. 'She was wicked. Wicked.' He lays back down, shuffles himself comfortable and prays, 'Dear Lord just let me get back to sleep. Just let me go there again.'

So Rubin closes his eyes, takes deep slow breaths and floats back to the party. But Jimmy, in his bunk below, can't get back to sleep. The time's crept on to four o'clock and Zilla is filling his head. At the site, Zilla is sitting on the step watching the same moon and thinking what a bastard Jimmy is. Well that's one part of what she's thinking, the other part is that she's missing him badly and she'd give the world for a beery kiss and a good cwch. Mind it's what she's had to endure ever since her and Jimmy got together. 'Every time,' she tells herself, 'every time he says it's the last time.'

She's trying to count all the trouble he's brought to their door, trying to list it and feel the righteous anger that'll dilute the pain of missing him.

What's she got out of all of this? Never enough money. A

struggle to manage. A static caravan that's hot in the summer and cold in the winter. There's a stifled sob to herself; a sparkling of tears in the moonlight. But still she sends a, 'Goodnight my Jimmy' on the night wind to him. She takes a deep lingering breath of the soft warm air and her head begins to fill with tomorrow – today now – when she'll be visiting him at Godstone jail.

It's in the early morning and a low mist is pooling in the hollows and filling the ditches. Zilla's watching from the window and Mikey is knuckling the sleep out of his eyes.

'You going to see Dad?'

'Yes.'

'Can I come?'

'You know you can't'

'Why?'

'You know why.'

'I want to see Dad.'

'He'll be home soon.' In her head she's adding the familiar, 'If he can stay out of trouble.'

Mikey says, 'But Mum . . .' and she thinks that they're going to have to go through the whole scenario again. Then from the outside Silas blows his horn and it means she can leave Mikey to his mood, and his cornflakes, and start the long trip to Godstone. She also leaves him with orders to at least get himself to school, otherwise there'll be more drama heading for the Penfold clan.

Mikey thinks that he'll call for Carter and they can have a mooch around Boarston, see what's about today. But as it happens, they get collared by Danny who's trying to teach them the rudiments of the noble art. He insists on giving them an hour's tuition in his tin-roofed barn where it's so cold they have to go at it full pelt on the bag just to keep warm.

Danny, fag in his mouth, shouts encouragement for jabs,

hooks and crosses and promises that, if they come back later, they can have the privilege of a proper sparring session with himself. They forgo this golden opportunity for a meet-up in the corner of Boarston Recreation Ground and a couple of cans of cider and a roll-up apiece.

For Zilla and Silas there has become a familiarity to these prison visits. She will take herself nervously into the entrance of the forbidding building and Silas will kill the waiting hour in the car park. He'll have a flask of coffee, the *Sun* on the dashboard, and his fags for company. From here he'll be watching the comings and goings of the residents' kith and kin. They range from loudly dressed skinny teenagers to the sixty-plus of the temporarily widowed. They are a mixture of the shady and the furtive, the worried and the downright brazen. But some have had enough; they don't want to be here because it's been too many times. They shuffle their resigned duty and feet in unison to yet another weary signing-in.

Silas, drawing heavily on his roll-up thinks that most of these straggled visitors could easily be on the other side of the fence – probably have been and probably will be. Then he thinks of his poor brother locked up behind these walls and how it always seems to be Jimmy who never quite makes an escape.

To their mother April, who keeled over in the chicken run at seventy-five, any trouble was never Jimmy's fault: he was far too trusting of people. He was her spoilt baby – the unexpected surprise when she was on the change (something that Silas shut his ears to when she recounted the details to her woman friends) and to Liberty, twenty years older than herself, it was even more of a surprise. Silas has a chuckle to himself about that thought then rolls up another tuvla and scans the *Sun*'s racing section for the name of a grai he's trying to remember.

*   *   *

Zilla doesn't like coming to Godstone HMP, doesn't like the high brick walls, the tiled floors, the tang of disinfectant, the screws who give her the once-over with their eyes, wondering, 'Who's keeping her happy while the old man's inside?'

She can't help being attractive; what with her blonde hair, green eyes, long legs, gorgeous figure. But she carries all this without the knowing, with hardly any awareness, and with little more than a sliver of self-consciousness. This might be because Jimmy's the only man she's known and because she was only sixteenish when he worked his magic on her. But whatever is between them, it's all that she needs, and she's going to stick with Jimmy for richer and poorer – probably poorer – and in sickness and in health. And it'll also be till death us do part because Zilla's never going to really change Jimmy; trouble is wired into his DNA.

Also on the way to Godstone this morning is a gleaming silver BMW 7 series. It's hogging the centre lane of the M6 at a cruise-controlled seventy miles an hour. If you happen to come up behind this car, you'll flash your lights then accelerate by with your middle finger stabbing at the BMW's driver. But only briefly, because this driver – Winston – is wedged into his seat like an African prince. Gold-ringed fingers are tapping a beat on the steering wheel and gold chains collar a thick neck. His bald dome is a polished black artillery shell and when he turns his head to look at you, there's a glimpse of Don King without the hair, or even Shaka from eight generations ago, and it sends a shiver down your spine. The finger is transformed into a wave. The scowl becomes an instant smile. Then your right foot pushes down the accelerator pedal because you don't want to be close to this guy, even on the motorway. This is the Winston that arrives at Godstone Visitors' Entrance just as Zilla is going into the search room for the intrusion of a quick pat-down for an unlucky recipient.

Zilla tenses at the stranger's hands on her body, wills it to be over, and always leaves the room a lot faster than she went in. She's already blaming Jimmy because this adds to his faults. If he hadn't been so stupid, so Jimmy, she wouldn't have to put up with this humiliation. If he could have kept himself sensible . . .

But then she sees him waiting at a table for two in the visiting room and she can't speak. She's sure she's crying as he holds her for the briefness of an allowed embrace before it's,

'Move apart you two. Now. I said now.' And the rough voice of authority separates the regretful couple.

They have to look at each other across the table and anyone who's been apart from a loved one for a while knows what they're thinking. They're young and fit and brimming with sudden want and it's a good job the furniture's between them. So they sit opposite each other and rokker of how things are going to change when Jimmy comes home.

Zilla says, 'Tell me this is the last time I'll ever have to come to a place like this?'

'On my mother's life my Zilla, never again.'

Jimmy knows his mother is six feet under but he swears on her life just the same.

At the other end of this meeting–greeting hall, Winston's impatiently drumming the table with his thick, gold-encrusted fingers. Rubin's late being brought through and Winston's taking a good butcher's around the room. It's what he does by habit because sometimes – quite a few times – his life has depended on his alertness and his observations. He sees Rubin pass behind Jimmy, give him an 'All right, bro', as Rubin squeezes Jimmy's shoulder and grins at Zilla. Then Rubin's raising his hand to high-five Winston and a wide grin is splitting his face in a welcome of, 'Hey man, how you doing?' And what Winston is doing is keeping tabs on connections, on the ones useful to him. 'Be better when you're back in the fold,' he says, like Rubin's a lost sheep. And then Winston nods his bullet head towards Jimmy.

'Is that him?'

'That's him,' says Rubin.

Christmas comes and goes and on a bitterly cold January morning there's snow in the exercise yard, and the prison boilers are running at full throttle. This is the day Jimmy's been dreaming of. It's not yet dawn and he's getting ready to leave his home of four months. He's thanking God for his time off for good behaviour. Well not God actually, he's thanking Rubin for keeping him on the straight and narrow, protecting his back and looking out for him. So for Rubin, there's a handshake and the heartfelt promise to him of, 'Anytime you want anything, anything at all, just ask.' And although Jimmy's certain he'll never clap eyes on Rubin again – he sees their relationship as a prison bromance – they swap numbers anyway.

After Jimmy's gone, Rubin's wishing it was his turn to step out into the morning air. He rolls himself the first fag of the day and lays back in his bunk. He thinks of his beautiful princess and wonders who's waking up next to her at this God-forsaken hour. Then he thinks of the dark streets and the shuffle of night-time deals, of the brutal enforcement of the rules of the manor. He thinks of all that he's good at. All that's made him valuable. All that's brought him here for nine months at Her Majesty's Pleasure. If it hadn't been for Winston he would have been looking at five years. Five years for GBH that changed, with a witness's statement, to over-enthusiastic self-defence. Man, he would have been old when he got out. So he owes Winston. He owes Winston big-time.

Outside in the prison car park, Silas is keeping the van ticking over, and the heater on full blast. Zilla has poured herself coffee from her Thermos and she's watching the prison door for Jimmy. She's moithering. 'Surely he should be out by now?'

'Perhaps he's staying for breakfast, Zilla,' Silas rasps. He laughs, adds, 'Be the last decent meal he'll have for a long time.'

Zilla doesn't think this is funny coming from a mush who can't even boil a yourri and then Silas says that maybe that Black guy is hanging onto Jimmy for a bit longer. ''Cos you know what they're like in prison and Jimmy is quite a pretty boy.'

Zilla starts to tell Silas how sick he is when Jimmy, his belongings in a carrier bag, steps out into the cold dawn. Zilla's out of the van, across the yard and into Jimmy's arms, sobbing into his shoulder and hugging him like she's never ever going to let him go. It's the same in the front seat of the van, and it isn't all one-way traffic because Jimmy more than returns her ardour.

Silas, with hardly enough room to change gear, sniffs, 'For fuck's sake, get a room you two.'

He has to say it several more times on the long journey home to Elm Hill.

Mikey's still away in town with Carter and so there's a snatching of some loving for the hungry couple. It's enough to say the caravan rocks, not like Romeo and Juliet's did – but it trembles very briefly (it has been a long time) later that afternoon.

In the afterglow, Jimmy makes the promises to Zilla that he has every intention of keeping at this moment. They are:

He's going straight.

He's going to work his fingers to the bone to look after his family.

He's going to save every penny he can, till there's enough for a plot of ground.

He's going to be a proper dad to Mikey.

He'd sooner die than go back inside.

He's going to do everything right for once.

Of course, Zilla has her dreams. She wants an easier life, a more normal life. She wants a brick house in the sun. She wants a square of lawn, a few lines of vegetables, a bathroom where she can lay and soak in hot soapy water. She can almost see Mikey in a few years' time, wearing a smart suit, driving a smart car, with all the pretty gorjer girls fluttering around him like butterflies. Yes, she wants to believe him, but she can't let herself go, because a quick peep in the form book is revealing. Reveals Jimmy. So she nods her head and swallows his impossible promises with enough salt to make her gag.

January moves on and leaves frost and ice for February to build on. Which it does with a vengeance. There's a heavy dusting of snow on the first Sunday of the month and if it wasn't for the social, things would be even tougher than they are. Most days are spent just trying to keep warm and watching the wind rattle the trees and sift the snow. A forty-gallon drum, holed into a brazier, burns anything and everything until it glows a cherry red. It's a place to congregate for a warm and a chat and a tuvla and a mug of meski and a moan at the world.

From the outside, the gathering looks like an old-time picket line keeping a watch for blacklegs. So in the coldness of this winter there's ice in the ditches, a frost in the fields and a deep chill that starts its creeping down from Elm Hill earlier and earlier each day. Woodburners, gas fires, electric fires, open fires throw out warmth into the living rooms of caravans and statics. Every burning attracts a huddling around the hearth – maybe a closer contact that not all would wish to subscribe to. By midnight, the air is super-cool and the site is dark, moon-shadowed, as still as the grave.

On this night, that stillness is subverted by Mikey, Carter and Will the Whippet, and a hundred-watt flashlamp with a beam that scythes through the darkness. We'll join them as they cut through the site and skirt the bottom of Elm Hill. Here the abrasive gorse grows in thick islands of cover and in the daytime you'd be lucky to get anywhere near the population of alert shoshis. They'd see you coming, hear you coming, their big ears would twitch, noses quiver, back feet drum the ground and they'd scurry into shelter, watch from their haven, until the all-clear is sounded. Mostly, it's a nice life for a rabbit; greens to nibble on, fur coat to keep you warm, sun on your back in the summer, plenty of company of your own kind. But it's night now and the night belongs to these hunters and these – Mikey and Carter and Will the Whippet – have the concealing darkness and the fitful surprise of a half-moon in a clouding sky to mask their intent.

That intent is released by Carter with the piercing beam of the flashlamp dancing across the landscape, searching into bush and clump and hollow, until there's a disturbance, a flurrying of movement and a panicked rabbit takes flight. It's jinxing run; a swerving, a doubling backwards and forwards, in a desperate attempt to shake off the harsh glare of revealment. But the spotlight won't let go; it stays glued onto the star of this snuff performance even when Will, hurtling out of the shadows, joins the production. The dog matches each dizzying twist and turn of avoidance in this coupling for a dance to the death.

Will is bearing down on the rabbit. Running it down. Clamping onto it and taking its life in a snap of jaws, in a squirm of live flesh. But for Brer Rabbit there are different ways of dying on this brittle cold night. One is to die quietly, instantly. One is to struggle briefly, hopelessly, and one is to scream the ending in an eerie high-pitched screech that's out of all proportion to a small furry animal. And this scream is what causes a fox to pause on his rounds, to prick his ears, cock his head and listen; perhaps even to catch a glimmer of a sweeping of light. He may also wonder that on a certain dark night there could be blinding brightness in his eyes.

Mikey and Carter are done now. The cold's seeped into their flesh, and bone-thin Will has started to shiver. It's enough. They've had enough of hunting, enough of sport and enough little bodies for a meal or two. They make tracks back to the site, as the snow starts to fall heavy and thickening. It will drift down steadily all night and into the breaking of a new day.

4

On this day, a hundred miles or more away from the Elm Hill site, the prison gates are being locked behind Rubin and soon he's heading up the M6 motorway in Winston's BMW. Winston hogs the centre lane, as usual, all the way to the turn-off into Manchester, into the bleak winter city where there's stale snow on the rooftops and leafless trees in the park.

These are the mean streets, the inner-city streets of gangs and drugs and the violence of knife and gun. This is where you'll walk by a savage beating in the road because it doesn't concern you. Even though there's blood in the gutter and three young hoodies are taking it in turns to kick the shit out of a transgressor. There's a peculiar rhythm to this savage beating.

Tap, tap, boom. Tap, tap, boom.

It's like two taps with the left foot and then a driving kick with the right foot.

This is the environment where only the strong survive.

And the clever.

And those who do what they're told.

This city is always in the news because here there's always a stabbing, a shooting, a bit of a riot or a brutal mugging. The impression is of chaos and rampant disorder. But the impression is wrong; there is order here. There's order from the packs of hoodies on souped-up mopeds circling in the road, to the Faces in sharp suits. Everyone has a place, everyone is a cog in the wheel; fat and thin, white and Black and all the shades in between. All Rubin has to do is slip back into his former role with Winston. And he does. It fits him like his Crombie overcoat. The weather changes from freezing to cold and wet while Rubin settles comfortably into his former life.

It's not quite the same for Jimmy at Elm Hill Caravan Park. He's finding things on the tough side and it's only lack of opportunity and the thought of a cold grey cell that's keeping him on the straightish and narrowish.

Zilla's trying so hard to manage. If she spends a tenner, she hides a bar. If she spends fifty pence, she hides a dino. For everything she spends, she saves something to add to her secret pot of dreams. And it is a secret for now because when Jimmy's got money in his hand he totals everything. If he's got a twenty in his pocket, he won't leave the pub until the last glass of livenner's drained. If it's a tenner, it's a pouch of baccy and a packet of Rizlas. A fiver, and it's a couple of meat pies and packets of crisps for him and Mikey. And that's what it is, pies and crisps, on this on a wet, cold, windy morning in March when Jimmy and Mikey are winding the van up a long drive to a big rambling house. This place is neglected; the garden gate's dropped on its hinges, the fencing's rusting through, the windows of the house are cobwebbed and the paint is peeling off the woodwork.

It's from here that old Mr Ashurst, eighty if he's a day, deaf as a post and not too steady on his pins, has been providing Jimmy with a bit of pocket money. There's been the odd fifty quid now and again, a bit more sometimes, for services rendered. The list includes clearing the gutters, unblocking drains, a slipped slate tingled into line; all the jobs that turn into ready cash.

Mr Ashurst, ancient and doddery, shuffles to the door on this cold, wet, March day. He says to Jimmy, 'I think it's a bit windy for the tree this morning.'

Jimmy says, 'It'll be no problem, Mr Ashurst', as the south-wester plucks the words from his mouth. Jimmy desperately needs some vonga and what they're referring to is a beech tree that's threatening the house's conservatory. Normally on tree-cutting there's Silas and Danny to cast an expert eye over the lean of the tree, over the weight of the boughs and the angle of the toppling cuts. They should be here on a three-way split but in the last month Jimmy's got himself in a mess; he's taken a step off the highway of dreams and, despite Zilla's close eye on him, he's managed to sink into debt. It's got to the stage where Jimmy's avoiding one or two people. But he's thinking that if he can drop this tree on his own, he can cane the old mush for a couple of hundred. It won't clear the decks but it'll help.

The beech tree carries thirty feet of trunk and a splay of thick boughs that are swaying and moaning and creaking in the strengthening gusts of the southwester. Jimmy, eyeing up his options, reckons if they rope it ten feet from the top and he nicks a V-cut on this side, does his main cut through the opposite side, and with Mikey taking the strain, he could drop it on a sixpence. So he sends Mikey up the tree to secure the rope – Zilla would have a fit – and they're all set to go. Mikey, feet firmly planted on the ground and a single loop of rope wrapped around a sturdy-looking fence post, is now taking up the slack. He starts a question,

'Dad are you sure that . . .?'

Jimmy butts into the unfinished query with, 'I've done this a thousand times.'

Which is more than a tad of an exaggeration. Then Jimmy starts the chainsaw that he's borrowed from Bob Lee and makes the first cut into the swaying tree.

On a day without the curse of this wind all the reasons for success might have worked. Even on this day it might have been possible but for the fact that the southwester is picking up considerably. After a particular hard buffeting there's a rebounding swirl of wet angry air that sucks at the bare beech. It couldn't have come at a worse moment because Bob Lee's chainsaw – operated by the overconfident Jimmy – has overcut the tree's point of balance and now that tipping point is beyond recall.

Mikey shouts a 'Dad!' and then an even louder 'Dad' in a frightened warning as he feels the weight of the tree on the rope. His feet start to slip and then it's a full-volumed alarm of: '*Dad! Help! Help!*'

Jimmy, who was thinking he's cut into the tree for the perfect fall, has taken a step back from his handiwork and is quickly realising that things are not going according to plan. He instantly drops the chainsaw and leaps over to his struggling boy. The scene is now of father and son in the pouring rain and wind, hanging onto the rope for dear life, desperately trying to pull the beech into the line of the drop. But the rope is relentlessly pulling through their hands as they're losing this tug of war. The rope scorches through four hands as the tree drags itself over the finish line. It collapses onto a conservatory that's withstood heat and snow and storm for a hundred years. There's the crushing of wood frame and the splintering of glass and that should be enough damage, but, as anyone who's ever felled timber knows, you always stand well away from the base of the tree because of the bounce. This bounce is when the tree settles on its branches and springs back. It might be inches, it might be a couple of feet and, unluckily, this time it's far enough and high enough to drop the tail end of the butchered beech onto Bob Lee's still-warm, top-of-the-range chainsaw. This is as bad as it gets. For today.

And, on this day, poor Mr Ashurst is left with a mangled conservatory, Bob Lee a mangled chainsaw and Jimmy Penfold with even more mangled finances.

Zilla will know nothing of this and Mikey will keep his mouth shut – he's already on his way to becoming a chip off the old block, and not only in looks. Jimmy will play it like he always has. He'll live in hope, still praying for a couple of good touches, until something turns up.

Then, like an angel that's been waiting in the wings, that something is his old cellmate Rubin calling up a connection on his phone. It's Friday night and Silas and Danny have pulled Jimmy out for a pint. It's not a usual haunt in their local town of Boarston on account that Jimmy's still keeping a low profile. The Unholy Trinity of Travellers are sitting at a pub table in the grubby bar of the Crown, pint pots in hand and chewing the fat over Danny's latest talk of retirement from the ring. This happens on a regular basis; it's very brief and as soon as vonga is mentioned Dangerous Danny Delaney laces on his gloves again. (Danny can say it's just for the money but if he was offered out on the street he'd be there for nothing. Danny is thirty-five years old and he knows, like every fighter does, that he's on the wane. But it's the letting go that's the hardest fight of all.)

'You know,' Danny says, 'sometimes I think I've had enough.'

Jimmy, playing along, says he's glad to hear it because he can't afford to bet on him anymore.

Danny says, 'Oh yea? You must have made a killing when I beat Masher Monty.'

This fight Danny had taken at short notice because of a late pull-out from Masher's scheduled opponent. It happened a lot with Masher because he was an animal in the ring; he never understood the rules so he didn't think there were any. Anyway,

Danny was offered the role of a stooge for eight hundred bar and he jumped at the chance. He also, when the bell went, took a running leap at a very surprised Masher Monty and caught him cold. So cold that Masher's hands weren't even up in guard. Masher, having a ruck with someone in the crowd, yelling threats through the ropes, didn't see the ref waving them in for the start of the action. And he certainly didn't see Dangerous Danny Delaney home in on him with the speed of an Exocet missile. Danny came charging in, head down and not really seeing ahead, and caught Masher with the full force of a shaven, rock-bone head and with a thud you could hear from fifty yards. You could say that Masher was so used to opponents backing away from him that this surprise added to him being totally unprepared. So thirteen stone of muscle and blood follows a hard, bony head in a percussion blow of such unintended accuracy and power it would have stopped a mule in its tracks. All the same, Danny rebounds off him and lands on his arse and Masher stands there, stock still, his gloved hands by his side and his eyes glazing over. Danny, hardly believing his luck and dazed himself, staggers to his feet and taps Masher with a jab that wouldn't have taken the skin off a rice pudding, but it's enough for Masher to topple straight over in a perfect line like a correctly felled tree.

Like Mr Ashurst's beech should have fallen.

The referee rules a knockout to Danny and outside the ring the usual rumpus starts and that's a lot more interesting and longer lasting than the twenty seconds of non-action that Masher provides. And Jimmy's right pissed off as well 'cos he should have backed Danny but he'd bet a hundred bar – social had just provided Jimmy with his monthly allowance – on the dead cert, Masher Monty. So he has to pretend to Danny – family loyalty and all that – that he's flush with vonga from his winnings even though the cupboard is nearly bare.

Jimmy's ordering up the beer, buying the round he can't afford, when his mobile rings. He's tempted to leave it in his pocket because contact has been on the negative side of late, he does owe a lot of money to a lot of people but, curiosity getting the better of him, he takes a quick dik at the screen. The surprise of Rubin's name is displayed and Jimmy ponders for a moment and then presses green for receive.

'Rubin?'

'Jimmy, my man. How are you?'

'Going on koorshti, Rubin.'

There's some more of the usual pleasantries between these reacquainted jailbirds before Rubin says, 'Look, I'm down your way in a couple of days. Fancy a meet-up?' He laughs. 'We could talk about the good old times in Godstone.'

Jimmy knows of a decent café in Boarston and Rubin says that he'll have to trust Jimmy's judgement and then he tacks on,

'Might have something for you. Bit of business. If you're interested man.'

'Could be, mush.' Jimmy knows the meaning of business.

The arrangements are made and, two mornings later, Rubin takes the road south. He takes himself an hour or so earlier than the appointed time because he wants a good look around Jimmy Penfold's stomping ground.

Rubin's driving a work vehicle – a fairly new 4x4 – in keeping with the trade that employs him. It's a black Range Rover Vogue with smoked windows and it's really more at home in the Manchester mean streets than coasting down narrow country lanes for a drive-by viewing of a gypsy site. Rubin slows down, stops on tick-over, at the entrance to Elm Hill Park.

He casts his eyes over the static caravans, the sheds and the huts; a shanty town that's grown comfortably into the landscape over the years. There doesn't seem to be anyone about, apart from a couple of dogs having a play fight and a rough-coated pony having a wander around. In the briefness of his observations, Rubin's thinking that now he'll at least know where to find his Traveller friend, if the need ever should arise. He moves on slowly and a hundred yards past this entrance there's the surprise of an old gypsy woman and a small black-and-white dog standing onto the verge to let him through.

Rubin lifts his hand in courtesy as he drives slowly by and, when he looks in his rearview mirror, she's standing out in the road watching him. He can feel the intensity of that stare boring into him and it doesn't let go until a bend in the road takes her away from his sight. Into his mind's eye comes a sudden jolting picture of his Nigerian grandmother, shrivelled with age, rocking in her chair, and telling the old West African tales of juju magic and voodoo women until Rubin's mother hushes her, telling her not to fill young Rubin's head with all that nonsense. With the echo of his mother's words the scene fades and Rubin drives on, picks up speed, shrugs his wide shoulders and fixes onto his rendezvous with Jimmy. His business meeting.

This meeting is at the Greasy Spoon Café – Jimmy is one of its best patrons – on the edge of Boarston where Fat Eddie, the Gourmet of Grease, and the balding, unshaven owner and cook serves up a mouth-watering breakfast of eggs, bacon, sausage, beans, tomatoes, black pudding, fried bread and toast. The works in fact, and it's complemented by a mug of strong, hot tea. All of this is pushing a tenner and guaranteed to put anyone in a good mood for the consideration of Rubin's proposition.

That consideration begins when they move to an outside table to enjoy a cigarette – the luxury of a king-sized tailor-made for Jimmy – and Rubin leans back in his seat and says,

'I think we may be able to help each other, Jimmy.'

Given his current predicaments, Jimmy's more than hoping that this will be the case. The gist of Rubin's offer is for Jimmy to pick up from A and deliver to B. It would sound simple enough, maybe even safe enough, to anyone listening in, but the cargo is an extremely valuable currency: the supplying of smack to the dragon-chasers. This is for a monkey a trip and the promise of maybe two trips a week. But Rubin doesn't pull any punches, doesn't spread honey over the reality of what's afoot.

'There's no fuckin' about with this, Jimmy. No mistakes,' he says. 'This is business.'

Jimmy's quiet for a minute or two and, while he's taking all of this in, he helps himself to another of Rubin's cigarettes, swallows down a mouthful of cooling tea and thinks about what a grand a week would mean to him and Zilla. Then he adds that grand onto their social security dividends and comes up with a very tidy sum. OK he should be looking for the pitfalls and the consequences but he's pissed off with scrabbling for pennies, sitting on wet roofs, for the occasional spot of pilfering (not to mention an unsuccessful attempt at tree felling). Jimmy feels that it's time he had an easier life, had a slice of koorshti bok. So it's a firm nod in Rubin's direction and a finger-crushing handshake from Rubin's mighty mitt to seal Jimmy's new line of employment. For this Jimmy receives a signing-on fee of a most welcome two hundred pounds in twenties, and a topped-up burner phone. Also included in the terms and conditions of his new job is the proviso that he must be on duty anytime day or night. Rubin says,

'Could be short notice, Jimmy. When they want it, they want it.'

'No problem, Rubin.'

Rubin puts his forefinger to his lips, points out that this is to be kept secret. No gobbing off to anyone.

'Not a word of this, Jimmy. Not a word. Nothing back to me. You understand?'

Jimmy's understanding all right because this is a changed Rubin who delivers this message. This Rubin's not his smiling mate; his tone is serious and his eyes are hard black stones. It's a jolting reminder to Jimmy that it's a dangerous unforgiving business that he's dipping into.

'You can depend on me, Rubin,' Jimmy says, convincingly he hopes. They shake on the deal in Fat Eddie's car park and that means that Jimmy's taken a first step in another direction leading to, well, wherever it's going.

On the drive back up north Rubin's phone conversation with Winston is simple and to the point.

Winston asks, 'How'd it line up?'

Rubin says, 'A dream, man. A dream.'

'Happy with the cover?'

'Perfect,' Rubin says. 'A gippo can go anywhere.'

Winston chuckles. 'We'll want him to.'

'Only need the word for the start.'

There's a moment or two of pause and then Winston says, 'We'll give him a run next week.'

So the job's on and it might be that Jimmy's landed on his feet at last. All he has to do is strictly adhere to the terms of his employment, keep his nose clean and everything should be hunky-dory. Although knowing the SP on Jimmy Penfold it might be better to touch wood on that thought.

The conversation's done now because Winston never wastes much time talking; he's too busy scheming and plotting and organising behind the steel doors of his fortified premises.

He's building up his network of runners, enforcers, dealers, suppliers and financiers. Winston's shell-encased brain is holding, manipulating, a hundred different deals, a score of alliances. And he thanks the Good Lord for sending him his right-hand honcho, Rubin.

It's Tuesday evening the following week on Elm Hill Caravan Park and Jimmy's bored out of his skull. He's sat through *Emmerdale*, *EastEnders* and *Holby City* and drank enough tea to float a battleship. Outside the trailer, Mikey and Carter are racing from end to end of the site on two mountain bikes that have mysteriously appeared. Also mysteriously appeared is a brand-new ride-on mower and a bush strimmer that's still wearing a security tag.

The boys are weaving in and out of dogs and children and debris and broken-up cars, and the language of pursuit is a bit loud, and a bit ripe, from these teenagers. And it's when Zilla goes out to hush them up that Jimmy's new shiny mobile phone shrills into life.

Jimmy's 'Hello?' is a cautious query, but all he gets in reply is a gruff, brief,

'Daniels' Park. Three quarters of an hour. Be there.'

'How will I know who . . .?'

'I'll know.'

And the phone goes dead.

Zilla's not too happy about Jimmy running off at this time of night. 'It's nearly nine,' she says. 'What's so important it can't wait?'

With just cause, suspicion has raised its head and Zilla follows him outside to his van and asks, 'What are you up to?'

'Nothing, Zilla. Honest. Just got to see a man about a job. Won't be long.' Jimmy starts the engine and clocks the fuel gauge. It's hovering on empty, like his pocket is right now. 'Don't suppose you could lend me a tenner for diesel, my lovely?'

The second word of Zilla's answer is 'off'.

*   *   *

Daniels' Recreation Park in Boarston is a ring-fenced area with a football pitch, a paddling pool, a kiddies' play area and a bowling green. At this time of the falling dusk, before the night owls appear with vodka, cider and potent skunk, the park's empty except for a Hoodie walking a stocky black Staffie.

This is the darkening view through Jimmy's windscreen as he sits out his waiting in the car park with two fags and some country music entertainment courtesy of the radio. Charlie Pride has just finished his 'Crystal Chandeliers' lament about being passed over for the gaiety of the well-to-do, when the Hoodie and his dog stop close to Jimmy's van. Under a lamp post on the verge, the dog squats and grimaces, and the Hoodie, hanging a Tesco's plastic bag from his hand, flicks a look at Jimmy and then leaves the dog to his business. He taps on the window and speaks as Jimmy's winding it down. 'Mr Penfold?'

It's been a while since Jimmy's been addressed as a Mr – probably when he was last arrested. 'Yeah, that's me.'

Now this Hoodie whose face is in shadow takes out his mobile phone and taps into a photo of Jimmy. He holds it where they both can see. Share and compare.

Jimmy's been caught on face view with a fag in his mouth and a grin on his lips. Jimmy's wondering when, where, who took the picture? But then Hoodie swipes the picture on and Zilla and Mikey appear in portrait. 'What the fuck . . .?'

Hoodie says, 'Insurance for us,' and chuckles like he's made some sort of joke.

'Insurance,' says Hoodie again. 'To make sure you're a good boy and never think of double-crossing us.' Then Hoodie thrusts the Tesco bag in through Jimmy's window – it weighs heavier than it looks – and says, 'This is to go to Aylesbury.' 'When?' 'Leave at five tomorrow morning.' 'Five? But . . . Where?'

Hoodie, ignoring the questions as though they haven't been asked, opens his jacket and produces a TomTom GPS and an address on an envelope. He also pulls out a monkey, plus a hundred for expenses. Hoodie says, as though he's explaining to a dinalow, 'And for fuck's sake, as soon as you're there wipe the GPS and eat the fuckin' address.'

So these are Jimmy's instructions for an early drive across the country, but he doesn't really have to eat the address, it's Hoodie's little joke that he uses on new recruits. And all of these arrangements for an illegal delivery have happened while the Staffie has been taking a crange on the grass verge. Hoodie leaves it there for someone else to pick up.

Before Jimmy leaves for home he stows the weighty Tesco carrier bag in the back of his van. He tapes it up and drowns it inside a twenty-five-litre tin of exterior emulsion, under a couple of bags of cement, a wheelbarrow and assorted tools. Jimmy, now with vonga in his pocket, stops for a much-needed pint at the Flying Horse and parks the van where he can see it. For the first time in their shared life he locks the doors of the vehicle.

It's pushing towards midnight and Jimmy, worse for wear, fumbles the door to home open, stubs his foot on the threshold, flops down on the settee. Zilla shuffles away from his beer fumes, takes her eyes off the telly and turns them onto him.

'Well?'

'Well what?'

'You going to tell me what's going on? What you're doing?'

She stands in front of him, so he can't avoid her searching look.

'Look, Zilla, I was going to—'

'Look, Zilla. Look Zilla.' She's straight onto him with her interruption, her mimicry.

She adds with a touch of fire when she says, 'D'yer think I'm a dinlow?'

Of course Jimmy doesn't think that and he can't avoid telling her the details of his new job. A grand a week for 'Two drops, that's all, Zilla.'

He's told her the simple version of his story though. Then, maybe slightly more theatrically than he intended 'cos the livener's still thick in his head, Jimmy digs out a roll of fifties from his pocket, spreads them out like a fanning of cards on the coffee table-cum-footstool.

'It's our chance, Zilla. Our chance.'

Zilla's staring at more money than she's seen in a long time. Perhaps ever. The notes are dealt out on the table like it's her fortune being told.

'But—'

'We won't get another one like this. Not us. Not me. It's easy money, Zilla.'

'But—'

'Every week, Zilla. Imagine this every week.'

Just think. Imagine no scrimping. No worrying about the bills. No stretching the social to its absolute limit. Imagine money — a lot of it — in the bank. Imagine dreams coming true. And then, as though it's justification for the tasting of the apple, she imagines that he'll do what he wants anyway. Yet all of this is not to be disregarded because every time a police car pokes its nose into Elm Hill Park from now on, Zilla's heart will take a God almighty leap in her chest.

As the weeks drift into months, through the seasons, for now it's an easy time for Jimmy Penfold. The best of times. It seems he's hardly turned around before it's a year to the day that he received his first wage packet from Winston and co. It's a similar sort of day really. The sun's already warm and the sky's a spotless blue. Jimmy's sitting on the step in the sun, sipping a mug of tea and drawing on his roll-up. He can hear Zilla singing along to the radio inside. She has a soft sweet voice and it seems unfair to interrupt her.

'You ready then?' he calls.

That's being ready for the regular run to a rapidly growing deposit account at the Halifax Building Society in the nearby town of Rootsham, away from the prying of local eyes. This saving has become a religion to Zilla and there's cajoling and threats and sulking until she's sure that she's had every last penny possible from Jimmy's pocket. Mind, it can be a bit of a struggle. In this time of twelve months, she's been at hand to make sure that the van's always taxed and insured and dieselled up for the road: Zilla's an unsleeping partner in an illegal enterprise.

Zilla checks her hair, her make-up, then her handbag for their passbook. And for the six hundred pounds in notes to add to her dreams. Then it's a clamber into the cab of the rather smart Iveco, with only eighty thousand miles on the clock, and a notable trade up from his tatty old van.

Jimmy sweeps fish and chip papers from the passenger seat. Zilla crunches a Coke can under her shoe and Jimmy says in laying false blame,

'Our Mikey's an untidy sod.' He gives Zilla a sidelong look, 'Must get it from his mother.'

Zilla laughs, 'No Jimmy, you're wrong. It's his brains he got from his mother.'

Sometimes, if it's handy for him, Jimmy puts the money in – it is a joint account – and he might flirt a little with the girl behind the counter. Only innocently mind, she's much too young for him.

Rhuta's the name on her badge and it's her mother's and her grandmother's name, and it's Polish. She tells him she'll soon be off to the land of those mothers for a three-month stay with cousins she's never met before.

Jimmy says, 'Three months eh? That's some holiday, Rhuta. Bring me back a stick of rock.'

This is deserving of a smile and a giggle from Rhuta as another deposit's safely accounted for. The future dream house, sitting smart and new in its own plot of paradise, is being bought brick by brick. And life is looking good for Penfold Enterprises.

5

While all this has been going on, Meg and her black-and-white jukal have been having a tour around the country in the Auto-Trail motorhome. They've been on their extended summer holidays down to sunny Sussex by the sea, up to the flatlands of East Anglia, where the warm breezes dusted her vehicle with a film of peat, and across the heart of England to the Welsh Marches and then back into the Midlands. They've been parked up in a field gateway at dusk, a kettle perched on a smouldering wood fire, sharing a hunk of bread and cheese and watching the stars come out. They've been stopped by the Flash Travellers on the side of the road, or they've pulled into a crescent of council houses and sat out on the green catching the gossip. They might have been seen virtually anywhere on their wandering route of travel.

On this particular day, they are in the office of A.H. Brown and Son (Birmingham), Chartered Accountants, attending a six-monthly meeting. Meg is sitting in a black leather chair, Wilma flopped sulkily at her feet. Meg's asking questions, listening to talk of accounts, of property values and of appreciating assets. She's nodding, querying, shaking her head, while the accountant, Mr Malcolm Brown, grandson of the A.H. Brown in the firm's title, tells her of rent collections and percentages, of short-term rates and ISAs – of all things of financial interest to Meg.

There's papers to sign, payments to authorise, money to shift from one account to another and then, when it's all done, it's a cup of coffee and two biscuits – one for Meg and one for an instantly alert Wilma – to end the meeting. How did it get to this, Meg in a plush office in Birmingham's Bullring going through details of her considerable finances?

This part of the story starts with a child and her mother in the late 1930s. It's a hot and sticky July afternoon on a Wimbledon Common that's thronged with people. The coming war is lurking on the horizon, but for now the funfair's in full cry: the swing boats are swinging; the tunnel of love is well loved; the dodgems are not dodging and the screams from the waltzers could curdle your blood. At the rifle range, hotshots are lining up to impress their girlfriends, little knowing that in a year or so's time they'll be lining up the bullseye for real. They'll be swapping flat caps, trilbies and baggy trousers for uniforms of army brown and hobnailed boots. They'll be swapping all the fun of the fair for the camaraderie of the company. And they'll swap the swirling of organ music for the haunting lament of the Last Post. And the girls will be swapping their brightly coloured dresses for the dark colours of mourning.

On the common of this scorching, bustling day is Meg and her mother. In this time Meg is eight years old and perhaps just under four feet tall, with thin bare legs and thick raven hair. She's outside a striped tent, under a banner that reads, 'Palms read – Fortunes told'. Here her mother, Madam Zingara, the Genuine Hungarian Gypsy, is beating up a bit of custom. She's standing alongside Meg – an older, darker, more striking version of her daughter – and she's delivering her coaxing patter.

'A silver sixpence, that's all. Cross my palm with a silver sixpence.'

Meg, doing her part, darts into the crowd, tugs at a sleeve, snares her selection. 'Please, sir. Want yer fortune told, sir?'

She's very persuasive is little Meg; a look into those brown eyes and the trap is sprung and then in the gloom of the striped tent, sixpence for the palm becomes a shilling for the crystal ball and sometimes, when curiosity is only half satisfied, a florin or even half-a-crown takes the punter further along the road.

There's good money to be made at Madam Zingara's trade of dukkerin. There's the palm, the crystal, the tarot cards, the tea leaves, the reading of the fire. There's private sessions in the drawing rooms of large houses, where questions are asked of fidelity, of parenthood, of missing sons and runaway brides and of secrets that have been buried in the grave. Afterwards in some rather smart guest house or hotel Madam Zingara asks Meg what she sees in the crystal ball and Meg tells her of the impressions, the blurred snapshots of fortune that were growing clearer by the day. 'You're learning, my lovely. You're learning.'

Madam Zingara is putting all of her considerable earnings into buying gold and silver. She's trading in the currency of refugees and stashing it in a bank deposit box somewhere in the Midlands.

Zingara and Meg spend the rest of the summer and into the autumn criss-crossing the country in a rather smart Morris van. In the back of this motor there's enough room to stow the tools and equipment of their trade. The striped tent is erected at fairgrounds, at race meetings, anywhere people congregate. Now while so many of the Travelling People are moving around by horse and vardo and flat cart, camping in muddy fields, chinning the cosh for pegs and watching the falling rain from the shelter of canvas benders, Zingara and Meg are touring in style and staying at the best hotels in Blackpool, Hastings, Liverpool, Sheffield and so many more. And they can afford to because an address, albeit temporary, adds a veneer of respectability to how they make their living. It's all part of the illusion of trust because there's another side to how they're amassing their money. And little Meg plays a big part in this.

Dear Meg, sweet quiet child that she is, is always there at a private reading in a large house when the curtains are drawn and the lights are subdued. In these sessions, Zingara sets the scene and there's the usual hypnosis of a flickering candle reflected in the crystal ball; the long slim fingers stroking, caressing, the cool glass; the hushed tones of enquiry, of disclosure; the setting up of intent in this room of shadows. And then the total concentration on softly spoken words to the exclusion of all else around.

Is little Meg even missed as she slips from the room, from the captivated clients? She's a shadow in the shadows and she can open a door with no giveaway creak of hinges. She'll take a slow deep breath, clear her head and let her gift of divining draw her to the hiding places of cash and jewellery at the back of deep drawers or under a loose floorboard. A hatbox can hold a month's wages and a tea caddy a handful of sovereigns. She doesn't take it all. She'll leave enough behind for doubt.

'I'm sure there was fifty pounds here, not forty. Or did I take out some for—?'

'After I wore Mother's brooch, didn't I put it back in the box?'

Uncertainty buys time, and realisation comes too late to apprehend the fortune-teller with the black or blonde or ginger hair, and with the northern or southern or Irish or indistinct foreign accent, and with the son in trousers and a cap on his head – or the pretty daughter in a bright dress. On this particular Saturday evening in the plush lounge of the Birmingham Railway Hotel, Zingara and Meg look like any respectable mother and daughter, not a pair of gippos on the make. Zingara is attractive and, underneath those fine features, and behind those coal-black eyes, there's a hint of fiery abandon.

She's turned the head of a young man, a newly qualified accountant who's desperate to set up on his own but lacks finance and clients. This young man, Alfred Herbert Brown, clever and good-looking in a bookish sort of way, is having a drink on this Saturday evening. He also has what is commonly called a gammy leg – the result of an Austin Seven driving over his foot in the street. This crippled foot is going to keep him out of the army; he won't be facing the bombs and bullets in the great retreat to Dunkirk.

On this Saturday evening, he's had a week of long hours, skipped meals and the stress of obeying orders when it's himself who knows best. He's been sitting on a hard wooden chair, behind a plain wooden desk, behind a soot-streaked window, occasionally glancing up at the miserable Midland mizzle drifting down from a low grey sky. What he needs is a few beers and a tot, or more, of whisky to make the world a better place.

He's already had a few when mother and daughter take a comfy sofa-seat opposite him. He can't resist a polite, 'Good evening ladies' – with a quick appraisal of Zingara. Her dark hair is pinned tightly to her head. Her colouring and finely drawn features carry a hint of the exotic and Meg, completely outshone, is hardly noticed except as a child in the background.

Zingara, quick on the uptake, quick on opportunity, is already onto him. 'Good evening Mr . . .?'

'Brown,' he says. 'Alfred Brown.' He leaves out Herbert; it's a middle name that he only uses the initial of.

Then from Meg's mother it's 'Zingara'.

'An unusual name,' he says. 'Is it foreign?'

'Hungarian,' she responds, when actually it's Italian as well.

This evening in the Birmingham Railway Hotel, after Meg is

tucked up in their room, Zingara shares whisky and water with Alfred H. Brown, the ambitious young accountant. He looks into those dark eyes and she looks into his soul and she draws out his dreams. And, if a little later this mysterious, erotic beauty draws him into bed – in his room, of course – well, they're two consenting adults cementing a deal in the best way possible.

They've chosen well, this ambitious accountant and fortune-telling lady. It's all to do with needs and provision and two-way traffic in the mutual benefits of finance and a bit of the other. The timing couldn't be better, thanks to the uncertainty Hitler is causing. If ever there is a period when opportunity is going to really rear its head, it's between 1939 and 1945. So the foundations are laid and investments are planned and A.H. Brown is soon to be established as a proper accounting firm. And Zingara's wealth has found a new and profitable home.

6

In the present day, back at the Elm Hill site, it's pushing on into the New Year and life there has been sweet lately. There's the regular weekly runs, and Jimmy's into this luxury of well-paid employment with minimal hours of effort. To him it's morning in the café, lunchtime in the pub, afternoon in the bookies and then home for tea. He's never had it so good, and if getting out of bed becomes a little bit harder in the mornings, it's because his weight has gone from whippet thin to Labrador fat. But what pisses him off is when the call comes in the middle of the night or when he's at the kitchema downing a pint of best. Or partway through a film at the local cinema.

'For God's sake Jimmy,' Zilla hisses as his phone vibrates and a text message flashes the order.

'Nag's Head. Quarter of an hour.'

'Back in a minute,' he whispers to Zilla and the rest of the row stand to grudgingly let him through. Jimmy mutters a dozen 'Sorry's as he steps on a dozen toes.

But this isn't going to be a minute. The Nag's Head is an old backstreet pub, split into a public and a lounge bar. The ceilings are yellowed with nicotine from long-dead smokers and the bar counter is a dull brown. And so is the barman, whose ancestors obviously came from a warmer clime than England's.

Within the ten minutes since he left Zilla mooning at Hugh Jackman on the barricades of Paris, Jimmy's taken a couple of decent swallows of a pint of Courage Best. He waits at a corner table of the virtually empty lounge and, because he's a bit of a thirst on, he's well into his second pint when the now familiar Hoodie, with his lead-less Staffie two steps behind him, mooches in. 'Mr Jimmy Penfold,' he says, 'another early morning for you I'm afraid.'

This is the first time Jimmy's caught a proper glimpse of Hoodie's ferret face as he, Hoodie, drops a Waitrose (must be shopping more upmarket now) carrier bag on the table. It thuds, the flat thud of a kilo of white lady.

Hoodie says brightly, 'See you in a week, Mr Penfold.' It's the nearest he's come to normal conversation and he slouches out with Staffie snuffling along behind him. But not before Staffie has cocked his leg and relieved himself of hot piss against the leg of the pub table. Then it's out to the van for Jimmy and, when he's at a convenient pull-off, he takes his Waitrose carrier bag and contents and sinks it into a tub of exterior emulsion paint and then seals down the lid. A few tools and the wheelbarrow piled around his crock of gold and it could be any old builder's vehicle.

Then Jimmy does what's expected of him, he goes into the nearest pub and orders another Courage Best, and it's only when he's halfway through that it suddenly strikes him that he's meant to be in the cinema with Zilla. All the same, he rolls himself a fag before he heads back to the closing scene of *Les Mis* that no one wants to miss a second of. Then there's more flapping of seats, more tutting and sighing before he settles back next to Zilla.

'Sorry,' he whispers and slips his hand into hers. 'Got held up.'

'Shush,' Zilla says, and the light from the screen glitters on her cheek.

'Why are you crying?'

54

Zilla just shakes her head because he won't understand. It's the same when he chances his arm later that night and Zilla pushes him away: he doesn't get it. Jimmy's fired up the Iveco, scraped the ice from the windscreen and he's heading into the rising sun, into the flat land of the Fens. It's a lonely drive this early in the morning on these long, straight roads. The van gobbles up the miles past the old dykes and pump houses, past countless acres of huge, frozen, empty fields. The postcode on the TomTom shows the route into Cambridgeshire and, after a two-hour journey, Jimmy drives into a small trading estate and onto the forecourt of a garage workshop, where he kills the engine. A Grease Monkey, in an oil-smeared boiler suit, steps out of a scruffy office and comes over to Jimmy. The Grease Monkey is badly in need of a shave and a haircut and a good wash and scrub-up.

'You the gippo with something for me?'

Jimmy shrugs, saying, 'This is the address.'

Grease Monkey scratches his head, nods towards his office. 'Fancy a cup of tea?' He turns and then throws over his shoulder, 'And bring the gear with you.'

To anyone looking in it would seem like Grease Monkey has bought a twenty-five-litre drum of Sandtex Exterior Emulsion off a shady pikey. Now Jimmy's not usually fussy, and he's gasping for a cuppa, but the tea is undrinkable and the cup nearly slithers through his fingers on account of its own coating of grease. Then Grease Monkey drops an envelope of cash in Jimmy's lap and asks if he wants a sandwich. That's a definite no.

As Jimmy's rolling up a cigarette before leaving, Grease Monkey asks, 'You want some baccy?'

Free it's not, less than half price is nearer to the mark, and Jimmy buys a ten-pack of Golden Virginia to keep him company on the haul homewards.

By early afternoon the Fenlands are behind him and Jimmy's into more familiar territory. He's also thirsting for a drink and, coincidentally, when he's at the outskirts of Boarston he spots Silas's van in the car park of the King George and pulls up alongside.

Inside, Silas and Danny are settling into a session and, because they're already on the chopsy side, they have one end of the bar to themselves. They're both flush; they've had a few good results lately – Danny's actually won another fight – he's delayed his retirement again – and they've picked up a few lucrative roofing jobs. Oh and the social security benefits have been increased in line with inflation. It's three cheers for the welfare state; it's putting food on the table and it's buying their beer today. It's buying several beers.

But while the cousins are enjoying their few pints of ale, some-thing important is taking place outside. This concerns someone who's been snooping around in the background. In fact this person is Investigating Detective Sergeant Thomas (Tom) Malone, late of the Metropolitan Police. He's young – right side of thirty – and determined to put his once promising career back on track after a rather unfortunate, and unforgettable, incident with his superintendent's wife in the back of an unmarked police car.

In this exile, far away from the Smoke, Detective Tom Malone, who's also trying to repair his marriage, as well as his future prospects, needs to break a case. He needs The Big One so that he can make his star rise again, because his good looks and charm can only take him so high. He's not happy at the moment though because there doesn't seem to be anything major on the horizon in this backwater of a town. He's putting in all the hours possible in his quest for the break, and that's not helping his marriage – the reasons why are stacking up one on top of the

other. Tom Malone's wife, Polly, ash-blonde hair and pale porcelain skin – one of those women who look slender enough, fragile
enough, to shatter – is really trying to make things work, but
she's in a strange new place with a husband who's rarely home.
She meets with other station couples and wives and girlfriends,
sips gin and tonic, swaps phone numbers for coffee morning
arrangements, listens to the gossip and the endless talk of shop.
But her bruised heart is postponing recovery and she yearns for
reassurances, for quiet evenings in front of the telly with Tom,
for taking her rightful place in their world.

This afternoon, on his own time, Detective Tom Malone is
casually checking out the vehicles in the King George's car park.
He knows this place is a bit of a rogues' den and that inside the
pub deals are being struck and jobs are being organised. Even
the landlord buys his optics on the black. Detective Tom Malone
would love to plant a bug in the bar; he thinks that would explain
the copper cables missing from the electricity depot, lead
stripped from the church roof, countless break-ins at the offies.
Also, why every other tobacco addict seems to be smoking duty-
free. There's an echo of 'smoking duty-free' as Detective Tom
Malone takes a sly look into the cab of Jimmy's Iveco. And what
he sees is the pack of 'For Export Only' that the Grease Monkey
sold Jimmy for a score. (Actually it's just the corner of the pack
that's not quite concealed by a scruffy jumper, but it's enough
for the dead-eye Dick.)

Now Detective Tom Malone knows that the owner of this
van is in the pub and he's thinking that it might be possible to
add a drink-driving offence to the one of denying Revenue
and Customs their slice of entitlement. But he has a little
problem in that he promised Polly he would be home in time
to take her shopping for a new outfit. There's an impending
wedding on her side of the family and she wants to look the

biz, or at least better kitted out than her sister. But this isn't top of Detective Tom Malone's priorities because he's focused on the work in hand, on bringing an errant felon into the welcoming arms of British justice. So he parks his motor – an unmarked police car – just up the road to watch for the Iveco leaves the pub.

He doesn't have to wait for long because Jimmy has every intention of going home to his loved ones on time for another cinema visit and an early supper of Kentucky Fried Chicken and chips. That'll be himself, the lovely Zilla and his son and heir, Mikey. Jimmy's also hoping that later tonight he's in for a good result in the conjugal stakes.

While he's been waiting, Detective Tom Malone has fired up his onboard police computer. He's asked who owns the Iveco and followed the criminal career of a certain James Peter Penfold. He's now following Jimmy's van and when it swings left, he can't believe his luck. It couldn't have been better planned if he tried. The not-so-innocent Traveller is actually going to drive right past Boarston Police Station. Well he was going to but Tom Malone's flicked on his siren and his stop now directive, cut in front of Jimmy and stopped him dead. Jimmy says 'Shit' to himself and tucks the baccy under the seat.

Detective Tom Malone comes to the driver's side of the Iveco and politely asks Jimmy, 'You do realise it's a thirty-mile-an-hour zone, sir?'

He receives a restrained, 'Yes, Officer,' from Jimmy who would really like to give this gavver a mouthful but has to err on the side of caution. Tom Malone, working on from the excuse of stopping Jimmy says, 'Have you been drinking, sir?'

This gets Jimmy asking himself, 'Am I over the limit? Was it two or three pints?'

Out loud he says, 'Just the one, sir.'

The last thing that Jimmy needs is to have to phone Zilla to tell her that he's been lelled by the gavvers for overdoing the livvener. That would please her for sure, and then he'd have to let Rubin and his cohorts know. There would be more than earache coming his way from them. Much more. They certainly wouldn't take too kindly to being let down.

The convenience of giving Jimmy a tug outside the police station means that intrepid Detective Tom Malone can escort the dejected didikai to the front desk. Here he hands Jimmy over to Duty Sergeant Dave Aubrey while he nips back and gives the Iveco a quick once-over. But this proves to be disappointing because the one pack of tobacco – from the Grease Monkey supplier – is all that he finds. It's hardly the crime of the century. So Tom Malone stands by the Iveco stroking his chin, hoping that a breathalyser test will be positive, or else he'll have more egg on his face.

A low grey cloud begins to settle over Detective Tom Malone's head; he needs some good luck to cheer him. And just then who should be coming back from exercising his springer spaniel, but PC Warren Davey of the area Drug Squad.

PC Davey manages to nearly complete his enquiry of, 'Got a live one then Tom? . . . Jesus!'

The 'Jesus!' is added because as they're talking, the spaniel's nose has twitched and he's taken a flying leap into Jimmy's cab. Lucky, the best drug dog in the business, has caught the scent of the package of white lady that sat briefly as a passenger along-side Jimmy. There's also a trail inside the back of the van to a perfect dried circle of Sandtex Exterior Emulsion on the plywood floor where the can once stood.

The two men exchange knowing glances and Tom Malone says, 'So that's how the crafty bastard smuggled it.'

PC Warren, nodding, says, 'It's the old paint dodge, Tom.'

PC Warren is more than familiar with the old paint job of

submerging and sealing the merchandise inside a container. He starts to tell Tom Malone of the time they stopped an articulated lorry loaded with ten thousand cans of . . . But Detective Tom Malone isn't listening because he is trying to mentally put his case together for the prosecution of Jimmy Penfold. But when he does, his initial enthusiasm falters and then nosedives.

On one: breaking the speed limit – the excuse for the pulling-over of Jimmy Penfold. No chance.
On two: contraband tobacco – yes. Physical evidence.
On three: drink-driving – might be. Not looking likely though.
On four: drug dog sniffs out where drugs have been – not enough to convict there.

If it even makes court, Jimmy Penfold will probably receive a slap on the wrist for the Golden Virginia; a year's driving ban for excess alcohol in the blood if proved; and the drug-related charge will be laughed out of court.

Bollocks. But Detective Tom Malone isn't anything if he's not a thinker, a schemer who would even now be locking up the big boys if it hadn't been for the unfortunate incident with the superintendent's lovely lady – the woman with a penchant for Merlot and good-looking young police officers out of uniform. So Detective Tom Malone leans on Jimmy's van and probes his old grey matter, loses himself in ifs and buts, winds through scenarios in seconds until a light bulb flickers into life, grows stronger, grows brighter, grows a plan, a hopeful solution, because he is a clever young man. He was top cadet in his class and he was expected to go far. Which he has, but not in the way those expectations were envisaged.

Jimmy Penfold just can't believe his good fortune when he's

given a stern warning by the desk sergeant – *Next time you'll be in serious trouble, my son* – for the buying of illegal tobacco products. There's no mention of a breathalyser test and he's free to go with no charge, no caution. He hightails it out of the police station before any minds can be changed.

Detective Tom Malone pensively watches Jimmy leave. Jimmy Penfold, the sprat to catch a mackerel and a few more bigger fish further up the food chain . . .

As Jimmy drives away from his close shave he wonders why trouble always seems to ambush him. He hasn't even begun to wonder if it's anything to do with his lifestyle because, just now, his main concern is the non-stop messages on the voicemail of his mobile. It's Zilla trying yet again to find out why he's so effin late when he promised that it was going to be the flicks and then a Kentucky Family Bucket. And Mikey's been looking forward to it all day and it's just not fair to break a promise to their chavo. And not to mention that she's had a shower and done herself up for him. And they've been waiting since three o'clock but now Mikey's gone off with Carter and his mates. And now the whole effin day's ruined. And what did she expect because a tiger never changes its spots. And he, Jimmy, might just as well stay in the kitchema where his effin buddies, and the effin livvener, mean more to him than his effin family. Best pleased she is not. She's also very surprised when he rolls into Elm Hill Caravan Park at a quarter past five and as sober as a judge. 'Sorry, my Zilla. I got held up.' Jimmy spreads his hands in the gesture of nothing to hide. 'I was worried,' she says and shakes her blonde hair that's washed and soft and rippling to her shoulders. She's out of jeans and into a black dress that shows off the slimness of her waist, the two good handfuls of breast and that so strokable derrière. And those legs. God, she takes his breath away.

Jimmy says hopefully, 'We could stay in tonight; I could get a takeaway.'

Reading him like a book, Zilla replies, 'We're going out. You get yerself a wash and shave. Spruce yerself up a bit. Make yerself respectable.'

Evening replaces the short afternoon and wraps itself around our happy couple as they catch a showing of *Iron Man 3* at the multiplex and a supper of a Kentucky Family Bucket. Then this frosty but friendly night settles over Elm Hill Park as the lights from the mobile homes go out one by one.

In Winston's city it's a different sort of night. It's bitterly cold and hard and sharp, and pitch darkness lurks in the shadows of the back alleys, the derelict factories, the wasted ground, the spaces between the streetlamps. And in Winston's HQ, where the man with the growing reputation holds his court, business is in progress. Orders are being checked by his crew. Trustworthiness and loyalty is being assessed, beatings are being arranged, and there'll be no fingers for anyone who's caught with their fingers in the till. And worse, much worse than this, are the acid facials being planned for the double-crossers. There's no redeeming features in this organisation, and Winston is in a tearing hurry and he's not taking prisoners. And the man who's helping make all of these terrible things possible is the likeable charmer and consummate lady-killer, Rubin the Enforcer.

On this same night – even later now – Detective Tom Malone is driving home along a lane that glitters with frost and is spotted with flurries of snow. He's yawning, rubbing his eyes and yearning to rest his handsome head on his pillow. He's spent the last eight hours putting together his proposal, his special plan, his career saver. He's copied it to his documents and first thing tomorrow morning he'll download the file and present it to his superior. Tom Malone is tired but satisfied, excited but apprehensive. But when he arrives at the little rented cottage that's home, there's not a light showing, not a glimmer in the window.

Even though he's knackered and he'll have to wake Polly, he wants to share his special plan with her. She's been through a lot lately – he's put her through a lot. And now he wants to make it up to her because suddenly everything has a chance of falling into place with this second chance. It's like he's bubbling with ideas and he desperately wants her to hear them, make her understand. Make her look up to him again like she did in the early days. Admire him like she used to. Like the WPCs at the station do.

Detective Tom Malone lets himself into their cottage. He goes in quietly, goes through to the kitchen, switches on the light and the kettle. He frowns at Polly's phone on the worktop because he was meant to sort out a new one for her today – now to be tomorrow – another black mark for him, because Polly's mobile had slipped from her fingers and taken an early bath in the loo bowl this morning. Now he'll make two mugs of sweet drinking chocolate and take it up to the bedroom. There he'll gently wake her and she'll smile that sleepy-warm smile of surprise and pleasure of seeing him. And they'll sip their drinks and then he'll take a shower and slip in beside her and she'll fall to sleep in his arms.

The kettle boils up and there's chocolate and milk in the cups and then sugar; two spoonfuls for Polly because she's a sweet girl with a sweet tooth and once she had a sweet nature. Before what happened happened.

A frown appears on that too-handsome face as Tom Malone spots a page of folded notepaper on the kitchen table. It's propped against a vase of bright, cheerful flowers that have begun to wilt. The note is not exactly a 'Dear John' letter but it's damn close.

Polly's note says that she's going to stay with her mother; she's taking a break from their relationship and needs time to think things over. But impatience is a fault of Tom Malone's and, in spite of the hour, he's going to contact his wife to try and sort this out. So it's a deep breath and a dialling to his mother-in-law's number.

Polly's mother picks up and she's straight into the attack. 'Don't you know what the time is, Tom?'

'I'd like to speak to Polly.'

'It's late. She's in bed.'

'I just want to talk to her.'

'If only talking was all you did.'

'I won't keep her long.'

'No. She's in bed.'

Polly's mother is more than curt because the situation is reflecting her own life with a philandering man. An untrustworthy man. A man who left her with an unforgivable bitterness to, well, men.

Then Tom Malone hears Polly's faint voice, 'Mum? Mum? Who is it?'

The phone is quiet for a few seconds except for a round of suppressed whispering. 'Yes.' 'No.' 'Yes.'

Polly's sweet, sad, tired, hurt voice comes on the line and Tom has a sudden remembrance of her wounded eyes. 'Tom,' she says, 'I needed to get away.' She corrects it with, 'I had to get away.' She sounds on the edge of tears. 'It's hard, Tom. It's late and I can't do this tonight.'

'I'll call tomorrow night, 'bout seven,' Tom Malone says.

'I don't know, Tom. I don't . . .'

'Tomorrow, Polly. I love you,' Tom Malone adds – and thinks he gets it in before the phone cuts off.

At the station, late that next afternoon, Tom Malone gets the call to his inspector's office where his proposal is opened on the desk. Chief Inspector Isaacs, once a beefy but now frankly a fatty ex-rugby player of boiler-house status, says,

'As I shouldn't have to remind you, our budget is tight. You're going to have to take on the spade work yourself. I can cover a couple of months or so, Tom. That's all.'

He spreads his palms in a generous 'I'm giving you everything I can mate' gesture but Tom Malone's toes are in the starting blocks. He's been given permission, means and a free rein that could find him tracking, quite soon, Jimmy's Iveco on his bi-weekly deliveries. Tom Malone hopes to pull together a case that will curtail the gypsy's wanderings, and also snare a few more big cats. In the meantime, it's watch and wait for Tom Malone.

Many miles from Boarston, in the early hours of the morning, Meg is parked down a gravel track on the edge of a lonely moor and, in the bed, Wilma is curled up to Meg like a warm, contented, sleeping baby. In this last fling of night, the clouds have cleared and a cold, bright moon glisters the frost that's settled onto the motorhome. Meg is into a dream that came to her in the darkest of the night, that slunk over her in the hour before dawn. And this is the dream. This is what she sees.

Elm Hill Park is asleep, the dogs are snoring and Harry Potter is a lonely sentinel scuffing the frozen grass. Meg's walking slowly into this world where things are as they are and they're not as they are. The air is thick and heavy and colder than ice. It cloaks Meg, squeezes between her toes in her surprise of bare feet, nips at her ears, pours in her throat. She knows she's going to Zilla's vardo (the old word is in her mind, even if there's no grai to haul it and it isn't really a vardo) where's there's soft lamplight in the window. Then it's up the steps to a door that opens to her touch, to a scene in this parallel world.

Inside here the light is soft and there's a pale eiderdown smoothed over the bed. Zilla, a tumble of blonde hair on a snow-white pillow, is stirring restlessly; not awake but not asleep. But there's also a stranger in this room, in this bed. There's a stranger with red hair and a bruised, cut face. He's laying on his back and his unblinking eyes are staring at the ceiling. He's laying in the stillness of death under the cover and his body is twisted and bent. And then Zilla eyes flutter, start to open. Her hand goes to her mouth and she sits up in bed, looks at this man beside her. On her face is bewilderment, incomprehension, the horror of being snared in a nightmare.

Then she's saying, 'I don't want this. Please, Meg. Help me. Help me.' And her hands are reaching for Meg, imploring for an embrace to draw herself into the familiar world. But Meg is being pulled slowly out of this dream and their fingers only brush together in the briefest of contact between dream and reality.

Then this scene starts to recede into the distance. But not before Meg has seen a splash of red blood formed on Zilla's heart; a poppy that drips a scarlet tear onto the pale eiderdown.

Meg wakes suddenly, joltingly, in the bitter cold under the moon-shadow of the moor. Wilma is whining softly in her sleep and dawn is still an hour away, but Meg steps out into the night, shakes the slumber out of her clothes, and prays to the moon and the stars and to all the heavens above her, that for once she could be wrong. And then she prays to the God she doesn't believe in because there's no one else left.

7

It's time for the world to wake now; the morning's coming over the hill and people are crawling out of their beds, visiting the loo, putting the kettle on, dropping slices of bread into the toaster. Cleaning the barrel of their Glock 19 Gen4. All the things that people do at the start of a bright new day. All the normal people and all the not-quite-normal people.

One of the normal people, Captain Surgeon Benjamin Day of the Royal Army Medical Corps, has taken a cup of coffee onto his garden patio. He's really an ex-captain because he's recently been retired from the service, at the ripe old age of fifty, and he's slowly starting to get used to civvy street. But what he can't get away from is the habit of rising early in the morning. Captain Benjamin Day is tall and upright with a smoothly ironed shirt, well-pressed trousers and polished shoes. He's clean-shaven and his hair is short and combed back from his forehead. He's served in every conflict that the British army has been involved in since he was eighteen and because of that he's an expert on injuries of the battlefield: shrapnel wounds, bullet wounds and the carnage that improvised explosive devices cause. And on this bright new day Captain Surgeon Benjamin Day – Ben to his friends – is standing on his patio drinking his coffee in the freezing stillness of this early morning. Behind him, the patio doors crash open and his two young daughters, nine and eleven, in pyjamas and slippers, skip out to him. If they were birds, they'd be a pair of fluttering chattering magpies. And they're chattering now because there's a trip planned today for a visit to Longleat house and safari park, and these two high-spirited sisters can hardly wait. They've planned the route, estimated the time of arrival, gone through the guidebook and ticked off everything, and more, that they want to see. Oh, and they want One Direction, full blast, on the CD player all the way there.

Now it's 'Daddy this' and 'Daddy that' and 'Daddy, when are we going?'

It's obvious that these two clean, polite, well-nourished, well-educated, well-spoken children are Daddy's girls. It's difficult to imagine a curse, or worse, slipping from between their well-brushed pearly teeth. Then their mother calls these perfect little madams in for breakfast and it's no surprise that it's a glass of fresh orange juice, a healthy bowl of cereal and a slice or two of wholemeal toast and marmalade.

While they're eating, she – Vanessa – joins Ben on the patio and lights up her first Silk Cut of the day. She coughs the dry cough of the seasoned smoker and, through pursed lips, blows the blue smoulder into the frosted morning. She's an angular dark-haired woman in her late thirties with a cut-glass accent that was honed to perfection at Westonbirt School for Girls. Just a glance at her would tell that she's strict with her daughters, that she first reads the 'Style' section of the *Sunday Time* and that she goes to town at least once a month. There's not much to associate this woman with the girl she used to be except when she fires up in bed.

By eight o'clock this family are travelling in their Volvo V90 estate along the A36 – the Salisbury–Warminster road. The girls are into non-stop chatter against the background of One Direction's 'Best Song Ever'. There's a smile on Ben's face that shows he's happy with his family. He's happy with his pretty girls, his striking wife, his new taking-it-easy lifestyle. He's content with his lot. But he'll occasionally grimace because there's still a stab of pain, just under his ribs. And sometimes, when he's alone, he'll trace the scar of combat and wonder which god smiled down on him on that day.

The two little never-sit-still sisters, who for now are strapped into their seats, are operating at full volume behind their parents. Their mother's lips are pursed but Ben is laughing along with them. Vanessa says, in exasperation, 'For God's sake, Penny and Julia.' Then to Ben, 'I need a cigarette. Will you pull over please?'

Ben draws into a lay-by and kills the motor, and Vanessa takes herself and her packet of Silk Cut and lights up outside the car. She takes a long pull on her cigarette, savours the nicotine hit and exhales in a sigh of blue smoke.

Inside the car, Ben's answering his mobile phone. His voice has dropped into a lower pitch and his words have quickened and, as talking becomes listening, he turns to his daughters behind him and puts a finger to his lips.

'Nantee,' he says and the girls turn down the volume slightly and momentarily. Overhearing Ben's word of shushing, Vanessa's sourpuss of a mouth sours even more. And when she catches the name Meg in the conversation the expression on her face could curdle milk. But what's interesting here is if these two high-spirited girls of Captain Surgeon Benjamin Day's were to be dressed in raggardy clothes, with a smudge of dirt on their faces, and then set down in Elm Hill Park, they wouldn't look out of place. Nor would their father. The same can't be said of Vanessa, the colonel's daughter.

Less than sixty miles away from this nearly happy family there's a rather smart ground-floor flat in Bournemouth's Triangle area. It has two bedrooms, a reception room, a kitchen, a bathroom, and it's only a five-minute walk to the sandy beaches. The property is in a highly popular area with a thriving night-life, or more cultural pursuits, if desired. The New Forest is a fifteen-minute drive away, and Poole harbour is just down the road.

Inside the kitchen a youngish man of medium height with a modest haircut, and quietly fashionable clothing, is sipping a Carte Noire and biting into a slice of toast. He's reading a local rag and clocking the cinema programme because he enjoys a good film. Now, if at a later date, the neighbours are asked to describe him, this is probably what he'd come out as. Average.

Height?

Average.

Dress?

Average.

Build?

Average.

Looks?

Average.

Any distinguishing features?

No.

Still, why would anyone be asking the neighbours about Roland Knight, aka Peter Jones, aka God knows who else?

In fact his real name is Veryll Evans and he's a boyo from the deep valleys of Cymru.

When he's finished his breakfast, Veryll Evans goes to his bedroom and draws the curtains. Then he lifts a length of floor-board and searches out a soft heavy bundle. He unwraps it carefully, slowly, in a striptease of revealment and, when all is exposed, a Glock 19 Gen4, the weapon of the assassin, is laid out to the light.

For what seems an age, Veryll Evans stares at the gun, then

he picks it up and cradles it, before laying it down again and slowly, lovingly, disassembling this weapon. He takes each part and oils and cleans and wipes, in an act of perverse affection for this Hermes from Hades, this perfection of deadly engineering.

Throughout, his eyes are ice cold and as clear as the day. There may be the beginning of a bitter smile plucking at the corner of his mouth but those cold eyes never change an iota. They only narrow when he raises the reassembled Glock, takes a sure-shot aim at himself in the mirror and imaginary blows himself away.

Then he does what he always does when there's something in the offing, when his head is filling with a contract. He opens his cupboard door and takes out all he has left of his mother: a faded photograph. His mother is hugging his small frame as only a mother can. For a fraction of a second that time breathes again. And in that time Mrs Evans vanishes out of the lives of Mr Evans and her only child. And the last, the very last thing, Veryll remembers of his mother is when he's awakened by the usual arguing, the usual shouting, the usual screaming, the usual crashing of furniture and the usual smashing of crockery in a maelstrom of noise. But what's not usual is his mother's pleading, plaintive cry and her last words on God's earth. *'Don't. Please don't.'*

And then there's a silence. A long, deep, deadly silence that seems to go on forever and little Veryll has to put his pillow over his head to shut it out.

Veryll's father tells everyone that his wife had left suddenly, without a word. Took her case and her clothes and walked out of their lives. 'Without a reason,' Veryll heard his father say a hundred times. It's always accompanied by a regretful shake of his head. But at school, Willie Williams reckons that Mrs Evans ran off with a bloke because, according to his father Dai

Williams, she's always liked a bit of fresh cock. Gavin Hughes says that Mrs Evans has eloped with an Englishman, which is much, much worse.

Veryll takes all of this. He doesn't bite, he doesn't blow up and launch himself at his mother's insulters. It's as though the words wash over him, don't really seem to affect him. But after school he takes his .22 calibre SMK air rifle up to the dense woods behind his lonely cottage home and, on the steep hillside, he plays his favourite game. His killing game.

He kills anything that moves and anything that doesn't move. He kills all he can of these small creatures of the forest: feather and fur; jackdaw and rabbit; pigeon and feral cat. Each one has a name, sometimes several names, that he whispers through his thin lips while he lines them up in the cross-hairs of the gunsights. He lines up Bret, David, Alison, Alwyn, William, Chas, Davina and Mrs Davis his teacher – all his real and imagined tormentors. Then he blows all of them away because young Veryll Evans is serving his apprenticeship, his NVQ, in serial killing and these innocent beasts of the forest will have to do. For now. And then there's silence after the dispatch as though the earth knows of it, the woods know of it. The breath is held fast alongside the racing heart and the deep, deep hush that only comes after a death, a slaughter, settles over the hillside.

In this two-bedroomed flat in the respectable retirement town of Bournemouth, Veryll Evans, with a slight tremor to his fingers, shuts his mother and all the dark things back into the cupboard.

For now.

And as carefully as he assembled the Glock 19 Gen4, he now disassembles it, wraps it in its funereal shroud and inters it under the floorboards until it needs to be exhumed.

8

There's a month or two to pass now, a saying of au revoir to the cold weather. It's late afternoon at the Elm Hill Park and Jimmy's off to pick up his mail for a delivery. He nods a 'Good day to you' at Harry Potter – he's been tethered a little further along the fence today – and he's munching out a new moon in the grass. It's been a warmish spring day – cooling into dusk now – and Jimmy is happy as he follows a winding right of way. This path takes him along the scrubland base of Elm Hill and over the rise of a grassy hillock and, although it's only two or three hundred yards of uphill climbing, Jimmy puffs a bit. And this is because he's really getting out of condition; too much livvener, too much scran and not enough exercise. Or graft.

Zilla's been saying, 'You've put on some weight, Jimmy.'

'I never hear you complain when I'm on top.'

Zilla's also been saying, 'That's 'cos I can't talk, you've squashed all the breath out of me.'

Jimmy has promised to cut down on all the fatteners he's gobbling up. Well, all except for the necessary beers on the week-end and the very tasty pizzas from the Italian's that just opened up in Boarston.

At the top of the rise above Elm Hill Park, Jimmy takes a breather before starting the downhill run – another couple of hundred yards – that leads him to the gateway of a narrow lane. This is the new venue for the passing over of illegal substances.

A usurper of the previous faceless Hoodie now meets Jimmy here with the bag of goodies. He's still one of the hooded tribe but he turns up in a smart black Volkswagen Passat, with a sound system that could shatter eardrums. This lad, Sparky, is actually quite friendly and although he shouldn't by rights hang around, he sits on the bonnet of the motor and smokes a tuvler with Jimmy. Then he opens the boot, raises the lid on the spare wheel compartment and casually lifts out a 'Save the World' hessian bag. Inside there's two slabs of paradise white, two ten-thousand-pound bricks of Columbia's best in a waterproof overcoat of sealed polythene. Then Sparky gives Jimmy the brown envelope of expenses and he tears away in a deep boom of bass that chases him out of sight.

These products are for a next-day delivery in the suburbs of Huntingdon and so Jimmy carries them home and stows them in a twenty-five-litre tub of special offer interior emulsion. (Sandtex have priced themselves out of the market.) It's just about dusk now and the working men are returning home. The site is lighting up for the evening and the lights are framed in the windows of the caravans and the static homes. There's a couple of jukals on the prowl and as usual they're nosing the bins for a few titbits. A waft of cooking bacon is on the air and it nips at Jimmy's stomach but he knows his dinner will be a while; it'll be sandwiched between *Neighbours* and *Emmerdale*. He reckons that he's got time to slot in two – only two mind 'cos he's driving – pints of best bitter before Zilla's ready to serve up another one of her culinary delights that she's been copying from a Jamie Oliver cookbook. This thought doesn't fill him with delight and he thinks he might treat himself to a frowned-upon takeaway from Singapore Syds and eat it in a lay-by.

But first a cool beer with the usual suspects and that means that later in the Flying Horse there are three familiar figures lounging at the bar. The Three Musketeers they most definitely are not. Old Alex Dumas would have a job creating swashbuckling heroes from this raw material: good-looking Jimmy Penfold, gravelly voiced Silas Penfold and bald-headed Dangerous Danny Delaney. Silas is fishing as usual. He's trying to dig out exactly what Jimmy is up to because, considering past occasions, it's not like Jimmy to withhold information from him. Bit worrying in fact.

'Few bits and pieces,' Jimmy offers.

'Where?'

'Here and there.'

'Here and there? You're all over the Wreking.'

This is not a new conversation and it ends like it usually does because Jimmy's sworn to silence and according to the old lags' lore, 'If you don't know, you can't tell.'

So he doesn't tell even if it puts Silas's nose out of joint.

And Jimmy can't really have anyone knowing so he keeps mum and knows that walls have ears and that careless talk costs lives. (Jimmy's been watching *Britain at War* on the gogglebox, so he keeps his schtum.)

The Flying Horse owes its high ornate ceilings to the overwrought style of the late Victorian era, and its inadequate lighting to the inefficiency of modern low-energy bulbs. The counter is long and narrow with brass-handled pumps, and the room itself is deep and shadowed enough for anyone to sit and observe without really being noticed. And that anyone is Detective Tom Malone. His smart detective's suit and tie have been replaced by a dark bomber jacket and saggy-arsed, multi-pocketed trousers. A black woollen beanie covers his poll and is yanked down over his ears. He hasn't shaved for a day or two, so he looks like a prime example of mauzey lowlife. And he does bolo a bit – being unwashed is par for this course. He couldn't be further removed from the impeccably turned-out policeman he usually is. Or rather was. Tom might, for a night or two, get a few suspicious looks as a stranger in town but by the time he's bought a bit of draw and skinned up in the gents, he'll be part of the background; one of those drifting nondescript no-hopers who live by the dole and small-time dealing.

It's not often that distant cousin, and old friend to the Traveller trio, Divi Denny Vincent passes through Boarston, but tonight he does. He's been to the race meeting at Sandown and he's making, albeit slowly, his way back to Peterborough. He's as tall as Silas but stooped in his back and his is a sudden presence at the bar. The boys are on their eighth beer – so much for the quiet drink – and chorusing 'Sweet Sixteen' in a broken and not very melodic order. 'It's Divi,' says Danny, like no one else would recognise him. 'Get him a pint, Silas.'

Silas says it's Danny's round but, to save an argument, Jimmy calls to Sammy the barman: 'One for my cousin here.'

Now Jimmy, already well-oiled and his need for food drowned by the ale, pulls a wad of twenties from his pocket and peels one off. Divi's eyes clock the roll and in that glance you can see the mind of a skint man working overtime. He had bet everything on the last race and, sure enough, his horse had come in last.

'Christ,' Divi's thinking, 'that must be over a thousand bar.' Divi Den, in desperate need of a few quid to tide him over till the next dead cert, begins to drop the odd hint into the conversation about his site-rent arrears, about how he's dreading going back to the missus because she's going to skin him alive. 'Dordee, my Jimmy, she can breathe fire that one.'

Silas reckons that his jukal loves him more than his wife does 'cos if he shut his dog and his missus into the boot of his car, and then let them out after an hour, he knows which one would be most pleased to see him. Danny says, speaking on the bitter experiences of being snuffed out more times than a candle, that women are more trouble than they're worth. 'And I should be going,' he says as he tips back his bald head and takes a huge swallow from his glass. The reason he should be going now is that he's fighting in two weeks and he's got to look after his body.

'But one more won't hurt,' he says as Jimmy calls in whisky and beer chasers. But not for Divi. 'I've got a way to go. Can't afford to lose my licence,' he says and then drops in, 'it's hard enough to earn a living . . . So if anything comes up?'

This is how he's doing it, never direct, not yet. He's preparing the ground as the whisky bottle shrinks on the optics and even Sammy the barman, who's been included in most of the rounds, has given up trying to calculate cost because every circuit of drinks is now exactly a tenner when it should be considerably more. This is the scene for another hour, until there's just the five of them in the bar and the clock's picking out one after midnight.

Mobile ring tones have been ignored, texts demanding to know 'Where are you?' have been left unopened because, as the Irish say, 'The craic is too good for the leaving.'

But leave it they must because when Sammy's full to the brim, he calls time, while he can still walk and talk, still usher our protesting gypsy quartet out into the night. He locks the door behind them and fumbles the lights off and sits in the dark bar. He smokes a cigarette and wonders how he's going to balance the books to his boss. He's also got the beginnings of a thumping headache and he knows there's an even bigger one on its way. He's not looking forward to the morning.

Outside in the rear car park, the long goodbyes have started and it's another twenty minutes before Danny and Silas leave Divi standing, and Jimmy swaying, on the gravel under the starlight.

Jimmy's also feeling distinctly unwell and he thinks he may have eaten something disagreeable during the evening. Of course it's nothing at all to do with the whisky or the excess of Courage Best or the bags of crisps with a pickled egg in the top.

Then Divi starts to make his move, to ask if Jimmy can lend him a couple of hundred. He wheedles out, 'Just till the weather breaks, my Jimmy. You know I wouldn't ask, but . . .' Jimmy is already reaching into his pocket but it's not for his roll of blue-backs, it's because it's *that* phone ringing. The one that must never be ignored.

The message is brief and precisely to the point. 'They want it now. Right away. You know where it is. Don't fuck up, Mr Penfold.' Jimmy, despite his inebriated state, knows that 'now' really means 'now or else'. He manages to get out a convincing, not drunk-sounding 'OK'. And that, to his relief, ends the call.

Now no sane person would take a chance of getting arrested for driving under so much influence, especially not with two kilos of the best of Columbia inside a tub of emulsion paint. And so for Jimmy the solution is standing right in front of him.

He says to Divi Den – not so much says as slurs,

'I'll give you two hundred bar if you drive me to Huntingdon now.'

'What now?'

'It's got to be now.'

Divi Den ponders for a few moments and says, 'All right, Jimmy. But . . .'

'But what?'

'Could yer make it two-fifty? 'Cos you know I've got a lot going on.'

There's a quick smack of hands on the deal – money to be passed over on successful delivery – before the transference of the tub of interior emulsion from Jimmy's Iveco to the back of

Divi Den's grey Vauxhall estate. But also in the car park the plain-clothed detective, in his plain but well-equipped police motor, is watching and noting as Divi Den and his inebriated passenger set off. In the blackness of these early hours they're driving off on a journey of, hopefully, mutual benefits.

On this dark journey of the night the problem for Jimmy is that his stomach's revolting. It's gurgling, leaking gas, threatening to throw up its contents. He's never felt so ill in his life – well maybe once after a long, long session after his granfer's funeral – but never when things have been this important. Jimmy just wants the delivery over. He wants to be in his warm bed at Elm Hill Park snoring for England but, and provided everything runs smoothly, that's over three hours away.

Following from a safe distance, Tom Malone is also shattered. He's been trying to keep tabs on Jimmy Penfold. He's been trying to keep the peace with Polly. He's been doing the work of two tecs and getting paid for one. At the moment Tom Malone is on his police radio giving a running commentary on direction of travel and putting in a word for stand-by back-up.

At this hour and away from the dark empty roads, and because he's well up the food chain, Rubin is at a private club in a less than salubrious part of his city. It's quiet in here and the lighting is subdued and the music's smoky blue. The place is chilled out and Rubin is relaxing – on a wide comfy sofa with the princess of his prison dreams. This relationship is not as hunky-dory as it appears because Freedom had found it more than difficult waiting for Rubin while he was keeping all male company and she was getting none. Freedom had missed being spoilt, being petted, being told she was a princess. It could be said that she was in a vulnerable state when Donny the Dancer hit on her. It could also be said that she was more than impressed by Donny's fancy footwork and his pelvic thrusts. She'd tossed her head and just asked to be kissed. And more, of course.

In this dimly lit club, she's snuggled up to Rubin like it's all forgotten but people like Rubin, they never forget. It's marked down in his repayment book as a debt to be paid at a future date of his choosing. But for now Rubin's enjoying her gratitude of his forgiveness. She really is a little minx who'll do anything to please him, especially after what happened to Donny the Dancer. It's such a shame that he can't dance anymore; someone took a sledgehammer to his legs and now he needs crutches to even hobble to the corner shop. Pity, he was such a lovely mover.

In this club, Rubin keeps the tabs on his posse of trusted operators. He sips a Jack Daniel's, ice and Coke, with his purring princess cuddled up to him. He also lights up one of Havana's best because the tobacco ban doesn't apply in this territory. In fact very few of the usual rules of society are adhered to in this place. And in this place, people, make a path, melt away, as Winston the bullet-headed leader displaces Freedom on the wide comfy sofa. This is Winston's court, this dimly lit nightclub with its background of rap music, gorgeous girls and the muscular studs who'll pull a chiv at the drop of a hat.

Winston starts with the questions, the review of the night's ongoing operations: Who's where? Who's doing what? It's like a friendly chat, a casual conversation that could be about the weather, but it's about the tracking of mules, the fulfilling of orders and the settling of scores in a violence that's never listed in police records. Business is running smoothly, things are going well and Winston's grin of satisfaction is broad and pearly white in this dimly lit club-cum-office.

Rubin asks of Winston, 'Did Mickie Taylor come across?'

Winston's grin broadens even more. 'Signed and sealed, my man. Signed and sealed.'

This means that a contract to supply Mickie Taylor of the Midlands Mafia with lots of goodies has been approved. Mr Taylor is a good man to have on side but a terrible man to cross, hence his nickname of Mental Mickie. It's rumoured that he takes a special delight in amputations and he's given a whole new meaning to the nursery rhyme 'This Little Piggy'. All that's got to be hoped for is that Jimmy Penfold does not get himself involved in a cock-up; a cock-up that might cause any sort of trouble for Winston or his clients. They're a bad lot with a new very important person on the client list.

The problem tonight is that the drunken, and extremely unwell, gypsy postman is breaking the two most important rules of the delivery business. One is to never, not ever, involve someone else in the operation. The second rule is to make sure you're not being followed. But Detective Tom Malone is tailing the operatives and is well on the way to setting up the monster bust that'll boost his career and put him back where he was before his little adventure with the superintendent's wife.

In Divi's car it's hot and stuffy because he reckons his blood is thin; he needs to keep warm. He also reckons that if their gypsy forefathers had stayed in Spain, he wouldn't have to freeze his balls off here every winter. Jimmy mumbles that Divi's never been to Spain so how would he know what the weather's fuckin' like. He wants to say a bit more but this high temperature is bringing the stew in his stomach from a simmer to a boil. It's a bubbling potage of those four packets of cheese and onion crisps – not forgetting the pickled eggs, enough Courage Best to float a battleship and several hits too many of Scotland's finest whisky. What happens now is that Jimmy, not concentrating on the road, concentrating more on his guts, nearly misses a turning. They're very close to their destination and Jimmy just manages to croak out through his fingers and an impending flood of vomit, 'Left. Left now . . . Now.'

Divi brakes harshly and his car slides around the corner, nearly skinning a lamp post and definitely clipping the kerb.

Tom Malone had crept up a bit closer to his prey than he intended because, for the last few miles, his eyes have been lazily closing, lazily opening. Tom Malone has been swigging Red Bull, driving with the window down, but he's still been slipping into the haze of half-sleep, and that's why he suddenly finds himself almost up the arse of Divi's estate car. And that's why he overshoots the turning and loses sight of them.

By the time he's swung around in the road they've taken a sharp right. Tom, panicking like fuck, misses another one of their turnings and, by the time he rejoins his watch, Divi and Jimmy must have been out of his sight for perhaps thirty seconds or more.

Now a lot can happen in half a minute in the dark suburbs of a country town; they should have been lost to him, impossible to find, but they've not gone that far because Jimmy's stomach's on the point of a major exploding event. That's meant a screech to a halt in an emergency stop for Jimmy's imminent, emergency. There's only a briefness of time for the reiteration of, 'Don't forget. The big place – Fen View. Sign. End of the road.'

Divi is sent on because there is no way that Jimmy can deliver in his state and Himself is left standing, not exactly upright, on the pavement. Not for long though because there's a couple of dustbins at the entrance of a short, hedged drive and one of them is just the right height for relief. Then Jimmy, feeling like death, takes refuge behind a low garden wall and, flat on his back in a bed of daffodils, gazes up at the stars that are spinning around his head. 'Jesus,' he says to himself over and over again as he loses time, and a stretch of consciousness, in the swirling of the universe. This means that ten minutes later he's only vaguely aware, if at all, of the flashing of blue lights and the speeding police vehicles racing to the house called Fen View.

This rapid unexpected response seems to be more than a stroke of luck for dashing Tom Malone. It's come about because there's been an aborted raid on an illegal tobacco ring. Two vanloads of Her Majesty's finest had geared up and prepared for a monumental dust-up with a dozen Poles who've muscled into a Romanian smuggling operation. The police squad were extremely disappointed at missing a punch-up and were on their way back to the station when the call came through to divert them to Huntingdon. This call cheered them up no end and within minutes they were on their way.

These frustrated coppers like nothing more than getting stuck in – there's even three elderly veterans from the miners' strike riding shotgun. In fact, there's also the nucleus of the police Eastern England rugby team, and they're not a nice bunch as anyone who's played against a police team will verify.

Tom Malone is parked discreetly near to the target where Divi Den's estate car disappeared up a hedged driveway. He's on the blower to Chief Inspector Isaacs and he, Tom Malone, is now not very happy.

Chief Inspector Isaacs is telling him to hold fire until the cavalry arrive. 'Chief Inspector Searle will take over the operation.'

Tom says, 'Chief Inspector Searle? What?'

Isaacs replies, 'Just direct them in Malone.'

'But, sir . . .'

'Just do it Malone. I repeat, Chief Inspector Searle is taking over.'

'But, sir . . .'

Tom Malone knows the politics of the police force, and he knows where he stands in the pecking order. Oh he'll get a mention, maybe even a commendation, but the kudos, the spoils of war, will go to Chief Inspector Searle and Chief Inspector Isaacs. So instead of an aborted tobacco bust, Chief Inspector Searle will be headlining the drugs raid in the newspapers, on the back of Tom Malone's long hours and diligent application to his duty. And also on the back of something Chief Inspector Searle never knew existed until an hour ago. He's been handed it on a plate and he'd do the same for his very good friend of the Old Boys Network if the opportunity merited it.

Chief Inspector Isaacs says, 'Get yourself home as soon as you can, Tom.' His tone has now changed, like he's really concerned about Tom Malone's welfare, 'We'll sort out the details later.'

If Tom Malone had been a weaker person he would have laid his head on the steering wheel and wept. Fucked off doesn't do justice to how he feels as he drives slowly away over the Great Ouse river.

But Tom Malone doesn't go back to his lonely cottage; he goes to Boarston Station and loads up his computer. He selects his file on Jimmy Penfold and brings it up to date with the night's events. By the time this is completed and he's printed a hard copy, the day shift has started clocking in, including Chief Inspector Isaacs.

'Tom,' he says, 'have you been here all night? You look shattered.'

'Report, sir.'

Tom hands over the paperwork and Chief Inspector Isaacs says, 'Look Tom, you've worked your arse off lately. Why don't you take a few days in the sun?'

'Sir?'

Chief Inspector Isaacs taps the report with his forefinger.

'No one in here is going anywhere Tom. But you can. Take the little woman with you. Treat yourselves.'

Tom Malone thinks that the chief inspector seems a tad insistent on his partaking of leave, but then he's had a few heavy weeks and, also, this might be a way to tempt Polly back into their marriage. So he takes the time offered and the knock-on effect is that he won't get to see the arrest and charge sheets for over four days. But for now, he's going to spend his vacation – thanks to Lastsecondholidays.com – at a resort in Spain putting his own sunscreen on, and without the consolation of a reunion with Polly. (On the phone, she says, 'I can't come with you Tom. It's still too soon.' Tom Malone has the impression that Polly's mother's standing behind her and working her strings.)

A few hours previous to this, and not too long after Tom Malone had driven over the Great Ouse, Jimmy Penfold, shrammed to death in the damp air, and after spending the darkest hours in someone's front garden, has found his feet and his mobile among the flattened dykers. Through the mother of all hangovers he calls his loving brother Silas who's nursing the father of all hangovers. And this morning Silas is not a paid-up member of the Jimmy Penfold Appreciation Society.

'Fuckin' hell, Jimmy, it's only just gone five.' Silas's voice at this hour could file iron. 'Where the fuck are you? Where? Huntingdon? What the fuck are you doing there?'

Jimmy says, 'Market Square, Silas. Be quick, pralla, I'm done in.'

Silas grabs a mug of meski and leaves his sleeping family, his wife Amey, and Carter, the nearing life-sized version of himself, and winds his tall frame into his van. He takes his tea with him as he drives carefully out into the empty lanes and then onto the main drag. He's a quarter of an hour into this drive, and keeping a weather eye open for the gavvers, before he lights up his first fag of the day and promptly coughs his heart up.

Meanwhile raggedy Jimmy Penfold is making slow progress towards Huntingdon Market Square and the Thinking Soldier, where his bleary-eyed caring brother will meet him, greet him, with open arms or a bollocking. The smart money's on the latter, and it's right.

As soon as Jimmy's in the van Silas reckons that Jimmy stinks like a polecat and he rolls down the windows, turns the fan on max and lights up another tuv.

'My God,' he coughs, 'what the fuck have you been up to?'

In the everlasting excuse for postponement, Jimmy mumbles in a sigh of revolting breath, 'Tell you later.'

An hour and a half later, Jimmy is safely home. He's face down on Zilla's pearly sheets, smelling like a sewage worker and snoring like a pig. All of Zilla's slamming of doors and rattling of pots won't rouse him. And although Jimmy's sleeping away his hangover, he can't sleep away the consequences. They're out of his sight and they're gathering together and nudging each other into some sort of order before they clap into his ears.

In police matters, there's shit flying everywhere this morning and just now it's splattered, like pebble dash rendering, over the wall of the interrogation room at Boarston nick. This is where Divi Denny Vincent – delivered to these premises by Chief Inspector Searle and company – is repeating, over and over again, that he met a man in a pub and gave him a lift into Huntingdon.

'And where is this man with no name?'

'I dropped him off. He was ill. He said to deliver the drum.'

'What? A drum of paint?'

There's a rather quiet, lisping excuse of, 'He said it was urgent.'

Divi is lisping because he has a split lip. And a black eye. And cuff burns.

'Where did you drop him?'

'On the road.'

'Where?'

'I don't know – it was dark. In the street. He was spewing like a dog.'

'So you give a complete stranger a lift in the middle of the night?'

'For,' Divi Den thinks about this, 'two hundred pounds.'

'Where is it, the two hundred?'

'I didn't get it.'

'And it seems that all we've got is you, Mr Vincent.'

That's not really true because there's half-a-dozen other bods under questioning at the same station. But what's pissing off the investigating officers is that no one's talking.

'Not one fucker. I didn't expect the gippo to – you know what they're like – but the other lowlife . . . I thought they'd be singing like canaries.' All the while that no one's singing, time is being bought, tracks are being covered, computer files are being erased, alibis are being established, fall guys are being set up and some are being shut up. And if all this is not bad enough, the merchandise halted in Huntingdon was due to be passed on to Mental Mickie; he's not a pretty sight when he's upset and he tends to lose what little control he has. And perhaps that's why no one seems keen to take a chance on whispering into PC Plod's outsize ears. So the day after the event drifts into the afternoon and its aftermath. Everyone's laying low, keeping mum, because there mustn't be any panic in the criminal ranks.

It's all trickling along without anyone yet realising that the gypsy who's being charged in possession of class A drugs isn't the didikai they think he is. Chief Inspector Searle's content with his catch and Chief Inspector Isaacs, with too much on his plate, shelves the file for Detective Tom Malone's return. (Tom Malone would have known immediately but he's not in the loop, he's thirty-five thousand feet up in the azure blue.) But the others, Winston and Rubin et al., are going to find out very soon and they'll find out because there's another set of big ears in the station – that's besides the aforementioned Noddies – and she's one disgruntled, middle-aged Sergeant WPC Connie Williams, who's been passed over for promotion more times than should be permissible. But she also has problems; a gambling addiction that has cost her a marriage, a house, several relationships and too many sleepless nights that only a bellyful of booze – another addiction – can address.

Then Casino Karl, the welcoming proprietor of Lucky Place, whispers into the ear of one of the untouchables about Connie's enormous gambling debts, and what a chance it would be to get someone sympathetic to their causes on the inside. This means that for Connie there's an empathic ear late at night at a local nightclub, a beginning of a bar-stool romance carefully nurtured by a brutally handsome roughie-toughie who's not fazed by age and weight – he's starred in a couple of porn movies: *Monster Mama* and *Porking the Pig*. Then there's too much drink, too much pillow talk and too much sleeping with a known felon; troubles to add to her troubles. When the lonely, mixed-up woman is in too deep to get out, she stops swimming and sinks slowly down to the bottom. The roughie-toughie, who's filmed some of their extremely revealing sexual exploits, milks besotted Connie for info, and she feeds him useful titbits. Nothing too heavy, nothing too serious. That is until now – the big bust that Jimmy Penfold should have attended – and Roughie-Toughie wants a bite on a big juicy bone. He bares his teeth and Connie fills her lover boy in on the details of the raid at Huntingdon. She supplies names, charges, copies of statements and all the evidence that she can access from the police computers. Thanks to the power of the internet, it only takes a click of the mouse for an instant betrayal to be instantly transmitted. Connie Williams passes all of interest on to her good-looking rogue who forwards it on to all involved for the usual fees. Because in this business, money can buy anything.

In the evening after the arrests Winston is shaking his head in disbelief because it's not Jimmy Penfold locked up and under questioning it's 'Dennis Vincent. Who the fuck is *Dennis Vincent?*'

Rubin, shifting uneasily on his feet, says, 'There must have been a swap.'

'Swap? What do you mean a swap?'

'They must have traded places. You recruited the Pikey,' Winston says slowly and quietly, putting the onus onto Rubin.

'I'll sort it Winston. Leave it to me.'

'How?'

'He'll have to answer with a punishment.'

'A fuckin' punishment? The bastard's cost me an arm and a leg.'

Rubin, seeing the way this is heading, says, 'OK, it'll be an arm and a leg then. I'll get onto it.'

Winston shakes his head at the suggestion of the usual in-house enforcer. 'We need someone from outside. Don't want everyone knowing my business.' So the outcome for Jimmy Penfold's misdemeanours is that he's on the waiting list to receive two surgical small-bore bullets: one delivered with precision through his kneecap and the other with the same specification through his rotator cuff. An arm and a leg.

It might also be expected that Winston blows a fuse and goes berserk, banging that great head against the wall. But he doesn't. He pours himself a drink, lights up a cigarette, leans back into his chair, closes his eyes and says casually, 'Take a break, Rubin.'

Rubin thinks, 'Thank fuck for that,' and leaves Winston to what he's good at, organising violence.

Winston lets the cogs whirl for a while longer and then he taps in a number on his phone that reaches quite a nice flat in the Triangle in Bournemouth. A youngish man with a strong Welsh accent answers and listens very carefully to what Winston has to say. When the youngish man puts the phone down, he's smiling softly to himself. Also smiling is Winston, when he gives Rubin the message and the order,

'All set for tomorrow morning. Sort out the meet, my man.'

And so the plans are laid.

9

Jimmy's been waiting for a call from Rubin. He's worked out that something must be very wrong; there has been no word, no sight of the hide or the hair of Divi Denny Vincent.

'He must have been lelled. Must have.'

In the pit of Jimmy's still queasy stomach a couple of snakes are having a wrestling match. Christ, whatever has he done? Or not done? Jimmy can't settle; there's no mention of anything on the telly – not what he's interested in – and going for a pint is the last thing on his mind. He keeps looking at his business phone, his useless fuckin' phone that only takes incoming calls; the barrier between the errand boy and those further up the food chain.

Zilla says, 'Why don't you go and lie down, my Jimmy. I'll bring you some cocoa.'

She means well but Jimmy's on edge and snaps at her that he's not an effin invalid. She, quick to fire up, snaps back that he might not be an invalid, but he's still an effin dinalow and always will be.

After this barney Jimmy does go for the suggested lie-down because Zilla's got a mighty cob on. He'll be in the marital bed all on his lonesome and Zilla'll be on the sofa because Jimmy's stomach is still not the healthiest. Their boy, Mikey, is on

Snapchat in his darkened room and catching up on the latest news in Boarston and the surrounding area. But he does seem almost over-engrossed in some of the pictures that are coming through. Anyway, for Jimmy, at a quarter past ten *that* phone goes. It rings and rings and rings till a befuddled Jimmy, fumbling in his coat pocket, manages a third attempt at pressing green.

'Jimmy, my man.'

'Rubin.'

'Jimmy, there was some trouble then?'

'Yes.'

'You never made the delivery?'

'I was ill.'

'Ill?'

'You know. Guts and that.'

'So you subbed it out?'

There's a few seconds of silence before a subdued Jimmy's, 'Sort of Rubin.'

'Sort of? You either fuckin' did or you fuckin' didn't. Which is it?'

'It's did, Rubin. But I need to explain.'

'And we need to meet up, Jimmy. You got to give me all the details.' And to ensure that Jimmy just doesn't up sticks and disappear in alarm, Rubin drops his snappiness, lowers his voice, adds some sympathy to his tone and sets the trap. 'Look Jimmy, anyone can make a mistake. I got another drop for you. Chance to put things right. A double bubble, Jimmy. And it's nice and close.'

'Close?'

'Four hours tops, my man. There and back.'

Jimmy's worries start to recede in the thoughts of absolution and of earning an easy thousand pounds.

Then sweetening his tone a bit more, Rubin says,' I'll bring it over in the morning. It's got to be early, about seven. OK?'

He gets an OK back from Jimmy and then there's only one more detail for Rubin to address.

'Ditch your phone,' he says. 'Wipe it out. It's time for a new one.'

Rubin hangs up and mutters to himself, 'Jesus Christ. What a fuckin' mess you've made, Jimmy.'

Now the beautiful Zilla, unwittingly involved in this 'fuckin' mess', has been woken by the ringing of Jimmy's phone; the thin partition wall between them doesn't really qualify as a sound barrier. She's heard the muffle of conversation and, to tell the truth, she's had enough of Jimmy's ways these last few months. Zilla's thinking that her beloved is spending more time in the kitchema, more time in the bookies, more time with Silas and Danny, than he is spending with poor neglected her. A week ago they'd had more than just a few words about the situation; they'd had a stand-up row that most of the site must have heard. In this row Jimmy has wolfed down his breakfast, grated back his chair and has nearly made it through the door before Zilla stops him with a demanding and harshly impolite question of,

'Where is it?'

'Where's what?'

'The vonga.'

This is the day for visiting the Halifax Building Society with the proceeds of Jimmy's employment and unemployment.

'Later, Zilla. I got to be somewhere. We'll sort it out later.'

Jimmy's impatient to be gone and his voice goes up several notches. But evasion's not on the menu this morning and Zilla raises her voice way above his. (Close-by dogs and people twitch their ears and pause to listen. Everyone loves a good row if they're not in it.)

'No. Not later. We'll sort it now.'

In his bedroom, Mikey turns his music up as Zilla plants herself in front of the door. Jimmy can see she's not for the stirring.

'For Chrissake, Zilla,' says – it's more like a shout now – the frustrated and cornered Jimmy. Zilla, easily winning the noise and volume stakes, tells him that she's not moving until every effin penny is on the table. She's counted his trips and she knows what the social amounts to.

The conclusion of this set-to is that Jimmy, well down on the usual income, has some explaining to do and some promises to make. They include the usual suspects of cutting down on the drinking, cutting out the gambling, and giving Zilla the keys to the treasury.

'Soon as I get paid, it's yours Zilla.'

Of course he'll have to keep a bit back for expenses but he doesn't say that out loud.

So there's an offer to placate Zilla to which, although still extremely miffed, she spits out an acceptance and a warning.

'But no more of this, Jimmy. No more or else.'

Or else nothing because there's nothing she can do. Jimmy'll try for a while, they'll get on for a while, and the stash will grow, and then Jimmy will have a relapse. It's the pattern of their lives but the good times will outweigh the bad because of the unbreakable, and sometimes fiery, love that tilts the scales. But neither of them expected such a relapse before the week was out.

So that's why on this night Zilla lies on the sofa in the dark and broods about all of his examples of unfairness. She can add to the list his latest escapade of staying out all night – not even a phone call – and coming home smelling like he'd slept with a family of ferrets. To say she's on edge is an understatement. But she's also on edge because it's the time of cramping in her stomach, of a hot-water bottle needed on her belly. So she begins to seethe on her makeshift bed, resents being out here when Jimmy is comfortably sprawled out on *their* double bed. Zilla broods and resents and holds her stomach until, God knows how, she falls into sleep. But it seems that she's only just closed her eyes when Jimmy barges into the kitchen area, slashes the light on, fills the kettle with an avalanche of water and crashes it down on the stove. She squints an eye at the clock and it's reading a six.

'For Christ's sake, Jimmy.' Her voice is high and raised.

'What?'

'You know what.'

He doesn't know what, and a scowling Zilla, blanket draped around her, gets up to claim her rightful place in the marital bed.

Jimmy says, 'I'll bring you a cup of tea.'

Zilla snaps back, 'If you want to bring me something, bring me a bit of peace.'

Jimmy takes that as a no and leaves her to simmer on her own.

He takes his tea outside, slips the SIM card from his phone and grinds it into the ground. Job done. (Or it will be when the handpiece is drowned in a watery ditch.) Jimmy sits on his steps and kills time watching the stars fade in the sky until he gets to his feet and lights up his first tuvler of the day.

And this is also a day when other important things are being set in motion in the dirty trading that pays the wages of Winston and Rubin and Jimmy Penfold and the like. The major thing is that Rubin and Winston, in the noiseless, luxurious, big, black BMW, are driving into a partly derelict industrial estate on the outskirts of Boarston. Here the roads are unfinished – no money's put by for maintenance – and where the pitted tarmac changes to potholed gravel they pull in behind an average-looking family car. Winston flashes his lights and an average-looking man steps out. He's carrying a small holdall and he slides into the back seat of the BMW without a word.

Winston growls, 'Everything all right?'

Veryll Evans says, 'Perfect. Just perfect.'

'It fuckin' better be, the money he's being paid,' Winston mutters to Rubin.

Rubin grunts a reply. He's not saying much this morning and, if truth be known, he's perhaps hoping his old cellmate's read something suspicious in the situation and done a runner.

By the time they're into the lane at the back of Elm Hill Caravan Park, Veryll Evans has carefully and lovingly assembled his weapon of choice, and the sun is starting to poke its head over the low ground. Winston is impatiently drumming his fingers on the steering wheel and on the dashboard the clock shows a quarter to seven.

Winston says, 'He'd better not be late,' as though there's a punishment worse for Jimmy than the one waiting for him. His punishment a drilled bullet to the kneecap – an operation practised to perfection in the Troubles – and the disabling shot to the rotator cuff that'll leave Jimmy's arm dangling for a long time. At least that's how Rubin understands the situation; a lesson for Jimmy Penfold that he'll never forget – and a lesson for anyone else who might think that a consequence will not come back on them.

A mile up the lane from Winston and co., someone else is running late. He's a farmer's boy and he's not in the best of moods. Last night he had a row with his girlfriend and took it out on a gallon of rough scrumpy cider. He's overslept by an hour and he now has a hangover of immense proportions. He shouldn't even be thinking about driving his huge, shiny tractor until lunchtime at the earliest, but he'd promised to pick up a trailer load of straw at seven this morning and, come hell or high water, or hangover, he'll be there. A farmer's word is his bond.

Now in the early hours of the morning as Farmer Boy's staggering back to the homestead, belly slopping with potent apple juice, Reynard's been prowling in and around the perimeters of Elm Hill. This mangy fox has mooched around the site most of the night upsetting the local canine populace. Reynard has been doing a bit of scavenging here, and there. And tonight he's struck lucky. He has a good sniff around and then his sharp teeth split open a black polythene bag and, in moments, he's burrowing his head into the remains of a chicken vindaloo. That's soon wolfed down and then the pungency of it is followed by a good mouthful of a madras and the soft bones of a set of spare ribs. There's plenty here because everyone always orders about twice as much as they can possibly eat. So Reynard has a rare old feast, topped off with a third of a loaf of mouldy wholemeal bread which should aid his digestion. And it certainly does. And that's because this healthy-choice bread in his stomach soaks up the spicy juices of the Indian cuisine. Then the bread swells, the bran starts to work and not far from his home, Reynard has to coopy down for an enormous bowel explosion. Feeling mightily relieved, he trots back to his den to sleep off the rest of the after-effects of his self-indulgence.

In the gateway of the narrow country lane where Jimmy's been picking up his packages of late, Winston and co. are parked up and killing time. There's not a lot of conversation on their watch and, to tell the truth, Rubin just wants to get it over with. He's not looking forward to this because of his soft spot for his ex-cellmate. But it has to be done. It's the administering of the law of example and there can't be any commuting of the sentence.

Not too far away from the hit squad, Meg and Wilma are taking a breather. They've paused on their early morning walk on the edge of the beechwood copse that now tops Elm Hill. Here, Meg rests on a tree stump and surveys the land. She scans down into the park where there's morning movement now: a few faint shouted goodbyes, a couple of vans nosing out of the site, dogs on the loose.

Meg's lost count of the times she's sat up here, thin cigarette in her thin lips, and watched the site come to life. She's come up here when a gale's been roaring through the trees, when a whisper of breeze has been a sigh of relief on a scorching day, when the bright moon glittered the frost in the middle of a winter's night. And when the snow has settled, and her footprints have traced her passage on the trail to the hill.

Meg can taste these times of heat, of frost, of wet, of snow, and she shakes her head to stop past and present merging into one. She takes a deep pull on her cigarette, calls a foraging Wilma to her heel, stretches out her aged limbs. But then her sharp eyes scan across the scrubland maze, over a row of tall trees, to the lane where the black BMW is parked in the gateway. She squints through the distance, holds her gaze in her curiosity because this vehicle doesn't belong here; a luxury motor that's lurking like a predator on the edge of the narrow lane. Meg shivers, shakes her head, as a cold unease taps her on the shoulder and Zingara whispers to her of unbalance, of things not quite in place, of something vague, something that's poised to fall. And now there's Jimmy Penfold into this scene and he's picking out the weaving path between the prickly gorse and clumps of hazel, heading to where the black motor is waiting. Zingara's unease is still softly ticking like a clock in Meg's head but when she catches a glimpse of Zilla's blonde hair it erupts into a drumbeat. An alarm of sound.

No. Zilla shouldn't be here. No. They can't be here.

* * *

98

Then Meg's on her feet and, although she tries to summon it with all of her strength, she knows that her old worn voice won't carry that far in a warning for danger. Oh she tries, tries with an effort that causes a sear of pain across her chest. But her desperate shout is captured in her throat, caught fast in her breath, as she can only watch and will that somehow she'll be wrong this time.

Jimmy's been following the ups and downs of the track across the wild ground to the rendezvous at the gateway. He's making it in no particular hurry, making it more like a Sunday walk. At least that's what it seems from the outside; inside himself there's more of a turmoil and a not-too-happy feeling bubbling away in the pit of his developing paunch. But progress is being made and he's been up the rise and now he's on the downhill run. Winston's BMW is fifty yards away and closing and Jimmy's coming out of cover and he's raising his hand in a greeting. 'Just want this over,' he thinks.

Rubin is resting his arse on the wing of the car, watching, arms folded, Jimmy's approach. Winston's bulk is occupying the driver's seat and the smoked glass of the back window is slowly winding down revealing the dull metal barrel of Veryll Evans's Glock 19 Gen4. The Welsh marksman is sighting the straightest line in the whole world and the unknowing Jimmy Penfold casually strolls into that perfect line of sight. Like a lamb to the slaughter.

In the few seconds before the cough of the shot, a bird is singing a sweet, sweet song of the early morning from somewhere in the white blossom of the blackthorn. And floating across the field from Elm Hill site, there's a snatch of the booming bark of a large dog. And in the high trees, roosting like sentinels, silent and watchful, are two score of coal-black birds; a funeral of crows.

From the shelter of the beech copse a quarter of a mile away, Meg sees the dark forms clouding those high trees, hears a whine forming in Wilma's throat. And the fragrance of this morning before everything must change is sweeter than the birdsong. It's the scent of bluebells and the white May and the spring grass; all things that are in the first breath of a new day.

Zilla's not here to enjoy, or even notice, anything of nature. Her simmering in the bedroom has now graduated into a furious boil-up that's blown the lid off the pot. She'd heard Jimmy clatter his cup into the sink and waited for at least an enquiry of, 'How're you feeling?' or 'Can I do anything for you?' but there was nothing, just the slamming of the door and he had gone.

And I bet he'll disappear for most of today and I bet he'll be down Ladbrokes, then the Flying Horse, filling his belly with beer till he sees his time to come home.

Zilla's really got a cob on and she's going to tell him what for. She's flung herself out of bed, thrown on her coat over her nightdress and followed her erring man out of the site. Zilla's a picture of wildness; her hair is flowing free and in those beautiful green eyes there's a hint of the temporary insanity that the full moon sometimes brings. She's a little behind Jimmy but gaining on his start, unseen and shielded by the straggled heights of gorse. She doesn't want the favour of a patronising stopping for her, so Zilla's striding it out, ready to present herself to him when *she* chooses. She'll catch him on the lane, stop him in his tracks. She'll stand in front of him, tell him to his face just how it is. Make him listen. She wants some attention. She wants to be taken notice of at any price. And the poor beautiful gypsy rawnee doesn't know how high that price will be. And then she hears a sound like the crack of a whip cutting through the early morning.

* * *

The exact line that Veryll Evans has sighted is on Jimmy's poll, right between his lying eyes. And Veryll Evans is a man who's rarely wide of the mark; it's his profession and the success rate for this snappy Welsh dresser is good. In fact he's top man in his trade. So now there's the squeezing of the trigger and the sharp cough of the Glock in this once peacefully still morning and then the stunning impact of a 9mm bullet delivered exclusively to Jimmy Penfold. His head snaps back and his legs skid from beneath him. He sprawls on his back, face up to the sky, sixty feet from his former cellmate Rubin. He doesn't hear that former cellmate explode with, 'What the fuck . . .?' as weapon in hand, Veryll Evans slides out of the back of the BMW. He calls to Winston, 'I'll just make sure,' in his soft Welsh accent.

Jimmy's on his back with blood beginning to cowl his face as his body lies deathly still in the dewed grass. Veryll Evans has taken three steps out of the twenty needed to make sure when through the green gorse Zilla steps into range. She sees and is seen in the same instant of time and in Zilla's instant a series of images scald into her eyes.

There's Jimmy, her Jimmy, laying crumpled on the ground. There's a black car, a Black man, and there's someone else pointing at her. Pointing at her with both hands. Pointing at her with a gun. Zilla, torn between running away or running to Jimmy, does neither.

Veryll Evans is nothing if not quick and, of course, very very accurate. The Glock is up, is directed in an almost casual precision at Zilla, held in his hands and the trigger is squeezed gently, and slowly, and for the second time on this beautiful morning. Now it seems like time has taken a suck of air and is exhaling slowly, breathing out this tableau, breathing out the execution of the innocent.

It's more than a good shot because the distance must be thirty metres before it hits Zilla exactly where it was aimed for. And the last thing Zilla ever sees on God's earth is that wisp of smoke from the Glock. Then there's the whistle of the bullet streaking towards her at the velocity of death, reaching her before the bark of the gun. There's the numbing whack of impact and the deep scorching penetration of hot metal into yielding flesh and bone and a soft, soft heart that falters, slows, stops. Zilla's chest is torn open to the morning sun and the bright red of her blood marks a scarlet blooming between her breasts. But she doesn't instantly collapse, she sinks slowly, almost in dignity, to the green grass. It's as though death is a little reluctant to claim her.

Above Zilla the black-feathered crows have taken to the air. They're wheeling and diving, climbing and tumbling, as Zilla's bruised and bewildered soul flutters from her body and seeks the freedom of the heavens. This soul twists, it turns, it soars in avoidance of the hard, cruel beaks of these birds of carrion. Its shape, its passage is formed by these spiralling catchers of the spirit and only a few folk – the ones with the gift – might hear a faint, distant voice calling out for something familiar in this strange new world.

Rubin is angrily shaking his head in disbelief at the double cross, at the replacing of two limbs for two bodies. But now it's done and Veryll Evans has taken another couple of steps towards Jimmy Penfold, who is lying deathly still and bleeding like a stuck pig.

In a recap from last night, foxy friend Reynard had been rummaging through the bins and had discovered the delights of Asian cuisine. Unfortunately, and fortunately, it also gave him the most upset stomach in the history of scavenging, and he dumped the ample proceeds of that escapade on the descent to the lane, about sixty feet from where Winston was to park his car for the execution of Jimmy Penfold. What were the chances of Jimmy stepping onto that slippery pool of pollution and his feet kicking from under him at the exact moment that the Welsh marksman lined up Jimmy's head for a dose of hot lead? What would that be? A million to one? More? Well, Jimmy's won the lottery, gone through the card at Ascot and is holding a royal flush in his hand. All at the same time.

He still took a stunning, creasing blow that knocked his head back and left him with a permanent centre parting through his thick dark hair. (In the future he'll look like a matinee idol from the 1930s.) But to anyone observing, he's been dropped. Finished. Yet if that anyone was to kneel down and put their ear to his mouth, they would hear the rise and fall of life.

As Veryll Evans starts to take another step towards Jimmy's prone form to deliver the coup de grâce there is, from further up the lane, the diesel roar of a tractor and the clattering bounce of a trailer. This is Farmer Boy, with his cider-hangover, bombing down the road like a bat out of hell. He's tried to phone the object of his desires this morning but she's not picking up. So he's pissed off . . . His foot is hard on the accelerator and the huge wheels of this monster tractor are sucking at the tarmac. The long flatbed trailer is being dragged around the bends and the whole carnival is bearing down on Winston's gleaming BMW at a frightening rate of knots. They need to get a move on, because the body count is rising and what was a single contract killing has the potential to turn into a mass slaughter.

Winston is revving up the motor and bellowing at Veryll Evans to get in the car. 'Now! For fuck's sake now!'

Veryll Evans pauses in his stride, even though what he'd really like to do is hold that Glock right up against Jimmy Penfold's head; he'd like to take a long slow pull on the trigger. But he's seventeen paces from Gypsy Jimmy and there isn't time, because

Winston's bawling again, 'For fuck's sake now! Now!' Because Farmer Boy is actually in sight above the hedge line.

Rubin's holding the door open for a quick getaway and the Welsh assassin swivels in his stride and sprints to the motor.

So Veryll Evans is in the car, Rubin's in the car and Winston's wheel-spinning from the off. They're only just in front of the wurzel who's hit the brakes and is skidding, snaking, up behind them. And this concentrated avoidance means that Farmer Boy goes sailing past the gateway, mouthing obscenities at the boot of the rapidly departing BMW, without a glance into the killing field. That also means, that apart from Meg, there are no witnesses for the prosecution. This country lane won't see the mailman for at least another hour and the milk tanker won't be doing its pick-up until tomorrow. All in all it looks very much like there's been a clean getaway. And all this has happened in less than the thirty seconds from when Veryll Evans lowered the smoked glass window of the BMW and levelled his Glock at Jimmy Penfold's poll.

What Winston and company have left behind is the beautiful Zilla, torn and bloodied and broken in the wet grass. All that loveliness is gone to waste, all her hopes and dreams are draining with her warm blood into the cold earth. It's going to be some-one's thankless task to tell Jimmy what's happened. And then there's young Mikey to think of, who at this moment is pouring the last of the milk over a bowl of four Weetabix.

What should occur now is that there should be a call to the police and to the ambulance service. This piece of ground should be requisitioned behind 'Police Crime Scene. Do not cross' tape. It should be crawling with gavvers and a tent should be pitched over Zilla. Jimmy should being stretchered off to hospital to be attended to. All of this in the usual process of these matters. So this is what should occur in a predictable, civilised world where everyone does everything by the book, where everyone is a law-abiding member of society with a duty to inform the authorities of any misdemeanour. That's how it should be.

But this is a different world and in this world someone wanted Jimmy dead. And because he's not, that someone will come back to finish off the job. So he may just as well be dead. Or seen to be dead, and that's not quite the same. Life would be a lot easier, a lot safer for Jimmy if the earth was shovelled onto a pair of coffins and a headstone erected to a couple that death could not separate.

Jimmy and Zilla Penfold
Taken so cruelly from us.
Together Forever.

Putting distance between them and the scene of the crime, Winston, Rubin and the psychopathic Welshman are driving away more steadily than you would have thought. There must be no attracting of attention, no breaking of speed limits, nothing to allow a slip twixt cup and lip. Inside the quietly running motor, Rubin's voice is loud. He whacks the dashboard and says, 'You said a lesson, Winston. An arm and a fuckin' leg. Not this.'

Winston says quietly, 'Mind the upholstery, Rubin. And mind your mouth; this is my show.'

'But—'

'Don't disrespect me, Rubin.'

Rubin shuts his mouth because he's trapped; there's no chance of avoidance for him in this. He was the bait, Winston was the planner and Veryll Evans the executioner. There's silence in the car now because a seething Rubin knows that in the eyes of the law he's as guilty as they are in a murder of joint enterprise.

In the back seat of the motor the Welshman, smiling softly to himself, is enjoying the ride in this luxury BMW, the only sound the swish of the tyres on smooth tarmac. Then it's rutted tarmac. And then it's pitted gravel. And then it's the exchange of money for the spilling of blood.

Winston hands Veryll Evans a fattish brown envelope and says, 'Half now and half when the heat's off.'

Veryll Evans says, 'That wasn't the agreement.'

Winston says, 'It is now.'

Veryll Evans says quietly, 'Two weeks, Winston. Then the rest.'

He gets into his car. Veryll Evans is not smiling now.

10

At Elm Hill the beautiful Zilla is being lifted gently, lovingly, into a bed that still holds a little of her fragrance, a residue of the warmth of her life. She's being lifted in by Silas and Danny and to say they're upset would be playing things down to zero. Silas can't get past muttering, 'The bastards. The bastards,' over and over again under his breath. Danny just shakes his head in time with the words. Then, alone with Zilla, Meg lifts a quilt over her, covers her body and her wounded heart. Meg sits beside Zilla, strokes her face, smooths her hair. And she talks to her of Jimmy and Mikey and how Zilla's not to worry about them and how, one day, they'll all be together again. Then she kisses Zilla softly on her cheek and gently closes the bedroom door on beauty and the stillness of death.

Mikey, the part-orphaned chavo, is standing bewildered outside his home. There's smears and spottings of his mother's blood on the steps, and he's staring at them like he can't believe what's happened. Carter, tall and lanky cousin that he is, has his arm around Mikey's shoulders and he's talking quietly to him. But it doesn't seem as though Mikey understands or even hears the words being spoken. Of course, there's the other Travellers here – there's nothing like a murder to get people out of bed. Romeo and Juliet are among the scene of sad, shocked faces who whispered into silence as Zilla was carried to her bed, and when a stunned, bloodied Jimmy Penfold was stretched out in Fred and Emma Flowers' park home, ruining their sheets and mattress. (Emma's pretending that it doesn't matter but secretly and guiltily, because she's extremely house-proud, she's wishing Jimmy was lying next door where they're so mauzey a bit of blood and gore wouldn't make much difference.) There always seems to be an unholy amount of bleeding from a head wound and Jimmy's sticky mass of reddening hunnel hides the fact that the wound is a flesh one. There may be a newly constructed runway over the top of his poll, and a concussion to his brain, but there's no deep damage. Nothing that a man skilled in treating injuries on the battlefield couldn't put right as a matter of course. So although not badly hurt, Jimmy Penfold must receive medical attention and Meg's slipped away to make an early morning call to Captain Surgeon (rtd) Benjamin Day.

And at this time of the day, where else would he be found except on his smart patio at his smart house on a smart estate. It's breakfast time al fresco and the girls are eating toast and marmalade – and Herself is already on her third cigarette of the day when the phone rings and one of the girls – Penny the eldest – beats her sister through the patio doors in the very important race to be first to answer.

Penny picks up the phone, politely recites the family's number and then asks, 'To whom do you wish to speak?' in a perfect parody of her mother. Posh Penny listens and then reverts to type as she shouts very loudly, 'It's for you, Dad.' And Dad, Captain B. Day, gets up from the table, takes the phone from her sticky little fingers and says,

'Hello?'

'Kushti duvus, drabengro.' He answers immediately, automatically in the rokkering that nowadays he doesn't hear or speak that often.

'Kushti duvus, Meg.'

He says it at normal pitch but in the quiet of this morning it carries to Vanessa who freezes mid-drag on her Silk Cut. *That* woman again. So soon? She looks at Benjamin sharply; she may not know what he's saying but recognises the intensity of his listening. She knows it can only mean one thing – trouble.

Inside of ten minutes, Benjamin's in his car with his medical bag – both of them belted to their seats. Vanessa is not looking best pleased as she lights a cigarette off the stub of her last one and asks, 'Will you be long?' through his driver's window.

'Can't say, Vanessa.'

In exasperation, she says, 'You don't have to go.'

'You know how it is, they're my family.'

She wants to scream at him, 'And we're your family too,' but she doesn't because she's a polite well-bred lady who just happened to marry into one of those dirty, low-down, didikai families. This isn't strictly true because she didn't *just happen* to marry him. Theirs is a long story that weaves together the lives of a colonel's daughter and a brave medical doctor. But it's enough to know for now that he's on call to Meg; she has a private line to her personal physician.

The connection to Meg started on a stormy afternoon over forty years ago. It's sultry and hot and the world's been waiting for the weather to break. Which it does with a vengeance. The heavens open and the rain bounces off the trailer roofs of this Travellers' site in the middle of not-so-sunny Sussex by the sea. The rain also bounces off the roof of an open tin shed where there's a pot of strong, stewed tea, along with tinned milk, sugar, crusty loaf and a melting saucer of butter, sitting atop of a forty-gallon drum. Lounging in this shelter from the storm is Eddie and Marion Day and two of their many brood, Jack and Jill (that's not funny for the chavees). There's also Meg, and this Meg of forty-odd years ago, is a bit of a looker. She's got meat on her bones and her hair is raven black. At Meg's side is Wilma's great-great- (God knows how many greats) grandmother.

Eddie Day says, 'But Meg, you know how difficult it is for the likes of us.'

Marion Day says, 'I'm worried for him; if he goes he won't know no one.'

What Marion Day is concerned about is that the future Captain Surgeon Benjamin Day, barely eleven -years old, has been offered a scholarship to a well-known school – a public school that encourages public duty. The boy's headmaster has recognised the potential of a young Traveller boy, nurtured him to the top of the form and put him forward for this once in a lifetime chance. But what Marion and Eddie Day are also worried about is affording the expense of this strange new world. There's too many mouths to feed, too many bodies to clothe and money is beyond scarce for them. But it's not scarce for Meg and she quietly takes the reins for provision, adopts the cost. And so for Benjamin Day, it's not a life of field work through the seasons, the cold wet, the hot dry, the brewing-up under the bor, the knocking on doors of the kennas. He'll rub shoulders with a different sort of people and he'll step in and out of his different lives. But Benjamin Day is of the type who will never forget where he comes from and that the helping works both ways.

* * *

On call, Captain Surgeon Benjamin Day pulls into Elm Hill Caravan Park in his shiny Volvo and takes his bag of tricks into the Flowers' home. There, laying on the once clean sheets, his head a mess of bloody matted hair, Jimmy, with the worst headache in all the universe, is moaning softly. What follows is a cutting away of hair down the pathway of the bullet's passage, a gentle washing and cleansing of the wound, a potent injection, and Jimmy is sleeping like a baby.

Not sleeping like a baby is Frank McFarlane – Gingerman to everyone that knows him on account of his hair colour – because he, like Zilla, is in eternal sleep, but his is for a more accidental reason.

The last day of Gingerman's life, two weeks before, began fairly ordinarily when his alarm went off at six and his wife, short and a bit on the plump side, with a flare of red hair, mumbles,

'Ohhh, turn it off.'

Mrs Gingerman is on the plump side because she's pregnant. Again. There's already, in the bedroom next door, two curly-haired, freckle-flecked boys soundly sleeping. In the room next to them, two curly-haired, freckle-flecked girls are also sleeping soundly.

Gingerman goes down to the kitchen and boils up the kettle while he's cutting up his sandwiches for work. Then he makes two cups of coffee and carries them up to where his wife is sitting up in bed, savouring a few minutes' quiet before the kids wake up and squabbles start. They share the five minutes of peace.

She says, 'You won't be late back?'

He's a delivery driver and he has a run to Newcastle.

''Bout six, if I'm lucky.'

What they don't know is that he'll never be back and these words that he's saying now will be the last she hears from him.

And the light kiss on her lips will never happen again. (She'll kiss him once more but it'll be when he's so cold to touch it makes her shiver.)

Then he's down the stairs, the front door shuts behind him, the van starts in the drive and his last day ticks remorselessly onwards.

Mrs Gingerman comes downstairs and lays out four bowls of cornflakes. She calls her brood to breakfast and then puts her hand to her belly because she feels a kick from the unborn. She wishes Mr Gingerman could have felt it before he went to work but she'll tell him tonight, and he'll put his hand on her stomach and they'll both hope to feel it together.

But they won't.

All this is happening barely a dozen miles from Elm Hill Caravan Park. In fact they're in the same local paper area – the *Boarston Bugle* – so the did and Gingerman families read and share the same news. Also television's *Spotlight* falls on places they know, people they know. But they don't know each other and probably never will.

Mr Gingerman takes the M5 and then the M6 to deliver machine parts to a suburb of Newcastle that's not important, and also what's not important is the rest of his day until he's fifteen miles from home on his return journey.

It's a cool day for May and there's a misted rain sweeping into the afternoon; visibility on the road isn't that great. Gingerman has the radio on loudly – *Steve Wright in the Afternoon* – and the heater's set low, pushing a gentle sleepy warmth around the cab. He's following in the slipstream of a monster lorry with Polish plates that's throwing up dense clouds of spray. This lorry's in the middle lane to overtake a Land Rover that's towing a horse trailer that's glued to sixty miles per hour in the slow lane.

Now Gingerman might have avoided his fate if an old biddy, who's braved the fast lane for the first time on a hundred-mile journey, hadn't found herself doing eighty mph. There's a black Jag up her arse pushing her on and she panics, just enough to pull sharply in front of the Polish juggernaut which has to hit the brakes and . . . it's wet and slick and the wheels lock. It draws the vehicle into a snaking skid that sideswipes the horsebox. All of this happens in a couple of blinks of the eye and Gingerman misses the first blink because he's doing what so many do when they're driving; he's on his mobile. It's not even an important call; it's some prat trying to sell him an upgrade.

What Gingerman has to briefly worry about is trying to avoid the rapidly slowing melee in front of him. But he clips the left-hand side of the lorry trailer and takes the back of the horsebox on his front wing. That impact crushes the wing onto his tyre which blows out like a cannon shot. And this takes away what little control Gingerman has and the van, now broadside on to the road, begins the initial roll of three roof-denting, glass shattering turnovers at the end of which Gingerman will be no more of this mortal earth. Meanwhile the old biddy has sailed on, oblivious to the chaos unfolding in her rearview mirror. (When she hears about the accident on the ten o'clock news, she'll say to her hubby, 'How lucky for me, I must have just missed that.' Also on this news item there'll be more time spent bemoaning the putting down of two injured horses – cue sad-faced animal-loving presenter. Then it'll be mentioned, almost as an after-thought, that a van driver died at the scene.)

A fortnight after this terrible accident, it's late in the after-noon on the day of Zilla's killing. Meg's sitting in her motorhome sipping a cup of tea and wishing it was something stronger but she needs her head to be as clear as a bell. She's cast her thoughts out far and wide, thrown them to the four points of the compass, let them soar with the swallows in the open blue sky. But there's nothing, coming back to her. Not even an echo. Wilma, picking up on Meg's mood, slinks out of the door; she doesn't fancy being a whipping dog today. Meg's thinking hard, scheming hard, trying to put everything together. But the jigsaw has pieces missing; and it won't meld. And also, there's no service on the crystal ball; it's been fogged up for hours. There's a breeze coming in through the window and it's rustling the pages of today's *Boarston Bugle*. It's peeling them over, shuffling the news of the area in and out of view. And then the breeze stills and a page settles down, smooths itself out, and Meg, cup of tea in her hand, sits to read. She reads of the forthcoming funeral – tomorrow – of local man Frank McFarlane – known to his friends as 'Gingerman' – who was tragically killed in a road accident two weeks ago. He's left behind a pregnant wife and four children under the age of eight. His widow says, 'He went to work and he never came home. I don't know how to tell the kids.'

There's a rather nice press photograph of Gingerman posted alongside the text. It's a head and shoulder shot and so well defined that anyone who knew him couldn't fail to recognise him. In this picture his hair is standing up as only ginger hair can do; it looks like he's seen a ghost. But it's Meg who goes cold. It's Meg who says to herself as she traces his features with her finger, 'You. It's you.'

And then suddenly clear in Meg's mind is that sad, sad dream with a bewildered Zilla reaching out for help, for an escape from the future.

11

Jimmy is stretched out on Mr and Mrs Flowers' double bed, being watched over by Benjamin Day. He's been cleaned up and the stripe of raw flesh through the middle of his hair has been treated by the battleground expert. The worst thing that he could now do is regain consciousness and so, of course, he does. He tries to sit up.

Benjamin Day puts his hand to Jimmy's chest, pushes him gently back down.

'Easy,' he says. 'Easy.'

Jimmy mumbles, 'What happened?' and then in his mind's eye there's a clear scene of himself walking towards the black BMW. A tall tree in the hedgerow is holding an audience of sable watchers which flutter and cajole, like they're arguing for the best seat in the house. In this scene Rubin's lounging on the bonnet of the car but also there's the movement of the smoked rear window sliding down. And then what Jimmy sees and hears in the same instant of time is the dull glint of the metal barrel of the gun and the cough of the discharge. There might be a millisecond of time before he's laying face up to the morning sky and he can't move and his eyes won't close and, before the blackness rolls in, he's sure he hears Zilla calling, screaming, his name.

'My Zilla?' he asks urgently. 'My Zilla, Ben?'

Ben Day, with his soldier's training and his first-hand know-ledge of the dead and dying, slowly shakes his head. 'Mullered, Jimmy. Mullered.'

'Dead? How can she be dead?'

But she is.

Zilla is laying in the marital bed, cooling into her death, and her long smooth limbs are setting into rigor mortis. Ben Day lights up a tuvler for Jimmy, pours him out a mug of sweet meski and watches as Jimmy grapples to understand the enormity of what's happened. He whispers,

'I want to see her, Ben. I want to see her.'

It's more than a want, it's a must see, and with Ben's support, he enters his home for the last time.

Zilla is in eternal slumber. She's lying in their bed and she's been washed and her hair has been brushed out. There's fresh make-up on her face and her lips are painted with bright lipstick. All this has been done by Meg who's sitting beside Zilla, stroking that beautiful face, smoothing that thick blonde hair and whis-pering in the language of the dead. Black-and-white Wilma is lying at Meg's feet, curled up comfortably against her toes.

Meg whispers, 'Here, Jimmy,' and she gives him her place, lets him seat himself on a watching of the dead; a touching of lips on cold flesh in this ending of it all. That's as clear as it gets for now because the sedation and concussion is putting such a tiredness into him that his eyes are clouding and his head is drooping.

'That's enough, Jimmy.'

Ben draws him away, helps him back to the Flowers' abode where he can sink into a temporary forgetfulness for a few hours.

Up in the north of England, Winston and Rubin are listening out for news. But it's too early yet for any confirmation of the misdeed. There's nothing on the radio, nothing on the internet.

Winston says, 'For fuck's sake Rubin, there's got to be something soon.'

What's going through Winston's head are the reassurances of cast-iron excuses; the witnesses that will, if needed, cover their tracks. These professional alibis will lie for reward without consequence, suffer the consequence if they don't. Winston goes over and over and over it because something doesn't seem quite right. Nearly but not quite. It doesn't quite add up to perfection. And vivid in his mind is what Veryll Evans was halfway to doing before Farmer's Boy loomed up in his roaring, bucking, monster tractor and frightened the shit out of them. What was missing was that coup de grâce; the insurance of bullets in the head for Mr and Mrs Penfold. *Just to be sure. Absolutely sure.*

So while Rubin is skinning up on the sofa and thinking, 'What a fuckin' lousy mess,' Winston is waiting for a confirmation of success, a few words from the media that a heinous crime has been committed. Completed.

As he waits, Elm Hill Caravan Park is on virtual lockdown. Eyes are peeled for strangers. There won't be text messages flashing from phone to phone; no tributes on Facebook to a *Wonderful Friend*, a *Beautiful Mother*. All this has to be kept secret, buried deep from the light.

12

The next day, handsome CID man Tom Malone is back in the country. He's taken an early flight and he's in Boarston by late afternoon. That means that he turns up at his mother-in-law's house with a bunch of flowers and a box of chocolates from a Tesco's garage while the night's still young.

Polly spots him through the window and watches him walk up the driveway. She wants to rush to the door, melt into his embrace, feel his strong arms around her, taste his mouth. But her mother gets to the door first and she wants none of these things. She fixes Tom Malone with the gorgon look and he freezes in his tracks.

'Yes?'

'Polly in?'

'Yes?'

By now Polly's joined her mater in the doorway. 'Tom,' Polly says. The pleasure of seeing him is in her voice – there's a side-long glance from Mother as she tuts and retreats inside.

Tom holds out the flowers and the chocolates and that's enough to entice Polly into his car.

The uncoupled couple take a drive out to a quiet country pub, the New Queen, where they have an early evening meal of steak and ale pie, peas and chipped potatoes. The waitress, young and shapely and so sure of her looks, sashays from kitchen to bar to table. Every male eye follows her movement except for Tom's; he sees only his china doll opposite with her pale hair, pale skin and, under her dress and what he can't see, her pale porcelain body. But if the waitress catches the male eye, when Tom Malone crosses the floor to the gents, there's almost a hush in the female conversation and so-sensitive Polly picks up on this. But, for the first time since the trouble, she feels, amid the jealousy, a tinge of pride at the envy of others. While Tom Malone drinks halves of Guinness, she sips quite a nice Merlot. Actually she has three glasses and it goes straight to her head. She relaxes, basks in Tom's attention and puts, temporarily, their trouble to one side. He tells her that his Spanish holiday was a miserable experience without her and Polly's secretly happy that he was unhappy. Then she has the irresistible urge to slide her leg under the table and tickle Tom's tackle with her toe. Irresistible it is and it causes Tom Malone to nearly choke on a mouthful of barley brew. That's because it's been so long since Polly made a move on him, and it causes an instant acknowledgement to her interest. The bill's paid in record time and the car is heading towards the local common at slightly more than the speed limit.

It's the time of twilight on this track – one of many that wind through the trees – and there's still a few hound walkers about, but descending night and a pattering of rain will soon send them off home. Also it's a bit early for the dogging brigade to be out in force so Detective Tom Malone and Polly get down and dirty with indecent haste. A stronger word than urgent would be needed to describe the pent-up longing between them. It seems to Tom Malone that things must be back on track now and normal service will be resumed, that they'll go back to her mother's, pick up Polly's belongings and head off to the little cottage of their dreams.

A sated Polly is now adjusting her dress, clipping up her bra and pulling up her white panties. Tom Malone is tucking himself away and thinking about knocking on his mother-in-law's door, giving her the good news, and watching for the horror and disbelief on her face.

That'll be a moment for Tom Malone to savour indeed. But then from the rear of the car there's a small, sad voice that quivers with the question of, 'Did you do it with her in the back seat too?'

No preamble to this shock of words. Polly has suddenly gone from hot totty to weepy wronged woman in the wink of an eye. Mother Nature has had what she wants for now and things are running back into recent course.

'I just can't stop thinking about it, Tom. It won't go away.'

'But it wasn't like that, Polly.'

But in effect this mentioning means that the evening's over; his single taste of infidelity has raised its ugly head yet again and ruined a reunion.

A silent and tearful Polly is dropped at her mother's and Tom Malone travels back to his lonely bed in his lonely cottage. Still, Tom Malone feels that he's made progress and the drive home is not one of thwarted desire. It's not perfect but optimism is knocking on his door so he's actually humming along to the radio as he drives.

Tom Malone is still humming as Mrs Gingerman is sitting alone in her deathly quiet lounge and reading aloud the poem she's going to recite at Gingerman's funeral. She wants to say it from her heart, without a stumble, without a tremble in her voice. Without notes. It's a task she's set herself to fill the chasm between the accident and the burial and every day she's added one more line. She's sitting with Christina Rossetti in her lap and she's going over and over the poet's words.

Remember me when I am gone away,
Gone far away into the silent land . . .

She whispers it over and over again, this eulogy to her flame-haired husband. She's pictured herself on a wet Sunday afternoon standing by his gravestone and hearing herself speaking the sweet sadness of these words.

. . . Better by far you should forget and smile
than that you should remember and be sad.

Mrs Gingerman checks on her sleeping children and she goes up to their – hers now – bedroom and brushes out her red hair until it hangs just like Elizabeth Siddal's. She wants to look her best for her husband's funeral and he always loved her hair.

Right now Mr Gingerman is in the funeral parlour of Messrs Bury and Pitt, and he's laid out in the dark of his pitch pine box. He's dressed in his best suit – his only suit – the one for weddings and funerals, and the coffin's lid has been screwed down on him. Gingerman is prepared for his final journey to Saint Mary the Virgin on the lower side of the town.

The premises of the aptly named Messrs Bury and Pitt consist of a level yard behind two wrought-iron meeting gates. Inside the perimeter there's two open garages where the hearse and the trailing cars are parked up. And then there's the funeral parlour-cum-carpenters' shop; an old brick building with a sharply pitched slate roof and a thick-planked padlocked door.

The hour is sometime between one and two o'clock in the morning and the moonlight is soft in the chilling night air. The surround of the whole town sleeps and dreams and snores like Llareggub. But inside the funeral parlour it's as quiet and as still as the grave. There's the smell of planed wood and clear varnish and of rather a strong disinfectant. The corners of this room are deep and dark and the ghosts of a hundred burials are watching from the lime-washed walls.

There's some light filtering through the barred windows and it glitters onto the simple brass nameplate:

Frank 'Ginger' McFarlane
1984–2018

There's not a breath of sound in the air until there's the intrusion of a metallic clash and the sharp snap of a bolt cropper clipping through the padlock on the door. Then there's a smattering of voices and a gleam of a bald head and of a tall, lanky figure stooping through the door, dragging a tarpaulin sheet. It's loaded with two stuffed sacks of logs and straw packing – approximately twelve stones, coincidentally the weight of a man. These two intruders are straight into the purpose of their visit; a quick flash of a torch over the workshop and then the sound of the unscrewing of the coffin lid. This is achieved with an erratic electric driver that Silas bought for a tenner off one of the Irish boys in the pub. But on the last screw erratic becomes kaput.

Gingerman has been dead for quite a few days now and, although he's not starting to smell too badly as yet, he has the scent of death on him. He's also as stiff as a board and anyone who's ever lifted a two-week-old body will know that it doesn't bend, doesn't give a fraction, and that there's a chill to it that sucks the heat out of your fingers. Silas reckons they could stand him up in the corner while they have a smoke, but Danny just wants to 'get the job over with 'cos this place gives me the fuckin' creeps'.

Five minutes later, the coffin's packed with the wood and straw and the lid's screwed back down. This screwing down is now courtesy of a nearly new Bosch drill that a brevitting Danny has discovered in a tool cupboard and it, along with a plunge router and two impact drivers, will be taken to a new home very shortly. (The Irish boy's dead drill is to be interred in the box with no body.) Mr Gingerman is wrapped in a stretcher of tarpaulin, carried by the gypsy bearers furtively across the yard and heaved into the back of Silas's ubiquitous white van. All this is taking place in the light of the fitfully shining moon that's waning its way to the end of a month that's been life-changing and life-taking.

Silas's van is soon over its rather short journey from Boarston to Elm Hill Caravan Park and it rolls to a halt outside Jimmy and Zilla Penfold's static home. Meg's waiting there at this ungodly hour, cigarette glowing in the dark and, under her instructions, Silas and Danny heave Gingerman up the steps and into an adulterous scene of the dead.

Gingerman and Zilla, this unlikely couple, strangers in life and death, lie in a comprising situation of lovers sharing a white-sheeted bed. On their still, cold bodies the gentle glow of the side lamps shows the red hair and the blonde hair of this unsuited pair.

Meg pushes Jimmy's platinum ring onto Gingerman's third finger on his left hand, and then steps back and appraises the scene; the scene that's a fulfilment of her premonition.

The illusion must now continue and it commences with a chip pan full of cooking fat, bubbling away over a full-on gas ring. Bubbling away. Boiling away. Spitting over the sides of the pan and becoming hotter and hotter until, like in those now outdated TV ads for safety, a quick-thinking mother throws a damp towel over the flaming pan and starves the fire of oxygen.

Only this isn't a TV ad; this is a contrived conflagration that is going to consume with a speed that's virtually unimaginable. Molten fat drips to the floor, pools on lino, gathers its yellow strength and then eats into the floor, the kitchen cabinets, into the extremely combustible comfort of the furniture. Already the kitchen window has popped out and the ceiling is buckling towards the floor. Partition walls crumble and in the bedroom the onrush of this furnace blast pours up the draping duvet and into the bed of deceit. Gingerman's hair, Zilla's hair, become instant halos of flame. Then smooth flesh and freckled flesh start to sizzle and cook in a banquet for the Devil, in an all-consuming roar of cremation.

They watch the burning in silence. It's in a silence full of sadness, shock and, for Jimmy, remorse. He's propped himself up in a chair like an old man, with a blanket around his shoulders. He's in the glow of the flaring of the firing, the sparks spiralling into the night sky from this flaming beacon of lies. And by God, does it burn. It falls in on itself, fuses vinyl, wood and plastic, and emits the pungency of the furnishing and the stench of melting rubber.

The flames of this funeral pyre are lighting up the night sky and it must be visible for miles around so it's time for Meg to phone the fire brigade. Within thirty minutes, a gleaming red fire engine with flashing blue lights is on-site, and a team of hunky, uniformed, helmeted men are shooting jets of water onto the smoking remains of Jimmy and Zilla's home.

The firemen have arrived too late to be of any use and the man in charge asks Meg if there was anyone in this inferno. She states simply that it was a Mr and Mrs Penfold and that it was lucky that their boy wasn't in there with them. Ten minutes later a police car draws up with two officers who proceed to tell everyone to stay as far away from the fire as possible. Then it's the same question that the fireman in charge asked and not much else besides. There's an interruption to this when the ambulance finally arrives. Silas says, 'No use turning up now,' to the immediately defensive crew. They've been covering from the next town and could do without any aggro. Then Meg says that she'll make a brew of tea and the fireman in charge says that would be most welcome. The heat's killing him.

At first light, the fire is out and all that's left of Jimmy and Zilla's home is a heaped and blackened spread of wet, burned spoil. Sheeting is being erected around the scene and fire officers are starting their investigation. They're already picking at the edges of the burning, sifting and prodding at melted metal. And soon they'll be prodding at blackened bone.

On the morning of the fire, Tom Malone's already had a shave and he's softening his Shredded Wheat in hot milk. He's about to flick the telly on for the early news and he's wondering how he's going to fill his day when, like providence has been watching him, his phone rings and he clocks his station's number.

'Detective Sergeant Tom Malone speaking.'

Chief Inspector Isaacs, bluff and hearty, says, 'Tom, I was hoping you'd be back. Been glad of a break, I'll bet? Look I know you're still signed out for a couple of days but we're a tad overloaded at the moment and we could really do with you back in harness. You remember that gippo you were trailing? . . . Penfold. That's it. Well his caravan's gone up in flames and, unfortunately, he was in it so it means there'll have to be some sort of investigation. You know all the usual bumf, liaise with the fire service, etc. So if you can get yourself down there sharp-ish and get the ball rolling it would be much appreciated. Oh, and tread carefully; ethnics and all that. Oh, and his missus was in there with him. See you when you get here, Tom. Make it asap. I'm up to my ears with appointments today. '

The phone goes down and Tom Malone, not having got a word of reply in, sits with his spoon of Shredded Wheat nearly to his mouth, wondering what the fuck is going on – or rather what the

fuck went on while he was sunning himself in Spain. He's thinking that surely Jimmy Penfold was taken into custody in the
Huntingdon raid? And, surely, he wouldn't have been bailed yet?

Tom Malone gets himself down to the station in double-quick
time to an extremely hasty meeting with Chief Inspector Isaacs
and then pulls the up-to-date report of the Jimmy Penfold investigation – *his* investigation – out of the files. And what reading
that makes when he sees that a certain Dennis Vincent, whom he
knows nothing about but presumes was Jimmy's driver, is banged
up. There's no mention at all of Jimmy Penfold. Odd doesn't
explain it. Tom Malone leans back in his chair and mutters,
'Jesus Christ.'

'He won't help you, sir,' says WPC Maria Fiore. This WPC,
young and very keen, has been assigned to help Tom Malone in
investigations into the fire at the Elm Hill site. She'll be doing
the cross-checking, a lot of the footwork and also riding shotgun in the motor that Tom Malone has been issued with from
the carpool. Earlier, in their hasty meeting, Chief Inspector
Isaacs had presented Maria as the perfect choice as Tom Malone's
assisting officer because, as Isaacs put it, and with a not-so-
subtle reference to the cause of Tom Malone's fall from grace,
'You shouldn't get up to any of the funny business with this
one.' This delivery is accompanied by a grating guffaw. The
reason Tom Malone shouldn't be able to get up to any 'funny
business' is because WPC Maria Fiore is a respectable married
woman. She tied the knot a year ago with the super-athletic
WPC Carol Oates, a tall and spare football player of renown
who is pushing for a position in the national team.

They're happy these two, they're building careers together, and
now Maria has the chance of putting herself forward with the
attachment to DS Malone. Carol, five years older, and

considerably more experienced in police work, gives her the benefit of that experience.

'Watch him,' she says. 'Learn from him. He's good at his job.'

'I'll keep him under close surveillance.'

'Not too close I hope,' Carol says in mock seriousness.

'As if,' says Maria and they laugh together.

In Manchester the news of Mr and Mrs Penfold's demise puts the lid on any lingering doubts niggling at Winston. He nods his great shell-shaped head in relief and says to Rubin, 'Hey man, it's cool. It's cool.'

Rubin supposes it is but all the same he'll miss his pikey pal. He'll think about him, perhaps imagine him, when he drives past a scruffy gippo's site. But now it's back to business proper; there's no room for sentiment because there's orders to fulfil, merchandise to move, imports that are riding the night waves of the dark sea and looking to dock in a lonely Cornish bay.

Life has to go on and Mental Mickie is screaming blue murder because his delivery is several days overdue and he's got a family to feed. And why the fuck is he dealing with a bunch of fuckin' amateurs when he only has to make a call to Ali the Turk and he can get what he wants on time? Winston has to gently, carefully, remind Mental Mickie that they are in a contract and he promises a filled order with a sweetener attached. Now things are settling into some sort of order after the upset, Rubin's found someone a bit more, actually a lot more, reliable than the deceased Mr Penfold to make the deliveries.

The deceased Mr Penfold is being moved over thirty miles away from Elm Hill. He's being driven carefully by Silas and watched over by his personal physician, Benjamin Day. Captain Day has been absent from his family for longer than Mrs Day wants and she's texting her pissed-offness at his continuing absence.

Do you know how much longer you are going to be away? The girls have been invited to Abigail's party on Saturday and it would be good if you could make it home before then.

There's no text language from Vanessa; she's too posh to abbreviate and she doesn't have to use coarse vocabulary to put her point across. But she's addressing a man who has applied field-dressing under enemy bullets, so he does what he always does: he soldiers on and ignores the incoming fire. Soon he'll pack up his bag, though, and tell Jimmy to keep his head clean, before leaving his people to their ways. Until he's needed again.

These three men are jolting slowly along a rough, gravelled track in the van. It looks like a road to nowhere but, in fact, it leads to an old, stoned yard where a roofless farmhouse and tumbledown farm buildings sandwich two static caravans. A holiday park this isn't but the statics are clean and serviced and liveable. All of this sits in about thirty acres of high-grown hedges and forsaken fields. A running band of wild-looking horses and a dozen shaggy and fierce-faced cattle roam up to the boundaries of this unworked land. Magpies clatter their displeasure at any intrusion and skudgies take to their flimsy treeline pathways in aeriel acrobatics. Generations of rabbits are holed up in overgrown borders and at night in the fields, there's the flashing of a lamp in the coursing of hares. This place holds firmly onto its remoteness and secrecy – bit like Doone Valley – and it should be a perfect hiding place for the recovering Jimmy Penfold.

The proprietor of this neglected homestead is Little-John Wells. His father had reputedly won this property on the turn of a card in the year before the Second World War. The father had pulled his vardo and his family into the stockyard on a cold afternoon in the first snow of that winter and Little-John, born the following January, was named in contradiction because he was a bouncing ten-pound baby. Age has stooped him over the years but he still stands at six feet four, is as wide as a door and bears a remarkable resemblance to Hagrid. He's a bachelor and the last surviving member of his family. He's buried his mother, his father, his sister and his brother, not on the farm but in a proper churchyard with slate-grey tombstones to mark their time on God's earth. His company now is a couple of monster Irish wolfhounds whose eyes follow his every move.

Jimmy sits by a log fire at night with Little-John and his dogs. They share a few beers and twists of Old Holborn. There's not much chat, Little-John is not renowned for his conversation, and most of the time Jimmy is silently brooding on recent events. He's lost the love of his life (his fault) and has had a permanent parting put through the centre of his hair (not all his fault). He's contributed to Mikey becoming an orphan (well, half an orphan and half his fault) and now he can't even go out to the kitchema in the evening because he's supposed to be dead. All of this sounds rather flippant when it's put against the cold killing of the beautiful Zilla but it's easy to imagine how guilty Jimmy's feeling. He needs some time to adjust to what's new and pick up the threads of his life again.

Also picking threads up, but for different reasons, is Meg. On a morning visit, and on a slow walk in Little-John's wildlife park, she says to Jimmy, 'I want you to tell me; I want you to tell me it all. Everything. From the first day.'

They stop the walk and Jimmy thinks for a minute, and then begins to talk.

Meg listens, sees Jimmy's world through her glittering eyes. She lives it with him, absorbing Rubin the cellmate who cast the line, the glimpse of shell-headed Winston at visiting time, the hooded scrote who supplied the merchandise, the drops at far-off places, the swap with poor Divi Denny Vincent, who will be looking at a curtailing of his freedom. And Jimmy tells her the lot. No stumbling over details. No hiding of names or identities. It's like a session with a psychiatrist, or confession before the Communion, for Jimmy. There's a mighty relief after all the words have tumbled out. Petered out.

Jimmy says, 'If I could have known where all this would end, my Meg. If I could . . .'

Then he shrugs because it's not ended yet, not for him, and the sentence doesn't need a finish to it, because Meg's already thinking about, and already addressing, the issue of unfinished business.

She'd started that addressing three days ago when, from the edge of the graveyard of St Mary the Virgin, she'd watched the ceremony for Gingerman's funeral in a mark of respect.

Ashes to ashes and dust to dust don't really suit the burial of a couple of sacks of logs. It certainly wouldn't suit Mrs Gingerman if she knew she was grieving for sawn beech, split oak and a bulking of straw. It's she who scatters a handful of earth onto Gingerman's coffin and then leads her bewildered red-headed tribe out of the graveyard.

13

Back at Elm Hill Park, the remains of the burning show a patch of scorched concrete that no one'll walk over because it may bring diss bok; it's unlikely that anyone will pull a waggon onto this cracked hardstanding for a while. But life, as it must, goes on and a pack of screeching, shouting, mixed-sized, mixed-aged and mixed-sex chavees are racing their bikes hell for leather around, and in and out of, Elm Hill Park. The circuit is a figure of eight across the site, through some non-existent fencing, past a totally disinterested Harry Potter. (The other two ponies are taking refuge at the furthest point away from the clamour.) There's no finishing line to this Tour de Park but numbers drop off with each circuit, until there's more watching than riding. There's also the smell of the cooking pot in the air and the jukals are raising their noses and sniffing the breeze. Not all of them though because a certain black-and-white collie-cross is sitting in the front passenger seat of Meg's motorhome. The engine's idling and Meg is chewing the fat with Dangerous Danny Delaney.

And this is a Danny who's being told to wait by Meg because he's threatening to take an eye for an eye and a tooth for a tooth. The trouble is he doesn't know who the enemy is and he could fuck things up if he goes off not fully cocked, asks the wrong people the wrong questions. So Meg reins him in, gives him a severe talking-to.

When Meg has gone, Danny slips his feet into his trainers, puts on his tracksuit and runs a circuit along the lanes of just over five miles. This circuit ends with a climb up the rise of ground to the summit of Elm Hill. It's not quite Rocky Balboa powering up the steps of the Philadelphia Museum of Art but the aim's the same. But Danny's no Rocky and he's not going to be fighting Apollo Creed. In fact he's agreed a six-rounder with Sinbad the Tailor for a ton a round. This scrap is scheduled in three weeks' time so a bit of extra – or even some – training might give Danny an edge. And that's a might, because at the moment he's mopping the sweat off his bald poll and wheezing like a set of bagpipes. The wheezing isn't helped when Danny tugs out a packet of cigarettes and lights one up. He takes a sigh of contentment and nicotine and feels he deserves it after all that exercise.

For now, Danny's sitting on his damp arse on the hill and thinking if he can get an early dig into Sinbad, catch him cold like he did Masher Monty, he could get an extra century as a KO bonus. He's also thinking that this exercise has given him a raging need for the taste of a long, cool pint of Wadworth 6X. He stubs his cigarette and trots down the hill for a quick wash and brush-up.

An hour later, Danny's standing at the bar of the Black Horse in Boarston with his morl wrapped around his second pint of the aforementioned Wadworth.

Bert the landlord says, 'Christ, Danny, you've got a thirst on tonight.'

Danny grunts, he's not in the mood for talking, 'Been a long day,' and takes himself and his drink to the quiet end of the bar.

In fact the whole room is quiet – it's midweek – and Danny sits at his table in the Black Horse, nurses his beer and broods. He broods about the hurt done to his cousin. He broods on finding the man who pressed the trigger and put Jimmy under the doctor and Zilla under the ground. And while he's brooding, he's drinking; by the time Silas brings his lanky frame into the kitchema, Silas is already three pints behind.

Early the next morning, while Danny's nursing an aching head, Meg and Wilma are in the glades of green in the beautiful royal county of Berkshire. They're driving down a winding drive between a pillared gateway, off the Nine Mile Ride, Finchhampstead, to a large house set amid an acre of mature trees and lawn. This house is built of pale facing brickwork with a style that could be interpreted as over-detailed. Every opening is arched, every corner picked out in Staffordshire blues, every window Georgian framed. It's built on money that had been carefully gleaned from businesses that it's best people keep their beaks out of. And it was built, nineteen years ago, by Ollie Cooper, who's now opening the front door to Meg and her jukal.

This grey-haired mush must be seventy if he's a day and his face is a giveaway of a life lived to the full. He's a tall, well-built man and his nose is bent to one side. On his neck there's a half-round scar, the result from a thrust with a broken bottle. These are the reminders of his past life, what he sees in the mirror every morning. And surely, no one should be wearing as much gold as Ollie Cooper? Thick gold chain around his neck, a thick gold bracelet on each wrist and a thick gold hoop in his left earlobe. Christ, he even shows two gold teeth when he smiles his greeting to Meg. This is a man who's not afraid of being noticed.

In the kitchen of this rather splendid house, Wilma gets a bowl of water and a bread crust to chew on and Meg gets a nice strong cuppa.

Ollie says, 'It's been a while, Meg.'

'It's about Jimmy Penfold,' she says.

Ollie looks straight at her. 'Jimmy Penfold?' he says and narrows his eyes, 'I heard that he'd been mullered, Meg?'

'Not exactly, Ollie,' says Meg. And she begins to tell the story of Jimmy's decline and fall. She tells it through two cups of tea and two thick slices of toast and butter, and continues it on a walk around the property.

It's so quiet here, so peaceful here, so green here, in these grounds of mowed lawns, bright early summer flower beds, gravelled paths and trimmed hedges. It's so peaceful apart from a shrieking blackbird that warns of human presence and a pair of pigeons moaning and a dog that's caught a whiff of Wilma and marks its territory with a deep bark from a hundred and fifty yards away.

In this garden there's a wide patio, a twenty-five metre swimming pool and a summerhouse big enough to house a cricket eleven. The main house and this garden are the epitome of middle-class success and taste except for the siting of a twin-wheeled Westmorland Star caravan that's parked up on a hard-standing. Its polished chrome is gleaming in the morning sun – even more than Ollie's bands of gold – as they take the step and go inside.

Ollie says, 'We've come a long way since the old days, Meg,' and Meg replies, 'We have, Ollie,' and they talk about the way life has changed in all the years that have flowed under the bridge. There's an easiness to their talk, a closeness of intimacy that might suggest, if anyone was a tad gossipy, that they had a bit more in common than a shared lifestyle. But if they did, it lays unspoken between them. They come back onto the subject of Jimmy Penfold and Meg says, 'If they know he's alive, they'll come for him.'

Ollie's shaking his head because he knows of Winston and Rubin and the Black Mancunian Mafia and the price that's paid for crossing their path. 'They're a bad lot, Meg. I'm glad I'm out of all that.' But he's not, not really. OK, he isn't doing the dirty work anymore but there's always a contact, always a favour to honour. And it's no big deal for what Meg wants; a passport for a man and a boy to be *bichedy pardee o pani* to the lovely country of Ireland, to the land of forty shades of green.

Ollie says, 'Give me a bit of time to sort it, Meg.'

'And what will be the cost, my Ollie?'

He looks at her. 'For you,' he says as he holds out his hands, opens his palms, 'it's nothing, Meg. Nothing at all.'

Meg steps out of the Westmorland Star and calls up her black-and-white jukal. Wilma's slow to answer because she's found a rather interesting deceased and rotteningly melting rabbit in the hedgerow and the smell is out of this world. If she could just scrabble that thorny blackthorn to one side, she could get a taste of heaven, but a commanding 'Wilma. Now,' intrudes and sullenly, resentfully, with ears flattened and tail dragging the ground, Wilma slinks back to the fold.

There's another element to be included in this meeting and it happens when Meg starts up her motorhome. She's dropped her window down and Ollie's saying to her 'to visit again and don't leave it so long next time'.

Meg says, 'There's just one more thing, Ollie,' and Ollie, a broad smile showing his gold-capped teeth, says, 'Anything yer want, Meg.' It's a jocular, light-hearted affirmative that nothing's too much trouble for an old friend. But it's strange how a few words can wipe that smile off Ollie's face, can freeze him in an instant.

Meg says quietly, barely audible above the tick-over of the engine, 'I want the name of the man who killed my Zilla. I want the man who pressed the trigger and the man who ordered it.'

Ollie says, quietly, 'Meg, this is best left alone. They don't fuck about, this lot.'

Meg says, 'Just names and details please. That's all, Ollie.'

As Meg drives away, she can see Ollie receding in the mirror. He's standing outside the fine brick-built symbol of his successes, slowly shaking his head. But without Meg's help a long, long time ago, he'd probably be looking out of a barred window and yearning for the freedom of the world. He owes her. And that is why, four days later, Meg's phone pings and all she needs is on her screen. It contains the answers to her request for names and a couple of lines telling her the passports and tickets are being sorted. And for her to be careful. That last line makes her smile. She copies the text into her book of secrets and presses delete to wipe the message. Then she leans back in her chair, closes her eyes and slowly begins the weaving of a new thread.

14

A month later back at Elm Hill Park things are getting back to normal. The bodies, or what's left of them, of the beautiful Zilla and the supposed Jimmy Penfold, have been released for burial and are in the premises of Messrs Bury and Pitt. (For the Gingerman, it's like a second home.) The coroner's passed her verdict of accidental death and issued the usual warnings about checking smoke and heat detectors, and also delivered a monologue on the dangers of chip-pan fires and the relative high incidence rate among the poorer families in our communities.

The local paper, the *Boarston Bugle*, reports:

Local Traveller identified by his platinum ring. Virtual cremation in caravan fire. DS Thomas Malone told the inquest that the intense heat of the conflagration had made it difficult to obtain any DNA samples. The coroner, Ms Jane Moody, accepted the evidence of a platinum ring to confirm the identity of Mr James Penfold. Mrs Zilla Penfold was also identified by her jewellery.

For the Fire Investigation Service, FO David Symonds said the cause of the tragedy was almost certainly a classic chip-pan fire which spread rapidly through the mobile home.

What's to follow is that now that the bodies – bones really – have been released, the funeral can take place. And this is a Travellers' funeral and that'll mean there'll be a very good attendance with the usual fleet of pick-ups, vans and small lorries. These will be haphazardly parked on verges and on pavements, and there'll be a lot of rough-looking folki discharged onto the streets and into the cafés and the pubs.

The service is at 2 p.m., which means that there's plenty of time for a few livveners before the interment. And beer means drama so there'll be occasional flurries of trouble in the local hostelries. Nothing serious and at the end of the day everyone will go back to their homes. And the filled graves – side by side – will be a mound for a score of wreaths and crosses and bouquets of bright flowers.

Much later the graveyard's emptied of the living and the moon's risen above the church tower. The rows of tombstones are pointing out the lunar sky, and the scent of the funeral flowers and fresh earth are hanging heavily in the still air of the night. The only sounds here are the hoot of an owl from a dense yew tree, and the clock that chimes the lonely hours to the field of the dead. It chimes the two strokes after midnight and then there's a slow crush of footsteps on the gravel path.

It's no surprise that this person furtively approaching is Jimmy Penfold. He has a titfer on his poll and he's buttoned into a voluminous black overcoat with the lapels turned up to his cheekbones. Jimmy stands on the damp grass in front of Zilla's resting place and lights up a cigarette behind a shielding hand. And then he rests his jacksy on a convenient tombstone. Jimmy slips a flat bottle of Lamb's Navy Rum from his pocket and in the moonlight of this cool and silent place he draws on his cigarette, sips the alcohol and talks to Zilla. He tells her of their story that began at Elm Hill Caravan Park one very early morning in a June of sixteen years past.

And in this remembering

the sun's barely tickled the foot of the gateposts and Jimmy's packing a mattress into the back of his newly, and proudly, acquired Transit van. Then there's the hitching of Silas's trailer to the towbar and Silas, now making an appearance, is rubbing his eyes and yawning,

> *'Christ, Jimmy. What time do you call this?'*
>
> *'Early,' says Jimmy.*
>
> *'Too fuckin' early I'd say.' But that doesn't stop Silas lighting up a cigarette and barking like a dog. Then Silas says for Jimmy to be careful and not to forget that he needs his trailer back in one piece. There's a shaking of hands and Jimmy drives out of Elm Hill for a fortnight on the drom. He reckons to pick up a bit of trade, scrap metal or anything he can turn a few bob on, and return hopefully richer than when he left. He'll have a drive around, camp up here and there, make his own way and his own luck in these weeks of travel. So that's the plan and that's what should have happened but young Jimmy, a slightly flash Jimmy, behind the wheel of his fairly new Transit, calls into a Travellers' camp south of Bedford. His intention is for the staying of a couple of nights on this small site before he drifts slowly back to Elm Hill. But he hadn't reckoned with the attraction of Amos and Violet Williams' extremely attractive granddaughter, Zilla. And the attraction is two way because Zilla is soon taking the passenger seat on Jimmy's business forays into the surrounding districts. She's a worker, this young woman. She doesn't mind getting her hands dirty, she'll help with lifting, with sorting metal, with knocking on doors. So Jimmy's couple of nights*

become a couple of weeks and they become an inseparable couple. It then follows that when Jimmy's van and trailer pull out of the Bedford site that Zilla's taken complete ownership of the passenger seat.

Amos and Violet Williams weren't exactly unhappy about losing their granddaughter because, just lately, Zilla had become a blooming beauty and was in danger of becoming a bright beauty, just like her mother, Lois, who'd caused no end of problems for them, especially when she had run away with the son of the local Chinese takeaway owner and left them holding baby Zilla, the daughter of Paddy Maguire (who'd only stayed one potent night in Lois's arms before taking himself off to the old country and promising to be back in a month, to never be seen again). So, it's with an almost sorry relief that her grandparents find out Zilla's in the good hands of the young and fairly respectable Jimmy Penfold. So for the two lovebirds, it's a slow rambling journey across Dorset and Somerset.

Jimmy's a good-looking boy, almost man, with his thick hair desperately searching for, and not finding, a parting. And Zilla's a stunning girl, almost woman, young and fresh and more than pretty.

In these early days, she's squeezed up to him in the front of the vehicle as closely as she possibly can. Behind them, in the towed trailer, there's a muddle of scrap metal: copper pipe, lead trays, brass fittings, a couple of cast-iron manhole covers. This is the home of their working capital and the Transit is their living van. Inside this vehicle there's a mattress, bedding, Calor Gas bottle and ring, a galvanised bucket, a plastic washing-up bowl and a silver churn of water. There's also an orange box full of bread and tea and all the groceries of needs.

The Undead Gypsy

They dwell on the road, young Jimmy and Zilla. They camp for a couple of days here and there, living from hand to mouth, and plenty (the jealous might class it as an excess) loving. It's a wandering existence from jobs on farms and metal salvaging to the odd bit of choring on opportunity.

This is a dry hot summer of sweltering days and star-filled nights. Their oodrus is the thin mattress and a summer quilt and, for Jimmy, there's the waking in the small hours when the air is chilling down and the drawing of the covers over his sleeping beauty. In the morning, the kharvi goes on the gas ring and sweet tea is brewed and sipped and Jimmy rolls up his first tuvler of the day and then takes a walk for his functions and to give Zilla time to wash and dress. She's a clean girl is Zilla; she fills the plastic bowl with warm water, wipes herself down with a soapy flannel and dries herself with a well-worn towel. Then she buttons herself into her dress for all occasions. And sometimes she wears something underneath it, sometimes she doesn't. And sometimes she shows him when they're driving along the lanes. Somewhere, towards the end of this glorious, glorious carefree summer, Mikey is conceived.

Jimmy tells the rest of their story, of their years together, in a long prayer of remembrance. He tells her in a low monotone, a mumble really, and it's like he's reminding Zilla so that she will hear and never forget. In this story, she ages from sixteen to thirty-two, and there's where it stops because there's no life left after that. And guilt sidles alongside his words. It slithers into his sentences. Accompanies his apologies. It won't let him go when his body's drained, his head's drained, the bottle's drained. Jimmy doesn't want to go, to leave her in the deep, damp earth, but the sun is biting into the eastern skyline and a choir of sparrows are nagging at the dawn. He's shrammed and he's shivering in the morning air and it's time to disappear before the world wakes up. Before he leaves, Jimmy whispers a goodbye from the undead to the dead and he makes an oath to his wife and a promise to himself. That promise concerns what's stowed in his inside pocket and carries a magazine of eight bullets – courtesy of Little-John Wells and his connections.

The object of Jimmy's oath – arguably the best-looking Black man in town – is attempting to put the bite on a certain Angel Ashanti. This girl he is trying to pull is seventeen years old. This object of his not-so-honourable intentions is still at school. Or would be if she went, although with respect to Rubin, he didn't know her age when he first spotted her through the dim, smoky atmosphere of Smokey's Bar.

Rubin's had a lot going on lately – there's been a God almighty bust-up with Freedom and they've bitterly called it quits – and also on this day, there's a row with Winston about a distribution deal that he'd – Rubin that is – set up with a street gang from Wolverhampton, aptly named the Wolverines.

Winston says, 'You should have checked it with me,' and he shakes his great head slowly. Rubin says, 'They had to have an answer,' but he's thinking that Winston's been on edge recently 'cos there's been some testing forays into his territory; some scumbags from Stockport have been beating up a few runners and choring the merchandise. Winston's putting together a plan to draw them in and he needs a juicy worm on the hook, a sacrificial lamb named Larry to lure the Stockport Scumbags to a secluded meeting and take them out of the game and, while this is being formulated, he's like a bear with a sore head.

Rubin says, referring to the previous matter, 'The man had to get back; there were people waiting.'

Winston says, 'You should have cleared it with me.'

Rubin, over-emphasising his patience and speaking really slowly, responds, 'It was deal or no deal. There and then.'

'You should have . . .' Winston stops, taps his bald skull. Taps into what's really bugging him. 'Fuckin' Scumbags,' he says. 'Gotta teach them not to mess with me.'

Rubin, now unsure of the status of the Wolverines says, 'Winston, do you want me to call it back?'

'What? No. No, that'll be all right.' Winston waves Rubin away. 'Let me think, man. Just let me think.'

Then he starts to talk through the luring of the Stockport Scumbags and Rubin's pulled into a plan for a vicious, disabling beating and also, because that's the way it is now, a take-out of the leader of the pack with a bullet to the head. Winston and his mob have to be more ruthless than the enemy, have to send out a message by delivering a lesson that'll frighten the shit out of all and sundry. They have to be badder than bad. But it won't be delivered in these clichés; it'll be something original, something that'll reverberate throughout this world and enhance a growing reputation. While Winston carries on with the thinking and planning, Rubin's had enough and he takes himself off for a stroll in the evening drizzle.

And a smoke.

And a steady drink.

Only it's more than a steady drink – he's working his way through every bar and club within the confines of the manor. In this time the drizzle turns to a hard pelt of rain from the invisible sky beyond the streetlights. This rain bounces off the pavements, fills the gutters and gurgles down the drains. It's a night that so far hasn't added anything positive to Rubin's mood.

About midnight, he takes himself down a concrete flight of steps, past a disinterested bouncer who's sheltering in the

entrance, to a basement establishment. The bouncer is nonchalantly pulling on a joint the size of a finger and he waves Rubin
inside with, 'Yeah. Go on in. Barman will be glad to see someone.' Then he laughs at his own joke. But the small, dimly lit
establishment isn't entirely empty and the barman isn't a man.
It's a girl and it's the very lovely Angel Ashanti.

Angel's an interesting girl. She's got a dog of a single parent, a
dad, Smokey, who's just about keeping his head above the water
and who is, at the moment, lying on his bed, staring at the ceiling
and listening to old-time ska – think Prince Buster – and partaking of a toke. Angel's an only child and her mother left for heavenly pastures when little Angel could barely walk. Now people
leave for many reasons: brutality, infidelity, boozing, gambling,
drugging. It usually takes a hard woman to leave her child and
the reason has to be an exceptional one. But Angel's mother
wasn't a hard woman but she was a strong woman, strong enough
to take a lift to the top of a high-rise car park and step out onto
a cloud of misty morning air. For Angel's mother there was no
other way to still the voices that were whispering away her sanity.
    Smokey never speaks of her to Angel but he keeps her picture
by his bedside and every night puts his lips to the cold glass.
Sometimes Angel will sneak into his room, hold her mother's
image and try to remember her. She'll look for life in a fading
photograph.

All these years after the tragic event this chance encounter
between Angel the Barmaid and Rubin the Punter has come
about. And it's because Rubin's had that bit of a ruck with
Winston and he needs a few drinks to dull his frustration, his
anger that he might be first lieutenant but he's not always up to
making first choice.

The other coincidence is that Angel's father is laying on his bed with a swirl of good old ganja smoke misting the ceiling, clouding his thoughts about his missing wife. Some nights he can't be bothered to make the small talk when he's serving out the drinks and he'll call his under-age daughter to take over the bar.

'Angel,' he'll yell up the stairs, 'give me a hand.' Angel'll sigh, close the laptop on her Facebook and take her place behind the pumps, in front of the optics and the rows of soft drinks and bottled beers.

'An hour,' he'll say in passing, 'an hour to clear my head.' But Angel knows that the hour will become two hours, three hours, all of the hours. She'll put the shutters down, cash up the till while Benny the Bouncer checks the doors and windows. But all the cashing up in the world can't hide the facts that the bar is treading water. This place needs investment. The walls could do with a lick of paint, the floor could do with new staining to cover the old staining, the light fittings could do with new bulbs: and a few more regular customers of an evening would be a godsend.

Although not exactly that godsend, Rubin drags up a stool to the counter while Angel's serving, along with some good-natured chat – a trio of young braves who are talking loudly. Rubin doesn't really notice her yet because she has her back to him and he's distracted by the catching of his own reflection in the mirror on the wall behind the optics. He's giving it the once-over. Christ. Just look at me! Four hours on the piss, a designer stubble he wasn't planning on displaying, added to a crumpled, damp jacket, doesn't make for a smooth operator. Rubin grimaces.

'Seen something you fancy, sir?'

He turns to a sweet voice, a sweet smile and a face that's openly – maybe deceivingly so – innocent and he says, 'I have

145

now.' The soon-to-be-known-as Angel laughs. 'I'm not for sale, sir.' But in this laugh there's a sense that she might be just a little wary of Rubin. He's a big guy with wide shoulders and scarred hands, and he has the look of a man who could, possibly, be involved in some bad shit. But he's also very good at working his magic on the susceptible, so who could possibly blame Angel Ashanti for daring herself to take a bite of the apple. And what chance does young Angel really have against this experienced man of the world? Conversely though, what chance does Rubin have against this unspoilt beauty?

The night moves on. New custom is non-existent and it's still pissing down outside and Benny the Bouncer has pissed off, the young braves have finished their pow-wow and left on a hunting expedition. There's only Rubin and Angel in the bar and Rubin buys her a drink and they sit together and talk. And it's all in the easy talk, the same wavelength talk, that turns into that all-important, all-revealing, first conversation. Rubin gets to learn that Angel's father is living here, running this bar for fuck-all wages, because he's working off a bad debt to Imperfect Pete – so called on account of his outsize flappers. In a year or maybe two, Angel's father should be unshackled. But Smokey knows, and Angel knows, that it won't be long until another scheme leaves the offing and he'll be back owing money to the wrong sort of people yet again.

So, that's the initial meeting between Angel and her hand-some suitor. From now on, most nights in fact, this close to thirty-year-old man and this young girl spend as much time with each other as they can. It's not always easy to arrange because of Rubin's commitments to Winston and the fact that he's on a permanent call. But when Angel's lying on Rubin's bed with her black hair spread on his pillow and his big brown muscular arms around her, he might let the phone ring on.

Now Rubin could be classed as an arch seducer of a young and innocent girl because that's how it might appear. But that would mean that this relationship is only being taken at face value and that beauty is really only skin deep. But the fact is that Angel is not exactly innocent – she's had boyfriends ever since she developed boobs and bum and if anyone knows how to take advantage of her looks, it's Angel. While her suicidal mother partook of the black dog and a high step into the morning mist, Angel is the opposite. She loves life; she loves the thrill of being the girly-friend of a Face, hangs onto Rubin's arm in the street, onkers to join him at venues of restaurant and club. She resents the long hours that he has to put into his profession.

'But I want to be with you all the time,' she purrs at a lustful Rubin as she pirouettes around the room, holds a dance pose in the mirror.

Rubin says, 'There's places you can't come, Angel.'

Angel replies throatily, 'I can come anywhere, Rubin.'

And she can, and she does.

She comes in the back of Rubin's car. She locks her legs around him in a dark doorway at three o'clock in the morning. She's unexpected, surprising, in her loving and right now they're spending more time together than apart. So Rubin's not at all concerned when he comes home one afternoon to find her sitting on his doorstep with all her clothes in a couple of bin liners. It's the next logical step into their relationship.

Angel's so excited to be moving in with Rubin that she accidentally forgets to take her pill. At least she tells herself that it's an accident when she finds that it's a whole week's supply that she's missed. 'Cos she wouldn't be calculating an insurance policy in the form of a miniature Rubin, would she?

15

While all this is going on Jimmy Penfold is still holed up with Little-John Wells, but he's becoming restless. In this time of nothing much to do Jimmy's mind replays *that* early morning time and time again. He goes through every second of the walk towards the gateway, towards the BMW where Rubin's lounging on the bonnet.

'A trap,' Jimmy thinks. 'The bastard set me up.'

This obviousness he repeats to himself over and over until there's a rhythm to the words, to the images, right up to the moment when the Glock barks. Jimmy'll sit by the evening fire with a fag in his mouth and a bottle of beer in his hand. Sometimes he'll be there for hours until the night is deep and dark, just thinking. And planning. Thinking and planning.

And pissing off Little-John Wells, who phones Silas and moans, 'You gotta take him out for a while; get the mush outa my hunnel. He sits by the yog like a mulla. He's driving me fuckin' dinilow.'

Jimmy's not daft though; he knows he has to pull himself together. It's like he's been waiting for his mind to strike a spark and fire up the old Jimmy. He could also, provided he keeps well away from his old stomping grounds, slip away for a beer or two. It would help and it wouldn't be too much of a risk 'cos everyone thinks he's been well and truly barbecued anyway. Well, not everyone, because folki at Elm Hill know he wasn't in the fire. And then there's Silas. And Silas's wife. And Danny. And of course there's Meg who's told Ollie Cooper. And so on and so on. But there shouldn't ever be a reason why anyone mentioned would want to dob Jimmy in, should there? And if they were going to, they'd have to be quick because Jimmy Penfold and son will soon be in receipt of passports and tickets for the free land of Eire.

So what circumstances might possibly make young Ricky Ward, small-time crook and user of stolen credit cards, even consider such an action? Especially not him because he's a resident of Elm Hill Caravan Park and a cousin twice removed from the unlucky widower. And blood – however diluted – should always be thicker than water. This Ricky Ward is one of those immoral characters who really doesn't know right from wrong. Just can't tell the difference. He was a pain as soon as he could walk, as soon as he could seize anything shiny in his grasping little fingers. His parents – with enough to do looking after another three children – should not be blamed for leaving him on his own at the tender age of seventeen. They'd had enough of him even before they pulled their long trailer onto the Elm Hill Park several summers ago. Mrs and Mrs Ward, bitterly ashamed after young Ricky chored a hundredweight of lead from Silas's scrap heap, exiled him from the family home. Ricky's father, a man as honest as the day is long, had sited a caravan on the edge of the site and banished his unpopular son to it. But as if that wasn't hard enough for the poor misunderstood lad, young Ricky comes back from Boarston early one evening to find his family have deserted him; they'd shaped up and shipped out. There was only a couple of dustbin bags left behind to show they were even there. So young Ricky has lived a lonely existence and fed himself out of tins, packets and microwave meals. But he's not as clever with his mind as he is with his fingers and he disappears regularly to alternative accommodation in the nearest place of incarceration for young offenders. So you can see that Ricky Ward, felon of growing distinction, is not a man you would entrust with compromising information.

Lanky Silas and Dangerous Danny, like the good fairies, grant Little-John Well his wish for some solitude. They turn up on a cold wet evening to take Jimmy to a backstreet kitchema where the bar's virtually empty and the beer's so good that it's soon sliding down gullets smoothly and quickly. The two unlikely minders are here to watch Jimmy and to keep him out of the public eye. That is to make sure he doesn't get a bit leery and cause any drama. But there's not much chance of that with Jimmy. He's hardly smiled all night and his conversation's been non-existent. (Earlier, he barely registered a thank-you when Silas and Danny delivered his beloved Iveco van to him.) So they sit and drink and it's so quiet that Danny reckons there'd 'be more life in a morgue' which isn't the choicest of phrases he could have selected.

Silas says that they're going to bring Mikey over for a few days now that things have calmed down. Jimmy just nods as though he's got more on his mind. And he has, much more. Jimmy Penfold takes a deep breath and starts the telling of his thoughts. 'There's something that's got to be done.'

Something that's got to be done? Two sets of ears prick up.

'What?' says Danny. 'What's got to be done?'

Jimmy Penfold shows them what's in his head, what he's brooded over every night in front of Little-John Wells's smoky yog.

Silas makes the mistake of asking him if he's thought it through and Jimmy, firing up a little, says he's thought of fuckall else since *it* happened. Silas reckons it's a shit plan and it would be suicide going into the lions' den. Danny, up for some action, doesn't agree. He says who'd expect a dead man to turn up on their doorstep?

Now to anyone looking in – the barman in this case – it's easy to see there's some sort of disagreement going on between these rough folk. Their conversation is in harsh whispers and the body language is ten times louder. This continues for another hour – or two pints in liquid time – until they start to sort it out and things start to simmer down. Then there's the nodding and shaking of heads on an ever-decreasing scale until the settlement is reached. The talk stops and there's handshakes all around and the deal is done, and the man with the permanent centre parting – hidden under his trilby hat – gets his way.

And to finance the newly agreed joint venture?

Jimmy Penfold says, 'I need to get my vonga out.'

Now this is the vonga that's sitting in the Halifax Building Society savings account, (maximum withdrawal five thousand pounds a day unless there's an arranged closure) at Sinners Street, Rootsham. These monies would be liable to a probate order if anyone had bothered, or realised, that Jimmy Penfold was officially mullared. But there's no all-embracing system of official notification. Just think how many times, and for how long, the benefits of the deceased have been cashed in by relatives? So, if that observation is added to the upwards of twenty thousand bar that's quietly sleeping in the Halifax Building Society, it won't be that great a risk for Mr Penfold to draw his cash out. His driving ID is in the glove compartment of his Iveco van and also in there is the HBS passbook. This is because a few days before Jimmy's beautiful wife breathed her last, Jimmy paid in a deposit of four hundred and fifty pounds in notes. (It should have been five hundred but Jimmy was looking forward to a night on the livvener and he dipped out a bullseye.)

There's no point in hanging about, and the next morning the Iveco is parked in a side road just along from the Halifax. Silas is in the driving seat with the engine ticking over. Just in case. Inside of the Halifax Jimmy, trilby on his head, is up to the counter with his passbook in his hot little hand. He's also getting a friendly welcome from Rhuta.

'Mr Penfold, what can I do for you?' She's a broad smile on her face, and a flick of her hair as she speaks shows she's still into the flirting game.

The last time Jimmy spoke to Rhuta, before all of his troubles, she was off on a two-months' sojourn to the land of her mothers. Now because she did just that, this good-looking young girl with high cheekbones and wicked eyes has missed all the drama. By the time she flew back into Heathrow, the caravan fire story was as cold as its ashes, and had been usurped by a long-running scandal concerning two *Love Island* celebs.

Behind the glass, Rhuta counts out Jimmy Penfold's five thousand pounds – he will in fact be drawing out the maximum five thou a day until there's nothing left. She's counting it out with a smile and Jimmy can't help noticing that the tip of her tongue is protruding slightly from her generous lips like . . . like a fresh pink young nipple.

Christ almighty! What a thought! What a bastard thought to come into his head when Zilla's grave doesn't even have a headstone yet.

All the same, he can't help watching, staring at her mouth when she says the next day, 'You again, Mr Penfold. Are you treating yourself to something nice?' She tilts her head slightly to one side in her question.

Jimmy's a little slow on the uptake and it takes him a moment or two to answer,

'What? Oh yeah, a holiday.' He almost adds, 'To Ireland,' but instead mutters, 'Spain. I think.'

'You think? Mr Penfold. What are you like?'

Then because he can't help it, and because there's a flash of the old Jimmy still on the simmer, he repeats the old joke, the old lie, 'If I was ten years younger I might be showing you what I'm like.'

Rhuta laughs at this and the customer behind him, an elderly woman with grey roots in her hair and carrying a hemp shopping bag, says, 'I'd be quite happy if you were ten years older and knocking on my door, young man,' in the camaraderie of the queuing people.

Jimmy mustn't be judged too harshly for this banter because that's all it is. Banter. This man laughing, joking, in the Halifax Building Society is the same man who gets up in the middle of the night to make a brew, to roll a fag, to stir the embers of the fire into flame, and sit and think of past days, past nights and promise, to a distant cold bright moon, a revenge, a levelling of the score. And there's always a trespassing into his sleep, a haunting that taints his slumber and will startle him into a sudden awakening.

And this is what he dreams.

It's night and in the flickering firelight Zilla is dancing slowly, gently swaying, and she's teasing him in a one-button-at-a-time exposure, wanting to be daring and shyly sensual. With the last undoing she shuffles her dress down her shoulders down her body, down her legs and steps out of her raggedy clothes.

And then she stops, suddenly shudders, and then stands as still as a ghost except for the ripple of the night breeze through her shoulder-length hair. And then she looks at herself, looks down to her chest, looks at him, and she says in a whisper of her voice,

'Look what they've done to me, Jimmy. Look what they've done.'

Her fingers are between her perfect breasts plucking at a gash of a wound that streams bright red blood over her stomach.

'It hurts,' she says. 'It hurts so much, Jimmy.'

Her voice holds a pain and her eyes hold a bewilderment that will forever haunt him.

So if Jimmy garners some light relief with a joke and a touch of mild flirting in the Halifax perhaps he shouldn't be judged too harshly. This could be his first stirring of a recovery because, bluntly speaking, Jimmy Penfold is back on the market. (Mind, in a couple of weeks when he's dossing down in Wythenshawe, Manchester, Jimmy won't be looking like future lover material. There'll be a beard on his face and the now permanent item of headwear, over his centre parting, will look even more battered. Accompanying Jimmy will be Silas and Danny. They'll be watching his back because the area is rough as fuck.)

A loose end to tie up is poor Divi Denny Vincent. He's now on remand in Winson Green and he's facing a four-year stretch, less remission, for his involvement with delivering class A substances that he didn't really deliver. A positive for Divi being locked up means Mrs Vincent will now find herself receiving her full monthly entitlements from the social security. Denny won't be deducting any allowances for betting, for beer, for the occasional lady of the night; she'll be much better off without him and she might even decide to make the separation a permanent feature.

16

At Elm Hill Mr Ricky Ward, this runt of a young man who's well on the way to establishing himself as a career criminal – albeit a not very successful one – is specialising this month in debit and credit card theft. His partner-in-crime, Knobby, a native of Boarston, has just got his grubby little hands on a host of cloned, plastic cards care of local lady, Simple Sally. Knobby reckons they'll have to use them as quickly as possible before the block goes down on the accounts. These two skinny toerags, suitably camouflaged by the ubiquitous uniform of face-hiding hoods, take Knobby's boy-racer Polo to a park-and-ride on the outskirts of Wolverhampton. Then it's into the centre and as many hits on the cash dispensers as they can make in an hour. The hits are two hundred a shot and nets the best part of two grand before the hour's up. Barclays gets a hit. HSBC gets another one. Nationwide contributes their share and so on. Some even get two hits because the boys can't exactly remember which ones they've done. Then they just can't help popping into the Wulfrun Shopping Centre to catch up on the latest Xbox games.

But their bony frames and white trainers are being tracked on CCTV. This is because some of the cards they bought from Simple Sally – which she most definitely is not – for a ton a time have raised an instant alert. What our bumbling duo of wannabe didn't know is that Sally and her cohorts have already done the rounds the day before and primed the alarms. The skinny pair have been sold a pup. Talk about honour among thieves.

So now that alarm's been raised, the balloon's gone up – although the local police really didn't expect a rerun at the same dispensers within twenty-four hours. They'd half-heartedly watched the line (picture two overweight PCs, size twelves on the table, ties undone, sweat patches under their arms, chewing on peanuts, eyes flicking to the computer screen and bored out of their skulls) for a nibble. What they get is a full-blooded bite.

A tail's put on the two little sprats; a nondescript-looking weasel in his own face-concealing hoodie who sits a row back from them on the park-and-ride. Then of course he clocks the Polo's number plates and that gives away the ID of one Knobby Clarke and then the known associates check confirms Ricky Ward as his accomplice in crime.

Just like that: name, address, record, in the blink of an eye off his iPhone.

There is one problem for the police and that is Wolverhampton Wanderers FC, riding high in the table for once, are due an evening visit by Cardiff City, a few rungs below them. Now, as nice as the Welsh supporters are, the police chief feels all available resources should be concentrated on herding the fans to and from Molineux. This is bound to be a tight game and the Welsh will be a bit miffed if their team come a cropper.

This is why Chief Inspector Isaacs finds himself 'asked' to intercept Knobby Clarke and Ricky Ward on his patch. Which means he passes it on to overloaded detective Tom Malone and his sidekick, Maria. So, they pay young Ricky Ward a visit at his ramshackle home on the Elm Hill Caravan Park. This visit is at 1700 hours and just as he's getting ready to go out to the pub. On his person, they find a thousand pounds in banknotes that will most certainly be traced back to the withdrawals, made that very afternoon, from various cash dispensers in Wolverhampton city centre. Before pulling in Ricky Ward, they'd found money and the cloned cards, along with Knobby Clarke, in a bedsit in Boarston. Knobby is now languishing in a single cell in Boarston Police Station, protesting that someone must have fitted him up 'cos he's 'no idea where the money and that come from'. And Boarston Police Station is where young Ricky Ward finds himself at what should be the end of Tom Malone's shift. But this has pushed the detective into an overrun on his time and this will also put a sharp bend in the reunion road to Polly.

Tom Malone has promised Polly a romantic meal for two this evening and he was going to pull out all the stops. Already there's a bunch of roses sitting on the back seat of his car, along with a box of Belgian chocolates and a rather soppy 'I Love You' card. These gifts of persuasion are belted up and ready to go. But Detective Malone isn't.

He phones Polly and gives her the news and she says, 'Oh, but you promised, Tom. You promised.'

'I'm sorry but something's come up, Polly.'

'Something always comes up. Why is it that your work comes first every time? Don't I matter, Tom?'

''Course you do but I can't get out of it. Tomorrow night, we'll do it tomorrow night.' But Polly doesn't hear anything about tomorrow night, she's put her phone down and now she'll be deaf for the duration.

Mr Ricky Ward is sitting at the table in the interview room. His hood is down and he looks about twelve years old and very vulnerable. He's got a nervous twitch in his right leg and he could kill for a fag. He also knows the game is up and he can't bear the thought of prison again because on his last visit he was adopted by Big Daddy, a hairy mammoth of a long-termer, whose price for protection meant Ricky couldn't sit down for a week.

Simple Sally's offer had seemed such easy money, such a simple exercise for profit, and it's only now that Ricky Ward is realising the extent of the stitch-up. Him and Knobby are going to cop it for everything, every penny of Simple Sally's drawings. The lot.

Watched by WPC Maria, Detective Sergeant Tom Malone deals out the counterfeit debit and credit cards and adds a value to each. It totals almost three times as much as Ricky Ward can account for.

Tom Malone says, 'This is a lot of money, Mr Ward.'

Ricky Ward replies, 'Look it was today. Only today. I don't know nothing about nothing else.' He's stuttering and he's nearly crying. Tom Malone, briefly, feels a needle of sympathy for this young man whose life is going to be one not-too-clever petty little crime after another. But this flash of sympathy does not prevent him saying, 'You get done for this lot and you'll be sent down for three years, Ricky.'

All the time this interview is going on, WPC Maria is watching Tom Malone from beneath lowered lids. My God, how assertive he is. How confident. How professional. Like Carol says, 'Look and learn, Maria.' So she does. She watches like a cat watches a mouse. Only that mouse is poor Ricky Ward and every avenue of escape is being cut off from him by the sharp claws of the detective sergeant.

Tom Malone is saying, 'All that money, Ricky. We can stick it on you.'

'But . . .'

'Just admit it Ricky and I'll have a word with the CPS to go easy on you.'

And it would be a lot easier for the police – and look good in the clear-up figures – if Ricky Ward and Knobby Clarke were to carry the can for Simple Sally's misdemeanours as well. But Ricky is adamant that, 'We didn't do it. Not that.'

Tom Malone just says, 'Admit it Ricky, else it's three years.' Then he looks to Maria and with a slight nod draws her into the conversation, and she says,

'At the least, Ricky. Three years at the least.'

Tom Malone offers the slightest of grins in approval and Maria nearly flushes with pleasure.

Now there's someone missing from this interrogation. There should be a solicitor in attendance. But this is what the police call a pre-interview, a little chat before the one allowed phone call to the brief. By the time that call's been offered, Tom Malone is hoping he'll have all that he needs for the convictions of Ricky Ward and Knobby Clarke.

If Tom Malone says three years once he says it a dozen times and each time it batters Ricky Ward nearer to submission. The accused's voice weakens, his answers weaken. His head drops and now could be the time that he'll take the offer of a deal. It's also the time that Maria thinks that an offer of a coffee might be just enough 'good cop' to clinch an agreement with this poor young man. She can see he's close to breaking and an act of kindness could push Ricky Ward over the tipping point.

'Sir?' she asks Detective Malone as she mimes drinking from a cup.

'What? Oh, yes,' he says, and to Ricky Ward Maria pleasantly asks, 'Tea or coffee?'

Ricky Ward plumps for tea and asks if there's any biscuits 'cos he's starving and he's had nothing to eat all day. WPC Maria, all smiles, says she'll see what she can do.

Now it would be presumed that an offer on a deal would come from Detective Malone and it might well have done if Ricky Ward hadn't suddenly held his hands up the moment WPC Maria was out of the door. He lifts his frightened face to Tom Malone and says, 'If I tell yer something, something really important, could yer make things right for me?'

'That's a big ask, Ricky.'

'It's worth it, Mr Malone.'

'How will I know until you tell me?'

'Please, Mr Malone. Say you'll help me.'

Because it's only words – and it's not being recorded – the handsome policeman says tiredly, 'Just tell me, Ricky, and I'll make it right for you.'

'Promise me you won't let on to anyone.'

'Just tell me, Ricky.'

The troubled young man looks about himself just like Judas Iscariot must have, even puts his hand over his mouth as he mumbles the betrayal, 'He's not dead.'

'Who's not dead?'

'Jimmy Penfold's not dead.'

Tom Malone, completely taken aback for a moment, says, 'Not dead? And how would you know he's not dead?' He speaks very softly in his enquiry because if this were to be true then it might be the greatest comeback since Lazarus. And not just for Jimmy Penfold.

The story that Ricky Ward spills to Tom Malone is of that black morning of wheeling crows and blood in the grass. And bodies – one breathing and one stilled in death – being lifted onto the bed of a pick-up, and then a wounded Jimmy Penfold being treated in Mr and Mrs Flowers' static and of a burning that disguises a killing. He tells nearly all that he knows with a frightened sincerity that should suspend disbelief.

As Ricky Ward stumbles through his narrative, Tom Malone thinks that if this is possibly true, he could be looking ahead to a career saver, to being a rising star again by cracking the big one of drugs and murder. Of a mystery man in a gypsy's grave. But first the cat has to be bagged and Tom Malone interrupts his own two-way consciousness with, 'And where is he now Ricky?'

'Don't know, Mr Malone.'

'Come on, Ricky. You can do better than that.'

Ricky Ward says that he doesn't know but if they have a deal, he's sure he can find out.

Tom Malone says it better all be true, 'Or else there's definitely nothing doing.'

'I swear, Mr Malone, that I'm not lying.'

And it's not a lie because most of Elm Hill Caravan Park knows where Jimmy is. As does Ricky Ward, supplier of goodies and tobacco to all and sundry, including Little-John Wells.

'You let me go, Mr Malone and I'll call you tomorrow. Tell you where he is.'

WPC Maria brings a tray of hot drinks and biscuits into a concluded agreement that she was not a party to. She raises her eyebrows to Tom Malone. He nods and says, 'Ricky's made us a promise. He's going to help us. Aren't you Ricky?'

'Yes, Mr Malone,' says young Ricky Ward.

A bit later on, Little-John Wells is going to receive a phone call from young Ricky; a warning to give the place the once-over because a little bird has told him that the gavvers are coming a-calling. Little-John Wells will thank the informant for the warning and promise to put some business his way.

So Ricky Ward could, if he wanted, give DS Malone the info right now. But Ricky's not a total quisling. As yet.

Tom Malone would like to share the good news with Polly, but she's still not picking up and instead of the romantic dinner there'll be flowers in a dustbin, a few beers in town and then a late-night takeaway and home to bed.

So Tom Malone's up and down at the same time. But he's feeling even more down with the coming of nine o'clock; it's after he's taken a stool in the Turk's Head and sat there for a drink or two on his lonesome. He's debating the usual choice of a lonely Indian or a lonely Chinese or maybe just taking a solitary walk home. But these thoughts are interrupted when WPC Maria Fiore walks into the bar and she's not looking exactly happy with life either.

Maria's not looking happy because when she'd finished her shift at Boarston Station, she was thinking of preparing a quick tuna bake for dinner, then a curl-up on the sofa in front of the telly with Carol. A few glasses of wine and a night in sounded heavenly because, just lately, their work patterns haven't coincided, one always leaving as the other was arriving home. But tonight, and with the weekend on its way, there's going to be plenty of time for each other. Right? Actually no. Carol's home all right but her suitcase is packed, her football kit bag is bulging and there's a train ticket to London in her wallet.

'Darling,' she says to Maria excitedly. 'There's been a couple of injuries and I've been called in.'

'Called in?' Maria's still trying to take it in.

'As a replacement. For the Fulham game.'

Maria, caught on the hop, says, 'Oh, but I thought we were—'

'A congratulations would be nice.' Carol's voice now has the beginning of an edge.

'Well . . . congratulations.'

'It's my big chance. You could say it like you mean it.'

'I do. I do. But I thought we were going to have some time together and . . .' Maria's disappointment is as obvious as Carol's defensiveness.

'We'll catch up when I get back on Monday.'

'Monday? But . . .'

It's another unfinished sentence because Carol runs her hand over her cropped hair and says, 'Look it's only for three days.'

Maria's questioning *'Three days?'* comes out much louder than she intended, sounding more of an accusation.

'Yes, three days. That's all.' And then Carol adds rather impatiently, and perhaps unnecessarily, 'Don't make such a fuss, Maria,' like a mother scolding a child. It's followed by an instant, 'Sorry.'

Maria, stung and ignoring the sorry, says a bitter, 'I suppose Maisie will be there?'

Carol delays the answer just long enough to make Maria think that it wasn't going to be information volunteered. Now that is probably because Maisie is Carol's ex-girlfriend, an excellent midfielder and her previous partner of two years standing.

Carol snaps, 'Yes, of course she'll be there. She's part of the team.'

Maria snaps back with, 'I bet she is.' She's fired up now because her evening and weekend plans are kaput, but before things can escalate further there's an interruption of a car beeping from the road.

'Taxi's here. Look I've got to go.' Carol couches it so that it sounds like an apology for leaving.

Then there's a quick breath-stealing hug – and the trying of a kiss to Maria's averted face. Then, as she's hefted her gear and is going out the door, Carol pauses and says, 'Love you Maria. I'll phone later.'

'Yeah, if you can be bothered to make the time.' Maria shuts the door on her partner rather abruptly. Sometimes her Italian temperament intrudes at rather inopportune moments.

Maria prepares the tuna bake, slams it in the oven, takes a quick shower and opens a bottle of wine. She has one glass. Then another. The tuna bake, overbaked by now, stays in the oven as Maria and her bottle of Merlot brood on the injustice of being alone, of feeling neglected. Deserted even. And then she broods about Maisie.

Maisie with her slim wiry body winning a tackle, hoisting the ball across the goalmouth and Carol rising like a gazelle to head past the keeper. Goal. Celebrations. Hugs and kisses. And reliving the moment in the changing room after the ref has blown time. What a pass. What a finish. What a partnership, a joint enterprise. And still talking about it as wet and muddy shirts and shorts are stripped from toned bodies. And still talking about it in the hot and steamy showers when she's standing face to face with a naked ex-lover.

Stop it, Maria! For fuck's sake, stop it!

Another tilt of the bottle. Another red cascade of liquid. And then the house seems too small to contain her feelings; the reminders that she's sitting in on her own while Carol is having a good time at some bar with her friends and *her*. And there's still no phone call. She's not even bothering to confirm a safe arrival. Well fuck her.

Maria, dressed to go out, spends a few minutes in front of the mirror. She brushes her dark hair, touches up her eyelashes and riffles in her handbag for the lipstick that Carol says makes

Maria look tarty. She applies it liberally as she waits for a taxi to take her to the first destination that comes to mind: the Turk's Head. (The taxi is another little protest because Carol always reprimands, 'A taxi, Maria? We'll stroll, it's only a mile.')

These are the reasons, the whys tonight, after the best part of a bottle of vino, Maria walks into the same pub where Tom Malone is deadening his frustrations. He's sat alone at a table for two, nursing the dregs of his pint and wondering about making a move towards a spicy supper. He's staring into his beer and doesn't see Maria until he looks up at her as she says,

'Hello sir.' Her voice is soft, subdued.

'Maria.'

He offers her a seat, a 'Call me Tom, we're off duty,' and a drink and, by what he can see of her, she's had a few already. Her face is becomingly flushed and her dark hair is lightly windswept. Her lipstick is a shade on the bright side and she's five feet seven of arresting, Italian attractiveness. And, like Tom Malone, she's alone tonight, although not for exactly the same reasons. So they sit and talk about station stuff; Ricky Ward, Jimmy Penfold and the like. Time moves on and one drink becomes two, three, and it's pleasant and warm and quiet in the Turk's Head. There's no telling of anything personal on the menu until Maria's phone makes the ping that she's been hoping for.

'I've got to take this.' She scrabbles in her bag for the phone and answering she says, 'Give me a mo. I'm just going somewhere quieter.' She mouths a 'Sorry' to Tom Malone.

Outside, in a mouth of the alley alongside the pub, Carol's saying,

'Maria, I tried the home number and . . .'

'I'm out. Just having a drink.' She adds, 'With DS Malone.'

'Oh. You didn't say.'

'Didn't feel like staying in.' Then pointedly, 'On my own.'

'Well we're having a coffee and an early night.'

'We?'

'Me and the girls of course.'

Me and the girls. Me and Maisie who know everything there is to know about each other. Maria should put a lid on it then but her Mediterranean temperament, helped by wine consumption, causes her to fire up.

'Of course! You and the girls.' Her tone bleeds the words into an accusation which are delivered several decibels up the scale. This well and truly lights the blue touch paper and the conversation escalates to a blame game of 'You this' and 'You that' until Carol, now really pissed off, reminds Maria that it's she who's out on the town with DS Malone and she could get upset about it if she chose to.

Maria says, 'But he's a man and it's only a harmless drink.'

Then Carol makes another reminder to Maria that drinking with a man wasn't always that harmless, was it? There's a silence then because some things of the past should never be dragged back into the light. All a shocked Maria can get out in answer is,

'But since you there's been . . .' before her voice changes into a sob of disbelief and she stabs off her phone. She leans against the alley wall and has a quick cry. She's hurt and all she wants to do now is to go home and curl up in bed, hide from the world. But first she has to retrieve her handbag.

Tom Malone's been lounging back in his chair and studying pictures of old Boarston framed on the wall of the bar. They're images of a bygone age, softened romantic images that contrast sharply with Maria's running mascara and her snotty nose.

'I'm sorry I need to go, Tom.'

She's scooted up her bag before a puzzled Tom Malone has hardly started to wonder what the matter is. But Tom Malone, ever the gentleman, is to his feet, arm around her, ushering her to the door. Then he calls up a cab, asks her no questions in the waiting, and sees her safely to her doorstep.

That should be that for this evening; no more than a few social drinks, Tom playing the Good Samaritan to the upset Maria, and then the taking of a head-clearing walk back to his lonely cottage and his empty bed. That's how it should unfold but Maria is feeling a little foolish about the night's events. Now it's important that he knows she's normally an efficient, level-headed officer at all times; a policeman, or a policewoman, is never off duty. So Tom Malone gets the invite for a nightcap and thinks that one for the road shouldn't hurt. A bottle is opened, glasses poured, and Maria starts off with all the good intentions of a brief 'You know how it is' explanation. It is brief, two words at the outset.

'Woman trouble' and then thinking that could be miscon-strued as something else, she says, 'I mean between me and Carol.'

Tom Malone suggests that they're sharing the same problem because he has woman trouble too and Maria has to laugh. And then she shouldn't be laughing because she's unhappy and Carol is miles away and they've had a terrible row and she's in a desperate need for comfort. That's Maria's side of it. Tom Malone's view is that Maria's eyes are spilling tears and there's a hunched sadness to her. Maybe he puts his arms around her, draws her in, with the intention of providing solace. Maybe. But the road to adultery is paved with acts of care and here there's no exception. Maria is soft and warm and vulnerable and needing. There's also only one place this is going, and that's into the bedroom that has only known Sapphic love. Until now.

We'll leave it there for an hour until the deed is done and Tom Malone starts making his lonely way home. Maria, needs supplanted by realisation, sobs into her pillow and into sleep until the alarm shrills out seven o'clock. It yanks her, none too gently, into the day.

She's thinking as she showers, 'What have I done?'

She's thinking as she carefully dresses into her smart WPC uniform, 'Carol must never know.'

She's thinking as she sets out for the station, 'It will never happen again.'

It's not exactly a coincidence that DS Tom Malone is thinking the same – he only needs to substitute Polly for Carol. Mind, his previous 'It will never happen again' rings a little hollow considering what's happened. But now there's another ringing and it's his phone and it's Maria straight on with the subject of a drunken loving,

'Sir, about last night. You won't say anything, will you? To anyone?'

'No Maria, I won't.'

'Only if Carol found out . . .'

(Or Polly.)

'It's OK Maria. It's our secret.'

Tom Malone wonders if 'our secret' might sound a little pervy but it's already said.

'And Maria?' he says.

'Yes sir?'

'You can still call me Tom, you know.'

Maria says, 'Yes sir, I mean Tom. Sir. Tom.' And they laugh and the air's cleared and Maria's not dreading meeting him this morning. She thinks that he's a nice man and she quite likes him again. Then she scrolls down to Carol's number and it's another apology for her jealousy. Carol says not to worry because she'll forgive Maria anything. This truth may well have to be tested sooner than she thinks because when Maria signs into the station, ten minutes after DS Tom Malone this morning, she's already eight hours pregnant.

17

This new morning at Boarston nick, Tom Malone – admittedly a little sluggish – is spending a few of his hours catching up on paperwork. Maria, now also his partner in a tacit agreement as well as at work, passes over a call from their current number one nark – a very nervous Ricky Ward – who gives the address of Little-John's homestead to Tom Malone. Tom, livening up in an instant, is on to it like a doberman. But first he has to fill in Chief Inspector Isaacs on Ricky Ward's off-the-record disclosures.

'Sounds a bit far-fetched to me, Tom,' says the inspector.

'I know, sir, but he's over a barrel. And I can sort it out. Sir?'

But Chief Inspector Isaacs is not some swooning female to handsome Tom Malone's lead.

'He's a petty thief, Tom. Bit of a fantastic story. Why should we believe him?'

It's obvious that Chief Inspector Isaacs is not exactly convinced of Ricky Ward's revelation. There's also the problem that the Home Office is pressurising all forces to act on the newly recognised problem of county lines. A recently appointed home secretary has vowed in cliché – 'to rid this country of the evil cancer growing in our midst.' Taking that cue, senior by several ranks – Chief Constable Donald Niven – has thundered down the line his order of 'Prioritise' to all station commanders.

'We must have results,' he thunders again, as if his future knighthood depends on it.

Results is what Chief Inspector Isaacs must deliver and he's feeling the pressure. So what to do with Detective Tom Malone? Chief Inspector Isaacs leans back in his chair and fingers one of his chins. He feels a little guilty about the Huntingdon raid; he quite likes hard-working, always respectful Tom Malone. He wishes he had a few more officers like him and Chief Inspector Isaacs knows that a little indulgence now and again can only improve relations and performance.

'OK, Tom.' He relents, 'Don't suppose it'll hurt to check it out. I can spare you the bus driver and two uniforms,' says the inspector.

'But sir, I was hoping . . .'

'One shift, Tom. That's all. Be ready tomorrow morning. And I need that team back here as soon as.'

That's the end of the discussion and Chief Inspector Isaacs stamps down his authority the same way he used to stamp his muddied boot into the ruck on a wet Saturday afternoon. He's more abrupt than he usually is and it might be because he's showing around the latest addition to his force: a young, big, fleshy man whose similarity to Isaacs doesn't end with his size and looks. It's Isaacs' sister's boy, his nephew Harvey Harris, a boiler-house star of unflinching, uncompromising character on the rugby field, and beyond. Just like his uncle in fact; just like the son Isaacs never fathered. And it looks like favouritism and nepotism might soon be holding hands in Boarston's cop shop.

The next day DS Tom Malone is in receipt of a search warrant and he's briefed his men, passed around a photo of Gippo Jim and given them the back story. There's time for a quick bite in the canteen, then by early afternoon Tom and his crew are bumping along the track to Little-John Wells' neglected smallholding. They pull into the old stockyard and Little-John and his pony-sized wolfhounds emerge from one of his tumbled barns. Little-John glowers in Tom Malone's face and demands to know,

'What the fuck do you want?'

'Jimmy Penfold. Where is he?'

'Never heard of him, so piss off.'

'We have a warrant to search the premises, Mr Wells.' What Tom Malone is told to do with the warrant would bring tears to his eyes. Completely ignoring that comment, Tom Malone says,

'Unless you want to be arrested, I'd advise you to stand aside. Sir.' (The 'Sir' is added on like an afterthought with no reverence in its delivery.)

Little-John looks around at the numbers he's facing and his silent highly strung dogs are tensed each side of him. It seems for a moment as though he's weighing up the options of a frontal assault. But two of the uniforms have slipped out their batons and WPC Maria has a can of Mace ready and cocked in her hand. There might even be a Taser in the offing so Little-John shrugs his massive shoulders, keeps his jukals at heel and sits himself down on a stone trough to watch the proceedings.

The search starts proper and Tom, while the rest of his workforce poke their noses into barns and sheds, starts with the static caravans. He doesn't spend much time in Little-John's; it's basic for a bachelor's dwelling. The other static is clean and smells of disinfectant. A quick search through reveals that the bed's made and there's shining pots on the cooker and clean dishes on the draining board.

Back outside he says to Little-John, 'Who's staying there?'

'Staying where?'

Tom Malone sighs because everything is an explanation or an obstruction with this bear of a man. He says, 'In that caravan.'

'A cousin.'

'Where is he?'

Little-John says, 'Gone. Could be anywhere.' He spreads his hands, and the pair of wolfhounds track his gesture. Then they turn to fix their eyes on Tom Malone in an unblinking, unnerving stare, as though they're daring him to make a move towards their master. A single word, maybe just a sign, from Little-John would be all that's needed to set them loose on the detective.

But there'll be no more questions from Tom Malone. All he wanted, needed, was a sign or a clue that the supposedly deceased Jimmy Penfold wasn't actually mullered. And now there's just the beginning of a doubt that Ricky Ward might have spun him a yarn to gain a bit of time before his miserable little carcass was remanded in custody. Well, Tom Malone would see about that.

After a three-hour search they leave empty-handed, bump back down the track where, by the entrance, a Traveller boy pulls his bicycle onto the grass verge to let them by. Tom Malone, head full of disappointments, hardly gives him a glance. It's just a fleeting glimpse of an intrusion but it's enough to niggle his memory into starting a slow recall. But with all that's going on, the police vehicle is well on the way back to Boarston nick before the realisation dawns in Tom Malone's addled brain. Now he has a picture in his head of the three of them together: Jimmy Penfold, the lovely Zilla Penfold and last, but by no means least, the boy on the fringes, Mikey Penfold. This boy, whom he hadn't given a thought to before now, is the connection to the man who may not have been burned to a crisp in the furnace of the caravan fire. So Jimmy Penfold might be a bird that's flown but there's bound to be a contact, a connection, to his boy. Suddenly Tom Malone cheers up and he's thinking that Ricky Ward is going to be invaluable;

he'll be the eyes and ears of the police investigator. But first Tom Malone has to tell Chief Inspector Isaacs that the search of Little-John Wells' premises yielded zilch.

There's an almighty sigh from Tom's superior. 'You've come back with fuck-all, and we've got fuck-all, Tom.'

'But we have, sir. We still have leads. Strong leads, sir.'

Tom Malone gets in that if he can keep tabs on Mikey there might – in fact, he's sure – there will be a path to Mikey's unexpired father. But the chief constable has been on the blower again. He's demanded an update on inquiries and delivered a pep talk at ear-numbing volume to Isaacs. This has left the chief inspector dubious to anything that might remotely detract from the prioritised ongoing county lines operation.

'Sir, he's still our lead to bigger things. I need more time.'

'More time is more money, Tom.'

'I'll work it in sir. We'll keep it on the back burner.'

'I don't want this interfering with county lines.'

'It won't, sir. I promise you it won't.'

'The second it does, Tom, I'm pulling it. OK?'

'OK, sir. Thank you, Sir.'

DS Malone doesn't waste time or sweat on a near miss; he's straight onto Ricky Ward and piling on the pressure. So young Ricky gets an invitation to attend an interview at Boarston Police Station. It's a front row seat, with transport provided, just to make sure he doesn't miss the occasion. At Boarston Station, he's the lucky recipient of an extremely aggressive in-your-face going-over by Tom Malone. It's putting the fear of God into the young hoodlum; Ricky Ward is shaking in his shoes. Maria, assisting in the interview, can't but help compare this Tom Malone with the man who gently kissed her, held her tightly in her hour of need and . . . and that's enough of that, Maria Fiore.

Tom Malone says, 'You lied to me, Ricky.'

'No, Mr Malone. I didn't. I didn't.'

There's several minutes of backwards and forwards of this until Tom Malone takes a deep breath and says, 'You've got one last chance to make this right. You've got to find Jimmy Penfold for me.'

Ricky Ward snivels an immediate, 'But he could be anywhere now, Mr Malone.'

'You've got to keep an eye on the boy, Ricky.'

Then in the only disclosure of the evening Ricky Ward quietly says, 'Mikey'll be back here by the weekend, Mr Malone.'

'You sure? Because if I don't get Jimmy Penfold, you don't get a deal.'

'Yes I'm sure Mr Malone. I heard he'd be back.'

Detective Tom reminds Ricky Ward yet again of the extras that'll be pinned to his head if he doesn't comply this time. Then Ricky Ward asks if he's all right for a lift back to Elm Hill 'cos it's getting late and he ain't got a penny in his pocket. Tom Malone says that the walk home will do him good and he can think about his last chance on the way there.

But Ricky Ward has told the truth because a few days later he reports that Mikey Penfold has returned to the fold at Elm Hill Park. 'He came back this morning, Mr Malone.'

'On his own?'

'Little-John brought him, Mr Malone.'

'No surprise there then,' thinks Detective Malone, but he's well pleased because things are adding up. It means that as soon – although there is still an if about it – as Jimmy Penfold pokes his snout into Elm Hill, he'll be nabbed. Then, at last, Tom Malone will find out just how the elusive gypsy escaped the Huntingdon ambush and exactly who the John Doe who was burned to a crisp.

Perhaps his luck is on the turn because Tom Malone is taking out Polly occasionally – cinema, drinks, something to eat. Maybe even a bit more sometimes. At the station, WPC Maria is becoming invaluable at lightening the load, of being a part of a – more closely than originally intended – two-man team. She puts in the extra effort, the extra hours, as the days turn into weeks. County line results are looking good and Ricky Ward keeps them up to date on the Elm Hill situation. Yes, life is good for Maria at present, she's happy in work and happy in love, so she could well do without a serpent slithering into her little Eden and whispering of trouble brewing, and that's because, as the French ladies used to say in medieval times, the English haven't arrived for their monthly visit.

Since Maria and Carol moved in together their time of the month has regulated like clockwork; there's barely an hour's difference between start and finish for each of them. Carol reckons that it's because they're so in tune with each other.

'In tune and in love,' she says, wrapping her arms around Maria. Carol's love is pleasured by a smile, a kind word, a lingering kiss. If Maria lets fly with her fiery temperament it's Carol who calms her down, holds her. Shushes her. Strokes her long dark hair. 'You're my world,' she says. 'I don't know what I'd do without you.' Maria says, 'You'll never need to find out.'

There are special days when Carol, much the better housewife, cooks for Maria. This is one of those days and there's flour on her apron and she's stirring a sauce on the stove in the kitchen of their first home together. Garlic is soaking into the air and the rain is pattering on the window as Maria, fresh in from her shift and still in her topcoat, laughs, 'You're fattening me up.'

Carol says, 'There'll be more of you to cuddle,' and then it isn't a joke between them and the cuddling is more than that. And Maria's coat is on the kitchen floor and then her skirt and then her blouse and then her bra and then her knickers and then Carol is on her knees before her. And the sauce is burning on the stove. And Carol is murmuring, 'I love a woman in a uniform.' And Maria is laughing and saying, 'And out of it.'

There's a score of times like this; a hundred times like this. There's a slow dance in a dim nightclub. There's a high on a roller-coaster with the wind in their faces and the lights of the fairground rushing up to meet them. And then there's hot sweet endless love in a tumbled bed. That's how it should be for Maria, a happy ever after.

So the days and weeks have sped on by since the 'Blame it on the alcohol' episode (that's been locked away and gathering dust in the file of One-night-stand mistakes) and on this Friday evening Maria arrives home with a takeaway for tea. She's on her own tonight – has been for several days – because Carol is away attending a course on the subject of unconscious bias in modern-day policing. (This separation was unavoidable and Maria's gritted her teeth and accepted it.) Now all Maria feels like doing this evening is putting her feet up on the settee. God, she feels tired today. Come to think of it, she's been yawning her head off for the last week or so.

Maria turns up the heating, switches on the telly, flops down on the settee and opens a chicken chow mein – third one on the trot this week. She's munching through her meal when the phone rings and Carol's warm voice is in Maria's ear.

'I'm missing you so much.'

Through a chomping of chow mein, Maria says, 'I'm missing you too.'

'You can guess what else I'm missing?'

'No idea,' laughs Maria.

'I've been shopping and found the most amazing underwear. It's smooth and silky and—'

'And that's enough!' Maria laughs again. 'Save it. I'm trying to eat my tea.'

'Can't wait until tomorrow night,' Carol says. 'We should be clear then.'

'Clear?'

'Clear of . . . you know. Bloody nuisance in more ways than one.'

Maria, cottoning on quickly, says, 'Oh yes. Me too,' when she realises it's not been her too.

Then there's a babble of voices in the background of Carol's phone and she says,

'Have to go now. Love you. See you tomorrow.'

Maria says, 'Love you too,' and then she sits and counts her dates back through all the busy days of investigating with DS Malone. There's the sinking, jelly-legged, feeling as the Virgin Mary receives an offering of prayer for assistance Maria's a good Catholic when she needs to be – and of her situation being a retrievable mistake.

Maria hotfoots it down to the late-night chemist and buys three pregnancy home-testing kits. In her bathroom, she squats over the loo and follows the instructions. And tests. And tests again. And, just to be sure, one more time. They're all quite a nice shade of blue, but it's a damning blue. A 'look what you've done' blue.

The next day is a Saturday – no work this weekend – and Maria's walked herself into the town, back out of the town, sat in the cinema for an hour with no clue as to what the film was about. Maria's not had a bite to eat when she should be eating for two and she's counting the hours and minutes until Carol brings her pure love home to the adulterated one.

Carol's key has opened the front door into the lounge, and she's nudged the door shut with her firm, shapely rear before she sets her case on the mat. She calls, 'Maria, I'm home.'

Maria's in the bathroom making sure that there's no visible evidence of the pregnancy home-testing kits. (She feels like one of the criminals she meets in her everyday life, covering her tracks like this.)

Maria calls, 'I'm coming,' and, as an alibi, the flush of the toilet follows her into the lounge and into the enveloping embrace of her wife. Now this should be the right time for disclosure, for honesty. Maria might be explaining, apologising, almost throwing herself at the mercy of her one true love. There could be tears, anger, perhaps even a hardening of expression and heart. But there's none of this because Maria can't utter the words of destruction. She can't watch the light die in Carol's eyes.

It's afterwards, after the tenderness of a welcome home loving, and Carol is softly sleeping. But that sleep won't visit Maria and she's lying awake as the digits on the bedside clock flick further into the night. Maria's fingers are stroking, gently kneading her stomach, where a speck of life is slowly but surely forming. Maria's saying silently to herself,

'Could I do this?' and her hand pauses, seems to stop of its own accord. 'Could I do this to you?' Because that's what's in her head, a termination; an early termination within the cover of her next cycle so that no one will ever know. Except her. Somehow it doesn't seem right to ask the Virgin Mary for help on this one but she still chances it. In the darkness of the night she waits for an answer to come to her. She waits and waits until it's seven o'clock and she can't lay in the bed an instant longer.

18

At this same seven o'clock, and some distance from Maria and her growing problems, Meg is sitting at the table in her motorhome and Wilma is snoring gently on the floor. Here in the Vale of Evesham a heavy morning mist is soaking into the hedges, dripping from the sheltering trees and onto the roof of Meg's motorhome in an irregular beating of the passage of time. Outside of her stopping place are villages, fields and woods that are recognised in her memory. She remembers the old atchentans, where families would camp and work and live all those years ago. She remembers the banter and laughter around the smoky yog, the bubbling kharvee, the grubby chavees, having to lag under the bor, and the dust and the heat of a June day in that past time.

'It was a long time ago,' she sighs to Wilma. 'A long time ago.'

But Meg has allowed nostalgia of place and time to seep its interference into what she should be addressing. So she takes a deep breath, straightens her stooped back and focuses her concentration onto the information that Ollie Cooper has passed to her. She opens her notebook, flattens the page and slowly traces out the name 'Veryll Evans' with her forefinger.

This Veryll Evans, clever killer, psychopathic killer, killer of the lovely Zilla, awakes with a start as his mobile alarm opens the day with a loud blast of 'Land of My Fathers'. He's not had a very good night because the unfinished business with Winston has been pecking at his head. It's not just the five thousand pounds, it's the fact that he thinks he's getting turned over like a nobody. Him. Made to look a fool . . . A man who holds life or death in the crook of his finger. So for Winston, it's an early phone call to be reminded that debts are to be paid. And Winston's not happy.

'Do you know what the fuckin' time is?'

'Quarter past seven, Winston.'

'What do you want?'

They both know what he wants but it still has to be said.

'I want my money, Winston.'

'You'll get it.'

'It's overdue, Winston.'

Winston says that he'll decide what's overdue or not and that he didn't expect 'buy one and get one free.' 'You're not fuckin' Tesco.'

Winston tells the Welshman that if there's an all-clear in a month or two he'll get his money.

Veryll Evans says, 'It's clear to me now, Winston. But if that's the way it is . . .'

Imagine a shrug of the shoulders to finish off the sentence, a casual gesture that's belied by the bitter coldness of his eyes. This could almost make anyone think that the money might be incidental to Veryll Evans personal satisfaction and if someone with a score to settle were to approach Mr Evans he may well be open to a deal of mutual benefits.

Meg is cradling a mug of meski at her table as the sun floods into this Vale of Evesham. She's shaking her head to clear the images that visited her in the deep dark night. They are images of the past. Images of the present. Images of the future. The living, the dead and the unborn dance together. They swirl, they join, they hold hands in a perverse ring o' roses. Meg shuts them down one by one, switches off the brightness of their faces, takes away the form of their being. And then Wilma's whining insistence at the door draws Meg out into the low mists of the morning. It puts her on an early walk along an ancient footpath between untrimmed hazel hedges. It takes her on a visit to a graveyard beside a small country church.

By the time she's at the grave, the heavy dew has soaked into Meg's shoes and it's soddened the hem of her long loose skirt. In this overgrown churchyard Meg kneels in front of a standing slab of marble that's pockmarked with lichen and spotted with birds' droppings. The inscription carved into this stone reads:

> *To my loving Mother and Friend,*
> *Zingara, taken from me . . .*

Meg scratches, cleans the rest of the wording with a handkerchief while Wilma, who has now finished snuffling around the beds of the departed, sits on her haunches, eyes on Meg, who speaks to the grave in this early morning.

'It's been so long Mum. So long.'

She's running her hand over the carved letters, feeling out the words, the dates of birth and death on the day of interment in 1955.

Nostalgia wraps itself around Meg and she's living again her time as a young woman. And this young woman is slightly taller than medium height, slightly underweight for the postwar period and slightly more striking than pretty. What you maybe notice about her is her ability to appear and disappear. She might suddenly be at your side, picking up your footsteps, giving you a few words of conversation. Then you'd turn your head from her for a few seconds and she'd be gone. And you'd miss her presence, and perhaps watch for her at Pershore market, or pick her out from a group of Traveller women and sprawling children sipping glasses of cool shandy in the yard of a local pub. Meg has something of the mysterious about her, this offspring of the fortune-teller. There are whispers about black cats and tarot cards, the misted crystal and the casting of the runes under the light of a full moon.

Zingara and Daughter – Purveyors of Portents,
Servants of the Fates, Tellers of your Future.

And Zingara knows what her future is because, in this time, she's come home to die in the place where she was born, inside a waggon, in the fields of Worcestershire. It's because Zingara has a pain in her lungs, a searing pain beneath her breasts. And of course she coughs; she coughs day and night. She coughed throughout her appointment with a Harley Street specialist. And his prognosis was not good. In fact it was dire.

In fact it was terminal.

And there'll be a gypsy's funeral in the autumn of this year of 1955.

Meg comes back to this place when she needs to clear her head, when the world is confusing and she wants to think clearly. She needs to put an order, place a solution, to the problems in the lives of her people. And they are her people. Her family. Her children. And, without a doubt, her liabilities.

On this day, Meg sits by her mother's grave as the sun starts to warm the earth and dry the dew from the grass. She thinks and she schemes and when she leaves the churchyard a plan is firming up in her fertile brain. And the action to the plan starts with Meg dialling a certain number. The number is to a mobile phone and it's answered in a voice with a soft Welsh accent and it starts the ball rolling.

Unbeknown to Meg, another ball is in motion. This one has revolved up north to where Jimmy Penfold and co. are spending some time in the Wythenshawe district of Manchester. This ball rolls through the entrance of a trailer park, 'Homes to Rent All Year Round', and stops where the number nineteen is screwed to an ill-fitted front door. The park home has seen better days. In this cheap retreat there's boarded-up windows, litter in the gutters and an epidemic of jukals – bull terriers and mastiffs mostly – which means that someone's always traipsing dog shit into the living room.

This is a site of workers on the black, of nightshifts in cold, dark factories where you will never hear a word of English spoken. People – men and women – have been imported here in the backs of lorries for the gangmeisters to pick up in early morning minibuses to labour in buildings where none of the rules of health and safety apply. It's the subworld, the hidden world, that's easy to pass by.

Now Jimmy and co. have been visiting the parts of Manchester frequented by Rubin and Winston. There's been no problem locating the two local bad asses, because Winston's name is on the streets and wherever he is, Rubin won't be far behind. Winston's name might be out there but it's not referred to fondly. It's mumbled, muttered, cursed and it's heard in the clubs, in the bars. And, in this world, the word is that it's better to play in his team than against it. If you cross Winston, you must be prepared for a swift and brutal retribution in a dark alley and, although Rubin might have a hand or foot in that retribution, Rubin's thought of as being a bit different.

Rubin's the sort of guy people want to like, to make excuses for. He looks that part; the sort of guy you could easily forgive, even as he's giving you a good hiding, because he's only doing his job. It's not personal like, and he'd probably shake your hand afterwards. But Jimmy Penfold doesn't subscribe to this rose-tinted perception. His view is of Rubin lounging against a motor, drawing him into a trap with his casual and deadly presence. Because of Rubin, Zilla's not walking this earth. That's what Jimmy believes, dwells on. So he's after chasing the biblical interpretation of an eye for an eye, a tooth for a tooth. A life for a life.

If tabs were kept on the gypsy trio in the last week or so, they would have been found mooching around the streets, and partaking of the odd pint. They slip into the underclass because they're of the same. They look the same, talk the same and the conversation barely falters when they walk into a pub. Our Romany Rag, Tag and Bobtail have now cased Rubin's abode; they're aware that the delectable Angel is his housemate. They know the street, the house block, the first-floor flat itself, what time Rubin stretches his legs in a morning walk to the Co-op for a newspaper and a bar of Fruit and Nut for his sweet-toothed lover. (He has to carefully skirt the builders' skip and associated rubbish, the result of ongoing renovations at this rather elderly residence.) In fact Rubin and Angel's flat is the only one occupied on their floor. Rubin might have a moan about plaster dust, holes in walls and dangling wires but he's not too concerned because him and the lovely Angel won't be here for much longer. They're due to move upmarket very soon to a rather luxurious apartment with CCTV covering the entrance and the landings. It offers a degree of protection he doesn't have in his present, frankly run-down, accommodation. The new modern apartment has been bought and paid for by Winston; he's diversifying his businesses, investing in property, and spreading his bets, like any ambitious player would.

The action of this day begins when Jimmy Penfold slips quietly from the rented Park home into the cool wet blackness of the early morning. He leaves Silas and Danny snoring like a pair of walruses and steps out into the six o'clock hour of a new day.

Anyone who knows Jimmy would have a job recognising him straight away. He's developed a hunched-up walk, a face-concealing beard and a titfer on his poll to hide his permanent parting. But the inside of him is even more of a contrast to the carefree man of a while ago because burning him up, eating him up, are the constant thoughts of what a let-down he's been to those who depended on him, loved him even. If he hadn't fallen into any of this . . .

He would be waking up at Elm Hill Caravan Park just about now to a mug of sweet meski and to Mikey moaning about having to get up so early and to Zilla asking him if he had any vonga 'cos some bastard has taken the rent money from the cash draw and spent the effing lot down the livvenerkenna and doesn't that same dinilow realise that if he got off his fat arse and did a week's booti then at least they'd be able to . . .

That's the picture Jimmy's seeing. And, right now, he would love to be in that portrait of domestic bliss. Right now, he knows who's to blame and can only think of what should, no, what *must* be done. In the name of honour and revenge. His honour. His revenge. It must belong to him alone, not Silas, and not Danny. It must be his finger on the trigger.

19

In this early Manchester morning there's a dark drizzle settling
on Jimmy, damping the pavements, hazing the car lights. He's
sheltering in a doorway and the rain's dripping off the brim of
his hat, running down his nose. Jimmy's eyes are narrowed and
he's sucking desperately on a soggy cigarette for a pull of nicotine. Across the road from Jimmy, the entrance door to Rubin's
residence is wedged open to welcome the builders. Jimmy's
hunched and tensed, wet and waiting, until there's Rubin, stepping out into the damp gloom of the morning. Rubin scans left
and right, shakes his handsome head at the black sky and starts
himself on his errand. (Angel, sleepy-warm in their bed, had
pouted, 'Don't forget my chocolate,' and he'd asked what it was
worth. And she'd said that was for him to find out, but for him
to hurry back in case the mood left her.) From his vantage point
Jimmy, knowing what's ahead, slips his hand to his inside pocket,
seeks again the heavy cold reassurance of his weapon of intent.
He huddles further into the doorway soaking up the rain and the
minutes until Rubin returns. As soon as Rubin's put a foot inside
the entrance Jimmy's across the road and perhaps five or six
yards in Rubin's slipstream. He silently tracks Rubin as he's
climbing the stairs, closing the distance, and shadows him along
the passageway. And it is shadows because the lights are on the

blink. Off, on, and now completely off. (At close of play yesterday the contractor's electrician, in a mighty rush to get home, had temporarily, and quickly, taped up a mess of connecting cables. 'Sure that'll be just fine for now.' But it hasn't been.)

Rubin, key in his lock and starting to push his door open, checks himself. Now it could be that he's picked up a soft footfall, the creak of a floorboard. Or it could be the sixth sense that helps his survival in a cruel and violent world. But whatever the reason, he's aware of someone behind him in the passageway and, in the quickest of glances, he takes in a blurred figure – courtesy of the lackadaisical electrician – of someone in the gloom. Someone who's paused when he paused, who's standing silently a dozen feet from himself. This vague figure seems to have an arm raised pointing at him. Pointing? There's only one thing that stance could mean and Rubin hurls himself through his door, slams it behind him, sprawls to the floor as the crack, crack, crack of small arms fire follows him in, showers him with splintered wood. Rubin slides across the floor, retrieves his own gun from its hiding under the sofa. Then he crawls back to the door and listens. But there's nothing to hear, it's as silent as the grave. Rubin, keeping his low-level profile, pulls the door open an inch. Two inches. More. He squints into the twilight and then suddenly, without a flicker of warning, every ceiling light is instantly ablaze and he can see the length of the passage. The empty passage.

'Man, that was close,' Rubin mutters to himself.

And it was also quick because the timeline from Rubin putting his key in the lock to checking out the hallway is barely half a minute. Then Rubin taps on the bedroom door, thanking the Lord that Angel was out of the way of the ruckus.

'It's OK, Angel. It's good,' he's saying into the silent room as outside in the passageway there's heavy-booted footsteps. If Rubin could hear, decipher, the murmur of voices, it would be the foreman builder saying that first job for Ed the electrician 'is to get these fuckin' lights working properly before someone trips over and breaks their fuckin' neck.'

But Rubin won't hear anything because the silence in the bedroom is deafening.

Jimmy, desperate to be well away from the crime scene before the blue lights arrive, sets himself into a fast walk back to trailer town. He makes one quick pit stop, a detour down a black back alley, because he has a desperate need and he doesn't want to wet his pants. He pisses behind a monster bin of restaurant waste and it's into the bin he drops his weapon. This should be where no one could ever possibly find it because the refuse collection lorry is only a block away and closing last. Then, it's back to the trailer park where Silas is making a cup of tea and Danny is making a roll-up and hacking his lungs clear to receive his first salvo of nicotine.

Silas says to Jimmy, 'Where the fuck have you been?' and then he catches the look on Jimmy's face as Jimmy slumps, wet and bedraggled, onto the sofa, asks again, 'Where have you been? What the fuck's been going on?'

The fuck's been going on is that Silas and Danny, meant to be acting on a joint enterprise ticket with Jimmy, have been dropped for the final performance. Jimmy's gone solo and neither Silas nor Danny can do anything about it now. Oh, there'll be a bit of snapping but what's done is done and there's no altering that. There's also no altering of the fact that Jimmy, like someone else mentioned earlier, botched the job and it's not common knowledge just yet because the answer to 'Did you muller the mush?' has to be a 'Not sure'.

To know for certain what exactly has happened time needs to be rewound to Rubin leaving Angel, still in bed and warm and sleepy, for his morning shop.

Angel's heard the slam of the door and now that she's awake proper she lays in the warmth of their bed until the nagging need for her morning pee becomes a matter of urgency. After which she flicks on the light and stands for a minute in front of the full-length mirror. Angel knows she's beautiful and she admires her body, admires the fact that her breasts look ever so slightly fuller and that her belly has not yet begun to stretch. She looks and admires and thinks that today she'll tell Rubin the good news. She's still thinking of this when she hears his key in the lock, and perhaps only hears the first of the three discharges from Jimmy Penfold's weapon. This first bullet had found the gap between door and jamb and had travelled through the partition wall that separates reception from bedroom. Weak lime plaster, slices of chestnut lathe, do nothing to deflect its deadly journey.

Poor Angel stands in front of the mirror a fraction of a second too long. If she hadn't been in that exact spot, and at that exact moment, the bullet from Jimmy Penfold's misaimed pistol would not have entered her back at just above kidney height. And it would not have mushroomed out through her still-flat stomach and she might not have met her dying eyes in the mirror as it cracked from side to side.

Angel collapses onto the double bed where love and lust have combined every night and morning for a month or more. As she's falling, her hands clutch to the mess of her stomach in an instinctive futile protection of the unborn.

That's how Rubin finds her, the love of his life and the remains of a child he'll never hold, never even know of, soaking blood red into the duvet. What he can hold, and what he does hold, is the wreckage of the lovely, still-warm, Angel. It's a perverse fulfilment of evening up the scores for Jimmy Penfold's wish of an eye for an eye, a tooth for a tooth. An innocent for an innocent. And Jimmy doesn't even know it yet.

In this bedroom Rubin holds Angel close to him, strokes her face, strokes her hair, closes her eyes, kisses her mouth. Kisses her goodbye. Then he must lay her gently down and begin to prepare for an ambulance, for the questions of the police. But before that it's a phone call to Winston and the clearing of any incriminating paraphernalia. Drugs, memory sticks, an iPad, two knives and the gun are all passed into the care of a hot-footed courier for concealment elsewhere. Then with all doors closed and dead ends sealed, Rubin reports a murder. The perpetrator of this killing, and his accomplices, have already packed their bags and taken the high road and the first reports of the shooting, then a fatality, then the sex of the victim, filter through to Jimmy and co. via the radio and Silas trawling on his phone. Danny's at the wheel of the getaway vehicle with Silas as co-pilot and roller-upper of cigarettes. This mainly benefits Jimmy who, slumped in the back, is lighting up one fag after another. So the news is collated, put into order and fact and Silas, shaking his head, and saying with disbelief,

'You must have mullered the rakkli, Jimmy.'

'I can't have. Fuckin' can't have. I didn't see anyone else, just fuckin' Rubin.'

Danny comes in with, 'We should have gone together, like we agreed,' which is not at all helpful after the event. Jimmy says that it wouldn't have made any difference, it was his shout, and for Danny to keep his yoks on the drom 'cos the last thing he needs now is to get pulled by the gavvers.

The undeniable truth is presented later on the evening news when they're parked up at a safe house – the whereabouts of which are not for the disclosing but it has no near neighbours – and a special report on violent Britain is underway. (This is pre-empting tomorrow morning's papers which will front page with,

Innocent Angel victim of gangland vendetta. Mystery gunman kills teenage lover of Manchester businessman with suspected criminal connections. Local MP, Lucy Plover, calls for community cohesion in the face of what could be interpreted as a racist murder.)

For Jimmy, it's a strange unreal feeling watching the television and knowing that it's him they're talking about, a callous killer who fired through the door of a flat, 'in complete disregard for anyone's life,' says the presenter as she positions herself for her maximum benefit in front of a screen-filling image of Angel's face. The presenter's face is set in empathy as she says,

'This beautiful teenager, standing on the threshold of her life, was the victim of a horrific killing. Innocent Angel' – this is to become a much-overused couplet – 'didn't deserve to die; she was simply in the wrong place at the wrong time.'

There'll be a couple more minutes of eulogy and then a brief discussion with her co-host – dyed dark hair, middle-aged male running to fat – on the requisite homely sofa. Then they'll flirt a bit before moving on to the very important questions of whether toilet seats have become smaller or have our butts become bigger?

At the safe house three pairs of eyes are glued to the telly and Danny's slowly shaking his head and muttering, 'Christ, Jimmy. You did hit the girl.'

Jimmy's staring at the screen like it's a horror movie. He's seeing the face of the girl he killed for the first time and she's so lovely, so young, she'd barely give Mikey two years – so innocent-looking. She's someone's daughter and she's collateral damage. Just like Zilla was. Silas says for the fourth time,

'You sure there's nothing? You didn't touch nothing?'

Jimmy hadn't touched anything, not even the wall in the staircase or the passageway of Rubin's flat. His feet had trod on the stairs and floor but his shoes are now charred wrecks, his morning attire cinders, in the first job when they got here. So the only connection is the gun and that's been safely disposed of into the monster bin of kitchen waste that was as good a dumping place as any. At least it should have been but there always seems to be something that may be a problem for Jimmy. In this case, it's that he wasn't alone in the dark alleyway. Someone saw him lifting the lid of the bin, saw him drop something into its mess of an interior.

This someone was Homeless Man, who's spent yet another typical night in Manchester – gusting wind and drifting rain – and Homeless Man has borne the last five of these typical Mancunian nights in this alley doorway. This has been one of his better shelters; it's off the main drag and the door in its recess – peeling paint and nailed shut tighter than a duck's whosskit – seeps a little warmth from the steamy kitchen behind it. Homeless Man is sharing his alley haven with the monster wheelie-bin that, in the early hours of the morning, lifts its lid to swallow the leftovers from the Chinese takeaway out front. He delves into the bin, feeling for spare ribs, a grasping of special fried rice, a pottage of sticky Eastern dishes. This well-cooked and well-mixed food – and reasonably fresh with it – fills his belly and drives energy into his tall, bony frame.

For the first time since God knows when, Homeless Man is warm and dry and properly fed. Here, in his sheltered doorway, he's been settled into the sleep of the contented, where the wet and the cold and the bluster of the wind doesn't wake him. What does wake him in this damp dawn is the acute sensitivity of the old soldier. It's a startle into wakefulness, a sudden yank from the depth of sleep, a return to an awareness honed in the dusts of the desert. As still and as silent as a statue, invisible in the deep shadow, Homeless Man watches as the furtive figure raises the lid of his larder long enough to plant something inside, and then leaves with the hurried pace of the guilty.

The now curious Homeless Man gives it a few minutes and then looks to see what has been delivered. He has a brevit among his foodstuffs, a root about into fried rice and sweet and sour chicken balls. But as soon as he touches the cool, smooth, rounded barrel he knows what his present is. There's a catch to his breathing, a pounding to his heart, as he lifts his find into the dim light of the dawning day.

How long is it since he felt the reassurance of a weapon like this? Five years? Ten tears? Blurred years. But it fits to him. Perfectly. Moulds to his hand. Belongs to him. God, it feels good to hold; the last time he felt like this he was young and strong and burned by the desert sun. And that was when his mind was complete and working well and his thoughts didn't slither away from him like snakes in the grass.

'Mine,' Homeless Man says to the handgun. 'You're mine.' And he feels like a complete person, like he's whole again.

It's a good job Jimmy and co. have packed up and left because Winston's sending out runners on a search across the city for the accidental assassin. They're on the lookout for strangers, some-one who doesn't fit. These runners watch, they ask questions, they put their ears to the ground. They beat people up, thrash them for a result that can't be realised because the trail is too vague and is already cooling, because Jimmy, Danny and Silas have hit the road south. They've vanished into the maze of contacts and safe houses and caravan parks that belong to the travelling people. Over the next few days they'll work their way quietly down the country and within this time Jimmy phones Meg.

'It didn't go well,' is his understatement.

Meg already knows: she's read the papers, seen the news, connected the dots.

Jimmy says, shaking his head to himself, 'I fucked it up, Meg.'

And because he failed in that duty, young Angel is laying stiff and cold on the mortuary slab. That's the part that's unreal to Jimmy. It's like he's almost removed from the event. Like he hadn't done it. He's never spoken to Angel. Never saw Angel in the flesh. Never knew Angel. Although she's more than just a name, more than just a picture on the TV screen, she's an accidental killing that's evened up the score. An Angel for a Zilla. A measure of satisfaction to know that Rubin must be feeling what he's been feeling.

20

At Elm Hill Park, Mikey, receiver of brief phone calls every few days from his feral father, spends some of his time helping Caleb Smith, general dealer and building contractor. At least that's what it says on the door of his lorry.

And if Mikey is a little quiet at times – every day he passes the blackened patch of concrete that was home – and if sometimes Caleb only receives a grunt as an answer to a question, it's understandable. He's lost his mother, his dad's on the run and he's under the wing of a man who thinks that work ends when the pubs open. This man, and the missus to him, also provide a home for young Mikey in the shape of a six-metre-long touring caravan that gave up touring years ago. It's in a tight space between Caleb's static and the boundary fence and has just the single mod con of an electric connection. This well-hidden home – screening bushes east and west – provides Mikey with a bit of privacy and somewhere to lay his weary head.

Caleb Smith has a daughter Charity – eleven years old and thin as a rasher of bacon, hair carelessly framing her sharp features – who doesn't usually say a lot. But this afternoon it's a knock on Mikey's door and the offering of a hunk of bread and cheese on a dinner plate.

'Mum said you might like this.'

Then she stands in the doorway and lapses into silence as her bright magpie eyes flit around Mikey's abode, not settling on anything in particular until they settle on him. Mikey's drawn into the strangeness of her gaze and the huskiness of a voice that's much too old for her child's face. She's stroking her throat and she's saying for Carter to keep his jukal inside tonight. Then she turns around and she's gone and Mikey wonders about the oddness of this child. But he doesn't have to wonder for long because early the next morning, when he goes to Carter's for a cup of tea, Silas tells that Carter is out the back. His prized jukal, Will the Whippet, choked on a bone last night and Carter's digging a hole for him.

'Pheasant bone,' Silas says to Mikey. 'A fucking pheasant bone caught up and he couldn't breathe. We couldn't do nothing. Couldn't fucking reach it.'

Then Silas puts his hand to his throat just like Charity did. Like Charity does when Mikey sees her walking down the site on this same morning. She's holding a handkerchief to her mouth, stifling a cough, swallowing with pain as though she's got something sharp caught in her gullet. 'You all right, Charity?' gets a hoarse, 'Gonna see if Meg can do something. Throat's mullerin me,' in response. But she's not going to be mullered like the jukal because Meg takes a dusty bottle from a shelf in her vardo, wipes it clean, draws the cork, and says for her to take a swig and, 'Gargle it, my Charity. Swill it around. Spit it out.' And Charity does as she's bidden, spits it onto the poove where Wilma has a quick sniff and recoils abruptly.

Now this last year Meg's been watching the daughter of Caleb Smith because there's something about her that draws the eye, makes you want to hear her voice. Charity Smith is pushing twelve and her clothes hang on her bony frame, and her hair reaches down to her shoulders. This girl's a loner; she doesn't look for company. She's content to wander, to appear and disappear, to drift quietly into view and drift quietly out of view. You'll find her in unexpected places, sitting by a dew pond in the shade of a willow, walking down a quiet lane, sipping a Coke in a café and watching the street through the window, or then she might be reaching above the door of Lavinia's vardo and tracing the wording of the name with her forefinger. She'll ask Meg 'Who is this?' and Meg will recreate the passage of the present to the past, as to why the blood that joins the living and the dead beats the same in both of their hearts.

Sometimes on a wet day Charity will tap on the door of Meg's motorhome, take a cup of tea and a slice of cake. And sometimes in the dusk of the day she'll climb Elm Hill with Meg and they'll watch the sun setting over the low ground. And sometimes she'll tell Meg of the strange dreams that she's not sure are dreams and Meg will nod her head and say very gently,

'Tell me, my child. Tell me what you see.'

Charity will speak slowly, haltingly, as she describes the world that startles with its insistence into her eyes. Into her mind. It's the world that Meg dwells in, that Zingara read of in the casting of the runes, that caused Lavinia to mourn before due time. It's a world that drifts between past, present and future and sometimes it's a curse that you wouldn't wish upon your worst enemy, a gift that you can never part with. A gift until the sweep of the Reaper's scythe takes it all away. Perhaps.

Mikey's days when he gives school a miss are filled with mornings of erratic labour and afternoons spent in some bar room. He's rapidly becoming sick to death of cheap beer, packets of crisps and games of pool, although it's Caleb's idea of a heavenly existence. He likes it best when he's on the knocker, calling at folki's houses to see if there's rubbish to clear, scrap metal to take away or loose slates to fix.

On this particular morning Mikey is doing the rounds, sounding out potential customers, and due to meet Caleb at the pub on the corner in a couple of hours. It's wet this morning and there are puddles in the grey streets, and the trimmed hedges of suburbia drip with the falling of the rain. At number 42 Estcourt Drive – a detached four-bedroomed house with a double garage, gravel drive and large rear garden – Mikey taps on the pale-blue entrance door. Now Hannah, the girl who opens the door and should also be at school, can't help gazing at him framed in the doorway. Mikey's tall for his age and his hair, curled by the rain, is longer than the norm. He's fifteen-going-on-sixteen and looks about three years older. He's a bit on the rough side. Like Heathcliff perhaps, a bit wild, a bit romantic.

Hannah Aubrey is clean and smart in sprayed-on jeans and a T-shirt. Her long blonde mane is pulled gently back from her face and her feet are bare. She's fifteen-going-on-twenty-one.

She looks at her gypsy visitor and says, 'You'd better come in out of the rain.'

Now it might seem unusual inviting a didikai into her mother and father's spotless home – they'd have a fit if they knew who was sitting at the breakfast table dipping digestives into Yorkshire Gold tea – but this is no coincidental meeting. It's been arranged in exchanges of texts and messages. Mikey and Hannah have been spending time together inside and out of Boarston Comprehensive. She's even a picture of Mikey on her iPad screensaver and when her mother, who prides herself on being her only child's confidante, asks who this handsome youth is, Hannah shrugs her shoulders and says nonchalantly, 'Just a boy from school, Mum.'

That explanation doesn't do justice to sweet wet kissing in the cinema, for Mikey sneaking into her room when there's a home-study afternoon and her mum's out and her dad's at work.

Mrs Aubrey is one of those mothers who just has to be involved in every aspect of her daughter's life. She's the type that gushes over Hannah's friends, wants to be included and be a part of their conversations. In fact, she wants to be one of them. She engages them on fashion, on music. She'd be better off leaving the youngsters to themselves because the world's moved on in the twenty-five years since she was a giggling schoolgirl.

'You can tell me, Hannah.'

'You can tell me anything, Hannah.'

'I'm interested in who you know, Hannah.'

'I want to know everything, Hannah.'

'At least tell me his name, Hannah.'

She's gifted the moniker, Mike, and she's away with, 'Mike? Mike who?'

Wouldn't anyone become a little pissed off with this incessant questioning? Wouldn't you raise your voice and give Mummy what she wants just to see the shock on her face? 'Penfold, Mother.'

'Penfold? He's not one of—?'

'Yes, Mother. He lives at Elm Hill, the caravan site.'

Inside Mrs Aubrey's head there's a confused state of mind between her right-on liberal views and the fact that her only child is mixing with that lot, who don't even live in houses. The site where the police are always visiting and where there was that terrible fire. Then she composes herself and says brightly,

'Still, it's not serious is it, Hannah?'

Hannah, clever Hannah, knowing which buttons to press, says with mock seriousness and a catch in her voice, 'It might be, Mother. It might be.'

Mummy Aubrey hugs her daughter. 'Oh my poor darling,' she says as she thinks back to the first boy that broke her heart.

My mother told me that I never should play with the gypsies in the wood.

But she did.

At Boarston nick, Chief Inspector Isaacs has called Tom Malone into his office to tell him,

'I'm putting Harv . . . I mean DC Harris into your team, Tom. I want him kept in the loop.'

'But, sir—'

'No buts, Malone. You've been chasing expensive shadows for too long. A fresh face, a fresh look at this Penfold inquiry might push it on a bit.'

'But, Sir, all we need is an exhumation—' This subject has been broached several times.

'What we need is more evidence, a lot more before we could do that Malone.'

'But, sir—'

'Where is this elusive Mr Penfold now? Eh?'

The only thing Tom Malone's sure of is he's not under his headstone. 'But, sir—'

'That's all, Malone.' Isaacs delivers this with a dismissive flick of the hand to a seething Tom Malone.

This meeting has put Tom Malone on a hell of a downer, not at all helped by Polly cancelling an evening meeting because she's, 'Feeling a little poorly. Picked up a sickness bug.'

Also suffering from the effects of sickness, though definitely not through a bug, is Maria. She's going to great pains to keep her pregnancy secret with her pretend period and her reliance on the excuse of 'It must be something I ate' every time she has to run to the loo. At home, her occasional morning throw-ups are masked by the shower and the radio both on at full bore. At the station restroom she'll sit in a cubicle, holding her throat closed until she's sure there is no one else in there, and then she'll perform a gut-wrenching vomit as quickly as she can get rid of it. But there are times, days in fact, when her stomach only produces a belch with no follow-through of a debilitating retch.

What surprises Maria is that she can be two people. She can be the loving wife, the tender wife who sits with Carol's head in her lap as they plan out the years to come. Or she can be the deceitful, unfaithful, pregnant bitch of a wife who's lying to conceal the truth, the lie that's dated to end with a vacuum aspiration. Maria wants it over, wants to wake up one morning with all of this behind her. Finished for good. She wants her life to be uncomplicated, fresh and guiltless like it used to be. She wonders if she's dreaming the impossible dream.

21

At Boarston nick, the newcomer DC Harvey Harris is already getting too big for his size twelve boots. His large frame sits at every desk, his budding cauliflower ears hear every pin drop and his outsize fingers tap his keyboard to access every file of misdemeanours, every case running. His big mouth reports every morsel of information back to his uncle. Very little that goes on escapes the eyes of the favoured nephew, Harvey Harris, and by proxy, Chief Inspector Isaacs. They're empire building, and Boarston Police Station belongs to them. Their noses are poked in places noses shouldn't be poked and if the premises were dusted for fingerprints, nepotism would be spelt out in black carbon powder on every surface. The only case that they're not seeing quite as much as they should is the one that Tom Malone's holding closest to his chest. And the person that the case is stalled on for now is in a murky backstreet pub near to Bristol's dockside, as dusk is falling.

Jimmy's sitting with Silas supping a pint of bitter. Danny's not with them. He's shot through a couple of days ago to catch up on his training – he's contracted to fight in a week's time and he's got to lose seven pounds of flab from his midriff. There's about as much chance of that as him beating an up-and-coming fighter who's never lost; fifteen out of sixteen on savage stoppages and the other one on points against a teak-hard man who'd never been dropped. He's known by the sobriquet of Berserker Billy Best. Judging by the man's reputation, the best thing for Danny to do would be to trip over the rope on his entrance to the ring and not get up again. But Danny is Danny, and his pride and his overriding desire for a few bar won't ever let him duck out of a fight.

About nine o'clock on this Thursday night, and after a couple more beers, Jimmy goes into the pub yard for a smoke and to phone Mikey, who answers under a background clatter of laughter and overloud voices.

Mikey, shielding his mobile against the noise, says, 'I'll call you back. Give me a couple of minutes.' He so nearly tags on the 'Dad' who's not meant to exist, because it's a natural answer, a natural flow of their conversation. Or it used to be. Dad and Mum. Jimmy takes a seat, settles himself into the waiting with a pull on his drink and a few deep draughts of nicotine. His phone (it's not actually his, it was bought by brother Silas) is in his lap and as soon as the screen lights up he's on to it.

Jimmy says, 'Where you to Mikey?'

'In town with a few mates.'

But there's more to this conversation than enquiries about whereabouts or a 'How're you doing?' Mikey has now become sole concealer of a pair of ferry tickets and two passports. (These were delivered in an A4 package – courtesy of Ollie Cooper – to Meg at the site by a motorbike courier who could easily pass as a member of Satan's Slaves.) They're currently residing beneath Mikey's pants and socks in his underwear drawer.

So if all goes to plan, the leaving to Ireland should begin at Pembroke Docks in the early hours of this coming Wednesday. It's a definite for Jimmy, but Mikey does have a choice and

Jimmy's been thinking about this, about dragging his boy across the water. Mikey isn't carrying anything on his head, he could stay at Elm Hill where there'll be Silas, Danny, Carter and all that he knows. And it's not too late if he wants to change his mind? But no, Mikey doesn't want to change his mind and he says,

'Well Mum wouldn't have let you go on your own,' and they share a laugh that's not as sweet as it's bitter. 'It's all arranged. I'll see you there then.'

'See you there.' Mikey does tack a 'Dad' on this time and there's a comfort in the familiarity of that word. Like when Mum and Dad fitted as a couple. Before all of this shit happened.

Now the reason that Mikey couldn't talk that first time was because he was sitting with Hannah at one of her friend's houses where the vodka bottle is being passed from mouth to mouth, tilted for a burn of spirits. It's more of a gathering than a party – the host's parents are out for the evening – and by 11 o'clock it's breaking-up time and Mikey's walking Hannah home. She's been making plans for the following weekend because there's a film she's just been dying to see and Mikey may not like it 'cos it's a bit soppy so she could go with her friends and meet him at Burger King afterwards and she was going to ask her mum if he could stop over and . . . and then it's like she realises Mikey's not interrupted her flow of intentions.

'You're quiet,' she says and he could joke about not being able to get a word in edgeways. But he doesn't. He tells her that he's going away for a while and she stops in her tracks, looks into his face.

'Away? What do you mean away? Mikey?'

Of course he has to tell her that the away is to Ireland, 'Mum's family,' he says. 'I should go and see them after – you know – what happened.' Mikey's slightly hesitant in this delivery because it doesn't feel right to be using his mother in a lie.

Then of course it's the unanswerable question of,

'But it won't be for long, will it?'

'It'll be a little while, Hannah.'

'What? A few days? A week?'

But they're talking of a long time because Mikey's loyalty is to Jimmy, to the family. Him and Hannah will stay in touch. He promises he'll phone regularly. Without fail.

Hannah's silent, taking it all in, and then she asks,

'When, Mikey? When are you going?' And when he tells her he thinks it's going to break her young and tender heart. He feels a bit choked himself; he's not just some whistling gypsy that's come over the hill to steal the heart of Hannah.

At Number 42, Mrs Aubrey has been waiting for her daughter to come in. She'd given herself an early night on account that she's been carrying a mild headache all afternoon but, like most parents of young girls, she's laying in bed and won't settle until her daughter's home. Mrs Aubrey has heard the back door open and close and what should normally follow is a footfall on the stairs, maybe a humming of the latest tune, the flick of a light switch, the flush of the loo. Mrs Aubrey listens and there's none of these sounds and so she goes down to the kitchen to find Hannah slumped at the table, her head in her hands, crying softly to herself.

'Boy trouble,' Mrs Aubrey thinks immediately, and slips her arms around her daughter's shaking shoulders. 'What's the matter, darling?' she murmurs.

'Oh, Mum,' Hannah cries, and then she tells her mother that her boyfriend, Mikey, is leaving, going to Ireland on the ferry.

This is delivered with barely a pause for breath.

'On Wednesday, Mum. It's so soon and I don't know when he'll be back.'

'My poor darling,' says Mrs Aubrey, the mother who's desperate to be a sister and an understanding friend to her daughter. She's also feeling guiltily relieved because now she's thinking that Hannah can find herself a new boyfriend. Hopefully someone more suitable, someone she'll meet at university. Someone with a future in the professions. Eventually Hannah goes up to bed, her attentive mother listening out for her until dawn streaks the sky and Mrs Aubrey hears her husband's key in the lock.

Sergeant Aubrey has been on night-desk duty at Boarston Police Station and he's had one hell of a night. All he wants to do is lay his head on the pillow of the nuptial bed and let sleep blot out the echoes of a screaming banshee who should be in an asylum, an alcoholic who pissed himself and of a free-for-all between two warring hen parties that leaves hair extensions and acrylic nails littering the station floor. Enough's enough for one night but it isn't enough for tired, worn-out Sergeant Aubrey because now he has to hear all the cares and worries of his wife and he will have to empathise, later on, with his heartbroken daughter.

On Friday evening Sergeant Aubrey – Dave to his closer associates – sits at the bar of the Falcon and ponders his sleeve of ale and the drama that's still being played out at Estcourt Drive. Sometimes, just sometimes, he thinks he should pack his bags and find himself a quiet little flat in a quiet little town and discover some peace in his life. But that'll remain a vague dream for him because of course he's not going to do that. He'll jog on in his job, pay up the mortgage on Number 42, retire at can be and slip into portly ageing. Mrs Aubrey will coincide her retirement with her husband's and then they'll downsize their house and take two foreign holidays a year – Greece and Spain probably, because Mrs Aubrey likes the sun.

Meanwhile, when he's doing his shifts at Boarston Police Station – front of house – Dave has to put up with Chief Inspector Isaacs and his overweight nephew chipping away at him. But for now it's another drink on this night off and he's thinking that he's barely forty and there's nothing exciting to look forward to.

Desk Sergeant Aubrey is already on his fourth pint when Tom Malone, after yet another terse telephone conversation with Polly, calls in for an off-duty drink. Polly has been blowing hot and cold and tonight's tête-à-tête has been more like a blast from the Arctic.

'Polly, please tell me what's the matter.' Polly's 'But you know what's the matter,' is followed by a deep sigh.

Tom Malone says, 'Then let me make it right. Just come home.'

'Oh Tom. I don't know. I miss you but –' Then, in the background, her background, her mother's calling, cooing almost, 'Polly dear, I'm home.'

'Look Tom, I've got to go. Phone me tomorrow.'

The handset goes down and DS Tom Malone mutters, 'Yeah, tomorrow' to himself and gathers up his car keys and heads for the boozer where Dave Aubrey is sinking pints for England.

They meet up at the bar, these two familiar faces from the same nick, and Desk Sergeant Dave Aubrey, in his near-kailied state, just needs someone to bore about his unsatisfactory life. This is certainly making Tom Malone's night a lucky one: he's had the brush-off from Polly and now he's being buttonholed by Dave Aubrey who's moaning to him about all the fuckin' interference he's getting from Chief Inspector Isaacs and his oversized nephew.

He's a talker, this police officer, and it seems he could go on for an eternity in his monotone monologue. Poor Tom Malone. Even a couple of swifties barely take the edge off the boredom of listening to someone else's troubles. But then his ears prick up. Dave Aubrey's saying something about his daughter who seems besotted by some 'little toerag from the gippo site'.

'Who did you say?' Tom Malone asks casually.

'Mike someone . . . Penfold, I think. Yeah, Penfold. Lost his parents in that fire.' Then Dave Aubrey stops his chat with a quizzical look at Tom Malone. 'Didn't you pull a Penfold in a few months back? Couldn't make anything stick? Same family?' He muses, 'Yeah. Course. I was on the desk.'

Tom Malone nods in agreement, and then Dave Aubrey, in his unloading sharing mode to a fellow officer, tells him that his daughter, Hannah, is heartbroken because this young didikai of a boyfriend is pissing off to Ireland.

Tom Malone, suddenly extremely interested, asks, 'When's that then, Dave?' to his new mate.

Dave Aubrey pauses, takes a swallow of his beer, 'This week sometime. Wednesday I think. And after all we've done for her,' Dave Aubrey moans, 'she'll probably end up living in a caravan making pegs around the fire.' He takes a long swallow of his pint and adds, 'And selling holly wreaths at Christmas.'

Then he starts droning on about life at the station and the pattern of his shifts and so on.

Tom Malone's not listening now, he's feeling that surge of excitement. Events are moving at last. He wonders if his spy in the camp has any info for him, info on the wandering Jimmy

Penfold. He gets himself home and comfortable and then thinks he'll give that spy a chance to redeem himself.

Ricky Ward's mobile phone has already informed him that it's dangerously low on battery life on account that young Ricky has been streaming down some hard porn when Tom Malone calls in for a catch-up on progress.

'You promised me a result, Ricky, and it seems there's fuck-all happening.'

'It's been a bit quiet, Mr Malone.'

'It's been too quiet, Ricky.'

The warning is in the detective's serious tone and Ricky gets a familiar feeling of dread in his guts.

'I'll sort it, Mr Malone. I'll sort it.'

'ASAP, Ricky, or else our deal's off.'

This call leaves a panicked, starting to sweat Ricky Ward thinking, '*I've got to do something. Anything*,' because he has that three-year stretch riding on the right result. This mugger of old ladies and snatcher of handbags is desperate enough to take a walk around the dimly lit caravan park to see if there is anything on offer. He's thinking that if he's going to pick up any useful information there's only one place where that's going to be. As luck will have it, Caleb Smith's home is in darkness and there isn't a light showing from Mikey Penfold's temporary abode. Ricky Ward, a shadow amongst shadows, taps gently on Mikey's door for confirmation of an empty residence which, luckily enough for Ricky Ward's intentions, it is. He slips the door catch with his own perfectly legitimate credit card and he's inside in a flash. Now Ricky Ward is looking for that something, anything, that'll fulfil his contract with the constabulary. He draws the curtains and risks a wall light and starts his searching.

There aren't many hiding places in a caravan and furtive Ricky is quick and thorough, even if he doesn't know what he's looking

for. And that should be the hand-delivered plain brown A4 envelope containing two passports in the names of Frederick Field
and Roy Field respectively – new ID for a new life and fitted to
the faces of father and son Penfold – and a printed email confirming those two tickets for foot passengers on the *Isle of Inishmore*.
This ferry is leaving at 2.45 a.m. on Wednesday morning and
travelling across the Irish Sea from Pembroke to Rosslare.

Mikey should perhaps have taken more care to hide the package, but who could have guessed that someone would be giving
the place the once-over? So, at the back of Mikey's underwear
and sock drawer, Ricky finds Ollie's favour to Meg and brings it
into the light. This is a find, a gold-nugget find. For Ricky Ward,
it's his get-out-of-jail-free card that he can't wait to deal to Mr
Malone. He'll photograph the evidence and send it through to
his keeper. But there just isn't enough power for the snapshots;
Juicy Lucy on Porn for Free has drained more of Ricky's battery
than he realised. There's a 'shit' and then a couple of 'fucks' as
he searches for a pen, a pencil. Anything to write with. Now as
luck would have it, Mikey's been keeping a check on his working
hours – Caleb Smith can err on the vague side when matching up
time and money – and Mikey's notebook and Biro are sitting in
company on the worktop. Ricky, sweating a bit now, snatches
them up and laboriously copies out the Penfolds' – or Fields' –
planned trip to the Emerald Isle. He tears out the page of
jumbled upper and lower case words, pockets it, and piles
Mikey's smalls back into the drawer. Then he's out of there,
slinking back unseen and unnoticed to his caravan home. He
plugs his phone in to charge and gives it the time of a mug of
meski and a tuvla before calling up Tom Malone. Ricky Ward is
ready to share what he hopes, for him, will be a jail-evading
chunk of information.

* * *

Tom Malone had booked himself an early night. He's had a hot bath, a shot of whisky, and he's stretched out in the non-marital bed watching a bit of telly when Ricky Ward makes his call.

'What is it, Ricky?'

'Mr Malone, it's really important. I found something about Jimmy Penfold.'

'And what's that, Ricky?'

'I know where he's going to be, Mr Malone.'

Ricky then recites rather haltingly – his reading is as bad as his writing – but rather proudly, from his notes: 'Field – that's the name he's using, Mr Malone. Isle of Inishmore. 2.45 a.m. Wednesday at Pembroke, Wales.

'It's when they're leaving, Mr Malone. They got passports an' all.'

'They? Who's they?'

'Mikey's going with him, Mr Malone.'

Tom Malone, now with his silver Parker pen – a birthday present from Polly in happier times – poised for action and a police force notebook in his lap, says, 'Tell me again, Ricky.'

Ricky Ward reads through his scribblings once more, as it's written down and carefully digested by Tom Malone who gives him a 'Well done, Ricky. Well done.'

Ricky says, 'But you haven't forgotten our agreement have you Mr Malone?'

'Of course not, Ricky,' and Tom Malone ends the phone call with a reassurance that his word is his bond. Then he has his best night's sleep in a long time and he's up bright and early the next morning. It may be a Saturday but he's at his desk while most of the force are still abed. Keen is Tom Malone and he's sorting out the week's agenda, making sure that all the case files in his realm are up to date. That's all except the one that belongs to Jimmy Penfold. (He's now titled this file 'JP. The Undead

Gypsy' because he's sure he is.) He opens the file, goes to the 'To add' section and begins to type in 'At 11.03 p.m. on Friday the 17th I received some info on Mr James Penfold from an associate of his. Mr Penfold will be at . . .'

Tom Malone stops, looks at what he's written, at what it means. And that's the sharing of this case, equal shares for doing nothing, half a cake for someone who bears an uncanny resemblance to Chief Inspector Isaacs. Tom Malone thinks back to the bitterness of the Huntingdon double-cross. Then it's an internal 'Fuck them' and he grits his teeth and presses the delete button and wipes out the words. This case is his. He's pursued it and he owns it.

If this plays right it should mean the longed for promotion, a move away from the backwater of Boarston, a reunion with the inconsistent love of his life, sweet Polly Malone.

And talking of Polly, Tom Malone is going to book a table for tonight at their favourite restaurant in Boarston. He'll wine her and dine her, show her the works and hope for a favourable result.

22

While DS Tom Malone is encountering some success in his investigation into Jimmy Penfold, there's no such luck for Winston. It's a frustrating time for him. He has a violent reputation to uphold and the justice administered should be swift and deadly to let everyone know, as Winston colourfully puts it,

'No fucker shits on my doorstep and gets away with it.'

Winston's put ten grand on the head of the nameless man and the word spreads like a virus through the criminal internet. But unless there's a God almighty cock-up for Jimmy Penfold, that ten grand will stay safely in the bank. With all of this on his plate now is certainly not a good time for Veryll Evans to call Winston and ask for the remainder of monies owed for services rendered. Winston says, 'I'm busy, I'll call you next week.'

'You said that last time.'

'Don't bug me, man. I got a lot going on.'

'I want what I'm owed,' says Veryll Evans in that softly deceiving Welsh voice.

Winston says, 'I said when the dust settles.'

'It's taking a long time to settle.'

'I'll decide when that is.' Winston, losing his patience, abruptly curtails the conversation with the stabbing of the off button. Veryll Evans speaks to his phone as though the call is still connected, as though Winston will hear the words, 'I think you should be showing more respect to me.' A ripple of anger deepens the greyness of his cold, cold eyes because for Mr Evans the killing isn't, and it will never be, just about the money.

Veryll Evans sits for ten minutes staring into a faraway place, reliving a long-ago playground in a little Welsh school. He shakes his head to clear it and then dials out a number on his phone. On the pick-up, he simply says, 'I'll do it.'

It's Saturday night in an intimate little restaurant in Boarston and things have been going really well between Tom Malone and the pale and pretty Polly. In fact they're going so well that the romantic candlelight flickering onto the table is also flickering onto the twining of their hands.

Polly is saying, hesitantly, 'Perhaps you're right Tom, perhaps we could try again.'

Tom Malone says, 'It's all I've ever wanted.'

Polly whispers, 'If we could start again Tom. A fresh start for us.'

'I'd do anything for that, Polly.'

'Would you, Tom? Anything?'

Tom Malone, full to the brim with love and hope and thinking of this fresh start in a new place. He could put in for a transfer just as soon as Jimmy Penfold is in the bag. Life hasn't looked this good in a long time. He promises his wife,

'Anything in the world, Polly. Just say the word.'

Polly hesitates, takes a mouthful of her wine, and then says, 'For me, Tom. Would you give up the force for me?'

Tom Malone is suddenly aware that this may not be a hypothetical question and he says, blurts out really,

'But it would never come to that, surely Polly?'

His words carry his disbelief and it's not exactly what she was wanting to hear. Her light pink lips start to tremble in her pale porcelain face. Her face falls and there's a choke in her voice as she says that she could hardly ask him to choose between her and the police, could she? Because the police would win every time, that's for sure. And now shed like to go home – that's to her mother's of course.

On that journey Tom Malone does most of the talking and all the apologising.

'You took me by surprise, Polly. I need to think things through.'

But there's not a lot coming back from Polly and it's only when she's getting out of the car that she says,

'I can't forget what happened, Tom. I try, I really try.'

All she wants is Tom to herself. She wants her perfect life back, to before the chief superintendent's wife took a punt on her handsome husband. For this she blames Tom Malone with justification, and she blames the police force without justification.

And Tom Malone blames their marriage problems simply on his one stupid mistake. (It's actually two because Maria must also go on the charge sheet.) He dwells on this in his lonely cottage, surrounded by mementoes of his and Polly's life together, and he can't quite convince himself that she may have given him a straight choice between her and the force? How could he possibly live without either?

He gets himself into bed but he knows it's going to be a restless night and it's a good job that tomorrow's the Sabbath.

It's about time to catch up with the travelling Travellers. Jimmy and Silas have moved on from Bristol and further west across the Severn Bridge. They've arrived at a nice, big, private house in the Cardiff postcode. This private house – secluded, four bedrooms with en suites, dining room and spacious lounge with comfortable seating and glimpses of the bay – is owned by Eddie and Selina Wood. It's a pleasant building with a huge garden in a wide road on the far outskirts of Caerdydd. This is a class area and neighbouring houses sit comfortably apart from each other. Top-of-the-range cars are parked in double and even treble garages, but there's to be no parking in sight for the pikey van. Eddie Wood, a powerfully built man in shirtsleeves, swiftly guides it to the back of a high-hedged rear yard. It's here where the loading and unloading of vehicles can be carried out without anyone knowing or seeing. And it's here that Eddie Wood greets Jimmy and Silas with a strong handshake and an enthusiastic enquiry as to the goodness of their journey. Then they follow him to the house, to a more reserved welcome from Selina. Her voice is half the volume of her brother's as she says, 'Glad to see you again, Jimmy.' She laughs, 'And not forgetting you of course, Silas.'

Selina bears a striking similarity to the woman buried next to a stranger in Boarston churchyard. (This could be because she and Zilla actually share a great-grandmother, circa 1920.) Selina has sorted out some fittle for the weary Travellers and they eat at the kitchen table and drink a couple of cool livveners from the fridge.

'Too early for me.' Eddie nods to the beer. 'Stuff to do.'

He goes off to finish a bit of booti in his garage workshop. In fact the workshop is all of his triple garage and the spacious loft above. The inside of the building is set out as a joiner's shop. There are countless chisels and planers and turning lathes and fretsaws and jigsaws and tenon saws. There are brushes and cloths and pots. And there's racks of pine and oak and walnut, light woods and dark woods and sheets of veneers. The floor is crowded with cabinets, chairs, cupboards, an unstuffed sofa, a

Welsh dresser, two oval mirrors – old, old furniture in various states of repair and renovation.

All of this is cloaked in the pungencies of sawn wood, paint and stain, glue and lacquer – a sniff-addict's paradise. It's in the territory of a master carpenter, someone who can replicate seasoned antique furniture; a mush with a flair for creating distressed dressers of the correct period. This coshengro is accomplished in the artistry of deceit for the gullible. (And the not so gullible because some of his pieces have even fooled the experts on *Antiques Roadshow*.)

Selina features in this, too. She'll bid at an auction, work her way carefully through a house effects sale, scan the local papers, tap into the internet. She picks class from tat, jewels from the rubbish heap, with an eye that's been honed with over thirty-years' experience. (That might be a slight exaggeration because she's only thirty-four.) Selina doesn't need any more of a physical description except to reiterate that she's a dead ringer for a dead wife and that's why Jimmy can't help that his eyes keep drifting to her.

Selina and Eddie Wood were born in Dublin. Their father was a dealer in second-hand furniture who kept a yard and a shop and a wife and six chavees on the proceeds of buying and selling and dubious deals. Selina, and especially Eddie, learnt how to spot a fake antique, how to fake an antique and how to sell a fake antique before they left school.

As soon as the siblings were old enough and had saved a wedge of vonga, they left the family and crossed the sea for the rich pickings to be found in England. And Scotland. And Wales, where they've set up a permanent base.

This evening the newly formed quartet are taking a meal in the Welsh Archer. This is one of those pubs – quiet on this night – which provides comfortable seating and just enough light to eat your meal by. The scran's tasty but Jimmy's not got much of an appetite and his drinking's on the swift side, so the beer goes quickly to his head.

Silas rasps, 'You got a thirst on, my pralla,' as Jimmy slots another one away.

Selina says with a laugh on her lips, 'Slow down, we don't want to be after carrying you home, Jimmy.' The Irish is still thick in her accent even after all the years away from the old country.

Jimmy, languishing in the fug of alcohol, feels more relaxed than he has in a good length of time. This shows when he's at the bar and the barmaid, not understanding his accent properly, begins the pour of a cider instead of a bitter.

'Sorry, sir, but I thought you said cider.'

Jimmy, elbows on the counter, says to her, 'I'll forgive you this time,' and she smiles sweetly at him and meets and holds his eyes in more than passing interest.

'Only this time, sir?' She flicks her hair. Her interest might be because Jimmy's scrubbed up well for tonight: clean-shaven, clean shirt, hat cocked, Eddie Wood's best leather coat and pressed strides, choklas polished, air of casualness. Or it just might be because he's a fine, slightly rough, slightly wild-looking man who, for a while at least, has stepped away from all the shite of the last few months. At least for as long as his head will let him before the dreams come a-whispering in. So he laughs at the mort and says, 'Depends on what there is to forgive,' and she replies, 'You'll never know, will you, sir?' Which might be the opening to an invitation.

Now this is the first time Jimmy doesn't get that stab of guilt, like he's deceiving Zilla. She's not standing at his side; she's left him for a while, drifted away with things past. So it's not Zilla but Selina who's soft-footed to his elbow, and she says, 'I'll help you carry the drinks over, Jimmy. Don't want you spilling the valuables.' Then in a low tone to his ear and her eyes towards the barmaid, Selina laughs and adds, 'She's young enough to be yer daughter, Jimmy.'

It's late when the quartet come back to the house and for a while they sit in the dark conservatory sipping nightcaps, smoking cigarettes, spotting satellites through the glass roof, and chewing the fat.

After an hour of this Eddie reckons, 'It's time for oodrus,' and Silas, with a rare stab at humour, says he's had enough as well and he thinks he'll join Eddie, 'But not in the same bed.' And that leaves just Jimmy and his dead wife's cousin sharing a long, wide sun sofa and watching the night sky through that glass roof.

For a while there's a contentment in the silence and Jimmy thinks that Selina might have fallen asleep but then she leans towards him and whispers into the gloom, 'Tell me how it happened with Zilla, Jimmy.'

Her face is a pale ghost of features in this light and she's so close he can feel the warmth of her breath on his face. And he tells her; he talks in a low murmur of all that has been learnt. The story pours out of him, and as Jimmy speaks, the burden eases. It lightens on his shoulders, and although it'll follow him aboard the *Isle of Inishmore* at 2.45 on Wednesday morning, it won't be dragging him back to the dark places tonight.

To anyone who's never experienced the relief, the release, of utterly safe disclosure, it's like a satisfying session with a really good shrink. It's secret and it's safe and it's shared. That's how it is for Jimmy.

Selina, filled with such a tenderness, puts her hand gently to his face and says she's sorry for all that he's been through and she hopes that Ireland will heal him, will give him and Mikey a chance to start again. Then she kisses him with her soft, soft mouth. She kisses his vulnerability and she kisses the nights he's watched the lonely moon steal across the sky and she kisses the bitter loss of a wife and mother. And without knowing it, she kisses the innocence of a Black Angel. Then they lay the full length of each other and her body is firm and warm, and there's the taste of her skin, and the scent of her hair, and there's the shutting out of this world. All except for a moment of such clarity when it's Zilla clinging to him. Zilla whispering her love. And he so nearly speaks her name out loud.

23

Meg is somewhere in Laurie Lee's territory as Silena is enticing Jimmy to break his untaken vow of celibacy. Her motorhome is parked outside an old stone cottage well off the beaten track. This is a lonely building of a single room and a fireplace, a shepherds' shelter from when these hills of the Cotswolds were strewn with sheep. The thick walls are raised in flat masonry and the roof tiles are split slabs of limestone, and it'll easily see out another hundred years. Inside, Meg has lit a yog in the fireplace and yellow flames dance on the bare walls, the shuttered window, the rotting plank door. Outside, pale smoke is drifting up into the heavens of the night; a night that's speckled with stars and a bright moon that's a-spying over the hill. This is a place of light and shadow and silence except for the bovel sighing gently through the rookars.

Meg is in her usual attire – long loose skirt, slack blouse, knitted cardigan, scarf around her hunnel, sturdy chorklars on her feet – except for thick, rubber, elbow-length gloves. In this night she carries a sharp-tined fork to the edge of a deep dark copse where she stops and from her mouth slips a low hoarse question.

'Akai?' she rokkers, and she cocks her poll like she's listening for a confirmation. Wilma, watching from a couple of yards away, shrinks back, flattens her ears to her skull and forms a whine in her throat as Meg drives the fork into the poove to dig, to loosen, to gather, a web of thick roots; finger-thick tubers that should never ever see the light of day. When she's enough of these Meg tugs a Tesco's bag from her pocket, gathers her gardening proceeds together and packs them carefully, gently, into the plastic carrier. And then they, she and the jukal, head back towards the warmth of the fire on the hearth.

In the morning Meg stands on the cold step of the little house, sipping a steaming mug of meski and watching the sun rise over the misted green of the hills and the depths of the woods. She's thinking about what needs to be done, what has to be done and how it doesn't become easier with the passing of all these years.

'Mum,' she says, 'how I wish you were here.' And she cries softly to herself; a skinny old gypsy rawnee weeping for the company of her long departed mother.

In Manchester, Winston's checking out his manor. He's the lord of the feudal system in the area and he makes sure that he's the face, a constant visible reminder. He misses nothing on these streets, in these clubs and pubs and cafés of his territory. He has a duty of protection to these premises and his clientele pay him in hard cash for services rendered. They might grumble but they still pay their monthly dues because it's better the Devil you know. They also pay for their orders of wines and beers and spirits, and base, china white, and whatever is trending in the marketplace.

Whenever Winston's out and about he always has a couple of heavies with him. These are massive men, eighteen or nineteen stones of muscle and bulk. They watch his back, and keep the riff-raff out of his face as Winston strides about barking his orders like he's a resurrection of Idi Amin. But watching him, trailing him, is Veryll Evans. He sees who Winston calls on, who he meets, where he meets them. He's good at not being noticed is Veryll Evans. He's one of those guys who sits next to you on the tube and you're only vaguely aware of someone, a shadow of a person. He's still young enough to carry off the wearing of a baseball cap or to flick his hoodie over his head. Veryll Evans doesn't draw a gaze. The man's nearly invisible, which is a good thing in his line of business.

Also not very visible of late is Rubin, that fine example of attractive manhood. Although he's been a bad, bad boy, involved with violence, extortion, drugs and all sorts of criminal activities, he deserves sympathy for what happened on that dark, wet Manchester morning. For now, he's been taking a back seat in Winston's Enterprises Ltd.

Winston says, 'It'll pay to keep your head down for a bit longer. Just in case someone wants another pop at it.'

For Rubin, keeping his head down means spending his working day at Winston's Administration Centre. In this time and place, Rubin, behind the metal-plated door and barred windows of the building, checks on the progress of the lines of supply and communication. He makes sure the money keeps flowing in and flowing out. There's cash for the buying and cash from the selling deposited at the Bank of Winston, and it takes some believing of the sheer amount of the stacks of fifties, twenties, tens and fives.

Inside this air-conditioned counting house, with its double-locked, plated-steel door, there are two females – both trustworthy cousins of Winston's. There's one you wouldn't want to argue with – think a big mama on the *Jerry Springer Show*; the other's a complete contrast – think of Whitney Houston in *The Bodyguard*. These two ladies are locked inside and only they can open the door. Rubin presses the buzzer and demands into the monitor, 'Let me in.'

Whitney says, 'What's the password?'

Rubin says, 'What fuckin' password?'

Whitney says, 'The polite one.'

Rubin says slowly and carefully, 'Will you open the door?' And then twigs the password of 'Please.'

And when Rubin's inside, Big Mama says, 'That wasn't too difficult, was it handsome?'

And when Rubin says 'Fuck off', they laugh at him and he has to let a smile briefly crease his face and maybe lighten his heart just a little.

So Rubin's cushy job, before he's due to return to the front line, is to make sure everything's running smoothly at Winston's fortified house. He checks security, the exits, the entries, the sentries. Checks his head to see if his mind is still functioning. To see if that last picture of Angel is still crystal clear.

He's focused is Rubin; he's moving his life on in his own way without the helpful literature on coping with loss, and alleviating grief. Rubin's managing because his is a rough, tough world where the dead are buried and the grave is smoothed over and sealed with scarred but loving fingers. And where life goes on no matter what. Transactions, cash transfers, deliveries on rainy nights, addicts shooting-up in bedsits that stink of soiled bedding, unwashed armpits and feet; shooting-up in dim alleys among overflowing rubbish bins; shooting-up on the beach, under the pier, in the bogs. And then there's blood on the pavement, teeth in the gutter, hands in vices and fingers and toes cropped off by bolt cutters. Not nice is it, the way some people spend their hard-earned lives thanks to facilitators like Winston?

For Veryll Evans, it's been a week now, a week of watching from the shadows. Veryll Evans sees Winston and his two heavies leave Winston's abode and take a morning walk through the tented market stalls of veg and meat and past reduced prices on dresses and coats.

Just off the market is Jamaica Jerry's Eating House where a huge breakfast of the full English is on daily order for Winston. This is how Winston likes to start his day in this building of a hundred covers – with a monster meal and a pot of strong, black coffee in front of him. He eats, chews, thinks and talks as he munches his way through several rashers of bacon, a couple of fried eggs, a ladle of baked beans, a shovel of fried potatoes and four slices of buttered toast.

When he's finished his breakfast, Winston leans back in his seat, burps and pats his stomach. He's ready for the day ahead. Ready for anything. But right now, courtesy of the discipline of a year's stretch in Feltham Young Offenders' Institution, he's ready for a visit to the gents. You could set your watch by the regularity of Winston's morning visit to the khazi, and you can guess that the Welshman has timed these regularities. Winston burps again and says to his minders, 'Give me five minutes.'

This has happened a hundred weekday mornings and Winston's escorts will sip another cup of coffee and have a moan about their babysitting salaries, while Winston answers the call of nature.

Veryll Evans is in cubicle number two – the middle of three. And three is where the creature of habit will sit again this morning. The barrier between the cubicle is the usual 2.1 metres high of water-proof board, which means that anyone standing on the toilet seat could easily see over it, reach over it, to the next cubicle.

This is the fourth time that Mr Evans has occupied number two on false pretences, and on each of the previous occasions there have been aborted attempts of reckoning because there's been someone else in here having a piddle or washing his hands or having a crange. But this morning as Winston's settling himself comfortably into his easement, there's not a sound as Veryll Evans, with the stealth of a cat lithely and silently, steps himself up onto the toilet seat.

Winston's sitting on the lavatory, trousers around his ankles and his hands at his sides. His eyes are closed and his mouth is forming a strain of a sigh and his head, that great-skulled bald dome that holds a thousand and one secrets, is tilted slightly off orbit as the silenced Glock – from a metre above – spits twice. And that's it. All that Winston's worked for, sweated for, committed terrible deeds for, counts for nothing. It ends here in the gentlemen's convenience of Jamaica Jerry's Eating House.

Winston tips forward, wedging his seventeen stones against the door while his drilled skull sprays twin fountains of blood onto the walls, onto the cistern. And even as Winston's body is still settling into the twisted floppiness of death, Veryll Evans is casually leaving, casually walking away. He's out the door of the gents, out the door of the building, and slipping onto the street. Unnoticed.

In this café, the only connection to Mr Evans is a barely sipped cup of tea, and that's being cleared away by a keen young waiter who's hard-up and working his way through university. This young man might wonder for a second what the point is of ordering a drink and then not finishing it, but it won't become a mystery to him. And anytime soon the tables will begin to fill and he'll be rushed off his feet.

By the time Winston is discovered his deadly acquaintance will be onto his removal route. There'll be the train to Brummagem, a vehicle picked up from a used-car dealer, a long-ish drive to a night-time meeting in a secluded lay-by twixt Tetbury and Bath.

In the meantime, one of Winston's bodyguards is informing Rubin that Winston's done for, soaking up his own blood, with his trousers down to his ankles.

'Man, we had to break the door down.' The minder shakes his head. 'Not a pretty sight, Rubin. Not nice.'

At this very moment Winston's still warm, still leaking blood and the police, with all their usual alacrity, will eventually be wanting to talk to Rubin. But it'll be a couple of hours at least before they come looking. And that's because the cop who's meant to be in charge of the fight against organised crime in the city is nine holes into his favourite golf course. Oh, and he's also inadvertently left his mobile in the clubhouse. When the police eventually get to Winston's, what will they find in the house of ill-repute? Not as much as anyone would think because Winston's is a modern operation. Of course, there are records they will probably never discover: incriminations on laptops, memory sticks, a master ledger. But the most important of all the information is leeching from Winston's brain onto the bog floor at Jamaica Jerry's Eating House.

Every situation needs an element of luck and Rubin's luck is that eighteen bricks of white lady has been shipped out that very morning and the drugs' cupboard in Winston's HQ is bare. The second stroke of luck is that there's a record number of our finest on sick leave and this has meant for the last month even occasional surveillance has been virtually curtailed. It won't take much risk, or effort, to gather up any incriminating evidence and take it to a place of concealment until there's such a time as it'll be needed again. This should mean that when the fired-up custodians of law and order arrive cut through the steel-plated door and into the deceased's abode, they'll find nothing of value to them.

The chief super, still wearing his golfing socks in his size eleven boots, is informed over the radio by the SWAT team commander that there's 'No one here, sir. Quiet as the grave.' The chief groans to himself because this is going to take some explaining away. He thinks that it might be some time before he's on the links again and wonders whether he could possibly wrangle a long-term sick note off his force's quack.

What's also gone from Winston's vaults is the money, the vonga, the filthy lucre. This is because Rubin, with his two very able assistants, has packed every last banknote into a couple of very large holdalls and it is now en route to somewhere safe in the boot of Rubin's motor.

With all that money in his hands, Winston mullered, confusion in the police ranks, all Rubin has to do is head for the nearest air or ferry port before an alert goes out. But it's not that simple, it never is, because some of that money is owed to people who must be paid regardless. Or else someone will come looking for Rubin and they'd find him wherever he might be. For now, Rubin needs time to think, to work out a salvage operation for Winston's rudderless, and now ownerless, concerns.

Rubin makes for a familiar bar with its doors flung open and with its mausy, dingy interior of peeling paint and yellowed ceiling. This is where Rubin goes and he remembers every detail of the first night he walked in here out of the rain. And Angel was behind the counter.

And he can see her now and she smiles him the sweetest of smiles and Rubin feels the pain of a knife twisting in his heart.

But it's her father, Smokey, broom in hand, saying guardedly, 'Rubin. What brings you here?' In Smokey's face, there's not a trace of his beautiful tragic child. Angel was her mother's daughter completely in looks and tragedy. Smokey is pulling mightily on his third joint of the day and looking for Rubin's answer.

Rubin says, 'I need to lay up for a while, keep my head down.'

Smokey thinks for a minute, shuffles from foot to foot, eyes Rubin's luggage. 'How long?'

'Couple of days.'

'You and Winston had a fall-out?'

'Winston's dead.'

'Dead? . . . You?'

'No. Not me.'

Smokey considers this for a minute and then says, 'Have to be Angel's room,' and it's only then he raises his head high enough to look directly at Rubin and Rubin can see the bleakness in his eyes as he slows her name, savours the syllables.

Then Smokey says, 'Don't want no one following you back here.'

'I'll be careful.'

'Couldn't stand no more trouble Rubin.' Smokey shakes his head as he turns away and mutters to himself, 'Couldn't stand no more trouble.'

In Angel's room, laying on his back on Angel's bed, staring at Angel's ceiling, Rubin plans the next stage of his life. He needs to think deeply and quickly because it won't be long before there'll be a tug on his collar and an invitation to attend an interview down the local nick. That'll come when he puts himself out there again in a day or two. Or more. At the moment he assumes he's safe; hidden away in a young woman's room where there's still the reminders of her life.

In this room Rubin spends hours scribbling names, notes and doing the maths. There's an endless number of phone calls, of setting up and knocking down meetings, and the putting together of new arrangements. Rubin's head is aching and he's chewing through double the recommended quota of Nurofen Plus. He works until he's worn out and desperately tired and now a dose or more of speed is joining the Nurofen Plus.

Smokey's not touched much in Angel's room. On a cupboard top, there's a framed photo of a laughing Angel, with three of her friends. There's another picture of a baby Angel in the arms of her mother with a very young-looking Smokey, thick fag in his fingers, looking slightly spaced out. One day soon, when Smokey can't delay his debts any longer, someone else will move in here. The furniture will be flung into a skip in the road, the walls will be emulsioned a plain cream, the woodwork painted, the floor carpeted. And it'll be like Angel never was.

It's time to leave Rubin on his undersized bed with his oversized problems and take a breath of air far away from the northern city and the suffocation of the streets. The stop will be at Elm Hill Park where Danny – sporting panda eyes courtesy of a third-round defeat by Berserker Billy Best – is sitting under the stars with young Mikey. They've pulled a couple of wooden chairs up to a smoking yog of burning tree limbs and Danny's saying, 'We'll jaul early tomorrow morning. Give us plenty of time, that will.'

Danny coughs, winces and puts his hand on his ribcage because Berserker Billy Best had driven a sledgehammer left hook to the body followed, a split second later, by the straightest of right hands. This punch had plastered poor Danny's nose a trite more to his face before a peach of a left hook dropped the not so Dangerous Danny Delaney to the canvas.

Danny says, 'He caught me. No denying that, but it was touch and go for a while and to tell you the truth,' he nods conspiratorially to the yog, 'I think he's a bit terashed of mandi. Now if I could get a return, get someone to put up the purse . . .' Danny's off on his Rocky Balboa dreams and they'll keep him occupied while young Mikey arranges a farewell meeting with Hannah. Danny keeps the fire going, keeps pushing the kosh on, as the night closes in and he steadily works his way into a dozen cans of Carlsberg Export and, because he's now out of training, he lights up a good wholesome Old Holborn twist.

* * *

Not too far away – from Elm Hill Park there's the secluded lay-by twixt Tetbury and Bath. This pull-off is on the old road, part of the winding route left behind when improvements for progress took the character away from the path of centuries. Here the trees are high and the bushes are a shield against the run of tonight's sparse traffic. There's also the rush of water under an old stone bridge, a strong bore of spring and drainage from the climb of the surrounding hills.

At this place of rest for weary drivers it's now pushing eleven o'clock and there's a faint glow from the interior of Meg's motorhome. And this is what Veryll Evans sees and he pulls up close to the glow.

It could be said that Veryll Evans has had a bit of a day: he's drilled two bullets into Winston's bald dome, trained it down from Manchester, picked up a dodgy car in Brummagem and driven eighty miles to a hidden lay-by off the old Bath road. His eyes are drooping and the euphoria of the kill is gently simmering in his heart, whispering its pleasure to his senses. He's tired and thirsty and he could do with laying his head onto a soft warm pillow but first there's the matter of payment due.

Veryll Evans parks his car behind Meg's motorhome and taps gently on her door. There's slivers of light shining through her blinds and Veryll Evans stands for a moment or two breathing in the night air. But it seems there's more than just the breath of this night in this air because leaking from Meg's vehicle is a waft, a scent of sweet delight. It's like a mist around him, this fragrance that makes his mouth water, makes him hunger for its taste on his tongue. His mind is searching for an association through the blurring of the years. And then the mist parts, clears, and he's back to that bare, humble cottage near Cowbridge. And then he's drinking the memory of a mother's warmth, of sitting barefoot on the stone hearth as she's warming a pan of Christmas wine and crushed cloves and sliced lemon on the edge of the fire. Her arm is around his thin body and she's holding him as only a mother can. And then, with a teacup she feeds him sips of sweetness in the flickering light of the fireside on a wet afternoon.

And this is heaven.

And it's heaven until they hear him kicking the mud off his boots in the porch.

And heaven's left them as the room darkens, as his mother's arm that's been holding him so gently, so tenderly, tenses and tightens around him. The moment's gone and soon she'll be gone.

Then it's today again, and it's night. Veryll Evans shakes his head as his dream dissipates, as he taps on the door and is welcomed in by, 'Sit yerself down for a minute,' from the confinement of the motorhome.

Meg is stirring a shiny steel saucepan on the cooker and on the table there's a thick, brown envelope. Veryll Evans's thick, brown envelope. But now it seems to him that there's no hurry to collect and to leave at the moment; it's so warm in here, so comfortable, so dreamy. And it's so like that long-ago day of his dreams that when Meg says, 'Do you want a drink, young man?', it could be his mother asking him. He nods and this gypsy queen very carefully dips a mug of heaven from her bubbling saucepan. Veryll Evans cups it in both hands and tastes and sips and takes the urge to swallow and drain and then . . .

He's a boy again with a ghost of his mother warm against him and her arm around his thin little body.

Veryll Evans feels it in his toes first, a tingling sensation like pins and needles. It makes him want to stand up and stamp his feet. But his legs are not listening, not acting for him. Then the mug drops from his frozen fingers, shatters on the floor and the dream moves into a nightmare because his mouth won't open and he can't take in his breath. For nearly an eternity, he can still see and hear and think, before the veil of a black curtain slowly creeps over his eyes and muffles his ears until his thoughts are his only company.

And those thoughts fade like stars, one by one in the darkness. And the last thought is,

'So this is what it's like.'

When Meg's sure, really sure, that the Welshman's on the road to hell she taps a message into her phone. Then she waits, as the deceased Welshman sits at the dinner table and stares open-eyed at his own reflection in the glass of the window.

While this murder's in progress, Wilma's been leashed to the front bumper of the Auto-Trail motorhome. She's whining softly to herself and feeling more than a bit pissed off. She's had her muzzle full of the most tempting of aromas for an hour or more and, right now, she'd just love to be sticking her nose in the pot. But Wilma's going to have to wait for a while longer to be freed because Meg will have to get rid of her tasty dish – and the saucepan and the shards of the broken crockery – in the strong current under the stone bridge. OK, so a few gudgeon might float to the surface. And a couple of perch. And maybe a couple of dace, and a pair of slimy eels, might join them. But Mother Nature will dilute potency with volume and hide the sins of the vengeful in the waters of Furina.

Meg sits on the step of her travelling home for an hour – with a sulky Wilma snuffling around a rancid rubbish bin. There's only Meg in this secluded lay-by and she's killing time until Ollie Cooper in his large Vauxhall van pulls in, steps out and says, 'All done, Meg?'

'All done, Ollie. All done.'

It's a good job though that Veryll Evans isn't a huge man. Ollie might be a big strong old boy but he is getting on in years, and to carry the deceased into his van is not exactly an easy job. Recently dead people are floppy dummies; they collapse in your arms, drag their feet and emit the most obnoxious of smells and slimy fluids. Ollie certainly has need of his throwaway protective suit and gloves which he hastily peels off after he's rolled Veryll Evans into a polythene shroud and taped him up so thoroughly that even if he was alive Houdini couldn't have burst him from his bonds.

The assassinated assassin is now ready to take a journey back to his Cymru roots dropped down a deep black mineshaft that itself leads into a huge, flooded gallery. He'll end up three-hundred feet below ground, floating around with a few more of the disappeared. They might gently bump into each other, nodding acquaintances in this subterranean graveyard of silent currents in coal-black water. But before that, before Ollie heads for the Severn crossing and the land of Veryll Evans's fathers, there's the little matter of firing the Welshman's car. Ollie empties five litres of diesel over the motor's seats and Meg throws in the seat cushion where the Welshman last sat. Ollie Cooper chucks in his protective suit and gloves and then it's a burning torch of the *Sun* newspaper thrust through an open window; a quick retreat and a boom of flame.

Now because of the circles these people move in, and the fact that the car's a knock-off on false plates, the police are not ever going to know who its last driver actually was. The law will cruise in, warm themselves for a minute or two, call the fire brigade, fill out a half-hearted report and file it away in the 'we've got better things to do' cabinet.

In the flaring of the fire Ollie says, 'That's it, Meg. We'd better jaul.'

There is a strong need to be on the move, to put a bit of distance between act and escape and, as he climbs into his van,

Ollie says, 'Don't leave it too long next time, my Meg.' He adds, shaking his head to his words, 'But not like this.'

Meg says, 'No Ollie. Never like this again.'

She's exhausted. She's tired and old and she's had enough for one day. For a lifetime. But she's also thinking that *never* might not ever be the final word. Then Ollie pulls away in his vehicle, Meg drives away in her motorhome and Veryll Evans's car burns brightly away all on its lonesome for now.

An hour later, in the deep of this night, Meg is on her way to Elm Hill. Wilma is sitting on her haunches in the passenger seat, sniffing out the streams of air that are drawn in through the quarter-open window.

'Enough.' Meg's voice is shaking with her tiredness. Wilma cocks her head, twitches her ears, listens for the rest of the words to come. And when they do, it's a repeat of the 'Never again' she said to Ollie and then it's, 'Oh, I'll be so glad when we're home, Wilma.'

24

It's several hours later at the greying end of the night at Elm Hill Park. It's quiet and still and there's only a bit of regular grunting, and faint squealing, and slight rocking, coming from Romeo and Juliet's waggon. At this hour you won't even see the glow of a cigarette end unless you look into the window of the quisling Ricky Ward, who's at present the sufferer of a heavy phlegmy cold. Now he's watching because he's providing the alert for Mr Malone and he's not going to risk losing his chance of avoiding a stretch at Her Majesty's Pleasure. He's still watching when Dangerous Danny's van fires up and stops outside Mikey Penfold's (actually Caleb Smith's) caravan. Then, with a clothes bag for company on this Tuesday dawn, young Mikey stows his bag in the back of the van. Before he settles himself into the front passenger seat, there's the appearance of Carter, a rough embrace and Carter saying, 'Give us a call when you get there.' Then Danny tickles the throttle and they roll out of the site. They're gone and Ricky Ward is still on his fag, and Romeo and Juliet's waggon is still a-rocking as Mikey heads towards the meet-up in Wales.

Ricky Ward stubs his cigarette out and dials Tom Malone's number. He drags the detective from the warmth of his lonely bed with, 'He's gone, Mr Malone, Mikey's gone. 'Bout five minutes, Mr Malone. Don't forget what you promised, Mr Malone.'

Tom Malone says he'll do what he can and that doesn't exactly inspire Ricky Ward with confidence.

'You did promise, Mr Malone.'

Tom Malone says, 'Yes I know I did, Ricky, I said I'll do what I can,' and an uneasy feeling sinks a root inside Ricky Ward's head. He lights up another fag, coughs up a mouthful of thick warm phlegm and spits it down the sink and thinks 'I'll do what I can' is not exactly a promise. He prays for a light bulb moment: he thinks he might need a plan B pronto.

What Ricky doesn't know is that an edgy Tom Malone has deprived himself of sleep for most of the night. He's been replaying his dinner date with Polly, seeing her eyes flooding, seeing the trembling of her lips. Hearing her ask, 'If you had to choose?' He's only just managed to sink himself into a deep slumber when petty criminal Ward gives him the heads-up about Mikey Penfold, curtailing any further thoughts of sleep.

A little later Tom is standing at the open back door of the cottage. His cottage. His and Polly's cottage. He has his mitt around a cup of hot coffee and his head is full of what Polly said: his career is on one side, Polly on the other. Tom Malone is remembering his boyhood dreams: his watching of every detective show that was on the television, his first case in the plain clothes unit, the thrill of working on a major incident. And the living and breathing of a life before Polly. And you know what? It's a seesaw. One side down, one side up. But his career just shades it by the thickness of a fag paper. It's so close that if a fly were to settle on poor Polly's side, it would be enough to bring it down in her favour.

It's now twenty hours before the *Isle of Inishmore* ignites her engines, slips her mooring and steams into the cold black Irish

Sea. Jimmy Penfold will soon be on the road to Pembroke as
Mikey Penfold is. And, as soon as his day shift finishes, Tom
Malone will have Maria and her yet-to-be-born (and disclosed)
bambino keeping them company. All of this should culminate in
a meeting on the dockside and the arrest and charging of Jimmy
Penfold. All matters done and dusted. A satisfying end to the
case.

Should. That's what should happen.

That Tuesday evening, Detective Tom Malone signs out of
Boarston Station with Maria, who's wearing that bloom of
enhanced beauty that comes with early pregnancy.

'We have to go to Wales,' Tom says to her.

'What now?'

'Yes.' Then the explanation of, 'I've received some info on
Jimmy Penfold.'

'But—'

'It's all cleared Maria.'

That's a lie – this is Malone's call only – but any trouble
should be cancelled out when he brings that Jimmy Penfold to
Boarston Station in the back of the car.

Maria, perhaps not as enthusiastic as Tom Malone would have
thought, says she'll have to phone her wife, let her know, because
on a Tuesday evening – Carol's non-training night – she always
prepares a sumptuous meal and she's going to be mightily disappointed at Maria's crying off. But Carol's in a good mood, says
that they both understand that work has to come first, and that
it'll have be a special breakfast instead. It's times like these when
Maria thinks that she loves Carol more than life itself.

The journey starts and the car's warm, the night's darkening and
the roads are emptying by the time they're close to Worcester.

The satnav's showing the route past Cardiff, past Swansea, and clocking down the three hours and the hundred and seventy-five miles to the docks. But Maria's not watching the screen, she's desperately praying that there's not going to be a throwing-up emergency.

Tom Malone flicks her a glance. 'You're quiet, Maria?'

But Maria's not only quiet, she's tired out. She's had a week of restless, guilty nights and she's sure that she can feel that guilt growing in her belly, gnawing at her strength, nibbling at her energy. In the deathly silence of the small hours when, unable to sleep, she's crept down the stairs to the kitchen, Maria sometimes thinks she can hear two hearts beating within her body. Of course Carol notices the difference between a bubbly, happy, sometimes fiery Maria and the lethargic one with smudges of soot under her eyes.

'You look tired Maria. You're not yourself. Is DS Malone pushing you too hard? Because if he is, I'll have a word.'

That's the caring protective side of Carol that causes Maria to well up and say,

'I just love you so much,' and seek the shelter of Carol's warm and strong embrace.

But don't squeeze too hard, Carol. You'll hurt my baby.

That's the baby that's due for eviction at 11 a.m. on Friday morning at the clinic for sexual health that's conveniently attached to the county hospital.

And thinking about what's impending is probably why Maria dreams what she dreams.

On the length of this night-time foray they've stopped once for coffee, and the loos, at the services. Apart from this, it's been a fairly quiet outing. Maria's pushed her seat back, stretched her legs out, relaxed herself. She's actually comfortable and that comfort leads to relaxation, dropping her eyelids and softly slipping into slumber. By Carmarthen she is well and truly residing in the arms of Morpheus.

In this dream world Maria's beautiful boy child is tottering towards her, arms outstretched. She bends, she scoops him up, feels his hard little body, buries her face in his mass of curly hair, drinks in the fragrance of him.

'So this is you, this is what you're like.'

Then he's on her lap, in the crook of her arm, and she's tracing the softness of his features with her finger. And these moments seem to be lasting forever.

Until the intrusion of Tom Malone saying, 'Won't be long now, Maria. Nearly there.'

She starts awake at his voice.

'Sorry, sir. Tom. I fell asleep,' and Tom Malone laughs and tells her she was snoring and she laughs and wonders if she snored *that other time*. But that's not a question for the asking, is it? Then she watches the black road unfolding in the headlights and she puts herself into remembering her dream and it's still so vivid, so real to her, that she knows that she's held her child, felt his warm sweet breath on her cheek. And she also knows that she could make the dream come true if she chooses. But whatever she does decide, Maria knows that her life will never be the same again.

25

Now there's something going on at Elm Hill Park that is going to bust wide open the outcome of what this should be building into. It concerns that snake in the grass, Ricky Ward and what he's been up to. He's concocted his plan B because if he's not careful he could be robbed, could be unrewarded for the part he's playing in the capture of Jimmy Penfold. He's going to phone Boarston nick and let them know what an honest and upright citizen he is and remind them that DS Tom Malone has promised him an amnesty from prosecution 'cos he's been so helpful on the case and he's just checking that everything's OK because DS Malone was very short with him earlier like he wasn't going to keep his promise and after all he's done to help and . . .

He does phone Boarston nick and, as luck would have it, the duty sergeant has gone for a crafty drag in the backyard and Chief Inspector Isaacs is on his rounds of checking on the night-shift operatives so it's him who picks up the phone. It's barely to his ear before a panicking Ricky Ward has filled that orifice with his convoluted tale of Jimmy Penfold.

A confused Inspector Isaacs, trying to make any sort of sense of Ricky's not-very-articulate presentation of his case, starts with,

'Jimmy Penfold? but he's supposed to be dead, Mr Ward. Is this a fuckin' wind-up? Because wasting police time is a . . .'

'He's not dead, sir. I told Mr Malone, sir.' There's a desperation in Ricky Ward's voice that prevents Chief Inspector Isaacs finger from cutting him off. And the mention of Malone holds his attention.

'OK, Mr Ward,' he says. 'Tell me from the beginning and slowly, please.'

Ricky starts again and rambles on through his story until it peters out with, 'And you see I need to know that I'll be all right, sir. You know. After what Mr Malone promised.' He adds on another respectful 'sir'.

'Of course you will be Mr Ward. I'll see to it personally.'

Chief Inspector Isaacs thinks that Ricky Ward has been a useful idiot and that he's as much chance of getting what he wants as setting a foot on the moon. First thing in the morning a uniform will be tapping on his caravan door and hauling him in to face cashpoint fraud. For this offence Ricky Ward will undoubtedly be sentenced to three years of being someone's bitch.

Isaacs is writing the befuddled details on the desk pad as Ricky Ward is mumbling out his story. He's writing down 'Jimmy and Mikey Penfold', the name of the ferry – Isle of Inish something? Departure time, two or three something in the morning from Pembroke, 'Which is in Wales somewhere, sir.'

But Frederick and Roy Field's monikers are not scrawled on the police desk pad. The Judas gypsy, confused and heavily dosed-up on Night Nurse, short-term memory shot to pieces, and not the best communicator in the world, has smothered that info deep inside his addled brain and it's beyond digging out. His scrappy note for DS Malone has been through the wash inside his crummy jeans and is now whiter than white and totally illegible.

Chief Inspector Isaacs puts the phone down and says to himself, 'You bastard Malone. You fuckin' bastard. Thought you'd have one over on me eh? Cut Harvey out. Well we'll see about that.'

He joins the dots of the *Isle of Inish(more)*, the Welsh docks of Pembroke and 2.45 a.m. in a few minutes of internet searching. Then he accesses the troublesome gypsy's police file, finds that there's been no status change or even a recent entry. Tom Malone gets another mention of being fatherless and then Chief Inspector Isaacs goes to the canteen to find his nephew.

DC Harvey Harris is having a coffee and filling his developing paunch with sandwiches and cake in a late supper – or early breakfast – on his night shift and with the sudden presence of Chief Inspector Isaacs he stands up smartly.

'Sir,' he greets his uncle, like he always does in company.

'Harvey,' says Uncle Isaacs, 'I've got a little job for you.'

'Sir?'

'I need you to go to Pembroke Dock. It seems that Jimmy Penfold – the one that Malone's been banging on about – is going to be making a guest appearance.'

'Penfold? But DS Malone hasn't said anything sir? Shall I contact him?'

'I think you should surprise him, Harvey.'

The details are passed from uncle to nephew with an incentive for Harvey because, and in another one-in-the-eye for Tom Malone,

'You're going to make this arrest Harvey. It's yours.' Chief Inspector Isaacs pauses before he tacks on, 'And it won't do your prospects any harm at all.'

All that's missing here is a sly smile and a conspiratorial nod and wink.

'Thank you, sir. I'm on my way.'

In ten minutes Constable Harvey Harris, supported by a uniformed officer, will be on the increasingly busy road to Cymru. Looking at the time scale, he should arrive to deliver his uncle's surprise present with thirty minutes to spare before the boat sails out.

So if all goes to plan there should be benefits for both oversized schemers. Chief Inspector Isaacs is thinking about a resurrection, an exhumation in a graveyard under a white tent, acres of press coverage. Perhaps a TV interview. Then he's considering his own career – and what just one step up would mean:

Chief inspector to superintendent.
Pension enhancements.
Early retirement with all the benefits.
Fishing in The Cut.
Following his beloved rugby team from the touchline to the bar.
Golf days with monumental booze-ups at the nineteenth hole.

This could be a life in heaven brought so much closer by the extremely unsuspecting – although not for much longer – DS T. Malone. This poor overworked, and overwrought, police officer will have the indignity of having the rug pulled from under his feet yet again, and the prospects for the advancement of his career – unlike that of the chief inspector and his overweight nephew – will be severely curtailed. After all he's invested in the case Tom Malone will be left eating the shite just like he did on the Huntingdon raid.

The main objects of everyone's attention, the unsettled Traveller and his son, have been carefully making their way to the early morning seaside rendezvous. The goodbyes are over, the man-hugs from Danny and Silas, and a rather different adieu from Selina Wood for Jimmy. Theirs was a hesitant, almost formal briefness of an embrace, like two people who aren't sure where a single act of physical comfort leaves them at. If you were watching, just sort of looking, you could be forgiven for mistaking that it was Zilla close up to Jimmy. That would be because Selina has the same hair, same features, same slender form. Same beauty. Same space that Zilla used to own.

Anyway, for Jimmy and Mikey there'll be a bit of sitting and waiting in the killing of time before the off, and before the long arm of the law starts its encirclement. Jimmy'll smoke a couple of cigarettes, Mikey'll send a couple of texts, and they'll count the hour into quarters and then they'll pick up their bags and ready themselves for fifteen minutes of queuing. Now if there's only fifteen minutes to embarkation then PC Harvey Harris should surely have burst upon the scene by now? And he would have if there hadn't been an upset on the motorway.

They've been making good time, DC Harris and his driver, and their journey has been a steady comfortable progression to their destination. Harvey Harris has bought a pack of sandwiches, a pasty, crisps and three cakes to see him through the journey. Oh and two bottles of diet cola, 'cos he's watching his weight at the moment. Now he's reclining, and as replete as he ever can be, in the passenger seat. He's practising to himself the process of arresting the promised felon on a plate. He's also hoping that there's going to be a struggle because he's not averse to violent restraint, feels that it keeps him on his mettle. But his thoughts of a satisfying conclusion are very loudly interrupted when his driver suddenly let's out a yell of,

'Fuckin' hell, Harvey,' and he stamps on the brakes.

The 'Fuckin' hell' is because an articulated lorry has turned broadside onto the motorway and split its sides. The result is that there's ten thousand cartons of Ambrosia Rice Pudding and twenty thousand cartons of Ambrosia Devon Custard across all the lanes of the M4. Harvey's driver hits the blue lights and slithers to a halt into the pottage of the world's biggest dessert. The outcome of this unfortunate accident is the safety buffer of thirty minutes' leeway is prised off the clock. There's no way now that DC Harvey Harris is going to deliver Tom Malone's surprise present on time and he calls back to base, gives his uncle the not-so-good news.

'Shall we turn around, sir? Come on back?'

Now Chief Inspector Isaacs didn't get to that rank by being slow on his feet. His objective is to gain his nephew an arrest on his say-so. So it's easy for him really to make the decision that they're to continue and Malone can hold Jimmy Penfold until Harvey's late arrival. There, it's simple. Well, except for one thing, and that's that the 'Bastard Malone' has his phone switched off; Her Majesty's Constabulary phone that any detective worth his salt would never think of disabling. Well, that's unless he didn't want distractions of any sort while he was partaking in a career-changing coup. But Chief Inspector Isaacs is not a man to be denied.

Unaware of this background drama, DS Tom Malone is currently drinking a strong cup of coffee and he's just outlining his requests to the acting head of Revenue and Customs at Pembroke Dock. This acting head is a friendly little Welshman – the antithesis to the poor departed Veryll Evans – with a roving eye that keeps roving over the very fetching Maria. (Her uniform really becomes her, even though she is looking slightly green about the gills.)

This trio are gathered together in a warm, plain white room with ceiling strip-lighting, two bare tables and six plastic chairs, a stainless-steel sink and, on a furrowed draining board, a kettle, coffee and milk. There's a heating radiator on full bore and the clock is fast approaching embarkation time. Even though they're indoors, the night still steals its breath into this room. The darkness pushes at the windows in these small hours and, outside, the swelling waves are crested with foam. The wind is freshening and the moon fitfully shows its face between ragged clouds. In the olden days, canvas would have been slapping in the breeze and the mooring ropes would be loosening for the catching of the tide.

Ron Davis, this acting head of Revenue and Customs is saying, 'Always glad to assist the boys in blue. We're in this together, Tom.' He's straight into the familiarities of we and us.

Tom Malone says, 'I'll identify him in the queue,' and he's about to inform Ron Davis about the passport status – ghosts in the name of Field – when Ron's phone rings.

'Just give me a minute,' Ron Davis apologises. He's duty bound to answer his work phone immediately; border control is a serious business.

With that phone to his ear he nods his head for a couple of yeses and says, 'All the help I can, sir.' Then a pause and a listen, 'Malone, sir? I'll pass you over right away,' and to Tom Malone he says, 'It's your boss.'

There's no holding back from Chief Inspector Isaacs and he's straight in with,

'What the fuck do you think you're doing with this Penfold business, Malone?'

Tom only has time to register that the inspector's in the know before he blurts out,

'It came up suddenly, sir. I had to act, sir. No time.'

'No time? You knew, Malone. You've known about this for days.'

'Sir?'

'Don't play the dumbass with me, Malone. I've spoken to Ricky Ward.'

'Sir, I can explain.'

'You can't explain fuck-all. I didn't authorise this, Malone.'

'No, sir. But . . .'

'But I am authorising DC Harris to pick up the pieces. He'll make the arrest.'

'What?'

'You heard me. Hold Penfold till Harvey – I mean DC Harris – gets there. Then hand him over.'

'But . . .'

'But my butt, Malone, and call me when it's all done. I haven't finished with you yet.'

That's the end of the conversation and Tom Malone hands the phone back to Ron Davis. The deflated detective looks so dejected that it causes Maria to say, 'Sir? Is everything all right, sir?'

But at the same time as she's asking, Ron Davis interrupts with, 'Foot passengers are coming through.'

He has the passenger list in his hands and is ready to start scrolling.

'Right. What names are you looking for?'

Tom Malone hesitates, then says,

'Penfold. James and Michael Penfold.'

Well, there's no doubt that was a mistruth because he knows they're under a name change but, as luck will have it, the only other person here that could assist in a personal identification has suddenly put her hand to her mouth and is rushing to the ladies. She'll be absent for the duration because it is morning and it is sickness. So while Maria's throwing up in the toilet there's only Tom Malone who can do the picking out of the felon. But what picking he's doing is on the carcass of his seven years as a cadet, as a policeman on the beat, as a plain-clothed investigating officer. And onto that carcass drops the fly that was buzzing around earlier. It was considering which side of the scales to alight on and it reluctantly plumps for the pale prettiness of Polly.

Jimmy Penfold and son – aka Frederick and Roy Field – have now joined the shuffling queue of embarkees. This shuffling queue, with its obligatory hacking coughs, is moving steadily through Passport Control and Baggage Check.

Jimmy's tipped down the brim of his titfer – still a bit sensitive about his centre parting – and speaks out of the corner of his mouth to his son, 'Mikey, don't forget yer name is Roy.'

Mikey shrugs his shoulders and says, 'I won't forget, Fred,' and they have a little chuckle about their new names. Then Mikey adds, 'Mum would've laughed,' and that stops them laughing because to Mikey it's an image of smeared blood on the caravan's steps, and to Jimmy it's the lingering taste of ice-cold lips and an everlasting guilt that squeezes his heart.

Now Jimmy is offering his passport to be checked. The line officer looks at Jimmy's photo, squints and says, 'Could you remove your hat, please, sir?'

This is the time, or it should be, for DS Tom Malone to make his grand entrance. He should leap out from the watch room and firmly grasp Jimmy Penfold's shoulder and say the words that viewers sync to every time they watch a TV cop show: 'You do not have to say anything. But, it may harm your defence . . .'

But we're not going to need this because DS Malone isn't going to speak. Yes, he's out of the watch room and standing behind the counter, beside the officer, and yes, he's fixed Jimmy Penfold with a cold hard stare.

A shocked and almost stunned Jimmy Penfold is frozen in motion. His mind is flashing into the scenarios that if the gavver lells him it'll put an end to the story of his demise. And then that might link him to the mullerin of Angel. Then Black bad asses will certainly come looking for him. Not to mention all the other charges he could well be facing: running of drugs, involvement with a stolen cadaver, burial of the same, and so on, and so on.

That's if things had gone to the original plan of DS Tom Malone. If Chief Inspector Isaacs had kept his big beak out of the case, it would have ended for Jimmy Penfold with a long miserable ride back to Boarston Police Station. But at Pembroke Passport Control, Jimmy Penfold is handed back his documents with barely a glance and only an 'OK, sir,' from the official at the desk. Jimmy shuffles onwards, anticipating his imminent arrest and wondering if he should make a break for it. His eyes flit from side to side and he even risks a backwards glance at his would-be nemesis. But there's nothing out of place, no sign of any interest in him. And nothing is going to happen because Tom Malone is not going to dob in Jimmy Penfold. He continues unobstructed and the only other person who could have influenced proceedings is throwing up in the ladies' toilet.

Still a little shaky as he walks up the gangplank, as a force of rain-spattering wind tugs at his hat, Jimmy Penfold mutters the disbelieving words, 'It was the gavver who knew me, Mikey. The gavver who knew me.'

The *Isle of Inishmore* slips with a fair bit of buffeting into the dark stormy Irish Sea as Tom Malone, gritting his teeth, makes the call on his reactivated work phone to Chief Inspector Isaacs.

'What do you mean, Malone? Not made a show?'

'Wrong info, sir. He didn't turn up.'

There follows a minute's rant from Chief Inspector Isaacs about what a waste of fuckin' funds chasing shadows and doesn't Malone know how much valuable time's been used up and that there's no real evidence that the pissin' pikey is even alive. And he's had a fuckin' bellyful of smart-alec cops who can't tell the difference between arse and elbow. And he can whistle for the overtime pay because he's not going to sign it off . . . And it's a mess, a fuckin' mess. And he wants to see Malone in his office the second he gets back to the station.

Then there's a pause for breath and into it Tom Malone says, 'I'll be handing in my warrant card.'

'Warrant card? What for?'

Tom Malone wants to say to stick it up Chief Inspector Isaacs bottom but he's much too polite so he says, 'I'm resigning, sir.'

'Resigning? For God's sake Malone, you can't . . . I'm up to my fuckin' eyes. Think about this, Christ almighty, Tom . . .' But even the insertion of the familiarity of 'Tom' hasn't stopped DS Malone from hanging up and Isaacs is blaspheming to himself.

This could now be presented as the ending of this rambling tale because Jimmy and son are travelling safely across the water, Rubin's sitting on a huge cache of vonga, Veryll Evans and Winston – soon to be headline news for the public to devour – have paid their dues and it looks quite likely that Tom Malone is giving up the force and going home to Polly. It seems that Maria is the only one left in a predicament and that's due to be sorted at 11 a.m. on Friday morning. So that should be it. The finish. Except that it's not the ending. Not just yet anyway.

We'll pick it up on the road home for Tom Malone and a rather sickly-looking Maria. They're breaking the journey in the motorway services drinking the shite that passes for coffee and nibbling sandwiches that defy categorisation. Soon to-be-ex DS Tom Malone has had enough time to miserably reflect on his decision and he's thinking of the way Polly will react to his news. Her face will light up with pleasure; she'll throw herself into his arms; she'll be like an excited child.

'Oh Tom. Really? Really?' she'll say, and she might cry a bit and he might choke up a bit because it's going to be hard for him. He'll tell her that he'll get a job in private security where the money might be less but the hours, and the holidays, will be regular. So should all of this occur then it would cap a satisfying exit for Mr and Mrs Malone.

On this roadside stop, Tom Malone sits opposite to Maria and makes his confession about his gamble on the unauthorised operation. He says, 'I shouldn't have dragged you in, Maria. This is all my doing; the mess is all mine and I'll make sure that I take the blame.'

He shakes his head and Maria widens her brown Italian eyes and says,

'And Jimmy Penfold never even showed. It was all for nothing, Tom.'

All for nothing. Jimmy Penfold slipping through the net, his own career likely slipping through his fingers. That nothing certainly amounts to something, although he nods his head in agreement with Maria, adding another lie to the rising heap in his life. Then he says, slowly drawing out the words, 'There's one other thing you should know, Maria. I'm out. I'm done.'

'Done, Tom?'

'Resigning. Leaving the force.'

'Oh. But why?' Maria says, and then it's out before her brain's properly engaged, 'It's not because of . . .' and pauses because she can't say 'us'. There is no 'us' despite what's in her belly.

Instead it's, 'Only I'd feel guilty if it was because of me. What we did.'

'No, Maria. It's nothing to do with that. With you.'

He sighs and he looks so sad, so unhappy, that it touches her heart and she has a sudden reminder of why they did what they did. And for a brief instant she wishes she could offer him the comfort he gave to her. Maria gets as far as lightly touching his hand and saying,

'I shall miss you, Tom,' and he says that he'll miss her, and that there's notice and stuff to work out and it'll be ages yet, but afterwards they'll stay in touch.

Because that's what you always say. Even when you don't mean it.

Then there's a gurgle in her stomach, a taste of bile in her mouth and Maria says, 'Sorry Tom but I feel sick,' and her hand's to her mouth and she's up and into the ladies. When it's done she wipes her mouth, splashes her cheeks with cold water, looks at herself in the mirror, thinks what a fool she's been and looks for the fool in her face.

When she's back in Tom Malone's company she says, 'Sorry Tom. Must have a bug.'

Then she wishes him well for his plans and the words bubble in her throat and for one awful second she thinks she is going to throw up over the table.

Back at Boarston, Tom Malone drops Maria at the gate and she takes her lovely pregnant self down the path to where a light shines through the window. It shines out as if someone's been waiting up all night to welcome her home safely; a someone who truly loves her, who will dry her tears, who will run her a hot bath and towel her dry. Someone who will hold her in strong comforting arms. And that someone will have to listen to a confession of deceit and consequence, and then be told that there's a cancellation of a Friday appointment and that, with or without her, a life is going on. It's as certain as can be that Tom Malone won't see the lad grow up, won't buy him birthday presents, won't take him to school. He won't know him at all unless, in eighteen years' time, an extremely handsome young man of Mediterranean extraction knocks on Tom and Polly Malone's door. But for now, a very tired Tom Malone is signing into Boarston Police Station with the intention of typing up his resignation notice and handing it to Chief Inspector Isaacs personally. But there's going to be a delay to that passing over because Tom's superior – bulging briefcase and armful of papers – is tearing out of his office and rushing off to an emergency meeting with the National Police Authority.

'Up all night and now this,' he moans to Tom.

'But, sir . . . I need to talk about my resignation . . .'

'Haven't got time now, Tom. I'll be back in a couple of days.'

'But, sir—'

'We'll sort out your trouble then. Just hold the fort for me, Tom.'

There's just time for one more 'But, Sir . . .' before Chief Inspector Isaacs eases himself into the back seat of his chauffeured car, slams the door, and is on his way.

DS Malone, now forced to leave the matter of his resignation until another day, decides to take his sleep-deprived self back to his cottage. Before he catches up on his slumber, it's a quick phone call to Polly and the offer of an Indian takeaway at his – well, at theirs technically – for evening dining. But Polly says, 'I'll cook us something nice if you want, Tom.'

There's a gentle sweetness in her voice, a soft flavouring to the way she says his name, to the way of, 'We will talk tonight, won't we Tom?'

He lays his weary head onto his pillows for the luxury of a

long sleep, and then awakes for a hot shower and the closest shave he can apply. At six o'clock he drives out to pick up Polly and her bag of provisions for their dinner.

Polly seems different this evening. She's relaxed. Confident even. There's a faint flush to her pale cheeks and she's humming to herself as she peels potatoes, chops carrots, checks the meat in the oven. She's dressed simply, casually, and she sounds so happy it bubbles from her mouth. And she touches him in the passing, in the laying of the table, the pouring of his drink.

They don't talk properly until the meal's finished and they're sipping coffee. The unsaid had flitted between them and now Tom Malone captures it and starts to go through his plans of leaving the force. He tries to sound enthusiastic, really tries, but he's sure that his tone starts to falter as he faces up to his reality. 'I've got a few contacts and I can start phoning around tomorrow and . . .'

But Polly doesn't seem to be listening. She's looking at him like she's not hearing his words. Not properly. Her eyes haven't flooded with tears; she hasn't thrown herself into his arms for the sacrificing of his career. Instead she's taken his hand across the table and she's interrupting him and saying, 'But you can't give up the police. Not yet anyway, Tom.'

'Not yet?'

'It's a good job, Tom. Secure. Good money. It's not the time to be leaving.'

What?

A baffled Tom Malone finds himself repeating her words like a parrot, turning them into a question of, 'Not the time to be leaving?'

Polly, eyes now swimming with tears and clutching his hand with remarkable strength, says, 'That night . . . you know when we went for a meal, and . . . and you know what happened. Well the thing is, Tom, I'm pregnant. You're going to be a father.'

Going to be a father and maybe not leaving the force?

Tom Malone's heart does a double beat with the twin shocks. It seems that Polly now has different, and perhaps more important, priorities than worrying about Tom Malone's life at the station. He can hardly believe the cards that Lady Luck has just dealt to him across the table.

Life has suddenly become a whole lot rosier for DS Malone.

Several hours later in the middle of this eventful night, Meg is leaving her bed. But it's not her bed in the modern motorhome. She's in Lavinia's vardo, facing the rising of Elm Hill and she's awoken in this living van – she slept with the door open and Wilma at her feet – with the moon bright onto her face. She pulls a coat around herself and climbs, with the dog at her heels, to the top of Elm Hill. Up here, with the rustling shadows of the night around her, she smokes a cigarette and looks down onto the sleeping site, onto the changes made in the years past. She's watched the nights, the days, the folki come and go, from this high ground. Meg doesn't even have to close her eyes to imagine a scattering of tents and waggons at dusk, the heavy tang of horses and ponies in the air, the woodsmoke curling from the vardo stoves, the women bent over the flickering yogs and the rattle of the kharvis, an odd bark from a wary dog and the shrill laughter of children in play.

Sometimes Zingara's voice is so close, so clear to her, that Meg thinks that if she was to turn suddenly she would see her. They would sit beside the smoky fire again. The painted tent would be erected in the showground again and for a settling of silver, secrets would be exposed. Fortunes would be told.

Zingara and Daughter – Purveyors of Portents,
Servants of the Fates, Tellers of your Future.

Zingara, the daughter of Lavinia whose name is carved above the doorway of the old living waggon.

On this night, while most of the world sleeps, Meg sits in the moonlight and rolls herself another thin cigarette. She hunches up her shoulders and watches until the sky lightens in the east and the coolness of the morning seeps into her body. Then she calls up her jukal and makes her way slowly back down Elm Hill. Here, with the old ways still fresh in her head, she lights up some kindling outside the vardo and feeds it into a healthy fire, warm enough to take the chill out of her old bones. But she can't shake the past out of her mind. And she feels so old, like she's been on this earth forever. Meg has days like this, especially lately. But then sometimes she'll wake in the night and she's a child and the warmth of her mother is beside her, her hands stroking her hair. Soothing her to sleep. Stilling her dreams.

In the earliness of the day, Meg's sipping from a mug of meski that's tainted with woodsmoke and peppered with wood ash. Meg's free hand is smoothing Wilma's head, who's daring to get as close to the warmth as is dogginly possible. And then, although Meg's not asked for this, pictures begin to form in the cherry-red heart of the fire. She looks away. Looks back. Looks away. *Not now. Please God not now.* But a soft breeze fans the glowing timber, and it pulls her into the reading of the Rosetta stone. The compulsion to know – a lifetime long – is too hard to resist. She looks into the oracle, tries to meld together an understanding of a warning. But then it fades, it's gone, and the fire is just a tumble of burning wood. But in this time Meg has seen enough, caught enough, to make her sigh tiredly to Wilma,

'It's not done yet, Wilma. It's not done.'

26
DECEMBER 1938

It's still and bitterly cold on this grey morning of winter. A fine mist of snow is drifting down onto a patch of bare trees and scrub and withered grass. This siting, leeward of the gentle – and now rapidly whitening – hill, could be called a lonely place. But it's not an empty place because there is life here; not just deer and rabbit and fox and badger, and not just frozen jackdaws waiting for some casting-out to pick over.

The light snow's falling, settling over all of this, settling on the cold metal of a black motor-van; a vehicle that's big enough to live in. At the rear of the van, a Primus stove is hissing like a snake, boiling up a kettle of water for two mugs of tea. And these mugs of tea, paled and sweetened by a spoonful of condensed milk, are cupped in the hands of a young girl and her mother. There's a warmth from the mugs and there's warmth – paraffin tainted – from the Primus. Then in the back of the van, the bedding's rolled up and there's talk of a breakfast of bacon and bread. But before this the girl pulls her boots on, drapes a blanket around her shoulders and steps out into the bitterness of this morning. She finds herself a shelter of a bush and, checking no one – as if there would be anyone – could possibly see her, she squats for her morning relief. Then she stands, hitches her skirt comfortable and takes a deep breath of the chilling stillness. And it's then that she sees the footprints; fresh footprints that are small and deep and alongside them are the scuffed paw marks of a dog. The girl's thinking that someone's passed close to them, passed by them, and in her thoughts is a curiosity for this person. And it's like the footprints are saying to her, 'Follow me' and there's the drawing of her alongside those tracks. A drawing of her up the hillside like she's following a scented trail in an irresistible compulsion.

She slows to look back, look down to the van, to where her mother, in that paraffined warmth, will be taking another mug of tea, perhaps laying down the tarot cards, picking out their path for the coming year; a path that will lead to the summer showgrounds, the fairs, the pub bars and the knocking on doors in the telling of fortunes.

The girl stops, cocks her head like a bird to listen, because there's something else up here, something that knows of her. It's like a murmur not quite to be heard under the rustling, sifting falling of the snow. But it is there and it's guiding her to a clearing on the edge of the wood that caps this hill.

And this is it.

In this clearing, long-skirted and heavy-coated, is a woman whose face is etched by countless years. She's settled on the trunk of a toppled tree and her thin lips are sucking on a thin cigarette. This woman is hunched and pinched and cold and old. At her feet is a black-and-white dog and this dog's nosing the scent of the girl, watching her intently. It's tail is slowly thumping the ground in a welcome as the woman, sharp eyes in her aged face, says,

'Sit with me for a while.'

And the girl, sharp eyes in a young face, sits herself beside the woman like she's known her all of her life. The woman reaches out, touches the girl's hair and it's the touch of the familiar, a gentle caress of the loving. And the girl's eyes close, shut out the winter's morning, as the woman talks soothingly in words that'll only be recalled in the darkness of night.

How long the girl sits there she can't say. It could be minutes, or it could even be hours, but when she opens her eyes there's no old woman and there's no dog. And when she picks the trail back down the hill, there's only her footprints in the snow.

27

Time has to move on and it's now a year to the day since Rubin's Angel ascended to heaven and as much as Rubin's dreaded waking up to each morning, this one's the worst. Five o'clock has found him in the kitchen, mug of black coffee in one hand and cigarette in the other. He's watching the dawn slide down the slate roofs, glitter on the windows and slowly sink into the streets. He's tired, he doesn't sleep well and he works most of the hours that God sends. He's still in the game – what else would he do? – but he's a different Rubin than the man of twelve months ago. And how different still if Jimmy Penfold's bullet had struck a foot or so in either direction. Because then there wouldn't be the ghost of Angel standing beside him, whispering to him of the child in her arms. 'Rubin,' she's saying, 'look at him. Look at your son.' But Rubin can't look, can't see what lives on in another world. But he feels it sometimes, a brush of her fingers on his arm, the warmth of Angel breath on his face in the black of the night. Once, in the very early hours, he even thinks he hears a baby's cry.

Sometimes, on warm evenings, Rubin will go up to the roof of his building. He'll sit out with a glass of the strong stuff and look up to the bright stars in the dark sky. Now he knows it's an illogical thing to do, but he looks for a new star because sometimes he's a little boy and his mother is telling him that his daddy's gone to heaven.

They're standing in the back yard among the dustbins and bike frames and she says, 'There Rubin, that's him. That star,' and she points a direction into the sky and he pretends he can see when he doesn't. Just to make it better for her.

Now in the night sky of northern England, Rubin looks for an Angel in heaven. He pretends that he finds her among a million stars. Just to make it better for himself.

It's later on in this day of a year to the day that one of Rubin's contacts phones him with the news that, 'The law's pulled the bastard who did your missus, Rubin.'

Now these words should really spell the curtailment of Mr Penfold's travels. Unless the bastard they've got is not the one and the same Mr Penfold.

But to find this out we need to go back to the Manchester of a few months ago to yet another damp depressing night. Although it's meant to be summer, the dark's filled with a drifting rain that settles like a sheen of mist on the head and hair and on the long buttonless over coat of Homeless Man. It's very late and he's laid himself for the sleeping in the now foreclosed British Home Stores' doorway. Homeless Man has wrapped his out-thrust legs in an extremely grimy sleeping bag that's sapped with stale urine and stained with unmentionable discharges. He's had a nice psychotic smoke of some decent skunk – courtesy of a shared, very soggy, joint with Pete the Paddy – downed several cans of Special Brew and swalloped from a bottle of Bristol Cream sherry until he put himself in *that* place; a place where the cold doorway, the wet night, can't touch him.

In his half-trance, half-sleep, Homeless Man feels under his coat for the reassurance of his protection, his smooth-metalled, cool-barrelled friend of confidence. And so he dozes, waiting for the early noises of the city to draw him into a new day while the rain sweeps in ever heavier from the west, and its fall streams down the gutters and drains. He dozes until three young bucks, Tyson, Nelson and Luther – fourteen, fourteen and fifteen respectively – who really should be tucked up in bed at this late hour, come a-calling.

They're out here in the early hours because a night that had started well at a party, in a second-floor flat of the Edith Cavell tower block, had ended up with Luther – top dog in the year of his school – and his two sidekicks having to back down in a confrontation with Woolly Eddie, who tells them, 'We don't want fuckin' schoolkids here; this is for grown-ups, so fuck off back to your mama's tits and have a good suck.'

They have to leave the party with their tails between their legs and the dreaded disrespect hovering over their heads. It hovers most distinctly over Luther and he says, 'Man, he was out of order. I should've shanked him.' He scuffs his feet on the kerb-stones as Nelson and Tyson nod to his words.

'Yea man, he would've shite himself if you'd pulled on him.' But these are words without meaning because Woolly Eddie is a bad man with a bad mind, a woolly mind in fact, that just can't tell the difference between right and wrong. He's more than a cut above them, he's leagues above them. Woolly Eddie is in the Premiership and they've not even made League Two. They, in particular, Luther, desperately need to earn some respect so they swagger around the town centre, kick the 'Keep Left' bollards, show their arses to the security cameras and look for trouble that isn't here on this god-awful night. They're abrasive and loud and there's no one in the deserted centre to know or care or confront three miffed young Black lads trying to gain a reputation.

The trio skin up a special in the shelter of a bus stop and then, although no one says it, it's time to go home. That should have been that and they should have made their way to their respective beds and their single mums but —it's then than Nelson catches sight of Homeless Man curled up in his sleeping bag in the doorway of BHS. He sees outstretched legs in the dark doorway that's running with damp and smelling of stale piss. And it's about to smell of stronger, fresher piss because Luther, finger to his lips, sidles up to the sleeping Homeless Man, stands over him, unzips his flies, flops out his todger and takes a horse-piss of mighty proportions onto the man of no abode. Homeless Man's awoken from his slumber by a splashing salty stream of wet warmth, and he's not in the least happy at the three young bucks who're laughing their heads off, clapping their hands, at his discomfort.

'What the fuck . . .?'

Homeless Man twists in his sleeping bag and wriggles to his feet to the applause of the mocking laughter. And then he makes an understandable – maybe justifiable – miscalculation in his reactions.

He spits out, 'You cunts. You fuckin' Black cunts.'

There's a sudden silence and into that silence Nelson and Tyson look to Luther 'cos this is a bigger disrespect to them than Woolly Eddie delivered. Now it's down to Luther to start the party and so he pulls his knife and Nelson and Tyson follow suit. That's three blades reflecting the dull glimmer of the nearest halogen light. It's also three blades that have never tasted warm blood because these boys are still at the wannabe stage in their fledgling careers. But this is the chance to take a step up the ladder of respect.

Luther says, without a hint of irony, 'No white pig is going to call us Black cunts.'

But Homeless Man has slid up the door and his sleeping bag is at his feet and his big overcoat is slitted open in the front and his hand is inside his coat and his forefinger is bent onto the trigger of his gun.

Homeless Man is preparing himself for combat and he needs to issue the last warning before opening fire on civilians. He should be saying, 'Back off. Back off.' But it comes out as, 'Fuck off you cunts. Fuck off.' It also comes out at a very loud and definitely at an unmissable volume. This is enough for Messrs Nelson, Tyson and Luther, the point of no return has been breached. Even though Homeless Man is clearly not right in his head, he has definitely disrespected them and no one does that. (Well, except for Woolly Eddie.) So they're going to shank him. One of them – or maybe all of them – are going to slide a blade into Homeless Man's bony frame.

'You gonna get it, man,' says Luther, pushing himself into the vanguard of the intended assault to claim the first slicing of the cake.

Luther's excited and nervous. He's about six feet away from the Homeless Man and leading with his knife. Then Homeless Man draws his weapon from his voluminous overcoat in one smooth professional action. The gun cracks, spurts a flame and Luther stops suddenly, instantly, in his tracks like he's walked into a glass wall. The knife falls from his hand, clatters onto the polished-concrete floor of the shoppers' entrance. Luther's eyes bulge out of their sockets, his hands clutch at his chest and a scream doesn't quite make it out of his mouth. He topples backwards, crumbles to the ground with a hell of a smack to the back of his head. Nelson and Tyson freeze in their forward assault. They've heard the gun, seen the spit of flame and watched their comrade fall to the hard wet concrete. But to Homeless Man it's like it's the old days. Like he's ten feet tall. Like he's not frightened of anything on this earth. He's training his weapon onto Nelson and Tyson. He's loud – a shout – with his,

'Come on you bastards. Come on.' Homeless Man is alive and suddenly young and strong and fired-up for combat, as he was in those hazy faraway days that keep him company in his dreaming times.

Nelson and Tyson don't waste a fraction of a second in turning and racing away at greyhound speed. They don't stop for several hundred yards, until they've dodged down a couple of side streets and are desperate to draw some breath. Nelson, bent over with his hands on his knees, gasps out, 'Luther. Christ, Luther. Ambulance. Call an ambulance.'

Tyson, not quite as knackered as his partner and a cooler thinker, says, 'And police.' And it's him who makes the call, who tells the 999 operator that his mate's been shot and that they weren't doing nothing and this guy pointed a gun at them and shot Luther.

This is also the impression that Nelson and Tyson give to the police, plus a distortion that tells the constabulary of them joshing with Homeless Man when he suddenly pulls out a gun and threatens them with it. Luther puts up his knife to protect himself and gets shot down and they, Tyson and Nelson, only just escape with their lives. (They also slip their blades down a convenient road drain 'cos they never carry nuffin' . . . Honest.) All the police have to do now is to turn up to tidy up. Which they do in numerical superiority and, inside forty minutes, Homeless Man has three red laser spots on his heart. He hasn't moved from his doorway and he still has his weapon in his hand. A hero PC slowly approaches Homeless Man and from a safeish distance calls on him to, 'Lay your weapon down please, sr. Nice and slowly.'

And because the PC has asked nicely, and because the PC's Anglo-Saxon through and through, Homeless Man lays down his gun. He offers his surrender in a place he's not sure of because he's more than a little confused; he's been holding his position and waiting for back-up. And now what he thought was his back-up has ordered his cease-fire. And his mind has misted up again and somewhere a clock is ticking, adding seconds of dread to his unsure consciousness.

He asks, 'What the fuck's going on?' and he's not sure if he's said it aloud but there's an answer of, 'It's all right, sir. It's all right.'

Then there's more of a friendly voice and he's being led past a blanketed body – from where blood is pooling and trickling to the gutter – and guided towards the back seat of a police car by strong firm arms and polite instructions to be, 'Careful, sir. Careful. Mind your head, sir.'

And it's a waste of time the ambulance screeching up, with blue lights flashing and siren howling, because Luther has spilled all of his short life onto the polished concrete at the entrance to BHS.

The upshot of all of this upset is that Homeless Man is carted off to Manchester Central Police Station by the boys in blue. He's given a change of clothing, an all-in-one virginal overall and then he has a friendly chat with two interrogation officers who glean that his surname is Hawkins, The duty solicitor has also been drafted in and he's a bit pissed off because he's due to fly out to Sardinia in four hours' time. The last thing he needs is to be sitting in on a murder inquiry and advising Homeless Man to, 'Just answer the questions, Mr Hawkins.'

But no matter how many times Homeless Man goes over the events of the night they always want it one more time.

The male DS says, 'Let's start from the beginning Mr Hawkins. Now where did you get – find – the gun?'

'It's Private Hawkins, sir. Number 25232301, sir. In a bin, sir.'

The female DS says, 'Whereabouts? Where did you find it?'

'In a bin . . . madam.'

The male DS says with impatient patience, 'Now what I mean Mr Hawkins is where . . .?'

'It's Private Hawkins, sir. Private Hawkins. Number 25232301, sir.'

After an hour of this, the two police officers and the solicitor leave Homeless Man in the interview room and grab a coffee in the canteen.

'Jesus,' says the DS to the DS. 'He's as nutty as a fruitcake.'

The other DS says, 'This is going nowhere fast.'

The solicitor looks at his watch. 'My advice is to contact the mental health team and get him sectioned.' He adds, 'And you can't use anything that he's disclosed in court.' But Homeless Man hasn't disclosed anything that can possibly be used against him. The DSs have hardly finished agreeing with the solicitor's suggestion before the legal eagle takes flight. He's just enough time to go home and pack and get to the airport to take a later flight and lose very little from his holiday.

The only good thing that this night has brought is that Homeless Man won't be homeless ever again; he'll be locked away. He'll be safe and warm. He'll spend nearly all of his day in his secure room in a secure unit. He'll be kept away from anything sharp, anything that could be construed as harmful to himself or others. He'll serve a life sentence without a trial and he'll see very little of the yellow sun that used to burn him brown when he was a hero in the desert. And sometimes those desert days will scythe through the veil of his protection and he'll taste the dust in his throat, smell the hot blood of the dying. Sometimes.

So, Homeless Man – ex-Private Hawkins – can't really help with the investigation and it seems it's all finished. The only thing that warrants some more investigation is the firearm that ended Luther's young life. The gun and the spent bullet – it's been dug out of Luther's torso and its passage tracked through his aorta to a lodging place in his spine, mullerin two vertebrae in the process – are desultorily offered into the system where they join a list as long as your arm.

Homeless Man's gun will be labelled to be prioritised – the same as all the rest of them. It'll sleep on a shelf in the waiting room until Ballistics check the rifling on the barrel, the bullet, and the hammer-strike impressions. Then the monster database will fire up, find a match and give out an almighty 'Hallelujah' for the identification of the gun that fired the projectile that killed Angel Ashanti. All of this will happen in good time – several months in fact – and then the beautiful Black girl will be front-page news again. Homeless Man will be attributed with a killing that he did not do – and knew nothing about – because it fits him like a glove. Time and place and opportunity will have coincided for the solving of a killing, and the implementation of Homeless Man's lifetime detention. There's no question that this is an open-and-shut case that will suit everyone and every-thing. Everything except truth and justice.

Also receiving the news on this dark anniversary is Jimmy Penfold. He's parked – van and caravan – in a lay-by near Doolin, and Mikey is buying two breakfast baps and two teas from a mobile canteen. Jimmy's phone lights up and Silas is in his ear and straight on with giving him the glad tiding about Angel.

'They've lelled a dinlow mush for it,' Silas tells Jimmy. 'Seems he's going around shooting people.' This is obviously an exag-geration but the guts of the story are there.

Jimmy says, 'You sure?'

'The word is out, Jimmy.'

But it's more than just a word because Angel's picture will soon take precedence on the front page of the daily newspapers. Her face will be once again on the television, her tragically short life will be replayed with a religious reverence. Innocent Angel will be the catalyst for the implementation of tougher gun laws and the 'something must be done' brigade. There'll also be a résumé of the life of the killer: a homeless drifter, a veteran of service. Someone who had slipped through the net. And killed two young people.

In the lay-by at Doolin, Jimmy's thoughtfully chewed through his bacon bap, drank his tea and lit a roll-up. But Mikey can see his father's distracted; he's been staring out at the grey sea. Hardly blinking. Finally, he turns to Mikey and says, 'I had a call from Silas.' What Jimmy doesn't say is that he's just been cleared of a secret slaying, that his life has been reprieved. Changed. 'Things are not as bad as they were.'

Mikey says, 'Not as bad?'

'Circumstances have changed. The heat is off.'

'How much heat Dad?'

Jimmy, still thinking deeply says, 'It might be enough.'

Into Mikey's voice comes the hope that he's kept clamped between his teeth for the whole of the time they've spent in Ireland. He asks, 'Enough? Does that mean we can go home, Dad?'

Can we go home? Time has passed. Winston has passed. The killing of Angel has passed. But the questions of disappearance, of an unlawful interment, are still standing; they'll be there for the duration and who knows when that'll end. So Jimmy measures up and weighs up, smokes his tuv down to a dog-end, flicks it out of the window into the salty Atlantic wind and says, 'Maybe it is time, Mikey.'

And sitting in their van in damp clothes, with condensation trickling down the windscreen, the ashtray overflowing with cigarette butts and crunched Coke cans underfoot, maybe it *is* time.

Maybe it is time to be driving into Elm Hill Caravan Park.

There'll be hands raised in greetings, inquisitive chavees dikking at the motor with Irish plates, Silas's broad grin, Danny,

271

sweat-stained T-shirt jogging into view, Mrs Flowers saying that Jimmy still owes her for new sheets, Romeo and Juliet having a stand-up row, Meg and her jukal sitting in the sun, watching them and an even taller and thinner Carter looking to Mikey for a visit to the town. But, of course, there's someone missing. There always will be a shadow in the window.

But maybe it is time.

'Dad?'

'Yeah, it's time, Mikey. It's time.' Jimmy points the Transit in the direction of Rosslare.

So what are they leaving behind in the old country? (Apart from their shipwrecked caravan in the lay-by near Doolin – a gift for the magpies to pick over.) What have the months on the run been like for Jimmy and son? It's not exactly been a successful tour; it's been mainly two-night stands and short stays out of the public eye. Jimmy's lost weight, his face is thinner as well as his body and it suits him. He looks a better, healthier specimen, than the gypsy who boarded the Irish ferry in what seems a lifetime ago.

And Mikey? Mikey is now into his seventeenth year and he's thickened, broadened out a bit. His is a confident walk, a confident tap on a stranger's door, a striking up of a conversation for a cleaning out of gutters, a patching of a yard. There'll be a friendly smile, a compliment, a putting of ease with, 'Only what you can afford, lady. I won't take a penny more.'

Mikey's into that transition between boy and man that appeals so much to the older woman, but he's also still appealing to Hannah Aubrey. If we were to take a peek into Hannah's room on a Sunday evening, we'd find her curled up on her bed, phone to her mouth, keeping things smoking between her and Mikey. This is to the chagrin of her mother who had hoped that distance would more than dilute contact for the unsuited twosome. But that doesn't mean that Hannah doesn't have a love life; she's young and lusty and there's no shortage of suitors. Lately she's been giving one of these much more attention that she normally would. This might be because he's three years older than Hannah and quite good-looking in a soft-featured way. Also he – Edward, never ever shortened to Eddie – occasionally drops her at school in his father's BMW, takes her to dinner at Boarston Country Club, sources the best tickets for a touring musical. And he buys her thoughtful gifts – a bottle of her favourite perfume, a box of expensive Swiss chocolates, a necklace of gold. He's one year into a law degree and his parents – an estate agent and a solicitor – are funding his course from their business returns. Put all of this together and Edward is the perfect permanent choice that Mrs Aubrey would like to make on her daughter's behalf. (She has already decided on a church wedding, should the big day occur.)

So what could possibly upset Mrs Aubrey's dreams of advancement – via her attractive daughter – up the social scale? The answer is that hour that Hannah spends curled up on her bed on a Sunday evening. She's been keeping tabs – and sending some rather interesting pictures on Snapchat – to someone who's been constantly shifting around the Emerald Isle, someone she hasn't seen for the best part of a year. But this night is different in that Hannah comes flying down the stairs, bursts into the room, throws her arms around her mother and, with a loud excitement, she says, 'He's coming home, Mum. Mike is coming home.'

Mrs Aubrey, trying desperately not to let her disappointment show on her face, offers a rather lame, 'That's nice for you dear,' when inside her thoughts are saying, '*For fuck's sake, what are you thinking of Hannah?*' And that's the same question that usurped Edward will be asking when his phone calls and texts are unanswered.

*   *   *

And so to the driving home for Jimmy and son, to the boarding of the *Isle of Inishmore* again, this time at Rosslare, and watching Ireland fade away on the horizon. It's an afternoon crossing on a heaving sea that pitches and rolls the ferry into the dusk of evening. Jimmy, not suited to a life on the ocean wave, is mightily relieved to hear the call for Pembroke and the reassurance of a landing on the safe and solid and dry land of Wales. This night they'll spend in Cardiff with the Wood siblings on an unexpected stopover.

Selina had said on the phone, had said softly at his asking, 'Of course you're welcome to stay, Jimmy. You're always welcome here.' There's the pleasure of a surprise in her words, and he hears her shout to her brother, 'It's visitors we're having tonight, Eddie.'

And when they get to the destination there's a warmness to Selina, a welcome in her eyes. Now it's not as though there hasn't been an occasional mobile call to keep track of Jimmy and his travels, but it's not the same as her standing there saying in her soft lilt of Irish,

'So you're here then Jimmy.'

He's here all right and he's looking at this woman who's the dead spit of his dead wife. But, it's been a long time since he held a woman. In fact the last time was Selina. And a couple of hours later it's going to be her again.

From their considered dealings, Eddie and Selina have kept the very best of their finds for themselves, for their house. It's a treasure trove of the finest pieces from over the last few centuries. These have been gleaned by guile and cunning and selection from manor house and auction and backdoor deals. These pieces fit together, belong together, complement each other in an impeccable placement of taste. Now if Selina and Eddie's long-departed grandfather could look through the smoke of the simmering yog from some long-ago atchen-tan, he'd put down his knife, pause in his chinning of the kosh and wonder at the luxury of this kenna where his breed live like the gorgers. He'd probably shake his head in disbelief and call to his romni, point through the smoke and then they could both marvel at what the future has become for two of their own.

Tonight the moonlight is strong and it gently lights the upstairs hallway, takes a vain peep at itself in a hanging mirror. It listens as a quiet footfall keeps perfect step with the tick of a grandfather clock, a matching creak of a floorboard; the path to the turning of a door handle and to the sliding in beside a warm sleep-soddened body.

'I thought you'd never come,' Selina says, and Jimmy can't tell her he so nearly didn't. He can't say that he hasn't confused the image of a dearly departed with a likeness so near that it could be the same. He's allowed himself into the world of pretence. And the beauty that's clinging to him, whispering his name, is the woman in his dreams.

At the early leaving of the next morning there's the shaking of Eddie's hand, the briefness of an embrace from Selina. The goodbye to man and boy. Eddie says, 'When it's all done Jimmy, you bring yourself back here.'

Selina says, 'Make sure you do.' And adds, 'And yerself, Mikey. You visit anytime.'

Eddie Wood slaps the side of the van like it's a pony and the countdown to Elm Hill Park begins.

In a few hours they're over the English border and well into their journey, when Mikey breaks ten minutes of silence to tell what he's been thinking.

He says, 'Selina looks so much like Mum,' and Jimmy guiltily nods an agreement. Then they're both silent again for a few miles until Jimmy asks Mikey to roll him up a cigarette. Mikey makes up two tuvlas, one for each of them, and Jimmy reckons that smoking will stunt his growth. Mikey laughs 'cos he's already down on his father.

They're into home territory as the day's slipped into dusk and Jimmy's glad that his entry into Elm Hill is camouflaged by the dark. He's not ready for a reception but he's back, he's home, and this old atchen-tan welcomes him with a brotherly embrace and a rasp of a voice.

'Thought you'd got yerself lost, my pralla.'

So what's going to happen here? Is this going to be a time for concealment, for being the man in the hat in the darkest corner of the kitchema; for looking over the shoulder, for waiting for a careless word to bring it all crashing down? (Although that word won't be delivered by young Ricky Ward. His slim, almost girlish form, is residing in Birmingham jail where it's hopefully not the the receiver of particular attention from some desperate long-termer.)

But for tonight, for Jimmy and Mikey, it's a step into Silas's static and in here it's bright and warm and a pot of stew's simmering on the stove. A new dog is in Will's place, stretched out in front of the fire, much too settled to raise a growl of greeting, and Amey's setting out the bowls around the table. She says to Mikey that Carter should be back soon; she thinks he's got some rakkli in tow.

'But you know what he's like. Won't tell me nothing.'

Silas says that it's because she'd pester him to death if he even gives her a clue.

Later, Jimmy's drifting to sleep and the last year and Ireland begin to dim, start to recede into the past. The caravan stops swaying in the wild Atlantic winds and the pounding rain on the roof becomes a light patter of memory that soothes into a deep and dreamless slumber.

28

This next morning at Elm Hill Park, Jimmy's up with the dawn. It's misted and chilled in the breaking of this day and he wants to get moving, warm himself up – he's spent the night under a thin blanket on Silas's sofa. There's no one stirring yet – not even Mikey who's in with Carter – courtesy of more than several bottles of Danish lager. And so Jimmy lets himself out quietly, stands for a few moments and breathes in the stillness of this early morning before the site starts to stir. He breathes in the good times and the bad times, and then takes himself for a walk past an oblong of scorched and blackened concrete, edges softened by a ragged invading of grass and weeds. An unkempt plot.

In the coolness of a different early morning, he thinks that he'll leave Zilla sleeping for an hour. Then they'll share a pot of meski and a bite of breakfast and he'll make his delivery. It should be a simple trip of a few hours there, a few hours in the return and home in time for lunch. And to ease this guilty feeling that perhaps he's not been the most attentive of husbands of late, he's planning a trip into town for him and his beloved. He's going to spoil her. Treat her. He'll wait in the pub while she spends some time going around the shops and then they'll have a meal, a couple of drinks together and be home in time to watch the Saturday-night film. A nice relaxing day when everything in the garden is rosy. But the road to hell is paved with good intentions.

Jimmy Penfold skirts the grazing Harry Potter – who hardly raises his head – and thinks to follow the path across the field. He just wants to aimlessly wander for an hour, stretch his legs, think about things, but he pauses at the tasting of burning wood in the air, at the rising of a thin plume of smoke. It draws him to Meg and Wilma, who are alongside her vardo and leaning over an open fire. Meg's lifting a boiling kettle from the heat and she says,

'*Koorshti duvas*, my Jimmy.'

And he gives her a 'Good day' in return and seats himself on the steps of her vardo, under the lettering of Lavinia. Then Jimmy silently waits while she fills a teapot and places it to a low table that's already home to milk and sugar. And two cups.

They sit quietly for a while as she takes a sip of tea, sets down the cup and rolls herself a thin cigarette, passes him the makings and pulls a light from the fire.

There, in the stillness of this morning, Jimmy tells her of his intention, of what he's going to do with his life.

'Because I want it ended, Meg. I don't want this running, hiding, anymore.' He doesn't want to be the man in a hat in the corner of the pub. The whys and wherefores don't have to be spelled out; they've been more than weighed within his judgement, in the time away from his people. Away from Elm Hill. And in the hostage loyalty of his own flesh and blood.

Jimmy rises, drains his tea and flicks his cigarette end into the fire, stoops to tickle a prone Wilma behind her ears, and sets off on his lonely walk. Meg watches him until he's out of her sight, sees his figure fade into the distance, then sits herself down for a drop more tea and the rolling of another cigarette.

Then she murmurs to herself, and to Wilma, and to the departed Jimmy, 'This will be an end to it.' There's a resignation in her words, an acceptance that from now on, what will be will be and there's nothing that can stop it.

If we do a catch-up on Detective Sergeant Thomas Malone, we'll find that he's worked like a dog – and all the hours that God has sent to him – to get back to where he was before the Pembroke Dock' disaster. And Polly doesn't seem too worried about him reverting to type; she has a baby at home now who fills all of her time. It's almost like this blonde-haired child who falls asleep in her arms, lays against the warmth of her chest, depends on her totally, is enough for her. It means the father of two can set himself on a course of hard work, playing everything by the book and aiming for success in his career.

Tom Malone is focused and he's attracting attention for his keenness to the task and his high rates of detection. Just this morning Chief Inspector Isaacs called Tom into his office for a chat, for a briefing of how well things are going, and for the subtle placing of their differences in the past.

'You're my right-hand man, Tom,' he says.

Which is probably true because first choice, Harvey Harris, has been exiled to Cornwall on account of a late-night fracas after a rugby match. So poor Harvey's deportation left the way clear for Tom Malone to return to the number one spot at Boarston Station. And he's made the most of it. No job is turned down, cases are pursued around the clock, and the pressure alleviated considerably for Chief Inspector Isaacs. The results are also being noticed at Metropolitan level and DS – almost certainly soon to be Inspector – Tom Malone is on the way back to fulfilling his earlier promise. All of this is so touchable that he's already started his dreaming. He's been checking up on his old haunts within our capital city. He's even sounded out previous comrades on current criminal issues; he's been seeding the ground. Yes, there's so much within his grasp.

That's only if no one ever finds out that DS Malone lied to a superior officer, set a suspect free on Pembroke Dock, and subverted the course of justice. And all of this on Chief Inspector Isaacs' watch too – it wouldn't look good on his record either. So it really needs to be kept under the police carpet and quietly forgotten in a silent truce of the interested parties. Which it will be unless . . . Unless a wayward gypsy fella takes a stroll into Boarston Police Station on a hot summer day and says to the acting, and slightly startled, Desk Sergeant Dave Aubrey,

'Will you tell Mr Malone that Jimmy Penfold wants to talk to him.'

ACKNOWLEDGEMENTS AND THANKS

To my gorgeous wife Debbie who has helped make so many things possible in this writing game.

To the support of all my nearest and dearest – even though Greg can't read my stuff because he says there are too many Dadisms in it – including Craig, Matty, Danny, Bertie, and Karen.

To the rest of the family too numerous to mention. Especially my daughter Carrie whose wicked and irreverent sense of humour has lightened the load on many a dull day.

Many thanks and appreciation to my agent Peter Buckman at Ampersand for his unerring judgement and continuing encouragement when it's most needed.

I'd like to make a special mention for my editor at Coronet, Hannah Black, whose discernment and professional advice has helped to enhance the text of this book. My gratitude also to the rest of her team who have contributed to the publication of this novel. They are: Erika Koljonen, Becca Mundy, Sahina Bibi, Claudette Morris.

A last mention must go to fellow novelist Karen Hayes whose enthusiasm for my fiction has kept me focused over the years.

INDUSTRIAL ORGANIZATION

Giles H. Burgess, Jr.
Portland State University

PRENTICE HALL, Englewood Cliffs, New Jersey 07632

Library of Congress Cataloging-in-Publication Data

Burgess, Giles H.,
    Industrial organization : a study of market structure and strategy
/ by Giles H. Burgess, Jr.
        p.   cm.
    Includes index.
    ISBN 0-13-462458-0
    1. Industrial organization (Economic theory)   I. Title.
HD2326.B77 1988
338.6--dc19   88-25533
                                                    CIP

Editorial/production supervision
  and interior design: **Carolyn Kart**
Cover design: **Lundgren Graphics, Ltd.**
Manufacturing buyer: **Margaret Rizzi**

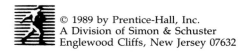 © 1989 by Prentice-Hall, Inc.
A Division of Simon & Schuster
Englewood Cliffs, New Jersey 07632

Printed in the United States of America

10   9   8   7   6   5   4   3   2   1

0-13-462458-0

Prentice-Hall International (UK) Limited, *London*
Prentice-Hall of Australia Pty. Limited, *Sydney*
Prentice-Hall Canada Inc., *Toronto*
Prentice-Hall Hispanoamericana, S.A., *Mexico*
Prentice-Hall of India Private Limited, *New Delhi*
Prentice-Hall of Japan, Inc., *Tokyo*
Simon & Schuster Asia Pte. Ltd., *Singapore*
Editora Prentice-Hall do Brasil, Ltda., *Rio de Janeiro*

This book is dedicated to my parents, Hal and Betty Burgess.

CONTENTS

PREFACE

The field of industrial organization, like the markets and firms which it studies, is subject to change. In this book, I have attempted to catch the outlines of the field as it is now defined; I have tried to reflect the growing interest in firm strategy and the market dynamics which derive from it.

The book is intended first as the text for an undergraduate course in industrial organization. It also might be of interest to graduate students in economics and to students in business or law. I assume that the reader brings a basic understanding of economic principles and a keen interest in seeing how they help to explain the "real world"—why markets are organized as they are and behave in they way they do, to be specific. I have also tried to relate the organization of the market and the behavior of some of the firms in it to the economic policies (antitrust) to correct "flaws" and to thwart "misconduct." Among the book's distinctive features (or those which were intentional, at any rate) is the use of illustrations, placed near the beginning of each chapter, to help define the primary subject of the chapter or certain aspects of it before attacking the matter head-on.

My interest in industrial organization stems from graduate school courses taken from Corwin D. Edwards and Robert E. Smith. I am also greatly indebted to H. T. Koplin for demonstrating the sheer power and usefulness of economic analysis. My perspective of industrial organization is that it provides some explanations missing in "pure" theory. For example, in theory, we may assume a market with non-homogeneous products, but in IO, we can account for the existence (and the form) of product differentiation—a feature of the market is neither an accident nor a mystery, but a piece of evidence about underlying structure and the strategy of the firms who contest one another in it. Industrial organization is both the search for understanding "real world" markets and the application of that understanding to policy formulation.

In the preparation of this book, I am greatly indebted to the three anonymous reviewers who offered much useful advice and to Carolyn Kart, Production Editor, Bill Webber, Executive Editor and Kathleen Dorman, Executive Assistant, for their help. I am also indebted to Nelson Crick, Mort Paglin, and Thomas Tuchscherer, three colleagues who listened patiently to various ideas I tested on them during the writing process, and who provided advice which helped to improve the final product. I take full blame, however, for any errors and omissions which survive the screening process.

The plan of this text is divided into 4 parts.

Part I is intended to serve as an introduction to industrial organization. The first two chapters on the market and the firm emphasize the importance of the two critical institutions in the organization of industry. The formation of markets and firms is explained by their ability to facilitate transactions which, in turn, are ultimately responsible for the economic welfare of the participants involved. And the structure of markets and firms is to be explained by a combination of market conditions and behavior. Industrial organization is not static; it incorporates a process of change in which markets (and firms) are created, grow, mature, decline and sometimes eventually disappear.

The third chapter provides a brief, formal introduction to industrial organization. It provides a sketch of how the various key elements of organization are defined, measured, and analyzed. And it provides a brief explanation of the framework most often used and associated with industrial organization studies.

Part II is a survey of market structure, the first of three basic elements in the structure-conduct-performance framework of industrial organization. In Chapters Four, Five, and Six, the principle dimensions of market structure are defined and their importance is analyzed. Chapter Four deals with scale economics and barriers to entry, factors which are capable of limiting the number of market participants. Chapter Five deals with market concentration, a factor which can explain the level of real or perceived interdependence between rivals found in some markets. Chapter Six, deals with product differentiation, a factor which can account for the apparent lack of interdependence in certain markets, even if rivals are few in number and concentration is high.

The last chapter in Part II, chapter Seven, provides a brief review of the possible relationships between market structure and performance. The discussion includes the problems of definition and measurement of performance. It concludes with a small sample of studies used to estimate structure-performance relationships and to test for statistical significance.

Part II, taken by itself, is representative of the so-called "structuralist" approach to industrial organization. However, Part II is not intended to be seen in isolation; it is intended to set the stage for the rest of the text; it is an integral part of a more comprehensive and dynamic approach to the organization of industry.

Part III is a survey of market strategy, the second element in the structure-conduct-performance framework. In the set of chapters which include Eight, Nine, and Ten, pricing strategy is examined; to be more specific, price behavior is examined in the context of oligopoly markets. In Chapter Eight, the theory of oligopoly provides a survey of the strategy of conflict between rivals, existing and potential. In Chapter Nine, the discussion turns to the strategy of cooperation to resolve conflicts between rivals and to achieve a certain degree of control over price. In Chapter Ten, a third alternative is considered, the strategy of independence; if firms should price simply to cover costs, rather than to increase their own shares of the market at the expense of their rivals, they may be able to avoid destructive rivalry.

Chapters Eleven and Twelve survey the non-price aspects of competitive strategy, advertising and product development. In Chapter Eleven, advertising is examined as a part of the overall strategy of the profit-maximizing firm and as an implication of certain features of market structure. In Chapter Twelve, design and development of products is examined in the same fashion. The role of non-price strategy in the dynamics of the marketplace is also examined.

Chapter Thirteen provides a somewhat different view of the firm and its strategy; it examines the relationship between the internal organization of the modern corporation and the emphasis upon growth and diversification. And Chapter Fourteen provides an overview of the interrelationship between market strategy and structure.

Part III attempts to accomplish two ends. It is intended as a survey of market and firm behavior. It is intended to show how structure-conduct performance is really a loop-like interrelation and how the organization of industry is an on-going process.

Part IV is a survey of those policies which are intended to alter industrial organization. U.S. Antitrust law is unique in the sense that it represents a broad policy, to be applied in a piece-meal fashion, to correct the "defects" in the structure of industry and to eliminate the "misconduct" of firms. Part IV is a source of examples of how industrial organization analysis can be and has been applied to public policy. Chapter Fifteen takes in the Sherman Act, which declares that all restraints of trade and monopolization are illegal. And Chapter Sixteen covers the Clayton Act, which declares that certain specific actions may be illegal if their effect should lessen competition.

Giles H. Burgess, Jr.

THE MARKET

1

In this chapter we examine the meaning and implications of the market. Starting with a workable definition, we turn next to examine cases of the birth of two markets. Then, we take time to distinguish between the market and the collection of producers who supply the market—that is, the industry. These topics all are preliminary to the major subject of the chapter which is the role of the market in the market-based economy. We begin with a look at the basic functions of an economy—the determination of what goods will be produced, how it will be done, and who will consume the end products—and at the price system. Demand and supply are presented as the price behaviors of those buyers and sellers who make up the market, and competition is compared to monopoly to illustrate how different market structures affect behavior and alter market performance. Finally, we consider the distinction between (1) perfect competition, where price is all that matters and (2) imperfect competition, where product development and the promotion of goods are important elements of market strategy. In this final discussion, we attempt to explain how some attributes of market structure called "imperfections" account for the emergence of nonprice competition.

What is the market? The market is the place where a buyer and a seller can meet and strike a bargain over a transaction which is expected to be mutually beneficial. There are all kinds of markets—those which trade in goods and those which trade in resources, those involving barter and those involving the use of money, those which involve or require personal negotiation in price between buyer and seller and those which merely involve acceptance by one party of a predetermined bid or offer price put forward by the other, those which represent the operation of competition in price, and those which represent the exercise of market power, and so on. In this book, we are particularly interested in markets which deal in the manufacture and sale of a product—that is industrial markets.

How does a market emerge in the first place? What determines the identity of the market participants? What are their objectives? How well does the market succeed in satisfying them? This chapter is a starting point. Questions introduced here are the subject of the entire book. Before we take on the whole list of issues let us consider how two markets got their start in the twentieth century in the United States.

TWO CASES OF MARKET EMERGENCE

The automobile is the symbol of the twentieth century prowess of American industry. In fact, when the influx of Japanese imports began to make significant inroads into our domestic market, we began to doubt seriously our place in the world. Automobile production is the single largest manufacturing activity in the U.S. The development of the assembly line for automobile production has given the world the prototype for the organization and operation of mass-production technology. The tremendous acceptance and widespread use of the automobile transformed society and created the distinctly American lifestyle—one which is highly mobile and largely suburban. But did this industry and the market it serves always exist? Of course not. How did it begin?

The automotive industry advanced rapidly from the stage of invention of a working prototype of a motorized carriage to the commercial production of the automobile. The early development occurred in Europe. From the first experiments with various self-propelled vehicles to the construction of a gasoline-powered carriage by Daimler and Benz in 1885, the automobile was distinctly European; it would take until 1893 for the Duryea brothers to build the first motorized carriage in the United States and until 1897, for the commercial manufacture of autos to begin here. Still, the automobile passed from experiment to production after migrating to the New World. So, who were the auto makers in 1897? They were an assortment of inventors who were associated with ongoing concerns; there were inventor-entrepreneurs, while one was an inventor hired by an enterprising firm which saw promise in the automobile.[1] The connection between their prior experience and application to the automobile was rather direct. The early automakers either had prior experience in vehicles—bicycles in some cases, carriages in others—or prior experience in engineering. Ransom E. Olds, for example, made stationary gasoline engines. Henry Ford, a particularly enterprising inventor, soon joined the growing ranks of automakers when he founded Ford Motor Company in 1903.

The way in which the American automobile industry began—and the speed with which it made the transition from tinkering with a product to manufacturing it—appears to support one important contention about the genesis of the new car market. Technology must be regarded as the primary explanation for the supply of the product and for the market upon which it is based. This is not to slight the importance of demand; Americans rushed to embrace the "horseless carriage"; and sales (and production) increased from 4,000 in 1900, to 187,000 ten years later. But the invention of the first successful working models created the industry, and the invention of mass production techniques, adopted

---

[1]John B. Rae, *The American Automobile* (University of Chicago Press: Chicago, 1965), pp. 20-22.

in 1913 by Henry Ford, so lowered the price of the car that it brought automobile ownership into the reach of a vast number of American consumers. By 1920, production was nearly 2,000,000, and there were more than 70 automakers. In less than two decades the industry grew from infancy to a position of leadership in U.S. manufacturing.

Now consider the ready-to-wear dress. In 1850, the apparel industry was one of the largest employers in the United States. But the industry served almost entirely the men's trade. The production of women's clothing was largely a domestic activity. The early clothing industry was operated at two levels: (1)expensive, high-quality goods were the product of a shop, made by a master tailor or dressmaker, and (2) inexpensive, low-quality goods were often the product of a "putting out" system. However, after 1850, several changes began to take place. Factory production of clothing began to appear. First, the invention of the sewing machine by Howe in 1846 and the improvements which followed shortly thereafter, changed the technology of the trade. Second, the influx of immigrants from Europe provided a supply of low-cost labor to operate machines in a true clothing factory. The production of new, inexpensive, high-quality ready-to-wear clothing flooded the market. Employment in the apparel industry more than doubled before the end of the nineteenth century, and the production of women's clothing became an ever increasing portion of the total industry. But were women's dresses a part of these changes? No, they were not.

Just before the turn of the century, there was substantial growth in the production of the ready-to-wear shirtwaist—a popular style of a woman's shirt, with details similar to those of a man's, to be worn with a skirt. Shirtwaist manufacturing grew to the point where 18,000 workers were employed in New York City by 1899-1900. By the end of the next decade, the shirtwaist shops would also be producing ready-to-wear dresses in volume, and by 1929, dress manufacturing would become the single largest segment of the women's apparel industry. And what brought about these changes? Tuchscherer[2] has argued convincingly that the best explanation for the emergence of the ready-to-wear dress industry was a change in style.

Fashion dictated that women's dresses of the Civil War era would affect the hoop skirt. Shortly thereafter, a style was adopted which remained in vogue for the rest of the nineteenth century. And for more than thirty years, fashion demanded that dresses have a tightly corseted waist and an expanisve skirt, featuring a bustle in the back. In the spring of 1907, however, fundamental changes began to appear in popular dress fashions. French couturiers had just recently introduced radically new styles. They featured a simplicity of line and a natural drape, in contrast to the tailored waists, exaggerated shapes, and abundance of frills characteristic of the 1897 dress for example. The new style was incorporated in the ready-to-wear dress designs which the shirtwaist manufacturers began to produce in substantial numbers between 1907 and 1909.

---

[2]Thomas Tuchscherer, *Fashion and the Development of the Dress Industry, 1890-1930* (unpublished doctoral dissertation, Northwestern University, 1973).

Tuchscherer offers three arguments for the hypothesis that style changes made the industry. First, the timing is correct. Second, the earlier designs would have been difficult for the producer and the retailer alike—the tailored fashions of 1897 would make it difficult to create standard sizes for a line of ready-to-wear dresses. Third, the cost of producing the style of dress popular in 1897 would have made the garment prohibitively expensive. It was estimated that, with 1929 technology, the 1897 style would have to be priced in excess of $25; in 1929, only six per cent of the ready-to-wear dresses sold were priced at that level.

So we have an interesting contrast. The automobile industry was born as soon as technology permitted. Inventors of motorized carriages, or the motor car, began to produce commercially almost as soon as they had a feasible product. But the women's ready-to-wear dress industry had to await a change in tastes. Technically, the bustle-back dress could have been made in a factory, but economically it would not have made sense to do so. In the first case, supply considerations determined when the market could be established, while demand considerations were the responsible factor in the second.

DEFINITIONS: THE MARKET AND THE INDUSTRY

In the preceding discussion we used "market" and "industry" almost interchangeably. But are they identical? No. First, they are defined in terms of different basic activities. The industry features production, while the market features exchange. The American automobile industry refers to the group of domestic producers who manufacture cars in the United States. The industry may supply products for the domestic market or for export. On the other hand, the American automobile market refers to the domestic trade in new cars, regardless of the home of their producers. The market may be supplied by imports as well as by the domestic industry.

Second, the market and the industry may be defined in terms of different products. An industry is defined by the technology and the materials used in a particular product by the group of suppliers who make it. The market is defined by the products which compete for the business of a set of buyers. At the turn of the century, the automobile and the horse-drawn carriage were substitute products vying for the same customers. And when the price of the car was cut in half by Henry Ford's invention of mass-production, the ascendancy of the automobile in that market became a fact—the carriage market ("horseless" or horse-drawn) eventually became the automobile market.

Thus, the emergence of a new industry, whether arising from changes in technology or changes in taste, may herald the disappearance of an aging industry from the market. The ultimate success of the automobile (and gasoline-powered trucks and farm tractors) was bad news for the makers of carriages and for the producers of harnesses, the breeders of horses, and the operators of livery stables as well. In the same sense, the success of the ready-to-wear dress was not a welcome sight to the manufacturers of dress patterns.

THE MARKET AND THE PRICE MECHANISM

In the United States, as in the other western industrial nations, the market plays an extremely critical role in the functioning of the economy. It is the very core of a system which coordinates the behavior of millions of independent individuals, each seeking to make the most of the scarce resources available. The production and consumption of private goods[3], from life-sustaining foods and life-saving pharmaceuticals to popcorn and motion pictures which entertain and thus enrich lives, are provided for by this system. Taken all together, the collection of markets which make up the system determines the answers to some basic economic questions: What goods will be produced? And how much of each? How will they be produced? And who will consume which goods? Taken by itself, each market will determine partial answers to the same questions: How much of one particular good will be produced? How will it be produced and by whom? And who will consume it? But the answers may continually be evolving since, by its very nature, each market is open-ended. The identity and number of market participants, who are self-selected after all, and the character and extent of the participation by each are constantly subject to change.

To understand the process better, let us consider a single, representative market. Who are the participants? What is their motivation? How does that relate to their dealing with one another? On one side of the market are private consumers; these are the individuals who want to use the goods which are traded in the market. On the other side are private firms; these are the entities who want to produce the goods traded in the market. The private consumer and private firm make up an informal coalition[4]; collectively they are willing to bid away resources from other uses in order to provide the one good which the former wants to consume and the latter wants to supply. But how does such a coalition actually work? It works automatically by means of the *price mechanism*: (1) the consumer who is willing and able to purchase the product at the going market price will benefit by exchanging a given sum of money for a product that he or she values more highly, and (2) the firm which is willing and able to produce the product at the market price will benefit by exchanging it for a sum of money that is greater than its value to the firm, i.e., the price of the product exceeds its cost of production. The consumer is in search of the satisfaction that results from consumption of the good; the firm is in search of the profits that result from producing it. The two are brought together through the price mecha-

---

[3]Private goods are those which are produced for and consumed by individuals for their private satisfaction. In contrast, public goods are those which are supplied by government for the benefit of the general public and which are financed by taxation rather than by sale to the beneficiaries. In a market economy, private goods are ordinarily provided by private suppliers although such items as the delivery of mail or the collection of garbage may be supplied by government to private consumers on a self-financing, user-fee basis.

[4]Whenever a product is sold, the sale represents a contract which binds the buyer and seller together, if only for a moment in time. But in the case of a long-term supply contract, the buyer-seller coalition is actually formalized.

nism of the market place, and as each side pursues its own self-interest, it also aids the other, its "partner" of the moment.

This seems too easy. It is clear that there is a mutual interest when there is one consumer and one firm who can agree to deal with one another, but how about the more general case when there are many buyers (consumers) and many sellers (firms)? The result turns out to be the same, although to understand it, it is necessary to develop an analytic device to represent the process. This device is the familiar model of supply-and-demand.

Demand and Supply

Let us begin with demand for a particular good. How does a product's price affect the behavior of all consumers towards it? At any given price, some consumers will be willing and able to buy and some will not. We merely identify the quantity which all consumers taken together would buy at each possible price, and when that information is compiled, it results in the demand curve for the product. It ought to look something like the D curve drawn in Figure 1-1. What does the D curve tell us? It indicates that the quantity demanded will be larger, the lower the price charged for the product because buyers do not have to sacrifice as much at the lower price—some buyers will buy more than before, and some will buy for the first time. The number of buyers who are active and the extent of their activity will, therefore, be price determined.

Now consider supply of a particular good. How does a product's price affect the behavior of all firms towards it? At any given price, some firms will be willing and able to supply and some will not. We merely identify the quantity which all firms would supply at each possible price, and when that information is compiled, the supply curve is the result. The supply curve ought to look like the S curve drawn in Fig. 1-1. What does the S curve tell us? It indicates that the

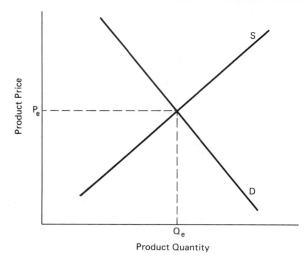

Figure 1-1 The demand curve D shows what quantities consumers will buy at various prices, and the supply curve S shows what quantities suppliers will sell. The competitive market mechanism determines an equilibrium price and quantity, P_e and Q_e, satisfying both.

quantity supplied will be larger, the higher the price received for the product because more firms will have an opportunity to cover their costs of production and make a profit[5]. Some firms will supply more than before, and some will supply for the first time. The number of firms which are active in supply and the extent of their activity will be a function of the price mechanism.

Now we can really explain the price mechanism. Recall that we were able to describe how a buyer and seller could be brought together by a mutually attractive price, but that we made no effort to account for how such a price was determined. Now we can complete the explanation. The supply and demand curves taken together represent the forces of price determination: (1) in our Fig. 1-1, there is only one price at which the quantity demanded is equal to the quantity suppied, (2) at any other price, there will either be a surplus (when price is greater than P_e, quantity supplied is greater than that demanded) or a shortage (when price is less than P_e, quantity demanded is greater than that which is supplied), (3) it may be assumed, therefore, that whenever price is other than P_e, the disappointed market participants[6] will bid against one another to change price, and (4) it may be assumed that when price is equal to P_e, the market is in a state of equilibrium. The price mechanism is such that price explains the behavior of the market participants, and the behavior of the market participants explains price. Does the price mechanism always work in the way which we have just described? No.

Competition Versus Monopoly

There are markets in which the buyers and sellers are always "price takers." That is, they react to price in the manner that we described in Fig. 1-1 by the demand and supply curves. There are other markets, however, in which a buyer or a seller functions as a "price maker." That is, one who has the ability to manipulate price rather than merely to react to it. And what are the implications? These markets also serve to benefit both buyers and sellers, but they do so on unequal terms.

Suppose that we have a monopoly—a market with a single firm in it. And suppose that the firm, the monopolist, decides to create an artificial "shortage" by supplying less output than Q_e. It is then able to push price to a level higher than P_e. What happens? The firm can earn higher profits than it would earn at

---

[5]The supplier needs only to cover its variable costs in order to be willing to supply in the "short-run" (or production period)—the firm's fixed or sunk costs must be borne whether it produces or not. Thus, a price which covers the firm's variable costs and, perhaps, only a small fraction of its fixed costs is still sufficient to make production "profitable." As price increases, the amount of profits for "profitable" firms will increase, and the number of "profitable" firms will increase too.

[6]Disappointed market participants are those who are unable to buy or sell as much as they would like at the prevailing price. They are, respectively, the consumers when there is a shortage and the firms when there is a surplus. When a shortage exists, consumers will bid up the price. When a surplus exists, firms will bid down the price.

the competitive price: (1) total revenues ($P \times Q$) could rise if the price increase outweighs the resulting decrease in quantity, and (2) total costs would surely fall because production is cut back. And even if total revenues should decline, the monopolist would never raise price too far. That is, it would never allow revenue losses to exceed cost savings.

The price mechanism would not correct for the "shortage." Notice we call this a "shortage" to indicate that output has been reduced, but actually monopoly has the effect of creating a surplus in capacity, and since monopoly has only one supplier, there is no competition to force the use of it.

In addition, the consumers would lose. The loss of opportunity to buy the product at the competitive price means that less would be bought and consumed, implying that consumers enjoy less satisfaction. It also means that higher prices must be paid for the amount of the product actually bought, implying that consumers would have less income left over after buying the monopoly quantity (Q_m in Figure 1-2) with which to buy other goods and so lose again. To summarize, the effect of monopoly is to increase benefits to the supplier at the expense of the buyer. Yet, there is another effect. Compared to competition, society loses under monopoly. But how?

Monopoly is inefficient; it wastes scarce resources. Let us consider Fig. 1-2, which may be used to explain both how and why. Suppose the monopolist reduces output from Q_e to Q_m and increases price from P_e to P_m. When this happens, consumers lose and the monopolist gains, but the inefficiency of

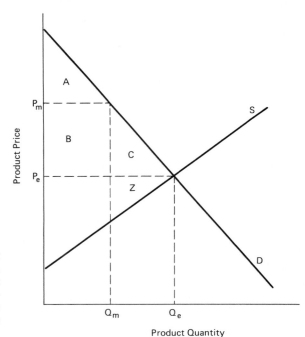

Figure 1-2 The monopolist restricts its output to Q_m, raising price to P_m. Raising price gives a monopolist additional profits, but it sacrifices overall efficiency. The monopolist gains by taking B away from consumers by increasing price, but the gains are less than the losses (B + C).

monopoly is related to the fact that consumers lose more than the monopolist gains. To understand this point, however, we must develop an understanding of two new concepts, "consumer surplus" and "producer surplus."

"Consumer surplus" measures the net benefits accruing to buyers which result from their opportunity to purchase the good on the terms offered by the market, and it can be estimated from their demand curve. It can be measured by the difference between what consumers pay and what they would be willing to pay. If price were equal to P_e, "consumer surplus" would equal the total area in the triangle in Fig. 1-2 above the price line (P_e) and below the D curve; it would equal the sum of the areas labeled A, B, and C in that figure.

In a similar fashion, "producer surplus" measures the net benefits accruing to sellers which result from their opportunity to sell the good on the terms available. It is the difference between what they receive for supplying the good and what they would be willing to supply it for.[7] Now, when the monopolist raises the price from P_e to P_m, "consumer surplus" is cut to the amount included in the area labeled A, and "producer surplus" is expanded by the amount included in the area labeled B. But to obtain B from the consumers, the monopolist cuts back on output, and that means that one segment of "consumer surplus," which was labeled C and which was enjoyed at the lower price, is simply lost. But there is additional loss, one which is measured by the area Z and represents the "producer surplus" given up when quantity is cut from Q_e to Q_m. Since the monopolist gains B and gives up Z and since $B > Z$, the monopolist is willing to make the tradeoff. The total loss to society—the inefficiency due to monopoly—can be measured by the sum of C and Z. Therefore, we can see why and how and to what extent monopoly is inferior to competition.

Perfect Competition Versus Imperfect Competition

There can be little doubt about the comparative virtues of competition and monopoly. But what would we think of a market which has elements of both competition and monopoly in it? This is the case in many markets which are imperfectly competitive.

Suppose that we take the situation in which a firm improves its market position by changing its product. If the firm profits by changing products, one may be justified in presuming that the new product is an improvement since consumers treat it as one. The automaker who introduces "weatherproof" paint, for example, provides a product which lasts longer and needs less maintenance. It may also take customers away from rivals who do not offer the improvement. But does an increase in sales necessarily mean that something better has been offered? No. Consumers may accept as an improvement a product change with-

---

[7]Producer surplus has another rather obvious interpretation. It is the sum of total revenues less the direct or variable costs of production since fixed costs do not figure in the firm's shortrun decision to produce. Thus, "producer surplus" equals the sum of the firm's profits and its fixed costs.

out a difference—the firm may change the packaging of a product, for example, to boost its sales.

Or suppose that we find that a firm increases its share of the market and its profits by advertising. If the firm attracts more customers by advertising, one might conclude that certain buyers had previously lacked information that it existed at all, and that advertising supplied them with it. For example, one who makes and distributes prescription eyeglasses might just attract a larger number of better informed customers if it advertises in the local newspaper and publishes its prices. However, an increase in sales does not prove that consumers are better informed. It might merely indicate that some buyers, lacking information before the advertising campaign and afterwards, were persuaded to buy from the firm.

Or suppose that we have a firm which increases its profit margin and its capacity to produce by building a larger-scale, lower-cost production facility. If the firm lowers cost and improves profits by adopting a larger-scale plant, one might easily conclude that the change improves efficiency since the same product is provided at a lower cost using less resources. When Henry Ford adapted the assembly line for the manufacture of automobiles, he was able to cut costs by more than half, increase the quality of the finished product, and double the pay of his workers.

For competition in product improvements and improvements in production technology, it is quite possible that the firm and the consumer are both made better off. And even for competition in advertising, it is possible that the consumer benefits along with the firm, when useful information is given and received. In such cases "competition" takes a different shape. Price takes a back seat. The questions of how high price is and how it is set are no longer quite so important. And in the second place, when competition involves product improvements or improvements in information in the form of advertising, the seller who is responsible may gain an edge over its rivals. In such cases, the meaning of "competition" is changed.

When we compared competition and monopoly above, we used the concept of "perfect competition." We were describing a state of the market in which (1) firms are so numerous and so much alike that no one of them is able to influence the market price, (2) the competitive effect of any one firm on any other is so small that they do not even regard one another as rivals, and (3) the quality of the product is so uniform and information about it is so complete that quantity of output is the only thing over which the firm can exercise control. But take "imperfect competition." It is a state of the market in which (1) firms compete in terms of products or productivity or in terms advertising, (2) firms can control the quantity of their output, and (3) the "better" firm who makes a "better" product can profit at the expense of its rivals. As such competition is associated with improvements in products and information, "imperfect competition" is clearly identified with good things. But the "imperfect" market also has a dark side.

The seller who has a better (or more popular) product or a cheaper method of production may also develop a certain ability to control price. The economist calls this ability market power. And what does it imply? In most instances it is like a miniature monopoly with the most modest of consequences, but on occasion it may be quite powerful. Is that bad? Not necessarily. When we deal with the case of an entirely new product in an entirely new market, the firm responsible for it may even have a monopoly for a period of time. But without such a monopoly, neither the product nor the market might exist. In the case of the "modern" automobile industry, Henry Ford's invention of the Model T and the mass production technology to manufacture it gave Ford a virtual monopoly in the market for low-price cars, and it made him the dominant producer for more than a decade.

The changes which may be attributed to imperfect competition may be a source of great benefits for the consumer. Nevertheless, there is a lingering tradition of suspicion of the process. It is felt that the firm may gain more market power than it deserves and that by advertising or "improving" products in minor ways, it may establish, even for a period of time, the ability to practice monopoly. But whether imperfect competition is the only means to generate improvements or another means to monopolize the market, it is clear that not all markets are "perfectly competitive" all the time. For that matter, it may be that some markets will never be "perfectly competitive." What is the explanation?

"MARKET FAILURE"

"Perfect competition" is an ideal state of the market. But is it a realistic one? Perhaps it is not. Before a market can function "perfectly" several conditions must be met. There must be (1) large numbers of sellers and buyers, (2) free entry and exit from the market, (3) a homogeneous[8] product, and (4) free and complete information. A failure to satisfy any of these conditions is therefore regarded as a "market failure."

Consider the first of the conditions for a "perfect" market, a large number of sellers (or buyers). The number of sellers in the market may actually be determined by the nature of production technology. On the one hand, a small-scale production operation may be economically viable; it may be able to produce a product as cheaply as large-scale operations. On the other, large-scale production may be necessary in order to compete. What are the implications? If there are important scale economies, a "perfect" market may be an illusion. The choices are either (1) a large number of small, inefficient firms or (2) a small number of large, efficient firms. At one time, the auto industry was notable for the small scale of the typical firm in it. The number of automakers was quite

[8]A homogeneous product is one which is identically the same for all suppliers and is so treated by perfectly informed buyers. It necessarily follows that dynamic changes do not occur in markets with homogeneous products since change implies there is, at least at some point in time, a difference between a product of the firm which innovates and those which do not.

large (more than fifty), and there was free entry of new competitors and free exit of old ones. However, it all changed. New mass-production techniques were discovered which were cheaper than prior methods of manufacturing parts and assembling them in overgrown machine shops. And large-scale distribution and product development became linked with large-scale production. In the end, the auto industry became the prototype of modern manufacturing industry, and the few surviving automakers rank among the largest manufacturing enterprises in the nation and the world. The automobile industry no longer has a chance to be "perfect," but that seems simply to be one of the natural characteristics of the industry.

Now consider the second of the conditions for a "perfect" market, free entry and exit. If there happens to be one source of a raw material necessary to produce a good, and if one firm happens to own it, competitive entry may be impossible. Nature can be blamed for certain "market failures." However, government is sometimes responsible as well. If government should grant to one firm an exclusive right or license to operate in a market, such as a product patent or a public utility franchise, it would bar entry to the market. And that would create a monopoly. "Market failures" are, therefore, sometimes just part and parcel of the environment surrounding the market, an environment which is both natural and institutional. They are sometimes attributable to very human factors.

Consider the third condition for "perfect competition," the existence of a homogeneous product. The homogeneity of products may be determined by the tastes of consumers. There are markets where different consumers want different things. And these can provide opportunities for the enterprising firm. To illustrate, in the teens and twenties, Henry Ford tried to make and sell one good car for the "common man," the Model T, while General Motors chose to differentiate[9] its product line at the same time. GM's proved to be the better strategy. Automobile buyers did not all want the same thing, and GM's diverse product offering helped it to gain the larger market share and to establish its leadership in the market. Ever since, product design and a reputation for "quality" have been among the chief competitive factors in the market—interestingly enough, in the 1980's, U.S. producers may be accused of having forgotten how to compete and of losing business to foreign automakers who have not.

Consider the fourth condition for "perfect competition," the existence of free and complete information. In a modern economy, the sheer volume of information needed to satisfy this condition is overwhelming; the consumer cannot know everything. Information is scarce and it costs something to obtain.

---

[9]Differentiation refers to the deliberate act of making one's product different from those offered by others. It can refer to making several products which are different from one another, as a soft-drink manufacturer may produce one cola, one lemon-lime, one orange-flavored drink, and so on. In some cases, the differences between differentiated products may be more apparent than real. Then, success or failure to differentiate will depend upon how well (or poorly) informed consumers are.

But this too is an opportunity for the enterprising firm. If a seller can attract enough attention to its product so that the consumer responds by purchasing it, and if the consumer is sufficiently pleased with the product and does not want to bother with experimenting with others, the seller may establish itself as long-term supplier of a loyal customer. A successful advertising campaign may do the same thing as a long-term contract may do. The market may cease to be competitive for the business of the loyal buyer. There are limits to such loyalty and if competitors offer much better terms or perhaps a new and better product than the designated supplier, they may take business away. Nevertheless, the consumer's lack of information and his or her responses to it account for significant departures from perfect competition—that is, where every seller charges the same price and every buyer is indifferent about who supplies him or her.

So, what have we learned about market failures? It would seem that they are the conditions, the imperfections, which shape the market in significant ways. They might limit the number of sellers, they may account for the variety of products, and they may determine what the consumer knows or thinks and how he or she behaves. It would also seem that firms must first exploit these market failures in order for them to be effective. Firms must adopt the large-scale production plants in order for large-scale production technology to limit the number of sellers, differentiate their products in order to create product variety, and advertise their products in order to establish the closed supplier-customer relationships. In other words, there is both a *structural* dimension to market failure, related to the natural environment of the market, and the *strategic* dimension, related to the behavior designed to take advantage of what nature provides. It is this combination of structure and strategy associated with market failures which makes individual markets both unique and interesting.

Now for some final observations. Market failure may be an imperfection in the market, but the term is often overstatement. It seems to indicate disaster when we really mean to suggest the failure to achieve perfection. There are, of course, the cases of monopoly where the allocation of resources is quite distorted. Even then markets do serve to improve the position of all who participate—both the seller who monopolizes and the buyers who are exploited by it are better off for taking the opportunity to trade than by not doing so. The imperfection is that monopoly limits the number of buyers participating and the extent of their participation.

However, market failure may simply be pure misstatement at times since it is used to describe the condition of imperfectly competitive markets, as well as monopoly, and since such markets are sometimes responsible for generating product innovations or improvements in production technology. The very sort of dynamic competition which provides a constant source of change, such as life-saving drugs or time-and-resource-saving machines, is just not possible in the perfect market. Thus, perfect competition is really only perfect in a static world, where everything that is possible already exists and everything that there is to know is known.

We began this chapter by describing the beginnings of two markets, one for automobiles and one for ready-to-wear dresses. We explained how the emergence of each market was dependent upon the establishment of certain preconditions. In the case of automobiles, the market emerged almost as soon as the technology would permit the manufacture of a horseless carriage. In the case of ready-to-wear dressses, the market emerged soon after a change in tastes made the manufacture of a dress economically feasible. The important point is the following one. Structural factors and the strategy of competitors may be used to explain the existence of a market. They may also explain how the market will be organized and how that might change over time.

THE FIRM

2

In this chapter we examine the meaning and implications of the firm. After establishing some basic definitions, we examine two cases where ownership changed the organization of the firm to cut costs and improve efficiency. Next, we develop the central theme of the chapter: the firm may be more efficient than the market for certain transactions where the buyer of resource services is systematically less informed than the seller about the quality and quantity of services, and where the seller may exploit that advantage. As a result, the firm relies upon hiring and internal supervision of suppliers, rather than the external checks and balances incorporated in market contracting.

*We then examine a secondary theme: the modern economy is dominated by large-scale corporations which are organized and controlled by hired-management. The **managerial firm**, the firm controlled by individuals whose objectives may be different from and in conflict with the interests of its owners (namely, pursuit of maximum profits), does not fit traditional price theory. We examine two of the nontraditional models which do fit. Finally, we conclude by observing how the organization of the firm (or the market) quite generally is shaped by and reflective of imperfect information.*

What is a firm? What gives it a shape and a purpose? The firm is a place where exchanges of resources services occur which are mutually beneficial to the buyer (the firm) and to the sellers (its employees). Now if this definition sounds a bit like the definition of a market, it should. For some kinds of transactions the firm is an alternative to the market. And when the parties involved prefer to utilize the firm as a medium for exchange, it is apparently a better one. However, the firm, as a substitute for the market, deals only in certain transactions. And the buyer and seller are bound together in an enterprise which involves more cooperation than just exchange. What are these special characteristics of firm-exchange which set them apart from market-exchange?

We commonly think of the firm as a unit of production. Production of some good or goods is the joint enterprise involving the firm and its employees—the sellers (i.e., the employees) supply the resource services which are transformed into the buyer's (i.e., the firm's) product. Is production the essential activity of the firm? If it were, why would the firm be necessary at all? What would prevent the suppliers, who contribute the services and materials necessary for production, from acting as independent contractors to supply the same things to each other as they do to the firm?

It is obvious that there are certain services, which are associated with the marshalling of resources to be used in production, and which are performed by the firm. But it is obvious as well that the firm does a better job in handling these activities than the market. Otherwise independent contractors would deal directly with one another through the market. In this chapter, we shall attempt to answer certain questions. Why does the firm take precedence over the market? How is the firm organized in order to perform its duties? What are the firm's objectives? How does it operate? First, we shall look briefly at the factors which shaped the organization of two American firms during their formative years.

TWO CASES OF FIRM ORGANIZATION

In 1900, Harvey S. Firestone formed the Firestone Tire & Rubber Company of Akron, Ohio.[1] It was the first enterprise in the United States, specifically established to manufacture rubber tires. It would turn out to be a timely decision. Firestone went into business to serve the infant automobile industry, and he reaped the benefits of its growth. In 1905, Firestone signed its first contract with Ford Motor Company, and the relationship became a lasting and profitable one. In the early twenties, Ford would become firmly established as the dominant auto producer and Firestone would serve as Ford's major supplier of tires.

Firestone, like the other U.S. tire manufacturers, was dependent upon raw rubber produced in the Far East. The British and Dutch had developed vast colonial rubber plantations in Asia and supplied the majority of the world's rubber—Britain alone supplied 70 percent from its operations in Ceylon and Malaya. The recovery following the First World War was uncertain and the world economy slid into depression during 1920-1921. The price of raw rubber collapsed, and the British Parliament developed a plan to "stabilize" the price of rubber. Adopted by the British Cabinet in 1922, the Stevenson Plan sought to establish a tight cartel to control the production and export of rubber. While it sought to enlist the cooperation of the Dutch, they refused to take part. Nevertheless, the plan was successful—prices climbed from a low of $0.11 per pound in 1921 to $1.20 in 1925.

Harvey Firestone was offended by what he felt was the arrogance and unfairness of the British action. His company was hurt by the swift increase in costs. And he was not a person to suffer indignity and injury lightly. Since the United States used most of the world's rubber, it would pay most of the bill for a monopoly price in rubber. Firestone tried to get some concerted action by other

[1]Alfred Lief, *The Firestone Story* (McGraw-Hill: New York, 1951).

manufacturers without much success. He also sought Congressional support to survey the feasibility of a domestic rubber industry, but the cultivation of rubber in North America would not prove to be successful. However, his most important action, from our present perspective, is the one which would change the organization of his company. Firestone Tire & Rubber Company began to produce and supply its own raw material, instead of relying strictly upon outside supplies. In 1924, the firm acquired a lease on a small plantation in Liberia to test the feasibility of commercial production. Ultimately, Firestone's rubber plantations in Liberia would become fairly sizeable. And while other factors would eventually bring an end to the British efforts to manipulate the world price of rubber, their initial success was enough to convince Harvey Firestone to establish an alternative to the market in order to secure his raw materials at a reasonable price.

In 1855, the Winchester Repeating Arms Company was founded. From the outset the firm was organized on the basis of an **inside contract** system. The ownership of Winchester provided the plant and equipment, purchased the raw materials, and sold the finished product. The firm also provided the specifications for the product. However, the manufacturing tasks were performed by independent contractors. They were the producers in the normal sense of the term. But Winchester gradually reorganized, with the greatest changes taking place in a relatively short period of time around the turn of the century. The process of the firm's metamorphosis has been well detailed by Buttrick[2].

The Civil War and technological change were two exogenous factors increasing the number of contractors needed to supply Winchester. The War increased demand for guns significantly. And technological change improved the methods for manufacturing interchangeable parts. Contractors were added in response both to the increase in scale and to the increase in specialization. As a result, the burden on the firm was increased; Winchester was forced to exercise more control over the sequence of activities in order for production to operate smoothly.

Other factors, inherent in the contract system itself, were a source of strain to the operation. Given the independence of the contractors and the unique bargains which each of them struck with the company, significant differences would appear between contractors in their earnings and in the wages which they paid their employees. Jealousies developed which could hinder the firm in the long run. Further, the independence of contractors and their self-interest encouraged secrecy. They would not share information with one another or with the firm, since that could weaken their bargaining position whenever new contracts were let for bid. Because the system did not afford a close and continuous check on the materials used by individual contractors, there was little to deter

---

[2]John Buttrick, ''The Inside Contract System,'' *Journal of Economic History*, XII (Summer 1952), pp. 205-221.

waste and much to encourage it, assuming piece-rate output could be increased at the expense of spoilage.

When the management of Winchester passed from the founder and his generation to his son-in-law, another change took place. The younger man brought more technically competent persons into the firm. And they were more interested and informed in matters regarding the design and manufacture of arms and more inclined to assert their authority over contractors than their predecessors. As a result, the firm began to reclaim certain initiatives which always had been delegated. For example, direct monitoring of the contractors increased. And there was a slow replacement of the regime of pure contracting with one in which the firm's superior authority overlay the operations of the independent supplier. Of particular note, in 1903, the firm asserted the right to oversee hiring by the contractors; it was the most significant challenge, up to that time, to their autonomy. Winchester had virtually established two layers of management and the time had come for completing the reorganization.

There were a number of reasons which together seemed to argue for replacing the contracting system. However, Buttrick indicates that the final one had an external origin. The federal arsenal at Springfield had adopted a *scientific* system based upon the principle of hierarchy. The model management was not to be ignored, and on the eve of World War I, with orders for arms soaring, the firm took the final step. The internal contract system at Winchester was finally discarded, after having been gradually transformed over many years.

MARKET IMPERFECTIONS AND THE EXISTENCE OF THE FIRM

The market is not always perfectly efficent. As a result, certain added costs may be borne by those who must depend upon the market for their supplies of goods or services. We noted, in Chapter 1, that a supplier monopoly can take away some of the gains which would otherwise accrue to buyers—in effect, monopoly can impose a *tax* on them. In the case of rubber, we saw that the exercise of market power by the British increased the costs to the buyers of rubber, including the tire industry, by a substantial amount. We also saw that Firestone Tire & Rubber Company took direct action to limit its exposure to manipulation of the rubber market. The company substituted internal production for external purchases of the raw material. Is resource monopoly the only reason for reliance upon the firm rather than the market? No. Firms use internal sources, rather than the market, to secure factor inputs and product components in all sorts of circumstances, while resource monopoly is quite rare.

If monopoly is not the only, or even the most important, source of market failures associated with the supply of resources and intermediate products used in production, what is? That distinction is held by imperfections in information. Whenever there is complete information regarding the quality and quantity contained in a standard unit of a service supplied to the buyer (i.e., the firm), price is the only remaining economic variable, and we may assume that the buyer is fully informed about that. When perfect information is combined with competition, the market is an efficient source of supply. But what happens when there is a lack of standardization? Whenever the quality or quantity of a service is subject to variation from time to time or from supplier to supplier, there are added costs for buying inputs. On the one hand, information is a scarce commodity; on the other, the lack of information is a serious threat to efficiency. For example, in the case of the Winchester Repeating Arms Company, we saw that the parent firm was not fully able to assess the conduct and performance of its independent contractors. The latter would hide certain information which could improve the firm's overall operations if it were known. What part, if any, of the Winchester Company's experience has general implications? What are the sources of the information problem? And, most important, how does the firm lessen its impact?

A very few elements may account for the most serious of the information problems. First, the quality (and/or quantity) of an input may be difficult to measure prior to its purchase and use by the buyer. For example, tests and interviews may provide some information about the skills and motivation of a prospective employee, at least enough to screen applicants, but they are not adequate predictive devices to determine precisely what the firm will get if it hires the individual. Prior specification of standards for subcontracting a product component may provide the guidelines for supplier performance, but their enforcement by the firm may require constant monitoring and testing. Second, the supplier of a resource service or a product component is in the position to vary its quality (or quantity) to satisfy his or her own private interest. Third, the supplier may benefit by holding back—that is, by willfully failing to deliver less to the firm than he or she is capable of providing and/or has contracted to supply. For example, the assembly line worker may lessen tension or lighten the workload by taking extended breaks away from the line or simply by relaxing concentration in place. Either may result in an overall slowing of production, while the latter may also result in an increasing rate of defects. And the outside contractor may lower costs, by substituting inferior materials or workmanship, in order to increase profits. The result may be to lessen the quality of components delivered to the parent firm.

How is the firm to combat *privateering* by those who supply it? The solution involves replacing market transactions for services and components with internal transactions. But what is the distinctive character of the internal transaction which makes the firm superior to the market? How is this related to the organization of the firm? Williamson[3] suggests that the firm operates as a hierarchy. While the market functions on the principle that parties to a transaction deal with one another as equals, the firm functions on the principle that an employee is subordinate to his or her supervisor. It is significant that the superior-subordi-

[3]Oliver Williamson, "Markets and Hierarchies: Some Elementary Considerations," *American Economic Review*, LXII (May 1973), pp. 316-325.

nate relationship embodied in the firm provides certain advantages for the supervisor to gain information and to remedy *deviant* behavior by the subordinate. First, supervision affords the direct observation of employee performance. It is not necessary for the firm to be able to predict an individual's productivity prior to hiring; that can be ascertained after the fact. If an individual slacks off on the job, the direct monitoring of performance can detect it. Second, supervision provides flexibility in the employer-employee relationship. The firm has the power to reassign an individual to a different job and to change (increase or decrease) his or her wage. Thus, the firm can penalize inferior work and can reward excellence. In other words, the firm is able to adjust the conditions of the contract to the performance of the contractor.

Do the same principles apply to the supply of components as to the supply of labor services? Yes. In the first place, the firm is better positioned to gain information about the performance of a subdivision than of a sub-contractor. In the second place, the supervisory power of the firm enables it to channel the activity of the subdivision into conformity with the interests of the parent—in short, internal transactions may all be brought to serve a single purpose, the profitability of the firm as a whole. While a market is a loose coalition between a buyer and a seller, it does have a weakness. Each party has an interest in altering the distribution of the gains. Unfortunately, self-interested manipulations of the market can reduce the sum of the benefits which are divided among the participants. A firm, however, may have an organizational advantage—all the benefits of exchange are thrown into a single pool.

Are there limits to the effectiveness of the firm? Yes. What accounts for its limitations? First, supervisors probably could not perfectly measure the performance of their subordinates. Even if they could, the direct monetary costs of supervision would impose an economic limit on the effort which the firm would choose to make. There are indirect costs to consider as well. Overly close supervision may cause resentment and be self-defeating. Second, and much more fundamental, a hierarchy is not a perfect institution. Someone must be at the top, subordinate to no one. Thus, there is a question about the ultimate performance of the firm. Will the chief executive act out of self-interest? If so, will it harm the effectiveness of the firm?

ORGANIZATION AND BEHAVIOR

The firm is a hierarchical organization. As it is viewed by the rest of the world, the firm is a single unit, guided by a chief executive with power over a staff of subordinates. How is it organized internally? What difference does it make?

Alchian and Demsetz[4] argue that proprietorship is the most efficient mode of internal organization for a firm. Their view of the firm is similar to Williamson's—the firm functions as a hierarchy to minimize the cost of monitoring

---

[4]Armen Alchian and Harold Demsetz, "Production Information Costs, and Economic Organization," *American Economic Review,* LXII (December 1972), pp. 777-795.

resource services supplied by individuals whose private interests are not necessarily in perfect harmony with those of the firm as a whole. Alchian and Demsetz believe that monitoring and discipline are the chief means used by the firms to minimize *privateering*. So they come to the question, who monitors the monitor? And their answer is, under the best of circumstances, the owner of the firm. In the proprietary firm, the owner is ultimately responsible for making decisions. The owner has the best economic incentive to see that everyone works hard. Since the owner has claim to all the profits of the firm, the owner is the perfect self-monitor.

By comparison, all other forms of organization, including partnership and corporation, would seem to be inferior. It is certain that Alchian and Demsetz would regard them as being constitutionally less effective than the single proprietorship for performing the task of monitoring. So, can we assume that the proprietorship is the most important form of organization? We would be wrong if we did. In the United States, proprietorships outnumber corporations 48 to 46 percent in the manufacturing sector.[5] However, corporations supply more than 98 percent of the total value-added; proprietorships supply less than one percent.[6] These numbers suggest that there are factors involved in the organization of the corporate firm to compensate for its inferior ability in monitoring and which account for its success in competition with the proprietorship.

What accounts for the dominance of corporate organization? What are the implications of it? The first question is easier to answer than the second. There are a number of factors which favor the corporation over the proprietorship, including the following. First, the owners of a corporation are protected by the limited liability of share ownership. Their personal wealth is protected from any legal claims which might be brought against the corporation. Second, the corporation is a perpetual entity. The life of an incorporated enterprise is independent of its founder(s), while a proprietorship or partnership must be reorganized upon the death of its owner(s). Third, the corporation is open-ended in terms of financial participation. Thus, it is the superior organization for attracting capital needed for growth and for securing amounts of capital in any instance.

What are the implications of corporate organization? It depends upon the basic nature of the corporation. Many of them are tightly-held units which are, except for legal purposes, proprietorships in all but name. However, the largest and most important of them are virtually all publicly-held corporations. Ownership is widely distributed and, often, is divorced from the management of the firm. For these, the form of organization has certain interesting and important implications.

Recognition of the **managerial enterprise**—the firm directed by a management and staff who do not possess a substantial proprietary interest—has brought about a change in the way economists view things. First, the new perspective brought fresh emphasis to the fact that the firm is a coalition of

[5]*Statistical Abstract of the United States, 1985.*
[6]*Census of Manufacturers, 1977.*

individuals, rather than a single entity. Second, the new perspective challenged the most fundamental of propositions about the behavior of the firm. The profit-maximization assumption was questioned; it was no longer accepted as self-evident. But what could be used to replace it? Several hypotheses have been proposed but none have achieved universal acceptance.

There are really two questions to consider relating to the behavior of the managerial enterprise. One involves the behavior of the owners, the stock-holders in the corporation. What are the interests of the stockholders? How are these translated into control over the management of the firm? The other involves the behavior of the managers of the corporation. What are the goals of the management? How are these related to the behavior of the firm?

Let us first consider the interests of the shareholders. There are a number of instances in which a small group holds a sizeable and permanent minority interest in a corporation. Such a group is often descended from the founders of the firm, and its members often bear a deep concern for the long-term success of the firm. They are likely to be well-informed about the firm due to their lengthy ties and personal connections with individuals inside. Their importance may far exceed the proportion of stock which they own since they are likely to be influential in swaying other stockholders. In short, they may be positioned to dictate to the management in important matters. For example, they may be able to affect personnel decisions and policy at the highest levels. In that event, the corporation is subject to **ownership control**.

However, most stockholders are interested only in the firm as a financial investment, and many *public* firms are subject to **management control**. The majority of stockholders own shares in a particular firm temporarily—they will sell their stock to either capture capital gains when the stock has appreciated in value or to cut off capital losses when it has not. For most investors, a position in any one stock is only part of a larger portfolio. The owners stand at a great distance from the decision-making center of the firm and have but a vague notion of its operations. They are most likely willing to let management vote their proxies to maintain its control of the firm.

Does this mean that there is no check on the management? No, not exactly. There will always be an external or market check on the performance of a firm, and in the case of the market for ownership, discipline can be exercised via *takeover*. When a corporation has *underperformed*, the stock will sell at prices which are low compared to its potential, and outsiders may purchase enough of the stock to elect a new board of directors and to take over the management of the firm. The performance of management may be improved as a result. Does this mean that the takeover is a perfect substitute for ownership control? Not at all. We argued above that the firm is created because internal sources of information and internal methods of discipline are superior to the control of the market. Assuming that to be so, as a general proposition, it follows that the takeover threat provides a weaker form of discipline than ownership control.

Let us now consider the interests of the management. Those who manage the firm may derive benefit from their activity in a number of ways. Income is undoubtedly a major consideration. Other factors are also likely to be involved. What are they? Power and prestige are likely to be very important. A position of authority is a desirable end in itself for one who enjoys the recognition and respect that go with high office. But how can such intangible factors as power and prestige be put into meaningful terms? And for that matter, what determines the income of managers?

The power of one in management is often measured by the amount of resources over which one has command. For example, the size of the work force and the amount of capital are indicators of power. The prestige of one in management can be measured by the success of the firm over which one exercises control. For example, the market share of the firm is an indicator of prestige. Is it possible to capture all such considerations on a single measure? Perhaps. Indeed, it might be possible that such a measure could be identified as the determinant of managerial income as well. At least that is the assumption of certain new models of the firm.

A Model of Managerial Control

One model of the managerial firm is based upon the idea that total sales (or revenues) represent the objectives of the managers, and therefore, the objective of the firm. A case can be made for the proposition that sales are directly related to and represent a good proxy for both the power and prestige of the manager. Sales (determined by output and price) reflect both the quantity of resources controlled and the degree of success achieved by management. Moreover, it is not unreasonable to presume that managerial compensation is correlated with total sales.

Baumol[7] proposed a model of sales maximization, such as the one illustrated in Figure 2-1. The model consists of two parts: (1) a function relating total profits of the firm to its total revenue or sales, and (2) a constraint upon the decision-maker, which represents the lowest level of profits acceptable to the owners of the firm. The model was designed to illustrate the behavior of a large, publicly-held firm with some degree of market power. The profit function is presumed to be determined by supply and demand conditions, such as those discussed in Chapter 1. The firm will be subject to the effects of an increasing supply cost and a decreasing demand price. At some point (R^*), an increase in sales can be achieved only at the expense of lower profits, resulting from higher production costs (and, perhaps, advertising costs as well) and lower prices. In the absence of better information, the owners' control over the management of the firm is imperfect—the profit constraint is presumed to be given by an esti-

---

[7]William A. Baumol, "On the Theory of Oligopoly," *Economica* N.S. 25 (August 1958), pp. 187-198.

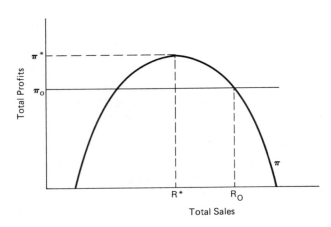

Figure 2-1 The firm which is directed by hired managers may pursue an objective, such as gross sales, other than profits. Discretion to do so may be subject to a profit constraint π_O, however. If profits are a function of sales, the sales-maximizing firm would choose R_O, the largest amount of sales consistent with π_0.

mate of what the firm may be able to achieve under good management. Thus, the managers will select R_0, the highest possible sales consistent with the profit constraint, $\pi = \pi_0$.

What are the implications of the model? First, profits will fall short of the maximum attainable level. Thus, the firm will not fully exercise its market power; it will produce more and charge less than a profit-maximizing monopolist. Second, control over costs will be the same as if the firm acted to maximize profits since excessive costs will reduce the level of sales which can be achieved for any level of profits. Thus, management will not be prodigal in its spending in spite of the fact that it is not primarily motivated by profits. In short, the managerial enterprise would be expected to behave in a fashion which is more socially acceptable than the profit-maximizing monopolist.

Does this mean that managerial models of the firm suggest that management control will result in an overall improvement in efficiency, compared to ownership control? Not necessarily. The performance of the firm depends upon the behavior of management. There are as many alternative specifications of the managerial firm as there are objectives which can be attributed to its management. Included among them are the following: (1) growth in firm sales (as opposed to the absolute level of sales specified by Baumol), (2) level of managerial utility, and (3) level of specific *managerial goods* which yield utility, including salary and other monetary compensation, the number and quality of direct subordinates, and the quantity and quality of the perquisites of office, and so on. While each of these objectives could be cast in a model similar to Fig. 2-1 above, they would have very different implications for efficiency.

A Model of Ownership Constraint

Baumol's model of sales maximization and numerous other models of the managerial firm all shared a common assumption, that the ownership of the firm would establish a fixed profit floor. Does this make sense? It is reasonable to

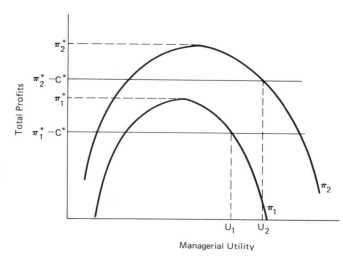

Figure 2-2 The firm controlled by hired managers may seek to maximize managerial utility. Ownership wants maximum profits π^*, but due to market imperfections, will miss its target by the amount C^*, representing costs of information. For its part, the firm would choose the highest managerial utility consistent with $[\pi^* - C^*]$.

assume that ownership does not possess perfect knowledge and cannot exercise perfect control over management. Is it necessary to carry the effect of those limitations this far? The potential level of profits will not be constant; there will be different profit functions, such as depicted in Figure 2-2, for different market conditions. In a banner year for an industry, the ownership of a firm in that industry could be sufficiently well informed to expect profits to rise. In down years, the owners could understand a fall in profits.

How can this be captured in a model of the firm? Yarrow[8] accomplished it by introducing a variable constraint. The model shown in Fig. 2-2 above illustrates the effect of changes in the level of potential profit on the performance of the firm via changes in the profit floor imposed by ownership. Yarrow assumed that the measure of stockholders' ignorance could be represented by a constant, C^*, which would account for the difference between potential performance and what owners could enforce. Thus, when the profit function is π_1, the profit constraint is $\pi_1{}^* - C^*$, and when the profit function is π_2, the constraint is $\pi_2{}^* - C^*$. As a result, a tighter control could be exercised by the owners than would be the case if they could not differentiate between states of the market.

General Limitations on the Large-Scale Firm

Much has been made of institutional failures which limit the efficiency of the large-scale firm. And much has been written about the internal conflict between management and ownership in the large corporation. Is managements' indifference to profits the heart of the problem? There are good reasons to argue otherwise. In the first place, management goals may not be so very different

[8]George K. Yarrow, "On the Predictions of Managerial Theories of the Firm," *Journal of Industrial Economics* 24 (June 1976), pp. 267-279.

from those of the owners. If they seek to maximize sales or growth of the firm, for example, and succeed, the firm's management team may produce maximum profits in the long run. Or if they seek to maximize their personal income, there may be no conflict at all when performance bonuses and stock options make up the major portion of their compensation. In the second place, a significant theme of the managerial theory of the firm deals with the impossibility of maximizing anything.

Consider the organization of the large-scale firm. It is a hierarchy, constructed like a pyramid with many layers. Top management can directly control only its immediate subordinates. And they, in turn, can directly control the next layer, and so on. Communication will necessarily be imperfect—both time and information will be lost through a succession of filters as orders are passed down through the chain and as performance assessments are passed up. How serious is this? It is very serious because, in a hierarchy, communication is control.

Consider the complexity of the large-scale firm and the uncertainties which surround it. It is one thing to construct a model of profit-maximization in which the firm is perfectly informed about the conditions of demand and cost, and in which production and sale of the product occur instantaneously. It is quite another to imagine the less-than-perfect operation of a firm which must guess what demand and cost conditions will be when it commits to production, which must sequence the stages of production in order for goods-in-process to flow smoothly, which must lay aside inventories of materials and finished goods in order to deal with interruptions which could occur at any time despite all precautions, and so on. To complicate matters, the fact that such elaborate planning is needed to coordinate all the activities associated with the production and sale of a product is, in itself, a hindrance to maximization. The nature of any optimization process is that it simultaneously *solves* all the constraints imposed upon it; given a change in even a single condition, a new *solution* is required. However, the planning of the firm will resist change. This has two significant implications.

A major contribution to the concept of the managerial firm was the notion of **satisficing**. Simon[9] proposed that the firm's logical response to a hostile environment—complexity and uncertainty in combination—would be to establish a system of targets and to seek to satisfy (or exceed) each of them. The firm may establish target levels for such things as unit costs, labor productivity, and inventories. And, most important, the firm would establish a target level of profits! Thus, if a single condition should change, the firm could deal with it in isolation, by accepting a "localized" failure or by modifying the corresponding target. However, the firm would not redraft its entire plan. Thus, one of the implications is that profit-maximization is sacrificed to the necessity of establishing a rational order in the management of the firm.

[9]Herbert A. Simon, "Theories of Decision-Making in Economics and Behavioral Science," *American Economic Review* 49 (June 1959), pp. 253-283.

What is the other implication? If the internal order of the firm is so inflexible that it cannot respond to external change, then efficiency will demand that certain limits be placed upon the size and the scope of the firm. That is, the market will be substituted for the firm as a means of coordination and control. And so there is a symmetry. Institutional failures associated with the market explain the existence of the firm. Institutional failures associated with the firm explain the limits to its ability to replace the market. There is a role for both in industrial organization.

INDUSTRIAL ORGANIZATION

3

In this chapter we examine the meaning and applications of the field of study known as industrial organization. Beginning with a brief comparison of certain aspects of the field of biology, we offer a definition of industrial organization and descriptions of three representative IO studies. At this point, we introduce the traditional conceptual framework for industrial organization analysis. The way in which the market or the firm is organized reflects certain environmental conditions and their consequences: environment helps to determine structure, behavior is in turn shaped by structure, and performance is the product of everything else. We provide some details about what the structure-conduct-performance building blocks are and how they are likely to be interrelated. We also point out that there are feedback effects. For example, the firm which succeeds in innovating may create a product monopoly so that performance (in contributing to progress) determines market structure (a patent monopoly).

Finally, we explain how the field of industrial organization may be described as having different schools of thought. There are some who emphasize the importance of market structure, while others emphasize the importance of market conduct or firm strategy. Both have contributed to the understanding of industrial organization.

The markets for industrial goods and the industrial firms which populate them seem as diverse and interesting as the animal world produced by nature. The markets are large and small, they come in various shapes and are designed to perform various functions, and there are many new ones and some which are quite ancient. Even industrial organization, the study of markets and firms, has some similarities to biology. We can talk about the development of certain forms of organization, the modern corporation, for example, as a *natural* adaptation to the tasks undertaken by a modern firm. The corporate organization seems necessary to coordinate the activities of the large numbers of employees and to attract the huge amounts of capital required for large-scale production. We can attribute an evolutionary character to the market as well. The market evolves when there is a purpose, an opportunity for both buyers and sellers to benefit from it. Moreover, the market will be shaped by *environmental* factors,—a lack of free and complete information, for example, may explain why the market turns out to be *imperfectly competitive*.

But the analogy between industrial organization and biology of natural selection may be stretched only so far. Industrial organization involves more than adaptations to nature; strategy is also involved. New products and new technologies are introduced by design. The firm may plan to acquire a monopoly position and may succeed in doing so, at least for a period of time. It is no longer a simple contest between animal and nature, with a random process for introducing potential changes and a survival of the fittest. The lion may be the king of beasts, but it did not design itself. DuPont did, and therein lies the difference.

What is industrial organization? It is the study of markets for goods and of the firms which produce them. It is the study of industry. Industrial organization shares many common concerns with the field of microeconomic analysis, yet it is not the same thing. Price theory (micro) is concerned with operation of the market in the abstract. For example, with the implications for pricing and resource allocation of monopoly versus competition. In contrast, industrial organization is more concerned with why markets are structured the way they are and behave the way they do.

Industrial organization is a study in search of answers to a number of interesting questions. Why are some markets monopoly-like while others are competitive? Why do the rivals in some markets compete vigorously while those in other markets appear to act in concert? Why are products in some markets differentiated while those in other markets are not? Why are the firms in some industries vertically integrated while those in others deal with outside suppliers or agents? Moreover, industrial organization is interested in policy implications related to a greater extent than pure theory. Industrial organization is an applied field; it is different from the pure theory of price.

In this chapter we shall attempt to complete the groundwork for the remainder of the book. In the first two chapters, we sought to explain the basis for the roles which the market and the firm play in our economy. Now we seek to explain the basic approaches and objectives employed in industrial organization. But before we begin in earnest, consider the following sketches of three industrial organization studies which illustrate the nature of work done in the field.

THREE EXAMPLES OF INDUSTRIAL ORGANIZATION STUDIES

The case study.   In 1958, Twentieth Century Fund published a two volume work entitled, *Antitrust Policies*.[1] It was the result of a lengthy project, financed by the Fund and written by Simon N. Whitney, to study the organization and significance of big business and the effectiveness of antitrust policy to preserve competition. The first volume presented a collection of general eco-

[1]Simon N. Whitney, *Antitrust Policies* (Twentieth Century Fund: New York, 1958).

nomic studies of eight major industries in the United States—meat packing, petroleum, chemicals, steel, paper, bituminous coal, automobiles, and cotton textiles. The second volume was comprised of economic studies of landmark antitrust cases in twelve other industries. Let us confine ourselves to the first volume.

What is the nature of such a case study? In general, it represents an application of the historical method. That is, facts are collected and arranged in an **orderly** fashion and **causal** relationships are identified—for the industry study, order and causation are drawn from or suggested by economic theory.

Consider Whitney's study of the steel industry. It begins with a description of the industry, including physical size and market positions of the major steel producers, the characteristics of the various stages of steel production, the product and geographic markets served by the industry, and the significance of the integrated producers—that is, firms which make pig iron, steel ingots, and rolled and finished products. The study continues with a history of industry conduct involving antitrust actions including the formation of the **steel trust** (the consolidations leading to the creation of United States Steel), the early price-fixing efforts fostered by USS through the so-called "Gary dinners," the establishment of a unified geographic pricing system (Pittsburgh plus) for the industry, the later merger activities in steel, and so on. The study concludes with an assessment of the competitive status of the industry including factors such as the size and number of manufacturers, the control of iron ore supplies by major firms, the practice of price leadership, and the incidence of secret price concessions to buyers.

It is the nature of the case study to *explain* each case as the conjunction of all the conditions and events surrounding it. Each case bears some important and universal implications, but it is also likely to contain implications which are unique. A case may truly be one of a kind, which is the case with Whitney's study of the American steel industry, 1900-1950.

The statistical cross-section study. In 1951, Joe S. Bain published his seminal paper, "Relation of Profit Rate to Industry Concentration."[2] In it, certain issues of real significance were addressed. Price theory makes a strong case for the superiority of competition over monopoly, all other things being equal. There are reasons to believe that oligopoly markets will behave more like monopoly than competition, under some conditions. What are those conditions? Can one devise some sort of scale to distinguish degrees of oligopoly?

Bain's study involved the testing of one simple statistical hypothesis: that the average profit rate for firms in an industry will be a direct function of the level of seller concentration. In his study, concentration was measured by the percentage of total industry sales supplied by the eight largest firms taken together, and the profit rate was measured by the ratio of net revenue to stock-

[2]Joe S. Bain, "Relation of Profit Rate to Industry Concentration: American Manufacturing, 1936-1940," *Quarterly Journal of Economics*, LXV (August 1951), pp. 293–324.

holder equity. Thus, Bain examined the profit-concentration relationship for a cross-section of 42 industries, selected on the basis of the availability of the data and the suitability of the industry definition. In the latter instance, Bain was concerned that the industry definition was consistent with the product and geographic dimensions of the market (see Chapter 1 for the significance of this point). What did Bain discover? He found that concentration made a difference. Specifically, he found that a threshold level of 70 percent in the concentration measure distinguished higher average profit rates from the lower, and that the difference was significant.

The effect of this study was far more important than any direct conclusions which might be drawn from it, however. It established a new method for studying issues of importance in industrial organization. One could ignore the numerous factors which distinguish one industry from another and could instead rely upon one or two quantifiable characteristics to estimate a **universal** or cross-sectional relationship—one which could be applied, to a greater or lesser extent, to all industries. Thus, the empirical study became an important part of research in the field of industry analysis.

The theoretical study. In 1978, Richard Schmalensee published a paper entitled, ''Entry Deterrence in the Ready-To-Eat Breakfast Cereal Industry.''[3] The study sought to provide an explanation for one aspect of structure in the market for RTE cereal, the fact that the market was dominated by four large firms, Kellogg, General Mills, General Foods, and Quaker Oats. It was Schmalensee's conjecture that this dominance was the result of the conduct of the four major firms—a conjecture which stood at the heart of an FTC complaint in an antitrust case brought against the four (a case which was eventually lost by the FTC). Schmalensee argued that the market positions of the leading producers were *artificial* in the sense that they could be maintained only by a successful strategy of deterring new competitors. The scale of production was small enough and the technology of production simple enough that there was room in the market for a much larger number of firms. And yet, the level of profits enjoyed by the leaders in the industry was high enough to attract competition, at least under normal conditions. So what explained the *majors* continued dominance of the market? Why were they not faced with an onslaught of new competitors for this profitable business? Schmalensee argued that it was the result of the established firms preempting the *space* needed for new competitors to do business. Schmalensee argued that the *majors* introduced so many brands of cereal products, some 80 or so in all, that there was no segment of the market left for new firms to exploit. They had already been exploited by the old firms.

The theory developed and applied to the RTE cereal market by Schmalensee was an extension of earlier concepts dealing with spatial competition and with entry prevention. Was his analysis correct? There is no satisfactory

[3]Richard Schmalensee, ''Entry Deterrence in the Ready-to-Eat Cereal Industry,'' *Bell Journal of Economics* 9 (Autumn 1978),pp. 305–327.

answer to such a question. It is a plausible conjecture, but there are equally plausible conjectures that brand preemption will not work. Whether the theory is internally consistent and correctly applied to the case in point is not our primary concern here. What is important is that the study of RTE cereal does serve to illustrate a third method of analysis used in the field of industrial organization.

THE INDUSTRIAL ORGANIZATION FRAMEWORK

What, if anything, do these three industrial organization studies have in common? Actually, they share several things. First, the unit of analysis is the same in each case. The market for a product, or the industry which supplies it, can be regarded as the basic unit of analysis in all three of the studies cited. In two instances, one industry was examined, while in the third, a cross-section of industries was the subject of concern. Is this always the case? No. There are studies in industrial organization which are based on the firm as the unit of analysis. In the preceding chapter, for example, we reexamined the theory of the firm and suggested that its existence and organization can be explained by regarding the firm as a substitute for the market. Second, all three studies employed a technique known as partial equilibrium analysis. That is, each market or industry was treated as if it were independent of all others. Is this unique to industrial organization? No. Marshall introduced the technique, and it has been widely used in microeconomic analysis. Third, each study cited above—Whitney, Schmalensee, and Bain's—makes use of a paradigm known as the industrial organization framework.

What is the industrial organization framework? It is just a general expression of relationship between the attributes which seem to characterize (or are associated with) an industry. It can be illustrated by a diagram as depicted in Figure 3-1. The industrial organization analyst assumes that certain attributes, designated as **basic conditions**, are given and that all the other attributes are

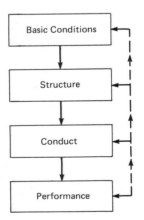

Figure 3-1 Industrial Organization Paradigm

logically determined by a chain of causation as follows: (1) the basic conditions are the primary determinants of the market or the industry **structure**, (2) the structure of the industry is the primary cause of the **conduct** by the participants in the industry, and (3) conduct explains or accounts for market **performance**. Thus, markets are analyzed or classified by the way in which their attributes fit into the framework. What are the contents of the boxes in Fig. 3-1?

Basic conditions.   Basic conditions are taken to include the many factors which shape the market or the industry. They define the human and physical environment which is relevant to it. Consumer demand is a key factor among the basic conditions. However, many things shape the demand for a product. Consumer tastes are affected by personal likes and dislikes and by social mores and trends. For example, in Chapter 1, we demonstrated the importance of style in the emergence, just prior to 1910, of the ready-to-wear dress industry in the United States. The level and distribution of income is important. Equally important are the geographic and demographic factors which can account for the spatial- and age/sex-distributions of the population. Information has a powerful influence on consumer behavior. Mere human ability to acquire and process information is progressively strained as the number, complexity, and variety of products grow; preferences for certain brands may have been shaped by their advertising; and the consumer may become more a creature of habit than of discernment.

The market is also shaped by the basic conditions in supply. For example, in Chapter 1, we recounted the importance of technology in the sudden emergence of the automobile industry in the 1890s. Technology provides a potential for a product to be made at all, and the state of technology determines how a product will be produced. Technology can be important in other ways. The development of cheap and rapid transportation, for example, widens the market, and a larger market opens up opportunities for more efficient production. Economic historians have often argued that, among the changes critical to the industrial transformation of the nineteenth century, was the vast railroad construction in the United States and Europe during that period of time.

The basic conditions also include the political environment. There are numerous ways in which government and its institutions are influential. In some cases, the effects are direct. Federal Antitrust Laws are intended to halt the spread of monopoly. The antimerger provisions have severely limited mergers between large competing firms. They have had other effects as well. Since horizontal mergers (combinations of firms in the same industry) are widely prohibited, firms became diversified as they grew, often by conglomerate mergers (combinations of firms in different industries). In contrast, Federal Patent Laws were intended to encourage the development of new technology, but they protect the monopoly position, at least for a period of time, of the firm that succeeds in discovering a new product.

Does the fact that basic conditions are taken as given mean that they are immutable? No, this is obviously not the case. We have described a number of ways in which new conditions appeared which led subsequently to changes in the market(s). Yet the term, basic conditions, does suggest that they are assumed to be exogenous to the market itself. Is strict independence of basic conditions a necessary requirement of the industrial organization paradigm? Not necessarily. It is possible that *feedbacks* are embodied in the industrial organization process, as indicated by the dotted lines in Fig. 3-1. These may imply that performance affects market structure and conduct (or even basic conditions), but we shall add some of the finer points of the analysis after introducing the other elements of the paradigm.

Structure. Structure is taken to include those attributes which are next in the order of primacy. The structure of an industry is taken to mean the set of characteristics which give definition to the supply-side of the market, such as the nature of the firms which produce a product, the characteristics of production cost and entry, the relative size and number of producers, and the nature of the product which they manufacture and distribute, and so on. These serve to give the same definition to structure as do the classifications of industry structure familiar to pure theory—namely, perfect competition, perfect monopoly, monopolistic competition, and oligopoly. Why was it necessary for industrial organization to develop something new? The answer is that analysis in industrial organization intends to predict or explain behavior in specific cases, while theory seeks merely to generalize. Moreover, except for those extreme cases—perfect competition and monopoly—the theoretical structures are quite indefinite. For example, there are apparent different degrees of oligopoly, depending upon the number and the size of rivals. And there are different degrees of monopolistic competition as well, depending upon the amount of product differentiation. Thus, the industrial organization model is intended to substitute a system of continuous indexes of significant and measurable attributes of market structure for the system based upon broad classification. What are these structural attributes?

Economies of scale are an important dimension of structure. They may result from the adaptation of technology to production, and scale economies are derived from one of the basic conditions identified above. There are other sources of economies of scale as well. Some tasks which complement production—coordination, resource acquisition, research, promotion, and distribution—are often performed better by the firm itself than they are by outside contractors. Why? Lack of perfect information is a basic condition as well. Adaptations by the firm to the need for better information could account for its expanding its role.

Barriers to entry are another structural attribute of real importance. They represent the natural and artificial limits to access in the market faced by potential competitors. And they are the result of basic conditions. For example, the physical supply of a particular resource may be so limited that one firm may control it all. Or the technology, developed by an existing firm for producing a product, may be protected by a legal patent, and thus, may be denied to all others.

Industry concentration—that is, the number and relative size of firms in the market—is widely regarded as the most important market structure attribute. What accounts for it? Scale economies are an important determinant of firm size. Barriers to entry are a major limit on the ability of *outsiders* to challenge established firms in the market. Together they may represent the crucial determinants of concentration, and they are themselves derived from basic conditions.

Product differentiation is the final element of structure with which we shall be concerned. It represents the absence of *pure* competition—competition based solely upon price—in the market. Instead, the products supplied by different firms are not perfect substitutes for one another, and competition may take the form of shifting demands. What accounts for this? Differences in tastes, differences in location, and imperfections in consumer information are all preconditions for some form of differentiation. Where they are found to exist, differentiation may be the result. Thus, differentiation is the market adaptation to certain **market imperfections**.

Now that we have enumerated the structural attributes, let us consider the following question: Is there any trait in common among them? Yes, there appears to be. Each of the attributes may be regarded as a *market imperfection* or as the result of one. Suppose that there were no scale economies, no barriers to entry, no concentration, and no product differentiation. What sort of market would we have? Presumably it would be a perfectly competitive market. To the extent that some degree of scale economy, barrier, concentration, or product differentiation can be found in a market's structure, we would probably describe the market as one which falls somewhere along a continuous scale of imperfection.

Conduct. Conduct is the term used in reference to the behavior of firms in the market. Sometimes we are interested in the interior motivation and conduct of the firm. For example, in Chapter 2, we examined the profit-maximization question in relation to the internal organization of the firm. However, we are most often concerned with the market behavior of the firm—that is, how the firm reacts to the conditions imposed by the market structure and interacts with rivals. In the extreme cases of market structure, interaction is not very interesting. The monopolist has no rivals, and the perfect competitor is not aware of any. However, in intermediate cases of market structure, where there are varying degrees of *imperfection*, it is. What are the significant aspects of market conduct?

Pricing behavior is certainly regarded as the most important aspect of conduct. Direct control of price—the existence of market power—is what distinguishes monopoly. The complete absence of market power—a condition where price is set by the market itself—is what distinguishes perfect competition. What happens when there are only a few firms in the market? In such a case, pricing behavior takes on strategic implications. The firm is aware of its rivals and is aware of the fact that its actions will affect them. Thus, a price change introduced by the firm may have consequences far beyond the immediate effect on the firm's revenues and profits. There is a range of possibilities. At one extreme, the firm may view interdependence with rivals as a constraint on its ability to forge a price of its own so that it is willing to cooperate with the competition. While at the other, the firm may view interdependence as an opportunity to use price as a competitive weapon in its strategy to eliminate rivals. A third possibility also exists. If there is some degree of product differentiation, the firm may price independently on the assumption that any adverse reactions to its initiatives will be so long in coming or so ineffective that the immediate gains are worth the risk. In the **imperfect** market, pricing could be relegated to a minor role in market conduct.

What would replace pricing? Rivalry may take any of several forms. Each of them is related, in some fashion, to product differentiation. Competition in product design is an alternative to competition in price. The firm might seek to offer a brand of product (or group of brands) which is more attractive than those supplied by its rivals. Moreover, advertising may complement the firm's product design strategy. The firm might seek, through a variety of means at its disposal, to inform consumers about the existence of its product or to persuade them of its superiority. The firm may even seek to use research and development to develop entirely new or substantially improved products. So, competition may take new form. Is that the only importance of non-price conduct? No. In conducting its product strategy, the firm may be able to forge a certain degree of market power which insulates it from competition. In short, product manipulation by the firm may result in changes in market structure.

There are other aspects of conduct which may affect the competitive position of a firm relative to its rivals. Consider the question of internal organization. A change in the size or scope of activity may result in an increase in profitability for the firm. After all, this would be expected whenever there are economies of scale involved. This alone could be a source of competitive advantage if rivals fail to make similar changes in their own internal organizations. It is even possible that such a change would directly result in the firm gaining market power. For example, consolidation of several existing competitors via a series of mergers could create, at least for a time, a monopoly in the market. An acquisition by one firm of exclusive access to important supplies of resources or channels of distribution may eventually lead to an elimination of competitors provided no other markets are developed to replace those foreclosed. On the other hand, this is just the sort of change which can lead to the development of a new market.

So, what are the implications of conduct and its position in the industrial organization paradigm? The role of conduct may be exactly as shown by the primary connections in Fig. 3-1. That is, one part of a top-to-bottom process.

There conduct is shown to be constrained by the market structure and the basic conditions which define it. On the other hand, the role of conduct may sometimes be reversed—at least in certain cases of *imperfect* market structures. Conduct is capable of altering the market environment. It is one of the *feedbacks* mentioned above and is indicated by dotted lines in Fig. 3-1. We just now described how conduct may affect market structure, but it may affect basic conditions as well. A research and development strategy can ultimately alter the state of existing technology, and we did assume that technology is a basic condition. Nevertheless, the most immediate effects of conduct, as depicted in Fig. 3-1, are expected to be seen in performance, feedbacks notwithstanding.

Performance.   Performance is the description of and, often by implication, a judgment about the results of market behavior. Performance stands at the very end of the chain of cause and effect described by the industrial organization paradigm. We are interested in how well the market works. But what do we mean by this? How well for whom? In Chapter 1, we observed that a market is created to serve both buyers and sellers. Therefore, it is clear that performance should be judged first in terms of the interests of the market participants. How about the rest of society? Non-participants may also have an interest in the market's performance. If production or consumption of a product results in lowering (or raising) the well-being of the rest of society, there are *spillovers* from the market. In that event, the description or evaluation of market performance would not be complete without taking into account all the results. What are the specific aspects of performance?

The dimensions of market performance about which industrial organization analysis is concerned include efficiency, fairness, and progress. Efficiency involves how well the market makes use of available resources. Fairness involves how equitably markets distribute the benefits of economic activity to the participants. Progress concerns how effectively the market nurtures the changes which yield new and better products and production techniques.

The economist is one whose scientific interest is tied to efficiency. That is, getting the most out of a limited supply of resources. It follows that industrial organization analysts take efficiency to be the single most important dimension of market performance. What is efficiency and can it be measured? First, there are two forms of efficiency, efficiency in allocation and efficiency in production. In Chapter 1, we found out that perfect competition was an appropriate structure to provide allocative efficiency. Using concepts of consumer- and producer-surplus to indicate the economic gains from trade accruing to buyers and sellers, we demonstrated that the total surplus would be maximized at the competitive price and output. In Chapter 1, we also noted that sometimes the attainment of productive efficiency is inconsistent with perfect competition. If there are large–scale economies, the minimization of costs—the objective of productive efficiency—may require a small number of large firms and that may mean an oligopoly structure. It is possible that cost minimization may preclude allocative perfection and vice versa; it is quite possible that **optimal efficiency** is a compromise, or what has become known as the *second best*.

Second, the measurement of efficiency is no easy matter. We need to know the gains in surplus to index allocative efficiency and the reductions in cost to index productive efficiency. We would require knowledge of not only what did happen, but what would have happened if the market had been perfect. These are however, impossible information requirements. It is possible that the economist has to make compromises in measuring efficiency. It is common practice to use proxies. Bain's study, for example, used profits as the measure of the efficiency aspects of performance. The justification was the following: exercise of market power by suppliers will simultaneously reduce consumer surplus and raise profits, so high profits are taken to indicate inefficiency. But there is a problem. High profits might also be an indication of low costs, other things being equal.

Efficiency aside, the economist is interested in the other dimensions of economic performance including fairness. But what do we mean? We may mean both fairness in process and fairness in outcome. On the one hand, the market seems intrinsically fair as a process. As we pointed out in Chapter 1, the market advances the interests of all participants and participation is completely voluntary. On the other hand, the end results are not always so laudable. The market does not guarantee that the weak, the old, and the otherwise disadvantaged will share adequately to survive and enjoy a *reasonable* economic life. This is, in fact, one of the fundamental principles of the modern **welfare state**—that government exists to make adjustments in income distribution to the end that economic well-being will be improved. While it is important, it is not a particularly relevant consideration to an understanding of *performance* in the industrial organization paradigm. Why is that?

In industrial organization we are concerned with *fairness in the small*. That is, does the particular structure of the individual market, not the overall system, produce fair results? Assuming that an individual has something to trade, and is not disadvantaged from the start, every market participant will be better off after trading than before. Not all traders will benefit on equal terms as we saw in Chapter 1. A monopolist will get more than its fair share of the trading surpluses by manipulating the price and by extracting some of the consumers' surplus. Therefore, for *fairness in the small*, competition will always be better than monopoly. As for fairness in the large—concern for the adequacy of income to ensure the survival of each individual—market structure may be irrelevant. One who is severely handicapped may not be able to compete, so the presence or absence of competition is of little importance.

The industrial organization economist must also be concerned with progress. This means that the market does more than transform resources into goods; it develops the potential for such a transformation. This is what happens when a product innovation is introduced. Obvious changes have taken place in the world economy over the last two centuries. The ability to produce more and better products has contributed to a spectacular advance in the average level of economic well-being. To a large extent, technological change is an exogeneous force responsible for economic progress—science develops knowledge independently, and applications are found in business. Yet, market structure, conduct, and performance can be important for economic progress also.

The invention of the electric light bulb was, for example, the source of many dramatic improvements. It was responsible for making the consumer's life more comfortable in the home. It was responsible for making the economy more productive as well. The development of high-quality artificial lighting directly improved the safety and productivity of the work-place. It was virtually necessary for the development of the modern department store and other large, low-cost retail establishments. It was clearly critical to the institution of multiple shifts in the factory, so expanding the productivity of all other capital. It was also the cause of a **market imperfection**. After all, the invention became the source of the product monopoly captured for a time by the inventor, Thomas A. Edison, and the Edison companies.

Monopoly may or may not accompany the introduction of a new product, but one thing is certain. Innovation is accompanied by upheaval. Competitive positions are likely to change; some will benefit; some will lose. In that sense, perfect competition is not an environment for progress. By definition, it has only one dimension for change—the entry and exit of firms, each of which can only offer an identical, existing product.

What can we say in general about performance? One thing is clear. Different dimensions of performance may compete with one another. Allocative efficiency and fairness, at least in the narrow sense of fairness of results, seem to favor the markets which are most like perfect competition. On the other hand, the dimensions of productive efficiency (when there are economies of large scale) and progress seem to favor the markets where there are too few firms and too many products for perfect competition. This can be very frustrating for the person who might wish that the world were simpler and lines more clearly drawn. It is further compounded by the fact that good universal measures of efficiency, fairness, and progress elude the best of attempts. Under the circumstances, comparisons of any two markets, where one has poorer performance in efficiency and better performance in progress, may be difficult. They may amount to little more than one person's subjective assessment.

We have traced through the industrial organization paradigm, from basic conditions to structure, conduct, and performance. In terms of its application, however, we have to develop a much more complete knowledge about the attributes of the market and their relationship to one another.

THE FIELD OF INDUSTRIAL ORGANIZATION

Let us presume that all industrial organization draws upon a model such as the one illustrated in Fig. 3-1. Does this mean that there is no controversy in the field or that all the work done is very similar in nature? The answer is no. Consider the question of controversy. Knowledge of how the market works, or might work, is far from complete. In the absence of perfect understanding, it is only natural to speculate. With many diverse facts to explain and only the general logical structure borrowed from economic theory for guidance, it is a relatively easy matter to develop a fair number of hypotheses. Do these form any patterns? Or, to put it another way, are there identifiable *schools* of thought? Yes.

There is a **structuralist** approach which places the primary burden for an *explanation* of the facts upon market structure. The study by Bain, on the relationship between concentration and profit rates, is an excellent example of this approach. In its purest form, market structure is taken as given and is presumed to explain or account for the level of market performance—for its part, market conduct, particularly pricing, is taken to be so completely determined by structure that it may be ignored.

In contrast, there is a **behavioralist** approach which places the emphasis upon market or firm conduct. The study by Schmalensee, on the relationship between product strategy and barriers to entry in RTE cereal, is an excellent example of this approach. In its purest form, market conduct is taken as given and is presumed to be responsible for certain imperfections to be found in the market's structure.

Does this mean that you will have to choose sides? Not at all. The earliest work in industrial organization certainly tended to be structuralist in approach. The schematic design in Fig. 3-1 is a reflection of the original industrial organization paradigm. Yet, there was always recognition of the fact that conduct could alter market structure. More recently, the potential for conduct to shape the market has been more rigorously investigated. Now structure and conduct receive more equal weight than they once did. While much of the work is eclectic, emphasis on one or the other may seem appropriate for a particular industry or a particular relationship. Still, *school* differences do persist.

Consider the nature of the work which is done in the field. There are some who are primarily interested in the objective side of the organization of industry. For example, What is the present structure of the steel industry? What accounts for it? How is it different from textiles? What are the implications of those differences? There are others who are primarily interested in the normative side of industrial organization. For example, how well does the steel industry function? What can public policy do to improve it? What are the best achievements of Antitrust? What are the major failures?

Again, the differences between the two forms of analysis—the positive and the normative—are easily overdrawn. In the two studies cited at the outset of this chapter, by Bain and by Schmalensee, we have examples of work that is primarily objective in nature. But both have close ties to normative questions. In fact, the Bain study and others like it have subsequently been used to justify enactment of a radically new Antitrust Law. The proposed piece of legislation, the Industrial Reorganization Act, would declare any market structure unlawful in which the four largest firms supply 70 percent of the market. Similarly, the Schmalensee study was developed in conjunction with a Federal Trade Commission action taken against members of the RTE cereal industry.

Thus, there is room in the field of industrial organization for considerable diversity in both subject and texture. We all use the same general model, but we do different work, have different interests, and harbor different opinions. Yet, we all function as economists who are concerned with applying ourselves to issues of market and firm organization.

THE PLAN OF OUR TEXT

The objective of this text is to introduce the student to the field of industrial organization. It seeks to develop an understanding of the concepts used in the field and an interest in the work done by specialists in it. So, where do we go from here? We begin with a section on market structure; the subjects include scale economies and barriers to entry, concentration, and product differentiation. We continue with the section on market conduct; the subjects include pricing (with an emphasis on theory and practices under oligopoly conditions), advertising and other product promotion behavior, product development and innovation, and the growth and development of the firm. In a final section, we review the basic elements of Antitrust Policy, with emphasis on applying our knowledge of structure and conduct to the law.

Some texts emphasize market institutions and public policy, while others emphasize analysis. This text emphasizes the latter.

ECONOMIES OF SCALE AND BARRIERS TO ENTRY

4

*In this chapter we examine the meaning and measurement of economies of scale and barriers to entry, two critical elements of market structure. Beginning with a basic definition of scale economies, we examine four brief illustrations of the phenomenon. Next, we distinguish between the two dimensions of **size** in the firm, scale, and scope. Then, we explain the source of economies, how indivisibilities in capital and/or labor may account for **plant economies**, and how integration of activities which support production (designing, marketing, and delivering the product to the final user) may yield **firm economies**.*

*Understanding scale economies may help to generally account for the large size of certain firms in certain industries, but in industrial organization, we seek to explain the specific forms of organization in specific industries. Thus, we turn next to the question of measurement of scale economies, reviewing briefly the different techniques used for that purpose. For plant economies, these include statistical cost estimates, engineering estimates, and inferences drawn from the principle of survivorship. Among these, the engineering estimate of **minimum efficient scale** or **MES** has been the most widely used to date. Finally, we observe that the initial efforts to measure firm economies employ a form of the engineering estimate.*

*Next, we address barriers to entry. Beginning with a brief definition and description of barriers, we summarize three cases in which established firms seemed to hold a strategic advantage over potential entrants. Then, we examine the different types: (1) There are barriers which result whenever certain firms have better access to natural resources than others and which explain their **absolute cost** advantages, (2) There are barriers which are sometimes found when certain firms have better market positions than others and which account for their **relative cost** advantages, and (3) There are barriers which sometimes favor the established firms and which are based upon the **high fixed costs** of entry. As we examine each, we see that it is not simply a matter of market structure; there may also be relationships between the **natural** conditions which support the barrier and the strategy employed by the firm to exploit it.*

*We next consider the recent challenge to the notion of fixed cost barriers. If large fixed investments are needed to enter a market, and they are not "sunk" once they are made, and if they can be liquidated rather easily, there may be no barrier to entry. If this happens, the market is called **contestable**.*

Finally, we review the measurement of entry barriers. Two different techniques have been used. Engineering estimates of the overall cost advantages for certain firms were used first. More recently, these have given way to statistical inference of the specific advantages resulting from large scale, high fixed cost, and established market position.

Economies of Scale

Economies of scale are the cost advantages enjoyed by the large enterprise when compared with the small. What is the nature of large size? What is the source of cost advantage? Actually there are several dimensions to the scale or size of the enterprise and, therefore, several sources of economies. In this chapter we shall attempt to explain the economies to which large scale might give rise and to examine the means which might be used to detect and measure them. Before we undertake this task, however, let us consider certain scale economies which appear to be well illustrated in the automotive industry.

EXAMPLES OF SCALE ECONOMIES IN AUTOMOBILES

First, the scale of an operation can affect the choice of production technique. Consider the extremes of the British auto industry, Ford Motor Limited and Aston-Martin Lagonda. The two are old and established firms, but the former is the largest automobile manufacturer in Great Britain while the latter may be the smallest. In 1983, Ford produced 414,000[1] cars while Aston-Martin Lagonda made about 200.[2] The disparity between the two firms in the size of their operations is matched by an equally wide difference in their approach to production. Ford employs a mass-production technique, which is more or less representative of the current state of industry technology. Aston-Martin Lagonda builds a handcrafted product using an outmoded, labor-intensive technology. An indication of the difference in the two production functions is given by the following:

INPUT/OUTPUT	FORD MOTOR LTD.*	ASTON-MARTIN**
labor/unit	0.15 workers	1.90 workers
capital/unit	2,420 £	12,500 £

* Estimated from reports in *Moody's International, 1984*, Vol. 2, p. 3677, and *Moody's Industrial Manual, 1984*, Vol. 1, p. 3677.

** Estimated from *Automotive News* of (September 6, 1982), p. 71 and (November 12, 1984), p. 14.

[1]*Moody's Industrial Manual, 1984* (New York: Moody's Investment Service, 1984), Vol. 1, p. 1403.

[2]*Automotive News* (September 6, 1984), p. 14.

Since it obviously requires more capital and more labor (to say nothing about material inputs) to build a Lagonda than an Escort, it is reasonable to conclude that Ford enjoys a tremendous cost advantage. Any cost advantage can be attributed directly to a *better* set of technological opportunities—those available to the large scale operation. Of course, any real comparison is complicated by the difference in the products of the two firms as well as the difference in their relative size. This is only natural; such a high cost operation as Aston-Martin Lagonda could not ordinarily be expected to survive under conditions of direct competition. The fact that a few buyers can be found who are willing and able to pay 20 to 30 times as much for an exceptional automobile as for a merely utilitarian one explains the survival of an outdated technology and the firm which employs it.

Second, the economy achieved in production may be affected by the length of time a given operation has been up and running. Consider the way in which Ford Motor Company in the United States was able to exploit its accumulated experience to increase productivity. From 1908 to 1926, Ford produced one basic car, the Model T, with one basic engine.[3] While the product remained more or less unchanged, the production process did not. For example, by 1913, mass production techniques—combining a moving assembly line with an elaborate division of labor—had been widely adopted in the manufacture of the Model T engine.[4] Nevertheless, Ford and his engineers continued to tinker with the division and sequence of work in the engine plants. Ford workers would become more experienced in operating the assembly line. As a consequence of improvements in design and operation, the labor input per engine fell from 35 hours in 1913, to 23.1 hours in 1914, to 17.3 hours in 1916, to 14.3 hours in 1922.[5] The improved performance of the line workers is an example of what is called the **learning effect**: the more experience one has in performing an activity, the more skillful one becomes at it.

Third, costs may be affected by adding to the siting, rather than simply to the size, of an operation. Consider the way in which various U.S. automobile manufacturers followed the early lead of Ford in establishing regional assembly plants throughout the nation. In 1955, the cost for shipping a fully assembled Dodge from Detroit to Los Angeles was $299. In contrast, the cost of shipping crated components from Detroit for assembly in Los Angeles was $124.[6] Transport savings were significant. However, determination of the net cost savings for a multiplant firm must consider the possible additional costs of branch operations, as well as transport cost reductions. It has been estimated that, in 1955, the additional costs for running a multiplant operation in automobiles could

[3]William J. Abernathy, *The Productivity Dilemma* (Baltimore: Johns Hopkins Press, 1978), p. 13.

[4]*loc. cit.*, p. 24.

[5]*loc. cit.*, p. 178.

[6]Charles E. Edwards, *Dynamics of the United States Automobile Industry* (Columbia, S.C.: University of South Carolina Press, 1966), p. 175.

amount to $15 per car.[7] Thus, expanding the geographic scope of the Dodge operation could yield net savings of $160 per unit for automobiles marketed in the West, an amount equal to about 6 percent of the 1955 retail price.

Lastly, the attainment of large scale may yield benefits to the firm in areas which complement production. For example, all major automobile makers in the United States maintain large and expensive advertising campaigns in order to market their products. Large scale appears to reward the successful firm with low unit cost for advertising, as indicated below:

Firm	1984 ADVERTISING EXPENDITURE*	ADVERTISING/CAR**
	(millions)	
General Motors	$764	$170
Ford	559	287
Chrysler	317	330
American Motors	121	640

* Reported in *Advertising Age* (September 26, 1985), p. 1.
** Estimated from expenditure data plus data on 1984 factory sales reported in *Automotive News* (March 11, 1985), p. 53.

Given the nature of media advertising, it would seem that General Motors achieved a greater saturation of the market than any of its rivals by purchasing a greater absolute volume of space in print and time on the air. This, together with other factors which might account for differential success in sales, appears to yield increasing returns to scale in product promotion. GM sold more cars per dollar of advertising in 1984.

DEFINITION OF THE SCALE OF THE ENTERPRISE: SCALE AND SCOPE

Economies of scale are the reductions in average total cost which result from increases in the scale of the firm. What precisely do we mean by scale? The most common usage refers to the size, in terms of production capacity, of a single plant. When the firm prepares to invest in new plant and equipment, it is likely to consider a range of options, given by the different scales or capacities of plants which it might build or purchase. These alternatives, and their cost implications, may be depicted as in Figure 4-1. Some specific alternatives are represented by the short-run average cost curves ($SRAC_1$, $SRAC_2$, $SRAC_3$) for discrete scales of plant. The full range of alternatives is summarized by the long-run average cost curve (LRAC). Economies of scale are reflected in the fact that: (1) the SRAC curves show progressive reductions in the minimum unit cost for progressively larger capacities (up through $SRAC_3$), and (2) that unit cost declines continu-

[7]*loc. cit.*, p. 173.

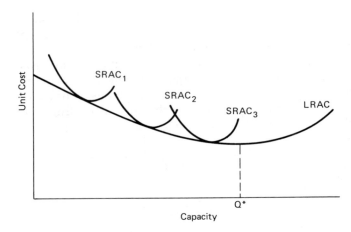

Figure 4-1 Economies of scale are represented by decreases in unit cost with increases in the size of plant. The $SRAC_1$, $SRAC_2$, and $SRAC_3$ short-run average cost curves demonstrate the effect of scale for three successively larger plants, while the LRAC long-run average cost curve traces unit cost for all plant sizes. Scale economies can be enjoyed up to the level of optimal capacity (Q^*).

ously with increases in capacity along the LRAC curve until the scale of plant reaches Q^* (diseconomies of scale are indicated by the rise in LRAC after that).

The size of plant (or production capacity) is not the only definition of scale. Scale is often used to refer to dimensions such as the number of activities—products, locations, stages of production, and so on—in which the firm is engaged. It is also used to designate the total amount of experience or volume of output which the firm has accumulated over time. Given this frame of reference, *scope* may be substituted for *scale*. It is a term which is possibly more accurate and less confusing when used to describe the breadth or depth of the firm's activity. A firm which produces two goods with **joint costs**[8] more cheaply than a pair of competitors who produce them separately is exploiting an economy of scope.

Economies of scope might be depicted as shown in Figure 4-2. The two short-run average cost curves ($SRAC_1$, $SRAC_2$) represent the unit cost function for two different ways of operating a specific activity. For example, in slaughtering cattle for beef, $SRAC_1$ may be used to illustrate the cost of producing beef alone, and $SRAC_2$ may be used to illustrate the cost of producing beef in combination with hides. The costs of the slaughtering operation may be divided in some fashion between the buyers of beef and the buyers of leather goods. The meat packer who also deals in leather goods may have an advantage over the rival who does not. Economies of scope are reflected in the fact that the unit costs are diminished when the scope of activity is broadened.

[8]If certain costs of producing two goods cannot be separated, they are joint costs. If the products themselves are produced in fixed proportions, they are joint products. In this case, it is cheaper (and more profitable) to produce and market both goods together than separately. Failure to take advantage of such economies would amount to throwing away one of the goods—or throwing away the opportunity to produce it at least cost.

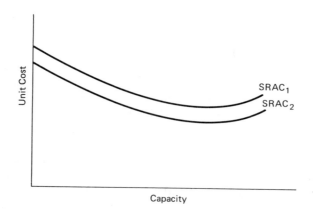

Figure 4-2 Economies can result from combining one or more activities into a single operation; these may be called economies of scope. Such an economy may be shown by the downward shift in the short-run average cost curve for one activity as another is added.

SOURCES OF SCALE ECONOMIES

What are the sources of scale economies? What dimensions of large scale (or scope) are specifically responsible for the cost reductions? There appear to be many. The examples which we drew from the automobile industry above merely serve to hint at the diversity of cost savings which might be exploited by large scale firms. Nevertheless, a simple taxonomy—classification system—can be used to sort and tag them. It has but two categories. First, **plant economies** are those which are associated with the organization and operation of a single production facility or plant; plant economies are explained by the scale (or the scope) of the production process itself. Second, **firm economies** are those cost savings which are not directly attributable to increases in the scale (or the scope) of the single plant; they are the result of the organization and operation of activities which support the production process. For example, the marketing and distribution of products and the acquisition and management of resources. It is when we think of the firm merely as a production unit that we tend to overlook the latter.

Plant Economies

The old saying, "There is more than one way to skin a cat," is aptly applied to manufacturing. There are, indeed, different technological possibilities for producing a good. For example, it may take a fixed amount of cloth to make a pair of jeans, but the cutting and sewing tasks may be accomplished in any number of ways—hand tailoring and robotic manufacturing may be taken as extremes. In economics, we depict the technological alternatives by a function which shows all the combinations of capital and labor required to produce a unit of output—an increase in the amount of capital would substitute for a decrease in the amount of labor. However, there is more to it than that. A change in the quantity of capital used per unit of labor often may mean a change in the form of the input as well.

Indivisibility is a real and significant characteristic of capital equipment. For example, a large die press for stamping out auto body sections may have a capacity for producing 200,000 units per year. It may be indivisible in a sense: a machine costing half as much or a machine producing half the volume may not be a feasible extension of the same technology. The choice of a particular technology—and a particular quantity and form of capital—may dictate a specific production capacity, or vice versa. Assuming that technological advantages do exist, the operator of a large scale plant would benefit from a lower cost of operating its installed capital equipment than it could expect from the alternative of equipment which would be designed for and used by a small scale plant.

Indivisibility is a real and significant characteristic of labor as well. A high-speed assembly line for automobiles may have the capacity for producing 400,000 cars per year. It may also be indivisible in the sense that a line with half as many workers or a line with half the capacity could not be set up with the same technology. The smaller assembly line may require a significantly different assignment of jobs for the workers and a significantly different collection of job skills for the work force. The choice of a particular technology (and quantity and quality of labor) may dictate a specific production capacity and vice versa. This indivisibility is more commonly associated with the specialization of labor. The large scale plant with a mass-production technology may have the opportunity to assign members of its work force to highly specialized tasks and may enjoy increased labor productivity—and lower costs—as the result. It may have the opportunity to employ less-skilled workers, hired at lower wages, to produce the same products as their higher-skilled counterparts do—at higher costs—in a smaller plant a more *primitive* technology. Either way, labor costs would be lower for the large scale plant.

Therefore, the scale of plant determines the technology to be used—the quantity and form of capital and the size and the composition of the work force. We may assume that the economies depicted in Figure 4-1, where $SRAC_2$ was lower than $SRAC_1$, and $SRAC_3$ was lower still, represent the cost advantages of crossing certain thresholds of capital and labor indivisibility. Is there a limit to scale economies? It is reasonable to assume that, for any given state of knowledge, there exists a scale at which all the limits of indivisibility in capital and labor have been exceeded. That limit is represented in Figure 4-1 by the capacity level labelled as Q^*. However, are diseconomies of scale, as shown in Figure 2-1, encountered immediately upon attainment of optimal scale? Perhaps not. After reaching the scale which incorporates the ultimate state of technology in production, the LRAC may flatten out. This is illustrated in Figure 4-3. In such a case, the critical threshold is known as the Minimum Efficient Scale (MES). Note that, for any plant size less than MES, economies of scale will apply, but for any plant size which is equal to or greater than MES, there will be constant costs of production.

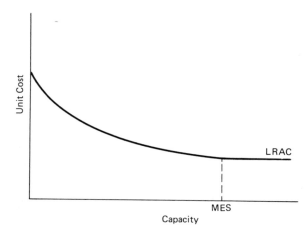

Figure 4-3 Increasing scale may reduce unit costs as long as there are scale improvements yet to be exploited. For a given technology, however, a threshold exists after which variation in scale has no effect. Optimal efficiency can be achieved provided capacity is at least equal to the minimum efficient scale (MES).

Indivisibility of capital and specialization of labor are the prototypical sources of plant economies. They are not the only ones. Earlier, we described the *learning effect* gains in productivity achieved in Ford's manufacturing plants for the Model T engine during the period 1913-1922. In ten years, labor productivity on the assembly line more than doubled. Passage of time allowed for experiment and improvement in the design of the assembly line by Ford's production engineers and for experience in its operation to be acquired by Ford's workers. The increases in the volume of experience led to decreases in cost. This relationship between time and learning is a special form of an indivisibility. When sufficient time has passed, the firm may experience a once-and-for-all economy as a downward shift in the SRAC, such as that shown in Fig. 4-2.

Joint production can also be the source of plant economies. When production yields goods that are perfect complements, such as beef carcasses and hides in a slaughterhouse operation, cost economies can be achieved, provided a market exists for selling both products. There are often by-products in production but less often chances to exploit them commercially. Less dramatic, but probably more common than pure (beef/hides) joint products are those situations in which (1) overhead[9] costs may be shared between products, while (2) direct (or production) costs may be separable. Consider, for example, a frozen food processor which produces several lines of goods. Plant size may be designed to manufacture the expected volume of its national brand of goods. It can also run off quantities of private label products to spread the fixed cost burden. Consider a telecommunications company. Fixed costs in lines, relays, and switching systems which are determined by the capacity requirements for

---

[9]Overhead costs reflect indivisibility in certain inputs. In the service station, for example, one worker may double in auto repairs and pumping gas. As long as there is unused capacity in its service station attendant, the firm can profitably take up the slack by offering additional services and generating added revenues.

the peak-load or daytime market can be partially offset by providing a service to the late-night (or off-peak) market.

A multiproduct plant may also be one that is vertically integrated. Vertical integration is also a potential source of economies—from savings of production inputs. For example, if molten steel, as it comes directly from the furnace, can be molded or rolled into products, the consumption of energy in the production of finished goods can be cut. The heating of steel in one stage of production can provide an economy in the next. The integrated firm would enjoy a cost advantage over a pair of independent firms, one in ingots and the other in finished goods. The same principle would apply to any cost savings resulting from elimination of storage and shipment costs for intermediate products, or from the elimination of delays, whenever the firm integrates successive stages of production into a single plant operation.

For each of these examples of plant economies, those which result from learning effects, multiplant operations, and vertical integration, the appropriate model for the scale (or scope) economies is not the traditional one. Instead, it is that given by Figure 4-2. As a firm expands the scope of its operation, the average cost for any one of its products or activities shifts down. Is this really a scale economy? Yes, the concept of scale may have been stretched, but the economic implications are the same as those associated with the traditional case.

So, what scale or scope of plant will the firm choose to operate? In the short run, of course, the firm does not control plant size—it is hostage to past decisions. In the long run, it might seem reasonable to expect that the firm would want to choose a plant of a size at least equal to minimum efficient scale (MES). The same principle would seem to hold for the adoption of the optimal scope of the enterprise. It might be reasonable to expect that the firm would choose to establish the level of multiproduct and vertical integration which minimizes costs. However, the firm's decisions on scale are not entirely technological. They must also be conditioned by the size of the market. We have seen that Aston-Martin Lagonda operates a sub-MES plant to supply the tiny market for ultra-luxury autos. The technology involved may be primitive, but it may also be the best technology for AML's own particular niche in the automotive industry. Optimal size is an economic decision. It necessaril, incorporates, but will not be limited to, consideration of the technical possibilities available to the firm.

Firm Economies

Not all the cost savings associated with large scale are the result of plant (or production) economies, important though they may be. Included among our illustrations of the economies in the automobile industry we found that Chrysler Corporation could save on transportation costs by operating a regional assembly plant in Los Angeles. We observed that General Motors, which often outsells its nearest competitor by a margin of more than 2 to 1, enjoys a tremendous advantage in advertising costs compared to the rest of the automakers. What does it mean? It means that certain economies accrue to the firm as a result of how that firm is organized and how it operates, not just how it produces.

The manufacturing firm is a unit performing many functions in addition to production. It: (1) designs and develops products and the means for producing them, (2) purchases resources from independent suppliers and provides other inputs of its own, (3) distributes products to wholesalers and retailers who market them, (4) nurtures the market for its own products through the activities of advertising and promotion, and (5) organizes and manages the whole operation. The size and scope of an enterprise is affected by the range of ancillary activities—activities which support and/or complement production—undertaken by the firm. Significant cost savings (or additions to revenue) may accrue to the firm as a result of expanding its scope. Is there any alternative? Yes. The nonintegrated firm might purchase all its resources from outside suppliers and might sell all its product, *sans* promotion, to be distributed by independent jobbers or wholesalers. For the integrated firm there are economies from carrying out ancillary activities. We call them **firm economies** to distinguish them from the plant economies associated with the scale (or scope) of the production unit.

Let us begin with transportation. How should a firm handle the shipment of products to market? The firm might deal with this question by asking two related ones: How many plants should we operate? Where should they be located? In distributing the products to the ultimate consumer, there are often diseconomies of centralization—the wider the geographic market served by a single plant, the greater are the transportation costs. The solution to the distribution problem may be for the firm to take advantage of multiplant economies. The firm may find that it can profit by trading off between transportation and production costs as shown in Figure 4-4. The long-run average cost function associated with the scale of the production unit (as in Figure 4-1) has been labeled average production cost (APC) with Q^* as MES or optimal scale of plant, consid-

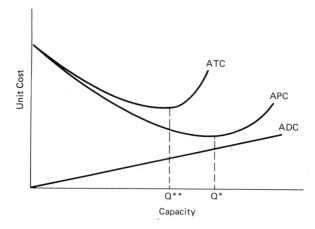

Figure 4-4 Spacing of plants may be important. The APC curve reflects economies of scale in production, and the ADC curve shows cost of transporting goods to market as a function of distance. The ATC curve sums all costs; the firm may minimize costs with less-than-MES plants and locating production closer to markets.

ering production costs alone. The average cost function for transporting goods to market from a single point source is represented by the average distribution cost curve (ADC). In this case we have assumed that transport cost is a linear function of market (and output) scale. So, when production and transportation costs are combined, the result is average total cost (ATC), with Q^{**} representing the optimal scale of plant and market served by it. For the firm which has a large market, the implications are significant. It may pay to set up a larger number of smaller plants than a production engineer would regard as optimal. The multi-plant firm is common in a number of industries in which transportation is a significant cost item. Regional assembly plants in automobiles and regional breweries in the beer industry are merely two examples. There is one related point to consider, however. If transportation costs account for the existence of regionally scattered production plants, rather than a giant central plant, what prevents the market being served by a set of regional, single-plant firms? That is, what prevents the market from being organized along the lines of monopolistic competition, instead of oligopoly? Is that not an equally valid way to balance production and transport costs? Yes. In fact, many markets have long been organized in that way. However, some have changed. In the beer industry, for example, the market has changed from a large number of independent, local breweries to a smaller number of national firms with local brewing plants.

Let us now consider the matter of research and development. How should the firm handle the problem of satisfying its need for scientific input into the production process? The answer to this question may be provided by finding answers to two related ones. How large should the firm's research unit be? How may the firm best utilize the output of its research operation? In R&D, a given increase in the size of the staff and in the scale of the research facility may yield a disproportionate increase in the capacity to design and test new products. There may be sizeable scale economies in R&D. What implications are there in this for firm economies? Where distinctly different products share common science, the firm might be able to exploit the potential for economies of scale in R&D operations by expanding a product line. Is there evidence of this? Yes. In nearly two centuries of existence, DuPont has changed from a gunpowder manufacturer to a maker of many chemicals, plastics, textiles, paints, and so on. When DuPont began the process of changing its product line, it used expertise in nitrocellulose (used in gunpowder) to begin its move into artificial fibers, cellophane, and other products.[10] And if the firm would not or could not sell its R&D output to other manufacturers, it could lose the opportunity for cost savings whenever it confines itself to the production of a single product. Thus, there may be incentives for the firm in a research-intensive field to diversify, as DuPont has done. The case is very similar to the joint products explained above. Whenever there are joint products, the firm can exploit the cost savings only by producing both goods.

[10]Alfred D. Chandler, Jr. and Stephen Salsbury, *Pierre S. Du Pont and the Making of the Modern Corporation* (New York: Harper & Row, 1971), pp. 248–249.

Let us take this matter one step further. Why should the firm have to produce a wider line of products in order to capture the cost advantages afforded by large scale R&D? Why wouldn't the firm merely sell or license its discoveries to other firms? It could and, perhaps, it would choose to do so. Markets are made whenever there is something of value to buyers and sellers. There are exceptions. As a strategic matter, the firm may find that it is advantageous to keep the technology out of the hands of a potential rival. Or, the firm might find that the return from selling inventions to other manufacturers is otherwise lower than the return from their internal use. In any case, the firm might simply find that internal R&D transactions are optimal.

The theory of the firm, as outlined briefly in Chapter 2, provides a theoretical basis for firm economies. Coase[11] and Williamson[12] have developed the concept that the firm is a substitute for the market. Up to a certain scale or scope, the firm may be a more efficient instrument than the market for organizing the activities which attend production—those which are either prior or subsequent to it. Imperfect information, in combination with misrepresentation or deception, may interfere with an efficient operation of the market. As a result, the independent contractor may pay more for services bought and/or receive less for services rendered than integrated firms for the same transactions. When certain activities are integrated, the firm may realize significant cost savings. The general case of firm economies—actually a case of vertical integration—might be depicted as in Figure 4-2. The costs of the integrated enterprise ($SRAC_2$) are shown to be lower than the costs of the nonintegrated enterprise ($SRAC_1$).

Finally, let us consider the firm as a buyer of inputs. The large scale buyer may possess a cost advantage, particularly if it is large relative to its rivals and relative to the suppliers with which it does business. Suppose that a large firm uses its favorable market position, in the form of threats to withhold its favors from suppliers, in order to obtain price concessions from them. Is this possible? Yes. In fact, in the trial of Standard Oil Company of New Jersey for monopolization in violation of the Sherman Act §1, evidence showed that Standard had squeezed rebates out of the railroads for shipping petroleum products, in spite of the fact that rate cutting was a violation of the Elkins Act of 1903.[13] That is, the Standard Oil "Trust" not only forced rail carriers to sacrifice potential revenues but also to violate the law to keep its trade.

Suppose that there is a cost advantage which is derived from ability to control price, rather than efficiency. The cost advantage is called a pecuniary economy to distinguish it from the real thing, and it does not benefit the consumer. Why not? In the case of ordinary scale economies, we may assume that the firm would adopt the absolute scale necessary to obtain the lower costs. If

[11]Ronald H. Coase, "The Nature of the Firm," *Economica* 4 (November 1937), pp. 386–405.

[12]Oliver E. Williamson, "Markets and Hierarchies: Some Preliminary Considerations," *American Economic Review* 63 (May 1973), pp. 316–325.

[13]Simon N. Whitney, *Antitrust Policies* (New York: Twentieth Century Fund, 1958), Vol. 1, p. 102.

competition between an input buyer and its rivals is rigorous enough, we may assume that a firm would have to be large and would have to share benefits of efficiency with the consumer just to survive. By contrast, in the case of pecuniary economies, we may assume that the firm would attempt to become large in a relative sense—large relative to its rivals, if any, and relative to its suppliers—in order to gain control of input prices. Since competition would be imperfect, there are no guarantees that consumers would share the benefits of lower costs.

So, how may we depict pecuniary economies? Since its cost advantage originates in the price which the firm pays for an input, and since it depends upon the scale of the firm's input purchases, the pecuniary economy may be illustrated as in Figure 4-5. The average cost of buying an input is shown as a decreasing function of the volume of inputs purchased, rather than the quantity of goods produced. It is important to note that the relevant dimension of large scale may reflect the fact that the firm is vastly larger than any of its competitors in a single product market or may reflect the fact that the firm is simply a large buyer by virtue of the scope of its activities spread over many markets.

Scale economies in advertising have a similar effect, but a somewhat different origin. Where they exist, the cost advantages are enjoyed by the firm simply because it has greater sales than its rivals. For example, the advertising advantages enjoyed by GM, as noted earlier, are among the benefits of GM's large and loyal market share. The nature of advertising is such that the total expenditure on advertising is determined by the number of persons which the advertiser desires to reach. Advertising cost per unit is determined by the number of sales—and sales may or may not be generated by the current advertising effort of the firm. General Motors and Chrysler may each purchase a one minute commercial to be aired during the Super Bowl, and the two firms may reach the same number of viewers for the same outlay. If GM has a base of loyal customers four times as large as Chrysler, and if four times as many viewers buy its products, it would appear that GM's advertising costs are only one quarter as high as Chrysler's. The resulting cost advantage of the large scale firm may be illustrated by Figure 4-5. They look the same as pecuniary economies.

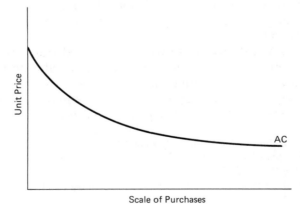

Figure 4-5 Purchasing inputs is an activity of the firm which may also yield cost savings for the large scale operation. The AC curve is drawn to reflect economies from volume discounts.

MEASUREMENT OF SCALE ECONOMIES

The measurement of scale economies is an important task. Economies of scale can be a significant determinant of market structure. The cost advantages of large scale may account for the large size of firms in many markets. Conversely, the question of whether or not the actual size of firms is dictated by economic efficiency can be an important consideration for policy. Resolution of these matters will not be easy. Why is that?

The measurement of scale economies is not an easy task. It requires finding the solutions to two different sub-problems: (1) defining scale in a manner which is both meaningful and capable of measurement, and (2) measuring the cost advantages which are *caused* by large scale. Our survey of the sources of scale economies should have prepared us for the fact that the first-stage problem—the definition of scale—varies considerably in difficulty between the case of simple plant economies and the case of complex firm economies. For plant economies, scale may be defined by the capacity of a single production plant. For firm economies, scale must be defined in terms of a more elusive target—the level or scope of integration. Let us begin with the simpler case.

Measuring Plant Economies

The scale of the plant is obviously given by its production capacity. So, why not use the quantity of output as a measure of scale? Or alternatively, why not use the size of the work force or some other measure of input? These are often used as a proxy measure for scale, and with a certain amount of qualification and care they may do. We should recognize the potential dangers. The design capacity represents the level of output (or input) at which production costs are minimized for a given scale of plant. In the short run, the actual level of output may either exceed or fall short of plant capacity. In either case, the observed level of average unit cost would exceed that for which the plant is designed. In either case, the observed level of output would not represent an accurate picture of scale. Having noted these limitations, let us consider the methods used to measure plant economies. There have been three different methods or techniques of estimation: (1) the **statistical estimation** of cost curves, (2) the **engineering estimates** of *minimum efficient scale*, and (3) the statistical inference of optimal scale using the **survivor method**.

Statistical Cost Estimation.   In principle, statistical cost estimation would be the ideal technique. The objective is, after all, to find the long-run average cost curve as depicted in Fig. 4-1. If statistical methods were successful, we would accomplish just that. Moreover, the statistical technique would also permit testing the results for significance. To illustrate, if the cost function estimated for all automobile assembly plants implies that the unit cost for a plant producing 400,000 cars per year was $50 less than that for a typical plant producing

100,000 cars, we would be able to determine whether or not the difference was statistically significant.[14]

Despite the obvious appeal of the statistical cost estimate—it is a straightforward response to measurement—there have been no widespread efforts to use the technique since the early work of Johnston[15] and Walters[16]. One of the liabilities of the statistical method stems from the problems with the quality and availability of data. Why should there be any problems? An LRAC function represents the complete hypothetical set of plant scale options facing the firm. A statistical sample is drawn from the set of actual plants built and operated by the firms in an industry. The latter may be a poor choice from which to infer the former. First, as noted above, we depend upon plant output rather than design capacity to measure the scale of the operating plant. Second, we rely upon the assumption that scale is the only determinant of cost. We assume that each plant is operated under equal conditions and is equally representative of the *ideal* of a plant for the industry. Apart from scale, other differences are likely to exist. Some firms may be better managed than others. Some may pay lower wages for labor and/or lower prices for materials. Some may have built or purchased buildings and equipment at lower prices at an earlier date than others. Thus, there may be significant unexplained variation in costs. There may also appear to be scale economies which are not the result of productivity differences—the firm with a large scale plant may enjoy pecuniary economies—so the estimate of the LRAC may be seriously biased.

Another of the liabilities of the statistical method stems from an even more profound shortcoming. Statistical estimation of the relationship between scale and cost relies upon an actual variation in scale. Assume that scale economies are really substantial, that the cost savings associated with large plants represents a major competitive advantage. In that case, small scale plants are unlikely to survive. Without small scale plants in the sample population, the data necessary to estimate the LRAC would be missing. The most compelling cases of plant economies, where the unit costs decrease significantly with increases in scale, could not be statistically confirmed. In that case, scale economies might be observed and measured only when competition between firms is not a factor. For example, the contrast between Ford Motor Ltd. and Aston-Martin Lagonda is very extreme, but since the two firms do not compete, they are able to coexist. A similar contrast may be found among firms when there is governmental intervention or a concerted private action, such as cartelization, to neutralize competition. So, what could be done?

[14]Given the random errors contained in a statistical sample, the nominal differences between points on an estimated cost function cannot be presumed to represent real differences. They may well fall within a *zone of ignorance* which results from the random variations.

[15]J. Johnston, *Statistical Cost Analysis* (New York: McGraw-Hill, 1960).

[16]A. A. Walters, "Production and Cost Functions," *Econometrica* 31 (January-April 1963), pp. 1–66.

Engineering Estimates. Engineering estimates of plant scale economies were devised as a solution to the *tainted* cost data embodied in statistical estimations of LRAC curves. The logic of the engineering estimate is that it provides *pure* information on the effect of scale on production costs. That is, management effectiveness, factor prices, and capacity utilization can all be controlled, at least in principle, in the hypothetical experiment which asks a production engineer to develop estimates of the unit production costs for plants of various design capacities, and in which scale can be varied by increments. In actual practice, the engineering estimate has taken a somewhat different form. For a selected industry, plant managers and other insiders are surveyed to determine the scale at which a hypothetical state-of-the-art plant becomes capable of achieving optimal cost efficiency. And the estimate is taken to be the minimum efficient scale (MES), as shown in Fig. 4-3. The pioneering work in this method was done by Bain for twenty industries in the United States.[17] Others have employed a similar survey technique to determine the MES for selected industries.

The Bain-style engineering estimate does sacrifice some information by examining unit costs at only one or two points on the LRAC. For example, costs may be estimated for an MES plant and for a plant of lesser magnitude, one that may be one-half or one-third the scale of the threshold optimal plant. On the other hand, this approach has certain advantages. The measurement of scale and cost can be transformed into universal terms, and then, comparisons between industries are possible. How can this be done? Suppose that scale is expressed in percentage terms by the calculation of the apparent fraction of total industry output to be represented by one MES plant. Of course for the comparisons to be valid, this assumes that each industry always operates at the full utilization of capacity. Cost can be expressed in percentage terms by estimating the relative cost advantage of MES plants compared to a standard alternative, such as plants one-third the size. An example of the application of the engineering estimate technique to measure plant scale economies is given by *Table 4-1*.

Has the engineering estimate solved the problems which we noted earlier? Not necessarily. It did solve some, but it introduced new ones. As a research technique, it must rely upon *expert* opinion rather than observation. The quality of the estimates are therefore dependent upon those who make them. And the plant managers and others who are surveyed are likely to have perceptions colored by their own experience and interests. They are likely to view the decisions they have made on plant size to be just about right. Moreover, since MES estimates for different industries are made by different experts, there may be a serious problem in consistency. Finally, the MES estimates have been provided only for selected industries and at selected times. Thus, there are limitations to the engineering estimate approach. On the other hand, it is useful for the infor-

[17]Joe S. Bain, "Economies of Scale, Concentration and Conditions of Entry in Twenty Manufacturing Industries," *American Economic Review* 44 (March 1954), pp. 15–39.

TABLE 4-1   ENGINEERING ESTIMATES OF PLANT SCALE ECONOMIES:
SELECTED INDUSTRIES FOR 1967

INDUSTRY	MES (% 1967 SALES)	ECONOMY (% COST SAVINGS)*
Beer brewing	3.4	5.0
Cigarettes	6.6	2.2
Cotton & synthetic fabrics	0.2	7.6
Paints	1.4	4.4
Petroleum refining	1.9	4.8
Shoes	0.2	1.5
Glass bottles	1.5	11.0
Portland cement	1.7	26.0
Integrated steel	2.6	11.0
Antifriction bearings	1.4	8.0
Refrigerators	14.0	6.5
Auto batteries	1.9	4.6

Source: F. M. Scherer, A. Beckenstein, E. Kaufer, and R. D. Murphy, *The Economics of Multi-Plant Operation* (Cambridge, Mass.: Harvard University Press, 1975), pp. 80 and 94.

* Cost advantage compared with ⅓ MES plant.

mation it provides on how widespread and significant scale economies have been (or have not been). Is there another alternative? Yes.

Survivor Method.   The **survivor technique** is an indirect method of estimating the optimal scale of plant. Stigler[18] proposed the technique for the following reasons: (1) to avoid the problems inherent in the statistical estimations of the LRAC function, and (2) to eliminate the problems of subjectivity which are inherent in engineering estimates of MES. The survivor technique presumes that the optimal scale of plant may be inferred from observation of the size distribution of firms in an industry. Given a size classification system, the distribution of industry sales (or its capacity) by class is examined over time in order to identify any shifts in the distribution. Growth in its position or share of industry activity by a size class is presumed to indicate its superior cost efficiency. *Table 4-2* illustrates the principle.

In this particular case, Stigler inferred that firms which fell into the market share (s_i) classes, where $2.5\% \leqslant s_i \leqslant 25\%$, appeared to enjoy the advantage of economies of scale since the relative industry capacity accounted for by the firms in these classes expanded during the period between 1930 and 1951.

How well does the survivor technique work? In principle, it can be applied to a complete listing of industries. In practice, however, it ought to be applied with considerable caution since it is subject to its own limitations on data quality.

[18]George J. Stigler, "The Economies of Scale," *Journal of Law and Economics* 1 (October 1958), pp. 54–71.

TABLE 4-2 DISTRIBUTION OF OUTPUT OF STEEL INGOT CAPACITY BY RELATIVE
SIZE OF FIRM

FIRM SIZE (MEASURED AS % OF INDUSTRY)	SIZE CATEGORY IMPORTANCE (MEASURED BY SHARE OF INDUSTRY)		
	1930	1938	1951
Under 0.5	7.16	6.11	4.65
0.5 to 1	5.94	5.08	5.37
1 to 2.5	13.17	8.30	9.07
2.5 to 5	10.64	16.59	22.21
5 to 10	11.18	14.03	8.12
10 to 25	13.24	13.99	16.10
25 and over	38.67	35.91	34.50

Source: George J. Stigler, ''The Economies of Scale,'' *Journal of Law and Economics* (October 1958), p. 60.

First, the fundamental proposition of survivorship—that survival can be taken as evidence of efficiency—is a tenuous one. It assumes competitive market behavior. However, if firms in an industry behave in a cartel-like fashion, their behavior may invite new entry. If that should occur, the resulting growth in the share of the market supplied by new entrants, often smaller firms, should not be presumed to be evidence of their superior efficiency. Second, many applications of survivorship employ data on firm size rather than plant size. In that event, survivability could reflect numerous influences in addition to those associated with plant scale—these include the economies of joint production, vertical integration, multiplant operations, and so on. Third, the survivor technique provides quantitative information only on the question of optimal scale. It tells us nothing about the size of the cost advantages—if there are any—of plant size classes which are identified as optimal. On the other hand, there may be qualitative evidence on the magnitude of the cost advantages if large and rapid changes are observed in the size distribution of plants in an industry. It may be inferred that the *surviving* class of plants (or firms) has a strong cost advantage over the competition.

Despite some of its disadvantages, variations of a survivor principle can be found in a number of studies which investigate effects of scale. In Comanor and Wilson[19], for example, a class of *optimal size* was identified from the group with the largest plants which collectively accounted for 50 percent of total industry output—and the MES was taken to be the average plant size within that group. Why should that be a measure of the optimal scale? About the only explanation that can be provided is that it is easy to apply. And the fact that such a proxy is used is evidence of just how difficult the measurement of scale economies can be.

[19]William S. Comanor and Thomas A. Wilson, ''Advertising Market Structure and Performance,'' *Review of Economics and Statistics* 49 (November 1967), pp. 423–440.

Measuring Firm Economies

The scale of the plant is given by its production capacity; it is a measure of the opportunity to produce output, whether or not it is used. Can we imagine anything comparable to fit the scope of the firm? Perhaps, but with some problems. Unlike scale of plant, where size is measured in terms of the magnitude of a single activity, the yardstick for scale of firm is not so apparent. Firm economies are presumed to result from increases in the number of activities in combination and in the degree of their coordination. The transport cost savings from multiplant operations, the advantages from combining R&D activity with the production of technically-related products, the cost savings from joint production, the exploitation of large scale in advertising, and so on. In short, the plant represents a single process which can be defined in a single dimension. The firm represents a very complex system in which there are opportunities to produce more efficiently, but in which there is no obvious dimension to size, that is, to the scope of integration.

Until 1975, there had been little progress in tackling the problem of firm scope. However, the study by Scherer et al[20] managed to accomplish major breakthroughs. First, *The Economics of Multi-Plant Operation* undertook to examine the full scope of the firm's activities: advertising, distribution, procurement, vertical integration, management, research, and so on. Second, the study of twelve selected industries attempted to identify a MES for each of the firm's activities. The particular method used was a form of the engineering estimate, interviewing insiders in the twelve industries and in six nations. Third, Scherer et al adopted as a unit of firm scale, the number of MES plants required for a firm to achieve a threshold of optimal efficiency in each of its activities. So, have all the measurement problems been solved? Not necessarily.

Multi-Plant Operations revealed quite a lot about the extent of firm economies, but not everything. Why was this? First, the advantages enjoyed by the large scope (multi-plant) firm are sometimes intangible, and the estimates of the cost savings which flow from them are subjective. Note that *Table 4-3* below merely gives a qualitative estimate of economies. Second, estimates of the optimal firm scope treat a single product market as the focal point of the firm's activity. But firms may achieve economies of scope by exploiting opportunities in several markets. This may be true especially in cases where activities, such as research and advertising, have significant spillovers between markets or the products in them. Third, the technique itself is extremely research-intensive. It seems doubtful that it could be used to develop estimates of firm economies over a full range of markets in the economy. Finally, since each large, multiproduct firm represents a unique system, in which cost savings derive from a unique combination of activities, the **multi-plant technique** may not generalize beyond estimating firm economies for the few selected industries to which it does fit

[20]F. M. Scherer, A. Beckenstein, E. Kaufer, and R. D. Murphy, *The Economics of Multi-Plant Operation* (Cambridge, Mass.: Harvard University Press, 1975).

TABLE 4-3 ENGINEERING ESTIMATES OF FIRM SCOPE ECONOMIES: SELECTED
U.S. INDUSTRIES

INDUSTRY	OPTIMAL FIRM SCOPE (NO. OF MES PLANTS)	FIRM ECONOMY (EST. COST SAVING)
Beer brewing	3 - 4	slight to severe
Cigarettes	1 - 2	slight to moderate
Cotton & syn. fabrics	3 - 6	v. slight to mod.
Paints	1	slight
Petroleum refining	2 - 3	v. slight to mod.
Shoes	3 - 6	slight to moderate
Glass bottles	3 - 4	slight to moderate
Portland cement	1	slight
Integrated steel	1	very slight
Antifriction bearings	3 - 5	slight to moderate
Refrigerators	4 - 8	moderate
Auto batteries	1	slight

Source: Scherer, et al., *loc. cit.*, p. 336.

well. Let us put aside its limitations for a moment and consider the results, as shown in Table 4-3 below. It is interesting to compare them with the results in Table 4-1 above.

Where do we stand with the measurement of economies of scale (and scope)? It would seem that the best we have been able to accomplish so far is to develop some measures of the *size* of the optimal plant (or firm), using either the engineering method or the survival technique. And the estimates of the cost savings associated with the MES plant (or MES firm) have been tentative at best. So, does this mean that economies of scale (or scope) are not important? Not at all. It only means that, thus far, it has been difficult for economists to establish good, independent measurement of the phenomenon.

Barriers to Entry

Barriers to entry are those economic factors which may give certain firms an advantage over the competition. Ordinarily, the advantage is viewed in terms of its long-run consequences. Firms which enjoy barrier to entry protection may be able to generate economic profits indefinitely without giving up market share to existing rivals or attracting new entry to the market. But what is the nature of the advantage? Why should some firms enjoy such a benefit? It is essentially a matter of access. The firm which enjoys a barrier to entry advantage may be able to produce its product at a lower cost than its rival, or it may be able to market a product more easily and successfully than they do. And in extreme cases, it may possess sole access to the market. We shall ultimately attempt to explain the sources and/or causes of barriers and to examine the attempts to measure them. First, let us consider a few examples.

ILLUSTRATIONS OF BARRIERS TO ENTRY

There are times when cost conditions will favor an existing firm. Is this simply because the existing firms exist? Not necessarily. Consider steel. The most basic natural resource in the production of steel is iron ore. In 1890, very rich and extensive deposits of ore were discovered in the Mesabi Range of Minnesota. Mesabi iron ore lay near the surface in soft deposits which were nearly 65 percent pure.[21] Ore could be strip mined, shipped by rail to Lake Superior ports, and transported by water to blast furnaces in the East, where it could be used to make pig iron for less than one-half cent per pound. Given the ease with which it could be mined and given its strategic location, Mesabi ore could be delivered to the lower Great Lakes ports at a cost savings of $1 per ton—roughly one-third cheaper than competing ores.[22] Much of the cost advantage could be attributed to labor savings. For example in 1901, U.S.- Steel underground mines produced less than five tons of ore per man-day, while the open pit mines produced more than 21 tons.[23]

For all their apparent advantages, Mesabi mine holdings were generally acquired by a few large firms at bargain prices. First, the soft ore tended to gum up in blast furnaces, unlike the hard ores for which they had been designed. Until a new technology was developed, the costs saved in mining ore could be lost in refining it. Second, the strip mines were economic to operate only with capital-intensive techniques. The small mine operations overextended themselves and, in the panic periods of the 1890s, were bought out by larger and better financed firms. Thus, Hanna, Mather, Jones & Laughlin, Republic, Picklands, and Inland Steel all acquired extensive holdings. Most important of all, U.S. Steel acquired nearly two thirds of the Mesabi mines with its purchase of the Oliver Iron Mining Company.[24] The large existing steel manufacturers acted to acquire access to cheap and abundant iron ore resources—resources which were subsequently not available to others on equal terms. It would give them a barrier to entry advantage over new competition, or at least it would do so until the development of processes which now make it cheaper to manufacture steel from ferrous scrap products than from pig iron.

There are also times when being established is an advantage all by itself. That is, the existing firm has an edge simply because it exists. Consider the

[21]William T. Hogan, *Economic History of the Iron and Steel Industry in the United States* (Lexington, Mass.: Lexington Books, 1971), Part 2, p. 367.

[22]*loc. cit.*, Part I, p. 198.

[23]Kenneth Warren, *The American Steel Industry, 1850–1970* (Oxford: Clarendon Press, 1973), p. 116.

[24]Harlan Hatcher, *A Century of Iron and Men* (Indianapolis: Bobbs-Merrill, 1950), pp. 168–192.

automobile industry. At the end of World War II, the opportunity seemed to be ripe for entry. No new cars had been built for over five years. The production had been halted in order to save resources for the military, and the established automobile makers had, instead, been making aircraft, tanks, trucks, and guns. A long pent-up demand—the absence of new car purchases combined with the presence of a new confidence from having defeated the Axis powers and having seen the Great Depression through to the end—had created a public willing and eager to buy automobiles. There was a shortage of capacity to supply them. In this setting, Henry J. Kaiser—the man who had built a considerable fortune in heavy industry during the war by making ships, jeeps, steel, and so on, was determined to become the first new American automaker since the twenties. Wall Street wanted to sign on to the venture; the original issue of Kaiser auto stock, an amount equal to $53,500,000, was sold easily and quickly in January 1946.[25] By 1948, Kaiser was able to manufacture and sell 5 percent of the new cars in the United States, and the prospects looked good. Yet, less than five years later, Kaiser was out of the business. What happened to the promising newcomer? It appears that there were a number of obstacles to entry. First, there was a matter of materials bottlenecks; the parts manufacturers tended to supply their old customers first. For example, Kaiser had difficulty purchasing transmissions from independent manufacturers, but GM came to its rescue by supplying automatic transmissions and gearboxes. Second, there was a problem with capital attraction. Kaiser found it very difficult to issue the stock which was needed to build a firm large enough to compete on an equal footing with the largest automakers; the initial capitalization had been too small to do this, and later, the market was much less enthusiastic. Nevertheless, Kaiser got help from the federal government through RFC financing. Finally, there was a matter of consumer resistance to the offerings of a new producer; product differentiation would appear to favor the existing automaker over the new one. In this matter, the auto industry historian, John B. Rae, has observed that the critical failure made by Kaiser Motors was that the firm failed to offer the buyer anything new.[26] Given a choice between nameplates, a buyer would prefer one which was known to one that was not.

Finally, there are times when markets favor an established brand name, pure and simple. Proctor & Gamble has long enjoyed an overall position of leadership in household products markets with a wide array of products. P & G's many brands of detergents and household cleansers sell extremely well. In an industry in which advertising is the major competitive weapon, P & G has no peers. Nevertheless, in 1957, the leading firm in the market for liquid bleach was a relatively small, independent manufacturer—the Clorox Corporation. Clorox sold half the liquid bleach purchased in the United States and enjoyed a signifi-

[25]*Fortune* (July 1951), p. 69.

[26]John B. Rae, *The American Automobile* (Chicago, Illinois: University of Chicago Press, 1965), p. 170.

cant price premium to boot. The Clorox brand had established a strong position in a market where the product's image and customer loyalty seem to be all important—as a chemical entity, bleach is bleach. Product differentiation stood as the only significant barrier to P & G's entry into the market for bleach. Procter & Gamble arguably had all the skill and resources necessary to launch its own brand to challenge Clorox. Instead, P & G chose to purchase Clorox by an exchange of Procter & Gamble stock which had a market value in excess of $31,000,000.[27] The price paid for Clorox was an amount nearly $20,000,000 greater than the value of its tangible assets, so the latter figure provides an estimate of the barrier to entry advantage enjoyed by Clorox. To complete the story, P & G's entry by acquisition was soon halted by the FTC, a decision upheld by the Supreme Court ten years later [*FTC vs. Procter & Gamble Co.*, 386 U.S. 568 (1967)]. Since Procter & Gamble must have known that this was a possibility, it is just one more indication of the advantage held by the established brand.

SOURCES OF BARRIERS TO ENTRY

What are the sources of barriers to entry? Several may be identified, including: (1) those which may be attributed to *natural* causes and are part of the market structure, (2) those which may be attributed to superior performance of the firm engaged in competition, and (3) those which may be attributed to strategic behavior and are the intentional result of a course of action designed to limit competition. Even in the case of natural barriers, however, the behavior of the firm can play a role. How can this be?

Assume that a firm is favored by a gift of nature. It has lower costs than others. Assume that it seeks to delay or even to bar competitive entry. It may succeed in limiting entry by its own discretion. But how? Consider a situation, such as that depicted in Figure 4-6, in which the costs of one firm are substantially lower than the costs of any of the potential competition. Given constant long-run costs (C_i for the incumbent and C_e for the potental entrant), the incumbent may successfully bar entry as long as it keeps the price below C_e. It is able to earn an economic profit, equal to [$P - C_i$] per unit, which is explained by its unique cost position.

What if the firm could not or would not limit entry in such a fashion? Can there be a barrier to entry in a market in which existing competitors are present and in which new entrants appear? The answer is yes. What is crucial is the existence of some initial cost advantage; it provides an opportunity for the firm to earn economic profits which competition cannot erase. We see that pricing strategy can affect the amount and time pattern of the firm's profits resulting from the cost advantage—a firm can sacrifice some near-term profits to increase

---

[27]*Moody's Industrials, 1957* (New York: Moody's Investment Service, 1957), p. 484.

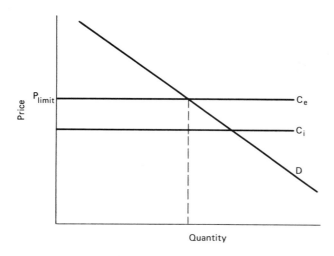

Figure 4-6 Barriers to entry result when incumbents have lower costs than entrants. The incumbent which establishes a limit price based upon the costs C_e of its potential rivals makes more than normal profits without attracting entry.

its market share in the long-run. Its ability to earn any economic profits at all depends upon the prior existence of a barrier to entry.

Now let us consider those factors which can account for the competitive advantages held by established firms whenever there is a barrier to entry.

Absolute Cost Barriers to Entry

Natural conditions are presumed to be responsible for many of the advantages held by incumbent firms in the market. But is should be noted that nature can be broadly defined; it might be used to describe everything which is part of a market structure. For example, the entry restrictions which were created by the Motor Carrier Act of 1935—barriers which are quite artificial in fact—were characteristic of the natural environment of the motor trucking industry from 1935 to 1980.

Ownership by a manufacturer of a critical natural resource may serve as the source of a barrier to entry. Suppose that an established firm is the owner of a mine, richer in ore or better located than all other mines currently in existence. That firm would have an *absolute cost advantage*. Its resource costs would be lower than any existing or potential rival. As a result, its production costs would be less. Absolute cost advantages can be used to bar entry, as depicted in Fig. 4-6, provided that the firm's quantity of cheap resources are sufficient to supply the entire market demand and provided that the firm prices its product below the costs of the competition. Is it necessary to satisfy such rigorous conditions in order to benefit from the barrier to entry? No. It seems unlikely that an established firm would ever possess a supply of a basic resource large enough to eliminate all competition. In the case of Mesabi iron ore, for example, the US Steel holdings were very extensive, but rivals owned Mesabi deposits too. And even if US Steel should somehow have acquired it all, Mesabi range mines did not produce enough iron ore to enable USS to meet total national demand for steel. Yet the rich ore was a barrier to entry. With it, US Steel and certain other firms could make steel at a lower cost and could earn higher profits than the competition. The same could be said for an existing firm's ownership of another type of resource such as a license which is granted by government.

Relative Cost Barrier to Entry

Are unique resources and the absolute cost advantages they convey the only natural barriers to entry? No. Possession of an established share of the market may also serve as a barrier to entry. The firm which has a large share of the market and which can exploit the potential for scale economies has a clear advantage over a competing firm in a weaker market position. Assuming the difference exists, the large firm would have a *relative cost advantage*. Suppose, for example, that the established firm can utilize a large plant with low unit costs, while the entrant can only make efficient use of a small plant with high unit costs. The difference may be illustrated by the comparison between $SRAC_3$ and $SRAC_1$ in Figure 4-1. The firm which is experienced in production and which enjoys the cost savings that result from learning has an advantage over the newcomer. The difference may be illustrated by comparison of $SRAC_2$ and $SRAC_1$ in Figure 4-2.

Is a relative cost advantage permanent? Is incumbency secure? Not necessarily. If an entrant can survive and become established, the relative cost advantage will disappear. There have been serious arguments over the following question. Can a relative cost advantage bar entry? Stigler[28] has argued that a rational entrant would never choose to be smaller and less cost-effective than the incumbent. That might be, but the entrant may not have a choice. Prior disadvantages—being a latecomer or having no established market—may handicap the entrant; it may face, at least temporarily, a very unattractive pair of choices: either to build a small plant for a small market and suffer the cost disadvantage, or to build a large plant and suffer the cost disadvantage, at least for a period of time, of underutilization of capacity. So, is there a relative cost barrier or not? If there is, how strong is it?

Superior performance in competition may be responsible for the barrier to entry. If all products were homogeneous, and if competition were limited to price, relative cost advantages could not exist. In some markets, competition is mostly concerned with product design and marketing. If a firm can outperform its rivals in the competitive arena, it can establish a position in the market which is superior to theirs. The position which Clorox held in the market for liquid bleach—a position which Procter & Gamble was willing to pay $20,000,000 to acquire—represents a form of superior performance.

Product differentiation may be the primary reason for the successful firm's relative cost advantage. Having captured the largest share of the market, the

[28]George J. Stigler, *The Organization of Industry* (Homewood, Ill.: Irwin, 1968), p. 67.

successful firm has the ability to operate at a larger scale and a lower cost than its rivals. In fact, without a product differentiation barrier, it is simply incomprehensible that a relative cost advantage would exist at all. If there were significant economies of scale in production, all the firms in the market, and there may not be many of them, would be the same size, provided the product is homogeneous. A relative cost advantage implies a product differentiation barrier. Otherwise, we can return to Stigler's point—that no rational firm would ever choose to be smaller and to have higher costs than its competition.

Again, how secure is such a barrier? In some markets, incumbents seem to hold permanent positions of dominance. In others, leadership is fairly fleeting. Why the difference? In some cases it may be attributed to the superiority of the incumbent, but in some cases it might be attributed to the inferior entrepreneurship of those who could challenge but do not.

The prospect of a temporary cost disadvantage may be cause for serious reflection on the costs of challenging incumbency. Nevertheless, the entrant might be willing to invest short-term losses in an enterprise if it offers profits in the long-run. It may take some time and considerable expense for developing a product or for winning the loyalty of a sufficient clientele to establish a position in the market and to challenge an incumbent. The problem for the entrant is a clear one. It must take risks. How about the incumbent? If it was really a pioneer in the development of a product, or if it had to develop a clientele in order to achieve its present position, the barrier to entry did not fall in its lap; it must have faced a risky venture too. As a result, it is reasonable to assume that relative cost barriers—or product differentiation barriers—are vulnerable as time passes and new entrants squeeze their way into the market.

In the meantime, does this mean that every barrier to entry advantage which befalls the incumbent firm is just the reward for its competitive excellence? Not necessarily.

High Fixed Costs as Barriers to Entry

Strategic behavior is presumed to be responsible for those barriers which are intentionally thrown up by the established firm. These barriers are attributed to preemptive actions taken to hasten the exit of existing rivals and to bar the entry of new ones. The nature of such barriers continues to be a matter of some controversy. Where do you draw the line between barriers resulting from superior performance in *honest competition* and barriers resulting from a successful campaign to *monopolize*? A strategy to preempt the market is not without risk—its success requires some skill and luck, as well as a bloodthirsty disposition. However, let us consider one example of preemption where the purpose and effect of the action seems to be reasonably certain.

Spence[29] argues that excess productive capacity held by the established

---

[29]Michael A. Spence, "Entry, Capacity, Investment and Oligopolistic Pricing," *Bell Journal of Economics* 8 (Autumn 1977), pp. 534–544.

firm acts as an effective deterrent to entry. Assume that a product can be produced under conditions of constant cost, so that the long-run competitive supply curve (LRS) can be shown as a horizontal line as in Figure 4-7 below. Also assume that the market demand is given by D. The established firm may be able to deter entry by building its capacity, Q^*, large enough to supply current market demand at the long-run competitive price (equal to LRS). Q^* is the point where the established firm's short-run supply curve (SRS) intersects the market's long-run supply curve and the current market demand. Having installed enough capacity to satisfy market demand at the competitive price, the incumbent can behave as a monopolist. It can restrict output to Q_m, and so raise price to P_m, without fear of entry. How can this deter entrants? Since competitive entry would shift the market's short-run supply curve to the right of Q^*, the existing firm could make certain that price falls below the break-even level whenever it chose to do so, that is, whenever it chose to stop restricting output. The incumbent's threat to act in this fashion may be sufficient to convince the potential entrant that it would not be able to recover its investment, including a normal return. Is it a credible threat, however? The incumbent would lose money as well as the entrant. Yes it is credible. Preemptive actions do work because the existing firm has already made its commitment. The entrant is the only one in the position to back away from a destructive price war.

Aside from the strategic aspect, does this illustration open up any new ground regarding the sources of entry barriers? Yes. Bain[30], who contributed most to the development of the analysis of entry barriers, added the category of *high fixed cost* to those of relative and absolute cost advantages. A firm might be deterred if the admission price were too high. In the case of Kaiser Motors, for example, remember the firm ultimately encountered trouble in attracting capital.

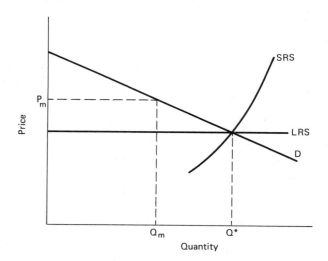

Figure 4-7 Barriers to entry also result from strategic behavior. If an incumbent builds "excess" capacity, shown as Q^*, large enough to supply the market at the long-run competitive price, it might convince potential entrants that there is no room in the market, in spite of the monopoly output Q_m and price P_m.

[30]Joe S. Bain, *Barriers to New Competition* (Cambridge, Mass.: Harvard University Press, 1956).

But is this related to strategic behavior? Yes it may be. If the entrant is faced with a risky decision involving a large sum, and if it would have to pay a premium for capital, it could be deterred by the prospect of never recovering its investment. If entry was possible on a small scale, however, the risk would be limited. Besides, there could even be a strategic advantage to being small. Suppose a small entrant challenges a large existing firm. Would it be rational for an incumbent to carry out its threat to *destroy* an entrant if the former has already committed to a large fixed cost—and has so much to lose if price falls below the LRS—while the latter has but a small one? No. Therefore, a strategy of deterrence may rest on the existence of a **fixed cost** barrier. This introduces another question. What do we mean by *fixed cost*?

Contestability and Sunk Costs

Suppose that a substantial investment is required to enter an industry. If the entrant survives, all is well and good, no matter how much is involved. However, if the attempt fails, what is the end result? If a capital investment is really fixed, entry can be very costly. If its investment is easily liquidated, the firm could withdraw without sustaining heavy losses. In such a case, the risk of entry would be small, and the probability of entry would be large whenever the incumbent restricts output and raises price—strategic behavior would not work. The concept of the case of a liquid *fixed* investment has been developed by Baumol[3] and the market structure has been termed contestable. It is used to emphasize that neither scale economies nor large fixed investments would deter competitive entry if a new firm could profit from hit and run tactics. A **contestable** market invites strategic behavior on the part of entrants whenever and wherever established firms attempt to exploit their control over price. It is a market in which barriers to entry are not likely to be found.

A contestable market is one where fixed costs, however large they may be, are not *sunk*. Instead, they are liquid, so that a firm can enter, try its luck, and if necessary, exit without taking a loss. Interestingly enough, it is the absence of barriers to exit which account for the lack of barriers to entry. In such a market, capital may easily become available to the entrant since investors would covet the lack of risk. Is a lack of *sunk* costs a realistic case? Yes. The airline industry, for example, has shown that where capital is extremely mobile, in the economic as well as the physical sense, entry is highly volatile and excess profits are extremely vulnerable. By contrast, in the domestic automobile industry, the combination of high fixed costs and strong product differentiation apparently contribute to very high barriers to entry.

We have seen that, in certain cases, barriers to entry are simple matters of market structure. The absolute cost advantage is the *pure* example of structural

---

[31] William J. Baumol, "Contestable Markets: An Uprising in the Theory of Industry," *American Economic Review* 72 (March 1982), pp. 1–15.

barriers to entry. In other cases, where the advantage rests on the relative costs or prior commitments to high fixed costs, the barriers depend on behavior—which may either be competitive or strategic in nature—as well as structure. The question of just how *natural* barriers are as an element of market structure is not so easy to answer.

MEASUREMENT OF BARRIERS TO ENTRY

The measurement of barriers to entry is not an easy task. Why? The fundamental problem is one of concept—how do you quantify a barrier to entry? In contrast, scale of plant (or plant capacity) is relatively straightforward. As we observed in the case of scale economies, measurement consists of two parts which are: (1) defining an index of the structural attribute, in this case the barrier itself, and (2) measuring the amount of the advantage resulting from it. How have the two problems been resolved? For the most part, they have not been. It would seem that the solutions have sought to deal with one or the other, but not both. Some index the attribute, without measuring the cost (or price) advantage that goes with it. While others measure the cost (or price) advantage, without directly indexing the quantity of the attribute. Consider the following.

Bain[32] made the first real effort, a heroic one, to measure barriers to entry. In his book, *Barriers to New Competition*, Bain published the results of an intensive study of the conditions in twenty industries. The same technique was used for measuring barriers as was used for measuring scale economies—a reliance upon judgment and expert opinion to form engineering estimates. Bain fit the disadvantages of the entrant into four categories: absolute cost barriers, relative cost barriers, fixed investment cost barriers, and product differentiation barriers. For each category, Bain estimated the size of the cost disadvantage faced by an entrant. The sum of the cost disadvantages—assuming they were additive—was the source of the total barrier for an industry. Thus, while he made no effort to develop an aggregate index of attributes, Bain did estimate the total cost (or price) effect. How confident was he in his estimates? Bain decided to group the estimates of industry entry barriers into three broad categories reflecting qualitative differences. They included: (1) *very high* barriers which gave the incumbent the ability to sell at a price which was estimated to be at least 10 percent above cost without attracting entry, (2) *substantial* barriers which gave the incumbent a price-cost advantage in the neighborhood of 7 percent, and (3) *moderate-to-low* barriers which gave the incumbent an advantage of 4 percent or less.

Later efforts were turned to indexing attributes which Bain had identified as potential sources of entry barriers. By working with single attributes, the aggregation problem could be avoided. For example, Comanor and Wilson[33]

---

[32]Bain, *loc. cit.*
[33]Comanor and Wilson, *loc. cit.*

studied the effect of barriers on profitability by defining three different attributes: plant scale, investment requirements, and product differentiation. Scale of plant was measured by the ratio of MES plant size, determined by a form of the survivor method (see page 00), to total industry output. Fixed capital requirements were determined by estimating the value of an MES plant. Product differentiation was measured by a ratio of advertising to sales. That is, Comanor and Wilson used three different indexes instead of a single one. Did they really measure barriers? Or did they measure attributes which may or may not act as barriers to entry? There is no clear answer to such a question.

Since Comanor and Wilson used their *barrier* variables in statistical tests of the relationship between market structure and profitability, they attributed any significant and positive relationship they found between the former and the latter to the effect of **barriers to entry**—higher profit rates *prove* that incumbent firms have cost advantages. Is that a satisfactory way to resolve the question of measurement? No.

Orr[34] examined the effect of a similar group of attributes representing barriers to entry—size of investment, advertising intensity, research intensity, risk, and so on—directly against a measure of the net rate of entry into an industry. An increase in the number of corporations doing business in an industry was taken to be evidence of the degree of entry. Thus, Orr was able to develop a quantitative measure of entry. He was able to avoid using profitability as a proxy for the entry barrier. When the group of barrier attribute variables were regressed against the entry variable, the regression showed that higher values of barrier attributes were associated with lower values of entry. So, do the combined effects of investment, advertising, research, and risk *cause* low entry? Perhaps, but it is easy to confuse relation with causation.

Where do we now stand with the measurement of barriers to entry? The answer, it would seem, is on shaky ground. Should we take this to mean that barriers to entry cannot be considered to be important in the study of industrial organization? No, not at all. In the next several chapters, we shall take the opportunity to discuss how barriers to entry and scale economies are related to the other elements of market structure and to the character of market conduct and performance. With a better perspective of their importance, overcoming the measurement problems may seem to be worthwhile.

[34]Dale Orr, ''The Determinants of Entry: A Study of the Canadian Manufacturing Industries, *Review of Economics and Statistics* 56 (February 1974), pp. 58–66.

MARKET CONCENTRATION

5

In this chapter we examine the meaning and implications of concentration. We start with three historical cases of markets which had been dominated by a single firm and, later, seek to develop a workable definition of concentration. We then turn to the problems of measurement which include defining the market as well as measuring the degree of its concentration. We define and compare the concentration ratio and Herfindahl index, and we examine summary data on concentration in the U.S. economy.

*Next, we examine the sources of concentration. They include **natural** market conditions such as scale economies and barriers to entry, **artificial** conditions such as those which result from mergers and other practices, and those conditions which can only be explained by **random** processes. Finally, we point out that the level of concentration in a market is not fixed for all time; it can change and often does over time.*

We conclude this chapter by considering the implications of concentration for market behavior, especially for pricing—high market concentration suggests oligopoly (or even monopoly in the extreme case), and oligopoly suggests a style of behavior that is different from perfect competition.

Concentration measures the degree of market **domination** by a few traders. What does domination mean in this context? It means that of all the buyers and sellers who trade in a single commodity, only a relative few account for the majority of the goods which are bought and sold. Concentration is important. It can mean that the dominant sellers or buyers have market power, that they have the ability to control price. In concept, measures of concentration could refer either to sellers or to buyers or to both, but in practice, market concentration nearly always refers to the level of domination in production or sales. Small numbers are more often characteristic of supply than of demand, but there are markets for very specialized factors of production (i.e., resources) where a few buyers dominate. For example, leaf tobacco is supplied by a relatively large number of producers to a small number of tobacco processors who may contol the price.

In this chapter we seek to answer several questions: What are the sources of market concentration? What difference does it make if a market is concentrated? And how is concentration to be defined and measured? But before we begin in earnest, let us attempt to develop a better feel for the subject by briefly examining three cases of market concentration.

THREE CONCENTRATED MARKETS

In 1937, ALCOA supplied (by domestic production or by imports from foreign subsidiaries) roughly 64 percent of the aluminum available for fabrication in the United States. In 1902, US Steel produced 65.4 percent of the steel manufactured in the United States. In 1980, General Motors produced 64.5 percent of the American cars for the U.S. market. At a certain point in the history of each of these major industries, it appears that aluminum, steel, and automobiles might be regarded as equally concentrated. Are the numbers comparable? Did the leading firm in each case possess the same degree of market power? Did the same factors account for the high level of concentration in each industry? Were the prospects for keeping its dominant position in the market the same for each of the firms?

Consider first the manner in which each of these industrial giants acquired its position of dominance. US Steel became the dominant firm in the steel industry by the consolidation of the nation's six largest steel firms in February 1901. By means of this merger and by the succession of mergers leading up to it, the market for steel became progressively more concentrated prior to 1902. ALCOA, by contrast, was born into its position of dominance. Beginning in 1888, the firm became the sole American producer of primary aluminum; it held the U.S. patent rights for the process of reducing aluminum oxide to aluminum; and it maintained its position for a period long after its patents had expired. Neverthelesss, change finally did come to the market for aluminum. ALCOA's share of the U.S. market was diminished by two forces: (1) imports from non-affiliated foreign manufacturers, and (2) production by independent domestic smelters who supplied secondary or recycled aluminum. Lastly, General Motors became the dominant firm in its industry, although in a less dramatic fashion than either US Steel or ALCOA. Through several mergers prior to 1920, General Motors had positioned itself as the second leading producer behind Ford. Then, GM overtook Ford during the mid-twenties, with superior management and with greater success in product design and product promotion. Subsequently, the ranks of domestic automakers thinned while GM's position of leadership widened. By 1980, only four domestic automobile manufacturers survived. In that year, General Motors managed to sell nearly three times as many units as Ford, its nearest competitor.

Next consider the ability of each of the dominant firms to maintain its position in the market. ALCOA had remained the only U.S. producer of primary aluminum for the half century preceding 1937. Some argued that there were substantial barriers to entry of an absolute cost nature—access to bauxite deposits and to low-cost electricity may have been difficult to obtain. Further, it was alleged that ALCOA had acted to exclude competitiors by building excess capacity. During 1941, however, ALCOA's monopoly ended. Reynold's Metals, a major fabricator of finished products made from aluminum, opened its own primary aluminum facility in that year. Shortly thereafter, a series of exogeneous factors produced significant changes in the industry: (1) the Department of Defense ordered the construction of new aluminum plants and smelters to supply the war effort, more than doubling ingot capacity, (2) in 1945, a Federal Circuit Court panel overturned the 1941 trial court decision in which ALCOA had been cleared of charges of monopolization, and (3) pursuant to court-ordered remedies in this case, the Defense Department's aluminum plants were subsequently sold either to Reynold's or to Kaiser, thereby further reducing ALCOA's dominance in the supply of primary aluminum.

In 1901, US Steel became the dominant steel producer by the merger of a number of independent firms, the mere existence of which argues against barriers to entry. Almost from the outset, US Steel's position began to decline. By 1920, the firm's share of domestic output had fallen below 50 percent, and by 1980, it was little more than 20 percent. From 1900 to 1950, a number of mergers took place among the other firms in the steel industry, and the effect was to replace the dominance of the industry by a single firm with dominance by a few. In spite of the structure of the industry, measures of long-term profitability indicate that optimal firm size was rather small—in the range of 1 to 4 percent of the market.[1] Numerous changes in technology and organization have subsequently taken place in steel, and evidence now suggests that the **minimills** are among the most efficient and competitive in the present market environment.

In the American auto industry, General Motors served as the leading producer for more than fifty years. During that period, certain important changes have taken place: (1) the scale of production and the significance of scale economies has grown dramatically, (2) the number of domestic producers has been trimmed from more than 50 firms in 1925, to only four firms in 1980, (3) potential domestic entrants appeared to be effectively barred from competition, (4) the relative market positions of the domestic producers appeared to be entrenched, (5) the U.S. market became increasingly more vulnerable to the aggressive and innovative competition provided by foreign manufacturers beginning in the late 1970s, and (6) during the 1980s Ford replaced GM as the most successful domestic firm; with better management and with better products—a reversal of the roles the two firms played in the twenties—Ford had become more profitable than General Motors even though it sold fewer cars.

[1]Walter Adams, "The Steel Industry," in W. Adams, ed., *Structure of American Industry* (Macmillan: New York, 1977), pp. 91-92.

Thus, the *equality* of 1937-ALCOA, 1902-US Steel, and 1980-GM is subject to important qualifications. We have seen that each of the three reached its position in a different fashion. We have also seen that the security of its position was different for each of the dominant firms. It was fleeting for US Steel, and although it had seemed so permanent for General Motors and ALCOA, it was overturned by a combination of events for both. However, the differences do not end there. First, the position of the leading firm is only one component of concentration; it is also important to take account of the number and relative size of the remaining firms in the industry. Considering the *other* firms as well as the leader, automobile and aluminum markets were substantially more concenrated than steel at the key dates chosen to make these comparisons. Second, concentration can be affected by the definition of the market. We took certain liberties in order to make the three markets appear to be equal in the degree to which the leading firm was dominant. For aluminum, the market was so defined as to include all aluminum smelting, both primary and secondary processes, and to include imports as well as domestic production. For steel, the market was defined in terms of output rather than capacity. In 1902, US Steel held slightly less than 50 pecent of industry capacity but enjoyed a much higher level of capacity utilization than the average for the rest of the industry. The automobile market was defined in terms of domestic production rather than domestic sales. By 1980, more than 20 percent of the cars sold in United States were imported, and GM actually supplied about 49 percent of the latter.

The chief lesson to be learned from this brief comparison is the exercise of caution. First, concentration is not permanent. Changes can and do occur which alter that which we regard as the single most important measure of a market's structure. Second, concentration is sensitive to definition; it can be changed by how the analyst chooses to define the market and to measure the extent of domination. But these are preliminary observations. Let us begin a more complete and orderly development.

DEFINITION OF CONCENTRATION

Concentration, as we have indicated above, measures the degree of market **domination**. That was sufficient to begin our discussion, but it is necessary to be more precise in defining terms. Consider the data contained in the concentration curve illustrated in Figure 5-1 below. Concentration is affected by two factors: (1) the number of firms in the market, and (2) their relative size. The concentration curve shows the cumulative market shares for all the firms in the market, ordered by size from largest to smallest. Thus, the steeper the slope of the concentration curve, the higher the degree of concentration. Considering the extremes of market structure, a monopoly would have the highest level of concentration (100% of the market supplied by one firm), while a perfectly competi-

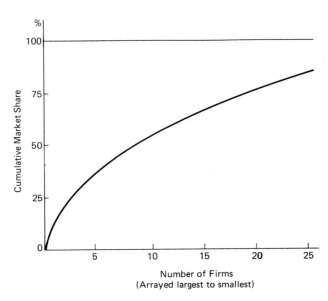

%

Cumulative Market Share

Number of Firms
(Arrayed largest to smallest)

Figure 5-1 Concentration can be represented by the concentration curve, which shows the cumulative market share supplied by the firms in the market arrayed from largest to smallest.

tive market would have the lowest level (100% of the market supplied by N, a large number of firms). Generally, concentration is a function of the number of firms and the degree of inequality in their size. For a given number of firms, concentration increases with inequality. For a given degree of inequality (assume all firms in a market are the same size, for example), concentration decreases with number.

Note that when we described concentration in the aluminum, steel, and automobile industries, we treated the market share of the leading firm in each industry—ALCOA, US Steel, and General Motors—as equivalent to an index of concentration. For an industry dominated by one firm, the market share of the dominant firm is not a bad indicator of the general degree of concentration. We were not incorrect to use it as we did. On the other hand, it is not a precise index either. The number and market shares of the other firms affect the concentration curve also.

Thus, concentration represents the massing of production or sales in a few firms. The level of concentration can be depicted by a concentration curve, as illustrated in Figure 5-1. Does this mean that there exists an unambiguous measure of concentration? No. Assume that Alpha industry has one large, dominant firm and 50 smaller firms; assume that Beta industry has only five firms but each is identical in size. The concentration curve for Alpha may exceed the height of the concentration curve for Beta for the first two or three firms in the industry, but Beta's concentration curve will necessarily exceed the height of Alpha's after some point. Remember that five firms in Beta will account for the total output or sales, but we have assumed that there are 51 firms in Alpha. Which industry is more concentrated? That is a difficult question. On the one hand, concentration is not so well defined as to provide a single answer. On the other hand, there are various measures of concentration which have been designed to supply one. Let us consider the rules or designs used for indexing concentration.

MEASUREMENT OF MARKET CONCENTRATION

Concentration is the single most important attribute of market structure. More research has been based upon concentration and its apparent effects than on any other factor in the field of industrial organization. Therefore, the measurement of concentration is a matter of the highest importance. Published data on levels of concentration is readily available. Does this mean that all of the problems of measurement have been put behind us? Can we simply pick up concentration data for the markets in which we are interested? Unfortunately, the answers are no in both cases.

Definition of the Market

Concentration measures the degree to which the market is dominated by a few traders. But what defines the market? We are so accustomed to thinking in terms of hypothetical markets—the product and all of its buyers and sellers are taken as given—we sometimes overlook the difficulty of *finding* a market in the real world. There are numerous problems which have to be solved.

The Product.   One of the dimensions of a market is the product which is the object of trading. How can a product—a unique commodity or service—be defined? In the world of homogeneous products, nature solves the problem for us. A rose is a rose. However, in the world of heterogeneous products, we have to fend for ourselves. Cellophane is not waxed paper. Are they both items in a broader classification of goods? Are they both flexible wrapping materials, for example? Is the common class a meaningful definition of a product?

It is reasonable to attempt to define a product in terms of the characteristics which it contains. But which characteristics count? Both cellophane and waxed paper have certain properties which make them suitable for wrapping food. Both diesel fuel and high octane gasoline have certain properties which make them suitable for fueling motor vehicles. Both diet cola and buttermilk have certain properties which make them suitable as a beverage. Is each pair of goods a product? It is reasonable to argue that a single common property, even an important one, is not sufficient to define a product. But where does that leave us? If it is necessary to identify a set of relevant characteristics and to aggregate them in order to define a product, how is this to be accomplished? There may well be instances in which the objective observer cannot possibly make an a priori definition of the product that is satisfactory. What then? Perhaps the best solution may be to observe buyer behavior.

The Buyers. The question of whether or not two goods are part of the same market may be resolved by observing buyers. Do the same buyers seem to be willing to substitute one good for another? If the product is one which is purchased frequently, and if behavior can be observed for individual consumers, this question might be answered directly. If the buyer purchases and consumes cola on one day and fruit punch on the next and treats them as the same thing, it might be inferred that the pair of goods belong in the same market, at least for one buyer. If many buyers behave in the same fashion, the problem is settled. If the product is not purchased frequently or if individual behavior cannot be observed, we may have to resort to the use of a statistical test of product substitutability.

The measure of the **cross elasticity of demand**, the ratio of the change in quantity demanded of one good to the change in price of another, where both changes are measured in percentage terms, is regarded as an accurate index of the degree to which one good may be substituted for the other. When the measure of cross elasticity exceeds some given value, the two goods are treated as substitute products. In concept, this is a workable test for market definition. In practice, there are difficulties with it. First, what is the critical value for the test of substitution? An arbitrary judgment must be made in order to interpret the results of the experiment. Second, what happens if prices of both goods tend to change at about the same time? In that case, it is not possible to measure cross elasticity—when relative prices of the two goods remain constant, there is no experiment in substitution. Of course in this case, the near-simultaneous movement of prices (evidence of a linkage in supplier behavior) may settle the question of market definition outright.

In defining markets, one might also consider the effect of buyer differentiation—the hidden presence of differences of time, place, and circumstance. Geographic differences, for example, may result in a segregation of markets. If buyers are widely dispersed, and if the costs of transportation are substantial, there may be several markets for a single product, instead of only one. In a similar fashion, differences in circumstance may subdivide the market. Consider the sales of industrial products, for example. If certain firms are vertically integrated, it may not be appropriate to treat internal and external sales as part of the same market. What about time? In the short-run, the substitution in the household sector between natural gas and heating oil may be insignificant—furnace conversions are both costly and time consuming. In the long-run, the two goods are very close substitutes.

The Sellers. Throughout the present discussion we have often used the word industry almost interchangeably for the collection of firms who supply a market. Is this accurate usage? The firms who supply a product market may correspond closely with an industry. However, they may not. They may represent only a segment of an industry, or they may represent the sum of several industries. Given the discussion above on the definition of a market, in terms of a product and the buyers of that product, we should have a pretty good notion of what we mean by the sellers who make up a market. What do we mean by an industry?

An industry is a collection of producers. Primary emphasis is placed upon the activity of production. The producers in the group may or may not all compete against one another in the market for their products. The entire group may or may not comprise the entire population of those sellers who do. The industry is really a census concept. In the United States, the Standard Industrial Classification (S.I.C.) is a system employed by the Census Bureau. At the highest level of aggregation, the definition of an industry is based upon the nature of the raw materials or the technical process involved in production. For example, fabricated metals (Major Industry Group 34) is one of twenty groups which define the manufacturing industries. At a lower level of aggregation, industry definition is based upon products and product characteristics. For example, sheet metal work (SIC Industry 3444) is one segment of fabricated metals.

How appropriate are census industry classifications for use in defining markets and in measuring concentration? They can be very poor at times. In some cases, product substitutes come from far afield. For example, residential metal siding is one of many of the products included in SIC Industry 3444. Metal siding competes in the same market with wood siding, which is classified in SIC Industry 2421 (sawmills, and planing mills, general)—the two products are not even in the same Major Group, let alone the same Industry. In other cases, certain goods competing in the market originate in the same industry, in a technical sense, but are the product of a foreign nation. Because they are not produced by domestic manufacturers, they cannot be part of the domestic industry. If this was a minor oversight, it would not be troublesome. Given the significant increase in imported manufactures during the 1970s and 1980s, market concentration figures based upon Census Industry classifications and data have become progressively more suspect. To illustrate, we observed earlier that, in 1980, General Motors produced 64.5 percent of the cars in the U.S. auto industry. However, GM supplied slightly less than 50 percent of the cars sold in the United States during that year. Automobile imports have continued to build.

Are there any other problems with industy definition? Unfortunately there are. First, an industry defined in terms of raw materials and technology may be over-inclusive in view of the large number of products produced within the industry or even within a single plant. For example, the sawmills and planing mills produce a variety of products which do not compete for the trade of the buyers of residential siding. But is this a fault? It can be argued that even mills which are not currently producing wood siding could affect the market because they are potential producers. This is a case of substitution on the supply side of the market, rather than substitution by the consumer. Second, a national industry may be over-inclusive in view of the regional subdivisions of the market. For example, we had observed earlier that Clorox sold roughly 50 percent of the bleach in the United States. However, there is no national market for liquid bleach, only regional markets. Among Clorox's competitive advantages was the fact that it was the only major brand capable of competing in all of the regions because it alone had plants located throughout the nation. In some markets, its share might greatly exceed 50 percent, while in others, its share might be much smaller.

Let us rephrase an earlier question. Are census industries necessarily imperfect as definitions of the market? Not at all. The census industry often provides good definition of the market. When errors do exist, they are often minor. Morover, the census data have one very important virtue—they are always readily available.

Measures of Concentration

Concentration measures the degree of market **domination** by a few traders. How do we measure concentration? How do we construct an index that measures domination? In an earlier discussion on the definition of concentration, we introduced the concentration curve which illustrates the cumulative distribution of market shares for all the firms in the market, ordered from the largest to the smallest. The concentration curve is a good indicator of concentration because it reflects the two dimensions which affect it, the number of firms, and their relative size.

The effect upon the level of concentration of the number of firms in the market may be illustrated with a simple hypothetical example. Compare two markets in which all firms are of equal relative size. The market share of each firm is, of course, equal to $1/n$ in both cases, but one market has ten firms while the other has only five. Concentration curves, C_5 and C_{10}, shown in Figure 5-2,

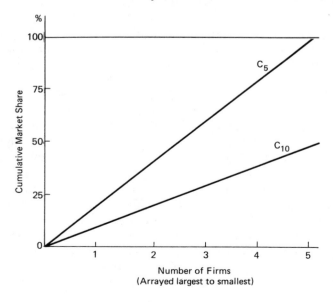

Figure 5-2   Concentration is affected by number of firms. A market with five firms of equal size is twice as concentrated as one with ten firms of equal size.

illustrate the distribution of market shares in the two cases. As noted above, the slope of the concentration curve is an index on the degree of concentration. In this case, the concentration curves for both markets are linear, but the slope of one curve equals 1/5 while the slope of the other equals l/10. The market with half as many firms as the other is twice as concentrated as it is.

Is the measurement of concentration always so easy and unambiguous? Unfortunately, it is not. Consider the effect upon concentration of differences in relative size. Compare two markets in which the number of firms is the same but the size distribution of firms is different. Let us assume that in one case we have an **egalitarian** market—the market shares of all firms are equal to 1/n. Let us assume that in the other case we have a **dominant firm** market—the market share of the leading firms is roughly three times larger than the market share of any other firm. An illustration is provided in Table 5-1 below.

TABLE 5.1 ILLUSTRATION OF FIRM SIZE INEQUALITY ON MARKET CONCENTRATION

	FIRM MARKET SHARES		CUMULATIVE MARKET SHARES	
Firm By Rank	"Egal" Market	"Dom-Firm" Market	"Egal" Market	"Dom-Firm" Market
1	.20	.45	.20	.45
2	.20	.16	.40	.61
3	.20	.14	.60	.75
4	.20	.13	.80	.88
5	.20	.12	1.00	1.00

Which is more concentrated? The **egalitarian** market or the **dominant firm** market? Considering only the leading firms, the latter is clearly more concentrated—the dominant firm is more than twice as large as any firm in the other market. Looking only at the remaining firms, the former is the more concentrated. The firms in the egalitarian market are larger in each instance. How can we resolve this issue? Consider the two concentration curves, C_e and C_d, shown in Figure 5-3. The skewed distribution of the dominant firm market causes its concentration curve to bend upward from the linear path of the curve representing the egalitarian market. C_d lies above C_e at all points except the extremes. The dominant firm market is, therefore, the more concentrated. If two markets have the same number of firms, the one in which there is a greater degree of inequality is the more concentrated.

As useful as they are, concentration curves are not the solution for measuring concentration. What are the problems? First, an index should be quantifiable. In the case of the concentration curve, however, that is not possible. We can say which of two markets is the more concentrated when the curve for one of them lies outside or above the curve for the other, such as illustrated in Figures 5-2 and 5-3. However, we cannot say how much more concentrated it is. Second, an index should be consistent. In the case of concentration curves, that

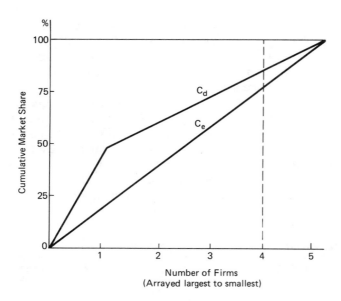

Figure 5-3 Concentration is affected by inequality in firm size. For a given number of firms, a market dominated by a large firm is more concentrated than one with firms of equal size.

is not always possible. Consistent ordering between an egalitarian market with five firms and a dominant firm market with six or more firms, for example, cannot be achieved. While $C_d > C_e$ for the first few firms, the curves would ultimately cross and the order would reverse.

There are several different indexes of concentration which have been constructed. Why are there so many measures of concentration? Are they based upon the same information? It is useful to observe that all measures of concentration are based upon market share data such as illustrated in Table 5-1 above. Therefore, the differences between one index and another are explained by the system of weights used in their construction. Thus, the possibilities abound. However, let us concern ourselves with the two most popular measures—the concentration ratio and the Herfindahl index.

Concentration Ratio. The concentration ratio is a measure of concentration which reflects both the number of firms and the inequality in their market shares. The concentration ratio, CR_n, is an unweighted sum of the market shares of the n largest firms in the market. Alternatively, the weighting scheme could be described as one in which a weight of 1 is assigned to the market share of the firm when it is among the n largest in the industry and a weight of 0 is assigned otherwise. CR_n is expressed in percentage terms so that values range from a maximum of 100, when the number of firms $\leq$ n in the market to a minimum approaching 0, when there are a high number of firms and there is little or no inequality. In the United States, the Census Bureau reports concentration ratios (when possible) for the four-, eight-, twenty-, and fifty-largest firms in an industry. While the value of n used as the basis for measuring

CR_n is clearly arbitrary, the number four was adopted by the Census as the smallest aggregate consistent with protecting the privacy of those surveyed. Since Census data are easily available and since it may not be possible to obtain data independently on the market shares of firms from other sources, a bureaucratic decision has settled matters, and CR_4 and CR_8 have become standards for the concentration ratios used in the United States.

Herfindahl Index. The Herfindahl index is a measure of concentration which also reflects the number of firms and the inequality in their market shares. The Herfindahl index is a weighted sum of the market shares of all the firms in the market. However, the actual weights are determined by the market structure; the weight assigned to each firm's market share is the particular value of the firm's own market share. The Herfindahl index is given by:

$$H = \Sigma s_i{}^2.$$

Until recently, data for the Herfindahl or H-index has been more difficult to obtain than data for the concentration ratio has been. Census reports formerly supplied only information on the concentration ratios of census industries so that, in the past, the researcher who desired to use the H-index had to be quite resourceful in finding data on individual firm market shares and in constructing his or her measure of concentration. Beginning with the 1982 Census of Manufactures, however, the Herfindahl index was included along with the concentration ratio.

Which of these two measures of concentration is the better one? Among economists and statisticians, the Herfindahl index is widely regarded as superior to the concentration ratio.[2] First, the H-index takes into account all the firms in the market, while CR_n includes information only for the largest n firms. It should be noted that the Census version of the Herfindahl ratio is based only on the fifty largest firms—if there are that many—in an industry. However, the exclusion of the smaller firms will not significantly affect the accuracy of the index. Second, the H-index reflects the existing inequality between each firm in the market and every other one, while CR_n reflects only the inequality between two groups of firms, the leading n firms and the rest. Are these differences important?

Consider the two hypothetical markets illustrated in Table 5-1 and Fig. 5-3 above. The four-firm concentration ratio has a value of 80 for the egalitarian market and a value of 88 for the dominant firm market. In relative terms, the latter is 10 percent more concentrated than the former. This rather minor difference is reflected in Fig. 5-3. When C_d and C_e are compared at the four-firm level, along the dashed line, the distance between them is quite small. It is important to note that the distance is much smaller here than it is at one- or two-firms. In contrast, the Herfindahl index has a value of .200 for the egalitarian

[2]Leslie Hannah and J. A. Kay, *Concentration in Modern Industry* (Macmillan: London, 1977).

market and a value of .279 for the dominant firm market. In relative terms, the latter is 39.5 percent more concentrated than the former. In this case, the difference between the two measures is substantial. The difference between the concentration ratio and the Herfindahl index is most clearly seen with measures of concentration for a dominant firm market structure—the former does not discriminate between single firm dominance and dominance by a small group, while the latter does. Is single firm dominance very common? Is the example shown here representative? There is evidence that this is an unusual case. Nelson[3] estimated that, for a sample of 91 industries, the correlation between CR_4 and the H-index was .936.

It is obvious that the concentration ratio has gained far wider use than has the Herfindahl index. This preference is an understandable one. It has been explained by a comparative advantage in ease and cost. Does this mean that great sacrifices in accuracy have been made? No. Such popularity also indicates that the concentration ratio has served sufficiently well as an index of dominance to make it acceptable. The concentration ratio is the measure upon which most applied work in industrial organization in the past has been based, but this may change as the Herfindahl index becomes more accessible. A sample of the 1982 Census of Manufactures data on concentration are given below in Table 5-2. Note the level of concentration for aluminum and steel has fallen, but we cannot be certain about automobiles as the data are not available due to disclosure limitations.

TABLE 5.2   CONCENTRATION IN SELECTED INDUSTRIES

SIC	INDUSTRY DESCRIPTION	CR$_4$	H-INDEX
2011	Meat packing	29	.0325
2082	Malt beverages	77	.2089
2346	Soft veneer and plywood	41	.0619
2721	Periodicals	20	.0175
2813	Industrial gases	75	.1530
2911	Petroleum refining	28	.0380
3275	Gypsum products	76	.1993
3332	Blast furnaces and steel mills	42	.0650
3334	Primary aluminum	64	.1704
3652	Phonograph records and tapes	61	.1153
3674	Semiconductors	40	.0597
3721	Aircraft	64	.1358

Source: 1982 Census of Manufactures (1986).

CONCENTRATION IN U.S. MANUFACTURING

How concentrated is American industry? Is dominance of the market by a handful of firms the typical situation? No, although there are a number of heavily

[3]Ralph L. Nelson, *Concentration in the Manufacturing Industries of the United States* (Yale University Press: New Haven, 1963).

concentrated markets which are highly visible, the majority of markets are not so concentrated. Let us close this discussion by using four-firm concentration ratios to describe the levels of concentration in the 449 Census Industries which made up U.S. manufacturing in 1977.

TABLE 5.3 DISTRIBUTION OF 449 CENSUS INDUSTRIES: FOUR-FIRM CONCENTRATION RATIOS, 1977

VALUE OF CR	PERCENT OF INDUSTRIES
80 to 100	4.9%
70 to 79	3.6
60 to 69	7.4
50 to 59	12.6
40 to 49	15.1
30 to 39	15.5
20 to 29	21.6
— to 19	19.3

Source: Census of Manufacturers (1981).

SOURCES OF CONCENTRATION

Concentration is a major dimension of market structure. Is the level of concentration a permanent feature of the market? Not necessarily. Concentration changes. Thus, we are faced with a new question: what leads to concentration? There are several factors which influence both the number and the relative size of the firms in the market. Some are natural; they are related to the underlying structural forces such as economies of scale in production and organization. Some are artificial; they are related to acts of strategic behavior where the purpose is the elimination of competitors or competition. Not all sources of concentration are known or knowable; they are stochastic or random determinants of concentration.

Natural Forces Supporting Concentration

Scale Economies.   Economies of scale are the cost advantages enjoyed by the large firms as compared with the small. Such cost advantages can be an important economic factor in determining the size of the viable firm in the market—the efficient firm can survive in competition where the inefficient one cannot. In the preceding chapter, we discovered that scale has many different dimensions—the size of the plant, the amount of experience acquired through learning, the degree of integration between production and support activities, and so on. We also discovered that each is associated with a distinctive cost advantage. But there is no point in repeating that discussion here. However, in the present context we may reasonably narrow our perspective of scale economies. The natural level of concentration can be affected only by those dimensions of scale where cost savings favor the firm which attains a large size in a single product market.

Firm size is only half the picture, however. The size of the market bears equal responsibility for concentration. What determines the size of the market? The obvious answer is product demand. In the absence of other factors, such as geographic barriers which create subdivisions of the whole, the size of the market is given by the fundamental determinants of demand. Population and per capita income are most important. Tastes (or technology in the case of producers' goods) are often taken as given. The population of the United States is much greater than that of any nation with a comparable level of per capita income and the per capita income of the United States is far higher than that of any nation with a comparable or larger population. Therefore, the United States is (taste differences aside) assured of having the largest national market. This fact is important for international comparisons of concentration—large markets mean low concentration, other things being equal. Once the size of the market is given, the size of the firm determines its market share, and by extension to all firms in the market, the level of natural concentration.

The concept of **natural monopoly** is a familiar one to the economist. It represents the extreme case of concentration being determined by the presence of scale economies. Examine the situation illustrated in Figure 5-4. Assume that demand and costs are given such that the long-run average unit cost (LRAC) declines throughout the range of output that is relevant. With the price set equal to average cost and output determined by the corresponding quantity demanded, the firm continues to experience increasing returns to scale. Under these circumstances, monopoly is a natural or equilibrium state: (1) if there were more than one firm in the market, the larger would have a cost advantage over the smaller and would have the incentive and the ability to seize monopoly by undercutting the rival's break-even price, (2) if there were more than one firm in

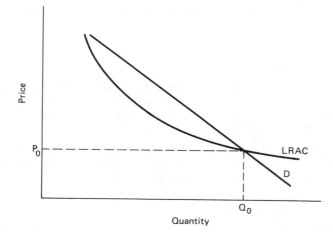

Figure 5-4 High concentration may be explained by the market structure. When scale economies extend over the entire range of a market, as shown by the D and LRAC curves, **natural monopoly** is the result.

the market and they were equal in size, they would have the incentive to combine in order to seize the cost advantages of a natural monopoly, but (3) if there was only one firm in the market and if it were to price its product in the fashion indicated in Figure 5-4, no entrant would be willing or able to challenge its position of monopoly. Natural monopoly may be unusual in the United States, but we regard it as an important exception to *normal* market structure. It is taken to be the hallmark of the public utility industry, and it is made socially acceptable by direct regulation so that the advantages of natural monopoly may benefit the consumer as well as the supplier.

How about the less concentrated **natural oligopoly**? The concept is straightforward. The real issue has always been a matter of application. Are the observed levels of concentration justified by nature? Beginning with the work of Bain, who developed the engineering approach for estimating scale economies, industrial organization specialists have sought to establish whether or not concentration in the United States, particularly in manufacturing, is supported by the presence of scale economies. In his study of twenty industries, Bain found that minimum efficient sale of plant (MES) might justify the existing level of concentration in no more than one or two cases, while the rest appeared to be excessively concentrated—by a magnitude of at least two and, in a few instances, more than twenty.[4] Does this mean that the vast majority of the markets surveyed by Bain were *over-concentrated*? Not necessarily. The scope of Bain's investigation may have been too narrow.

Large scale has many dimensions; the size of the production unit is only one of them. For example, Bain's study indicated that a final assembly plant in the automobile industry could achieve optimal efficiency with a capacity no larger than 3 percent of total U.S. output (and perhaps as little as one percent). In the preceding chapter, we noted that cost savings could be enjoyed by a much larger firm. The operation of multiple plants can provide the opportunity to save on transport costs for a firm serving a national market in automobiles. The attainment of large size, in terms of total sales, can provide the opportunity to save on advertising costs. In the case of General Motors, the dominant firm enjoyed much lower costs than any of its smaller rivals. Finally, to reinforce our point, Bain also estimated that a fully integrated plant would serve between 5 and 10 percent of the market.

There have been a few attempts to estimate the economies of the large scale firm (as opposed to the large scale plant), but none have been as thorough or successful as the work by Scherer and his colleagues, noted in the preceding chapter. In their study of twelve selected industries, Scherer et al undertook to examine the full scope of the firm's activities, including advertising, finance, distribution, procurement, vertical integration, management, research, and so on. What were the results? In eight of the twelve industries, efficiency might

---

[4]Joe S. Bain, ''Economies of Scale, Concentration, and Conditions of Entry in Twenty Manufacturing Industries,'' *American Economic Review* 44 (March 1954), pp. 15-39.

require the firm to operate multiple plants.[5] In three of the twelve cases, the observed level of concentration was warranted by firm economies. However, in the remaining cases, scale economies could not account for the concentration in the market (and in two of these, the size of the leading firms was nearly ten times larger than warranted).

Apparently, scale economies cannot account for the level of concentration in many markets. Does this mean that concentration is excessive? Perhaps not. In the first place, there is no reason to believe that nature dictates that firm size must be no greater than minimum efficient scale. The median size of the fittest firms in the market may well exceed MES, provided that scale may be increased beyond the lower threshold of optimal size without sacrificing efficiency. In the second place, there are other natural forces which might affect concentration.

Barriers to Entry.   Barriers to entry are those economic factors which give certain firms an advantage over rivals. As a support to concentration, entry barriers are important in two respects: (1) they may limit the number of firms entering the market, and (2) they may preserve or protect the market shares of those firms already established in it. Does this mean that barriers to entry could support a level of concentration which is higher than might be warranted by scale economies alone? Yes it does.

What is the nature of barriers to entry? What gives rise to them? The essence of the barrier is a matter of access to the market. The firm which enjoys a barrier to entry advantage is able to produce its product at a lower cost or to market its product more easily than the competition. Often, it is a matter of who got there first or who staked out the better position for itself from the outset. Barriers are, therefore, a form of market imperfection. When they are present, changes in market structure take place slowly even though they may seem to be warranted. Thus, barriers to entry will tend to preserve the status quo in terms of relative firm size and overall market concentration. In the preceding chapter, we distinguished between barriers which are natural and barriers which are the result of strategic behavior on the part of the incumbent. At this point in the discussion, we shall limit consideration to the former.

Consider the automobile industry in the United States. As noted above, the U.S. auto industry was dominatd by General Motors for a long period of time. The relative positions of the leader and its smaller rivals did not change from the mid-fifties until the early eighties. Are barriers to entry responsible for the high concentration and stability in the market's structure? It would seem so. At the end of World War II, a new competitor challenged the market, the first new automaker since the twenties. Henry J. Kaiser was regarded as the mid-century Henry Ford, a brash entrepreneur who was willing to take risks and make changes. Wall Street reacted favorably in January 1946, snapping up the

---

[5]F. M. Scherer, et al., *The Economics of the Multiplant Operation* (Harvard University Press: Cambridge, Mass., 1975), p. 336.

new stock issue and supplying $53,500,000 for the new venture.[6] Kaiser's timing seemed perfect. The American public wanted new cars and there did not seem to be enough capacity to supply its appetite. In 1948, Kaiser supplied 5 percent of the new cars sold in the United States. Within five years, however, Kaiser sold the famous Willow Run plant, which it had originally acquired from Ford, to General Motors and ceased production. What was the barrier responsible for Kaiser's demise? To some extent, it was a matter of bottlenecks. In the postwar recovery many producers competed sharply for scarce materials, and suppliers tended to favor their old customers. Nevertheless, Kaiser received help from strange quarters. When Kaiser encountered difficulty in purchasing transmissions from parts manufacturers, General Motors supplied it with automatic transmissions and gearboxes. To some extent, it was a matter of capital—Kaiser issued too little stock when the market was hungry for it and could not attract capital later when more was needed. On the other hand, Reconstruction Finance Corporation did supply what the private market did not. Most fundamentally, Kaiser faced a product differentiation disadvantage—one which was mitigated by the early shortages of new cars but which became more pronounced as time passed. As *Fortune* observed: "Disguise a Chevrolet effectively and slap a new name on it, and you'd find it as hard to sell 200,000 a year as [Kaiser] finds it to get rid of 200,000."[7] Auto industry historian, John B. Rae, attributed the failure to the fact that Kaiser offered the buyer nothing new—the entrant supplied a conventional car, built by conventional methods.[8] The lesson seems to be that if the buyer wants a standard automobile, he or she wants it to be a well-known make. Under these circumstances, the newcomer faces an inherent disadvantage. This explanation of auto industry barriers has the added virtue that it does seem to be consistent with the success in the 1970s and 1980s in the American market of the low- and medium-priced Japanese cars and of the luxury cars of European manufacture.

Are barriers to entry capable of explaining high levels of concentration in a number of industries? Or is the auto industry merely an exception? Research on barriers to entry seems to indicate that they are important and that natural concentration relies heavily upon them. For example, Bain's study of twenty industries concluded that in twelve of the industries (or, in some instances, important product groups within an industry) the barriers to entry were either very high or substantial.[9] Highest barriers were found in automobiles, cigarettes, fountain pens, liquor, tractors, and typewriters, while substantial barriers were found in copper, farm machines, petroleum refining, shoes, soap, and steel. Bain attributed the barriers to four sources: (1) economies of large scale, (2)

[6]*Fortune* (July 1951), p. 69.

[7]*op. cit.*, p. 158.

[8]John B. Rae, *The American Automobile* (University of Chicago Press: Chicago, 1965), p. 170.

[9]Joe S. Bain, *Barriers to New Competition* (Harvard University Press: Cambridge, 1956), pp. 169-170.

product differentiation, (3)absolute cost disadvantages for entrants, and (4) large capital requirements for entry. It is especially interesting to note that very high product differentiation barriers were identified for every one of the consumer good industries with high levels of concentration—automobiles, cigarettes, soap, and liquor. Finally, it should also be noted that some of the factors which are termed barriers to entry by Bain are identical to those which are treated as multi-plant scale economies by Scherer and his colleagues.

Thus, natural concentration is vindicated, at least in part, by scale economies and barriers to entry. There may be other explanations for the differences in size and success achieved by competing firms which contribute to concentration as well. The emphasis upon the technological and other physical attributes of the firm and its environment often ignores human factors. The organization and operation of a firm is a human, not technological endeavor. Human differences can be important. It is reasonable to presume that some firms are abnormally large—neither ordinary scale economies nor entry barriers can explain their size—because they are managed by persons with superior skill or because their personnel in marketing and product development do a better job. Other firms are small because they lack these natural advantages.

A final caution should be registered about concentration that is based upon market structure—what we have called *nature*. Such concentration is by no means permanent. Changes in technology and growth in demand may eliminate the influence of scale economies and barriers to entry. Indeed, rapid growth and high concentration are not likely to coexist. Changes in tastes and the development of new products may neutralize the advantages enjoyed by incumbents from product differentiation. Changes in the leadership of a dominant firm—or of its much smaller competitor—may bring about a reversal of fortunes and change the level of concentration. Nature is no more permanent in the economic world than it is in the physical world. This does not mean, however, that *natural* forces can account for all observed levels of concentration. Concentration is also affected by market conduct. However there are times when this distinction is hard to maintain. How much of the product differentiation advantage of GM is natural and how much is created?

Artificial Forces Supporting Concentration

When the market position of a firm is altered by its conduct, and when this has a material effect upon concentration, we may regard the resulting market structure as **artificial**. Does this mean that the behavior is wrong? Not necessarily. Remember that firms do not automatically become the right size to exploit economies of scale; their size and efficiency is the result of actions taken by their management. In the case of internal expansion, we are willing to presume that the firm, in building a large and efficient scale of plant, is merely seeking to maximize profits. However, if a firm seeks to increase its production capacity through mergers and acquisitions, we are more likely to regard its actions with suspicion. Perhaps, this too is merely an effort to increase profits. Does it really matter what the firm is after? Yes it does. The motivation of the firm which seeks to increase its size and strengthen its market position is important. We shall have the occasion to consider it at length in later chapters dealing with public policy. At this point, however, we are interested in other questions: What actions might alter the level of market concentration? Is the change a permanent one?

Mergers. Consolidation of the stock or assets of competing firms will decrease the number of firms in the market and will increase the market share of one of them. Such an action must necessarily increase concentration. It is called a horizontal merger. At the turn of this century in the United States, a wave of horizontal mergers took place unlike any other. Over a short period of time, near-monopolies were created in a number of industries. The creation of US Steel, as described at the outset of this chapter, was part of this movement. Indeed, it was the largest combination ever established up to its time; it was the world's first billion dollar corporation when a billion dollars represented real money. The steel merger was also prototypical in the sense that it was intended to concentrate the market. An impression of the short-term success achieved by certain mergers is given in Table 5-4.

TABLE 5.4 RESULTS OF TURN-OF-THE-CENTURY MERGER WAVE: TEN SELECTED INDUSTRIES

| | MARKET SHARE | | | |
| | Post-Merger | | Later | |
Firm	%	Date	%	Date
Standard Oil	88	1899	67	1909
American Sugar Refining	95	1892	49	1907
National Starch Manufacturing	70	1890	45	1899
Glucose Sugar Refining	85	1897	45	1901
International Paper	66	1898	30	1911
American Tin Plate	95	1899	54	1912
American Tobacco	93	1899	76	1903
American Can	90	1901	60	1903
US Steel	66	1901	46	1920
International Harvester	85	1902	44	1922

Source: Yale Brozen, *Mergers in Perspective* (American Enterprise Institute: Washington, 1982), p. 17.

This sweeping merger wave had an effect upon market structure in a number of industries. The post-merger levels of concentration were exceptionally high, as can be seen from the first two columns of Table 5-4. How significant were these mergers in the long run? Did they permanently alter concentration? Opinions on this issue differ. Nelson[10] points out that the early merger wave created dominant firms—such as US Steel, American Tobacco, International Harvester, and du Pont—which have maintained leading positions in their respective markets. He argues that the effect of the merger wave has endured. Brozen[11], on the other hand, points out that the artificial giants quickly lost their market positions to competition. The ten firms, as shown in the last two columns of Table 5-4, experienced an erosion of market share, giving back from one-third to one-half of their acquired positions within ten to twenty years (and as little as two years in one case). And these, Brozen argues, were the successful cases; many of the early combinations were business failures.

Who is right? Probably both of them. Brozen suggests that the mergers which "took" are those which represent efficient reorganizations of the merging firms. Nevertheless, one might agree with Nelson that the mergers which significantly changed the relative market positions of firms were, in the proximate sense, responsible for what followed. Mergers will increase the level of concentration in the short run; that much is certain. However, mergers alone will not alter concentration in the long run; that would seem to require some sort of barrier to entry. If the merger should take place in a market where entry is not perfectly free, however, it may render a permanent change in concentration. Thus, the merger history may be useful in explaining the structure of the market. This is not to say that internal growth could not and would not produce the same end result under certain circumstances.

In any case, the dramatic changes which took place in the first merger wave produced a long-lasting political result. It caused U.S. Antitrust Laws dealing with horizontal mergers to be toughened. That has resulted in a much diminished role for the horizontal merger as a means for increasing the market share of the combining firms. During the 1960s, the standards of the antimerger law were so strict that a combination of two local supermarket chains in Los Angeles, with roughly four percent shares of the local market each, was forbidden.[12] During the 1980s, these standards were relaxed some and the horizontal merger reappeared to regain a certain degree of importance.

Other Practices.   Strategic behavior by the well-placed firm may also be responsible for erecting barriers to entry. There are numerous practices which have been cited in the case law on monopolization as evidence of "bad" conduct—the resort to predatory pricing, introduction of "fighting brands" (cheaper product lines to undercut the competition), foreclosure of retail outlets to competitors through the signing of exclusive dealers, proliferation of products in order to exhaust all opportunities for an entrant to find a niche in the market,

[10]Ralph L. Nelson, *Merger Movements in American Industry, 1895 - 1956* (Princeton University Press: Princeton, 1959), p. 34.

[11]Yale Brozen, *Mergers in Perspective* (American Enterprise Institute: Washington, 1982), pp. 16-21.

[12]*U.S. vs. Von's Grocery Co. et. al.* 384 U. S. 270 (1966).

and so on. Are these acts of strategic behavior? Perhaps. Does strategic behavior have an effect upon concentration? Probably, under the right circumstances. However, there are a few problems.

The first problem is proving that the predatory practice—whatever it is, is the principal cause of the *insider's* advantage. It is unfortunate that there is so little hard evidence upon which to base measurement of the effects of strategic behavior. In the Antitrust cases involving allegations of predatory practices, the evidence is used to prove monopolistic intent on the part of the defendant, not the effect on the market. Aside from the problems of proof, there are also problems with the theory of predation. Assuming that strategic behavior results in weakening competitors or limiting the competition, its success is dependent upon the predator having a prior advantage of superior strength. For example, if a firm sells its product below cost to drive out a competitor, it is the firm with the largest market share that takes the greatest risks and suffers the greatest losses. Thus, the predator needs extra resources—a deep pocket—in order to wage economic warfare. Which comes first, the position of power (structure) or the strategic behavior?

The second problem is proving that the firm is really practicing predation. It is sometimes very difficult to distinguish between a firm which is resourceful in waging hard competition and a firm which is bloodthirsty in crushing the competition by any means, fair or foul. In the case of ALCOA, for example, the Court was concerned with the fact that the firm had expanded its capacity to meet the growth in demand.[13] This was seen as a matter of preempting competition. Instead, it may have been evidence of superior foresight and industry, to paraphrase Judge Hand who found ALCOA to be guilty of monopolization.

What is the role of strategic behavior? It would seem to be an adjunct of or partner with nature. In the case of mergers, strategic actions may directly increase concentration, but some natural advantage(s) may be necessary to preserve the state of heavy concentration, once established. As for the case of predation, strategic actions may tend to reinforce nature in maintaining a given state of concentration. Nevertheless, one can imagine a circumstance, a merger strategy, in which conduct alone could account for a high level of concentration. Artificial concentration would require constant tending—the old firms buying up the new firms as soon as they enter the market. As we saw in the case of US Steel, when it failed to do this, its market share gradually eroded. Such a strategy may prove to be too expensive, in any case. Once the intentions of a leading firm became known, entry could become a growth industry, and asking prices could skyrocket.

If strategic behavior is only of marginal importance, why is so much attention given to it? Two factors may be involved. One is that it does exist. Firms do attempt to strengthen their positions in the market by strategic moves. Secondly, nature—or market structure—cannot fully account for the existing levels of concentration. Thus, those who require a deterministic explanation, turn to

---

[13]*U.S. vs. Aluminum Co. of American et. al.* 148 F.2d. 416 (2d. Cir. 1945).

behavior. There is an alternative, however. Consider the possibility of random forces.

Random Forces Affecting Concentration

If market success reflects survival of the fittest, it can also reflect survival of the luckiest. Anyone who has spent an evening at the poker table knows what usually happens—there are winners and there are losers. Indeed, that is the attraction of gambling. A poker game may begin around 8:00 p.m., with five players who have equal skill and who start with identical stacks of chips. Sometime after midnight, if not before, one the players may sit smugly behind a huge pile of chips, having won them all. The game is over. Can the outcome be explained? It is the expected result of a game of chance and it is not possible to predict the winner.

Is the poker game analogy applicable to the workings of the market? If natural and artificial forces—market structure and conduct—fail to account fully for the level of concentration, it is reasonable to seek other answers. The **random process** is certainly a candidate—the market may operate somewhat like a game of chance.

Some have taken the hypothesis of a stochastic or random process rather far. Gibrat[14], for example, observed a common pattern in the size distributions of firms in the market—the pattern of a few large firms, a larger number of medium-sized firms, and a substantial number of small firms tailing off at the end. What could produce this distribution? Why was it so common? Gibrat offered the hypothesis that, behind the size distribution, was a universal process of random growth common to all firms. That process had the following properties: (1) each firm was expected to grow in the same proportion as every other, and (2) each firm's actual growth rate was determined by a random variable term. This process is called the **Law of Proportionate Growth**. Because firm growth is random, the process can generate differences in firm size. Growth is also proportional and the process will tend to make large firms progressively larger (and small firms progressively smaller) relative to the others over time.

Consider the following example. Assume that a group of firms begin with equal market shares. Assume that the expected growth rate is zero and that there are equal probabilities that a firm will either grow, remain unchanged, or decline in a given period of time. Assume that the firm which does grow (or does decline) during a ten-year time period will do so at a rate equal to 50 percent per decade. Finally, assume that the rate of change experienced by a firm in any given decade is independent of the change it will experience in any other decade. The expected effects of a Gibrat-like random growth process upon the distribution of firm size are recorded in Table 5-5.

[14]R. Gibrat, *Les Ineqalites Economiques* (Recueil Sirey: Paris, 1931).

TABLE 5.5 ILLUSTRATION OF THE EFFECT OF GIBRAT'S LAW (DISTRIBUTION OF 216 CUSTOMERS AMONG 27 FIRMS)

TIME PERIOD	NUMBER OF FIRMS DISTRIBUTED BY NUMBER OF CUSTOMERS																										
	1	2	3	4	5	6	7	8	9	10	11	12	13	14	15	16	17	18	19	20	21	22	23	24	25	26	27
0								27																			
10				9				9				9															
20		3		6		6		3				6						3									
30	1	3	3	3		6		1	3			3						3									1

This table was constructed on the assumptions of the **Law of Proportionate Effect**. Assume that 27 firms begin with equal market shares. Assume that random changes occur which have the following properties: (1) there are equal probabilities that each firm will grow, stay the same, or decline in a given period of time [Pr(+) = Pr(0) = Pr(−) = ⅓], (2) the rate of change will be the same (proportional) for every firm regardless of its size, and (3) the changes which do occur will take place over a ten year period and the growth (or decline) will increase (or decrease) the size of the firm by 50 percent during that time.

The hypothetical market is assumed to contain 27 firms to supply 216 customers. For each triple of firms, it is assumed that one will grow by 50 percent, one will shrink by 50 percent, and one will stay the same in each and every decade. Thus, after ten years, 9 firms have 12 customers each, 9 firms have 8 customers each (the same as when they started), and 9 firms have 4 customers each. And so the process goes. After 30 years, the scatter of firm sizes is dramatic—the largest firm is 27 times as large as the smallest. During that period of time the market becomes progressively concentrated. In the beginning, market concentration is assumed to be $CR_4 = 15$; after ten years, $CR_4 = 22$; after twenty years, $CR_4 = 31$; and after thirty years, $CR_4 = 39$. The concentrating effect of the Law of Proportional Growth can also be shown by concentration curves as in Figure 5-5. Note that, for the three decades of growth history, the concentration curves become progressively more distended with the passage of time, in contrast to the linear concentration curve of the base year.

How significant is Gibrat's Law? That has been a matter of fierce debate. One thing is certain. It is useful as a device to demonstrate the ability of a random process to alter the size distribution of firms in a market. However, Gibrat's Law is a radical proposition. The insistence that the level of concentration and the changes which are observed to occur in it are to be explained solely by a random process of proportional growth seems to go too far. It is one thing to assert that some differences in firm size can only be explained by chance, having exhausted all the alternatives, and it is another to assert that firm size (and the firm's market success or failure) is merely the result of a mechanical process.

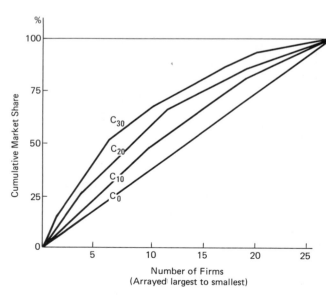

Figure 5-5 High concentration may be explained by the cumulative effect of random forces. Gibrat's Law, applied to a hypothetical market with a fixed number of firms, demonstrates that concentration may increase with time. Over thirty years, $C_{30} > C_{20} > C_{10} > C_0$.

Stability and Change in Concentration

Is the level of concentration a permanent feature of the market? No it is not. Technology may change, and with it, the significance of scale economies as an explanation of firm size. Long distance communications was a **natural monopoly** in 1975, but there were many competitors vying with AT&T in 1985. Barriers to entry may either appear or disappear. For example, product differentiation may be as important in bringing about change as it can be in resisting it. In the case of automobiles, General Motors suspected that Americans did not all want to drive the same car and, therefore, designed and built a line of autos to differentiate according to what the consumer could afford. As a result, GM became the new leader of the U.S. auto industry, and Henry Ford's determination to make an inexpensive, universal car—the Model T—changed from an advantage (Ford had enjoyed cost savings from producing large volumes of a single model for a long period of time) to a liability. Artificial market structures are also subject to change. For example, a dominant position in the market, which had been established by an earlier merger, may erode in the face of subsequent events—the entry of new firms and the growth of others can erase a near-monpopoly. US Steel and many other giants of its era witnessed such a change in their fortunes. Of course, random change brings about a shift in the level of concentration. Thus, when concentration is stable for a long period of time, it is reasonable to presume either that the underlying structural features— the advantages of large size and the presence of barriers to entry—have remained relatively unchanged, or that the strategic behavior which built up the position of the leading firm continues to preserve it. When significant changes are observed in the level of concentration or in the relative positions of firms in the market, it is reasonable to presume that change is underfoot. What is the point? The level of concentration and the change or stability in it are indicators of the past history and present trends in market structure and behavior. An analysis of a market is never really complete unless it looks at past levels of concentration as well as the present levels.

CONCENTRATION AND OLIGOPOLY

Concentration is widely regarded as the most significant single attribute of market structure. Oligopoly, perhaps the most interesting of the four elemental market structures, is virtually defined in terms of concentration. Such terms as **tight oligopoly** and **loose oligopoly** are used to differentiate between greater and lesser degrees of concentration. What are the primary behavioral implications of oligopoly? How are they related to concentration?

Pricing in the oligopoly market can be an enigma. At one extreme, oligopoly pricing may resembly monopoly. At the other, oligopoly pricing may produce results that are the same as one would associate with perfect competition. In any case, it is assumed that oligopolists recognize their interdependence, and that this recognition is the result of concentration. If there are but a few firms in the market, each firm must be aware of the implications of its actions. First, an increase in the output of one firm, unless it is roughly offset by a decrease in output by one firm, will tend to depress price. Second, an increase in the market share of one firm will necessarily be accompanied by a decrease in the market share of another. Thus, the behavior of the oligopolist is predicated upon assumptions about the nature and timing of rival reactions to any initiative taken by the firm. In some cases, the firm may assume that any action it takes will trigger a response by others, and the expectation may be sufficient to restrain the firm. Price may tend to remain unchanged if all firms are of a similar mind. In other cases, the firm may assume that rival prices are set and that it may well get away with an improvement in its relative market position, at least for a period of time sufficient to make the effort pay off. Price competition may prevail. In some cases, an understanding of mutual interest may be assumed by the firms in the market—a pattern of price leadership may emerge as a result.

Price leadership and concentration are closely associated in oligopoly theory. There are two cases to consider. In the first case, if the number of firms is small and the market share of the respresentative firm is large, each firm may realize that cooperation among them will enable the group to exercise market power—to raise price and to increase profits to their mutual advantage. Moreover, fewness has other implications for the case of cooperative price leadership. With a small number of firms, it may be easier to find a price that is mutually acceptable to all the members of the group. With a small number of firms, it may be easier to keep a check upon one another, making certain that each firm maintains the group price. In the second case, if the market share of the leading firm is very large, the dominant firm may realize that it has the unilateral ability to control price in spite of what the lesser firms in the market do. The *others* may accept the leadership of the *dominant* firm as a matter of course, in the belief that (1) they have little or no ability to control price, and (2) they have no reason to exercise self-restraint in supply since the leader will make whatever adjustments are necessary to maintain the price.

The relationship between concentration and price behavior may clearly be seen in the markets for steel, automobiles, and aluminum which we considered at the outset of this chapter. Consider the steel market in which US Steel was the leading firm from the time of its formation. Certain actions taken by US Steel may be seen as efforts to enlist the cooperation of others in the industry to maintain supracompetitive prices in the market. For example, **Pittsburgh Plus** was a basing point pricing system established by US Steel in 1903 to provide a simple and common standard for pricing in the industry. US Steel would quote prices to its customers as though all steel mills were located in Pittsburgh and as though the buyer were held fully responsible for paying rail freight charges from the point of production. Since US Steel was known to be good to its word, to sell at prices announced rather than to offer secret rebates or concessions, the basing point pricing system was an effective means to enlist cooperation of others in the industry, and the practice continued until the Federal Trade Commission forced the company to halt the practice in 1924.

In another example, US Steel acted as the instigator of the **Gary dinners** from 1907 to 1911; these were social/business affairs hosted by the Corporation's board chairman, Judge Gary. The object of the Gary dinners was to encourage the cooperation of others in the steel industry to maintain a discipline in stabilizing the price of steel. These two illustrations represent some of the more obvious acts of leadership, but the overall record of behavior of US Steel speaks even more strongly. US Steel was intent on supporting a price that everyone could live with that (1) the Corporation set its prices high enough to support even the weakest of firms during periods of normal demand, and (2) the Corporation was even willing to sacrifice market share to the more aggressive of its competitors. The example of the steel industry shows that the conceptual distinctions between types of price leadership are sometimes sharper than those which can be found in practice. US Steel acted as a dominant firm price leader *and* an emissary for cooperation, with the support of others in the industry. Thus, the Corporation's influence did not disappear after its dominance of the market had been transformed into a position of being the largest of the steel giants in the United States. Concentration continued to play a role in the price behavior in steel until the domestic industry, especially the large integrated producers, failed to keep pace with the productivity gains achieved by foreign producers.

Concentration was also extremely important for pricing in the automobile market in the United States, but the pattern of pricing behavior in autos appeared to define certain variations on the theme of dominant firm price leadership. In the early period, during the twenties and thirties, Ford was the price leader. For a while, Ford held the largest market share in automobiles, and the pattern of behavior fits the standard mold. Even after it had sunk to second place in the industry, Ford continued to exercise leadership because Henry Ford chose to be the low-price producer in the market. However, when domestic production was resumed after World War II, General Motor's dominance in the industry was unchallenged, and GM set its prices to fulfill certain profit targets which the firm established for itself. Since GM's market position was so superior, the others in the industry seemed to have little choice but to go along. They were reluctant to undercut GM's prices for fear that the leaders's market position was so well entrenched, and they were reluctant to sell at higher prices for fear of losing even more market share to the leader. More recently, auto imports have become a significant factor in the market, which is one of the reasons for automakers' pressure on Congress for import restrictions. Finally the respective fortunes of Ford and GM have reversed. Domestic concentration may not have changed much, but the price setting behavior of the industry has changed rather dramatically.

Finally, what can be said about the relationship between concentration and the pricing behavior in aluminum prior to the structural changes brought by the antitrust actions against ALCOA and the wartime boom in new plant construction by the Defense Department? When ALCOA was the only producer of virgin alumimun ingot, the prices for aluminum in the United States revealed a secular trend downward. ALCOA set its price (1) to yield a target profit of 10 percent and (2) to enlarge its market at the expense of other metals. It has also been suggested that ALCOA used price as a weapon to discourage new competition. If that were true, then price behavior might explain the concentration in the market rather than the reverse. In any case, it is clear that steel, automobiles, and aluminum provide some interesting and fruitful examples of the relationship between concentration and oligopoly behavior.

PRODUCT DIFFERENTIATION

6

In this chapter we examine the meaning and implications of product differentia-
tion. We look at evidence of differentiation in three markets. Then, we seek to define it.
Next, we examine the conditions which can account for differentiation; these include
differences in location, differences in tastes, and lack of information. The consumer
may prefer to buy from the nearest seller, may choose the product best suited to his or
her tastes, or may select that product which he or she knows the most about. In each of
these cases, the product is **differentiable.** *That is, the product appeals to a special*
segment of the market.

Next, we examine the market implications of differentiation—the ability of firms
to exercise some degree of independence and control over the demand for their prod-
ucts. We relate this to the measurement of product differentiation, using measures of
price elasticity or comparing price differentials between brands, for example. We
observe, however, that many have chosen to focus narrowly on advertising intensities
to measure differentiation. Finally, we note that product differentiation tends to
diminish the importance of price competition. The seller may have some independent
control over price or, at the very least, may resort to some nonprice strategy to achieve
better positioning in the market.

Product differentiation measures the degree of independence possessed by
a seller in the market. What do we mean by independence? We mean that the
supplier of a product which is differentiated has the ability to set its price,
independent of the prices which competitors have established for their own
products. Obviously, monopoly represents the ultimate in product differentiation. There are no substitutes. However, a degree of monopoly-like market
power is possessed by any seller who has a differentiated product. So, what
explains or accounts for this market power? Consider the buyer.

Product differentiation measures the degree to which a buyer is *attached* to
a particular product and to the seller who supplies it. What do we mean by
attachment? Perhaps it is helpful to compare the case of product differentiation
with the case of homogeneous products. When all products are identical (or are
perceived to be so), a buyer will be indifferent between sellers. The choice of

supplier will be determined by price if there are any price differences, or will be determined by chance if there are not. When the products—or the agents selling them—are different in some way (or when they are at least perceived to be different), a buyer will become attached to a particular product or supplier, and the buyer's choice will reflect the presence of a differentiating factor or factors.

In this chapter we seek to answer several questions including: What are the sources of product differentiation? What difference does it make if a market contains differentiated products? How is differentiation to be defined and measured? Before we begin, let us consider three cases of differentiation.

THREE DIFFERENTIATED MARKETS

In the market for home heating oil, location seems to make a difference. Different regions of the United States are supplied by different sources of oil. Some regions are more dependent upon oil as a source of heating than others. New England and the Middle Atlantic states consume a large part of the #2 distillate used for home heating, and a major source of the oil consumed is from the Persian Gulf. In contrast, the Pacific Northwest relies more heavily upon cheap hydroelectric power and upon natural gas for home heating, and the heating oil comes largely from Alaskan and other domestic sources. Consider the following:

STATE	1985 PRICES
New York	$1.112
Massachusetts	1.069
Connecticut	1.080
Oregon	.970
Washington	1.011
Idaho	.971

Source: U.S. Department of Energy, *Monthly Energy Review* (January 1986), pp. 96—97.

On average, the cost of heating oil—exclusive of taxes—was 10 percent higher in the East than in the Pacific Northwest during 1985. What accounts for such a price differential? As noted above, demand conditions seem to be different for the two regions, and the Northeast relies upon different sources of oil than the Pacific Northwest. Is that sufficient to explain a difference in price? It is not if oil could be shipped at zero cost from a low price region to a high price region. However, shipment of crude oil and finished products is costly. There are even relatively large price differentials between Oregon and Washington, for example, or between New York and Massachusetts. Location is a factor in differentiating regional markets for home heating oil.

In the market for automobiles, style seems to make a big difference. While there are only four U.S. firms which dominate the domestic auto industry, each produces a number of styles or models, ranging from station wagons to sports cars. The American consumer can choose from dozens of models of cars supplied by the domestic industry and by foreign automakers. Why is there so much diversity? The automobile may be utilitarian, at least in part, but it also seems to be an important extension of the ego. Consider the following:

MODEL	PRICE
Aston-Martin Lagonda, 4-dr.	$167,000
Chevrolet, Chevette CS 4, 4-dr.	5,959

Source: Automotive News, 1986 Data Book Issue (April 30, 1986), p. 53.

On March 15, 1986, the price differential between the Chevette and the Lagonda was 2700 percent, using the lower price car as the base. What is the meaning of such a price differential and how can it survive? Prices merely reflect differentiation. Thus, a 2700 percent price differential is undeniable evidence of the fact that buyers do not regard the two products as substitutes, in spite of the fact that both are motor vehicles. This example serves to emphasize a much more general point—the style (and quality) of the car is a differentiating factor.

In the market for prescription drugs, the identity of the drug manufacturer and of the druggist filling the prescription seems to make a difference. Compared with most other purchase decisions, the choice of the product is virtually dictated by someone else—the prescribing physician will determine for the consumer what product to buy. The consumer may choose a pharmacy to fill a prescription without giving the matter a second thought. Consider the following prices for filling prescriptions for 250 mg of tetracycline from a sample taken in 1974;

CITY	PRESCRIPTION	LOW PRICE	HIGH PRICE
Sacramento, CA	50 tablets	$2.95	$16.50
West Flatbush, NY	16 tablets	0.80	3.20
Cedar Rapids, IA	30 tablets	0.90	3.60

Source: Staff Report to the Federal Trade Commission, *Prescription Drug Price Disclosures*, submitted January 28, 1975.

For the samples in both Cedar Rapids and West Flatbush, the price differential was equal to 300 percent between the highest and lowest price prescriptions, and for the sample in Sacramento, there was a price spread of 459 percent. What can account for such large variations in price? One factor is the existence of the brand/generic differential—some physicians might prescribe a brand name drug, such as Achromycin, while others might well indicate the generic drug, tetracyline hydrochloride. Often the brand name drug, protected by a trademark and promoted through advertising aimed at and by personal contact with the physician, may be sold at a premium of two or three times the price of its chemical twin, the generic drug. If the physician is not aware that the same compound may be obtained at a lower price or is convinced that the generic drug is inferior, the patient will pay a premium for the brand name drug. Another factor is the conduct of the pharmacy. Some pharmacies might price on a standard mark-up over cost, while others might act as discount houses, selling at a lower margin than the competition. If the patient is not aware that drugs are available at some pharmacies at a price discount, he or she may pay a second premium, whether the product is branded or not.

DEFINITION OF PRODUCT DIFFERENTIATION

Product differentiation implies that the seller of a product enjoys a degree of independence. Also noted was the fact that differentiation implies that the buyer exhibits a degree of attachment towards a particular product or seller. When we described the examples above—heating oil, automobiles, and prescription drugs—we associated product differentiation with price differences. It would seem, therefore, that price differences are evidence of both the seller's independence and the buyer's attachment. Is a difference in price a reliable indicator of the existence of product differentiation? Perhaps it is not.

We compared the Oregon price of #2 distillate (residential heating oil) with the New York price and found that they were different. Is that product differentiation? In the case of heating oil, we actually encounter another phenomenon—market differentiation. The New York and Oregon markets are regional (i.e., spatial) markets for an otherwise homogeneous product. Location can be a differentiating factor. Within each state or community heating oil supplied by any one dealer may be a perfect substitute for heating oil supplied by another. Thus, the national market is subdivided (differentiated by location) into numerous local markets, while each of the latter may be completely undifferentiated.

In the case of automobile price differences, we see the evidence of product differentiation *per se*. Certainly it is true that the example we chose—the comparison of the Chevette with the Lagonda—also involves market differentiation as well as product differentiation. Identifying segments or submarkets, such as the market for inexpensive cars (including the Chevette) and the market for luxury vehicles (including the Lagonda) is not unlike identifying geographic segments in the market for heating oil. However, there is a difference. Within any one market segment, the product of a particular seller is still uniquely defined. For example, the Escort and the Chevette are distinctive products in the market for inexpensive cars. Note that differentiation of the automobile make and model is actually based upon many product characteristics while only one is involved in the definition of the market segment.

Thus, price difference is not a sufficient condition for product differentiation. Is it a necessary one? There are any number of markets—such as those for magazines, soft drinks, and cigarettes—in which competing brands may sell for the same price but are differentiated. Even when price is identical, the market for differentiated products is distinguishable from the market for homogeneous products. *Time* magazine has enjoyed a much larger market share than its competitor, *US News and World Report*. The colas routinely outsell all the other flavors of soft drinks combined. Moreover, these differences in market shares may be more or less permanent characteristics of the market structure. They are evidence of the attachment or brand loyalty of consumers to given sellers. They are evidence (just like price differences) of product differentiation.

So, what is product differentiation? It is a condition in which the products of individual sellers are treated, either by the buyers or by the sellers themselves, as being unique.

NATURE AND SOURCES OF PRODUCT DIFFERENTIATION

Product differentiation is, along with concentration, a major dimension of market structure. Does this mean that certain markets are predestined to a trade in differentiated products while others are not? Is it all a matter of basic conditions? There are significant factors which, when present in the background, will lead to product differentiation. The level of product differentiation is not preordained. In some cases, market participants have a great deal to do with determining how much differentiation there will be and what form it will take.

Product differentiation, more than any other element of structure, is affected by conditions on the demand side of the market. Characteristics of buyers—where they live, what their tastes are, and how much they know about rival products and the sellers who supply them—are extremely important. They determine the extent, if any, of the attachment of the buyer to his or her chosen supplier. They determine whether or not the firm will be able to achieve some degree of independence from rivals by differentiating its product.

Are demand conditions alone sufficient to explain the existence of product differentiation? No. It is also necessary that certain supply conditions, such as transportation costs and economies of scale in production, are present and are part of the structure of the market as well.

Location and Product Differentiation

Why is location important? It is important because it affects access: (1) the access of any one buyer to various potential suppliers, and (2) the access of any one seller to various potential customers. It is interesting to note that the model of perfect competition is defined without any spatial dimension. It implies that all buyers and all sellers share a common location. But is that realistic? It is only in the exceptional case, when special care has been taken to *organize* a market in a manner such as the Chicago Board of Trade or the New York Stock Exchange. More often, however, buyers and sellers are widely scattered. Why?

Location is ultimately a general equilibrium phenomenon. The population settles where there are economic opportunities to support it, and industry settles where there is a population for it to serve. So, why doesn't all activity concentrate at one location? The answer involves land resources. Agriculture requires arable land and water for farming. Manufacturing requires raw materials for processing. Economic activity must be located where natural conditions are favorable. Indeed, even residential activity imposes certain resource requirements in order to support a comfortable existence. And, most important, nature has scattered resources unevenly. Thus, location is an adaptation to nature—land resource is the exogenous variable in the general equilibrium process determining population and industry location. So, where does this leave us in our quest to explain product differentiation in specific instances?

In order to understand how product differentiation may emerge from geographic factors in certain industries and not in others, it is necessary to establish how certain things interact: (1) the location of the population as a condition of demand, (2) the location of industry as a condition of supply, and (3) the presence of other structural factors which are significant.

Let us begin with the location pattern of the population.[1] How is the population of the United States distributed? It is very widely scattered. The population is heavily concentrated in urban areas. In 1980, there were more than 8,765 urban places with 73.7 percent of the total population, as indicated in *Table 6-1*. Two things should be noticed about this: (1) the number of urbanized areas and other urban places is large, and (2) the amount of land area in the United States is vast. The 1980 population density exceeded 5,000 persons/square mile in the largest urbanized areas such as New York and Los Angeles, but was only

TABLE 6.1   RESIDENTIAL DISTRIBUTION OF POPULATION: UNITED STATES, 1980

TYPE OF LOCATION	NUMBER OF PLACES	PERCENT OF POPULATION
All Urban	8,765	73.7%
Inside Urbanized Areas		
Central Cities	(431)	(29.6)
Urban Fringe	(4,507)	(31.8)
Outside Urbanized Areas	(3,827)	(12.3)
All Rural	13,764	26.3

Source: Census of Population, 1980, Population and Land Area of Urbanized Areas for the United States and Puerto Rico: 1980 and 1970, p. 31.

[1]It is reasonable to apply partial equilibrium analysis to this problem since it may be assumed that location of any one industry will not substantially affect the location of the population.

63 persons/square mile for the nation as a whole. Thus, there were a few large urban clusters but many more of a modest size, and there was a great deal of *empty* space in between.

Now consider the location of industry. In some cases, strong centralizing tendencies may be observed. Why is this? Certain industries are notably **resource-based**. That is, location of activity is determined by the location of critical raw materials used to produce the product. The steel industry concentrated around the Great Lakes region because rich deposits of iron ore were discovered in the Mesabi Range in the period of time just preceding the explosion in steel, a big part of the twentieth century industrial development of the United States. The aluminum industry concentrated in the Pacific Northwest because great surpluses of cheap hydroelectric power, necessary for the aluminum reduction process, were developed in the period just preceding the expansion in aluminum brought on by World War II. However, our present interest is in those industries where location is widely scattered. These are the **market-based** industries. That is, location of activity is determined by the location of the buyers for the product. Here, industrial location conforms to the pattern set by population. The distributive trades are obvious in their market-based orientation. So are certain industries which make consumer goods. For example, newspaper publishing, flour milling, and brewing are (or were) all examples of this effect. (At this time, we shall ignore the multiplant firm.)

We have shown that population is scattered, and that certain industrial location patterns adapt to the population. That is, we have provided an explanation for the emergence of geographic markets, such as those observed earlier in this chapter in the case of home heating oil. We must still account for locational product differentiation. What more is involved?

Consider the influence of certain structural factors which can and sometimes do limit the number of suppliers in any market—economies of scale and barriers to entry. Economies of scale can be the critical factor in determining the number of suppliers who can serve the local market. Natural monopoly is not that uncommon in a spatially differentiated market—one newspaper, one bakery, one dairy, one sand and gravel operation, and so on, may serve the community. Of course, the regulated public utility is the classic case of a local natural monopoly. On a wider geographic scale, a single cement plant or one fertilizer factory may supply an entire region, due also to the effect of scale economies. Moreover, entry barriers can be significant in limiting suppliers. Control by one firm over the supply of a critical natural resource is more likely to occur in the small area than it is for the nation as a whole. Once again, the regulated public utility provides the perfect example, given its exclusive legal franchise to serve the public convenience and necessity.

Is such a local monopoly complete? In cases other than the public utility, there may be competitors for the local monopolist. They would necessarily be at a disadvantage. Transportation costs are a factor with which the more distant competitor must contend.[2] So, what is the effect? How strong is product differentiation based upon location?

Spatial differentiation can be illustrated with the help of a model such as the one shown in Figure 6.1. Three factors are crucial in this analysis: (1) the location of the consumer or group of consumers, as indicated by point A, (2) the location of suppliers, as indicated by the points S1 and S2, and (3) the existence of transportation costs for shipping the product from the seller's location to that of the buyer, as indicated by the isocost curves encircling A. For ordinary consumer goods, such shipping costs are more likely to be incurred when the buyer travels to the seller's location to complete a transaction, but the effect is the same as any other transportation cost. The more distant supplier is at a disadvantage relative to the nearer, *ceteris paribus*, and the wider the distance between them, the greater the disadvantage. Let us consider an example.

Assume that S1 and S2 are two cement plants, producing an identical product at an identical cost. Suppose that cement can be produced at either site for an average total cost (including a normal return on investment) of $5.00 per cwt. Assume that the transportation cost for shipping cement from the factory to the consumer at point A is equal to $0.50 per cwt. for every isocost line crossed. Thus, the costs of delivering cement to a buyer located at point A are as follows: (1) $5.50 for S1, including transportation costs of $.50, and (2) $6.50 for S2, including costs of shipping of $1.50. What is the implication of this fact? The implication is that product differentiation will be very strong. First, the consumer located at point A will be a loyal customer of S1, other things being equal. Second, the supplier (S1) can exercise a significant degree of independence from the competition (S2) when pricing in the market at point A. S1 can expect to raise price by as much as 20 percent (i.e., one dollar out of five above the competitive F.O.B. price) and still enjoy the loyalty of buyers at point A. How about the

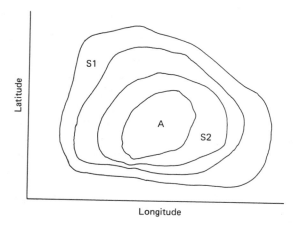

Figure 6-1 Differentiation can be explained by location and the cost of transportation necessary to supply the buyer. A buyer at point A chooses between sellers at S1 and S2. Since costs increase with distance, A chooses to buy from S1 as the cheaper alternative.

[2]In fact, the pattern of market-based location for certain industries is the result of transportation costs.

second supplier? Independence and attachment runs both ways. The cement plant at S2 will enjoy the advantage when selling to customers located in its **sphere of influence**. In fact, the location of S2—as with the location of S1—is based upon the existence of a regional market for the plant to serve, as well as the existence of transportation costs.

Product differentiation is very easy to understand in the case of location. The relationship between location of the buyer and access to the seller is obvious. Is this true of other types of differentiation?

Tastes and Product Differentiation

Why are tastes important? The answer lies in the fact that differences in taste call for differences in product design. Since not all consumers want the same thing, not all products will be the same. When there are different products to choose from, the consumer will choose the one which most closely corresponds to his or her ideal. Moreover, if the design of that product happens to be unique to one firm, the consumer will **bond** to the firm. The supplier of the differentiated product will have a *local* monopoly. The implications are similar to spatial differentiation. In fact, the design of a particular product may be imagined to describe the location of the firm which supplies it and the taste for such a design may be thought of in terms of the location of the consumer who demands it. What determines consumer tastes?

Consumer desires for certain product designs (consumer tastes) and producer actions to supply them are undoubtedly interdependent. Which comes first? Or is it possible to answer such a question? It is certainly reasonable to argue that there is a general rule: sellers offer, buyers respond. Do producers really dictate to consumers? Are consumers at the mercy of their suppliers? No. First, consumers do exercise independent judgment about producers offerings; they often reject them. Second, there are some powerful forces, largely independent of any one seller, which often appear to be responsible for shaping the tastes of the consumer. Some are physiological. For example, a craving for sweets or an allergy to wool will condition the tastes of an individual. Some forces are social. For example, in 1984, writers began to notice the emergence of the "Yuppie". The *Baby Boom* generation had traded in one conformity for another. The antiestablishment style of the early 1970s had been replaced by the proestablishment style of the 1980s. Finally, some forces involve the complex psychology of the individual. What one believes is beautiful, exciting, or comfortable is highly individual. How much importance one attaches to each of these characteristics is really a matter of individual taste.

Thus, the products which are appealing to consumers are more likely to be a response to their tastes than to be a determinant of them. There appear to be major exceptions—those cases in which *style* changes are introduced to stimulate a demand for the product. The annual model changes of the automobile are an obvious case in point. Even in this case, however, it must be noted that some firms, those which we might identify after the fact as the *style leaders*, are successful in their efforts, but others may fail.

The traditional approach in economics to consumer tastes involves an application of Gestalt psychology. That is, the consumer prefers Product X to Product Y. It is an approach which provides no insight as to the source of the preference: Why does the consumer choose one rather than the other? Another approach has emerged in an effort to provide answers to this and other questions. Lancaster[3] introduced the concept that a product is demanded by the consumer because of the attributes contained in it. There is an advantage to the Lancastrian method for our present purposes. We can describe the distribution of consumer tastes in terms of product attributes; we can maintain and expand upon the spatial analogy.

Let us consider an example of a popular consumer product, the soft drink, as described in Table 6-2 below. The product design alternatives may be described by identifying the important product attributes. Table 6-2 lists five illustrative attributes of soft drinks: flavor, sweetener, caffeine, package, and brand. Also indicated are some of the variations available for each attribute. For some products, design variations may be discrete and limited in number, but for others, variations in an attribute may be virtually continuous. In any case, the pattern of consumer tastes could be described by filling in such a table as this with the appropriate percentage of product sales. The effect is to map the apparent distribution of tastes, as revealed in the behavior of consumers towards specific attributes. This corresponds to the population distribution described above in our consideration of locational differentiation.

TABLE 6.2 DISTRIBUTION OF PRODUCT ATTRIBUTES: AN ILLUSTRATION
USING THE SOFT DRINK MARKET

| ATTRIBUTE | VARIATION | | | |
	#1	#2	#3	#4
Flavor	cola	lemon-lime	fruit flavor	. . .
Sweetener	sugar	artificial	——	——
Caffeine	yes	no	——	——
Package	12 oz. can	16 oz. bot.	. . .	. . .
Brand	Pepsi	7up	Crush	. . .

How is the industry organized relative to this pattern, where tastes are distributed in favor of different attributes? Does each firm maintain multiple positions, offering a wide range of product designs and serving different consumers? Or is each location in the market served by a local monopolist? Do the differences in taste support product differentiation? Or do they merely result in a situation similar to the one we described for the market in home heating oil?

[3]Kelvin Lancaster, "A New Approach to Consumer Theory," *Journal of Political Economy* 74 (April 1966), pp. 132–157.

Product design differentiation is a stable condition only when there are market factors present which prevent rivals from supplying the same product design. In principle, each design could become the homogeneous product around which a competitive market is organized, provided there were enough sellers. What prevents this?

We return again to basic conditions and market structure. We would look for economies of scale and barriers to entry that apply to the production of a single product design. Let us first consider scale. Is there a natural monopoly in the production of a single product design? Perhaps, but it does seem much less likely than in the case of spatial differentiation. Why? It is a matter of flexibility in operations. To illustrate, compare the options of supplying different product designs with those of serving different locations. Let us assume that a soft drink bottling plant is located in Phoenix. As long as the plant stays in its present location it cannot feasibly compete in Denver—the transportation costs are too great. With some difficulty and given sufficient time, the entire operation could be moved to Denver. The plant could serve one market or the other, but not both. What about product design mobility? The same Phoenix soft drink plant can be transformed from bottling a sugar-free, caffeine-free, orange drink to bottling a sugared, caffeine-rich cola in a matter of minutes. The lesson would seem to be the following one: If the market is large enough to support different firms supplying different product designs, it may be large enough to support competition if each firm could divide its time and resources among several product designs, like the soft drink plant.

Barriers to entry are more likely to be a factor. Legal constraints are important in protecting product design. Consider the effect of product branding. Brand names are unique and are protected by law from trademark infringement. Brand loyalty may be important. In the case of soft drinks, market shares of the leading brands are abnormally large and extremely stable. An even stronger form of protection may be afforded to the supplier of a product which is patented. The seller of a patented product has a legal right to exclude competition from the market for a period of seventeen years. In terms of our present discussion, the patent holder may have a product design so unique that several valuable attributes contained in it can be found in no other product. In that case, production differentiation—that is the degree of attachment of consumers to a particular product and the degree of independence of the supplier in pricing it—may be extremely high. Are the legal protections of trademarks and patents the only factors which are distinctive to the barriers in product design? No.

Barriers to entry are also associated with the various time lags which prevent rivals from immediately copying the product design of a successful competitor or improving on it. Consider what happened to the U.S. automobile industry in the period following the 1974 oil embargo. The American public suddenly became energy conscious, the fuel consumption characteristics of the automobile suddenly became an important attribute, and U.S. automakers soon lost ground in the market. Did American industry rebound quickly to adversity?

No, it clearly did not. Why was this? The production of any specific car design requires specific tools and dies, and the switch from the production of full-size cars to sub-compacts requires a complete transformation—from the basic platform and body shell to the engine and transmission. To complicate matters, Detroit had not prepared itself for completely redesigning and reengineering the American car—and the tools and dies to produce it—to meet radically different design requirements. As a result, a large share of the market was lost to foreign competitors, producers who were better located to satisfy the change in tastes. In spite of their vast resources, the giant U.S. automakers could not easily overcome the barriers associated with changes in product design.

Differentiation based upon product design differences can be illustrated with the help of a model such as the one shown below in Figure 6-2. The analysis shown here is derived from two basic assumptions: (1) the consumer's tastes are taken to be given and are reflected in terms of the *ideal* product, point A in the attribute space, and in terms of the iso-utility lines which encircle A, and (2) the product offerings of competing firms are taken to be given and are represented by the points S1 and S2 in the product space. What are the implications of the model? When there exists a product such as S1, which more closely fits the consumer's tastes than any other available in the market, the consumer will become attached to it, *ceteris paribus*. Such an attachment would be revealed to the observer, including the seller at S1, through the loyalty of the customer. Such an attachment would permit the seller of S1 to charge a premium for it over and above the price of S2 and still retain the custom of the buyer at A. Why is this? It is the result of the fact that substituting one product (S2) for another (S1) involves a cost to the consumer in terms of utility. The iso-utility lines shown in Figure 6-2 describe psychic costs which, like transportation costs, isolate the consumer from less desired product locations.

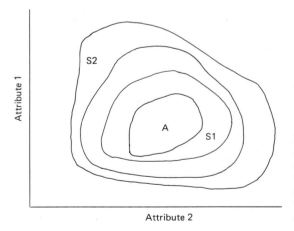

Figure 6-2 Differentiation can be explained by product characteristics and consumer tastes. **Location** in the product space is defined for a buyer at A. Since utility decreases with distance, A will choose to buy from S1 as the preferred alternative.

For all the insight into consumer behavior provided by the Lancastrian approach, it does leave us with some unanswered questions. What are we to make of the one attribute which seems to be different from all the rest, the product brand? The brand or trademark often appears to symbolize *quality* in a fashion which seems to serve either of two purposes: (1) to elevate the status of the buyer as in the case of conspicuous consumption goods or (2) to reassure the buyer as in the case of prescription drugs. When the brand is a status symbol, it is like any other product attribute which yields utility. When the product brand serves as a proxy for quality in the latter sense, this implies that other product attributes are not known or do not provide sufficient information upon which to base a judgment of the product or do not matter. In these instances, the product brand seems to symbolize the product design in some general way, rather than being a specific ingredient in it or component of it. In these instances, treating the brand as an attribute seems to trivialize the basic theory rather than to confirm it. What does the brand really represent? It may be evidence of information failure.

Information and Product Differentiation

If the brand conveys information to the consumer, we must attempt to understand why it is so. Let us first consider the model of perfect competition. In it, complete information is presumed. We assume that the buyer is fully apprised of the existence of every seller and of the composition of every product, and as a result, every seller is compelled to supply the best quality product possible at the lowest possible price. There is no reason nor room for product brands. But is that realistic? No. In virtually every market situation, information is an economic good. That is, it is scarce and it is costly to acquire. Are buyers in all markets equally ill-informed? No. Thus, there are some interesting questions to answer: Under what conditions is the lack of information most likely to be a significant element in the market structure? How will it affect behavior?

Lack of information is a basic condition of demand. It is more likely to be a factor in markets for consumer goods than for producer goods. Why is this? In the first place, when there is an information problem in the market for producer goods, when information is scarce but is critical to efficient operation of the firm, the firm may respond by becoming its own supplier. In Chapter 2 we described how Winchester Repeating Arms replaced inside contracting with integration. This is not an economic option for the consumer. Specialization and scale economies have eliminated self-sufficiency in the modern economy, as economists have argued since Adam Smith. Moreover, the consumer faces a much more daunting task than the firm. There are so many more goods to purchase and so much less in resources and expertise to apply to purchasing them. In fact, we might reverse the assumptions of the model of perfect competition and consider the following one: in a state of nature, each consumer would be randomly assigned to a unique and isolated location, knowing nothing about the products available in the market nor the producers who supply them. Are we then forced to assume that the task of the consumer is hopeless?

The consumer is neither condemned to a perpetual state of perfect ignorance nor is he/she likely to attain a state of perfect knowledge. It may be presumed that the consumer will seek to gain more information. Stigler[4] and Nelson[3] contributed to the development of a theory of information which they applied to consumer behavior. That is, they each developed some of the elements in a theory of consumer self-sufficiency for the supply of information. Stigler examined the implications of an economic search procedure. That is, a process by which the consumer obtains information about a product and evaluates it prior to purchase. For example, when a consumer buys a stereo system, it is possible to acquire a great deal of information by shopping around. The product is one which lends itself to such an effort since many of the product features and performance specifications may be discovered in a search which may include reading through reviews and product comparisons in magazines, and listening to various competing systems in dealer showrooms. In fact, this is a case in which the product can be judged reasonably well by the attributes contained in it.[5]

Nelson amended search theory to allow for experience. That is, a process by which the consumer obtains information about a product and is able to evaluate it by the consumption experience itself. For example, when a consumer buys a box of breakfast cereal, it is nearly impossible to gather information through the standard search procedure. Nor is it worth the effort. The price of a single box is relatively small, and it will soon be used up. If the consumer does not like it very much, there is no great loss. Therefore, the product is one which lends itself to experience—buy the product, try it, and form a personal judgment on it.

How does search theory apply to product differentiation? What, if anything, does it reveal about product brands and the information which they represent? We might employ a model, such as the one shown in Figure 6-3, to illustrate the search process. Let us assume that the consumer is initially located at point A, with no knowledge about any of the products in the market. Let us assume further, that the process of gathering knowledge—either by search or experience—can be summarized by the series of isocost curves which are shown

---

[4]George J. Stigler, "The Economics of Information," *Journal of Political Economy* 69 (June 1961), pp. 213–225.

[5]It is possible to take a narrower view of search, one which would not include products such as a stereo as a "search good" on grounds that product durability cannot be ascertained prior to purchase. That is, it might be argued that search does not provide full information. This view suggests that a stereo or an automobile or any similar product is an "experience good". It has merit, but the counterview has merit as well. It is a logically sound proposition that the information search, if it is based upon the large samples used for and the expert opinions embodied in product ratings to be found in publications such as *Consumer Reports*, can predict product durability better than personal experience.

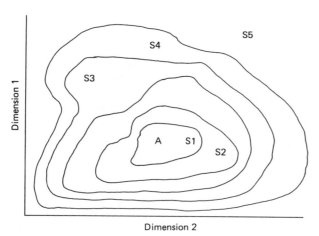

Figure 6-3 Differentiation can be explained by information, or the lack of it. **Location** in the space is defined relative to ability of A to obtain information about different products. Since search costs increase with distance, A will choose to buy from an S1 or S2 rather than an S4 or S5.

to encircle A. Finally, let us assume that each product location (S1, S2, . . .) is taken to represent the fact that the consumer located at A could acquire relevant knowledge about the corresponding product—the very existence of the product and its supplier, the price of the product, the product attributes contained in it, and so on—at an expenditure indicated by the isocost curves radiating out from point A.

The model suggests that the consumer is able to choose how far to extend the boundary of his or her information; the consumer may acquire knowledge about a greater number of products by a greater expenditure in the search for information. The consumer who is knowledgeable about more goods is likely to make better consumption decisions—eliminating the overpriced goods and the products of inferior quality which have been identified in his or her sampling experience. The consumer must decide how much to sacrifice to obtain a better command of product information. For example, if the consumer at A places a very high value on time, he or she may halt the search after becoming informed about only the first product, S1. In contrast, if the consumer places a very high value on information, he or she may continue the search to S5, or beyond. However, decision on the scope of the search need not be *a priori*. The consumer may decide to devote more effort to the search once it has begun if it proves to be productive. The first few discoveries might reveal a substantial spread in price or a significant variation in quality. On the other hand, the initial search may yield just the opposite. It might turn up little or no difference and thus encourage the consumer to cut short the process.

Is it reasonable to assume that the initial conditions—the location of the consumer (A) relative to the locations of specific products (S1 and S2, for example)—are independent of the behavior of suppliers? No. The supplier may achieve prominence in the market by advertising its product and establishing brand-name recognition for it. What do we mean by prominence? What does it mean in terms of our model? It means that the average cost to the consumer to discover the well-known brand may be assumed to be lower than the cost for obtaining information about other goods. It also means that the best-known brand occupies the prime location in the market—that of S1—in the information space for more buyers than any other brand. Is this important? Yes, it certainly can be. Consumers may exercise their own judgments about the quality of the name-brand. If they are more apt to try it than any other brand and if it is a product that is comparable, it is reasonable to presume that the product with the familiar name will capture an abnormally large share of the market.

If one firm can reap dividends from developing brand-name familiarity in a market where information is scarce, will all firms attempt to do so? Not necessarily. Some firms sell no name products, basing the appeal of their product on a lower price. In fact, much of retail or local advertising is designed to announce the lower price of a particular dealer or a particular no name item. In such instances, the dealer helps the consumer tremendously in his or her search for information. On the other hand, some firms may sell inferior unbranded or misbranded goods, exploiting the consumer's lack of information. They are the "fly-by-night" operators who enter a market, sell a bargain product or service, and exit quickly before the buyer comes to realize that he or she has been taken.

What can we conclude from all this? First, the consumers' lack of information leads directly to a form of differentiation. The consumer may develop an attachment to a particular seller out of ignorance. Price differences may exist in such a market, in spite of the absence of any real product differences. For example, videotape rental stores operate only blocks apart with price differentials as great as 100 percent, comparing the least with the most expensive. This is a case with obvious similarity to a natural form of spatial differentiation. Second, suppliers may alter the natural differentiation in such a market with the information they supply to consumers. In some cases, they supply objective data, such as information on the price and product attributes of their goods. This normally occurs in the market for **search goods**. In other cases, the information they supply is subjective, attempting to create a favorable image for themselves. This normally occurs in markets for **experience goods**.

Finally, let us ask two questions: Do the efforts to brand and advertise a product serve only the interests of the seller? Do these efforts serve to increase the level of product differentiation? The answer to the first question is no. When the seller advertises prices or other *search* information, the answer is obvious. Merely branding the product can assist the consumer. In a market in which there is both an absence of information and the presence of variation in product design and product quality, the brand can be important. At the very least, it provides an important adjunct to the experience process. When the consumer has personally experienced several products and found that one seems to suit his or her tastes better than any other product sampled, the brand name permits the consumer to exploit this information. Even prior to experience, it does indicate that the product will meet certain standards of quality, having been tested and found acceptable by others. How important is this? It is not unusual to find studies which show that many consumers cannot identify a favorite brand of beer, cola, or cigarettes in a blind test. Of course, the same studies do show that some can. Some individuals simply have a more acute sense of taste or smell than others, and the trademark can be an aid in getting more satisfaction from consumption.

There is no adequate way to answer the second question. Without advertising or branding, there is a lack of information, and there is a natural level of differentiation. When sellers advertise or brand their products, it will change things. It is quite likely to provide some rational order to the search and experience activity of consumers and to produce some improvement in information. It is certain to produce some artificial differentiation, which *bonds* the consumer to a particular supplier. Finally, the change may even produce a net improvement in efficiency—increasing profits for the successful firm and increasing utility for the consumer. How can we interpret this. Does the introduction of advertising result in more differentiation or in less?

STABILITY AND CHANGE IN PRODUCT DIFFERENTIATION

Is the level of product differentiation a permanent feature of the market? As we have indicated, existence of product differentiation depends first upon a presence of certain basic conditions affecting demand—either the dispersion of the population, or a wide variation in consumer tastes, or a general lack of information about products and suppliers. It also depends upon the direct and conscious actions of sellers—to locate in patterns which serve spatially separated markets, to manufacture different product designs which appeal to different tastes, or to brand and advertise them which alters information available to consumers—in order to establish the pattern of product differentiation with which we are familiar. Since differentiation is derived from market conditions in demand and supply, it can change when they do. How could this happen? There are several possibilities.

We have noted above that product differentiation of any sort must be protected by scale economies or other barriers to entry, limiting the number of suppliers and making the differentiated product unique to one of them. In some cases, exogenous change occurs removing the barrier which limits entry. Thus, growth in local population could eliminate a regional monopoly. A change in the technology of production or transportation could produce the same result. The former could permit smaller local firms to enter the market, and the latter could permit interregional imports to compete. The passage of time may be the crucial factor. Patent protection—in some cases, the best protection against competitive manufacture of a firm's own product design—is specifically intended to lapse after seventeen years. Time may be all that is necessary for rivals to develop substitutes for a specific product design. Time may be helped along by other factors. The incentive to **clone** a product is stronger when it is one which is especially profitable for the incumbent local monopolist.

Finally, barriers that have been artificially created by the firms enjoying them can be undone by others. We seem to think that the *images* of established firms are invulnerable to competitive assault. That is not always the case. In the network television market, the epitome of the experience good, CBS and NBC were the only major firms until 1953. The entrance of ABC was regarded by virtually every expert as a foolhardy venture. The "Big Two" were certain the new network would never sign a sufficient number of local affiliates to survive, and even if it did, viewers would largely ignore its "minor league" programming. The veteran networks were not far off in their assessment of the difficulty which their new competitor would face. However, by 1978, ABC had not only reached parity with its older rivals, it had taken over the largest share of the American television audience.

What do we make of this? We must keep in mind the fact that differentiation is not static. In fact, many of the forces which ultimately give rise to differentiation are dynamic by their very nature. In Section III of this text, which is devoted to market conduct, we shall take up the subjects of product design, product research and development, and product promotion. There, we shall see how the competitive strategy of the firm seeks to alter market structure and to provide the firm with advantages relative to its competitors and even relative to the process of competition itself. At this point, however, it is enough to note that market structure can change over time and that the behavior of firms can bring it about.

MARKET EFFECTS OF PRODUCT DIFFERENTIATION

What are the effects of product differentiation? How can we best depict them? We must begin with the realization that product differentiation is a characteristic of demand. And the important effects of differentiation can be illustrated with the aid of demand curves. How? Let us assume that the demands for products can be expressed as functions of prices, with income and with all those demand factors which differentiate products—location, tastes, and information—taken as given. Let us assume that the set of differentiated products is fixed. Now, consider the two cases which follow.

Vertical Product Differentiation

Vertical differentiation describes a market situation in which the products vary in quality, or at least are perceived to do so, and which vary in price accordingly. We may analyze the process by considering the demand curve (D1) for a differentiated product, such as that shown in Figure 6-4. Note that price of the product is expressed in relative terms. Price is shown as an index number, which compares the price of a single product to the *standard* or average price of goods in the market. If the total revenues for all brands is R, and if the number of units sold by all firms is equal to M, the average price is R/M, and the index number

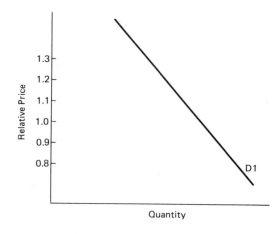

Figure 6-4 Product differentiation may provide the seller the power to control price. The demand curve D1 demonstrates this dimension of product differentiation; a high quality brand may command a price significantly higher than the average for the market.

for such a price will be set equal to 1.0. The price of an *upscale* product, such as that shown in Figure 6-4, will be some multiple of R/M and its relative price will be indexed accordingly.

Earlier in this chapter, we noted some examples of vertical differentiation. In the case of prescription drugs, we observed that a large price spread between the brand name drug and its generic equivalent is common. Differentiation in pharmaceuticals could be illustrated by a demand curve, such as D1 in Figure 6-4, which shows that significant quantities of the good are demanded at prices far in excess of P1 = 1.0. The demand curve indicates several things: (1) its general position indicates how consumers value the particular product design (or location or image), (2) the gradient or slope of the demand curve indicates how strongly attached the consumers are to the particular product, and (3) the **elasticity of demand**—functionally related to its gradient—indicates how much market power the seller has over price.

The vertically differentiated market is easy to identify by the hierarchy of products which are to be found in it. The sellers of the most highly prized or upscale products in such a market would appear to possess a high degree of market power. Are they highly profitable? Not necessarily. That depends upon the costs as well as upon demand. Differences in product value may be greater than, equal to, or less than differences in cost. Recall the example of the Aston-Martin Lagonda, which sells for nearly thirty times the price of the Chevette. It is not surprising, however, to find that Aston-Martin has had a long history of losing money manufacturing the world's most expensive and exotic production cars. There are very few buyers who are willing and able to pay the price for such a costly car, and so it is difficult to cover all the fixed costs of producing it. Even so, the example is instructive about the significance of vertical product differentiation.

In markets for homogeneous goods, it is necessary to supply a product at a cost low enough to be able to survive. For this reason, scale economies and barriers to entry may be extremely important in determining the structure of the market and deciding who is a factor in the market and who is not. In markets for vertically differentiated goods, the survival of the individual firm is based on its own ability to market a product the public will accept. If enough buyers place a high enough value on it, the seller will succeed. In that sense, Aston-Martin has been a success, although just barely most of the time.

Vertical differentiation in pharmaceuticals illustrates the extremes of competitive success. The strongly differentiated brand-name drug is often a big profit-maker. The generic drug is usually not. While it costs substantially more to promote, it often costs about the same to manufacture, and a brand-name drug will normally yield the firm which makes it significantly higher returns than will a generic equivalent. Why? It would appear that value is increased by more than cost in differentiating them. In this sense, Parke-Davis has been more successful than Aston-Martin has been in differentiation.

Does the comparison of a firm such as Parke-Davis in the prescription drug industry with a firm such as Aston-Martin in autos reveal another side to differentiation? Why can P-D sell enough products to cover more than its costs of differentiation while A-M cannot? Let us consider **horizontal differentiation**.

Horizontal Product Differentiation

Horizontal differentiation describes a market situation in which products differ in popularity—quality is not the issue in this case. The differentiated product contains, or at least is perceived to contain, unique product attributes. The image of a popular product can be a very important attribute in such a market. The degree of differentiation is indicated by the breadth of a product's appeal, not the depth of the consumer's attachment to it. We may analyze the process by considering the demand curve (D1) for a leading brand, such as that shown in Figure 6-5. Note that quantity of the product is expressed in relative terms. Quantity is shown as an index number, which compares the quantity of a single brand to the standard for the average brand in the market. If the total sales for all

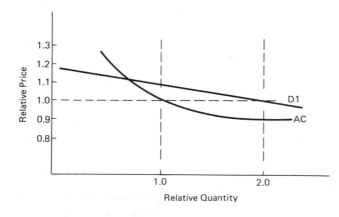

Figure 6-5 Product differentiation may provide the seller the power to control its market share. The demand curve D1 demonstrates this dimension of product differentiation; a popular brand may hold a significantly larger share than the average for the market.

brands in the market is Q, and if the number of brands in the market is N, the average brand will sell Q/N, and the index number for such a quantity will equal 1.0. Thus, the leading brand in the market will sell some multiple of Q/N and its relative quantity will be indexed accordingly.

What are the implications of horizontal differentiation? Does the leading brand have market power? We have drawn the demand curve (D1) with a very shallow gradiant. We have presumed that the firm has only a weak ability to control price. This is clearly different from the case of vertical differentiation. Does this mean that horizontal differentiation does not count? No. The leading brand has a strong market position—we have assumed that the leader sells more than twice the quantity of the average brand in the market when all prices are equal, i.e., when the leader's relative price is equal to 1.0. Market position may be a source of substantial profit if costs are favorable. How may this be explained when the leading firm commands no premium price?

Recall the discussion in Chapter 4 on the cost advantages of the large firm. We observed that certain costs, including the costs for advertising and for product design and development, are **fixed costs**. To differentiate its product, the firm must make a certain commitment to product development or promotion. The successful firm—the one which sells a large quantity of goods compared to its rivals—will be able to spread such costs over a large number of units. To illustrate the point, we observed that General Motors—the leading U.S. automaker—has enjoyed advertising cost advantages over its smaller rivals, ranging from $100 to $470 per unit.

The GM experience may be demonstrated with Figure 6-5. In our figure we show a declining cost curve (AC) as a function of the index of quantity. Let us assume that if Q1 = 1.0, the firm will break even. If the firm supplies the leading brand, it will make a substantial profit. Thus, horizontal differentiation may yield extra profits, due not to higher prices but rather to lower costs. Market position may be just as profitable as market power.

Is the model shown in Figure 6-5 meaningful? Does it illustrate an important aspect of differentiation? There are numerous markets for consumer goods, from the simple goods such as soft drinks to complex goods such as autos, where firms compete in horizontally differentiated markets. For example, Coke and Pepsi sell for the same price as 7up and Dr. Pepper, but the market shares of the former brands are two to three times the market shares of the latter. If the leaders could get a premium price, it certainly seems that they would. Instead, they exploit their market positions via a larger price/cost spread than that which is enjoyed by rivals.

Is a leading market position always a profitable one? Not necessarily. It is possible that a strong market position does not come cheap. It appears that the Cola wars of the 1980s have been costly to sellers in the soft drink industry; profits have suffered as the result of intense competition between Coke and Pepsi for market leadership. In fact, a leading position in a market may be tenuous if there is little upon which to base differentiation. Images which are created artificially can be destroyed by the same means. Challengers are forever reminding the public that their products "are just as good as #1", and possibly they speak the truth.

Are the two cases of vertical and horizontal differentiation so completely separate that a product is either one or the other? No, but it would seem that experience goods are more likely to fall into the latter category, while search goods are more likely to fit the former. Yet there are exceptions. Recall the position of Clorox bleach, as it was described in Chapter 4 above. When Procter & Gamble sought to acquire the firm and its brand-name, Clorox held the loyalty of half the consumers in the market and commanded a premium price as well. Here is a case of a good—an experience good at that—which enjoys the benefits of both horizontal and vertical differentiation.

MEASUREMENT OF PRODUCT DIFFERENTIATION

Product differentiation is an attribute of market structure which is widely regarded as more important than any other, with the exception of concentration. In spite of this, much less is known about the effect of product differentiation on the market than is known about concentration. There has been much less research done on product differentiation than on concentration. Why? The most obvious answer is that measurement is more of a problem with product differentiation. Why should that be? There are two factors involved. First, there is no published summary statistic for product differentiation which is comparable to the concentration ratio. Second, there are far more problems inherent in measuring differentiation than concentration.

Differentiation is a matter that involves the status of the individual product—a particular brand or product design or dealer location—rather than the status of the market (or the industry) as a whole. For example, the market for prescription drugs contains both brand-name drugs, which are differentiated, and generic drugs, which are not. This is a source of real difficulty. It means that there are conceptual problems which have to be dealt with in order to analyze the differentiated market. One solution is to deal with individual products as separate markets, while the other is to develop a meaningful form of aggregation to deal with the entire market. There are serious operational problems as well. Getting price and quantity data on individual products is a serious problem—it may be manageable for a case study of a single market, but it could prove to be virtually impossible for a cross-sectional study of markets in general.

Putting aside the problems of data for the moment, what are the measures of differentiation? How are they related to the theoretical aspects of differentiation to which we have devoted much of this chapter?

Measures of Seller Independence

The measures of seller independence gauge the degree to which the supplier of a particular product or brand is able to control its price. What is involved in this? It is an aspect of vertical differentiation. The measurement of it is quite straightforward. Consider two measures—the price elasticity of demand and the relative price index. These are illustrated, in Table 6-3 below, for the market for regular, ground coffee—an inexpensive, nondurable consumer good.

TABLE 6.3 MEASURES OF DIFFERENTIATION FOR FIVE
BRANDS OF REGULAR COFFEE: APRIL 1954 – MARCH 1957

BRAND	PRICE ELASTICITY	RELATIVE PRICE
A	−2.32	1.072
B	−4.60	1.037
C	−0.21	1.050
D	−4.23	1.044
E	−1.63	0.897

Source: Lester G. Telser, "The Demand for Branded
Goods as Estimated from Consumer Panel Data,"
Review of Economics and Statistics (August 1962), p. 321.

From the information provided above on price elasticity, it would appear that only the seller of Brand C is in the position to exploit—or perhaps, to further exploit—the independence to control price. With such an inelastic demand (−0.21), the price of Brand C could be increased while total sales would be slightly affected. In relative terms, quantity would fall only by one fifth as much as the rise in price, with the result that total revenues would rise dramatically. By contrast, the sellers of Brands B and D would appear to have little power over price since the estimated elasticity of demand for their products is so high.

From the information in Table 6-3 on relative prices, it would appear that there is little vertical differentiation in the market for regular coffee—the highest price brand sells for a modest seven percent premium over the average for the market, while the lowest price brand sells at a ten percent discount.

Are the findings made in the Telser[6] study representative? Is there so little vertical differentiation in most markets for consumer goods? We may not be able to know. It is difficult to generalize because there is so little direct information. Telser based his study on data acquired from a market research firm. In principle, this could be done for many markets, but access to such data is so limited that it is not practical to do so—the costs of proprietary data are very high and the constraints placed upon its use are very severe. However, casual observation seems to suggest that differentiation is much higher in other markets. At various points in the preceding chapter, we have suggested that there are substantial price spreads to be found in automobiles, prescription drugs, and videotape rentals. These are only a few cases in which significant differences in design, information, and/or location appear to be present, and they may be taken to indicate that vertical differentiation is often much greater than that which Telser found in regular coffee.

[6]Phillip Nelson, "Information and Consumer Behavior," *Journal of Political Economy* 78 (April 1970), pp. 311–329.

Measures of Buyer Attachment

The measures of buyer attachment gauge the degree to which the consumer is *bonded* to a particular product design or brand (and to the seller of it). What is involved? It is one aspect of horizontal differentiation. Ideally, we would like to have information based upon the behavior of individual consumers and to measure loyalty in terms of the probability that the individual routinely repeats the purchase of a product. Is that practical? No. Continuous observation over an extended period of time for a large sample of consumers would be required to gather the necessary data. Are there alternatives which are more feasible. Consider the measures of attachment, indicated in Tables 6-4 and 6-5 below, for the market in instant coffee.

In Table 6-4, we illustrate one facet of buyer attachment—the stability of consumer loyalty. Over a period of five years, the ranking of brands of instant coffee changed somewhat. A brand which was in fifth place in 1978, had risen to second place by 1982, and a brand which had been in second place in 1978, had fallen to fourth by 1982. In a larger sense, however, there was substantial stability in the market. The six top brands in 1978 were the six top brands in 1982. In the market for coffee, it is interesting to find evidence that horizontal differentiation may be important, even if the market power we associate with vertical differentiation is missing.

TABLE 6.4   MEASURES OF DIFFERENTIATION FOR SIX LEADING BRANDS OF INSTANT COFFEE: RANKINGS IN 1978 AND 1982

BRAND	1978 RANK	1982 RANK
Maxwell House	1	1
Taster's Choice 100% Coffee	2	4
Sanka	3	3
Nescafe Regular	4	6
Folger's	5	2
Taster's Choice Decaffeinated	6	5

Source: Advertising Age (May 9, 1983), p. 82.

In Table 6-5 below, we illustrate another facet of consumer loyalty—the popularity of certain products or brands. In this instance, we compare the top sixteen brands of instant coffee in terms of the relative quantity which each sold in 1982. The leading brand sold four times as much as the average of the top sixteen brands. It also sold twice as much as the second place brand. At the other extreme, the four least-selling brands taken together sold less than one average brand. Is this important? It certainly may be. If a brand is able to establish a position in which it commands the loyalty of a large segment of the market, it indicates that the seller has a strong competitive advantage.

Another aspect of differentiation can be seen in the fact that three firms, the leading producers of instant coffee, supply an average of five brands each. This proliferation of brands is evidence of the strength of the leading firms. That is, the leader may increase its market share and its market position by introducing new products. It is also evidence of the dynamic aspect of differentiated markets. That is, there is a gradual turnover of products and product images in such a market. This is a matter which we shall develop presently in Section III.

TABLE 6.5 MEASURE OF DIFFERENTIATION FOR SIXTEEN LEADING BRANDS OF INSTANT COFFEE: INDEX OF RELATIVE QUANTITY, 1982

BRAND (AND MANUFACTURER)	QUANTITY INDEX
General Foods	
Maxwell House	4.05
Maxim	0.57
Sanka	1.86
Yuban	0.23
Freeze Dried Sanka	0.44
Brim	0.76
Mellow Roast	0.18
Proctor & Gamble	
Folger's	2.03
High Point	0.97
Nestle	
Nescafe Regular	1.24
Nescafe Decaffeinated	0.37
Taster's Choice 100% Coffee	1.68
Decaf	0.09
Taster's Choice Decaffeinated	1.27
Sunrise	0.18
Borden	
Kava	0.18

Source: Derived from information contained in *Advertising Age* (May 9, 1983), p. 82.

Are the implications of Table 6-5 general ones? Is it common to find that certain products will enjoy the loyalty of a larger number of buyers than their rivals? Or is the market for instant coffee an aberration? While it is often dangerous to generalize, casual observation seems to suggest that horizontal differentiation of the type seen here is rather common in markets for both consumer and producer goods. We have repeatedly stated that differentiation stems from a variety of causes—product design, dealer location, and product image. Perhaps, it is more likely than not that products will differ in their ability to appeal widely. For reasons both real and perceived, some will do better than others. When they do, a measure of buyer attachment will indicate it clearly.

TABLE 6.6 MEASURE OF DIFFERENTIATION FOR EIGHT CONSUMER
GOODS INDUSTRIES: 1967

CODE	INDUSTRY DESCRIPTION	ADVERTISING/SALES (PERCENT)
2043	Cereal Preparations	18.43
2086	Soft Drinks	4.83
2251	Women's Hosiery	1.01
2771	Greeting Cards	0.34
2844	Toilet Preparations	28.77
3651	Radios and Television Sets	3.74
3751	Motorcycles, Bicycles	2.68
3911	Jewelry	1.06

Source: Stanley I. Ornstein, *Industrial Concentration and Advertising Intensity* (American Enterprise Institute for Public Policy Research: Washington, 1977), pp. 81–82.

Now let us consider one final question. Does it appear that the measures of seller independence and buyer attachment provide a useful index of differentiation? They show the effect of differentiation well—they reveal the character of product differentiation. However, their weakness is one of application—it may not always be possible to obtain the data necessary for estimating the seller's market power or the buyer's loyalty. So, what can be done?

Measures of Seller Effort to Differentiate

Differentiation is a natural phenomenon to the extent that differences in location and tastes and a lack of information all contribute to the Balkanization of the market. There is an artificial side to it as well—sites are developed, products are designed, and images are created. It is unfortunate, but there is often a tendency in discussions of differentiation to emphasize the latter to the exclusion of the former. Is that a problem? Not necessarily. It seems that such an emphasis, coupled with the obvious difficulties of indexing the effects of seller independence or buyer dependence, had led to the almost exclusive reliance on indexing artificial differentiation. What are these measures? Consider advertising intensities, as shown in Table 6-6.

What does Table 6-6 show? It shows that advertising effort does vary widely between one market and another. The ratio of advertising expenditures to total sales revenues ranged from almost 30 percent to less than one half of one percent for the selected industries shown above. It indicates that there is a substantial difference between types of products in the degree to which advertising affects the *information* available to the consumer and the product imaging which is associated with it. It also indicates that there is a wide variation between markets (or industries) in the degree to which competitive effort is channeled into advertising. But does it show the differences in the degree of product differentiation?

Advertising intensity measures only *one* aspect of differentiation.[7] What does the extremely high level of advertising intensity indicate? Does it show strength in the differentiation of the product, or does it show weakness? Most likely it shows that, in cases such as cereals or toiletries, differentiation is highly artificial and that heavy doses of advertising are needed to create and maintain the image which the seller seeks for its product.

Despite its obvious limitations, advertising intensity is used more as an index of differentiation than any other measure. Why is this? Two things are involved. First, a good deal of research attempts to compare large cross-sections of industry. As a result, there is less concern with measuring the relative strength of different product designs or brands and more concern with measuring the **aggregate differentiation** of whole markets or industries. Second, the data are relatively easy to obtain—operational considerations are very important.

Finally, we might ask: How strong is advertising intensity in the U.S. economy? The answer is, that it is rather modest overall. Ornstein[8] calculates the average ratio of advertising expenditures to sales to have been 1.7 percent in 1967, with a substantial difference between consumer and producer goods industries. The former averaged 3.8 percent, while the latter averaged 0.9 percent. It would seem, therefore, that the forms of differentiation which are associated with image and derived from advertising are more prevalent among consumer goods. Does this mean that producer goods are less differentiated? Not necessarily. The answer to that question would require more knowledge than we have about differentiation; it would require solving the many problems of measurement.

PRODUCT DIFFERENTIATION AND OLIGOPOLY

Product differentiation is recognized as a major attribute of market structure. Certainly the definition of monopolistic competition is dependent upon it. Differentiation gives the seller who is more or less directly in competition with many others the ability to price independently. At least in the short-run, differentiation may be regarded as a source of market power for the monopolistic competitor. What about the case of oligopoly? What are the implications of differentiation for behavior in a market in which there are only a few competitors?

[7]We might assume that transportation intensity could measure the tendency towards spatial differentiation, and R&D intensity could measure the tendency towards differentiation based upon innovation and product design, in the manner that Comanor and Wilson or that Orr have done in measuring entry barriers, as we indicated in Chapter 4. If it were possible, an overall index of product differentiation might be used to aggregate all the expenditures which are directly or indirectly comparable to advertising.

[8]Phillip I. Ornstein, *Industrial Concentration and Advertising Intensity* (American Enterprise Institute: Washington, 1977) p. 60.

In the preceding chapter on concentration we dealt briefly with the issue of oligopoly. We noted that concentration is a cause of interdependence among competitors and a reason for the firm to anticipate rival reactions and to take them into account whenever it initiates a price change. As the result, the presence of concentration can raise the level of competitive tension. However, if product differentiation is mixed in, tension may fall. Why is this? The pricing independence which may accompany product differentiation is an obvious answer. Differentiation, where it is strong enough, simply gives each firm some room in which to operate. That is, the firm may be able to adjust its price without significant effect on a competitor and, therefore, without triggering a retaliatory response. In the pharmaceutical industry, for example, each brand name drug occupies a unique niche in the market. The manufacturer of each drug enjoys a limited monopoly in it.

Product differentiation may soften the edge of price competition, without replacing it with monopoly. In the first place, given the existence of differentiation, competition need not be limited to pricing. Secondly, differentiation may directly or indirectly affect oligopoly price behavior.

In the pharmaceutical industry, for example, competition takes the form of product development and product promotion. Research and development plays a substantial part in competition among drug firms. It is also costly. Many chemical substances are screened to discover if they have potential and most are rejected. Those which have promise must be subjected to lengthy testing for their effectivenes and safety in use. And those which pass all the preliminary tests must apply to the Federal Drug Administration for approval for general distribution and use. The legal monopoly attached to the patent on a new "miracle" drug may be so valuable that the firm is willing to invest a great deal of money and time in order to win the race with the competition. However, the costs of research and development pale in comparison with the expenditure made on advertising and promotion. In 1958, it was reported that 22 of the largest drug manufacturers spend 6.3 percent of sales revenues on R&D while they spent 24.8 percent on product promotion.[9] The drug firms advertise heavily in medical publications, but their greatest promotional costs are incurred in the direct contacts between their representatives and physicians. The practice is known as **detailing**.

In the pharmaceutical market there are a great number of products, but they do not compete nose to nose. In fact, the market may be made up of layers of products, some brand name and some generic, so that vertical differentiation is a major characteristic of the structure. In such an environment, pricing is not likely to be seen as the significant competitive factor. Survival is more a matter of successfully developing acceptable products (or acceptance of them) than a matter of successfully controlling costs and seeing that price is high enough to cover them. In such an environment, pricing tension is not so likely to occur, whether

---

[9]U.S. Subcommittee on Antitrust and Monopoly, *Report on Administered Prices: Drugs* (Washington: U.S. Government Printing Office, 1961), p. 31.

the market is concentrated or not. Also, costs are not likely to form a barrier to entry and to raise the level of concentration.

In the automobile market, product differentiation has a much different implication for oligopoly behavior. As we noted in the previous chapter, the auto industry has been characterized by a form of oligopoly price behavior known as price leadership, and in particular, a type of price leadership in which the dominant firm in the market may more or less dictate the price. How is product differentiation related to this phenomenon? In the past, General Motors enjoyed a position of price leadership due to its widespread success in *selling* its brands and models to the public. GM had won such a large market share and such strong brand loyalty that it was able to establish the general level and structure of prices from the top to the bottom of the market for domestic cars.

In the automobile market, horizontal differentiation is one of the chief characteristics of structure. Each manufacturer has an established share of the market which is more or less stable from one year to the next, barring major product changes. The manufacturer with the largest market share has an advantage over the competition, *ceteris paribus*. So, does this mean that the other automakers have no say in pricing? No. Again, the effect of product differentiation can be seen. Each make and model is unique to a certain degree, and may be priced with some degree of discretion. Indeed, nearly every year, each automaker will normally make minor adjustments in prices to the dealer according to changes in its supply and demand conditions. During the recession which hit the industry hard during 1981-1982, Chrysler and Ford—normally the followers in the market—were the instigators of significant price cuts in the form of rebates paid directly to buyers.

Finally, we might take note of a particular form of market differentiation which has implications for oligopoly pricing. In markets for homogeneous industrial goods, we might expect that price uniformity would necessarily exist and that, if the market is concentrated, oligopolistic tension would be extremely high. Is that always the case? No, it is not. In certain markets, such as steel, the buyer and seller meet directly and may agree to a price for a particular transaction which deviates from the manufacturer's list price. Because the transaction is hidden, prices charged by other firms and involved in other transactions are not directly threatened. In this case, differentiation of a sort—each transaction can be isolated—may support both real price competition and nominal adherence to the oligopoly price.

There is much more to say about the relationship between product differentiation and market behavior, but we shall wait until later to elaborate on it. Parts III and IV focus upon various aspects of market behavior including pricing, product design, product development, and advertising. Here, we merely seek to establish that certain relationships exist between product differentiation and conduct and to begin to suggest how they work.

MARKET STRUCTURE AND PERFORMANCE

7

In this chapter we examine the relationship between market structure and performance. Starting with a simple comparison of three industries, we are introduced to the sort of data commonly used in industrial organization (IO) studies. Next, we see that the typical IO study seeks to establish a statistical relationship between measures of market structure—concentration, barriers to entry, and product differentiation—and measures of market performance. While efficiency and economic progress are the most obvious dimensions of performance, we have had to rely instead on something more observable; profitability is readily available and has been most widely used as the measure of performance. We see, however, that it is far from perfect. On the one hand, monopoly profits would be an indication of inefficiency, but on the other, profits resulting from a cost-saving innovation would be just the reverse.

Next, we survey the form and content of a few IO studies in order to better understand the field. We examine some early work on the concentration-profitability relationship and some of the extensions with additional structural variables to explain the performance. We examine certain later work which uses firm market share position, rather than concentration, as the key explanatory variable.

Following the chapter is an appendix with a brief account of the use of regression analysis for the estimation and testing of structure-performance hypotheses. Finally, we review a sampling of industrial organization studies just to get the flavor of the technique.

We have developed some understanding of market structure—that is, barriers to entry, scale economies, concentration, and product differentiation. Why should we have been so concerned about it? One answer is that structure is interesting all by itself, that structure tends to vary from market to market (or from industry to industry), and that structure reflects some important differences between them in terms of the underlying conditions or prevailing behavior. Another answer is that structure is interesting as a determinant of performance. What exactly do we mean? What is market performance? How is it determined by market structure? In this chapter, we attempt to deal with such questions. In doing so, we must be able to answer certain others: How can performance be measured? How can the structure-performance relationship be explained? Finally, what proof is there of the existence of a relationship between market structure and performance? The field of industrial organization has produced a great deal of research on these questions. We shall attempt to summarize some of it here. Before we begin in earnest, let us consider three abbreviated case studies of market (or industry) structure and performance.

THREE CONTEMPORARY INDUSTRIES

Let us consider three industries which have certain similar structural attributes, as well as certain differences, but which have exhibited very different performance characteristics during the period of the seventies and eighties. We will examine each of these three industries—steel, computers, and prescription drugs—in turn. First, let us summarize the present status of each with attributes which can be measured, as shown in Table 7-1 below.

TABLE 7.1 AN ILLUSTRATION OF THREE INDUSTRIES

CHARACTERISTIC	STEEL	COMPUTERS	DRUGS
Concentration, 1982 (CR$_4$)[a]	42	44	26
Advertising/Sales, 1982 (Percent)[b]	—	0.2	1.9
R&D/Sales, 1981 (Percent)[c]	0.6	6.4	5.3
Profits, 1975–1984 (Percent)[d]	2.8	21.1	16.7

Sources:
[a] *1982 Census of Manufacturers.*
[b] *Advertising Age Yearbook, 1984*, p. 85., for IBM (computers) and Pfizer (pharmaceuticals), from the 100 largest U.S. advertisers.
[c] "R&D Scoreboard, 1981," *Business Week* (July 5, 1982), pp. 55–74.
[d] Fortune 500, 1976–1985, for US Steel, IBM, and Pfizer, averaged over ten-year period.

Steel was the heart of American industrial might at the turn of the century. It was at the center of the early merger movement which created the firms which were dominant, at least for a time, in many industries and which increased concentration levels in many markets. From the time of its formation, US Steel dominated the steel industry, and together with the other major producers, it set the example for pricing, modernization, and other aspects of conduct. For more than twenty years, US Steel controlled roughly half the production capacity for the nation. In 1906, US Steel built the largest and most modern steel plant in the world, located in Gary, Indiana. In 1907, the firm sponsored the **Gary dinners**, designed to coordinate price among the members of the industry. While the *dinners* were abandoned to defend against an antitrust suit, US Steel continued to play its role as the price leader for the industry, always setting an example of output restraint in order to control price. Did conditions remain the same? No.

The market structure in steel was different in 1982, than it had been eighty years earlier—it was much less concentrated than before. "Big Steel" was much less profitable than it had once been. So, can we take this to mean that the structure had *improved* and that performance had too? No. In fact, they reflect just the opposite. Low profits reflect the high costs of the steel giants. The diminished levels of concentration are the result of a failure of "Big Steel" to compete. Why did it come to this?

Adams and Mueller[1] blame the leading firms in the American steel industry for failing to keep up with modern technology. What is the evidence of this failure? Two new processes—the basic oxygen furnace and continuous casting—were developed in Europe and were adopted most rapidly in Japan. The U.S. firms lagged behind both Europe and Japan in modernization and, as a result, lost heavily to foreign competition—U.S. exports of steel diminished tremendously and foreign steel began to pour into the domestic market. Finally, when Big Steel lost the ability to control price via price leadership, its profits fell. Did the entire American steel industry suffer? No, it did not. Some firms were able to adopt new technology and were able to compete profitably under the new market conditions, but they represent the relatively smaller firms or **mini-mills**. What is the lesson of the steel industry? The behavior of "Big Steel" exposed it to outside competition, both foreign and domestic—the failure to compete in price seemed to spill over into the failure to innovate as well. That failure ultimately led to the loss of its ability to control price.

The computer industry is much younger—it really began in the early fifties. It is an industry created by technology, and as often happens, the pioneers dominated the market for a period of time. The Univac Division of Remington Rand built the first commerical computer, but it faced strong competition from IBM. The latter successfully branched out from the manufacture and servicing of data processing equipment for business—a market in which IBM had been well positioned—to capture the lion's share of the market in computers. For nearly two decades, IBM held a near monopoly in **mainframe** computers, but wholesale changes in the market have occurred more recently: (1) in the mainframe segment of the market, compatible components of various manufacturers could be purchased separately and linked together by the buyer to form a system, (2) substantial growth occurred in those segments of the market for minicomputers and microcomputers, and (3) the opportunity for new entry into small and specialized segments of the industry has led to a population of hundreds of firms. As indicated in Table 7-1, the level of concentration in the electronic computer industry (SIC 35731) has fallen dramatically.

So, how do we assess the computer industry? There are now a few larger firms—although IBM is still in a class by itself—and a great number of smaller firms. In fact, IBM's market position is still such that it yields a greater than

[1]Walter Adams and Hans Mueller, "The Steel Industry," *The Structure of American Industry*, ed. by Walter Adams (MacMillan: New York, 7th ed., 1986), pp. 74–125.

normal profit. It is not a perfectly competitive market. How well does it perform? Brock[2] suggests that its performance is good. Technological change has been rapid, as indicated by the data in Table 7-1. Research and development activity is high in the computer industry. Price competition has been responsible for dramatic price reductions in the market. Rivals, new and old, have forced IBM to cut prices and to innovate in order to maintain its position of leadership. IBM, for its part, has been a far more aggressive force in the market than US Steel had been, for example. It is no mere coincidence that the United States has maintained its position of leadership in the world market for computers, in sharp contrast to steel. What about IBM's supracompetitive profit levels? "Big Blue" appears to enjoy a position of vertical differentiation—a public perception of superior quality which allows IBM to sell its products at a premium in spite of competition from many lower-priced **clones**. The structure of the market for computers has its imperfections—both concentration and differentiation. It performs rather well, however, given the dynamic character of competition.

The third industry, ethical drugs, is younger than steel but older than computers. As a specialized branch of the chemical industry, it is more than a century old. Yet in its present form, the pharmaceutical industry is less than half that age. Until the discovery and widespread use of the "miracle drugs"—sulfa in the 1930s and penicillin in the 1940s—the industry supplied medical-grade chemicals to the pharmacist, who prepared the compounds and dosages prescribed by the physician. The wartime exigencies encountered in World War II created a need for the manufacture and supply of preparations, ready to administer in life-threatening situations under the worst of conditions. The efficacy of the miracle drugs proved the value of research and development to doctor and patient alike. When the war ended, the pharmaceutical houses had discovered a new way of doing business, one which emphasized technology in developing new drugs and quality control in marketing existing drugs. The firms began the use of brand names to identify and differentiate their products, as they sold ready-made compounds to the pharmacist and **detailed** (or marketed) their goods to the prescribing physician.

The levels of concentration—as can be seen in Table 7-1—are not particularly high in the pharmaceutical industry, and there are two dozen or more firms which develop, manufacture, and market branded drugs. Differentiation is so strong in many cases, that ordinary competition is nonexistent. As we saw in Chapter 6, great differences in price are frequent, even for apparently identical products, because consumers and their physicians lack information and drug firms exploit the opportunity afforded by ignorance. Differentiation—vertical and horizontal—is the only really important element of market structure in drugs. The only real barriers to entry—the brand names and patents protecting existing products and the FDA rules limiting the introduction of new products—have been created by government.

[2]Gerald W. Brock, "The Computer Industry," *loc. cit.*, pp. 239–260.

How well has the pharmaceutical industry performed? Those who have studied the industry, such as Walker[3] and Measday[4], suggest that it is both good and bad. Much good has come from the research and development efforts of the industry. And competition to discover and introduce new products is strong. However, the promotion and pricing behavior associated with branded drugs leads to excessive costs and high prices; in this respect, competition has had an adverse effect upon the consumer. How can this be seen? In spite of the fact that the major firms spend one quarter of all their revenue on promotion, their profits tend to be abnormally high. Thus, it would seem that the industry has two faces. One is progressive, the other is inefficient, and the overall performance is hard to assess.

RESEARCH ON PERFORMANCE

The case study—far more detailed than the brief sketches provided above—had been the chief staple for research in the field of industrial organization until the appearance of Bain's[5] study on the relation between profits and concentration in 1951. From that point on, however, a great deal of research took the form of the cross-section study. What is a cross-section study? It is the search for a general pattern of behavior or relationship, which is based upon the analysis of numerous cases—each market or industry is treated as a single observation in a sample taken from the population of all markets or industries. Why did the cross-section study become so popular? There are certain advantages, real and perceived, which it affords. First, it is (or at least it would seem to be) more likely to lead to the discovery of general truths than the case study. Second, it is (or at least it has the appearance of being) more objective and scientific than the case study. Third, it makes use of the econometric and other statistical techniques which were growing in popularity in economics.

The cross-section study also extracts a price. The very nature of the study creates a need for exact specification of the variables and of the relationship between them. Why should this be a problem? In the first place, there has been a tendency to focus upon a single dimension of performance. Why should this be the case? The answer is very simple. Most studies are based upon the hypothesis of a single equation: $PERF = f[STRUC]$, where the former is taken to be the dependent variable. With one equation, there can be only one dependent variable (performance), which is explained by one or more independent variables (the attributes of structure). In the second place, there is always the need to

[3]Hugh D. Walker, *Market Power and Price Levels in the Ethical Drug Industry* (Indiana University Press: Bloomington, 1971).

[4]Walter S. Measday, "The Pharmaceutical Industry," *The Structure of American Industry*, ed. by Walter Adams (Macmillan: New York, 5th ed., 1977), pp. 250–284.

[5]Joe S. Bain, "The Relation of Profit Rate to Industry Concentration: American Manufacturing, 1936–1940," *Quarterly Journal of Economics* 65 (August 1951), pp. 293–324.

adopt a specification which works. This means that the measure of performance will most likely be chosen because it is practical, rather than theoretically correct. If there is no conflict, this latter point is irrelevant. Is it?

Measurement of Performance

Beginning with Bain's paper, most cross-section studies have adopted *profitability* as *the* index of performance. The data are available to construct a variety of measures of profitability—profits as a return on equity, profits as a return on total assets, profits as a percentage of sales, and so on. Each of them has been used. An alternative, the profit margin, has also been quite widely used. The *profit margin* measures the average difference between prices and **direct costs**, where the latter includes the costs of labor and materials but excludes all **overhead** expenses—costs of research, costs of advertising, and costs of management are all bundled together with capital costs in overhead. The fact that various measures have been adopted is evidence that researchers have had misgivings about the spurious effects of factors, embedded in the ratio of profits to any given base, which have nothing to do with performance—the age (and original cost) of assets, the capital intensity, the degree to which expected profits have been capitalized into the asset base, and so on. Measurement questions aside, are profits an accurate indicator of performance? What do they indicate?

What is market performance? Performance is the description of and a judgment about how well the market works. What do we mean by this? How well for whom? As we observed in Chapter 1, the market is the creation of buyers and sellers to serve their mutual interests. Assuming that there is no external effect or spillover to alter the well-being of other members of society, the market should be judged in its own terms—market performance should measure how effectively it serves to advance the economic welfare of market participants. What are the specific dimensions of performance? There are three: efficiency, progress, and fairness. Just exactly how are they related to profitability? Let us begin with the first.

Profits and Efficiency   How do we conceive of efficiency? What does it mean? Let us assume that buyers and sellers are rational agents of their respective self-interests, which may be depicted by the demand and supply curves in Figure 7-1. The market will provide maximum allocative efficiency[6] if (1) price and output are established at the levels P_c and Q_c, respectively, and (2) producer and consumer surplus—measures of economic gain resulting from the opportunity to trade in the market—are set at the levels of X and C, respectively.

Suppose, instead, that price had been fixed at P_m. Assume that price is set by a monopolist. In that case, **producer surplus** would be larger than before—as

---

[6]Allocative efficiency is to be distinguished from efficiency in production, which refers to minimizing the cost for the quantity produced.

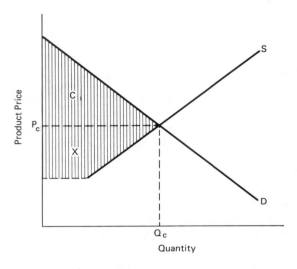

Figure 7-1 Market performance can be represented by the total benefits accruing to buyers and sellers. The competitive mechanism which sets price equal to P_c and quantity equal to Q_c yields a maximum benefit. The sum of consumer benefits C and producer benefits X is at a maximum under competitive exchange.

shown in Figure 7-1, $X_m > X$. Consumer surplus would be smaller, $C_m < C$. Most important of all, the gain enjoyed by the seller would not cover the loss suffered by consumers. Monopoly pricing implies that there will be a net loss in allocative efficiency, and the drop in efficiency will be directly attributable to monopoly.

Profits are used as an index of efficiency because we cannot observe or measure surplus. The justification for using profits is as follows: the exercise of market power by suppliers will simultaneously lessen efficiency and raise profits. The increase of producer surplus from X to X_m, as illustrated by comparing Figure 7-1 to Figure 7-2, will be directly reflected on the income statement. Thus,

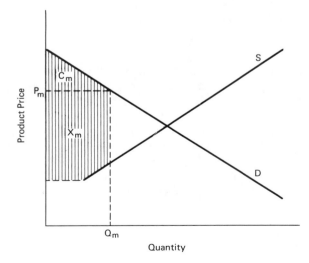

Figure 7-2 The effect of imperfect market structure on performance can be shown by the cost of monopoly. A monopolist sets price at P_m and quantity at Q_m. The seller gains by increasing its benefits from X (in Fig. 7-1) to X_m, while the buyers lose—going from C to C_m. However, monopoly gains are less than consumer losses.

high profits will be an indication of inefficiency, other things being equal. Can we count on the neutrality of other factors?

When the choice is between competition and monopoly, there is little doubt—in the example above, market demand and cost conditions were assumed constant, so that the increase in profits comes solely from the restriction of output and the manipulation of price depicted in Figure 7-2. Suppose that there are cost advantages of large scale—large firms might achieve levels of productive efficiency that smaller firms cannot and the former may be more profitable because of it. Or suppose that there are demand advantages associated with product differentiation—the consumer may derive more satisfaction buying (and consuming) a favorite product design than from buying a generic product, and the producer may derive extra profits from supplying it. Do these really represent an increase in efficiency? Yes they do. An improvement in efficiency is involved any time that a larger quantity of goods or a greater amount of utility can be squeezed out of available resources. If both the buyer and seller are better off, it would appear that efficiency has improved, even when profits are higher than under pure and perfect competition and even if some degree of monopoly attends the change.

So far we have focused upon the external environment—elements of market structure such as scale economies and product differentiation. What about the internal environment? Suppose that firms differ in terms of their organization and management. One firm may be more profitable than its competition because it is more efficient. Its organizational superiority may also lead to its attainment of a dominant position in the market, so that it becomes difficult to separate one from the other. In light of such effects, can we rely upon high profit rates—or profit margins—to signal high levels of efficiency? Under the appropriate conditions, we can.

It can be argued, however, that profitability due to lower costs or better products or better management will disappear in the face of competition. Other firms may adopt a larger scale or produce a similar (or better) product or hire away (or at least bid up the price of retaining) a good manager. In the long run, competition may tend to equalize profits (after adjusting for differences in risk) across firms and markets, only the existence of barriers to entry could reasonably be expected to halt this leveling process. What is the long run? Is it five, ten, or even twenty years? What about the fact that the leading firm may be a moving target—it too can upgrade its position? The profit-equalization hypothesis rests upon static conditions. If the market is changing, is it appropriate? Probably not.

Profits and Progress Progress is a second dimension of market performance. What do we mean by it? Progress means change in the sense of making new use of knowledge to reduce the costs of producing old products or to permit the introduction of entirely new ones. What are the implications of change? The successful innovator will enjoy, at least for a time, a level of profits which exceed the norm. The "process innovation"—a change in the way in which an existing product is produced—will lower production costs, relative to the technology which it replaces. The innovator may realize either (1) an increase in the profit per unit if prices and market shares remain the same, or (2) an increase in total profits if it cuts prices and increases its market share, exploiting its new cost advantage over rivals. The product innovation—a change in the nature of the product itself—will raise the market power of the firm. The innovator may realize an increase in profits as a direct result of either (1) a higher price if it exploits the advantage of vertical product differentiation, of (2) a greater market share if it exploits the advantage of horizontal product differentiation.

Is it always true that the innovator will profit? Of course not. Attempts to change the production process involve risk. The costs of development may exceed the gains. For example, it has so far proved to be less efficient to produce electricity using free wind or solar power than to produce it using conventional means. Attempts to change product design may not succeed either. The consumer may fail to appreciate the improvement—for example, the Edsel. On the other hand, when an innovation does succeed, when the product or process is accepted by the consumer and profitable for the seller, it would seem to constitute an improvement in efficiency.[7] As we argued above, an improvement in efficiency simply requires that a larger quantity of goods or a greater amount of utility can be produced from available resources. Does this mean that progress and efficiency are the same thing? No, not exactly. It does suggest that progress is the means to improve efficiency, notch by notch, in a nonreversible process over time.

So, where does this leave us? Is there a relationship between performance and profitability? Yes there would seem to be. At the beginning of this chapter, we examined three cases. In two of them, computers and prescription drugs, innovation is a real and positive factor in performance—average expenditures on research were greater than the norm, and profit rates enjoyed by the leading firms were greater as well. As for the third industry, the failure of the leading U.S. steel firms to adopt new technology as it developed appears to be reflected in their profits in the negative—US Steel's low profits can certainly be attributed, at least in part, to its failure to keep up with the competition, foreign and domestic. Are these few cases illustrative of anything? Do they represent a general condition or three odd exceptions? Proof may be difficult to muster, but it would seem that a good case can be made for the proposition that innovation is profitable: (1) innovation involves additional costs, (2) it also involves uncertainty, and (3) therefore, it must offer the promise of extra profit in order to induce the rational firm to invest. Reversing the case is also instructive. What happens to the firm which does not seek the opportunity to innovate? In dynamic markets, doing nothing may be a guaranteed way to lose. At least in terms of progress, high profits may be associated with superior performance.

---

[7]It may also be argued that innovation can be used strategically to limit entry and that this could negate or offset the apparent improvement resulting from the change. This is an issue to consider in Chapter 12, dealing with market conduct.

Profits and Fairness   Fairness is the third dimension of market performance. What do we mean by fairness? Normal usage in economics seems to suggest that there are two ways to judge it: one involves the process of the market and the other involves the end results. Both, however, appear to reinforce the judgment that monopoly is bad. A seller with market power has an ability, within the limits proscribed by demand, to dictate terms to the buyer, and the use of such power transfers some of the consumer surplus to the seller. The ability to exercise power, since it implies asymmetry, constitutes an unfairness of process, and the actual exercise of power implies unfairness in the results. Therefore, monopoly profits and unfairness are linked.

So, what are the implications for profits as a measure of market performance? To the extent that a high profit rate is simply due to monopoly, it is evidence of poor performance. In this respect, fairness and allocative efficiency go hand in hand. Are they the same thing? No. Fairness is a distributive notion, involving the manner in which both power and the *gains from trade* are distributed among participants in the market. Efficiency is a quantitative one, involving only the size of the gains from trade, the sum of producer and consumer surplus.

In some instances, high profits may be an indication of bad performance. In others, they may signal good performance. Without knowing the source— whether profits result from restricting output and raising price or from producing a better product at a lower cost—we cannot really say much of anything. However, it is extremely hard to avoid the conclusion that profits are just not a good comparative measure of performance, widespread practice notwithstanding.

Determination of Performance

We have discussed measurement—the measurement of scale economies and barriers to entry, of concentration, of product differentiation, and finally, of profitability. Why is this? The answer is that it reflects the emphasis to be found in much of the contemporary research in industrial organization. What is that? The industrial organization paradigm assumes that a relationship exists between the organization (the structure) of the market and the way in which the market performs. What form would we expect the relationship to take? What would it mean?

The general form of the structure-performance relationship can be written as PERF = f[STRUC]. The variables typically will include (1) a measure of profitability to represent performance and (2) one or more variables to represent structure. In most cases, the relationship is taken to be linear. The test of the relationship is based upon whether or not a correlation can be established between structure and performance. A variety of specifications and numerous samples of data have been used for this purpose. What has been the result? The result has been to show that, in a cross-section of industries or firms, there is normally some correlation between profit rates or profit margins and the industry or firm structure. These findings have led to various and sometimes conflicting claims being made about the determination of market performance. So much research has been produced, in fact, that the most we can hope to accomplish is to summarize and illustrate some of the findings and interpretations which have been generated over the years.[8]

Concentration and Profitability   The first hypothesis to be tested, and the most popular, is that profit rates or profit margins are determined by market structure. In 1951, Bain[9] published a study on the concentration-profitability hypothesis: the average profit rates for firms in concentrated markets or industries will tend to exceed those in unconcentrated ones.

What precisely were Bain's findings and what was the method used to produce them? In Table 7-2 below, we reproduce the evidence of the concentration-profitability hypothesis.

TABLE 7.2   BAIN'S STUDY OF THE JOINT DISTRIBUTION OF INDUSTRY AVERAGE PROFIT RATES AND CONCENTRATION

CONCENTRATION RANGE (BASED UPON CR_8)	NUMBER OF INDUSTRIES	AVERAGE PROFIT RATE (BASED ON INDUS. AVER.)
90 – 100.0	8	12.7
80 – 89.9	11	10.5
70 – 79.9	3	16.3
60 – 69.9	5	5.8
50 – 59.9	4	5.8
40 – 49.9	2	3.8
30 – 39.9	5	6.3
20 – 29.9	2	10.4
10 – 19.9	1	17.0
0 – 9.9	1	9.1

Source: Joe S. Bain, "Relation of Profit Rate to Industry Concentration: American Manufacturing, 1936 – 1940," *Quarterly Journal of Economics*, 65 (August 1951), p. 313.

What precisely did Bain infer from these data about the relationship between the industry average profit rate and the industry concentration ratio? First, he found that there was a rather weak correlation between them, and he concluded that any hypothesis of a linear relation of concentration to profit rates was unwarranted. Second, he observed the discontinuity in the concentration decile averages of industry average profit rates that appeared to occur at $CR_8 =$

---

[8]Most research on the structure-performance relationship has been based upon econometric techniques. In an Appendix below, we do provide a brief explanation of the estimation and testing of linear regressions of industrial organization relationships.

[9]*loc. cit.*

70. Bain calculated the simple averages for the 22 industries with $CR_8 > 70$, and for the 20 industries with $CR_8 < 70$. They turned out to be 12.1 percent and 6.9 percent, respectively. This difference proved to be statistically significant at a high level of confidence. Bain concluded that a threshold effect of concentration on profit rates appeared to separate market structure into two discrete categories: (1) those oligopoly industries with "high" levels of concentration and (2) all other industries. But what does it mean?

Several important inferences have been drawn from Bain's findings, but we might concern ourselves with just two of them. First, the relationship of concentration to profitability was presumed to be causative. That is, the level of concentration was assumed to determine the industry profit rate, other things being equal. Second, the results were taken to demonstrate the validity of oligopoly theory. Oligopoly would somehow restrict output and raise price (the high profit levels were taken as the evidence of this) by means of a process of mutual understanding or forebearance or fear. Weiss[10] later justified the proof by summarizing many of the particular theories of oligopoly which, while inconsistent with one another, predicted that oligopolists would exercise some control over prices and profits.

A great many studies have been undertaken to validate Bain's discovery of the concentration-profitability relationship. Some sought to confirm the existence of a critical threshold at which concentration took over and affected the behavior of the market. Others examined linear relationships between profitability and concentration. Typical of the latter was a paper by Miller[11], which found that there was a positive, statistically significant relationship between the two variables. Miller interpreted the results as evidence of the price-raising effect of oligopoly interdependence. So, what is the problem with this? Like so many others, Miller's linear regressions demonstrated that the relationship was weak—less than seven percent of the total interindustry variation in profit rates could be explained by the variation in concentration levels.

Many appear to have been impressed by Bain's discoveries—and by those in a number of subsequent studies which seemed to bear them out. Are they persuasive? Not necessarily. In the first place, there is a great logical leap to make from the finding that a relationship or correlation exists between two or more variables to the conclusion that it is a causative one and to the conclusion that it bears upon some particular theory of causation. In the second place, there is a need to distinguish between the hypothetical relationship one has in mind— in this case, oligopoly interdependence—and the variables used to test it. We have already expressed doubts about the meaning of the profitability measure. We might add to those, doubts about the oligopoly measure, the eight-firm

[10]Leonard W. Weiss, "The Concentration-Profits Relationship and Antitrust," in *Industrial Concentration: The New Learning*, ed. by Goldschmid, Mann, and Weston (Little, Brown and Company: Boston, 1974), pp. 184–233.

[11]Richard A. Miller, "Marginal Concentration Ratios and Industrial Profit Rates: Some Empirical Results of Oligopoly Behavior," *Southern Economic Journal* 34 (October 1967), pp. 259–267.

concentration ratio. Is there any *a priori* theory of oligopoly which states that eight-firm concentration ratios are critical? Not really.

Recall that the eight-firm concentration ratio is merely the aggregate sum of market shares for the eight largest firms in an industry. There are many different forms of oligopoly market structure where $CR_8 = 70$. At the one extreme, one firm with 50 or 60 percent of the market might dominate, while at the other, the industry could have an **egalitarian** structure in which eight or more firms each have market shares of less than 10 percent. Moreover, there are many different forms of oligopoly behavior, as we shall see in Chapter 8.

Thus, the concentration-profitability hypothesis may be an *ad hoc* interpretation of the sample of data examined by Bain, or it may be a significant implication of market structure. Can we tell which it is? No. Additional evidence must be examined to try to determine why concentration is related to profitability—if indeed, that is the general case. Much subsequent research has been undertaken with that purpose.

Market Structure and Profitability   From the outset, Bain suggested that the concentration-profitability relationship was only one in a larger complex of relationships involving market structure and performance. He was often more careful about the inferences to be drawn from his study than others who cited its results. Bain sought to explain why concentration caused high profits. Economic theory suggests that whenever profit rates are abnormally high, new entrants will be attracted to the market. Entry will increase supply relative to demand and will weaken the ability of any group to restrict output, it will lower prices and profits, and it will lessen concentration. Thus, the existence of barriers to entry may be necessary to explain the concentration-profitability relationship. To put it another way, without barriers to entry we may observe neither high profit rates nor high concentration, except in the short run as temporary conditions in a changing market.

Bain[12] produced a detailed study of entry barriers, as we described in Chapter 4. His interest extended beyond the measurement of barriers to the examination of their effect upon profitability and concentration. What did he find? In an intensive study of twenty industries for two time periods, 1936-1940 and 1947-1951, Bain found that the level of barriers to entry—he used a three-way system of classification for measuring entry, based upon "engineering estimates" of the cost or price advantages of the leading firms—was related to both concentration and profits. Significantly, he found that when entry was most difficult, concentration was always high. He found that the reverse was not true—concentration could be high even in the absence of high barriers to entry. Finally, he found that there appeared to be an interaction effect—within any barrier to entry classification, the average profit rate was higher when con-

---

[12]Joe S. Bain, *Barriers to New Competition* (Harvard University Press: Boston, 1956).

TABLE 7.3 BAIN'S STUDY OF INDUSTRY ENTRY BARRIERS AND INDUSTRY CONCENTRATION LEVELS ON THE PROFIT RATES FOR LEADING FIRMS IN AN INDUSTRY

CONCENTRATION Classification	BARRIER TO ENTRY CLASSIFICATION		
	Very High	Substantial	Moderate to Low
1936–1940			
High	19.0	10.2	10.5
Moderate	—	7.0	5.3
1947–1951			
High	19.0	14.0	15.4
Moderate	—	12.5	10.1

Source: Derived from Joe S. Bain, *Barriers to New Competition* (Harvard University Press: Cambridge, 1956), pp. 45 and 192–195.

centration was greater. In Table 7-3 above, we summarize the findings of that study.

The relationship between market structure and profitability appeared to be a rather complex one. Many sought to examine it. The study by Comanor and Wilson[13] provides a good example of research which was stimulated by Bain's pathbreaking efforts. It sought to examine the effect of various dimensions of market structure on profit rates. In particular, Comanor and Wilson sought to advance the analysis in three ways: (1) they defined specific variables—the absolute amount of capital investment and the relative scale of plant for the leading firms in an industry—to represent the technical barriers to entry, (2) they introduced advertising intensity variables—the absolute amount of advertising expenditure per firm and the relative advertising/sales ratio—to measure product differentiation, and (3) they employed the technique of multiple regression analysis to identify and isolate the specific effects of each structural variable, including concentration, on profitability. What did they find?

In a study based upon a cross-section of 41 consumer goods industries, Comanor and Wilson discovered that market structure was important. For various specifications of the structure-performance relationship, the multiple regressions could explain roughly half of the interindustry variation in profit rates. In comparison to simple linear regressions of profit rates on concentration, the improvement in explanatory power was significant. In the multiple regressions, a new discovery was made. The barrier to entry and advertising variables bore the weight of the correlation of market structure to profitability. The concentration variable, using either a threshold measure as did Bain, or a continuous index of CR_4, was not statistically significant. What could be made of this?

One inference might be that concentration did not really matter at all. This

[13]William S. Comanor and Thomas A. Wilson, "Advertising, Market Structure and Performance," *Review of Economics and Statistics* 49 (November 1967), pp. 423–440.

is inconsistent with the findings that, for the sample used, the simple correlation between concentration and profits is statistically significant. Another inference might be that concentration is correlated with other variables in the regression, and that significance tests on concentration are biased as a result. Comanor and Wilson separately tested the relationship between concentration and the two barrier to entry variables and discovered strong intercorrelation. Capital requirements and scale economies could explain 80 percent of the interindustry variation in concentration. Obviously, the relation between the structural variables themselves is stronger than that between structure and profitability. Should this be surprising? No. Industry structure deals only with the supply conditions in the market. Profitability may be affected by demand as well as supply. Thus, intrastructural relationships—particularly between concentration and those factors which are commonly presumed to account for it—might be expected to be stronger than relationships between structure and profitability.

What of the inferences about performance and structure? Comanor and Wilson felt that their study shows that barriers to entry—due to technical conditions and product differentiation (that is, advertising)—establish a position of market power and that profit rates show the effects of its exercise. Are they correct? Not necessarily. There are two problems. First, they assume that high profits are the result of high prices. It may be right, of course. Another possibility exists. High profits may be the result of low costs. Indeed, much of their argument supporting their specification of barriers to entry is based upon assumptions that scale economies yield cost savings—the large firm may have an advantage in production and promotion activities. Second, they assume that **causation** runs from the structural attributes to profitability. Are they correct? It is one thing to show that there is a relationship, but it is quite another to prove that a chain of causation exists at all, let alone that it exists in a particular form. In fact, Comanor and Wilson acknowledge that high profits could be responsible for the high levels of expenditure on advertising. In that case, is product advertising representative of structure or behavior? Is it cause or effect?

It may be well to observe that not everyone subscribes to the popular doctrine that oligopolistic market structure creates market power and results in excessive prices and profits. For example, Demsetz[14] argues that the positive correlation between concentration and profitability may be accounted for by variation in firm size—large scale firms dominate the industry profit rate averages and boost the industry concentration levels. The large scale firms may be more efficient, enjoying cost advantages including those associated with scale economies and earning higher profits as the result. Also, it may be well to observe that some of the more recent research has produced evidence that relative firm size, not industry structure, explains profitability.

---

[14]Harold Demsetz, "Two Systems of Belief About Monopoly," in Goldschmid, et al., p. 178.

Firm Position and Profitability   Using a new source of data[15], Gale and Branch[16] published a paper comparing the relative **explanatory** power—the relative correlation with profits—of firm market share and industry concentration. In 1982, Gale and Branch examined simple linear regressions of the competing explanatory variables taking profit margin to be the dependent variable. Their results showed that the firm's position in the market—its market share—was ten times as successful as the level of market concentration in explaining cross-sectional variations in profits. What does this mean? Like so many others before them, Gale and Branch did not shrink from drawing strong inferences from their own results. They declared that the market share effect on profits reflects the cost advantage of the large scale—that superior profits were due to superior efficiency. Are they correct? Perhaps, but the regression cannot prove it.

Two things should be noted about Gale and Branch's findings: First, the correlation between market share and profit margins was much stronger than between concentration and profit margins, but it accounted for only 20 percent of the variation—most of the variation in profits was unexplained. Second, the relationship between market share and profits could represent something other than cost savings; the leading firm or firms in the market could have product differentiation advantages over their rivals which permit them to charge price premiums and to earn higher profits. At the beginning of this chapter, we saw that the profitability of IBM in computers and Pfizer in pharmaceuticals seemed to be unusually high. There is a market share advantage held by the former, but is it one in which the benefits are derived only from scale economies? No, probably not. It would seem that IBM's ability to charge higher prices than its rivals for comparable products is responsible for part of its profit success. As for Pfizer, the markets for prescription drugs are so strongly segmented by differentiation, one could argue that each firm has a 100 percent share of the market for its brand name product. That is, once the physician prescribes a specific brand, there is no substitute for it. Is market share dominance a source of efficiency in scale in such a case? No. Product differentiation is responsible for the high profits and for the high market share.

The Gale and Branch findings were very important. They shed new light on the concentration-profitability hypothesis, and they are very damaging to the proposition that concentration directly and unambiguously leads to price coordination in oligopoly. They also introduce a new controversy and leave other questions unanswered.

[15]Information supplied by more than 200 firms (most included in the Fortune 500) was broken down into more than 2,000 specific businesses. The activity of individual components—specific lines of products—could be examined in competition with rival products in the context of well-defined markets, rather than in broadly-defined industries. This is the data base known as PIMS, which is the property of the Strategic Planning Institute.

[16]Bradley T. Gale and Ben S. Branch, "Concentration Versus Market Share: Which Determines Performance and What Does It Matter?" *Antitrust Bulletin* 27 (Spring 1982), pp. 83–105.

In 1983, Martin[17] published a study on the effects of firm and market structure on profitability. It was based upon **line of business data** collected by the Federal Trade Commission and was similar to the PIMS data used by Gale and Branch. That is, a *line of business* is the activity associated with a specific product line within the firm. It was a far more elaborate study. It introduced numerous variables into the analysis: (1) market structure, including concentration and market share, (2) firm structure, including the share of the line of business in the total firm activity and a measure of overall diversity for the firm, (3) advertising and other sales efforts for the line of business and for the firm and the industry, (4) scale economies, (5) research and development activities for the line of business and for the firm, and (6) demand conditions, in terms of whether the buyers were consumers, industry, government, and so on. Martin also investigated the relationship between past profits and the current market share and current firm structure. That is, he examined the possibility of causal relations which run counter to the usual structure-performance hypotheses. What were his findings? Let us consider only those which touch on matters of structure and performance which we have previously examined.

In the regression of profit margins on the other variables, Martin found that the firm's market share had a positive effect and that industry concentration had a negative effect; both were statistically significant. The finding that there was a negative relationship between concentration and profits was unexpected and difficult to explain. Martin suggested that profit margins in certain concentrated industries might have been unusually hard hit by the recession and oil shocks—as a dependent variable, profits were measured for the one year, 1975. Advertising for a line of business and for the firm was not significantly related to profitability, although the lagged industry advertising/sales ratios were. Scale economies seemed to have a significant relation to profitability. Aside from finding that concentration was negatively correlated with profitability, however, Martin's results were rather consistent with earlier studies. Some significant new discoveries were made.

In certain regressions in which profit margin was treated as one of the explanatory variables, Martin found that past profitability in a line of business has a twofold effect: (1) it tends to reduce the average firm's current market share of that line of business, and (2) it tends to raise the average firm's current share of activity devoted to that line of business. What was the significance of this finding? Martin pointed out that the regression results are consistent with the role which we normally attribute to profits in the theory of allocation—high profits attract new resources. This, in turn, implies that performance and behavior will reshape structure. The fact that the relationship involved a lagged effect of profits was all the more persuasive. This was not a matter of a simul-

---

[17]Stephen Martin, *Market, Firm, and Economic Performance* (Monograph Series in Finance and Economics, Monograph 1983-1: Published by Salomon Brothers Center for the Study of Financial Institutions, Graduate School of Business Administration of New York University).

taneous and possibly interactive correlation—high profits occurred first, then structure changed. Martin's study added to and helped to clarify some of the previous controversies. Did it resolve all of the questions? No.

Martin was far more cautious in drawing inferences from his results than some earlier researchers had been. Where some of the earlier claims had been extravagant, Martin suggested that the relationship between market share and profitability could be due either to the cost-reducing effects of larger scale or to the price-increasing effects of differentiation and the market power it affords. He did not oversell the negative relationship discovered between concentration and profit margins. The most important contribution of all may have been Martin's discovery that the relationship between structure and performance appears to run in both directions.

MARKET STRUCTURE: IN REFLECTION

The structure of the market is extremely important in the study of industrial organization, whether we are interested in the case study of a single market or a cross-sectional study of a major sector of the economy, such as manufacturing. Our theory tells us that structure is important. Our empirical research tends to bear that out, even if we must often satisfy ourselves with results which are less categorical and absolute than we would wish them to be. Structure does not answer everything. There are markets in which there are only a few rivals, but the few seem to compete fiercely. There are markets in which there seems to be no natural basis upon which to differentiate products, but competing sellers spend heavily on advertising. How can we explain such aberrations? Can we explain them at all? We can get only so much mileage out of market structure. If we are to advance further in our understanding of markets, we must expand our horizon. We must consider market conduct.

APPENDIX

Elements of Regression Analysis

What is regression analysis? There is some temptation to leave this question alone. If the reader really needs an answer to it, he or she will need more explanation than this short appendix can provide. On the other hand, yielding to that temptation would not be fair to the student who needs some help in understanding how statistical research is conducted in economics. Let us consider some of the basics.

Assume that we have a sample of twelve observations, representing a cross-section of industries, which contains information on the concentration ratio and the profit rate for each industry. Assume also that we are given a hypothesis: profits will increase with concentration. Can we test that hypothesis? If so, how would we go about it? The first thing we must do is to transform the general concept of a relationship between concentration and profits into a specific functional form. For example, let us assume that there is a simple linear relationship between the two variables, such as:

$$PR = \beta_0 + \beta_1\, CR_4, \qquad\qquad \text{(Eq. 7A-1)}$$

where PR is the profit rate, CR_4 is the four-firm industry concentration ratio, β_0 is the value of the profit rate for an industry with zero concentration, and β_1 is the slope of the relationship between profits and concentration. We can depict the sample of data and the relationship with the assistance of Figure 7A-1.

Observations for the twelve industries in the sample are plotted and are shown as twelve points in the figure. Our hypothetical regression line is drawn in position to represent the average relation between industry concentration levels and profit rates. What about the scatter of points above and below the regression line? That scatter is also significant; it reflects the fact that there are random forces, or at the very least, unidentified factors which also account for the location of the points which we have plotted. So, how does regression analysis work? Without involving ourselves in the specific details of the technique, regression analysis attempts to use simple statistical estimating procedures to get the most out of what is known. That is, to use the sample data efficiently. How is that accomplished? In layman's terms, the regression line is placed in Figure 7A-1 in a position that best represents the center of the scatter of points. Thus, estimates are made of the two parameters, β_0 and β_1, which fix the position of the regression line.

Let us assume that we have estimated the two regression line coefficients, the β's. How do we use this information to test our original hypothesis? There

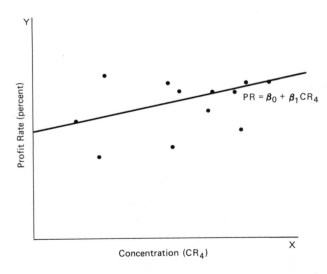

Figure 7A-1 Linear regression is the process of *fitting* a hypothetical straight-line relationship, such as $PR = \beta_0 + \beta_1 \cdot CR_4$, to a given sample of observations on profit rates PR and concentration CR_4.

are really two separate tests of the regression. One is called a test of **significance**. It provides a measure of the confidence we have that there is some relationship between the two variables. That is, that profit rates and concentration move together in some fashion, and that the regression line reflects this fact in that β_1 is shown to be either positive or negative. The other is called a test of the **goodness of fit**. It provides a measure of how closely the observations track to the estimated regression line. That is, how well the regression line explains the variations observed in the dependent variable. We will explain these two tests a little more fully—or at least illustrate their use—when we examine the first of the concentration-profit studies below.

Let us assume that our tests are positive, that they show a significant relationship between concentration and profit rates, and that profits increase with increases in concentration. Does that mean that we have proved our hypothesis? No, it does not. There are two objective statements which can properly be made: (1) the tests of the regression show that a relationship exists between concentration and profit rates, and (2) the tests of the regression fail to reject the hypothesis that concentration affects profitability. The former is obvious, but the latter needs some explanation. Formally speaking, it is *never* possible to prove that a hypothesis is correct, but it is possible to prove that it is incorrect. When the statistical results are favorable, one can go no further than to say that they are consistent with the hypothesis. Why is this? The answer is quite simple. Take the same sample of data, and reverse the hypothetical relation. That is, assume that profit rates are the cause of concentration. The new regression will be different from the first because the relationship has been inverted, but the tests of significance and goodness of fit will be exactly the same. If we were to claim that they *proved* any hypothesis, we would have a dilemma. The regression tests would have proved two competing hypotheses, and that is logically impossible.

Finally, we have described the linear regression process for the case of two variables. What about multiple regressions. That is, what about the case of several independent variables being used to explain a dependent variable? Actually the same comments apply to multiple regressions as to simple regressions. Similar techniques are used to estimate the β's—where there is one coefficient for each independent variable plus one for the intercept term—and to test their significance. There is one difference which should be noted, however. With a multiple regression, the overall relationship may prove to be significant, but some of the independent variables may fail to contribute to the explanation of the dependent variable. When that occurs, does it mean that the nonsignificant variables are uncorrelated with the dependent variable? Possibly, but not always. It could also mean that they are correlated with the dependent variable in the same way that one of the significant variables is. Recall the Comanor and Wilson study. In their multiple regressions, concentration was not statistically significant in explaining profitability, but in simple regressions, concentration was significant. They later showed that the problem was due to the correlation among several of the variables. Concentration was highly correlated with scale economies, for example, a variable which tested significant in the multiple regressions and in such a case, significance tests on individual explanatory variables are not reliable.

This is, admittedly, a very sketchy review of regression techniques. It is intended only as a guide to interpret the findings of studies cited in the preceding chapter and detailed briefly below. Let us now consider a few of the structure-performance studies in which the authors have employed regression analysis for estimation and testing of various hypotheses.

A Sample of Applications of Regression Analysis

In 1967, Miller published a study which was designed as an elaboration of Bain's concentration-profitability hypothesis. Among other regressions performed on his sample of manufacturing industries, Miller reported the following[18]:

$$PR = 3.89 + \underset{(0.010)}{0.030} \ CR_4, \text{ with } R^2 = .068 \qquad \text{(Eq. 7A-2)}$$

Here we have shown the test results, along with the estimates of the regression coefficients. The value in parentheses below the estimated coefficient for the concentration ratio variable, is used for the test of significance. In this case, the statistic shown is the value of the standard error in estimating β_1, and because the value of β_1 is three times the value of the standard error, we can conclude that β_1 is significantly different from zero. That is, the regression is statistically significant. The value for R^2 is used for testing the goodness of fit. It is a measure of the percentage of the total variation in the profit rate variable which can be explained by the regression. In this case, $R^2 = .068$, which means that 6.8 percent of the variation in profitability can be accounted for by variation in concentration. Is this unusual that so little can be explained by the regression? Not necessarily. There are so many factors which account for interindustry differences that cross-section studies often show a poor fit to a regression.

In 1967, Comanor and Wilson published their study of an expanded specification of market structure on profitability. We might illustrate one of their regressions, leaving out the insignificant variables, with the equation below[19]:

$$PR = 0.049 + \underset{(2.4)}{0.424} \ ASR + \underset{(3.0)}{0.000281} \ AKR, R^2 = .47. \text{ (Eq. 7A-3)}$$

Profit rates are regressed on two significant variables, ASR for the advertising-sales ratio, and AKR for the absolute capital requirements. Comanor and Wilson interpreted the two variables as measures of the barriers to entry (due to differentiation and technical conditions, respectively). In this case, the values

[18]Miller, *loc. cit.*, p. 262.
[19]Comanor and Wilson, *loc. cit.*, p. 431.

reported beneath the regression coefficients are the ratios of the respective β_i's to their standard errors. While both are statistically significant, the capital requirements barrier is more significant than the advertising barrier. The test of goodness of fit indicates that 47 percent of profit rate variation is explained by the regression.

In 1982, Gale and Branch published their study comparing the strength of firm market share to the market concentration in accounting for profitability. We can show the results of the two simple regressions on profit margins below[20]:

$$\text{(Eq. 7A-4) PM} = 16.6 + \underset{(0.02)}{0.10} \text{ CR}_4, \text{ R}^2 = .017, \text{ and}$$

$$\text{(Eq. 7A-4') PM} = 10.5 + \underset{(0.026)}{0.492} \text{ MS}, \text{ R}^2 = .198.$$

The dependent variable, the profit margin (PM), is more closely correlated with the market share variable (MS) in the second equation than with the concentration variable (CR_4) in the first. This is reflected in the test of significance—the values reported below the regression coefficients are the standard errors estimated for the coefficients, and while the regression coefficient for concentration is five times greater than the standard error, the regression coefficient for market share is roughly twenty times greater than its standard error. The test of goodness of fit also indicates that market share is a better explanatory variable than concentration in this sample of data.

In 1983, Martin published his study of the effects of market and firm structure and performance. We can illustrate a portion of his results by extracting from one of his regressions the estimated regression coefficients for concentration and market share as shown below[21]:

$$\text{(Eq. 7A-5) PM} = 13.1962 + \underset{(3.1213)}{9.8198} \text{ MS} - \underset{(5.9726)}{0.1145} \text{ CR}_4 + \ldots$$

In this regression, firm market share was found to be positively correlated with profit margin while industry concentration was negatively correlated. In the tests of significance, shown by the estimates of the ratios of the regression coefficients to their standard errors, concentration was more significant as a negative influence than market share was a positive influence.

Martin also demonstrated the influence of profitability on market share, using PM74 on MS75 to demonstrate that 1974 profits affected 1975 market shares. A portion of one of his regressions is shown as follows[22]:

$$\text{(Eq. 7A-6) MS75} = -0.054530 - \underset{(3.2905)}{0.000076} \text{ PM74} + \ldots$$

[20]Gale and Branch, *loc. cit.*, p. 90.
[21]Martin, *loc. cit.*, p. 54.
[22]*loc cit.*, p. 35.

In this regression, the lagged effect of 1974 profits appear to reduce the level of 1975 market share. The effect is shown to be statistically significant.

These few cases are presented to indicate the nature of research on the structure-performance relationship. That is, to provide some impression of the findings made and the techniques employed. The interested student will find that many studies have been performed and that the results have been somewhat diverse. However, they have all shown that, in some fashion or another, the relation between structure and performance is robust and interesting. Perhaps, this short presentation will also serve as a warning against reaching hard and fast conclusions about the meaning of such relationships. Empirical research can be extremely useful, but it can also be easily misused to serve to reinforce preconceptions.

OLIGOPOLY PRICING: THE THEORY

8

In this chapter we examine the meaning and implications of oligopoly. Starting with some basic definitions, we begin with a brief review of classical theories of oligopoly, and then follow with some background on modern game theory. In the course of the overall review, we discover that oligopoly market structures give rise to strategic behavior, but the possibilities are numerous. They range from peaceful coexistence at the one extreme to all-out price warfare at the other. We discover that game theory has given new life to the oligopoly equilibrium introduced by Cournot.

Next, we consider a different aspect of oligopoly strategy, pricing to deter entry of new rivals. We examine the original models of deterrence as well as more recent versions, where both explain how firms may try to exploit real or perceived advantages to maintain their position in the market and how effective they may be in their efforts.

Finally, we consider how potential entry may limit prices set by existing firms. **Contestable markets** *is the name given to markets where entry is presumed to be so free that it would keep prices in check, regardless of how few competitors there were.*

What is oligopoly? Oligopoly is a structure in which a few firms of relatively large size supply the market. In our terms, oligopoly is a concentrated market. Of what importance is such a structure? The importance of fewness (or concentration) is that it fosters interdependence in the marketplace. That is, a mutual recognition among competing firms, particularly in terms of pricing plans and actions, of the fact that one's competitive gains come at the expense of another's losses. Perhaps the best way to begin to understand the meaning of interdependence is to consider those situations in which there is none.

For the other market structures, sellers act as if they are independent and price determination is straightforward. Price is determined by an internal decision process in the monopoly market; the monopolist takes the market demand for and production costs of its product as given, and sets the price. Independence is an obvious condition of monopoly. How about competition? Price is determined by an *auction* process in the competitive market; the interaction of all buyers and sellers taken together establishes the market price. Each buyer and seller accepts it. No one seller feels the pressure or presence of rivalry in the process. To illustrate this latter point, we may note that it is not unusual, for example, for one farmer to help another build a barn or harvest a crop. Both regard themselves as competing with nature—a hostile, impersonal force—but not with one another.

In contrast, the classic oligopoly market operates in a different fashion. Suppose that the market is supplied by a few firms. Suppose that their products are either perfectly interchangeable or are differentiated only slightly. Under these conditions, two important facts emerge: (1) each firm has the responsibility for setting its own price in the sense that there is no impersonal price-setting mechanism, unlike the competitive market, and (2) each firm lacks the unilateral ability to control price in the sense that the demand for its product is seriously affected by the prices of rival products, unlike the monopolist who has no rivals. In short, the oligopolist must have a price policy (unlike the competitive firm), but the individual firm in an oligopoly market does not possess market power (unlike the monopoly firm). So, what does it mean? Under these conditions, pricing will ultimately be affected by interaction between the individual firms. Under these conditions, the firm's price plans are likely to reflect this fact.

It may be clear why oligopoly implies interdependence—the market structure dictates that to be so. Is it equally clear what style of behavior results from it? No it is not. Indeed, there is not one general theory of oligopoly. There are many special theories. Some deal with the matter of interdependence on the assumption that sellers incorporate it in their plans. Some theories deal with it on the assumption that sellers ignore it. Some deal with interdependence on the assumption that sellers accept the presence of their rivals and accomodate them in their plans. Some theories deal with it on the assumption that sellers seek to cripple or eliminate their rivals. In this chapter, we shall attempt to sort through this diversity. First, let us consider a few hypothetical examples of oligopoly interaction.

THREE HYPOTHETICAL CASES OF OLIGOPOLY PRICING

In some cases of oligopoly, the market may demonstrate a tendency towards price instability. Imagine that airline traffic on the normally busy route between Los Angeles and New York City has dropped off so that flights operated by the two competitors, Alpha Airlines (AA) and Beta Airlines (BA), are currently operating at a 50 percent *load factor*. That is, they are only half full. AA may consider that it has two preferred options: (1) cutting back in the number of flights in the hope that its passengers adjust their flight schedules rather than change their carrier, or (2) cutting price in the hope that a lower fare, whether matched by BA or not, will fill the existing flights. BA may prefer to let things stand for the present, but if AA chooses to cut its fare, BA will either match or better the offer. In this market, a single price cut by Alpha may touch off a price war. Once ignited, the war may be driven forward by a tenacious rivalry for position in the market by two firms, each of whom acts as if it expects to be able to achieve the upper hand.

In some cases of oligopoly, the market may demonstrate a tendency towards price stability. Suppose that the automobile industry has experienced a deep slump in demand so that filling orders for new cars produced by the two competitors, Alpha Motors and Beta Motors, can be accomplished by operating at no more than 50 percent of capacity. Both AM and BM may be willing to make modest price concessions to clear away excess inventories of new cars, but both firms may be willing to cut back on production in order to maintain a level of price approximately equal to the one established at the beginning of the model year. In explanation, each of the automakers may believe that a price inducement can affect the timing of a purchase, assuming that a buyer is already in the market, but that demand for automobiles is rather price inelastic on the whole. Equally important, each of the automakers may perceive that its rival has the same belief. Unlike the first case, neither firm may be perceived to challenge or threaten the position of its rival, even when it makes a price adjustment. Peace may be maintained by each firm acting as if it expects peace to be maintained.

Finally, in some cases of oligopoly, the market may show a real tendency towards dynamic instability. Suppose that the chemical industry has been dominated historically by a single seller, Alpha Chemicals. Further suppose that a barrier to entry—an absolute cost advantage associated with AC's ownershp of critical resources—is responsible for Alpha's domination of the industry. Under ordinary circumstances, Alpha Chemicals uses its market power to establish monopoly prices and to enjoy the resulting monopoly profits. However, whenever a would-be rival, a potential Beta Chemicals, threatens to enter the market, Alpha changes its pricing strategy. Alpha cuts price to a level below the costs of production of the potential entrant, exploiting the advantage of its lower costs. Even if some entrant should happen to make the mistake of ignoring Alpha's warning and should enter the industry, AC's devotion to a limit-pricing strategy would ultimately succeed in driving BC out of business in the long-run. In this case, price warfare is a crucial element in the price behavior of the market. It is the basic weapon used by Alpha Chemicals in its strategy to control the structure of the market and it will be waged by AC each time there is a threat to the *status quo*.

While these three cases describe widely different patterns of behavior, there is an important element common to all—Alpha behavior affects and, in turn, is affected by Beta behavior. The interdependence of oligopolists, like the Alphas and the Betas above, ultimately implies that pricing decisions are made in an environment of uncertainty. Each firm must take price decisions without knowing the consequences, because it does not know how its rival will react. Each realizes that a rival's reaction, whatever it turns out to be, could have a significant effect on its own position. Only in the case of limit-pricing—the case in which market has endowed the incumbent with an absolute cost advantage over all potential rivals—can any firm be presumed to know in advance how things will ultimately turn out. Even that is limited knowledge; the incumbent does not know how often it will be called upon to wage price warfare, for that depends upon the behavior of potential rivals.

CLASSICAL THEORY OF OLIGOPOLY

What exactly do we mean by oligopoly interdependence? What form does it take? How do we relate it to the behavior of the firm? Beginning with the classical theories of Cournot and Edgeworth, specific answers have been given to such questions. Over the years, efforts have been made to make oligopoly theory more realistic and precise. Nevertheless, the perfect oligopoly theory—that is, one which is applicable to all cases and is acceptable to all observers—continues to be elusive. Why is that? We have already seen a reason for it in the three hypothetical markets which we considered above. What we call oligopoly behavior is, in fact, a collection of behaviors which are shaped by expectation and strategem. This means that oligopoly, in the larger sense, is indeterminate. It has led to a multiplicity of models of oligopoly. So, how can we approach oligopoly theory? A chronological approach may work best. Let us begin with the classical theories, which contain the simplest assumptions about expectations and strategy.

Classical theory captured the essence of the interdependence we associate with oligopoly. First, the attribute of *fewness* was taken to the extreme by assuming that the market contained but two firms—formally, we call this a duopoly. Second, the attribute of rivalry was taken to the extreme by assuming that the product supplied by the two firms was perfectly homogeneous. In such a market, there can exist only one price at any given time. The demand for the product of one firm will depend upon the price charged by the other. And given market demand, price will be equal to $P = f(Q) = f(Q_\alpha + Q_\beta)$, where Q_α and Q_β are the quantities of the good sold by Alpha and Beta, respectively.

The Cournot Oligopoly Model

Cournot[1] was the first to investigate the implications of duopoly. By explicitly introducing consideration of rival behavior into the firm's decision-making process, he became the father of modern oligopoly theory. In his model, Cournot hypothesized that each seller would act on the assumption that the rival's position in the market is fixed. Each seller would, in turn, examine the rival's present position and would take the most favorable position afforded by it. As a result, the Cournot model produced a chain of moves, each of which proceeds directly from the last move made by the rival firm. If only one price can logically exist in such a market at any point in time, what dimension of the rival's position can be taken as given, and what is the nature of the firm's reaction to it?

[1]Augustin Cournot, *Researches into the Mathematical Principles of the Theory of Wealth*, translated by N. T. Bacon, (Homewood, Ill.: Irwin, 1963).

Cournot hypothesized that each seller, in its turn to move, would act in the following way: (1) it would take the rival's current quantity of goods supplied to be strictly determinate, and (2) it would choose to supply that quantity of goods which would maximize its own profits. Cournot's model of oligopoly has often been illustrated with a diagram such as the one shown in Figure 8-1. We assume that market demand is given by the linear function, FD, and that the marginal cost of producing the good is constant and equal to zero. Let us begin with the assumption that $Q_\beta = O$. Beta might be on the horizon, prepared to compete with Alpha, but has not yet made a move. As a result, Alpha chooses to supply a quantity equal to OA—exactly the same as the chosen position of a monopolist since, under the Cournot assumptions, Alpha sees itself as a monopolist—and the market price settles at the level of OB. Is the market in equilibrium at this point? No. It is Beta's turn to move. If Beta assumes that Q_α may be taken as fixed at the level OA, Beta perceives its demand to be represented by GD—that is, the total market demand less the quantity supplied by Alpha. As a result, Beta chooses to supply a quantity equal to AC—exactly the same as the chosen position of a monopolist facing a demand curve GD. Since $Q = Q_\alpha + Q_\beta = OC$, price must shift downward to the level OE.

Thus, each firm has chosen a position in the market on the basis of observing the rival's position and assuming it to be fixed. Is the market in equilibrium now? No. Alpha's decision turns out to have been made on a faulty assumption. Alpha must adjust its output to meet the new conditions and the new expectations to which they give rise. When that is done, Beta must adjust its output, since its previous decision would turn out to have been made on a faulty assumption. Assuming that it starts in a position of nonequilibrium, the Cournot model works like a perpetual-motion machine to generate round after round of

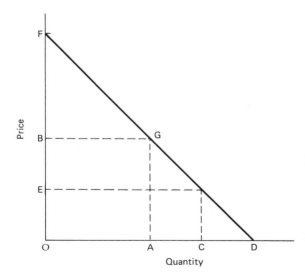

Figure 8-1 A classical oligopolist assumes that rival positions are fixed. One firm sees no competition and supplies OA, given the demand FD and zero marginal cost. A second firm enters, claims the unfilled demand GD, and supplies AC. The lack of foresight gives rise to an endless cycle of action and reaction.

adjustments in position, as each duopolist in its turn reacts to its rival's last move.

Cournot oligopoly behavior can be generalized in the following fashion: (1) each firm will take the quantity supplied (Q_r) by its rival to be given, (2) each firm will presume that its own demand is the residual ($OD - Q_r$) given by the difference between total demand and rival supply, and (3) each firm will choose to supply the profit-maximizing quantity [$\frac{1}{2}(OD - Q_r)$] derived from the residual demand. For any given starting point, we can generate the whole sequence of supply decisions for Alpha and Beta. Illustrated in Table 8-1 below is the sequence which is appropriate to the case described in Figure 8-1, the case in which Beta enters a market previously monopolized by Alpha.

TABLE 8.1 SUPPLY STRATEGIES FOR COURNOT DUOPOLY

	ALPHA		BETA	
Round	Own Demand	Own Output	Own Demand	Own Output
1	OD	1/2(OD)	1/2(OD)	1/4(OD)
2	3/4(OD)	3/8(OD)	5/8(OD)	5/16(OD)
. .	. . . .	. . . .	. . . .	. . . .
∞	2/3(OD)	1/3(OD)	2/3(OD)	1/3(OD)

So, what can be said about the Cournot model? What does it predict? How realistic does that seem to be? First, the model would eventually produce an equilibrium, provided that there is an infinite amount of time to make the infinite number of moves necessary to reach it. Second, the model is such that the equilibrium shown in Table 8-1 would be reached, regardless of the initial positions of the two rivals. The final line of Table 8-1 would apply to all Cournot strategies. Third, the properties of the equilibrium are such that duopoly peformance falls between the extremes defined by monopoly and competition—the duopoly price would exceed the competitive market price by two-thirds the amount which the monopoly price would do so.

There are certain aspects of Cournot's model which are very appealing. Most important is the fact that it demonstrates the possibility that equilibrium might be achieved under conditions of extreme interdependence, even for a noncooperative strategy. What do we mean by **noncooperation**? We mean that each firm acts independently of the other, without communication with or obligation to the other firm(s) in the market. The character of that equilibrium, in which the oligopoly price falls in between the monopoly price and the competitive price, is also important. Together these imply that, under certain conditions, oligopoly market structures can generate noncompetitive behavior without collusion. These are plausible results. The Cournot model also requires that oligopolists act in a fashion which does not seem at all plausible. What is this?

In order to reach the Cournot equilibrium, it is necessary for duopolists to act as if they never learn from past mistakes: (1) they are presumed to plan their next move on the assumption that the rival will not make a subsequent move, and (2) they are presumed to have observed an infinite sequence of moves and countermoves which would directly contradict such an assumption. Is that plausible? Not really. Is such a complaint unique to Cournot's model? Not at all.

The Bertrand-Edgeworth Oligopoly Model

After Cournot, the next formal analysis of oligopoly was undertaken by Bertrand.[2] It was Bertrand's belief that Cournot had been wrong. Bertrand objected to the fact that quantity, not price, was taken to be the principal decision variable in the model. Bertrand argued that a model of interdependence which did not feature competition in price simply lacked realism. Bertrand reformulated the model of oligopoly by replacing Cournot's behavioral hypothesis with one of his own, one in which each firm chooses its price on the assumption that the rival will maintain its present price. So Bertrand assumed, like Cournot, that the rival's position was fixed, but it was price, not quantity, that was taken to be fixed. How important was this change.

Let us assume there exists a market in which the supply of a perfectly homogeneous good is provided by two sellers, Alpha and Beta. Now if Alpha and Beta follow a noncooperative course in pricing, one of two outcomes will occur: (1) if the two rivals offer to sell at different prices, the effective price will be the lower of the two with the lower-priced firm supplying the whole market, or (2) if the two rivals offer to sell at the same price, sales would be divided equally between them. So, is there any difference between the noncooperative strategy based upon price and the one based upon quantity? Yes.

Bertrand's theory of oligopoly may be explained as follows. Suppose that two firms begin in the position where price is equal to the monopoly price, with Alpha and Beta each selling one-half the monopoly quantity. Is joint profit maximization a stable equilibrium in the Bertrand model of oligopoly behavior? No, it is not. Under Bertrand's assumptions, Alpha would be tempted to cut price whenever it assumes that Beta's price is fixed (and the same would apply to Beta). A slight price cut would marginally reduce profits in one's own share of the market, but then profits would nearly double by taking the other's share of the market as well. The Bertrand model of oligopoly leads naturally to a **cutthroat** price war. Does this mean that there is not equilibrium in the Bertrand model? No.

One competitive price cut would follow another until price is forced to the level of marginal cost. Once that position is reached, there would be no further

---

[2]Joseph Bertrand, ''Theorie mathematique de la richesse sociale,'' *Journal des Savants* (September 1883), pp. 499-508.

movement—the market would come to rest in a state of equilibrium with an outcome which is identical to that of the case of perfect competition. So, what can we make of this result? To Bertrand, the outcome resulting from non-cooperative behavior was so obviously contrary to the self-interest of the duopolists, as to ensure their cooperation. Bertrand felt that his analysis, substituting price for quantity as the decision variable, established that Cournot had developed a useless concept. It demonstrated that oligopoly was not really a meaningful market structure, distinguished from competition and monopoly. If two firms competed openly, the result would be the same as the one reached under conditions of perfect competition, and if two firms acted in concert, the result would be the same as under monopoly.

Did Bertrand's analysis succeed in eliminating the oligopoly market structure and oligopoly theory from serious consideration by economists? Obviously it did not. But it began a tradition in which numerous models of oligopoly are put forward to explain the variety of behaviors which are observed to occur when there are a few competitors. It did suggest another modification of the oligopoly model to Edgeworth.[3]

Edgeworth took the Bertrand model and inserted one change, an assumption that Alpha and Beta faced capacity limitations. In effect, Bertrand had assumed that there was so much excess capacity available that either seller was capable of supplying the entire market single-handed. Edgeworth felt that this was unrealistic and modified the model accordingly. Let us assume that the Alpha and Beta think and behave as Bertrand-duopolists. If the two firms begin from the monopoly (collusive) position, each firm stands to profit by a stategy of undercutting its rival. In this case, price cuts yield less profits than the Bertrand model. Why? Consider the position of Alpha. It may benefit at first by taking sales away from Beta by cutting price, but at some point it will be unable to engross all of Beta's market because Alpha can never sell more than its capacity to produce will permit. Thus, when price edges down and quantity edges up, Alpha will realize fewer gains by raiding the Beta market. It is possible that price could fall all the way to the competitive level, but it is possible that before price falls that far, the capacity limit effect will bring a halt to further price reductions. Yet there is more to the Edgeworth model than this slight difference.

Whenever Beta becomes committed to using its full capacity (or vice versa), it is no competitive threat to Alpha, whatever price Alpha chooses. In such a case, it is possible for two prices to coexist in the market. So, Alpha could exploit Beta's total inelasticity of supply by raising its price to the monopoly price level. The same applies to Beta.

What are the implications of all this? Edgeworth was able to demonstrate that whenever a firm prices its product on the assumption that the rival's price is fixed at some given level, it is always profitable to change price. When prices are

[3]Francis Y. Edgeworth, *Papers Relating to Political Economy*, vol. I (London: Macmillan, 1925), pp. 111-142.

at the monopoly level, rivalry will reduce them, and when prices are at the competitive level, rivalry will increase them. This sounds as if there would be no equilibrium. Indeed, that is precisely what Edgeworth concluded. Non-cooperative strategies would lead, not to a competitive equilibrium as Bertrand had suggested, but to continual oscillation in price beween monopoly at one extreme and competition at the other. In Edgeworth's analysis, oligopoly was very different from other market structures. Unlike monopoly or competition, it promised no state of equilibrium. Price would wander between the levels which are taken as benchmarks of the other market structures.

TRANSITION TO MODERN OLIGOPOLY THEORY

Classical theories of oligopoly, as different as they are, share one common attribute. Each is based upon the behavior of a firm whose perception of interdependence is asymmetric. That is, the classical theory of oligopoly failed to perceive the reflexive nature of interdependence. Each duopolist is shown to behave on the assumption that its rival will continue to do what it is doing presently. The duopolist reacts to its rival. However, the duopolist does not act as if it expects the rival to do the same. Instead, he/she acts on the assumption that a rival has no stategy at all except to stay where it is.

Does this seem reasonable? Not as a universal assumption. Under certain circumstances, the duopolist may believe that it can *one-up* its rival. The firm might, for example, be able to initiate a secret price cut. Even in that case, however, the clear implication is that the firm would not "get away with it" under other circumstances. The classical assumption seems all the more unreasonable in light of the fact that, in the models of Cournot, Bertrand, and Edgeworth, an endless chain of action and reaction proves the assumption to be unwarranted. So, what is the implication for oligopoly theory?

The strategic nature of oligopoly has been aptly compared to the contest of intellects between Sherlock Holmes, the fictional master of deductive logic, and Professor Moriarity, the fictional archcriminal and equally worthy opponent of Holmes. Each one is fully capable of developing a strategy which anticipates every move and countermove, ad infinitum. "If he does this, then I'll do that, then he'll do this, then I'll do that, ..." Unlike the classical theories of oligopoly, the model of the struggle between a Holmes and a Moriarity assumes that each contestant attributes rational behavior to his rival. As a result, it fully recognizes the bilateral nature of interdependence.

Can this be incorporated into a model of oligopoly? Consider a homogeneous product duopoly of the sort defined by Bertrand. That is, one in which competitive strategy is based upon the relative price positions of the rivals except for the following modifications: (1) assume that Alpha now expects that Beta would match any price cut which it initiated, and (2) assume that Alpha expects that Beta would refuse to match any price increase, preferring instead to capture the entire market merely by maintaining the old price. Now let us consider the demand for the Alpha-side of the market, given the existing price for Beta as P_b, as illustrated in Figure 8-2.

Our modification of the Bertrand model can be characterized by a kinked demand curve—Alpha's demand curve (ADD') shows a discontinuity at the present price and quantity (P_β, Q_α)—so that quantity demanded falls to zero for any price above P_b, and that demand is relatively price inelastic for prices below P_b. Does this make a difference in the behavior predicted for the model? Indeed it does. In this case, Alpha is willing to accept Beta's price (and vice versa). Price is stable and determinate in this model for the simple reason that it never changes. In the true Bertrand model, price is always changing, and the market reaches an equilibrium state only at the competitive price. Is this a satisfactory model of oligopoly? Not entirely.

Our modification of the Bertrand model has a very unusual property for a theory of oligopoly price determination. In the first place, the model does not explain price, but only explains why the existing price will remain unchanged. In the second place, it is an equilibrium model in which there are an infinite number of potential equilibria. The model which we have shown here was formally introduced in a slightly different form by Sweezy.[4] But the essential character of the Sweezy model has been preserved. It shares the strengths and weaknesses of the Sweezy model: (1) the model provides an oligopoly strategy which is more acceptable in form—one attributing rational behavior to the rival firm—than that which the original Bertrand model provided, but (2) the model provides an oligopoly strategy, the implications of which are not very interesting in content—one predicting preservation of the status quo in any and all circumstances.

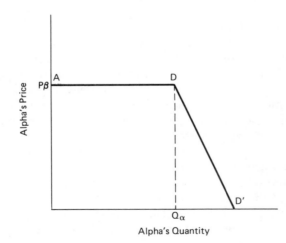

Figure 8-2   A **modern** oligopolist takes rival reactions into account. In the case of a "kinked" demand curve, the firm is immobilized by its expectations. If Alpha raises price, it expects Beta to take over the market at its old price. If Alpha cuts price, it expects Beta to protect market share by following. Since Alpha expects to lose with any change, it keeps price at $P\beta$.

[4]Paul M. Sweezy, "Demand Under Conditions of Oligopoly," *Journal of Political Economy* 76 (July/August 1939), pp. 568-573.

Where does this leave us in the evolution of oligopoly theory? Is it possible to model oligopoly in such a fashion as to incorporate rational expectations of mutual interaction and to produce results which are interesting. Or is it necessary that a model of rational oligopoly behavior degenerates into inaction?

GAME THEORY AND OLIGOPOLY

Traditional oligopoly theory had advanced the analysis of interdependence up to a point. Then, game theory was proposed as a means to finish the job. Moves planned and countermoves anticipated by competing duopolists could be fully developed as strategies in a game. The application of the mathematical theory of games to economics, accomplished in the monumental work by Von Neuman and Morgenstern[5], was designed to analyze the play of strategic contests such as those posed by oligopoly. How? What precisely is game theory?

R. G. D. Allen has provided some help in defining the basic elements, as follows:

> A *game* is the whole set of rules and procedures of play; a *play* is one particular realisation of the game, a particular application of the rules leading to a definite result. A *move* is a point in the game where the players are faced with alternatives; a *choice* is the actual alternative picked in a play of the game. Payments are made at the end of each play according to the outcome. . . .[6]

Thus, the oligopoly game may be defined by: (1) the number of players, assumed to be equal to 2 in the duopoly case, (2) the set of moves or strategies, S_i, for each player i = 1 or 2, and (3) the payoff functions, $\pi_i(S_1, S_2)$, which transform each of the possible plays into the corresponding payoff which would accrue to the ith player. Each player may be presumed to act in pursuit of its own self-interest by choosing a particular line of play (or a particular strategy) to maximize its payoff, contingent on the rival's line of play. Thus, the game may be specified to represent, as fully as one desires, the mutual interdependence of oligopoly behavior. Does this mean that the game theory approach will advance beyond the mutual inaction of the Sweezy model?

If it is assumed that the players—either a Holmes and a Moriarity or a pair of duopolists—both play full-contingent stategies which are designed to be set in motion in reaction to the play of the rival, and if it is assumed that both players act so as to maximize their own payoffs, the game may deadlock. Why? Assume that each player has devised an optimal series of moves, given an initial move by its opponent. Then, each player waits for the other to initiate the action. But neither moves. An impasse such as this makes for a dull mystery and an even duller model of duopoly. So, what can be done? The inventive mystery writer

[5]John Von Neumann and Oskar Morgenstern, *Theory of Games and Economic Behavior* (Princeton, N.J.: Princeton University Press, 1953).

[6]R. G. D. Allen, *Mathematical Economics* (New York: Macmillan, 1960), pp. 494-495.

or economic theorist will devise a means to avoid it. Von Neuman and Morgenstern did just that. They suggested that rational players, for the sake of the game, may be willing to pursue a more conservative (or less ambitious) objective as a substitute for the objective of maximum payoff.

Suppose that each player selects a line of play which will minimize the damage inflicted by its rival, regardless of the rival's line of play. The player will ensure that it achieves at least the maximum of all the minimum payoffs. Under these conditions, the logical impasse in the oligopoly game can be avoided. This is precisely the nature of the *maximin* strategy of games suggested by Von Neuman and Morgenstern. Without prior information, a player simply assumes the worst and does its best in reply. Just as Sherlock Holmes and Professor Moriarity survive their encounter in one story only to be locked up again in a later one, duopolists could assure their own survival in a noncooperative game by choosing a maximin strategy or line of play.

A Simple Game Theory Model

To demonstrate the application of game theory to a very simple case of oligopoly, let us assume that Alpha and Beta are two rival sellers, supplying a differentiated product to a market which regards them as significant, yet imperfect substitutes. Let us assume that the strategies of the two sellers, which are designated by S_α and S_β, are given by the alternative values at which each seller would be willing to price its product. Let $S_\alpha = (8, 7, 6)$ and $S_\beta = (9, 8, 7)$. Finally, let us assume that the payoff functions, $\pi_\alpha = f_\alpha(S_\alpha, S_\beta)$ and $\pi_\beta = f_\beta(S_\alpha, S_\beta)$, are given by Tables 8-2a and 8-2b. How can these payoff functions be interpreted? Let us suppose for the moment that the game has been played so

TABLE 8.2A   A SIMPLE GAME THEORY MODEL—ALPHA'S PAYOFF FUNCTION

ALPHA'S PRICE	BETA'S PRICE		
	9	8	7
8	8	6	2
7	2	3	5
6	6	4	7

TABLE 8.2B   A SIMPLE GAME THEORY MODEL—BETA'S PAYOFF FUNCTION

BETA'S PRICE	ALPHA'S PRICE		
	8	7	6
9	12	4	1
8	10	7	5
7	12	10	3

that $P_\alpha = 8$ and $P_\beta = 7$. Then, the payoffs will be as follows: (1) Alpha's profits will be 2, as shown in Table 8-2a, and (2) Beta's profits will be 12, as indicated in Table 8-2b.

Now let us consider the play of the game. Assume that Alpha employs the maximin strategy. That is, plays so as to ensure itself of the best possible result in the event that Beta should play that particular strategy most damaging to it. What is the maximin choice for Alpha? Examining the various rows in Table 8-2a, Alpha's safest move is to choose a price of 6—the worst that could happen would be a payoff equal to 4, while the payoff could be as low as 2 if Alpha should choose either of the other alternatives. How about Beta? Assume that Beta also employs the maximin strategy. Examining the various rows in Table 8-2b, Beta's safest move is to choose a price of 8—the worst that could happen to Beta would be a payoff equal to 5.

So, the game defined by the strategies and the payoffs attributed to the two players, Alpha and Beta, has a determinate outcome: $P_\alpha = 6$, $P_\beta = 8$, $\pi_\alpha = f_\alpha(6,8) = 4$, and $\pi_\beta = f_\beta(6,8) = 5$. Is the solution to the game an equilibrium? Yes it is. Consider the actual payoffs as compared to the maximin payoffs. In this case, both Alpha and Beta earned exactly their maximin returns. There were no surprises. Both firms got what they feared they would get, expecting the worst from their rivals. Since the game turned out precisely as expected for both players, it would be played in the same fashion over and over again until the rules are changed. That is, until the firms' strategies and payoffs are altered by exogeneous factors.

A Few Variations on a Simple Game

What is the nature of this game? Does noncooperation, and the play of a maximin strategy seem to affect the character of the results? To answer this question, consider what would have occurred under a strategy of cooperation. To illustrate this alternative, we have summarized the information relevant to a joint profit-maximizing strategy in Table 8-3. There we have written down the total payoffs which would result from all possible combinations of Alpha and Beta prices. If they were to cooperate, Alpha could agree to set its price equal to 8, Beta could agree to sets its price equal to 9, and the total payoff could be equal to

TABLE 8.3 A SIMPLE GAME THEORY MODEL WITH COOPERATION—JOINT PAYOFFS FOR ALPHA AND BETA

ALPHA'S PRICE	BETA'S PRICE		
	9	8	7
8	20	16	14
7	6	10	15
6	7	9	10

20, which they would have to agree to split in some fashion. With a maximin strategy, Alpha unilaterally sets its price equal to 6 and Beta unilaterally sets its price equal to 8, and the total payoff turns out to be equal to 9. It is obvious that noncooperation makes a difference, particularly when it takes the form of a maximin strategy. Indeed, maximin (or minimax) guarantees a result very unlike monopoly. On the other hand, profits and/or prices could have been lower than they turned out to be. In this sense, the model of the oligopoly game is similar to the Cournot model.

Does this mean that there will always be a game theory equilibrium? Will it always be Cournot-like? The answer to both questions is no. Consider the question of equilibrium. If we change the game only slightly, equilibrium may be impossible. To illustrate, let us alter Beta's payoff matrix by increasing the value from 3 to 6 for the cell in the bottom-right corner of the Table 8-2b. This is a substantial improvement from Beta's point of view. Beta's maximin strategy would yield a payoff of 6 rather than 5 as before, and would call for setting P_β equal to 7 instead of 8. Since in the play of the game P_α will still be 6 (Alpha's strategy is unchanged), Beta's actual payoff turns out to be the amount given by the new maximin value. Beta would not be surprised. On the other hand, Alpha would be surprised and pleasantly so, with $P_\alpha = 6$ and $P_\beta = 7$, Alpha's payoff would be equal to 7, rather than Alpha's maximin value of 4. What could be wrong with this? Very simply, this surprise could upset the state of equilibrium. Once Alpha discovers that Beta's chosen line of play does not inflict the maximum possible damage, Alpha could abandon the maximin strategy in the play of the next game. Indeed, Alpha may "shoot the moon", setting its price equal to 8 and hoping that Beta sets its price at 9—something which Beta would not do at this point, having earned its maximin payoff in the last game. If the switch in behavior by Alpha results in Beta's earning a payoff higher than the maximin in that next game, Beta may abandon its maximin strategy in the play of the one which follows. With disappointed expectations, the games may proceed with new plays developing in each round and with no equilibrium in sight.

Suppose that we have a noncooperative, equilibrium game. Is it possible to design a game which could turn out like the Bertrand model? Yes it is. Our first game was based upon the assumption that Alpha and Beta supplied differentiated products. What if we had assumed that the product was homogeneous? In that case, it is reasonable to assume that Alpha's sales would cease and its payoff could be zero whenever Beta's price were lower, and vice versa—in fact, the payoff would be negative if the high-priced firm had sustained any fixed costs. Let us assume that both Alpha and Beta limit their strategies to the set of prices, $S = (8, 7, 6)$. Let us assume that, given the market demand for the good and the costs for producing it, the payoff function for either Alpha or Beta can be represented by Table 8-4.

What is the line of play in this game? If Alpha employs the maximin strategy, it would unilaterally set its price equal to 6—Alpha is guaranteed a minimum payoff of 8 under the worst-case scenario, when $P_\alpha = P_\beta = 6$, while

TABLE 8.4 A SIMPLE GAME THEORY
MODEL WITH HOMOGENEOUS
PRODUCTS: ALPHA'S (OR BETA'S)
PAYOFF FUNCTION

ALPHA'S PRICE	BETA'S PRICE		
	8	7	6
8	10	0	0
7	18	9	0
6	16	16	8

at any higher price the payoff could be zero. Since Beta is faced with the same choice as Alpha it would make the same decision. The game would have a noncooperative equilibrium with a market price equal to 6, the minimum price allowed in the strategies considered by Alpha and Beta.

General Comments on Game Theory

Has game theory advanced the understanding of oligopoly? The application of game theory to economics has contributed an elegance and a degree of generalization that was previously lacking in oligopoly theory. This should come as no great surprise. The adaptation of game theory to economics brought some powerful tools of mathematics to bear on relatively simple and straightforward problems of conflict. Game theory models of oligopoly, unlike their more primitive antecendents, brought a realism to the way in which the conjectures of the oligopolist were represented, where the firm's pricing strategy was planned in full recognition of the mutual interdependence between itself and its rival.

For all this, game theory failed to provide that which many, perhaps unreasonably, expected of it. Why was that? There were many who sought definite answers to old questions. What market structures or levels of concentration, lead to unacceptable market performance? Which oligopolies will conduct themselves in a monopolistic fashion? Which will behave in a sufficiently competitive manner? Game theory did not answer their questions. It was not a predictive tool, nor was it ever intended to be.

Does this mean that game theory has been of little use to such applied fields in economics as industrial organization? Not necessarily. In an unexpected turn, game theory has proved to be responsible for resurrecting an interest in the Cournot model of oligopoly and some of the more useful predictions which can be derived from it.

Game Theory and the Rehabilitation of Cournot

At one level of abstraction, game theory provides the rules which define oligopoly, as illustrated by the simple examples we examined above. At another level of abstraction, game theory provides an insight into the very nature of equilibrium in the oligopoly situation, with or without providing a specification for the rules of the game. In his analysis of noncooperative games, Nash[7] observed that the requirements for the existence of an oligopoly equilibrium can be stated simply as follows: If each and every firm behaves in the way that all others expect it to behave when they planned and executed their own courses of action, the market is in equilibrium. How can this principle be applied to the Cournot model? It is very simple. When each firm simultaneously selects the output which it will place on the market, based upon the assumption that the output of all other firms is given, and when each firm's assumption is not betrayed, the market will be in equilibrium. What does this mean? While the Cournot-oligopolist may be incredibly naive—thinking that it can choose an output or a price without causing its rivals to react—when it happens to be correct, who is to argue with it?

Nash rescued Cournot's theory by making the implausibility of the Cournot strategy a dead issue. In this indirect way, game theory contributed to the development of a predictive model of oligopoly. The Nash-Cournot model can be used to derive estimates of the market price under various possible structural conditions.

Consider an oligopoly market with a homogeneous product, a fixed number of firms (N), and Cournot-type behavior. Now, if each firm selects its output (or price) on the assumption that the outputs (or prices) of all other firms are given, and if each firm's expectations are met, the market will be in equilibrium. Cowling and Waterson[8] have been able to show that the Nash equilibrium which results will have the following property:

$$[P - MC]/P = - H/\epsilon,$$

where H is the Herfindahl index of concentration and is exactly equal to 1/N when all firms are the same size (a reasonable assumption with homogeneous products) and ϵ is the elasticity of demand for the product. What does this tell us? It predicts that oligopoly price will be inversely related to the number of firms. That is, it will be directly related to concentration and to the price elasticity of demand. In order to develop some illustrative predictions, as shown in Table 8-5, let us insert some hypothetical values for the determinants of price. Assume that demand has a constant elasticity throughout. Let us assume that MC is equal to unity.

The Nash-Cournot model, with help from Cowling and Waterson, can be used to generate structure-conduct predictions which are related to oligopoly. With but a few firms and with an inelastic demand, prices are predicted to be significantly higher than MC. Do the results seem familiar? Yes, at least to a

[7]John F. Nash, Jr., "Noncooperative Games," *Annals of Mathematics:* 48 (1951) pp. 286-295.

[8]K. Cowling and M. Waterson, "Price-Cost Margins and Market Structure," *Economica* 43 (August 1976), pp. 267-274.

TABLE 8.5 PRICING IN A NASH-COURNOT OLIGOPOLY

ELASTICITY	NUMBER OF FIRMS					
	2	3	4	5	10	20
$-\frac{1}{2}$	∞	3.00	2.00	1.67	1.25	1.11
-1	2.00	1.50	1.33	1.25	1.11	1.05
-2	1.33	1.20	1.14	1.11	1.05	1.03
-3	1.20	1.12	1.09	1.07	1.03	1.02
-5	1.11	1.07	1.05	1.04	1.02	1.01

Source: Estimates derived for $[P - MC]/P = -1/N\epsilon$, with $MC = 1$.

certain extent they do. Recall the study by Bain[9], based upon examination of the relationship between industry profitability and industry concentration. In it, Bain found that $CR_8 \geq 70$ represented an apparently significant threshold for market structure: profits (and presumably prices) for industries with concentration levels above that threshold would resemble monopoly. While there are similarities, the present analysis differs from Bain on two important points: (1) the relationship between concentration and monopoly-like pricing in the Nash-Cournot model is one which is continuous, unlike Bain's threshold relationship, and (2) the Bain threshold level of concentration would include markets with at least ten or more firms of equal size, and that is too many to produce monopoly-like pricing under the Nash-Cournot model unless demand is quite inelastic. Does this mean that the Nash-Cournot model and the Bain study have different implications? Yes. The notion that a threshold may exist at which firms recognize their mutual dependence and cooperate to raise price may be traced back to Bertrand, who sought to disprove Nash's (or Cournot's) conjectures.

Let us examine the Nash-Cournot theory of oligopoly on its own terms. It appears that the model predicts that a form of quasi-monopoly behavior could be associated with certain market structure conditions, to be defined by demand elasticities and number of firms. For example, with $\epsilon = -2$ and with $N = 2$, price would be greater than marginal cost, one third greater in fact. However, the Nash-Cournot model can also explain existence of a zero-profit oligopoly.

Let us suppose that there is free entry to the market and that there are certain fixed costs associated with production. Then, the Nash-Cournot model can be used to explain the market structure. That is, the equilibrium number of firms—as well as the equilibrium market price. Suppose that free entry leads to a condition in which each of the firms in the market earns zero profits at the Nash equilibrium price—the market could not support another firm. This is illustrated in Figure 8-3 where the market equilibrium price, P_e, is equal to the average cost of production for the representative firm, AC_i, and the demand curve shown is

[9]Joe S. Bain, "The Relation of Profit Rate to Industry Concentration: American Manufacturing, 1936-1940," *Quarterly Journal of Economics* 65 (August 1951), pp. 293-324.

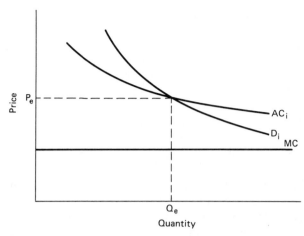

Figure 8-3 Entry can be included in the analysis of oligopoly. The long-run Nash equilibrium may describe a process in which the typical firm reaches the "break-even position," P_e and Q_e, and the demand D_i and cost AC_i determine the number of firms in a market, as well as the price and quantity.

the demand for the representative firm, D_i. To illustrate, consider the case when demand is $Q = 32/P^2$ and when the costs are such that fixed costs are equal to 3 per firm and $MC = 1$. Then, the number of firms in equilibrium will be exactly 2.[10] The Nash-Cournot model has simply been reversed to explain the number of firms rather than the market price.

So, let us suppose that we have a market with no barriers to entry. Let us also presume that the structural dimensions of cost and demand are taken as given. Finally, let us assume that the sellers act independently, in a non-cooperative fashion. Does this mean that, in equilibrium, the market will always have the number of firms given by the model described in Table 8-5 and the relationship between price and cost illustrated in Figure 8-3? No, not necessarily. There may be fewer sellers than predicted by the model. It is possible that the number of firms will be explained by the pricing behavior, and not by the market structure. Established sellers in the market may act to prevent or discourage competitive entry. They may succeed. As a result, it is a very different kind of market equilibrium. It is a very different form of oligopoly behavior. It leads us, nevertheless, to an important area of oligopoly theory—strategic pricing designed to protect the market positions of the incumbent firms.

PRICING TO DETER ENTRY

What do we mean by behavior designed to deter entry? How does it fit into the analysis of oligopoly? Let us first recall that oligopoly is used to refer to a market in which the element of interdependence is present and is significant in the plans and actions of the market participants. From our previous discussion, it is

[10]For the assumed degree of elasticity of demand and number of firms, $P_e = 4/3$ and $Q_e = 32/[16/9] = 18$. Thus, $Q_\alpha = Q_\beta = 9$, and $\pi_\alpha = \pi_\beta = \{[P - MC]Q - FC\} = \{[1/3]9 - 3\} = 0$.

clear that unimpeded entry will erode the market power of the older firms and will reduce their ability to earn economic profits—from the latter's point of view, entry will "spoil the market". An awareness of the potential dangers of entry to the position of the established firm is a reasonable extension of the concept of oligopoly interdependence. The concept of a strategy to deter entry is a reasonable extension of the concept of the general strategy of oligopoly games. Thus, it was predictable that oligopoly theory would ultimately be applied to strategic pricing behavior vis-a-vis potential rivals, as well as existing ones.

Where do we begin? Suppose that we begin with the case of the Nash-Cournot model we've just been examining. Suppose that the established firm, Alpha, seeks to develop a strategy for shifting the *share-of-the market* demand curve for the entering firm, Beta, downward and far enough to the left to ensure that Beta, if it should enter the market, would lose money. Can this be accomplished? Yes. It only involves two things: (1) a preemptive course of action, and (2) a state of mind on the part of the entrant which guarantees that this action will be seen as an effective deterrent. First, let us assume that Alpha—in a market in which total demand is given by $Q = 32/P^2$, and in which $MC = 1$ and $FC = 3$—takes preemptive action. Alpha sets price at 1.33 and supplies 18 units, the entire quantity demanded by the market at that price. That is, Alpha takes the initiative to establish the conditions, indicated in Table 8-5, for the Nash-Cournot equilibrium. Second, let us assume that Beta takes the existing firm's output as given. This is as critical as Alpha's preemptive action because it explains why Beta should conclude that entry would be an unprofitable venture.

Note first, that it is never profitable for two sellers to supply more than 18 units to this market: (1) given the condition $Q \geq 18$, then $[P - MC]Q \leq 6$, and (2) when that result is coupled with the condition that $\Sigma FC = 6$, then $\Sigma \pi \leq 0$. Because Beta believes that Alpha has already staked its claim to the entire quantity—in strict conformity with the Cournot tradition—Beta is forced to conclude that the market offers no prospects for its own success. Alpha is able to deter its entry into the market.

What does Alpha gain from this? The answer is simple—it gains profits. Alpha can earn a profit of 3 by successfully deterring Beta's entry. Its profits would be zero if Beta entered the market and if price and output were determined by a Nash-Cournot equilibrium process. Thus, we have a complete model of entry deterrence. Yet there are other questions to consider. Is there a sacrifice associated with deterrence? Could Alpha have adopted a different pricing strategy that costs less and could have been as effective? Are there limits to the general effectiveness of deterrence? The answer is yes to all of these questions. To answer them, we must ultimately deal with the details of the formal **limit-pricing** models.

There has been an evolution of the theory of strategic entry deterrence, just has there has been one for the general theory of oligopoly. We may begin with a model which is very similar to that which we have just considered.

The Modigliani Model of Deterrence

Modigliani[11] developed a model of entry deterrence which is based upon the assumptions of one oligopolist—or the potential oligopolist to be more precise—regarding the position and the behavior of another. It is taken directly from the mold of classic oligopoly theory. What are the basic principles of the Modigliani model? There are two. First, it assumes that large scale production is a necessary condition for success; thus, we shall assume that capital is sufficiently indivisible that entry commits the firm to a large fixed cost and that short-run average costs decline over the entire range of the firm's output until plant capacity is reached. Second, it assumes that expectations of the entering firm conform to the Cournot model of oligopoly; adopting what has become known as the **Sylos postulate**, we shall assume that the position of the existing firm is given, that its level of output will be the same in the future as it is now. Is it possible to construct a model of entry deterrence from so few elements? Yes it is.

Let us assume that the market demand and production cost functions are given by D and AC respectively, as illustrated in Figure 8-4. Let us further assume that when Alpha (the established firm) selects its output, that Beta (the potential entrant) will respect Alpha's established position and will expect Alpha to continue to supply the same quantity even after Beta's entry takes place, if it ever does. Certainly this is familiar; it is the Cournot assumption. Does it mean that there is nothing new in the Modigliani model? Not at all. While Beta is presumed to act as a classic oligopolist—never suspecting that its rival might change its position in response to changes in conditions—Alpha is not. Indeed, Alpha is presumed to select its output and price so that Beta will react by staying out of the market. How is this done? If Beta treats Alpha's supply as given, Beta

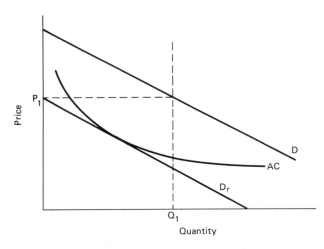

Figure 8-4 When an oligopolist prices to deter entry, it takes account of the position of potential competitors. Given market demand D and cost AC, the established firm may price at P_1, with quantity at Q_1. Assuming an entrant would have the "leftover" demand D_r and costs AC, it would have no chance of covering cost and would stay out of the market.

[11]Franco Modigliani, "New Developments on the Oligopoly Front," *Journal of Political Economy* 66 (June 1958), pp. 215-232.

will regard the residual demand curve, $D_r = [D - Q_\alpha]$, as the demand for its own output. Assuming that Alpha reads Beta's behavior correctly, Alpha will choose its rate of output, Q_α, so that the residual demand curve would not cover Beta's production costs, and Beta would regard its entry as an unwise and unprofitable venture. This is illustrated in Fig. 8-4, which shows that Alpha has chosen Q_α so that D_r lies below AC.

By employing a strategy of entry deterrence, Alpha could be able to accomplish two things: (1) it could enjoy monopoly-like levels of profit as indicated by the margin between price and cost, and (2) it could enjoy the peace and security of monopoly, not having to contend with a competitor. We may suppose that Alpha could choose a P_α just low enough (or Q_α just high enough) to deter entry. The Modigliani model is, therefore, a rational model of strategic behavior in which the firm is able to secure for itself both a level of performance and a market structure which is favorable to it. Is this an important discovery? Yes it is. It provided one of the first formal models in which the firm could rationally undertake to alter the market structure. It also demonstrated that the model of industrial organization would have to be flexible enough to allow for this reversal in the chain of causation between structure and conduct.

There were some misgivings with the model. There were questions about its basic assumptions. Could Alpha's position really be secure when it was based upon no intrinsic advantage vis-a-vis Beta? Could Alpha's pricing posture really make any difference unless such an advantage did exist?

The Bain Model of Entry Deterrence

Bain[12] developed a model of entry deterrence in which the principal explanation for the success the strategy to limit entry rests upon the assumption of an absolute cost advantage. That is, a barrier to entry held by the established firm. On the other hand, the behavioral assumptions in Bain's model were the same as in Modigliani's. In fact, Modigliani borrowed them from Bain.

Let us assume that the market demand and production cost functions are given by D and by C_α and C_β, as illustrated in Figure 8-5. The cost functions depicted there reflect two conditions regarding supply: (1) the absence of any fixed costs, so that unit cost is assumed to be constant over the entire range of output, and (2) the difference between Alpha and for Beta in their respective cost levels. The assumed cost advantage held by the established firm presumably reflects the existence of some factor, such as the possession of a superior resource supply or a patented production technology, which is not available to the entrant. Together, these conditions may also be taken to imply that while the established firm can be large enough to satisfy the entire market demand all by itself, there is no lower limit to the size of potential entrant so that, if entry

[12]Joe S. Bain, "Pricing in Monopoly and Oligopoly," *American Economic Review* 39 (March 1949), pp. 448-464.

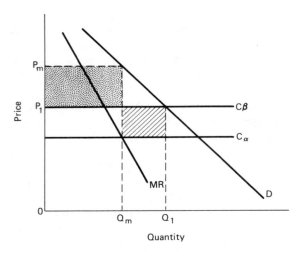

Figure 8-5 If an oligopolist prices to deter entry, it is a calculated sacrifice. Given market demand D and costs C_α, the established firm may price at P_1 to keep out an entrant with costs C_β, or it may set a monopoly price P_m and supply Q_m, inviting entry. The choices are between maximum profits now or a perpetual monopoly, with lower "guaranteed" profits.

should occur, it could involve the immigration of many firms. What would Alpha do under these circumstances?

Bain suggested that there were two lines of play for the established firm: (1) the short-sighted monopolist would choose to supply Q_m at the price P_m, the ordinary profit-maximizing level of output and price, but (2) the far-sighted oligopolist would choose to supply Q_1 at the price P_1, the entry-deterring levels of output and price. How would the latter deter entry? Since any Beta would accept Alpha's position as given, when Alpha takes the precaution of setting price just below Beta's cost of production, no Beta would venture into the market. In contrast, if Alpha's position had been (Q_m, P_m), Betas would have poured into the market until price had been depressed to the entry deterring level and would have supplied the entire increase in output, $[Q_1 - Q_m]$, in the bargain.

Which line of play did Bain think would best serve Alpha's self-interest? Bain believed that, in the example shown, the strategy of entry deterrence was best. The monopoly-profit increment—indicated in Fig. 8-5 by the dotted area bounded by P_m and P_1 on the top and bottom—would accrue to Alpha for only a short time and then be lost forever. The defensive-profit increment—which results from halting entry and is indicated in Figure 8-5 by the cross-hatched area bounded by Q_m and Q_1 on the left and right—would continue indefinitely. The strategy of securing a position in the market would yield larger gains than strategy of maximizing the level of profit. Indeed, the latter is a mere illusion in the face of entry.

Was entry deterrence always the best strategy? Bain conceded that there were two cases in which the firm could ignore it: (1) when the entry-deterring price P_1 was higher than the monopoly price P_m, and (2) when the entry-deterring price was much lower than the monopoly price. In the first case, the cost advantage of the established firm is so great as to make the market a natural monopoly of a sort. In the second case, the cost advantage of the incumbent is so small as to make the protection of the market a matter of no importance.

The Bain model of limit pricing, or entry deterrence, became the standard for analyzing questions of firm strategies which dealt with threats of entry. How plausible was it? To the extent that entry deterrence was founded upon a structural advantage of the incumbent—a cost-based barrier to entry—the model was far more credible than Modigliani's. A potential entrant must know that the incumbent is not merely posturing if it is to be deterred by a limit price. Does this mean that Bain had shown that entry deterrence was—with the exceptions noted above—the dominant factor in pricing strategy whenever the incumbent has a cost advantage? Not necessarily. There are considerations, which are either left out of the Bain model or have been assumed away, that could shape market behavior. What are these? There are three chief considerations: (1) the effect of time on entry and deterrence, (2) the ability of both the incumbent and the entrant to act strategically, and (3) the effect of information—or the lack of it—on strategic behavior. These have been the focus of subsequent revisions of the basic model of limit pricing.

Time and Entry Deterrence

The issue of time is unavoidable. It became so the moment Bain compared short- and long-run strategies. Why is that? Remember that Bain compared today's profit maximization with tomorrow's entry deterrence. How long will it take for tomorrow to arrive. What is the cost of waiting? If it is assumed that entry is a process which is time-using, the strategy of market-protection requires that a significant sum of near-term gains be invested in securing the long-term gains associated with entry deterrence. If it assumed that time imposes a cost, the established firm must discount future profits at a nonzero interest rate in order to compare them with current profits. As a result, the firm must give greater weight to the present than to the future. As a result, Bain's basic conjecture—that entry deterrence is a superior strategy to profit maximization—will be correct only when entry is rapid enough and the discount rate low enough to make it so.

Entry and the strategy to discourage it is essentially a dynamic process. It takes time for an entrant to develop the capacity to produce a product and the ability to market it. Yet Bain's model of entry deterrence was essentially static. There is a fundamental inconsistency here. Gaskins[13] sought to get rid of it by the explicit introduction of time into the analysis of *limit pricing*. He assumed that the amount of entry—the market share taken by new firms—would vary

[13]Darius W. Gaskins, Jr., "Dynamic Limit Pricing: Optimal Pricing Under Threat of Entry," *Journal of Economic Theory* 3 (September 1971), pp. 306-322.

with the passage of time. He also assumed that the *rate* of entry would be determined by the difference between the prevailing market price and the entrant's cost of production. These modifications yield new and interesting variations on Bain's major theme: (1) at any point in time, the incumbent's optimal strategy may be to set price at a level P_o, where $P_m \geqslant P_o \geqslant P_1$, and (2) over time, the share of the market served by new entrants may increase at the expense of the established firm and the price may decline as this process takes place. The strategy of the incumbent is no longer confined to the polar choices on deterrence—either to allow entry or to prevent it. Instead, in Gaskin's analysis, the strategy involves the determination of the optimal rate of entry—it is a more sophisticated tradeoff between short-run profits and long-run protection of market position. The strategy reflects a new concept of market power: that the power of the established firm to control price is time-dependent, and that it is likely to be stronger in the short-run than in the long-run.

Rationality and Entry Deterrence

Limit pricing models tend to be one-sided. They portray a market in which one group of sellers—the incumbents—think and act in a rational fashion while another group of sellers—the entrants—do not. The former anticipate entry and take precautions to make certain that it is not an attractive option for potential competitors to pursue. The incumbent is presumed to price with caution to achieve a better profit-position in the future but the entrants are presumed to act like lemmings. If the incumbent's price presently is high enough to cover the entrant's prospective costs of production, entrants will pour headlong into the market until profits are driven to zero. Is this really a model of strategic behavior? No it is not. It may be assumed that the incumbent has an advantage due to the structure of the market, but this is no justification for presuming that the incumbent is also of superior intellect.

Limit pricing is intended to be a model of strategy. Friedman[14] has argued that the actions attributed to the entrant should be as rational as the actions of the incumbent. What difference would this make in the end result? Possibly, it can make a good deal of difference. Let us assume that Alpha has a cost advantage over Beta, just as indicated in Figure 8-6. Let us assume that there is only one logical candidate for entry. What would happen if Alpha chooses to restrict output to Q_m and price at P_m? There are two interesting cases to consider.

Let us assume that Beta expects that even after entry Alpha will continue to supply Q_m. We apply the Sylos postulate once again. What would the rational Beta do? In such a case, Beta knows that its supply, when added to Alpha's, will depress price. Therefore, Beta will select that output which yields the maximum profit. Under these conditions, price will not fall to the level of P_1, and the

[14]James W. Friedman, *Oligopoly Theory* (Cambridge: Cambridge University Press, 1983), p. 181.

incumbent's postentry loss of profit would never be as severe as that presumed in Bain's model. What is the implication? Under these conditions, limit pricing may be an undesirable option for the established firm. We can go even further with this line of analysis. Friedman shows that a stronger conclusion is justified.[15]

Let us assume that Beta is fully aware of the cost advantage possessed by Alpha, and that Beta believes that Alpha would be willing to use it as a competitive weapon after entry.[16] That is, Beta expects that if Alpha should ever face an actual competitor, Alpha will cut its price from P_m to P_1 (or below) to force losses on Beta—assuming that there are certain fixed costs associated with entry—and to force it out of business. What is the implication of this? In the first place, Beta would never be tempted to enter, regardless of Alpha's current price position, since its expectations are that it would never realize a profit from doing so. In the second place, Alpha would never actually have to use a limit price to deter entry. The incumbent's cost advantage alone is sufficient to provide protection against entry.

Information and Entry Deterrence

Does this mean that entry deterrence is a dead issue? Not necessarily. Friedman's argument presumes complete information. But what would happen if Beta did not know Alpha's production cost and vice versa? It is obvious that a cost advantage—assuming that one exists—could not deter entry if the market were ignorant of its existence. Milgrom and Roberts[17] sought to analyze the strategy of limit pricing as a means to signal a warning to potential entrants. Specifically, if Alpha's price is read by Beta as an indication that the former's costs are lower than the latter's, entry may be deterred. Alpha may believe that it is necessary to price below its own monopoly price, P_m, in order to convey such a message to Beta. We can make the game of deterrence even more interesting. Alpha may choose to adopt a mixed strategy—pricing part of the time to extract monopoly profits and part of the time to demonstrate a cost advantage which it may or may not have relative to Beta. Does this mean that limit pricing works?

If Beta believes that Alpha is trying to sell an advantage it does not have, if Beta believes that Alpha is only posturing, limit pricing may backfire. Beta may be impressed more by a strategy which establishes a high and stable price. This might be interpreted as indicating a confidence on the part of Alpha that the incumbent believes it has a cost advantage and would be willing to use it to eliminate an entrant. Indeed, it could even be simpler than that. There is an incumbent advantage that can be attributed solely to primacy. The dynamics of entry account for an element of uncertainty for everyone—incumbent and new-

---

[15]*loc. cit.*, pp. 194-198.

[16]In this respect, pricing to deter entry is related to predatory pricing, which is discussed below.

[17]Paul Milgrom and John Roberts, ''Limit Pricing and Entry under Incomplete Information,'' *Econometrica* 50 (March 1982), pp. 443-459.

comer alike. Since the incumbent is already exposed to the danger, by having previously paid the price of admission to enter the market, only the potential entrant is in a position to exercise caution. If Alpha refuses to bend to the threat of entry, by setting P_m instead of P_1, Beta may regard the action as evidence of Alpha's resolve to fight—whether it has a cost advantage or not—and may decide not to enter. If Alpha's actions indicate a more defensive posture, by setting P_1 instead of P_m, Beta may see them as evidence that Alpha would back down in the face of actual competition. Limit pricing may make Beta a bolder and more dangerous adversary.

Predatory Pricing

We have considered a number of the implications of pricing to deter entry. A similar strategy applies to the behavior of the firm intent on eliminating existing rivals. Let us assume that Alpha is a firm with a cost or revenue advantage over an existing rival, Beta. If Alpha wanted to monopolize the market it shares with Beta, it could cut price to a level so low that the latter would be unable to cover costs. If Beta were to conclude that its losses would continue, a reasonable assumption particularly if the sole explanation for Alpha's price seemed to be a desire to eliminate Beta, Beta might reluctantly retire, a victory for predation. What would Alpha have gained? If it does pay off, the predator must earn more profits in the period after monpolizing the market than it sacrificed in eliminating the competition. If entry is too easy, that would not seem possible. So, what is necessary for predation to work? How likely is it to be employed?

For predatory pricing to work at all, it is necessary that the predator have either a cost advantage over its rival or a source of funds independent of the market shared with the rival to finance its economic warfare or both. If the predator really has a cost advantage, the natural condition of the market may be monopoly. The loser is more the victim of circumstance than of the "monopolistic" intentions of the winner. In such a case, predatory pricing may be a predictable response by the firm with a natural monopoly which had not anticipated the entry of new competition when it originally set its monopoly price but which is capable of meeting (and beating) competition now that it has appeared, and the predatory price is the same as Bain's limit price. So, does this mean that predatory pricing is never really monopolistic? No.

Take the case where the predator's advantage is independent funding with which to wage competitive warfare; the predator must have a monopoly in another market and must be willing to use the profits from it to subsidize its campaign of predation. This is often called **cross-subsidization**. If the predator does not have a cost advantage, is an artificial monopoly really worth the cost of such a subsidy? The mere fact that a firm has an ability to wage economic warfare does not mean that it will be willing to use it. Suppose that one firm can be ruined, only to be replaced by another every time the predator sets its monopoly price in the contested market. In such a case, rivals might be eliminated by predation, but not rivalry, and predatory pricing would never pay off. Does this mean that a predatory pricing strategy based upon cross-subsidization can never work? Not necessarily. Consider the matter of rational behavior by entrants once again. The firm considering entry must accurately assess its ultimate prospects. If an incumbent has established that it is willing to finance the ruination of any rival, it is irrelevant that the entrant would expect a profit at the existing (monopoly) price—the predator will surely cut price after entry. The predator may be able to profit by cultivating its reputation as a bully, provided that potential rivals can be deterred. Once again, predatory pricing is closely related to entry deterrence.

CONTESTABLE MARKETS AND OLIGOPOLY PRICING

We have seen how limit pricing may alter market structure by discouraging the potential entrants. Is it possible that the tables can be turned? Is it possible that a market structure that breeds potential entrants can limit the pricing option of the incumbent? That is precisely the proposition advanced by Baumol, Panzar, and Willig[18] for **contestable markets**. What are contestable markets and what are their implications?

In the traditional models of market structure, the number of firms (or the level of concentration) is extremely important as a determinant of behavior—as we have seen throughout the course of the present chapter on oligopoly. Suppose that entry was absolutely free and exit was absolutely costless. That is, if an entrant were free to adopt the same production technology as any and all incumbents and could expect to receive the same treatment as they do from the consuming public, it would be moved to enter the market whenever incumbents set prices above their costs.

Consider Figure 8-6. If the costs are given by AC and MC, and if demand is given by D, the established firm maximizing profits would restrict quantity to Q_m and set price at P_m. But the contestable market would see a competitor enter under the circumstances, and price would drop to P_c.

Pricing must necessarily reflect the contestability of the market. Incumbents will either price at cost so as to keep the entrants at bay, or they will price above cost, attracting entry. Either entry itself or deterrence will ultimately force price to the level of costs. Are the conditions sufficient to attract an entrant, assuming it is aware that price will soon be lowered to cost and assuming it is rational? Baumol et al argue that it is, provided that exit is costless. If the entrant can enter for a brief period of time, make economic profits until prices fall, and then exit without having to pay an admission price, entry is certain whenever incumbents elevate price above cost. Costless exit means that the entrant can liquidate all its fixed costs when it leaves, so that there is no *sunk* cost in the

[18]William J. Baumol, John C. Panzer, and Robert D. Willig, *Contestable Markets and the Theory of Industry Structure* (San Diego: Harcourt Brace Jovanovich, 1982).

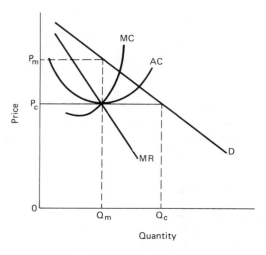

Figure 8-6 A **contestable** market
nutures competitive pricing since the
limit price is equal to P_c. The oligopolist
has no market power.

venture and, therefore, a zero price of admission. So, if there is free entry and
exit, oligopoly markets—defined strictly in terms of the number of sellers, not
their behavior—will be marked with behavior that is perfectly competitive. Is
this feasible? Some critics have argued that perfect contestability is not at all
possible. Baumol and his coauthors have countered that there are markets, such
as in the passenger airline industry, where it may be possible for competitors to
hit and run if prices for any particular route should get far out of line with costs.
They have argued that the principle of contestability is more important for its
general implications than it is for explaining behavior in the few odd cases of
perfect contestability.

Baumol et al argue that contestability is consistent with large scale economies and small numbers, things impossible under perfect competition. Yet, they
argue that contestability can produce optimal results, just as competition does—
efficiency in allocation. They argue that contestability has stronger implications
than competition does; it may determine the market structure, rather than
depend upon it. It may even assure that the existing structure is optimal, or
something close to it. A reasonable degree of contestability will make certain that
the number and size of firms is appropriate for keeping costs and prices low. In
this view, the critical market imperfection is a lack of free entry and exit and not
a lack of large numbers of firms. How free does entry have to be for the entrant
to be able to contest the incumbent and for the market structure to become
reasonably optimal? That is a difficult question. Even so, contestability may force
us to alter or, at the very least, to review our perception of oligopoly.

OLIGOPOLY PRICING: MECHANISMS OF COOPERATION 9

In this chapter we examine the meaning and implications of cooperative behavior. Starting with the historical examples of actions to end competitive price wars in two different industries, we seek to develop an understanding of cooperation. We begin by considering the more obvious benefits of cooperation—a group could enjoy monopoly profits—and we continue with some of the difficulties in enforcing a cooperative price—some firms in the group may want a larger share of the total and make price concessions to get it. We suggest that certain mechanisms are used to aid cooperation: (1) the cartel or explicit agreement and (2) price leadership. Cartels, or similar arrangements, are especially likely to be found in those markets where efforts at voluntary cooperation have tried and failed in the past.

In examining price leadership, however, we find that there are different cases. In some, price leadership may be a natural result of a dominant form setting its own price. In others, it may be the result of an understanding among a group of firms, at least implicitly, to set price above the competitive level. In still others, leadership may be the way we describe the process by which competitive prices change when cost and demand conditions change.

Evidence of **cooperation** can often be found in the behavior of oligopolists. To some, cooperative behavior, even more than the concentrated market structure itself, is the hallmark of oligopoly. Many have argued that cooperation is no more than the natural reaction of a small group of sellers to the high degree of interdependence which is presumed to exist in the oligopoly market. What do we mean by cooperation in this context? Is it truly as natural as some would contend?

Cooperation means that firms act in concert, a process which involves communication with or obligation to one another. It may include all sorts of arrangements—formal or informal, explicit or implicit, rigorously enforced or self-enforcing. How does the state of cooperation come about? What leads former rivals to put aside their past struggles for position and/or dominance in the market and to work together? How does cooperation work? Are there conflicts which threaten or limit its effectiveness? Or are there conditions which help to support cooperation, to make it work? There are a number of obvious questions which we must attempt to answer in the course of this chapter. Before we begin, let us consider two examples of cooperative pricing.

TWO EPISODES OF COOPERATION

In 1959, investigators from the Antitrust Division of the Department of Justice began to turn up evidence of a price-fixing conspiracy among the manufacturers of electrical equipment.[1] Before it was over, 29 firms and 44 executives would be charged with unlawful restraint of trade. What was involved and how did it begin? The price-fixing **conspiracy** was actually a string of agreements involving various products, which included insulators, switchgears, circuit breakers, transformers, and turbine generators. There were twenty products in all. The total industry was dominated by General Electric and Westinghouse—GE alone was involved in 19 different "cartels" but there were various smaller firms which manufactured one or two products and held minor shares in their respective markets. The roots of the conspiracy can be traced to a period of price slashing which had occurred about five years earlier.

Fortune[2] reported that, in 1954, the electrical industry was in a slump, with large amounts of excess capacity. At this time, Westinghouse appears to have surprised GE—suggesting perhaps that there had existed an understanding of cooperation and that it had been betrayed—taking a sizeable discount from its list price on a large order of turbine equipment. General Electric's reaction was angry, and the firm sought revenge. What followed was a price-slashing spree which came to be known as the "White Sale" of 1954-55. Prices were discounted by as much as 40 to 45 percent for certain industrial products sold by the electrical manufacturers. After a period of such vigorous price warfare, the industry was ready for peace.

The makers of various electrical products met over the next few years and a variety of arrangements were the result. In some cases, there were simple understandings about adherence to price lists. In other cases, there were complex formulas for dividing the market and/or for setting price in sealed bids. For example, in the market for circuit breakers, GE would get 45 percent of the business, Westinghouse would get 35 percent, and Allis Chalmers and Federal Pacific would each get 10 percent.[3] In the switchgear cartel an elaborate process was developed: (1) the right to a bid was rotated among seven producers over a fourteen week cycle, (2) the amount by which the winning bidder would discount from its list was specified by a formula which was designed to appear to be random so that the outside observer would be unable to tell that it was rigged,

---

[1]"The Incredible Electrical Conspiracy," *Fortune* (April and May 1961).

[2]*loc. cit.* (April 1961), p. 172.

[3]*loc. cit.*, p. 137.

and (3) the amounts by which various losing bidders would discount from their price lists were also predetermined in such a way as to appear to be randomly distributed.[4] In spite of it all, however, there were often occasions when cooperation in the electrical equipment industry would break down—while they all were able to escape the detection of antitrust authorities and violate the law for a period of time, some of the conspirators continued to cheat on their agreements as well.

In April 1962, prices in the steel industry were raised as US Steel announced that a price increase of $6 per ton would be put into effect for all products and as the other producers in the industry quickly fell into line. The price increase was soon rolled back, however, as President Kennedy exploded in public—the increase followed shortly after the Administration adopted a program of "voluntary" wage-price guidepoints—and his brother, the Attorney General, applied the screws in private. Aside from the reversal played out so publicly, the behavior of the steel industry in this incident followed much the same pattern as it had for sixty years. US Steel acted as the price leader for the industry; it accepted the responsibility for setting the price standard for the industry, and others followed its lead. There were seldom surprises. How had the process begun?

In the period between the end of the Civil War and the turn of the century, the U. S. steel industry simply exploded. It was the age of "steam and steel"; the construction of the railroads, the building of steel-hulled (and later, steam-powered) ships, and the evolution of modern industry created a huge, growing demand for steel. Hundreds of firms supplied the market, but their fortunes were not always good. Buyers of steel were very sensitive to the business cycle, and when demand was slack, the industry experienced wild, price-cutting sprees as manufacturers sought to regain full utilization of capacity at the expense of their competition. There were frequent attempts to fix price and allocate market shares, but they typically ended in failure since there was no discipline. In this environment, some sought to introduce a measure of order by taking over the mavericks and by consolidating smaller firms into larger ones. Did this strategy work? Not very well, or at least not until US Steel was founded by merging the six largest steel combines in 1901.

The creation of US Steel had an immediate effect on the market. With half of the total industry capacity and about 70 percent of the sales, it had the ability to control price. At least as important, US Steel had the will to control price. In 1901, the company quoted a price of $28 per ton for steel and the price held for fifteen years (from 1922 to 1932, the price held at a level of $43).[5] How was this stability accomplished? At first, US Steel explicitly invited the rest of the industry to go along. The *Gary dinners* provided a forum for the Chairman of US Steel, Judge Gary, to urge cooperation and for the industry to peg prices. Later,

[4]*loc. cit.*, (May 1961), p. 212.

[5]Simon N. Whitney, *Antitrust Policies* (New York: Twentieth Century Fund, 1958), Vol. 1, p. 308.

US Steel won the universal respect, if not always the emulation, of others in the industry. US Steel always charged the prices it quoted and vice versa. Thus, *Big Steel's* price quotations were a reasonable standard for the industry to follow. Did the others always follow? No, they did not. In fact, there were occasions in which the industry reverted to its old form; it is reported that steel experienced periods of cutthroat competition in 1911, 1921, and 1938.[6] Generally, the granting of secret price concessions became common business practice in steel. Through it all, US Steel worked to stabilize pricing. Indeed, it did so at a cost. US Steel held price, like an umbrella over the heads of the others, at a level high enough so that the industry could prosper as a whole, and in so doing, sacrificed its own market share. US Steel's share of the market declined from 70 percent in 1901, to less than 50 percent in 1920, and to less than 30 percent by the time of the 1962 flap over the steel price increase. To the extent that there was effective cooperation in the pricing of steel in the twentieth century, it was due in large part to the self-discipline shown by US Steel Corporation.

THE GENESIS OF COOPERATION

Do the electrical industry price conspiracy and the steel industry price leadership have much in common, aside from the fact that each served to advance the mutual interests of their respective participants? They do seem so. They appear to have arisen from similar circumstances; in both cases the industry had experienced periods of cutthroat competition prior to taking action. They also appear to have encountered some difficulty in maintaining cooperation, once a mechanism to fix price had been established. Perhaps the more interesting question is the following: do the conditions found in the steel and electrical industries and the behaviors spawned by them reveal something about the process of cooperation in general? Perhaps so. Let us consider the mix of opportunity and motivation which are likely to generate and/or to support cooperation.

Cooperation is a conscious decision. Rivals ordinarily compete. So, if oligopolists choose to cooperate instead, why do they do it? One answer is frequently suggested; one that can be found rooted in oligopoly theory as we observed in Chapter 8. Beginning with the classical duopoly model of Cournot and continuing through modern game theory, one observation appears again and again: noncooperative oligopolists will do less well as a group than a monopolist would have done. It implies that sellers who act independently will earn less profit than they would earn if they act in concert. Or to put it in economic terms, the implication is that cooperation is rational, noncooperation is not. Is it all that simple?

If the oligopoly market is a candidate for cooperation, what about the perfectly competitive market? Most oligopoly models—aside from Bertrand and Baumol et al—all tend to suggest that oligopoly behavior results in profit levels

[6]*loc. cit.,* p.310

that are below those found in monopoly but are above those found in competition. It is clear that perfect competitors have even more to gain than oligopolists. Indeed, logic suggests an even bolder step. If the maximization of group profits is presumed to be the motivation of rival firms, and if collective action is presumed to be perfectly costless (including the absence of legal restraints), cooperation would become the universal way of doing business. Then, monopoly profits would become the standard for all markets, despite the nominal differences in market structures. But that is not the case. Stigler[7] has suggested one explanation.

Cooperation is not really spontaneous. It takes an effort. There are certain costs associated with it. Why? The basic reason is that cooperation requires information; a group of firms can control price effectively if and only if they possess, as a group, the information necessary (1) to set a monopoly price and (2) to enforce it.

Let us consider first the task of setting price. We may illustrate the objective of cooperative price fixing with the assistance of a simple model, such as that shown in Figure 9-1. Given the demand and marginal revenues curves, D and MR respectively, group profits can be maximized by restricting the group output to the level of Q_m, determined by the intersection of MR and S, and by setting price at the level of P_m. The curve labeled S represents industry supply, the sum of the marginal costs for all the firms in the industry, but does not function as a supply curve when the firms cooperate. The results depicted in Figure 9-1 for cooperative behavior—the price set and quantity supplied—are precisely the same as those which distinguish monopoly behavior. There is one

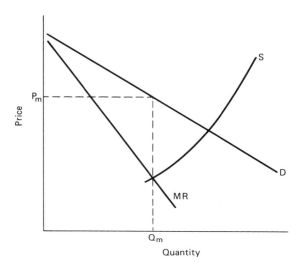

Figure 9-1 A cooperative group, which takes the collective view of the market, would have the perspective of a monopolist. Given market demand D, marginal revenue MR, and the collective supply curve S, the group would maximize collective profits by setting price P_m.

[7]George J. Stigler, "A Theory of Oligopoly," *Journal of Political Economy* 72 (February 1964), pp. 44-61.

difference which the model cannot depict easily. In the case of cooperation, it is far more costly to obtain the information necessary to make this choice.

In order to establish the profit-maximizing price, P_m, it is necessary to know—or to have a good estimate of—the demand and cost conditions, which are summarized in the D and S curves. Since the monopolist is the only producer and seller in the market, it is reasonable to presume that the firm knows how much of the good consumers have purchased in the past at various prices. It is reasonable to presume that the firm knows what its own production costs have been. While all of the information may not be at one person's finger tips all of the time, it should be a relatively simple task to collect it. With these pieces of information, the monopolist may be able to make good estimates of the D and S curves.

How about the group which attempts to maximize joint profits? In that case, the group must determine how much each of the firms has sold in order to establish how much of the good has been purchased in the past at various prices. The group must find out what the production costs of each of the firms have been in order to establish what the joint supply costs have been. Can the collective be as effective as the single firm in estimating the D and S curves? It does not seem very likely. Within the monopoly firm, lines of communication are short and information is passed quite freely. Within a group of firms, the lines of communication are longer and, we might presume, less open than inside any one of them. Even those firms which are most keen on price-fixing are likely to want to keep certain matters private. As a result, the transfer of information is likely to be more costly to accomplish—or the accumulation of information less complete—for the group of firms than for the single firm. The transfer of information is neither the only, nor perhaps the most serious problem facing the group.

Let us now consider the task of enforcing a monopoly price. We may illustrate the problem with the assistance of the simple model shown in Figure 9-2. In the panel on the right, we have merely duplicated the previous model to indicate the joint profit-maximizing price and quantity, P_m and Q_m, for the group taken as a whole. In the panel on the left, we illustrate how the group decision translates into a single firm imperative; in order to satisfy the conditions for joint profit-maximization, each firm must restrict its output to Q_{mi}, determined by the intersection of the group's equilibrium marginal revenue, MR_0, and the firm's own marginal cost, S_i. Will the firm do so? Not necessarily. From the firm's private point of view, Q_{mi} is not optimal. Given a price of P_m, the firm has an inducement to cheat its fellow price-fixers. The firm may perceive that its own marginal revenue curve is the same as the group price, P_m—or only slightly below it—for all quantities up to Q_{ci}, and that its private requirements for profit-maximization calls for it to supply the "cheater's" output, Q_{ci} rather than output, Q_{mi}, mandated by the cooperative agreement. If individual firms supply more than their allocated shares, their collective effort to control price will be

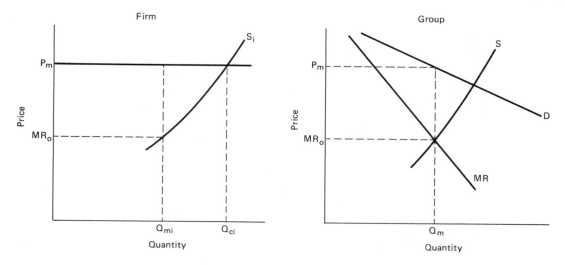

Figure 9-2 A cooperative group may have difficulty enforcing a monopoly price. Given P_m, the firm maximizes its profits when it produces Q_{ci} from its supply curve S_i, instead of Q_{mi}, its "fair share" of group output. If the members of a group indulge their individual self-interests, group output will rise and price will fall.

compromised. There is a conflict between the private interest of the firm and the public interest of the group.

A participant in a cooperative price-fixing scheme is placed in an ambivalent position: (1) each firm can be made better off if all cooperate to raise prices, but (2) assuming cooperation has raised price, each firm can improve its position on its own by cheating. Such cheating takes the form either of selling a larger quantity than the firm is supposed to sell according to the terms of the agreement or of selling at a price below the one the firm is supposed to charge in order to attract added sales. In either case, price will fall below P_m. The temptation for the individual to act independently is an institutional weakness inherent in the cooperative scheme. It is potentially strong enough to limit the effectiveness or even the survival of the price-fixing agreement.

Does this mean that cooperation does not work? There are circumstances which will favor mutual restraint on the part of those willing to cooperate. If there is a very small number of firms who can see the advantage in cooperation and who are quite content to share in the proceeds of a shared monopoly, rather than fighting over them, cooperation may work smoothly and with little effort. The Bertrand oligopoly theory suggests such a pattern of behavior, and the theory of collusive price leadership—discussed later in this chapter—shows how it might work.

In the absence of some such process, cooperation faces serious difficulties. For example, in the electrical industry price conspiracy, the elaborate rules may have been intended as much to cut down on cheating as to avoid detection by antitrust authorities. The bid rotation scheme in switchgears may have sought to distribute sales fairly among members of the cartel and to keep them all in line, as well as to deceive authorities. In the steel industry, the efforts by US Steel, including its sponsorship of the Gary dinners, sought to encourage a measure of self-discipline among steel makers in maintaining the fixed price. In spite of all efforts to the contrary, price cutting continued in both the steel and electrical industries. Is that surprising?

In the markets for most industrial goods, sales are made on the basis of individually negotiated transactions. In such cases, the conditions of sale, including price, are known only to the parties directly involved in the transaction. Under these circumstances it is difficult to enforce a cooperative agreement to fix prices. Even the detection of cheating is difficult. We have assumed above that the primary source of information to the members of a coalition is the membership itself—in no small part, cooperation depends upon the voluntary exchange of data. If a firm is cheating, it will certainly not volunteer that information to the others. Stigler[8] has suggested that detection must therefore rely on independently verifiable facts—those participating in a price-fixing scheme may use indirect evidence, such as large and sudden shifts in markets shares, to find the cheater. When there are shifts which exceed the normal, random variations in market shares, it may be assumed that the one who gains is secretly cutting price. How effective would such a test be? Stigler indicates that substantial diversions of sales may be accomplished without detection.

Even if the problem of detection is solved, there is the problem of discipline. How do the members of the group make the cheaters stop? Perhaps the most effective discipline would be to neutralize price cutting. If the group can identify each secret price cut, and if the group can match every such offer, there is no incentive to offer price concessions. However, this assumes that detection is quick and accurate and that the group response is immediate. That is, it assumes not only that information is complete, but also that the coordination necessary for the group response is highly developed.

In summary, decision-making is more difficult for the cooperative group than for the monopolist because it is more difficult for the group to obtain the information necessary to make decisions. Execution of decisions is more difficult for the group than for the monopolist because there are inherent conflicts between the interests of the group and the interests of individual members, while such conflicts do not exist within the single firm. So, what is the implication? It is reasonable to assume that, on average, cooperative price-fixing will be less effective—and perhaps much less effective—than monopoly. Is there anything that the cooperative group can do to improve its ability to control prices and profits? Yes there is. The existence of certain institutions is evidence of that fact.

[8]*loc. cit.*

CARTELS AND COLLUSION

What is a cartel? As defined by Simon Whitney[9], the cartel is "an agreement among firms to set prices, divide markets, limit production, or share technical knowledge on a broad but exclusive basis." The term may be used either narrowly or broadly. In the narrow usage, the word is used to refer to licensed and regulated agreements which have been officially sanctioned. In a number of European nations, institutions from the Middle Ages lasted well into the twentieth century, and the concept of the royal charter survived long after the royal heads had fallen. In a broader sense, the word may refer to any explicit collusive agreement to control the market price. For our purposes, we will use the word cartel broadly to describe all collusive actions.

OPEC, the Organization of Petroleum Exporting Countries, is undoubtedly the best known cartel in the world. Because so much has been written about it, the popular concept of the cartel has become synonymous with OPEC: (1) we have come to believe that the cartel has a formal organization, (2) we have seen that the cartel makes operational decisions at periodic meetings of high-ranking representatives of its membership, sometimes with a bit of discord but eventually with compromise ruling the day, (3) we have observed that the cartel has tremendous market power—in the case of OPEC, the official price of crude oil rose from $3 per barrel in 1973 to $36 per barrel in 1981, and (4) finally, we have seen that the cartel has limits to its power—dissent from within and competitive pressure from without forced OPEC to cut the official price by more than 50 percent in 1986 alone. The OPEC-inspired image notwithstanding, the institution neither requires formal organization nor implies tremendous market power.

When is a group most likely to turn to the establishment of a cartel? Would it so so when, without an agreement, it fails to achieve maximum profits? Perhaps. The weight of evidence suggests that collusion has less ambitious goals.

Asch and Seneca[10] examined the relationship of collusion to other factors for a sample of large American manufacturing firms during the period 1958-1967. They found that, in a multiple regression of firm profitability on a number of structural and behavioral factors—the degree of industrial concentration, the nature of product (producer or consumer good), the level of advertising intensity, the rate of growth in sales, and the presence or absence of collusion—collusion proved to have a negative effect on the rate of profit. How could this be? To understand the results, it is necessary to get the direction of causation right. The most plausible explanation for such a finding, and the one favored by the authors of the study, was that subnormal levels of profitability provide the incentive for collusion.

The cartel, or collusive agreement, is often the sign of distress. Its emer-

[9]Whitney, *loc. cit.*, p. 14.

[10]Peter Asch and Joseph Seneca, "Is Collusion Profitable?" *Review of Economics and Statistics* 58 (February 1976), pp. 1-2.

gence can often be traced to a period of severe price competition. In the United States, many price-fixing agreements are the product of efforts by the firms in an industry to achieve relief from price warfare. The electrical conspiracy of the late 1950s followed the so-called White Sale of 1954-55. The **Powder Trust**, the Gunpowder Trade Association, was created in 1872 to control the stiff price competition in the industry that resulted fom excess productive capacity left over from the Civil War.

Those who seek to establish control of the market, whether privately or with the aid of government, are likely to justify their behavior on the grounds that competition is destructive. What is **destructive competition**? How is it related to cartelization? A simple model is instructive. Assume a market may be characterized the following way: (1) firms operate under conditions in which the ratio of fixed costs to variable costs is unusually high, (2) market demand is depressed relative to its past history, (3) voluntary efforts to restrict output to levels sufficient to maintain higher industry prices and profits—as illustrated in Figure 9-2—are undermined by cheating, (4) in the end, hard price competition seems irresistable in view of the state of excess capacity, and (5) the entire industry suffers under low prices and low profits (or even large losses). The end result may be illustrated with the help of Figure 9-3. In it we show that competition leads to the price P_c, determined by the interaction of supply and demand, as illustrated in the panel on the right. At this price, the best that the individual firm can hope for is to minimize its losses by supplying the quantity Q_{ci}, as illustrated by the panel on the left. It is obvious that a stark contrast exists

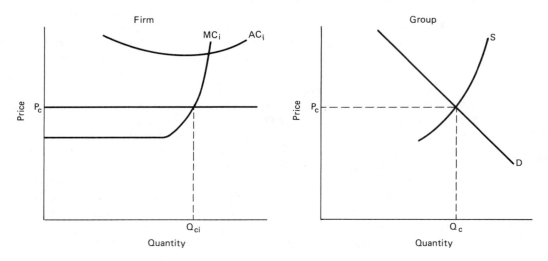

Figure 9-3 If voluntary cooperation does not work, the market may give in to **destructive competition**. With a low demand relative to capacity, firms may cut price to take on extra business. With a large gap between marginal and average costs, cutthroat pricing can produce severe short-run losses.

between the destructive competition shown in Figure 9-3 and the monopolistic cooperation shown earlier in Figure 9-2. At some time, it must occur to the firms involved that cooperation would be far less destructive to their interests than is competition. If past experience has demonstrated to them that voluntary cooperation does not work, a cartel—that is, some form of collusive agreement or understanding to control price—may be the answer to their competitive problem.

Does this mean than all cartels are the result of episodes of severe past competition? Not at all. In some cases, they may simply represent the realization that the group can do better if the members in it cooperate rather than compete with one another. When members of an industry take to slashing prices, it may be an indication that list prices had been pegged at a level above cost by some less complete form of cooperation—at least in comparison to the cartel—in the past. But we will have more to say about implicit cooperation later in this chapter.

Let us suppose that a group of firms has failed to achieve voluntary cooperation, has suffered from too much competition, and has determined to remedy its problem. Let us assume that the group is small enough for the firms in it to be able to organize effectively—oligopolists have a comparative advantage in the ability to band together. How does the group go about it? There are many possibilities, and some may involve a formal organization, but few would resemble the model of joint profit-maximizing cooperation that we presented in Figure 9-2. Let us consider some of them.

The group may simply act to restore the credibility in and compliance with list prices in the industry. In many cases, the experience of destructive competition is associated with a war of discounts; each seller attempts to shift the burden of its own idle capacity to its competitors by offering to shave a few cents more from the list price. As the competitive struggle heats up, the secret discounts mount up. In this situation, success in restoring the industry's list price qualifies as improvement, and while reestablishing the list price may not be as profitable as setting the monopoly price, it may be a more realistic objective. Why is this? First, the industry list price already exists. The information costs in establishing it are negligible, particularly when compared with the information costs of establishing a joint profit-maximizing price. Second, the historic list price would be a safer choice for a conspiracy than the monopoly price. The cessation of price warfare is likely to appear less suspicious to antitrust authorities and customers than the introduction of an industry-wide price hike, particularly when we assume that the industry is saddled with substantial excess capacity. Thus, we may reasonably presume that, under certain conditions, conspiracy seeks only to bring a halt to runaway price cutting. But can we find evidence to support this presumption? Yes we can.

After the White Sale of 1954-55, General Electric and its co-conspirators sought to restore a *reasonable* adherence to the list prices for a number of electrical equipment products. They met frequently with such a purpose, and they repeatedly sought to reach an understanding. So, did they succeed? No they did not. There is evidence to suggest that price cuts of 10 to 15 percent were often granted by individual firms to win additional business despite the existence of a conspiracy.

Let us assume that the agreement to halt secret price cuts is not self-enforcing and that at least some members of the group choose to ignore their commitments. Mutual interest and common understanding alone may not be adequate to secure the control of price. Let us assume that a group is determined to end its price warfare and to improve its profits. What can it do? The common reaction is to organize.

Consider a cartel which is constituted and governed like OPEC. Why does the agreement sometimes take the form of a quasi-governmental organization which has the authority to make decisions for the group and the power to police them? The answer should be apparent. When the terms of a lawful agreement are breached, the injured party normally seeks redress through the courts. If the agreement is itself a violation of law (or involves matters beyond the reach of the law, such as found in certain international cartel agreements), civil authorities will not aid in its enforcement. To achieve success in fixing price, the collusive group may find it necessary to establish both a contract and a government to enforce it.

How much government is necessary? It would seem that, other things being equal, the more elaborate the organization of a cartel, the more costly it would be to create and maintain. Therefore, it would seem that a cartel would be kept as simple as possible. Suppose an industry had experienced serious and persistent competitive problems. In that event, the firms in the industry may become willing to subject themselves as a group to some rather harsh and expensive forms of discipline. Let us consider some of the possibilities.

Suppose that a group of firms which comprise an industy has attempted to eliminate secret price cutting but has failed. Suppose that there exists an industry trade association to serve the legitimate interests of its membership. In this setting, the group may attempt to use the lawful association as a means to an unlawful end, the control of price. How can this be done? A trade association could require its members to report fully on all transactions. Its purpose may be twofold: (1) to acquire the information necessary for the detection of cheating on the agreement to fix price, and (2) to use the force of peer pressure to discourage cheating.

During the twentieth century, an institution called the **open price** association became very popular. The advocates of open pricing argued that making information available through the disclosure of the exact price and quantity involved in each transaction would serve to improve competition. It was claimed that exchange of information would advance the interests of buyers and sellers alike and would tend to stabilize price. When participants were charged with violating the law on restraints of trade, it was denied that open pricing was intended to fix pricing or could ever have such an effort. Nevertheless, the administrator of the price reporting plan servicing the American Hardwood Manufacturers' Association freely admitted that it was intended to establish uniform prices and to eliminate cutthroat competition.[11] In the thirties and forties, the Tag Manufacturer's Institute provided that the office of its Executive Director would be used for the exchange of published price lists and all off-list sales.[12] The Sugar Institute introduced a new wrinkle to price reporting. The Institute, which was organized to cope with secret price cutting, incorporated a "Code of Ethics" requiring its members sell only at their announced prices and terms.[13]

Suppose that there exists an industry in which location is an important factor—sellers and buyers are widely scattered and transportation costs are a substantial fraction of the price of delivered goods. In this case, the group may attempt to use the natural pattern of the competitive market—a tendency of any given customer to buy from the nearest supplier—to its advantage in controlling price. How would a cartel adapt to this situation? A division of the market may serve its end very well. If the group could agree to assigning each member exclusive rights to serve a certain geographic market, such as the area immediately surrounding the place of business of that member, competitive rivalry would be easy to control—in this case, any purchases from the wrong seller would be detected. Yet, when the contrived pattern of pairing sellers to buyers resembles one which would develop quite naturally, it would be more difficult for antitrust authorities to prove the existence of a collusive agreement.

During the 1893 recession, producers of cast iron pipe were faced with the exigencies of excess capacity and found themselves vulnerable to bidding wars in order to attract business; it was a very unprofitable experience. In the Southeast, Addyston Pipe and Steel Company joined with five other producers to form a pool in 1894. Operating under the name of Associated Pipe Works, the six firms devised a scheme for controlling price. One element of that scheme was the adoption of **reserved cities**, the name they used to refer to the territory assigned to one of the members of the cartel. Other sellers might bid for a contract in a reserved market, but their bids would be rigged in order to ensure that the right producer won the contract.[14]

Another variation of geographically-based cartels is that which uses a price formula to control cheating. Suppose that a common practice has been for a seller to quote a standard price for its product, plus a transportation cost for delivery to the customer. Suppose that market concentration is such that one seller—and one plant location—is dominant. In such a case, the natural tend-

[11]*American Column and Lumber* s. *United States* 257 U.S. 377 (1921).
[12]*Tag Manufacturers Institute* vs. *Federal Trade Commission* 174 F. 2d 452 (1st Circuit, 1949).
[13]*Sugar Institute* vs. *United States* 297 U.S. 553 (1936).
[14]*Addyston Pipe and Steel Co.* vs. *United States* 85 Fed. 271 (6th Circuit, 1898).

ency may be for the pricing pattern established by the leading firm to be imitated by others, whether or not they share the same location. What are the implications? Under these conditions, pricing may have a tendency to become geographically systematic: (1) the dominant firm quotes a price to a buyer based upon its own base price and transport cost, (2) the other firms quote the same price to a buyer, (3) the small producer can make extra profits when they pay for less transportation costs than they bill the customer, that is, when they are located nearer the customer than the dominant firm, and (4) the small producer can make less profits when they pay for more transportation costs than they bill the customer, that is, when they are more distant from the customer than the dominant firm.

Could such a pattern exist without collusion? Yes it is possible. The self-interest of producers could account for it. The dominant firm, the seller with the largest established market share, would have a strong interest in seeing others adopt its own delivered pricing formula. Their passive acceptance of its standard price would tend to stabilize prices and profits. The smaller firms would certainly enjoy the extra profits from charging "phantom freight"—billing for transportation costs that do not exist would be a real bonus. Smaller firms might even be willing to accept lower profits to bring in more business when sales are slack—absorbing freight costs for the marginal sales could contribute to the firm's total profits. Would such a pattern be rigidly observed without collusion? It is not likely. Whenever a seller could make an extra profit by charging the full formula price and matching the prices offered by every other seller, it would have an incentive to cheat a little bit to make certain that it wins that sale. The small firm would regard a 99¢ profit with a probability of 1.0 as a great deal better than a $1 profit with a probability of 0.01. When market conditions sour and sales become scarce, cheating could become irresistable.

In 1903, US Steel adopted a single basing-point price system with its Pittsburgh mills as the standard. The entire steel industry adopted the "Pittsburgh Plus" formula, using the system as the standard guide to pricing until it was ordered to halt the practice in 1924 by the FTC.[15] Afterwards the industry adopted a system of multiple basing-points, and again the pricing practices of US Steel guided the industry as a whole. A substantial number of other industries have, at some time or another, used formula prices, including cement, corn syrup, and plywood. In some cases of basing-point prices, the presence and role of collusion were firmly established. Nevertheless, geographic price formulas provide a weaker control over cheating than market division. Since it is common to see shipments of goods invading the home market of a producer, even when every seller is acting in full compliance with the system, it would not be obvious when one of them is cheating. For a market division cartel, the act of invasion of reserved territory has to be cheating.

[15]Whitney, *loc. cit.*, pp. 260-262.

Are cartels explained only by selfish private actions to secure better prices? No, there are also those which owe their existence to direct governmental intervention. During the oil glut of the 1930s, which resulted from the discovery of vast new reserves at the same time as the depression deflated the demand for oil, the states of Texas, Oklahoma, and Louisiana acted to restrict the output of crude oil and to raise price by laws which established production quotas for the nominal purpose of conservation. The Connally Hot Oil Act of 1935 was passed by Congress to support the oil states by prohibiting interstate shipment of oil produced in excess of such state quotas. Another depression-era law, the Agricultural Marketing Agreements Act of 1937, was adopted to support an establishment of producer cartels in agriculture. Marketing orders allow producers (1) to fix the minimum price which they will receive from processors for the sale of raw milk, and (2) to establish limits on the quantity of citrus fruits and certain other crops to be marketed. Athough collusive agreements are generally banned as restraints of trade by the Sherman Act, such special legislation was justified on the grounds that oil well operators and farmers were powerless to do anything about destructively competitive conditions in their respective markets, and that there was a public interest—in addition to the obvious private interest— in establishing the compulsory cartels.

We have discussed at length the problems and limitations of the price-fixing cartel. Is it inevitable that the cartel must struggle so hard merely to maintain a list price? No it is not. If it can operate with sufficient authority to control the actions of its members, the cartel does not need to struggle at all. In the domestic oil industry, the prorationing apparatus of Texas, Oklahoma, or Louisiana could exercise tight control over the oil supply in the state. Under the auspices of a federal marketing order, a California orange growers' cooperative could establish a joint sales agency so that the shares of output and profits could be tightly controlled; Sunkist can operate a very effective cartel. In these two cases we see illustrations of legally-sanctioned cartels. Does that mean that the illegal price-fixing agreement cannot be as effective? Not necessarily. It is a great deal more difficult to establish institutions with sufficient strength and to operate them effectively in the shadows, and those that succeed do not become textbook examples; they remain secret, known only to the participants themselves.

Let us assume that the group has solved—either with the sanction of legal authorities or without it—the internal problems of operating a cartel. Does this mean that the group will be able to manipulate price at will? No it does not. If entry is a possibility, the group may face outside competition. Indeed, the more successful a group has been in restraining its own members, the more likely it is to encounter competition from non-members. The OPEC experience is very enlightening. In 1973, the West was very dependent upon oil which it imported from the OPEC nations. The price increase imposed by OPEC was of such a magnitude, it invited entry. Exploration efforts by the West vastly increased, and substantial new fields were developed both in Alaska and in the North Sea. Also, new efforts were made to recover old oil; it had become profitable to pump oil from wells which had been abandoned as uneconomic in the days when crude oil was selling for less than $2 per barrel. These induced changes increased the world supply, and OPEC's share of the world market declined as the cartel cut back its own production and sales to maintain prices in excess of $30 per barrel. But in 1986, the cartel allowed the price to plummet. The OPEC nations increased their rates of production; and their action forced some of the high cost independent producers to shut down. In the end, OPEC found that it could maintain a dominant position in the world market or it could set the price at a high level. It could not do both—there were limits to its power.

So, what is to be learned from all this? First, a cartel is an organization born in adversity. If sellers suffer from an excess of competition in the absence of cooperation, and if they can succeed in establishing a cooperative regime, they will operate as a cartel. Second, the cartel may be a second-best choice. If it were possible to do so, the sellers would likely prefer combination to collusion. Monopoly is constitutionally superior to agreement as a means for controlling the market, but the law appears to be more effective in preventing monopoly than collusion. Third, the whole process has an important lesson for the student of industrial organization. The structure of the market—the cartel or the monopoly—may be determined by past conduct, such as past price warfare.

It should be kept in mind, however, that neither existence of oligopoly nor existence of profits in excess of competitive levels necessarily imply collusion. It is possible that in some oligopoly markets the sellers never have experienced cutthroat pricing. It is possible that they will cooperate in some manner without recourse to an agreement or an organization. Finally, it is possible that the structure of the market is important in accounting for—or helping to account for—such behavior, consistent with the traditional paradigm of industrial organization. Consider a new cooperative process.

PRICE LEADERSHIP

What is price leadership? Why does it seem to work in some circumstances and not in others? To answer these questions and those which follow them, is is useful to recognize that there is not one meaning for price leadership but several. Since Markham's[16] essay on the nature of price leadership, economists have been generally willing to agree that there are three main varieties: dominant-firm price leadership, collusive (or to use Markham's term, "in lieu of overt collusion") price leadership, and barometric price leadership. Each case is distinguished by certain structural and behavioral characteristics from the others. Does this mean that the three are mutually exclusive or that they exhaust all of the possibilities? Not necessarily. It is possible to form cases which are combina-

---

[16]Jesse W. Markham, "The Nature and Significance of Price Leadership," *American Economic Review* 41 (December 1951), pp. 891-905.

tions of the others. More to the point, it is possible that continued observations of an industry group will discover behaviors fitting different descriptions at different times.

What do we mean when we use the term price leadership? First, we use it to convey a form of behavior in which there is recognition of interdependence; there is a sense of cooperation implicit in it. Second, we apply it to a particular process for changing price in an oligopoly setting; the cartel is viewed more as a mechanism for enforcing a given price. Third, we apply it to a process of communication. Price leadership refers to those circumstances in which a price change (1) is offered as a signal by the leader and (2) is treated as a signal by the followers. Even so, neither the behavior itself nor the motivation behind it is necessarily collusive. In the appropriate setting, the signal may indicate nothing more than that, in the opinion of the leader, current market conditions warrant a change in price. The use of such signaling may signify nothing more than that the firms in the market are wary of their interdependence.

Dominant-Firm Price Leadership

What is dominant-firm price leadership? It is leadership of a form shaped by the structure of the market. It can occur only when there is extreme inequality in the size of firms or in their shares of the market. The dominant firm would typically control 50 percent or more of the sales, and the follower would typically supply a small fraction of that amount. What accounts for such an unusual structure? It is reasonable to presume that some combination of natural advantage, superior performance, good luck or historical accident, and contrivance may explain the big disparity in size between the dominant firm and its rivals—a critical patent or collection of patents, a large endowment of superior resources, a superior organization, a popular brand with strong customer loyalty, an inheiritance of being the pioneer in the market, a carryover from an early series of mergers, and so on.

What precisely is dominant-firm price leadership? Is structural dominance sufficient to generate the behavior? Dominant-firm price leadership describes a particular style or pattern of behavior in which (1) the leader behaves like a monopolist and (2) each of the followers behaves like a perfect competitor. The behavior can be modeled in the manner shown in Figure 9-4. Let us assume that market demand and the supply of the followers are given by D and S_f, respectively, in the panel on the right. Let us also assume that the demand and cost conditions relevant to the dominant firm are given by D_{df} and MC_{df}, repectively, in the panel on the left. Where does the dominant firm's demand curve come from? It is calculated as the residual demand for the dominant firm's product after followers have supplied as much as they want given the price chosen by the leader. It is derived by subtracting the quantity supplied by the followers from the quantity demanded by consumers at each and every price: $D_{df} = [D - S_f]$. What is the importance of the dominant-firm's demand curve? It explains how the market price determination process works. The dominant firm selects its profit-maximizing price and quantity (P_{df} and Q_{df}), determined by the inter-actions of MR_{df} and MC_{df}, as shown in the panel on the left in Figure 9-4. Given the price selected by the dominant-firm, the followers will choose the profit-maximizing quantity (Q_f), determined by the intersection of P_{df} and S_f shown in the panel on the right in Figure 9-4. Thus, the behavior of the leader is con-ditioned upon the behavior of the followers and *vice versa*.

Let us ask a key question again. Does the structure of the market dictate this behavior? No it does not. The model is so mechanical that it is easy to overlook an important behavioral element implicit in it. We take the dominant firm's demand curve to be a residual—$D_{df} = [D - S_f]$. That is so only because the dominant firm chooses it to be; the dominant firm does not require that followers share the burden with it in maintaining the level of price. As indicated in Figure 9-4, only the dominant firm has excess capacity available at the price D_{df}—the leader allows the followers to sell as much as they want. A dominant firm intent on maintaining as large a market share as possible could not serve as a price leader in this sense. In fact, the dominant firm who is greedy for more power and higher profits might resort to predatory pricing to eliminate followers rather than supporting them with a price umbrella, as some have so described this behavior.

Assuming, however, that the dominant firm establishes the price P_{df} and acts to support it by inviting followers to supply as much as they want, price-fixing can be achieved unilaterally. There is no threat to undermine the price

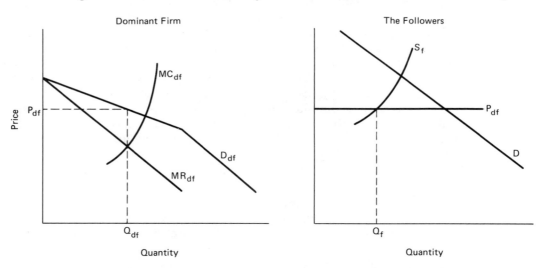

Figure 9-4 A **dominant firm** can set group prices single-handedly, if it unilaterally restricts group output. The panel on the right describes behavior of followers, given their supply curve S_f. The panel on the left describes behavior of the dominant firm. Given demand D_{df}, the residual from market demand D and S_f, the dominant firm acts like any monopolist, except that permits its followers to supply as much as they are willing and able.

since the only firm in the position to do so, the only one with slack capacity, is the dominant firm which sets the price. Indeed, it might be fair to ask if is this really oligopoly pricing at all. It may be more accurate to treat it as a variation of monopoly pricing and to treat the dominant firm as a monopolist with incomplete control over the market. To illustrate the last point, let us consider the effect of entry. If the number of followers or the size of their productive capacity should increase, the demand for the dominant firm—$D_{df} = [D - S_f]$— will decline. As a result of the change, the dominant firm would be forced to lower price.

Can we find examples of this pattern of behavior? In 1902, US Steel supplied nearly 70 percent of the steel in the nation. The newly-formed combine in steel had the market position necessary to act as a dominant firm. Its management chose to use that power to end the costly price warfare that hurt the industry in the past. In the early days, US Steel could operate as a dominant firm. It unilaterally raised the price of steel and set the pattern of Pittsburgh Plus pricing. Its performance as the price leader was imperfect, and its power was to become limited. In periods of slack demand, discipline can be maintained only by adjusting the price downwards. US Steel attempted to maintain stable prices. In these periods, secret price cutting would reemerge. One may say that the followers refused to follow, but it is more accurate to say that the leader failed to lead. As time passed, US Steel's share of the market declined—in this century, the firm's market position shrunk from a share of nearly 70 percent to one of less than 20 percent.

The OPEC experience in oil is much the same. In 1973, the oil cartel held a strong position in the world market, and it took advantage of that position to raise the price tenfold. OPEC set a price that the rest of the world followed. Price was high enough to attract entry and the followers' supply grew. In an effort to maintain the price it had set, OPEC reduced its own rate of production, but its share of the world market shrunk even more. In 1986, the cartel introduced major price reductions. In the short run, the action reestablished a position that had been eroding through entry. The action also exposed the limits to the market power possessed by the dominant firm; the price leader can exert no more control than the market structure will permit.

Are there other structural factors to consider? Perhaps there are. The model depicted in Figure 9-4 implies that (1) the product is homogeneous, and (2) the quantity to be sold by the followers, given the price by the dominant firm, is solely determined by their productive capacity. What if we modify these assumptions? Let us suppose that the dominant firm holds a strong position in a differentiated market. We may assume that the dominant firm has a market share several times the size of the typical follower. A large number of consumers may be loyal to the brand(s) supplied by the leading firm in the market, while a much smaller number may be loyal to each of the remaining firms. This is the type of attachment which we termed horizontal product differentiation in Chapter 6. Let us suppose that the dominant firm enjoys a cost advantage resulting from its market position. We may assume that the unit cost function for the differentiated product—a function which includes costs of production, marketing, distribution, and so on—exhibits important economies of scale. Under these conditions, the dominant firm may enjoy even more power than indicated by the previous model. Consider the situation illustrated by Figure 9-5. At the price chosen by the dominant firm (P_{df}) and at the quantities of goods which can be sold at that price by the dominant firm and the typical follower (Q_{df} and Q_f, respectively), the leader will earn substantial profits while the follower will just break even.

It should be noted that this model explains the result of the pricing decision taken by the dominant firm but not the means for arriving at it. We can offer a tentative explanation here and a more complete explanation in Chapter 10. Suppose that the dominant firm decides to hold an umbrella over the heads of the followers. The leader may attempt to set a price high enough, given the costs and expected sales of the follower, to keep it in business but not so high as to allow it to prosper or to attract new competition. The follower may accept the lead because it has no real alternative—a follower might be able to increase its market share and profits via a price cut if its reduction was not matched by the leader, but a cut in price might well cause a loss in profits for the smaller firm if the lower price was met by the seller of the more popular product.

What is significant about this model of the dominant firm? It is that demand, and not productive capacity, would limit the supply of the followers and would determine their willingness to follow. If differentiation also limits entry, the dominant firm price leader can exercise some control over price and enjoy a measure of protection from competition at the same time.

Can we find examples of this pattern of behavior? In automobiles, for example, General Motors had maintained a position of leadership in the U.S. market since the twenties. For many years, GM had enjoyed a market share which is more than double the size of the next largest automaker, Ford. The

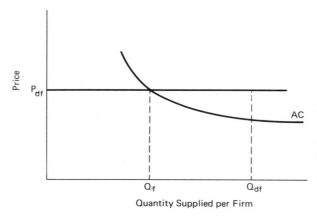

Figure 9-5 A **dominant firm** can price unilaterally, if it sells the "most popular" differentiated product. An extralarge share of the market and economies of scale may enable a dominant firm to set its price equal to P_{df} and supply Q_{df}. Others may be forced to follow as competition for market share may not allow them to cover costs at any other price.

advantage which GM holds over Chrysler and American Motors had been even greater. For much of this time, the relative profits of the rival automakers appears to reflect their relative market shares in a manner consistent with Figure 9-5. In the fifties, for example, when demand for cars was relatively stable and foreign competition was nonexistent, the "Big Three" were positioned as follows:

AVERAGE ANNUAL PROFIT RATE
(1950–1960)

General Motors	21.5
Ford	14.5
Chrysler	10.5

Source: H. Michael Mann, "Seller Concentration, Barriers to Entry, and Rates of Return in Thirty Industries," *Review of Economics and Statistics* (August 1966), p. 306.

Are automobiles unique in this regard? No. There are other markets in which a similar pattern of dominance can be found. Firms such as IBM, Kodak, and duPont appear to hold—or to have held at some time—more or less the same sort of position in certain markets in which they do business.

What is the implication of dominant-firm leadership? It would appear that the most important inference which can be drawn from either model, Figure 9-4 or Figure 9-5, is that price leadership can exist without the followers choosing to cooperate. Dominance can be used to compel imitation. Is it always true of price leadership?

Collusive Price Leadership

What is collusive price leadership? It is leadership—and followership—of a sort dependent upon the willingness of all to contribute to the maintenance of a cooperative price. It is, in fact, the very essence of cooperative pricing. Whereas the cartel is a contrivance, an artificial device designed to bring about cooperation, collusive price leadership is a natural state. What can explain it? Obviously, the members of a group have a shared interest in the control of price so that they can make monopoly profits. Just as obviously, individual members of the group often act to spoil it for the others.

Market structure is important. Markham identified five specific market conditions which he claimed were prerequisites to effective collusive price leadership[17]: (1) concentration must be high and firms must be roughly equal in size—it is important that each firm be large enough to perceive that its actions will have an effect on price, (2) entry must be difficult enough to enable the group to maintain control over price and to benefit from doing so, (3) the prod-

[17]Markham, *loc. cit.*, pp. 901-903

ucts do not have to be homogeneous, indeed, we will argue that some differentiation can help to hold price competition in check but they must be regarded as close substitutes so that the cooperating suppliers will consider their prices as strongly interdependent, (4) the market demand must be inelastic enough to make output restriction profitable, and (5) the cost conditions of the individual firms must be sufficiently similar so that the margin of price over cost for one firm is the same—or nearly so—for all.

A model of collusive price leadership can be developed by modifying the model of cooperative profit-maximization slightly. In Figure 9-2, we illustrated the problem of enforcing the group price, but in Figure 9-6, we assume that problem away by showing that the price and output position of the individual firm, shown in the panel on the left, is consistent with the group price, shown in the panel on the right. What is the role of market structure in providing for this consistency?

Two elements would seem to be important in distinguishing this case from other cases of cooperation. First, similarities in costs and market shares may help to minimize any differences among firms in their perceptions of the optimal price. When the price leader takes an action, it can be relatively certain of the willingness of others to follow. Second, if there is a degree of horizontal differentiation which helps to separate the markets of the members of the group and to stabilize their markets shares, it will act to make the individual firm demand and marginal revenue curves more inelastic—more like the industry curves—and to make price cutting less attractive. The D_i and MR_i in Figure 9-6 are shown for a case of the strongest possible separation of the markets of the members of the group.

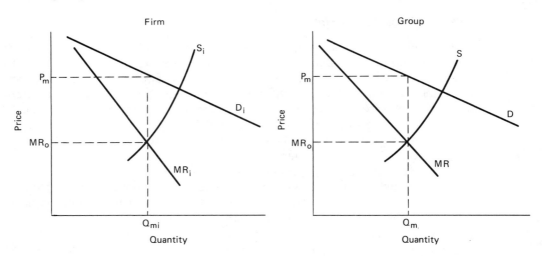

Figure 9-6 Collusive price leadership may yield maximum group profits, provided that the leader has a clear view of industry demand D and supply S and sets price P_m, and provided that the follower has the clear interest of the group at heart and treats Q_{mi} as its fair share of the sales.

Let us assume that the market fits the requirements Markham specified for collusive price leadership. Does this mean that the group will behave in the fashion described by Figure 9-6? Will the sellers always cooperate in establishing the monopoly price? Not necessarily. The model of price leadership "in lieu of overt collusion" implies that each and every firm is willing to act as if it were a dominant firm: (1) to concede to the other firms whatever share of the market they hold, (2) to accept the residual demand as its own, and (3) to be willing to keep its excess off the market. That is, the individual firm's demand curve is derived in the same way as the dominant firm's demand curve was derived; it is the difference between the total market demand and the supply provided by the other firms. It is one thing to attribute unselfish behavior to the firm who can control the price unilaterally and another to attribute the same to the collusive price leader and, especially, to its followers. Only if their markets were strongly separated is it reasonable to believe that they would always show the quality of self-restraint depicted in the theoretical model.

What about the role of the price leader? In the model described in Figure 9-6, the price leader is unimportant. As long as the group monopoly price satisfies the profit-maximizing needs of every firm, and as long as every firm knows its own interest, every firm might be relied upon to set the correct price, with or without a signal from a price leader. The group monopoly price would be the solution to a cooperative oligopoly game.

In real markets with collusive price leadership, the role and identity of the price leader are not mere details; they would be important. Followership is not something to be taken for granted. Nor is leadership for that matter. The discipline of the group price can break down if there is sufficient pressure on it. The examples of secret price cutting described earlier in this chapter are evidence that idle capacity, experienced during periods of slack demand, can test any price-fixing regime. Thus, the effective and trusted leader must act in a manner so as to maintain discipline. There may be secrets to leadership: (1) changing price infrequently and timing the changes so that there is universal acceptance of the need (or the opportunity) for the change, and (2) establishing a level for price that will lessen the temptation for cheating. Each change in price challenges the willingness of followers to follow. Thus, leadership may be more an exercise in statesmanship than the practice of monopoly. While it may be the responsibility of followers to comply with their implicit agreement, it is the responsibility of the leader to make compliance possible, even for the morally weakest of the group.

Are there certain conditions which make the task of oligopoly price leadership—and of followership—easier? Yes there are. When the overall demand for the industry product is strong and when industry capacity is heavily used, there is not much incentive for the individual firm to trim prices. Under these conditions it is easy to maintain high P/MC ratios. This is, in fact, the point made by Edgeworth on oligopoly behavior. Or, when the market shares of individual firms are fixed, or at least are relatively stable, compliance with the price lead is much easier. Horizontal product differentiation can account for this condition. Whenever consumer loyalty is strong enough, the competitive incentive for any firm to cut price is tremendously diminished. Indeed, it is an interesting paradox that whenever competition between firms emphasizes product, rather than price, price-setting is that much easier, other things being equal. In extreme cases, prices may be fixed at convenient levels for the sellers. In one version, there may be a common semi-permanent position for price, such as for candy bars and soft drinks. In another, there may be differentiated *full-cost* price positions for the individual sellers, such as for automobiles and stereos, but this is a matter that we will discuss in the next chapter. In any case, let us consider two examples of collusive price leadership.

The tobacco market was one in which product differentials between the major brands—Camels (RJ Reynolds), Lucky Strikes (American Tobacco), and Chesterfields (Ligget & Meyers)—led the industry to experiment with independent pricing for a period of time before the twenties. From 1922 until 1946, however, the "Big Three" were sold at identical prices at retail.[18] After 1928, they sold at identical prices at wholesale as well. During the entire time, RJ Reynolds acted as the price leader, with the exception of a period in 1933, when American Tobacco initiated two substantial price cuts. Over the entire period, there were only eight price changes and four of those took effect between 1931 and 1934. RJ Reynolds, the maker of the most popular brand, announced a wholesale price increase of $.45 per thousand in June 1931, which like all the other price leads was quickly followed by the other major manufacturers. The retail price, exclusive of state tax, increased from 14¢ to 15¢ per pack as a result. But the position of the majors was weakening as the depression wore on. The sales of economy brands, which retailed at 10¢ per pack, increased from one percent to over twenty percent of the market in less than two years. In January 1933, American Tobacco announced the first of two price reductions which cut the price of Lucky Strikes from $6.85 to $5.50 per thousand at wholesale. The others followed the new leader and the retail price of the major brands dropped by three to five cents per pack, and the market position of the leading brands was soon restored. In January 1934, RJ Reynolds led a price increase which raised the wholesale price $.60 per thousand and brought the retail price to 13¢ per pack. Over the entire period, the experience seems to suggest that, except for the competition from the economy brands, the industry relied upon price leadership to cooperate in setting and maintaining a satisfactory level of price. The record also seems to suggest that the sellers of major brands were only moderately concerned with price. They made infrequent changes in their base price, they did not chisel on it, and they became especially sensitive to pricing matters only when faced with outside competition.

The record of collusive pricing in the steel industry is very different. US Steel set out to be the price leader for the industry, whether other steel makers

---

[18]*American Tobacco Co. vs. United States* 328 U.S. 781 (1946).

were willing to accept the discipline of cooperation in pricing or not. While US Steel may have once held a position of dominance, it soon had to rely upon statesmanship rather than power alone. Did the other firms play their assigned roles on cue? No, it appears that they did not. The leader sought to establish prices high enough to make steel production profitable during normal demand conditions. The followers frequently offered secret discounts in order to win customers at the expense of their leader. Chiseling was a small but persistant vice in the good times and a major one during the bad.[19] Like the price leader in cigarettes, US Steel did not make frequent price changes—only when demand or costs had changed sufficiently that others would be inclined to follow, would US Steel be inclined to lead. Even then, followers in steel were disinclined to maintain the base prices which they nominally accepted.

There seems to be an irony. Pricing identity may be easier to achieve when products are differentiated—at least slightly—than when they are homogeneous. This implies that when competition is focused upon pricing and when cooperation is all the more important for the collective well-being of a group of suppliers, it is all the more difficult to achieve. In any case, collusive price leadership is not an automatic solution for controlling price warfare, assuming that that is the primary objective of collusion. It works only when it works. That is, only when rivals choose to accept their joint responsibilities to one another in maintaining a cooperative price. Suppose that they do not cooperate. And suppose that there is no dominant firm to compel them to do so. Is price leadership dead?

Barometric Price Leadership

What is barometric price leadership? Is it leadership at all? It is a type of price leadership, but the intent of the leader is not to control price in the same sense of the dominant firm and/or the collusive price leader. Consider the behavior in a market in which the current price is nonequilibrium—the sellers find themselves in a situation with a surplus or a shortage. What are they to do? Do they wait for a mechanical process to determine what price should be? Of course not. Sellers will have to find a new equilibrium on their own. The barometric price leader is one brave enough to act, given that recent shifts in demand or cost call for a change in price. The barometric leader quotes a price representing the cost of supplying that quantity which it *expects* to sell. If its lead is accepted, others will follow. What do we mean by the terms, leadership and followership, in this context? First, it is necessary that followers concur in the leader's reading of market conditions. If they do, they will adopt a leader's price change as their own. Second, it is necessary that subsequent events prove that the leader's judgment was good. And unless the leader was correct, the search for an equilibrium will continue. In that case, followers will abandon one leader for another.

[19]Whitney, *loc. cit.*, p. 291.

So, what is barometric price leadership? It is a process by which the competitive market can function. Unless the market is organized in such a fashion that an auction process determines price, something akin to barometric price leadership will perform that function. Strictly speaking, it is cooperative only in the sense that the barometric leader's price quotation signals the leader's judgment of market conditions, which others are invited to accept but are free to reject. Does this mean that the barometric price is always competitive? No, not necessarily. Just as the collusive price is not necessarily monopolistic. Nevertheless, it is fair to say that barometric leadership tends to be more competitive, as opposed to the price leadership of the dominant firm and collusive varieties.

Is market structure involved in explaining the differences? Yes, it would seem so. Barometric pricing is often associated with one or more of the following conditions: (1) a relatively low level of concentration, (2) a substantial fringe of small suppliers, (3) a high degree of substitution between the group's product and the products of outside suppliers, and/or (4) relatively low barriers to entry. What is the importance of these structural conditions? The first two involve concentration. They indicate that it is lower than in either the dominant firm or the collusive market cases, and they may be responsible for fostering a perception of independence on the part of at least some of the firms in the market. The result may be a lack of discipline. The first two conditions imply an internal weakness, limiting the ability to control price; the second two imply an external weakness.

Assuming that barometric pricing is an inferior form of price leadership, is market structure alone responsible for the fact that a group may come to rely upon it instead of something better? Not necessarily. In fact, the same industry may show signs of collusive price leadership at one time and barometric leadership at another. The lack of discipline in maintaining price is not merely a matter of low market concentration. Price leadership in the steel industry, for example, seems to fit the former pattern during good times and the latter during the bad. Moreover, control of price by the dominant firm or by collusion is affected but not eliminated by external competition. Price leadership in the cigarette industry, for example, seems to have withstood the threat of outside competition from the 10¢-brands in the early thirties.

PRICING INDEPENDENCE IN MONOPOLY AND OLIGOPOLY

10

In this chapter we EXamine the meaning and implications of independent pricing and its relation to oligopoly in particular. Starting with two illustrations of pricing independence, we then examine the source of the firm's ability to act independently in oligopoly. It is the result of product differentiation. Next, we find that the independent firm may seem to ignore its demand curve, pricing at the level of expected costs, including a target profit, instead of the profit-maximizing point along the demand curve. We find, however, that such pricing rules of thumb may be the most practical way to get ahead.

Next, we consider that the independent behavior involved in the full-cost price may serve as a substitute for direct forms of cooperation—rivals may live with each other's independence as long as it is seen as mutually nonthreatening.

Finally, we consider that pricing independence may be a part of a broader firm strategy. The firm may produce a wide line of products covering an assortment of markets, with the following two implications: (1) the diversification it represents gives the firm even more independence from rivals, and (2) it implies that opportunities may present themselves to discriminate in price and to enhance overall profits.

For all the attention paid to oligopoly pricing strategy—rivals eying rivals—in the previous two chapters, the market is filled with products, the prices of which are set by firms with some degree of independence. Ford sets the price of its Mustang, McDonald's sets the price of its Big Mac, and the Safeway Supermarket at 12th and Jefferson sets the price of its ground beef. Each of these firms has some degree of market power, especially in the short run, and each is accustomed to exercising it. Yet each also has close competitors which are both clearly identifiable and few in number.

In this chapter we shall attempt to answer several related questions. What do we mean by pricing independence? Is it compatible with oligopoly? What explains the market power held by the independent firm? How strong is it? Finally, if the firm has the power to set price independently, how will it use that power? Let us consider the first question only. We shall regard pricing independence as a condition under which the firm can set price or adjust it without the fear of retaliation by a competitor. Is independence the same thing as monopoly? Not necessarily. A monopolist must have it. An oligopolist may have it as well.

We shall endeavor to answer the remaining questions in due course; indeed, they are the subject matter for the rest of this chapter. First, let us consider two examples which involve pricing independence.

TWO EXAMPLES OF INDEPENDENT PRICING

In the early twenties, General Motors began the use of a new management tool which was termed standard volume pricing.[1] This involved setting price according to expected costs, including the cost of capital, i.e., the return on the fixed investment of the firm. Lanzilotti[2] reports that in the mid-fifties GM sought to produce a yield of 20 percent after taxes on its investment in automobiles and to maintain its position in the market. How well did GM succeed? From 1947 through 1955, General Motors averaged a 26.0 percent annual return, with 19.9 percent being the lowest yield during that period. The firm also maintained its market share at an average of 50 percent. It would seem that General Motors was very successful in its pricing. This is only part of the story, however.

In the automobile industry, annual model changes have long been a significant part of the scene. Planned price changes coincide with the introduction of new products at the beginning of the model year. Setting price is only part of a complex and lengthy process—one which is explained by Kaplan, Dirlam and Lanzilotti in their book, *Pricing in Big Business*.[3] In the fifties and sixties, General Motors (and the rival automakers) produced annual styling changes, but significant design changes of existing models—and the retooling which accompanied them—were introduced in a three-year cycle. Kaplan et al report that GM's decisions on designing, costing, and pricing of new models were taken over a thirty month period prior to the introduction of the new car and its price. The firm would take into account a number of factors simultaneously: (1) forecasts of the trend in consumer tastes and personal income which could alter the demand for automobiles in general, (2) anticipations of the changes in design and engineering which might be introduced by rivals and which would affect the ability of the firm to maintain its market share or expand it, given its own design and engineering plans, and finally, (3) estimates of the costs necessary to produce a competitive design. Thus, GM's price was set to cover costs, given its product

[1]Donaldson Brown, "Pricing Policy in Relation to Financial Control," *Management and Administration* 7 (March 1924), p. 283.

[2]Robert F. Lanzillotti, "Pricing Objectives in Large Companies," *American Economic Review* 48 (December 1958), p. 925.

[3]A. D. H. Kaplan, Joel B. Dirlam, and Robert F. Lanzillotti, *Pricing in Big Business* (Brookings Institution: Washington, 1958).

design. Product design was set, given the product offerings expected from Ford and Chrysler, the costs of producing GM's prospective design, and the forecast of consumers' willingness and ability to pay.

In 1960, Xerox introduced the 914 copier and, of course, had to set its price. The 914 was a unique product. At that time, it was the only machine which could produce copies on plain paper and Xerox had significant market power to exercise in setting its price. Over the years, Xerox's pricing of its 914 copier has reflected several different factors:[4] (1) initially, the possible reluctance on the part of prospective buyers to accept a new and untried product, (2) the inelastic demand for any one buyer for purchasing the services of plain-paper copying, (3) the inherent differences in the copying needs between potential customers, and (4) eventually, the potential for substituting copying services for duplicating services. As long as Xerox enjoyed a monopoly secured by patents, it preferred to lease the services of the machine for a monthly charge, rather than selling it outright. The schedule of charges for leasing reflected the firm's use of market power. At a fixed monthly charge of $25—plus added charges for copies—the user faced a minimal risk even if the product should prove to be undependable. Thus, Xerox was able to capture a large market readily. With a rental fee of 3½¢ per copy, the rental income generated by the lease of a machine was, at least at the margin, proportional to the intensity of use. Xerox was able to capture a large fee for renting a machine to a heavy user and yet was able to get the copy business of the more numerous, but smaller customer. It has been pointed out that the machine rental fees established by Xerox amounted to selling the 914 copier to different users at discriminatory prices, set to match each user's willingness and ability to pay. Capitalizing the rental income at a 10 percent rate of discount and assuming a five-year life for the machine, Blackstone has estimated[5] sample prices of $4,471 for the user who makes 2,000 copies per month and $17,650 for the user who makes 10,000 copies per month. In 1965, Xerox recognized the potential market for substituting xerography for duplicating services.[6] It established a price of 4¢ per copy for the first three copies made from any original, 2¢ each for the additional copies up through the tenth, and 1¢ whenever more than ten copies were made from a single original.

Xerox's pricing clearly reflected the exploitation of market power, taking into consideration the elasticity and intensity of demand for the product. Did it take cost into consideration in the same way as did General Motor's pricing? No, probably not except perhaps for minimum rentals. At the time the rental yield may have implied a purchase price of $10,000 or $20,000 or even more. The

[4]Erwin A. Blackstone, ''The Copying-Machine Industry,'' *Antitrust Law and Economics Review* 6 (Fall 1972), pp. 105–122.

[5]*loc. cit.*, p. 113.

[6]*loc. cit.*, p. 115.

manufacturing cost of the 914 copier—exclusive of the cost of fixed capital and the substantial costs invested in development—was roughly $2,500.[7]

Both GM and Xerox possessed—and do possess—a degree of market power. In their own way they each have used that power in setting price. In the case described above for GM, that use has implications for oligopoly. In the case described for Xerox, that use has implications for a more self-contained strategy of the firm, in terms both of price and product. Let us begin with the former.

INDEPENDENCE AND OLIGOPOLY

Throughout the last two chapters, we emphasized one critical aspect of oligopoly. We examined how interdependence shapes the behavior of oligopolists, in theory and in practice. Is it inevitable that, in markets with only a few firms, price will be a constant source of tension or concern among them? Perhaps it is not. Product differentiation is a condition under which there is a bit of room for the firm to maneuver independently, even if it has close rivals, and even if they are few in number. It is that aspect of market structure which tends to offset the firm's perception of and response to interdependence which we associate with high market concentration. What is the precise nature and importance of such independence?

If the firm has some degree of independence, it may adjust prices—and at least as important, allow its rivals to adjust their prices—without upsetting the "balance of power." This is important. Oligopoly equilibrium may be very stable. If so, it represents a significant departure from the predictions given by traditional and modern oligopoly theories. It provides an alternative explanation for the peaceful coexistence which is often found in oligopoly markets and is often attributed either to price leadership or to collusion, as we have described in the preceding chapter. Independence may have powerful implications for oligoply, but for the moment, let us consider how it works.

Let us assume that a firm can and does price independently. How much market power does that imply? Does independence mean that the firm faces a steeply sloped demand curve—that is, the firm enjoys strong vertical product differentiation—and is in the position to exercise considerable discretion over price? It can mean that, but not necessarily.

Consider the case of General Motors once again. GM designs, makes, and sells differentiated products. As a result, GM has some discretion in pricing individual models. Indeed, there can be no question about GM's long-held position as price leader in the market; it was dominant in the U.S. auto industry for a period of sixty years. Could GM establish any price level it wanted unilaterally? No, it seems unlikely that GM could set the price unless other automakers regarded the same as a legitimate basis for the whole industry and followed GM's lead. So, what was the nature of General Motor's control? Briefly,

[7]*loc. cit.*, p. 112.

it had been able to exercise sufficient control over its costs and over its market share—through horizontal product differentiation—to make modest independent control of prices pay off. Equally important, in the 1980s, it has been GM's failure to maintain control over costs and market share which has led to reversals. This does not just apply to General Motors and/or the auto industry; it has been the experience of a number of firms in a wide variety of industries.

What is the implication of this? It is common to regard market power and/or pricing independence simply as a matter of demand. Costs are important too. A common form of pricing under oligopoly—or even monopoly—reflects this fact.

Full-Cost Pricing

What is full-cost pricing? Why is it important? First, the *full-cost price* is one based upon the sum of average variable cost plus average fixed cost (including a margin for profit) for the expected volume of goods to be sold by the firm. Second, it is important because it is widely practiced in business, and because it has been the source of considerable controversy in economics.

General Motors uses a form of the technique, one known as *standard volume pricing*. Indeed, GM may well have introduced, refined, and popularized it, according to the series of 1924 articles in *Management and Administration*.[8] General Motors grew to dominate the automobile market, achieved a virtual monopoly in diesel locomotives, and established strong positions in markets for various home and industrial appliances. Full-cost pricing may either have helped or, at the very least, proved to be no great hinderance. In any event, GM appears to have been very successful. Its example seems to have given numerous other large firms a pattern from which to develop their own pricing procedures. What is surprising about all of this? Only this, for a long period of time, the community of academic economists appears to have been virtually unaware of the practice of full-cost pricing.

In 1939, Hall and Hitch[9] published an article based upon interviews with the executives of 38 British firms. The article reported that a substantial percentage of firms surveyed used a simple formula or rule of thumb, based upon cost, for setting price. Several implications appeared to follow directly from this finding: (1) the firms perceived themselves to have some degree of independence in making price decisions, (2) the firms seemed to regard the condition of demand to be of secondary importance in the matter, and (3) the firms seemed to be more interested in achieving satisfactory levels of profits, rather than maximizing. These implications, particularly the second and third, were contrary to accepted theory. The whole disclosure was a surprise. It led to lengthy debates. How do

---

[8]Donaldson Brown, *Management and Administration*, "Pricing Policy in Relation to Financial Control," 7 (February 1924), pp. 195–198; 7 (March 1924), pp. 283–286; 7 (April 1924), pp. 417–422.

[9]R. L. Hall and C. J. Hitch, "Price Theory and Business Behavior," *Oxford Economic Papers* 2 (May 1938), pp. 12–45.

firms use full-cost pricing rules? Why? Do they really behave in a non-optimal fashion or can firms maximize profits in ways other than those which seem more familiar?

Standard Volume Pricing

Standard volume pricing may be the most complex of the various full-cost techniques which have been applied. At least it would appear that more factors are separately and explicitly considered in standard volume pricing than any of the others. How does it work? Let us consider a hypothetical example of a firm such as General Motors pricing its 1986 car line.

First, we need to consider some of the basic parameters of the decision process. GM has accumulated a considerable amount of history: (1) it has seen what it has been able to accomplish with respect to market share, (2) it has discovered what it can expect to earn, on the average, when it maintains that position in the market, (3) it has learned how external factors, such as GNP and employment growth, affect total industry auto sales, (4) it has an idea about what product design changes are likely to be introduced by the competition and what it will have to do in order to stay competitive, and (5) it knows what the costs of producing current models have been and what the costs of future models are likely to be. Second, we need to consider what the firm establishes as its objectives. In the case of GM, it would appear that the firm has established two related targets: (1) it seeks to maintain a domestic market share of 50 percent, and (2) it seeks to earn a return of 20 percent on equity, after taxes, assuming normal conditions. Third, we need to consider how all of the pieces apply to the determination of product cost and price.

Let us assume that the firm starts the process of planning the product design, cost, and price early in 1984 for the 1986 model year. Let us assume that preliminary estimates of the 1986 model year market conditions dictate that retail price for the GM line be set at a level of $10,500 in order to ensure the firm's ability to hold its market share of 50 percent. In order to reach this figure, it is necessary to anticipate the basic design and production conditions which the future market will dictate and to cost them out in rough terms. Given the fact that the dealer margin has historically been set at a level of 24 percent of the sticker price, the factory price of the car must be set at $7,980. Thus, a car must be designed which can be produced for such an amount; the figure includes target profits of 20 percent, net of taxes, assuming that the firm is able to sell the number of units equal to its standard volume. For the purposes of this exercise, let us assume that 5 million units is the standard volume.

As the whole process moves forward, and as the final design of the product is settled upon, certain elements are determined. For given specifications, the tooling and production costs are set, subject to changes in factor prices. The firm is able to forecast how much additional investment in plant and equipment will be necessary to produce the future models. Depending upon (1) how the firm decides to finance this investment (by borrowing or by reinvesting retained earnings), (2) the amount of capital, net of depreciation, the firm will carry over into the 1986 model year, and (3) the cost of capital (the market cost of borrowing and the target rate return on equity), the fixed costs of the new line will be set. Now let us see how all of this fits together. The basic results are summarized in Table 10-1.

The forecasts of total expenditures on fixed cost items—the cost of administration and selling plus the cost of capital—are shown in the first section. If the firm achieves a volume of sales equal to five million units, these will amount to a unit cost of $2,042. The forecast of production costs—the cost per unit for all labor and materials used within the plant and for all purchases of finished goods incorporated in the final product—is shown in the second section. If the firm maintains strict control over its variable inputs and if the marginal production costs are constant, the firm plans on manufacturing its cars at a cost of $6,030 per unit. Thus, the full-cost pricing technique requires that the firm charge a factory price of $8,072. Will the firm simply charge this price and set the sticker price at $10,621? Perhaps it will, but there is an alternative.

Remember how we described the start of the whole process. We assumed that the firm anticipated that a competitively priced unit would carry a sticker price of $10,500 (and a factory price of $7,980). A firm such as General Motors may have sufficient independence to depart slightly from the competition if it comes to that, and its full-cost price is only $121 over the original target. However, the firm could still make a final adjustment in its product and the cost of producing it; it could design down the finished product by making virtually imperceptible changes in the specifications and by substituting cheaper components, such as a lower grade tire, than it had originally planned. In fact, the firm

TABLE 10.1 AN ILLUSTRATION OF STANDARD VOLUME PRICING

COST ITEM	TOTAL COST (BILLION DOLLARS)	UNIT COST (DOLLARS)
Fixed Costs		
Administration and selling	$ 3.5	$ 700*
Interest payments	1.0	200*
Target profits	5.7	1,142*
Variable Costs		
Labor and materials (including purchases of finished goods)	– –	6,030
Factory Price		8,072
Dealer Margin @ 24% of Sticker Price		2,549
Sticker Price		10,621

*Item unit cost calculated on the basis of a standard volume of 5,000,000 units in the model year

might offer as a recommended option, the equipment specified in the original design. Is this so different? No. It does serve to underscore an important point: the pricing and the costing of the product are all part of the same process. To take the argument one step further, the firm's ability to alter a differentiated product and its ability to control the price are all derived from the same fundamental condition. To do either, the firm must enjoy a degree of independence from its rivals.

What about demand? What are the limits to the firm's control over price? We have assumed, in the present case, that our firm expects to maintain its normal share of the market as long as its product is competitively priced. What do we mean by a *competitive* price in this context? How does it affect target return pricing? We have implicitly assumed that our hypothetical firm enjoys a market position in which loyal customers prefer its cars to those made by the competition and will buy them, *ceteris paribus*—horizontal differentiation is presumed to be present.[10] We might also assume that demand for the product of our hypothetical automaker looks something like that which is shown in Figure 10-1. In Figure 10-1, we have indicated that firm could expect to keep its normal market share—and its sales will reach the standard volume target of Q*—provided it meets the market price P*. We have shown that the market price is, in effect, a band rather than a point. Is there evidence to support this? Yes, one seller's product is frequently priced above or below the comparable differentiated product of a rival. Thus, the firm has some range of discretion in pricing. To illustrate this, we have shown that our firm's full-cost curve, AC, cuts through the band. If our firm believes that a factory price of $8,072, shown in Table 10-1 below, falls

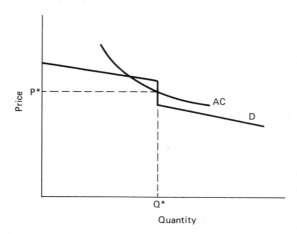

Figure 10-1 Target-return pricing is based upon costs AC, the standard volume Q*, and a demand D which allows some discretion in price. Rather than worrying about rival reactions, a firm looks inward. Price P* will equal cost, including the target profit, provided the firm makes its standard volume.

[10]In the actual case of GM, the strength of differentiation is shown by the breadth of the appeal for its products, by the fact that the firm has been able, year after year, to capture about 50 percent of all sales made in the United States.

within such a band, it will fix price at that level. If our firm believes that the corresponding sticker price of $10,621 is too high to meet the competition, it will find some way to lower costs.

Let us assume that our firm has sufficient market power to set its full-cost factory price at $8,072 (or its retail sticker price at $10,621) and to capture its share of the market. Does that mean that the firm will realize its target profit of $1,142 per unit, or a 20 percent return on equity after taxes? No, it does not. The firm would satisfy its goal precisely only if its actual sales volume turns out to be equal to its planned standard volume, which we have assumed to be five million units per year. If the firm were to sell four million units, *ceteris paribus*, its actual profit would be $912 per unit, or a 12.8 percent return on equity after taxes. If the firm were to sell six million units, its actual profit would be $1,292 per unit, or 27.2 percent return on equity after taxes.

So, what is the implication? It is that standard volume—or for that matter, any other full-cost pricing technique—is a tool which helps the firm to achieve its profit and market share targets over the long run. Variations in performance might occur from year to year. Indeed, they are virtually certain to occur since demand for the firm's product, along with aggregate demand, will swing back and forth with the business cycle. The firm has a limited ability to predict such changes, let alone control them. In such a case, the firm concentrates upon those factors over which it does have some control—the design and costing of its product. So, the firm's pricing decisions are based more upon the latter considerations than upon demand *per se*.

Fixed-Price Supply

Let us assume that the firm sets price at the level of its full cost. It is a price maker in the usual sense of that term. However, one thing is lacking from the more familiar case of the pure monopolist—the firm does not know in advance how many units it will actually be able to sell nor what its profits will be. What does this mean in terms of the behavior of the full-cost pricer? It means that the firm stands ready to meet the market demand for its product, whatever that turns out to be, at the price which it has chosen. The firm adopts what is called a fixed-price supply. That is, it acts as a quantity adjuster, rather than a price adjuster. We illustrate its behavior with the perfectly elastic supply curve, $S(P^*)$, as shown in Figure 10-2. The firm sets the full-cost price, P^*, on the assumption that output, Q^*, will be at standard volume, but the firm is prepared to supply output as the market dictates. If quantity demanded should exceed the standard volume expectations, the firm will earn more than its target return. That is, average costs, including a provision for profits, will be less than planned. If sales should fall short of the standard volume, the firm will not earn its target return. Average costs will exceed the supply price.

Can any oligopolist or monopolist who chooses behave in this fashion? Or will they? Apparently not, since there are many who do not. What is the expla-

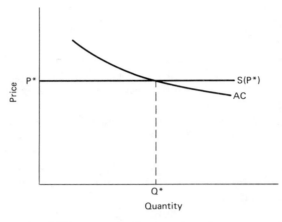

Figure 10-2 A firm's fixed-price supply S(P*)is a commitment to adjust quantity, not price, to compensate for changes in demand. Once it sets price P* through its internal target-return process, the firm is committed to a strategy of price stability.

nation? We must really examine the two questions separately: (1) would the firm choose to act as a fixed-price supplier if it could? and (2) could the firm set and maintain a fixed-price if it wanted? Let us defer the first and consider the second question here.

What is needed for the firm to be able to maintain a fixed-price with any real success? The most critical consideration, aside from the matter of pricing independence, is the ability to *control* costs. There are two factors which figure in such an ability: (1) the constancy of average variable cost over a wide range of output, and (2) the predominance of variable costs in the total of all costs. Consider the illustration of standard volume pricing laid out in Table 10-1 above. There we assumed that the hypothetical automaker could keep its variable costs at $6,030 per unit, regardless of the level of output, and that fixed costs (exclusive of profits) would be $900 per unit at the standard volume. In this example, if sales should increase by 20 percent, the drop in average total costs (not including the target profit) would only be 2 percent, and if sales should decrease by 20 percent, the rise in average total costs would only be 3 percent. Even if large absolute amounts of capital are necessary for producing certain types of goods, as they are in the auto industry, if the scale of operation is large enough, fixed costs may be a small and relatively constant percentage of average total cost.

Does control over costs apply to full-cost pricing formulas other than the standard volume? Consider the case of mark-up pricing. Let us suppose that a firm obtains a product—either by producing or purchasing it—at a constant cost and suppose that the firm markets the product at a modest overhead cost. It would be possible to use the model shown in Figure 10-2 to explain the pricing behavior for such a firm: the height of the firm's AC curve at Q^* is determined by the sum of the product cost plus the overhead cost, including a profit, and in turn, that is used by the firm as the basis for its price. Take the case of a retail establishment with a rapid turnover of inventory, where mark-up pricing appears to be the norm—the supermarket comes quickly to mind. The unit cost of any good which the supermarket retails is constant at any point in time; it is set by conditions in the wholesale market. The store's overhead costs are relatively small. They are treated as a more or less constant increment of unit cost. Supermarket prices are, therefore, generated by a formula which simply adds a mark-up to the wholesale price.

Is there any important difference between the standard volume price and the mark-up price? Yes there is. The retailer uses mark-up pricing as a tool for setting price on a day to day basis. When wholesalers increase or decrease their prices, the retailer does the same. The retailer has no general plan in pricing except to use the appropriate mark-up formula. The manufacturer uses standard volume pricing as a tool for planning the design and cost and price of a new product, perhaps several years in advance of its introduction. The fixed-price supply of the standard volume manufacturer represents a real commitment, while the mark-up price of the retailer represents little more than a temporary position determined largely by factors beyond its control.

What can be said about firms which cannot control costs? What happens when marginal costs have the traditional U-shape and fixed costs are a major proportion of the total? Price changes are most likely to accompany changes in demand, *ceteris paribus*, when the ability to control cost is missing. In the case of the monopolist, the firm is able to control price—it would set a new profit-maximizing price if demand should shift—even if it is unable to control cost. In the case of the oligopolist, matters are different. If the products are homogeneous, the oligopolists may find themselves in a desperate situation when demand is slack. The price warfare which we described in Chapter 9 and which we called *destructive competition* is endemic to those industries in which firms have little control over cost and have to rely upon price to attract and/or to hold customers. Let us consider, for the moment, the oligopoly which is subject to price warfare. Does fixed-price supply have anything to do with such a case? Surprisingly, yes.

When a group of firms comes to the conclusion that it has suffered enough from warring, it may well seek to restore peace by fixing price. The cartel is, after all, an institution designed to compel its member firms to adopt a common fixed-price supply. In comparison to the single, independent, standard-volume pricing firm, how well can the cartel really expect to perform? Not nearly as well, it would seem safe to say. The cartel must depend upon cooperation. However, the single firm can rely upon its own market power. The former must modify the behavior of its members and is likely to be only partially successful in order to make up for the structural advantage which the latter possesses all by itself.

Does this mean that the independent firm which controls cost and sets a fixed-price—a firm such as General Motors—has nothing to fear from swings in demand? No it does not. In the three year period from 1980 through 1982, the giants of the U.S. automobile industry, including General Motors, lost several billions of dollars. If there had been any illusions about the ultimate invulnerability of certain firms to unfavorable market conditions, this experience should have removed them. Full-cost pricing implies that the firm has substantial, but not unlimited market power.

We have answered, at least in part, why one firm can act as a fixed-price supplier while another cannot. We also posed a second question earlier: why would a firm choose to do so? Let us turn to that question now.

Full-Cost Pricing and Profit Maximization

When economists began to absorb the Hall and Hitch findings, that many of the largest firms in the economy employed full-cost pricing, they became embroiled in a new and heated debate. Did it imply that a widespread abandonment of profit maximization had taken place in the private sector? There was certainly evidence to that effect: (1) firms stated that they sought target levels of profit, sometimes expressed as a *fair return* rather than the maximum, and (2) firms acted in a semi-passive fashion by setting price and adjusting quantity to meet market demand. Why should a firm be willing to settle for less than the best? If indeed that was an accurate interpretation of full-cost pricing, it posed a most challenging question to economic orthodoxy.

In truth, full-costing pricing simply became the new focus for a longer-running debate over profit maximization. Several years earlier, Berle and Means[11] had challenged the traditional theory of the firm. They suggested that the typical modern firm, the corporation, was operated by proxy by a professional team of managers whose interests were not identical with those of their principals—while the owners may desire maximum profits, the managers may not. Ideas introduced by Berle and Means were later elaborated by advocates for **managerialism** in their feud with advocates for **marginalism**. The former term was used to describe the anti-profit-maximization faction while the latter was used to describe the pro-profit-maximization view. Precisely how did full-cost pricing fit into the picture?

The managerial view saw the firm as an instrument to serve a coalition of interests, rather than as a single entity. The firm did not have a mind and, therefore, could not choose to pursue an objective (or set of objectives). The person (or persons) in charge of the firm did and could. Managers could choose. Owners could act to hold them in check, but at a disadvantage of distance from the information about the crucial decisions. Thus, management could expect some free rein. What would rational managers choose to do with it? The manager would seek power and prestige. That would follow from claiming responsibility for the firm's record of performance. How would that be gauged, if not by profits? There are several dimensions of expansion—size, growth, and market share—as well as various expressions of stability in the firm's profit and market

---

[11]Adolph A. Berle and Gardiner Means, *The Modern Corporation and Private Property* (Macmillan: New York, 1932).

position which often seem to be used to measure the stewardship of a firm. These were proposed by the managerialists as objectives competing with or replacing profit-maximization. In this light, pricing formulas, which include either a target return or a mark-up rule of thumb as the profit objective, could be viewed as management decision tools in which profitability is important only to the extent that it keeps ownership happy and off the backs of the managers and/or is consistent with the other, more important objectives of the firm.

Is there a real conflict between the interests of the management and the ownership? Not necessarily. In the long run, attention to growth in sales and to stabilization (or growth) in market share may advance the position of the stockholder as well as the manager. Our intention here is not to introduce and then resolve the managerial revolution; it is to understand the use of full-cost pricing. So to the point at hand. The use of a price formula which is based upon a target rate of return—irrespective of the management of the firm—is not necessarily an indication that the firm has chosen to settle for less than maximum possible profits.

Consider the target rate of return. Do all firms use the same target or are there differences between them? In his study on pricing by twenty firms, Lanzilotti[12] reported a wide variation in profit targets: General Motors sought 20 percent after taxes, Johns-Manville sought 15 percent, International Harvester sought 10 percent, while United States Steel sought only 8 percent. Why should targets vary so much? Is it because the stockholders of GM kept a closer check on management than the stockholders of USS? That seems very unlikely. It is plausible, however, that GM was in a better market position than USS. That is, General Motors had the opportunity to make a higher return on its investment in automobiles than United States Steel—or any other firm, for that matter—could make in steel. In that interpretation, the firm's target rate of profit might represent its best estimate of its potential. What is more convincing, the corporation may assign different profit targets to different divisions.

In automobiles, as in many industries, manufacturers have long practiced a form of price discrimination, pricing cars in their luxury lines at much greater margins over unit labor and materials cost than cars in their standard lines. Innovative firms from a wide range of industries systematically build high profit margins into the prices of new products—charging "what the traffic will bear." The high margins are, in part, justified by costs when one considers the product development expenses. The high prices will gradually taper off over time, not so much because costs level off and decline but because competition increases. Both the luxury product and the new product represent opportunities for the firm to exercise greater market power. When the firm has more market power, *ceteris paribus*, it seems willing to shoot for a higher profit target.

Now consider fixed-price supply behavior. Do firms which employ a full-cost pricing technique ever depart from it and raise or lower their price? If so,

[12]Lanzilotti, *op. cit.*, pp. 924–927.

under what conditions? Yes, it appears that they do. In the study by Hall and Hitch,[13] it was reported that full-cost pricing firms will, on occasion, change price, either to follow a competitive price change or to respond to a depressed market. The pricing in automobiles and many other products seems generally to conform to this pattern. Price cuts to dealers, or sometimes factory rebates direct to buyers, are offered when the manufacturer has excess inventory on hand. Price increases are instituted when there is an excess demand for the product. On the other hand, price changes are most often represented as temporary departures from the norm; when conditions warrant, the standard price will be reinstated.

What conclusions may be drawn? It would seem that the use of pricing formulas, profit targets, and fixed-prices is perfectly consistent with profit maximization. But there is more.

Independence and Cooperation

When a firm such as General Motors sets a full-cost price, it requires a degree of pricing independence. Recall the prior discussion about how the product design, product cost, and product price all figure in. GM must still be concerned about being competitive with the rest of the industry with respect to each of these dimensions. GM's full-cost price may be a tool for obtaining maximum profits for the firm, but it may also represent a benchmark for and a barometer of the prices of all the firms in the industry. Does this mean that full-cost pricing behavior is a complement to oligopoly coordination? Perhaps it does. Should each firm adopt its own full-cost formula and should each control its production and overhead costs effectively, its vision of the "right" or competitive price should be consistent with those of its rivals. Assuming that a firm establishes its full-cost price correctly, it will necessarily satisfy the expectations of its rivals. This is the essence of the Nash equilibrium of Chapter 8, as well as the collusive price leadership of Chapter 9.

Of course the simplest pricing formulas are those which are blatantly intended to achieve coordination. Some prices cry out for uniform adoption, whether or not they are related to cost. Common even denominations such as a quarter or a dollar are often used by manufacturers in pricing goods, while odd denominations such as 29¢ or 99¢ are often the most popular with high volume retailers. Does such a practice have much to do with cost-based pricing, as we have described it above? No, at least not to the extent that the latter is an expression of independence.

However, it can be argued that full-cost pricing is really a substitute for oligopolistic cooperation rather than a complement to it. Whenever price is set

[13]Hall and Hitch, *op. cit.*, p. 29.

according to the firm's own costs, rather than the rivals' prices, it is clear that (1) the firm has a degree of independence, and (2) the firm chooses to exercise it so as to control its profit margin rather than its market share. Thus, price changes may be seen as consistent with the integrity of the oligopoly market structure—price changes may be seen as the necessary response to cost changes rather than as the effort to improve market position, and the independent price behavior of the firm need not ever be regarded by rivals as threatening.

Full-cost pricing plays an important role in the oligopoly market. It may serve to avoid the destructive competition, as described in Chapter 9, that is sometimes found in oligopoly, but does not always work that way. For example, manufacturers of undifferentiated products—USS in steel and GE in industrial electrical equipment are two cases in point—have less success with full-cost prices than do the manufacturers of differentiated products. Why is this? When competition is focused on price, as it is in the case of homogeneous products, rivals do not seem to be able to resist competitive price cuts, particularly with slack demand. How about those markets in which a cost-based price system works? It would seem that non-price competition—that is, reliance upon developing a better or more attractive product than the competition or promoting consumer acceptance of the real or perceived differences between one's product and those offered by the competition—is most often associated with the practice of full-cost pricing. That should not be surprising, however. When price is not the most important competitive factor, pricing is not likely to be a problem, even in the oligopoly market. Then what is cause and what is effect? Does price independence and the use of formulas in setting price lead to oligopoly coordination, or does the irrelevance of coordination in pricing explain price independence? Perhaps it is a bit of both.

INDEPENDENCE AND INTERNAL STRATEGY

So far we have stressed the importance of independence in reducing oligopoly tensions. We have also suggested that pricing independence often takes form in the application of a management tool, such as target return pricing. Where does this lead? It would seem that it leads to blurring the distinctions between differentiated oligopoly and monopoly—the difference between Ford pricing current Taurus or Mustang models and Xerox pricing its original 914 copier is merely one of degree, rather than of kind. It also leads to a new perspective on pricing. Ford is not interested in pricing just one product in one market; it has a long product line and sells in many segments of the market; it is interested in setting prices for the entire line. For many a firm, the fact that it has a position in a number of markets may be just as important as the fact that it possesses some degree of independence in any one of them. But why?

The Multiproduct Strategy

General Motors faced a desperate situation in the spring of 1921. It was the second largest auto producer behind Ford, but it was fast losing market share, and it was losing money as well. A new management had taken over, and a prime concern of the new team was the state of the product line.[14] The founding genius of GM, "Billy" Durant, built good cars but seemed to have no sense of direction in designing a product line (or in running a major corporation, for that matter). Most of GM's products including Chevrolet, its leading brand, competed generally with one another in the mid-price range of the market. So, after he had secured Durant's departure, the new chief executive, Pierre S. du Pont, assigned the Executive Committee the task of developing an overall product line policy. The result, like the development of target-return pricing, would provide a model for others to follow and would influence the behavior of the modern corporation.

When the Executive Committee delivered its final report, it recommended that GM offer products in six different price ranges—Chevrolet, Oakland, a 4-cylinder Buick, a Buick 6, Oldsmobile, and Cadillac.[15] Thus, GM established a plan for segmenting the automobile market. While it is such an obvious strategy now that we see it everywhere in markets for consumer goods, it was quite revolutionary at the time. Remember that Ford had achieved such great success in the industry with one car, the Model T, holding a virtual monopoly over the low-price, high-volume end of the market. The committee also attached a recommendation for GM's marketing strategy; General Motors should use quality, not price, as its competitive weapon. It was intended that GM products be priced at the top of their respective market segments. How well did the strategy work? In six years, GM would replace Ford as the leading automaker in the United States. It is an interesting tale, of course, but what is the general lesson to be learned regarding pricing independence?

First, product differentiation not only permits the firm to distinguish its own product from those offered by rivals but also to offer a range of products, distinguishing each from the other and making an appeal to different groups of consumers. In this fashion, the firm can—as General Motors proved could be done—build up a larger market share than otherwise.

Second, when the firm acts to segment the market—that is, to offer a line of differentiated products rather than a single one—it may build a larger market for itself without having to make a direct assault on the home market occupied by a rival. This, in turn, helps develop a feeling of independence which runs both ways. As GM broadened its product line, in terms of its total operation, it became less of a direct rival of Ford or a threat to Ford (with the exception of the

---

[14]Alfred D. Chandler, Jr., *Pierre S. du Pont and the Making of the Modern Corporation* (Harper & Row: New York, 1971), p. 513.

[15]*loc. cit.*, pp. 517–518.

Chevrolet Division). In a very real sense, the independence of both GM and Ford was strengthened, and each would be freer to price its own products without the disabling fear of retaliation. In the case at hand, as General Motors sought to offer higher quality products line by line than the competition, it further enhanced its own ability to control price independently.

Third, the ability to differentiate products in this fashion illustrates that the multiproduct strategy may permit the firm to improve its position and profitability on its own initiative. An ability to differentiate provides the firm with an alternative to *outpricing* the competition. In the following chapters we shall attempt to focus upon the details of such competition. At this point, however, we are really interested in the implications such a strategy has for pricing—it does provide a freedom for the firm to price as it so chooses. In contrast, if the firm cannot insulate itself from direct rivalry, either (1) it must deal with destructive competition on the one hand, or (2) it must depend upon the willingness of its rivals to cooperate on the other. It would seem that a multiproduct strategy, one which enhances the firm's independence and that of its rivals, is superior to the strategy of cooperation with rivals in a undifferentiated, single product market.

Finally, the multiproduct strategy also leads us to another facet of independent pricing, price discrimination.

Price Discrimination

What is price discrimination? Why is it important? To answer the first question, price discrimination is the practice of charging different prices to different buyers—or different prices for different sales to the same buyer—for the same good. To answer the second question, price discrimination allows the firm to increase its profits. It permits the firm (1) to secure a high price for those sales which it is bound to get in any case and (2) to use a lower price to attract added sales which increase volume, improve utilization of fixed resources, and yield the extra profit. In fact, price discrimination may enable the firm to make a profit under conditions in which it otherwise would be impossible to do so.

Consider the case illustrated in Figure 10-3. We show a demand and average cost curve for a monopolist who can charge any price it wants but cannot find a single price that yields a net profit. If the monopolist can charge P_0 for the first block of goods, a quantity equal to Q_0 units, and can charge P_1 for the second block of goods, a quantity equal to $[Q_1 - Q_2]$ units, the monopolist's average price P_a will exceed average cost for its total sales. Price discrimination permits the firm to fashion an average revenue curve, shown here as AR, which extends beyond the original demand curve and which accounts for the added profits—neither selling Q_0 at the higher price P_0 nor selling Q_1 at the lower price P_1 will yield as much revenue as selling some at one price and some at the other.

Discrimination necessarily implies pricing independence and requires market power. It is the natural extension of monopoly, but as we have seen,

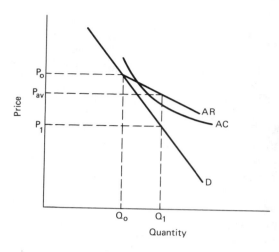

Figure 10-3 Price discrimination increases profits. If the firm could separate markets, selling Q_0 units for P_0, and additional units for P_1, it could sell Q_1 for an average price P_{av}, which is more than enough to cover the average costs of Q_1. Yet, the higher price, P_0, could not cover the average costs of Q_0 alone.

monopoly and differentiated oligopoly can be difficult to distinguish. Indeed, the differentiated oligopolist may employ a strategy enabling it to price independently. We have described how General Motors, like many other oligopoly firms, uses target return pricing to do so. Now we are interested in a related matter. How may GM or any other firm, monopolist or oligopolist, use its market power to gain maximum profits? Can the ability to extract additional profits be attributed to the multiproduct strategy of the firm?

Price Discrimination in Theory.   Suppose that a firm faces the market conditions shown by the demand and average cost curves of Figure 10-3. Is it clear that the firm will discriminate in the manner indicated above? No it is not. Monopoly power alone is not sufficient; two other conditions must be present. First, if the firm is to profit from discrimination, it is necessary that different buyers have different demand characteristics. That is, some buyers must have a more inelastic demand for a product—be willing and able to pay a higher price for the opportunity to buy the good—than others do. Otherwise, discrimination would not increase profits and there would be no reason to discriminate in price. Second, if a firm does discriminate, it is necessary that buyers who receive different price offers be separated from one another. That is, the buyers in one market must not be able to communicate and transact with the buyers in the other market. If there were no separation between buyers, and if the discriminating monopolist offered to sell to one at a price lower than the price it offered to the other, its entire scheme could be ruined. The first buyer could act as an arbitrageur—i.e., buying cheap and reselling dear to the other—and the original supplier could be closed out from the more profitable, high-price market. One part of the strategy (selling cheaply to buyers in a down-scale market so as to expand total sales volume) could interfere with another (exploiting the inelastic demand of the firm's up-scale market).

Let us assume that the basic conditions are met. How will the monopolist go about establishing a system of prices? Pigou identified three cases which have become a tradition in economic theory. Although they are only hypothetical alternatives, they should provide some insight into the actual practice of price discrimination.

First-degree price discrimination is the name given to the most profitable and least likely form. Imagine the result of the monopolist's being able to sell each unit of a good separately to the highest bidder. Each unit would be sold at a unique price. Since the monopolist would profit from each sale up to the point that the last unit auctioned off sold for a price just covering marginal cost, monopoly would supply the identical quantity that a perfectly competitive market would supply but would extract all the consumer surplus [see Chapter 1] in the process. What could account for such a degree of power? First, separation between buyers must be total, making it impossible for the buyer who pays a low price to resell the product to another who would be willing and able to pay a higher price. Second, a seller must be able to measure demand perfectly and costlessly—note that an auctioning process is never costless. Thus, this seems very unlikely. Nevertheless, first-degree price discrimination does serve its theoretical function; it establishes an absolute limit of monopoly power, *ceteris paribus*.

Second-degree price discrimination is the name given to a form which produces similar results, but one which imposes less stringent conditions for achievement of discrimination, provided that the typical buyer purchases several units of the product. Imagine the result of the monopolist's being in the position to sell the first block of units to a buyer at one price, to sell the next block to the same buyer at a little lower price, and so on. This could be depicted as in Figure 10-3, envisioning D as the demand curve for an individual, rather than for the market. The effect on the firm's average price would be the same as shown above, and the firm could generate more revenues and net profits by discriminating than by not discriminating.

Third-degree price discrimination is the name given to the most common form—setting different prices for sales made to different buyers. Imagine the result of a monopolist's being able to discriminate by charging a high price for the sale of a good to its customers who are willing and able to pay it and by charging a lower price for the sale of a good to its customers who would have been excluded from the market by the higher price. We may illustrate third-degree price discrimination as shown in Figure 10-4, in which it is assumed that two market segments are served by a firm with a constant marginal cost, labelled MC in both panels. It is assumed that the two demand curves, D_1 and D_2, and the corresponding marginal revenue curves, MR_1 and MR_2, for the two sub-

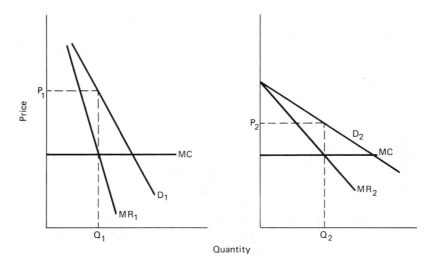

Figure 10-4 Price discrimination is a special case of monopoly. If the firm separates its markets, and if the market demands D_1 and D_2 are different, the firm would set two prices. Buyers with more inelastic demands would pay a higher price P_1, while buyers with more elastic demands would pay a lower price P_2.

markets are different. A profit-maximizing monopolist would, under these circumstances, set two prices for its product, P_1 and P_2.

Price Discrimination and Multiproduct Strategy.   As a practical matter, is it fair to say that the firm would consciously set out to discriminate in price? Perhaps. And would the firm carefully tailor its price structure in the fashion suggested by the theory described above? Would it be concerned, for example, whether to construct a system of prices based on second-degree or third-degree price discrimination and whether or not the prices it set were optimal? Perhaps not. It is likely, however, that a firm would search to improve its profit position. In so doing, a firm is likely to experiment with pricing schemes which turn out to be discriminatory.

What determines the workability of a scheme? We have already indicated that price discrimination requires that markets which are assigned different prices be separated, and that they have different elasticities of demand. Thus, the same efforts that lead to establishing the firm's product line are likely to produce its ability to discriminate in price. Differentiated products are designed to appeal to different segments of the market, and that implies separate markets with separate demand characteristics. Thus, pricing the various items in the firm's product line probably implies a form of discrimination.

Consider the case of General Motors. The designs of GM's various makes and models of automobiles were created in order to appeal to different individuals or groups within the car-buying public. A set of products could satisfy a population, which is naturally diverse in age, taste, and income, in a way in which a single product cannot. As we have seen in establishing its 1921 product policy, General Motors planned on offering six different models, appealing to different price segments to gain the widest possible access to the market. This decision merely marked the beginning of *product lining*. Later, automobile styles and models would proliferate, with coupes and sedans, convertibles and hard-tops, station wagons and pickups, and so on. Some would be designed along utilitarian lines (the Chevrolet Celebrity, for example), while others would appeal to the car buff seeking the thrill of high performance (the Corvette), while still others would be aimed at the person seeking prestige in an automobile (the Cadillac Allante).

It is obvious that at some point it became clear to the automaker that elasticities of demand varied significantly from one market segment to another, that some buyers were willing and able to pay a good deal more for a car than those seeking only basic transportation, because the auto manufacturers eventually began to practice a form of price discrimination. General Motors, for example, will price its luxury car or its performance car so as to discriminate for differences in demand, as compared to the price of its fleet car. How? We have assumed above that GM prices according to cost. It is quite simple. The full-cost price of its luxury or performance models will include a larger proportion of GM's target returns and other overhead costs than the full-cost price of the fleet models. General Motors, or any differentiated oligopolist, will assign a higher proportion of its overhead cost burden to customers willing and able to pay it than to its other customers.

The same general principle would seem to apply to products whose relative attractiveness can be explained by their newness. Kaplan et al[16] reported that the large, multiproduct firm which specializes in research and development for its product mix—a firm such as DuPont—controls price and product simultaneously. It will ordinarily seek the highest target returns from the most promising of its new products, it will seek a lower target from the more mature and competitive products in its line, and it will drop those products which cannot satisfy its own guidelines for a minimal return. What does this mean? It means that the profit targets or price-cost margins vary from one product to another, with the highest margins earned in supplying products which face the least competition. It means that discrimination is an important element in the price-and-product strategy of the firm, even if the form of the discrimination does not look much like that depicted in Figure 10-4.

Is such behavior exceptional? Or are General Motors and DuPont, and industries such as automobiles and chemicals, the rule rather than the exception? It would seem that, in cases of multiproduct firms which supply differenti-

---

[16]Kaplan et al. *op. cit.*, pp. 96–108.

ated products, price discrimination of some sort is a rather commonplace phenomenon. All things considered, it is likely that this is the most common form of discrimination—the discrimination that is practiced is a part of the multiproduct strategy of the firm. Are there other forms of discrimination in use? Yes, but these are often associated with pure monopoly rather than with differentiated oligopoly.

Consider the discrimination practiced by Xerox in the early years of its monopoly of plain-paper copiers. As we have indicated, Xerox was able to discriminate between different users of the same product, the 914 copier. So, how did Xerox accomplish this? It used second-degree price discrimination, with a pricing scheme that was uniform for all users. Xerox leased machines to users rather than selling them outright. It simply discriminated between customers according to the intensity of their use; those who had a heavy demand and produced large numbers of copies would pay large user fees, and those who copied relatively few items per month would pay smaller user fees. To accomplish the same result for a product sold outright, it would have to tailor the price of the machine to the particular demands of each user. In addition, it would have to prevent the resale of any machine to keep others from spoiling the high-price market. The firm could not legally prohibit buyers from reselling. Thus, Xerox accomplished by leasing two things which would otherwise have been impossible: (1) it could maintain the separation of markets necessary for discrimination, and (2) it could use the schedule of leasing fees to discriminate in price.

In application, price discrimination seems different from the theory. It would seem to be a far more common practice than we might have been led to believe. It would seem to be an important part of price behavior under oligopoly—particularly differentiated product oligopoly—rather than just monopoly. Indeed, it would really seem to be part of a larger strategy of the firm in an oligopoly market setting. It would seem to be related to those elements of non-price behavior that are designed to establish for the firm a stronger and more profitable position in the market.

COMPETITION IN SELLING EFFORTS: ADVERTISING AND RELATED MARKET BEHAVIOR

11

*In this chapter we examine the meaning and implications of advertising and other product promotion behavior. Starting with two examples of product promotion, we turn to the analysis of **selling**. First, we examine the relationship between selling and information. We discover how market failure in information accounts for differentiation of the product and how advertising provides information. Next, we see how advertising affects the sales of the product and its costs. We see how the two effects can be incorporated into a model of **optimal advertising** for a firm which acts independently of rivals.*

Next, we examine modifications of the model which might be dictated by an oligopoly strategy. We also consider how the firm may adopt a rule of thumb approach to advertising as a rational alternative to strategy based upon anticipations of and reactions to rival behavior. Rules may provide more peace of mind and a sense of independent control lacking in the latter. Finally, we consider the role of advertising in a strategy to deter entry.

A short appendix to the chapter is provided to examine the statistical relationships between concentration and advertising and between advertising and profitability.

What are selling efforts? They incorporate all those forms of competition in which the firm seeks to increase sales without changing either the price or the product itself. Are selling efforts important? Yes they are, at least in certain markets.[1] What precisely constitute selling efforts? They are defined as being any and all of the expenditures which promote the sales of a firm's product. Advertising is the most obvious. Much of the selling effort involves personal contact between seller and buyer: there is the person stationed at the cosmetics counter who demonstrates the newest product to passing shoppers; there is the

[1]Selling effort is one of three elements—price, product, and selling effort—identified by Chamberlin as controlling how much of a differentiated product consumers demand. He made the point that selling can be as important for certain cases of oligopoly as it is for the case of monopolistic competition.

auto salesperson who provides the pitch, the test drive, and the not-so-subtle twist of the arm to sign an offer sheet; and there is the manufacturer's representative for a major computer firm who spends months with a client, often together with a team of technical specialists, selling a concept.

In this chapter we attempt to answer several questions. Why do selling efforts work? Are there certain advantages to the firm which seeks to outsell—rather than to underprice—the competition? How is selling incorporated into the theory of the firm? How do firms actually behave in practice? Can selling behavior alter the structure of the market? How? But before we begin in earnest, let us consider two examples of the use of selling efforts.

TWO CASES OF SELLING EFFORT

In 1970, Phillip Morris purchased the Miller Brewing Company and brought a new aggressiveness to the marketing and advertising of beers. Miller, which was the seventh largest brewing company in 1970, almost immediately became the second largest advertiser in the industry, and by 1975, Miller's advertising expenditure had reached $3 per barrel. It was spending at a rate nearly double that of the next most intensive advertiser.[2] Was the effort worthwhile? Yes, it would appear to be. Miller Brewing Company had increased its share of the market from 4 percent in 1972 to 12 percent in 1975, and was challenging for third place in the industry.[3] Within two more years, Miller had again increased its market share, then 15 percent, and had established itself as second only to the industry leader, Anheuser-Busch.[4]

Was the quantity of its advertising expenditure the only factor in Miller's growth? No it was not. The new management junked the old Miller image—"the champagne of bottled beers"—for a new one. It introduced a number of innovations, both in product and in marketing strategy.[5] Miller introduced the "pony" bottle, a seven ounce container, to attract those who might not be "real" beer drinkers. It struck a deal with the European brewer to produce and sell under the *Löwenbrau* label in the United States. Most important of all, it successfully launched a low calorie beer, *Miller Lite,* which turned out to be the most important new product ever introduced in the industry.[6] The advertising campaign for *Miller Lite* also introduced one of the most popular and long-running series of television commercials, featuring an improbable, but loveable collection of ex-athletes and assorted oddballs.

Did Miller's success change more than its own position in the market? Very definitely. Other brewers were faced with the necessity of increasing their sell-

[2]"Miller's Fast Growth Upsets the Beer Industry," *Business Week,* (November 8, 1976), p. 58.

[3]*loc. cit.,* p. 60.

[4]"John Murphy of Miller is Adman of the Year," *Advertising Age,* (January 9, 1978), p. 86.

[5]"Miller's Fast Growth," *op. cit.,* pp. 58–67.

[6]*loc. cit.,* p. 60.

ing efforts. As the result, advertising expenditures rose for the whole industry. The intensity of competition in selling spilled over into pricing. Beer prices did not keep up with the increase in production and market costs, and profit margins dropped from 6 percent to 3.5 percent.[7] The other brewers were forced to adopt the marketing strategy introduced by Miller. In addition to their standard products, each of the major competitors followed the lead of Miller in offering a "pony" bottle and a "light" beer.[8]

In 1950, a successful manufacturer of business machines committed to build the first commerical computer, the IBM 701.[9] The technological problems of developing such a product were rather great, but they were tractable. The marketing problems were much greater. What was the potential for using high-speed data processing? How might that potential best be explained to and accepted by the customer? It would seem that IBM's first generation of computers were not really superior to competitive machines, such as the UNIVAC made by Remington Rand.[10] Two factors did differentiate IBM from early competitors: (1) the willingness to invest in rapid technological development (and in the rapid obsolesence of its own machines), and (2) the awareness that its customers were not interested in the hardware so much as the services which could be derived from it.[11] IBM seemed to do more than the competition in marketing the concept and the use of electronic data processing—a phrase which was coined by IBM.

IBM adopted the practice of direct selling, with a small army of sales representatives. It also relied upon leasing the machines to customers and upon *bundling* the services which it supplied to them. That is, the software, the systems design, the service and repair, and the education of the customer's EDP personnel were all provided in a package.[12] In fact, it is not easy to distinguish between the pre-sale marketing effort and the post-sale service. In the early days, few understood either the workings of computers or their potential applications. Even today, it may be necessary for the sales representative, together with the support of the systems engineer, to develop a feasible and attractive product to sell the customer. Was IBM alone in this practice? No it was not. However, IBM was willing and able to put more resources into the selling effort than rivals. That paid handsome dividends. In more recent years, various firms have had success in developing certain products for certain uses that are superior to those of IBM. Nevertheless, IBM has been able to maintain a position of market leadership—although not nearly as dominant as before—and to com-

[7]*loc. cit.*, p. 59.

[8]*loc. cit.*, p. 62.

[9]Franklin M. Fisher, James W. McKie, and Richard B. Mancke, *IBM and the U.S. Data Processing Industry* (Praeger: New York, 1983), p. 15.

[10]*loc. cit.*

[11]*loc. cit.*, pp. 94–96.

[12]*loc. cit.*, p. 23.

mand the loyalty of its customer base by virtue of the technical and marketing skills upon which it has always relied.

Does this mean that IBM has not changed the way that it sells computers? No it does not. While it did not have a hand in pioneering the development of the personal computer, IBM has not failed in that market. Again, part of the success was the development of a saleable product—the IBM PC is a good basic machine, but it does not overshadow the competition. Another part of IBM's success has been in marketing. In 1981, IBM signed contracts with both Sears and Computerland to market its personal computer line to the new class of retail customers.[13] The change in marketing technique seems to have paid off, but the overall success of the IBM PC is in no small measure due to its name, its reputation, and its intensive advertising campaign.

These two illustrations demonstrate how selling effort—advertising in the one case and direct servicing of accounts in the other—has affected the success of particular firms in particular industries at particular times. Selling the product effectively may be as important as producing it efficiently, if the firm is to maximize profits. Are other factors involved as well? Yes it would seem so. The successful sales strategies of IBM and Miller Brewing Company were also linked to successful product strategies. It may never be possible to separate one from the other. Let us assume that it can.

THE CHARACTER OF SELLING EFFORTS

Let us assume that the firm can and does increase its sales and profits by selling efforts. Is this a reasonable assumption? Yes, we have seen in the cases of Miller Brewing Company and IBM that the firm can better its position by selling. Why does it work? Why do firms sometimes prefer to outsell—rather than to under-price—the competition? To answer these questions we must consider the character of selling.

Selling Efforts and Independence

Advertising (or other selling efforts) may be strategically superior to price competition under certain market conditions, especially under oligopoly. It is not uncommon to find rivals—those who make toothpaste or breakfast cereal or perfume are but a few examples—who carry on a continuing war of words but who rarely compete in price. Why? Competition in advertising (or in other techniques of selling) appears more stable. That is, it seems less apt to invite destructive retaliation than competition in price. The firm which relies upon its selling effort to attract customers seems to enjoy a greater degree of independence than the firm which relies upon its price to do so.

As we explained in the preceding chapter, independence is a desirable characteristic from the point of view of the firm. In the case of full-cost pricing,

---

[13]Stephen T. McClellan, *The Coming Computer Industry Shakeout* (John Wiley: New York, 1984).

the firm may set its own price and maintain its share of the market, provided that the price and the product are competitive. In the case of advertising, however, the firm may set its own level of selling effort and might even increase its share of the market in the bargain. That is, the degree of independence enjoyed by the firm in selling may exceed that enjoyed in pricing. Why? One part of the explanation is that, unlike price, there is more than a quantity dimension to advertising. There is a dimension of quality or content as well.

Selling Efforts and Information

Selling is a form of behavior which we commonly associate with differentiated products, such as Miller Lite and the IBM System/360. Is product differentiation—at least nominal differences—necessary in order to make selling pay? No it is not. Yet it is necessary that differentiating conditions be present—i.e., if advertising or other selling techniques are to generate added sales for the firm, prospective buyers must behave as if the products are differentiated. What accounts for such buyer behavior? It is a simple matter of information or rather the lack of it.

Consider a hypothetical situation in which the consumer is not aware of the existence of a certain product. In that case, the consumer would act in the same way towards it that he or she would act if the product were not suited to his or her tastes. As long as ignorance persists, the consumer would never buy the product. Or consider a hypothetical situation in which the consumer is not aware of the existence of a price difference in the market. In that case, the consumer would act in the same way that he or she would act if all dealers in the product priced it identically. As long as ignorance persists, the consumer would never switch his or her custom from a high-price dealer to a low-price dealer. Advertising can break old buying habits if it can supply new information to the consumer. It can alter the demand for certain products and/or for certain dealers. The consumer can be made better off in the process, purchasing a more suitable product or getting a better price.

Are these merely hypothetical situations? No they are not. A dramatic finding was made by Benham[14] in a study on the effect of advertising on the prices of prescription eyeglasses. Benham based his study upon a 1963 survey of individual household expenditures. The sample could be divided into two groups: (1) purchases by consumers residing in states with no restrictions upon advertising of eyeglasses, and (2) purchases of consumers residing in states with total prohibitions of such advertising. The average price paid in states with unrestricted advertising (Texas plus the District of Columbia) was $17.98, while the average price paid in the only state with an absolute ban on eyeglass advertising (North Carolina) was $37.48.[15] There were, however, different degrees of

---

[14]Lee Benham, "The Effect of Advertising on the Price of Eyeglasses," *Journal of Law and Economics* 15 (October 1972), pp. 337–352.

[15]*loc. cit.*, pp. 340–344.

restriction. Benham found that price differences were not substantial—only amounting to $1.32—between the sample taken from states permitting advertising of some sort and the sample taken from states permitting nonprice advertising only.

What is the significance of this finding? It suggests that when information is in short supply, much could qualify as information. Advertising which merely informs the consumer that a dealer (or a product) exists may be of value. Can this be taken to mean that all advertising messages and selling efforts will improve the consumer's ability to choose products (or dealers) more wisely? Not at all.

Consider the hypothetical situation in which the products of competing suppliers are virtually identical but the consumer is not aware of that fact. In this case, the consumer might be persuaded, through advertising or as the result of a direct sales pitch, that the product of one supplier is better (or more suited to his or her tastes) than are competing products. That is, selling efforts might cause the consumer to behave in a manner inconsistent with his or her best interests: to pay a premium price or to invest a degree of loyalty to the supplier when neither is warranted. Or consider a hypothetical situation in which competing products are not of equal quality but the consumer is unaware of that fact. The consumer might be led to believe that the products are the same, even when they are not. The consumer might be induced to make an unwise purchase: to buy an inferior product when a superior product could have been purchased at the same price. As for its part, the firm might be able to create new buying habits if it supplies new information, even if it is false, to the consumer. By manipulating information, it is possible for the seller to benefit at the expense of both the consumer and the rival.

Are these merely hypothetical situations? No they are not. An interesting finding was made by Allison and Uhl[16] in a study based upon a consumption experiment with 326 beer drinkers and five popular brands of beer. Each of the participants had indicated, prior to the experiment, that one of the five tested brands was his or her favorite. In a *blind test* of consumer behavior, the survey participants were asked to sample each of the five brands, without their labels, and to rate them according to taste. Allison and Uhl found that no brand was rated by the panel as significantly higher than all the others, although some favorite brands were rated significantly higher than some of the others and some favorites were rated significantly lower than some of the others. In a second test of consumer behavior, the participants were asked to sample each of the five brands, properly labeled, and to rate them. In this case, all of the favorites were rated higher than they had been rated in the blind test and three of the favorites were rated higher than all the others.[17]

[16]R. I. Allison and K. P. Uhl, "Influence of Beer Brand Identification on Taste Perception," *Journal of Marketing Research* 1 (August 1964), pp. 36–39.

[17]loc. cit.

What is the significance of this finding? It suggests that whatever the consumer treats as being information has the same effect on his or her behavior as real information—the favorite beer appeared to taste better when the consumer was informed that it was his or her favorite.

Information vs. Persuasion.   What is information? Is it objective fact? Or does it also include subjective impression? Apparently it is both. In the case of eyeglass advertising, for example, the seller supplies the consumer with details such as the price of the product or the location of a dealer. These are objective data and the selling efforts which provide them are called **informative**. On the other hand, in the case of beer advertising the seller supplies the consumer with self-serving claims about the product. For example, "Blotz is America's best beer" or "Blotz drinkers have more fun in life." These are subjective data, difficult to verify and the selling efforts which provide them are called **persuasive**. Are they really such clear distinctions? In advertisements for eyeglasses in the newspaper or the telephone book, it is not uncommon to find that the layouts feature an extremely attractive model or models. Is this informative? Not really. It is intended to catch the reader's attention. It is a ploy through which Acme Optical hopes to be able to convey an informative message, such as its location and hours of operation, to the reader. Nevertheless, Acme Optical used beauty in much the same fashion that Blotz used fun: to get the consumer to consider its product and to seek more information about it.

So, how manipulative is persuasive selling? How much power does the seller who employs it hold over the buyer? That is a question which has triggered heated arguments in economics. At one extreme is the benign view that persuasive selling is a form of information. Nelson[18] has argued that the consumer may rationally accept the very presence of advertising as information about the quality of the product being advertised. On what grounds? Nelson's argument proceeds as follows: (1) a consumer of an experience good is ultimately sold by the quality of the consumption experiment itself. If experience indicates that a particular brand or product design tested yields more enjoyment than any of its competitors, the supplier of that product wins a loyal customer, (2) the seller of a high quality product could expect to capture the loyalty of a larger number of consumers who test its brand or product design than the seller of an inferior product, (3) the seller of a high quality product could expect its advertising or other selling efforts—efforts which attract the attention of the consumer and induce him or her to try the product at least once—to be a better investment than could the seller of an inferior product, (4) the seller of a high quality product would be willing to spend more to advertise its product than the seller of an inferior product, and (5) therefore, the rational consumer might

[18]Phillip Nelson, "Advertising as Information," *Journal of Political Economy* 82 (July/August 1974), pp. 729–754.

accurately regard relative advertising intensity as a rough proxy for product quality.

At the other extreme is the view that persuasive selling is a form of disinformation. If the consumer should ever accept uncritically all that he or she is told, the seller would have an interest in outdoing the competition with extravagant claims. To illustrate the implications of persuasion, Schmalensee[19] turned the Nelson argument on its head, suggesting that the relationship between advertising intensity and product quality could become an inverse one. What explains this twist? Consider what would happen if the consumer decided to abandon the practice of testing different products. That is, suppose the consumer used the size of the selling effort as the sole basis for determining which product to buy, without ever trying other products. Schmalensee argues that the rational producer might, in these circumstances, substitute spending on advertising for spending on quality. The level of quality would turn out to be lower than it would if the public were more sceptical—or better informed.

Differentiation and Information.   Why should the consumer be in a position in which he or she can be misled in the first place? It would seem that two factors are largely responsible. On the one hand, the lack of information is a direct result of resource scarcity. There are so many products of such great complexity—or in some cases, as when product qualities are difficult even to identify, ambiguity is a more apt description—that it is not possible to know everything about everything. On the other hand, ignorance or the lack of information is aggravated by the existence of spatial and product differences. That may help to explain why the consumer does not know the comparative virtues, or even the existence, of certain brands or certain dealers. The need for information is necessarily greatest where there is differentiation, when the products have different attributes or when dealers are widely scattered. Why? Consider this: if all brands were the same, consumption would be optimal whether or not the consumer really understood the product attributes of the goods he or she purchases—in such a case, information is redundant. Does this mean that selling effort will be most intense when differentiation is greatest? Not necessarily.

In certain markets where the product differences seem to be quite modest, the emphasis upon selling effort is very intense. The manufacturer of prescription drugs, for example, spends large amounts on the promotion of products via direct contacts between its representatives and prescribing physicians. It is a trade practice called **detailing**. Certainly some of the detailing represents an effort to inform the physician of new drugs offered by the pharmaceutical house, drugs which represent substantially differentiated products from those offered by the competition and for which the manufacturer has a legal patent monopoly. Much of the detailing represents an effort to persuade the physician to prescribe

[19]Richard Schmalensee, "A Model of Advertising and Product Quality," *Journal of Political Economy* 86 (June 1978), pp. 485–503.

the firm's own brand name drug instead of the brand supplied by competing firms or instead of a generic drug, both of which are chemically equivalent to the firm's brand name product. The evidence suggests that the expenditure on detailing by the ethical drug industry is roughly 25 percent of gross sales.[20] The manufacturer of ready-to-eat breakfast cereals spends large amounts on the promotion of products through media advertising. Some of this is spent on introducing new cereal products, but most involves promoting existing products. While there are differences between cereal preparations in terms of flavor and nutrition, the information contained in cereal advertising would not seem to warrant the intensity of the industry selling effort. Nearly 20 percent of revenues are spent on advertising.[21]

Why is so much spent on selling efforts in pharmaceuticals and cereals and similar products? Is it a matter of information supplied by selling? No, at least not directly. There are many products which are difficult to assess prior to purchase. These are referred to as *experience* goods. That is, the information about them is obtained through the consumption experience itself; it is highly personal and objective. If the consumer tries a product and is satisfied with the experience, he or she is very likely to repeat the purchase. So, what is the role of selling in this process? The seller—either through advertising or by direct contact—must persuade the prospective buyer to try the product. It is the consumption experience which must finally sell the consumer on the product. If the consumer likes the taste of a particular breakfast cereal, he or she may become a loyal customer, buying it frequently if not all the time. If the physician is satisfied with the results of a particular brand name drug, he or she may prescribe it for all patients for which its use is indicated.

Is this a common reaction? Yes, it seems to be. Consumers seem to be creatures of habit. Telser[22] found that purchases of branded goods—for a few tested products such as orange juice and instant coffee—appear to be repetitive. Quantity demanded for a given brand in any given month is most largely explained by the quantity demanded in the preceding month. There was more. Telser also found that the apparent loyalty enjoyed by some brands of orange juice and instant coffee was substantially stronger than that enjoyed by others. In multiple regressions to explain market shares for individual brands of orange juice concentrate, for example, the strength of loyalty as measured by the coefficient of the brand's lagged market share varied from a maximum of .79 to a minimum of .23.[23]

---

[20]Hugh D. Walker, *Market Power and Price Levels in the Ethical Drug Industry* (Indiana University Press: Bloomington, Ind., 1971), p. 143.

[21]Stanley I. Ornstein, *Industrial Concentration and Advertising Intensity* (American Enterprise Institute for Public Policy Research: Washington, D.C., 1977), pp. 77 and 81.

[22]Lester G. Telser, "The Demand for Branded Goods as Estimated from Consumer Panel Data," *Review of Economics and Statistics* 64 (August 1962), pp. 300–324.

[23]*loc. cit.*, p. 317.

What are the implications? They appear to be threefold. In the first place, the seller has a substantial interest in getting consumers to try its product because a certain number of those who do will become repeat customers. This is more than enough justification for the firm to spend substantial sums on a program of advertising and/or other selling efforts to build a base of loyal customers. Second, it must logically follow that the seller relies in part upon persuading customers who are currently loyal to rivals to switch their allegiance—to try the product at least once and, perhaps, to continue purchasing it after that experience. Third, having identified an aggressive aspect of the selling effort, it follows that there must be a defensive aspect as well—if any seller can gain by raiding the customer base of a rival, it can lose customers to rival raids on its own base. This would justify spending additional sums on advertising and other selling efforts to protect what it has already won. Thus, we can explain why selling efforts may become so intense when the product differences seem to be so modest. Rivals might get caught up in an advertising-war, similar in many ways to a price-war.

Selling Efforts as Capital

If the typical consumer had little or no information about the products in the market and no past experience upon which to draw, it may be reasonable to presume that either (1) the market shares of competitors would be roughly equal, in the absence of any selling efforts, or (2) they would tend to vary in roughly direct proportion with the selling efforts of competitors. What would tend to happen in the case of experience goods? It is not unusual to find that one firm (or its leading brand) has captured an unusually large share of the market. Does this mean that the leading firm is currently spending proportionally more in total on advertising than the competition? Perhaps, but not necessarily.

Consumer loyalty is a fact; consumers repeat purchases of a favorite brand. This is particularly true of the frequently purchased, experience good. The consumer has tried the product at least once and has been sufficiently satisfied to buy it, in preference to rival products, again and again. The product must ultimately sell itself, or so it would seem. What can explain the large number of loyal customers of the leading brand? Is it a superior product? Again perhaps, but not necessarily. In the past, the market leader may have outspent the competition by a large margin in advertising its product and may have induced a much larger number of consumers to experiment with its product as the result. So in the past, even if the leading firm were to have done no better than its rivals in converting those who try the product into those who stick with it, it may have established the basis for its present market dominance.

What does this imply about the nature of selling? It means that, under certain circumstances, expenditures on advertising or other selling efforts may have the character of an investment in what may be called **human capital**. Advertising may, at least in the indirect fashion described above, build a stock of goodwill among a certain segment of the population, the firm's clientele. To the extent that anything should happen to its customers—if they should either purchase a "lemon" from the firm or try the product of another firm and disaffect, or if they should die or otherwise leave the market for any reason—the firm's stock of goodwill will diminish. Human capital is, after all, embodied in the person and the behavior of specific individuals. For such reasons, even when the firm has a huge goodwill advantage over the competition, it may continue to spend on selling to maintain its capital and to replace those bits that wear out.

Is goodwill created only by experience? Or can it also be created by persuasion? It would seem that virtually everything we have said could be applied to the firm which persuades a number of individuals that its product is better than the competition: (1) the efforts to persuade are an investment in human capital, (2) if they are successful, they will yield returns in the form of future sales, and (3) if it is left untended, the capital stock will deteriorate as customers forget what they have been told.

How about the firm that doesn't have a huge endowment of goodwill? Is it forever doomed to live in the shadow of the old and established firms? Not necessarily. Recall the example of Miller Brewing Company. On the one hand, in the early 1970s, Miller Brewing probably spent a good deal more on advertising its products than it could have justified by the short-run impact on sales. On the other, Miller's expenditures on advertising, which were more than double the outlay per barrel sold of the industry as a whole, proved to be a good investment in spite of the risk. The firm virtually lifted itself from a position in which it had been lost in the pack of lesser U.S. breweries, to a strong second place position in the industry.

Analysis of Selling Efforts

Selling efforts—by supplying information to prospective customers of the firm—can boost the demand for a product and can increase profits. How much selling effort is warranted? What form will it take? Let us address the latter question first. We have suggested that there are various techniques which can be used to sell a product. For some purposes, advertising may be the most effective technique. For example, to inform a very large and widely scattered public about the location of a dealer or the existence of a product. For others, direct contact by a sales representative may be the best. For example, to explain and demonstrate to selected prospects how a product works. Under certain circumstances, the advertising or the direct sales pitch may be informative, but under others it will be persuasive. In every case, however, the selling effort aims a message at the buyer which is intended to trigger a response. There are no intrinsic differences between advertising and other selling efforts.

Is this fact reflected in the research on selling? No it is not. For whatever reasons, economists have focused almost entirely on advertising—the theoretical models and empirical studies all deal with that subject to the virtual exclusion of all else. For the sake of convenience, we shall do the same. From this point on, as we discuss the effect of selling efforts on the behavior of the firm and the structure of the market, we too will focus on advertising.

THE COSTS OF ADVERTISING

Advertising and/or other selling efforts increase the demand for a product, or at least that is the intent. What do they do to its costs? Does the law of diminishing returns apply to advertising as well as to production? Or are there economies of scale? There are a number of questions about advertising costs which are important, and some have led to serious debate. Is it possible to resolve them all? Probably not, but perhaps we can make some sense of the matter. To this end, let us begin with something familiar.

Consider the hypothetical situation, depicted in Figure 11-1, in which there are two firms with identical production costs (AC) and with an identical price (P_0). Let us assume that the first firm does nothing to promote its product and sells Q_1 units of it, while the second firm spends S dollars on promotion, sells Q_2 units of product, and bears the combined costs of production and advertising represented by $AC_{w/s}$. In this case, the second firm is in an obviously preferred position: (1) it sells a larger volume of goods, and (2) the average cost for the quantity that it sells is lower than the average cost for the quantity that the first firm sells. Assuming everything else to be equal, this illustrates a case in which there are substantial, positive returns to advertising. What can it tell us about advertising costs? Not a great deal.

Doesn't the cost advantage of the second firm and the convergence of the $AC_{w/s}$ curve with the AC curve as the quantity of goods increases indicate the presence of a scale effect? Not really. The former can be attributed to operating a production plant at a level closer to optimal capacity. As for the latter, it may seem to suggest that there is an advantage of spreading an S-dollar fixed outlay

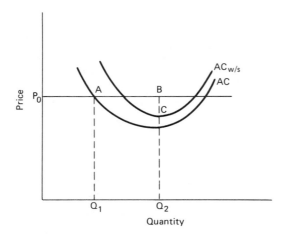

Figure 11-1 Advertising affects both demand and cost for the firm. In the monopolistic competition model, a firm could profit from its selling effort if the resulting sales increase allows the firm to tap previously unexploited scale economies and if unit costs fall in spite of the rise in the average cost curve.

over an even larger quantity of goods, but that is only an illusion. The expenditure of S-dollars can push the sales from Q_1 to Q_2, assuming that price is fixed at P_0, but C is the only point on the $AC_{w/s}$ curve that has any meaning.

So, how can the cost of advertising actually be measured and/or represented? Let us try to imagine running an advertising experiment: (1) from Figure 11-1, we know that Q_1 can be sold with a zero outlay on promotion and with price equal to P_0, (2) we can visualize finding the advertising outlay needed to expand sales by one unit, to $Q_1 + 1$, with price fixed, and (3) we imagine the result of varying advertising continuously to identify an entire function. Would we find *the* selling cost function? No, we would not, because we have examined only the relationship between quantity and advertising cost. Alternatively, we could examine the advertising cost of increasing the price the firm is able to charge, given a particular volume of goods to be sold. That too would yield an advertising cost function.

Both represent shifts in demand. Do we have any reason to believe that the first type of a shift implies the other? Not at all. It would be one thing to increase the market share for a soft drink, for example, but quite another to persuade a consumer to pay a premium price for it. On the other hand, the seller of a branded pain reliever may be able to charge two or three times the going price of an unbranded product. Why such a difference? Advertising might permit the firm to increase the price of its product relative to the competition only if the consumer were to perceive there to be significant differences between them— and these may be real, or they may represent ignorance of substantial proportion, unlikely to be remedied by search or experience.

Let us suppose, however, that we are interested only in the results of advertising on the revenues of the firm, that we are not really concerned whether advertising works to differentiate the product in a horizontal or a vertical fashion. Then, we might express the product of the advertising effort in terms of the effect on total sales revenue—that is, as $P \cdot Q$. In that case, we might use a relationship, such as that shown in Figure 11-2, to describe the costs of advertising.

How would such a function behave? It seems reasonable to presume that there would be two interesting properties of a total advertising cost function (TAC): (1) sales volume at the zero cost level, and (2) the effect on sales of increasing the expenditure on advertising.

What might we expect from zero-effort advertising? It is reasonable to presume that the firm will be able to generate some revenues without current expenditures on promotion—some level of sales, unlike output, may be a free good. These are shown as R_1 (and R_1') in Figure 11-2. Why should the firm be able to sell its product in a differentiated market without any effort? There are two main explanations. First, it may be the result of the consumer's willingness to search for products and to experiment with those encountered. Since unbranded goods are often shelved alongside the well-known products, there will be some consumers who will give them a try. A producer may capture a share of the market with a product whether or not an effort is made to promote it.

Second, it may be the result of the past accumulations of goodwill. In Figure 11-2, we show two advertising cost functions (TAC and TAC'), and we see them as having different zero-effort levels of sales (R_1 and R_1'). Why? It might be presumed that the latter function, with more free sales than the former, represents the position of a firm which has more goodwill. What explains this advantage? Several factors might be involved. It may be the result of past advertising investment. It may represent a coattail effect such as the multi-product firm might enjoy, as compared to its single-product rival, if advertising one line of products increases demand for another. It may even represent another form of goodwill—one that cannot be bought but is based instead upon popular recognition of and respect for the innovator. Some products can become institutions in society, and certain brand names can become a part of the language—Kodak for camera, Levis for denims, and Xerox for plain-paper copiers are examples of this phenomenon.

Consider the shape of the advertising cost curve. What can we say about it? The only certainty is that advertising costs must be an increasing function of sales; to increase sales beyond R_1, a firm must increase its outlay on advertising. Now consider the function labeled TAC. We have shown it initially to rise at a decreasing rate, but ultimately to rise at a steadily increasing rate. What explains the former? Some have suggested that an advertising threshold exists, and that until a certain level of saturation is reached, the firm sees little response from its efforts. Perhaps that is so, at least in some cases. What does it imply? It would seem to suggest that there are certain indivisibilities. Is this a possibility? Yes it is.

In the extreme case, potential customers for a product or a dealer may be widely scattered and may be difficult to target in advance. If we presume that the firm seeks to advertise the availability of its product or its place of business,

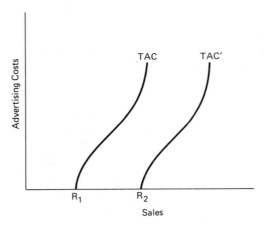

Figure 11-2 The total advertising cost function TAC describes how sales revenue may be functionally related to advertising expenditures. The TAC may reflect (1) the ability of a firm to achieve certain levels of sales, such as R_1, without any advertising, and (2) the effect of increasing- and decreasing-returns to advertising.

the firm may be able to reach its full market potential by purchasing a single unit advertisement in a directory such as the Yellow Pages. In that case, the TAC function could be represented by two points: R_1 at zero-advertising, and R_n at some cost level S, the cost of the advertising unit. Short of the threshold, the firm would realize no additional sales. At the threshold, the firm would generate sales equal to $[R_n - R_1]$ at MC = 0. What about additional advertising expenditures? Hypothetically, the firm could spend more than S, but it could never sell more than R_n. The TAC function for this firm in this market would jump discontinuously from zero returns to increasing returns back to zero returns again, all at the advertising expenditure level of S—it is the limiting case for a function like TAC.

At the other extreme, the advertising cost function may be continuous, with decreasing returns to advertising from the outset. Why? Two explanations can be offered, but one of them seems highly conjectural. First, let us assume that the potential customers are few in number and that the seller knows who they are and how likely each is to buy. Let us assume the firm targets its sales efforts so as to utilize resources most efficiently—it may even tailor its pitch to individual customers. Hypothetically, the firm could and would pursue the easiest sales first. What would such a case imply about advertising costs? The firm's marginal advertising costs would increase with each sale, and as a result, its TAC function would increase at an increasing rate.

Second, we assume that potential customers find the seller, rather than the other way round. We may assume that the TAC function reflects the fact that the well-positioned firm is able to exploit its stock of goodwill in making current sales. We may also assume that the well-positioned firm finds it more difficult to attract additional sales than its smaller rival: the easiest sales have already been made; the larger is the market share of the firm, the smaller is the remaining pool of potential customers; and it is progressively more difficult to capture the business of customers who have restricted earlier attempts to reach them and win them over.

So, what can we say about the advertising cost function? It would seem that a few generalizations are appropriate. First, it is necessary to establish precisely what we mean: the advertising cost is the outlay for increasing the sales of the firm. Second, it may be possible that decreasing marginal costs—or even zero costs—could be experienced over a narrow range of activity, if there were indivisibilities in the units of advertising for sale, or if there were some evidence of increasing consumer response to frequent repetition of an advertising message. Third, it is most reasonable to expect, however, that marginal costs will rise as a firm intensifies its efforts to increase sales via advertising. The TAC function of Figure 11-2 may provide a reasonable representation of the general case.

Are there implications for scale economies in advertising? Yes. Chiefly, the TAC function—or the assumptions underlying it—seems to suggest that true scale economies do not exist in advertising. The appearance of scale advantages may have much more to do with the goodwill effects, which could account for lower average advertising outlays per unit of sales that one might find for larger firms with established reputations, than with a condition of decreasing costs, *per se*.

So, do the largest firms have the lowest ratios of advertising to sales? Perhaps, provided that their market position is aided by goodwill and that all firms compete in advertising. Still, the firms with the lowest ratios of advertising to sales may be at the opposite end of the spectrum. They may be those small firms which produce and sell unbranded goods.

THE THEORY OF OPTIMAL ADVERTISING

How much advertising will the firm purchase? What factors will affect that decision? To understand that this is a problem like the one with which we are more familiar—that of choosing a price and a level of output—we need only to construct a simple model of the firm. Suppose that the firm finds itself in the position, shown in Figure 11-3, which is defined by two functions, one for cost and one for revenue. These are: (1) the total cost of advertising function, TAC, which is taken from Figure 11-2 and which reflects both the presence of a zero-effort level of sales, R_1, and the existence of decreasing returns as the TAC function eventually begins to rise at an increasing rate, and (2) the function representing total revenue net of production cost, TNR, which reflects the twin effects of changes in price and changes in quantity. Consider what accounts for increases in the firm's gross revenues. In the first place, when the firm is able to exploit decreasing production costs as illustrated in Figure 11-1 above, it will be able to increase net revenues simply by increasing output and gross receipts, but in the short run, it must eventually begin to experience increasing production costs. In the second place, when the firm exploits advertising to boost demand for its product, it might be able to raise the price for a given output so that

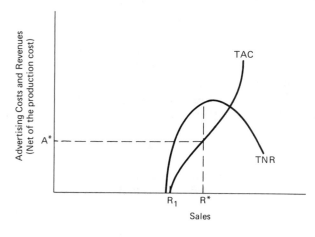

Figure 11-3 Advertising levels, like prices, may be set by the firm with some degree of market power. If sales are taken to be a function of advertising TAC, and if revenues net of production costs are a function of sales TNR, the profit-maximizing firm would determine an optimal level of advertising, A*/R*.

revenues net of production cost will rise, *ceteris paribus*. The combined effect will yield a TNR function—first rising, then falling with gross revenues.

What will the firm choose to do? As a profit-maximizing entity, the firm must select the level of gross revenues, R^*, at which profits—$\pi \equiv$ [TNR $-$ TAC]—are at a maximum. This implies that the firm selects the optimal level of advertising, A^*, necessary to produce R^*—that is, A^*/R^* is the optimal ratio of advertising expenditure to total sales revenues for the firm, given the relevant revenue and cost functions. Yet, models are mechanical. What does this one really mean? There are several implied assumptions, in addition to those which we noted in explaining the TNR and TAC functions. Two assumptions are most important. First, we assume that the firm is able to act in complete independence of rivals; it is free to choose its own A^* and R^*, taking note of the fact that the latter may also imply the discretion to set P^*. Second, we assume that the firm has perfect knowledge about the TNR and TAC functions; it has full information, while consumers are not so fortunate. Are these assumptions realistic? Probably not. Do they come close enough to be useful in understanding the behavior of the firm which employs advertising. Quite possibly.

Do we know anything else about optimal advertising? Or to put it another way, do we know what determines the shape of the TNR and TAC functions? Yes we do. Dorfman and Steiner[24] were the first to examine this problem. They found the relationship: $A^*/R^* = \sigma/\epsilon$, where σ is the elasticity of demand with respect to advertising, and ϵ is the elasticity of demand with respect to price.[25]

The firm's advertising intensity—its A/R ratio—will be greater, the higher is its advertising elasticity and the lower is its price elasticity. What explains the two elasticities?

Consider the advertising elasticity, σ. What factors seem most likely to cause consumers to buy more of a good in response to advertising? First, if a

[24]Robert Dorfman and Peter O. Steiner, "Optimal Advertising and Optimal Quality," *American Economic Review* 44 (December 1954), pp. 826–836.

[25]This can be shown by considering two functions: (1) the demand for a product, Q, as the joint function of price and advertising, $Q = f(P,A)$, and (2) the cost of the product as the sum of the production and advertising cost, $C = C(Q) + A$. The total profit function can be written as $\pi = P \cdot Q - [C(Q) + A]$. If we seek to maximize profits with respect to price and advertising we get the two first-order conditions:

(1) $\pi_P = Q + P \cdot Q_P - C' \cdot Q_P = 0$, or $Q_P \cdot [P - C'] = Q$, and
(2) $\pi_A = P \cdot Q_A - C' Q_A - 1 = 0$, or $Q_A [P - C'] = 1$,

where the subscripts on the functions for π and Q represent the partial derivatives with respect to the choice variables, P and A, and where $C' = dC/dQ$.

Now the two equations can both be expressed as functions of a common term, $[P - C']$. When set equal to one another we get:

(3) $Q/Q_P = 1/Q_A$, or $Q \cdot Q_A = Q_P$.

But since $Q_A = \sigma \cdot [Q/A]$ and $Q_P = \epsilon \cdot [Q/P]$, this gives us:

(4) $\sigma \cdot [Q^2/A] = \epsilon \cdot [Q/P]$

If we divide both sides of eq. (4) by Q^2 and ϵ, and then if we multiply both sides by A, we get:

(5) $\sigma/\epsilon = A/P \cdot Q$.

But since A, P, and Q are optimal values and since $P \cdot Q = R$,

(6) $\sigma/\epsilon = A^*/R^*$. Q.E.D.

product is new and public awareness of it is minimal, it seems reasonable to suppose that advertising could have a substantial effect in boosting sales. There is evidence to support this hypothesis. The motion picture industry is in the business of continually introducing new product. Each film is put into distribution for only a short period of time; it is necessary to inform the public of its existence quickly and to persuade them of its quality, or else the whole enterprise may fail. The advertising campaigns for new films reflect these considerations. They have the blitzkrieg character of a short, incisive war—to commit large amount of resources to capture a specific target and to move on. Backman[26] cites IRS data which verify that more is spent on advertising in motion pictures than in any other major service industry. The ready-to-eat cereal industry, in contrast, introduces new products or brands in a less frenetic fashion. A new product, if successful, will be around for quite awhile but may take some time to establish its position in the market. The advertising campaigns for new brands of cereal may reflect the longer perspective; it has been shown that the marketing costs of new cereal brands absorb two-thirds of revenues in their first year on the market and 30 percent of sales receipts in the second.[27]

Second, if a product is purchased for the first time or if it is purchased infrequently, the consumer's lack of information may be considerable. If search is costly, the consumer may come to rely upon advertising for information. In this case, the firm might increase its sales by advertising. There is evidence to support this hypothesis. Household furniture is one of those products (1) which is a search good, (2) which offers a wide variety in style, quality, and dealer location, and (3) which is purchased infrequently by the consumer. Indeed, the lack of information may be so great that, if the buyer can afford it, his or her decisions on furniture may be delegated to a professional agent, or decorator. The rest of us may rely upon advertising for our information, however, and Backman[28] cites IRS data which show that furniture dealers spend more on advertising per dollar of sales than all other retailers.

For new products and for those products which are otherwise unfamiliar to the typical consumer, advertising may be the major source of information. In such cases, owing to its ability to attract new business, advertising may be the supplier's most effective tool of competition. So, does this mean that the size of σ, the strength of advertising elasticity, is a function of the direct informational content of advertising? Not at all.

There seems to be a third category of products to consider, products for which brand loyalty is a major factor in consumer choice but for which product design differences are a relatively minor factor in differentiating them. These are the frequently-purchased, experience goods—that is, goods which are judged

---

[26]Jules Backman, *Advertising and Competition* (New York University Press: New York, 1967), p. 129.

[27]*loc. cit.*, p. 26.

[28]*loc. cit.*, p. 131.

by the individual only after purchasing and consuming them. If the product differences are merely cosmetic, based more upon packaging than content, a consumer's choice of which brand to try—and possibly to stick with—might easily be swayed. In such a case, the firm might be able to use advertising to advantage—to profit by capturing a significant share of the market, if it wages a successful promotional campaign. There is evidence to support the hypothesis. Backman[29] has shown that substantial changes in overall brand preference, as measured by shifts in rank and market share, take place among the leading sellers in the markets for such products as cigarettes, toothpastes, soaps and detergents, and ready-to-eat cereals. In each case, these were products which were heavily advertised. Can this be attributed solely to a high value for σ? Probably not.

The advertising intensity, A/R, is presumed to be a function of price elasticity, as well as advertising elasticity. The heavy expenditure on advertising for such experience goods as soaps, cigarettes, and cereals may be attributed in part to their low value of ϵ. What determines the price elasticity of a product? At bottom, ϵ is determined by the availability of good substitutes—if there are many good substitutes, demand for a product will be very elastic, but if there are few, demand will be inelastic. Generically speaking, it would seem that there are few close substitutes for soaps, cigarettes, and cold cereals for those who consume them. Could the same be said about many things? How about houses and automobiles, for example? It would seem that they play at least as unique and important a role in the life of the consumer as the perishable goods do. That is not the point. The purchase of a durable good can be put off. Because its price is high, relative to that of a perishable good, the consumer will be more price-conscious in buying a new car, for example. However, soaps, cigarettes, and cereals are such inexpensive items, the consumer will buy whenever he or she runs out. Elasticity of demand for a product is a direct function of unit price, *ceteris paribus*.

Is there evidence that this may be important? Indeed there is. Backman found that expenditures for all those products which are regarded as heavily advertised—cigarettes, soaps, beer, over-the-counter drugs, toilet preparations, candy, cereals, soft drinks, and so on—together total no more than 6% of the average family budget.[30] Apparently the consumer cannot be bothered to seek better information than that supplied by advertising and is, therefore, willing to be manipulated. The price is cheap. Brand loyalty may extract a small opportunity cost if brands are rather similar and may pay real dividends if they are not—in the latter instance, the consumer may benefit by repeating an enjoyable and proven consumption "experience."

Can the optimal advertising model be tested as a whole? Yes it can be.

[29]*loc. cit.*, pp. 70–75.
[30]*loc. cit.*, pp. 27–28.

Metwally[31] examined the advertising behavior of firms in eight Australian consumer goods industries to examine the question of whether or not competition in advertising tends to be excessive. The question led Metwally to estimate and to test a version of the Dorfman-Steiner model. Using annual data, 1960–1970, for the leading brands of instant coffee, cigarettes, beer, toilet soap, detergent, toothpaste, paint, and gasoline, Metwally estimated ϵ and σ for each of the eight commodities. The results are shown in Table 11-1, along with values of A/R—one value for the hypothetical $A^*/R^* = \sigma/\epsilon$, and one value for the actual ratio itself.

TABLE 11–1 COMPARISON OF ACTUAL WITH "OPTIMAL" ADVERTISING RATIOS: METWALLY STUDY OF EIGHT AUSTRALIAN MARKETS, 1960–1970

| | ELASTICITIES | | A/R | |
PRODUCT	ϵ	σ	A^*/R^*	ACTUAL
Instant Coffee	−3.509	.061	.017	.020
Bottled Beer	−3.640	.039	.011	.011
Cigarettes	−2.091	.037	.017	.046
Toilet Soap	−3.442	.027	.008	.012
Detergent	−2.701	.044	.016	.030
Toothpaste	−2.194	.041	.019	.059
Paint	−3.014	.031	.010	.019
Gasoline	−3.000	.043	.014	.016

Source: M. Metwally, "Advertising and Competitive Behavior of Selected Australian Firms," *Review of Economics and Statistics* (November 1975), p. 423 [Table 2, model iii].

For several of the products—coffee, beer, toilet soap, and gasoline—the estimated optimal advertising ratios were roughly equal to those which were observed. Does this mean that the sellers decided how much to spend on advertising by a process similar to the Dorfman-Steiner model? Perhaps. Would they really enjoy the monopoly-like independence, implicit in the model? That may seem doubtful. As for the other products—cigarettes, detergent, and toothpaste—the A^*/R^* values were a fraction of the observed A/R. [We may exclude the case of paint in this comparison, since one model (iii) predicted lower levels for the advertising ratio than that which was observed, but other models did not.] What are we to make of these cases, assuming that Metwally's estimates of the demand function parameters were accurate? It might seem that the optimal advertising model is out of place in oligopoly—especially in markets for "heavily" advertised, experience goods. It might appear that the behavior does not fit the predictions of the model. So, is it necessary to restructure the model of advertising behavior to better fit oligopoly? Perhaps.

[31]M. M. Metwally, "Advertising and Competitive Behavior of Selected Australian Firms," *Review of Economics and Statistics* 57 (November 1975), pp. 417–427.

OLIGOPOLY AND ADVERTISING

How much advertising would the firm purchase if it expected rivals to counter its every move? Suppose that we take the model represented in Figure 11-3, except for the following modification: now the TAC function will be drawn as a vertical line, placed at the zero-effort level of sales, R_1. What does this mean? It means that the firm cannot independently act to improve its sales or market share by advertising because its rivals will match its spending, penny for penny. Suppose that the oligopolist's demand is given by $Q = f(P, A, A_r)$, where A_r is rival advertising. Suppose that σ_r is one firm's elasticity of demand with respect to the advertising expenditure of its rivals, with $\sigma_r = -\sigma$.

Now suppose that the firm realizes this fact. Under these circumstances, the optimal advertising effort will be zero, and the firm's total revenues will be R_1. Why? The reason is that the firm can achieve R_1 whether or not it advertises, but the firm can achieve maximum profits only if $A = 0$. In terms of the Dorfman-Steiner model, $A^*/R^* = [\sigma + \sigma_r]/\epsilon = 0/\epsilon = 0$.

But if the oligopoly firm did not foresee the consequences of its actions, if it did not realize that rivals could match its efforts and would feel compelled to do so, it might unwittingly precipitate an advertising war. Under these circumstances, oligopoly costs could rise and profits could be squeezed to the competitive level.

In cases where the products are differentiable and where the rivals are few in number, do we find either zero advertising or zero economic profits to be the rule? Not at all.[32] Indeed, it would seem that nonprice competition—including advertising—is an important aspect of behavior. So, how are we to explain it? Our initial assumptions about the implications of oligopoly may have been wrong. The firm's own advertising campaign might never be completely offset by an equal effort on the part of the competition, the oligopolist's TAC function may look like the one we originally depicted in Figure 11-3, and the optimal advertising-to-sales ratio may be greater than zero. As a result, it is reasonable to speculate that the firm's rivals would neither seek to match every move nor succeed if they were to try. But why?

There are several factors to consider. First, the effect of an increase of advertising effort on sales, unlike a decrease in price, may be delayed. Consumers may take some time to react to a selling campaign, some time before they become *persuaded* to buy the product from a new seller. For this reason, the other firm may not feel compelled to respond immediately. Second, if and when the firm's advertising campaign begins to win over the loyalty of some new clients, it is likely to do so at the margin—rival firms who are being "outsold" may lose some market share to the aggressive firm but will continue to enjoy the business of their longtime customers. In contrast, an action to underprice a rival constitutes a direct assault, against which no segment of one's customary market is safe—hard price competition cannot be ignored. Third, even if those who lose

---

[32]Some of the support to this conclusion is summarized in the Appendix to the chapter.

customers decide to retaliate, they are not likely to do so immediately. It may take them some time to prepare an effective response to a new sales pitch. In the meantime, the firm which launched the first attack has time to enjoy its benefits. Finally, those who seek to retaliate may never fully succeed to regain what they have lost. Why? It is possible that the success of a selling effort depends upon content, as well as on the timing and magnitude. Miller Brewing Company's move from the seventh largest market share in the U.S. beer industry to second was accomplished by more than an excessive outpouring of money on advertising. It was abetted by the simultaneous introduction of a popular new product— the low calorie beer—for which Miller became the leading supplier. Advertising people would also say that Miller brought an expertise to competition in selling that had previously been lacking in the beer industry.

Does this mean that the Dorfman-Steiner model of optimal advertising explains nonprice competition under oligopoly? Not necessarily. While we have established that the firm may choose its own advertising intensity, we have also discovered that the firm may reasonably expect rivals to react to this choice. We may conclude that the optimal choice would take such reactions into account. What does this imply about oligopoly behavior?

On the one hand, the firm may develop a strategy based upon an assessment of: (1) its own advertising elasticity, σ, (2) the advertising elasticity of its rivals, σ_r, and (3) a coefficient, μ, which measures increases in rival advertising expenditures in response to the firm's own actions. Schmalensee[33] suggested that the profit-maximizing firm would choose $A^*/R^* = [\sigma + \mu \cdot \sigma_r]/\epsilon]$. Doesn't retaliation—or rather the expectation that it will occur—eliminate the firm's reason to advertise? Not entirely. Where $\sigma > |\sigma_r|$ due to the firm's expectation that the content of its advertising campaign will be more effective than that of its rivals', and where $\mu < 1$ due the firm's expectation of a time lag in the response, advertising may be expected to yield a profit in spite of retaliation. The level of optimal advertising would be lower than in the D-S model, *ceteris paribus*.

On the other hand, the firm may develop a strategy which is based upon balancing a modest degree of independence against the substantial level of uncertainty. Does the firm know σ, σ_r, and μ? Does the firm know what independent actions rivals might take on their own initiative? Is the firm more concerned with getting a larger share of the market or keeping what it has? There are several reasons why we may believe that the Dorfman-Steiner model—or the Schmalensee modification of it—does not quite fit. What do we use to replace it?

Target Advertising

What do we mean by target advertising? First, we mean that the firm employs a target to establish the amount to be spent on advertising. Instead of choosing an A^* where π is maximized, as illustrated in Figure 11-3 above, the firm may

---

[33]Richard Schmalensee, *The Economics of Advertising* (Amsterdam: North-Holland, 1972), p. 33.

budget advertising according to a target ratio of spending to total sales revenue. Second, we mean that the firm views its advertising as part of a semi-independent process by which it is able to accomplish certain internal objectives. For example, to achieve a target return on fixed investment or to maintain a target market share—given rival advertising behavior. It is a part of the same process as target pricing.

When the practice of full-cost pricing first came to light, it was discovered that the practice of relying upon certain rules was rather widespread. Many firms used formulas for pricing, but they also used them for other purposes as well—it was all part of a managerial revolution. For example, Lanzillotti has reported that General Foods used the following rule of thumb to price products: the unit price of each would represent, in equal parts, the sum of its production cost, selling cost, and profit margin.[34] That is, General Foods expected to spend one-third of its total revenues on advertising and other selling activities.

How would target advertising work? Let us recall the example of target-return pricing from Chapter Ten. Suppose that a firm has accumulated knowledge about pricing and selling strategy from past experience: (1) it has seen how large a share of the market it has been able to capture in the past, (2) it has discovered what it might expect to earn, on the average, when it maintains that position, (3) it has learned what to expect from the competition in terms of price, product, and advertising and what it takes to stay competitive, and (4) it has developed the means to forecast total industry sales. In terms of a defensive or conservative market strategy, the firm may believe that when its advertising-to-sales ratio is equal to the historic average value—let us call this $A/R = \alpha$—it will be able to maintain its position relative to the competition. It may act on that basis.

Assume that the firm wants to plan its advertising budget for the coming year. What would it do? In this case, the firm would plan to spend $A^* = \alpha \cdot R^* = \alpha \cdot [P^* \cdot Q^*]$, where P^* and Q^* are the target-return price and quantity, respectively. If we assume that the firm uses a full-cost pricing formula, price would depend in part upon advertising cost. In fact, if TNC is used to represent total non-advertising expenditure (including target profits), $P^* = TNC/Q^* \cdot [1 - \alpha]$. Consider a hypothetical case of General Motors. If GM took α to be 2 percent of sales revenues, determined that its non-advertising cost per unit will be $10,000, and forecast that its volume of sales will be equal to five million units, its target price, P^*, would be equal to $10,000/[1 - .02] = \$10,204$. Its target advertising budget, A^*, would be equal to $.02 \cdot [\$51,020,000,000]$, roughly equal to $1.0 billion. Consider another hypothetical case, for example, Seven-Up. If 7up took α to be 6 percent of sales, believed that price would be stable at 40¢ per bottle, forecast that total market volume would reach 20 billion bottles for the year, and felt that its market share would remain at 10 percent, it would plan to spend $A^* = .06 \{[.10] \cdot [\$8,000,000,000]\} = \$48$ million.

[34]Robert F. Lanzillotti, "Pricing Objectives in Large Companies," *American Economic Review* 48 (December 1958), p. 925.

Is this a reasonable strategy? Very possibly. In the market in which goodwill or buyer loyalty is very strong, the firm may believe that one course of action has been proven to be successful. Past experience may suggest that maintaining its investment in goodwill can be achieved by maintaining a target level of advertising expenditure—$A^* = \alpha \cdot R^*$—and that doing anything else would be unreasonable. The firm might consider an attempt to increase its market share by launching an advertising blitz, but it may reject that as being either too costly or too uncertain, given the rival reactions it could unleash. The firm might consider cutting costs by reducing its advertising outlay, but it may reject that as being too shortsighted.

So, what is the implication? It is that the firm determines how much it is willing to spend on advertising on the basis of a strategy for achieving its profit and/or market share target—it is a tool, like full-cost pricing, for decision-making. Does this mean that the firm's advertising-to-sales ratio will always be constant? Not at all. While advertising expenditures may be set according to a fixed ratio to *expected* revenues, the firm's *actual* revenues may turn out different. Swings in the business cycle, changes in consumer tastes, or sudden switches in rival behavior—in its pricing, product design, or selling strategy—may produce changes in the firm's actual A/R ratio. The α is a planning instrument, not an absolute requirement. If the firm's actual advertising-to-sales ratio remains quite stable, and that is often the case, it is likely to reflect the fact that the firm has been reasonably successful in its planning.

How widespread is target advertising? Schmalensee reports that various surveys taken on the behavior of large firms report that a substantial number of them plan advertising budgets using a rule based upon a fixed ratio of expenditure to sales revenues—as many as 75% of the firms surveyed indicated that they used an advertising formula.[35]

Target Advertising and the Oligopoly Equilibrium

How does target advertising affect the behavior of the oligopoly market as a whole? Do all the firms in the market have the same α? No, they do not. In general, it would appear that those firms which enjoy the largest shares of the market have an advantage in that they might spend more in the aggregate than the competition, but less in proportion to revenues. A leading firm may be able to maintain its market position at a lower unit cost than its closest rivals are able to do so. At the other extreme, a no name brand may be able to secure a position in the market and hold it without any advertising budget, competing instead on the basis of price. What are the implications? There are two which may be important.

Although the individual firm may act independently in planning its own advertising expenditure level, its behavior may foster a Cournot-type equi-

[35]Schmalensee, *loc. cit.*, pp. 17–18.

librium in advertising. How? If each firm decides how much it will spend on advertising on the basis that (1) the positions of the other firms—their markets shares and their behavior—are to be taken as given, (2) the objective is to maintain rather than to enhance its own position, and (3) the target can be achieved if it employs an advertising formula. Its success will reinforce a state of equilibrium. The firm is not likely to alter a system of behavior that works. In turn, as its own behavior becomes more predictable, other firms which base their decisions upon it are all the more likely to be successful in their own planning and execution of advertising strategy. Non-cooperative advertising strategies based upon a simple formula may, therefore, be mutually consistent. The result may be an equilibrium in behavior.

Also, it would seem that target advertising is likely to reinforce the structure of the oligopoly market. First, it will inherently play to the advantage of the entrenched leaders in the market. When there is a substantial amount of "goodwill" which is carried over from the past, the firm with the largest market share may be able to secure its position with a smaller relative outlay than others are able to do. If the small firm were to act to expand, if it were willing to break with the advertising formula, it would have to be prepared to commit a huge sum to the venture, particularly if the leader were to choose to defend its position vigorously. Second, target advertising is a style of behavior which will naturally preserve the *status quo*. If we assume that behavior conforms to its past pattern in spite of the fact—or perhaps because of it—that advertising may be a most effective means for altering market shares, target advertising would tend to be associated with structural stability.

Does this mean that advertising is not used aggressively in oligopoly? No it does not. Recall the example of the Miller Brewing Company. When a new ownership—Phillip Morris—took over at Miller, it introduced a new aggressiveness to the firm's marketing behavior. Advertising expenditures were increased so dramatically that Miller Brewing was spending almost twice as much per unit of sales as the next most intensive advertiser in beer. The competitiveness of the industry was affected as a result: (1) Miller eventually improved its own market share from four percent to over 15 percent, moving from seventh place to the position of second largest in the industry, (2) the rest of the industry was forced to increase spending on advertising, and (3) the competition in marketing carried over into price inasmuch as price increases failed to keep up with the cost increases and industry profit margins dropped from 6% to 3.5%.[36] In this case, advertising was the instrument of the increase in competition and of the change in the market structure. Was this unusual? Not necessarily. A similar change was brought about in the late seventies and early eighties by the Cola Wars. In this case, the two largest firms were primarily responsible as Pepsi sought to reduce, if not overturn, the market dominance of Coke. It was simply

[36]"Miller's Fast Growth Upsets the Beer Industry," *Business Week* (November 8, 1976), p. 59.

a matter of old rivals having a new run at "king of the hill." In the process, all the soft drink manufacturers—the colas and the others—found themselves in a war which involved price, advertising, and product competition.

We have treated target advertising as a possible means of mitigating the interdependence we associate with oligopoly. Is the quantity of advertising expenditure the only dimension in which rivalry matters? Probably not. As we noted above, the content of advertising may really be as important as the amount. Is there anything regarding content which seems to represent a mutual understanding among oligopolists? Yes. The Cola Wars provide an incident which seems to illustrate the point. It was an incident in which competitors became so inflamed that it seems that one of the firms must have violated an unspoken code of the industry. In the spring of 1982, 7Up began a campaign which injected the health issue into its advertising, an issue involving the caffeine contained in the colas and other soft drinks but not in 7Up. The President of 7Up explained the reason for the firm's new campaign: ". . . it appeared to us that there is a growing body of concern among consumers about negative health implications of this stimulant, especially with regard to children. . . ."[37] The competition was furious. Competitors took action, although more than a bit unusual. Sunkist petitioned the television networks to halt the ads, and Pepsi Cola threatened its franchised bottlers who also bottled 7Up with summary cancellation, if they were to give any support to 7Up's anti-caffeine campaign.[38]

Why all the excitement? It seems that 7Up had broken a tacit understanding. Health discussions are probably no more welcome among manufacturers of soft drinks than auto safety might be among automakers. [It would seem that there might be areas in which more information could be provided by rival advertising than the industry could stand.] In contrast, if a new campaign involving a series of television commercials for a soft drink were to stress fun or refreshment, it would likely be acceptable to the competition, even if it were very expensive. Indeed, such advertisements, although they are aimed at boosting the sales for a certain brand, could increase the sales for all brands.

Advertising and Barriers to Entry

We have seen above that advertising behavior may affect the structure of a market by maintaining the *status quo*, especially when all competitors accept their places in the industry and act merely to keep what they have. This involves the protection of mutual advantage, ignoring the disproportionate sharing of the gains between the larger and smaller firms, or the more popular and less popular products. Does advertising always offer a mutual advantage to all firms? Not

---

[37]"7Up Campaign Leaves Industry Feeling Mad," *Beverage World* (March 1982), p. 26.

[38]*Beverage Industry* (March 26, 1982), p. 1; As a postscript, within months after the incident Pepsi, Coke, and the others all introduced caffeine-free products.

necessarily. It may protect the incumbent firm from the potential entrant. It may act as a barrier to entry. How? What does advertising have to do with entry barriers?

Recall the earlier discussion on the costs of advertising. In it we argued that the established firm, with its goodwill, would be positioned to sell a larger quantity of goods than the newcomer for any given advertising outlay—the demand for the product of the incumbent would be significantly greater than the demand for the product of the entrant, *ceteris paribus*. Now let us suppose that there are economies of scale in production. If we combine these two elements, a larger market share and scale economies, the established firm might possess a great advantage relative to the newcomer, as illustrated in Figure 11-4. The AC curve indicates the effect of scale on cost, and the D_o and D_n indicate the goodwill effect on the demands for the old and the new firms, respectively. The established firm could price at P_o and sell Q_o, enjoying a substantial economic profit, but the new firm could not find a single price which would cover its costs of production.

What is the implication? It would seem that the entrant could be deterred by the prospect of losses, that the incumbent would enjoy the protection of a barrier to entry. Indeed, this looks a lot like the Modigliani model of entry deterrence, which is described in Chapter 8. There is a significant difference. In the Modigliani case, the newcomer conceded the market share advantage of the established firm. This was a conjecture; if we assume that the product is homogeneous, there is no reason why the incumbent would sell more than the entrant and no explanation of deterrence, except for that which rests in the mind of the newcomer. If the entrant were ever to challenge the established firm, it would discover that the latter had no inherent advantage. In the present case, however, deterrence is not a matter of conjecture; there is a real difference. The new firm cannot sell as much as the old.

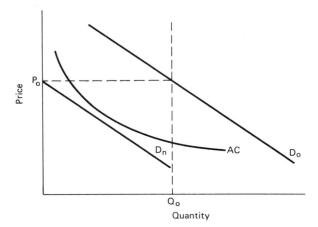

Does this mean that the goodwill advantage will act as a barrier to entry? Perhaps so. There is another possibility. While the entrant may struggle at a disadvantage for some period of time and incur losses in the process, it might eventually be able to accumulate its own stock of goodwill if it were to back its attempt at entry with a sustained advertising campaign of its own. Wouldn't that be a risky venture? Yes it would. And to the extent that the risk deters would-be entrants, established firms might enjoy the protection of a barrier to entry.

We have based the advantage of the incumbent who has a better *image* than the potential entrant upon production costs, rather than advertising costs. Is that really fair? Yes, it would seem to be. Consider an industry with constant long-run costs. That is, with no scale economies. Let us assume that the established firm can outsell the newcomer, so that D_o and D_n are taken as before. Is there a barrier to entry? No there is not. The entrant can only capture a small part of the market but it can do so without disadvantage. To illustrate, a firm may be able to survive by selling a no name brand of aspirin alongside competitors with well-known names and premium prices (and higher costs due to their advertising expenditures), but the possibility of an entrant surviving with a no name automobile seems out of the question. Nevertheless, the manufacturer of the well-known brand of aspirin will probably enjoy much greater profits than a no name competitor, owing to its goodwill. The incumbent's market, in contrast to the market as a whole, may still be tough to crack.

APPENDIX

Do oligopolists compete more heavily in advertising than do others? Does advertising have the effect of creating barriers to entry? Theoretical arguments can be offered either in support of or in contradiction to propositions which answer these questions in the affirmative. There is more than a passing interest in the answers. There are wormy policy issues at stake. How can the economist resolve such questions? Or is it even possible to do so? A great deal of empirical research has been devoted to provide answers, based primarily on econometric analyses of cross-sectional samples of industry-wide data. The results, taken together, tend to be inconclusive. Consider a few examples.

The Concentration-Advertising Hypothesis

Kaldor[39] argued in a 1950 article that advertising had been responsible for the widespread emergence of oligopoly structures in the modern market economy. Telser[40] performed a test of the hypothesis by estimating a linear regression of

---

[39]Nicholas Kaldor, "The Economic Aspects of Advertising," *Review of Economic Studies* 18 (1949–1950), pp. 1–27.

[40]Lester G. Telser, "Advertising and Competition," *Journal of Political Economy* 72 (December 1964), pp. 537–562.

concentration on advertising intensity over a cross-section of 42 three-digit consumer goods industries. The results may be written as:

(Eq. 11A-1) $CR_4 = 34.32 + 1.150 \ A/R,$
$\qquad\qquad\qquad\quad (1.057)$

with $R^2 = .03.$[41] CR_4 is the concentration ratio, and A/R is the ratio of advertising to sales revenues. Telser concluded that the absence of a statistically significant relationship failed to confirm the concentration-advertising hypothesis.

That was not the end of the matter. Others would test different relationships on different sets of data. For example, Greer[42] examined a quadratic relationship between advertising and concentration. While Greer used a similar data set to that used by Telser, the "best fit" was given by a sub-sample, made up of experience goods only. The results may be written as:

(Eq. 11A-2) $A/R = -1.856 + .1564 \ CR_4 - .0019 \ CR_4^2 + 1.3034 \ G,$
$\qquad\qquad\qquad\qquad\quad (5.71) \qquad\quad (-5.10) \qquad\quad (1.09)$

with $R^2 = .43.$[43] The variables are defined as before with the exception of G, which represents the growth in sales. And Greer concluded that the statistical significance of the CR_4 and CR_4^2 terms confirmed the concentration-advertising hypothesis. What exactly was the nature of that relationship? Greer argued that, on the one hand, advertising explained concentration, as Kaldor had claimed. On the other hand, he argued that this was an interactive relationship, and that high concentration created a market environment in which firms stressed non-price competition—and advertising in particular—instead of price competition. Even the tailing off effect of very high concentration, as represented by the negative sign associated with the CR_4^2 term, was consistent with this new twist: with a very small number of firms, recognition of interdependence would cause oligopolists to avoid those expenditures which could only invite retaliation and increase costs.

Why such a great difference in results? In part it may be due to the specification of the function, whether it is linear or quadratic. In part it may be due to the sampling. Greer found that the quadratic function did not provide the same good fit for the whole sample of consumer goods industries as it did for the experience goods sub-sample. Ornstein[44] later tested the two specifications for a larger and more inclusive sample of four-digit consumer goods industries, with the following results:

(Eq. 11A-3) $A/R = 1.1313 + .0646 \ CR_4, \ R^2 = .10,$ and
$\qquad\qquad\qquad\qquad\quad (3.05)$

[41]*loc. cit.*, p. 544.

[42]Douglas F. Greer, "Advertising and Market Concentration," *Southern Economic Journal* 38 (July 1971), pp. 19–32.

[43]*loc. cit.*, p. 26.

[44]Stanley I. Ornstein, *Industrial Concentration and Advertising Intensity* (Washington, D.C.: American Enterprise Institute, 1977), p. 50.

$$A/R = -0.1076 + .1324\ CR_4 - .0007\ CR_4^2,\ R^2 = .09.$$
$$\qquad\qquad (1.41)\qquad\quad (0.74)$$

While his linear specification was statistically significant, in contrast to the quad-ratic form, neither explained very well the interindustry variation in advertising-to-sales ratios. So, what does it mean? First, it would seem that concentration, at least by itself, is not the critical factor in explaining advertising. When Greer discovered a fairly strong relationship for his sample of experience good indus-tries, he may have confirmed that, when the product (or the market) is one in which advertising can be an effective instrument of competition, concentration may be quite important in determining the intensity of the advertising effort. Second, it would seem that advertising, at least by itself, is not the critical determinant of concentration. Even these conclusions should be taken lightly.

The Advertising-Profitability Hypothesis

An alternative hypothesis is that advertising boosts profit, that advertising rep-resents a means by which the firm may acquire and/or protect market power. Comanor and Wilson[45] were among the first to test this hypothesis, with a sample of data similar to the one used by Telser. The results may be written as:

$$(Eq.\ 11A\text{-}4)\ r_e = 0.042 + 0.362\ A/R + 0.0097\ K + 0.016\ G,$$
$$\qquad\qquad\qquad (2.4)\qquad\quad (3.2)\qquad\quad (1.6)$$

with $R^2 = .40$, and where r_e is the net return on equity and K and G are the logarithms of (1) capital needed for an efficient scale of plant and (2) growth in demand, respectively.[46] The multiple regression is statistically significant, and both variables which Comanor and Wilson took to represent entry barriers—A/R and K—are individually significant. How strong is the relation between advertis-ing and profitability? What is the nature of it? Does the former cause the latter, or *vice versa*?

Backman[47] tested the relationship for a sample of 102 firms taken from the 125 leading spenders in advertising, as listed by *Advertising Age*; 23 firms were removed from the sample for one of two reasons—either they were not in the manufacturing sector or their profit data was not publicly available. The results[48] may be written as follows:

$$(Eq.11A\text{-}5)\ r = 12.593 + .278\ A/R,\ with\ R^2 = .119,$$
$$\qquad\qquad\qquad (3.86)$$

[45]William S. Comanor and Thomas A. Wilson, "Advertising Market Structure and Perfor-mance," *Review of Economics and Statistics* 49 (November 1967), pp. 423–440.

[46]*loc. cit.*, p. 432.

[47]Backman, *op. cit.*

[48]*loc. cit.*, p. 215.

where r is the net return on investment. Backman concluded that there was a statistically significant relationship between the level of profits, and the level of advertising intensity. On the one hand, the regression explained only 12 percent of the variation in profits. On the other, the average profit rate for the sample firms—$r > 13\%$ for the group as a whole—would appear to be high. The leading spenders on advertising may earn more on the average than other firms do. Why? They may spend more because they are larger and more profitable. The direction of causation is still uncertain.

COMPETITION IN PRODUCT EFFORTS: INNOVATION AND RELATED MARKET BEHAVIOR

12

In this chapter we examine the meaning and implications of innovation and other product positioning behavior. Starting with two examples of product development, we turn then to an analysis of the firm's product design efforts and the consumer's response to them. Next, we consider the role of research and development in product innovation, and we examine the strategy of imitating a rival's products, rather than innovating. We continue with a review of Schumpeter's ideas on competitive dynamics.

*Next, we see how innovation affects sales and costs, and we incorporate both into a model of **optimal innovation**. Then, we consider how market structure may affect innovation intensities, a la Schumpeter, and how oligopoly in particular may shape overall strategy in product behavior. We also consider the use of **rules of thumb**, placing greater emphasis on the internal control mechanisms of the firm, as opposed to the external market environment. Finally, we examine innovation and the strategy to deter entry.*

A short statistical appendix follows the chapter to examine the relationships between firm size and market structure, and product innovation.

What are product efforts? They incorporate all those forms of competition in which the firm seeks to increase its sales by changing what it has to sell. Are product efforts important? Yes they are, or at least they can be in certain markets.[1] What precisely are product efforts? Innovation is certainly the most obvious. Innovation, or the creation of a new product, is the end of what might be a long and intensive effort devoted to research and development. Product efforts may be defined as being any and all of the expenditures which change the product offerings of the firm. They include such diverse activities as designing and engineering a model year changeover for a line of kitchen appliances, modi-

---

[1]Product effort is one of three elements—price, product, and selling effort—identified by Chamberlin as controlling how much of a differentiated product consumers demand. In all but the perfectly competitive market, product may be one of the key aspects of competition or even monopoly.

fying the formula of a soft drink to replace sugar with an artificial sweetner, relocating a new car dealership from the crowded central city to the suburban beltway interchange, and altering the design of the package for a box of detergent.

In this chapter we attempt to answer several questions. How do manufacturers bring about product changes? Why do consumers demand them? How can product efforts be incorporated into the theory of the firm? What advantages are there to competing in terms of product, rather than price? Does market structure shape product behavior? Does product behavior alter structure? Let us consider two examples of product efforts.

TWO CASES OF PRODUCT EFFORTS

In 1977, the Apple Computer company was born together with a new product, the personal computer. Its co-founders, Steve Jobs and Steve Wozniak, wanted to make something which interested no one else. Neither the industry giant, IBM, nor its many smaller competitors saw the market potential for a desktop computer. By default, two young men working in a garage were responsible for the innovation. Was it a tremendous technological breakthrough? No it was not. In fact, one writer on the computer industry has observed that Apple had made ". . . the most spectacular rise in the American business history . . . with a product that is probably less complicated than most toaster ovens."[2] Their first model, Apple I, was introduced in 1977 but was quickly discontinued when the firm replaced it with a vastly improved product, Apple II, in the following year. Sales really took off in 1979, after the firm pioneered a floppy-disk subsystem, replacing a tape cassette drive.[3] Before the end of 1981, it had sold 300,000 units of the Apple II.[4] Five years after its founding, Apple had achieved sales in excess of $1 billion, had gone public, and had seen some 300 of its employees accumulate a million dollars or more each.[5] However, Apple's success would soon lure many others into the market which it had discovered. In 1981, IBM entered the market with the PC, which offered some technological improvements of its own. IBM's 16-bit microprocessor, for example, was both faster and more efficient in using available memory space than Apple's 8-bit microprocessor.[6] Innovation had been responsible for creating a product market initially and for Apple's success, and innovation would continue to be important in reshaping that market and the success of those competing in it.

[2]Stephen T. McClellan, *The Coming Computer Industry Shakeout* (New York: John Wiley, 1984), p. 27.

[3]Ulrich Weil, *Information Systems in the 80's* (Englewood Cliffs, N.J.: Prentice-Hall, 1982), p. 160.

[4]*loc.cit.*

[5]McClellan, *op. cit.*, p. 217.

[6]*loc. cit.*, p. 215.

In 1981, while working on a formula for a new diet cola, a group of chemists for Coca Cola developed a mixture that seemed to taste "smoother" than Coke.[7] When these findings were turned over to the company executives, they produced a dilemma. What should the firm do? Coke was the most popular soft drink. However, it had been losing market share to Pepsi—by the end of 1984, Coke's market share was 21.7% to Pepsi's 18.8%.[8] Subsequent to the findings of the research team, the firm quietly invested $4 million on a massive taste-test in which Coke was pitted against the new formula, using a panel of 191,000 consumers. The results were rather emphatic—the new product was preferred to the old by a 55% to 45% margin.[9] In 1985, management decided to take a risk, to replace the old flavor of Coke with one which a "new generation" of cola drinkers seemed to prefer. New Coke was introduced to the public in April. Nevertheless, the company continued to be concerned after the switch, taking weekly surveys of buyer reaction, but as late as May 30, everything seemed to be going well for New Coke as 53 percent of those who were surveyed said that they preferred the new taste.[10] Still, the preference was not universal, and a rebellion of "old" Coke drinkers was soon to be heard from. Organized resentment began to build among those who were unhappy with the fact that their old favorite was no longer available.[11] The storm of protest became very loud—no doubt including the voices of some who really did not care that much but who found the whole thing very entertaining—and the company was forced to reverse its strategy of product change. On July 24, "old" Coke returned under a new name, Coca-Cola Classic, and a massive advertising campaign was launched to make the best of a bad mistake in product innovation.[12] In late fall of 1985, Coke Classic was outselling New Coke by 3 to 1.[13]

These two illustrations demonstrate how product efforts may affect the success of a particular firm in a particular market. On the one hand, they demonstrate how innovation may account for the emergence of a new competitor in an industry populated by old and established firms. On the other, they demonstrate how innovaton may be a dangerous, double-edged sword in the hands of the established firm. They also suggest that economic innovation—product change that affects the market in a meaningful way—does not necessarily require a substantial investment in research and development or imply a significant technological change.

[7]"Is Coke Fixing a Cola That Isn't Broken?" *Business Week* (May 6, 1985), p. 47.

[8]*loc. cit.*

[9]*loc. cit.*

[10]"Coke's Brand Loyalty Lesson," *Fortune* (August 5, 1985), p. 44.

[11]*loc. cit.*, p. 45.

[12]*Business Week* (September 9, 1985), p. 38.

[13]*Advertising Age* (November 18, 1985), p. 100.

THE CHARACTER OF PRODUCT EFFORTS

The firm can increase sales and profits with a successful product innovation. The firm can even use a new product as its ticket into the market in the first place— the case of Apple Computer is one example. Even more to the point, innovation may be the single most important factor in the organization of industry. It certainly may be argued that product quality and the innovations which provide it, has come to replace price as the most critical factor in competition. In 1921, while still trailing far behind Ford in the auto industry, GM established a new marketing strategy that would feature quality as its primary competitive weapon.[14] General Motors introduced a whole new line of cars and overtook Ford, while the latter continued to produce proven products (Model T's) and continued to feature low prices. It would seem that General Motors' strategy has become the model for much of modern industry—a lesson which some in American industry, including GM itself, seem to forget on occasion while others in Japan and elsewhere have not. Let us consider the fundamental principles involved. How does innovation work?

Product Efforts and Independence

Innovating—or perhaps, imitating—may be strategically superior to competing in price for the firm set in an oligopoly market. Why? The answer is much the same as that which we offered in connection with selling behavior. It derives from the same condition. If products are homogeneous, and if price is the only basis of competition, interdependence is everything. A change in price, which might allow one seller to capture a whole market and might bring disaster to another, cannot be ignored or left unchallenged. In such a case, no firm is in the position to act without considering the possible retaliation of rivals. Competitive tensions are necessarily high.

If products are heterogeneous, and if product change is only one of several factors in competition, the firm can enjoy a degree of independence. It may not discourage innovation. It may even intensify it if there are but a few close rivals.

There are at least two reasons to explain the independence which is enjoyed by the innovator. First, while a successsful product innovation may gain market share for the innovator, it certainly does not spell doom for the rival who loses. The fact that the product is differentiated in the first place tends to insulate one firm's market from another's. The loser is not compelled to respond or retaliate, as opposed to the case of the victim of a price-cutter. Second, even when the loser is moved to respond to a rival's innovation, it is unlikely to be able to do so instantaneously. In the meantime, the innovator can enjoy a

---

[14]Alfred D. Chandler, Jr. and Stephen Salsbury, *Pierre S. Du Pont and the Making of the Modern Corporation* (New York: Harper & Row, 1971), p. 517.

position which affords a temporary monopoly. The example of Apple's development of the personal computer illustrates both points rather well. Apple's innovation expanded the market for computer products, instead of simply taking sales away from the other manufacturers. It would take IBM two to three years before it became a significant force to rival Apple's ascendancy in the personal computer market.

Thus, independence is an important dimension of competition in product. Independence is also the result of other, more fundamental characteristics of the differentiated product and the product efforts which produce it. What are these?

The Product and the Consumer

What are product differences and why does the market respond to them? The short answer to the latter question is that there is a demand for product differences. Why? In Chapter 6, we dealt with the nature of product differences. We asserted there that there are two ways in which to describe and explain them: (1) some differences are represented by the spatial location of competing, but nonidentical sellers and are explained by the fact that the population is geographically scattered, and (2) other differences are represented by the physical attributes of competing, but nonidentical products and are explained by the fact that the population is made up of individual consumers who have different tastes and/or means.

Consider a hypothetical situation in which the consumer is assigned to a particular location. Further, let us assume that transportation is a significant element of cost. Now, if one particular seller were to locate closer to the consumer than any competitor, *ceteris paribus*, the locational advantage of the seller would guarantee that it could capture and hold the loyalty of our hypothetical consumer. What do we mean to imply with our use of *location* and *transportation*? In the first place, the terms may be taken quite literally. The geographic location of buyers and sellers can be used to define regional sub-markets in which the local seller always enjoys a monopoly in supplying the local population. The retail grocery industry provides an excellent example of this sort of spatial organization; a small, independent Mom-and-Pop store—and more recently, a small, franchised convenience store—represents the neighborhood monopolist.

In the second place, location and transportation may be figurative references to the consumer's tastes. A preference for a certain combination of product attributes could be taken to define the location of the consumer, while certain attributes contained in a product would be taken to define the location of the seller. The strength of a consumer's preference could be taken to define an in-kind transportation cost—that is, the utility which would be lost if the consumer were forced to substitute a less-preferred product for another. Loyalty to a favorite brand may be taken as a locational advantage of a sort. One product is simply located closer to the consumer than the product offered by any of the competition and will be purchased in preference to others unless there is either

(1) a sufficient price inducement leading to the substitution of a subjectively inferior product, or (2) a change in buyer (or seller) location.

How far can this analogy be taken? Is the firm's task of locating a product as simple as picking a good site from which to run a retail business? No, apparently it is not.

In the case of Coca Cola, the firm sought to introduce a new product which marketing research indicated would be *closer* to a larger number of soft-drink consumers than the old. New Coke was an innovation aimed at relocating by a firm concerned about the erosion of its market through a gradual change in popular taste. With the advantage of hindsight, we see that this particular innovation was not a huge success.

The Product and the Supplier

What is the product strategy of the firm? In simple terms, a product strategy might be described as locating its products in the most favorable positions in the market. How? Let us consider the matter first as a static question. Given perfect information, where would the firm choose to locate? The most obvious answer is where most of the consumers are located. What if consumers are scattered? In that case, the firm may want to have several products in the market. In the automobile industry, for example, an automaker may have different lines or name plates. Some may be specialty lines, such as the Chevrolet Corvette, while others may be full lines, such as the Chevrolet Caprice, and may contain a business coupe, 2-door and 4-door sedans, a station wagon, and possibly even a convertible. Why such proliferation? If may be a reasonable strategy if the market really is made up of many different market segments.

The full-line manufacturer can reach a larger proportion of consumers provided that it offers products which cater to the variety of tastes or market segments than the narrow-line manufacturer can. Other things being equal, the full-line producer can achieve a larger market share. In that event, other benefits may accrue: (1) certain costs of design and promotion may be jointly shared by various products in the line, so that the full-line producer may enjoy economies denied the single-line firm, (2) certain plant or other production facilities may be capable of switching from making one product to another as demand dictates, so that the full-line firm may enjoy better utilization of capacity than its single-line rival, especially if there are indivisibilities and/or scale factors involved, and (3) certain products in the line—the **luxury** models, for example—may command a higher margin of profit to cost than others, so that a full-line producer may exercise greater control over price by exploiting its ability to discriminate.

Now let us consider the matter of product location as a dynamic question. What are the factors involved when the firm seeks to enter a new market with a new product? Whereas the owner of a service station or a convenience store can identify its customers—or at least it can make a rough estimate of how many there are and where they will come from—in advance of selecting a new business site, the producer with a new product can identify its customers—if there are any—only after the fact. The automaker or the soft-drink manufacturer must first offer the new product for sale to explore for a new market. There are significant risks involved. What is the implication? It would seem that it may either encourage or discourage search for a new market.

Consider a hypothetical situation in which a new product could be introduced by two different firms, an established giant in the industry or a small, new rival. Do both firms have the same product strategy? Not necessarily. Who has the most to gain? It may be reasonable to conjecture that the established firm would place less value on a given new product than a recent entrant would do, *ceteris paribus*. Assuming the firm is already well-positioned in the market, the return on an investment in the new product may be viewed as rather small—in large part, this product may actually draw on sales which the firm already counts as safe. If the firm is struggling to find a position in the market, the return on an investment in the identical product may be viewed as very substantial. If the new product should enable it to take sales away from the established firm, the small firm would clearly regard it as a valuable asset. Is this merely hypothetical? Not at all. Indeed, it may be the explanation for Apple's pioneering venture into the personal computer while the existing manufacturers deferred. It also may help to explain why the introduction of New Coke was regarded as such a gamble by the firm and the industry, despite the fact that the development costs involved in the project were minimal.

Invention, Design, and Innovation: The Product Efforts

In a world of differentiated products, we may imagine that the consumer can become attached to a particular product design which corresponds most closely to his or her tastes. We may imagine that the supplier of such a product can enjoy a position of market power—it can count on the custom of certain loyal patrons as long as its price is competitive and as long as its location is unique. What product efforts are necessary to develop such a location in the first place? Are all new products generated in the same way? Let's try the last question first. No, they are not. Why?

Several processes may be involved in the development of a new product, but it is *innovation* that is common to all of them. It is the final stage, the commercial commitment to manufacture and market a new product design. In certain cases, the only risks for the innovator are those which are directly associated with testing the market. In New Coke, for example, the same production techniques and facilities could be used to make it as were used to make the product it was supposed to replace. In other cases, the risks for the innovator include the investment in major new production facilities. In the automobile industry, for example, a model changeover commits the manufacturer to an investment of hundreds of millions of dollars in new tools and dies. In the latter instance, a product mistake would be much more difficult to undo. If the public were to reject its 1988 models, it is unlikely that the automaker could or would change back over to the 1987 product line, unlike the sudden rebirth of Coca Cola Classic.

How does the firm develop its new product in the first place? We often tend to use such terms as invention and research and development rather loosely. We may casually refer to a new product as an invention. That is wrong. An *invention* is a prototype for a product (or for the process to make a product) which involves new technology; it is something which is new in some significant technical aspect and which works. On the one hand, many product innovations do not require invention. A new design, which is introduced by a Paris couturier for example, is likely to be innovative, but it is rarely inventive. On the other, many inventions never advance beyond the prototype stage. Technical feasibility does not always—or perhaps, most often does not—translate into economic viability.

If a new product is not based upon invention, what is it based upon? *Design* is a term we can use for non-original product development. Most often an innovation is the skillful product of the engineer or the designer. The Ford Mustang, introduced in the spring of 1964, was one of the most successful new cars ever offered by Detroit. It was a designer's dream of the sporty car of the mid-sixties: a long hood and a low, flat rear deck. It was powered by Ford's basic 289 cubic inch V-8, and it was built on the existing Ford Falcon platform. It became an instant success. Ford sold more than one half million units in both 1965 and 1966; its sales represented 78.2 percent of the U.S. market for small, sporty cars.[15] Is it always so easy to create a new product out of a redesign effort? Not at all. In 1957, Ford Motor Company had tried to launch an entire new line of cars—one built upon Ford and Mercury platforms—with the Edsel. It was to be a dismal failure. Ford took the decision only two years later to scrap the line, the product division, and the dealership network set up exclusively for it.[16]

A new product design may be difficult to distinguish from a new invention for the outsider; it is the process, rather than the final product that is important. The crucial difference is that, in the case of pure design, the project team works with existing technology—technical feasibility is never an issue. In the case of a new invention, the project team works with new technology. A further distinction is commonly made between two phases of inventive activity: (1) *research* is the term used to describe the highly speculative and wide-ranging search for new science, while (2) *development* is the term used to describe the more practical and narrowly-directed efforts devoted to the application of new bits of knowledge, together with old, to the making of an invention.

Thus, an innovation which is based upon discovering and applying new technology represents a significant pyramiding of risks. At the first level, the research efforts may or may not generate new knowledge. At the second level,

[15]Robert Lacey, *Ford: The Men and the Machine* (New York: Little Brown, 1986), pp. 512–513.
[16]*loc. cit.*, p. 493.

assuming that the research has paid off, the development efforts may or may not produce working prototypes. At the final level, assuming that both research and development are a success, the innovative efforts may or may not produce a product which finds its market and generates sufficient revenues to pay for the enterprise and to return a profit. So, what is the implication?

The firm is most likely to "play it close to the vest" and to channel its product effort most often into projects based on old technology, *ceteris paribus*. The firm is also more likely to be willing to spend on the application of knowledge to making new products than on the search for new knowledge *per se*. Indeed, data on research and development expenditures seem to bear this out. The National Science Foundation has reported that in 1979, total research and development expenditures were divided in the proportion of 1:3 between research and development; according to NSF definitions, less than 4 percent of all R&D was spent on **basic research** or the general search for knowledge, about 22 percent was spent on **applied research** or the search for the commercial applications of new knowledge, and 75 percent was spent on **development** or on innovations—that is, on products which are new whether the science upon which they are based is new or old.[17]

Innovation: Product and Selling Efforts

After the firm has developed a new product and the means to produce it, does it sit back and wait for the line to form? Not very likely. When we say that a successful innovation must find its market, we mean to suggest two things: (1) there does exist a potential market of consumers for the new product, and (2) there is a need to inform them of its existence, and perhaps, a need to persuade them of its superiority to something else. This means that the innovator must sell its new product, using advertising and/or other selling efforts. There are many cases in which the major expense of an innovation is advertising cost. For example, we noted in Chapter 11 that the marketing costs of new ready-to-eat cereal brands may absorb two-thirds of revenues in the first year. When New Coke was finally put on the market, Coca Cola spent more—a great deal more—on promotion than on its "discovery." Finding a market can be expensive, and it can take talents which are very different from those of finding the original idea upon which an innovation is based. It should not be surprising, therefore, to discover that independent inventors often turn to established firms for the commercial exploitation, including the promotion, of their inventions.

Imitation Versus Innovation

Will the incentive to innovate always be strong or will the process which produces change degenerate and be replaced by one in which the firm chooses to imitate the successsful product instead? Will product diversity ultimately disap-

---

[17]National Science Foundation, *Research and Development in Industry, 1979* (Washington, D.C.: Government Printing Office, 1981), p. 42.

pear? The idea that imitation is a threat to innovation is not new. So, let us consider the proposition.

The innovator is one who bears the risks of developing new science and of searching for new markets. Yet the imitator can profit from a much less risky strategy: (1) wait to see which products succeed and which fail, (2) borrow the technology and/or copy the design of the former, and (3) move into the market and take a piece of the action. Is the possibility of imitation mere speculation? No, we can easily find examples of it. After the cola became America's most popular flavor of soft-drink, Coca-Cola saw many imitators enter the market, including Pepsi, Royal Crown, Shasta, and even Jolt. After Apple discovered the personal computer—and especially after IBM introduced the compatible PC—an army of clones has entered the market. Yet, it is one thing to observe that imitation will rival innovation as a product strategy for the firm, and quite another to conclude that imitation will replace innovation.

Product Clustering.   What do we mean by **clustering** and what does it have to do with imitation versus innovation? There will be a cluster when the products of various suppliers are targeted for the same market and contain the same attributes. In spatial terms, a cluster exists when sellers occupy identical locations. Hotelling[18] analyzed a case of spatial competition in a duopoly and concluded that rivals would be inevitably drawn to the center of the market. Why? Let us consider Hotelling's model.

Hotelling sought to illustrate two things: (1) that products could be differentiated by a single attribute, location, and (2) that open competition would tend to eliminate product differences. Let us assume that there exists a homogeneous good, supplied by two firms at a noncooperative fixed price of P_o—let us assume that the product is a hotdog and the two rivals operate competing hotdog stands. Let us further assume that all consumers have identical demands for hotdogs. For each consumer, demand is given as perfectly price inelastic, with one hotdog demanded per day. Let us assume that there is a simple spatially-defined world in which consumers are evenly distributed along a stretch of beach, and in which the two dealers are located at specific positions, illustrated as x_1 and x_2 in Figure 12-1. Finally, let us assume that each consumer will buy from the nearest dealer—we might assume that each person faces a common transportation cost (c) per unit of distance between his or her location on the beach (i) and the nearest dealer, so that the "delivered" price of the hotdog will be the lesser of $P_o + c \cdot (i - x_1)$, or $P_o + c \cdot (i - x_2)$. Given the respective locations of the dealers, the market will be divided between them by the point d, which is equidistant between x_1 and x_2 as shown in Figure 12-1. Under these circumstances, what is the most profitable locational strategy? What does that imply about the market equilibrium?

In Hotelling's model, if the two hotdog stands are located at some distance

[18]Harold Hotelling, "Stability in Competition," *Economic Journal* 39 (March 1929), pp. 41–57.

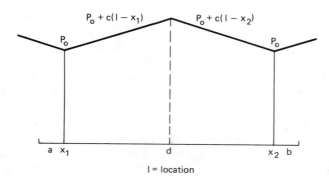

I = location

Figure 12-1 Rival locations determine how the market will be divided. If price is fixed and transportation costs are significant, one firm can increase its share of the market by moving towards the center, provided the rival does not. As a result, both rivals are likely to cluster at the center of the market.

to move towards the center of the beach. Each dealer sees that it can engross a larger share of the market if it narrows the distance between itself and its rival, given the location of the rival. Why? There are two relevant segments of the market: (1) the home market, made of beach-goers located in the shadow of one's hotdog stand and necessarily a captive market, and (2) the competitive market, made up of the beach-goers located between the two hotdog stands and necessarily divided equally between them. Strategically it is always profitable to increase the size of one's home market at the expense of the competitive market. Hotelling is led to conclude that spatial equilibrium dictates that the two hotdog stands be located side-by-side at the exact center of the beach. If not located at the center, a dealer can gain by moving towards it. Once located there, a dealer would lose market share by moving away from it.

Hotelling offered a strong argument for uniformity, and it has an intuitive appeal, given the clustering we can see about us—there are banking districts, theater districts, and so on. How convincing is the argument itself? It is derived from some very strong and questionable assumptions. If the dealer's price were not fixed, for example, the strategy of locating at some distance from the rival would be more attractive—it would afford the dealer the opportunity to increase price. If the consumers' demands were not perfectly inelastic, locational strategy would not necessarily reduce to a zero-sum game. If there were a larger number of competitors or entry or even multiple sites for the existing duopolists, diversity of location may be the result of competition.

Moreover, the question of diversity versus uniformity may not really be addressed best in static terms, as Hotelling has done. It may be a question of a dynamic process.

Imitation, Innovation, and Dynamics

Under what circumstances is innovation most likely to occur? Why? Schumpeter[19] offers us a most controversial hypothesis: that innovation depends upon monopoly. In the most basic terms, the Schumpeter hypothesis has two prongs:

[19]Joseph A Schumpeter, *Capitalism, Socialism and Democracy* (New York: Harper, 1942).

(1) the assertion that the monopolist, with its resources derived from the exercise of market power, is better able to supply innovation, and (2) the assertion that the monopolist, with its position constantly at risk to potential competition, has more at stake to justify its demand for innovation. Our current interest is with the latter point.

Precisely what does the Schumpeter hypothesis suggest about the relationship between imitation and innovation? It would seem that imitation spurs innovation, rather than discouraging it. A monopolist's market power, in Schumpeter's view, could be reduced to nothing by the entry of a plague of imitators, carried by the winds of "a perennial gale of creative destruction." Only by constantly improving its product, could the monopolist keep ahead of the competition and secure its monopoly indefinitely. In this view, monopoly was not something to be condemned, but instead it should be admired since the monopolist earned its position by superior performance.

Is Schumpeter's view universally held? No, it certainly is not. The justification for patent laws to protect innovators appears to take the opposite view. A patent is a grant of legal monopoly designed to protect the inventor from **free-riders**—imitators who copy an invention but who contribute nothing to its development—for a specific period of time in order to secure enough reward so that the inventor will be compensated for his or her risks and will be willing to take them. From this point of view, a threat of imitation is sufficient to eliminate, or at the very least, seriously to reduce innovation. Are these two views so different? No, in some ways they are not. Both regard monopoly as a necessary condition for innovation, and both regard competition as a fundamentally static—even stagnant—market condition. But many embrace neither the Schumpeter nor the patent-protection view of innovation.

Stigler[20] has argued that a dynamic view of competition is fully capable of explaining innovation. Introducing new products is one means by which firms can and do compete with one another, particularly since some markets are constantly changing. In this process of competition, past dominance is not necessarily the most reliable predictor of future success. Why should this be? A major reason has to do with incentives. The small firm or the new entrant may have a stronger incentive than the large, established firm to innovate. The established firm will have a natural advantage over the imitator if consumer loyalty plays any role in competition between them. A new or small firm will have as much chance of capturing a new market as the established firm. Again, Apple Computer provides us with an illustration of the potential for success of a tiny firm matched against giants. As was shown in that case, the investment needed to develop a new product may be completely within the means of the small enterprise, Schumpeter notwithstanding. Finally, the established firm may be slow or even reluctant to innovate. If it should fear that its offer of a new product

---

[20]George J. Stigler, "Industrial Organization and Economic Progress," in Harvey J. Levin, ed., *Businesss Organization and Public Policy* (New York: Holt, Rinehart and Winston, 1958), pp. 125–135.

would spoil the market, and if past success should lead it to believe—however falsely—that it has nothing to fear from the competiton, the leading firm may wait. In such a case, it may turn out to be the imitator.

THE COSTS OF INNOVATION

Innovations are undertaken to increase the demand for the firm's products. They also increase costs. But what exactly is the nature of the costs of innovation? To simplify matters, let us consider the question in terms of a single project. When the firm seeks to innovate, and whether or not it succeeds, it must commit to a fixed investment. A project undertaken now can pay off only after the passage of a great deal of time, at least in the case of a time-intensive innovation involving the research and development of a new technology. And the returns to certain innovative projects can begin only after the commercially-viable new product has been found—provided that one ever is—and only after it has proved itself on the market. Having made that point, however, let us begin by ignoring the dimension of time. Let us consider the effect of innovation on the costs of doing business in an otherwise static world.

Consider the hypothetical situation, depicted in Figure 12-2, in which there are two firms with identical production costs (AC) and with an identical price (P_0). Let us assume that the first firm does nothing to change its product and sells Q_1 units of it, but the second firm spends N dollars on innovation, sells Q_2 units of product, and bears the costs of production and innovation represented by $AC_{w/n}$. Of the two firms, the second is in the obviously preferred position: (1) it sells a larger volume of goods, and (2) its effective average cost—the unit cost for the quantity that it is able to sell—is lower than that of the first firm. All other things being equal, this illustrates the case of a profitable innovation.

The similarity between the present case and the analysis of advertising behavior in Chapter 11 is dramatic. Should this be surprising? Both deal with the firm's use of an economic, non-price tool for controlling its demand and profit position. Does Figure 12-2, explain how innovation would affect costs? No, it only illustrates the effect of an N-dollar expenditure for innovation on the average cost curve and on the quantity of goods sold, provided that the scale of the operation is taken as given and the price is fixed at P_0.

Let us suppose that we are interested in the total effect of an innovation on revenues, whether differentiation of the product affects the firm's price, its sales volume, or both. If the N-dollar expenditure should produce the product change which in turn results in shifting the firm's total revenues from R_1 to R_2, we might take total innovation cost, TIC in Figure 12-3, to be *the* cost function for innovation. Alternatively, TIC can be regarded as a revenue production function in which innovation is the critical input.

As with the total advertising cost function (TAC) from the previous chapter, the total innovation cost function (TIC) would seem to have two interesting

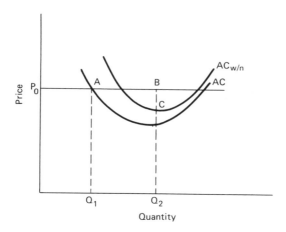

Figure 12-2 Innovation affects both demand and cost for the firm. In the monopolistic competition model, a firm could profit from an innovation if it allows the firm to exploit scale economies (or exploit a product monopoly). The firm's revenues could grow by more than its costs.

properties: (1) the sales volume at a zero-cost level of innovation (R_1), and (2) the sales volume with innovation (R_2), given the expenditure N_0. Let us consider the first of these.

What accounts for the zero-cost sales? We must assume that in the market for differentiated products any firm always has a choice of options: (1) it can continue to make and sell the style of product it is presently marketing, and (2) it can innovate in order to improve upon its present market position. Thus, zero-cost sales are those which are a *free good*, owing to the past development of a product and a place in the market. The old, established firm may count upon R_1 in sales revenue.

The same free good concept could be applied to entry into a segment of the market which an old, established firm had pioneered. The newcomer may copy the product and take a minimal risk since the technological problems—if there ever were any—have been solved and the commercial viability of the product has been proved. In this case, the entrant may regard R_1 as its prospective share of the established market, unless the pioneer were to enjoy an advantage of brand loyalty. Are there any other restrictions to free entry into the market? Yes, there certainly might be. It depends upon whether the entrant has in place production facilities which it could use to manufacture the existing product. Otherwise, non-innovative entry into the market by a copy-cat producer could not properly be regarded as free.

Now consider the sales resulting from innovaton. Suppose that the expenditure of N_0-dollars would automatically result in sales revenues of R_2 for the innovator, regardless of which firm that might be—the established firm or the entrant. Would the revenue gain attributable to innovation be the same for any firm which was able to beat the competition? Not necessarily. The sales of some new products would likely take sales away from older products. That implies that the more the firm stands to sell without troubling to innovate, the less it has to gain; the benefits of innovation, $[R_2 - R_1,]$, would seem to be smaller for the well-positioned firm than for the newcomer, and that in turn implies that the costs would be higher. Would that always be the case, however? No, it would not.

Consider the case of a strongly differentiated market: (1) market segments are clearly delineated, and (2) consumers will either buy the product which matches their tastes precisely or they will not buy the product at all, instead they would choose to substitute a variety of other goods. Under the circumstances, an innovation may not affect established markets, provided that it fits into the gaps left by the other products. The personal computer, for example, was the kind of innovation which expands the market as a whole since it increased sales at virtually no expense to existing products. In such a case, it would seem that the innovator—either an established firm or a newcomer—would stand to gain from the new product, without sacrifice to its other products. In that case, the cost function, Figure 12-3, could represent any firm in the industry.

How much difference does it make whether the market is strongly differentiated or not, and whether new products replace old products or complement them in the market? It really may not matter at all. If an innovation is important enough, and if it yields a product with substantially superior characteristics to that which it most closely resembles, so many new uses might be found for it that the growth of new sales may overwhelm the loss of the old. In the aircraft manufacturing industry, for example, a switch from reciprocating to jet engines appears to have led to a mid-century explosion in demand. With the arrival of the "jet age" in the late fifties, the commercial airliner seems to have replaced the steamship and the railcar as the preferred mode for passenger travel almost overnight. In such a case, it is the R_2 sales, not the R_1, which are likely to matter to the innovator. "Big" innovations—and many smaller ones, for that matter—stretch the logic of our model contained in Figure 12-3 beyond its limits. Certain revisions of it may be necessary.

The total innovation cost function (TIC) must reflect the fact that innova-

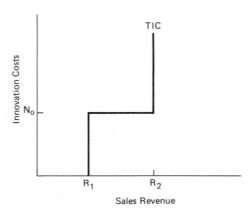

Figure 12-3 The total innovation cost function TIC describes how sales may be functionally related to innovation expenditures. If the cost to produce a specific innovation is N_0, the firm may supply an old product with sales R_1, or innovate with sales R_2. With many innovations, TIC could be a continuous function of N.

tion has a time dimension. First, the design or development of a new product may take seveal years to complete. Even in routine circumstances, such as the annual model changes for automobiles, the process begins years ahead of the deadline for production. Second, the successful innovation ordinarily does not "wear out" in a single year. If the innovator gets a long lead on the competition, it may take others several years before they can match the product or supply a better one. Until then, the innovator may realize significant profits from its product monopoly. How do these factors affect the TIC function? Until now we have treated the costs and revenues in the TIC relationship as current flows of funds. But if costs and/or revenues accumulate over time, and if they do not occur simultaneously, we can compare them only if we treat them as stocks of funds.

Suppose, for example, that a product could be developed in the current year at a cost of $2,000, and that it could increase revenues by an amount equal to $1,000 per year for the next five, beginning one year from now. Does this mean that we could treat the innovation as yielding a ratio of benefits to cost equal to 5:2? No, it does not, or at least it does not if we assume that the appropriate rate of interest is greater than zero. When we compare the current development cost to the future revenue gain, we must calculate the "present value" of those gains according to the following relationship: $PV = \Sigma R_t/[1 + d]^t$, where R_t is the revenue in time period t, and d is the rate of discounting future revenue gains to the present. If we were to assume the discount rate for risky investments in innovation is 10 percent, the PV of our hypothetical innovation would equal $2,984, in contrast to the sum of $5,000 in non-discounted future revenues ignoring the effect of time.

A similar calculation would be used to find the investment cost of an innovation. If a product innovation has taken several years to complete, its present value would be represented by the relationship: $PV = \Sigma C_t \cdot [1 + r]^t$, where C_t is the cost incurred in the past time period t, and r is the compound rate of return for such investments, the firm may well assume that $r \equiv d$.

Does this exhaust all the time-related factors associated with the TIC function? Not necessarily. The productivity of innovation activity may also be time related. Scherer[21], among others, has discussed the possibility that (1) increases in the rate of spending on a research and development project may speed up its completion date while adding to the total cost, on the one hand, and (2) hastening the whole process may lengthen the period of time during which the innovator enjoys a product monopoly and thereby increase its profits, on the other. Aside from the productivity effects, changes in the time-shape of the cost and revenue flows may alter the present values—future revenue may be discounted less and present value may be greater, for example, if the firm could move up the date at which it starts to enjoy the benefits of its innovation, *ceteris paribus*.

[21]F. M. Scherer, "Research and Development Resource Allocation under Rivalry," *Quarterly Journal of Economics* 81 (August 1967), pp. 359–394.

THE THEORY OF OPTIMAL INNOVATION

How much will the firm spend on innovation? What factors will affect that decision? We confronted similar questions in the case of advertising in Chapter 11. We might presume that we need merely to construct a simple model of the firm—as we did once before—in order to deal with them. Let us suppose that the firm faces the situation, shown by Figure 12-4, in which it must balance the costs of innovation against the benefits. These are illustrated as follows: (1) the function representing total cost of innovation, TIC, and (2) the function representing total revenue net of production cost, TNR.

Before proceeding further, there a few things to note about the model. First, we have assumed once again that we may ignore time—those efforts to produce innovation and those gains which result from it are all assumed to occur in a single time period. Second, we have assumed here that the quality (or quantity) of innovation is a variable—unlike the case illustrated in Figure 12-3 in which a given innovation was assumed to cost a fixed amount. Third, we have assumed that while net revenues accruing to the firm from introducing new products will reflect both increased price and quantity, at some point, the firm's TNR function must eventually reach a maximum due to increasing costs and falling prices as sales and output of the new product rise.

So, what will the firm choose to do? As a profit-maximizing entity, the firm must then select the level of gross revenues, R^*, at which profits—$\pi \equiv [\text{TNR} - \text{TIC}]$—will be at a maximum. This means that the firm will supply the innovation effort, N^*, which is necessary to produce R^*—N^*/R^* is the optimal ratio of innovation expenditure to total sales revenues for the firm, given the innovation cost and revenue functions represented by TIC and TNR. Therefore, Fig. 12-4 can be used to illustrate the optimal innovation strategy for the firm. What determines the shape and position of the TIC and TNR functions? Needham[22]

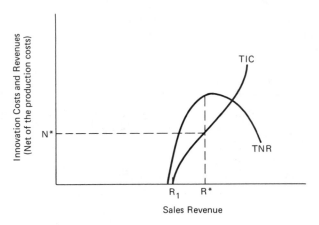

Figure 12-4 Innovation strategy may be defined for a profit-maximizing firm by taking account of the two relationships: (1) sales as a function of innovation expenditure TIC, and (2) revenues net of production costs as a function of sales TNR. Optimal innovation may imply N^*/R^*.

[22]Douglas C. Needham, "Market Structure and Firms' R and D Behavior," *Journal of Industrial Economics* 23 (June 1975), pp. 241–255.

has shown that the following relationship exists: $N^*/R^* = \theta/\epsilon$, where θ is the elasticity of demand with respect to innovation while ϵ is the absolute value of the elasticity of demand with respect to price. These two crucial parameters are derived from the firm's demand and cost functions, $Q = f(P,N)$ and $C = \Phi(Q,N)$, where N measures the amount of innovation expenditure. Should this result come as a surprise? Not at all. It is similar to the solution provided by Dorfman and Steiner's model of optimal advertising, which we examined in the last chapter.

The firm's innovation intensity, its N/R ratio, will be greater, the higher is its innovation elasticity and the lower is its price elasticity. What explains these elasticities? It would seem, if one can abstract from the accumulated discussions and investigations of innovation, that two factors are mentioned most often, technological opportunity and market structure. It would seem that these are related to the innovation and price elasticities of demand.

It is reasonable to presume that, at any point in time, the technological opportunities which exist in one industry will be different from those which exist in another. In the nineteenth century, great advances were made in applications of mechanical principles to commercial activity. The industrial revolution took root where the steel and engineering industries were among the most dynamic. And when the automobile was introduced at the turn of this century, the engineering age may have reached its peak. Since then many new industries have emerged and grown to prominence in the economy, especially

TABLE 12.1 INNOVATION EXPENDITURES: R&D FOR SELECTED INDUSTRIES, 1984

INDUSTRY	N/R (PERCENT R&D)
Aerospace	4.8
Appliances	1.4
Automotive (cars and trucks)	3.4
Chemicals	3.1
Drugs	7.1
Electronics	4.3
Food & Beverages	0.9
Computers	7.4
Computer Software	7.8
Machinery (tools, indus., mining)	3.0
Metals and Mining	1.1
Paper	1.0
Personal & Home Care Products	2.6
Semiconductors	8.2
Steel	0.5
Tobacco	0.4

Source: Reprinted from July 8, 1985 issue of *Business Week* by special permission, © 1985 by McGraw-Hill, Inc.

those which have borrowed from and contributed to the state of knowledge in aeronautics, chemistry, and electronics.

And the greater the opportunities for applying technology to new products—or to new production processes—the greater the revenue potential for innovative efforts. In terms of Needham's model of optimal innovation intensity, technological opportunity should directly increase the innovation elasticity of demand, θ, *ceteris paribus*. How might we detect this effect? To begin, it is necessary to devise a measure of innovative effort. As we have suggested above, innovation might involve anything ranging from a simple redesign of a product to a significant new invention. We might assume that expenditures on research and development are representative of the effort to innovate—and especially as it is affected by technological opportunity. Let us consider the industry spending averages for R&D, as shown in Table 12-1, as indicative of the inter-industry differences in technological opportunity. The *high-tech* group of industries do seem to support significantly higher levels of innovative effort than the all-industry average of 2.9 percent.[23]

The most persistent debate over innovation intensity has been that involving the role of market structure. We might start with the Schumpeter hypothesis: monopoly is a more fertile ground for the germination of a new product or a new production process than is competition. What support for that contention, if any, is provided by the model of optimal innovation? Let us consider the price elasticity parameter, ϵ. For a particular industry demand function, the monopolist has more control over price and, therefore, has a lower price elasticity than the more competitive firm. If we consider this factor alone, a monopolist would have more incentive to innovate than an imperfectly competitive firm would have. But that is not the whole story. Now consider the innovation elasticity parameter, θ. Innovation is a threat to take sales away from existing products. The market position of the firm, prior to innovation, could be a determinant in the net revenue potential of a new product. A firm which is currently a monopolist may have less to gain than one which is currently a competitor, *ceteris paribus*; it would have a lower value of θ. If we consider this factor alone, a monopolist would have less incentive to innovate than a competitive firm would have. Now for the total effect, if a monoplist has both a lower θ and a lower ϵ than a competitive firm, how do their respective θ/ϵ ratios compare? Is θ/ϵ larger or smaller under monopoly? That is the critical question. Unfortunately, deductive reasoning is entirely inadequate to supply us the answer. Whatever the relationship between market structure and innovation, discovering what it is turns out to be an empirical question.

We can learn something by examining the R&D expenditures of individual firms. *Business Week*,[24] reporting on the research and development activities of U.S. corporations, provides evidence to suggest that N/R is just not a simple

[23]"R&D Scoreboard," *Business Week* (July 8, 1985), pp. 88–104.
[24]*loc. cit.*

function of size. Many of the leaders in R&D, measured in percentage terms, are among the smaller firms in a given industry—firms such as Electronics Corporation of America and Cray Research are much smaller than the industry sales leaders, GE and IBM, with whom they compete. However, the evidence is mixed. In 1984, for example, General Motors and Ford were the co-leaders in the automotive industry, and in the oil service and supply industry, Schlumberger was among those with the highest ratios of research and development expenditures to sales revenues.

So, where do we go at this point? It would seem that there are two directions to investigate. First, we need to examine the theoretical effect of market structure more carefully. Our model of optimal innovation analyzes decision-making under conditions of independence—the θ and ϵ parameters (or the TIC and the TNR functions) are taken as given. That is sufficient for the firm in the case of monopoly (or even for the case of competition). Oligopoly may provide the more interesting case—and it is certainly the more important one for many markets. Second, we need to examine the empirical studies which have been undertaken to find the effect of market structure on innovation. Numerous efforts have been made to test the Schumpeter hypothesis—and variations of it—and we shall summarize them later in this chapter; additional details will finally be provided in the Appendix to Chapter 12.

OLIGOPOLY AND INNOVATION

The innovator, we may presume, will have a monopoly in its new product (or its new production process). For how long? Will that innovator take into account the behavior of rivals when it plans the unveiling of its product (or process)? Market structure is bound to have some effect. A monopolist would not be concerned about competition. However, the firm which is accustomed to interdependence in matters of price-setting is quite likely to consider a competitive reaction in matters of innovation as well.

Close rivalry introduces some interesting possibilities into the analysis of optimal innovation behavior. First, the firm may worry about the reactions to its new product. Suppose that sales of a new product should cut deeply into the sales of rival firms, as many consumers see it as an improvement over other products in the market. On the one hand, the innovator would regard this as a good outcome, the best that one might hope for. On the other hand, the innovator might also feel a bit uneasy about too much success. If it comes at the expense of the competition, they can not and will not allow it to go unanswered. An innovation which is successful in displacing other products—as opposed to one which is successful in expanding the **product space**—invites retaliation, or in this case, imitation of the product. The act of imitation, when and if it does take place, will reduce the θ parameter of the innovation. Retaliation will make innovation less attractive.

Second, the firm may worry about the product initiatives of its rivals. If it should allow itself to be left behind by new product innovations supplied by the competition, the firm may be out of luck and out of business. Thus, the firm may be compelled to spend some amount on research and development, even if it is only a defensive strategy. Imitation of a successful innovation—at least in a time frame that is competitively meaningful—may not be possible without a degree of technological skill and input comparable to the original effort.

So, what do these two concerns imply? The first might seem to suggest that less would be spent searching for innovations in the oligopoly market than in the competitive market, for example. The second seems to suggest that more would be spent just to remain competitive in the oligopoly market. Oligopoly, and the strategic behavior which is presumed to accompany it, introduces new and interesting complications in modeling innovation. We have only just scratched the surface.

Let us suppose that the firm believes that the technological abilities and efforts of the competition determine at what point they will be able to supply a new product. Scherer[25] analyzed an oligopolist's behavior under this Cournot-type assumption, and he concluded that oligopoly might intensify innovative efforts. The firm may be encouraged to pour additional funds into a project in order to hasten development and to prolong the period during which it enjoys a monopoly, increasing the value of its θ. Why would this increase expenditure as well? Scherer assumed that the total size of the monopoly profits was an economic good, that the costs of development were a function of time, and that speeding the process could be accomplished only by increasing the outlay. Indeed, there are added implications. Since larger firms may have more resources upon which to draw, they may be the more likely candidates to innovate. Market concentration might be a positive factor in innovation, due to the interdependence and the firm size considerations.

Suppose, however, that speeding up the innovation effort is only one of the firm's options; alternatively, it might gear up to imitate its rivals' products quickly when they appear in the market. In the first place, this precaution may insure the firm against severe market damage if a rival should ever succeed in developing a new product first. In the second place, it may be a strategy which returns more to the firm than if it should always be first out with a new product—this has been called the **fast second** strategy by Baldwin and Childs[26]. What advantages are there to being second rather than first? It may cost less and involve less risk to be second. As a technical matter, it may be easier to do *reverse engineering*—that is, to discover how something is done by taking it apart—than do the original job of invention, and the R&D for the imitation is likely to cost less as a result. As a marketing matter, the imitator may get a free ride. If

[25]Scherer, *loc. cit.*

[26]William L. Baldwin and Gerald L. Childs, "The Fast Second and Rivalry in Research and Development," *Southern Economic Journal* 36 (July 1969), pp. 18–24.

consumers should reject a new product, the innovator learns a costly lesson, but all the would-be imitators go to school for nothing. Does this mean that the fast second strategy is superior? Not necessarily. If it should take too long to catch up in technology, of if it should be too difficult to recover the market share it lost to the innovator, imitation may not be a good strategy. Provided that the firm has the technical and marketing ability needed to recapture lost ground rapidly, however, imitation may work to advantage. Baldwin and Childs have suggested that the dominant firm in the market often does have just such an ability. At the other extreme, innovation may be the most effective way for the small firm to move ahead. If so, innovators are more likely to be the smaller firms in the market, *ceteris paribus*, while "fast second" imitators are more likely to be the larger firms.

Even if imitation becomes a favorite strategy for some of the major firms in an oligopoly market, does this mean that less will be spent on innovation? Or that less innovation will be done? Not necessarily. In the first place, it may not be cheap to operate a fast second strategy. To keep from being left in the wake of more aggressive and innovative rivals, the firm may budget a substantial amount to its research and design activity. Thus, oligopoly may stimulate, rather than retard the level of spending on matters related to innovation. In the second place, the long-run survival of the strategy of imitation in oligopoly is necessarily dependent upon the success of innovation itself—if there should be a steady flow of innovations, the imitator is justified in maintaining its capacity to copy them.

Does this mean that the oligopoly firm will devote more to innovation than the monopoly firm? Not necessarily. Suppose we begin with our optimal model of innovation: the firm knows what its costs and revenues will be if it innovates and if no one else imitates the product—there exists a perfect certainty about the technical success of innovation. Now suppose that we assume away the gains of imitation: (1) the firm that is first enjoys benefits for as long as its product (or process) is unique, and (2) the firm that is second halts the flow of "monopoly" profits which accrue to the innovator, but realizes no gains for itself. What might be the logical implication for the oligopoly firm in possession of these facts and under the realization that others are in the same position as itself? One possibility is that the whole group of firms would decline to invest in the innovation. Kamien and Schwartz[27] report on game theory models of oligopoly which predict that stalemate may result: (1) each firm knows how much it would cost to innovate and how much it would gain from doing so, (2) each firm knows that others are similarly informed, and (3) each firm realizes that should they all proceed forward, not one of them would profit. Either no firm will innovate, or only one firm will do so, outguessing all the others. Is this really plausible?

Perfect technical certainty is not very likely to exist in a dynamic world. A

[27]Morton I. Kamien and Nancy L. Schwartz, *Market Structure and Innovation* (Cambridge: Cambridge University Press, 1982), p. 176.

firm cannot know whether it will succeed with an innovation, and certainly cannot be expected to know about a rival's prospects for success. Differences in timing are likely to produce time lags which benefit the innovator and at least some of the imitators. The quality of innovative effort is most likely to vary— some firms are likely to better than their rivals, or at the very least, believe that they are. And in the end, it may be the very riskiness of the innovation process that helps to save it from extinction.

It is possible that interdependence would discourage some innovative efforts under some circumstances. Innovation may be slowed as a result. But it is also possible that there is a substantial degree of independence in innovative behavior.

Target Innovation

What do we mean by target innovation? First, we mean that the firm uses a target to set its budget on new products. Rather than setting N* at the level where π is maximized, as indicated in Fig. 12-4 above, the firm may budget an amount on innovation which is consistent with some independent objective of the firm. The innovator may seek to maintain a target return on investment in the face of anticipated innovative efforts of its rivals. It may seek to hold a target market share. The effort may be all part of that same process in which the firm uses targets for pricing and for advertising, a process in which its targets are managerial tools, or rules of thumb, used in decision-making. Second, we mean that the firm's total outlay for innovation may be set according to a fixed formula in which the firm's ratio of innovation expenditures to sales revenues, N/R, is a constant. How realistic is this?

According to Mansfield et al,[28] it is not uncommon for the firm to rely in the short run upon a fixed N/R ratio. It can be explained in part by the difficulty in forecasting returns from individual projects. The firm can adjust the ratio over time if that should seem prudent. Why should the firm use targets at all? It is part of a larger issue of managerial control. The firm—that is, top management— may set the budget for research and development activities, establishing limits on the staff and resources available. Research personnel may play the major role in running their own shop. The creative people may be given a relatively free hand—with some general guidelines from above—in determining what to do and how to do it. In contrast, the decision on which projects will be allowed to proceed further is one more likely to be reserved for management. It is, after all, the entrepreneurial decision and it generally is the one, rather than research, which involves the most cost. The management of the firm will ultimately

---

[28]Edwin Mansfield, John Rapoport, Anthony Romeo, Edmond Villani, Samuel Wagner, and Frank Husic, *The Production and Application of New Industrial Technology* (New York: W.W. Norton & Co., 1977), p. 8.

decide, given the firm's N/R budget for innovation, (1) which projects to undertake and (2) how much to devote to each. What is the breakdown of an N/R budget?

In a sample of 39 innovations in the chemical, machinery, and electronics industries, Mansfield et al found that much more than half the cost was devoted to post-R&D activity: (1) 10 percent went to the applied research costs, (2) 8 percent went to design and specification cost, (3) 29 percent went to the cost of prototype design, (4) 37 percent went to the investment in tools and manufacturing facilities, (5) 9 percent went to startup costs for production, and (6) 8 percent went to the initial costs of marketing.[29] Are these representative? Perhaps not. It is possible that the sample may overstate the R&D costs of an average innovation, since so many are simply redesigns of existing products and are produced using existing facilities.

If management sets the agenda, and if target innovation is a strategy to be used in conjunction with other managerially-determined tools, such as target pricing, does this mean that all target innovation strategies are the same? No, not at all. Let us consider the difference between two firms which are credited with developing the target strategy to a fine art.

Du Pont is a major innovator in a high-tech industry. In fact, one case study of the U.S. chemical industry concluded that Du Pont outperformed the rest of the industry—producing more product innovations relative to its size than any other firm—over long periods of time, from 1930–1950 and from 1950-1966.[30] Why? Was this due to Du Pont's superior size? No, this study concluded that Du Pont's superior performance was most likely the result of quality factors, that the attitudes of its management and the quality of its personnel gave it an edge.[31] Innovation served the management objectives of the firm. How? Du Pont sought to maintain a target rate of return on investment. A steady generation of new products would give the firm the ability to achieve that objective. Lanzillotti notes that Du Pont felt that it had the ability to realize its target return, year after year, especially with its market power in pricing new products.[32] Du Pont has been quoted as follows:

> If our contribution of an improved or new product is an exceptional achievement because of long and expensive research and development . . . , we feel we are entitled to an exceptionally good return and we ask a corresponding price for it.[33]

[29]*loc. cit.*, p. 71.

[30]*loc. cit.*, p. 62.

[31]*loc. cit.*, pp. 204–206.

[32]Robert F. Lanzillotti, "Pricing Objectives in Large Companies," *American Economic Review* 48 (December 1958), p. 928.

[33]A. D. H. Kaplan, Joel B. Dirlam, and Robert F. Lanzillotti, *Pricing in Big Business* (Washington: Brookings Institution, 1958), p. 153.

Innovation—at least when it is successful—has another facet. It allows the firm to eliminate its older products which no longer contribute sufficiently to the firm's overall targets. Kaplan et al note that the Du Pont pricing strategy is based upon continuous turnover of products, casting out those which are now "worn out" in terms of profit production potential and replacing them with new ones.[34]

General Motors has been a sales leader in the American auto industry since the late 1920s. Not coincidentally, GM was the leader in making product quality, including the annual model change part of doing business in automobiles. General Motors saw product improvement in general and periodic change in particular as a means of meeting competition from rival producers and from the growing stock of secondhand cars.[35] General Motors was also the inventor of standard volume pricing. These two changes in business practice really are connected. Institutionalizing model changeover was a marketing strategy. GM's plan for stardard volume pricing—which relies upon coordination of the separate tasks of designing, engineering, costing, and pricing new cars—is directly related with marketing. In order for GM to achieve its target return on investment over the business cycle, it is necessary for the firm to maintain a certain standard volume of production. This, in turn, requires that the firm maintain its share of the market. The success of General Motors depends, in no small measure, upon its styling or designing cars that are "competitive" with the rest of the market. The firm learns over time how much effort is necessary, how much it must budget to the annual changeover, to achieve this objective.

Of the two models of target innovation—Du Pont or General Motors—which is more likely to be representative of managerial control in general? Both logic and history suggest the latter. Du Pont's successs depends upon pushing forward the frontiers of technology. How many firms in how many industries are likely to be able to do that? Not many, Schumpeter notwithstanding. On the other hand, General Motor's success depends upon changing the style of its products within the limits of existing technology—a much more feasible undertaking with a far more manageable risk. In the end, it is apparent that most new products are commercial, not technical innovations.

Does this mean that the existence of target innovation as a strategy—and the form that it takes—depends only upon the internal objectives of management and the external limitations of technology? Not necessarily. Targets in innovation may also be compatible with oligopolistic stability. Why? If the lead firms in an established industry follow a predictable pattern of behavior, it is possible to achieve a Cournot-type equilibrium—when a firm plans its innovation strategy on the assumption of a given rival strategy, and when its expectations are subsequently met, a noncooperative equilibrium is possible, provided

[34]*loc. cit.*, p. 151.

[35]John B. Rae, *The American Automobile* (Chicago: University of Chicago Press, 1965), pp. 98–99.

all the other firms do the same. If the major firms all tend to set constant N/R budgets, and if they all tend to limit innovations to regular model changes, these requirements can be met.

However, there can be surprises. A research effort, even of a routine nature, can turn up a new invention with promising commercial potential. The one who taps it can gain, at least for a brief time, a position of superiority in the market. It is not safe to presume that target innovation is an insurance policy against instability. For some, the uncertainty is seen as a threat. Those desiring security may act to eliminate surprises. How? It may be that a group would combine to fix products—i.e., to eliminate innovation—in just the same fashion as it would to fix prices. For example, four manufacturers of golf clubs—Wilson, Spaulding, MacGregor, and Hillerich & Bradsley—had at one time agreed with the leading manufacturer of steel golf club shafts to limit changes in shaft designs.[36]

Innovation and Barriers to Entry

We have seen the way in which market structure might affect innovation. How about the other way round? Can innovation be used in a strategy to affect market structure? There is, of course, the obvious case. The innovation which gives the firm a monopoly in a product (or a process) will alter the structure, at least for a brief time. This is the very essence of Schumpeter's theory of **creative destruction**. The innovator will be able to control price and quantity in the manner depicted in Figure 12-5—as long as the innovator prices its product below the cost, C_e, of any potential competitor's product, it can control the market.

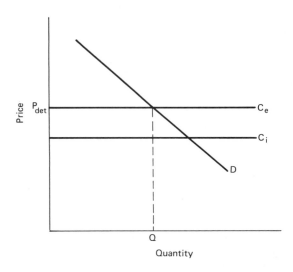

Figure 12-5 When an oligopolist prices to deter entry, it takes account of the position of prospective rivals. If entry requires that a rival innovate and if that, in turn, would make costs higher for the new entrant than for the incumbent, the established firm can deter entry by pricing at P_{det}.

[36]John M. Blair, *Economic Concentration* (New York: Harcourt Brace Jovanovich, 1972), p. 231.

What can explain the persistence of the monopoly? Since rivals will imitate a successful product given sufficient time to do so, what would keep them out? What accounts for the cost difference between the innovator and the imitator, which we have shown in Figure 12-5 as equal to $[C_e - C_i]$? The most obvious answer is patent protection. If the innovator applies for and is granted a patent for its new product (or production process), the innovator can maintain a legally protected monopoly. Imitators can be sued for infringement—a sort of trespass—for copying a product without the approval of the patentee, for the life of the patent. Imitators do have some choices however. They might be able to obtain the use of a patent in return for a payment of royalties to the innovator—this is one explanation of the cost difference shown in Figure 12-5. They may seek to "invent around" the original product. However, if it should cost more to discover the next best product, or if consumers should be less willing to accept an imitation, entrants would be at a cost/price disadvantage relative to the established firm, and the result is illustrated in Figure 12-5. Does this mean that patent protection is secure? Not at all. It is contingent upon those things which we have indicated. The innovator must succeed in protecting its property in court if some rival should infringe upon it. The cost of legally imitating an original product must be higher than the innovator's cost (or the public acceptance must be lower) if entry is to be barred by market conditions.

Does this mean that entry protection depends solely upon the patent granted by government as a reward to the innovator? Some have suggested otherwise. Schmalensee[37] and others have claimed that innovation can be preemptive *per se*. How? Suppose that established firms possess a productive capacity in excess of that which they need to supply the current market. Suppose that, in a market for undifferentiated products, excess capacity would be viewed as sufficient threat to prospective survival; entrants would be deterred granted our first assumption. We explain the strategy of entry preemption based upon these grounds in Chapter 4. But the market for differentiated products is likely to be another matter. Suppose that certain areas of the product space remain open and that entrants view them as an opportunity to penetrate the market, despite the disadvantages of small size and belated timing. The entry of Apple Computer is an example. Apple expanded the market by finding and filling a niche in it. Suppose, instead, that existing firms had filled in all the gaps as a precaution. What might have happened?

Schmalensee argues that entry might be preempted and cites the ready-to-eat cereal market as an example. Kellogg, General Mills, General Foods, and Quaker Oats collectively dominate the market and, along with the rest of the six largest firms, supply more than 80 brands of cereal. Is the argument complete? It is not. Preemption requires that scale economies severely limit the number of suppliers who can survive in any market segment. What does this mean? For the

---

[37]Richard Schmalensee, "Entry Deterrence in the Ready-to-Eat Breakfast Cereal Industry," *Bell Journal of Economics* 9 (Autumn 1978), pp. 305–327.

established firm to have a real advantage in product proliferation, the same production plant is used to make other products as to make the new one. This is a danger too. On the one hand, entrants may have also capacity in place, as long as their production plant and equipment can be converted with some degree of ease, to switch from one market to another and to copy the products of would-be preemptors. On the other, preemptive innovation may not be credible as a threat to forestall entry as long as the established firm has the option to exit from a segment of the market after being challenged by an entrant. The exit potential would seem to be implied in the original set of assumptions: (1) if established firms switch into producing new brands by using old equipment, they could as easily reverse the process, and (2) if established firms experiment with new brands to find empty segments of the product space and drop those brands which do not succeed because there are not enough customers, they could also drop those brands which do not succeed because there is too much competition.

Judd[38] argues that free exiting is a serious limitation to the preemptive strategy. So, where does that leave us? It would seem that innovation—at least without the protection of patent rights, or perhaps, of consumer loyalty—is not a particularly secure basis for controlling the structure of the market. It would seem that this, in turn, is consistent with the widespread practice of imitation of new products.

EVIDENCE ON MARKET STRUCTURE AND INNOVATION

Schumpeter had insisted that monopoly was the driving force behind innovation. There are several interpretations of the Schumpeterian hypothesis: some attribute innovation to firm size, and some attribute it to monopoly power. Some measure market power using an aggregate concentration ratio, so that if there is a relationship between market structure and innovation, it may be a reflection of oligopoly, not monopoly.

What does the evidence tell us? That is not entirely clear, but there are some generalizations which might be warranted. In Mansfield et al,[39] the authors report on findings which they have accumulated through a series of studies, including three previous volumes. Some of the most interesting include the following: (1) large firms do not appear to account proportionately more for the innovations introduced than smaller firms do, (2) when innovation is very costly, however, large firms do seem to account for it in disproportion to their size, (3) in chemicals, Du Pont had done more innovating relative to its size than any other firm, but it was the only case in which the authors found the largest firm in the industry to be the most innovative, (4) in other industries, the most active innovator was more often among the larger firms, but not the largest, (5)

[38]Kenneth L. Judd, "Credible Spatial Preemption, *Rand Journal of Economics* 16 (Summer 1985), pp. 153–166.

[39]Mansfield, et al, *op. cit.*, pp. 190–212.

imitation—i.e., the diffusion of new technology—did not appear to be positively affected by levels of concentration, (6) speed of diffusion of new technology seemed to be directly related to the level of R&D activity, however, and (7) in some cases of less concentrated industries, the diffusion or imitation of new technology was so rapid that the gains could not cover the cost of innovation and, had that been anticipated, the innovation would never have been made.

In their 1975 survey of the literature on innovation, Kamien and Schwartz,[40] report similar conclusions. In cross-sectional studies, differences in research intensity—N/R in our earlier discussions of firm behavior—do not appear to be associated in any systematic fashion with firm size. The authors caution the reader: (1) there are interindustry differences in innovation and firm size which may affect the statistical relationship but which are ignored in some cross-sectional studies, and (2) there are potential sampling errors since comparisons are made between firms of various size which are observed to conduct R&D, but the large firms are more likely to maintain R&D programs than small firms. The design of the cross-sectional study has not appeared to take account of differences in the R&D participation rates of firms of different size in spite of the fact that it attempts to explain innovation as a function of size. In studies conducted on the relationship between concentration and research intensity, however, Kamien and Schwartz report a wide diversity in results. Some research on cross-sectional data appears to show a positive relationship and some does not.

What can be made of all this? That is a difficult question, but it is fair to say that much of the difficulty can be laid to the problem of measurement. It is often not possible to measure that which is theoretically significant. In the present case, we are interested in innovation. How do we measure it? In the cross-sectional studies of innovation, it is represented by one proxy variable or another. In some cases, the research effort of the firm (or the average of the industry) is used—expenditure on R&D, or the size of the R&D staff. Suppose that there are scale economies in research and development. In that case, equal proportional efforts for large and small firms may translate into unequal outputs—large firms will be more innovative. In other cases, the research output is used—patents, for example. Yet, there are major patented innovations and minor ones, and some patents are stockpiled and never put to use except, perhaps, to keep rivals at bay. Finally, these studies tend to treat R&D—output or input—as equivalent to innovation. Innovation, as we have argued above, is not necessarily technological; it is any new commercial venture, so that even a new flavor for a soft drink or a new location for a business may qualify as one—an innovation is anything which may physically differentiate the product.

In any case, we should not just assume that the quality of entrepreneurship will vary from firm to firm in a fashion reflecting only size and market structure. In fact, a new firm often emerges so that the entrepreneur/inventor

[40]Kamien and Schwartz, *op. cit.*

will be able to introduce a new product or will be able to enter a market. Apple Computer was a new product and a new company. Cray Research was born in order to produce the supercomputer; the supercomputer was the brainchild of the firm's founder, Seymour Cray, begun when he worked in research at Control Data but left undeveloped at CDC as too unpromising.[41]

APPENDIX

Does size of the firm affect the level of innovation? Does market concentration increase the intensity of competition among firms with respect to their search for and introduction of new products? These are fairly representative of the questions which we find in statistical studies on research and development. They may be illustrated by two different but related studies by F. M. Scherer.

Firm-Size and Innovation

Scherer[42] tested certain relationships between firm size and innovation in a study published in 1965. Using a sample of data from the Fortune 500 industrial corporations, Scherer tested the overall fit between firm size in 1955 and the number of patents granted to the firm four years later, a time lag to allow for R&D work to come to fruition. The results were as follows:

$$\text{(Eq. 12A-1)} \quad G = 10.65 + 73.81\ R, \text{ with } R^2 = .422,$$
$$(4.09)$$

where G is the patents granted in 1959, R is sales revenues for the firm in 1955, and the figure in parenthesis is the standard error of the regression coefficient.[43] In his overall sample, Scherer did find a positive relationship between firm size and innovation, measured by patent grants. On the other hand, more than half of the variation in patents was not accounted for by firm size. How much was the result affected by interindustry differences in technological opportunity? Was the relation between size and innovation linear or nonlinear?

Scherer then tested a nonlinear relationship between size and innovation for individual industries. The objective was to eliminate differences not associated with size alone and to test whether or not there were constant-, increasing-, or decreasing-returns to size. To illustrate, the results of the electrical industry regression were as follows:

$$\text{(Eq. 12A-2)} \quad G = -21.9 + 583.87\ R - 177.41\ R^2 + 26.67\ R^3,$$
$$(98.16) \qquad (95.88) \qquad (22.13)$$

[41]Weil, *op. cit.*, pp. 29–30.

[42]F. M. Scherer, "Firm Size, Market Structure, Opportunity and the Output of Patented Inventions" *American Economic Review* 55 (December 1965), pp. 1097–1125.

[43]*loc. cit.*, p. 1099.

where $R^2 = .94$, and where the negative and positive values of the coefficients for squared and cubic terms of the firm size variable would suggest increasing returns at a very large scale, provided the values were statistically significant.[44] The cubic term is not significant at all and the squared term is only marginally significant. Disaggregation of the size-innovation production function was to produce better estimates—patent outputs were shown to vary considerably by industry. The industry regressions seemed collectively to suggest slightly decreasing-returns after a certain point was reached—patent activity had increased directly with the size of firm up to the level of $500 million in sales and decreased very slightly after that.[45]

Market Structure and Innovation

Scherer[46] also tested relationships between market structure and innovation in a study published in 1967. Using data from a random sample drawn from the 1960 Census of Population, Scherer investigated the relationship between innovation, as measured by employment of scientists and engineers, and concentration in 56 manufacturing industry groups in 1960. The primary results may be written as follows:

$$\text{(Eq. 12A-3)} \quad \ln E_N = -.03 + \underset{(.11)}{.95} \ln E_T + \underset{(.24)}{.94} \ln CR_4 + \Sigma \beta_i D_i,$$

with $R^2 = .83$, where E_N is the employment in innovation, E_T is the total employment, CR_4 is the four-firm concentration ratio, and $\Sigma \beta_i D_i$ is used to represent the combined effect of a set of dummy variables which Scherer used to account for interindustry differences in R&D intensity. In this case, the Schumpeterian hypothesis seemed to be confirmed. However, Scherer tested an alternative model in which the effect of firm size was removed and the results were as follows:

$$\text{(Eq. 12A-4)} \quad E_N/E_T = 16.4 + \underset{(.109)}{.155} \, CR_4 + \Sigma \beta_i D_i, \text{ with } R^2 = .728.$$

In this specification, the concentration effect is marginally significant; the dummy variables appear to supply most of the explanatory power of the regression—in particular, those dummy variables used to designate the chemical and electrical industries were very strong. So, what are we to conclude? On the one hand, the results seem to bring the market structure effect into doubt. On the other, there is evidence that the technologically progressive industries are also

---

[44]*loc. cit.*, p. 1107.

[45]*loc. cit.*, p. 1110.

[46]F. M. Scherer, "Market Structure and the Employment of Scientists and Engineers," *American Economic Review* 57 (June 1967), pp. 524–531.

more heavily concentrated than the all-industry average; the explanatory variables are intercorrelated. Why? It is possible that there is a relationship, that the markets may be progressive because of nonprice competition between oligopolists, or that concentration may be the result of the nonprice competition.[47] Then again, no causative relationshp may be involved at all. There may be nothing to the correlation. This is one possibility which we should always keep in mind when dealing with empirical evidence.

[47]*loc. cit.*, p. 529.

THE MANAGERIAL FIRM: ORGANIZATION AND STRATEGY 13

*In this chapter we examine the meaning and implications of the managerial firm. Starting with some working definitions, we continue with two illustrations of managerial control. Next, we set out to develop a model of the managerial firm, beginning with an analysis that includes the goals, organization, and workings of coalitions. We see how modern multidivisional structures emerged from the simple hierarchy; the so-called **M-Form** designs were intended to combine centralized strategic control over the direction of the firm with decentralized, semi-autonomous control over its operations.*

*Next, we examine how the M-Form firm seems inclined to adopt a long-term strategy of growth and diversification. This develops into an investigation of the Marris theory of **optimal growth** of the firm.*

*Finally, we examine how the firm's internal strategy to continue to grow and diversify is related to the merger behavior of the large, modern firm and to its diversified structure. The levels of **aggregate concentration** are explained by the strategy and structure of the modern corporate giants.*

The targeting behavior of the firm—that is, choosing some formula or using a rule of thumb for setting a price, determining advertising intensity, and/or establishing a research budget—is one of the most obvious and frequently debated characteristics of the managerial firm. Why? When such practices first came to light, there were those who expressed surprise at the apparent disregard for profitability. Since economics had traditionally presumed that the firm was an optimizing unit, a pattern of behavior that suggested otherwise was hard for many to accept. Is targeting really inconsistent with optimizing? Not necessarily.

First, targeting—or **satisficing**[1]—describes a process by which the firm establishes certain operational goals at which to aim. When a managerial firm

[1]Satisficing is the term adopted by H. A. Simon to represent a firm's decision rule that accepts any outcome which satisfies a self-determined performance goal, as opposed to a decision rule that accepts only the optimal level of performance.

attempts to satisfy a profit target, rather than to search for a profit maximum, it does not necessarily mean that the firm is willing to settle for less. It may mean nothing more than that the firm has found a different—and possibly better— way to achieve a maximum. Targeting may not *cost* the firm anything.

Secondly, and more importantly, targeting may make a positive and significant contribution to the success of the firm. How? Cyert and March[2] have observed that the firm is surrounded by uncertainty—there is uncertainty about the future of the market, about the behavior of suppliers, about the actions of competitors, and so on—and that this fact seriously complicates the decision process. Optimizing is a process which requires as much information as the firm can obtain, but it is a process hindered by uncertainty. On the other hand, targeting is a process by which a firm can avoid uncertainty or, more accurately, can work around it. The managerial firm may choose to employ short-term decision rules instead of deciding, in an uncertain future, which of many long-term options is best. As a result, the managerial firm may control its environment instead of being controlled by it. The firm may achieve a measure of independence.

Even oligopoly interdependence may not deter the firm from following its chosen course of behavior, a fact we noted in the chapters on price, promotion, and product behavior. Indeed, when the firm follows a strategy so predictable that rivals anticipate its behavior accurately and come to regard it as non-threatening, the uncertainty associated with oligopoly may be eliminated, or at least it may be reduced to manageable proportions.

What is the managerial firm? The managerial firm is one in which managers rather than owners set the directions. Yet why should they? In very large part it is a matter of organizational necessity. The modern corporation, with thousands and thousands of shareholders scattered far and wide, could never function as a pure democracy. The corporation has a representative government sitting as the board of directors; and in turn, the board of directors delegates authority to those whom it hires to manage. That authority is likely to be broadly defined and is likely to function with a significant degree of independence from those granting it. Thus, managerial control follows from three factors: (1) large size of firm: (2) wide subscription of equity capital which goes with it, and (3) difficulty in organizing an absentee ownership agenda and putting it into action—or alternatively, from ownership's point of view, difficulty in monitoring the behavior of managers. How significant is large firm size? In 1982, the firms with more than $250 million in assets supplied at least two-thirds of the output in the manufacturing sector, in the finance, insurance, and real estate sectors, and in the public utilities and transportation sectors.[3]

[2]Richard M. Cyert and James G. March, *A Behavioral Theory of the Firm* (Englewood Cliffs, New Jersey: Prentice-Hall, 1963), pp. 10–13.

[3]Internal Revenue Service, *Statistics of Income, 1983. Corporation Income Tax Returns* (Washington: U. S. Govt. Printing Office, 1986), pp. 44–45.

The managerial firm has interesting implications for the study of industrial organization. First, the managerial firm may tend to be more independent than the typical proprietorship. We have discussed how targeting emphasizes the autonomy of the firm—how it seems to operate on its own terms, rather than on those dictated by the market. Another dimension of independence is the result of diversification. A large firm is less constrained than a small one to the extent that it is structured in such a fashion as to be able to enter or leave a given market at will. Second, managerialism brings a new perspective to the study of industrial organization. We cease to look exclusively at external or market factors which determine firm behavior, primarily as constraints. Instead, we begin to look at some key internal factors: (1) the organization of the firm as a complex entity or a coalition; (2) the goals of the individuals who manage its several parts and/or activites; (3) the possibility of internal conflict, and (4) the institutions and actions to determine a common purpose and/or to resolve conflict.

How is the managerial firm organized? And what are its objectives? What are the roles of merger and internal growth in the plans of the firm? These are some of the questions which we shall try to answer in this chapter, but first let us consider two brief examples of the managerial firm phenomenon.

TWO EXAMPLES OF THE MANAGERIAL FIRM

Du Pont is consistently among the most profitable and dynamic firms in the U.S. economy, and it is easily the largest and most diversified manufacturer in the chemical industry. Unlike other dominant firms in other industries, Du Pont appears to have spent more effort on R&D and produced more innovations relative to its size than any of its smaller competitors.[4] The planning and expansion involved seem to have been coordinated in pursuit of an overall commercial strategy. For example, Du Pont has employed product improvements, as in the case of nylon, rather than price cuts to expand markets.[5] And Du Pont has used diversification by acquisition and internal growth as a means by which to be able to exploit more fully discoveries made in the research lab. Du Pont claimed, for example, that its earlier acquisitions of paint and varnish manufacturers gave it the ability to understand and utilize the discovery of a fast-drying automobile finish in 1923 and to develop Duco.[6] Has Du Pont always been organized with such rationality? Not at all.

In 1802, Du Pont was formed as a maker of explosives, and it remained committed to that one product for more than a century. Du Pont became a

---

[4]Edwin Mansfield, John Rapoport, Anthony Romeo, Edmond Villani, Samual Wagner, and Frank Husic, *The Production and Application of New Technology* (New York: Norton, 1977), p. 66.

[5]A. D. H. Kaplan, Joel B. Dirlam, and Robert F. Lanzillotti, *Pricing in Big Business* (Washington, D. C.: Brookings, 1958), p. 265.

[6]Simon N. Whitney, *Antitrust Policies* (New York: Twentieth Century Fund, 1958), p. 232.

member of the Gunpower Trade Association in 1872, formed to control price competition, and by 1902, the firm succeeded the "powder trust" by acquiring the last surviving member.[7] The Du Pont monopoly would not last long; the Government filed an antitrust suit against it in 1907, and the courts found it in violation of the law and ordered partial divestment of Du Pont's gunpowder holdings.[8] Certain changes within Du Pont—some moves towards a *modernization* of its management—began before the end of the monopoly; some of them began as a result of its formation. Pierre du Pont was closely involved with them.[9]

Pierre du Pont was the Treasurer of the big powder company and was responsible for many of Du Pont's managerial innovations, which included: (1) establishment of an executive committee, which was made up of the department heads of all functional activities in the firm, plus the president, and which collectively planned the firm's overall strategy; (2) establishment of a strong, centralized financial control of the enterprise, with an accurate and uniform basis for pricing and costing products of the many new plants and operations acquired by Du Pont, and with an orderly plan for acquiring and allocating the financial resources for further expansion; and (3) the establishment of a Development Department which would bear among its several duties the responsibility for experimenting with new product improvements.[10] Shortly, under the pressures arising from adversity and success—the antitrust case on the one hand and the huge wartime profits on the other—the Development Department became instrumental in changing Du Pont from an explosives maker to a chemicals manufacturer. For example, when the Executive Committee realized that it was facing a prolonged excess capacity in smokeless gunpowder, it ordered the Development Department to investigate systematically all the products, aside from gunpowder, using nitrocellulose or guncotton and to recommend a strategy of expansion. Development built and operated a small experimental plant for making artificial leather—one product which could be made from guncotton—at a closed-down gunpowder factory and demonstrated the feasibility of a *new* production process. Upon learning that an existing firm (Fabrikoid) already used the process, Du Pont offered to buy the firm in 1910, expanding both its assets and product line.[11] The Fabrikoid experience established a pattern for future development. Du Pont used research and finance to change with the times. In 1987, when DuPont sold its remaining explosives business to a Canadian firm,[12] it completed its diversification away from gunpowder.

[7]*loc. cit.*, p. 192.

[8]*loc. cit.*, p. 193.

[9]Alfred D. Chandler, Jr. and Stephen Salsbury, *Pierre S. Du Pont and the Making of the Modern Corporation* (New York: Harper & Row, 1971).

[10]*loc. cit.*, pp. 123–128.

[11]*loc. cit.*, pp. 248–250.

[12]*The Oregonian* (May 21, 1987), p. E16.

In the early twenties, General Motors became a pioneer in the use of standard volume or target return pricing. GM was portrayed in the management literature of the day—such as in the 1924 series of articles by Donaldson Brown[13]—as a paragon of the *modern* organization. Had General Motors always had such a reputation? Not at all. Indeed, this was a new and very different face for GM, which had been in serious financial trouble only a short time earlier. What had happened? What brought about the change?

William C. (Billy) Durant took over Buick Motor Car Company in 1904, built it into one of the most successful firms in the infant auto industry, and founded General Motors in 1908, adding a string of new acquisitions which included Olds, Cadillac, and Oakland to his new corporation.[14] But Billy Durant's wild drive to pick up every available auto company, apparently without much regard for the value of the acquisition, quickly got him into trouble. A syndicate of investment bankers rescued the firm and wrested control from Durant in the process. Subsequently, Billy joined with Louis Chevrolet to make a successful, low-priced car to compete with Ford's Model T. Durant's interest in his new enterprise turned quickly to using the Chevrolet Motor Company as a means to reacquire control of GM. He succeeded in 1916.[15]

When Durant returned to head General Motors, however, there was one real change. Pierre du Pont had been persuaded to become the Chairman of the Board and served as an independent mediator between banker interests and Durant's associates. Initially, du Pont had little concern with his position at General Motors; he was very occupied with the operations at DuPont and he had only a minor personal holding in GM shares. But two things happened to bring about a change: (1) the DuPont Company had accumulated a large amount of cash in the gunpowder operations during World War I, and GM was an attractive firm in which to invest, considering the growth potential in autos and the certain postwar decline in powder; and (2) Durant had gotten himself in financial trouble once again. In 1917, the DuPont company agreed to purchase $25 million in GM stock, while Durant agreed to establish a GM Finance Committee, which would be headed by du Pont and run much the same as the Finance Committee at the chemical firm, and which would be responsible for directing all the finances of GM.[16] Did this bring about a complete change in operations at General Motors? No it did not. Durant was still in charge, and he ran the firm as a one-man show in the same loose manner, much as he always had. He got into financial trouble again, much as he always had.

[13]Donaldson Brown, "Pricing Policy in Relation to Financial Control," *Management and Administration* 7 (February 1924), pp. 195–198; 7 (March 1924), pp. 283–286; and 7 (April 1924), pp. 417–422.

[14]John B. Rae, *The American Automobile* (Chicago: University of Chicago Press, 1965), pp. 42–43.

[15]*loc, cit.*, pp. 65–66.

[16]Chandler and Salsbury, *op. cit.*, pp. 450–456.

Du Pont rescued Billy Durant one last time. Du Pont money was used to cover Durant's personal debts and to force him out once and for all.[17] Pierre du Pont took over as President as well as Chairman of the Board. But it really was different this time; Du Pont interests no longer had to rely upon "outside" control—that is, on the Finance Committee—to reform the operations of General Motors. Du Pont entered directly into the management of the firm. Du Pont had longed to see GM run in a manner similar to his own firm, and he found a willing and able executive in the person of Alfred P. Sloan, Jr. In fact, Sloan contributed many of his ideas to the reform of GM, to go along with the concepts of management developed at Du Pont. In particular, Sloan wanted to combine divisional autonomy and central organization, a plan which could be accomplished if the firm would adopt a system of uniform statistical checks on rate of return and other measures of performance.[18] In Sloan's plan, the functions of GM divisions would be defined in terms of their relationships to the central organization, rather than their relations to one another. While division managers would have a wide latitude in operations, the Executive and Finance committees of the board would provide the over-all direction of corporate policy, as envisioned by Pierre du Pont. Managers of the vehicles, parts, and accessories divisions—with seats on the board of directors—would run the Operations Committee.[19] After tackling the reorganization problems, the new management team could move to solve inventory control, product, and financial problems which had long haunted the *old* General Motors.

A THEORY OF THE MANAGERIAL FIRM

The form of organization pioneered by du Pont and Sloan and incorporated into the structures of DuPont and General Motors has since been extensively adopted by large-scale enterprises in the United States and in Europe.[20] Why should that be? It might be argued that it is a matter of *survival of the fittest*, that the organizational form invented by du Pont and Sloan has proven to be a successful adaption to the requirements for the modern corporation. Again, why should that be?

The Firm as an Alternative to the Market

In Chapter 2, we observed that the firm is used to acquire and organize the resources necessary for production. It is an alternative to the market, and internal transactions are used in place of market transactions. Why? As we observed

[17]*loc. cit.*, pp. 485–491.

[18]When standard volume pricing was subsequently adopted by GM, it was seen as a tool to guide the product divisions in pricing so as to meet their corporate responsibilities.-

[19]*loc. cit.*, pp. 492–500.

[20]Oliver E. Williamson, *Markets and Hierarchies* (New York: The Free Press, 1975), p. 141.

earlier, there are several factors which combine to make market transactions costly. First, the quality (and/or quantity) of an input may be difficult to measure prior to its purchase and use by the buyer. Second, the supplier of a resource service may be in the position to vary the quality (or quantity) to suit his or her purposes to the possible detriment of the buyer. Third, the supplier may benefit by willfully delivering less service (or a different one) to the buyer than the contract stipulates. Can a firm do a better job of transacting? Perhaps it can.

There are really three obstacles to optimal efficiency: (1) the problem of independence; (2) the information problem; and (3) the problem of resolving conflicts. Each individual involved in a common undertaking, such as production, has a private agenda and an independent will. These factors are potentially in conflict with the interest of the group as a whole. But the firm has certain advantages in coping with such problems. First, it can audit the performance of individuals to obtain better information. Second, it can tailor the compensation to performance in the long run by promoting superior employees and firing inferior ones, and thus improve the level of firm performance over time. Third, it can adapt better, with its *ex post* information and its ability to exercise—at least to a limited degree—a supervisory control of subordinates, than any contract can do. Simon[21] has suggested that the labor contract assigns to the employer a certain range of authority to control or direct the actions of the employee.

Does this mean that the firm relies basically upon fiat for transacting? Not at all. In fact, Williamson[22] argues that, as a system, the internal labor market of the firm works best if it cultivates an atmosphere of cooperation.

The Goals and the Organization of the Firm

The first criticism leveled against **managerialism** and the managerial firm was that it does not pursue maximum profitability. But is this a fair criticism? Not necessarily. On one hand, it seems inappropriate to attribute profit maximization to a unit in which profit decisions are jointly made by a group of managers and often appear in the form of a target. On the other, it seems quite proper to attribute profit maximization to an owner/manager of the firm. However, does a proprietor attain the maximum potential for the firm simply by wanting it? Of course not. The owner who manages his or her firm must rely upon others within the firm to cooperate. Since the owner is not likely to be able to oversee personally each activity of the firm, he or she will be forced to delegate certain responsibilities to subordinates in order to manage the firm effectively. The larger and more complex the firm, the more thinly stretched will be the resources of the owner/manager and the more dependent upon others he or she will be. How is this done and what are the implications?

---

[21]Herbert A. Simon, *Models of Man* (New York: John Wiley & Sons, 1957), pp. 184–185.
[22]Williamson, *op. cit.*, pp.72–81.

A common resolution of the problem is the development of a simple hierarchy for the management of the entrepreneural firm: (1) the owner is installed as the general manager of the whole enterprise; (2) below the general manager, several subordinate managers are appointed; and (3) the sub-managers each bear the responsibility for running a functional subdivision of the firm. The typical organization may be represented as follows:

The functional division of the firm has certain advantages. It gives management personnel the opportunity to specialize in areas in which they have particular technical expertise, and the owner is left free to oversee the operation of the whole. The functional division of the firm has certain disadvantages as well. It almost certainly implies that the primary goal of the enterprise—let us assume profit maximization—is translated into operational goals for each of the subdivisions. That is, a divisional manager will be judged according to how well he or she achieves some meaningful objective.

To illustrate, production may be asked to produce, or to be prepared to produce, a certain target output at a certain target cost. Sales may be asked to generate a certain target number of units at a target price (or alternatively, a certain target of gross revenues). Research may be asked to develop a sufficient number of new products to achieve or maintain a target position in the market. Finance may be asked to acquire and allocate funding to achieve a target of profit. Are these targets supplied by the owner? Perhaps, but as we have indicated in the preceding section, efficiency within the firm may be improved by cooperation with subordinates. The general manager may meet with department managers and work out with them a list of operational goals. On one hand, this is likely to promote a better atmosphere of cooperation in which to pursue the interests of the firm. On the other, this is likely to involve some degree of compromise on the owner's part—possibly including some sacrifice of profit—to enlist the more active support of subordinates.

Without any intention of doing so, profit-maximization may be lost in the process of compartmentalizing firm activities and in delegating authority. *Managerialism* may be found, even in sole proprietorship, as a result of the compromises implicit in the owner's effort to establish a workable organizational design and operation. Is this what is normally described as the managerial firm? No, it is not.

Collective Decision-Making

The firm is an organization, comprised of many individuals whose primary economic interests are self-determined and self-centered. The firm is, therefore, a coalition of many separate interests rather than a unit in pursuit of a singular goal. Does this mean that there are no common interests among members of the coalition? No, it does not. The economic success of the collective body makes it possible to increase the welfare of its many members.

In this respect, the internal coalition of participants in the firm is similar to the cooperative oligopoly we described in Chapter Nine above: (1) the collective interest will be advanced by full cooperation, but (2) the individual interest of any one member of the group may be advanced by **privateering**, and thus (3) the coalition may need to be organized and operated so as to reward its members for behaving in a manner consistent with the collective interest.

Cyert and March[23] argue that the coalition of the firm—much like any coalition—is put together by means of a system of side payments. And the various managers within the firm are the ones who will receive the bulk of them. Side payments take many forms, including monetary compensation, perquisites of office, authority to direct a staff of subordinates, participation in policy making, and so on. Cyert and March argue that policy commitments to the managers of the firm's functional subdivisions may loom very large in the sum of concessions made to secure a workable coalition.

What are the implications of this? Each of the departments within the firm may negotiate with the central management—and with one another—to establish certain rights and privileges in the total organization. For example, the production department may want the firm to maintain large inventories of raw materials and to be willing to accept large inventories of finished goods so that the production lines may run continuously. In direct contrast, finance may want to keep inventories of materials and goods at a minimum in order to minimize costs. Thus, conflicts must be resolved within the cooperative managment of the firm. And how is this accomplished?

Cyert and March propose that the coalition sets operational goals by an internal process of negotiation.[24] These are presumed to involve: (1) production goals, including a goal to keep output running smoothly and a goal to achieve at least a minimum target output, (2) inventory goals, which prescribe inventory levels to keep the production and sales departments satisfied, (3) sales goals, which define the targets for both volume and revenue consistent with the other goals of the firm, (4) market share goals, which define the aspirations and the interests of top management, and (5) profit goals, which reflect the ownership's interest in the coalition and the financial requirements to keep the organization functioning as planned.

---

[23]Cyert and March, *op. cit.*, pp. 29–32.
[24]*loc. cit.*, pp. 40–43.

Thus, the formation and operation of the coalition is one in which decisions are reached by a cooperative, sequential decision process. What does it mean? It means that the firm does not search for a maximum profit—simultaneously setting the levels of production, inventory, sales, and market share to reach that point—but instead attempts to find some solution which satisfies the production, inventory, sales, market share, *and* profit goals. Operational goals are treated as constraints which the firm must satisfy, but they may be satisfied in any order—that is the nature of *satisficing*.

Does the cooperative decision-making process have any other important characteristics? Yes it does. To hold the coalition together, it helps to give permanent or semi-permanent status to the organizational goals or departmental targets. It strains the coalition to renegotiate terms over and over. A cooperative planning process is one which directly involves the budget. The members of the coalition compete for funding, so it is likely that cooperative mangement is associated with a degree of budgetary stability. Thus, an internal strategy of the firm may be important in explaining the relative constancy of the advertising/sales and the research/sales ratios which we discussed in Chapters 11 and 12.

If the firm is designed to operate on the basis of fixed targets and fixed budgetary allotments for each department, is it also prepared to deal with changes in the market as they arise? Or is the internal system so rigid that it will break down when exposed to stress? The short answer is that the managerial firm survives problems resulting from the external environment, such as shifts in the demand for its products and in the prices for its inputs. How? The explanation given by Cyert and March is that there is a cushion, which naturally exists in the core of the firm that is organized as a coalition, called **organizational slack**.[25] It is the result of the fact that total demand for side payments—which include the staff and resources allocated to unit managers to meet the organizational goals—will not always coincide with the firm's ability to meet them. But an institutional bias must exist towards having an excess of resources. Why? It is simple—a coalition which is unable to meet the demands will fail, but a coalition which is able to meet them will survive. As a result, within the internal market of the firm, $Q_s \geq Q_d$ and $[Q_s - Q_d] \equiv$ **slack** where Q_s is the supply of internal resources available for distribution among the members of the coalition and Q_d is the demand for them. To illustrate, if the firm should experience a sudden, unexpected increase in demand and if total sales should rise accordingly, the production department may be able to keep up, provided that it has sufficient capacity in reserve to handle the increase. If demand should suddenly decrease, on the other hand, the firm's production and sales departments would probably keep excess or slack personnel employed, rather than cutting back.

Doesn't the existence of organizational slack suggest that there may be something constitutionally deficient about the organization which must depend

---

[25]*loc. cit.*, pp. 36–38.

upon a collective management, or at least, that there may be a form of organization which is superior to it? Perhaps it does.

Quasi-Independent Decision-Making

A firm which is structured as a hierarchy and operated as a cooperative coalition may be effective as long as it is limited in scale and complexity. What happens if it becomes too large to control effectively? What if the organizational slack is bloated out of all proportion to the economies of scale based upon the firm's production and/or integration efficiencies? Williamson argues that this is precisely what happened to the leading firms during the late nineteenth and early twentieth century: (1) the typical firm was organized as a simple hierarchy, reflecting its origin as an entrepreneural firm, (2) large enterprises emerged, however, in a frenzy to establish giant single-product firms with control over markets, and (3) the wave of horizontal integration—often accompanied by vertical integration—brought about by merger produced tremendous changes in scale but left the form of organization unaltered.[26]

What happened? By trial and error, innovative executives—Pierre du Pont and Alfred Sloan, Jr. are examples—discovered forms of organization which have proven to be superior to the traditional hierarchy. To illustrate, consider the following:

How does this work? There are two basic principles of the multidivisional organization. First, the multidivisional firm relies to a much greater extent upon self-monitoring than the hierarchy can because each division is organized as a semi-autonomous profit center. Second, if the general management of the firm can rely upon the self-discipline of its operational divisions to perform efficiently, it will be free to focus upon strategic planning instead. In the diagram above, each of the divisions functions as an operationally independent unit, while the general office, with its supporting staff, audits performance and plans strategy. While each division may be organized on the lines of a typical hierarchy, the overall organization has certain advantages. Its lines of communication are shorter than those of the single large hierarchy which it replaces, so tighter control is possible. It avoids, with its multidivisional structure, some of

[26]Williamson, *op. cit.*, pp. 140–141.

the internal political games found in the collectively-managed firm. There is less "slack," *ceteris paribus*, in the multidivisional firm.

As we described earlier, Pierre du Pont sought to find a way to audit the performance of sub-units at GM. While it seemed promising to develop oversight and control through the financial apparatus of the firm, it was not until du Pont accepted Sloan's concept of divisional autonomy that an effective means was devised to do so. Does this mean that du Pont abandoned the idea that Finance was the key to central operation of the enterprise? Not in the least. On one hand, divisional profits were the means by which the central office could keep track of operations without becoming involved in operational detail. Finance would control the central auditing of operations. On the other, control over the allocation of funds—especially funds for new projects or products—was critical to strategic control. Thus, Finance would determine the direction at GM, just as it had done at Du Pont Chemicals. In this case, managerial control advanced the stockholder interests—no small matter to the du Ponts.

Williamson has argued that the organizational innovations represented here—the multidivisional organization or "M-Form"—are extremely important: (1) they are largely responsible for providing internal checks on the ability of management to exploit a position of trust at the expense of ownership, and (2) they are largely responsible for the conglomerate firm which has become an increasingly dominant force in the economy in the late twentieth century.[27]

Strategy in the "M-Form" Enterprise

The modern multi-product firm has strategic advantages over the single-product firm. The latter is constrained by the size and growth of the market for its given product, and even with a monopoly position, the single-product firm has a definite limit to how large and profitable it can become. To make matters worse, few markets provide a secure position for the firm over the very long run— changes in tastes, changes in products and in production technology, changes in resource prices, and entry of new competitors are all real potential threats to the firm. Is that true of the multiproduct firm? Not necessarily.

The basic strategy of the *M-Form* enterprise seems to be one that embraces growth and diversification. Why? There are several related considerations. First, diversification is a rational strategy and a direct response to the external factors which act as contraints to the firm. Diversification gives the firm the opportunity to expand sales beyond the absolute limits of any given market and to avoid the more immediate concern of the diminishing returns and/or increasing risks associated with outpromoting or underpricing the competition. It also supplies the firm with a means to increase size and profits without the dangers of antitrust

---

[27]*loc. cit.*, pp. 136–138.

liability. Du Pont provides a good example. After losing the "powder trust" case, and with the prospect of losing a large part of its sales of explosives at the eventual end of the World War, the firm became anxious to find new products to exploit. As a result, a new firm strategy was born. Second, diversification allows the firm to allocate internal resources so as to exploit the best opportunity available in the marketplace at any given time. It opens new doors.

Third, diversification is strategy which reflects internal considerations as well. There is a positive relationship—at least up to a point—between growth and diversification on the one hand and profits on the other. Management must maintain a good profit performance—one that meets certain standards of adequacy—to maintain the approval of ownership and to retain control. Growth and diversification also have implications for the internal success of management. In order to establish better levels of self-discipline within the ranks, Williamson has argued that it is necessary to reward superior performance and that this can be provided by promotion.[28] If the firm is growing, there is a reasonable opportunity to generate positions for promotion. And if the firm is growing, lower-level executives may perceive that they have a bright future within the organization.

Finally, keeping in mind that the firm is an instrument under their personal control, top mangement may push for growth for its own sake. Why? Several models of managerial control argue that the behavior of the firm can be expressed in terms of maximization—but maximization of managerial utility, instead of profits. It is frequently suggested that chief among the goods which yield utility are income, status, and power.[29] It is not difficult to project growth as a factor which produces, to a greater or lesser extent, all three. Executive incomes have been shown to be correlated with the size and growth (of sales) of the firm[30], and it seems reasonable to presume that status and power of top managers are directly related to the size and growth of the firm entrusted to their care and are measured by the firm's sales, assets, and employment.

Thus, there would seem to be a definite relationship between growth and overall success for the M-Form enterprise. Does this mean that any pattern of firm diversification and growth will do? Not at all. While successful M-Form firms seem to be widely diversified, there often seems to be a rational order to their product mix. For example, Du Pont's products—including a wide variety of chemicals, synthetic fibers and films, plastics, paints, and so on—are all related to Du Pont's expertise in research and development. Proctor & Gamble's products—including a vast array of soaps and detergents, paper products, soft

---

[28]*loc. cit.*, p. 77.

[29]Donaldson A. Hay and Derek J. Morris, *Industrial Economics* (Oxford, England: Oxford Unversity Press) p. 258.

[30]J. W. McGuire, J. S. Y. Chiu, and A. O. Elbing, "Executive Incomes, Sales and Profits," *American Economic Review* 52 (September 1962), pp. 753–761.

drinks, foods, and so on—are all related to P&G's expertise in advertising and promotion of inexpensive, consumer search goods.

Let us suppose that the strategy of the M-Form firm involves growth and diversification. How does it work? And why? Williamson[31] argues that the M-Form firm functions as an internal capital market. The implication is double-sided: (1) the external capital market functions at a disadvantage, owing to certain "market failures," and (2) the strategy of M-Form firms is closely related to capital allocations. In terms of the first of these, **outsiders** who are or would be interested in financing an undertaking lack the ability to assess and control performance to the degree that is possible within the firm. The organization of the firm, on the other hand, provides a direct means to audit behavior and to modify it—these are among the functions of the general office and its supporting staff, as depicted above—so as to produce a level of performance much closer to an investor's ideal of profit-maximization.

But as important as auditing and control may be, Williamson argues that allocation of financial resources—choosing what to invest in and how to do so—is the real *core* function of the M-Form enterprise. The general office, with its support staff, must determine which investments to make, which existing products to keep and expand and which to drop, which research projects to fund and which to develop commercially, and which acquisitions to pursue. These are all decisions which affect operating divisions but which cannot really be delegated to them. In some cases, a decision may lead to the creation of an entire new division, and in others, it may lead to the elimination of one. Chandler,[32] in describing Pierre du Pont's hand in shaping the strategy of the *new* General Motors after taking control in 1921, suggests that control of finance, determination of a rational product line, and establishment of a sound research and development capability were critical tasks for top management once the job of reorganizing GM had been accomplished. Was this new? No. In the operation of Du Pont Chemicals, Development had been given responsibility at some time earlier for the strategic expansion of the product base and the maintenance of the firm's level of profit.[33] This might imply that Du Pont would either enter the market *de novo* or would seek to buy a going concern. In either case, the firm would not proceed unless staff analysis indicated that the investment would yield a return $\geq 12.5\%$.

These two alternatives—internal expansion and merger—comprise the means by which the M-Form firm is able to achieve its strategic objectives of diversification and growth. And they have been incorporated into the Marris[34] model of optimal growth for the managerial firm.

[31]Williamson, *op. cit.*, pp. 141–143.

[32]Chandler, *op. cit.*, pp. 511–512.

[33]*loc. cit.*, pp. 381–385.

[34]Robin Marris, *The Economic Theory of 'Managerial' Capitalism* (New York: The Free Press of Glencoe, 1964).

A MODEL OF OPTIMAL GROWTH

What is **optimal** growth? It might be the profit-maximizing rate of growth for the firm, defined in terms such as the Dorfman-Steiner optimal advertising model. But in the model developed by Robin Marris it is not a profit-maximizing growth rate. In fact, the Marris model follows in a tradition established by Baumol in his model of the sales-maximizing firm (see Chapter 2) as it examines tradeoffs between profits and growth which corporate managers are willing and able to make.

Suppose that a large, multiproduct firm finds itself in a position, depicted by Figure 13-1, which may be defined by a pair of functions, **demand** and **supply**. Demand and supply of what? Why do they have the shape which is given them?

Consider the demand curve (D). We presume that growth in demand for the firm's products is a matter which, while subject to the usual external constraints, can be controlled by the firm itself. How? Sales—as we have observed repeatedly—are a function of price, product, and selling effort. The firm can increase sales by reducing prices and/or by increasing expenditures on product and advertising. Up to a point, sales and profits increase together, but eventually added sales will come at the cost of lost profit opportunities. The presumption of every profit-maximizing model of the firm is that there must be an optimal level for price, product, and promotion. This is consistent with the demand curve in Figure 13-1, but it is not sufficient to explain it. The growth model introduces another dimension.

Suppose that the firm has done whatever it can to increase the sales of its products. It has saturated the market—it may either have established a product monopoly or have reached the point where all intitiatives are expected to force the competition to retaliate in kind. While it might seem that additional firm growth could be achieved only through a natural expansion of the market, a

Figure 13-1 If the managerial firm seeks to maximize its growth rate, a function D of profits, it may be willing to trade off profits for growth. However, in the long-run, growth depends upon expanding its capacity to produce, and growth in capacity is a function of profits S (= * π). Thus, optimal growth and optimal profits are determined by the demand and supply curves in the Marris model.

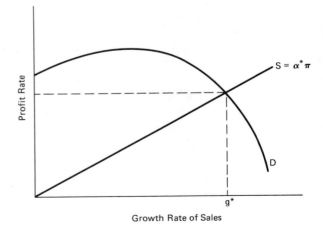

Growth Rate of Sales

limit to growth has not necessarily been reached. The firm which seeks to improve its growth rate can and will be expected to diversify. And in the long run, growth in demand necessarily requires the firm to add new products to its line.

Developing, pricing, and promoting new products will lead—once diminishing marginal returns to diversificatin has been reached—to the firm having to choose between a faster growth in demand on the one hand and a higher rate of profits on the other. Why should this be? There are two reasons. First, the introduction of virtually any new product or facility entails certain one-time costs. For example, in Chapter 11, we observed that the advertising costs for a new brand of breakfast cereal may absorb as much as two-thirds of its gross revenues. In Chapter 12, we noted that the total costs of starting commercial production of a new product—as opposed to costs of basic research—are often quite substantial. Even if the firm were to acquire a going concern rather than developing a new product internally, there may be significant legal and financial costs associated with the process itself in addition to the price paid to the owners of the acquired firm. Second, the introduction of new products or new operations places stress on the mangagerial resources of the firm during a period of break-in. Even the M-Form enterprise would face some period of adjustment.

The firm must choose between high rates of growth and high rates of profit. Who makes this choice? The mangers of the firm are the ones in the position to do so. The critical point is that management represents a faction in the coalition of the firm which is presumed to have a preference for growth and is willing to make sacrifice profits in order to achieve it. The long term growth of sales has to be matched with the long term growth in the capacity to produce. Consider the firm's supply curve (S). Growth in the supply of products is limited by the growth in productive assets. The firm must develop means to finance its expansion. How can this be done? Marris has recognized that the sources of funding include retained earnings, borrowed capital, and new equity. It might be presumed that, in the long run, an optimal mix may exist. Nevertheless the growth in supply will depend upon the growth in internally-produced capital—that is, in the amount of retained earnings. The slope of the supply curve of Figure 13-1 can be imagined to be determined by the inverse of the retention ratio (percentage of profits retained by the firm). For any given rate of return on the firm's past investment, any increase in the ratio of earnings paid out to stockholders will increase the slope of the S curve and lower the growth in supply. What determines a firm's retention ratio? What is the implication?

In the Marris model, stockholders are presumed to require that a certain minimum percentage of profits be distributed in the form of dividends. Why? It is presumed that the value of the firm's stock is a positive function of dividends paid so that stockholders earnings—dividends plus capital appreciation—are maintained at satisfactory levels as long as the critical distribution of profits is maintained. It is also presumed that, if stock prices are kept high enough, the ratio of market value to equity will discourage raids on the firm. Thus, the incumbent management team seeks to protect itself from both internal (share-holder revolt) and external (takeover) threats to its survival. It can do so by keeping the ratio of dividends to profits above the critical level. And finally, this implies that the slope (α) of the S curve $\geq \alpha^*$.

Now consider the Marris model, taken as a whole, over the entire range of permissable managerial discretion. Behavior of the firm is prescribed by the D and S curves. All profit and growth rates are possible in the areas contained in the space above the S curve and inside the D curve. What will the firm do? It will maximize growth, subject to the ownership constraint on retained earnings. With ownership dictating the slope of the S function $\geq \alpha^*$, the firm's *optimal* growth rate will be g^*, and by implication, the profit rate will be π^*.

How realistic is this? That depends upon the perspective of the question. On one hand, a process of growth seems to describe rather accurately the dominant strategy of the dynamic and well-managed business firm of the twentieth century. On the other, the **steady state** process of the Marris model is a tax of credibility. The opportunities for growth—presumably provided either by developing a new product or by acquiring an established business—are not likely to flow steadily. It is the basic process, with growth and profits interrelated in a rather complex fashion, which really matters. The form is just a detail. The Marris model can be useful to examine the process. What are the implications? There are really two: (1) those applying to the internal structure and behavior of the firm, as we have seen, and (2) those applying to the external market environment.

FIRM SIZE AND DIVERSIFICATION: EFFECTS OF MERGER AND INTERNAL GROWTH

When DuPont sold its North America explosives operation to Canadian Investment Capital Ltd. in 1987,[35] it completed a circle begun eighty years earlier. DuPont had been a single-product producer, with a monopoly in explosives acquired when it bought its last surviving competitor/collaborator from the Gunpowder Trade Association. The Government's antitrust action, which was filed in 1907, eventually forced DuPont to divest itself of half its powder plants and to begin a process of diversification. It led to DuPont's diversifying out of explosives. The final step—like the beginning one and many of those in between—was associated with merger. In this case, a merger by Canadian Investment, not DuPont, was the instrument of change.

Is there a lesson here? Yes. The firm has the ability to determine, over time, its positioning in the market. There will be certain areas in which the opportunities for profit and growth are expanding and others in which they are diminishing. And with skill and good fortune, the best firms will prosper most. They will grow larger and earn more than the average firm, and they will rely upon diversification to do so. Mergers and internal growth will be critically important

[35]*The Oregonian,* op. cit.

in this process. Where will it lead? Does it imply that the private economy must ultimately be dominated by a tiny handful of giant firms? Not necessarily.

Hay and Morris[36] describe a view of industrial organization in which the **active** behavior of the business enterprise shapes the market. Market structure is the effect of behavior, rather than the cause—it reverses the ordering upon which formal study of industrial organization was originally based. It also reveals a far more dynamic process. It involves many things: entry and exit, growth and decline, invention and replacement, consolidation and divestiture. The fact that a large firm buys out another does not necessarily imply that the market becomes any more concentrated over the long run. The increase in market power may lead to higher prices, and higher prices may lead to new entry—either in the same product or in the form of a new substitute. For example, even in DuPont's short-lived monopoly in gunpowder, noted above, new entry began before the antitrust action had run its course.[37] Thus, the measures of the firm's success in the long run—and its long-run impact on structure—may be determined by its size, diversification, and profitability, instead of its market share in a specific product or location.

This is not to say that the Hay and Morris view of **active** firm behavior replaces (or is meant to replace) the traditional view of the **reactive** or **defensive** character of behavior and its implications for structure-conduct relationships. Instead, it means that the two approaches serve to complement one another: (1) the traditional approach is static and provides short-run explanations of firm and market performance, which are so very important in microeconomics; (2) the "new" approach is dynamic and provides long-run explanations, even of structure itself.

Diversification

How diversified are firms in the United States? One answer may be given by observing the extent of diversification in the nation's 200 largest manufacturing firms, the firms most likely to diversify, *ceteris paribus*. In Table 13-1, it can be seen that over half of the 200 largest firms in 1968 produced in more than five of the possible twenty major industry (2-digit) group classifications and in more than ten out of the approximately 450 product (4-digit) group classifications. In fact, a small number of firms produced in more than 50 product groups. Is there evidence of change in the degree of diversification among the largest firms? Yes. The FTC tabulations indicate that, between 1960 and 1968, more firms became more diversified. In 1960, 69 percent of the top 200 manufacturing firms produced in five or fewer major industry groups, but in 1968, this class contained only 44 percent of the distribution. Over the same period of time, the percentage of large firms producing in more than ten out of the twenty major industry groups increased form 3.5 percent to 16 percent. Can there be any dispute in

[36]Hay and Morris, *op. cit.*, pp. 29–30.
[37]Whitney, *op. cit.*, p. 193.

TABLE 13.1 DISTRIBUTION OF 200 LARGEST MANUFACTURING FIRMS BY EXTENT OF DIVERSIFICATION: 2-DIGIT AND 4-DIGIT INDUSTRIES

	2-DIGIT MAJOR INDUSTRY GROUPS			4-DIGIT PRODUCT GROUPS		
Class	1960	1965	1968	1960	1965	1968
1— 5	138	120	88	57	38	16
6—10	55	66	90	52	42	38
11—20	7	14	32	60	73	70
21—30	*	*	*	19	24	37
31—40	*	*	*	7	13	19
41—50	*	*	*	2	5	11
51—	*	*	*	3	5	9

Source: Committee on the Judiciary, United States Senate, Staff Report of the Federal Trade Commission, *Economic Concentration* (U.S. Government Printing Office: Washington, 1969), p. 223.
*Class does not exist; there are only twenty 2-Digit Groups.

what the level of product and/or industry diversification is and how much change there has been in it? Yes.

The distributions, shown in Table 13-1, describe the number of product activities in which the 200 largest firms are engaged. But they fail to describe how much or how little the same firms are dependent upon any of their product activities. The possibility exists that a firm could be counted as active in ten different industry groups but could be concentrated in only one of them. How, then, can "true" diversification be measured? One means would be to adopt an index based upon the principle of the Herfindahl index (see Chapter 5). Berry[38] used the index, $D = 1 - \Sigma p_i^2$, where p_i is the percentage of the firm's total production supplied to the ith industry and $\Sigma p_i \equiv 1$. With $0 \geq D \geq 1$, in principle, $D \rightarrow 1$ for the fully diversified firm. Berry used his diversification index to measure and compare the level of and changes in diversification for the 500 largest U.S. industrial firms. What did he find? Berry concluded that, on the average, the firms were much less diversified than simple activity distributions would indicate. For the 2-digit industry groupings, $D = .361$ in 1960, and $.379$ in 1965, for the average large firm.[39] What does this mean?

To interpret the measure, let us assume that a firm has 80 percent of its total activity in one industry and the remaining 20 percent divided equally among ten others (2 percent each). Thus, $D = \{1 - [(.8)^2 + 10 \cdot (.02)^2]\} = \{1 - [.64 + .004]\} = .356$. Now suppose that, at an earlier date, the same firm had the same 80 per cent of its activity in one industry with the remaining 20 percent

[38]Charles H. Berry, "Corporate Growth and Diversification," *Journal of Law and Economics* 14 (October 1971), p. 373.

[39]*loc. cit.*, p. 375.

divided equally among five others. In that case, D = {1 − [(.8)² + 5 · (.04)²]} = {1 − [.64 + .008]} = .352. Looking at it from one perspective, a substantial diversification has taken place, but looking at it from the perspective of the D-index, it would seem that the change has been insignificant.

What would cause a significant change in the D-index? Suppose that we take the last case as a starting point, and then suppose that a change occurs in which we see the firm split 80 percent of its activity equally between *two* industries while the remaining 20 percent is divided equally among the *four* others—that is, the number of industries remains unchanged. In this case, D = {1 − [2 · (.4)² + 4 · (.05)²]} = .67. It is a value which is virtually double the original D-index! That is what we mean by diversifying: that the firm becomes less dependent upon its prime product market.

A widely diversified firm, such as DuPont, does not depend upon any one product market for its sales. This is reflected in its D-index. Using a classification system based upon 4-digit product groups, a value of D = .859 was calculated for DuPont, from data cited in Whitney[40], for its 1947 shipments. Whitney had observed just how diversified the DuPont operations were and how much this diversification was dependent upon research. How does DuPont compare with other large firms? It would seem to be substantially more diversified than the average. Berry has determined that the 4-digit D-index for the 500 largest firms was equal to .627 in 1960.[41]

Mergers and Growth

Merger activity has been one of the important means by which diversification has taken place. The data contained in Table 13-2 below seem to indicate that

TABLE 13.2 DISTRIBUTION OF LARGE ACQUISITIONS*
BY TYPE OF MERGER

	PERCENTAGE OF MERGERS		
Type of Merger	1948–1978	1978	1979
Horizontal	16.9	19.8	5.2
Vertical	10.2	11.7	5.2
Conglomerate	72.9	68.5	89.7
Product Extension	(43.0)	(33.3)	(42.3)
Market Extension	(3.9)	—	(2.1)
Pure Conglomerate	(25.9)	(35.1)	(45.4)

Source: Bureau of Economics, FTC, *Statistical Report on Mergers and Acquisitions, 1979* (July 1981), p. 109.
*Large acquisitions are those ≥ $10 million.

[40]Whitney, *op. cit.*, p. 241.
[41]Berry, *op. cit.*, p. 375.

fact. Over a thirty year period beginning in 1948, the vast majority of large acquisitions are classified as conglomerate mergers. This indicates that the acquiring firm had, in the majority of instances, used merger as the means to enter into a new line of business rather than to build upon activity in an old line—i.e., horizontal expansion or vertical integration appear to be less preferred. Why should this be?

On the one hand, conglomerate mergers probably indicate the attractiveness of diversification; strategic considerations may call for the firm to broaden its base. The acquisition of a going business may be the most cost effective means for the firm to do so. If entry into a new market requires development of a new brand and the consumer loyalty which goes with it, it may be easier to acquire an established firm (and its product) than to expand by internal growth. On the other hand, the appeal of conglomerate mergers probably indicates the effect of public policy as well. With fairly stringent guidelines on mergers, the large firm may be deterred from pursuing horizontal and vertical acquisitions (see Chapter 16). Hay and Morris[42] have observed that merger has played a larger role in the growth of the firm in the United Kingdom than in the United States; there are fewer legal restrictions on merger in Britain than in the U.S.

This has produced interesting results. As important as mergers have been to the growth and diversificatin of the large firm, there is considerable evidence that they have contributed a relatively small amount to the overall growth. In Table 13-3 below, we can see that over the thirty year period, 1950–1979, acquisitions have generally accounted for between ten and twenty percent of the growth of the nation's 200 largest manufacturing firms. And this continues. During 1970–1979, the unweighted average of acquired to new assets is equal to 13.0 percent.[43]

Large firms have grown, but by how much in relation to the others? During the 1970s, there were 786 large mergers (involving more than $10 million) in manufacturing and mining, and 31.3 percent of the total acquisitions were by the 200 largest manufacturing firms.[44] This is clearly out of all proportion with their numbers, but what does it mean in terms of their size? Did the 200 largest manufacturing firms increase their share of the aggregate assets in manufacturing? No. Consider the evidence provided by the historic data series measuring aggregate concentration, as shown in Table 14-4 below. It would seem that, given the historic share of the total business activity accounted for by the largest firms, growth has been just rapid enough to keep aggregate concentration at a constant level from 1963 onward.

[42]Hay and Morris, *op. cit.*, p. 536.

[43]Bureau of Economics, Federal Trade Commission, *Statistical Report on Mergers and Acquisitions, 1979* (July 1981), p. 115.

[44]*loc. cit.*, p. 113.

TABLE 13.3 GROWTH IN THE ASSETS OF THE 200 LARGEST U.S. MANUFACTURING FIRMS: ACQUIRED COMPARED WITH NEW INVESTMENT

YEAR	NEW	ACQUIRED	ACQUIRED AS PERCENT OF NEW
	(millions of dollars)		
1950	8.23	.19	2.3
1955	13.20	2.23	11.8
1960	16.39	1.73	10.6
1965	24.90	3.72	14.9
1970	33.84	6.60	19.5
1975	51.74	5.53	10.7
1979	83.82	16.03	19.1

Source: Bureau of Economics, FTC, *Statistical Report on Mergers and Acquisitions, 1979* (July 1981), p. 115.

TABLE 13.4 AGGREGATE CONCENTRATION IN MANUFACTURING FOR CENSUS YEARS, 1947–1977

Number of Firms	AGGREGATE SHARE OF VALUE-ADDED							
	1947	1954	1958	1963	1967	1972	1977	1982
Largest 50	17	23	23	25	25	24	24	24
Largest 100	23	30	30	33	33	33	33	33
Largest 200	30	37	38	41	42	43	44	43

Source: Bureau of Census, Department of Commerce, *1982 Census of Manufactures* (Washington: U.S. Government Printing Office, 1986) MC82-S-7, p. 3.

Management and Strategy Among the Giants

We should pause, at this point, and reflect upon some basic questions. Are all large firms well managed? Not necessarily. Do we mean to suggest that they are? Not at all, although that might have been the impression left by the preceding discussion. Some large firms are well managed, and they will outperform—that is, outgrow—the others in the long run. Some are not well managed, and they will struggle and possibly falter. To make the distinction, it is necessary to see what happens to the individual firms which make up the aggregates, the largest 100 or 200 firms.

For example, the largest U.S. steel firms—once the giants of the entire world—have long suffered from a failure to keep up with productivity advances made elsewhere. The U.S. automakers have more recently struggled with product; they have faced strong competition from the several Japanese manufacturers at the moderate-price end of the market and from certain of the European auto makers at the high-price end. As a result, USS (now USX) is not the giant it once was, and even General Motors has slipped a bit.

Yet this is not particularly unique or new. There has been a fairly constant turnover in membership in the club of the largest firms in the nation. Stonebreaker[45] has reported that only 21 of the top 100 firms in 1909 were still among the 100 largest firms in 1976. On average, there have been 23 entrants—and of course, 23 exits—from the list every decade. The turnover has reflected the growth and decline of individual industries, but it also reflects more than that. The surviving firms in the top-100 group outperform their primary industry base, as Stonebreaker has shown.[46] What does this mean? It would appear to mean that the consistently successful firms must either have diversified or have absorbed an increasingly larger share of the market. But since there are physical (and legal) limits to the latter, it seems most likely that diversification—and superior management—is the factor that separates the survivors from the other large firms on the list.

Let us consider another question. Are all the acquisitions noted above undertaken for the primary purpose of growth? Not necessarily. Mergers may have been motivated by other strategic objectives. Certain horizontal and vertical mergers may seek to improve efficiency. In some cases, there are economies of scale or intergration which might accrue to the acquiring firm. In these cases, technological (or market) considerations predominate. And in some cases, which may include conglomerate mergers, there are improvements in management or operation which might be felt by the acquired firm. In these cases, their "takeover" is motivated by a willingness and ability—perhaps it is just a hope—to replace an inferior management team with a superior one. On the other hand, certain horzontal, vertical, and even conglomerate mergers may seek to establish market advantage. It is possible—although not very likely, given the legal restraints—that such a merger seeks directly to establish a monopoly. But it is more likely that the merger seeks to establish an advantage over the competition, existing or potential, by raising the latter's costs or by reducing its opportunities—in this case, it is necessary to assume that there does exist some form of natural barrier to entry if the strategy is to succeed. In any case, the point is that growth is merely one of several objectives for merger, in spite of the emphasis given to it in this chapter.

[45]Robert J. Stonebreaker, "Turnover and Mobility Among the 100 Largest Firms: An Update," *American Economic Review* 69 (December 1979), pp. 968–970.

[46]*loc. cit.*, p. 971–972.

THE DYNAMICS OF STRUCTURE AND STRATEGY

14

In this chapter we reexamine the meaning and implications of industrial organization. Structure-conduct-performance is not a static explanation of a once-and-for-all state of organization, but rather, it is the continuing process of shaping and reshaping industry. We begin with a short case history of the automobile industry in the United States. Next, we reestablish the importance of the market imperfections which shape the organization of industry—the technological, institutional, and human factors.

*Having laid out the basic elements, we examine the cause-and-effect process once again. We begin with the **direct chain** from market structure to conduct to performance. We continue with the **feedback effects** from firm strategies (and success in achieving them) to market structure. We conclude with exogenous changes or **wild cards** which periodically reshuffle the deck—overturn an old position of dominance or create a new one in a new market.*

The purpose of the chapter is not merely to review earlier topics of industrial organization, but to see how they all fit together in one piece.

The organization of markets and of the firms which populate them is determined by an interplay of forces. Some are more or less directly attributable to nature—and we refer to them collectively as the market structure. Others are more or less attributable to the strategies of firms in the market. In the course of this text we have sought to develop understanding of structure and strategy, but we have followed the established tradition in industrial organization of looking at the structure-conduct-performance relationships in a more or less static way. This is a useful perspective to learn the basics of industrial organization, but it can hamper development of a more complete understanding of the relationships. In this chapter, we seek to correct this shortcoming, and to do so we shall emphasize the dynamic processes of the market. Before we begin, however, let us consider a brief case study.

A CASE STUDY OF THE AMERICAN AUTOMOBILE INDUSTRY

In 1987, Ford was the most popular trademark in U.S. car and truck sales.[1] It had been three decades since Ford last outsold Chevrolet, but that 1957 accomplishment was an isolated event. This time Ford's comparative success seemed to carry more weight. In 1986 and 1987, Ford Motor Company surpassed GM in profits, despite the fact that Ford sold fewer cars than its corporate rival. Several factors may have been involved in this latest chapter in the history of the U.S. automobile industry, but two seem to stand out. First, Ford seems to have been more successful than General Motors in its product developments, the former capturing a growing share of the market with profitable new product lines, while the latter was in decline. Second, Ford seems to have been more successful than GM in its management of production technology, increasing productivity and achieving a better control over quality. Ford had been more aggressive than General Motors in closing outdated facilities and computerizing and automating others, but then, Ford had been in that position before.

Ford first became the industry leader during the teens and early twenties, that critical period of time when autos became the symbol of American industry and the U.S. became the leading industrial power in the world. After all, Ford made the first "people's car," the Model T, long before there was a Volkswagen, and developed the first assembly line for automobile production. These two innovations were responsible for changing the face of the industry. Large scale was made both feasible and necessary. When automakers began to grow and integrate, their numbers began to decline almost immediately.

General Motors took over auto leadership in the late 1920s with another innovation: the development of a product line which offered some variety to suit different tastes and pocketbooks. GM demonstrated that success in the automobile market did not depend solely upon low price and mass appeal. Cars were differentiable, and it was possible to compete in style and quality, as well as in price. GM also introduced annual model changeovers, one more wrinkle in its new strategy. During the next forty years, the industry became more mature, surviving first the Great Depression and then flourishing in the post-war recovery. It was an industry which seemingly had become invulnerable to additional change. General Motors had become the increasingly dominant firm in an increasingly concentrated market. By 1955, only six U.S. auto firms remained in operation, GM manufactured more than fifty percent of all cars, Henry J. Kaiser finally abandoned his ill-fated attempt to crack the market, and foreign imports accounted for less than one percent of total U.S. sales.[2] And yet, change would come.

[1]*Automotive News* (January 11, 1988), p. 1.

[2]Simon N. Whitney, *Antitrust Policies* (New York: Twentieth Century Fund, 1958), Vol. 1, p. 432.

First, the post-war recovery contributed to the development of strong automobile industries in Europe and Asia. Former allies and enemies alike became important automakers, serving their own domestic markets and even beginning to serve the periphery of the American market. Second, the extraordinary post-war prosperity in the U.S. began to produce certain changes in demand. By the 1960s, a few of the more adventurous consumers began to show an interest in buying products which were a bit different from those bought by the next-door neighbors. In cars, sales increased for European luxury and specialty cars at one end of the market and for the ugly but affordable VW Bug at the other. Still, the U.S. auto industry seemed invulnerable. By the 1970s, however, the stage had been set for even greater changes. Conflicts in the Middle East led to the oil embargo of 1974, and to a series of dramatic price increases in gasoline, as OPEC emerged with a new sense of power and a determination to exercise it. It was at this point that the average American car buyer, who previously wanted only larger and more powerful machines, discovered the sluggish but fuel-efficient compact. "Small is beautiful" became the slogan of an era. Suddenly the foreign car maker had an advantage; Detroit was unwilling at first to believe that Americans would really accept compact cars, and later, was unable to build them. The trickle of foreign cars had become a flood. To make matters worse for Detroit, there was evidence that imported cars, at both ends of the market, were of better quality. Nameplates such as Mercedes and BMW became symbols of upper-middle class success, rather than Cadillac and Lincoln. Japanese car makers began to make and export inexpensive versions of the compact, European-styled sports sedan. The American automaker was the victim of a double-team, as Japanese and European imports seemed to attack both ends of the U.S. market at once.

When the 1980-82 recession hit, the U.S. automobile industry found the going especially difficult. Each of the auto makers lost billions of dollars. It was a challenging period, but Ford and Chrysler—the latter with a generous federal bail-out plus significant "givebacks" from the UAW—were especially successful in cutting costs and developing more competitive products. With a boost from the economic recovery of the 1980s and with further assistance from the restraints on Japanese imports, the American auto industry made a comeback. However, comeback does not mean an exact restoration of the past; there were changes. Ford had become the most profitable domestic producer, GM had its share of the market sliced to little more than one-third, American Motors had disappeared (acquired by Chrysler), and cars from more than a dozen major foreign manufacturers had managed to secure one-third of the American market.

What is the lesson to be learned from this brief history of the American automobile industry? It is just that no market is invulnerable to change, and that no leading firm—no matter how big and powerful it may seem to be—is completely secure in its position in the market. Or, to put it in industrial organization terms, market structure is not a given.

THE INDUSTRIAL ORGANIZATION MODEL REVISITED

The structure-conduct-performance model can be misleading if one is not careful. It is very easy to transfer habits formed in the analysis of markets in pure theory to the analysis applied to industrial organization. Specifically, it is very easy to assume that market structure is a given. Take perfect competition.

In the ideal world of perfect competition, there are no market imperfections. Everyone possesses perfect information. All buyers and sellers occupy a single point in space with the result that communication is perfect and transport is costless. Products are homogeneous. Production can be carried on under conditions of long-run constant costs. With free entry and exit, large numbers of small firms can compete. It must follow that, under these conditions, the firm has neither a real strategy nor the need for one. When the firm's price, product design, and production technology are predetermined, it only controls the rate of output.

Moreover, as long as the market is free from imperfections, a competitive structure would persist. It would be impossible for the firm to differentiate its product. It would be pointless to attempt to establish barriers to entry to limit competitors or create a monopoly. The real world is quite a different matter. Market imperfections—and imperfect competition—seem to be the rule. It would be accurate to say that the markets for most industrial goods, from automobiles to zoological implements, would be classified as cases of either oligopoly or monopolistic competition. The importance of this fact can be seen as we trace the structure-conduct-performance implications which follow from market imperfections.

Consider market concentration. There are technical and/or physical factors which are viewed as critical in determining the level of concentration. Economies of large scale may account for large production plants. Integration economies may provide the explanation for large firms. Absolute cost advantages, which we associate with the ownership and use of scarce natural resources, and relative cost advantages, which we associate with the large firm, may constitute barriers to entry. These factors help to explain why the number and identity of competitors in certain markets remains more or less fixed over time. Does this mean that concentration is entirely a natural phenomenon? No. The technology of the large-scale plant does not just happen. It has to be developed, and it has to be exploited. The same could be said about barriers to entry.

Consider product differentiation. There are human factors which may be seen as critical in determining the level of product differentiation. Differences in tastes, which divide consumers as a whole into semi-autonomous submarkets, seem to account for those differences in product design offered by otherwise similar firms in an industry. Information failures which tend to limit the knowledge of the consumer may explain the consumer's reliance upon the self-serving information supplied by the advertiser and the differentiation of products which results from it. Does this mean that product differentiation is the natural implication of taste differences and information failures? Not necessarily. Differences in product design do not just appear; they represent innovations by their respective suppliers. Moreover, as product designs are developed and offered to the public over time, it is quite possible that changes in tastes will follow—we consume and want to consume products which earlier generations could not have imagined. Neither are advertising messages dictated by an impersonal market environment; they represent strategies planned and executed by the advertisers themselves. Furthermore, as the number and complexity of products grows, the lack of information may become more pronounced. Differentiation may feed on itself.

Market structure is not necessarily the cause of everything else as it seems to be in the case of perfect competition. When market imperfections are present, the firm has more options and fewer restraints. The firm can possibly make more profits. It might even discover a monopoly of a sort. And the presence of market imperfections may provide the firm with something which is even more valuable than an ordinary monopoly, the opportunity to change the market structure itself.

STRUCTURE AND STRATEGY DYNAMICS

In industrial organization, we want to be able to use our understanding of structure-conduct-performance relationships to predict the behavior of firms in the market—and the resulting market performance—on the basis of knowledge about the market structure. But we also want to be able to use our knowledge to explain why the market is structured the way it is and changes the way it does. Such prediction of behavior relies upon the traditional approach to industrial organization, which is to examine a *linear chain* running from market structure to conduct to performance. However, explanation of structure relies upon a newer approach, which is to treat behavior as strategy and to examine the *feedback* which runs from the behavior of the firm to the structure of the market. We find that *cause* and *effect* in industrial organization are hard to separate. Nevertheless, we shall try to do so. Let us begin with the traditional view.

The Linear Chain of Structure-Strategy Implications

In the case of high concentration, we expect the behavior of firms to reflect the interdependence they feel between themselves and the small number of relatively large and visible rivals. How, precisely, will they behave? That is a question for which pure economic theory provides no clear answer. Oligopoly may produce a form of aggressive behavior, where a firm seeks to increase its market share and profits at the expense of its rival, or even to exclude an existing or potential rival—from duopoly models of Bertrand and Edgeworth to the entry-deterring models of Bain and Modigliani, we find a long tradition of attributing a cutthroat strategy to the oligopolist. Oligopoly may also produce a form of passive behavior, where a firm seeks to coexist with rivals—from the traditional duopoly of Cournot, to the Sweezy kink, to the theory of games, we find a counter-tradition of attributing some sort of *maximin* strategy to the oligopolist. Still, the state of oligopoly theory is no less ambivalent than the behavior which it is designed to model.

There is certainly evidence that concentrated markets often waver between periods of price competition (sometimes it is open, often it is secret) and price conformity. In some cases, where competitive pressures have been most severe—among industries such as steel, characterized by homogeneous products and, during slack times in the business cycle, by large amounts of excess capacity—there is a strong urge for firms to cooperate with one another in fixing price and an equally strong urge for them, or at least some of their number, to cheat by cutting price and increasing sales at the expense of rivals. Where cooperation has been most difficult to achieve, it is not unusual to find firms organizing cartels or other forms of explicit agreements to fix price. OPEC is simply a recent and the most visible example of this. In other cases, mechanisms of cooperation are far less apparent and often have far more modest ambitions. For example, the members of the U.S. oil refining industry sought merely to hold the line against price cutting in one scheme they hatched during the oil gluts of the 1930s. [*United States vs. Socony-Vacuum* (1940)]

In contestable markets, however, concentration does not seem to have an effect. When there are no sunk costs—that is, the fixed capital is either mobile or liquid or both—hit-and-run entry can force incumbents to price at cost. Markets for airline service have, since deregulation, demonstrated this effect. The airline industry seems to illustrate the case where entry, rather than concentration, is the real determinant of pricing behavior.

In other concentrated markets, price does not seem to pose a competitive problem for the firms. Cooperation of a sort may be involved, of course, but it may be a passive form of cooperation rather than collusion. In some cases, *price leadership* requires no more than the willingness of the dominant firm to set and maintain a price—followers are free to sell as much as they are willing and able at this price, so they have no reason to deviate from it. For example, when GM dominated the U.S. auto industry, GM set the general price level unilaterally. In other cases, price leadership requires a form of mutual self-discipline—the followers must be willing to accept the price set by the leader and the leader must be willing to set a price which will be acceptable. In the tobacco industry, for example, there was a period during which one of the two major manufacturers—either RJ Reynolds or American Tobacco—acted as the price leader, and it brought a long period of price stability and conformity to the industry. [*United States vs. American Tobacco Company* (1945)] Why is it that certain concentrated industries—tobacco is an example—seem to have no trouble in adhering to the leader's price or in maintaining price stability while others—steel and petroleum are good examples—seem to have difficulty? Product differentiation may be the critical factor.

Product differentiation is a facet of structure which may profoundly alter the strategy of the firm. In the first place, the firm which makes a differentiated product may exercise a degree of pricing discretion unknown to the firm which makes a homogeneous product. For example, *target return* pricing, the practice introduced by GM in the 1920s, reflects the ability to set internal parameters on price. This does not necessarily mean that the firm ignores its rivals. Rather, the firm may expect its rivals to understand that changes in price, set by a rule of thumb, are not aimed at strategic advantage and are not a threat to them. In fact, GM's target return price, based upon GM's cost of production, was the *lead* for the industry. So, certainty and stability can be achieved in an oligopoly setting, even without cooperation.

In the second place, if the products are differentiated, price may not be that important. Instead, competition may focus on product quality or service and on the information or perceptions which consumers have about the product. Non-price competition will tend to allocate resources to those activities and attributes which differentiate products—the firm will tend to spend on advertising and promotion to increase its sales and to spend on research and development and on innovation to improve its products and its market position.

Competition in advertising and product development seems to pose less threat to the stability and balance of power in the oligopoly market than competition in price. There may be several reasons for this: (1) the attack on a rival's market position is less threatening than is a price change in a homogeneous product market since changes in product or in marketing appeal are likely to divert only a fraction of sales from the loser to the winner, (2) the effects of non-price strategies are likely to be delayed and/or lagged since, without perfect information, consumers may not react to an advertising campaign or the product introduction immediately, (3) the reactions of rivals to the firm's choice of strategy are also likely to be lagged, partly because of the lag in consumer behavior and partly because of the lag in developing a strategic counter-move, and finally, (4) non-price competition may tend to be less of a zero-sum game than competition in price tends to be. On this last point, advertising for one brand may stimulate consumption for the product in general, and innovating may do the same—introducing a product so radically different from existing ones that, as it establishes a market, it does not materially reduce the sales of existing rivals.

In the linear chain of causation, market structure is seen as the explanation for behavior. Concentrating factors increase the sense of rivalry; and they account for the extreme reactions to it—that is, cutthroat competition and overt collusion. In a similar fashion, differentiating factors decrease this sense of rivalry as they increase the independence of the individual firm; and they account for the strategic behavior involved in non-price competition.

Does this account exhaust the structure-conduct-performance relationship? Not at all. While it summarizes the influence of structure on conduct—and, by implication, on performance—it does not reflect the influence of conduct on market structure. The *feedback* mechanism is important.

The Feedback

The structure of the market is not set once and for all by nature; it is also affected by the dynamic processes involving the past and present strategies of market participants. Actions can alter the market, sometimes for a brief time, sometimes more or less permanently.

Pricing and investment behavior of the incumbents sometimes determines whether or not firms will enter the market—barriers to entry are not just a matter of structure. If incumbents keep prices low enough or maintain a sufficient excess capacity, they may deter rivals from entering the market. The absence of entry may result from (or be evidence of) existing firms' willingness to sacrifice profits to maintain their market position.

There is the other side of the coin. If incumbents should ignore potential competition and charge very high prices, they may invite entry. To illustrate, consider the international market for crude oil. A side effect of the oil price increases engineered by OPEC during the 1970s was an increase in non-OPEC oil supplies. Others were induced to explore for new oil and to take extreme measures—often at very high cost—to extract old oil. As OPEC continued to maintain artificially high prices, its share of the world market shrank; to hold prices at their chosen targets, OPEC nations were forced to reduce their own rates of production, offsetting increases in production by other suppliers. In 1987, OPEC cut price and increased output; the cartel members conceded their inability—at least until they could rid themselves of excess suppliers—of maintaining a price discipline. Does this mean that OPEC made a strategic mistake? Not necessarily. The very same thing could happen to any monopolist which has no barrier to entry to protect it; the best strategy may be to mine monopoly profits in the short run, while it controls price, because such opportunities will not be available in the long run.

In the extreme case, the contestable market is presumed to exercise its own discipline—any attempt to raise price above cost by reducing output is futile, as entrants will immediately fill the gap. In any case, the entry of competitors and/or the level of concentration may accurately reflect the behavior of established firms, past and present. It is not uncommon to find market structures with a few large firms and a substantial number of small ones, known as the *competitive fringe*. This structure may be a reflection of a past practice (or present one) where the large, established firms—independently or cooperatively—set prices above cost. But in the long run, costs may tend to rise to the level of price, especially for the smaller entrants.

Product differentiation is itself a form of feedback; the products may be differentiable in any market in which there are imperfections, but the act to differentiate them is one piece in the strategy of the firm. Thus, there is a distinction to be made between differentiability (market structure) and the act of differentiation (firm strategy) and the product differentiation which results (market structure once again).

An advertising strategy may alter, at least for a period of time, the structure of the market. The successful firm may shift the demand for its product. As a result, it could (1) increase market share (horizontal differentiation) at the expense of its rivals, (2) increase its product price (vertical differentiation) independently of rivals, and (3) even deter entry of new firms if differentiation confers a competitive advantage over some new and unknown entrant. In any of these cases, the effects of market strategy may be to increase or maintain, at least for a while, the level of concentration.

A strategy of innovation—or, more properly, the feedback resulting from it—may have more important effects on product differentiation and more permanent effects on market structure than an advertising strategy would have. The strategy employed by General Motors in the twenties, to overtake the dominant Ford Motor Company, was based upon developing a line of cars rather than making a better low-price car and competing toe-to-toe with Ford on his own ground. The success of the strategy changed the automobile industry dramatically. *Product lining* has since then been copied by manufacturers in many markets.

Product innovations, where the new technology is embodied in new products, may explain the process of continuous change. The development of new products may cause the development of entirely new markets. In Chapter 1, for example, we described how this process worked in two cases, the auto industry and the ready-to-wear dress industry. The automobile was a technologically-driven innovation; the ready-to-wear dress was the result of independent changes in consumer tastes which were exploited by manufacturers of shirt-waists.

Suppose that the firm feels boxed in by competition—it is unable to exercise any control over the market and/or to make more than a normal profit. What can be done? One answer is that the firm might create a new product and establish a new market. Schumpeter's model of economic progress—a process he argues is unique to market economies—describes the process. Monopoly provides the reward for one successful innovation and a means for financing the search for another.[3] If the firm is successful in its search, it can establish a new market. But the creation of a new market—and its monopoly—will not end there. A market with a real commercial potential will almost certainly attract competitive imitation. The dynamic process will be endless.

Or suppose that a firm would simply like to enter a market. In the high-tech field of computers, Apple won success with the invention of a relatively

[3]Joseph A. Schumpeter, *Capitalism, Socialism and Democracy* (New York: Harper, 1942).

[4]In Chapters 15 and 16 below, we attempt to summarize the substance, procedures, and implications of antitrust law in the United States.

low-tech product, personal computers. Apple became a success in entering and competing with IBM, where several large firms had failed before, because it exploited one niche which IBM had not. Moreover, Apple was able to build upon its base by the successful upgrading of the personal computer. Product innovation may be important for entry through the back or side door.

Or suppose that a firm would like to improve its position in a market seemingly dominated by others. The auto industry is a continuing example. Product innovations were responsible for General Motors' success in the twenties in replacing Ford as the industry leader, for the success of imports in the seventies and eighties, and for Ford's success in outselling Chevrolet in the mid- and late-eighties.

Process innovations tend to be even more dramatic. When new technology is introduced, it becomes a part of the environment, and it may be an irreversable change. Consider the innovations in automobile mass production line technology introduced by Henry Ford. Until this technology was available, the relatively small market sustained a relatively large number of competitors, with a relatively high turnover. The new technology raised the limits of *minimum efficient size* considerably and reduced the number of firms. The assembly line revolutionized both the method of production and the organization of the industry—the number of competitors was quite literally decimated. This does not mean, however, that process innovations are necessarily concentration-increasing; some may have the opposite effect. The long-line telecommunications industry seemed to be a natural monopoly, at least until the microwave relay system was linked with the earth-orbiting space satellite. But after the technological change was introduced, the AT&T monopoly (or monopoly by some other carrier) became unnecessary. It was possible for the telephone industry to become more reliant upon competition (and less upon regulation of monopoly) than before.

In the long run, a strategy of diversification may, from the point of view of the firm, be even more important than strategies of deterrence, advertising, or innovation. And the feedback from diversification may be important for the overall market economy as well. Why? Consider the following.

It may be reasonable to presume that the market places many a restriction on the firm in the long run. In the first place, the firm is unlikely to make more than normal profits, with the passage of time, unless one of two conditions support a long-run control of price: (1) there is a natural monopoly, or (2) there is unusually strong and persistent cooperation among the members of an oligopoly group which is, in turn, sufficiently protected against entry to be able to control price effectively. In the second place, even if the firm should be able to make more than a normal profit in any given market position, it is unlikely to have room to grow as fast as it might want and/or is able to deal with. The firm's growth is constrained by (1) resistance to its expansion of market share—on one hand, competitors are certain to fight back, and on the other, antitrust authorities are also certain to resist monopolization, and (2) the growth capacity of the market as a whole, assuming the firm has achieved maximum share. The market may just be too confining to suit the firm and the desires and ambitions of those in charge of it.

If the firm should be unhappy with the prospects afforded by any single market, however, it has the ability to diversify into other markets. Diversification seems to have become the dominant strategy of the twentieth century industrial firm. It is a sharp contrast with the drive to monopolize found in the last century and the first few decades of the present century when the *trusts*, such as in oil, gunpowder, and tobacco, were formed. Why should this change occur? Substitution of a strategy of diversification for one of monopolization was certainly made more attractive by the strengthening of antitrust enforcement.[4] Widespread adoption of diversification was a matter of organizational feasibility as well. Diversification was made possible by certain changes in internal organization developed in the twentieth century. The M-Form organization made it possible (1) to centralize the control over the financial resources and the strategy of the very large enterprise, and (2) to decentralize operational control over the whole by establishing autonomous subdivisions. The end result was the emergence of the modern multi-product firm, doing business in many markets yet not depending too heavily upon any one of them. Diversification had another effect. It elevated the importance of mergers and takeovers.

Diversification has led to an organization of industry in which the conglomerate firm is more in control of its destiny. It is likely to experience a greater degree of independence than giant firms of the past since it is not confined to a specific arena with a given number of recognized rivals; instead, it has the ability to pick its spots—it can challenge others more aggressively for market share, it can differentiate its product to insulate itself from competition, or it can drop one product line and add another to minimize the competitive pressures. In the case of DuPont, for example, we find a firm with a very sound strategy: it sets overall target return parameters for making its investment decisions, it relies upon research and development to find new market opportunities, it prices new products as high as the market will bear, and it drops old products from the line if and when competition for them gets too severe or the yield too low. However, for every diversified firm like DuPont, there are probably dozens which do not allocate their financial resources wisely, which do not maintain adequate oversight of subsidiaries, which time their moves into and out of markets badly, etc.

Diversification has also led to an organization of industry in which aggregate concentration is quite high. The successful firms develop the financial resources necessary to expand. A few hundred large and diversified firms accumulate holdings which account, collectively, for a quite large percentage of the assets (or sales or employment) in manufacturing. This, too, is part of the feedback on the organization of industry.

To summarize, feedback is a process—or the sum of many processes—whereby the market structure is a record of the past strategic successes of the firms in it. In some instances, the feedback is continuous, and the market structure continues to change as the result. For example, if past advertising explains the market share of the leading firm (or constitutes a barrier to entry), the future success of a firm that expands market share (or the firm that succeeds in entering the market) may rely on advertising campaigns as well. Or, if innovation gives one firm a product monopoly, imitation may eliminate it, and/or innovation by another firm may replace it. What is "sauce for the goose may be sauce for the gander."

In other instances, feedback may represent a once-and-for-all change; the process innovation is an example. The feedback from behavior may account for changes in market structure which become permanent.

Does this mean that the structural change is the purpose of the strategy which caused it? Not necessarily. It is reasonable to presume that, in many cases, firms act simply to establish a more secure or a more profitable position in the market. Only in cases of a more blatantly aggressive strategy, such as predatory pricing, is it likely that there is a self-conscious objective to alter market structure. This does not diminish the importance of strategic feedback, however, and it may be too fine a distinction to make. Is it possible to draw the line between an action which is intended to improve the firm's market position and one which is taken to change or reinforce a market structure? Perhaps not.

The Wild Cards

Does the linear chain of structure-conduct-performance, plus the feedback effects which run in the opposite direction, exhaust the explanatory power of industrial organization? No. There are a number of exogenous changes which can alter the course of the market as well. We might call these the market's *wild cards*.

Markets benefit from externally generated science, as well as from that which is homegrown. Historically, some of the most important technological developments resulted from basic research conducted independently. In certain cases, new discovery is the product of the search for knowledge for its own sake; it becomes part of the public domain quite by accident. In others, it may be the product of targeted public programs such as research in defense or space. For example, major developments in radar and computer technology were the product of the Allied research effort during World War II. Is the external discovery process important? Yes. At least some of the time the research involved may be so costly or so risky that commercial innovation could never have become feasible or economic without it.

Markets also benefit from construction of social overhead capital. For example, the nineteenth century construction of a nationwide network of railroads led to the creation of national markets for the same goods which had previously been sold only regionally or locally. It changed market structures. The change in transportation brought many manufacturers, who had previously enjoyed protected local monopolies, into direct competition with one another.

Cheaper and better transportation redefined market boundaries, and this increased competition.

The market may also benefit from the competitive entry of foreign supplies. The domestic industry, which had long enjoyed control over the home market and which suddenly awakes to find imports pouring in, is often changed dramatically. Automobiles, for example, experienced such a change in the seventies, and the effect was quite profound. The control of the market enjoyed by the "Big Three" (or "Big Four," if we include American Motors), which had previously been dominated by General Motors, was badly shaken by the emergence of unexpected competition. The pricing and product development initiatives in the American market were largely taken over by foreign car makers for a period of several years.

Foreign competition would seem to be the most dynamic of all the exogenous factors in the recent past. Industries which had seemed impervious to threats of entry have become competitive—basic industrial commodities, such as steel, and sophisticated producer and consumer goods, such as machinery and electronics, have both been affected. It would seem that foreign competition has the same impact as does contestability. First, the ability of foreign competition to affect the U.S. market has little to do with the level of concentration in the domestic industry. Second, it has a great deal to do with a foreign producer's ability to hit and run, if necessary. For example, foreign steel makers would have no sunk costs at risk since they are already in business; the U.S. would just be another market to them. Their strategy could be to enter if price is above (marginal) cost, to exit if price falls below it. An analogous situation exists for the market in which product competition is important—to enter if the firm has a product which is able to compete in the U.S. market and exit if it does not. Under these circumstances, in the 1970s and 1980s, key U.S. markets have been subjected to a new discipline which can only be attributed to the wild cards.

To summarize, there are certain external factors—the wild cards—which can change market structure and/or affect behavior and performance. We have suggested that such characteristics of markets as the state of technology, the stock of social overhead capital, and the presence or absence of foreign competition are among them. These wild card changes can, in the extreme cases, totally remake the market environment.

CONCLUSION

The purpose of this chapter was to provide a quick review of the basic elements of industrial organization and to suggest how, taken together, they describe an interactive and dynamic system. The greatest difficulty with industrial organization—probably for students and professionals alike—is the fact that markets in the real world are never quite at rest and never completely determinate. It is in this respect that industrial organization is a more elusive study than the pure theory of markets. But it also makes industrial organization interesting.

MAINTAINING COMPETITION: THE SHERMAN ACT

15

In this chapter we examine the meaning and implications of the Sherman Act. We begin with a brief history of the passage of the law and follow this with examples of two early cases brought in enforcement of it. Next, we will have a brief review of procedures in antitrust and the legal standards applied to the Sherman Act.

Having established a background in Sherman Act law, we will examine specific elements in it. We will begin with the treatment of restraints of trade, including horizontal price fixing and the division of markets. These are the elements of the law which are used to combat the establishment of cartels in the United States. We will then examine the application to vertical restraints—the arrangements between manufacturers and their distributors.

Next, we will examine the treatment of monopolization under the Sherman Act. We will discover how important conduct is to the offense of monopolization. A violation of law involves both possession of market power and a strategy to achieve or maintain it, so that the sort of behavior involved in entry deterrence would not be a lawful practice.

Finally, we will consider how the Sherman Act represents a public commitment to maintaining competition.

What is the Sherman Antitrust Act? What does it do and how did it come about? The Sherman Act is a law which declares that (1) all contracts, combinations, and conspiracies in restraint of trade, and (2) acts of monopolizing and/or those attempting to monopolize are illegal. It is a law which establishes the right and duty of the government to control the structure and behavior of the marketplace. It is distinctly American. While many who came to the United States came from countries in which there was a long history of government granting monopoly privileges to a chosen few, there had been no precedent for a government which aggressively protected the privilege to compete to all who would do so. Economic independence can be seen as a natural extension of the political independence which had been won little more than a century before. But why pass such a law in 1890?

Two processes of change evolved to the point where they were joined in the passage of the Sherman Act. The first involved the economy itself; the other involved political ideology and popular movements of the day. Let us consider the first. At the time of the Civil War, the United States was a rich, but largely agrarian nation. By the outbreak of the First World War, the nation had become the world's largest industrial power. A tremendous change had taken place in a relatively short period of time.[1] There had been a rapid growth in manufacturing. Why? First, advances had been made in transportation, particularly with the expansion of rail, which translated into substantial reductions in shipping costs. Manufactured goods could be transported more rapidly and more cheaply over longer distances. This, in turn, opened up opportunities for manufacturers to pursue ever wider markets. In an earlier era, local markets—and often local monopoly—were the rule. Second, technological changes made it possible to gain from establishing large-scale business operations. Larger firms, wider markets, and lower production costs were all parts of the American industrial revolution. Third, there was a great influx of population, which supplied the unskilled labor needed by the growing manufacturing sector and which supplied the growth in the urban population necessary to demand the goods produced by the manufacturing sector.

Together with the changes in the economic structure, changes in behavior began to appear. During the periods of rapid growth there might be demand enough to keep all firms busy, but during the slack periods, competition became very intense. Cutthroat competition was not unusual; neither were the cooperative efforts to eliminate it. Firms would frequently form loose associations to control price and output within an industry. In other cases, the more enterprising firms—steel production, tobacco products manufacturing, and petroleum refining included—sought to find relief from the problems of competition by combination, that is, by offering to buy the stock or the assets of their rivals. And if that did not work, the threat of destruction might.

What about political change? The period which produced rapid industrialization also produced widespread sentiment for political reform. There were many causes. First, the reform movement reflected a transplanting of different attitudes. The newer immigrants from Europe came with a hope for a better life in the New World, the same as those who preceded them. They also brought the experience of a more turbulent, more radical age than those who preceded them. When they found the opportunities less than what they had imagined and the working conditions worse than what they had come to regard as fair, dissatisfaction arose. Some took up the newer, class-oriented political ideologies which were rooted in 19th century Europe. To some extent, socialism and anarchism began to surface.[2] The effect upon American political change was minor, except

[1]Douglass C. North, *Growth and Welfare in the American Past* (Englewood Cliffs, N.J.: Prentice-Hall, 1966).

[2]Eric F. Goldman, *Rendezvous with Destiny* (New York: Vintage Books, 1955), pp. 29–35.

that it contributed a more radical flavor to an urban discontent which arose periodically. Second, the political changes reflected the temporary reversals in the upward trend of economic growth and change, such as the recessions of 1873 and 1893. Economic distress, brought by periods of falling income and rising unemployment, produced temporary reversals in the popular acceptance of the *status quo*.[3]

Finally, political change—that is, reform—derived most immediately from the growing rural discontent.[4] What was the cause of it? Farmers complained that: (1) their farm prices had fallen more (or risen less) than prices of manufactured goods in general, which they presumed were all manipulated by monopolists, (2) the railroads (and grain elevator operators, and so on) exploited them unmercifully, and (3) banks were squeezing them dry with the hard money—the gold-based currency—which they had managed greedily to protect with the aid of government. Were their complaints legitimate? North[5] has shown that they were not. Yet that is beside the point. Farmers, who felt left out of the game of economic change and who were a dwindling fraction of the total population, became a political force. **Populism** was clearly more influential than any other contemporary reform movement. It had to be one of the major factors in the coalition which drafted and passed the Sherman Antitrust Act of 1890. That is not to say that the urban population was not concerned with the emerging power of big business—the antitrust law passed with but one dissenting vote in the Senate and without an opposing vote in the House of Representatives.[6]

The Sherman Antitrust Act declares that restraint of trade and monopolization are illegal. What do these terms really mean? How precisely have they been applied? What are the economic implications? These are questions which we shall attempt to answer in the present chapter. But before we begin, let us consider two cases of behavior which ultimately led to antitrust actions being filed against the parties involved.

TWO ILLUSTRATIONS OF SHERMAN ACT CASES

In the period following the depression of 1893, a number of industries were hard hit by lagging demand. Many markets were, at least for a time, overhung with excess capacity, and price competition became intense. Cast iron pipe was just one of them, but there was a difference. Six manufacturers of cast iron pipe who were located in Ohio, Kentucky, Tennessee, and Alabama acted to do something about their plight. In 1894, they formed a pool, which they named Associated Pipe Works, to control the sales and prices of cast iron pipe in their section of the country.[7]

[3]North, *op. cit.*, pp. 31–32.
[4]Goldman, *op. cit.*, pp. 32–44.
[5]North, *op. cit.*, pp. 137–142.
[6]Simon N. Whitney, *Antitrust Policies*, Vol. 1 (New York: Twentieth Century Fund, 1958), p. 5.
[7]Whitney, *op. cit.*, Vol. 2, p. 4.

A major part of the business in cast iron pipe was the sale of pressure pipe to municipalities and public utilities for the construction of water and gas lines. The Associated Pipe Works pool sought to devise a scheme of market division and price determination to eliminate competition among its members for bids on such sales. How did they accomplish this? It was a matter of controlling the bids and the selection of the winning bidder in a geographically-defined system with three divisions: reserved, pay, and free territories. The rights to supply reserved cities were assigned to members on an exclusive basis—each of the six manufacturers had its own reserve, usually close to the mill, for which it would serve as the designated winning bidder for the cartel. In return for submitting fictitious bids on a reserved city contract, all the other members would benefit by dividing up a fixed bonus (a tax), paid by the firm entitled to win the bid. The rights to supply pay cities were determined by auction in each instance—members would compete by offering to pay a bonus into the pool, and the member offering to pay the largest bonus would be selected. Again, fictitious bids would be submitted by the other members. In both the reserve and pay territory sales, the Association would determine the price of the winning bid. No rights were involved, however, in the supply to free cities; to the extent that members sought this business, it was entirely competitive.

How strong was this cartel? How much did it exploit its ability to control price? These are not easy questions. And it is reasonable to presume, however, that the market power of the pool was greatest in the reserve cities, close to the member mills: (1) transportation costs are always a real disadvantage to the more distant competitor in a market for a product, such as cast iron pipe, where value is relatively low per unit of weight, (2) in the pay territory, the Association had 56 percent of the productive capacity so that nonmembers would have had to been a substantial competitive force, and (3) in the free territory—i.e., the rest of the nation—the Association maintained less than 30 percent of total capacity so that the competitive status would have had to been dictated by others. And it is reasonable to presume that the cartel had some effect on price. When it was charged with a violation of the Sherman Act, the Association responded that it had sought only to set prices at a reasonable level and to halt the unprofitable cutthroat competition that had preceded.[8]

Early in 1890, after a period in which competition in price among the five leading tobacco firms had been unusually strong, a major consolidation took place—all firms merged into James B. Duke's American Tobacco Company. Duke had been in the business for less than ten years but had been an innovator in adopting the newest technology in cigarette making. Duke pressed the competition hard; his firm was responsible for creating the conditions which led to consolidation. Yet, control of the market proved to be somewhat elusive. Public taste grew for Turkish tobacco, and the tobacco trust's share of the market dropped substantially below its post-merger level of 91 percent. Not to be

[8]Milton Handler, Harlan M. Blake, Robert Pitofsky, and Harvey J. Goldschmid, *Cases and Materials on Trade Regulation* (Mineola, N.Y.: The Foundation Press, 2d ed., 1983), p. 86.

undone, however, the American Tobacco Company persisted; it introduced its Turkish blend brands and managed to build its market share back up to 86 percent by 1910.[9]

Up to this point, the story of American Tobacco sounds like a classic case of entrepreneurship and hard competition—some are simply better at it than others. The record also seems to contain evidence of a strategy to monopolize the industry. For example, American Tobacco Company bought out forty different tobacco firms in the period of 1891 to 1907, merely to close them down. The sellers were required to agree not to compete with the buyer for up to twenty years.[10] American Tobacco Company also engaged in predatory pricing—it sold **fighting brands** at a loss, subsidized by its other products, so as to force smaller competitors either to sell or to face bankruptcy.[11]

Both the Associated Pipe Works [*U.S. vs. Addyston Pipe and Steel Co.* (1897)] and the American Tobacco Company [*U.S. vs. American Tobacco Co.* (1908)] were tried under the provisions of the Sherman Act, and both were found to be in violation of the law. In the former case, the violation consisted of acts which were designed to eliminate competition among the participants. In the latter, the violations included acts which were designed to eliminate competition by destroying competitors. Is this a real distinction? Yes, because it is a difference in form, if not in result. In the one instance, the restraint of trade results from a voluntary combination of the participants, while in the other, it results from a forceful exclusion from the market. The latter is a distinguishing characteristic of monopolization.

PROCEDURES UNDER THE SHERMAN ACT

The words antitrust regulation are often used in reference to enforcement of the Sherman Act. What do they mean? Is it like public utility regulation? Is there some sitting authority with the power and/or the ability to oversee the behavior of each firm in the marketplace? No, there is not. Instead, the Sherman Act was modelled along the lines of criminal law, but there are no police officers empowered to arrest alleged violators. If a violation is suspected, as a result either of complaints by the public or of information developed internally by the Department of Justice, the Attorney General (or subordinate agent) may seek to have the allegations investigated by a Grand Jury. The Grand Jury, once empaneled, is free to issue subpoenas to obtain information of virtually unlimited depth and scope from the firm (or firms) under investigation. If it discovers sufficient, though rebuttable evidence that a violation has occurred, it may issue an indictment. Does this mean that the Sherman Act is a matter solely of criminal law? Not necessarily.

[9]Whitney, *op. cit.*, Vol. 2, p. 14.

[10]Handler, et al., *op. cit.*, p. 104.

[11]Whitney, *op. cit.*, Vol. 2, p. 15.

On the assumption that the Department of Justice has enough information to make a case, it has an alternative to the criminal prosecution. It may file a civil complaint against the alleged offender(s). Why would the Justice Department prefer this alternative to the other? In a civil case, the wrongdoer is not punished. This is correct in the strictly legal sense but it may be beside the point. In certain types of antitrust cases, a civil remedy—that is, an action taken pursuant to an order of the court in order to correct a civil inequity—may be far more significant than a criminal penalty ever could be. Consider the tobacco monopoly developed by the American Tobacco Company. After it was determined that American had violated the law, the court ordered the firm to divest itself of several of its properties. There were several dimensions to the restructuring, but important among them was the result that three large firms—a reorganized American Tobacco Company, a Ligget & Myers, and a P. Lorillard—were spun off from the original cigarette manufacturing assets of the defendant.[12] On one hand, in the case of a single-firm restraint of trade—where the firm monopolizes the market—it may be more important to redress the structure of the market than to punish the offender. On the other, forced reorganization of the firm may be a considerable penalty in itself.

The civil remedy may be quite ineffectual in the combination case, however. Consider the cartel/monopoly. In most cases, an injunction in a combination case would produce only one result, a court order to stop colluding with one another. The wrongdoers could enjoy the fruits of monopoly until ordered to stop, and at that point, their benefits would cease but no real cost would be felt. Thus, criminal sanctions are regarded as the most effective weapons against combinations in restraint of trade. In 1974, in an effort to strengthen the deterrence-effect of criminal prosecutions, Congress upgraded the violation of the Sherman Act from a misdemeanor to a felony, raised the fines to $100,000 per violation for individuals and $1,000,000 for corporations, and increased the maximum term of imprisonment to three years. In 1977, the Justice Department adopted guidelines which marked a significant departure from the past. It recommended imprisonment for all Sherman Act violations involving price fixing and market allocation.[13]

Does this mean that the Federal Government bears total responsibility for the enforcement of the Sherman Act? No, it does not. There is another important area which involves civil proceedings—the private treble-damage suit. When a plaintiff (ordinarily a firm) can prove both that violation of the law has occurred and that a personal injury has resulted from it, it has the right to receive payment equal to three times the amount of that injury. Why treble damages? The purpose of adding such a provision to the antitrust law is twofold: (1) to assist the government in eliminating illegal restraint by giving sufficient incentive to others to initiate actions on their own, and (2) to deter restraint of trade by

[12]Whitney, *op. cit.*, Vol. 2, p. 17.
[13]Handler, et al., pp. 138–139.

enhancing the punitive character of the civil remedy, making it more costly to violate the law.

LEGAL STANDARDS IN THE SHERMAN ACT

Consider the substance of the Sherman Antitrust Act [the Act of July 2, 1890, c. 617, 26 Stat. 209; 15 U.S.C.A. §§ 1–7].

> Section 1. Every contract, combination in the form of trust or otherwise, or conspiracy in restraint of trade or commerce among the several States, or with foreign nations, is declared to be illegal. Every person who shall make any contract or engage in any combination or conspiracy hereby declared to be illegal shall be deemed guilty of a felony, and, on conviction thereof, shall be punished by fine not exceeding one million dollars if a corporation, or, if any other person, one hundred thousand dollars, or by imprisonment not exceeding three years, or by both said punishments in the discretion of the court.
>
> Section 2. Every person who shall monopolize, or attempt to monopolize, or combine or conspire with any other person or persons, to monopolize any part of the trade or commerce among the several States, or with foreign nations, shall be deemed guilty of a felony, and, on conviction thereof . . . [the same penalty shall apply as under § 1].

Does this mean that any restrictive contract is illegal? If, for example, the legal profession determines—that is, members of the bar mutually combine and contract—that graduation from a certified law school and passing the state bar examination are necessary requirements for one to enter the practice of law, and that all others are barred, has a violation of the law occurred? Or does it mean that monopoly of any market is illegal? If, for example, a supermarket is first to establish a location in a new suburban development and has a grocery monopoly for a period of time, has it violated the law? Of course not. While the strict language of the law seems to make categorical prohibition of all combination and monopolization in restraint of trade, there has always been an understanding that reasonable discretion would be applied to interpretations. In the first place, Senator George F. Edmunds—who was chair of the Senate Judiciary Committee and was actually the chief author of the law—declared that the Sherman Act would not apply to a person who was able to take the whole of the market away from competitors by sheer superior skill.[14] In the second place, there was a long legal history regarding the various interpretations placed upon the concept of restraint of trade, and in particular, elaborate distinctions between legal and illegal restraints.

How were such distinctions drawn? In part, distinctions were based upon the intent of those involved in a restraint. For example, suppose that buyers of an established restaurant insist that their purchase of the business will be made

---

[14]Whitney, *op. cit.*, Vol. 1, p. 5.

on the condition that the seller agrees not to compete with them for a period of time following the transfer of ownership. In this instance, the restraint may be seen as a reasonable protection of significant, but intangible assets involved in the transaction, namely the goodwill of the established business. Indeed, the restraint may even be regarded as **ancillary**—that is, as an aid but otherwise incidental to the primary purpose of the contract—since the intent of the parties involved would seem to be the conclusion of a sale of property. Such contracts were accepted as valid in English common law.[15] In part, distinctions were based upon the effect of the restraint. In general, the courts were more likely to be tolerant of contracts which contained an element of restraint, if the overall effect was to increase trade and to enhance the value of property.[16] Still, American common law has been less tolerant than English law in certain matters, such as those involving price-fixing, market division, and so on, whatever the overall intent and effect of contracts containing restraints may seem to be.[17]

Just as there had been an emergence of rules for good and bad restraints under common law, there would emerge in the years to come rules defining legality and illegality of Sherman Act restraints. What are they? What is illegal restraint of trade? What is illegal monopolization? That is not such an easy question to answer. First, it would seem to depend upon the existence certain conditioning factors. A restraint that may be held to be lawful under one set of acts may be found unlawful under another. In the second place, it would seem to depend upon the time period. What had been lawful around 1910 may have become unlawful by 1945. The best that we can do is to examine general divisions of case law and to note the standards implied in each. At this point, however, we might note that a certain overall dichotomy has developed.

In the most general sense, the legality of each challenged restraint is tested by a **Rule of Reason**—that is, beginning with the opinion of Chief Justice White in *Standard Oil Company of New Jersey vs. United States* [221 U.S. 1 (1911)], the Court condemned only the unreasonable restraints of trade. How could this be determined? Applying tests established in common law, an agreement or combination would be judged on its purpose and effect and on the market power held by the parties involved. In certain instances, however, the form or content of an agreement is such that Court has held there is no real question of its intent and effect. Beginning with the opinion of Justice Stone in *United States vs. Trenton Potteries Co.* [273 U.S. 392 (1927)], the Court declared that certain types of restraints were illegal *per se*: "The aim and result of every price-fixing agreement, if effective, is the elimination of one form of competition." That established a new standard of case law, the **per se rule**, which was subsequently applied to certain classes of restraints.

[15]The lease of a bakeshop was so conditioned in a leading case precedent, Mitchel v. Reynolds, 1 P.Wms. 181, 24 Eng.Rep. 347 (1711).

[16]Ernest Gellhorn, *Antitrust Law and Economics* (St. Paul, Minn.: West Publishing Co., 3rd ed., 1986), p. 4.

[17]*Loc. cit.*, pp. 7–10.

RESTRAINT OF TRADE

Restraint of trade is a term that can cover a wide variety of behaviors, and the law has had to deal with quite a number. In no small part, however, the term is used most often to refer to agreements among competitors, and particularly, to agreements among them not to compete. We begin, therefore, with horizontal restraints of trade.

Horizontal Restraints

Horizontal restraint is the most fundamentally monopoly-like form of behavior, and agreements among competitors to fix price are the classic versions of it. Indeed, monopoly can be regarded as a special case of combination, since the consolidation of the market's productive capacity in a single firm results in a formal elimination of independent competitors and the ability to control price. However, with horizontal restraints, we deal with combinations which, in some fashion, eliminate competition between nominally independent enterprises.

Price Fixing.   As noted above, the Court has established that agreements to fix prices are illegal *per se*. Just what is it that constitutes price fixing? Is that term restricted only to a situation in which the combination sets a monopoly price? Is it necessary to show that P > MR, and MR = MC? No, it is not.

In the case involving the Associated Pipe Works, the group of six manufacturers of cast iron pipe did not have a monopoly over the market. Collectively, it had only 56 percent of the production capacity located in the pay territory, but it did set the price which would be submitted by its chosen bidder. That was sufficient to show illegal restraint of trade. In the *Trenton Potteries* case, the defendants were members of the trade association known as the Sanitary Potters' Association, which sold 82 percent of the goods produced in the industry in the United States, and were charged with fixing and maintaining uniform prices. While the defendants had been found guilty in trial court, the appeals court had overturned their conviction on the grounds of procedural error. The association denied that it had been involved in restraint of trade. It claimed that the prices it set were reasonable, that the government had failed to prove otherwise, and that the trial court judge had failed to instruct the jury properly on the issue of reasonableness. The Supreme Court found that combining to fix price was unreasonable in itself, and that any price set by group agreement, rather than by competition, involved restraint. [*United States vs. Trenton Potteries* 273 U.S. 392 (1927)].

Let us forget monopoly pricing. Suppose that the group has taken no action to set a uniform price—or at the least, no evidence is found to show that it has done so. Is it possible to prove restraint of trade in price without showing price fixing? Perhaps so. In the twenties, secret price cutting was widespread and competition was strong in the sugar industry. In 1927, the Sugar Institute was established to cope with this problem. Its members—responsible collectively for 70 to 80 percent of the sugar sold in the United States—agreed to a Code of Ethics which pledged, among other things, strict adherence to prices and terms publicly announced. It was this specific aspect of the agreement which the Court found in violation of the law in *Sugar Institute vs. United States* [297 U.S. 553 (1936)]. Is the decision good economics? Yes, it would seem to be. Assuming that there would be at least some voluntary adherence to the Code, such an agreement is a threat to competitive pricing; perhaps, as much a threat as any of the usual agreements to set uniform prices. See Chapter 9 for discussion on secret price concessions and cooperation.

How far would the Court go in outlawing agreements to fix or tamper with price? In *Trenton Potteries*, the Court declared that it was not necessary to show that the association had fixed unreasonable prices—that is, that a bad effect had taken place—as long as it had the power to do so. But in *United States vs. Socony-Vacuum Oil Co.* [310 U.S. 150 (1940)], the Court seemed to go much further. At issue in the case was a price stabilization scheme that had originally been endorsed by the N.R.A. An oil glut persisted in the thirties, due to large discoveries in East Texas. The major oil states had attempted to establish prorationing schemes to slow production rates, and the Congress had passed the Connally Hot Oil Act to help enforce the state proration laws. There was a substantial record of public endorsement of price stabilization measures in oil. The refining industry leaders, who collectively dominated the industry, sought to contribute their part—and to enhance their own positions in the bargain—by stabilizing the gasoline prices in the Midwest. Major refiners purchased tank-car lots placed on the spot market by independent refiners in order to maintain the general level and structure of prices to jobbers and retailers. When it found the scheme unlawful, the Court declared that combinations to fix prices were illegal *per se*— even if the participants lacked the power to fix prices.

Doesn't this mean that any private agreement which fixes price is unlawful? Not quite. In *Broadcast Music, Inc. vs. Columbia Broadcasting System, Inc.* [441 U.S. 1 (1979)], the Court delcared that the *per se* rule does not apply to every arrangement that might fix price. At issue was a practice adopted by BMI and ASCAP, organizations representing the copyright interests of the composers and publishers of music, to collect and distribute the royalties due to copyright owners for the use of their property. ASCAP and BMI ordinarily negotiated blanket licenses with radio and television broadcasters for over-the-air use of music. A broadcaster and the music agency would agree to the payment of a percentage of total revenues or a flat fee for use of all music during a given period of time, and the agent would distribute the proceeds to the rightful owners. A blanket license provided for an efficient enforcement of property rights, but it also meant that all copyright fees collected from the broadcaster would be fixed and equal. In determining that the arrangement was not in violation of the law, the Court obviously recognized that it was a reasonable solution to a complex problem. Does this mean that there is some life left in the Rule of Reason as it might apply to price-fixing cases? Perhaps. The Court has accepted the proposition that some who form combinations which affect price do not have *per se* price fixing in mind. It is apparent that the purpose of an agreement counts for something. Legitimate commercial combinations—such as the joint ventures of ASCAP and BMI which are otherwise lawful—will not be made unlawful simply because price fixing of a sort is involved.

Market Division.   Let us now consider a different question: is price fixing the only outlawed form of behavior in restraint of trade? No, nor should it be. The control of price is only one strategy for a combination which seeks to exercise market power. Division of the market is another. In fact, since it is difficult to set a common price and to enforce it (as discussed in Chapter 9), a group which establishes exclusive territories for each of its members—reserve cities in the Associated Pipe Works scheme are just one example of this—may control price more effectively than a group which seeks directly to fix price. Nevertheless, there are few market division cases on record. Why? On one hand, those divisions which have appeared often involve price fixing, and it has been customary for the prosecutor (or plaintiff) to treat them as matters of illegal pricing. Case law has been well established for price fixing. On the other, pure market division cases may be rare—exclusive territorial assignment may be very difficult to achieve in any but well-defined, spatial markets.

Market division was dealt with in the very first combination case in U.S. antitrust history, *U.S. vs. Addyston Pipe & Steel* [175 U.S. 211 (1899) affirmed]. In that case, territorial assignment was part of the joint price behavior of the industry association known as Associated Pipe Works, and a pattern was established. Most subsequent cases involving market division were treated as aggregations of restraint which included price fixing. The law which evolved produced similar standards to those applied to price fixing. Does this mean that the law was applied only to oppose cartel-like combinations such as the Associated Pipe Works? Not necessarily. In fact, the Court may have established stricter standards for the market division case than for price fixing alone.

Thirty small manufacturers of mattress and bedding products joined in a venture to create a "parent" company for a national brand of mattresses. Each of the firms was licensed to produce under the Sealy trademark, each was assigned an exclusive dealer territory, and each agreed to sell at the same price. The Court declared in *United States vs. Sealy, Inc.* [388 U.S. 350 (1967)], however, that the agreement for exclusive territorial assignment did not warrant a rule of reason inquiry. The ruling was made in spite of the fact that (1) the agreement may have been necessary for the joint venture to succeed, and (2) it may have resulted in increasing the competition between brands of mattresses, creating a brand to compete with the larger, established products such as Simmons. But the Court did not quite establish a *per se* rule for market division because price fixing was involved. It would do that soon, however—in *United States vs. Topco Associates, Inc.* [405 U.S. 596 (1972)].

Was Topco a cartel? No more so than Sealy. It was an agency established by twenty-five independent small and medium-sized regional supermarket chains to purchase and market private brand goods under a common label, Topco. The arrangement was one in which members had exclusive use of the private brand. From a small beginning in the 1940s, the collection of independents had managed to grow into a position to compete strongly with the three leading national grocery chains. The success of the Topco brand, although accounting for roughly 10 percent of their sales, had apparently helped the independents achieve a stronger position in the market and had certainly increased the competition among all supermarkets for privately-branded goods. Did the Court consider the positive side of the joint venture as it had in the BMI case? No, it did not. In spite of the fact that trial records in both the Sealy and Topco cases showed that (1) the joint ventures lacked the market power to restrict output or raise price, and (2) exclusive territorial arrangements were a necessary condition to promote the brands successfully, allowing the members to capture the benefits of promoting the product in their home territories as opposed to losing sales to free riders, the Supreme Court rejected a rule of reason. The Court insisted that these joint ventures—unlike the ones in BMI and ASCAP—involved *per se* restraints of trade. This insistence has been criticized by those who feel that the law has not been flexible enough to recognize that some arrangements, although restrictive in part, are procompetitive on the whole.[18] In certain cases of price fixing and market division, a rule of reason might be better law, and certainly better economics.

Exclusion.   Have we now exhausted the possible variations on horizontal restraint of trade? Not at all. The Associated Pipe Works plan contained only one type of cartel exclusion—mutual exclusion to eliminate the competition between the parties to an agreement. There is another type of restrictive exclusion— exclusion of nonmembers in order to keep them out of the market. This represents a form of predatory behavior, a strategy to take and/or keep control of the market.

The Associated Press is a cooperative association of member newspapers who, in order to gather news efficiently from all over the world, exchange information freely with one another. Rather than having its own reporters stationed around the globe, an individual newspaper simply covers the local news scene with its own staff, puts any local news of interest on the AP wire, and picks up important national or international news stories off the wire. The AP is a joint venture to share privately, a public good—indeed, that is precisely the character of all in the news business. So, what was objectionable about the AP's operation? The government complained in *Associated Press vs. United States* [326 U.S. 65 (1945)] that certain By-Laws of the association constituted a restraint: (1)

[18]*Loc. cit.*, pp. 206–211.

members were forbidden from selling news to nonmembers under penalties of fine or even explusion from the organization, and (2) members were granted a power sufficient to block the extension of membership to their direct competitors if they wished to exercise it. The Associated Press argued that it did not have a news monopoly and could not have excluded rivals from the market if it had tried to do so. The Court declared that the Sherman Act intended to prohibit the use of any association to limit competition. The offensive By-Laws—those limiting the member's rights to sell news and the nonmember's rights to gain membership status—were seen as barriers to entry and were declared to be unlawful. However, the joint venture itself would otherwise be unaffected.

The Associated Press By-Laws could be viewed as aggressive and unfair agreements to exclude competitors from the market—at least that is how they were viewed by the Court. Let us suppose that certain firms believe that they have been unfairly victimized by the competition and therefore combine for mutual protection. Would the Court treat defensive combinations any differently? Not necessarily. In *Fashion Originator's Guild vs. Federal Trade Commission* [312 U.S. 457 (1941)], the Court dealt with just that issue. The Fashion Originator's Guild of America (or FOGA) was a group comprised of certain manufacturers of women's clothing and certain manufacturers of textiles. Clothing manufacturers who were members of FOGA claimed to be the creators of original and distinctive dress designs, and the textile manufacturers who were members claimed to be creators of original fabric designs. FOGA maintained a Design Registration Bureau for recording claims to the designs of garments, and the Textile Federation maintained a similar Bureau for textiles. Both FOGA's garment and textile makers alleged that they were systematically victimized by many pirates who would knock-off their styles and undersell their fashions unfairly. To defend their property, members of FOGA combined to boycott any retailer who sold goods copied from the Guild members by independent manufacturers. As a result, there were nearly 12,000 retailers who signed agreements to refuse to buy from the fashion pirates. Many retailers who signed did so not out of sympathy but because they feared FOGA's boycott threat. The Court ruled that the purpose of the Guild's actions was to suppress competition and found, therefore, that the actions were unlawful. The Court also declared that it was not appropriate to hear the Guild's plea. Whether or not it was the victim of unfair competition from pirates, FOGA did not have the right to exclude competitors from the market.

Vertical Restraints

Less well known—and probably less well understood—are those vertical restraints which are dealt with under § 1 of the Sherman Act. What are vertical combinations? How do they affect trade? Unlike the horizontal restraints of trade, which involve cartel-like combinations of nominal competitors, vertical restraints involve cooperation between the manufacturer of a good and its chain of distributors. Are the vertical combinations monopolistic in intent or effect?

They may be in some cases, but more likely, they are similar to horizontal combinations such as *BMI* or *Topco*—in the former case, the members sought to improve efficiency, and in the latter, their ability to compete.

Price Fixing. What constitutes vertical price fixing? How is it accomplished? Typically, a manufacturer of a consumer good establishes a recommended retail price for its product. In the case of vertical price fixing, however, a manufacturer contracts with its distributors to fix the price at resale—this is known as a Resale Price Maintenance contract. Why? What possible purpose could be served by controlling the resale price? It has been argued that the manufacturer may only be acting on behalf of retailers who want to limit competition among themselves. In that event, vertical restraints would serve as substitutes for a horizontal restraint. However that taxes credibility. How likely is it that thousands of independent retailers could envision a price-fixing scheme in toothpaste, or would want one, let alone organizing to force the manufacturer to carry out their plan? It can also be argued that the manufacturer is the one who wants to fix price at resale. This would appear to be more likely. But again, why? There are two possible answers: (1) the manufacturer wants to limit price competition at retail in order to assist or comply with an agreement with its competitors to fix price, or (2) the manufacturer wants to limit retail price competition for its own product to enhance its position in the market. Let us consider the latter.

Suppose the firm manufactures a trademarked, experience good (see Chapter 6)—a differentiated product such as toothpaste—for which convenience, not price, is the key factor in making a given sale. Suppose that the firm feels that it can capture the largest possible share of the market by getting the widest possible distribution—the firm wants every drug store, supermarket, and convenience outlet in the country to stock its product. How can the firm accomplish this? If the product has already been established as the most popular brand in the market, this should be no problem. If it is not, the firm may make its product more attractive to potential dealers with contracts for Resale Price Maintenance which promise a handsome margin for the retailer. Even if its sales volume does not prove to be immense, the dealer may feel that the product "earns" its shelf space. An alternative, such as an expensive promotional campaign, might produce the same effect. It could increase retailer acceptance, and it would probably raise price. However, Resale Price Maintenance may be less risky or more attractive to the manufacturer.

Dr. Miles Medical Company, a manufacturer of proprietary medicines, established a system of Resale Price Maintenance with both wholesale and retail distributors. John D. Park & Sons was a wholesale drug distributor which managed to buy certain of Dr. Miles' products at a discount from other wholesalers—those who had signed RPM contracts—and resold them to druggists who retailed at cut-rate prices. Dr. Miles sued John D. Park & Sons for contract interference. The issue was simple: if Dr. Miles' contracts were lawful, John D. Park & Sons had acted wrongfully, but if the contracts were illegal restraints of trade, no wrong had been done. The Supreme Court found that such contracts did restrain trade. [*Dr. Miles Medical Co. vs. John D. Park & Sons Co.* 220 U.S. 373 (1911)]. The court expressed concern that a tightly-controlled system of vertical contracts would destroy competition between the 25,000 retailers who sold Dr. Miles' line. However, the Court did not choose to consider the effect of inter-product competition on such ability to restrain trade—an effect suggested by Justice Holmes in dissent. Finally, the Court's finding seemed to be unconditional; resale price maintenance was illegal *per se*. But was it?

Colgate developed a comprehensive resale price maintenance program for soap and toilet products which was based upon (1) a list of uniform resale prices for its products, and (2) a threat of dropping any dealer who failed to comply. The trial court found that, in the absence of restrictive contracts, Colgate had not violated the Sherman Act prohibitions on restraint of trade. Upon appeal to the Supreme Court, it was declared that: "In the absence of any purpose to create or maintain a monopoly . . . " Colgate could lawfully refuse to sell to whomever it chose [*United States vs. Colgate & Co.* 250 U.S. 300 (1919)]. Why the turnabout? In no small part, it may have been due to the fact that Colgate was the clear instigator of the plan, while in *Dr. Miles*, the Court took the view that a retailer conspiracy to restrain trade was at the base of the scheme. In *Colgate*, the Court declared that no monopolistic purpose was involved.

Was there really such a difference between Dr. Miles and Colgate? Probably not. It is likely that each firm acted out of self-interest to strengthen its distribution network using resale price maintenance, and it is unlikely that support for a retailer cartel was involved in either case. It is also certain that some price competition would have been sacrificed in both cases. It is clearly arguable as to whether or not the gains in product promotion would enhance competition between brands by at least as much as the loss in price competition between retailers handling the one brand. But in any case, the restrictive effects involved in the markets for Dr. Miles and Colgate products are not likely to have been very serious. So, is vertical price fixing a more or less harmless practice? Not necessarily. ·

In *Simpson vs. Union Oil Co.* [377 U.S. 13 (1964)], the Court dealt with a case in which vertical price contracts may well have been intended to support horizontal price cooperation. Union Oil leased stations to independent dealers on an annual contract that was renewable, provided the dealer took goods on consignment from the parent company and resold them at terms stipulated by Union. The lease agreements were an alternative to forward integration into retail markets by oil refiners. In this case, Union leased its station to Simpson on the condition that gasoline be sold at a price of 29.9¢ per gallon. When Simpson chose to sell for 27.9¢, the lease was not renewed. The Court found that neither consignment agreements nor unilateral refusals to deal could be used by Union to enforce resale price maintenance—it was a restraint of trade, however it might be accomplished. The Court said that it was significant that Union's actions were coercive. But coercion necessarily is involved—in the trivial sense—in any sale in which the contract requires the buyer (or seller) to do something that he or she would otherwise not do.

What distinguishes this case from the others? In the previous cases, resale price maintenance could make the product more attractive for a potential retailer by making the price-cost margin higher, and could help the manufacturer achieve a more all-inclusive system of distribution. However, Union Oil Company is likely to have found a lease-operator for each station it owned, with or without resale price maintenance. On the other hand, the consignment contract could produce sustantial benefits, with or without RPM—the contract made the firm the exclusive supplier for a whole chain of dealers and it reduced the firm's costs for handling accounts. Two questions arise: (1) why would Union insist on RPM in leasing? and (2) would it make any difference to the market? With virtual product homogeneity in gasoline, Union could not alter prices on its own. If the industry acted to stabilize refinery prices—and it had tried to do so before—industry-wide practice of resale price maintenance could make a difference. The issue was not considered, however.

Market Division.   Let us consider another vertical restraint, the market allocation agreement. A manufacturer may franchise dealers to serve specific territories. How? One way is to assign an exclusive territory to each dealer. Another is to assign a specific location to each dealer—in this case, dealer territories are not necessarily mutually exclusive since the typical buyer may have several options from which to choose. What is the purpose of territorial assignment? As in the case of resale price maintenance, the primary objective may be to establish a stronger distribution network—to be able to sell more goods in a market in which several brands compete for the business of the consumer. It has been suggested[18] that, without some territorial restrictions, the distributors who represent a manufacturer may compete in a destructive fashion with one another. If one distributor invests in the promotion of the product and develops a local market, another may attempt to exploit that goodwill as elsewhere without contributing to it. If the free ridership becomes rampant, promotion of the product will ultimately cease. Thus, exclusive territories offer protection to the distributor against free riders. It should be easier for the manufacturer to find willing distributors, and those who are appointed should be far more willing to invest in promoting the manufacturer's product.

One final question: why should one manufacturer, the one who uses resale price maintenance, want to get as many dealers as possible, while another, the one who uses territorial allocation, wants to limit their number? This can be explained by differences in the nature of the product. On one hand, experience goods are a convenience, and the wider the distribution, the better. Resale price maintenance may help to obtain wider distribution. On the other hand, search goods are purchased only after a certain amount of shopping around, and the greater the degree of local promotion, the better. Territorial allocation may help to generate a greater degree of awareness of the product and help the dealer who sells it to obtain wider sales.

How has the Court dealt with vertical market division? It has been rather ambivalent, but it has certainly proved to be more tolerant of vertical market division restraints than it has been of restraints involving either resale price maintenance or horizontal market allocation, as in *Topco*. In *White Motor Co. vs. United States* [372 U.S. 253 (1963)], the Court reversed the trial court ruling that contracts which limited distributors to assigned territories were *per se* violations of law. The majority argued that too little was known of the economics of territorial arrangements to outlaw them completely and that " . . . they may be allowable protections against aggressive competitors or the only practicable means a small company has for breaking into or staying in business. . . ." The minority stated, however, that White Motor's distribution system was a brazen violation of law.

In *United States vs. Arnold Schwinn & Co.* [388 U.S. 365 (1967)], the majority found that vertical restraints on territory involving products it sold to wholesale distributors were illegal *per se*. The Court treated the matter as analogous to *Dr. Miles* in this respect. However, the Schwinn case also involved a firm which had adopted a distribution system to help stem losses of sales to foreign manufacturers and to domestic mass distributors, such as Sears. The Court held that vertical restraints on territory involving the distribution of products sold on consignment were lawful. The Court was willing to apply a rule of reason in this respect, and it found sufficient interbrand competition to justify the practice. Finally, in *Continental T.V., Inc. vs. GTE Sylvania* [433 U.S. 36 (1977)], the Court upheld the right of a firm to contract for territorial restrictions, provided it did not unreasonably restrain trade. In this case, Sylvania acted to restrain the location of its dealers in order to build a stronger distribution network. Since Sylvania began with a small share of the market, the Court concluded that anticompetitive effects were bound to be minimal. If Sylvania increased its market share as a result of territorial assignments, the Court was willing to presume that it would necessarily improve competition.

To conclude, is it possible to generalize about contracts and other arrangements to restrain trade? Perhaps, but only in the very roughest of terms. First, price fixing has generally been treated as more restrictive than market sharing. Second, horizontal combinations have generally been treated with more suspicion than vertical combinations. Have the distinctions always made sense? No, unfortunately they have not.

MONOPOLIZATION

Monopolization is the term that applies to cases of grand restraint—in other words, it applies to the instances in which market structure is involved, as well as behavior. When the Department of Justice files a case against a large corporation, charging monopolization and threatening forcibly to restructure an entire industry, it is a major event. Does this imply that in the enforcement of the Sherman Act, the section which deals with monopolization (§2) is far more important than the section which deals with restraint of trade (§1)? Not necessarily. Why? It is simple. Restraint cases outweigh monopolization cases by more than 10 to 1, and it makes sense. The opportunities to restrain trade illegally by combination are likely to be far more numerous than those to monopolize, especially since all sorts of horizontal and vertical arrangements are included in the former. That fact notwithstanding, what is the law in monopolization cases? What is an illegal monopoly?

The first complete expression of the law on monopolization was provided in *Standard Oil Co. of New Jersey vs. United States* [221 U.S. 1 (1911)]. Standard Oil Co. of New Jersey (SONJ) was the corporation which, after 1899, held controlling interest in the many oil companies that John D. and William Rockefeller had acquired to dominate the American refining industry. SONJ was the successor to the Standard Oil Trust, which had been organized for the same purpose, but which had encountered legal problems for violating corporation laws in the State of Ohio. In fact, the Standard Oil Trust was the inspiration for the usage in which the word, trust, became synonomous with monopolies and other combinations in restraint of trade. SONJ, or its predecessor, had assembled the capacity to supply 90 percent of the oil refinery products in the U.S. Was control of the oil industry the basic issue for the Court's finding Standard Oil in violation of §2 of the Sherman Act? No, or at least it was not the sole issue.

In the Standard Oil case, Chief Justice White declared that Sherman Act violations—like restraints of trade under common law—would be judged by a Rule of Reason. It would be necessary to judge the intent, effect, and power behind an act of restraint or monopolization in order to determine its legality or illegality. SONJ certainly had the requisite power, but it was also necessary to consider how Standard had acquired that power. The record seemed to show that Standard had set out to dominate the industry: (1) from the earliest days, the Rockefellers seemed intent on buying out all their competitors, acquiring most of the nearly 40 refineries in the Cleveland area and shutting some of them down to limit production, (2) the creation of the Standard Oil "Trust" seemed intent initially on skirting the law against intercorporate exchange of stock, and eventually, on defying it altogether, (3) the inducement of rail carriers to violate ICC prohibitions on the payment of rebates seemed intent on gaining an unfair advantage over the competition, and (4) the resort to localized price cutting seemed intent on destroying the competition. White declared that the behavior of SONJ—deviant from the "normal" or usual methods of business conduct— demonstrated an intent to exclude others from the right to trade. Monopoly alone was not a violation of §2, but when monopoly was combined with an intent to exclude, it was definitely a violation of law.

The meaning of monopolization was given further definition in *United States vs. United States Steel Corp.* [251 U.S. 417 (1920)]. Two facts were important in finding US Steel not to be in violation of §2: (1) subsequent to its formation, the company lost market share until its share of industry sales had dropped below 50 percent, and (2) after its creation, US Steel sought to live in peace with others in the industry, unlike Standard Oil and American Tobacco, which had seemed intent on intimidation and eventual absorption of weaker competitors. Thus, US Steel did not have monopoly power, and it did not abuse its competitors—in fact, as we have seen in Chapter 9, US Steel did what it could to cooperate with them in setting supra-competitive prices.

Does this mean that the law on monopolization gradually became more and more distant from the law on restraint of trade, which established *per se* rules early on? To a certain extent it does. However, a dramatic change would eventually appear in the *United States vs. Aluminum Co. of America* [United States Circuit Court of Appeals, Second Circuit, 148 F.2d 416 (1945)]. What was the nature of this change? It established a different test for illegal intent than the one used by Chief Justice White. It had previously been thought that there were good monopolies and bad—where the difference would be judged by the behavior of the monopolist towards competitors—but only the latter were illegal. In the ALCOA case, however, there were no competitors; the firm had always held a monopoly position in the market. In this case, the market was determined to be production of virgin aluminum ingot, so that recycled aluminum was excluded. Therefore, how had ALCOA managed to exclude the competition? According to the presiding[20] Judge Hand, ALCOA excluded competition by building new plants and expanding existing ones to meet the growth in industry demand for aluminum; the ALCOA monopoly in aluminum ". . . could only have resulted, as it did result, from a persistent determination to maintain the control . . ." of the market. The firm was guilty of having a monopoly which it could have avoided if it had wanted to do so.

The *ALCOA* case is obviously a watershed. Judge Hand wanted to narrow the difference between restraint and monopolization. From his point of view, all agreements which had the power to fix price were illegal *per se*, so any firm which had the power to fix price ought to be illegal as well. But does that analogy really make good economic sense? A combination is obviously artificial, but what about a natural monopoly? The natural monopoly has the ability to sustain its position in the market, but only if it keeps its price below the costs of potential rivals; that is, the natural monopoly must *act* to keep its position, and if it does, it is artificial by Judge Hand's logic. A strict interpretation of Hand's rule of avoidable actions would declare that natural monopoly is illegal. In effect, §2 of the Sherman Act could be read to make monopoly power unlawful *per se*.

Where does *ALCOA* leave us? Two things may limit how far the changes will carry: (1) the definition of market power, and (2) the interpretation of the law on intent. Let us consider the first. Prior to the Aluminum case, the questions of defining the market and measuring the degree of market power were

---

[20]In lieu of a Supreme Court which lacked a quorum to hear *ALCOA*.

seldom given a second thought. In the Aluminum case itself, definition of the market was rather strange. Aluminum recovered from scrap was treated as a different product from virgin aluminum, in spite of the fact that no evidence was presented to suggest that it should be. Apparently buyers treated the products as identical. There always had been opportunity for the defendant to raise the issue: to claim that the defendant could not be held responsible for monopolization when it did not have a monopoly. There was a stronger reason after *ALCOA* to make that claim an issue. What happened? The so-called Cellophane case appeared to turn on the issue of market power.

The Department of Justice filed suit against DuPont charging monopolization of the manufacture of cellophane, in November 1946. DuPont's basic patent on its most advanced cellophane had expired only one year earlier; still, DuPont faced only one competitor in cellophane, the firm it had licensed to use its patent beginning in 1933. DuPont produced about 75 percent of all the cellophane in the United States, while American Vicose (Sylvania) produced the rest. Did DuPont have a monopoly? Did it illegally monopolize the market? These were the critical questions in the case. At the trial, the issue of market definition broke new ground. DuPont argued that cellophane was only one of several products competing in the market for flexible wrapping materials, which included greaseproof paper, glassine, waxed paper, aluminum foil, and Pliofilm as well. Evidence was presented during the trial that dealt with the comparative characteristics of various products, the functional interchangeability in use, the prices of various products, and measures of the cross-elasticities of demand. The judge in the case concluded, after a year of studying the record with the assistance of an economist as a law clerk, that there was no monopoly. The market was the market for flexible wrapping materials, and the relevant market share was 18 percent. When the government appealed the case to the Supreme Court, a majority of the Court upheld Judge Leahy's finding [*United States vs. E.I. DuPont de Nemours & Co.* 351 U.S. 377 (1956)].

A standard of **reasonable interchangeability** was born. If monopolization was to become an issue of market structure, it was necessary to deal with it directly. Interchangeability was a test for defining the market when a unique product faced some competition from one or more reasonable substitutes. Was it applied properly in the Cellophane case? It can always be argued whether flexible wrapping materials is the best possible market definition, but it is quite clear that some such concept of interchangeability became inevitable after *ALCOA*. In any case, it has been an appropriate development of the law on monopoly in an economy in which both innovation and other forms of behavior which lead to product differentiation are important factors in competition.

Suppose that cellophane had been found to be a separate market. What would have happened in the case? A minority of the Court wanted to overturn Judge Leahy's decision on both grounds. They held that: (1) DuPont had a monopoly in cellophane, and (2) it had illegally monopolized the industry. If the minority had won support on the first issue, it might have prevailed on the second. What was the basis for this position? It was based upon a pair of dubious propositions. First, the minority argued that DuPont's patents—conveying a legal monopoly—may have been tainted by earlier behavior connected with their licensing. Second, they argued that since DuPont's patents were of no consequence, DuPont had no defense for its near-monopoly, and since it had been able to enjoy a highly profitable business in cellophane, it must have excluded competition.

This is a highly speculative matter. The minority of the Court did not consider whether or not a lack of competition may have been due to a lack of initiative. The DuPont and ALCOA monopolies may both have been the result of their enterprise, rather than their suppression of competition. Moreover, who can say that there was no competition? After the District Court trial which had found ALCOA innocent of monopolization, and before the Court of Appeals review which overturned that decision, Reynolds Metals finally built its own aluminum plant—and ALCOA did not have a monopoly in virgin aluminum at the time of Judge Hand's decision. By the time of the DuPont trial, the production of plastic films had already begun, although the market had barely been developed. This was the product innovation that would become the next generation of wraps after cellophane.

The case law since *DuPont* has not produced decisions as sweeping as the minority position in that case might imply. Also, the level of controversy has diminished. In *United States vs. Grinnell Corp.* [384 U.S. 563 (1966)], the Court dealt with a case in which Grinnell was charged with monopolization in acquiring a controlling interest in three companies which provide a type of detection and reporting service to protect against loss due to fire and burglary. Justice Douglas declared for the majority:

> The offense of monopoly under §2 of the Sherman Act has two elements: (1) the possession of monopoly power in the relevant market and (2) the willful acquisition or maintenance of that power as distinguished from growth or development as a consequence of a superior product, business accumen, or historical accident.

In *Grinnell*, there was little controversy over the issue of how the firm achieved its dominance; assuming that it had monopoly power, its acquisitions were taken to indicate the intent of the firm. However, there was disagreement over the question of monopoly, which derived from the definition of the relevant market. The majority of the Court found that Grinnell controlled 87 percent of the national market in accredited (that is, approved by the insurance underwriters) central station services for break-ins and outbreaks of fire. The minority found that the market definition had several shortcomings. First, it disagreed with the majority on the relevance of the national position of the defendant. Since the central station detection system operates on a purely local basis, the geographic dimension of the market defined by the majority was inappropriate. Second, it disagreed with the majority on the product aspect of the market. Since central station systems are one alternative to guards, patrols, automatic proprietary alarms, alarm systems connected with the local police or fire station, and so on, the product dimension of the market defined by the majority may have been inappropriate. The majority dismissed all alternatives as irrelevant solely because they were of lower quality. The minority criticized the failure to demonstrate that clients did not regard them as substitutes. Finally, the minority of the Court criticized the majority for tailoring a definition of the relevant market to exactly fit Grinnell's corporate structure.

Another decision, which the Court refused to review, may be revealing. In *Telex Corp. vs. IBM* [510 F.2d. 894 (10th Cir. 1975)], Telex sued for damages resulting from the monopolization of the market for IBM-compatible peripheral equipment. The basis for the Telex complaint was IBM's action in cutting the prices of its disk drive units after IBM had suffered fairly significant losses of market share to Telex and other competitors. There were two issues to determine: (1) what was the definition of the market? and (2) did IBM monopolize it? The Court of Appeals found for IBM on both counts. The rule of reasonable interchangeability did apply, so that peripheral equipment that was compatible with non-IBM equipment would also be included in the market definition. Conversion of equipment could be accomplished at a modest cost and some manufacturers would convert at no charge to the customer in order to make a sale. IBM's competitive price cuts were not monopolistic because (1) price cuts were an ordinary business practice, typical of those used in a competitive market, and (2) these price cuts were not dependent upon the power and position of the firm. In the latter respect, the Court found that since IBM earned a 20 percent margin on the disputed sales, it did not rely upon predatory pricing or cross-subsidization from other business to finance its campaign to recapture its lost market share.

What was the importance of this decision? It seemed to find a reasonable limit to the application of the *ALCOA* ruling. The large firm might be permitted to compete activity—at least for as long as there were competitors in the market and for as long as it did not rely upon a superior market position to compete with them. The decision also seemed to reaffirm the concept of interchangeability established in the Cellophane case.

THE SHERMAN ACT IN PERSPECTIVE

What has the Sherman Act accomplished? Has it guaranteed competition? Has it eliminated all restraint of trade? No, of course not; no law could achieve that degree of perfection. Also, the enforcement of the Sherman Act is far from perfect. On one hand, the law has banned certain agreements because they are in the form of restrictions, whether or not they actually do restrain trade. On the other hand, the law has failed to ban certain cooperative restraints of trade because they are not in the form of agreements and proof of conspiracy cannot or has not been found. Yet, it is useful to see what has been done. The Sherman Act has made cartelization a crime; and it has made monopolization—the creation of monopoly by willful act or acts—unlawful.

The objective of the Sherman Act is to maintain competition, but it would certainly be naive to expect the government to do it alone. Antitrust—like public health—depends upon the self-interest of the public to be successful. It should work. If it is a crime to combine to restrain trade, those seeking to profit by cooperation must do so in secret and must do so without any assistance from a legal system to enforce their contracts. If it is more profitable to cheat fellow conspirators than to conform, self-interest of the conspirators is bound to weaken their combination. If it is a crime to monopolize, those seeking to remain in the market, or to enter, will help to enforce the law by their own determinations. The would-be monopolist may be required to limit its strategy to legal means in order to defend a monopoly position. If it does not, the competitor may sue for damages, and that may be a sufficient handicap to frustrate the attempt to hold a monopoly.

PROTECTING COMPETITION: THE CLAYTON ACT

16

In this chapter we examine the meaning and implications of the Clayton Act. We begin with a brief history of the passage of the law and follow this with cases which illustrate two different interpretations of protecting competition. Next, we provide a brief review of procedures under the Clayton Act, which involve both the Department of Justice and the Federal Trade Commission, and the legal standards applied to the law.

Having established a background in Clayton Act law, we turn to an examination of its specific contents. We begin with the treatment of vertical restraints, involving tying agreements and exclusive dealerships, and discover that certain practices have been treated as illegal per se. *Next, we examine treatment of mergers under the Clayton Act. We see that vertical mergers have been opposed when* **foreclosure** *of the market is feared, and that horizontal mergers have been denied when the resulting increase in concentration is believed to be too great. Finally, we review the treatment of price discrimination under the Clayton Act.*

Lastly, we consider how the Clayton Act has adopted certain concepts and standards of protecting competition which seem to be more concerned with providing a level playing field than with supporting competition itself.

What is the Clayton Act? What does it do and how did it come about? First, the Clayton Act is a law which was adopted to amend the Sherman Act. Second, it declares that certain acts—price discrimination, certain types of contracts, and mergers—will be unlawful if the effect harms competition. Why was the law adopted when the Sherman Act was already in existence and was able to deal with such acts, as well as many others? Why was it passed in 1914?

To understand the Clayton Act, it is necessary to understand a bit about the temper of the times. Recall that the Sherman Act had been passed by a Congress in reaction to political pressures arising outside the mainstream. The Populist movement was the leading call for reform in the eighties and nineties, but it was in serious retreat by the time Congress was debating the Clayton Act. Instead, antitrust had become mainstream. In part, this was due to its remarkable successes. In 1911 alone, the powder, oil, and tobacco "trusts" were broken when decisions were handed down sustaining the government in suits against DuPont, Standard Oil of New Jersey, and American Tobacco. In part, this was due to the perceived limitation of the Sherman Act. Why did it take so long to bring Standard Oil to justice? How effective was a law, in which the breakup of the tobacco trust produced three giants to succeed it?

In no small part, antitrust became an issue because of one very powerful personality. Teddy Roosevelt had been a very popular President. He was a progressive Republican and a self-appointed "trust-buster" who approached few things timidly. When he lashed out at "the malefactors of great wealth," the public was carried along in the excitement of it all. "TR" decided not to run for reelection in 1908, but he would come to regret that decision and reenter the race in 1912. When he failed to get his party's nomination, Roosevelt ran as a **Progressive** in a three-way race. Wilson, the Democratic candidate and major opposition, also took a progressive stance against monopoly and for free enterprise. Antitrust was no longer one of the slogans for the various groups of down-and-outers but a major issue for the major candidates for President of the United States. If Roosevelt was unable to carry his third-party banner to victory, he was at least able to dictate the agenda of the debate. The people had had a taste of antitrust and wanted even more reform in the marketplace. Congress would have to act. How?

The Clayton Act of 1914 is one of the answers. The Federal Trade Commission Act—establishing an agency with the power to administer the substantive provisions of the Clayton and FTC Acts—was another. The Clayton Act, in language that differs from one section to another in small degrees, declares that some specific acts are unlawful ". . . where the effect may be . . . substantially to lessen competition . . . or tend to create a monopoly." What do these terms really mean? Precisely how have they been applied? What are the economic implications? How well does the enforcement of the Clayton Act enhance the enforcement of the Sherman Act? These are among the questions we shall attempt to answer in the present chapter. Before we begin, however, let us consider two cases of price discrimination which were held to be violations of the Clayton Act. Their importance to us is that they illustrate how protecting competition can be given very different meanings in antitrust enforcement.

TWO ILLUSTRATIONS OF CLAYTON ACT CASES

The Cement Institute was formed as a trade association in August 1929, to establish a code of ethics for the industry. Why? Whitney[1] has observed that the industry's single *ethical* problem seemed to be the use of trucking for delivering cement—motor cariers had begun to create problems for the industry's delivered

[1]Simon N. Whitney, *Antitrust Policies* (New York: Twentieth Century Fund, 1958), Vol. II, pp. 295–297.

pricing system, based on uniform rail rates. A number of cement mills in Ohio and Pennsylvania formed an agreement in 1931, independent of the Institute, to ban the use of trucking. The Institute never went that far. However, the Institute and its members did seem intent on operating a multiple basing-point price system. In 1937, the Federal Trade Commission filed a complaint against the Institute and its price system, charging in part that its behavior violated § 2 of the Clayton Act (as amended by the Robinson-Patman Act of 1936) prohibiting price discrimination. What was involved? The Institute was an apparent effort to limit price competition, and given the price behavior of its members, cement was systematically offered for sale at different locations at prices which did not reflect the differences in costs of supplying it. The latter fact was the basis for the charge of price discrimination.

If the price system really was a restraint of trade, why was the matter not dealt with as a violation of § 1 of the Sherman Act? The reason is that there is a legal hitch—lack of proof that there was an agreement to fix price. If it could be shown that (1) there was price discrimination, and (2) it contributed to a lessening of competition, the FTC could order the Institute members to cease and desist. Because the Clayton Act does not require proof of illegal intent, only that there is a prohibited effect, the matter can be dealt with more easily.[2]

Did basing-point pricing in cement lead to a lessening of competition? The record cited in *Federal Trade Commission vs. Cement Institute* [333 U.S. 683 (1948)] seems to suggest that it did. There was considerable evidence to show that the price system did produce uniform prices, discounts, terms of sale, etc. Couldn't *real* competition produce the same results? Yes, but with a difference. Real competition does not usually work so that rivals know in advance what one another will do. The Federal Trade Commission found that identical sealed bids for government contracts were the rule, rather than the exception. For example, the U.S. Engineer Office in Tucumcari, New Mexico, received identical bids of $3.286854 per barrel, with a 10¢ per barrel discount for payment in 15 days, from eleven different mills located throughout the Southwest in a contract for 6,000 barrels of cement [see 157 F.2d at 576]. Thus, Clayton Act § 2 was a convenient means to strike at the heart of a conspiracy in restraint of trade without having to prove that it existed.

During the period stretching from 1958 through most of 1961, Utah Pie Company suffered as the victim of illegal price discrimination practiced by several national producers, according to the jury in a Salt Lake City District Court and upheld in the opinion of the Supreme Court in *Utah Pie Co. vs. Continental Baking Co. et. al.* [386 U.S. 685 (1967)]. What led to this finding? What were the facts in the case? It would seem that the defendants, Pet Milk, Carnation, and Continental, had intensified their pricing competition in a local market. Some of the time they sold their frozen dessert pies to dealers in Utah at prices lower

---

[2]Note that in Sherman Act law, the act of agreeing to fix price is itself taken as proof of illegal intent to restrain trade.

than they were sold in other markets. As a result, market shares of the defendants increased at the expense of Utah Pie. Where is the "lessening of competition?" It would appear that the only injury to competition was the loss of a near-monopoly previously enjoyed by Utah Pie. Consider the following:

DATE	UTAH PIE SHARE	UTAH PIE PRICE	UTAH PIE VOLUME
1958	66.5%	$4.15/doz.	38,000 doz.
1961	45.3%	$2.75/doz.	103,000 doz.

During the period of alleged wrongdoing, the price of frozen pies fell by 33 percent, the total quantity of pies sold rose by 298 percent (Utah's sales by 171 percent), Utah Pie's profit margin dropped from a level of 2.01 percent of sales to 1.56 percent, and Utah Pie's net worth increased by 117 percent. With a price elasticity which averaged 3.0, the new price competition produced some extraordinary results. Consumers' purchases grew rapidly, as did both producers' sales and profits, and prices were forced closer to cost. These are the very marvels of competition which economists praise at great length in the abstract. How can they be condemned when they appear in the real world? The answer, it appears, is that large firms were seen to be picking on a small firm—never mind that the latter seemed to be the healthier for it, and both the price elasticity and the apparent ease of entry into the market (given the existence of a midget) suggest a market in frozen dessert pies could never become truly monopolized. After all, Utah Pie did lose market share.

In *Utah Pie*, a different meaning was attached to protecting competition than in the *Cement* case. While both cases dealt with price discrimination, only one resulted in the restraint of trade. While in the *Cement* case, the law was used to protect the process of price competition, in *Utah Pie*, the law was used to protect a competitor, even if it meant the sacrifice of price competition in the bargain. This difference illustrates clearly the schismatic nature of Clayton Act interpretations.

PROCEDURES UNDER THE CLAYTON ACT

Is the Clayton Act administered in the same fashion as the Sherman Act? No, it is not. In the first place, no stigma of criminality is to be attached to violations of the Clayton Act. An illegal merger—or tying contract or price discrimination—is a violation of law because of its illegal effect alone. Each alleged violation is treated as a civil proceeding. In the second place, the administration and enforcement of the Clayton Act is shared by the Department of Justice and the Federal Trade Commission, which was also established by Congress in 1914.

The FTC—as well as the Clayton Act—was established in reaction to some of the perceived limitations of the Sherman Act and its enforcement. When Chief Justice White set down the rule of reason in *Standard Oil of New Jersey*, many worried about the future of antitrust, fearing conservative, business-oriented judges and justices would give business firms a free rein. But establishing an independent agency with the power to enforce antitrust law was a way of insuring against this threat. The FTC is administered by a commission of five, with a chairman and four others who are appointed by the President—with the advice and consent of the Senate—for staggered seven-year terms, and with the condition that no more than three commissioners may be affiliated with the same political party. Like the Department of Justice, the FTC acts largely upon public complaints to initiate investigations, although like the Department of Justice, the FTC also has staff who study market structure and behavior in search of potential trouble. The Federal Trade Commission does have wide powers of discovery, under § 6(b) of the Federal Trade Commission Act, to require corporations engaged in commerce (excepting banks or common carriers) to provide ". . . reports or answers in writing to specific questions, furnishing to the Commission such information as it may require. . . ."

There the similarity ends. Assuming investigators for the Federal Trade Commission find sufficient evidence upon which to act, commission proceedings are initiated by an administrative complaint and tried before an administrative law judge within the FTC—that is, findings of fact are made internally rather than by a District Court, as would be the case in a matter brought by the Department of Justice. Thus, the petitioner and the judge in these hearings are both FTC employees. Decisions reached by the hearing examiner may be reviewed—endorsed, overruled, or modified—by the Commission sitting as an administrative court. Does the defendant in such a proceeding have any right to an "independent" review? Yes, the defendant may appeal any adverse ruling reached by the Commission to the Federal Circuit Court of Appeals, and ultimately to the Supreme Court.

How has the dual jurisdiction over the Clayton Act been handled? In fact, enforcement is not really shared equally. The Federal Trade Commission has handled virtually all enforcement of the price discrimination provisions of the Clayton Act (§ 2 as it has been amended by the Robinson-Patman Act), and the bulk of the enforcement of the provisions of § 3, whenever illegal tying and exclusive dealerships are not related to Sherman Act offenses. In the area of mergers (§ 7 as amended by the Kefauver-Celler Act), however, jurisdiction has been shared.[3] Also, a system of liaison has been developed between the Justice

---

[3]A. D. Neale, *The Antitrust Laws of the U.S.A.* (Cambridge, England: Cambridge University Press, 2d ed., 1970), p. 373.

Department and the FTC to iron out potential problems of jurisdiction and investigation.

Let us assume that an action has been brought by either the Department of Justice or the FTC and that a violation of the law has been established. Since no criminal penalties can be levied, what happens next? A federal court can issue a decree designed to prevent and restrain violations of the law. The Commission can issue a cease and desist order. Since both have the force of law, the result would be much the same whether the Department of Justice or the FTC had proceeded with the action. Is it necessary to carry an action through litigation to achieve some satisfactory resolution? Not necessarily. In the first place, both the Department of Justice and the Federal Trade Commission can and will negotiate settlements at any point in a proceeding. Thus, relief can be achieved without full trial or hearing. In the second place, it is possible that the adversarial process can be avoided entirely. For example, the FTC and the Department are willing to confer with corporate officers or counsels and to give informal approval or disapproval of a pending merger. While it is not binding, such informal consultation is promising as a means to enforce the law more efficiently.

Is enforcement of the Clayton Act left solely to the two federal agencies? No, it is not. Private complaints for relief from injury can be brought under the Clayton Act, including those which seek treble-damage compensation for the plaintiff. Victims—even those with dubious claims of injury, such as in the *Utah Pie* case—may sue to collect damages when the damages result from violations of the Clayton Act. The private civil action has produced, as a result, a significant contribution towards the enforcement of the law.

LEGAL STANDARDS IN THE CLAYTON ACT

Let us consider the language of the three critical sections of the Clayton Act which define unlawful conduct [the Act of October 15, 1914, c. 322, 38 Stat. 730; 15 U.S.C.A. §§ 12–27].

> Sec. 2. (a) That it shall be unlawful for any person engaged in commerce, either directly or indirectly to discriminate in price between different purchasers of commodities of like grade and quality, where . . . the effect of such discrimination may be substantially to lessen competition or tend to create a monopoly in any line of commerce, or to injure, destroy, or prevent competition with any person who either grants or knowingly receives the beneits of [it]. . . .

> Sec. 3. That it shall be unlawful for any person engaged in commerce, in the course of such commerce, to lease or make a sale or contract for sale of goods . . . on the condition, agreement or understanding that the lessee or purchaser thereof shall not use or deal in the goods . . . of a competitor . . . where the effect of such lease, sale, or contract . . . may be to substantially lessen competition or tend to create a monopoly in any line of commerce.

Sec. 7. That no person engaged in commerce or in any activity affecting commerce shall acquire, directly or indirectly, the whole or any part of the stock or other share capital and no person subject to the jurisdiction of the Federal Trade Commission shall acquire the whole or any part of the assets of another person engaged also in commerce, where in any line of commerce or in any activity affecting commerce in any section of the country, the effect of such acquisition may be substantially to lessen competition, or tend to create a monopoly.

The Clayton Act deals with ordinary commercial practices—selling a good to one buyer at a price which may be different from that offered to another, negotiating terms so as to acquire more of a buyer's business, and merging with or acquiring another firm—which are not unlawful in themselves. The question of whether or not they are lawful turns upon a test of effect. The Clayton Act develops a statutory test of legality: behavior which is otherwise legal may be unlawful if the effect "may be to substantially lessen competition or tend to create a monopoly." What does this mean? Does it conflict with or complement the Sherman Act?

The Clayton Act was drafted, debated, and passed at a time when the abuses of recently dismantled monopolies were still at the forefront of the public consciousness. It was widely felt that certain actions, in the wrong hands, could be damaging to competition or could lead to monopoly. Indeed, trusts had gained control over markets by a variety of techniques: (1) by acquiring the stock of independent firms and dragging them into their web, (2) by tying up retail distribution for manufactured products to cut off rival manufacturers' access to the market, and (3) by slashing prices systematically to weaken competitors and drive them either into bankruptcy or submission. Under the Sherman Act, was it necessary to prove that practices were unreasonable or abnormal in order to prohibit them? This clearly was one interpretation of the Rule of Reason, which had established the standards in *United States vs. Standard Oil Co. of New Jersey* (1911). Under the Sherman Act, would it be necessary to wait until the monopolist had become firmly entrenched before anything could be done? This was an implication of the Rule of Reason, too, since Chief Justice White declared that power and intent, as well as effect, were involved in illegal restraints of trade and monopolization. Under these conditions how could competition be given adequate protection? It was apparent to many that new law was needed. The Clayton Act was one part of the response to this need.

As originally passed, the Clayton Act's concept of lessening competition was probably very close to the established concepts of restraint of trade found in common law—that is, anything which constrained choices and decreased trade was an undesirable effect. The one difference—and an important one—is that the Clayton Act concept would admit no consideration of intent. Did the original concept remain unchanged? No, it did not.

The eighties and nineties had been the era of the trusts, the era of giant horizontal combinations. During the twenties, however, another type of structural change began to take shape. The market saw the emergence of large retail chains as it became apparent that certain scale economies could be exploited in the resale business. For example, chains could order in volume, and suppliers would be willing and able to make price concessions to win such attractive accounts. Didn't this represent a real improvement? Didn't it mean that many consumers, especially in small towns, might be able to choose from a wider variety of goods at lower prices than ever before? Yes, it did have that result, but it also had another. The change made it more difficult for the independent retailer to survive and prosper, and the Great Depression placed even greater pressure on small businesses, or so it was argued. Small business interests lobbied Congress to provide relief from the unfair competition they faced from the large retail chains. What was the result?

In 1937, their efforts were rewarded with the passage of the Miller-Tydings Act, legalizing fair trading; Congress voted to permit the states to pass laws which could compel every retailer to sell at the manufacturer's recommended resale price. Miller-Tydings amended the Sherman Act to permit states to create legal cartels in retailing—price competition would be sacrificed in order to protect small business. Unlike the *Dr. Miles* case, in this instance, resale price maintenance really was inspired by a retailer cartel, but of course in this instance, the plan carried the approval of government. Fortunately, Congress repealed the Miller-Tydings Act in 1976.

In 1936, however, Congress passed the Robinson-Patman Act, which amended § 2 of the Clayton Act. Robinson-Patman formally altered the standards to be applied in testing the effects of price discrimination. In addition to the old, established test—"where the effect may be substantially to lessen competition or tend to create a monopoly"—there was a prohibition of price discrimination where the effect might be "to injure, destroy, or prevent competition." What did injury to competition mean? Was it the same thing as lessening? No, not at all. It soon became apparent that Robinson-Patman intended injury to mean a competitive disadvantage. Robinson-Patman would be applied whenever one firm—the firm discriminating in price or the firm receiving the discriminatory price—got an advantage over a competitor as a result. When *Utah Pie* established that injury might cover even the loss of market share suffered by a quasi-monopolist, it was easy to see the full extent of the change in standards. If the Clayton Act originally had been intended to protect the process of competition, the Robinson-Patman Act was willing to sacrifice the process to protect the individual competitor.

Did the change in emphasis constitute a complete break with the past? Not necessarily. In the Presidential campaign of 1912, both Roosevelt and Wilson preached a brand of progressive philosophy, but Wilson's was derived from Jeffersonian ideals of democracy—the United States was fundamentally a nation of the small farmer and the small businessman.[4] The Wilson antitrust agenda

[4]Eric F. Goldman, *Rendezvous with Destiny* (New York: Vintage Books, 1955), pp. 165–170.

always intended to serve twin purposes: (1) to limit the ability of the corporate giants to rule the economy, and (2) to provide the opportunity for small business to prosper. Thus, the "new" laws of the thirties had roots in the same ground as the Sherman and Clayton Acts. Populism and Jeffersonian Progressivism were ideologies consistent with Depression-era antitrust laws, whether or not the latter were consistent with past legislation.

But certainly this new standard would apply only to the price discrimination law, since § 2 of the Clayton Act is the only section with such wording. Not necessarily. In certain cases, other sections of the law—those dealing with mergers and with tying contracts—were interpreted as if they too had been amended to prohibit actions where injury to competition was involved.

What has been the result? The Clayton Act has evolved with a pair of standards, illustrated by the *Cement Institute* and *Utah Pie* cases, respectively. In one instance, the law may be used against an act of lessening competition (or restraint of trade), while in another, the law may be used to oppose behavior resulting in injury to competition (or damage to a competitor). But we may see the development of the Clayton Act more clearly by examining the case law which applies to each of its substantive sections.

VERTICAL RESTRAINTS

During the debates leading up to the passage of the Clayton Act, it was noted that certain practices had contributed to the monopoly positions of firms such as the American Tobacco Company and Standard Oil of New Jersey, and that these included contracts which tied up critical sources of raw materials and/or critical channels of distribution. In drafting the new law, Congress had intended § 3—which prohibited selling (or leasing) goods on the conditions that the buyer (or lessee) did not use or deal in the goods of a competitor—to prevent vertical restraints when they would lessen competition; Congress was concerned about the monopolistic use of contracts to exclude competitive access to the market. What precisely was the nature of such contracts? How did the law to deal with them actually evolve?

Tying Contracts

There is no explicit reference in Clayton Act § 3 to tying contracts. Nevertheless, this category of contracts has become one of the two major targets of § 3 enforcement. What is a tying contract and why is it illegal? A tying contract is one which conditions the sale of one item to the sale of another. For example, the manufacturer of a mainframe computer might lease the central processing unit (CPU) to users on the condition that peripheral equipment—memory units, tape drives, and so on—be bought or leased as well. Or the manufacturer of a punch card sorter might lease its equipment on the condition that users buy their punch cards from the same firm. The concern of enforcers of the Clayton Act is that the implied leverage of the seller (or lessor) of the tying contract (the CPU or the card sorter) can and will use its leverage to exclude competitors in markets for the tied products (the peripheral equipment or the punch cards). And the result may be a tendency for monopoly to creep insidiously from one market to another.

There is some potential for lessening of competition, in the standard restraint of trade sense. Leverage could be used to monopolize markets in tied products. But, do tying contracts always have a monopolistic effect (or intent)? Not necessarily. In fact, it has been argued that tying contracts often do not.[5] Why would the seller choose to tie the sale of one product to another if no *evil* strategy was behind it? There are several reasonable explanations. First, **bundling** of products may be nothing more than a way to improve the efficiency in marketing. The seller may lower its selling costs by packaging the sale of several goods. This may be a common practice in direct selling by the manufacturer for search goods, such as the computer CPU and peripherials described above. Or the seller may introduce a new product by offering it in tandem with an established one. This may be a common practice for a manufacturer in distributing consumer experience goods through independent retail outlets. Second, the tie-in may be used as a means to increase profits by a form of price discrimination. The seller may establish a promotional installation price [P < ATC] for the basic good in order to obtain wide acceptance, and may set a profitable user price [P > ATC], levied on amount of use and representative of the differential value to the individual customer in order to exploit the product for maximum profits. This may be the reason why the lessor of a card sorter might tie the use of its machine to the purchase of its punch cards. In this case, a tying contract may serve the same purpose as the two-part price which Xerox used for its 914 copier, described in Chapter 9. There we saw that with a low $25 per month rental and a 3½¢ per copy use fee, Xerox was able to sell its machine for prices ranging from the $4,471 paid by the user who makes 2,000 copies per month to the $17,650 paid by one making 10,000 copies per month. Third, it is possible that the tie-in may be used to protect the quality of products used as inputs with a machine, and thus to protect its serviceability. If a machine is leased or even is guaranteed, the manufacturer continues to have a legitimate interest in its maintenance. In short, tying contracts may either be efficiency-enhancing or exclusionary or both. Does that mean that the Court has applied a rule of reason to tying? Not necessarily.

In *International Salt Co. vs. United States* [332 U.S. 392 (1947)], the Court dealt with a tying contract which it declared to be unlawful under both § 1 of the Sherman Act and § 3 of the Clayton Act. International Salt Company was a manufacturer of two patented machines—the Lixator, which dissolved rock salt into a brine for use in various industrial processes, and the Saltomat, which injected salt tablets into cans in the process of canning foods and other prod-

---

[5]Richard A. Posner, *Antitrust Law: An Economic Perspective* (Chicago: University of Chicago Press, 1976), pp. 171–184.

ucts—which it leased to users on the provision that they purchased salt used with the machines from International. In its behalf, the firm argued that the tie was not an unreasonable restraint since the contract provided the opportunity for the lessee to purchase salt of equal grade in the open market, unless the lessor offered the client an equal price. The Company argued that the rock salt it supplied for use in the Lixator was of consistent quality—containing a constant 98.2% of sodium chloride—whereas the rock salt available in the open market was of variable quality—containing impurities in amounts up to 5% and disturbing the functioning of the machine.

The Court presumed that International's patents on the two machines conveyed to the firm a degree of legal monopoly, but not one which would permit it to restrain trade in salt or to act to lessen competition. Had trade in salt been restrained? Had there been a substantial lessening of competition? Didn't the Company have a right to protect its machines? The firm pleaded for a Rule of Reason judgment but the Court rejected it. The contracts were *per se* violations of the law on restraint, and the firm could adopt some less restrictive means, such as a quality specification on salt to be used, to protect its machines. As for the question of substantial lessening, the Court pointed out that the Company's $500,000 in 1944 sales of salt were "not insubstantial." Finally, the Court declared that all agreements which "tend to create a monopoly" are forbidden and that ". . . it is immaterial that the tendency is a creeping one rather than one that proceeds at full gallop. . . ."

What was the implication of the *International Salt* decision? It seemed to suggest that tying agreements would be judged on the same basis as contracts in restraint of trade. That implied that little consideration would be given to effect—the *per se* rule did not require it—in spite of the fact that the Clayton Act was specific in declaring that the question of legality or illegality was simply a test of effect.

The association of tying agreements with *per se* violations of § 1 of the Sherman Act was made more complete in *Northern Pacific Railway vs. United States* [356 U.S. 1 (1958)], where the Court declared that such arrangements ". . . are unreasonable in and of themselves whenever a party has sufficient economic power with respect to the tying product to appreciably restrain free competition in the market for the tied product. . . ." In the *International Salt* case, sufficient power had been shown by the fact that the firm had a patent monopoly. What was the basis for the conclusion that Northern Pacific had sufficient power to tie illegally the sale and lease of its land to a tenant's use of NP rail service? First, Northern Pacific's landholdings were large. The company received nearly 40 million acres in land grants for the construction of the railway. While NP had sold nearly 37 million acres, the terms of sale often included a preferential routing clause obligating the buyer to use Northern Pacific's services, provided its transport rates were equal to those of the competition. Second, the mere existence of the ability to impose a tying contract was taken to be evidence of market power. The assumption, of course, is that a buyer (or lessee) would accept a restraint on its ability to choose the tied service only if it placed a high value on the tying product, and that the seller (or lessor) would insist upon tying land to rail service only if it expected to exercise market power as a result. The Court, however, had little evidence to support any strong inferences. It did not establish whether or not NP had to make price concessions to get buyers (or lessees) to sign a preference clause, and it did not consider whether or not the clients really gave up anything since they could use alternative transport whenever Northern Pacific's rates were not competitive.

After *Northern Pacific*, it did seem possible that all tying contracts were illegal—the leverage theory presented in the case suggested that they were. Had the Court eliminated the necessity of establishing independently that a seller had market power in the "tying" product? Not necessarily. In *United States Steel Corp. vs. Fortner Enterprises, Inc.* [429 U.S. 610 (1977)], a building contractor complained that it had been forced to buy components for prefabricated homes from the Home Division of US Steel in order to obtain favorable credit terms from the Credit Corporation Division of the firm. US Steel had provided Fortner with 100 percent financing of the total development costs of the latter's subdivision at a very attractive 6% rate. But Fortner charged that it had been forced to pay prices for the components which ranged up to 15 percent higher than available elsewhere. The District Court held in favor of Fortner, based upon the fact that US Steel had sufficient power to effect the restraint. This was a pure case of applying the *Northern Pacific* leverage theory to a different set of facts, but the Supreme Court chose to reject a presumption of power without showing that financing offered by US Steel was unique. The Court found that since Fortner had failed to establish that US Steel had an advantage in financing which its competitors could not match, there was not an illegal tie-in.

Exclusive Dealership

The other major type of Clayton Act § 3 contract violation is the exclusive dealership. What is exclusive dealership? Why should it be unlawful? Those contracts which establish exclusive dealerships are, in some ways, the complement to the vertical arrangements which divide markets (see Chapter 14). In the latter case, the manufacturer establishes its own distribution network in which its retailers are assigned mutually exclusive territories. In the former case, the manufacturer establishes a distribution network in which it claims for itself exclusive territories in the person of individual dealers, who only sell its products and do not deal in the products of rival manufacturers. In either case, the residual competition, which remains in the retail market after the vertical restraint, is the competition which exists between brands of products. Exclusive dealerships have been compared to forward vertical integration; they do offer an alternative to the manufacturer who might want otherwise to build or buy a chain of distributors to market its products. Exclusive dealerships have been fairly common in providing opportunities for independent small businesses to be franchised to sell a variety of products, including automobiles, gasoline, ice cream, and hamburgers.

Like tying contracts, there is some potential for using the exclusive dealership contract to restrain trade. The powerful manufacturer may be able to exclude rivals' access to the market if it can tie up available retail outlets. But there are also legitimate commercial reasons for exclusive dealership. It certainly is one means to develop a stronger distribution system for a branded product. An exclusive dealer would have an obvious incentive to promote the manufacturer and its product. In fact, the interests of the manufacturer and the retailer would seem to be made one except, of course, for setting a distribution formula for sharing the profits from the resale of goods. Exclusive dealership could also produce other integration economies. With a single contract covering a period of time, the manufacturer and the dealer may receive benefits in transaction cost savings—it may be cheaper and less risky to secure a channel of distribution (or supply) than to rely upon the spot market. As long as there are outlets available for the resale of rival products, it is hard to see the harm from exclusive dealing—and easy to see the benefits.

Indeed, even if there are few existing outlets for the other manufacturers, the exclusive dealership contract need not exclude them from the market. Why not? There are two possibilities. First, the typical exclusive dealership contract is of quite brief duration, one or two years. Thus, the firm in search of an outlet may attempt to bid away a rival's dealer, providing that dealer with a better bargaining position in the process. Second, the manufacturer in need of an outlet always does have the option of building or buying its own dealership. There is no fixed limit to the number of outlets so that there is no absolute barrier to entry. On the other hand, the need to build one's own chain of outlets may mean that a new entrant suffers a temporary disadvantage. Even then, it may not be a serious one. Does this mean that the Court has tended to apply a rule of reason or to look favorably upon exclusive dealership arrangements? Not necessarily.

In *Standard Fashion Co. vs. Magrane-Houston Co.* [258 U.S. 346 (1922)], the Court established that an exclusive dealership contract between the manufacturer of a popular line of patterns for women's and children's garments and its agent—a dry goods store in Boston—was invalid. Magrane-Houston had signed a two-year contract to deal only in patterns made by Standard Fashion, but the retailer subsequently discontinued the line and began to sell another. Standard sued to enforce the contract, but a trial court refused to do so, ruling that the contract was in violation of § 3 of the Clayton Act. The lower courts emphasized the fact that Standard—together with two other manufacturers controlled by the same holding company—had 40 percent of the agencies in the nation. Thus, the potential for substantial lessening of competition had been established. The Supreme Court concurred with this finding.

What was the attitude of the courts to the principle of exclusive dealership Was the Standard Fashion contract invalid because the firm had so many agencies or because the exclusive agency arrangement itself was restrictive? The Court of Appeals had observed, along with the market share of Standard, the fact that in some small communities an exclusive dealership could be the same thing as monopoly. But the point is irrelevant to the dispute between Standard Fashion and Magrane-Houston since Boston is not a small community. Thus, why was this principle established and why was it cited by the Supreme Court in review, if not to suggest a general distrust of the practice? Would the courts make distinctions between tying and exclusive dealer contracts? All these issues are joined in *Standard Oil Co. of California vs. United States* [337 U.S. 293 (1949)].

Standard Oil Co. of California (SOCAL) and its wholly-owned subsidiary, Standard Stations, had entered into full-requirements contracts with a large number of independent service stations for the supply and resale of gasoline (and, in some cases, a variety of auto accessories). Defining the market as the "Western area"—the Pacific Coast plus Idaho, Nevada, and Arizona—it was found that: (1) SOCAL supplied 6.8% of the total gasoline sold in the West through its own service stations and 6.7% through its exclusive dealers, (2) SOCAL's six major competitors supplied another 42.5%, and (3) all other retail sales were supplied by more than seventy competing small refiners. The District Court held that the contracts were unlawful. The issue of actual or potential lessening of competition was settled by the evidence that the contracts tied up a substantial number of dealers and a substantial quantity of sales—the trial court seemed to make the test of legality in exclusive dealing the same as that which had been applied in cases of tying. The trial judge noted that the practice was widespread, that the number and sales of SOCAL dealerships had declined as a percentage of the market, and that the arrangements had been defended by claims of increased efficiency beneficial to the industry and the public. The trial judge came to the conclusion that all contracts which are restrictive in nature are illegal where they have an effect on a substantial amount of business—i.e., where they ". . . affect injuriously a sizeable part of interstate commerce. . . ."

The Supreme Court chose not to go quite that far. In its review of the case, the Court suggested that the tying contract, in contrast to the exclusive dealership contract, served only to suppress competition—the *per se* illegality of the former was apparently based upon inferences of intent, not just effect. The Court was willing to grant that requirements contracts could have beneficial effects which accrue to the buyer as well as the seller, and which may pass on to the ultimate consumer. The Court established a basis for applying a rule of reason to exclusive dealerships. Did it? No, it really did not. In its hesitance, the Court observed:

> "To interpret that section [§ 3] as requiring proof that competition was actually diminished would make its very explicitness a means of conferring immunity upon the practices which it singles out. Congress has authoritatively determined that those practices are detrimental where their effect may be to lessen competition."

The Court seemed to interpret § 3 of the Clayton Act as saying that restrictive contracts necessarily lessen competition, and improvements in efficiency or competition would not mitigate the negative effect. On the other hand, exclusive dealership was not *per se* illegal. The Court held that a complaint of lessening of competition would be sustained only if a substantial share of the market was affected—the 6.7% share of the Western market would satisfy that standard. Therefore, SOCAL's contracts for exclusive dealerships were illegal.

Standard gave us the test of **quantitative substantiality** and it has been applied to other sections of the Clayton Act, as we shall see. What is that test? There seems to be two parts to the fundamental logic: (1) the presumption that a forbidden practice is restrictive in itself, and (2) the presumption that it would have the forbidden effect of lessening competition if its use became sufficiently widespread. Suppose that the first assumption is mistaken. How many practices are presumptively restrictive? Certainly not all tying and/or exclusive dealership contracts will restrain trade, and certainly not all mergers and acts of price discrimination will do so either—in fact, that is one reason why there is a test of illegal effect attached to the Clayton Act. But it is especially difficult to apply this logic when a specific practice has both pro- and anti-competitive effects.

What are the implications? A practice which may be restrictive in one situation might be widely adopted in another without ever damaging competition. For example, from the facts of the Standard Stations case we know that, in the West, there were seven major oil refiners and over seventy minor ones with obvious access to the market in spite of exclusive dealerships. Since the plaintiff's theory of the case was that exclusion caused the lessening of competition in gasoline distribution, it is difficult to understand how the major presumption—that exclusive dealership contracts were restrictive—withstood the evidence. The majority of the Court, acknowledging that actual proof of lessening competition might be difficult, sought to justify the substitution of a simple rule for a proper analysis of economic effect. In his dissent, Justice Douglas expressed dissatisfaction with applying the rule to the Standard Stations case, not out of disagreement with quantitative substantiality in general, but because he feared that refiners would continue to build their own distribution networks and that greater barriers to entry would result. Douglas wrote: "Our choice must be made on the basis not of abstractions but of the realities of modern industrial life." It was a vain call which the Court—along with Douglas himself—often failed to heed.

MERGERS

In drafting the Clayton Act, Congress was greatly aware of the role which mergers had played in the Trust movement. In *Standard Oil of New Jersey* (1911), the Court broke up the holding company which had held controlling interest in a number of major corporations in oil—in fact, it broke up the successor to the original Standard Oil Trust. In framing § 7 of the Clayton Act, Congress intended to prevent any recurrence of the monopoly-building fury that had engulfed the economy in the late nineteenth and early twentieth centuries. Congress wanted also to avoid the possibility that a corporate giant would be found not guilty of monopolization—such as US Steel later was—simply because it had not quite achieved monopoly proportions or had not done anything really bad. Concentration on the past form and use of acquisitions led to some serious drafting errors in § 7. The original law prohibited mergers of stock ". . . where the effect of such acquisition may be to substantially lessen competition between the corporation whose stock is so acquired and the corporation making the acquisition. . . ." That is, in its original form, § 7 banned only *horizontal* mergers of stock.

Two changes began to take place shortly after its adoption. First, it did not take long to discover the loophole that had been left in the law. The takeover of a competitor could legally be accomplished by winning approval of its stock-holders to a plan to sell its assets to the "acquiring" firm and to distribute the proceeds to the stockholder. After the transfer of assets, the "acquired" corporation would exist only on paper. Second, a new generation of managers would soon discover a strategy different from that of the past. A greater independence of action and growth in sales and profits could be achieved without building monopolies—the corporation could diversify instead (refer to Chapter 13). The merger began to take new shapes and new names—the *vertical* merger and the *conglomerate* merger would dominate acquisitions in the U.S. economy. What would happen to the law? It would have to be amended. In 1950, the Kefauver-Celler amendment was passed by a new Congress which was concerned with the threat of "growing concentration of economic power" in the hands of a few. Attention had shifted from the issue of monopoly to the issue of aggregate concentration. The fear was that giant corporations by mere size and power alone would exclude tiny competitors, and by their appetite for growth would gobble up those who were not deterred.[6] How did the law deal with the new "problems" in protecting competition?

Vertical Mergers

While there is no explicit reference in the amended § 7 of the Clayton Act to vertical mergers, the first case to reach the Supreme Court after its passage was one which involved a vertical merger. What is a vertical merger and why should it concern the law? As we have just seen in cases of vertical contracts, the issue is one of potential exclusion. The firm which acquires a dealer (or a supplier) is presumed to have better access to the market than its competition. In fact, in the Standard Stations case, Justice Douglas dissented from the majority, stating a

[6]Ernest Gellhorn, *Antitrust Law and Economics* (St. Paul, Minn.: West Publishing, 3rd ed., 1986), pp. 340–342.

fear that, without the ability to sign exclusive dealers, SOCAL might just build a dealer network which would more permanently exclude the small competitor. How might that be done? The merger could certainly play an important role in it. Why would SOCAL be so intent on developing such a distribution system? Douglas, as well as the majority of the Court, was willing to concede that vertical integration may improve efficiency.

Indeed, in the general case, efficient operation is likely to be the major reason for a vertical merger. It would seem to be more likely that the acquiring firm would improve efficiency and/or expand sales than that it would benefit by denying access to a potential competitor. Indeed, the Court has recognized the efficiency advantages accruing to the vertical merger. Has this led the Court to adopt a conciliatory posture towards the vertical merger? Quite the contrary.

In *Brown Shoe Co. vs. United States* [370 U.S. 294 (1962)], a vertical merger case reached the Court under the newly amended § 7. Brown Shoe, the nation's fourth largest manufacturer of shoes, had acquired stock in G. R. Kinney Company, the nation's eighth largest retailer. The Government filed a complaint that the merger would unlawfully lessen competition. Was the shoe industry as concentrated as the oil industry had been? Not at all. At retail, Kinney sold about 1.2% of the shoes in the U.S. by value (or 1.6% by volume) through 350 stores located in 270 cities and towns. Brown had 1,230 outlets, including both stores which were owned (about 470) and those which operated as franchises selling Brown's shoes through department stores. For the industry as a whole, there were some 70,000 retail outlets—20,000 of which were classified as shoe stores, operating in the same fashion that Kinney did business. In manufacturing, Brown made about 4% of the total volume for the industry; Kinney made 0.5%. For the industry as a whole, there were roughly 900 manufacturers, but they were not all the same size. The largest twenty-four firms accounted for a 35 percent market share and the four largest manufacturers had a 22 percent market share.

If the industry was not concentrated in the aggregate and if neither Brown nor Kinney was really large in itself, how could the merger be a threat to lessening competition? The Court did not apply its own rule of quantitative substantiality in *Brown Shoe*. Instead, it sought to analyze the conditions of the industry and the trends in it. The trial court found that the merger was likely to foreclose the access to Kinney's stores which had previously been open to other manufacturers and that this "may substantially lessen competition." In other words, the trial court treated the acquisition as an exclusive dealership, although there was no evidence (1) that Brown had foreclosed its competitors, or (2) that the Kinney chain represented a necessary outlet for independent manufacturers in the industry.

When the Court reviewed the lower court's finding, it concurred with it on at least two grounds: (1) when it discovered that Brown had increased sales it made to the distributors which it had acquired in the past, it was willing to presume that the same would apply to Kinney, and (2) when it discovered that several manufacturers had acquired their own retail outlets, it was willing to presume that a trend towards vertical integration was established. That is, the Court depended heavily on projecting past trends into the future in order to interpret the meaning of the words "may be substantially to lessen competition." Mergers with probable (not certain) anticompetitive effects were to be banned under the new § 7. However, the Court still depended heavily upon the presumption that integration was anticompetitive. In this respect at least, its decision was based upon a logic similar to that in *Standard*, even if the rule of quantitative substantiality was not used.

How did the Court deal with the issue of efficiency? If a vertical merger should enhance efficiency, would it be regarded as a positive factor in the case? No, not at all. Instead, it could be regarded as another problem. Integrated retail chains would be able to obtain shoes for distribution by eliminating the wholesaler and could market their own brands at prices below the independent retailer. Isn't that increased competition? Not in the view of some. The Court, reflecting on it, observed that Congress sought ". . . to promote competition through the protection of viable, small, locally owned business." The Court found no inherent contradiction in the fact that "protection of competition" would result in higher costs and prices.

This brings us to what might be the most revealing side to the *Brown Shoe* case. In developing the meaning of the Clayton Act in general, and § 7 in particular, the Supreme Court declared itself solidly behind the preservation of the *status quo*. Trends in the economy seemed to lead towards increased concentration; it was important to stem them in their incipiency. Merger activity in shoes was just beginning to alter the structure—although in a vertical dimension—of a very unconcentrated industry. It was important to act in a timely fashion. The Court declared that it had a duty to serve: "Where an industry was composed of numerous units, Congress appeared anxious to preserve this structure." It was not seemingly concerned with the fact that the changes in the organization of the industry might reflect the market dynamics of a competitive process. In a competitive environment, firms are compelled to make adjustments which make them more efficient and better able to compete; they do not stay the same forever.

If the Court was willing and able to overturn a vertical merger between a manufacturer with a 4.5% share of the market and a retailer with 1.6% (or 1.2%) of the market in an industry which was not concentrated, does this mean that *Brown Shoe* brought a virtual halt to all vertical merger activity? Not necessarily. First, the Antitrust Division, which shares responsibility with the Federal Trade Commission in merger law enforcement, sets down guidelines for the information of firms contemplating merger and for the use of its own personnel. For example, in 1982, the Justice Department would not generally oppose a Brown-Kinney type of merger if the retail market after the merger had sufficient capacity to handle the distribution of two or more unintegrated manufacturers with minimum efficient scale (MES) plants.[7] Further, the FTC would not be inclined to oppose such a merger unless the structure of the manufacturing market had a concentration level with H > .18, where the Herfindahl (H) index of concentration, indicates a sitution roughly equivalent to a six-firm oligopoly.[8] Given the *Brown Shoe* facts, the Federal Trade Commission would not be likely to have opposed the merger in 1982.

Second, Gellhorn[9] has observed that lower courts have been rather skeptical of the foreclosure theory of vertical mergers, as so starkly represented in *Brown Shoe*. Of particular interest is the challenge to an important strategic assumption about the post-merger behavior of an acquired firm set down in *Brown Shoe*. The Court accepted the Government's contention that Brown might force its products on Kinney—making it an exclusive dealer. Would that have made good commercial sense? Given the market in general and the size of the two involved in particular, Brown was in no position to monopolize shoe manufacturing by denying access to the Kinney retail outlets. If Brown should force shoes on Kinney that were not what Kinney's customers wanted, it would destroy its own investment. In *Freuhauf Corp. vs. FTC* [United States Court of Appeals, Second Circuit, 603 F.2d 345 (1979)], a lower court challenged a similar assumption about the strategy of the firm. Freuhauf, the nation's largest maker of truck trailers, had acquired Kelsey, a manufacturer of heavy duty wheels. Among the FTC's contentions was that, in the event of a shortage in wheels, Kelsey would chose to favor Freuhauf over the other trailer manufacturers, in spite of an established policy of providing *pro rata* allocations to all its regular customers under such conditions. The FTC assumed that foreclosure was an imminent danger. The court disagreed, however, pointing out that by mistreating the firm's outside customers, Kelsey (or Freuhauf) would risk losing its future business for wheels and for other products. The firm's self-interest would prevent it.

With the passage of the Kefauver-Celler amendment to § 7, another type of merger was exposed to the law, the **conglomerate** merger. The conglomerate merger is a combination of firms who don't have any direct relationship with one another. If firms are related neither as competitors nor as successive stages in distribution, how can their combination lessen competition? The answer is, once again, the potential of foreclosure. However, it is more difficult to make a logical case for denial of access in a matter involving a conglomerate. Merger statistics (shown in Chapter 13) seem to bear this out—conglomerates are five to ten times as numerous as others. Nevertheless, there have been a few interest-

---

[7]Milton Handler, Harlan M. Blake, Robert Pitofsky, and Harvey J. Goldschmid, *Trade Regulation: Cases and Materials* (Mineola, New York: The Foundation Press, 2d ed., 1983), p. 888.

[8]*Loc. cit.*, p. 889.

[9]Gellhorn, *op. cit.*, p. 353.

ing cases, such as the one involving Procter & Gamble's intended acquisition of Clorox. Since the majority of issues are so similar to those in *Brown Shoe*, we have two real choices: (1) to develop the conglomerate merger law carefully to point out distinctions, or (2) to stop here, conceding that some important details are lost. We shall do the latter.

Horizontal Mergers

The Kefauver-Celler amendment did not change the language of § 7 with respect to the horizontal merger, but it did change the focus of concern. When the original Clayton Act was passed, the fear was that mergers would be used to create monopolies. It would seem that there was no very clear concept of the meaning of lessening competition, short of monopoly. A modern oligopoly theory had yet to be developed in 1914. In the debates over the amendment to § 7, however, it was clear that Congress wanted: (1) to halt the general increase in concentration, and (2) to forbid any merger which would adversely affect competition in a market.[10] Were these two objectives related in any way? Yes they were. By that time, a structuralist model of industrial organization—a model which tended to emphasize the ubiquity of oligopoly—had been developed and was well-known to the staffs of the FTC and the Antitrust Division, although Bain's 1951 seminal article on the concentration-profitability hypothesis (see Chapter 7) had yet to be published. The members of Congress had heard a great deal about administered prices—prices which were set in a non-competitive fashion in markets dominated by a few firms—since Gardiner Means had first begun to report his research to the U.S. Senate in the thirties.[11] The case law in horizontal mergers would reflect these considerations.

The *Brown Shoe* case would again provide the first landmark decision on horizontal mergers, and Brown-Kinney could be viewed as a horizontal merger either in manufacturing or in retailing. Of major concern in a horizontal merger case was the definition of the relevant market. In *Brown Shoe*, the trial court found that, in manufacturing, the market was the whole national industry devoted to the production of shoes. In retailing, it found that markets were differentiated both by location and product. The Supreme Court agreed, in large part, with the market boundaries so prescribed by the District Court, and the legality of the merger was tested by its effect upon markets (1) differentiated by product into men's, women's, and children's shoes, and (2) differentiated by location into all cities with populations exceeding 10,000.

In the manufacturing aspect of the case, the trial court found that the combined market shares of Brown and Kinney totaled less than 5 percent of the market, and that the combination was not significant enough to lessen competition. The plaintiff did not appeal this finding. However, in the retailing aspect of

[10]Posner, *op. cit.*, p. 99.

[11]F. M. Scherer, *Industrial Market Structure and Economic Performance* (Chicago: Rand-McNally, 2d ed., 1980), p. 350.

the case, the trial court found that in 32 separate cities, Brown and Kinney combined to sell more than 20 percent of all women's shoes, and that in 31 cities, the two combined to sell more than 20 percent of the children's shoes. In 118 cities, Brown and Kinney combined to sell at least 5 percent of the shoes in one or more of the product lines defined by the Court. Was this enough to invalidate the merger? The Court determined that it was. The Court held that, in those cities where both Brown and Kinney had outlets, the merger would have an effect whereby competition "may be lessened substantially." The Court explained its decision as follows: "If a merger achieving 5% control were now approved, we might be required to approve future merger efforts by Brown's competitors seeking similar market shares." The Court feared that it might end in the transformation of a fragmented industry into an oligopoly—a result that Congress would wish to avoid.

This was the first declaration of the oligopoly theory of lessening competition in merger law. Was there evidence of merger to oligopoly—that is, merging with the specific intent of limiting competition by increasing cooperation? Historically speaking, it seems fair to say that those mergers which created US Steel embodied a strategy to do just that. They were certainly successful in the sense that US Steel acted subsequently as the conscience of the industry in seeking to stabilize price (see Chapter 9). Was there such evidence in this case? It would seem that there was none at all. On the other hand, let us assume as the Court did that the Brown-Kinney merger would be followed by a series of others, producing a retail industry with 20 firms (each with a 5% market share). Would such an industry fix prices? Perhaps, but not necessarily. How much price discipline could it exercise? That would be very difficult to predict (see Chapter 9).

We do know, don't we, that the Court was concerned about the threat that the merger would raise prices in retailing? Yes and no. In the *Brown Shoe* case, the Court expressed concern that the integrated retail chain was more efficient than independent competitors; it would have a cost advantage and could undercut them in price. Only one fact was really clear—the merger was illegal. However, it was difficult to determine whether or not the reason was that Brown-Kinney would be too competitive, or not competitive enough.

Even as a pure horizontal case, the Court could not quite make up its mind whether it was more concerned with maintaining a high level of intense price competition, or with protecting a structure of the market which contained many small, independent firms. Wasn't it reasonable for the Court to take such a position? Couldn't it assume that (1) a group of oligopolists could price to drive out small competitors (who would probably sell out to the large firms), and (2) after accomplishing that, the large predators could control price? Yes, but the group of oligopolists could never really hold price at a level above the limit-price of small businesses without inviting new entry—that is, they could control the price or they could control the structure of the market, but not both.

Does this mean that subsequent case law placed as much emphasis on preserving small, independent firms as on preventing the market to become overly concentrated? Not necessarily. In fact, in *United States vs. Philadelphia National Bank* [370 U.S. 294 (1962)] the Court chose to determine that the merger between the second and third largest banks headquartered in the Philadelphia area was illegal almost solely because it produced a substantial increase in concentration in the regional banking market. The combination of Philadelphia National Bank and Girard Trust Corn Exchange Bank would give PNB 36 percent of bank deposits and 34 percent of bank loans, and the top two banks after the merger—PNB plus First Pennsylvania Bank and Trust—would have a total of 58 percent in both loans and deposits. In applying its test of quantitative substantiality to mergers, the Court observed: "Such a test lightens the burden of proving illegality only with respect to mergers whose size makes them inherently suspect in light of Congress' design in § 7 to prevent undue concentration. Furthermore, the test is fully consonant with economic theory." Is the merger which substantially increases competition more of a threat to competition than the merger which increases efficiency and, thus, threatens the small firm? Yes it is. As Posner[12] has observed, the *PNB* precedent, unlike *Brown Shoe*, does apply a widely accepted theory—than an oligopoly market structure is more likely to foster cooperation than any other—to enforcement of § 7, and it does provide a guide for the behavior of those contemplating merger. Both the FTC and Antitrust Division adopted guidelines on just such grounds. For example, the 1982 Antitrust Division guidelines distinguish between two extremes: (1) a market would be considered unconcentrated if there was room for ten or more equal-sized firms after a merger takes place (if the H-index $\leq$ .1), and (2) a market would be considered overly concentrated if there was room for six or fewer equal-sized firms (if the H-index $\geq$ .18).[13] The Justice Department would act to halt a merger, under ordinary circumstances, only if the market would become overly concentrated as a result. Under these rules, a Brown-Kinney type of merger would be permitted to stand.

If *Philadelphia National Bank* led to the adoption of a better theory of lessening competition, did it also herald the beginning of equal consideration to be given potential benefits of a merger? Did it allow some sort of a rule of reason? No it did not. But the Court did allow for ". . . evidence clearly showing that the merger is not likely to have such anticompetitive effects. . . ." What could satisfy that requirement? There is the failing company doctrine, which suggests that an acquisition of a firm about to go out of business may be granted on the grounds that the merger would not really alter the market structure.

Economists have not all been satisfied with these small concessions. Williamson[14] has argued for an adoption of merger standards which would allow for a tradeoff between enhancement of efficiency, on the one hand, and

---

[12]Posner, *op. cit.*, p. 105.

[13]Handler, et al., *op. cit.*, p. 961.

[14]Oliver E. Williamson, "Economies as an Antitrust Defense: The Welfare Tradeoffs," *American Economic Review* 58 (March 1968), pp. 18–36.

lessening of competition, on the other. After all, it might reasonably be argued that the prime attraction of a merger to those involved is likely to be either the change in efficiency expected from it or the growth in sales expected by the acquiring firm. If there is any "lessening of competition," it would benefit all firms in the industry and not just those directly involved in the merger. Has the law taken any notice of the efficiency argument? Yes and no. While the 1982 Antitrust Division guidelines recognize that mergers can be important in improving efficiency, they seem to presume that most efficiencies can be gained without exceeding the Division's concentration limits, and they seem to suggest that only in extraordinary cases would the Justice Department even consider enhanced efficiency to be a mitigating factor for a merger that violates the guidelines. Why has the Department been so reluctant to yield on this? It has been suggested that efficiencies are speculative—they may or may not exist and their magnitude could be very difficult to determine. Perhaps so, but it is a strange position, when one considers the Antitrust Division's own speculative theories of lessening competition.

Nevertheless, the *Philadelphia National Bank* decision did establish more reasonable grounds upon which to judge a merger than the *Brown Shoe* case. Does this mean that all subsequent cases before the Court would follow the new standards? No. There was one case, *United States vs. Von's Grocery Co.* [384 U.S. 270 (1966)], which seemed to be a throwback. The majority of the Court found that the merger between the third and sixth largest retail grocers in the Los Angeles market was unlawful—almost in spite of the fact that market concentration was low, the new "giant" had but a 7.5% share of the market, the chains in the market totaled 150 in number, and single-store outlets numbered nearly four thousand. What was wrong with the merger? It was *Brown Shoe* all over again. A *rising tide* of concentration threatened the competitive status of the market and the efficiency of the chains would make survival of independent stores more difficult. The Court chose to protect the *status quo*. But in *Von's*, the minority wrote a stinging dissent. It criticized the majority (1) for ignoring legislative intent to protect competition, choosing instead to sacrifice competition in order to protect individual competitors, (2) for ignoring the past case law, and (3) for ignoring the facts in the case: "Nothing in the present record indicates that there is more than an ephemeral possibility that the effect of this merger may be substantially to lessen competition." With the strong dissent in *Von's*, the case has not seemed to act as a standard for others. In horizontal mergers, *Philadelphia National Bank* seems to serve as the present model for determining legality.

PRICE DISCRIMINATION

The price discrimination law, the amended § 2 of the Clayton Act, is the most highly controversial of the antitrust statutes—at least among economists. It is a law which is supposed to protect individual competitors and which may be applied to gain unusual results, as we have seen in the *Utah Pie* case discussed earlier in this chapter. Let us rephrase the critical language of the law as simply as possible: it is unlawful to discriminate where the effect may be substantially to lessen competition, or to injure competition. The law may permit discrimination which makes due allowance for differences in cost, however. This raises an interesting question. What is discrimination in law? As economists, we know that a seller who sets prices such that $P_i/P_j = MC_i/MC_j$ does not discriminate—a difference in price making allowance for a difference in cost is not discriminatory at all. In economics, **postage stamp** pricing—selling at uniform prices for delivery at all destinations, regardless of differences in cost—does discriminate.

In law, price discrimination means only that prices are different to different buyers. It would be possible to cite a seller for practicing illegal discrimination when the behavior was neither monopolistic nor discriminatory.

Recall that § 2 was amended by the Robinson-Patman Act in order to provide protection to small, independent retailers, in spite of the fact that the original language and intent of the law applied only to discrimination that lessened competition between the producers of goods. In the parlance of antitrust enforcement, the original law applied to the **primary line**—competition in manufacturing—in order to avoid the strategic destruction of competitors attributed to Standard Oil, but the amended law applied also to the **secondary line**—competition in the resale of goods—when the manufacturer discriminated in price.

As we have seen above, in the *Utah Pie* case, injury to competition may be found whenever a firm—in the primary or secondary line—is placed at a competitive disadvantage as the result of illegal discrimination. What precisely amounts to injury?

In *Federal Trade Commission vs. Morton Salt Co.* [334 U.S. 37 (1948)], the Supreme Court established that it was not necessary to prove injury directly. It could be inferred from the price structure itself. What was the price structure? Morton sold its top brand of table salt on the basis of quantity discounts:

QUANTITY	PRICE PER CASE
Less-than-carload purchase	$1.60
Carload purchase	1.50
5,000-case purchase in 12 mos.	1.40
50,000-case purchase in 12 mos.	1.35

While Morton claimed that the discounts were non-discriminatory since they were available to all customers, the Court found this to be a fiction since few could avail themselves of the largest discounts. The results were discriminatory and that was what the Robinson-Patman Act was designed to eliminate. Without proof of a cost basis for the price differentials, Morton Salt's discounts were unlawful, provided injury could be shown. The Court proclaimed: ". . . there is a 'reasonable possibility' that competition may be adversely affected by a practice under which manufacturers and producers sell their goods to some customers substantially cheaper than they sell like goods to the competitors of these customers." Small retail grocers would be at a disadvantage selling products in competition with the large chains, who could purchase their stock at discounts amounting to 10 percent or more. The Court declared that in such instances, injury was self-evident. That is, the size of the discount is proof of illegal discrimination—another quantitative rule.

Is the Court's logic convincing? Not necessarily. In order for a corner grocery to suffer injury, it would have to be in competition with the supermarket. If the retail food market is differentiated, there is no necessary disadvantage of having to pay a higher price for stock. Since the convenience stores typically charge higher prices—which cover higher costs—than the supermarkets, the conventions of the industry would seem to establish that the market is differentiated. Also, the competitive injury remains to be proved. Thus, in *Morton Salt*, the Supreme Court's decision may have done more to deprive the ultimate consumer of lower prices than it was actually able to do to "protect competition," as the law has defined it.

Does the *Morton Salt* decision mean that substantially all price discounts are illegal? Not necessarily. There are two statutory defenses: (1) that the discrimination is justified by cost differences, and/or (2) that discrimination is justified by a seller "meeting competition in good faith." Neither the FTC nor the courts have seen fit to give unlimited sanction to discrimination whenever justification is offered, however.

THE CLAYTON ACT IN PERSPECTIVE

The Robinson-Patman Act intends to compel price uniformity at wholesale with the hope that it will protect the opportunity of small business to compete. However, that leads to strange results: (1) a local quasi-monopolist may have a right to protection from outside competition, as in the *Utah Pie* case, or (2) a group of manufacturers may be encouraged to exchange information with one another about prices offered to buyers prior to a sale to ensure that they are meeting competition in good faith. As a general proposition, these are the sorts of things which the Sherman Act was supposed to attack, but they are given protection by § 2 of the Clayton Act. It would be unfair to suggest that the Clayton Act—in protecting competition—has completely abandoned the spirit of the Sherman Act and the objective of maintaining competition. As embodied in various case decisions, however, that attitude pervades much of the law. The law has too often sought to provide a level playing field, rather than a true process of competition—where competition is a struggle for survival, and the inefficient are weeded out. And the law has too often sought to protect the *status quo*. Where changes in the organization of industry seem to be developing, such as encountered in the *Brown Shoe* and *Von's* cases, the determination to protect the tradition of the small business may hinder progress.

True lessening of competition is a legitimate concern, and the law should be used aggressively to prevent it. The main requirement is a development of better understanding and analyses of anticompetitive behavior involving price discrimination, tying and exclusive contracts, and mergers. From the economist's point of view, the replacement of certain *per se* rules and the related concept of quantitative substantiality with a rule of reason would be a good start.

INDEXES

NAME INDEX

"A man has absolutely no other duty than this: to seek himself, to grope his own way forward, no matter whither it leads. That thought impressed itself deeply on me ... Often had I pictured the future. I had dreamed of fulfilling roles which might be destined for me, as poet perhaps or as prophet, as painter, or some such role. All that was of no account. I was not here to write, to preach, to paint, neither I nor anyone else was here for that purpose. All that was secondary. The true vocation for everyone was only to attain to self-realization. He might end as poet or as madman, as prophet or as criminal — that was not his affair; that was of no consequence in the long run. His business was to work out his own destiny, not any destiny but his own, to live for that, entirely and uninterruptedly. Everything else was merely to shun his fate, to fly back to the ideals of the masses, to adapt himself to circumstances. It was fear of his own inner being. There rose before me this new picture, terrible and sacred, suggested to me a hundred times ere this, perhaps often already expressed, but now for the first time lived. I was a throw from nature's dice box, a projection into the unknown, perhaps into something new, perhaps into the void, and my sole vocation was to let this throw-up from primeval depths work itself out in me, to feel its will in me and to make it mine. That solely!"

——— Hermann Hesse

(Demian)

THE LETTERS
OF
THOMAS
WOLFE

BOOKS BY THOMAS WOLFE

Look Homeward, Angel
Of Time and the River
From Death to Morning
The Story of a Novel
The Face of a Nation
The Web and the Rock
You Can't Go Home Again
The Hills Beyond
Letters to His Mother
A Stone, a Leaf, a Door
The Letters of Thomas Wolfe

*My whole effort for years might be described as an effort to fathom
my own design, to explore my own channels, to discover my own ways . . . .
I have at last discovered my own America, I believe I have found
my language, I think I know my way. And I shall wreak out my vision
of this life, this way, this world and this America, to the top of my bent,
to the height of my ability, but with an unswerving devotion, integrity and
purity of purpose that shall not be menaced, altered or weakened by anyone.*
FROM THE LETTER OF DECEMBER 15, 1936 TO MAXWELL E. PERKINS.

THE LETTERS OF
THOMAS
WOLFE

Collected and Edited,
with an Introduction and
Explanatory Text, by

ELIZABETH NOWELL

New York

CHARLES SCRIBNER'S SONS

ACKNOWLEDGMENTS

GRATEFUL ACKNOWLEDGMENT is here made

To William B. Wisdom for making available the major portion of Wolfe's own letters and other papers, which he purchased from the Wolfe Estate and presented to Harvard University;

To Houghton Library, Harvard University, and to the following members of its staff: William A. Jackson, William H. Bond, Carolyn E. Jakeman, Mary Shea Goulart, Jean Briggs, Mary K. Daehler, Julie P. Johnson, Marilyn S. Schultz, Winifred Cadbury Beer, Arnold Weinberger, W. B. Van Lennep, Mary J. Reardon, George W. Cottrell, Leslie M. Oliver and Thomas Mathews; also to Widener Library and Thomas Little, and to the Poetry Room of Lamont Library and Mrs. Lydia Roberts and Robert O'Clair;

To Mabel Wolfe Wheaton and Fred W. Wolfe for making available letters written by Wolfe to them and other members of the family, for permitting quotations from letters of their own, and, in general, for their tireless and devoted aid;

To the University of North Carolina Library for making available the letters and other material by or about Wolfe in its possession; also to Charles E. Rush, Director, and to Mary L. Thornton, Librarian of the North Carolina Collection;

To Charles Scribner's Sons for making available their own correspondence with Wolfe and their records concerning him; also to the following Scribner employees, past or present: Irma Wyckoff Muench, Marion Ives, W. Gilman Low, S. Elizabeth De Voy, Whitney Darrow, Robert Cross, George Merz, David Randall, Wallace Meyer, Elizabeth Youngstrom and Fidelia Stark; and to John Hall Wheelock and the late Charles Scribner III for their sympathetic encouragement and affectionate paternalism;

To the late Aline Bernstein for making available certain letters written to her by Wolfe, for providing much background material, and for giving unstintedly of her own recollections concerning Wolfe;

To Pack Memorial Public Library, Asheville, and to Myra Champion of the Reference Department for her energetic and enthusiastic help;

To the New York Public Library and to Paul North Rice, Chief of the Reference Department;

To Newberry Library, Chicago, and to Stanley Pargellis, Librarian, and Amy Nyholm, Manuscript Cataloguer;

To Mrs. Sherwood Anderson for allowing the quotations from Anderson's letters to Wolfe of April 23, 1935 and December 17 and 18, 1937, and for supplying background material. Also to R. L. Sergel;

To New York University for making available the letters of Wolfe to Homer A. Watt and the records concerning Wolfe's employment at the University; also to Thomas Clark Pollock, Oscar Cargill, LeRoy Kimball, and Jean Webster;

To the Princeton Library and to Julian Boyd, Alexander Clark, and Alexander D. Wainwright, and to Mrs. Samuel J. Lanahan, daughter of Scott Fitzgerald, for allowing the quotation from Scott Fitzgerald's letter of July 19, 1937 to Thomas Wolfe.

To Mrs. George P. Baker for allowing the editor to examine Professor Baker's own correspondence, and for supplying background material;

To the late J. M. Roberts for allowing the quotation from Mrs. Roberts' letter of May 11, 1936 to Wolfe, and of her commentary on the letters which Wolfe wrote her;

To Robert N. Linscott for permission to quote from his letters of October 22 and November 17, 1937 to Wolfe, and for his recollections of the negotiations between Wolfe and Houghton Mifflin;

To Melville H. Cane for his encouragement and advice;

To Richard S. Kennedy for allowing the editor to read his "Thomas Wolfe at Harvard" and other writings concerning Wolfe before their publication, and, in general, for making available to her the results of his own research;

And to Edward C. Aswell, Administrator C.T.A. of the Estate of Thomas Wolfe, for his loyalty and devotion, and for his self-sacrificing expenditure of patience, strength, and time.

GRATEFUL ACKNOWLEDGMENT is also made to the following for letters by Wolfe, or information concerning him, or both:

Milton A. Abernethy, George Matthew Adams, Phoebe Adams, Walter S. Adams, Mrs. Charles S. Albert, Ruth and Maxwell Aley, Elizabeth Ames, Anne W. Armstrong; *The Atlantic Monthly:* Edward Weeks and Charles W. Morton; Caroline Bancroft, LeBaron R. Barker Jr., Stringfellow Barr, Hamilton Basso, Ralph A. Beals, Gweneth P. Beam, Alice Beer, Richard C. Beer, Alladine Bell, Pincus Berner, Arthur F. Blanchard, LeGette Blythe, Charles S. Boesen, Dr. Walter Bonime, Hilda Westall Bottomley, Mrs. James Boyd, Nancy Hale Bowers, Donald Brace, E. N. Brandt, M. A. Braswell, Joseph Brewer, the late Herschel Brickell, H. Tatnall Brown Jr., John Mason Brown, Mr. and Mrs. Struthers Burt, Witter Bynner, Gwen Jassinoff Campbell, Henry Seidel Canby, Henry Fisk Carlton, William D. Carmichael Jr., Mrs. D. D. Carroll, John Carswell, Lenoir Chambers, Harry Woodburn Chase, John W.

Chase; The Chatham, and Fred F. Holsten, General Manager; Richard S. Childs, Albert Coates, William J. Cocke, Allan C. Collins, Benjamin Cone, Pascal Covici, Ray Conway, Kyle Crichton; The North Carolina Historical Society, and Christopher Crittenden, Secretary; E. A. Cross, B. Crystal and Son, Mina Curtiss, Jonathan Daniels, Alfred S. Dashiell, Edward Davison, Mrs. Clarence Day, Frederic L. Day, L. Effingham de Forest, George V. Denny Jr., Byron Dexter, Robert B. Dow, Olin Dows, Dr. A. Wilbur Duryee, Dr. Eugene F. DuBois, Max Eastman, Duncan Emrich, Morris L. Ernst, Evangelical United Brethren Church, W. Ney Evans, Mrs. Raymond C. Everitt, Mrs. Marjorie C. Fairbanks, Dr. Achilles Fang, Thomas Hornsby Ferril, Mrs. Arthur Davison Ficke, Kimball Flaccus, Dr. John G. Frothingham, A. S. Frere, Daniel Fuchs, Charles Garside; Genealogical Society of Pennsylvania and John Goodwin Herndon, Executive Director; General Alumni Association of the University of North Carolina: J. Maryon Saunders and William M. Shuford; Charles Goetz, J. Lesser Goldman, Henry Gollomb, Edward Goodnow, Mack Gorham, Mr. and Mrs. Douglas W. Gorsline, Elaine Westall Gould, Frank P. Graham, Hans J. Gottlieb, Mrs. W. W. Grant, Paul Green, Kent Roberts Greenfield, Ferris Greenslet; The John Simon Guggenheim Memorial Foundation: Henry Allan Moe, Josephine Leighton and James F. Mathias; James J. Hankins, William E. Harris, Henry M. Hart Jr., Rupert Hart-Davis; Harvard University Archives: Miss Florence K. Leetch and Clifford K. Shipton; Charles M. Hazlehurst, George W. Healy Jr., Theresa Helburn, Dorothy Kuhns Heyward, Greta Hilb, Betsy Hatch Hill, Helen Train Hilles, Clayton and Kathleen Hoagland, Mr. and Mrs. Terence Holliday; Houghton Mifflin Company: Paul Brooks and Mrs. Dorothy de Santillana; James S. Howell, Arthur Palmer Hudson, Louis C. Hunter, Katherine Gauss Jackson, Dr. A. C. Jacobson, Belinda Jelliffe, Edith Walton Jones, The Rev. Arthur Ketchum, Donald W. Keyes, Kenneth J. Kindley, Freda Kirchwey, Mary Mathews Kittinger, T. Skinner Kittrell, Blanche Knopf, Mrs. Frederick H. Koch, Charlotte Kohler, Eleanor Lake, Dr. Else K. La Roe, H. M. Ledig-Rowohlt, Dr. Russel V. Lee, Elizabeth H. Lemmon, Edgar Lentz, Dr. Isaiah Libin, G. Linnemann, Louis Lipinsky, Marian Smith Lowndes, Mabel Dodge Luhan, Ralph E. Lum, Percy Mackaye, Dr. J. Donald MacRae, George W. McCoy, Thomas McGreevy, Lura Thomas McNair, Gertrude Macy, J. Carroll Malloy, Arthur Mann, Sam Marx, Mrs. Edgar Lee Masters, Robert D. Meade, Nina Melville, Mr. and Mrs. Edward M. Miller, Fred B. Millett, Cornelius Mitchell, Nathan Mobley, Doris Moskowitz, Anne Arneill Mueller, Herbert J. Muller, James Buell Munn, Hugo Münsterberg; National Institute of Arts and Letters, Felicia Geffen, Secretary; *The New Yorker,* and Mrs. K. S. White; Marcus C. S. Noble Jr., Paul Nordhoff; Northwestern University Alumni Association, and G. Willard King, Executive Director; Donald Olyphant, Paul Palmer, Hortense Roberts Pattison, Wendell L. Patton,

Charles A. Pearce, Marjorie N. Pearson, Norman H. Pearson, Bessie Peretz, Mrs. Maxwell E. Perkins, Frances Phillips, James Poling, William T. Polk, Garland Porter, Desmond Powell, George R. Preston, Henry F. Pringle; *The Raleigh News and Observer:* Mrs. Harry W. McGalliard, Librarian; Dr. James G. Ramsay, Mr. and Mrs. Robert Raynolds, Filomena Ricciardi, Mrs. Lillian W. Richards, Mrs. Lennox Robinson, Barnet B. Ruder, Phillips Russell, Thomas Sancton, Mrs. Dorothy Greenlaw Sapp, Mrs. A. P. Saunders, Mrs. Bradley Saunders, Mark Schorer, Edgar Scott, George Seldes, Mrs. Mary Shuford, Luise M. Sillcox, Mrs. Lora French Simmons, Beverly Smith, Harrison Smith, Mrs. Stella Brewster Spear, Mrs. Catherine Brett Spencer, Corydon P. Spruill, Stanford Alumni Association, Marion L. Starkey, George M. Stephens, Mrs. Martha Dodd Stern, Mr. and Mrs. James Stevens, George Stevens, Donald Ogden Stewart, James Stokely, Edward Stone, Jesse Stuart, Mr. and Mrs. James Sykes, Nathan R. Teitel, Arthur Thornhill, William Y. Tindall, Perry Tomlin, Mrs. Susan Hyde Tonetti, Jean Toomer, William Troy, S. Marion Tucker, U. B. Publishing Estab., Inc., The late Carl Van Doren, Mark Van Doren, Willard Van Dyke, Henry Volkening, Frank K. Wallace, Mrs. George Wallace, Margaret Wallace, Nathan Wallack, The late Dixon Wecter, Mrs. Emily MacRae West, Bruce William Westall, Caroline Whiting, Mrs. Dorothy F. Wiley, Mrs. Jeannie Colvin White, Mrs. Lenore Powell Whitfield, Max Whitson, John Hay Whitney, James Southall Wilson, Ella Winter, Edgar E. Wolf, Olivia Saunders Wood; Yale School of Fine Arts: Maude K. Riley, Registrar; Stark Young.

CONTENTS

INTRODUCTION

BY ELIZABETH NOWELL

SOME of Thomas Wolfe's most interesting letters were the ones he never mailed. Among his papers, now preserved at Harvard and the University of North Carolina, there are many of these letters, written with his typical wholeheartedness and eloquence and verve, but simply never sent. For this, there was a variety of reasons. For one thing, Wolfe was usually too absorbed in his own creative world to perform the routine acts of life, such as buying envelopes or stamps or pen and ink, let alone remembering to take a letter to the mailbox. For another, his life was a series of engrossments and of interruptions: if something intervened to prevent his completion of a letter, he would seldom have the time or inclination to go back to where he had left off. For still another thing, his utter trustfulness and lack of reticence were sometimes superseded by fits of caution, or even of suspicion: he might suddenly get a hunch that what he'd written was too indiscreet, and break off in the middle of a sentence. Then he would stride up and down his room in indecision, meditatively suck his upper lip inside his upthrust lower one, rub the nape of his neck or the back of his head, or thrust his hand inside his shirt and rub his chest, and say: "Well, I don't know . . . ," and turn to other things. Sometimes, if repeatedly goaded to anger or perturbation by the matter dealt with in his letter, he finally would grab it up and finish it and mail it and be done with it. Or sometimes he would rewrite it, over and over, until the version which he mailed was only a brief and non-committal note. But he had a chronic difficulty in arriving at decisions, so for the most part, he would never "get around" to doing any more about a letter, but would simply leave it lying on his writing-table.

Also, many of his letters were not written for his correspondents as much as for himself. He maintained that "a writer writes a book in order to forget it," and he might have said the same about a letter. From his youth, he had the habit of pouring out on paper all his thoughts, emotions and experiences, either in rough-draft notes for possible creative work, in diaries or letters—and the dividing line between these different forms of writing was often very thin. This outpouring was a psychological necessity: it was a solace for his loneliness, an apologia for the errors and confusions and difficulties of his life, and a safety-valve for his intense emotional reactions. Once off his chest and down on paper, "for the record," as he called it, an emotion or experience lost its first compulsive force and could be stored away and half-forgotten. It had had its primary effect on Wolfe himself: the communication of it to other people was a different, secondary thing.

Therefore, for one or several of these reasons, his letters might lie discarded on his table, together with manuscripts, bills, timetables, empty envelopes, shopping lists and other papers, till the accumulation grew so large as to leave no room for him to write, whereupon he would grab it up and move it to his mantelpiece, bookcase, bureau, chairs, or, lacking any other space, the floor. There it would remain for weeks or months or even years, growing grimy with the coaldust of New York, Brooklyn, London, or wherever he might be, until the time came for him to move into a new apartment, or to embark upon the feverish travels which were for him both a rest and a renewal. At the last possible moment, he would plunge into the dreaded task of packing, and would jam the entire hodgepodge mass of papers into battered suitcases or the big pine packing-boxes which he got from Scribners for this purpose. From that moment on, it became part of the vast accumulation of manuscripts and other papers which was his carefully-hoarded possession, in fact the only permanent possession which he had.

In *Of Time and the River*, Wolfe describes Eugene Gant's belongings: "the notebooks, letters, books, old shoes, worn-out clothes and battered hats, the thousands of pages of manuscript that represented the accretions of . . . years—that immense and nondescript collection of past events, foredone accomplishment, and spent purposes, the very sight of which filled him with weariness and horror but which, with the huge acquisitive mania of his mother's blood, he had never been able to destroy." Wolfe himself was no string-saver like Eliza Gant, but he had a strange reluctance to throw anything away, and this increased to blind possessiveness when the thing was a piece of paper—any piece of paper—with his writing on it. And so, just as Eliza slept in a room "festooned with a pendant wilderness of cord and string," Wolfe lived and worked, for the great part of his adult life, in a succession of small two-room apartments, encumbered with his battered suitcases and huge pine packing-cases full of manuscripts and other papers. Moreover, when he travelled, he either had to take this vast accumulation with him, or had to store it with his publisher or with some trusted friend. He would complain half-humorously about it—"This business of being a vagabond writer with two tons of manuscript is not an easy one," he said. However, if any of the well-intentioned friends who were always trying to bring order to his life suggested that he dispose of anything, he would become as desperately tenacious as Eliza Gant. "Here, give me that!" he'd cry in outraged panic. "I might need it! I might find a place to use it some time!"— and back into its crate the paper would immediately go. The fact was that he considered all of his vast hoard of papers, whether manuscripts or random notes or letters, as part of "the fabric of his life" from which his books were made. "It is, so far as I am concerned, the most valuable thing I have got," he wrote in 1937 to his brother Fred. "My life is in it—years and years of work and sweating blood."

This accumulation of Wolfe's papers, now preserved in the William C. Wisdom Collection at Houghton Library, Harvard, and at the library of the University of North Carolina, has been the chief source of material for this volume of his letters. The unmailed or rough-draft letters found scattered among his manuscripts have, for the most part, been included, and when there have been various versions of a letter, the most revealing has been chosen, regardless of whether it was the one actually mailed or not. In these letters, Wolfe seldom bothered to write in any heading of place or date, or even any salutation. This data has been guessed at after a study of Wolfe's diaries and other sources of information concerning him: when it is probably correct, it has been marked with brackets: when dubious, with both brackets and question marks. The same designations have been used for words which were illegible, either because of the tearing or decomposition of the paper, or because of Wolfe's too-hasty handwriting. Words always came boiling, pouring from Wolfe's mind too fast for him to get them down on paper, and because of this, his writing was a kind of shorthand: he would form the salient letters of a word with some degree of legibility, but would indicate the less important ones by a series of hasty undulations or by simply a straight line. As a result, one cannot read his writing by deciphering it, letter by letter: one must take a bird's-eye view of it through half closed eyes, get the general gist of it, and then be guided by one's intuition of what he meant, rather than by what his hasty hen-scratches may actually seem to say.

Also included in this volume are carbon copies of many letters typed by the stenographers who worked for Wolfe during the last eight years of his life; also letters from the files of Charles Scribner's Sons, and from those of his friends and other correspondents whose names are listed gratefully at the conclusion of Acknowledgments. Wolfe's letters to his mother have been omitted, since they have already been published in a separate volume:* also his more personal letters to Aline Bernstein have been excluded from this volume at her request since it was her intention to edit them herself. Also omitted are form letters written in reply to fan mail, legal or routine business letters, letters which repeat, almost word for word, material written to other people, or letters which concern the affairs of the people to whom Wolfe was writing, rather than those of him himself. In other words, the letters published here have been selected from the huge bulk of Wolfe's

* *Thomas Wolfe's Letters to His Mother*, edited by John S. Terry, Charles Scribner's Sons, 1943.

correspondence to tell the story of his life, with the immediacy of its successive moments.

As might be expected, many of Wolfe's letters deal with the personal relationships which influenced him strongly and also caused him bitter disillusionment during a great part of his life. For instance, there are letters expressing his early adoration of and subsequent compulsion to break away from, first, Professor George P. Baker, then Aline Bernstein, and finally Maxwell Perkins. Wolfe has been accused of "turning against" these influential people in his life, and even, by one somewhat sensational writer, of "betraying" them. However, there is no law which compels a man to enroll for the same course at Harvard for more than three successive years, nor to love eternally a married woman nineteen years his senior, nor to remain forever with one publisher, especially if he feels that his general reputation and his creative talent are suffering therefrom. A calmer, more judicious description of what happened would be to say that Wolfe "turned *away*" from these people, or outgrew them and their dominating influence upon his life. But it is hard to be calm or judicious about Wolfe: his own emotional intensity tends to be reflected by everything and everyone concerned with him.

Wolfe constantly became involved in these too-constricting personal relationships and these subsequent struggles to break free from them as a result of what he called "the search for a father." "The deepest search in life, it seemed to me," he wrote in *The Story of a Novel*, "the thing that in one way or another was central to all living, was man's search to find a father, not merely the father of his flesh, nor merely the lost father of his youth, but the image of a strength and wisdom external to his need and superior to his hunger, to which the belief and power of his own life could be united." This quest of his has been attributed to various causes: to a nostalgia for the security of his early childhood which was disrupted by the partial separation of his parents; to a simple feeling of bereavement at his father's death; to a desire to escape from the domination of his mother; to a subconscious yearning for her; and to a search for the God-the-Father of a religion which he intellectually could not accept but for which he still had need. There is something to be said for all of these interpretations, but it must also be remembered that the normal impulse of all adolescents is to attach themselves to people they admire, and that Wolfe retained many adolescent traits until comparatively late in life.

At any rate, in both his letters and his novels, he repeatedly described this search, and the disillusionment it inevitably led to. "Why was it? What was this grievous lack or loss—if lack or loss it was—in his own life?" he wrote in *Of Time and the River*. "Why was it that, with his fierce, bitter and insatiate hunger for life, his quenchless thirst for warmth, joy, love, and fellowship, his constant image, which had blazed in his heart since childhood, . . . that he grew weary of people almost as soon as he met them? Why was it that he seemed to squeeze their lives dry of any warmth and interest they might have for him as one might squeeze an orange, and then was immediately filled with boredom, disgust, dreary tedium, and an impatient weariness and desire to escape so agonizing that it turned his feeling almost into hatred? Why was it that his spirit was now filled with this furious unrest and exasperation against people because none of them seemed as good as they should be? Where did it come from—this improvable and yet unshakable conviction that grew stronger with every rebuff and disappointment—that the enchanted world was here around us ready to our hand the moment that we chose to take it for our own, and that the impossible magic in life of which he dreamed, for which he thirsted, had been denied us not because it was a phantom of desire, but because men had been too base and weak to take what was their own?"

Occasionally he would find a man or woman, such as Professor Baker, Mrs. Bernstein or Maxwell Perkins, who was remarkable enough to withstand this first onslaught of his scrutiny, and to seem to be a fitting "image of strength and wisdom . . . to which the belief and power of his own life could be united." Then he would be swept up on a great surge of strength and joy and certitude: he would literally idolize his friend, would proclaim his or her excellence to all the world, and would lay the entire conduct of his life into his hands, or hers, repeating, like an incantation: "If you'll just stand by me, everything will be all right." However, he could never rest content till he had probed deep into a person's character and decided what the very essence of it was: he seemed always to be searching for a flaw, although hoping fervently that he would fail to find one. But the men and women whom he worshipped were only human, after all, and when he finally did find faults in them, he felt a bitter disillusionment and a sense of having been betrayed. "I see every wart and sore upon them," he wrote in an unpublished passage from *Of Time and the River*, "every meanness, pettiness, and triviality . . . and I hate these mutilations in them ten times more cruelly and bitterly than if I saw them in people that I did not know, or cared nothing for."

Then would begin the period of his trying to break away which caused so many wounded feelings. Because of his emotional intensity, Wolfe could not drift casually away from an outworn friendship, as an ordinary person does. Instead, he felt a moral compunction to explain the causes of his disillusionment to his defective friend. Sometimes, as with Professor Baker, he merely wrote out his complaint in letters which he never mailed: sometimes, as with Mrs. Bernstein, he delivered it face to face in scenes of violent recrimination: sometimes, as with Maxwell Perkins, he both wrote and talked about it, endlessly, until the latter cried out in exasperation: "If you have to leave, go ahead and *leave,* but for Heaven's sake, don't talk about it any more!"

However, in spite of all these endless explanations and accusals, Wolfe's friends, as for instance Mrs. Bernstein and Maxwell Perkins, were usually thrown into a state of bewilderment and shock by his decision to break free from them. They were still devoted to him, and after constant contact with his vitality, emotion, humor, his enormous talent and his basic goodness and nobility, the prospect of life without him seemed intolerably drab and thin. But if they tried to cling to him, he would be overcome by a sort of claustrophobia of friendship and "a desire to escape so agonizing that it turned his feeling almost into hatred." To quote his favorite words from Martin Luther, he had to leave them, he "could not do otherwise." It was not until he had achieved his freedom from these too-close relationships that they could be reduced to any sort of norm, the first excessive hero-worship and the subsequent too-violent disillusionment balanced evenly against each other, and a final statement made of detached, nostalgic gratitude and love.

For stronger than "the search for a father" and entirely superseding it in the last year of his life, was Wolfe's need to grow, and to grow in complete freedom. "My life, more than that of anyone I know, has taken on the form of growth," he wrote in his "Credo" at the conclusion of *You Can't Go Home Again*. And again, in his letter of December 15, 1936, to Perkins: "My whole effort for years might be described as an effort to fathom my own design, to explore my own channels, to discover my own ways. In these respects, in an effort to help me to discover, to better use, these means, I was striving to apprehend and make my own, you gave me the most generous, the most painstaking, the most valuable help. . . . As for another kind of help—a help that would attempt to shape my purpose or define for me my own direction—I not only do not need that sort of help but if I found that it had in any way invaded the unity of my purpose, or was trying in any fundamental way to modify or alter the direction of my creative life—the way in which it seems to me it ought and has to go—I should repulse it as an enemy, I should fight it and oppose it with every energy of my life, because I feel so strongly that it is the final and unpardonable intrusion upon the one thing in an artist's life that must be held and kept inviolable. . . . I have at last discovered my own America, I believe I have found the language, I think I know my way. And I shall wreak out my vision of this life, this way, this world and this America, to the top of my bent, to the height of my ability, but with an unswerving devotion, integrity and purity of purpose that shall not be menaced, altered or weakened by anyone."

This collection of Wolfe's letters tells, in his own words, the story of his growth and his discoveries. The tragedy, of course, is that the story is unfinished—that his death at the age of thirty-seven has left us only to speculate on what he might have come to, had he lived.

THE LETTERS
OF
THOMAS WOLFE

I

CHILDHOOD AND CHAPEL HILL
1908–1920

The earliest existing letters written by Wolfe are to his eldest sister, Effie, who had married Fred W. Gambrell and moved to Anderson, S.C.

To EFFIE WOLFE GAMBRELL

Asheville, N.C.
October 23, 1908

Dear Effie:

I am sorry to hear you are sick.

Mabel [1] went to Anderson this morning.

It has been raining here for two or three days.

I got your letter the other day. If you don't get any better, write us and we will come down to see you. I am getting off to school in time every morning, and I am never late.

I want to see you very much.

We have got the house cleaned fine down at 92. [2]

But we can't get papa to go. But mama says soon as it stops raining she is going to move us down there any way.

I had better close my letter now.

It is time for me to go to bed.

Good by,

Your little brother,

Tell Fred [3] I will write him a letter next time.

---

[1] Mabel Wolfe, now Mrs. Ralph H. Wheaton, Wolfe's other sister.

[2] 92 Woodfin Street, Asheville, where Wolfe was born. In 1906, Mrs. Wolfe had bought her boarding-house, The Old Kentucky Home, at 48 Spruce Street, with the result that the children lived sometimes at one house, sometimes at the other.

[3] Fred Gambrell.

To EFFIE WOLFE GAMBRELL

Old Kentucky Home
Mrs. Julia E. Wolfe
Owner and Propr.
No 48 Spruce Street
Asheville, N.C.

May 16, 1909

Dear Effie:

How are you feeling?

I am selling Post [1] and won a prize last month and think i am going to win one this month. I sold 61 Post this week.

Fred is going to give the boys who sell the most Post this week 50 cents, but i ain't in it, if i was i would beat them all to pieces. So he don't want me in it. The boys would not feel like working if I beet them.

We are going to have a pretty good crop of fruit this year. We will get out of school in two or three weeks.

Good by,
Your brother

The following letter to Ralph H. Wheaton, the husband of Mabel Wolfe Wheaton, was written by Wolfe just before he entered the University of North Carolina. At this time Wheaton was a salesman for the National Cash Register Company with an office in Raleigh, N.C. He had offered to drive Wolfe out to the University at Chapel Hill and to help him enroll there.

To RALPH H. WHEATON

48 Spruce Street
Asheville, N.C.

September 10, 1916

Dear Ralph:

Mabel received your telegram saying you would meet me Tuesday. I realize this is an imposition on you, but I think you could better arrange matters at Chapel Hill than I, that is, if it is possible for you to leave your work. I arrived at my decision to attend our state university last Wednesday night. Perhaps I should say *forced* instead of arrived. For that was

---

[1] Wolfe was selling the *Saturday Evening Post* on the streets of Asheville under the direction of his brother, Fred W. Wolfe, who held the local agency for it.

what it amounted to. For I had held out for the University of Virginia in spite of the family's protests. But when no reply came from the University of Virginia, I consented to go to Carolina. Two days later a letter did come from Virginia telling me to come on. However, it was too late. But, nevertheless, Carolina is a good school, and perhaps everything is for the best. Will at least be near you and Mabel. If it is possible for me to connect with a train at University Junction, I think that would be best. However, do as you judge right. Will be on the lookout for you at University Junction, which is, I believe, a few miles from Durham. Will leave here Tuesday morning at 8:00. Expect to reach Durham about 5:30. Mabel will not be on until Saturday.

As to the news, there is none of importance. All the home folks are well. The town is emptying itself of summer visitors fast. Monday will see nearly everybody gone from this house. Hope you are well and enjoying a good business.

To FRED W. WOLFE

[Chapel Hill, N.C.]
[September, 1916]

Dear Fred:

I wrote you a letter a while ago. Received your other postal. I was unable to know where you were living.[1] I wrote home and just received your postal, with a notation on top of it. You mentioned money matters in your postal. Please don't worry about it and take your own time as I have plenty.

Papa has been most kind in regards to everything. I have made only one mistake so far. Am located at ——'s, an Asheville lady. The food is splendid and costs $15 a month. This is cheap enough, as cheap as may be had in town, although Swain Hall, run by University costs only $12.50 a month. I room also at ——. This is where I am being "stuck." My half of the room costs me $7.50 a month which is exorbitant. The University Dorm. costs only $3. Papa sent me a check soon after my arrival and advised me to pay board and room two months in advance. If I'm held up here until November, I will then seek cheaper quarters. Have met all my "profs" and they are fine fellows. I hope I will do well in all my studies and my guess is I'll have to "bone" on math.

Have met and made many friends. I have enrolled a week ago with a frat whose membership is 137.[2] It's the custom of older members of this

---

[1] Wolfe's brother Fred was working in Dayton, Ohio at this time.

[2] The Dialectic Literary Society, which was really not a fraternity at all. In *Look*

society to put the freshmen through a mock initiation in which they try to get their "goats." They have instruments to shave our heads, etc. After the poor freshman is frightened half out of his wits some "soph" calls on him for a speech. I was the first called on. The society hall is lined with the pictures of the distinguished men once belonging to this society. The portrait of Zeb Vance hangs right over the rostrum. In my little talk I told " 'em" I was both happy and proud to be in such distinguished company. I ended by telling " 'em" I hoped they would have the pleasure some day of seeing my picture hang beside Zeb Vance's.

Just address mail c/o University Post Office, Chapel Hill and I'll get it.

The following letter to James Holly Hanford, a professor of English at the University of North Carolina, indicates that Wolfe's desire to go to a larger and more distant college than the University of North Carolina had persisted through his freshman year. In a previous letter, now lost, he had evidently asked Professor Hanford to recommend him to Princeton, which Professor Hanford had agreed to do. Wolfe's father refused to let him make the transfer, however, and he remained at the University of North Carolina for the full four years' course.

To JAMES HOLLY HANFORD

92 Woodfin Street
Asheville, N. C.
August 15, 1917

Dear Professor Hanford:

I received your letter yesterday and I can't begin to tell you how much your writing it is appreciated. But that is what I expected you to do. Not "feeding you taffy," sir, but I knew that you would direct me impartially as "a friend and not as a professor." That is why I wrote you instead of anyone else.

I have not brought the matter before Father as yet. I am collecting my forces in order to deliver a crushing blow. My sister [1] has enlisted in my brigade and her influence will count. Have two letters from the registrar at Princeton and when I receive a third in a few days, I will make the attack. If I am repelled it will not be due to defective generalship. But if Father

---

Homeward, Angel, Wolfe describes this incident with embarrassment: "He was the greenest of all green freshman, past and present: he had . . . been guilty of the inexcusable blunder of making a speech of acceptance on his election, with fifty others, to the literary society."

[1] Mabel Wolfe Wheaton.

should refuse, nevertheless, a beginning will have been made and, I have no doubt, I will be able to finish my last two years at Princeton—a proceeding upon which I am now decided.

I do not know if what you said in the letter concerning myself is true. I hope so and I have tried to be a boy of "honor and ideals." At any rate, it's not so very hard to go straight as long as you have friends who say these things. I sincerely hope the boy will one day become a man who is a man, and thereby justify the faith of his friends.

I have just returned from the depot. A crowd of young officers from the camp at Oglethorpe came in this morning. They were a fine looking set of men. Among them I saw "Nemo" Coleman—last year's football manager, Leicester Chapman, who, as you remember was in English I last fall, and "Cy" Parker, the cheer leader.[2] I believe the old University, if personified, would feel proud of her sons who have stood up to their work so well. I am a little envious and wish that I were older.

By the way, my uncle, Mr. Henry A. Westall,[3] lives in Boston. His residence is in one of the suburbs, I think. He is Harvard, '79, having graduated for the ministry, but went into real estate business because it paid better. He is very eccentric but interesting. If you have the time or the inclination, look him up.

I will write you shortly and inform you how matters turn out. If I get to go, I suppose poor old U.N.C. will in time manage to lift its drooping head and bear up under its loss. If I don't go, I'll be back next year and work like fury.

Wolfe's brother Ben has been immortalized in Look Homeward, Angel. *The following letter to him was written soon after he had taken his father to Johns Hopkins Hospital for treatment of the cancer which caused Mr. Wolfe's death in 1922.*

To BENJAMIN H. WOLFE

Chapel Hill, N.C.
February 18, 1918

Dear Ben:

I have intended writing you for some time but exams have kept me busy until recently and even now various activities are taking up my

[2] James M. Coleman and Samuel I. Parker were members of the Class of 1917 at the University of North Carolina: Leicester Chapman was a member of the Class of 1918 but left the University to enlist in 1917.
[3] Henry A. Westall was Mrs. Wolfe's brother.

time. I hope you enjoyed your stay in Baltimore and that you left Papa progressing nicely. It is indeed fortunate that he was persuaded to go and the whole outlook is much more cheerful now.

I am happy to say that my year so far has been most successful (I averaged 91% in work) and I look forward to an exceedingly busy Spring. I go out to-morrow for track and will try to make the quarter mile. I have only one competitor and he has the advantage of having had more experience. However, I have the strides on him and if I can get away at the beginning I see no reason why I shouldn't make the team and perhaps my letter this spring. This quarter mile is a very devil of a race. It is just long enough to be tiresome and just short enough to keep you sprinting all the way. If I don't make it, the other fellow's going to know he's not had any evening stroll. I've found out one thing down here that ought to be invaluable to me some day when I get out and root for the shining shekels. You don't get anything handed to you on a silver platter. The man that is most popular and the best-liked is the man that goes out and takes what he wants by his own efforts.

I have received a card and a letter from Fred. He seems a little raw just now but I'm sure he's going to like it immensely when he gets more accustomed to surroundings. Think he did the wisest thing. He didn't have a chance in the army.[1]

They're giving us blazes in this military stuff. Military engineering, bomb throwing, trench warfare, bayonet fighting are a few of the things we are doing. By the way, we're going to have a big summer camp at Bingham. Quite a number have signed up already.

I believe you mentioned Christmas that you had an old suit of clothes you were not using. Of course, I wear my uniform on drill days, but Tuesday, Thursday and Saturday afternoons we have no drill. Most of my stuff is getting frayed except the new suit, so if you don't need this particular suit I would be more than thankful to get it. But please don't send it if you need it at all.

Write and let me know how you are getting on and I will send you all the news down here. I hope you are in good health and enjoying a good business.

The following letter from Wolfe to his father was written on a page of the March, 1918, issue of The University of North Carolina Magazine, *in which appeared a poem by Wolfe called "The Challenge" and a story by him called "A Cullenden of Virginia." In a speech made at Purdue University in May, 1938, Wolfe says that these were his first creative efforts to be published.*

[1] Fred Wolfe had enlisted in the navy.

To WILLIAM OLIVER WOLFE

[Chapel Hill, N.C.]
Wednesday, March 27, [1918]
2:00 P.M.

Dear Father:

I have just received your letter and your check for $40.00. Please receive my thanks. I was initiated into the Pi Kappa Phi Fraternity Monday night after taking a 12 mile march in the afternoon. It is the greatest thing I ever did and will mean much.

Through my work for the magazine *Tar Heel* [1] I have just received a bid from Sigma Upsilon, the great national literary fraternity. See Hiden Ramsey [2] and he'll tell you about it. The expense is small and it is a big honor to belong to it, only about 15 members in school.

Will write later.

Wolfe's letter of May 17, 1920, to Lora French was written one month before his graduation from the University of North Carolina. Miss French, now Mrs. Clarence R. Simmons, had met Wolfe when she spent a few weeks in Asheville during the summer of 1919, and had soon afterwards moved to Los Angeles.

To LORA FRENCH

Chapel Hill
Monday, May 17, 1920.

My Dear Lora:

. . . I haven't been working a "hold out" game on you, waiting for you to write, but I wanted some definite information as to your residence. Hereafter I'll communicate direct to Los Angeles. Do you mean to say that you have received only *one* issue of the *Tar Heel* and *three* of the *Baby?* [1] Something must be sadly amiss and I'll go gunning for my business manager immediately. I'm sending you a copy of our latest *Tar Baby*—the

[1] The student paper at the University of North Carolina. Wolfe became managing editor of it in his junior year (1918–1919), and editor-in-chief in his senior year (1919–1920).

[2] The general manager of *The Asheville Citizen and Times*.

[1] *The Tar Baby*, the undergraduates' humorous magazine at the University of North Carolina. Wolfe was Guest Editor of the April 10, 1920, issue which burlesqued the *Raleigh News and Observer*.

burlesque on the *Raleigh News and Observer,* Josephus Daniels' paper. Jo is an old Carolina man and he took it with a grin, although we treated him rough at times. I edited this issue and, in fact, wrote most of the stuff. The *News and Observer* gave us a good write-up in its Sunday edition, which I'm sending you. Tar Baby, Inc. wants me back next year to edit the issues. May accept. Graduate in another month.

I hate to leave this place. It's mighty hard. It's the oldest of the state universities and there's an atmosphere here that's fine and good. Other universities have larger student bodies and bigger and finer buildings, but in Spring there are none, I know, so wonderful by half. I saw old Carolina men home Christmas who are doing graduate work at Yale, Harvard and Columbia. It would seem that they would forget the old brown buildings in more splendid surroundings, but it was always the same reply: "There's no place on earth can equal Carolina." That's why I hate to leave this big, fine place.

The seniors are going to have a glorious time Commencement. One of our features will be a "Dinner Dance." We'll have girls down and between courses pull off a cabaret stunt between the tables. Also a program of the Playmakers and a Senior Stunt, which I'm working up at present.

I've read about the Los Angeles moving picture craze from such infallible authorities as the *Saturday Evening Post* and others, but this is my first experience with a young lady who has been hypnotized or, shall I say, Los Angelized? Don't sign a contract, please, for less than a thousand a week. After reading the *Post,* I am sure that even the bathing girls get that much.

It's good to know that you've missed me. I miss you also, and I know that this summer will only bring back the memory of the short days I was with you in Asheville. I can only hope that time and space (some three thousand miles of it, I believe) will be generous to me and that we will soon meet on that beautiful shore (Los Angeles, of course, if it's on the shore; if not we'll move the ocean).

II

HARVARD AND THE 47 WORKSHOP

1920–1923

The following letter, giving Wolfe's first impressions of Harvard, was written to Professor Frederick H. Koch, the founder and director of The Carolina Playmakers at the University of North Carolina, under whom Wolfe had begun his career as a dramatist, and on whose recommendation he had enrolled in Professor George Pierce Baker's English 47 at Harvard.

To FREDERICK H. KOCH

[48 Buckingham Road]
Cambridge
Friday, Nov. 26, 1920

Dear Prof:

I wonder if you'll accept a letter written on the leaves of a note book and with a pencil, the ink having fled from my pen. When I get through I'll go back and write a gloss (à la Coleridge) with suitable annotations, in the margin. Out of the chaos of interesting things that come crowding forward to be told, all of which, I know, won't go into one letter, I want to tell you first of the joy with which I received news of your glorious success in the Raleigh pageant.[1] Coates [2] and I are waiting now for the book which, like the production, is said to be "a thing of beauty and a joy forever." I hope you don't get a foot taller and with a softly modulated accent tell the world that "I'm a creative artist"—the last being quoted from some of my "Neat Particular" "ass"-ociates in English 47. And now

[1] *Raleigh, the Shepherd of the Ocean,* a pageant drama written by Professor Koch for the Tercentenary of Sir Walter Raleigh, was produced on October 19, 20, and 21, 1920, at the amphitheatre of Baseball Park, Raleigh, N.C. It was published in 1920 by the North Carolina Historical Commission.

[2] Albert Coates, a graduate of the University of North Carolina, was studying at the Harvard Law School and had a room at 48 Buckingham Road, as did Wolfe.

to tell you about Eng. 47, Prof. And about Mr. Baker who is one of the best friends you have. He is enthusiastic about you and the work you're doing (I had a half-hour conference with him this morning) and he has suggested putting on some of the plays you sent him. He likes my "Buck Gavin" and says it is a more finished piece of work than my "Third Night," [3] which he said absorbed him at first but lost in interest as he went on.

I'm happy since my talk with him this morning, Prof, because I don't feel quite so useless. I wrote a letter to Horace [4] the other day when I was in a gloom that covered me "deep as the pit from pole to pole" but, with startling swiftness, my attitude has changed again. And the reason, to wit: Mr. Baker's first task for the budding Pineros is to put them to work on an adaptation of a current short story. My first attempt was rotten; I knew it when I handed it in. It followed the story up bit by bit and ended with many tears in the last scene where the father conveniently dies of heart failure offstage. I was completely lost at first, Prof; didn't know where to turn. My associates in this class (there are a dozen of us) were mature men, eight, ten and in one case twenty years older than I am. When they criticize, it is as follows: "Sir Arthur Pinero takes that scene and treats it with *consummate art.*" or "The remarkable literary charm of this play seduces my admiration." Prof, so help me, God, these are direct quotations. Imagine a raw Tar Heel who, with native simplicity has been accustomed to wade into a play (at Chapel Hill) with "that's great stuff" or "rotten"—simple and concise. Why, one man the other day made a criticism of a play as follows: "That situation seems to be a perfect illustration of the Freudian complex"; and it gladdened me when Mr. Baker, the most courteous of men under very trying conditions, replied: "I don't know about the Freudian complex; what we are discussing now are the simple human values of this play." At any rate, you understand the atmosphere, and they are all sincere earnest people at that, but with that blasé sophistication that seems typical of Harvard.

At any rate, Prof, I went through hours of bitterness and self-condemnation, finally drawing into myself and trying to forget the others. On the revision of my adaptation I cut loose from the story and made my own play, which now is not at all like the story. Mr. Baker read it the other morning and likes it. He says I've struck a keynote greater than that the short story author thought of, and that I have the beginnings of one of those curious comic tragedies. In the meantime, Prof, I'm at work on my

[3] Professor Koch had sent to Professor Baker the manuscripts of Wolfe's two plays which had been produced by the Carolina Playmakers: *The Return of Buck Gavin* and *The Third Night.*

[4] Professor Horace Williams, head of the Department of Philosophy at the University of North Carolina.

original one act play [5] and I'm exalted—that's all—pure exaltation. It's a North Carolina play and, Prof, I believe I've struck gold, pure gold. Of course it may turn out rotten in Mr. B's estimation, but now I think I've got something. He asked me this morning what kind of plays I wanted to write and I told him promptly that what I didn't want to write were these blasé, high society dramas (à la Oscar Wilde) in which divers wise epigrams are flourished about the differences between man and woman, etc. I hit the bullseye, for he " 'gins to be aweary of the puns" and tells me he has too many "high society" plays now by authors who know nothing of high society. Prof, I'm going to play fair with myself and I'll make a go of it, I think. This thing has seized me with a deathlike clutch, with few friends to take my time away, with no more delightful "bull sessions," I have turned to work and I'm really working, Prof. I'm reading voraciously in the drama, stocking up with materials the same as a carpenter carries a mouthful of nails: I am studying plays, past and present, and the technique of these plays, emphasis, suspense, clearness, plot, proportion and all the rest, and I've come to realize that this doctrine of divine inspiration is as damnable as that of the divine right of kings. Coleridge, certainly one of the most inspired imaginatively of the poets, did more research work for "The Ancient Mariner" than does the average chemist in writing a book. I had almost got to the point of sneering at the Facts, and laughing at those who grubbed for them as little worms, and of course this is true if you submerge in a sea of Facts. But to paraphrase Kipling, "If you can dig and not make Facts your master, You'll get along in writing beaucoup faster." This is rotten, I know, but I couldn't resist it.

But when all's said and done, Prof, what you said last year is pretty true: "Harvard teaches you to appreciate the Hill more." This is a great place, no denying it, but Chapel Hill holds much that Harvard doesn't. Vice versa, also. You can get what you want if you want it: if you don't, nobody worries. In the graduate schools one finds real men fit to be classed with our Tar Heels on the Hill. As to that species of knickerbockered, golf-stockinged, Norfolk-jacketed, lisping ass that is turned out with machine-like regularity by the college, the species for which Harvard receives much odium everywhere now—to those I say: "Why don't you get a college education instead of coming to Harvard?"

Prof, I've hurled myself at this letter viciously to relieve myself, and if you can read it, you have one on me. I realize that, to a certain measure, the fair name of the Carolina Playmakers at Fair Harvard rests with me, and the Carolina type of play is what I'm going on with. But, Prof, realize that Mr. Baker welcomes this, he wants me to do it, he sincerely admires you and your work, and he says your plays are remarkable. The man is

[5] *The Mountains.*

tired, I'm sure from what he said this morning, of an excess of light froth—a class of stuff the embryos around here dote on.

For heaven's sake, what do we go to the theatre for? I go to be lifted out and away, and if that sensation leaves as soon as the curtain falls I don't think the play worth a single curse. It's a species of fairyland, I think, this theatre, and I want fairyland to last with me even after the players have passed off the stage. I don't think we go to see life as it is in all its minutiae —to h— with all the "realists" as they style themselves (pardon my French)—if a play hasn't some lifting quality besides bare, sordid realism, then it becomes nothing but a photograph of life, and what place has a photograph in art? I don't mean that it has to end happily, or that you have to use any cheap trick at all to please your audience, but just as "Macbeth" and "Oedipus the King" become something bigger than men, they become monuments of Gigantic Ideas—so should the play become something bigger and finer than drab, sordid, commonplace, everyday life. And in spite of all our pathetic optimism, Prof, that's just what everyday life is—drab, sordid, and commonplace. And I'm not posing as one who has lived and suffered either. At any rate, that's my ideal for the theatre—it lifts you up just as a great picture lifts you. A great landscape artist one time remarked when looking at a beautiful sunset that "it was a pretty good imitation, but you should see one of mine." Voilà—there you are, Prof. And I'm going to keep that in mind. Write and let me know what you think about it.

This has been a feverish, wild letter, hasn't it? I've written at terrible speed, as you've found to your sorrow, I suppose, and for startling beginnings and tame endings, my epistle has all the qualities of that amazing grammatical construction: "The man threw the horse over the fence some hay"! I groan for Chapel Hill at times—many times—but I know my bolt there is shot. I got away at the right time. Here, as there, I am a Carolina Man, learning with sorrow to-day that Va. beat us. It's the greatest place in the world, Prof. That sums up all my findings.

Mr. Baker took me into his course even before you sent the plays, solely because I had worked under you. I use "work" here with poetic license.

Please forgive my laxness in writing—I've really worked hard—and write me a good letter. Give my regards to the Class, tell them I'm a sadder, and I hope wiser man, and that I no longer wade in with glittering eye and inflated nostrils to flay the quivering brain-child of some hopeful author. I have mellowed and grown sweet under adversity—a great example of chastened pride. But tell them—for I can even now see the eagerness on their bright young faces when hearing of me—that my spirit is high, my head, though "bloody is unbowed," and though a tadpole with 6000 others,

I cannot refrain from 'aving 'opes. And if they bear up bravely under this, give them, the male members, my continued felicitations.

Love and Kisses for the Co-eds. (More Power to 'Em.)

Your whilom loafer,

The first and last parts of the following letter have been lost, but it was evidently written to Frank C. Wolfe, Wolfe's eldest brother, in the early summer of 1921.

To FRANK C. WOLFE

[Cambridge, Mass]

[Early Summer, 1921]

. . . Personally I'm always ready to root for the spectacular, the running, twisting slashing teams,—but Harvard is out to win.

All that has been said of *some* Harvard under-graduates is true and more, but I wish you could have been here with me Commencement, and seen the old grads back to their class reunions. They were the finest looking group of men I ever saw. The real thing. Something must happen to them after they leave.

I suppose Asheville is again overrun with pretty girls. They're all right if you can just look at them without having to talk to them, but when they open their mouths all is lost. I am convinced that the average girl around Asheville (aged 20 or over) has the brain capacity of a fourteen year old child.

There's one thing we're deadly afraid of in North Carolina and that is appearing highbrow. If you use a word of more than one syllable around an Asheville girl she will roll her eyes, look up to heaven and say, "Look it up in the dictionary." If you happen to know the year Columbus discovered America you're a bookworm. This is slightly exaggerated but it's true in its essence.

And the hell of it is that the damn-fool boys pander to the girls, deal with them in their own silly childish talk and in time become empty vessels themselves. Consider what a vacant life young people around Asheville lead. Five dances a week throughout the summer at night and Patton Ave. all day. What imbecilic slop this is! I don't want to make professors out of everyone but it is possible to mix a certain amount of purpose and pleasure in life and be better for it.

If I get home and use a new word and the boys look at each other and wink and say, "Aha—Harvard did that," I'll tell them to go to hell. The biggest crime one can commit is to check their own development because of some weak-kneed desire to appear as vain and shallow as the rest.

We've boasted about our Southern beauty long enough. It's foolish! There are pretty girls everywhere, thousands of them here who prove it is possible to have brains as well as beauty. I am not speaking of education but of intelligence—an entirely different matter. Shop girls here are more intelligent, I believe, than most Southern girls. They have definite ideas and show they have done some thinking for themselves. Personally I don't believe the presence of brains in a female detracts from her charm although many down South fear it more than they do a double chin.

Every town has a definite personality. I sometimes wonder if that little town of Asheville has a soul or if it is like its young people, shallow, vain, inconsequential. There's a good play in Asheville—a play of a town which never had the ordinary, healthy, industrial life a town ought to have but instead dressed itself up in fine streets and stuck hotels in its hair in order to vamp the tourist populace. There's a good play in the boy who lets the town vamp him, who sees the rich tourists and their mode of life and thinks he must live that way, who gets a job without enthusiasm or ambition in order to pay his way around at night and who finally settles down a dull, plodding, month-to-month fellow till he dies. The town got him. The octopus drew him up. It sucked away his youth, hope, ideals, ambition and left a clean shirt front. You and I have seen that fellow—dozens of times. I believe there's a play there. There's a play in everything that lives if we only had the power to extract it. . . .

To FRED W. WOLFE

42 Kirkland Street
Cambridge, Mass.
[July, 1921]

Dear Fred:

. . . My transatlantic steamer plans fell flat due mainly to the fact that employment is given out mostly at the New York offices of the steamship lines operating from here.[1] I wish you could have come to Mass. Tech for your summer course [2] . . . At any rate Atlanta will prove no hotter than Bean Town which, despite its northerly location, is quite an inferno in summer. It's the humidity more than the heat, the humidity that doesn't

---

[1] Wolfe had considered trying to work his way across the Atlantic on a steamer during summer vacation, but had finally enrolled in Summer School instead.

[2] Fred Wolfe had enrolled for a summer course at Georgia School of Technology.

allow the sweat to evaporate and keeps one sticky and uncomfortable. You should hear our Uncle Henry curse Yankee weather, Yankee honesty and everything Yankee in general.

He and Aunt Laura [3] are a great pair; they are giving me materials for a great play which I shall write some day. Each waits till the other is out of the room and then asks if you've noticed how childish he (or she) is getting. Isn't that a pure, 100% cross-section of human nature for you? They have been very kind to me, however, although Aunt Laura spends a great part of the time in telling me what a fearful handicap it is to be born a Westall, how I must watch myself at every point to keep the family traits from cropping out, and what an unbalanced, lopsided clan we are in general.

I got a card from Frank when he was home. About all he said [was] nerves and pus under a tooth. . . . I don't see why nature doesn't fit us with durable cast iron teeth and do away with all this damned business of cavities, nerves, pains, aches, which haunt us from the cradle to the grave.

I hope you won't wait as long to answer this as I did to answer yours. Give my kindest regard to all my friends who inquire about me.

To WILLIAM OLIVER WOLFE

[Cambridge, Mass.]

[August, 1921]

Dear Papa:

I got your letter along with Mama's this morning, and coming in the midst of my lonesomeness, it was thrice welcome. I put in five weeks of hard study in the Summer School which closed August 13, and although I have heard nothing yet as to my grade I am reasonably certain it is high—a B plus at any rate.

Do not think I feel no call from home, that I have no desire to go back to see my people and my home town. That call has been loud and long ever since Christmas, and this summer when my friends were gone and I was alone here in a big city—and, as you know, even the solitude of a desert is companionship when compared with the loneliness of a city—during this time in particular have I thought of you all and wanted to see you. My friends and you and Mama have had such faith in me that you can hardly realize how powerful the will within me is to justify your faith: so strong is that will that I believe I would use the last rasping breath. . . .

[THE LETTER BREAKS OFF HERE, OR THE REMAINDER OF IT HAS BEEN LOST]

[3] Mr. and Mrs. Henry A. Westall.

The following letter was written in answer to one from Margaret Roberts who, with her husband, J. M. Roberts, had conducted The North State School in Asheville where Wolfe had been a pupil from 1912–1916. Mrs. Roberts had written Wolfe to ask if he would recommend her for a teaching position to Frank Wells, Superintendent of Schools in Asheville. Wolfe's letter to Wells is chiefly a repetition of what he wrote to Mrs. Roberts, and has therefore been omitted here.

To MARGARET ROBERTS

Cambridge, Mass.

Sept. 2, 1921

Dear Mrs. Roberts:

Your letter finally came a day or two ago and I am getting a glowing testimonial under way to Mr. Wells. *Glowing* I say, and the term is mild: if I didn't restrain my leaping pen it would be a red hot paean. And I find the difficulty in writing such a letter is the tempering it down to a point where the man won't think you hired me. I know you were joking when you asked me if I would do this as a *favor* but I wonder if you really have any idea what a joy and a privilege and an honor I esteem it. I only fear I may hurt your own cause by my own fervor. Under any condition I fear the letter will have an over-eulogistic flavor to one who doesn't know me—or you. I am therefore making the letter informal, as I know Mr. Wells slightly, for I feel I will better create the impression of utter earnestness I am so desirous of creating.

But I shall certainly tell him that I have had only three great teachers [1] in my short but eventful life and that you are one of these. Harvard, fine as it is, has as yet been unable to submit any candidates to my own Hall of Fame though I hope within another year to nominate and elect a fourth.

This 'point system' of selecting teachers is a relic of barbarism—when I compare you not only in actual culture but in the more vital quality of stimulating and inspiring the love of fine and beautiful literature in the heart and mind and soul [of] that boy lucky enough to claim you for a teacher (my sentence is becoming attenuated; I'll have to get a fresh breath)—when I compare you in these respects to the average college grad, comparisons, as Mrs. Malaprop says, become odorous.

Mrs. Roberts, there's no estimating the influence you've had on me and the whole course of my life; what's done is done, each day causes me

[1] The other two were Horace Williams, head of the Department of Philosophy, and Edwin Greenlaw, head of the Department of English, at the University of North Carolina.

to see more plainly how tremendous an influence that was, and I know I shall be even more emphatic on this score the last day of my life than I am now.

Your friendship, and that of Mr. Roberts, and your faith and hope in me, one of the most cherished possessions of my life, causes me ghastly suffering at times when I doubt myself and wonder if you are fooled in me. Yes, I have actually writhed in my sheets in the dead dark night thinking of this and this alone. It has been my yoke and will. . . .

It goads me to fury to hear the cant and the clap-trap daily bandied about which would divorce a man like Shelley from Life and Reality and call him a cloud-gatherer, and laud a writer of debauched plays such as Wycherley or Congreve for his *infinite* knowledge of life. What rot! Those who spend their lives searching around pigsties, bask in the favor of the unthinking, while those who take a [——?] view of things or, as Shelley did, identify themselves with the wind—"timeless and swift and proud" —are hooted at because they won't stay to be shod!

Francis Thompson was a unique figure and had a good deal of the Coleridge mysticism about him. I have read his "Hound of Heaven" and some of his other poems. He too was a drug addict and a street waif, the people who finally unearthed him and supported him finding him almost barefoot. I suppose he could have satisfied the utmost desires of the worldly with "knowledge of life" if he'd cared to exhibit that "knowledge" but fortunately the glory and significance of things struck him as more important.

Well, I mustn't rave any more or I'll be at it all night. I am desperately tired and weary of limb. We are having another hot spell—it was almost 100 to-day. I want to go home. I've *got* to go somewhere, but I'm afraid they [2] won't want me to come back next year and I've got to do that also. Give my kindest regards to Mr. Roberts.

To HORACE WILLIAMS

[42 Kirkland Street]
Cambridge, Mass.

Sept. 9, 1921

Dear Mr. Williams:

As I write this I suppose you are preparing for another busy and fruitful year and, in order to wish the thing that will bring you most happiness, I

[2] Wolfe's parents, who had agreed that he should go to Harvard to "try it for a year" but who, at this time, had not consented to his demands that he be allowed to re-enroll for 1921–22.

hope that Logic [1] is filled with the most disputatious, questioning crew ever.

I had a good year at Harvard and am about to return for a second under the urging of my professor of dramatics, Mr. Baker, who has strongly encouraged me and thinks that now is the time for me to continue. I didn't go home this summer but stayed to the summer session where I took another course toward my master's degree. Since then I have done nothing but rest but I rather regret not having gone home as I feel it would have rested me more.

I have tasted to the full this summer the philosophic sweets of solitude but I find it not an unmixed blessing. It is something one enjoys, I think, when one has friends to run from; but when enforced, it loses much of its charm. The poet seems to find communion with nature; I could imagine Wordsworth having a lively time on the Sahara desert but in a city where he knew no one, never! There one finds not solitude but loneliness. But I am not at all as melancholy as I sound. I am quite cheerful, indeed, and as school draws on I don't regret the summer a bit, for it was inevitable that a restless fellow like myself would do considerable thinking in that time to keep himself company. That I have done with some profit, I believe, and never have I been in more need of such a period of contemplation, for last year, as you would know, was a great seed-time to me, filled with new questionings, new surveyings, new and varied attempts to penetrate and devise. All of which left me in a muddled state. It has been said that men desire order before freedom, and indeed, human experience seems to argue this. To some small degree perhaps I have achieved order: now we shall see . . .

Mr. Williams, at times my heart sickens and sinks at the complexity of life. I know I haven't looked through yet; I am enmeshed in the wilderness and I hardly know where to turn. Your words keep haunting me almost even in my dreams: "How can there be unity in the midst of everlasting change?" In a system where things forever pass and decay, what is there fixed, real, eternal? I search for an answer but it must be *demonstrated* to me. Merely saying a thing is not enough. The other night I was reading "Adonais" by Shelley, a really great poet, I think. The beauty of his lines . . .

[THE REMAINDER OF THIS LETTER HAS BEEN LOST]

Wolfe's one-act play, The Mountains, *was produced at the Agassiz Theatre at Radcliffe on October 21 and 22, 1921, and was received unfavorably. The*

[1] One of Professor Williams' courses at the University of North Carolina.

following two letters, found among Wolfe's own papers and perhaps never sent to Professor Baker, show Wolfe's reaction to the criticisms of the play which, according to Workshop custom, were written by the audience.

To GEORGE PIERCE BAKER

[Cambridge, Mass]

[October 23 (?), 1921]

Dear Professor Baker:

After reading the numerous *remarks,* euphemistically called criticism, on my play, and some few criticisms which I consider worthy the dignity of that title, I feel compelled to make some rejoinder in defense of my play. It is useless, of course, to try to argue my play into popular favor; if the people didn't like it I shall play the man and swallow the pill, bitter as it may be.

Many of the audience seem to be of the opinion that I conspired to make them as uncomfortable as possible for thirty-five minutes. One of the catchwords which these people are continually using is that a play is "depressing." My play has been called "depressing" so many times in the criticisms, and with so small a store of illuminating evidence that I am even now in doubt as to just what has depressed these gentle souls.

My play is wordy, I admit [but I] take it they didn't mean exactly this. The play itself, the theme, more than the manner and the execution, depressed them.

Now let us analyze the cause of this depression. Is it due to some monstrous distortion of character? I think not. Richard, as he now is, may be a little the prig but he is not unworthy of sympathy. Dr. Weaver, a tired, worn, kindly man, is surely deserving of a warmer feeling. Can we feel nothing but repugnance and dislike for a poor ignorant devil like Tom Weaver, who feeds on hate because he's never known anything else? Do Laura and Mag and Roberts turn us to loathing? No, I think not. The thing that shocks these good people is the ending. It is such a pity that Richard must go the way of his fathers. One can understand it of his Uncle Tom, but Tom hasn't got the fine understanding about these matters that a Harvard man would have. But to see Richard, whom they continually dub "the idealist" (because, I suppose, he preferred to practice his profession rather than go out and shoot his neighbors—surely a normal desire)—to see him crack after all his fine talk, is more than they can bear. Dear me!

All I have to do to please these people is to change the ending slightly. Richard can go out with Roberts instead of with his father. Tom Weaver can slink off with a beaten look on his face, and the curtain speech can be given to Dr. Weaver, who might look upward and say: "Thank God! He wins where I have failed." The cause of depression having been thus removed by these slight changes, the curtain can descend leaving an audience to go home in a happy frame of mind, knowing that virtue and the higher education has triumphed, and myself—to go out and jump in the Charles River. This can never be! My show is over, they will not have to suffer again, but, even now, they can't egg me into changing the ending.

If the audience is depressed over my play, I am depressed over my audience. Good God! What do they want? What would they have me do? Are these people so wrapped in cotton-wool that they are unwilling to face the inevitable fact of defeat in a struggle like this? Let me write a contemptible little epic to small-town mean-ness (a favorite theme nowadays) in which the principal goes down to defeat from the parlor-and-gate slander of spinsters, and they will applaud me to the echo: "This is life! This is reality! This is a play of great and vital forces!" But let a man go down in a monster struggle with such epic things as mountains, and it is merely depressing and sordidly realistic. They can see no poetry to such a fight.

Why should I bother myself about all this anyway? I would like to be lofty and above such criticism, to feel like a statue attacked by a swarm of wasps, but these things [——?] and goad me. I sweated decent honest blood on what I thought was a decent, honest play. If my motive was that, I at least deserved a decent, honest criticism. I'm no pachyderm.

There was also considerable talk about my "psychology" and my "philosophy" in this play. If I've got to deal with this jargon, let me make my peace with all the "subtle-souled psychologists" straightway. Must I be accused of expressing my own personal philosophy in every play I write? Must an opinion uttered by one of my characters be taken from his mouth and put into mine, as an official credo? One critic found fault with a statement of Richard's to the effect that "a man may leave the sea or the town or the country, but it isn't often he leaves the mountains." Why blame me for such a statement? I didn't say it. Richard said it. Yet the critic would debate with me regarding the truth of an opinion uttered by a person with an antipathy toward his environment occasioned by what he believes to be the very holding power of that environment. Richard said he hated the mountains. I've never said any such thing. Weaver saw no beauty there. I see great beauty. Tom Weaver expressed faith in the curative quality of gun-shot to heal inter-family disorders. I hope I may be accused of no such "philosophy" for it seems that every stray observation is sure to be dignified as philosophy.

Others don't understand what they call the "psychology" of Richard. They can't understand how he could express the opinions and convictions he had, and yet give in at the end. If we must fool with "psychology" here, let me say that Richard's giving in has not to do with the psychology of an individual. It has to do with the psychology of a circumstance and a situation. To listen to such criticism, one would think that Richard was free to do as he chose, yet the whole struggle of the play is the struggle between his inner conviction and the outer pressure. And the outer pressure wins.

If even this is lost on them—this, the one vital thing in the play—then indeed I am the most wretched and miserable of bungling pen-pushers and should know enough to quit now before I get to the point where people will say: "You had better have died when you were a little boy."

I don't know whether it be ungracious and unbecoming to fly my colors in the faces of my critics, but if they expect me to sit quietly by and chew the cud in the face of such nincompoop criticism, they are far wide of the mark. The crowning insult of all came when my play was put in the same category with "Time Will Tell." I thank God that the far-reaching wisdom of the founders [1] saw fit to remove the names from the criticisms, for if I knew who wrote that, I would no longer be responsible for my actions.

The following letter was probably written to Gladys B. Taylor, whom Wolfe had evidently met at Harvard. It was found in rough draft in his own files and may or may not have been rewritten and sent to her.

Probably to GLADYS B. TAYLOR

208 Craigie Hall
Cambridge, Mass.

Sunday Morning, Nov 13, 1921

My dear Gladys:

I was about ready to write you and tell you that if you were waiting for me to write twice to your once you had the victory, and I wish you joy of it. Last night, however, I slept at 42 Kirkland for the first time in six weeks and I found a most welcome letter from you which the good landlady had saved for me for over a month. You will therefore be able to forget and forgive.

I did not go home at all. But just as school started I got a call to go to Baltimore; my father and mother were there. He is sick, you know, and

[1] The founders of the 47 Workshop.

goes to Johns Hopkins every year or so. I went to Baltimore and stayed there two weeks. My father is feeble but in better condition, the doctors say, than he was two years ago.

I stopped in New York long enough to see several shows:—"Liliom," "The First Year," "Daddy's Gone a-Hunting," and a revival of "The Return of Peter Grimm"—which someone suggests should be called "Daddy's Gone A-Haunting." Not bad. I saw the Follies when I got back to Boston. Fanny Brice is an artist.

There have been several good shows in Boston. Lionel Barrymore does a wonderful piece of acting in "The Claw"—a French play of Bernstein's. I also saw sister Ethel in "Declassée," an artificial play but enhanced by lovely and touching acting on her part. Saw Holbrook Blinn in "The Bad Man," a subtle and very funny satire, and Margaret Anglin in "The Woman of Bronze," the world's worst play (including those I myself write or try to). If you get to New York try to see "A Bill of Divorcement" and "The Circle." Both are highly recommended by no less an authority than our own Professor Baker.

Boston has two capable stock companies now, one engaged in producing English plays, the other American. I manage to see their programs quite often and have regaled myself with "The School For Scandal," "A Woman of No Importance," Galsworthy's fine new play "The Mob," "Three Faces East," and "A Cure For Curables."

We also have an Experimental Theatre which has planned a most ambitious program for the year (if they can only carry it out). Last night I saw them present what is probably our greatest native play, Eugene O'Neill's "Beyond the Horizon" and it is seldom I have been so stirred and moved. The play has somewhat of the spirit in it of my own one-act play, "The Mountains," which, by the way, ran here for two consecutive nights on Oct. 21 and 22, just a day after I returned. I have been reading a batch of the criticisms which an ironic Fate has deluged me with and I feel much as the tailor must have felt when requested by the tramp to "please sew a suit of clothes on these buttons." However I think my play was successful. It made either friends or enemies which speaks volumes for it, and I hope the friends outnumbered the enemies. I am setting to work to make a three act play of it. . . .

C. is going to see a girl in Brookline that he met in the bank last summer and it seems the Ohio girl has been ditched and after all his fine talk about the true delight of connubial relations and so on! These young fellows never learn. I, myself, am, as usual, a free-lance and will continue so, I fear. Cambridge has some fearful and wonderful women. They call me up on the telephone without divulging their identity, show the utmost familiarity with all the family skeletons and then ring off with a mocking laugh.

I am comfortably located at #208 Craigie Apartments but I am preparing to move again. My room mates are nice boys—when they're sober—which is about twice a week. I can't get my intellect to functioning properly with the fumes of alcohol and girlish shrieks of laughter coming to me from other parts of the apartment. However, I must fold up my tent like the Arab (I believe it was the Arab who folded up his tent).

I hope you're meeting success in conveying knowledge to your classes and I believe you will. I went out to Columbia while I was in New York and visited all your old haunts (if you did much haunting there this summer).

I want to hear from you and I don't want to wait the time I have kept you waiting—for reasons which I have satisfactorily explained, I hope.

You may write me here: if I'm not here the mail will reach me.

Yours in the bonds of Amity,

To MARGARET ROBERTS

[67 Hammond Street]
[Cambridge, Mass.]
Sunday night [February (?), 1922]

Dear Mrs. Roberts:

I am still paving the infernal road with my good intentions. Yet failure to answer promptly letters from one who never fails to send hope and to invigorate me with new strength is not merely bad manners but bad judgment. If the press of work and examinations recently ended cannot come to my aid by way of excuse, nothing else can.

Yesterday the secretary of the Graduate School sent me a note saying he was "happy to inform" me that I would get my M.A. with distinction upon removing the French requirement.[1] I am sure his happiness cannot equal mine. I have heard from only one course—but that is the one course I need. By their generosity my grade was A, although I would hardly have dared to mark myself so well. So far, I have made but one B and that was B plus last year in the Workshop. The rest have been A's. When the year is over, I will not only have completed the four courses required for the

[1] Wolfe had come to Harvard with no credits in French, and was therefore obliged to take French A or to pass the elementary French admission examination with a grade not lower than C before being eligible for his M.A. degree. He took the examination in June, 1921, but received a grade of only 60. He therefore took it again in May, 1922, and passed it satisfactorily.

degree but will have received credit for two more as well.[2] Six in all. This does not include the French. My second year in the Workshop didn't count for the degree, since not more than *one* composition course may be counted and, of course, 47 last year went down for that.

I am reading heavily. I will give you some idea of my labor for I take a great delight in counting the victims of my insatiable bookishness, though I despair at ever really knowing anything. To-day is Sunday. This morning I finished Wells' "Undying Fire," which I began last night. This is one of the few moderns I have had time for, but rarely have I been more stimulated. He's not a profound man, but he's a very sound man. Not, i.e. what Emerson would call a "primary man" but one who is a living proof of the benefits of a broad and intensive education applied to the training of a first-class mind. But to go on with the tally: this afternoon I took a walk and read half through Swift's "Tale of a Tub." Tonight I have read two essays of Emerson's and will finish Leslie Stephens excellent life of Pope before I retire. I suppose I make a mistake in trying to eat all the plums at once, for instead of peace it has awakened a good-size volcano in me. I wander throughout the stacks of that great library there like some damned soul, never at rest—ever leaping ahead from the pages I read to thoughts of those I want to read. I tell you this in all its monotonous detail because it is illustrative of the war that is being waged within me now— between what forces? For it brings me acute discomfort even in my writing. Still, as ever, I am seized with these desires to scribble, but this thing wiggles at me like some demon and says: "not yet, not yet. In two, three, or five years! Then you'll be ready." But this is folly! If it continues, the weight of my ignorance will fall on me like a stone, to crush me.

There is something in that splendid serenity of Emerson that gives me courage. I reread for the second time to-day his essay on Books. . . .

[A PORTION OF THIS LETTER IS MISSING HERE]

. . . with death" The reference, of course, is plain, namely that the drama cannot deal successfully with the supreme moment. But is not this a little unfair? I know of no other art form which can treat the subject with more truth. The interesting thing about "Liliom" is that this play gets off to a new start in interest after the hero kills himself. The next scene is the suicide court in Heaven (as he thought it would be). But I will tell you no more. There is humor, even farce comedy, while he dies; there is comedy almost of a slapstick variety in the Heaven scene; but all the time one says "Why not?" For if we look at life intelligently, we realize what a curiously woven fabric it is. The calloused police officers in "Liliom" drag the body

---

[2] He had taken the other courses necessary for his M.A. in 1920–21 and in Summer School.

of the dying man out to an open place, and while he lies there groaning his life away, talk about the heat, curse the mosquitoes, the new wage-scale, etc.

Let me add a gruesome touch of my own. When my brother died a few years ago, I went around to the undertaker's with Fred to see him. The particular undertaker who met us, a pious, mealy-mouthed man, took us back, asked us to wait a moment, as an artist would ask his friends to wait until he got the light adjusted on his picture. Then he called us back and showed us Ben's body. As we stood there watching, filled with emotions and recollections of indescribable pain, the man began to talk. He was proud of this job. It was one of the best he had ever done. No other under-taker could do a better one. Then, with true artistic pride, he began to point out the little excellencies in his finished work that showed the hand of the master. It was too much for me. I went into howls of uncontrollable laughter. It was no doubt a reflex of my condition at the time, but to this day I think of the incident with a smile.

That is one reason I defend Sir J. M. Barrie whenever he is criticized. I think Barrie is the most significant dramatist in the English-speaking world to-day because he really is carrying on the great tradition of our drama. This is an arch-heresy here, where some of my young critical friends consider him as "sentimental." Is it not strange how the academic, critical point of view shrinks nervously away from the sympathetic? I have never read a play of Barrie's that didn't give me this curious "mixed" feel-ing. He is not trying to "prove" anything (thank Heaven) but, like Shakespeare and other old fogies, is more interested in the stories of human beings than in the labor problem. That's why I believe his plays will outlast those of his contemporaries, because people at all times can understand and appreciate the emotion of other people. Sceptics are re-ferred to "The Trojan Women." This is the universal, eternal element in drama. After all, the conditions of which John Galsworthy wrote in "Strife" are becoming changed already; in twenty years we will still have a labor problem no doubt, but it will be one altogether different from the one "Strife" sets forth.

During the most inventive and mature years of his genius, G.B.S. ex-pended his great powers of satire on the one thing he thought worthy of drama—the thesis. Then a war comes along that kills twenty million people and destroys nations, and suddenly we can't convince ourselves that "Mrs Warren's Profession" or "Widowers' Houses" deal with the big-gest things in the world after all. If I were Shaw now, I think I should feel as if I had been equipped with a mighty bludgeon but had spent my life braining gnats.

I agree with you about Eugene O'Neill. He's the beacon light in our own drama to-day: he's kept his ideals and now seems in a fair way to prosper by them. Two new plays of his are shortly to come to New York; "Anna Christie" is there now enjoying a popular success. I saw "Beyond the Horizon" not long ago. It is a fine play. O'Neill is still a young man, c. 35, I think. I don't believe he has reached his greatest development yet. When it comes! There's one thing that worries me: in a forecast of his new play, "The Hairy Ape," which is to be produced soon, I see the subject is to be a stoker on an ocean liner. During the successive stages we will see him go back steadily to the primitive man. I hope O'Neill won't let this tendency run away with him. You see, he was "looking backward" in "The Emperor Jones" and, to a degree, we find this in other plays. Tragedy if continued in this vein, will become sordid and brutal. Surely this does not represent his outlook on life. Great tragedy, I think, must look ahead. . . .

J. S. Mill, whose autobiography I was reading the other night, said the greatest lesson the Greeks taught him was to dissect an argument, as did Socrates, and find its weak spot. If men ever needed to use that method, now is the time. There is so much claptrap, so much nonsense veiled behind intricacies, that we need all our sanity and common sense to tear the arguments of these buffoons to pieces. Oh, for a Swift to flay the free versists . . .

Well, I really must be going. I hope Mr. Roberts is feeling well. Give him my kindest regards. . . .

Your criticism of the last scene in my play [1] was unerringly accurate. I've cut Mag's speech. I've written the first two acts of the play as a three act, (also a prologue).

To HORACE WILLIAMS

67 Hammond Street
Cambridge, Mass.

[February (?), 1922]

Dear Mr. Williams:

. . . I have worked hard this first term and feel that I have accomplished more in an unseen way than in a visible manifestation. I remember one incident plainly in connection with my summer's work at the Langley Flying Field in Virginia three or four years ago.[1] Crews of negroes were grading and levelling the field that the flying machines might land there.

[1] *The Mountains.*
[1] Wolfe had worked as a time checker at Langley Field in the early summer of 1918.

Trees had been blasted out of the ground, which was right at the water's edge and filled with water rapidly. It was the duty of the negroes to fill these holes. It was depressing work. I have seen an entire crew throw dirt into a hole for a day, and as night came, there was little progress to show for their labor, for the water had devoured the dirt as if it were sugar. The effort to fill one's mind is like that, only more so.

I have one thing in common with Henry Adams. I do not feel at home when I am there, and I never feel at home anywhere else. Quanta patimus pro amore virtutis! I have decided to devote my life to the drama, if I have any gift in that direction. Therefore to go home now is impossible. I must be where I can read plays, see plays, and study plays. I think this is absolutely necessary if I'm ever to become an artist. A man may be a philosopher in Chapel Hill but hardly a dramatist. Again the limitations of my art are driven in on me.

Philosophy is gnawing me again. I read the other day of a star riding free and far in the universe, so that a ray of light from that star, travelling 186,000 miles a second would be 40,000 years in reaching the earth. That makes the head swim, doesn't it? Philosophy seems determined to make man the centre of the universe and a pretty important figure, and I suppose it's best to look at it that way. The other way leads to madness. Still, who can say but that life may express itself in many ways; can we affirm that we are the chosen vessels of that experiment?

I would like to see an "undying fire" of human progress in history but I am mighty dubious. I confess I have difficulty in seeing a projection of the Greek philosophy in Christianity, or a perpetuation of the Hebrew theology of vengeance in the Christian doctrine of mercy. Do philosophy, religion, or art really grow eternally, or do they grow to a certain point and then decay? Why shouldn't Greece have waxed stronger and profounder after Pericles, and Socrates, and Plato? Why should men regard Christianity as historical rather than living: i.e. something that was finished two thousand years ago and interpreted (or misinterpreted) ever since.

Finally, when literature produces a Shakespeare, after a period of steady fulfillment, why shouldn't the one who comes later be greater than Shakespeare? After the Elizabethan drama, why the decadence of the Reformation drama? Is this progress? If it is, it is surely a progress that seems to contradict itself.

Most everyone seems to waste his life in false attempts: a show of fine energy foully misplaced. Time after time it has seemed as if mankind was about to come upon the Absolute: to plunge into and discover the ultimate, impenetrable mystery; and then they quit, or turn to something else, to baffle and foul themselves anew. I tell you, Mr. Williams, I have become almost fanatically convinced that if the good and the wise and the great men would all turn to solving one problem at a time, all working in unison, searching together, and letting the false, misleading things go hang, something might be done. It is an insane dream, but I would be willing to obliterate my personality to work with men in that attempt. First we would try Religion, then Art, or Philosophy and Science. One by one we would drive them to the corner, Argus-eyed would we watch them, to prevent ducking or dodging, and if God could then escape us, my belief in the miracle would be established and I would ask no more questions but eat, and sleep and die!

It was William James, I believe, who said men knew as much of the universe as cats and dogs in a library know of the contents of the volumes therein. Yet, by no rational conviction can I convince myself that such ignorance is inevitable, or that such a problem can not be solved. What virtue is there in such ignorance? We are taught that knowledge is a liberating force, to increase and enlarge ourselves spiritually. Is it then reasonable to suppose that a definite knowledge of the supreme end of life would have a baneful influence, or that our efforts are being mocked, our paths twisted by an unseen hand? Surely, such belief is malignant.

The very nature of a philosophy, to me, is speculative. It must ever be on the hunt. Show me a man who has evolved a philosophy which, he says, has solved the problem of his life, and I believe you'll find a man who has surrendered to it. I have no use for a system which says that, after all, some things defy knowledge, and the only thing to do is to look around at the facts of life, never going beyond your vision, and work out a plan from these. Many a man, after running up blind alleys all his life, cries: "I have found it," and then tells you the answer is to read good books, develop a sense of the beautiful, enjoy the few and fleeting years to the utmost. He might as well have saved his breath, for he could have come to the same conclusion in high school.

The thing that continually chafes me in this highly cultivated community is the continual emphasis that is put on what they call "culture" as a means for attaining that divine consummation, a sense of the beautiful. But if this is all "culture" can do for one, teach one to enjoy and discern beauty, then I am ready to call it off. We don't need a "sense of the beautiful" any more than we need a "sense of the ugly," for the world is full of ugly things, Mr. Williams, and we've got to face them with our heads up. I have no use for the kind of "culture" that could discern the hand of a great artist in a painting but would withdraw into itself and cringe from the dirty, ugly, sweating crowd; that could read Sappho's poems and enjoy them and be shocked and resentful at the harsh voice of the subway guard, bawling to mason and professor alike to "Step Lively there—wheredyathinky'are?"

This is one thing that makes the matter hard. It is comparatively easy to imagine a kinship with the perfect and divine essence if we are forever handling and seeing and reading beautiful things, but we're put to it to find this relation in that which outwardly, at least, is ugly. I can read one of Walt Whitman's poems about the nobility and dignity of labor and the universal brotherhood, where Walt affectionately claps each artisan on the back and calls him "camerado," but when I go out, filled with a great desire to clasp mankind in my arms, the subway guard, or the man behind the counter can, by a few ill-timed remarks, change my desire to call him "camerado" to a desire to punch him on the jaw. So much for the universal brotherhood!

I hope the book [2] is going well. Count me in for an advance copy. I hope they're giving you the time you need so badly and that the class is not keeping the trail hot to your house at night. Please let me have some news when you are conveniently able.

To EDWIN GREENLAW

> [67 Hammond Street]
> [Cambridge, Mass]
> [March (?), 1922]

Dear Professor Greenlaw:

I write you without the impertinence of expecting a reply for I know the times and you are busy. I am sorry you're not coming here this Spring term after all. Someone told me you were going to the University of Chicago.

I will get my M.A. now as soon as I remove the accursed French requirement. I'm putting in an application to teach but I don't expect to return South for a time. I feel the necessity of being where I can watch the theatre, of seeing what is going on, and you know the conditions at home. We must do something to remedy it. More and more, it seems to me, our Southern people are so much better adapted to an appreciation of fine things than these shy, clumsy Yankees, but it seems to be a case of the hare and the tortoise over again.

There are good plays being written. I've seen "Liliom" three times, remembering M. Arnold's injunction about "the good things two or three times." So I'm epicurean.

It won't be long now until America has a drama. If we have three or four men of the caliber of Eugene O'Neill, each with a capacity for a different form, our drama has arrived. I don't feel as if I'm walking toward

---

[2] *The Evolution of Logic* by Horace Williams.

the sun but as if I could almost touch it. The thing will surely happen soon.

The English are getting brittle. Their little social plays, and comedies of manners are hard and brilliant. They leave an unpleasant taste. . . .

The war seems to have torn away the foundations of our old beliefs. And we haven't much to tie to yet. We've got to build something new, something we can see and almost handle. If I'm ever to be a dramatist I must believe in struggle. I've got to believe in dualism, in a definite spirit of evil, and in a Satan who is tired from walking up and down upon the earth. These are things I can visualize. When we erase the struggle, our power of visualization seems to fade. I have the utmost difficulty in bringing into my mind the picture of Professor Williams absorbing a negation. (Confidential.)

You remember the story or legend of how the medieval monks, by the very intensity of their reflection, could bring out upon their foreheads and hands the sign of the cross, the nail-wounds of the Crucifixion. I feel deeply the necessity of symbols like these to tie to. This is no mere windy talk with me. I'm beginning to know the kind of thing I want to do now. And it calls for a grasp on the facts of life. When I attended philosophy lectures (and I rate these lectures very highly) I was told that there was no reality in a wheelbarrow, that reality rested in the *concept* or plan of that wheelbarrow. But the wheelbarrow is the thing you show on the stage and, so far am I from denying the reality of the fact that it must be admitted when we kick a stone it bruises our toes.

Professor Lowes' book on Coleridge [1] (not published yet, I believe) which he read to the class last year, had a great effect on me. In that book he shows conclusively how retentive of all it reads is the mind and how, at almost any moment, that mass of material may be fused and resurrected in new and magic forms. That is wonderful, I think. So I'm reading, not so analytically as voraciously.

[THE LETTER BREAKS OFF HERE]

The following letter to Professor Baker announcing Wolfe's intention of withdrawing from the 47 Workshop may never have been sent, since it was found in Wolfe's own files and is not to be found in Baker's files. Wolfe made out his application for a teaching position with the Harvard Appointment Bureau on March 24, 1922, but his heart was still set on writing for the theatre and he completed the three-act version of The Mountains *and submitted it to Baker in April or May.*

[1] *The Road to Xanadu* by John Livingstone Lowes. Wolfe had taken Professor Lowes' course, Studies in the Poets of the Romantic Period, in 1920–21, and was taking his Comparative Literature 7 in 1921–22.

To GEORGE PIERCE BAKER

[Cambridge, Mass]

[March (?) 1922]

Dear Professor Baker:

I am writing you to notify you of my withdrawal from your course. Having received some assurance from the university of teaching employment somewhere next year, and gaining my family's permission to continue the year here and get my masters degree, I shall finish up the term.

The conviction has grown on me that I shall never express myself dramatically. I am therefore ending the agony by the shortest way; I would not be a foolish drifter promising myself big things.

I can not find words to express the gratitude I bear toward you, not only for your kindness and encouragement but for the inestimable benefits I know I have derived from your course. I shall never forget nor cease to be grateful to you.

The letter which appears below was evidently sent to Professor Baker with the new three-act version of The Mountains.

To GEORGE PIERCE BAKER

[Cambridge, Mass.]

[April or May, 1922]

Professor Baker:

When one writes a play one feels there are a thousand ways of saying a thing and that one usually selects the worst. But when one rewrites the play it is found that a very definite mould has been formed which it is difficult to break. I believe I have broken the mould in the last act— whether for good or ill I dare not say. Not once in the rewriting have I referred to the original one-act.

The introduction of the romance element will not cheapen the thing, I hope. I did it not to popularize the piece but to make a more living figure of the girl, Laura, who was somewhat wooden before. It will be said, I know, that a love affair with a member of the opposing clan is a somewhat conventional device, but all plotting is somewhat conventional and I can not see why the device is not a good one if I have made a true and honest lover of Will Gudger and a more human figure of the girl Laura, "torn between" (as the saying goes) love for her beaten father and the blunt young apple grower. Thus, also, it seems to me I am able to deal at the end what you would call a "swingeing blow." . . .

[THE FRAGMENT BREAKS OFF HERE]

Through the Harvard University Appointment Office, Wolfe had been offered an instructorship in the English Department at Northwestern University, but in evident reluctance, had postponed accepting it. He was waiting for Commencement, at which he was to receive his Master's degree, when he was suddenly summoned home to his father's deathbed. The following postcard to Miss McCrady, head of the Appointment Office, was mailed by him in New York en route to Asheville.

To LOUISE McCRADY

[PENNY POSTCARD]

[New York City]
[June 20, 1922]

Dear Miss McCrady: A telegram announcing the expected death of my father has forced me to go home. I left on two hours' notice and was unable to see you—I will send the Northwestern people my photograph as soon as I get home. Would you send them a note explaining the circumstances? I will write you a letter as quickly as possible.

To LOUISE McCRADY

48 Spruce Street
Ashville, N.C.
Saturday, Aug. 26, 1922

Dear Miss McCrady:

I was informed, in a letter from your office, that you had gone to Europe for the summer. I trust you had a very pleasant holiday. . . . I regret nothing more than my delay in giving you and the authorities at Northwestern University an answer to their offer of an instructorship in the English department. However, when I have explained the circumstances which occasioned this delay, I am sure you will understand and pardon it. Matters at home were in an extremely unsettled condition following the death of my father, and it was not until very recently that I knew definitely whether I should stay at home with my mother, accept the offer from

Northwestern, or return to Harvard for another year with Professor Baker. My finances are now in such a condition as will permit me to return for another year to Harvard.[1] Professor Baker has been so unfailingly kind and encouraging that I believe this extra year which is now made possible will be of the utmost importance to me.

The only thing that could disturb my happiness at the prospect of returning would be to think that my delayed answer had caused any serious inconvenience to my friends at the Harvard Bureau, and to those at Northwestern who, by their extraordinary kindness and sympathy, have made me long to know them.

It is a pleasure to think I will renew my acquaintance with you in a short time.

To MARGARET ROBERTS

[Asheville, N.C.?]

[September, 1922?]

. . . Coming home this last time I have gathered enough additional material to write a new play [1]—the second fusillade of the battle. This thing that I had thought naive and simple is as old and as evil as hell; there is a spirit of world-old evil that broods about us, with all the subtle sophistication of Satan. Greed, greed, greed—deliberate, crafty, motivated—masking under the guise of civic associations for municipal betterment. The disgusting spectacle of thousands of industrious and accomplished liars, engaged in the mutual and systematic pursuit of their profession, salting their editorials and sermons and advertisements with the religious and philosophic platitudes of Dr. Frank Crane, Edgar A. Guest, and *The American Magazine*. The standards of national greatness are Henry Ford, who made automobiles cheap enough for us all, and money, money, money!! And Thomas A. Edison, who gave us body-ease and comfort. The

---

[1] Wolfe had evidently secured his mother's consent to enrolling in the 47 Workshop for a third year. The financing of his three years at Harvard was a complicated matter which is best explained in his letter to Fred Wolfe of January 22, 1938. He had originally persuaded his mother to let him go to Harvard for one year by suggesting that the expense be deducted from the legacy of $5000 which was left him in his father's will. Later, when he stayed at Harvard for two additional years, no mention had been made of deducting these additional expenses from his legacy. However, when Mr. Wolfe's will was settled, his estate was found to have shrunk so much that the bequests of $5000 to each of his children could not be paid. Wolfe accordingly signed a paper waiving any claim to his $5000, in return for the money which he had received during his three years at Harvard.

[1] *Niggertown*, which finally became *Welcome to Our City*.

knave, the toady, and the hog-rich flourish. There are three ways, and only three, to gain distinction: (1) Money, (2) more money, (3) a great deal of money. And the manner of getting it is immaterial.

Among the young people here there is one who spends two-thirds of his time in the drug store, and who announces boldly, and as a kind of boast, that he is going to "marry money." This boy's father is . . . an honest, industrious, straightforward sort of man who walks to his work every morning with a tin dinner-pail swinging from his hand. Meanwhile the boy rides through the streets of the town, in pursuit of his ambition, in a spick-and-span speedster which he has enveigled from these hard-working people . . . Another boy, of good but common stock, who had all his advances repelled to within a few months back, with contempt or indifference, has unlimited money and with a part of it has purchased an expensive roadster, like a foolish fellow. Now they cluster about him like flies, and feed upon his bounty.

These are but mean and petty things, which I could multiply indefinitely. But what of the darker, fouler things? What of old lust and aged decay, which mantles itself in respectability, and creeps cat-footed by the stained portals of its own sin? What of the things we know, and that all know, and that we wink at, making the morality we prate of consist in discretion? I assure you I am not barren in illustrations of this sort. The emotion I experience is disgust, not indignation. Moral turpitude on the physical basis does not offend me deeply—perhaps I should be sorry to confess it—but my attitude toward life has become, somehow or other, one of alertness, one which sustains and never loses interest, but which is very rarely shocked or surprised by what people do. Human nature is capable of an infinite variety of things. Let us recognize this early and save ourselves trouble and childish stupefaction later. I desire too much to be the artist to start "playing at" life now, and seeing through a rosy or vinous haze. Really I am un-moral enough not to care greatly how the animal behaves, so long as it checks its behavior within its meadow. The great men of the Renaissance, both in Italy and England, seem to me an amazing mixture of God and Beast. But "there were giants in the world in those days," and they are soon forgiven. What do their vices matter now? They have left us Mona Lisa. But what of this dull dross that leaves us only bitterness and mediocrity? Let pigs . . .

[A PORTION OF THE LETTER IS MISSING HERE]

I suppose the alarmist means that the time will come when the strength of our national life will wither and decay, just as all preceding national lives have served their times, and have withered and decayed, and passed on. But what is there in this either to surprise or alarm us? Surely a nation has no greater reason to expect imperishability than has an individual. And it is by no means certain that a long life, whether for man or nation, is the best one. Perhaps our claim to glory, when our page is written in the world's history, will rest on some such achievement as this: "The Americans were powerful organizers and had a great talent for practical scientific achievement. They made tremendous advances in the field of public health, and increased the average scope of human life twelve years. Their cities, although extremely ugly, were models of sanitation; their nation at length was submerged and destroyed beneath the pernicious and sentimental political theory of human equality."

I do not say that this is utterly base or mean or worthless. It will be a very great achievement, but it has left no room for the poets. And when the poets die, the death of the nation is assured.

Well, I have returned to all this at midnight. The fires of the hearth have burned to warm, grey cones of powder. There is a roaring in the wind to-night, the streets are driven bare, and my "autumn leaves" are falling already upon the roof in a dry, uncertain rain. The annual taint of death is in the air. . . .

[THE REMAINDER OF THIS LETTER HAS BEEN LOST]

According to the recollection of William E. Harris, who was a member of the 47 Workshop at this time, Wolfe submitted the first acts of six different plays to Professor Baker in the early fall of 1922, before he settled down to work on Niggertown *(which finally became* Welcome to Our City.*)The play discussed in the following letter is probably one of these six. Fragments of it found among Wolfe's papers concern a hero named Eugene Ramsay whose thirst for knowledge is very similar to Wolfe's own, and a Professor called Wilson or Weldon who somewhat resembles Horace Williams.*

To GEORGE PIERCE BAKER

[Cambridge, Mass.]

[September or October, 1922?]

Dear Professor Baker:

I am leaving herewith the first act of a three act play with a synopsis of the rest. I am on so unsure a footing, so troubled with doubt and misgiving that I feel the necessity of waiting your opinion before going on.

This is my first attempt at what is called the "problem play." But the play, as I conceive it, deals with a spiritual and a human problem, rather

than with a social or economic problem for which I have small use. I will
state it, as I see it, and it is unfortunate if the language seems involved and
complicated. In a system where things are forever changing, where is the
fixed, immutable, unchanging principle to be found? That is—where is
the Absolute? Moreover, by the very exigencies of this vast, mechanical
civilization we have built, life becomes bewildering and overpowering in
its complexity. In the last chapter of that remarkable book, "The Education of Henry Adams," Adams voices this sentiment when he returns to
New York after a long absence and looks at that terrific and chaotic skyline. Civilization has exploded. In this chaos of force and disorder, where
is to be found that principle of unity, order, which his spirit seeking
"education" (which is but knowledge of unity) is on the hunt for. He goes
to Washington and finds his friend, John Hay, a man of splendid ability,
already drained and sapped of his vitalities by the demands of this monstrous new world. Now, as I interpret it, Hay represents the finest we have
to offer to combat the demands of our present life. But he is not adequate.
A new type of man must be created. And so he leaves it up in the air.

But how, how? In the first act of my play I try to present the problem.
When the young man, Ramsay, tells Professor Wilson, the philosopher,
that he feels at times he is on the earth seven centuries too late, he is
giving expression to a sincere conviction. Adams mentions the mighty gap
that yawns between the unity of 1200 and the multiplicity of 1900. Consider the case of the young man Ramsay. He too is on the go for "education"—that is the quality of understanding and grasping present life in its
entirety. He knows the limitations of the Middle Ages, their comparative
ignorance and superstition, but he also knows the promise of fulfillment
they held open to the student. Ramsay could picture himself taking orders
and going into a monastery in the 13th century. There he could have spent
the years in his cell going through the monastery's precious collection of
manuscripts—not too many, however, for a life time. He would have
known Plato and Aristotle almost by heart, he would have been well-read
in the scholastic philosophy, and perhaps sub rosa (safe from the prying
eyes of a fat abbot) would have refreshed himself, in moments of relaxation, with Homer and the dramatists.

I do not expect people to be greatly interested in Ramsay's account of
his trials in the world of books. For this reason, I mention this problem only
in passing, believing that, for dramatic purposes, his trials in the world of
action will be more appreciated. Yet when Ramsay tells of wandering past
the countless, loaded shelves of the library like some damned spirit in
search of the unattainable, he is voicing that which has caused him acute
pain. How infinitely little of the contents of those pages can be made his
own: he, with a passionate thirst for knowledge, cannot become master

even here. It goads him to fury to think that some idle woman gorged to the gills with the latest output of fiction, can speak knowingly of this, that or the other book, which he has not come to. Ramsay feels passionately that instead of there being too little science . . .

[A PORTION OF THE LETTER IS MISSING HERE]

. . . knows that once he loses this, he too is lost. Then we find him being swept into the current. The bewildering cross currents of this life to which he makes a frenzied effort to apply his philosophy, and for which he finds his philosophy incomplete and inadequate, begin to sweep him about. He realizes that he has so adapted his philosophy to each occurrence that denies it, that it has lost its original quality and has become a mere agent of expediency, through which he is trying to find—what?

Ramsay, as I should have stated, wants to interpret life through the medium of literature. In the city he works for a newspaper (however I have no newspaper scenes in the play). Time and again he writes, but tears up what he has written, with a terrible sense of its incompleteness. A cross-section of life will not content him; he wants to show in each type the universal, in the one the many. At first he says "I will write nothing now. But in five years I will know enough. Then I will be able to give a broadside view of things." But the conviction grows that in five years this knowledge of imperfection will be more oppressive than ever. It disgusts Ramsay to hear the perfection of universal understanding of humanity ascribed to such a writer as Dickens, for instance. He admires Dickens but he sees plainly that Dickens, as so many other writers, had a very limited point of view. He knew one particular side of life and he knew it well.

It would perhaps be much better for Ramsay if he could limit himself thus. His own common-sense tells him that a sure limitation is the only solution in the present frame of things. But the daemon goads him on.

As you have doubtless surmised, there is much that is personal in this statement. But let there be no confusion between Ramsay and myself. I am trying to portray a figure bound by his own strength, not by his limitations. In this, it seems to me, there is a tremendous irony. Consider the cases of Coleridge and Wordsworth. Coleridge was a man of far deeper and more varied genius. But this was his undoing. The brilliant promise of his youth, which produced "Christabel" and "The Ancient Mariner," was baffled and checked in his later years by the expeditions of that devising mind which tried now poetry, now science, now philosophy—ever beginning and never ending anything. Wordsworth, possessed of less profound but more single-minded genius, devoted his life to the production of the one kind of poetry he could write well. And I will not deny that (on paper) he's the greater poet.

Or there is Leonardo, who painted so little because of his other activities and researches as engineer, canal builder, geologist, speculator upon flight of birds and flight of men, astronomer, physicist, etc.

[THE LETTER BREAKS OFF HERE]

The play discussed in the following letter was probably another of the six which Wolfe considered writing in the early Fall of 1922.

To GEORGE PIERCE BAKER

[Cambridge, Mass.]
[Autumn, 1922?]

Sir:

The figure around whom this play revolves will suggest strongly to those who know him Jonathan Swift. But I wish to make it clear that this is not a biographical play. Swift is responsible for [it]—it is true, but out of his character I have drawn my own play. On reading Leslie Stephen's "Swift" recently, I was powerfully impressed by the tremendous humanity of the man. Here we have a really savage misanthropist. He regards mankind with none of the noble or patient scorn of Alceste, but with a terrible hate: he rakes them with the withering fire of an unequalled satiric talent. But —when I say he hated men, I mean that hard cold accretion that makes up the world.

The tremendous antithesis appears when we consider Swift's remarkable love and loyalty toward his friends; his extreme personal parsimony which he practices in order to be more generous to friends and dependents. Consider the pathetic contrast in this grim, bitter old man who yet, with almost womanish fear and trembling, keeps a letter from a sick friend unopened for five days because he fears bad news: or the grief he hides under harshness, at the death of a friend, when he tells us never to choose a sick or feeble person for a friend, because the danger and worry at losing them is so great.

[THE LETTER BREAKS OFF HERE]

The following brief fragment is evidently part of a letter which Wolfe submitted to Professor Baker with a play entitled The People. *This was probably one of the six which he began in the Fall of 1922.*

To GEORGE PIERCE BAKER

[Cambridge, Mass.]

[Autumn, 1922]

Dear Professor Baker:

In this play I hope to incorporate certain ideas that have been stirring about in my mind concerning the eternal warfare that is waged between the Individual and Society. The fiction I have invented to dramatize these ideas is fairly evident, I think, in the first scene. I will hastily sketch out the rest of the play, as follows: in Scene II we see the Fair and the People, who are a sort of chorus in the play. In the various tent shows and booths, under the guise of "bally-hoo men" and spielers, I propose to show in turn . . .

[THE LETTER BREAKS OFF HERE]

The following letter from Wolfe to his cousin, Elaine Westall Gould, the daughter of Henry A. Westall, was evidently called forth by a criticism of Welcome to Our City *which she had made at Wolfe's request.*

To ELAINE WESTALL GOULD

[21 Trowbridge St]
[Cambridge, Mass.]

[January 14 (?) 1923]

My dear Elaine:

Your letter was read with great interest and I return my thanks for the many valuable contributions you have made. I do not think, as you suggest, that there is any fundamental difference between us as to what constitutes a play; there is rather, I think, a misunderstanding as to the *kind* of play I have written, and as to what that play was primarily about. I have no doubt, when I come to the criticisms, that I shall run into the same difficulty with other people and I know that it is a difficulty to be reckoned with, since I can not hope to reach a general audience of any such intelligence.

First of all, I want to impress the fact that the play is not about any problem—least of all about the negro problem. I try to settle nothing, I want to prove nothing—I have no use for solutions.

My play is concerned with giving a picture about a certain section of life, a certain civilization, a certain society. I am content with nothing but the whole picture, I am concerned with nothing else. The racial aspect of the picture is deliberately diffused with the other elements at first, it gradually comes to the surface until it overshadows the whole picture at the end. There is no need of assuring you, who have lived in the South, that the part that element plays is not disproportionate. It is not.

So here, I think, you struck your snag, and you thought I had written two plays instead of one. It is sometimes difficult, of course, for people who have been trained in the theatre of the last twenty years to adapt themselves readily to the looser and more expressive structure of such a play as I have written. The mind is accustomed to the old forms, to the three, four, and five act forms, and adapts itself hardly.

[THE LETTER BREAKS OFF HERE]

Welcome to Our City *was chosen for production by the 47 Workshop, and was actually put on on May 11 and 12, 1923. Wolfe evidently wrote the following letter to Professor Baker when the selection of the play was first announced.*

To GEORGE PIERCE BAKER

[Cambridge, Mass.]
Sunday night.

[January or February, 1923]

I am submitting herewith a list of people and of sets required for my play. As I say, I think it can be done with two dozen people, perhaps with fewer.

I am letting you have the play in my fearful scrawl and with no revision whatever. I feel that many of the scenes may be strengthened by the introduction of more satirical material, most of which I have written.

Anyone, I think, is a little dubious about the matter of revision. Often it is nothing but a hit or miss sort of thing. I know of only one rule and think it covers the whole business. Revise with the sole purpose of writing a better play. This means, if possible, the making of each scene better, briefer, more direct, and more economical in the use of people. That I can do this *in time* I have not the slightest doubt: of doing it in twenty-four hours, or two days, or half a week, I am not so sure.

I think this states my position with this possible addition: I would be sorry to think that a close eye on the relevancy, the direct bearing of each scene and incident on the main problem, that of the negro, would conceal from you the fact that I knew what I wanted to do from the beginning to the end. With what success I did it, I can not even venture a guess. But will you please remember this: a play about the negro, a play in which each scene bore directly upon the negro, a play in which the negro was kept ever before you, might be a better play: it would not be the play I started to write. I wish you would bear this in mind when you read the mooted scene (VIII)—the cubistical, post-impressionist politician scene. It needs revision, but I'd hate to lose it. It's part of the picture; part of the total.

I have written this play with thirty-odd *named* characters because it required it, not because I didn't know how to save paint. Some day I'm going to write a play with fifty, eighty, a hundred people—a whole town, a whole race, a whole epoch—for my soul's ease and comfort. No one may want to produce it but it will make an interesting play.

And the next I do will have eight, ten, certainly no more than a dozen.

If you need a translator for my manuscript—I suspect you will—call me. I will be at your service when you want me.

To MABEL WOLFE WHEATON

[Cambridge, Mass]

[April or May, 1923?]

Dear Sister Mabel:

I am deeply sorry I have neglected writing you for so long, and in especial, to thank you for your beautiful gift Christmas. It's a pretty time to acknowledge it I know, but better late than never and I want you to know I've worn it daily and got great service. I know you're tired and I can appreciate your position. I don't think we'll ever forget what you have done [1]—I'm sure I won't, and if there's any poor consolation in this, perhaps I shall write a play someday about my family [2] in which it will be seen we're not all of us heroes nor all of us villains, but that we're all pretty human people, with more virtues than imperfections, and capable (you, in particular) of actions that make the heart beat a little faster.

Families are strange and wonderful things and one never sees the mystery and the beauty in them until one is absent from them. When one is present, the larger values are obscured sometimes by the little friction of daily events. I sometimes wonder for instance, if two people constituted as differently as are Fred and I could ever live together in perfect harmony?

---

[1] In her devotion to her father until his death.

[2] There are fragments of such a play among Wolfe's papers, using some of the material which finally appeared in *Look Homeward, Angel*.

Fred's generosity and his many acts of kindness to his younger brother are often remembered with deep emotion, but if ever we've lived together so much as a week without friction, I can't remember it. I would do anything in my power for him; he would do that and more for me but the plain truth is—when we get together we're apt to irritate one another. Once or twice —God help us—we were on the verge of fighting. It would have been a calamity. . . .

Mabel: don't think I overrate myself or have any false idea of my ability. I have no illusions about that and you may be sure if I ever do anything worthy [of] the name of Genius, I will not be too modest to admit it. Two or three times in my short life, I have had flashes that caused me to think for a moment that I had a spark—a very small one—of Promethean fire in me, but at present you can cover it all and more, if you say: I believe I have some *talent*. The one big hope I have now is that Professor Baker has more confidence in my abilities than I have. That sentence is badly stated. I mean, the fact that he does believe in me gives me hope. But if ever you thought I was given to puffed-up conceit, I entreat you to revise that opinion now, for I know that if you could have been with me at times this year, out of the very kindness of your heart you could not have forborne telling me I was not quite as bad as I thought.

[THE LETTER BREAKS OFF HERE]

It would seem impossible to date the following letter correctly, or to guess to whom it was addressed. However, the decomposed state of the paper on which it is written, the general flamboyant style, and the reference to "every drunken Sophomore, to every paunchy pickle salesman" seem to indicate that it was written while Wolfe was at Harvard, probably in 1923.

To AN UNKNOWN GIRL

[Cambridge, Mass?]

[1923?]

My Dear:

When I saw you first, and heard you speak, I loved your voice. It was low and husky, and strangely tender. It had little notes, and shades in it. There was something steadfast and fine about your carriage; I noticed your breasts when you walked—they were firm, and sprang forward.

I heard you speak a second time, and I asked the other girl—Margaret —to get you for me. I thought of Cordelia, King Lear's daughter. I think I have always loved her. When she died the old mad king [leaned] over her, and said:—"Her voice was ever soft and low—an excellent thing in woman."

That, my dear, is great poetry—simple, sensuous, passionate, poignant and beautiful. And your voice was like that, I thought. Or, rather, that queer false romantic part of me thought so—the part that is always lying to me. The other—the real, hard, practical part—said "Cigarettes and booze."

But—no matter what, I met you. You came to my room and said, "Well, where's the liquor? You're the first Southerner I've ever seen"—and so forth. I grew sick with horror, and fear, and shame. I'd heard that so often before and, somehow, I felt that I had lost you. To complete it, you need only have said: "My companionship for your booze. Is it a bargain?"

It was a blow, an insult to my intelligence—but I didn't mind that. I knew you had said it to every drunken Sophomore, to every paunchy pickle salesman you had known—but I didn't mind the classification. It was the fact that I had lost something; and I couldn't call it back.

So I got the booze, and you sat there on the bed with your hard, wise, knowing little manner, displaying all the shameful and degrading symbols with which this brute-blind world has marked you—what silly and vicious people call "worldly wisdom." That was when I began to love you, my dear. That surprises you, doesn't it? You have lovely eyes—and they looked at me now and then—it seemed with a frightened question in them. I thought I saw a child whom the world had bewildered: all the common hardness and pertness and flippancy of the "digger" was a protective covering.

Meanwhile, you were fulfilling your function as "the life of the party." With a sudden revulsion, I wondered how many times you had been "the life of the party." You told your filthy stories, I told mine. Only, you told yours beautifully. And I didn't mind. I wanted to kiss you. It was really amazing. I have never cared for a woman with a dirty mouth, even if she were a street prostitute—but I didn't mind it in you. Foulness dropped from your mouth like honey.

Strangely, I have no shame, because, I think, you will be tender, and sad, and will not boast of your conquest. I offer myself for a day, a week, or a month. I shall grow tired and forget you; you will be another beautiful phantom—and I shall ask of you not even so much as a picture, a garter, a handkerchief, a bit of perfumed lace to remember you by. I never do.

I shall kiss your lips—your beautiful mouth, your fine, soiled prettiness, tainted with so many foul and drunken kisses. I shall pour golden song— what my maddened heart has wrought and made lovely—into those ears which have heard every bawdy ballad in the country from countless drunken Sophomores. Only, my dear, when the time comes, you shall forget my poetry, and remember the ribald ballads.

Life has left his dirty thumb marks on you; you have been pawed over —yet, somehow the pity and the beauty. . . .

[A PORTION OF THE LETTER IS MISSING HERE]

. . . love you, and—at the end—I shall give you back into the vicious slimy sea from which you came.

Love me for a time, my dear. Hold me in your arms, and say to me: "You are fine, you are good, you are great, you are beautiful. You are my god—and I love you"—and, by God, I will be.

This

X

is a Kiss, my dear.

(If you don't destroy this letter you
will be shot at sunrise)

The letter below was found in Wolfe's own files and was evidently addressed to Merlin McF. Taylor, who was a graduate student at Harvard from 1921 to 1923, and a member of English 47 in 1921–1922. The last two paragraphs of the letter were written on a separate sheet of paper, and may be part of the letter to Taylor, or part of one to someone else.

Probably to MERLIN McF. TAYLOR

[Cambridge, Mass.]

[July, 1923?]

My dear Merlin:

Your letter came this morning to revive my fainting spirits from over the red Hell of a beautiful Cambridge day. I drew sustenance from the tidings of your fruitful industry. Know, then, that I, too, have not been inactive. I have written a prodigious amount which is piled here about me, on the floor—but nothing as yet which looks like a play. That is not to say the thing [1] won't dramatize—I think it will—I have merely attacked most of the juicy spots and left out the conjunctive ifs, ands, buts.

Summer School arrived in a swirl of petticoats and lilac-coloured drawers. Some of the arrivals are passably fair—the remainder teach school. There are a number of old women, of both sexes. . . .

I read prodigiously. The Widener Library has crumpled under my

[1] *The House* (later *Mannerhouse*).

savage attack. Ten, twelve, fifteen books a day are nothing. And, now and then, I write. With you away, I see few people that I know. Raisbeck [2] is here with his dog—or vice versa—but I rarely see him. Prof. Baker is reading manuscripts in the wilds of New Hampshire: the rest of the crew is missing. . . .

. . . I think my play "The House" will "pack a punch" for it is founded on a sincere belief in the essential inequality of things and people, in a sincere belief in men and masters, rather than in men and men, in a sincere belief in the necessity of some form of human slavery—yes, I mean this— and it deals, moreover, with the one period in our history that believed these things and fought for them and was destroyed because of its belief in them. This I am working out in my new play. I find it very interesting.

I have been reading the *Amores* of Ovid this morning. It is beautiful Latin and beautiful poetry—although it is altogether concerned with two topics: How am I going to get it and How fine it was when you let me have it. If our modern romanticists could be as honest, I'd make no kick. Ovid would never have written a verse to the Virgin Mary as an indirect address to . . .

[THE FRAGMENT BREAKS OFF HERE]

To KENNETH RAISBECK

[Cambridge, Mass]

[Early August, 1923]

My dear Kenneth:

I hung around your doorway yesterday like a second Laddie Boy. I have done everything but bay the moon. From your letter I infer that you left Thursday about midnight. I went by your lodgings at one o'clock, and concluded that you were in bed. Your letter was a shock,—a shock which has spurred me into feverish activity. I am packing! This is the last and heaviest calamity—for the present. I'm going up to Carlton's [1] for three or four days—though God knows why. Perhaps it is to see the kingdoms of my world from an exceeding high mountain,—if I only could! Misfortune has fallen like rain since you left. Last night I was caught in the Harvard Yard with a girl . . . doing the worst I could. The yard-cop was fat, and portentous.

[2] Kenneth Raisbeck was Professor Baker's assistant in the 47 Workshop, and a close friend of Wolfe's.

[1] Henry Fisk Carlton was a member of the 47 Workshop from 1920 to 1922, and had invited Wolfe to visit him in Madison, New Hampshire.

"Mister," says he, breathing heavily through his mouth, "this has got to stop."

I scrambled to my feet, and asked him what he meant, because I couldn't think of anything better to say.

"You were spooning with the young lady, she was sitting on your lap. The university doesn't allow that."

"You will please confine your remarks to me and to Harvard University," says I, as lofty as you please.

"I'm sorry," says he. "Them's my orders. I am only doing my duty." Here he threw back the lapel of his coat and displayed a badge as large as a small saucepan. "That's my authority," he says. When I saw it was official I made my exit.

Well, I came back to all this at midnight Sunday. I leave here to-morrow at six—vespers—on the Portland, Me. boat—that is if I can tear myself away from the —— girl. Again, I am in the toils, and fast nearing the breakers, physically and mentally. What shall I ever do? . . . How can I stick with anyone in the present state of my affairs? It is mad, mad, mad. I tell you there is no escape! And I, who fear and live in utter horror of this thing, am most in need of someone to supply the sheer physical wants—to provide me with decencies, mended sox, bleached linen, clean sheets, pressed trousers, and all the other trivialities by whose want I may sink!

There is a mighty conspiracy everywhere abroad—the more terrible because silent, and veiled in holy words—which crushes us slowly and relentlessly into the [souls] of the domestics and the Pure Young Men. Any suggestion that a male may hold physical communion with a female without first propitiating the priest and the Holy Ghost is met with invective, hatred, and relentless opposition.

By the way I saw Fritz Day and his wife in the Georgian last night. They are still living happily and Cathi (?) has apparently heard the play, because she told me it was 'awfully good'—probably because my eyes looked queer when I got the news. No! It is not about her! Fritz spoke of Art while I, in recent vein, spoke of Commerce. But Fritz has dwelt too long with his ear tuned to the rustling of the angel's wings: I could see he thought the conversation sordid.

They are going up to the Bakers' to play with the proteins for a few days. No doubt I will see them and hear the play,[2] which is now cut to eighty pages. I am going to send my play [3] in from New Hampshire. We can only hope for the best. Perhaps if I can get up there in the woods for a few days, with a little peace of mind, I can do considerable revision. I

[2] A play of Day's, *The Sea*.
[3] *Welcome to Our City*.

should never have met that girl! And who do you think introduced me? Brewster.[4]

The following fragments to Professor Baker were found scattered among Wolfe's papers, and were evidently written during his period of final disillusionment with the 47 Workshop which began with the failure of Welcome to Our City in May, 1923, and culminated in his acceptance of an instructorship at New York University in January, 1924. Since many of them were obviously written in the Summer or early Fall of 1923, they are included all together as of that date, although some may have been written a little earlier or later.

To GEORGE PIERCE BAKER

I feel that the time has come for me to speak to you, as becomes our friendship—freely, frankly and earnestly. You have something more than a play to deal with, sir. You have the fate and destiny of 190 pounds of blood, bone, marrow, passion, feeling—that is, your humble servant, in your keeping. I hope that's not an undue responsibility—but it's true and you must know it.

I admit the virtue of being able to stand criticism. Unfortunately it is a virtue I do not happen to possess. Last year my unfortunate play returned to let my blood; the springs of creative action froze and in the blackness of my despair, I doubted if they would ever return. They returned because my father died, because I was subjected to deeper tragedies of love, hatred, and contempt. These things dwindled and lessened the others. But according to the system . . .

The ability to take such criticism you said not long ago might make the difference between a second-rate artist and a great artist. I do not believe this. Being a great artist depends no more on such callousness than does his ability to swallow castor-oil, or blue-point oysters, or fried pork chops. It has nothing to do with it. You, or no man else, can make me a great artist, or a second-rate artist, or any kind of artist. That is a matter which was settled in my mother's womb—she, whose blood fed me, whose heart and whose brain lighted me and gave me being. That part of our destiny, believe me, is fixed, and nothing save death or madness can check or change it. And worldly wisdom on life, from the experienced traveller, is of no

[4] W. R. Brewster, who was a member of the 47 Workshop Company at this time.

avail. If there is genius, the thing is a marvellous intuition, little dependent on observation. If there is no genius, I'd as soon draw wages from one form of hackery as another.

I have no doubt that if I set myself to it and worked long and earnestly, I could ultimately be successful in writing plays which only the dramatic critic for the *Boston Transcript* could understand. Unfortunately for those who like myself are indolently inclined, the way out is not so easy. [Inch-brow (?)] drama deserves, and will get, a speedy, damnatory death. High-brow drama about low-brow people deserves an even quicker and more painful decease: I refer to plays like *The Hairy Ape*.

Dear Professor Baker:
I settled the affair with the typist as soon as the news of your award reached me.[1] I thank you very much for acting. You were made referee, I must tell you, at no instigation of mine. Indeed I was informed only after you were named.

In frankness, I do not consider the woman's services worth $88.00. I consider the original $75.00 as not only ample but generous. But, even so, I have beaten this unpleasant person from bonnet to bootstrap and when she gets through paying her attorneys she will be fortunate indeed to realize $50.00. I would be ashamed of my vindictiveness if I had not been forced to suffer from her false and perjurous tongue. . . .

It is a shameful commentary on our civilization that I, after seven university years, and the consumption of thousands of books, may earn barely $2000 a year—if I am fortunate—by teaching, while this creature is paid at the rate of $22.00 a day for incompetent, slipshod work. But when I speak of incompetence, let me, in shame, draw a veil over my own. Everyone is earning, procuring, achieving a measure of independence, it seems, except myself. A pretty little girl I picked up in the Yard the other night . . . earns $2200 as a school-marm—and $35 weekly for extra instructions. Can I hold my head up longer?

[1] Wolfe had engaged a stenographer to type one of his plays, and had been horrified to find that her bill was more than he could pay. He had done nothing about it and the matter had dragged on, until she finally brought suit against him. According to a letter written by his uncle, Henry A. Westall, who acted as his attorney in the matter, they let the typist get judgment against Wolfe, and then informed the court that he was still a minor when he had ordered the work done, that Mr. Westall as his "guardian pro tem" had not authorized it, and that the claim was therefore invalid. Professor Baker was then asked to referee the case, and a settlement was made.

There is a chagrin in my [youth?] threatening my happiness, making me bitter, morose. The brute is Money. With money I'll throttle the beast-blind world between my fingers. Without it I am strapped; weakened: my life is a curse and a care. If God had only made me with the soul of a villager! Then might I like Cowley—a gentle poet—see life in a thimble and be content. But I have the heart of a far-wanderer and a farer-forth into unknown places. And so begins my vagabondage.

By God—no one knows me—no one knows my capacity. Those who liked my play looked on it as a fortuitous accident—as something which might not happen again. But already I have a bigger play under construction—I do not say it will be better because my heart and my mind is bitter-sick—but the concept was bigger, truer, nobler.

I am leaving here as soon as I pack my junk to send it home. Where I am going I do not know, but I hope the journey will be far and long. I am an observant, fairly intelligent person, with an insatiable desire for this thing called life—and I will learn.

[The] world is a large, large oyster—but I do not think I will choke when I swallow it.

Good-bye, and may God bless you, and bring prosperity and fine accomplishment to your work.

Dear Professor Baker:

I am leaving here to-morrow—journey, as yet, unknown. I have hopes, however, that it will take me far and keep me going. I am destroying all my manuscripts. My apprenticeship has drawn to an end.

I am going to add to my manifold indebtedness to you by asking you to write, at your leisure, a short letter to my mother, in Asheville, North Carolina. She is a shrewd woman, of great discernment and penetration: she will understand and appreciate what you write in honesty and sincerity. If you can tell her with some measure of conviction that you do not think my time here has been wasted, that you believe, in time, there is some promise of fulfillment, you will render me (and her) a service of inestimable value. I ask you to do this because, I fear, she will be subjected to unpleasant criticism from people who look on my career here as a failure, and on the money which has been spent as wasted.

I could earn my living by teaching, I believe. Indeed I was offered an instructorship at Northwestern University last year, and I suppose I could go somewhere else even yet. But I have forsworn this course: I believe it is a false compromise. I do not know how I am suited to vagabondage, but I know myself for an observant and fairly intelligent person who ought to learn several things by the experience.

Life does not come to me evenly or gently. Do not deceive yourself. You can teach me no balance, equipoise, or moderation. Nothing will be gained by putting a fence around me: I will but burst forth the more intemperately at the end. My life is a rude, rash gamble—a curse and a care. I shall see presently if something useful may not be done with it. My affections were all too strong, my aversions too fierce—odi et amo— tells the whole of it.

Be of good cheer when you think of me. If the ship goes down it will be far enough out, I promise you, not to sadden the watchers by the shore. And we may, I hope and believe, swim through bravely at the end.

The world, by Bacchus, is a large, large oyster, but since I'm bent on opening it, there's nothing to be done but wait and see if it defies gustation. I am fairly strong, and of boundless energy. If anything, I have the odds and a dreadful fear of the mute, inglorious, to whip me on.

I think you are really a fine, good man, and when I consider the excellence of the fibre which has caused you to persist here in the face of disheartening conditions, resisting the lures of more seductive offers and greater personal opportunities, it seems to me you are an individual who has maintained himself on an impressive level of character—the most impressive level of character that I have ever known. Now, this is what I understand by the term *morality:* it seems to me that on the moral level you deserve to be called a great man.

If this is true, I want you to give me credit for actually seizing upon the fundamental and essential thing about you—something, I venture to think, which few people have discovered about you. Because we must fight against a whole background of tradition and convention when we consider your personality on the moral level. In the first place, morality at once associates itself with physical stability. That is, it is much easier to associate morality with Immanuel Kant who never travelled 100 miles from the place of his birth, who ate the same breakfast for 30 years, and whose morning walk was so minutely punctual that his neighbors set their watches on his appearance—this is much easier than when we have to consider the individual who is here this week, in New York. . . .

But I think I also feel this: a man on your level of conduct is apt to give the appearance of being more devoted to the abstract than to the concrete, to the ideal more than to the individual, and, if that ideal is expressing itself through an organization, to the organization more than to the individual who is a part of that organization.

One of your students recently said to me: "He's like us all—he's looking out for himself. You can't blame him—Jesus Christ, that man can't spend much time thinking of us—he's got too many things in his mind to think of."

It is difficult for me to escape the reflection that while you have been able to provide some tangible opportunity for everyone who has needed it—from Carlton to Brink to Raisbeck to Daly [1]—you have been generous to me only in words. I do not say that I would have accepted such aid:— I do not think I would at any time, certainly not now—but I would have felt considerably better about the whole thing. I have even heard you speak with deep emotion of the sacrifice Fritz Day [2] is making "for his art" —on $15,000 a year. Really, how does he do it?

I think that my complaint against you, and very nearly everyone else who has proffered advice during the past year concerning the management of my life—and, God knows, that advice has been copious enough —is that all of it has been beautifully indefinite, amazingly lacking in substance. If I meet you again soon, and breakfast or dine with you, I think I can foretell, from invariable experience, the result: There will be [an] other verbal outpouring on my part: I [will] talk freely and openly, and at the [end you] will say, as you have said each [time in] the past two years: "Now, you know [that you can] come to me at any time, don't [you?]." And when] I assure you that I do know that I can, you [will nod] as if satisfied, and say: "Good, I want it that way." Really I despair of ever knowing you any better. You get so far with an individual and then you come up against a wall, and you can't get over it. You impress me at times as a man who is trying hard to get over his own wall, but who has never succeeded. Well, then, to get back to the point, you have told me the things I ought not to do, but you have left me adrift in the void as to the method of doing those things that I ought to do. No Europe, you say, at this time; no New York, no North Carolina; no [teaching] school; no outside work, as it [would take] too much time and energy. But [what, then?] You must write. You would be [unhappy] doing anything else. Quite so. [But you are a wise] and travelled citizen of this small [world, and it has] surely not escaped your observation that a young man of my age and growth [must eat.]

[1] Henry Carlton, Roscoe Brink, Kenneth Raisbeck and James Daly were all members of the 47 Workshop.
[2] Frederic L. Day was another member of the 47 Workshop.

If anyone in the future, should manifest enough interest in my life to ask you what I am doing, I hope you will not lift your shoulders and with a twisted little smile, impart the information that I am selling pickles, or laundry soap, or real-estate as the case may be, nor that you will add: "I did my best, but it was no use. He would see things that way." Rather, I hope you will say something like this: "Tom Wolfe, who was a poet and a dramatist, has begun to face life boldly and with courage. He was faced with the necessity of earning his own living, and he is doing well, representing the famous Katzenjammer Pickle People. Everybody had free and copious advice for Tom Wolfe except advice on the very simple matter of how he was to sustain the breath of life in his body. As we failed there, where the Katzenjammer Pickle Company has so splendidly succeeded, Tom Wolfe has quite properly rejected all our former exhortations as pretentious and windy bunkum. We may draw some sustenance from the fact that a few of us—a very few—believed he could write, and told him so, but this, too, is of very little importance since he knew the scope and depth of his talent so much better than we."

My energy—at one time vast, sustained, seemingly inexhaustible—is waning fast into its Indian Summer. It has proved no match for the mongrel sneer, the apathetic attention, or the misguided efforts of my friends who, honestly desirous to preserve and enhance the worth in me, tried to discipline, to subdue, to tame those things which were not consistent with their notions of balance and respectability! What, I take it, you were after was a thoroughly respectable, thoroughly balanced, thoroughly canny person, with artistic proclivities, who, upon demand would turn on the spirit and let the energy run out and express itself in three acts and a prologue. Drop a penny in the slot and I would turn out a golden sunset; for a five or ten cent piece, romantic love, or a tragedy of the soil; for a quarter (my top price) a bit of lashing satire.

Wolfe did not re-enroll in the 47 Workshop in the Fall of 1923. Instead, he went to New York at the end of August, to submit Welcome to Our City *to the Theatre Guild, who had asked to see it on the recommendation of Professor Baker. While waiting for the Guild's decision, he went to Asheville, then returned to New York where for six weeks he had a job soliciting donations from University of North Carolina alumni for the Graham Memorial Building. The following letter to George Wallace, a former member of the Workshop, was written when Wolfe first reached New York and was visiting a friend of Wallace's, Harold Duble of the Holland Advertising Agency.*

To GEORGE WALLACE

[Pleasantville, N. Y.]

[August, 1923]

My dear George:

I am writing you at greater length, as I promised. You see I occasionally keep my word. I am spending the night at the Dubles. I called them up and Mrs. D. invited me out. I came. That is how I treat your friends. Mrs. Duble asked me to stay longer, but I refused for a variety of reasons. The chief one is that I feel the impropriety of accepting the invitation of these kind and hospitable people who have come to know me solely and simply through you, and casually, at that. Lesser reasons are the typing of my play which is being done at the Remington Typewriter office on lower Broadway and which demands my daily attention now. I expect to give it to the Guild by the end of the week but when I shall hear from them only God, in his infinite wisdom, knows. My dear old friend, add a few lines to your prayers for me and my play. And burn the candles, boy, burn the candles.

Another consideration against my staying here is that it would cost two dollars a day going in and out, plus the time. I was out to Taylor's [1] at Mountain Lakes until this morning, but last night it was murmured that relatives were due to-day. So you see I've been kept moving. I shall try to make my own time now for such time as I shall be here, but where, I can't say. If you still think enough of me to write, address your letter to the Holland Advertising Agency. Hal will look after it.

George, if you come down before I leave, please let me see something of you. I feel like Horatio Alger's boy hero: alone in the cit-ee—which has no pit-ee—and that kind of thing, you know. I am flippant but, my dear old George, I represent the boy-hero in more than one way. God knows I'm poor enough, and my fortune at the present is tied up in my handkerchief, in the shape of a play in ten scenes—very badly typed. Unfortunately I have not the money-making penchant which all of Horatio's boy-heroes seemed to have. George, if anyone should ever tell you that "money doesn't matter," apply a length of lead pipe above his right ear with my kindest regards. Poverty is an awful, eventually a degrading, thing, and it is rare that anything good comes from it. We rise, old friend, in spite of adversity, not because of it. The unheated garret is *not* as favorable a place for the artist as the well-warmed study, cheese and crackers is *not* the fare on which great poetry is fed—and those who say it is so are fools and sentimentalists. War! War! War to the death on twaddle! Of course great poets

[1] Merlin Taylor's.

have lived in garrets; great poetry *has* been written on cheese and crackers, but to advocate this as the true artistic environment is as much as to say that Mordecai Brown, having only three fingers, was a great base-ball pitcher, and that all base-ball pitchers should immediately therefore, have two of their fingers cut off.

But enough of this worldliness for the present. I have one monster at the present—that is money. I have one idol—commerce—and whoever prates big to me of "Art" and "Sacrifice" (words continually in the mouths of wretched little people who know the meaning of neither)— when they speak thus, I say, I shall fall upon them, and smite them hip and thigh. I will never respect my brains until I pick a few gold coins from them. That may be a shameful confession, but it represents the true state of my feeling. . . .

Goodbye, then, for the present. I shall hope to see you but if I don't, you will continue to find me . . .

To ALBERT COATES

[New York City]

[Early September, 1923]

My Dear Albert:

Just a few lines to tell you I'm on my way home and hope to see you on the Hill [1] before many more weeks have elapsed. I will not stop by on way down, but expect to go by as I return. I was in Cambridge until mid-August, working on my new play [2]—two acts of which are completed. I went to New Hampshire then for a week with Prof. Baker or other friends and have been in New York for three weeks now, part of the time with Lacey Meredith and Bill Folger,[3] who have an apartment on 123 St. I am now staying there. I have spent my time here getting my play [4] revised and retyped and will submit it to the Theatre Guild tomorrow or next day. Then—home.

Remember me—or rather that play—in your prayers, Albert. It's about all I have now, except my mother's confidence and Prof. Baker's belief in me. He wrote her a corking letter in my behalf, and then wrote me if she didn't "place the entire family fortune at my disposal and beg me never again to mention any career save that of dramatist, he missed his guess."

[1] Chapel Hill.

[2] *The House* (which became *Mannerhouse*).

[3] Two graduates from the University of North Carolina with whom Wolfe shared an apartment at 439 West 123rd Street that autumn.

[4] *Welcome to Our City.*

So, you see, I'm one of these people poor in money, but with some other things of value, one of which, of course, is your friendship.

I will be glad to get back home, if only for a little, glad to see my folks, Asheville, the Hill, you! You know, if you were writing plays, Albert, I think I would be jealous of you—they'd be such damned good plays. As it is, I take almost as much pride in your achievements as if they were my own, which is going pretty far. I see such certain success for you, whether as teacher [5] or practising attorney, that the prospect must at times seem monotonous to you. I hope you will try, every now and then, to fail at something, in order to give a little spice and variety to existence if it palls. I wonder if, in some respects, I'll ever cease being a child. I want to see the Hill unutterably, but the thing that has held me back has been the desire to go back with some definite achievement behind—namely, the *selling* of a play. Please God I get my wish before another year—another month!

Write me a line or so in Asheville. The address is 48 Spruce St. Should I close wishing you success? I might as well say farewell to Hercules and wish him health.

[5] Coates had returned to the University of North Carolina as Assistant Professor of Law, and is now Professor of Law and Founder and Director of the Institute of Government there.

III

NEW YORK UNIVERSITY AND EUROPE

1924-1926

In December, the Theatre Guild declined Welcome to Our City, *although they offered to reconsider it if Wolfe would shorten and tighten it. In despair, he returned to Cambridge for the Christmas holidays. He made no serious attempt to revise and resubmit the play, but finally faced the fact that he must become a teacher to support himself. The following letter to Professor Homer A. Watt, Chairman of the English Department at the Washington Square College of New York University, is his application for the instructorship which he was to hold for the next six years.*

To HOMER A. WATT

> 10 Trowbridge Street
> Cambridge, Mass.
> January 10, 1924

Dear Professor Watt:

I am informed that there will be several vacancies in the English department at New York University on the opening of the new term, in February. I have requested the Harvard Appointment Bureau to forward my papers, including letters and scholastic grades, to you. Mr. Dow,[1] formerly of Harvard, and now an instructor at the uptown branch of the university, may also be consulted.

I was graduated, as you will note, from the University of North Carolina, in 1920, and received my master's degree in English from Harvard in 1922. The appointment office secured me an offer from Northwestern University

---

[1] Robert Bruce Dow had known Wolfe at Harvard in 1922–23, and had then become an instructor in English at the University College of New York University. Dow is now Associate Professor of English at the Washington Square College, and Assistant Director of Admissions.

in 1922, which I ultimately refused, in order to return for another year under Professor Baker at the 47 Workshop. Thus, I have been a student in the Graduate School for three years.

I have had no experience as a teacher. It is only fair to tell you that my interests are centred in the drama, and that someday I hope to write successfully for the theatre and to do nothing but that. My play is at present in the hands of a producer in New York but, even in the fortunate event of its acceptance, I feel the necessity of finding immediate employment.

I am twenty-three years old and a native of Asheville, North Carolina. I do not know what impression of maturity my appearance may convey but it is hardly in excess of my age. In addition, my height is four or five inches over six feet, producing an effect on a stranger that is sometimes startling. I think you should know so much in advance, as the consideration may justly enter into any estimate of my qualifications.

If New York University feels justified in offering me employment as an instructor in English, and if I am satisfied with the offer, I promise to give the most faithful and efficient service of which I am capable.

I hope you will find it convenient to reply to this letter at some early date.

To HOMER A. WATT

[Telegram]

Boston, Mass.
January 21, 1924.

Accept instructorship. Will report Feb. first. Will you acknowledge wire.

To MARGARET ROBERTS

Hotel Albert, Room 2220
Eleventh St. & University Place
New York City

Sunday, Feb. 10, 1924

Dear Mrs. Roberts:

I am writing at length to answer your last heartening letter, which was written after I left home, and which has grown old, but more precious. I have seen a great many people, witnessed a number of events, and, like Satan, have grown, for the moment, weary of my goings to and fro and up and down the earth. It seems now that I will be fastened for several

months in this great madhouse of a city—for good or ill, who can say?—
but I think I have chosen wisely.

Briefly—since I saw you, I have been in New York for six weeks, when
I was busy with the Graham Memorial Fund at the University; later I went
to Boston and Cambridge for the holidays and remained a little more
than a month. The Guild held my play [1] for three or four months, as you
perhaps know,—held it until I was on the verge of madness and collapse
—and finally returned it, after wining and dining me, telling me I was "a
coming figure," and so on, and trying to extract a promise that all my
future work would be submitted to the Guild for consideration before any
other producer got hold of it. Of course, I made no such promise.

Before I left the city, however, one of the Guild directors,—a Jew by
the name of Langner,[2] and, I believe, a very wealthy, patent lawyer, had
me in to his apartment. He wanted me to cut the play thirty minutes—a
reduction I concede it needs. He wanted me, also, to cut the list of characters (this means cheaper production) and to revise—he insisted it
needed no rewriting—with a view to "tightening"; that is, to develop a
central plot which will run through each scene, and which would revolve
around a small group of central figures: Rutledge, the Negro, the girl, etc.
Of course this would mean a more conventional type of play. I told him I
had deliberately tried to avoid writing such a play; that I had written
a play with a plot which centered about the life and destiny of an entire
civilization, not about a few people. If I consented to this revision, Langner
promised his support and added that he was fairly certain he could place
the play. He observed, cheerfully, that he had really asked for very little;
that I could make all necessary changes in a week. This was a bit of
optimism in which I did not share. However, I promised to make the
effort, and departed for Cambridge.

Professor Baker was properly horrified when I communicated the evil
tidings. Not only, he said, would the proposed revision greatly cheapen the
play, but it was also impossible, since my play had been hailed and praised
as a new departure in American drama; its fate was on the rails. Thereupon, he read to me from a book on the American Theatre just published,
by Oliver Sayler,[3] in which my play is described at some length as "the
most radical and successful experiment ever made in the American Theatre." The Workshop comes in for its share of praise for doing my play.

This is, of course, sweet music to my ears, but my heart is assuming
a flinty cast, and the sound of the shekel is not unpleasing. I told Professor
Baker as much, as gently as I could, and he accused me of having allowed
New York to "commercialize" me in my six weeks' stay. This opened the

---

[1] *Welcome to Our City.*
[2] Lawrence Langner.
[3] *Our American Theatre.*

floodgates; I had heard enough of such talk. All the old and cruel sentimentality of the world, in its relation to the artistic, struck me with a bitter
blow. It was not a question of desiring cake and wine, I told him; it was a
question of naked need: Bread! Bread! Bread! Was this commercialism?
Then, indeed, was Christ a materialist when he multiplied the loaves?
Christ, by the way, unlike many of his present followers, was base enough
to recognize that men and women must be fed.

I broached the question of my future again. What must I do? The answer
came, as always: Write! Write! Do nothing else. Yes, but how? I had been
told this for three years: it was all, no doubt, very true, but not very helpful. I suggested teaching. At the suggestion, he looked as if he were being
rent limb from limb. Of all possible suggestions, this was the worst—and
he seemed to think that all of mine were incredibly bad. Finally—suprem-
est irony of all!—he confided that, after mature consideration, it seemed
to him that a year abroad was the very thing I needed most. The full
humor of this is apparent when I tell you that no later than August he had
descended on me in his wrath when I suggested this very thing, and he
had told me this would be colossal stupidity at the time. Now, plainly, he
has forgotten he ever made such a statement; the wind, for unknown
reasons, has veered from another corner, and he has tacked.

At any rate I began to understand—a bitter draught it was—that Professor Baker was an excellent friend, a true critic, but a bad counsellor. I
knew that, from this time on, the disposition of my life was mainly in my
own hands; that one profits, no matter how good the intention, not by the
experience of others, but only by such experience as touches him. At that
time I heard that New York University needed several new instructors for
the February term, and I directed the Harvard Appointment Bureau to
forward my letters, grades, and papers. I applied; I had friends in New
York speak for me. In two days I had their answer. An instructorship was
mine if I wanted it. I came to New York on a flying trip. I liked the men.
The offer was more than reasonable: $1800 for seven months over an
eight-hour-a-week teaching schedule; my work was to be concerned entirely with English composition. The men here at the University assure
me that I should easily complete my work, in and out of class, with three
hours a day. If this is true, I should have time to write.

There is one other advantage—a decided one. The college—this branch
of it—is but eight years old, and has no traditions. I am given great liberty;
personal idiosyncrasy is recognized and allowed. The students, moreover,
mainly Jewish and Italian, have come up from the East Side; many are
making sacrifices of a very considerable nature in order to get an education. They are, accordingly, not at all the conventional type of college
student. I expect to establish contacts here, to get material in my seven
months' stay that may prove invaluable. I am here until September; I must

teach through the summer. I am here where the theatre is—the theatre
I love—and if I can't write plays, at least I can see 'em. What Professor
Baker will say, or has said, I don't know. I never told him my decision.

But I have taught for two days now, and I am living; and nothing about
me, so far as I know, has "suffered a sea change."

And this is all that I have to tell you for the time—over that which you
know already: that you wax immensely in my affections and that, as ever,
I am

Faithfully yours,

P.S. And—glory of glories—I'm free. The world is mine, and I, at present,
own a very small but satisfying portion of it—Room 2220, at the Hotel
Albert, where I hope presently to have the joy of reading one of your
letters.

The new play [4] comes; I read it to a friend [5] in New Hampshire, who also
writes 'em. He said I would sell it in spite of "hell and high water." The
words are mine. And, by the way, I was in New Hampshire for four days
and fished through the ice of the lake. This is the history.

*The following letter to Frederic L. Day was found among Wolfe's own
papers and is evidently a rough draft of a letter which was rewritten and
mailed. Words in brackets denote those made illegible by the decomposition of the paper: double spaces denote separate fragments which may
or may not follow in the order given them.*

To FREDERIC L. DAY

Hotel Albert
New York
[April, 1924]

[With an arrow pointing to the picture of the Hotel Albert on the Letterhead]
Aint it perty, Fritz?

My dear Fritz:

Your letter is about the pleasantest thing that could have happened; if
my pen trembles a little, remember it comes from eagerness. I've just
finished reading yours. I noted, with a pained start, that you "hardly expect a reply"—and here one is off on the first mail. If this doesn't destroy

4 *The House* (later *Mannerhouse*).
5 Probably Henry Fisk Carlton.

for a time your faith in yourself as a character judge, you are safe [in] your own conceit. But you have little of [that], Fritz.

I don't know how long this letter will be but when I begin to sling ink, there's no stopping me. So, do your Daily Dozen now, take five deep breaths, and begin.

I have no intention of discussing here the wisdom or the folly of my decision to come to New York. I am more at peace than in four years, and during the moments when I have time to write, I write like a fiend. . . . I have over one hundred people in [my] classes here—boys and girls—mixed [in] race, but ninety per cent Jewish. Many of them come from New York's East Side. I believe I am making a contact which shall prove itself to be of the greatest value to me. I came without racial sentimentality—indeed with strong racial prejudice concerning the Jew, which I still retain. I shall learn—I am learning—a great deal.

Of one thing, of course, I am convinced. I am no school teacher. This, I think, will not occasion surprise in Cambridge. But *this* may surprise you —my little devils like me: I am "popular." And—keep this under the rose, Fritz—I am told that the girls—some of them are very pretty, you know— have a "crush" on me. The language is another's, I quote. A girl came to the English office late the other day—for what is technically known as "a conference." Nothing was wrong. She was passing her work. She was very pretty. On a sudden, however, she began to sob convulsively, ended by covering her face by her pretty little [hands]. Before I knew what was what, she was over on my shoulder. I looked around and saw that the head of the department was nowhere in sight. We continued the conference. Now, this is an amazing thing. Nothing was wrong: but it is April and something is stirring in their blood. And "in mine, in mine, so I sware [by] the rose." . . .

I am, I fear, an incurable romanticist cursed with a sense of humor. No true romantic should be able to see comedy, Fritz. You are forever "kidding" your own emotions, you know. And, certainly, it is not . . .

Perhaps you wonder, Fritz, what I have done with my ten-scene play— whether I have rewritten, revised, recast, cut, added, changed. No—I have done none of these things. As a matter of fact, I was hectored, badgered, driven, [harried?], to such a degree before, during, and after the play by commendation and criticism—none of which agreed—that I am wholeheartedly and completely tired of my first huge opus. I leave it to all the glory of its imperfections. My world has moved; I am writing a better play—I'll have nothing to do with the old.

Now, all this, I know, violates the Workshop standard of proper conduct for an "artist." If I were an "artist"—Thank God I'm not!—I should work unceasingly for five years until I had my play in that mythical state of perfection toward which every true 47-er is tending. But, unfortunately, I can not operate with such restrained decorum. I have a crude lusty young talent which is kicking up its coltish heels, and I have all I can do in keeping it within the pasture as it is. I have new ideas—I tire of a thing almost as soon as it's written. No man, I believe, writes solely to express himself— the idea of some kind of audience is always there—but, I suppose, I come as close to writing for pure expression—simply, that is, to get it out of me —as anyone you know.

Of course I realize that this is not likely to fill my wallet.

New York has been a stimulus, it has increased my enthusiasm for some things, my contempt for others. My love of the theatre has grown: my dislike of most of the people I have met who are concerned with the theatre has grown, also. If a play of mine is done, I think I should prefer Belasco or Geo. M. Cohan to do it rather than the Guild or that abominable little clique at the Provincetown. The latter, by the way, have had my play over four months now. I have gone to them repeatedly, pushing my way through the crowd of short-haired women and long-haired men who fill their rooms, in order to get news, news. Each time an evil-looking [hag?] with red hair has gone into a little room, shuffled some papers, and returned with the information that the playreader had the play, that "you shall certainly hear next week." Each time I have been asked for my address, and it has been noted piously. A month ago I went back for the last time. Escaping the red-headed harpy and a few of the degenerates, I got into the little room and asked the typist. She opened a cabinet and found my play—under an inch of dust. Ah God! It had been returned. I was honestly glad: I wanted it back. Besides, what would one of their productions, in their lousy little theatre, net me? Nothing.

But no. It had not been returned. It had not even been read. But,—she was sure that "in another week"— Groping blindly for the door, I staggered out. Of course I have heard nothing since. But I have almost finished a long and vitriolic letter which I end with three words: *Go to Hell* and which I conclude "with renewed assurances of my warm personal detestation." Of course, I tell them that I am young, I am unknown and that, therefore, they have been insolent. Such people know only two moods— insolence and servility. After all, as I tell them again, the problem is simple:—

it is one of fundamental honesty.

Perhaps this will shock you. It is not a good beginning when one is obscure and needs patronage. Unfortunately, Fritz, I have not the spirit to bow before such insults as these. In adversity I grow more stubborn. But— I am beginning to see that a mere course in play-writing is not enough. There should be a sister course in peddling, auctioneering, servility, fawning, licking, and whining—a kind of sales-course, you know.

They tell me constantly that one must have the friendship of such people. It is not true! It may be harder but, by God, this inner *daemon* of mine is not at the mercy of their knavery; this flame, once fired, may not be taken lightly, and, so help me God, the day will come when, unaided, I shall hammer them down upon their creaking knees.

This is big boasting, but men grow modest on prosperity—

it's a dishonest virtue. And I have sense to understand there's something schoolboyish in my ravings.

It amounts to this: they withhold the trumpet, but poetry remains: they cannot take it from me.

And that brings me to the proposal of Miss Helburn that I look her up. What for? I am not good at self-introduction. What is she going to say to me? Will a look of wonder greet me when I tell her that I have come at her suggestion? Will it be supplanted by vague recollection when I tell her she spoke of me to you—that it was through you. Will a perfunctory conversation ensue, in which she remembers vaguely that my play showed "promise"? By God, Fritz, I won't stand for it. A talky woman is bad enough; a woman organized artistically is to me—who am a feudalist— intolerable. Lemon and Langner were nice to me; I remember them with affection.

But the Gods in Olympus spoke by messenger through the clouds. Therefore, for all of me, they may go to Hell. They had my play four months; they drove me frantic by their inaction. Finally, they returned it with wretched evasiveness: "good—but doesn't fit in with our program now"— "perhaps you were a little prejudiced in Scene IX—but, then, perhaps you weren't."

And then, this charming Miss Helburn, whose lily-white hand has this far never clasped mine, asked G.P.—on a train somewhere—if I was making any of the changes suggested. Why do they pry around so? It goads me to fury. They could have talked to me if they had had any genuine interest. And now, damn them, they'll come to me—or not at all.

$150 every month, Fritz, gives one a tremendous sense of confidence in his [profanity?].

And by the way—I am being paid in twelve monthly instalments rather than in seven or eight. That means that in September when I finish, I shall have $750 due me. I'm going to England in October—[——] steerage. My plan is to go to Cornwall, to some little village where it's cheap—and stay a month or two—writing, writing, writing. I'm going to Heaven, that is, in October.

I am charmed, delighted to know that my disappearance has been completely successful—that the frantic efforts of the 47-ers to discover me have been foiled. Pray don't give me away, Fritz. It's die, dog, or eat the hatchet for me now. Alone or nothing. I want to do it unbeholden to anyone or anything. I feel like the Count of Monte Cristo who already has [——] "The world is mine," and who is to return twenty years later with fortune and a noble name.

As for 47, I don't think it will experience great difficulty in forgetting me. Its mind functions from day to day; to-day's masterpiece is forgotten to-morrow; yesterday's lion is not remembered to-day—last week's culture is outmoded and supplanted by a new already. There's good, kindly, foolish, futile Miss Loveman. Last year she pursued me. If I didn't go to her terrible teas on Sunday I was reprimanded Monday. I was Milton, Shakespeare, Keats—and more. At Christmas this year I saw her at the Opera House. A look of vague recognition lighted [up her face]. Somewhere she had met [me] before. I started to speak. She held up one finger admonishingly. "Don't speak! I know you! I have your name on the tip of my tongue. It will all come back in a moment."

And there, dear Fritz, spoke 47. Esau's skin, you know, but Jacob's voice.

I shall cut myself away entirely—from G. P. and all the others. However, he seems to have severed the cord already. For me the wine dark seas send coiling enticements; my bark puts out and as Columbus I shall find a green new world, where my spirit shall quicken, [and like] Odysseus, I shall come upon the enchanted isles—perhaps to eat the Lotus and sink Lethewards into a drowsy obliviousness of this present actual existence [————].

I must decide for myself. Everything for myself—and the wonder and the glory of that has not yet faded. For it was but recently that I put utter dependence in the power of older men to decide for me. A few quick words, an authoritative setting to rights and the wounding business of my life would be adjusted. And yet, in over two years, I never suggested a plan for my future to G. P. that was not condemned; nor did I get one from him which was practicable or which would devolve on him [————]. Lately for my future. I suggested *home, New York, teaching, Europe* —all, particularly *Europe,* were condemned. And now, at Christmas, when the thing is impossible, and as if the idea had never been suggested,

Professor Baker said: "You know, I think it would be a good thing for you if you took a year abroad now."

[THE LETTER BREAKS OFF UNFINISHED HERE]

To GEORGE WALLACE

Hotel Albert, New York

Friday, April 11, 1924.

My dear George:

I am sending you a pome—writ by me. It has the full flavor of the romantic ironist, you see. If you will give it to the girl from New Orleans [1] with my compliments, and wait until she reads it, noting her comments and reactions, I promise to buy you a horse's-neck at Steve Bozzanetti's.

And, believe me, George, with renewed assurances of reverence and respect, and all that sort of thing, I am

A.D.—2024

The great drums of the world may beat,
And the trumpets of earth may blare.
But, beneath the thunder of the feet,
Silent, I shall not care
Or stir, unless you come, my sweet,
With lilac or rose in your hair
And twice in pain, and thrice again,
The earth may be cloven through,
And my statue may get down and walk
From its place in the avenue.
I shall not know, I shall not care!
But I *shall* know if you
Should stir the grasses over me
    With feathery, airy tread,
Should pass with the rustle of scented silk
    Above my earthy bed;
And one of my bones would stand erect,
    To show you I am not dead.

(Cetera Desunt) Know what that means, son?

[1] Efforts to identify "the girl from New Orleans" have met with no success.

To MARGARET ROBERTS

Hotel Albert
New York
May 5, 1924

Dear Mrs. Roberts:

This, briefly, to thank you for your fine letter, and to render my poor judgment on the subject nearest to your heart— ——'s future. I think I understand his position. Did you know I fell in love when I was sixteen with a girl who was twenty-one?[1] Yes, honestly—desperately in love. And I've never quite got over it. The girl married, you know: she died of influenza a year or two later. I've forgotten what she looked like, except that her hair was corn-colored. A woman five years older can make putty of a boy of eighteen. In one way, she is as old as she will ever be, and a great deal depends upon her own quality. . . . It seems that at this period man comes to grips with something elemental—beyond him. I'm beginning to question the wisdom of mixing education with adolescence, Greek with Seventeen, literature with love. Perhaps the academics should come later when we have leavened our madness with a grain of method. I'm not sure, and I suppose there's not time enough. . . .

You speak of Harvard. That's most difficult. I don't know what to say. But I'm sure of this:—if I had gone to Cambridge instead of to Chapel Hill—when I was sixteen—the result would have been catastrophic. Of course, —— is a big, fine, strapping fellow, well-grown, mature in appearance, with associations with wealthy boys which may have given him a kind of balance. But this, I think, is *now* true of Harvard: no boy should go there now until he is ready to mine his own ore. If he is still in need of dependence on someone or something—a *very* real and honest need, by the way—Harvard is not the place, I think. A sensitive young Southerner, fond of companionship and warmth, will find the sledding rough, I'm afraid. Of course, with a student of one of the great academies—Andover or Exeter—the situation is different, I believe. He is graduated with his class and accompanies them to Cambridge. This occurs as naturally as the transition, say, from Asheville High to Chapel Hill. But I have seen hundreds of boys submerged in the student life of Harvard. Unknown they enter—are swiftly appalled by the vastness of the system and its impersonality—and unknown they leave, at the end of four years, with a feeling of disenchantment and futility.

The quality of Harvard instruction is very high—the highest, I believe—but, again, many succeed in evading all attempts at education on the part

[1] Clara Paul.

of the University faculty. It is not difficult to slide through; and, in addition, you must prepare to calculate the probable effects of a metropolitan community of over one million people upon a fascinated young stranger thrust suddenly in from the provinces. A change of climate and geography might be intensely valuable . . . now. Remember, there are a number of first-rate small colleges in New England, beautifully located, with admirable scholastic standards. There is Amherst, for example, which still demands Greek, I'm told. And Williams, a lovely place, walled in by mountains not unlike our own. And Bowdoin—and, of course, Dartmouth, one of the best. In all these places a young fellow might assert himself, and grow. . . .

As for me, I work and am fairly happy. Really, I'm having a wonderful experience. This place—particularly the University—swarms with life, Jewish, Italian, Polish. My little devils like me. I tell them every week that I'm no teacher. I suppose they can see that for themselves; and perhaps that is why they like me. The head of the department [1] has asked me to come back next year, but I have given him no answer. The desire to write— to create—has, for the first time, become almost a crude animal appetite. And this is because of the obstacles thrown in the path of creation. During the few hours left to me, I write like a fiend on one of the finest plays [2] you ever saw. My first term is almost over—two weeks more, in fact—gone like a flash!

And did you know that I'm going to Heaven in September. That is, to England. From September 1, six months pay will be due me—September through February. This is $900. With economy I can stay over five or six months. I'm going down to Cornwall first—it's very beautiful, I'm told —and bury myself in a country village for two months. There I shall write my heart out. Then over the country, into London for a few days, Scotland, and France.

This is all for the present. I've snatched Time to write this. But, during the examination period, you shall have greater detail. The Provincetown Theatre has had my play [3] five months. I can hear nothing. One of the editors of D. Appleton left a note at the hotel this morning. He wants my play [4]—the Theatre Guild suggested it—to read for publication. I shall let him read it; I doubt that I shall let him publish—even if he wants to. Certainly, not as long as someone may produce it.

The new play is an epic. I believe in it with all my heart. Dear God! If I but had the time to write.

[1] Professor Watt.
[2] *The House (Mannerhouse).*
[3] *Welcome to Our City.*
[4] *Welcome to Our City.*

Professor Koch of Chapel Hill bounded into town a week or so ago, and looked me up. He wants to put one of my juvenile one-acts—the *Buck Gavin* thing—into his new book [5] which Holt is bringing out soon. He is insistent, and has just sent me a copy of the thing. I'm not ashamed of the play, but I wrote it on a rainy night, when I was seventeen, in three hours. Something tells me I should hate to see my name attached now. Of course I couldn't tell Koch that. Besides, he had his chance two or three years ago, when he brought his first book out. Please don't *publish*—but I'll give you my honest opinion: I believe his eagerness to publish the little play now comes from a suspicion that I'm going to get famous in a hurry now—God knows why!—and he wants to *ticket* me, so to speak. This is a rotten thing to say, but it's my honest opinion. I sent Koch an act or two of my new play [6]—you heard the prologue—and he did everything but break down and weep. It was the greatest thing ever; I was the American Bernard Shaw, etc.

Everyone, you see, is enthusiastic, but I notice that *I* earn my own living. The Theatre Guild is cordial. When am I going to bring my new play in? Their officials want to know me. Will I have lunch? Their play reader Lemon,[7] trumpets my name abroad. He told me recently he had spoken of me at the banquet of some dramatic association. I am grateful, but how I wish someone would *produce* one of my plays. . . .

But—I learn. I am acquiring patience. And I'm quite willing to wait a year or two for the unveiling exercises. Do you know, all that really matters right now is the knowledge that I am twenty-three, and a golden May is here. The feeling of immortality in youth is upon me. I am young, and I can never die. Don't tell me that I can. Wait until I'm thirty. Then I'll believe you.

I never hear from you but my respect for your intelligence waxes. You are a lovely, beautiful woman. Other women I have known—young and old—who wanted to mother me, to ruffle my hair when it's curly, or to feed me. But you mother the minds and spirits of young men until they grow incandescent. That is a nobler, finer thing.

So, it seems, you are a great woman.

To you all, as ever, my deepest love,

[5] *Carolina Folk Plays, Second Series.*
[6] *The House* (*Mannerhouse*). Probably Wolfe had read the prologue to her when he was in Asheville in October, 1923.
[7] Courtenay Lemon.

To GEORGE WALLACE

Hotel Albert, New York

Monday, Sept 8 [1924]

Et tu Brute:—One would think, from the insolent silence that has greeted my letters to hypothetical friends, that a man of my kidney has no higher purpose than to submit in silence. But 'ware the tiger! If I don't get some answers I shall turn and rend the world. Now, I charge thee, George, do thou as I desirest, and show thyself a good lad, a tall fellow.

Some days agone I writ to Mistress Ann Macdonald,[1] pleading pressure of time, and the exigencies of an impending voyage, and desiring her to get for me both copies of my play. Mistress Ann hath not suffered to answer yet, and I commission thee to go to her, lay siege, and take the play by frontal attack.

The point is, I must make haste, my dear boy, for time presses; and I infer by their silence, and the one letter, which I showed you, that they have no profitable intentions toward my play, but would cheer me with sounding praise and apparent consideration. (T'Hell wit dat stuff, George.) I must send the play out before I go: there *really* is a producer who wants to see it, and you might hasten its return if you hinted as much.

I wrote Miss M. about a week since, urging the necessity of speed: but in this hustling, go-ahead, up-and-coming theatrical business, speed means anything within six months. My letter, I fear, was full of proud and vaunting speech, courteous enough, however, as regards Miss M. Among many other things, I remember saying I was tired tossing gold nuggets at folks' heads, and that when Caesar returned to Rome again, (God help me—I said that, too) the people would come to him at the gates. If she is disposed to look askance, or do some other angry thing, you might say that I have been drunk these six weeks past, and have added hysteria to irrationality. That should protect you, my boy.

All this, of course, is written on the supposition that you have not drowned in a New Hampshire lake, and are again working your garden in Pleasantville.

Really, my dear George, if you would see me you'd best come in soon. I've had my last class, and was the recipient (that's the word, eh?) of a Dunhill pipe from one of my adoring classes; I give the final examinations Friday, and hope to *leave* somewhere around the twentieth, possibly a bit la-tah. . . .

Cordially, though in view of your perverse, unfriendly, and revolting silence, you deserve no such greeting,

[1] Miss MacDonald was a reader and translator with The Neighborhood Playhouse, to which Wolfe had submitted *Welcome to Our City*.

The following letter was evidently never presented to Professor Baker, since there is no trace of it in his own files.

To GEORGE PIERCE BAKER

On board the Cunard R.M.S. *Lancastria.*

Wednesday, October 29, [1924]

Dear Professor Baker:

On shipboard I have had the pleasure of the acquaintance of Mr. ——. ——. . . . His interests, he tells me, have always been creative—in short, he has wanted to write. He was faced in his thirties by that very blunt and very terrible economic necessity which most of us must face, and now that he has overcome it, he has the great good sense to abandon the profession which has always been hostile to his genuine interests. . . . I have given you so much of Mr. ——'s more intimate history because I know such material interests you, and may influence your decision toward a prospective applicant; and further, it is because Mr. —— feels he may apply for admission to 47 that I write this letter, hoping it may be of some small service to him should he ever care to present it.

As I write you, we are limping comfortably along through the North Atlantic at 300 miles a day, with an injury to the starboard engine that may delay us a day or two. I am taking with me the prologue and three acts of my new play, "The House." (Perhaps not my potential best, but better than anyone else's). At any rate, everything looks good when you do it. I am going, after my year in New York (in the "Latin Quarter" at the University) like a discoverer: the world is opening before me like an oyster, and valiant deeds are in me. . . . Ideas are simply boiling in my pan; the next one is a most tremendous thing. Also, I started my new birthday on 1500 words a day: and I shall continue.

I don't know where this will find you, since this is your sabbatical year, but I have heard that you are going abroad, and if you are near me, I shall ferret you out; and you may caution me on my lack of discipline, and on my heart affairs, and I shall promise faithfully to heed your warnings— haven't I always *promised?* At any rate, I may send the new play—if you'll stand for it—and prove all my boastings.

I have been silent a period of months—perhaps you've wondered why. I was in the furnace there in Jerusalem—I sponged up a million impressions; I admired, loathed, loved a million things; and in between the damnable corrections on Freshman papers, I wrote like a fiend—quite honestly the best work I've ever done. I cut myself away from all of which I had been a part; I went like a nameless ghost at night along the streets of the City—but I [got her?]

It was simply hell at times, but I'm older and wiser, and that counts.

I think you know how I really feel toward you. You are just about the best friend I ever had, and no year passes that does not compel renewed and increased affection for your character and courage.

P.S. Some of the most amusing people in the world are on this ship. There's an English cockney who has confessed to an interest in the theatre, and who asked me if I had ever seen "The Eyesiest Wye."

Wolfe's letter of November 8, 1924, to George W. McCoy of The Asheville Citizen *was written in an attempt to sell material describing his European trip to that newspaper. His journal of the voyage over, "A Passage to England," was never published, but a short piece entitled "London Tower" appeared in the Sunday, July 19, 1925, issue of the* Citizen.

McCoy had attended The North State School in Asheville, but did not actually meet Wolfe until he entered the University of North Carolina in Wolfe's senior year there. Later, when he was working on the Citizen, *he became a good friend of Wolfe's, who liked to drop in at the news room late at night to see him. He is now Managing Editor of the* Citizen, *and Secretary of The Thomas Wolfe Memorial Association.*

To GEORGE W. McCOY

The Imperial Hotel
Russell Square
London

Saturday, November 8, 1924

Dear George:

I am writing you this in the most extreme haste, in the hope that it shall bring us both to better fortune. I arrived in London on Wednesday after an amazing voyage, and I am now lost in the beauty and mystery and fascination of this ancient and magnificent city. I came over on the *Lancastria*, a 17,000 ton Cunarder. . . . The cabin list was small—ninety-six—but in that number were knaves, fools, aristocrats, tradesmen, fat Americans . . ., English traders and gentlemen who had traversed the seven seas many times, and who thought nothing of a two weeks' voyage to Chicago and back.

George—I put it all on paper from day to day; I let nothing escape me, and even when the sea made me feel a bit sorry for myself I put it down. Now that voyage—the poignant emotion of it all, and the astonishing differences in habit and custom and opinion of different races, English and American—is recorded hastily, it is true; sometimes clumsily. But it is there. I don't know what to do with it. I might send it to some American magazine, but it is a conglomerate of so many things—drama, comment, incident, opinion—that I scarcely know what to call it. I have given it a title: "A Passage to England." It is written, George, in my own hand on sheets of white and yellow paper. And my penmanship is poor.

Now to the point. Some of the *Citizen* people suggested that I send them a weekly letter. No pay was suggested, and perhaps none was intended. At any rate, I give and bequeath outright to you this letter with certain conditions. If it is suitable for publication in the *Citizen*—I don't know that it is—take it to Mrs. Roberts at once, read it to her, and ask her to censor it, if necessary. Much of it is so personal, written so rapidly, and I am so *close* to it—not enough detachment—that I don't know whether I work myself an injury (in the eyes of the burghers, you know) at times. Let her word go: if she gives the word to print it as it is, and the paper wants it, print it.

Now to brass tacks again. If this letter gets published and is of sufficient interest to call for others, see if you can get me some money for them. What I am doing from day to day now, primarily for my own use later when I shall create from these sources, is to watch people—their manners of eating, drinking, sleeping, acting. For these are the things that count. I have learned more of England on that boat by watching a Cockney at mortal sword-play with an English aristocrat—we were all at the table —than I ever did in reading the articles on political opinion and elections of all the Philip Gibbses and David Lawrences in the world. And people everywhere—their drama, their emotion, their humor—are interested in people everywhere else. Perhaps if I can do the thing plainly and clearly and honestly, without fear or favor, people at home may be interested.

I need the money—I want to stay a year, if possible. I have the utmost faith in your integrity and character—that is why I write you this foolish but very *earnest* letter, leaving the whole matter at your disposition. . . .

I am sending along the manuscript of the voyage over to-morrow.[1] Answer me as soon as you are able to let me know what you can do with it. Perhaps it might be Sunday feature stuff. If you sell my letters to one or many papers, you get your own cut-in, of course. If the paper doesn't want the stuff, give it to Mrs. Roberts to keep for me.

Since coming to London I have walked the queer, blind, narrow, incredible, crooked streets of the city, looking at the people, hearing them

[1] Wolfe did not actually send the manuscript at this time. In March, 1925, he sent the Prologue of it to Mrs. Roberts, but it was never published.

talk, getting them. Late at night, early in the morning, when the streets are deserted, I traverse great sections of the city, going down narrow alleys, stopping at small refreshment wagons, at pubs, taxi stands, anywhere, listening to them talk. And all the time I am making notes—London and New York, England and America.

I was twenty four a month ago, George. I would to God I might be twenty four forever. This is a magnificent adventure and the world is opening like an oyster.

Answer P.D.Q.
American Express Co.,
Haymarket St.,
London.
Sending mss. to-morrow.

To HOMER A. WATT

[Paris]

Jan. 15, 1925

Dear Professor Watt:

I am conscious that the letter I promised to write you has been long delayed; I shall tell you the extraordinary reasons for the delay.

I have had an astonishing voyage—I spent 1 month in England, went down almost every back alley in London, and into most of the disreputable pubs; about six weeks ago I came to Paris and settled in a small hotel in the Latin Quarter. I went to this place with my bags very late at night—one o'clock—the concierge who admitted me had been wounded in the war, and gave a great groan when he saw the baggage, and when I told him my room was five flights up. He pointed to his crippled leg, and hobbled around painfully; I suggested that he keep one of the bags until morning; I would take the other two myself; he agreed to this gladly. The story is that during the night a man entered, asked for a woman formerly resident of the hotel, and on the way out, stole my bag.

The bag was old and battered, the articles in it were not of great value; what it did contain that could not be replaced was the prologue and two acts in manuscript of the play [1] I had lived with for more than a year. I know it sounds silly, but nothing has hit me like this since the death of my brother Ben six years ago. I moved to another hotel the next day: I bought paper and swore that I should rewrite the play in two weeks—by

---

[1] *The House* which finally became *Mannerhouse.*

New Year's—and on January third I had not only recreated what was lost, but completed an entire first draft. Since then I have been re-writing. For three weeks I saw or spoke practically to no one; then I met friends, and have passed the time very pleasantly since. Good or bad, what I have done in these past five weeks is the best I have ever done. I am rather glad the thing was stolen: it has helped me.

The hotel people, after a very nasty scene, paid me 500 francs for the loss of the valise: they suggested it was a conspiracy (which they knew to be false), and I told them they were dishonest scoundrels—after I got my fingers on the 500.

Since very charming friends—including two attractive ladies—have purchased a car, and want me to go South with them for two or three months, I think I shall do this.

You spoke to me early about the February term; later you suggested that the matter was uncertain, because of larger enrollment, and so on. At any rate, although my own money is nearly gone, I feel that everything that is happening to me now is too important to be checked violently. I shall stay over, if possible, some months longer: my mother, I believe, will help me.

In five weeks time I have acquired enough French to read very easily —and to speak very badly, but comprehensibly, without the necessity of beginning all over. I am entering a new world of art and letters; during the past two weeks I have been to some incredible places—working men's dance halls; all night lodgings where the wretches are huddled in sleep, a hundred to a room, over long tables, drugged by their own weariness, and by the over-powering stench of the bodies, breathing as one like a great terrible organ.

If I didn't make it sufficiently plain before I left, let me emphasize now the gratitude and affection I bear toward you for your kindliness, patience, and forbearance last year—for me, just hatching out, a genuine anno mirabilis. When I come back I shall certainly be in to see you. If you only have time, meanwhile, to write me a line or two, you would give me a great deal of delight and pleasure.

If this seems to you to be hastily scribbled by a man coming out of a dream, I think your intuitions will be correct. But I'm all right now, and beginning to live.

The following letter was written by Wolfe in reply to one from his brother Fred which informed him that Mabel Wolfe Wheaton had undergone an operation, reproached him for having lost a check sent him by his mother,

*and suggested that it was about time he came home. In a comment made
later on this letter, Fred Wolfe says: "I condemned Tom then, for I truly
did not understand what he was about . . . I plead guilty that I and also
perhaps other members of the family (certainly not Mama) misunderstood
him then and 'bore down' too hard on him. I think Tom and I understood
each other fully later."*

To FRED W. WOLFE

Paris

January 27, 1925

Dear Fred:

I have just received your letter which contained the news of Mabel's
operation; I am writing her at the same time I send you this. I appreciate
the motives which kept you from writing me at the time. I am deeply
thankful that everything has turned out so well, and that she is recovering.

Also, let me thank you very much for your contribution to the check. I
have thanked Mama in a letter which should be home at this time. That
letter also contains explanations of the loss of the first check and that I
stopped payment here, and that it is absolutely safe.[1] It also gives an
account of my activities here and in England. I think you may understand
when you read it that there has been no foolishness on my part, and that I
have been hard at work.

You speak of my three months in Europe, and conclude that I will be
ready to come home about this time. I do not think you quite understand
the circumstances: I am going to try to explain them to you now.

I think you understand, Fred, that I have the greatest respect and admiration for you—I do not believe you have always understood my motives,
or a certain purpose in my life towards which I am striving. I want you
to know that I am ready and willing at all times to earn my living, and
that I am able to do this by teaching as instructor in some university. I
want you to know that I have worked faithfully and hard upon this trip,
and that until I received the check so generously sent by you and Mama, I
was using my own money. That it should be necessary for me to ask for
any help to anyone is a matter of the deepest regret to me. It is not my

[1] In a letter to his mother dated January 20, 1925 (see page 98 of *Thomas Wolfe's
Letters to His Mother*) Wolfe wrote: "What happened was this: I got your check
in January. It was made payable to you and drawn on the American Express, Paris.
. . . Your name was *not* on the back. I went to the American Express Co. here to
cash it. They explained that it could be cashed by no one but Julia E. Wolfe, and
not until her endorsement was on the back. . . . Somewhere, somehow—where,
when I don't know—I lost your check . . . but I am quite sure no one can cash it."

intention to ask anyone, particularly members of my family, for any considerable help on this trip. As I believe I told you, it will be possible, in May or June, for me to procure assistance, if I need it, from a friend who will inherit money at that time.

You must try to understand that I am working very hard, practically alone as to friends, because I believe in myself and in my eventual capacity to succeed. You must try to understand, furthermore, that the road I have chosen is not an easy one, and that the purpose of this trip abroad is to prevent the necessity, if possible of my return to teaching—teaching which is critical work, and which sometimes kills, or injures badly, a creative talent. It was my purpose when I came over here to stay as long as I could—eight or ten months, if possible, and in that time to finish my play, and to try to write some short stories for the commercial market. This was the last chance I gave myself before my return to teaching. As you know I had about $400. I mentioned this to Mama; the understanding was that I should go as far as I could upon it. I have been for three months in France and England: England is expensive. I have done as much travelling as I could. I have spent about $150 a month, travel and all, including the journey from London here.

Now it is my purpose to go to the South of France where I shall settle down in a small place and do my work. I expect to do this on less than $100 a month. When I return to America I shall come third class on the *Leviathan;* the fare is only $90.

If I return to America now, I return without a job—instructors at New York University have already been appointed for February, and it is the only place I know of where instructors are employed in the middle of the year. Furthermore, I know I can live a great deal more cheaply here than in New York.

I know that I have no right to ask anything from any of you, but I do feel that I set out with a certain understanding as to my plans and the length of my stay; I think I am entitled to this final chance to come through, without enslaving my time and what talent I may have as a writer, for years to come, or for all time, as a teacher.

If I can secure $500, I shall be able, I think, to complete my time, and to do my work. I am sorry my trip should cost anyone anything, but I do not believe it is costing a great deal.

I want you to remember, Fred, that I have believed in something in myself enough to put all the money I had, all that was given me, all that came to me from Papa's will, in my education and in my development. All I have to-day are two ragged suits of clothes, a few articles of apparel, and the manuscript of two plays. I submit that it has taken some courage to do this; a great deal of belief. It would be rather easy to be hard now;

I am not in a position to defend myself. But from you I expect no such treatment.

Somehow or other, the health of my family permitting, I intend to stay over here four or five months longer. If I do not succeed by that time in making my way alone, none of you will have cause to complain thereafter that I had not supported myself wholly and alone.

I trust that this will find you all in good health, with Mabel fully recovered from her sickness. With much love to all,

I am sorry the cable cost so much—it came to about $5.00; but at that time I thought I was going South with friends in an automobile. Your letter changes a good deal of that; I think I shall continue to stay here in Paris until I hear again from home. Good luck.

The following letter to Mabel Wolfe Wheaton was evidently never mailed, but was found among Wolfe's own papers.

To MABEL WOLFE WHEATON

[Paris]

[January 28, 1925]

Dear Mabel:

Fred's letter came to-day which informed me of your illness. I am terribly distressed and shocked to hear of it, but I pray God your trouble is now over; that you are on your way to perpetual health and happiness. God knows you deserve it.

You rarely—hardly ever—write me, Mabel, but I ask of you earnestly that you do it now. You may think it strange that I turn to you now, but it is quite honest and instinctive with me. I believe in you as one of the few women I have ever known to whom one could turn when one was in trouble: that, I believe, is why Papa loved you so.

And for God's sake, say nothing of what I am going to tell you either to Fred or Mama. Don't be worried. I haven't disgraced myself. I have worked hard and written, I believe, my best play—the unfinished play which was stolen with my old valise.[1] That doesn't matter: it was a good thing, for it made me work. And it is true also that I have run out of my own money and have had to appeal to the family for help; but I shall not be travelling hereafter, or living in big cities, and if I can get as much as $500 these next five months, I shall be able to live, travel in Italy and work.

[1] *Mannerhouse.*

And although I have no right to ask it, I hope from the bottom of my heart that Mama can spare it; because I am taking this last desperate chance to save myself from teaching. It is not my own money now—nothing is my own, except my belief and courage—but I believe it is the chance that will put me through.

And, my dear, I want you to know that I would not willingly take a cent that belongs to you or Fred—if the hope of repaying you were also taken. I am a mad fool who loves a vision, who has pursued a dream; it is harder than real estate or cash registers, I believe, but I know in my heart it will one day—very soon, I hope—come true.

But I come to you for another reason. This letter is so different from others I have written you that you may think me drunk or crazy—I am certainly not drunk—I want to say "my dear" to you for the first time, because I am badly hurt, and I believe in that thing in you which comes to the aid of people who have been hurt. And for God's sake, Mabel, don't laugh at me when you read this, because I'm a man now, and this thing is quite real. I'm hopelessly, madly, desperately in love with a woman who doesn't care a tinker's damn about me. She's in love with someone who doesn't care a tinker's damn about her. To make it harder, I know him: he's one of my best friends. Don't think I'm wasting my time mooning about it: there is only one impulse in me now—to work like a fiend, to cut her out of my heart, to forget. She has gone now—out of Paris. I shall not see her again—never; for there is something in me that won't break.

I wish to God there were something in me that would break, that would break down completely; but all I can feel now is that I should like for my heart to burst, but there's too much granite in it—it will never burst.

And if there's anything great in me I believe it's coming out now. I believe love is making a man of me. I hope you won't laugh at that, either. I took the thing without a whine; I told her good-bye; I told her not to worry—that I was the kind of person to whom these things mean very little; that I should be over it in a few days. Then I went away and left her.

Well, I shall get over it in the same way proud passionate fools of my sort get over these things. . . . You must not think anything of this woman that is not true: I tell you now, and I will always be ready to affirm it, that she is a great, good, and beautiful person. Also, because I suppose you always tie up love and marriage, I tell you that I never had the faintest intention of marrying her, or anyone. She is five years older than I am; as regards the world, she is a child. She's from a rich old Boston family who have kept her under lock and key all her life.

[THE LETTER BREAKS OFF HERE]

The following unfinished letter to Kenneth Raisbeck was probably never sent.

To KENNETH RAISBECK

[Paris]

[January 30 (?) 1925]

Dear Kenneth:

I was very sorry not to see you before I left. You told me you would see me before I went. I'm getting out of Paris as quick as I may, because the exchequer holds only about enough to take me where I'm going.

My dear old boy, as I get poorer, I get more grimly-gay. Perhaps I shall not be thoroughly happy until my last shirt has gone. Then I have visions of a tall ship along the docks of Marseilles, and a roaring life across the wine dark sea; to Quinquireme, or Nineveh, or Ophir, or wherever a fabled sea breaks on a fabled shore with perfumed waves. You've got to wrench the rhythm if you read that last one right.

I have had a terrible letter from home, and have spent these last few days quite pleasantly in hell. When I want gaiety, I refer to our little comic opera for a background. So much for contrast!

For God's sake, see that you get some work done on this trip. And don't moon—not until the time comes. It is quite surprising, you know, how much steel one's heart can hold; a good twelve inches is driven in, you break off six of them that stick out, the rest is grown over, and you go on quite nicely, thank you. I think if I were ever thrown into the pot, like the unfortunate gentleman in Jim Daly's "Crucible," [1] I should realize quite a tidy sum in pig iron.

[THE LETTER BREAKS OFF HERE]

The following unrelated and undated fragments were found in Wolfe's own files and were evidently never mailed, or recopied into final drafts and mailed. Since there are many variations on the same general theme, a selection has been made from the great mass of them to give the gist of the material. They were all evidently written between January and April, 1925, and are all undated. Therefore, they are arranged according to general tone and subject matter rather than in any definite chronology.

[1] One of the 47 Workshop plays.

[Paris]

[January 29 (?) 1925]

My dear ——:

I am on my way South with more money than I had hoped to have. I had 300 francs left and had to pay my hotel bill with part of that sum. Third class passage to the South is 135 francs. I went in and talked with the woman next door—the same one who had invited me to lunch. She loaned me 500 francs. It was an action of a very high order: I shall not forget it even when the debt is paid.

These past two days your humble servant has passed very pleasantly in Hell. A letter came from a brother at home: my youngest married sister had an operation January 12—a very serious and painful operation. She is getting over it now. I want to tell you something about her: she is ten years older than I am. Since she was ten years old she was the only person who could manage my father; he was bigger than I am, and quick as a cat; occasionally he drank terrifically. During the last eight years of his life, he was dying palpably—a huge, magnificent machine going to pieces: she gave her strength to him. She has lived in a constant state of nervous irritation and excitability: she is fierce, tender, angry, biting, caressing, by turns. Her voice breaks in sheer desperation. She is 5 feet 11 tall, and thin as a rail. She blazes with restless energy. Strong commonplace people drink her vitality like wine: they never forget her, and they return to her. I have never known her to be "brave" about anything. I have seen her weep, fret, and despair; I have seen her face death two or three times. She would die if she had nothing to spend herself on: nothing to weep, fret, despair about. She wants to be told she is generous, good, thoughtful. She likes adulation. But when one suffers a hurt, her voice is low and gentle: she has large wonderful hands, and all the pain goes out under their touch.

The simple and terrific fact is that with all her fuming, fretting, weeping, her love of adulation, I have never seen her do a selfish thing. I mean it is simply not a part of her. I say it is a *terrific* fact: it is. There's nothing beyond it. She has more human greatness in her than any woman I've ever known. I suppose, honestly, that's why I sometimes get tired of the women I meet—particularly women who are carefully calculated. You're not: that's why I liked you.

My brother also suggested in his letter that I come home: three months of Europe, he thought, was enough. . . . Beside this pleasant little communication the events of the past three weeks provide a rosy, pinky background. So much for contrast. God forgive me for ever playing golf with my emotions: yet, God knows, we must take our comic opera seriously, or how the hell do we face the other? I wrote a painful and humiliating letter home, in which I pled for $500, a few months time, and a final chance to save myself from the deep damnation of Freshman composition.

I am engaged at the present time in the composition of a story with the magnificent title of "Pigtail Alley": [1] try as I may, parts of it look good.

I owe you money and I've got to write you. I take pleasure in it, too; in this one, at least. Don't be a fool and not answer. You'd cheat yourself of some good letters, perhaps some damned good letters, at another time. Besides, I may run into some interesting things—it often happens with me. I'm really terribly upset by the news from home, and you're one of the few people near enough to listen. It's a rotten confession, but you've no idea how soothing it is to let things run out on paper.

On second thought, I shall stay here in Paris until I hear from home. If the wheat arrives, it's to the road again. I don't know where, but I've had an eagle eye fastened on Munich and beer, and robust blondes for some time. I want the South, too—honestly not so much, except that South that knows only two colors—the sea and the sun—the sky and the temple—the eyes of the Argive men above their robes—blue and white, blue and white, blue and white. And, for God's sake, an end to your curled moustaches, and your rapid hands, and your black hair, and your gleaming dark eyes. Blue and white, blue and white.

[Early February (?) 1925]

Dear ——

Thanks very much for your pleasant letter. I am still, as you see, in Paris waiting for funds to arrive from home, which may be ten days or two weeks longer. My friends in the South [1] have wired me several times, and written once, asking me to go to Italy and Spain with them, after that, if I can, to Austria and Czecho-Slovakia—but I will set out under my own steam. They are waiting a week longer, but I'm afraid it's useless.

Paris has not very many "distracting influences," as you put it, for me; but I am beginning to enjoy it thoroughly for the first time, and to get my teeth in it. I am buying books once more, thank God—Voltaire, Gérard De Nerval, Flaubert, Edmond Goncourt—and beginning to speak badly, and with some fluency.

You know, I am a very suspicious person *when I get started*, and you may remember you did nothing to allay my suspicions: I believe you poured

[1] Perhaps some of this material appears on pages 97–98 of *Look Homeward, Angel*.
[1] Professor D. D. Carroll of the University of North Carolina and his family, who were staying at St. Raphael and had invited Wolfe to join them there.

oil on them. It began to dawn on me that I was being asked to go along as a kind of stimulant and travelling companion to Kenneth. I pressed you on this the last day or so. I saw you, and you agreed, adding, as I recall, that I was "merely a happy fourth." Now my dear girl, that was really too much. I got in quite a rage about it. I felt dishonored and insulted. In a series of prolonged conversations with myself, I asked myself what kind of donkeys and fatheads would ask a battleship to convoy a fleet of Gloucester fishing smacks; Sir Launcelot to go a-jousting for the inmates of a Baptist school for girls; Caruso to act as Court Minstrel to the Governor of South Dakota. I assured myself that there were only three people to whom I would doff my colours and act as interlocutor, and that they were all dead. They are Sophocles, Samuel Taylor Coleridge, and Jesus Christ. I think I will do as much for my friends as almost anyone you can find, but I won't wipe their little nosies, take them to the little room where one goes all alone, or kiss them lovingly before [they go to bed(?)]

You were all having important things done to you. Your life, in this great new world of pulsing freedom and unrestraint, was opening like a flower—let us be big and say a sunflower. Kenneth's bleeding soul was being nurtured for the gestation of the opus, Marjorie was displaying her usual magnificent courage, with an occasional brave tear for baby, and a day or two in the wilderness to "think things out" alone. That sounds rather bitter—and I don't feel at all bitter. I am simply sorry, regretful. I had hoped for so much. When I met Kenneth, I had no idea he was with anyone here. This was New Year's Eve, I had an idea he was terribly alone and was cracking under the pressure. As we drank more and more, before setting out on our expedition, he began to hint darkly of some dark secret thing in his life—something of burning horror which had happened, no doubt, at Cannes. Next day we went to the studio, slept, and you returned with Marjorie. When I came downstairs I saw a woman whom I took for his Cambridge aunt or cousin—I don't know why, but for a good week I persisted in this error. When we went to Montmartre that night I saw in Marjorie an older person being nice to the boys, tolerantly amused at our pleasures.

Well, it's no good dishing it up again; in the days that followed I heard much talk of honesty by people who have had to think about being honest; much talk of unconventionality by people who have had to think of it—and who can never do anything but flutter around the safe edges, with a rather kittenish feeling that they are getting very *near* at times. It's simply no use. All the emotion was too carefully calculated; too carefully staged. All genuine contact with the world and with acquaintance is arid and stale because the genuine perception is missing, and people fall victim to the malignant evil of listening to the tickings of their own pangs and quivers, feeding their emotions with their beliefs about things, spinning, re-spinning; seeing, understanding, feeling very little of the most important reality—which is objective—beyond and without us.

In a word, my respect for the dignity and value and goodness of most people is such that I will not truckle to the device of planting in them qualities which they do not possess. I believe enough in most people to accept, without bitterness or despair, those things which are in them— those alone. Any other attitude has always seemed to me the deepest and most dishonorable insult to our fierce and secret honor.

I am going on Thursday night, in company with a man I met in a café at the side of the Opera, to a place where, so he assures me, the criminals of Paris are wont to come: they will be augmented that night by one rogue more. This, since you left, is my sole concession to E. Phillips Oppenheim.

I want you to understand that I hold nothing lightly; that I do not underestimate the importance of having met you all when I did. Someone has said that every man should see Paris before he is twenty-five. I came at twenty-four, the stage was set, not only by the magical place, but by the fortuitous and satanic theft of the manuscript. You were all given magnificent background to set yourselves in my life: there are terrific reasons why no man may forget his first Paris; and his last twenty-four. Very well. You may rest assured that you filled three weeks of that Paris, and may not thereby be forgotten. It is a grievous thought that there was a blazing inner life during that time which none of you quite reached, the sword was in your hands, the sword that pierceth very deep, and you did not plunge it to the hilt. And thereby, God help us all, I may say at 40, if I say aught:—"When I was in Paris for the first time, I met some friends— Americans."

My dear ——, when the fire blazes, the wood must burn: but only the fire remains. I have made cinders, ashes, dust of forests: only the flame is eternal, only the flame is enduring, only the flame is absolute among the Change. Oh God, for something outside of me to last.

I haven't the slightest intention of remembering any of you with anything but affection and regard. It is because of you that I am in Paris now— and that, which seemed at first a penance, has turned into a happy event.

[Later in February?]

My dear ——:

Your letter dishonors us both. I am returning it to you in no bitterness, but merely in order to let you read again, in a more generous and representative moment, what you have written apparently in pique and resentment. Out of that sad and weary meeting in Paris, so long ago that it is now, happily, only a dim horror, I think nothing more grievous has come than this little letter.

I am going to talk gently and painstakingly with you to-night, ——, because the old fires have burnt out—whatever fires you may have known —and I can speak to you, I think, with a calm weariness and horror. For that is what I feel. And I have been reading to-night great pages written by a great man, "La Rotisserie de la Reine Pedauque" of M. Anatole France; and I think something of the old tired gentle balance of spirit, which men call philosophy, and which flows through these gracious lines, has been inherited by me, who have read philosophy, but who am too young to be a philosopher.

But what I am going to say to you now will bring you no joy; and each word of it will become more hateful to me as I go on. And yet I feel an awful necessity in what I write, a necessity which may not be stopped.

You do me the honor to suggest, if I read your intent properly, that you feel some hurt at my proposed suspension of correspondence. And I thank you for this evidence of your interest. But this has caused in you a petulance of spirit, which seems to be a deliberate failure to understand and accept, and a corresponding desire to wound which I observed in you once or twice in Paris, and which I know is no true part of you: it is part of your evil inheritance from God knows what culmination of degrading experience.

You quote me as saying that I shall write you no more love letters, and you say you have never asked for such letters; but you know exactly and definitely, ——, that I have never written such a letter since I saw you: you know perfectly well that these letters of mine, foolish and mad, perhaps, but such letters as you will never receive again—were filled with a deep and earnest affection for you, and with nothing but that. When I think now to what purpose I have spoken, I am filled with a humiliation that knows no limit or no depth.—My God, I tell you truly, I am filled with repulsion as from a leporous blotch, with a visible shrinking away of the flesh.

In Paris toward the end the thing became comic and terrible. In Paris, ——, a long time ago, a young man—lonely, desperate, for he had been recently robbed of something he had distilled his blood in,[1] in a strange country and ignorant of customs and language—met a friend whom he had known well formerly, but not as well or as intimately as he had known other people, but a friend for whom he would have done a great deal. And this friend had told him he had come to Paris alone: he spoke of some

[1] His play, *The House* (*Mannerhouse*).

shadowy horror in his recent life, and he said that he had but 700 francs for the entire next month, but that he did not care. And he was willing to aid this friend under any circumstances, to any extent. It was in this way that he met you next day. He felt a terrible isolation; he lacked the comfort and the solicitude and the affection that might have been his elsewhere, and he turned to you. And he spoke to you without reserve of his affection for you; he explained to you exactly what this meant to him— that he found in you a primitive source of shelter and strength—and you, fastened in every wretched dogma of your kind, had the essential uncleanliness of mind that shows again in your letter. You could not think of an avowal of affection except as an exhibition of carnality, of physical contact—and you began at once to say: "You have not known me long enough to talk like this," etc. Finally, you began to talk of "friendship"— and rather wearily your young man agreed. It was a word you thought you understood. But you were not content: even when he had said "Very well, we shall be friends," you kept recurring to the other motif, harking back to it eternally, dragging it in by the horns, saying: "I'm sorry, but it is impossible"—long after, if you can remember, he had ceased to mention the possibility. And indeed, if you will be fair, he did not [really mention it at all(?)]

It is degrading to be led to these revelations, but you must know that you exerted very little physical attraction for me—you must know my affection for you was of quite a different order. Physically, I was repelled as I am repelled by most Boston women. On the one occasion that I remember touching you with any affection, I had the terrible internal shame, that feeling of wanting to cover my face with my hands and turn away that I have had only once before—when, as a child, I saw two very cold reserved people, a man and his wife, break down under emotional stress one day, and go into each other's arms. It is a terrible horror of the flesh. And you are not cold; I know that you must be physically attractive—it was my revulsion of the kind, and not of the person, that mattered. And that thing is deep in me—when I touched you, I felt your own shame and your own terrible awkwardness—and I couldn't stand it. That generous warmth of spirit that lies in you I felt like a definite flame, and that is what drew me to you. This is all so simple and honest that you cannot help seeing the truth of it. I shall tell you again what I mean, and I know that at my illustration you will not show the loathsome delicacy of the well-bred vulgarian, for you are not common.

Formerly in my life, ——, I knew a man of great courage and character, for whom, in spite of all the repellent coldness, and in spite of too much of the woman under a fairly masculine exterior, I had a deep affection. In fact, I think I loved this man. He was . . . a native of New England. One day, after I had known him for two years, we had had a talk of a most intimate and poignant nature—he saw in me, I think, a certain warmth and fire and spontaneity, and I saw his fire under the ice. On this day, I say, as I left him, in a terrible effort to get over his fences, he slapped me on the back, and when I got back to my room I writhed in such shame and torture as I have rarely known. I felt that there had been an indecent revelation. Later, one evening, I was dining at his home, and one of his sons was present. His wife came in and talked. I had tried to imagine them as man and wife before, and I had failed. Now for the first time, I saw them in family, with a son he had begotten on her; and as I looked at these two fine people, each walled eternally behind ice, the old horror of that dead cold Northern flesh came on me again. For the first time, I dared to think of this man in bed with his wife; and unutterable shame for him came on me again.

I render it to you as my solemn, and doubtless worthless, judgment of the New England temperament—about which I may know quite a great deal, because it represents the antithesis of nearly every *feeling* process I own myself—that there is generally something great about it: always something blasted, twisted, limited. When you consider it in its relation to our civilization—I know this sounds a bit pompous—you are forced to salute it for going so far: you are forced to regret its not being able to go far enough. You take its greatest representation, perhaps, in the world of spirit and thought—Emerson—and at one moment you are convinced you have someone you may place beside Plato and Kant and Hegel: the next moment, you see you have someone who lived near Boston.

There is very little in beauty and creation that escapes its eye—there is very little that is able to reach its heart. Thus you have the Boston ladies and the Browning Societies of a past generation—the sharp keen Northern head and eye sees, a little before most of the others, that another great original is writing poetry: and they begin to interpret what they can never fully apprehend. A little before New York and Chicago, there are articles in *The Transcript* on the German Expressionist plays, and pretty good plates of the scenes [when] the Dramatic Club does a play with experimental settings.

Likewise, a little before the rest of the people, your women understand that there is a great impulse astir in the world—an impulse toward the liberation of women in the social relation. So they go in for it. But their tragedy is that having torn down fences, they can not do without walls; they can never go beyond a half thaw; the fire never burns completely through the ice.

I feel about your people in a million different ways, that they know so much and understand so little. For example, I have eaten with them excellent food—splendid thick tender steaks, splendidly cooked, and I have been forced to agree with their unerring rational judgment that the food was good. But in my heart I have known what they could never understand—that the food was disappointing, somehow. Submit it to analysis, and you must admit it is an excellent steak—good as New York, Paris, anywhere—but the soul is out of it.

I wish there were more passion in what I am putting down here: if there were passion, there would be prejudice, and the likelihood of my being wrong. Unfortunately—for me—there is no such likelihood. I am too far away in spirit from something which I have comprehended too completely, with *almost an absolute objectivity*, for me to be wrong. What I feel, with appalling certainty, is the utter uselessness of my trying to *find* truth—as the saying goes—by some inward crucifixion of spirit. The truth is not for me either to discover or miss or define—it is there, outside me, a solid, unchangeable block of granite. There you all are; there you all stand—utterly damned because there is nothing in you that can possess utter damnation; you can not quite go mad; you can not quite grow satanic; you can not quite grow great.

It is quite useless to talk about vulgarity when one is trying to communicate a straightforward but yet a finely tapered state of mind. To illustrate: I could not hear of a liberated Boston lady going to bed with an unconventional Boston gentleman, without thinking: "Oh, hell! They've thought it all out!" I could not imagine bed with a liberated Boston lady anyway. I know that the steak would be excellent—but disappointing.

It strikes me now as comically illustrative of the whole weary business that I should again be making patient explanations about a thing so simple that only honesty and intelligence can grasp it. And I wonder— because my mind is so infinitely tired of it all—why I should explain anything. I am in somewhat the same position as God, called on to explain his gifts to his dunderpated subjects. And like God, with whom I am on very good terms at this writing, I could blast you with lightning or wither you like a blade of grass in my wrath. But I am not enraged; I am only weary—and I understand now why Zeus, Theos, Jahveh, Jupiter, Adonai, and Allah—calling Him by certain of His titles—does not exercise His royal prerogative of destruction oftener. He is bored, bored as I am bored—vanquished by His mightiest enemy, Supreme and Invincible Dullness. My dear girl, you win; to you are the bays and laurels; to you are the golden apples; yours is the jewelled coronet of all of the former Empresses of Night, who are small beside thee. The owls grow blind before thee; and the ground hogs belie their prophetic souls at thy approach, for thou puttest out the sun. On you falls the mantle of the lamented McFlecknoe who never had a lucid interval; to you as well goes Hooligan's Hat, the justly celebrated Wooden Derby, the Fur Lined Robe de Nuit, and the Cut Glass Frying Pan.

Huntress, on suppliant knees I sue for peace. Make an end to this uneven warfare—you are impregnable; you were dipped in the waters of oblivion long ago but, unlike Achilles, you have not even a vulnerable heel which may be assaulted by the Arrows of Comprehension.

Well, I really get some pleasure from this kind of thing, for it eases my weariness, and makes me grin a little as I write it, for I do see vaguely a large, grim body clutching this paper with murderous hands. That pleases me and makes me like you yet. And it is better than weariness.

I think that even in my most serious moments you have always inspired me a bit to bear-baiting; I observed a certain large and dogged determination, nay, more, an elephantine resolve, to do life thoroughly, taking an occasional note. Your pious reflection, in your horrid little letter, that after your forthcoming voyage to Alsace Lorraine you will know your France, touches in me pleasant springs of indulgent laughter.

I write you letters which ought to convince you that you drew at your birth the first prize in the Olympian Lottery, and you remark that you have enjoyed them very much. I know, of course, that you know only a few words, but it is as if Homer had read the Iliad to a young lady at the Misses Pringle's School, and had been told it was very pretty.

Your defense of a friend is worthy of you: but it is also thoughtless and unworthy treatment of a more or less innocent person. It is good to defend those you care for, even when they have acted badly, but a secret honor toward everyone in the world, known or unknown to us, should forbid our defending friends who have acted badly at the expense of other people who have acted well. You must do me the kindness of remembering that all I asked was to get away: I made no accusation against him, I make none now. That is past, and between us. I believe a time will come when that part of him which is fibre, and in which I believe, will supplant completely that other part of him which is jelly. But these things take time.

That terrible and degrading friendship which defends another for the flattery and unction of one's own soul—which says: "I will, I simply will believe in him," for the sake of appearing forthright and loyal against the world; which says: "Ah, but you have not known him as I," for the sake of a soothing overplus of pride for a greedy but incompetent ego; and which always takes that which it has degraded and humiliated as an object of defense, as the means of diverting the necessity for defense of oneself. My God, how have I suffered from this thing, first from my own blood brother, whose terrible selfish soul went wrapped in flattery for years; who converted each of his ignoble acts into a means for tribute, and who met my savage passionate accusals either in a great but wounded silence, or with a smile mixed with pity and pain.

You want, you say, my friendship; yet when you have it, you use it as a means to wound and degrade me. Somehow I do not hate you for it. I see you as you are, good and beautiful, disturbed by a hundred complicating things, groping desperately through the jungle of your will, inarticulately, desperately, inchoately, and ending finally by stabbing. Formerly I asked you not to try to understand—for I saw then how cruelly contorted things would get for us—and you saw in that only a foolish and vain desire to remain in mystery. I do not want nor do I desire mystery; but my instinct then was a right one, for all your efforts at comprehension have brought you to conclusions about me which do no honor to either of us. And I suspect, too, that once or twice you were kind enough to talk about me with our friends.

For the first time in my life I resent being talked about by acquaintances, even when, as you suggested, your talk with Kenneth about me was of a friendly nature. For the first time in my life I have a sense of shame for my honesty. Outside of certain bits of false emotionalism and of false romanticism, the result, no doubt, of a previous creative effort in real romance, I was terribly honest.

May I not suggest, if you want my friendship, that you seek it honorably upon your own account, and not on account of anyone else. That is the only basis on which any enduring or worthy affection may be established.

I knew you at a time and under circumstances which I do not care to recall. That I should care to see you again at all is a tribute to you. And I do care to see you again. But if you honestly do me the honor of wanting my friendship, you must come to it squarely on your own feet: you must not come to it bringing arguments, defenses, reasons for things that died a bloody death with me long since. In other words, I choose to know you without intrusions.

I think this is the last time I shall ever write you—I have forgotten the sound of your voice; your smile; the colour of your eyes—all except your generous largeness.

I offered you my affection—you gave me shame, humiliation, and dishonor. You have in you great qualities: you have in you also the qualities of a peasant woman. . . . I remember these last and I do not want to see you again. I do not like you now.

> Paris, Tuesday night at
> Ten of the Clock—
>
> [February 23 (?), 1925]

Really a short one now to greet your last. Oh God, but this is the very ecstacy of joy—after a foul confinement I am free; I have dropped from the monastery window in the moonlight: and I hear laughter by the distant fountains. I am not mad: I am not talking in the moon. But I am free—the wind has lodged in my wings (I am an angel) as in a sail—and I am bellied up. . . .

A week ago I cabled. No answer. A slow spine-putrefying conviction came to me that the infernal chessmen were strangling me with tiny cords in the hands of petty people: I wanted to go like a tree in a high wind—I was being slain by the thousand tiny arrows, Sebastian-like, which pierce but do not kill. I was doomed to stay, to rot, to flow off in corruption here before a vast [chorus?] of high, evil sniggers.

To-day, God reft the sky in two in his great hands: Christ looked down on me and wept joyously, tears of golden blood; the bushes burst into lilac bloom; the great bells struck all through the town and bronze by bronze; the swallows and the larks flew from the towers with a gentle thunder—

In short, $125 came from home and I am drunk. Oh Gentle Jesus, there's a moon in Paris and the clouds make patterns round it.

Of all the worlds that I have known, this is the best. I rushed to pay the people of the hotel—the old man, his wife, the girls. I have given them nothing in almost a month—to-day they didn't want it, thinking I needed it. . . . They said it didn't matter when I paid: that I was a good boy—they thought I was much younger—bien gentil, who had fallen among thieves. The girl is lovely, peasant stock: I dined with her to-night, convent bred in Ireland.

You can purchase madness for ten francs: and a titled head of a goddess for forty.

To-night the drawn blinds and the coverlet of red, and Thursday to the world again.

[Early March, 1925]

. . . the peasants. And, all I knew now was "What does it matter—Orleans or Nowhere—I am going." I did not care. At times I rubbed the frost from the window and looked at the flat land, and at the sky. The girl kept looking at me under her shaded hat, and shivering, and smiling in a strange drowsy fashion: I could stand it no longer, and I put my arm around her—we said nothing—and came to Orléans. The peasants seemed not to mind it, or to be over-curious: they kept shouting and laughing among themselves.

At Orléans she got out: I said, "Pardon, Mademoiselle," when she almost fell over my suitcase. She waited outside for me, as I walked across the street to a hotel with a porter, but I did not speak to her.

Three minutes later at this hotel I had met the Countess Constance Hillyer de Caen, and I am at present engaged in collecting materials for a great and compassionate satire. She had been in my town, she had been everywhere in America making speeches to Rotary Clubs, Lion Clubs, Gold Star Mothers—she had been called "Little Mother" by thousands of Americans over here, and she puts flowers on their graves. She had expended all her fortune, her money—the French government did nothing.

She saw me, and pounced upon me as I entered the hotel; in two minutes she had given me the history of her entire war experience, had spoken of her 17 trips to America, and had given the names of everybody of prominence in my home town.

"I will show you the clippings," she [said]

Blois.
Monday night.
[Early March, 1925]

Dear —— :

Another enchanted week in my Mens Mirabilis. You are become a blurred sweet dream of which the lines, the notes, the shades are forgotten: it is a pleasant thing—I can be faithful only to the shades. I write you with no thought of your actual presence, somewhere on some dot of land—it is as if a woman in the moon is waiting on my letter. . . .

I have written you two or three times: I can't remember exactly what I said, but much of it, no doubt, was nonsense: some of it was golden numbers, golden numbers—and too good. But the deepest purest ray it is which sometimes finds the depth of the darkest mine. (Je ris, I jest—O beati pauperes spiritu, quoniam ipsorum est regnum coelorum. Pardon. C'est Chartreuse!)

But a wonderful week—a week of wonders. I have come to Blois in my journey of blunders. I hope you fathom my smooth profondeurs.

But to our tale—

The night was long, the way was cold: the minstrel young was over-bold: he carried in his great valise, two pairs of socks and one chemise; and in his hand, to stay the curse, the Oxford Book of English Verse. Under a sky of leaden grey, he went from Chartres unto Potay, and from that point he journeyed on, until he came to Orléans.

I am infinitely touched and moved by your honest letter, ——, if at any time in my letter I seem to be *writing*—God knows I'll try to avoid it—never doubt the sincerity and earnestness of what I say. Simply attribute anything that seems a bit too fine to an instinct to handle words, and never make the mistake of thinking that is not as much a part of me as my right hand.

At any rate, I can't be dishonest. Honesty with me is not a virtue, but a fact. This was true in Paris, when I was *asked* to be honest. I have a sort of shame in insisting to you now that I am honest, for I know that none of you are worth it; and yet I'm so fond of you that I keep on explaining.

I'm afraid that I'm a bit mad—I mean actually off. I think I have been since the first week after I came to France, when the play [1] was stolen. But I'm not afraid of it. I know that a week in England later with people I know will bring me back. Lately the fear of my madness has lost what terror it possessed, and has been tinged with a beautiful quality. Everything makes me dream. People look at me with a friendly interest, although few of them, save some of the women, speak to me.

[Middle of March, 1925]

You can understand, of course, that this life has become a great deal more tolerable to me than it was at first. For a number of years I have drawn a great deal of my strength from my ability to absorb innumerable

[1] *The House* (*Mannerhouse*).

experiences in books, in the streets, with women. Wildly, recklessly, and dangerously I burst suddenly into a new country, a new speech of which I knew nothing, a new life. I was oppressed with loneliness which had lost the power to be confident: I was crushed with a feeling of futility and despair. Well, in three and a half months, I have learned enough of their speech to read it rapidly, to understand it when it is spoken to me, to mangle it conveniently enough for all purposes, and to absorb a good part of that which goes on around me. And I have become a good Frenchman in a great many of their delightful habits of life. I shall never become a good Frenchman in other respects—shall we say a good American-Frenchman, who seems to me to be a very detestable and third rate person.

The Frenchman is lacking in true wisdom: he is tragically poisoned in his art, his life, his education by provincialism. He wastes himself in useless hatred and dislike of other nations: despite his great reputation for hard reasoning power, he is able to reason clearly not so well as he is able to reason sharply and shrewdly.

[Probably after March 16, 1925] [1]

I am enclosing a small sum of money—all I can afford to send at the time—and you must understand that there is nothing at all insulting in my action. I simply want to conclude an episode which fills me now with weariness and horror. I was told that I was expected to pay a certain sum, and I believe you vouched for it—but I am unable to determine whether it was $80 or $90. However, as it may be—as it no doubt will be—some months before I am able to settle the full obligation, there is no haste in knowing.

It would give me great pleasure to be able to pay you out of the receipts from my work for *Snappy Stories*, which you specify as the future receptacle of what I write. I should welcome the royalties a great deal more than I welcome your remark, for I can not smile at a jest—if such it was—when I no longer believe in the goodness of heart of its author. You, who will never know the dignity and secret courage of the work I have been doing, will never be able to realize the affront you have offered. But if you believe in gods and demons, I beg of you to go down before the mightiest of them and ask remission of your offense—you who have so terribly and stupidly mocked the poor song that was written for your glory and honor, you who have come to secret poetry with unclean ac-

---

[1] In a letter to his mother, dated March 16, 1925 (see page 108 of *Thomas Wolfe's Letters to His Mother*), Wolfe wrote "Both your checks came by way of the Nat. City Bank." He therefore probably began paying back his debt.

cusations, you who made a sty of Arcady and who have poured vitriol in what was all of honey and a song for sirens. I write this finely, not simply, in order that you may smile at it—for then you will know that you have really died.

Probably to KENNETH RAISBECK

[March (?) 1925]

The wind and the rain has come and gone a great many times since. I have not room enough here to examine these reasons: but I could explain them now, I believe, with fullness and clearness. That is not at all important. It is enough if I have understood the intent of your letter—I believe you ask if a renewal of our friendship is possible. It is not only possible, I believe, but desirable. Again, I understand you to intend friendship between us—not communal friendship. Life is too short and too disastrous for any love-me-love-my-dog obstinacy. Believe me when I say that I have only respect and good will for any of your friends. But I know of no way out of this except by a sword cut. As I told you, there is no room here to go into the web: it is only manifest that we did very well together until I was brought in with your two ladies in Paris. Then things went wrong. My dear boy, for me that is finished. Your own relations with either of these women will not be affected in the slightest: your only need is to keep us separate in your mind. I am a good butcher because I know . . .

[THE FRAGMENT BREAKS OFF HERE]

To MARGARET ROBERTS

Avignon, France,
March 21, 1925

Dear Mrs. Roberts:
My only plea for my tardiness is that my own life has had a little private Hell and Heaven of its own and I have been involved in my own wonder, my own emotion, my first bewilderment at a new civilization, at a new tongue, which is now beginning to unfold magically as I take hold. I am wandering across France like a ghost, alone and glorious in loneliness, knowing not at all my next step, save vaguely; trusting to miraculous accident to find the enchanted harbor for me—and at times it does. . . .
I have an enormous manuscript of my voyage—enormous notes.[1] I do

---

[1] Perhaps "London Tower," which was published in the July 17, 1925, issue of the *Asheville Citizen*, was originally part of this manuscript, or perhaps it was written separately by Wolfe when he returned to London in June.

not know where to peddle it—my one impulse is to write—and to send it to you. If you care to—you, mind, are my only literary executor and censor—you may give it to George McCoy for the *Citizen*, with this one condition which I make absolute: my name is not to be mentioned or published under anything I write. This is the one binding restriction, and I insist on it.

A few days ago, from Paris, the day I departed for Lyon, I entrusted the prologue of the *Passage to England* to a lady, a friend, giving her your address and requesting that she send it at once. In that prologue, about 10,000 words I judge, I said nothing of my actual voyage; I indulged, under a rather fantastic plot-work, [in] certain speculations of mine on voyages—the true voyages. The idea came to me when, on going over the notes of the actual voyage, it occurred to me that the account I gave of events and people, if ever published, might get the author and the publisher into trouble. I had honestly made these notes while at sea, and while feeling none too gay; but I wanted even then to do what, to my knowledge, had never been done: to isolate a transatlantic voyage, beginning and ending abruptly the moment the ship docks or sails, acting upon the belief that the sea and a ship disorganize the whole social scheme for a few days, and that the social scheme reorganizes a new pattern before the voyage is over. I did this absolutely without malice; you may accept the whole when you get it as a mélange of fact and fiction, with fiction emphasizing the truth of the business as I saw it.

That explains the subtitle: "Log of a Voyage That Was Never Made." This occurred to me at first purely as a device to escape libel; I changed the name of the ship and the characters. Then I remembered that I had not sailed on the day I had originally planned—that I had remained in Asheville [2] a week longer, and that during that time I had had a queer feeling that I was or should be on the Atlantic. This led to the fantastic prologue, and my own growing conviction in the spiritual need of true voyages.

The whole, when you get it, will amount I believe to 40,000 or 50,000 words—a short novel. It is queer journalism, I know, but since I *give* it, I feel that I am able to do and speak as I please. You may tell George that I have amusing and interesting notes on England (I believe they are), and a story of Orléans, France—a true one—about the town and a genuine countess who drinks horse's blood for anaemia, and an old villain of a Marquise, which, if I told it well, would make my future. I think, also, I may say things about people, about politics, about social differences, which may be superior to the banalities of the greater part of foreign

[2] Wolfe had gone to Asheville for a short visit in October, 1924, before sailing for Europe.

correspondence, which, nevertheless, earns its authors a good living. The reason for all this is simply that I am tired of writing for the four winds; I realize the desperate lack and hypocrisy of pure expression. We are children—we must have an audience; and if my audience may be the people of a little North Carolina town, well and good. That is my whole desire for the present—perhaps there is a tiny feeling that if any of it is at all good it may reach the ears of the gods.

I shall send you lots of manuscripts. I want to write—nothing else—and I have neither the patience nor the time nor the inclination to pull wires with literary agents, and so on. And honestly, I know of no one who would publish my account now; because, as I said, I shall write this once as I please. Let him put it all in print, if he wants, but my name must be absent. Some of it may be fiction; most of it may be fact seen imaginatively—it should have the same relation to reality as most autobiographical novels, as "Childe Harold" if you like. I appoint you censor: I have not been careful of myself in what I have said or am going to say—careful, that is, of what the townsfolk may think. That would be too petty, too dishonest. You must not be careful of that either in going over the manuscripts—it is not at all important. I think the sole thing—the *principal* thing—is the relation any of it may have to my family, to their position in the community. I shall never be too "advanced" to respect that.

It may be before I am done that I shall say something important—that in the mad rush to get it down, something of high worth may come out.

A letter has come, a very flattering and friendly letter, which asks me to return to N.Y.U. in September at $2000—Composition and Soph. Lit. I shall accept, hoping that the heavens may rain manna before, or that a syndicate of county newspapers will appoint me representative at the councils of the League of Nations. For God's sake, say a word to my people, and get them to extend sustenance as long as my period of sufferance lasts.

I am reading French like mad. I came here alone, ignorant of the language, and for two months wretchedly unhappy. Now I am jabbering villainously but adequately, and the world is brightening again. . . .

The duty I impose on you is arduous and long—but I turn to you in trust and hope in this, as in all things. Do not hesitate to deny the responsibility if it's too heavy. I'll understand that, and if the paper doesn't care for the stuff, keep it for me. After all, I'm *embalming* the moments for future exhumation.

To you all my deepest love. Forgive me again if I send no cards, no letters. I'll give them to you on my return. Meanwhile, read and accept my chroniclings as for yourself. It has been mad, bold, unhappy, lonely, glorious!

To HOMER A. WATT

St. Raphaël

[April, 1925]

Dear Professor Watt:

I am sending you a hasty scrawl here in answer to your letter of several weeks ago, but I shall follow with another of a more explanatory nature. I want to get this off on the day's mail. I am on the Riviera, in a little town possessed mainly by the English, and I am writing as if pursued by devils. This will perhaps show in my writing.

Let me say here that if I were methodical enough to keep a scrap book, your last letter would occupy a position of honor in it. I am very proud of it: proud and pleased to know that I am wanted for something and that I am worth as much as $2000 to anyone.[1]

I was in Tours when your letter came to Paris—my mail was being held for me, and I did not get your letter for several weeks. I departed almost at once for the South of France.

First of all, I am terribly shocked at the confusion that resulted when I did not return. I did *not* get your earlier letter offering me a place in February: you say that you sent it to my "American address," and I have wondered whether you meant the Albert, or Asheville, N.C. If you sent it to Asheville, it should have been forwarded by my brother, although my mother closed her house and departed for Miami early in the Fall.

Today I heard from home, and my family is evidently desirous that I return in August. I am therefore writing you to tell you that I accept with the deepest gratitude your offer of a post in September.

You have always shown the utmost patience with me, Professor Watt, even in circumstances where my greenness must have been excessively trying to your patience and good nature. But I have had one instinct towards you that has been a happy and a right one: I have never had the slightest hesitation in speaking to you in absolute honesty, without concealment. That is why I am going to give you certain information now about my domestic background and my present circumstances which I feel it is necessary you should have, in order to understand my present state of mind.

My mother is a very extraordinary woman in her middle sixties, small, strong, intensely vigorous, and uncannily canny in business affairs: she is part Scotch. Since my father's death a few years ago she has, by shrewd investment at home and in Florida, more than trebled her estate. For

---

[1] Professor Watt had asked him to return to New York University in September as a member of the regular September-to-June teaching staff at a salary of $2000.

every cent I spend I am, at the present time, absolutely dependent on my mother.

I spent the few thousand dollars that came to me following my father's death at Harvard. My other brothers and sisters, following my mother's advice, have profited hugely. And everyone, you understand, has been beautifully loyal to me. They seem to have a touching belief in me without knowing very well what I am doing. And what I am doing is to write, write, write—it may be the most frightful muck, but I can't help putting it down. At times I grow slightly bitter at the idea of having to stop writing, even temporarily, to do something of a more profitable character. I feel at such a time that my own destiny has been matched against that of a piece of black earth in Carolina, and a piece of sand in Florida, and that the land always wins.

At the same time there is another impulse in me which makes me rather fiercely independent: I have a horror of becoming like those wretched little rats at Harvard who are at the mercy of their pangs and quivers, who whine about their "art," who whine that the world has not given them a living. I'll be damned if I'll become a "chronic unemployable." It was this that Professor Baker could not understand; he protested that I was making a serious blunder in coming to the university,[2] he seemed absolutely unable to comprehend my reasons, he said "You must keep on writing," and he kept on saying this with a sublime disregard for circumstances. I settled the business for myself—the only possible settlement, as I found—and I lost, I fear, the friendship of a man who had stood by me for two years: at any rate, I have never heard from him.

That is why, even now, I doubt; and that is why I seem to hesitate. I observe a rather widespread tendency among older people to condemn the conduct of young people as headstrong and obstinate, but I do not observe a widespread tendency to give a plain answer to some of the questions young people ask.

I should like to think, frankly, that something I have written or am writing might in these next few months relieve me of the necessity of doing anything else. I keep hoping for a little more time, but I know that you need time as well. You may be assured, however, that, my word being given, I will come through to the scratch, death or disease excepted.

And I want to repeat what I believe you already know: for innumerable reasons I prefer to be at N.Y.U. to any other place North or South. There is, at the present time, one possible means for me to keep on with my work. If it is not too late, will you drop me a line, and let me know how much time for further meditation you can allow me? I beg of you not to be too impatient at what seems to be my indecision:—I am in a

[2] New York University.

web of tangled and troubling events, only the barest outlines of which I have been able to indicate to you. I hope you have not been bored with the recital. . . .

I am living here in a land of opulent Springtime, of incredible color. I should like to tell you more about it, but I'm not sure it's really true. My address continues at the American Express Co., Paris. Mail will be forwarded. I go from here to Italy, then to England.

To HOMER A. WATT

> Brasserie Vetzel
> 1 Rue Auber
> Place De L'Opéra—Paris
> June 22, 1925

Dear Professor Watt:

I went to Italy almost immediately after receiving your last letter; and I have been travelling and living with one valise since, returning to Paris only a day or two ago. I shall go back to America in August, and want to spend a few weeks at home before returning to the University. I believe the date of the term's opening is around September 20, and that you want, generally, the instructors to return a little in advance. If the request is not extravagant will you absolve me from this preliminary work of registration? I desire this solely because of the exigencies of time.

You asked me my preferences concerning hours. I have none, save a prejudice against nine o'clocks. I am incurably and unfortunately night-owlish, doing a good part of my work when most of the world, even in New York, is silent; getting Satanic inspirations from the dark.

I think you will understand that I express something stronger than a perfunctory regret when I tell you that I am profoundly sorry to hear that you will be absent next year.[1] My decision to return was not utterly contingent on your own presence, but it was considerably strengthened by the expectation of again working with you.

I await with great pleasure my association with Professor Munn.

Italy was for me the core of the world's loveliness; and this I take to be a miraculous thing, because that great current which draws some men toward the Latins does not draw me, who have fog in my soul, and think grey the best of colours, and London the most unfathomable of cities.

I stayed there until my money was gone; and I ended at last in Venice,

---

[1] Professor Watt was to teach as a visiting Professor at the University of Southern California during 1925–26, on leave of absence from New York University. In his absence, Professor James B. Munn was to be chairman of the Department of English.

which I shall remember not as a place which may always be reached by train, but as one of those cities that never were, formed in magic by the sweep of a wizard's arm.

I am going to England in a day or so, and I shall remain there for the remainder of my time. If you have any further communications, I suggest that you send them to the American Express Co., London. I wrote you before in pencil because I had no ink; I write you now upon the only paper provided by Vetzel's: it is used, generally, I believe, by young men and women naming a time and place. This is no reason why it should not Serve a Worthier Purpose.

I am thoroughly disreputable in appearance. I have no clothes, and I shall have none until more money comes from home. At the present moment I am drinking nothing stronger than beer; there is, five feet away, a Frenchman, all whiskers, with a glowing cigarette tip blooming dangerously in the midst of the foliage, an old man and his young mistress just beyond, two Americans drinking cognac across, and an amorous couple at the back, kissing each other with solid smacks between draughts of beer.

I've done my best to give you a picture of Parisian life.

The letter below to Mrs. Mildred Weldon Hughes, whom Wolfe had known in Paris, was found in his own files and may never have been mailed. Exactly what the "serious and disquieting news" about his health was is not known. In a letter to his mother dated July 27, 1925 (See page 119, Thomas Wolfe's Letters to His Mother) Wolfe wrote: "I took cold shortly after my arrival, and for the better part of three weeks I was a great deal more dead than alive." Probably he had consulted a doctor and been frightened by his diagnosis, but it is doubtful that the tubercular lesion on his lung was discovered at this time.

To MILDRED WELDON HUGHES

[London]

[Early July, 1925]

Dear Mrs. Weldon,—

Your black rimmed stationery is fairly familiar to me now; but if you use it with any expectation of putting *me* in mourning, your intent is frustrated.

Merry England has not been merry for me these past four days: I have come down with a most damnable cold—not this time blameable on the

English climate, which has been dry and warm, but on my restless toes which filched the cover from my bosom at dead o' night—and only by means of copious draughts of John Walker am I now able to wash it into Hell.

London is little better off than Paris, I judge, for tourists—the American Express here twangs with their squeaky voices; but London is bigger and one may lose them, or get lost.

Today I spent in very melancholy fashion at Wembley, which bored me infinitely. It was too big, too crass; and it repeated itself mechanically: nowhere was there gaiety.

I have lived quietly enough here, seeing only a few acquaintances. The night I came, on going into the Hotel Imperial for a drink, I was accosted by my friend K,[1] who used to stumble up and down the stairs in Paris. I let him pump me up to a point; but I asked him no questions concerning himself or his friends—I have lost the interest.

I am going down to the English country shortly. I have received serious and disquieting news about myself here this past week. Health—heart, all else quite sound. I have youth enough yet, I hope, for any-thing. . . .

Remember, my most cordial remembrances cross the Atlantic with me. Please write me again.

The following fragment is evidently a rough draft portion of the first letter which Wolfe wrote to Aline Bernstein, whom he had met on the ship coming back to the United States, and who was to have the greatest influence on him for the next five years, during which time Look Homeward, Angel *was written and published.*

To ALINE BERNSTEIN

Hotel Albert
New York

[September 1925?]

. . . me now with a profound sense of wonder and unreality. Through you, I slid back into America again; since then, my spirits have bounded, and my sense of the greatness and capacity for madness of this people has quickened beyond all measure.

I am just back from Boom Town, where everyone is full of Progress and Prosperity and Enterprise, and 100,000 by 1930, and Bigger and Greater

[1] Kenneth Raisbeck.

Asheville. Everyone is growing wealthy on real estate, and there is a general tendency to slap everyone on the back and call everyone by the first name. I did not know what it was all about, nor do I know yet, except that it is all perfectly useless along with everything else; but it made me glad to see them all so happy, and the enormous vitality of that town and of this country charmed and fascinated me.

For three weeks I went wherever they went, and made their ways my own: I drank their corn whiskey, and joined their parties, and was involved in their generous falsehoods which are so full of hope and good will for all things. They love success, these people, or what they conceive success to be; they put in their papers announcements that I was a professor and that I held the "chair of English" at N.Y.U.

I am no longer so arrogant, cruel, and so contemptuous of all this as I was a year ago: I think I like people a great deal better than ever before. . . .

[THE FRAGMENT BREAKS OFF HERE]

To FREDERICK H. KOCH

[Hotel Albert]
[New York]

Sunday night.
[January ?, 1926]

Dear Prof:

Your Playmaker pamphlets and folders came to-night, including your note suggesting that I go around to see Sheldon Cheney.[1]

The Guild has my new play,[2] and has had it for two months:—a letter a day or so back from Lemon, the play reader, in reply to a rather sharp one of my own in which I asked the return of the play, informs me that he read the play, passed it on to members of the board, and that it is now in the hands of Lawrence Langner. The board, he says, is going to vote on it finally. In view of this, I have consented to let them keep the play until a final decision is reached. Although I have several other copies of the play, I promised Mr. Lemon that I would not send it out until the Guild had seen it. I really have only the most trifling hopes of the play's production by the Guild, but when it is returned, I shall take a copy to Mr. Cheney and several other people who have asked for it.

Let me thank you very sincerely for the interest you show and have

---

[1] Cheney was with Equity Players (The Actors' Theatre), which, however, was discontinued around this time.

[2] *Mannerhouse.*

shown for years in the fortunes of my life. For two years now I have worked and travelled alone, ordering the events of my life as courageously and honestly as I could, compromising for my existence by teaching in order to escape the more odious restraints incurred by demands on my family. In that time, some people who disapproved of the compromise, and others—the honey flies who found me lacking in the promise of instant victory—have turned away and forgotten me. But a few people have never forgotten: they have given unbounded loyalty to a mad fellow who made loneliness his mistress, and among them I am happy to believe I may include yourself.

It would give me infinite pleasure to witness the success of my new play, because it was written in the silences, and because it would give me the chance, if necessary, to repel obligation where no obligation is due; but whether it is produced or not, or whether I succeed or not, I have the most unwavering confidence in the integrity of your friendship for me. For that, believe me, you will not find me lacking in affection or gratitude. . . .

My communication is infrequent, but my interest in you and in your work unwavering.

The following is the letter of submission sent with Mannerhouse *to The Neighborhood Playhouse. It was written on the stationery of the Hotel Gralyn in Boston, where Wolfe had gone for the third week in January to visit friends, and may have been intended for either Alice or Irene Lewisohn, since they were both directors of the Playhouse. Judging from Wolfe's letter of June, 1927, to Mrs. Roberts, it was probably addressed to Alice Lewisohn.*

To MISS LEWISOHN

The Gralyn
20 Charlesgate West
Boston, Mass.

[January, 1926]

Miss Lewisohn, this play belongs to no world that ever existed by land or sea. For it, I have created a medium as special as the one Coleridge used for "The Ancient Mariner."

This is what the play means to me:—one, three or four years ago, when I was twenty-one or twenty-two, and wanted to prove things in plays, I wanted to write a play that should describe a cycle in our native history—

I should show by it the rise and fall of a powerful Southern family. I was going to call it "The Wasters." I made a draught of it and destroyed it. Later, still significant, I called it "The House"—my house was to be the symbol of the family's fortunes—you saw it put up and torn down.

Finally in Paris, after that script had been stolen, and I was alone, I knew that I cared little for that, and beginning anew, I created this play— which has no relation to problem, none to history—save that any one may guess when it is supposed to occur, but no one, I think, will confuse it with realism. It became the mould for an expression of my secret life, of my own dark faith, chiefly through the young man Eugene.[1] If you would know what that faith is, distilled, my play tries to express my passionate belief in all myth, in the necessity of defending and living not for truth— but for divine falsehood.

That, simply, is what I mean; that has come as truly from me as anything I ever wrote; and I am a young man who read the Greeks at 15, and who read Kant and Hegel at 17, and who, like every other fool, thought himself wise when he saw God as a sea, himself as a drop of water on the way; but who knows now, at 25, that he had merely substituted an ugly superstition for a beautiful one.

I have no more time. You complained of a certain *diffusion* in my first play:[2] I do not believe you can complain of it here. There is certainly the focal power of one idea, developed with enormous concentration—I do not believe any speech is vague, but the whole is packed.

I have not tried to be smart or wise, nor have I adopted a cheap easy obscurity. I tell you again, this thing came out of me—even in its fierce burlesquing of old romanticism, it defends the thing it attacks.

Finally, of course, it contains the first complete expression of that thing that has fascinated and terrified me since I was a child. Are we alive or dead? Who shall tell us? Which of the people in this play are ghosts, and which are living?

Read it carefully, Miss Lewisohn. Certainly men must have felt like this, but I have never seen it expressed.

In the following note to Olin Dows, Wolfe speaks quite optimistically about the possible production of one of his plays. Probably he wrote this when he had high hopes that the Neighborhood Playhouse might do Mannerhouse, *or perhaps he was simply whistling to keep his courage up.*

[1] The Eugene of *Mannerhouse* is not the autobiographical Eugene of Wolfe's novels, although Wolfe sometimes uses him as a mouthpiece for his own ideas.
[2] *Welcome to Our City.*

Dows had first met Wolfe at Harvard in the spring of 1923, after having seen and admired Welcome to Our City. *He painted Wolfe's portrait there soon afterwards; then left Harvard to go to the Yale School of Fine Arts. From 1924 to 1928, Wolfe often visited him at his family's house in Rhinebeck, New York, and in June 1927, he lived in a small cottage on their estate.*

To OLIN DOWS

[New York City]

[Spring 1926 ?]

My dear Olin:

I was very glad to get your note. It gave me what I had lacked—a New Haven address by which I could reach you; and it served to deny what I was beginning to fear—that I had become too scandalous a fellow for a decent, respectable lad. . . .

There's little about me to tell you—little that *can* be told. Make the most of that. It seems a theatre here may do one of my plays next season. Meanwhile, I seethe with the finest ideas I've ever had, and little time for writing. It's England in June, and the Continent for the next year or two.

Let me see you more often, Olin. I very honestly would like to have you as my friend; and very honestly I tell you that I have never been wholly sure I had your friendship. This is because you are fundamentally decent and courteous to everyone, and because you have a great deal of gusto for people. It cheers me to think that you may have ever found me interesting or strange or stimulating, but one sometimes grows a bit tired of existing as the Man-Mountain, the Wild-Haired-Wonder, and the like. Beneath the homespun shirt, and so on, as some one has said so beautifully, beats the heart of a man. At any rate, no matter how you feel, I get a great deal of pleasure from seeing you, and I will willingly perform my stunts for you, including thirty-seven hair-raising, awe-inspiring, and reason-defying novelties, exhibited to all the Crowned Heads of Europe (both of them) but never before upon this Continent.

Words in brackets in the following letter are only guessed at, since they have been eradicated by the tearing of the paper at one edge.

To MABEL WOLFE WHEATON

[Hotel Albert]
[New York]
Saturday [May, 1926]

Dear Mabel:

I have your letter; today is my best opportunity to answer it. I finished my work at the university yesterday, save for examinations. I give all my Freshmen examinations Monday and Tuesday, but I must wait around until Thursday, May 27, to give my [final] examination to the school teachers. During [the interval] I shall go up to [Boston], talk to Elaine who is going to Europe and wants information, and see old Henry,[1] in order to get my books from him. I suppose [Mama] has returned from Florida. After May 27, I should like to come [home] for a few days, if you are able to put me up. I am going abroad early in June. I think I shall leave my books here in New York, stored in the house of a friend who lives here.

I have heard from Mama, and I wrote her, and telegraphed her, too, the other day. Things seem to have gone badly with her—apparently she has [lost] money in Florida [real] estate. I know you are all . . . upset by the whole wretched business, but let us try to keep down [bitterness] and recrimination as far as we can.

I am sorry for her, if she has lost money, because she cares [for] money a great deal, and was happy in the belief that she was making money. But if she has lost part of it, it may be a good thing for the happiness of us all; for I have observed that people who make an end rather than a means of money, and even lower their own standard of living in order to have more of it, sometimes do a right-about-face when they find how insecure a foundation their life is built on: in other words, when they lose part of their coin, they become more liberal with what is left, and get more comfort from a little than formerly they got from much.

It seems a little pathetic to me now as I think of you all, and of Asheville people I saw Christmas—you were all hypnotized by the talk of Florida and Asheville, you were all full of convincing facts and figures, you were all secretly proud of "business ability," although everyone elsewhere knew you would have to wake up sooner or later—the sad history of these affairs has always been pretty much the same, I believe: everyone makes a million on paper and in pipe-dreams, until one day somebody calls for a dollar in cold cash, and things blow up.

I know things are not so bad as this at Asheville—the town probably

[1] Henry A. Westall, Wolfe's uncle.

has a certain assured growth, and if you never get $5000 an inch for property, you may in time get an honest price. If your boom returns this summer in full blast, the town will eventually get done in the eye—it always happens. The people who gain apparently are the near-swindlers and the near-thieves who stay within the letter of the law—the ——s and ——s who, at the top of the dope-dream, are reputed by the admiring boobs to be worth at least $200,000,000, or some such figure, but who usually get away with two or three million. And, of course, it is the Boob, the eternal cocksure Boob, who loses his (or her) shirt. Inasmuch as the last census listed some 97,500,000 specimens of the American Boob, the pickings for the ——s and ——s should continue to be soft and easy. For the Boob never learns, he never changes. Steal his shirt this year by [a] scheme for manufacturing gasoline from Florida grapefruit, he will cheerfully give next year his socks, trousers, and B.V.D.'s to a project which proposes to capture the American clothing trade by importing Bulgarian wool grown on cactus bushes. They never learn and they always lose. Quote a few figures to them and they will believe anything. If you told one of them that the population of Asheville would be a half million by 1930, you would not be believed; but tell him that the town has grown fifteen thousand during the last year, and that therefore it is bound to grow thirty thousand next, sixty thousand next, and so on, and he will give you the gold out of his teeth. The Boob believes anything he hears or sees, as long as he is given a few meaningless statistics. Print a picture in the newspaper of Washington Crossing the Delaware, and sub-·title it "President Coolidge on his way yesterday to greet the Pope at Ellis Island," and he will swallow the bait, hook, line, and sinker. There is no limit to his ignorance, stupidity, and gullibility, but since he sometimes has good intentions, I side with him rather than with the crooks who rob him.

I hope the effect of the present slump in Asheville will be a corresponding slump in wise-acre real estate chatter during the time I am at home, but it will probably be my luck to get there just as the thing starts again, and just after —— has persuaded the surrounding boobery that Asheville is the logical place for the National Capital, and that a majority in the House of Representatives has already decided to start excavations on Battery Park hill for the Treasury, the Department of State, and the Congressional Library.

That everyone will be rich in his own mind I have no doubt, for all that is needed to persuade the suckers that they are rolling in wealth is to take $250 of their money in exchange for a piece of paper telling them they are the owners of Lot 693 on Haywood Heights, said lot being worth $3000 (on paper); to buy it back at the end of six weeks for $300, paper value now $4500; and congratulate them on having made $1500 without turning over a hand. And the sucker not only believes he has made it, but he begins to flatter himself on his cleverness, business foresight, and all round shrewdness. All that is needed after this is to walk up to him, take the greenbacks from his pocket, cut the buttons off his coat, and steal the chewing gum out of his mouth, leaving him a nickel for carfare home. He is ripe for plucking. . . .

Perhaps we dead may awaken someday and manage to get ten times the comfort from one tenth the money we thought we had. I assure you I am not disgruntled in writing this. I have no very selfish designs upon the family treasure, in spite of any dissenting opinion: money has always been to me only a necessary convenience, and fortunately I am going to be able to make it now without home help. But I really like you all too much to want to see you made unhappy by this mad folly. . . .

I am not being bitter, Mabel. Let us admit, before I close, that I have had more out of it than the rest of you; let us admit, too, that I will never be ungrateful for it. At any rate, what I was told was mine, I spent myself as I damned pleased, on the thing I wanted to do. For what was given beyond, my fervent thanks—but now that I speak as a free agent, asking no more, let us try, you and Fred and I, to forget about it, so far as we may, and to step upon the rotten poisonous thing that has never been anything but a source of bitterness, accusation, and suspicion. In other words, since few people we know will ever care for us more than we ought to care for one another, let us try to change the system by which huge sums for dirt are kept in secrecy, but a donation of a few dollars to feed hungry children is brandished about as if it were the war debt.

This may be cheek, since I can give nothing; but it also happens to be the truth—which ought to make it worth something. At bottom, I believe, we are all fairly decent and honorable people—somewhat given, perhaps, to parading our virtues—but with enough kindliness and loyalty for anyone. Mama is old; she has had a hard bitter life, and her sense of values has become distorted. But she, too, I have always believed, has our welfare at heart. In short, I believe she would do almost anything for any one of us, if she realized the necessity; but, as you know, it has been her tragic fate to realize that necessity sometimes too late—sometimes to the tune of clods of frozen earth upon a wooden board—the last venture in real estate, I might add, any of us will ever make. There's nothing to be done about that. She's too old; but she too is fundamentally a decent person.

I want very much to see you all. If you have room for me, drop me a line.

And, in spite of all I have said, which you will treat, of course, with discretion, I sincerely hope that none of you have been hard hit by this depression.

You'd better let me know right away.

To MARGARET ROBERTS

Hotel Albert
New York

June 1, 1926

Dear Mrs. Roberts:

I was away in Boston when your letter came, during a vacant interval in the examination period at N.Y.U. I came back Thursday for a final examination. . . . I shall see you perhaps in a few days. I may come home, although invitations have not been marked by their warmth or frequency, nor am I driven by my own inclination. . . .

Two years ago I was forced into work for which I had no affection, at the penalty of what talent I had. It may be said that I was not "forced," but I insist that money has been held over me like a bludgeon. Recently what little help I have secured from home to eke out my salary (and, I confess, my own lack of economy) has been withdrawn. Meanwhile, I get insane attempts at falsification—dark hints at "the poor house" and "old age" and the insistence that everything has been done "for the children" or in order to secure "a few dollars for old age." My uncle,[1] sniggering, told me he supposed my mother had not told me (she was too cautious) that she is building a $100,000 hotel at Brevard. This a week after a letter telling of pinch and poverty. These are the facts, and are prefatory to your letter. You are certainly wrong in supposing I took your letter badly. I honor the motive, and I trust in your friendship too much to wear a chip around you. But I will be forgiven, I know, and understood, I believe, if I say that a brief, but very intense and varied life has told me that all advice is bad—even that of so wise and understanding a person as you are.

Further, if, in this affair, you see only consequences of future unhappiness for me [2]—what, pray, should unhappiness mean to me who called for wine, and was given the sponge, and whose bread as a child was soaked in his grief. Am I so rich, then, that I can strike love in the face, drive away the only comfort, security, and repose I have ever known, and destroy myself just as my mind and heart, aflame with hope and maturity, as they have never been before, promise me at length release.

[1] Henry A. Westall, whom Wolfe had seen in Boston.
[2] This probably refers to Wolfe's having fallen in love with Mrs. Bernstein.

Well, I'm in no debater's mood. Thank God, I have escaped, at any rate, from *odious* bondage, and I shall come home and depart thence, free, because that ugly monster, money, which breaks the will and kills courage, has been banished for me. I expect nothing from my family—now or hereafter. I have given my life to the high things of this earth—I am free to say that I consider any debt that has been made has been repaid by the effort and example of my life; and I assure you that from now on, I shall strike a blow in the face of insolence, confessing no obligation where none is due, and repelling any hostility toward my life and my creation with all the energy and violence I command.

Of this you may be sure: I believe you have been my constant friend, that you have never stooped to the common daily treachery of the village, that in your heart you have believed in me and trusted in me. Be assured, then, that *you* at least I shall want to see when I come home.

I am sailing on the *Berengaria* June 23. Until we meet, then,

With great affection,

IV

EUROPE AND THE WRITING OF
LOOK HOMEWARD, ANGEL
1926–1928

To MARGARET ROBERTS

Bath, England
July 19, 1926

Dear Mrs. Roberts:

Here are just a few lines—a short record of my doings since I left you. I was in Paris ten days, in Chartres two days, in London a week, and here two days. I am on my way to the North of England—to Lincoln and York for a few days, and finally to the Lake District, where I settle down to work. My trip has been fuller, richer, more fruitful than I had dared hope. I looked, and looked so fiercely the first time that I return now to something which seems to be opening itself for me.

I have begun work on a book, a novel, to which I may give the title of "The Building of a Wall" [1]—perhaps not; but because I am a tall man, you know perhaps my fidelity to walls and to secret places. All the passion of my heart and of my life I am pouring into this book—it will swarm with life, be peopled by a city, and if ever read, may seem in places terrible, brutal, Rabelaisian, bawdy. Its unity is simply this: I am telling the story of a powerful creative element trying to work its way toward an essential isolation; a creative solitude; a secret life—its fierce struggles to wall this part of its life away from birth, first against the public and savage glare of an unbalanced, nervous brawling family group; later against school, society, all the barbarous invasions of the world. In a way, the book marks a progression toward freedom; in a way toward bondage—but this does not matter: to me one is as beautiful as the other.

---

[1] This was an early title for *Look Homeward, Angel.*

Just subordinate and leading up to this main theme is as desperate and bitter a story of a contest between two people as you ever knew—a man and his wife—the one with an inbred, and also an instinctive, terror and hatred of property; the other with a growing mounting lust for ownership that finally is tinged with mania—a struggle that ends in decay, death, desolation.

This is all I've time for now. I wish I could tell you more of this magnificent old town, held in a cup of green steep hills, climbing one of them, made on one plan from one material—the finest place really I've ever seen.

Write me, American Express Co., London. God bless you all.

Henry Fisk Carlton, to whom the following letter was written, was a member of the 47 Workshop in 1920–1922, and a fellow instructor of English with Wolfe at New York University from 1925–1928. Since then, he has been a free-lance writer for radio.

To HENRY FISK CARLTON

[32 Wellington Square]
[London]
[September 3, 1926]

Dear Henry:

I enjoyed everything in your letter except its brevity. I put *that* down to New York heat. While you were sweltering at Washington Square, I suppose I was being fanned by the chill breezes of the English Lakes, and Scotland.

I am living now in London's Chelsea, a so-called Bohemia, though why it should be, I don't know. Certainly none of the gay artists hereabouts are afflicted with any form of Exhibitionism. I have two rooms, a bedroom and an ample sitting room at Number 32 Wellington Square, in a house that looks exactly like all the other houses in Wellington Square, save that one of them, just opposite, is painted yellow. Thus far, I am sure you believe me—the rest, so help me God, is also true.

I am brought a cup of tea and a newspaper at 8:30 every morning by an old man who was formerly a butler—now with his huge, fat, one-eyed wife, proprietor of this establishment. I arise, dress, shave, and have a simple breakfast of tea, toast, marmalade, one fried egg and two slices of bacon. Later I read the paper again; depart at ten o'clock for my morning walk along the Thames, during which time my rooms are cleaned;

return; go to work until lunch, when I take a bus for the American Express where I hope to find mail. Then lunch near Piccadilly and Soho, a stroll about London, and back to work. I am in bed by midnight.

I have finished a very full and complete outline of my book [1]—the outline itself the length almost of a novel—and at present I am writing about 3,000 words a day, which I hope to increase to 4,000. The novel will be Dickensian or Meredithian in length, but the work of cutting—which means, of course, adding an additional 50,000 words—must come later. . . .

The best friend,[2] I believe, that I ever had went home almost two weeks ago. We came here from Glasgow two weeks ago yesterday. . . . She is a very exceptional person—the grit, determination, and executive capacity that men are mistakenly supposed to have, but good-humored and kindly always. "She knew what she wanted."—I saw the opus, by the way, the other night in London, as it finished its run here: it gives me additional proof of my error in trying to write plays. What is, is not; the Good is Bad; the Stupid Brilliant; the Shallow Profound; the Mediocre Significant. . . .

I am completing this several days later. England has had an unprecedented summer, warm and sunny, the dryest August in almost thirty years; but starting punctually on September 1, as if scheduled, leaden, misty, drizzly days have set in. It is now September 3: in just one month, Henry, I will have marked off another year of my life. I have hoped for much: the lurid phantasies of my young twenties of fame, wealth, and honor have become, if not less modest, more mature; but I believe I can tell you honestly my desire for excellence in my work has grown more intense—where once the Golden Apple was going to drop into my lap in some more or less miraculous way, I am now, for perhaps the first time in my life, engaged seriously in trying to pick the fruit. I am writing from five to six hours a day. . . .

If in any way possible, I will stay over here until I have written my book—perhaps, although I hope not, until I have been forgotten. But I believe the thing is as hard for me as for anyone. I have had for a year now companionship, affection, and the inestimable comfort of human belief. I am here now without resources of friends, without the pleasure of having my work either known or recognized, and with no establishment save what I fashion myself. I would not attempt to conceal from you the genuine hole this makes in my life. I have had, and given up, what I never had before: but I am not at all despondent, and I am doing my work. . . .

[THE LETTER BREAKS OFF UNFINISHED]

[1] *The Building of a Wall*, later called *O Lost*, and finally *Look Homeward, Angel*.
[2] Aline Bernstein.

To ALINE BERNSTEIN

· Brussels

Wednesday, Sept 22, [1926]

My Dear:

. . . I have been in this very gay city for ten days now; in over a week I have not spoken in my own language, or talked with one of my own nation. My talk with nearly everyone has been impersonal—a matter of buying and paying. It's not bad, save at night. I get rather lonely, then.

I have done a great deal of writing—my book is going to enormous length, and I can't get done as quickly as I thought. To-day is the only day I haven't written—I am writing you this at dinner (8 o'clock) and shall try to get my day's work done to-night.

I took the day off and went to Waterloo in a bus—the first trip I've made. There were seven or eight of us only—two or three English, two or three French, and your old friend, James Joyce.[1] He was with a woman about forty, and a young man, and a girl. I noticed him after we had descended at Waterloo—I had seen his picture only a day or two ago in a French publisher's announcements: he was wearing a blind over one eye. He was very simply—even shabbily—dressed. We went into a little café where the bus stopped to look at the battle souvenirs and buy post-cards: then we walked up what was once the Sunken Road to a huge circular building that had a panorama of the battle painted around the sides; then we ascended the several hundred steps up the great mound which supports the lion and looks out over the field. The young man, who wore horn-rim spectacles, and a light sporty looking overcoat, looked very much like an American college boy: he began to talk to me going up the steps— I asked him if he knew the man with the eye blind. He said he did, and that it was Joyce. I commented briefly that I had seen Joyce's picture and read his book; after this the young fellow joined me at every point. Walking back down the road to the café, I asked him if Joyce's eyesight was better—he said it had greatly improved. He said Joyce was working on a new book, but thought it impossible to say when it was finished. We went back to the café—they sat down at a table and had tea—the young man seemed about to ask me to join them, and I took a seat quickly at another table, calling for two beers. They all spoke French together—he told them

[1] Mrs. Bernstein had known Joyce when his play, *Exiles*, was put on in 1925 by the Neighborhood Players, of which she was a director and stage-designer. She says that in 1926 she called on Joyce in London, to pay him his royalties from the play in American dollars. As she remembers it, Wolfe called for her there and was introduced to Joyce hastily in the dark hallway where he could not clearly see his face.

all about it, and they peeked furtively at me from time to time—the great man himself taking an occasional crafty shot at me with his good eye. As they had tea, they all wrote postcards. As they got up to go into the bus, the young man bowed somewhat grandly to me—I don't blame him; I'd be pleased too. I judge the people are Joyce's family—he is a man in the middle forties—old enough to have a son and a daughter like these. The woman had the appearance of a thousand middle class French women I've known—a vulgar, rather loose mouth; not very intelligent looking. The young man spoke English well, but with a foreign accent. It was tragic to see Joyce—one of the gods of the moment—speaking not one word of the language his fame is based on. The girl was rather pretty—I thought at first she was a little American flapper.

Joyce was very simple, very nice. He walked next to the old guide who showed us around, listening with apparent interest to his harangue delivered in broken English, and asking him questions. We came home to Brussels through a magnificent forest, miles in extent—Joyce sat with the driver on the front seat, asked a great many questions. I sat alone on the back seat—it was a huge coach; the woman sat in front of me, the girl in front of her, the young man to one side. Queer arrangement, eh?

Joyce got a bit stagey on the way home, draping his overcoat poetically around his shoulders. But I liked Joyce's looks—not extraordinary at first sight, but growing. His face was highly colored, slightly concave—his mouth thin, not delicate, but extraordinarily humorous. He had a large powerful straight nose—redder than his face, somewhat pitted with scars and boils.

When we got back to Brussels, and stopped in front of the bus office, the young man and two women made a little group, while Joyce went inside. The young fellow was looking at me, and I was swimming in beer. I made a dive for the nearest place, which was under a monument: they are more respectable here than in Paris.

Anyway it was too good to spoil: the idea of Joyce and me being at Waterloo at the same time, and aboard a sight-seeing bus, struck me as insanely funny: I sat on the back seat making idiot noises in my throat, and crooning all the way back through the forest.

I think really they might have been a little grand about it if they had known they were discovered. But they were just like common people out sight-seeing.

I'm going on to Antwerp to-morrow, Bruges the day after, London Sunday or Monday. . . . My life is utterly austere, utterly remote. I have eaten well here—some of the restaurants are excellent. But I have not sat at table or anywhere else with anyone, save a little English merchant who came over on the boat with me: he was a funny little man, . . . who conducted me, with many a sly wink to a table at a most respectable dinner hall: we drank orangeade, the little man looked at the girls, and winked at me, going off into fits of silent laughter.

You get nothing to drink in Brussels but beer and wine unless you buy *bottles* of the stronger stuff at stores. I drink beer mainly: there are places here where you get iced sparkling champagne for twelve cents a goblet.

Last night about midnight—I had gone out from my room after working, for a walk—a woman stopped me, and began to wheedle me. She was a large strapping blonde prostitute. I gave her money for a beer and sent her on. A few minutes later, I noticed a fearful commotion across the street. Prostitutes, with their eager delight in a brawl, came in magical hordes. My lady had cut a sizable hunk out of a drunken gentleman's neck with a razor, and was fiercely mauling a small man all over the pavement. There were several minor brawls going on between the whores and their pimps. Finally, someone yelled "Police," and the army disappeared up four separate alleys. The police came up and arrested magnificently the man who had been cut. . . .

I am going back to England to try to finish the book—it is a far vaster thing than I had thought, but it grows in clarity and structure every day. This letter is stupid—all my energy . . . has gone into the book. I may go to Oxford next month. Meanwhile I shall try to get back my old apartment in London. . . .

Good-bye—God bless you, my dear.

I'm tired after Joyce and Waterloo. Forgive a stupid letter. I just thought that I shall probably be 26 years old when you get this. At 23, hundreds of people thought I'd do something. Now, no one does—not even myself. I really don't care very much. . . .

To OLIN DOWS

Harvard Club
New York.
Thursday night.

[January, 1927]

Dear Olin:

I've just had your note—I've twenty minutes to answer it but I'm quite willing to take the rest of the night if my reply will fetch you to see me, or me to see you.

I came back from Europe January first: I am living in a huge garret at

13 East 8th Street (not the *village*) over a tailoring shop. I am writing a huge book, on which I started while in England. I write from eleven o'clock at night till six in the morning, and get up at one or two o'clock. For the first time in my life, I'm seriously at work. It is mad, drunken, wild— but it makes good reading.

Let me get this in—breathlessly. I have thought of you, my fine fellow, several thousand times, and I have wondered why I have lost you. I wondered if I had written something in a letter that offended you, or whether you were disgusted at my manner of life. Because, somehow or other, I imagine I may suggest to the thoughtful person the worst excesses of Nero, Caligula, or the most evil devotee of Gomorrhaean lechery. Let me reassure you: you will find me respectable, hard-working, poverty-stricken, dirty—and, I'm afraid, somewhat dull. A few friends from the old sunken world climb the steps to see me—beyond them, I see no one, go nowhere.

I may be forced back to teaching next September [1]—they want me back, God knows why (no modesty)—and I may go abroad this summer if I can get Moby Dick launched.

If you were waiting for me to write you, you would have had (as Sam Johnson said) the victory long ago. But I did not know where to find you. I thought of Yale, but didn't know the address, and I didn't think of Rhinebeck. The master mind again.

[THE REMAINDER OF THIS LETTER HAS BEEN LOST]

To MABEL WOLFE WHEATON

> Harvard Club
> New York.
> Monday, Jan. 24, [1927]

Dear Mabel:

I got your letter to-night, and I saw Ralph off last night.[1] Your letter to him came an hour or two before the boat sailed, and it was so full of love and kisses that he was unable to speak for five or ten minutes. Then he began a long oration celebrating your goodness, greatness, beauty, and so on, which ended when he ran out of breath and the boat sailed. Also, he was fairly sober at the time. But more of this later. . . .

I wouldn't have missed Ralph and his playmates for anything. It was

[1] Wolfe did not teach at New York University during the spring, 1927 term, but went back in September.

[1] Ralph Wheaton had gone on a cruise to Cuba conducted by the National Cash Register Company for their salesmen.

the first time I had ever seen several hundred up-and-coming go-getters together. I went down to the dock at five o'clock. Sleety icy nasty weather! Beautiful little boat, kept beautifully clean by the Dutch who run it. But it won't last. Ralph had a berth on B deck with an agent from Memphis, and Mr. ——, the —— Knockout. I found Ralph in his room, S—— doing a wild Charleston at the piano on the landing, and everyone else looking as if he had just come from Cuba.

I was touched by the manner in which the boys greeted each other after a year's absence. As they came aboard and spied their friends, their mouths would drop open in an expression of astonishment, they would drop their bags, let out a loud whoop, and rush forward roaring with laughter, shouting such pleasantries as:

"Joe, you old bastard, how the hell are you!"
          or
"Well I'm Goddammed if it ain't Pete—you lousy bum!"
And so on. The Company had presented each of them with a new walking stick, the hat of an Admiral of The Fleet, with a star for each trip—Ralph had nine—and $85, I believe, in cash. I went off the boat about six o'clock with Ralph, S——, the Miami agent, and the man from Hagerstown who thought he knew where we could get it. Only he didn't, and I took them to one of my places, an Italian restaurant, where we could. All of us ate the enormous dollar dinner, and put away a good amount of America's fine old table wine—synthetic booze—in the shape of rye, rum, beer, ale, and cocktails, of which last I, four, your husband two or three.

Poor devils, they were pleased as children because it was what they called "good stuff," but I've been worried over the state of their health all day. —— bought a bottle of Baccardi Rum which we took back to the boat and pretty well killed with the aid of the aforementioned Brother ——, who took a long pull, belched loudly, and remarked that it was damned good Scotch. He had apparently been in training for the last two or three days, and I saw no particular reason why he should go to Cuba at all since he seemed to be doing so well in New York. He was in love with all the world: his way of showing it was to pull an eight inch pocket knife from his trousers, open it, go off in a fit of insane laughter, and announce that he was going to cut your goddammed heart out. But there was no harm in the boy—he took a great fancy to me, informed me that I looked like a damned pirate, and was worse than my brother Fred— which was all he could say for anyone. By this time the effects of New York hooch had worn off a little from other members of the passenger list, and they stood about thirstily waiting for the ship to sail and the bar to open. I informed them that a ship's bar does not usually open until the next morning, if she sails at night, at which 437 voices yelled that she had better open (By God!) or they'd break the damned door down. So I suppose she opened. . . .

[THE REMAINDER OF THIS LETTER HAS BEEN LOST]

To HOMER A. WATT

Hotel Hemenway
Boston
Monday Night, March 7, 1927

Dear Professor Watt:

I have come to Boston for a few days to see some friends and to get several dozen volumes of divine poetry, relics of my youth, which . . . I left with my uncle, three years ago. . . . I had your letter several weeks ago: I have thought it over many times. Later, Carlton [1] told me that he had talked with you, and that you suggested that I accept the appointment to teach next September, with the understanding that I might withdraw my acceptance provided I informed you within reasonable time.

I know you will be glad to hear that I have worked hard and steadily in my garret, and that I hope to have my huge book on paper by May, and in the hands of a publisher (I hope!) by summer. I think you understand that what I want to do with my life is to live by and for my writing. That independence—I had better say that slavery—is the highest desire I have ever known. To hope for it at present is precarious. I thank you again, fervently, for your patience, your kindness, and your encouragement. May I assume that if the miracle (of publication and royalty) does not happen, I can have employment in the September division, and if it does, and I am able to go on under my own steam, that I may decently (before the term's beginning) withdraw?

I am returning to New York day after tomorrow. My mail address is still the Harvard Club. I shall come in to see you during the month.

Life is many days. But I'm at a time when it seems very short. My twenty-six years weigh on me and, rather desperately, I feel my lack of achievement. I surrender myself again, therefore, to your extraordinary indulgence, which has been unfailing.

This is a bad, groping, fumbling letter. I've said what I wanted to say, but badly. I've been roaming over Concord all day and climbing the tower in Hawthorne's house. I'm tired.

[1] Henry Fisk Carlton.

To MABEL WOLFE WHEATON

Harvard Club
New York
Sat. night, March 26, 1927

Dear Mabel:

. . . Your apples came while I was away in Boston. They were splendid apples, but they had been en route for some time, I believe, and a great many of them were getting soft. Mrs. B's [1] chef, therefore, converted the sick men into apple sauce—there were some for me too, when I got home. Don't feel badly about them—if I didn't cram them all down my own gullet, you can have the satisfaction of knowing they gave pleasure to a very great lady, the best friend I may ever have. . . .

I am working like a horse. I go nowhere—not even to the theatre. I am in my garret all day, and come here sometimes at night for mail, and to do a little reading. I hope to get my book written, revised, and typed this Spring. It has been suggested to me that I go abroad this summer, but I shall not budge from my present residence until the book is done and in the hands of a publisher.

My health is good, although I've lost weight since I came back, and no longer have my jolly red English complexion—a combined effect of rain and John Haig. Also, I am no better than an idiot usually by midnight, because I drink some dozen or eighteen cups of coffee during the day of my own brewing. It gets me simply crazy with nerves, but it keeps me alive and cursing. Like many of my more famous associates I work best at night, and I am not often in bed before three thirty or four o'clock in the morning. But I'm getting my work done, which is all that matters.

Thanks for your words of good cheer. I shall probably do something someday—soon, I hope. My greatest deficiency is a total lack of salesmanship—a quality that is quite as important in profitable writing as anywhere else. I never sent my plays to more than two or three managers and if I got no answer within a month I wrote insulting letters demanding their return. I have never known where to go, where to turn, or what to do. This time, certain friends will probably attend to that part of it for me.

The University job is open for me in September, and I have also been offered work with the radio,[2] and with an advertising company that's

---

[1] Mrs. Bernstein's.

[2] At this time, Henry Fisk Carlton was doing several free lance radio programs for WJZ and WEBF, and had suggested that Wolfe try doing some shows for his programs, also on a free lance basis. Carlton says Wolfe had similar offers from other people but never did any actual writing for the radio.

lousy with money.[3] I could probably make a great deal more from the advertising than from teaching, but it would take more time.

This is a bad, stupid letter. It's midnight, I've been at work all day. I'm fagged out. I'll write you again when I'm in better fettle. I'm glad to hear of your improved health. We may all live yet to die of old age. Give my love to Mama, Fred, and Ralph. Tell me what's happening as soon as you can.

I've been out once to parties of the great and near-great in New York— writers, poets, actresses—another effort of my friends to help me. Went to one terrible studio party where I met a man named Van Vechten, novelist, a . . . woman named Elinor Wylie, who is all the go now—she writes novels and poetry—and her husband, Will Benét—I hated them so that I managed to insult them all before the evening was over. So, if I get there, I shall probably have to depend on my own steam. . . .

To MARGARET ROBERTS

Harvard Club
New York

[Early June, 1927]

Dear Mrs. Roberts:

Forgive my long silence and the shortness of this letter. I have poured my life, my strength, and almost all my time for almost a year into my book, which is now nearing its end. I think it is the best thing I've ever done: certainly it is the only thing I have ever really worked on. I have learned that writing is hard work, desperate work, and that (as Ben Jonson said) "Who casts to write a living line must sweat." I have lived since I came back to New York in a deserted ramshackle building that trembles when a car passes; I have lived in its huge dirty garret, without heat, without plumbing—without anything but light. My mother wrote me several weeks ago—I hear from at least one member of my family every two or three months—congratulating me on the possession of "rich friends." Well, I suppose I have rich friends—a few of all kinds, rich and poor, have shown me amazing devotion—but I have taken only what was necessary for the barest existence. I have lived closer to poverty this year than ever in my life. And I do not regret it. I have had all I needed. The world for me was ghost when I wrote.

I don't know what the outcome will be. I have no power to peddle my wares, and I strike patronage a blow in the face. The other day word reached me that a rich woman who has supported a famous little theatre

[3] The J. Walter Thompson Company.

here for years (Miss Alice Lewisohn of the Neighborhood Playhouse) had told one of the directors last year that she would have done my play ("Welcome") but that I was the most arrogant young man she had ever known. The news gave me pleasure: my proud foolish words to her of disdain and contempt came back to me and I felt that I had acted well— I who will never be dandled into reputation by wealth. I have forsaken all groups; I live, save for the affection of a few friends, as much alone as anyone can live. And I know I am right! I believe—they believe—I shall come through. . . .

I wish I could tell you more of my book. I meant alone this: I think I shall call it "Alone, Alone," [1] for the idea that broods over it, and in it, and behind it is that we are all strangers upon this earth we walk on—that naked and alone do we come into life, and alone, a stranger, each to each, we live upon it. The title, as you know, I have taken from the poem I love best: "The Rime of the Ancient Mariner":—

> Alone, alone, all, all alone,
> Alone on a wide, wide sea!
> And never a saint took pity on
> My soul in agony.

My state is not bad—in spite of the fact that I am considered arrogant and proud (the protective coloration of one who was born without his proper allowance of hide). I am told, by someone who loves me, that I could have what I wanted of people—"the city at my feet," and so on—if I let myself out on them. Perhaps not—but, what's better, my friends like me.

I'm very tired; my health has stood the pounding beautifully. I don't know what I shall do when I finish. I may go abroad for a short trip. . . . Good-bye for the present. Write to me soon. You are one of the few people that will never become a phantom to me. God bless you all.

To MARGARET ROBERTS

Harvard Club
New York
Monday—May 30, 1927

Dear Mrs. Roberts:

. . . You say that no one *outside* my family loves me more than Margaret Roberts. Let me rather say the exact truth:—that no one *inside* my family loves me as much, and only one other person, I think, in all the world

---

[1] Another early title for *Look Homeward, Angel.*

loves me as much. My book is full of ugliness and terrible pain—and I think moments of a great and soaring beauty. In it (will you forgive me?) I have told the story of one of the most beautiful people I have ever known as it touched on my own life. I am calling that person Margaret Leonard. I was without a home—a vagabond since I was seven—with two roofs [1] and no home. I moved inward on that house of death and tumult from room to little room, as the boarders came with their dollar a day, and their constant rocking on the porch. My overloaded heart was bursting with its packed weight of loneliness and terror; I was strangling, without speech, without articulation, in my own secretions—groping like a blind sea-thing with no eyes and a thousand feelers toward light, toward life, toward beauty and order, out of that hell of chaos, greed, and cheap ugliness—and then I found you, when else I should have died, you mother of my spirit who fed me with light. Do you think that I have forgotten? Do you think I ever will? You are entombed in my flesh, you are in the pulses of my blood, the thought of you makes a great music in me— and before I come to death, I shall use the last thrust of my talent—whatever it is—to put your beauty into words.

Good-bye for the present. This is Decoration Day. I am decorated with weariness, but I am going to try to get it all down on paper in the next few weeks and then I may go abroad for a short time. My attic is getting hot—my friend, Olin Dows (almost as great a saint as you are) came down from his 80 rooms and 2000 acres on the Hudson Saturday and asked me to finish the book in the country. But I'm afraid of the big house and all the swells. He's had it alone all winter—but now his mother's coming from Washington (with all the legations) and his sister from Sweden; they're in for a big summer. But there's a lovely little cottage of two rooms, with a bath, deep in the woods, by the bathing pool, and he's offered this to me, together with as many acres of land as I need, forever, if I should ever care to stay there near him. He paints, lives like a Spartan on vegetables, and is a Bertrand Russell Socialist (much to his father's sorrow).

Write as soon as you get this. When I pluck up more strength, I'll write a good one. Excuse the gibberings. Good-bye. God bless you all.

The following letter to Mrs. Roberts was never finished and never mailed. Instead, Wolfe sent a brief letter dated July 11, which is omitted here since it only duplicates this in much briefer fashion.

[1] His father's house at 92 Woodfin Street, Asheville, and the Old Kentucky Home at 48 Spruce Street.

To MARGARET ROBERTS

Harvard Club
New York
[July 8 (?) 1927]

Dear Mrs. Roberts:

I read your letter this afternoon a few minutes after I had purchased second class passage on the *George Washington,* sailing Tuesday. Thus, I will not be here to greet you if you come in August: I am returning in September. All this I decided at once on Sunday, after mulling the business hopelessly for months. I had thought before that I would finish the book here and go abroad in the autumn to stay for a year in Italy. Several considerations prevented me. First, I have exhausted my wits on a gigantic piece of work—and I shall not want to write more, I think, for several months. Second, I should be here in New York next winter to try to launch the thing and some of my plays. Third, my going away for a long period of time would cause the deepest pain to the one person on earth who has the greatest claim to my love.[1] There is nothing in my life as important as this: I was a lonely out-cast, and suddenly I became richer, in the one true wealth, than Maecenas.

I am going to Paris for a short time—then on to Prague, Budapest, and Vienna, all lovely and unvisited. I shall be back in Paris for a few days in September. . . .

I have been in the country several weeks with my friend Olin Dows. I'm much restored physically, but my brain is falling apart like over-scrambled eggs. Hence this stupid letter. I refused to live in the big house with the swells: he gave me the gate-keeper's lodge—a little bit of heaven with a little river, a wooded glade, and the sound of water falling over the dam all through the night. Beyond, the stream widened into the mighty Hudson—the noblest river I know of.

I had to dress up in my dinner jacket almost every night, which was good for me because I'm somewhat afraid of people, and sometimes conceal my fear by being arrogant and sneering magnificently. On the Fourth of July, in the evening, I went with Olin to a neighboring estate of one of his rich friends, a young man named Vincent Astor, who is one of the richest young men in the world—his chief claim, I believe, to distinction. The young man likes to play with every kind of steam engine (he has a miniature railroad on the place) and to set off fireworks. He set off several thousand dollars worth for our delight—they were the loveliest things I've ever seen and did incredible things, whistling like

[1] Mrs. Bernstein.

birds, bursting in cascades of color, changing their lights, and so on. The simple villagers—some hundreds or thousands—sat on the lawns, and all the swells upon the verandahs. How they stared at me! I looked very well in my clothes, but they knew I was an alien of some sort. I have a kind of notoriety among them, I believe, as Olin's wild Bohemian friend: whenever they met me, they asked if it were really true that I stayed up all night and was writing a book—and what was it all about! But they were all very lovely—I'm afraid if I had to do it I'd find them dull.

Astor's grounds were huge and beautiful (thousands of acres magnificently kept), his house was huge and ugly—a stone Victorian thing that belonged to his father—the rooms were also huge and ugly, stuffed with ugly red plush furniture. After the fireworks we went inside to the dining room and ate ice cream and chicken salad and punch with the assistance of eight or ten flunkies. I'm sure I'd go murderously insane and kill a few of them if I had them around long. Astor's wife is a tall, blonde, slender young woman—very elegant and beautiful, and cold. Olin told me it was the first social position in America: the big rooms, the people around her really gave one the sense of a court. (But I've heard them talk— opinions that would disgrace an English Tory.)

But I lived very simply at the lodge house—by myself—going to the big house once a day, or having one good meal brought to me, and poisoning myself on my own cooking the rest of the time. As for Olin, he is in many respects the finest young man I've ever known—a very great person. . . .

To MABEL WOLFE WHEATON

Harvard Club
New York
July 10, 1927

Dear Mabel:—

. . . Mama and Mrs. Roberts have both written me that you have not been well. I am sorry to hear this; I hope you are better now and will write me how you feel. I think of you all with loyalty and affection; I wish you all health and the good life with all my heart. If I have been different from the rest of you, and you thought me "queer" and a "freak," please remember that my fundamental nature is something I could neither help nor change, and that I have never lifted a finger to injure or molest any of you. I am older now, and perhaps not so unpleasant as you thought me when I was a child. The hostility and bitterness that was shown when I was in college and at Harvard ought to be dead now; I want nothing that belongs to any of you except your good will. I want to know very much that you are well and happy and at peace with life. . . .

I have been up in the country with the swells for three weeks or more. . . . I found a card from Donald MacRae [1] when I got back: I looked him up last night at the maternity hospital where he's in training, and stayed until four o'clock in the morning watching a baby get born. The doctors dressed me up in a long surgeon's dress (they laughed like hell!) and took me in to the operating room. I saw everything; they explained everything. It was one of the most terrible and beautiful things I have ever seen. I shall never forget it. The result of everything was a fine eight pound boy with a very healthy set of lungs. The mother was a big husky Irishwoman. She screamed like a maniac, and every time she did, I screwed my face into a knot and clenched my teeth—which the young doctors thought very funny. But she did not really suffer as much as it seemed; she wouldn't help them, she fought them, things weren't getting along; so Donald finally put the lady to sleep and they took the kid with forceps. Wonderful! Wonderful! Wonderful! I was bothered at first by the rough-and-ready talk of the doctors and nurses—it seemed brutal; but I saw later they are really very good and kind people, doing a humane service to poor and common people. If their talk was rough, their hands were gentle—everything was beautifully clean, and the poor woman's baby came into this world with more care and skill and comfort than you and I had.

I wish I could tell you more—it's more thrilling than any story: the chief doctor kept coaxing her along by saying: "Come on, momma! Do your stuff now! Give us some help, momma! Push! Push! Do you want to have this baby, momma, or not? It's your kid, momma, not mine! Be a sport." and so on. Finally—ether, forceps, baby. It was ugly, bloody, messy, horrible—but somehow beautiful: when I saw the little skull begin to come, and then the little body, and the doctor held him up by the heels and spanked him, and he screwed his face up and let out his first yell (a good loud one), I could restrain myself no longer: I gave a yell of my own and said "Come on, baby! Come on!" That made them laugh: they did not understand why anyone should get so excited. The ugliness, the horror, the pain is gone now: all that remains is that little perfect child, and all the mystery and tragic beauty of life, which now seems greater to me than ever. I have been so excited and stirred all day that I cannot eat for thinking of it—I could hardly get to sleep when I got home this morning. You

[1] J. Donald MacRae had been a fraternity brother of Wolfe's in Pi Kappa Phi at the University of North Carolina, and was at this time an intern at Manhattan Maternity and Dispensary in New York. He is now radiologist at Highsmith Hospital, Fayetteville, N.C.

will understand me when I tell you that this thing has made a great music in me: something gathers in my throat and my eyes are wet when I think of all the pain and wonder that little life must come to know; and I hope to God those feet will never walk as lonely a road as mine have walked, and I hope its heart will never beat as mine has at times under a smothering weight of weariness, grief, and horror; nor its brain be damned and haunted by the thousand furies and nightmare shapes that walk through mine. This is no sentiment—but the stark truth, from a very deep place in me.

This is all I can write—I'm terribly tired. Write me at Paris, if you can. Keep yourself well, lift up your heart, be happy.

P.S. I think Donald is going to be a good doctor. He has much kindliness and gentleness. When it was over last night I went downstairs with the doctors and nurses. We sat down and told one another dirty stories. It sounds bad—but it is their escape, healthy and harmless: I was more convinced than ever that they are fine people. If I get sick let me have such people around me—expert and calm-tempered roughnecks. No weeping bunglers. This is a bad letter: too tired to write well.

To HOMER A. WATT

Vienna

Aug. 11, 1927

Dear Professor Watt:

This is just a line of greeting and a reminder of our conversation several weeks ago about my schedule. I hope you have finally managed (from the distressing network of schedules you have had to arrange) to give me the hours you thought possible. By this arrangement, I would have night classes M. T. W. Thurs: my free time would be lumped together—highly desirable to me.

I have been in this charming town of Vienna for two days: I came on from Munich and the Bavarian mountains. There was a revolution here three weeks ago in which four hundred people lost their lives, but you could not tell it now from the gaiety of the city's life. These people seem to belong to an entirely different civilization from the Germans. There is a lightness, a delicacy, and a charm in the life here which is as un-Teutonic as anything can be. The whole town is much more French in its appearance—a smaller Paris, but I believe the gaiety of the people is more spontaneous than that of the Parisian—there is a much more honest cordiality here: they lack the very bad Gallic hardness.

I am going from here to Prague, and from there back to Paris. I expect to sail for New York about September 10. This has been a quiet and very rich little voyage. I am devouring the German language in gluttonous gobs and buying books with both hands. Do you know that I talk German to these people—very bad, clumsy, halting German, it's true, but they understand me. I have very little facility for speaking a language well, but I have a real talent for understanding it and soaking it up. I can now speak French with a bad fluency and read and understand it as well as English. Before another year has gone by I'm going to do the same for German. Then I'm going to get Italian. It's simply fascinating to be sunk in a new language and to have the names of all the things you want—tobacco, soap, matches, veal cutlets, and so on—printed and spoken around you in a new tongue. In this way it soaks in through the pores of your skin.

The papers are terribly excited here (and all over Europe) about the Sacco-Vanzetti case. The entire front page is given to it. There seems to be a universal demand for the pardon of the men. I do not know enough about the case: I think it is likely the men *may* be guilty, but I think also the trial was long, fumbling, and prejudiced. The great pity is that a thing like this suddenly coalesces and *symbolizes,* so to speak, the terribly bitter feeling that is felt for America throughout the world today. I am finishing this letter, by the way, several days after I began it: I have been in Vienna almost a week, and the enormous charm of the place has invaded me. When I come again, I'm coming here for several months to get the language. Munich was a magnificent town, with some of the greatest things in it I've ever seen, but there's simply no denying it: there *is* a sort of German—young gentlemen with dueling scars on their face, and older ones with shaven bullet heads, small porky eyes, and three ridges of neck over the back of their collars—that I do not, I do not like! I gave over carefully and quietly on the pavements until I found that these gentlemen had an unhappy (and I believe unconscious) habit of taking not only the four yards which was theirs, but the eight inches which was mine. All that I had ever felt about the sacredness of liberty and the rights of men boiled over, I kept grimly on my way, increased my stride just as I got upon the startled Hun, before he could retreat. God forgive me for this meanness of spirit: let me assure you that my prejudice, if I had any, was in their favor, because of the war's vicious propaganda. They are a very powerful and energetic people, quite ignorant, I believe, of their unpleasant qualities; they have tremendous creative and intellectual power: huge, profound, murky, and earth-shaking (like Kant and Wagner), but they are lacking in the fine delicacy and urbanity of these Viennese.

I've got to end abruptly. I hope you've had a pleasant summer. Please get me the schedule, if you can.

The following letter was submitted to various publishers with the manuscript of O, Lost (Look Homeward, Angel).

NOTE FOR THE PUBLISHER'S READER.

[Late March, 1928]

This book, by my estimate, is from 250,000 to 280,000 words long. A book of this length from an unknown writer no doubt is rashly experimental, and shows his ignorance of the mechanics of publishing. This is true: this is my first book.

But I believe it would be unfair to assume that because this is a very long book it is too long a book. A revision would, I think, shorten it somewhat. But I do not believe any amount of revision would make it a short book. It could be shortened by scenes, by pages, by thousands of words. But it could not be shortened by half, or a third, or a quarter.

There are some pages here which were compelled by a need for fullness of expression, and which had importance when the book was written not because they made part of its essential substance, but because, by setting them forth, the mind was released for its basic work of creation. These pages have done their work of catharsis, and may now be excised. But their excision would not make a short book.

It does not seem to me that the book is overwritten. Whatever comes out of it must come out block by block and not sentence by sentence. Generally, I do not believe the writing to be wordy, prolix, or redundant. And separate scenes are told with as much brevity and economy as possible. But the book covers the life of a large family intensively for a period of twenty years, and in rapid summary for fifty years. And the book tries to describe not only the visible outer lives of all these people, but even more their buried lives.

The book may be lacking in plot but it is not lacking in plan. The plan is rigid and densely woven. There are two essential movements—one outward and one downward. The outward movement describes the effort of a child, a boy, and a youth for release, freedom, and loneliness in new lands. The movement of experience is duplicated by a series of widening concentric circles, three of which are represented by the three parts of the book. The downward movement is represented by a constant excavation into the buried life of a group of people, and describes the cyclic curve of a family's life—genesis, union, decay, and dissolution.

To me, who was joined so passionately with the people in this book, it seemed that they were the greatest people I had ever known and the texture of their lives the richest and strangest; and discounting the distortion of judgment that my nearness to them would cause, I think they would seem extraordinary to anyone. If I could get my magnificent people on paper as they were, if I could get down something of their strangeness and richness in my book, I believed that no one would object to my 250,000 words; or, that if my pages swarmed with this rich life, few would damn an inept manner and accuse me of not knowing the technique for making a book, as practiced by Balzac, or Flaubert, or Hardy, or Gide. If I have failed to get any of this opulence into my book, the fault lies not in my people —who could make an epic—but in me.

But that is what I wanted to do and tried to do. This book was written in simpleness and nakedness of soul. When I began to write the book twenty months ago I got back something of a child's innocency and wonder. You may question this later when you come to the dirty words. But the dirty words can come out quickly—if the book has any chance of publication, they will come out without conscience or compunction. For the rest, I wrote it innocently and passionately. It has in it much that to me is painful and ugly, but, without sentimentality or dishonesty, it seems to me, because I am a romantic, that pain has an inevitable fruition in beauty. And the book has in it sin and terror and darkness—ugly dry lusts, cruelty, a strong sexual hunger of a child—the dark, the evil, the forbidden. But I believe it has many other things as well, and I wrote it with strong joy, without counting the costs, for I was sure at the time that the whole of my intention—which was to come simply and unsparingly to naked life, and to tell all of my story without affection or lewdness—would be apparent. At that time I believed it was possible to write of all things, so long as it was honestly done. So far as I know there is not a nasty scene in the book—but there are the dirty words, and always a casual and unimpeded vision of everything.

When I wrote the book I seized with delight everything that would give it color and richness. All the variety and madness of my people—the leper taint, the cruel waste, the dark flowering evil of life I wrote about with as much exultancy as health, sanity, joy.

It is, of course, obvious that the book is "autobiographical." But in a literal sense, it is probably no more autobiographical than "Gulliver's Travels." There is scarcely a scene that has its base in literal fact. The book is a fiction—it is loaded with invention: story, fantasy, vision. But it is a fiction that is, I believe, more true than fact—a fiction that grew out of a life completely digested in my spirit, a fiction which telescopes, condenses, and objectifies all the random or incompleted gestures of life —which tries to comprehend people, in short, not by telling what people did, but what they should have done. The most literal and autobiographical part of the book, therefore, is its picture of the buried life. The most exact thing in it is the fantasy—its picture of a child's soul.

I have never called this book a novel. To me it is a book such as all men may have in them. It is a book made out of my life, and it represents my vision of life to my twentieth year.

What merit it has I do not know. It sometimes seems to me that it presents a strange and deep picture of American life—one that I have never seen elsewhere; and that I may have some hope of publication. I do not know; I am very close to it. I want to find out about it, and to be told by someone else about it.

I am assured that this book will have a good reading by an intelligent person in a publishing house. I have written all this, not to propitiate you, for I have no peddling instinct, but entreat you, if you spend the many hours necessary for a careful reading, to spend a little more time in giving me an opinion. If it is not a good book, why? If parts are good and parts bad, what are they? If it is not publishable, could it be made so? Out of the great welter of manuscripts that you must read, does this one seem distinguished by any excellence, interest, superior merit?

I need a little honest help. If you are interested enough to finish the book, won't you give it to me?

The following letter was sent to Professor James B. Munn with the manuscript of O, Lost (Look Homeward, Angel) *which Wolfe had asked him to read. Dr. Munn was Professor of English and Dean at Washington Square College, New York University, from 1928–1932, and had been Assistant Professor and Assistant Dean during Wolfe's earlier years as an instructor there. He is now Professor of English at Harvard University.*

To JAMES B. MUNN

[New York City]

Tuesday, March 27, [1928]

Dear Doctor Munn:

I give you my book with a feeling of strong fear. When you read my play [1] two or three years ago, you spoke about it in a way I shall not forget. The one criticism I remember concerned a page or two of dialogue which was tainted by coarseness. You spoke mildly and gently of that, but I felt you were sorry it had been written in. Now I give you a book on which I have wrought out my brain and my heart for twenty months. There are places in it which are foul, obscene, and repulsive. Most of those will come out on revision. But please, Dr. Munn, believe that this book

[1] *Mannerhouse.*

was honestly and innocently written. Forgive me the bad parts, and remember me for the beauty and passion I have *tried* to put in it. It is not *immoral*, it is not *dirty*—it simply represents an enormous excavation in my spirit. Saying that, I feel better. My energy is completely exhausted—I felt as if I should drop dead when I came to the last comma. I feel as if my life were beginning again, and what I shall do for a year or two, or where I shall be, I don't know.

But remember that I give you this for no other reason than for the tremendous regard I have for you. The thought that I may have written anything that will cause you to change any good opinion you may ever have had of me makes me pause.

But I can't go on explaining forever. Please read the "Note to The Publisher" [2] before you begin.

Here it is—my heart is in it.

To HOMER A. WATT

Harvard Club
New York
April 1, 1928

CONFIDENTIAL

Dear Professor Watt:

I am writing you this letter before I speak to you, because I feel you may want a formal record for your files.

After long consideration I have decided not to accept a teaching appointment at the university for next year.[1] I think the time has come when I must make a bold venture with my life: in some way—not, I am afraid, very clearly defined yet—I want to get the energy of my life directed towards the thing it desires most. In short, I am going to try to support myself by writing—if necessary, by hack writing of any sort, stories, advertising, articles—but *writing* of a sort. If my book should be accepted I should, of course, immediately start work on a new one. I know that this is a gamble, but it occurs to me that we can afford to gamble once or twice in an effort to get at the heart of our desire. The most reckless people, I believe, are those who never gamble at all.

During the last few days, in the tragic misfortune of Mr. Powell,[2] I have

[2] The "Note for the Publisher's Reader."

[1] Wolfe did not teach the Fall 1928 term at New York University, and only taught half-time in the Spring 1929 term. He accepted appointment for the academic year 1929–1930 and taught the Fall term, but resigned in January to devote himself entirely to writing.

[2] Desmond Powell had been an instructor in the English Department at New

seen again the splendid generosity which shows that New York University is not simply a group of buildings with elevators. And since an action of this sort must come from men, and not from brick and stone, I am inclined to place the credit for it where I have myself the deepest cause for gratefulness—with you and with Dr. Munn.

I have been more tired this Spring than at any other time of my life—I have felt, along with the finishing of my book, such damnable weariness of my brain and heart as I did not know existed. And often, I am afraid, I have been surly, ill-tempered, unable to join happily with other people. For this, if I cannot plead justification, I can at least ask pardon. But there is one assurance I must give you: once or twice, when I was in a chafed and bitter temper, I have heard some of the young men say that I occupied the position of a privileged character—that I was the departmental "wild oat," and any laxity or extravagance would be permitted me. Now this, I am sure, was harmless joking, but it touched rawly on me at the time. I think no one knows better than I do my deficiencies as a teacher —among which I would name a lack of orderly arrangement, an extravagant and useless expenditure of energy on all things, and a constant belief in miracles—but please believe that within my limits I have given you honest and faithful service.

It is perhaps childish for me to mention this, but I am childishly proud of this—that being notorious for a lack of discipline and regularity when I came here, I have, in my three years, missed only one class. That happened my first year, and was caused by the lateness of a boat returning from Boston. And I think I have never put a grade on a student's paper without trying to add a few lines of sensible and honest criticism. If you have ever had cause to doubt that, I think a very simple investigation would bear me out.

Will you please understand, Professor Watt, that I am not crying myself up vainly and boastfully? Most earnestly I want you to know, now that I'm leaving, that I have not tried to pose as a Bohemian or a temperamental fellow in order to get out of work—within the trap of my nature I have done all things I could to fulfill my obligation to you. It would cause me very real distress to think you doubted that. I have been at times a very difficult, a very moody and extravagant person, but I do not believe I have been a cheap or common person.

I think one of the chief reasons for my leaving now is not that I dislike teaching, and find it dull, but that I may like it too well. I find that it takes from me the same energy that I put into Creation: if this is true,

York University, and had been obliged by ill health to go to Colorado in March, 1928. Professor Watt had told him that the University would continue to pay his salary for the rest of the academic year and would also pay his travelling expenses.

and there is anything in me worth saving or having, I draw comfort from the belief that my classes must have got some of the best of me during my three years.

This is a bad and clumsy letter from a tired man. But none the less it comes from a very deep place in me. Three years of my life have been spent here. I know that they have carved a mark and left a deposit. Let me assure you that I will never forget your kindness, and your generous comprehension, and that if any *good* distinction ever attaches to my name, I shall be proud to acknowledge my connection with this place—if any *bad* one, I shall keep silent.

P.S. Will you please treat this as a *personal* communication?

To MARGARET ROBERTS

> Harvard Club
> New York
> April 6, 1928

Dear Mrs. Roberts:

Forgive this long silence—I finished my book and sent it to a publisher [1] for reading ten days ago. This means nothing more than that it will get read, and that I will get an answer in another three weeks. I am completely, utterly exhausted—the last twenty pages were agony—but I have a feeling of enormous relief to know that it's done. I have done a rashly experimental thing—the publishing firm said it's the longest manuscript they've had since "An American Tragedy"—but like Martin Luther, I couldn't do otherwise. Hereafter I'll keep more within prescribed limits.

The dean of Washington Square College [2] (N.Y.U.), who is a young man, a millionaire, an idealist, and a sensitive, romantic person, has just finished reading it. He wrote me a magnificently honest letter about it: he was terribly shocked at the pain, the terror, the ugliness, and the waste of human life in the book—he thought the people rose to nobility and beauty only at the end (in this he is terribly wrong!). But he said the book was unique in English and American literature, that if it is published it must be published without changing a word, and that he felt he had lived with the people in it for years.

Whether any publisher can be found who is willing to take the chance, I don't know. But, for good or bad, I'm going the whole distance now. I shall not be back at N.Y.U. next fall. They have been splendid and offered

[1] Boni and Liveright.
[2] Dean Munn.

me a raise, and finally told me the latch string was out at any time—that I could come back any time I needed the job. . . .

After the sap has risen in me a little more, I'll write you a longer and better letter. This is just a filler-in. Let me hear from you when you have time. Give my love to all the family. And tell me something about mine. I write, but I don't always get answers.

How is Asheville? Still, I hope, repentant.

To JAMES B. MUNN

[New York City]

Monday, May 21 [1928].

Please read this at your leisure.

Dear Dr. Munn:

I have tried to reach you several times during the last two or three days, but your very capable office force has fended me off. I'm going to Europe next month, and I'm trying to get all the money I can together. I believe your sanction will carry a long way with the Bursar—I don't know if he'll give me *all* the remainder of my salary in one lump or not, but will you say a word for me?

I've got a *new* book in mind.[1] I thought I should not write again for several centuries, but there's no cure for my own kind of lunacy. I don't see how this one can fail—it has everything: rich people, swank, a poor but beautiful girl, romance, adventure, Vienna, New York, a big country house, and so on. Also, after a careful examination of 4,362 modern novels, I have decided to make it exactly 79,427 words long. Will you please order your copy now? But honestly, I'm excited about it. In spite of my summary, I've got stuff for a good and moving book—also, perhaps, stuff for a bad and trashy, but possibly successful book. Now what's a poor young guy to do, Dean Munn? I've got to do it one way or the other—straddling the fence is no good.

About the Monster—"O, Lost." I had bad news of it, and then a bit of good news. The good news came last. I sent it to Boni and Liveright first. After five weeks they rejected it. I had a polite but very firm note from Mr. T. R. Smith, the manager. It had been given three readings, he said—much of it had quality and originality. He had to admit, he said, he enjoyed reading much of it. But it was "so long—so terribly long." Besides, it was autobiographical. They had lost money on four books "of this type"

---

[1] *The River People,* which was never published, but of which a portion appears on pages 500–596 of *Of Time and the River.*

last year. Others would no doubt be published, and might even sell, but for the present, as far as B. and L. is concerned, etc.

Meanwhile Ernest Boyd, the critic, was giving it a private reading. I heard from him—rather, from his wife [2]—the other day. Boyd said he thought the book could not be published in its present form because of "crudities." I don't know what that means—I'll have to see him. Perhaps his sensitive soul recoiled at some of the *langwidge*. He grew up in Dublin, you know, with James Joyce. But Mrs. B.—who is a big fat Frenchwoman (I hear)—did not agree with her gifted spouse. She translates French novels, and is a literary agent, and knows everyone. She seems to think there's a chance for it. As for me—I think nothing. I'm still in a stupor when I try to think of it. I'm going to see her to-morrow.

Harcourt Brace is reading it now. I've heard nothing from them. Could you talk to me for a few minutes before I go? The irony of it is that the book—which may get me kicked out of doors by every highbrow publisher in America—has landed me a good job with an advertising company [3]—if I want to take it. God knows what I shall do! I want to write the other book.

To GEORGE WALLACE

Harvard Club
New York
Monday June 25, 1928

Dear George:

I am going to Europe Saturday on whatever boat I can get on—but I hope a German one, so that I can get the beer. I want you to write me, if you can, before July 15, and send the letter to the American Express Co., Paris. I am asking this of a half dozen other people also, because I know that one of the ugliest feelings in the world is to come away from a foreign mail window empty handed. I do not know where I shall be—I shall be in Paris only a few days—but that mailing address is most convenient. Was going to Vienna, but I heard the other day that a great music festival is on, the town is full of our fellow countrymen, and prices, of course, have hit the ceiling. So I must look elsewhere. If I can get second

---

[2] Madeleine Boyd, who became Wolfe's literary agent at this time, and who sold *Look Homeward, Angel* to Scribners.

[3] In a letter to his mother dated June 7, 1928 (see *Thomas Wolfe's Letters to His Mother*, page 159), Wolfe wrote: "The J. Walter Thompson Company . . . has offered me a job writing advertisements for them. . . . They want me to begin in October—but they also want me to promise to stay for three years. . . . I don't like the three year business."

class passage on *Ile de France,* I'll get off at Havre, and go up the pleasant Seine to Rouen. And Brussels—that's a good place, too. Pretty girls and cheap champagne. Or München again. Or Buda-Pest—I have a typed list of all the good things to eat and drink there, given to me by Mr. Beer, the writer's brother.[1] And if it weren't so hot I should like to try Florence. I get no thrill from Spain, although everyone is doing it. I'm usually three or four years behind the moderns.

I haven't answered J. Walter Thompson yet. They gave me more time to think it over. But what I want to do is to write a new book. I've got one outlined that stinks with swank and money and romance.[2] It'll be just the length and everything. But honestly I think I can get a very good and moving story out of it.

About the first one—the *monster:* Mrs. Ernest Boyd has appointed herself my agent—at 10%. She says it's a good book, miles too long, but thinks she can find publisher. Says I must cut. Also, Mr. Melville Cane, attorney for Harcourt, Brace and member of the firm, says it's a *good* book—a fine, moving, and distinguished piece of writing. He says it's miles too long—he opened a copy of "Elmer Gantry," which his firm printed, and set that as *my* maximum length.[3] If I cut, he thinks it will get published. Mrs. Boyd gave the book to a young firm of publishers— just out.[4] When she heard about Harcourt Brace, she called up and said I would do much better to stick with new firm. She said they wanted first option on my second book and would publish if writing is as good as the first, and the book *of a reasonable length.* Does this at last sound like anything to you? I don't see why they should kid me. . . .

This is all for the present. Went home for a week, and found everyone with lots of real estate and no money. Was going to Europe Saturday but dentist made fascinating operation on tooth and jaw. Hurt like hell, but good job.

Please write me a good letter to Paris, and I'll try to answer in kind. Love to the family.

[1] Richard Beer, who had been an American Vice Consul in Budapest in 1922 and 1923.

[2] *The River People.*

[3] Mr. Cane was not a "member of the firm." He did serve as a director of the corporation. He did not prescribe "Elmer Gantry" as the maximum length but simply offered it as an example of a good-size novel.

[4] Covici-Friede.

To ALINE BERNSTEIN

Savoy Hotel, Frankfurt A.M.
Begun last Saturday and
finished today, Friday Sept 7 (?),
[1928]

Dear Aline:

Here I am at another stage of my travels—a very short one, for I came on here from Wiesbaden, which is only thirty miles away, to-day. . . . I got here as it was growing dark to-night—the ride was not interesting: the beautiful Rhine country ends about Wiesbaden, and the trip was through a flat fat-looking country full of crops and grapes. I love to come to a strange city along towards darkness—you get an impression, a suggestion of things which is half magic: sometimes it fades completely next day—you see how wrong you were. Again I have walked up and down new streets—great broad avenues, filled with great broad solid buildings, and rich shops. Have you ever noticed how all Germany seems to be built in just *two* styles of architecture? There is the lovely Albert Durer and Nurnberg style—great delicate gables, cross timbers, and lean-over upper stories, and then there is the Kaiser Wilhelm Deutschland uber Alles style—great rings, and avenues and boulevards filled with these solid ugly masses—all bulging in front with bays and balconies and round turrets. It is impressively rich and powerful and ugly—it seems to have been done (most of it) between 1880 and 1900, about the time, perhaps, it was becoming evident to them that the rest of the world ought to be colonized and given the advantages of a *real* civilization. That sounds like a malevolent speech full of the spirit that we ought now to put away —but I did not mean it against Germany alone. The way she felt about her excellence and her duty to enforce it on others is only the way England has felt, and the way a great many of us in America are feeling now. . . .

I get very tired taking it in, and I really believe I am taking a great deal in. But I feel like a great blundering child—I am feeling my way along by myself, and what I get is good and lasting, but it does not come in that brilliant and triumphant way I like to think it should. My life has been full of bitter strife and spiritual labor—a great deal of it, you very correctly say, unnecessary—but then, things come to me in that way. . . .

Now I'm going to tell you a Great Big One—you won't believe it, but it happens to be true. I made the Rundfahrt of the city to-day in a big bus: when I got in at the Bahnhof Platz at 3:30, it was crowded with large solid Germans—there was one vacant seat, and another opposite in which a gentleman was sitting. He looked up quickly as I came down the aisle, smiling in a nervous sort of way, and said very rapidly in English, "Sit down here." I sat down beside him: he pulled up his knees and crowded over against the side of the bus as if he was afraid of me. The man was James Joyce. I think he may have recognized me from the time we went out to Waterloo from Brussels just two years ago this September. He looked much older, he was quite bent, but very elegantly dressed—that is, better than he was last time, and instead of the single eyeshade, he wore black glasses in the sunlight; and he had another pair of plain ones for indoors.

We went into the Rathaus and Goethe's House: both were fine. In the Rathaus, which is called the Römer, everyone had to stick his feet into huge felt slippers before going into the Main Show, which is the huge Kaisersaal. He wandered around by himself peering at things while a German woman gave a long-winded lecture to the sightseers; then he got interested in the beautiful polished floors, and went skating up and down in his slippers in a very absent-minded way. We had not said a word to each other; but we kept smiling nervously and insisting by gestures that the other go in first through doors. We left the bus at Goethe's house, and after we came out again into the street he said to me that it was "a fine old house." I said I thought it was one of the finest houses I had ever seen—as it is—and that they were not able to do it any more. I said I was going back to the Old Town, which is right near the House, and which is as close to Elfland as we'll ever come. He said he thought he'd go "and get lost there for a while." Like a fool, I was too awkward and too shy to ask to go along—I am sure he would have let me: he wanted to be kind and friendly, and it would have been a grand thing for me to have gone with him. But I didn't, and I must wait now for the third time we meet—The Magic Third!—which will be in Dresden or in Heaven. Then I can speak. Joyce carried his right hand in a sling of black ribbon when he sat beside me in the bus, but he took it out when we got out of the bus.

After I left him I walked down one side of the street and he the other, both towards the Old Town. I peered into windows and looked at him from the corner of my eye; finally I went back to the Market Place, where the Rathaus is, and sat in an old house out of Grimm's fairy tales, where they sell the best Apfelwein and Frankfurters in the world. I had two orders of both. But all the time I kept thinking of James Joyce and the chance I had missed. I am not as certain as I was two years ago, when his son was with him and told me it was he; but the only reason I doubt it now is because *twice* seems so incredible. You won't believe it was if I tell you one item of his costume—he wore an old French beret, which he pulled off and left on the bus seat when we got out anywhere,—but it did not seem out of place. Besides, his "Portrait of the Artist"—"Jugendbildnis" here—is in a great many of the book windows; and the face of the author, I am sure, is the face of the man I was with to-day.

Wednesday Evening. My heart and soul have been at war with this German City, and now a kind of peace and certitude has come out of it. Last night when I came in, I saw scrawled on a slate in the hotel's lobby a notice in English which said that "Members of Tour 105 should be ready by nine o'clock to-morrow morning for the tour of the city, after which lunch will be served. The departure for Cologne will be at 12:30." Thus in a day and night these people traverse the country I have spent a month in . . . I talked to two old ladies from Ohio who were on this tour—they were very sweet, and told me all the things they had seen in their ride around town during the morning. One of them kept talking of "Goaty's House," and I wondered what in God's name it was until it occurred to me she meant Goethe's House. I wonder what Goaty would say if he could hear them—he has one of the handsomest and noblest heads I've ever seen, but there doesn't seem to be much humor in it. . . .

Thursday Evening. This has been a dull letter: I have wanted to tell you too much, and there is no room for it. The deeper, inner things I put in my little book: [1] I have filled one and begun another. . . . The world is very strange to me during these days—I have only been alone for two months among strange people, but the kind of *aloneness* I go in for makes that seem very long, and everything very far away. . . .

I lay down and slept for three hours—from eight to eleven—here; because I was up most of last night investigating the Old Town by moonlight. It was magical. This town has not the magnificent unity of Nurnberg; nor the grand quality that Nurnberg has. The Old Town here is a labyrinth of elfin houses, quainter and more like Grimm's than anything you will find elsewhere. I sat in the square before the Römer last night; the moon was blazing down. I was on the terrace of one of these houses, drinking a glass of Rhein wine. When you are tired, you can go to one of these faery tenements and drink apple wine—cold and heady—and eat hot frankfurters.

What else is here? A Volker museum, that has a magnificent collection of Asian, and Chinese, and African and Malaysian things. . . . Also a magnificent old church here—the *Dom,* with one of the richest interiors I've ever seen; and Goaty's house and museum; and the picture and sculpture galleries; and the Kunstgewerbe, which I have not seen—and Lord knows what else.

Their night life is heavy and brutal—I took it in last night—went to a couple of cabarets and bars and spent $1.25. A very poor and very heavy imitation of Paris—if anything can imitate an imitation. There is an im-

---

[1] The little notebook which he always carried in his pocket and in which he wrote down his random thoughts.

pression of variety everywhere: their life, however, is much more stand-
ardized than ours, no matter what they say. All over Germany they are
drinking beer and eating great slabs of pork and veal covered with heavy
sauces. The markets are filled with the most beautiful green vegetables
and fruits—enormous cucumbers, great clusters of grapes, peaches, plums
and so on—but you never get them on the menu. I am tired of the
heaviness and monotony of the food—to-night I had a beautiful inspiration and ate two soft-boiled eggs. I almost wept with joy, recovering one
of those simple and magnificent things I had almost forgotten. Then I
went to an enormous Bier Keller nearby in the Balonhof Platz, and watched
them. This is their *real* night life—Beer. There was an orchestra that
made a terrible noise, dressed up in the Bavarian costume: the leader
grimaced and went through antics and the crowd roared with laughter.
Someone would buy him a great mug of beer, and his band would play and
sing "Ein Prosit! Ein Prosit!" and the crowd would all join in, holding up
its glasses. Most of the people were large and heavy, they swilled down
quarts of beer, the air was heavy and thick, the band banged and
shouted, the crowd sang, now a sentimental song, now a smashing beer
song—the great tune of "Trink, Trink, Trink, Bruderlein, Trink." This is
the real Germany—it is impressive and powerful, and yet, after a time, I
dislike it. Nevertheless, I think this country interests me more than any in
Europe—can you explain this enigma? Here is this brutal, beer-swilling
people, and yet I doubt if there is as much that is spiritually grand in any
other people in Europe as in this one. This beer-swilling people produced
Beethoven and Goethe, the greatest spirits of modern times. And it produced long ago those faery and enchanted houses in Nurnberg and here.
And at the present time it has such men as Wassermann and Thomas
Mann writing for it. Also in its books—particularly in its thousands of
art books, magnificent books on Gothic, and the painters, and on everything—it far surpasses in delicacy and understanding any other nation.
Can you understand it? When I get up from a meal now, I feel that I have
eaten something brought dripping to me from the slaughter house. The
quantity of meat they consume is enormous—it has almost made a vege-
tarian of me: I did not know there was room enough in all Germany to
support so many cows and pigs; the air is filled with the death-squeals of
butchered swine.

Friday evening. Well, I've done it: I've devoured the city—almost—
enough for this once, and I'm on my way to Munich to-morrow morning.
I will not be sorry to leave here—it is a big, flat, dirty place, full of noise
and bustle, but intensely interesting. . . . Now I am thinking of Munich—
my heart begins to pound when I think of the letters I hope are there.
To-morrow is Saturday; I shall therefore not get my mail until Monday—
it will then be *seven* weeks since I've heard from anyone. . . . What has

happened in my world since I dropped out of it, I do not know. It has been only a short time, but I believe it has been a time of spiritual recuperation. I look wild and crazy and ragged, but I believe I am almost as sane as I can hope to be. I get a great draught of strength from looking at Goethe's lovely and tranquil head, and at Beethoven's fierce and all-sufficient one . . . I get, you see, a good part of my courage from better and greater people, but that is as it should be.

I still have moments of insanity when I rush into a big book shop and call for the name of some book in English which I know they haven't got, or which I invent, insisting that it is in the Tauschnitz edition. Then while they look, I stagger around like a drunk man from one shelf to the other, thumbing over countless volumes, leaping from one place to another, until they all begin to follow me around, to keep me from doing damage. And I have other charming little fancies—such as buying out all the sausage shops in Frankfurt, together with all the preserved fruits and plum-cakes in Rumpelmayer's here, and bringing it all back to America with me. Sometimes in the old market place here and in Mainz, or at the fruit stalls, I have grown mad to buy up all the wonderful fruits and vegetables. I have rushed from one stall to another, buying a peach at one, a bunch of grapes at another, and at Mainz, even a huge cucumber which I began to devour before all the yelling peasant women. But these fits are rare—I am calmer and more secure, and trying somehow to get at my picture of life. . . . I shall write again from Munich—but not a history next time.

P.S. . . . I've had nothing to eat to-day but two soft-boiled eggs and coffee which I had at Wiener Sacher's branch here. Now I'm going out to the pig-pens again. I think I shall have a dainty Vorspeisen—say, a Schwedish Gobelbissen—this is only a little cavair, a couple of Eggs à la Russe, some sardines, a piece of Bismarck herring, a slice of liverwurst, one of ham, and some tomatoes and—Kartoffel Salat. After this, I should have a good appetite for three or four slices of roast pork with mahogany sauce, and side dishes of Rotkohl and Bratkartoffel. In spite of their culinary skill, I know stage designers who cook better than the Germans do!

To ALINE BERNSTEIN

Munich
Thursday, Oct 4, 1928

Dear Aline:

. . . To-day is the first time I have been for mail since Saturday. I went to the hospital Monday and got out this afternoon. I had a mild concussion of the brain, four scalp wounds, and a broken nose. My head has healed up beautifully, and my nose is mending rapidly. . . . I am shaven as bald as a priest—in fact, with my scarred head, and the little stubble of black hair that has already begun to come up, I look like a dissolute priest.

What happened I am too giddy to tell you about to-night. I shall begin the story and try to finish it to-morrow. I had been in Munich three weeks —during that time I had led a sober and industrious life—as I have since coming abroad. It is now the season here of the Oktoberfest. What the Oktoberfest is I did not know until a week or two ago when it began. I had heard of it from everyone. I thought of it as a place where all the Bavarian peasant people come and dance old ritualistic dances, and sell their wares, and so on. But when I went for the first time, I found to my disappointment only a kind of Coney Island—merry-go-rounds, gimcracks of all sorts, in-numerable sausage shops, places where whole oxen were roasting on the spot, and enormous beer halls. But why in Munich—where there are a thousand beer-drinking places—should there be a special fair for beer? I soon found out. The Oktober beer is twice as strong as the ordinary beer— it is thirteen percent—the peasants come in and go to it for two weeks.

The Fair takes place in the Theresien Fields which are on the outskirts of the town, just before the Ausstellungs Park. . . . I went out to see the show two or three times—these beer halls are immense and appalling— four or five thousand people can be seated in one of them at a time— there is hardly room to breathe, to wiggle. A Bavarian band of forty pieces blares out horrible noise, and all the time hundreds of people who cannot find a seat go shuffling endlessly up and down and around the place. The noise is terrific, you can cut the air with a knife—and in these places you come to the heart of Germany, not the heart of its poets and scholars, but to its real heart. It is one enormous belly. They eat and drink and breathe themselves into a state of bestial stupefaction—the place be-comes one howling, roaring beast, and when the band plays one of their drinking songs, they get up by tables all over the place, and stand on chairs, swaying back and forth with arms linked, in living rings. The effect of these heavy living circles in this great smoky hell of beer is un-canny—there is something supernatural about it. You feel that within these circles is somehow the magic, the essence of the race—the nature of the beast that makes him so different from the other beasts a few miles over the borders. . . .

This is what happened . . . There is an American Church in Munich. It is not really a church—it is two or three big rooms rented in a big building in the Salvator Platz—a place hard to find, but just off the Promenadeplatz. They have six or eight thousand books there—most of it junk contributed by tourists. But you can go there in the afternoon for tea—if you are lonely you can find other Americans there . . . There was a young American there with his wife and another woman, his wife's friend. . . . I was delighted to talk to these people; they asked about rooms, life in Munich, galleries, and so on. . . . I told them about the Oktoberfest, and suggested that they go there with me during the afternoon, as the good museums were closed. So we went out together: the weather was bad, it began to rain. There was a great mass of people at the Fair—peasant people in their wonderful costumes, staring at all the machines and gimcracks. I took them through several beer halls, but we could find no seats. Finally, after the rain had stopped, we managed to get in at a table some people were leaving. We ordered beer and Schweirs-wurstt . . . and I was beginning to desire only to get rid of these people, who were full of quotations from the *American Mercury*. . . . I was nauseated by them, I wanted to be alone. I think they saw this; they suggested we all go home and eat together; I refused and said I would stay there at the Fair. So they paid their share, and went away out of all the roar and savagery of the place.

When they had gone, I drank two more liters of the dark Oktober beer, singing and swaying with the people at the table. Then I got up and went to still another place, where I drank another, and just before closing time—they close at 10:30 there at the Fair, because the beer is too strong, and the peasants get drunk and would stay forever—just before closing time I went to another great hall and had a final beer. The place was closing for the night—all over the parties were breaking up—there were vacant tables here and there, the Bavarian band was packing up its instruments and leaving. I talked to the people at my table, drank my beer, and got up to go. I had had seven or eight liters—this would mean almost a quart of alcohol. I was quite drunk from the beer. I started down one of the aisles toward a side entrance. There I met several men—and perhaps a woman, although I did not see her until later. They were standing up by their table in the aisle, singing perhaps one of their beer songs before going away. They spoke to me—I was too drunk to understand what they said, but I am sure it was friendly enough. What happened from now on I will describe as clearly as I can remember, although there are lapses and gaps in my remembrance. One of them, it seems to me, grasped me by the arm—I moved away, he held on, and although I was not angry, but rather in an excess of exuberance, I knocked him over a table. Then I rushed out of the place exultantly, feeling like a child who has thrown a stone through a window.

Unhappily I could not run fast—I had drunk too much and was wearing my coat. Outside it was raining hard; I found myself in an enclosure behind some of the fair buildings—I had come out of a side entrance. I heard shouts and cries behind me, and turning, I saw several men running down upon me. One of them was carrying one of the fold-up chairs of the beer hall—it is made of iron and wood. I saw that he intended to hit me with this, and I remember that this angered me. I stopped and turned and in that horrible slippery mudhole, I had a bloody fight with these people. I remember the thing now with horror as a kind of hell of slippery mud, and blood, and darkness, with the rain falling upon us several maniacs who were trying to kill. At that time I was too wild, too insane, to be afraid, but I seemed to be drowning in mud—it was really the blood that came pouring from my head into my eyes. . . . I was drowning in oceans of mud, choking, smothering. I felt the heavy bodies on top of me, snarling, grunting, smashing at my face and back. I rose up under them as if coming out of some horrible quicksand—then my feet slipped again in the mud, and I went down again into the bottomless mud. I felt the mud beneath me, but what was really blinding and choking me was the torrent of blood that streamed from gashes in my head. I did not know I bled.

Somehow—I do not know how it came about—I was on my feet again, and moving towards the dark forms that swept in towards me. When I was beneath them in the mud, it seemed as if all the roaring mob of that hall had piled upon me, but there were probably not more than three. From this time on I can remember fighting with only two men, and later there was a woman who clawed my face. The smaller figure—the smaller man—rushed towards me, and I struck it with my fist. It went diving away into the slime. I was choking in blood and cared for nothing now but to end it finally—to kill this other thing or be killed. So with all my strength I threw it to the earth: I could not see, but I fastened my fingers and hand in its eyes and face—it was choking me, but presently it stopped. I was going to hold on until I felt no life there in the mud below me. The woman was now on my back, screaming, beating me over the head, gouging at my face and eyes. She was screaming out "Leave my man alone!" ("Lassen mir den Mann stehen"—as I remember). Some people came and pulled me from him—the man and woman screamed and jabbered at me, but I could not make out what they said, except her cry of "Leave my man alone," which I remember touched me deeply. . . .

These people went away—where or how I don't know—but I saw them later in the police station, so I judge they had gone there. And now— very foolishly perhaps—I went searching around in the mud for my hat— my old rag of a hat which had been lost, and which I was determined to find before leaving. Some German people gathered around me yelling and gesticulating, and one man kept crying "Ein Arzt! Ein Arzt!" ("A Doctor! A Doctor!") I felt my head all wet, but thought it was the rain, until I put my hand there and brought it away all bloody. At this moment, three or four policemen rushed up, seized me, and hustled me off to the station. First they took me to the police surgeons—I was taken into a room with a white, hard light. The woman was lying on a table with wheels below it. The light fell upon her face—her eyes were closed. I think this is the most horrible moment of my life . . . I thought she was dead, and that I would never be able to remember how it happened. The surgeons made me sit down in a chair while they dressed my head wounds. Then one of them looked at my nose, and said it was broken, and that I must go the next day to a doctor. When I got up and looked around, the woman and the wheeled table was gone. I am writing this Saturday (six days later): if she were dead, surely by this time I would know. . . .

Sunday morning. I do not think I have told you what happened to me after the police doctors had looked at my wounds and dressed them that night at the Oktoberfest—or how I found doctors to look after me, and so on. From the doctors I was taken before the police next door where they asked me many questions which I did not answer. They also had two of the other men there, looking very bloody, also—and perhaps others I did not see. Then they let me go, when they could get nothing out of me. I had lost my hat, and was one mass of mud and blood: it was raining hard and wet: a young man I did not know went along with me, and when I asked him what he wanted, he said he "had no role to play." We got a street car and came back to the center of town where I got off and shook him— at the Odeonsplatz.

That day at lunch with the three people who had gone to the Fair with me, I had met a young American doctor who had come here for special study. Now I was going back to their place to get his address. I found the married pair in bed, and the other woman out with the doctor. They stood around and gasped and looked scared—the woman made me a cup of tea —and in a few minutes the woman and the doctor came back. He gave me the address of another American doctor who was working in a famous clinic here, and told me to see him the first thing the next morning.

I got a taxi and drove through town to the clinic. My appearance almost caused an earthquake in the pension, and people in the streets stared at me. I had been directed to Dr. Von Muller's clinic—and Dr. Von Muller is one of the greatest doctors in the world. His picture was in all the papers the other day—on his seventieth birthday. . . . I found the great man in the office, and when I asked for his American assistant—Dr. Du Bois,[1] whose name I had been given—I was told he was at home, and that

[1] Dr. Eugene F. Du Bois who at that time was working as a volunteer in the clinic of Dr. Friedrich von Muller. He is now Professor of Physiology, Emeritus, at Cornell University Medical College.

I should go there. I felt low-spirited and was on the point of asking old Von Muller himself to look at my head (which would have been a great breach), when in came this man Du Bois. The name is French, but you never saw anyone more prim and professorily American. He was very tidy and dull-looking, with winking eyeglasses, and a dry prim careful voice. I felt done for. I told him what had happened and where I was hurt, and he listened carefully, and then said in his precise careful way that we ought perhaps—ah—to see what can be—ah—done for you. By this time, I thought I was dead.

But here let me tell you the truth about this man, Dr. Du Bois, who is, I found later, a professor in the Cornell Medical School (hence the professorly manner). He is one of the grandest and kindest people I have ever met. In this dry prim way he showed me for days the most amazing kindness—and then refused to accept anything for his services, although he had come to my pension with me in a taxi, to help me pack, when the German doctor said I had to come to the hospital, and had gone back with me, and had visited me once or twice a day, and brought me books during the time I was there in the hospital. At any rate, he asked the great Von Muller first of all where we should go, and the great Von Muller had said that we should go across the street to the Surgical Building and see the great Lexer, who is the best head surgeon in Germany.

Monday night

Midnight—Salzburg

My dear, I held my breath until I got over the blessed border to-day— I have escaped. To-night—in spite of a desperate cold that is making me blind—I feel that life from now on is going to be freer and happier and wiser—and although I've had this silly feeling before, I believe somehow it's going to be true. Munich almost killed me. It scarred my head and broke my nose, and last of all smote me in ten wretched seconds with a deadly cold which burned like fire along the membranes of my nostrils, and then made a sour lump in my throat. Munich almost killed me—but in five weeks, it gave me more of human experience than most people get in five years. . . .

The Herr Geheimrat, I believe, has made a bad job of the nose. It looks to me hopelessly crooked, although people in Munich insisted it looked all right. My hair is out in a wolly nigger fuzz, and my scars shine through the brush. . . .

P.S. The accursed weather of Munich cannot be described. Snow fell there the other day—mid-October! And God! how I came to hate the

leaden sky, the wet thin sunshine. But the magic that is around Salzburg—
all white—and lovely!

To ALINE BERNSTEIN

Vienna
[November 1, 1928]

Dear Aline:

About the only thing I want to write during these days is a letter to
you—and I want to write that all the time now. It is my only way at the
moment of talking to the only person I care about talking to—my being-
alone-ness has become a kind of terrible joke—I have somehow lost all
power of breaking my own silence. . . . I live in a strange world—I will
brood for an hour over a map of Vienna that I carry in my pocket, studying
the vast cobweb of streets. Then suddenly I will rush into the Ring, seize
a taxi, and yell out some address on the outer rim of the city that the
driver has never heard of. He has to study my map—we go out and out,
across the great outer girdle—to-day it was a great bare spot marked Sport-
platz; when we got there, it was a huge field with a fence around it and
turfed banks, which is used as a football field. All around the place were
shabby looking buildings with small shops downstairs and people leaning
out of windows above. The man was surprised and looked back at me to
see if a mistake had been made. But I jumped out and paid him, and ran
around the corner of the fence till he had gone. Then I walked on and on,
straight up the long sloping street that seemed to reach to the Magic
Mountains—the soft hills of the Wiener Wald looming against the horizon.
It was All Saints Day: most of the shops were closed and the people were
out in force. They were almost all walking in the same direction as I was
—towards the Magic Mountains. The shutters were down on most of the
little shops, and everything had a strange quietness, it seemed to me.

It was amazingly like a dream I used to have of a dark street, and dark
shuttered houses. There was only one bit of light and sound in the street
that came from a carnival. I was in this carnival riding the merry-go-round,
surrounded by noise and lights and many people. Then it seemed that I
was looking through the bars of a bright wooden gate into the dark street
(from the carnival). In this street, there was no sound, no vehicles, no
traffic except a great crowd of people all walking silently and steadily in
the same direction. They did not speak with one another, they turned their
faces neither to right nor left—not even as they tramped past the gate of
the carnival and the white light fell over them. I know that in that white
light the faces of these people looked thin and ghastly-sallow and damned;

and what their march meant, and all that silence I could not say, but I felt that death and doom and the end of all things was there in that place; but whether it was I who was dead in that carnival, or these strange phantom shapes from whom I was cut off, I could not say either.

This dream came back to me to-day as I walked up that long street with the people all tramping steadily towards the country. And strangely enough, when I got into the outskirts of the city, and the buildings were uneven and scattered about with much open ground, ugly and messy as the outskirts of great cities are, I began to come on shabby little carnivals—only a little merry-go-round and a few swings, grinding out old Schubert and Strauss tunes incessantly. Then I went on and on; the hills were very close and beautiful now; I was on their fringes; and I could see the edges of Vienna right and left, vast and smoky and roughly circular.

I came to a place where there was a whole colony of stucco houses, all alike, all ugly, with gardens behind, and trying to look like the Austrian equivalent for an American suburban stucco "English" cottage. I sometimes think that the enormous difference we think we see between Europe and America is not as deep as we believe—when you see these cottages all alike, it is not hard to imagine an Austrian Arnold Bennett or Sinclair Lewis writing a book about the people in them. The things you and I have liked best in Europe—the grand pictures, the buildings, and so on—belong mostly to an order of things that has gone: the world—the world that has to eat and drink and labor—is probably being "Americanized." At least, they groan about it, and deprecate it, but I think they earnestly want it for themselves. To be "Americanized" is simply to be industrialized in the most complete and serviceable fashion. America is the apex of the present industrial civilization, but that is the only civilization the modern world has got. The European who carries a really good load of hate against America, nearly always hates because America is rich and Europe is poor; because America is strong and Europe is weak. But the European does not always put it so honestly: he salves his pride by picturing himself as a lover of the good and beautiful, a defender and patron of the arts, and a despiser of filthy money, while the American cares for nothing else but money, and so on. A great fat boy in one of the big beer houses in the Neuhauser Street in Munich one night poured all this into my ear while he swilled down liters of beer and gorged himself with the fourteen different meats and sausages of a delicatessen aufschnitt. There is not a picture or a book in the world for which he would have foregone a liter of his beer.

Budapest
Thursday, November 8

Dear Aline: I have been here since last Friday night, and I have already heard of Hoover's election. The news seems to be authentic, and his election to be overwhelming. This only makes me sorrier than ever that Smith didn't get it. Why is it that the good people, the right people are so often the underdogs? From this great distance it looked as if the whole nation had gone mad in an effort to strangle the man. Now, what are they going to do with him? His intelligence for government will be wasted while small incompetent people thrive in great jobs. And now that it's over, the people who voted against him because he is a Catholic will insist that this had nothing to do with it. The only American paper I get to read over here is the *Paris New York Herald,* and this filthy little sheet, together with all the filthy little people who write letters to it, has nearly convinced me that most of the good Americans have stayed at home. We are a people who ought not to live out of our country too long—the attempt to make Europeans of ourselves succeeds in producing loose and abortionate idiots. But America is also a very difficult country for many people to live in, unless one can with a great hurrah join in the rush to elect the Hoovers and Coolidges. And think where you find yourself in this rush? With the Ku Klux Klan, and the Anti-Saloon League, and Senator Heflin, and John Roach Straton, and the Methodist Church, and the Rockefellers. My part of America is not with this. It is somewhere perhaps with the part that voted for Smith—and he got beaten four to one.

But I am coming home. I am an American and I must try to take hold somewhere. I am not burning with indignation or revolt, or anything. I am tired of struggle and should like to fall in step if only I knew how. But how? . . . I am a citizen of the most powerful and interesting nation of modern times—and I wish to God I knew how to make something of it. . . .

Monday Evening. My Dear: If all the rest of my journey has been waste and if I have done very little for myself with it, I think what I have seen these last two days might almost make up for it, not for what I may get from it, but for the news that I can now pass on to you. . . . Yesterday morning at six o'clock I got up here—with the aid of the hotel staff— and went to the East Station. At seven o'clock I left the station on an express train bound for the village of Mezö-Kövesd, about 100 miles away. Away *where* I do not yet know, for I had failed to look the place up on the map before I started, and have been so charmed by my fancies that I have not dared to do so since. . . . My belief now is that I was on the Bucharest express—for a ticket man in the station asked me if I was going there—and that Mezö-Kövesd is eastward or southwestward from Budapest. It was a grey, wet, foggy day of the sort that seems to afflict all Europe from England to Hungary—and farther perhaps—at this time of year. And the landscape was wearily depressing. For a while after leaving Budapest there were low hills and rolling dismal looking country— possibly everything looks dismal now. Then, for the greater part of the journey there was a vast muddy plain, stretching away infinitely until it was lost in the steam and haze of the horizon. This great plain is one vast farm: the land is striped with bands of plowed field and bands of green unploughed field, and these long bands stretch straight away as far as the eye can travel. This also adds to the impression of hopelessness. . . .

I got there a little before ten o'clock—the train stopped at a dreary station surrounded by the vast muddy fields. At first I did not know where the village was—there seemed to be scattered houses away in the distance—I walked away from the station around a huge field of mud. A great many of the young men of the village were assembled on this field: there were bugle calls and they were lining up in military formations—from little boys to young fellows of 18 or 20. The rain had collected in pools all over the place and the big fat ducks and geese were everywhere: in the muddy streets, the fields and yards of all the houses. I was terribly depressed. I wondered what I had come for—the place seemed so barren, so lost, that I thought Russia must be like this. But I heard a churchbell ringing away in the distance; and women, dressed up in these amazing costumes, began to hurry along, coming from the little white houses that bordered the road. Finally I came up to what seemed a main street—it was another mudhole, but it seemed originally to have been paved. I turned off to the left in the wrong direction, away from the main part of the town, and I walked straight along this street for a good distance until suddenly the last white houses of the village ended, and the great wet fields began, with the muddy road running straight into eternity. I realized that most of the people I had seen were going in the opposite direction. I turned and went back as fast as I could. All the people stared and whispered and frowned and snickered; little children, in their strange costumes, giggled at me—any one of these people would have stopped the traffic in New York. The children found me strange and comic, yet the men with their embroidered aprons and their ridiculous derby hats stuck straight off of their heads, and the women in their bewildering costumes, did not seem at all strange to the children.

Presently I saw the church ahead of me, and began to pass the little shops of the village. It is a very sinful place—everything was open and doing business—I suppose the people work during the week and that Sunday is their best day for selling and trading. The street opened into a kind of square before the church: it was obvious that this was the center of the town. There was a brisk business going on in the market place among the fruit and vegetable peddlers, and dozens of men hung around in groups, loafing and gossiping as they do in our small towns. I made straight for the church, after having provided the whole market place with a new subject for gossip. I went into the church and found it crowded. In the cold little vestibule outside the doors several old women were crowded muttering responses to the service, or kneeling on the dirty concrete near the doors. I went into the church and stood near the doors. A priest in gorgeous robes was making his sermon. The church was crowded: all of the aisles and bare space, as well as the seats, were filled with people. In one solid section of the pews sat all the married women, with black conical shaped bonnets, and sober costumes. The old men, the chief men of the place, I suppose, sat in another part wearing those wonderful robes which are among the beautiful things I have seen in Hungary—for what I have seen here seems to me to be wild and strange, for the most part, rather than beautiful. I have pictures of this wonderful robe in the great book I have bought for you—it is a garment in which every man looks an emperor. It is a great block of thick stiff white wool or felt with short sleeves, although most of the old men wear it as a cape. It sits upon the shoulders of a peasant in the most regal and splendid way. It can be embroidered along the edges and the arms and shoulders in any way that suits their barbaric fancy—and some of the decorations were magnificent. Most of the old fellows wear a kind of turban—very handsome—of fuzzy black wool, with this robe, and of course the stiff high boots that nearly all the men wear. And God, but they're dirty! After church I looked at some of the old fellows—some with the faces, moustaches, slant eyes, of the East—and their hides were stiff and caked with dirt.

The young unmarried women were together in all their splendor in another part of the church, and I suppose the young men elsewhere—although most of the young bucks were loafing around in the market place outside. The priest finished his sermon and left his cage in the wall; then the long Catholic ritual before the altars began. The people knew the order perfectly: they listened faithfully, made all the responses, began to sing from time to time, then listened again while the priest sang out Latin in a high, false, annoying voice—what he said was indistinguishable, and seemed calculated only to make a weird reverberation in the church. Old women remained on their knees on the hard cold floor during the whole service; there were wretches there in filthy rags; over the whole place there was a close warm odor of hay and manure—the place had an unmistakable smell of a stable. Nowhere have I ever seen the simple animal nature of men so plainly as in this church—I kept thinking of this as they all stood there with their smell of the stable, hearing of their kinship to God.

When it was over they all streamed out slowly—and immediately two men in blue uniforms outside the church began to beat rapidly upon small drums. The crowd split in two and gathered in two great circles around the drummers. Then when all was quiet, the drummer put aside his drum, pulled a slip of paper from his jacket, and began to read rapidly. The old fellows in the woolen robes stood around, looking wise and puffing thoughtfully at their funny pipes. The announcement, I learned later and guessed then, is a kind of weekly official journal—probably with decrees, laws, tax announcements, and so on.

When the reading of this was over, the two crowds broke away and streamed rapidly down the street, probably to gossip or to eat, or to their homes. But I began to look for a restaurant. I had been warned that it was hopeless—that I had better take a few sandwiches along, because I could not eat the food I might find there—but so much preparation is not in me. There was a place on the square marked Etterem—that means Restaurant—and I went in. I am sure it is the Swell Place of the town, for none of the gorgeous peasants were there; but a fat dirty waiter with a dirty stiff white shirt and greasy black hair, also several of the town Dandies (they must be all over Europe, just as Maupassant put them in his French country towns): a man with spats, and a Hungarian-English tailor, and a sensual barbered face with pointed moustaches, and a luscious smile showing his old-pearl teeth: I am sure he went to Budapest often and was a great Rounder. There were several of this kind there— one came in with a bald knobby head, a golf suit of loud checks, stockings to match, spats, and elegant brown shoes you could see your face in. He was the damndest looking monkey I've seen. A young fellow was drawing their caricatures at a pengo—17 or 18 cents—apiece. They all gathered around, looked knowing, said it was very good, ordered their own portrait, and roared with laughter when they saw the result. Then they took the drawing all over the place, showing it to their friends. I had him draw me—I recognize myself, but it is as if I have been in hell for several years. . . . I thought I would eat something, but an unfortunate visit to the urinal destroyed my hunger. I ordered a bottle of beer, knowing they could not do anything to this.

Then I left the place and began to explore the village. I walked out by the church along the muddy main street or road in a direction opposite the one I had first taken. I went straight on past the cemetery, past the little white houses, until I came again, abruptly as before, to the open country. Nothing but the land—the vast muddy land stretching away to nowhere. There were hills over to my left. But I was terribly depressed—the barrenness, the greyness and monotony of this life frightened me. It seems to me that the life of people in a middle western village must be gay compared to the life here, and I still think it may be. And the road stretched straight away until it, too, was lost in the fog and steam of the horizon.

I turned around and walked back towards the church. But instead of going the whole way, I turned off the main road, and went down a muddy road to the right. Here was the main body of the village which I had not before suspected, spread out behind the church. It is one of the strangest places I was ever in. All of the streets that I had seen heretofore running off the main one had been straight muddy alleys with the little white houses punctually spaced along the road. This straightness, and the feeling of open space, with the awful unending land all around had depressed me. Back in this part, however, I immediately became more cheerful. The muddy little roads that serve as streets wound and twisted about and met each other in a labyrinthine pattern. The little white houses were covered with roofs of dry reeds bound together, and of the thickness of a foot. On these reeds, patches of green moss were growing. The houses were one-story, with perhaps a half-story attic above—this upper part was often of wood with carved designs on it. The end of the house faced the street; the doorway, with a very narrow wooden porch that ran the whole length of the house, faced the side yard. This mudhole was full of quacking geese, and at the back there was always what seemed at first to be several stacks of beautifully rich hay, mellow and odorous. Then I discovered that these were not haystacks at all, but that they cover their pig pens and barns with hay—the pigs were rooting and grunting in the slime.

In the middle of the muddy street, people were drawing water from a well. These wells are as familiar in Hungary as that strange device in the pictures of Peter Breughel—I mean the wheel on top of a pole. The well is a bucket attached to a long pole which swings up and down, by weights and balances, I suppose. Back in this part, as I say, I lost a great deal of my depression, although the streets were mud-holes and the geese and swine were quacking and grunting everywhere. The little white houses with their thick walls and small windows, on which moisture was gathered, showing warmth therein, and the reed roofs, and above all, I believe, the mellow sweet hay covering over the barn and sty, shut out the awful emptiness of the plain all around, and gave a close warm look to things. They were huddled together here with their pigs and geese, but I felt that they must get a great satisfaction out of the elaborate ritual and convention of their lives. How elaborate it is I did not then know, nor do I yet know fully.

My train back to Budapest—the only one before night—passed at 2:30. It was now 1:30. I found the Turkish spire of the church above the houses and made my way towards it, knowing the public square was there. When I came into the square again, I saw one of the most extraordinary spectacles I have ever seen—it is as bright and strange and wonderful to me now as it was the moment I saw it. When I had left the restaurant an hour or so before, the square had been almost deserted. Now it was crowded with hundreds of people, some standing, others walking back and forth. But what caught you immediately was that these people were not mixed into the great shuttle of a crowd. They were divided into groups and companies with military formality—the blazing color and pageantry, all regimented, made me think of one of the old pictures of a battle, in which you see the companies all drawn up in blocks upon a plain outside a city. The young men in groups of twenty or thirty were stationed at various places around the square; the married women elsewhere; the older men still elsewhere; and the young girls, likewise in groups of twenty of thirty, marched back and forth and around and up and down. Of course this explosion of color that simply turned that grey day into a pageant came mostly from the girls. I can't go on to describe the costumes, for they were infinitely varied—the one uniform detail came in the wonderful shawls they wore over all the rest of the bewildering business. These shawls were of some delicate material—silk, probably—with a great variety of patterns around the neck. Then they were fringed with a great thick border of woolen thread—this was a solid color and was either a brilliant yellow, or crimson, or red. Curiously enough, those groups with yellow, and those with red, and so on, seemed to keep together. As to the rest of it, you can see it better than I can—the long plaited skirts, covered with strange designs—the skirts are one thick mass of ruffles, and when the girls walk, the skirts billow and undulate and show inches of thickness where they are kicked up by the feet. Over this they wear the apron—similar if not exactly the same as that worn by the young men—and I am told the apron on the young man is a sign of bachelorhood. It is black or blue, this apron, but it has across it a strip of embroidered flower and leaf work, which is sometimes over half its length. As the girls go up and down in groups, the young men stand together, or march off in columns of twos—they all grin and snicker among themselves, but they act otherwise as if the other is not there. I did not find this funny. I did not find it naive and delightfully childlike. I had a feeling of terrible disgust and revulsion against this elaborate and evil ritual. The great swathings of pleats and ruffles and shawls which concealed the bodily lines of the girls were only foils to the evil, searching curiosity of the young men, whose talk—I will bet my nose, because I was born a villager myself—was mainly of breasts and fornication. The huge sexual rituals of society are weakened and dispersed in great cities because they exist mainly through close public observation. And they are all-powerful in the village for this reason—if you try to break a custom you will very likely break your heart as well. It is for this reason that I believe in cities more than in villages: I think there is greater good in them, and higher life, and a greater spiritual freedom. I am simple enough to understand the city and urbane life: I have never been complex enough to understand the village. That is what I felt at Mezö-Kövesd the other day—there was an evil and barbaric complexity about this that I loathed. But I recognized it as one of the most remarkable things I have ever seen. The thing that brings *wonder* is not the *strange* thing alone—it is the touch of the familiar with the strange thing: that is what makes it strange. And all the time I was feeling the strangeness of this parade the other day, I was simply being pounded all the time by its fundamental likeness to *all* village life.

When I was a college boy in the South, the young men used to go to a neighboring town on Sundays, a town where there were two or three girls' schools. The young men would line up in groups outside the churches where the girls attended, and wait for them to come out. Then they would snicker and talk among themselves, as would the girls. But they would not speak. Later in the day, or in the evening perhaps, they would go courting. And in Asheville, and in all American small towns, the young bucks line up before the drug store, or the post office, and watch the girls go by.

I looked at this parade in Mezö-Kövesd as long as I dared. I will never forget those blocks and company formations, with the Virgins marching up and down with rhythmically billowing skirts. Of course, I harmonized with this scene about as well as would a Chinaman at a meeting of the Ku Klux Klan, and I got many unfriendly glances; but my curiosity was stronger than modesty or good manners—I took it all in gaping. Then I had to run for my train and just got in, sleeping as well as I could most of the way back across that dreary misty plain upon the hard bench of a third class carriage. . . .

I have written these last pages on Wednesday night. About a thousand and one other things: the theatre, gypsy music, Hungarian literature (O yes, O yes, they have a literature), Hungarian food (which is very good as well as full of all kinds of colors)—I must tell you later. The people here have been very kind to me. They want to do all they can to interest the world in their cause, and of course they have been murderously treated. They had 20,000,000 people before the war, now they have 7,000,000. Over two-thirds of their country has been given to the Czechs, the Rumanians, and the Jugo-Slavians. How they can continue to exist they do not know. They despise the people who now have most of their wealth and land—the Rumanians, Czechs, and so on. They call them peasants and barbarians and speak of themselves proudly as "a highly cultivated people." And the Austrians speak of the Hungarians as barbarians! So it goes! What do we know? We say the world is a small place —but the fact is, it is much too large a place. What does the man in Nebraska know, or care, about this people or their troubles? Yet they have an extensive literature, a great capital, a history thousands of years old, and the honor of saving Europe twice against the Turks who came storming up out of the East. They were themselves a nomad Eastern people who settled upon these plains many hundreds of years ago—and now their young village men wear embroidered aprons, and the old men great coats of white wool, and the young girls are swaddled in elaborate costumes, every stitch, every pattern, every design of which has some meaning.

And here in Budapest, the Singer Sewing Machine has agencies, and Cadillac and Chrysler; and the people read Jókai and Herczeg Ferencz and Bibó Lajos and Molnar Ferenc and Lewis Sinclair, and Wallace Edgar and Bennett Arnold and Takáts Sándor, and a whole raft of other Hungarian writers. But what do they know about this in Newark; or what do they know about Newark here? What's it all mean? I think I have found a little meaning, a base of culture and understanding that is universal. Someday I shall tell you what it is.

I am going back to Vienna to-morrow. Then I want to get to the sea and a ship again. I seem so far away from it now that I can hardly believe I shall ever find it. . . .

When Wolfe returned to Vienna from Budapest in November, 1928, he found a letter waiting for him from Maxwell E. Perkins, the head editor at Charles Scribner's Sons, who was to become the greatest influence upon him and his work. This letter dated October 22, 1928, said in part: [1] *"Mrs. Ernest Boyd left with us, some weeks ago, the manuscript of your novel, O, Lost. I do not know whether it would be possible to work out a plan by which it might be worked into a form publishable by us, but I do know that . . . it is a very remarkable thing, and that no editor could read it without being excited by it . . . What we should like to know is whether you will be in New York in a fairly near future, when we can see you and discuss the manuscript. We should certainly look forward to such an interview with very great interest." The following letter is Wolfe's reply.*

[1] For the full text of the letter, see page 61, *Editor to Author, the Letters of Maxwell E. Perkins, Selected and Edited, with Commentary and an Introduction,* by John Hall Wheelock. Charles Scribner's Sons, 1950.

To MAXWELL E. PERKINS

Vienna,
Saturday, Nov 17, 1928

Dear Mr Perkins:

Your letter of October 22 which was addressed to Munich, was sent on to me here. I have been in Budapest for several weeks and came back last night. I got your letter at Cook's this morning.

Mrs Ernest Boyd wrote me a few weeks ago that she was coming abroad, and said that you had my book. I wrote her to Paris but have not heard from her yet.

I can't tell you how good your letter has made me feel. Your words of praise have filled me with hope, and are worth more than their weight in diamonds to me. Sometimes, I suppose, praise does more harm than good, but this time it was badly needed, whether deserved or not. I came abroad over four months ago, determined to put the other book out of my mind, and to get to work on a new one. Instead, I have filled one notebook after another, my head is swarming with ideas—but I have written nothing that looks like a book yet. In Munich I did write thirty or forty thousand words, then I got my head and my nose broken, and began to have things happen thick and fast with a great many people, including the police. I have learned to read German fairly well, and have learned something of their multitudinous books. But I had indigestion from seeing and trying to take in too much, and I was depressed at my failure to settle down to work. Now I feel better. I have decided to come back to New York in December, and I shall come to see you very soon after my arrival.

I have not looked at my book since I gave a copy to Mrs. Boyd. At the time I realized the justice of all people said—particularly the impossibility of printing it in its present form and length. But at that time I was "written out" on it—I could not go back and revise. Now I believe I can come back to it with a much fresher and more critical feeling. I have no right to expect others to do for me what I should do for myself, but, although I am able to criticize wordiness and over-abundance in others, I am not able practically to criticize it in myself. The business of selection and of revision is simply hell for me—my efforts to cut out 50,000 words may sometimes result in my adding 75,000.

As for the obscene passages and the dirty words, I know perfectly well that no publisher could print them. Yet, I swear to you, it all seemed to me very easy and practical when I wrote them. But already I have begun to write a long letter to you, when all I should do is to thank you for your letter and say when I am coming back. Then the other things can come out when I see you.

But your letter has given me new hope for the book—I have honestly always felt that there are parts of it of which I need not be ashamed, and which might justify some more abiding form. I want you to know that you have no very stiff-necked person to deal with as regards the book—I shall probably agree with most of the criticisms, although I hope that my own eagerness and hopefulness will not lead me into a weak acquiescence to everything.

I want the direct criticism and advice of an older and more critical person. I wonder if at Scribners I can find someone who is interested enough to talk over the whole huge Monster with me—part by part. Most people will say "it's too long," "its got to be cut," "parts have to come out," and so on—but obviously this is no great help to the poor wretch who has done the deed, and who knows all this, without always knowing how he's going to remedy it.

I am sorry that Mrs Boyd sent you the letter that I wrote for the reader. She said it was a very foolish letter, but added cheerfully that I would learn as I grew older. I wish I had so much faith. I told her to tear the letter out of the binding; but if it indicated to you that I did realize some of the difficulties, perhaps it was of some use. And I realize the difficulties more than ever now.

I am looking forward to meeting you, and I am still youthful enough to hope that something may come of it. It will be a strange thing indeed to me if at last I shall manage to make a connection with such a firm as Scribners which, in my profound ignorance of all publishing matters, I had always thought vaguely was a solid and somewhat conservative house. But it may be that I am a conservative and at bottom very correct person. If this is true, I assure you I will have no very great heartache over it, although once it might have caused me trouble. At any rate, I believe I am through with firing off pistols just for the fun of seeing people jump— my new book has gone along for 40,000 words without improprieties of language—and I have not tried for this result.

Please forgive my use of the pencil—in Vienna papers and pen and ink, as well as many other things that abound in our own fortunate country, are doled out bit by bit under guard. I hope you are able to make out my scrawl—which is more than many people do—and that you will not forget about me before I come back.

My address in New York is the Harvard Club—I get my mail there. Here in Vienna, at Thomas Cook's, but as I'm going to Italy in a week, I shall probably have no more mail before I get home.

V

THE ACCEPTANCE AND PUBLICATION OF
LOOK HOMEWARD, ANGEL

1929

To MADELEINE BOYD

Harvard Club
New York
Jan 8, 1929

Dear Mrs. Boyd:

I got your letter from Paris tonight—it had been sent from the Harvard Club to Paris, Munich, and Vienna, and back again. I was ready to write you anyway—I got back here New Year's Eve, and I am sure I have telephoned you at least ten times since. On two occasions I talked with your maid, left my name and told her to tell you.

Mrs. Boyd, I am terribly excited about the book. I have seen Mr. Perkins twice, and unless I am quite out of my head they have decided to take the book. I saw him first the day after New Year's—at that time it seemed to me there was little doubt about it, but yesterday he confirmed it. I told him I should like some definite news—that there was one friend I should like to speak to. He told me that I might go ahead; he said their minds were "practically made up." I told him I needed money and he said they would give me an advance. Now, don't be mad at me—I did *not* talk money; I asked him to get as much as he could for me, and he said he did not think he could get over $500, and that that was unusual for a first novel.

It is perfectly understood at Scribners that you are my agent and that I shall do nothing, sign nothing, until I have seen you. I also want to see Mr. Melville Cane the lawyer.[1] As you request, I am sending you a written

---

[1] For approval of the contract before signing it.

statement authorizing you as my agent. All that was said at Scribners I can not put into a short letter—I must see you and talk to you—but they have been amazingly generous, it seems to me, in what they are willing to print. Of course I must set to work, and work hard, but I have a very clear idea of what is wanted—they had made very full notes, and we talked the thing over in considerable detail.

Mr. Perkins told me to set to work at once and I have promised to deliver the first instalment of the revision in ten days. He said that I would get a letter from Scribners in a few days—I suppose business must be done in this way. It seems to me, Mrs. Boyd, there is no doubt of it.

Of course, I realize exactly how great a part you have played in this, and if I get rich nothing will please me more than to see you get prosperous. (This is a kind of joke, but I wish it would come true.) I am full of energy and hope—I know I have a big job ahead, but with this encouragement I can do anything. Although this is a business matter I can't help having a warm place in my heart for you, and I hope to God we both prosper.

This is all for tonight—it is past midnight and I haven't eaten. On another piece of paper I am writing out a statement authorizing you as my agent. When and where can I see you? I've almost given up hope of finding you at home.

I've taken a place at 27 West 15th Street (2nd Floor Rear—no telephone yet). You can phone or write here to Harvard Club, and leave a message. I'll do nothing until I see you.

To MAXWELL E. PERKINS

> Harvard Club
> New York
> Jan 9, 1929

Dear Mr. Perkins:

I got your letter this morning and I have just come from a talk with Mrs. Madeleine Boyd, my literary agent.

I am very happy to accept the terms you offer me for the publication of my book, *O Lost*.[1] Mrs. Boyd is also entirely satisfied.

I am already at work on the changes and revisions proposed in the book, and I shall deliver to you the new beginning some time next week.

Although this should be only a business letter I want to tell you that I look forward with joy and hope to my connection with Scribners. To-day

---

[1] The terms for *O, Lost* (*Look Homeward, Angel*) offered in Mr. Perkins' letter of January 8, 1929, were an advance of $500 against royalties of 10% on the first two thousand copies sold, and 15% on all copies sold thereafter.

—the day of your letter—is a very grand day in my life. I think of my relation to Scribners thus far with affection and loyalty, and I hope this marks the beginning of a long association that they will not have cause to regret. I have a tremendous lot to learn, but I believe I shall go ahead with it, and I know that there is far better work in me than I have yet done.

If you have any communication for me before I see you next, you can reach me at 27 West 15th Street (2nd Floor Rear).

To MARGARET ROBERTS

This is a horribly long letter. I'm as limp as a rag. I pity the people who have to read it and I pity the poor devil who wrote it.

> Harvard Club
> New York
> Saturday, January 12, 1929

Dear Mrs. Roberts:

Everything you write has power to touch and move me and excite me. My heart beats faster when I see your writing on a piece of paper, and I read what you write me over and over again, exultant and happy over every word of praise you heap upon me. Nothing you have ever written me has so stirred me as your letter which I got today. I have mounted from one happiness to another during this past week since I came back from Europe, and the knowledge that you are now so generously sharing with me my joy and hope just about sends the thermometer up to the boiling point. For several days now I have felt like that man in one of Leacock's novels who "sprang upon his horse and rode madly off in all directions." I have literally been like that—at times I have not known what to do with myself. I would sit in the club here stupidly, staring at the publishers' glorious letter of acceptance; I would rush out and walk eighty blocks up Fifth Avenue through all the brisk elegant crowd of late afternoon. I am gradually beginning to feel ground again, and it is occurring to me that the only thing to do is to get to work again.

I have the contract in my inner breast pocket, ready to be signed, and a check for $450 pinned to it, $50 having already been paid to my literary agent, Mrs. Ernest Boyd, as her 10 per cent share. There is literally no reason why I should walk around New York with these documents on my person, but in a busy crowd I will sometimes take them out, gaze tenderly at them, and kiss them passionately. Scribners have already signed the contract. I am to sign it Monday, but, with their customary fairness, they have advised me to show it to a lawyer before I sign it. I am therefore going with Mrs. Boyd on Monday to see Mr. Melville Cane, a lawyer, a poet, a member of Harcourt, Brace and Co., and the finest attorney on theatrical and publishing contracts in America. I have met him once, he read part of my book, and he has since been my friend and well-wisher. He told the person who sent me to him sometime ago [1] that I represented what he had wanted to be in his own life, that I was one of the most remarkable people he had ever met. And when he was told yesterday that I had sold my book he was delighted.

I am filled at the moment with so much tenderness towards the whole world that my agent, Mrs. Boyd, is worried—she is a Frenchwoman, hard and practical, and she does not want me to get too soft and trusting in my business relations. I wrote Scribners a letter of acceptance in which I could not hold myself in. I spoke of my joy and hope, and my affection and loyalty towards the publishers who had treated me so well, and my hope that this would mark the beginning of a long and happy association which they would have no cause to regret. In reply I got a charming letter in which they told me I would never have to complain of the interest and respect they have for my work. Mrs. Boyd herself was almost as happy as I was—although she is agent for almost every important French author in America, and publishing and acceptances are the usual thing for her— she said the thing was a great triumph for her as well, as Scribners consider me "a find" and are giving her credit for it.

It is all very funny and moving. Seven months ago when she got the book and read parts of it, she got interested—it was too long (she said), but there were fine things in it, she thought someone might be interested, and so on. Now I am a "genius"—she is already sorry for poor fellows like Dreiser and Anderson; she told the publishers that "this boy has everything they have in addition to education, background, (etc, etc,). Of course, poor fellows," she said, "it's not their fault—they never had the opportunity"—and so on and so on. Also, she pictures the other publishers as tearing their hair, gnashing their teeth, and wailing because they are not publishing the book. She gave it to one or two to read—they all said it had fine things in it, but was too long, they must think about it, etc.— and meanwhile (says she) Scribners got it. She said she was talking to one of them (Jonathan Cape, his name is) a week ago. He said at once: "Where is your genius, and when can I see him?" She told him Scribners had it and (groaning with grief, no doubt) he begged her to let him have first chance at the next one. We must salt all this down—her Gallic impetuosity, I mean—and I've got to come to earth and begin work.

I've had to tell several people, and everyone is almost as glad as I am. The University people are throwing a job at my head. I can stop in June if I want, they say. This is absurd. Of what earthly use would I be to them

[1] Mrs. Bernstein.

for only a half year—but they will give me more money, I think, than last year, fewer hours, (eight or ten) and almost no paper work. Now that this thing has happened, I feel kinder toward teaching than ever. Of course, my $450 will not last forever, and even if the book goes well I must wait until six months after its publication (so reads a *regular* clause in my contract) for my first statement, and every four months thereafter. The University people are genuinely friends and well wishers—the dean,[2] a wealthy and fine young man (of thirty-eight or forty) would give me a job at any time—but I think this rather increases my value to them: it is a big swarming place, fond of advertising.

The people at Scribners want me to set to work on revision at once, but they told me they thought I would have to find work later. No one knows how many copies the book will sell, of course, and besides, I must wait eight or ten months after publication for my first money (if there is any, but perish *that* thought.) Mrs. Boyd says the contract is fair, regular, and generous—giving an advance of $500 on a first book is unusual—of course that $500 *comes out* later from my first royalties. The contract offers me 10% of the *retail* price of the book up to the first 2,000 copies: after that 15%. As the book is a very long one, it will have to sell, I think, for $2.50 or $3.00. You can estimate from this what it is possible to make—but for the Lord's sake, don't. This is a fascinating weakness I have succumbed to, and everything is too uncertain. There are also clauses covering foreign translation and publication, and publication in any other than book form. That means serial and movies, I suppose, but *that* won't happen to me on *this* book—but if it does, the publisher and author split the profits.

Mrs. Ernest Boyd is also recognized as my agent and business representative and all checks are payable to her. This may make my thrifty friends squirm—she also gets 10% of all my profits (I hope, naturally, her share is at least $100,000)—but it's the best arrangement. How hard she worked to bring this about I don't know. Nevertheless she did it and I'll pay the 10% ·cheerfully—that's the regular agents' rate. Also, I think it is just as well that I am managed by a practical person who knows a little business. Although it is a business matter and I ought not to get sentimental, I can't help having a warm spot in my heart for the old girl who brought it about. I might have done it by myself sooner or later, but she certainly helped enormously at the present.

Finally, I want to start and continue my life by being decent and loyal to those people who have stood by me—whether for business or personal reasons. If we muddy and cheapen the quality of our actual everyday life, the taint, I believe, is bound to show, sooner or later, in what we create. Mrs. Boyd is so happy that Scribners took it. She said I should be very

2 Dean Munn.

proud of that; she said they were the most careful and exacting publishers in America—others publish fifty or a hundred novels a year, but Scribners only ten or twelve, although they bring out many other books. They are also trying to get the younger writers—they now have Ring Lardner, Scott Fitzgerald, and Ernest Hemingway (to say nothing of Wolfe). They were reading sections of my book, they told me, to Lardner and Hemingway a week before I got home—I'm afraid somewhat coarse and vulgar sections.

Finally, I must tell you that the ten days since I got home on the Italian boat have been the most glorious I have ever known. They are like all the fantasies I had as a child of recognition and success—only more wonderful. That is why my vision of life is becoming stranger and more beautiful than I thought possible a few years ago—it is the fantasy, the miracle that really happens. For *me* at any rate. My life, with its beginnings, has been a strange and miraculous thing. I was a boy from the mountains; I came from a strange wild family; I went beyond the mountains and knew the state; I went beyond the state and knew the nation, and its greatest university, only a magic name to my childhood; I went to the greatest city and met strange and beautiful people, good, bad, and ugly ones; I went beyond the seas alone and walked down the million streets of life. When I was hungry [and] penniless, anemic countesses, widows . . . —all manner of strange folk—came to my aid. In a thousand places the miracle has happened to me. Because I was penniless and took one ship instead of another, I met the great and beautiful friend who has stood by me through all the torture, struggle, and madness of my nature for over three years, and who has been here to share my happiness these past ten days.[3] That another person, to whom success and greater success is constant and habitual, should get such happiness and joy from my own modest beginning is only another of the miracles of life.

Ten days ago I came home penniless, exhausted by my terrible and wonderful adventures in Europe, by all I had seen and learned, and with only the hated teaching—now become strangely pleasant—or the advertising, before me. The day after New Year's—truly a *New* Year for me—it began: the publisher's demand over the telephone that I come immediately to his office; that first long conference, as I sat there wild, excited, and trembling as it finally dawned on me that someone was at last definitely interested; the instructions to go away and think over what had been said two or three days; the second conference, when I was told definitely they had decided to take it; the formal letter of acceptance, with the terms of the contract, and finally the contract itself, and the sight of the blessed check. Is not this too a miracle?—to have happened to a penniless unhappy

[3] Mrs. Bernstein.

fellow in ten days? Are a child's dreams better than this? Mrs. Boyd, trying to hold me down a bit, said that the time would soon come when all this would bore me, when even notices and press clippings would mean so little to me that I would not glance at them. So, she says, does her husband, a well-known critic and writer, feel and act. But isn't it glorious that this should have happened to me when I was still young and rapturous enough to be thrilled by it? It may never come again, but I've had the magic— what Euripides calls "the apple tree, the singing, and the gold."

Of my voyage in Europe this time, of all that happened to me this time, and of how all this began, I can do no more here than to give you a summary: of my adventures on the ship, of my wanderings in France and Belgium and Germany, of all the books and pictures I saw and bought, of my new book,[4] now one third written, of my stay in Munich and the strange and terrible adventure at The Oktoberfest (with all its strange and beautiful aftermath). . . .

Then, of how, still battered and blue, with a dueling student's skullcap covering my bald head I went to Oberammergau; how one of my wounds broke open there, and I was nursed by the man who played Pilate (a doctor) and by Judas, and by a little old woman there, almost eighty, whom I had known in Munich—almost as mad as I was, no husband any more, children dead, even the name of her village in America only a name she couldn't always remember; a vagabond at seventy-eight around the world, hating the Germans she once loved, and loving only the Oberammergauers who had known her for forty years. She had written one book about them and was at work on another, but she was afraid she was going to die and wanted me to promise to write it for her. When I refused to do this we had fallen out and she had left Munich in a temper at me.

Now, all battered up, I was coming to see her again. She was the daughter of a Methodist minister, and despite her long life in Europe and the Orient she had never lost the stamp of it—she read insanely all the statistics concerning illegitimate children in Munich and Oberammergau, going almost insane when she discovered the guilt of her adored Passion Players. Her treatment of me now was a mixture of old Methodist intolerance and "it serves you right" combined with love and tender mercy.

Of how I left Oberammergau; of how she followed me up to Munich in a few days; of how the police almost drove me mad with their visits, questions, and inspections; of how the poor old thing became my accomplice, almost driving me mad with her advice and suspicions, seeing a policeman looking for me behind every bush, and rushing over to warn me at my pension at all hours of day and night. Of how finally she saw

[4] *The River People.*

the great Zeppelin over Munich early one morning and came to pull me out of bed twittering with excitement; of how from this time on she lived only for the Zeppelin, staying in her cold pension nearly all day long with the radio phones clamped to her ears, her old eyes bright and mad as she listened to news of the flight to America. Of how a night or two later the pension people had tried to get me when I was at the theatre, and of how the old woman had died that night with the phones to her ears still.[5]

Of how they got me next morning and [I] went over and saw her there, and old Judas and his daughter Mary Magdalene who had known her for thirty years—they had come up that morning from Oberammergau —they were weeping gently and softly, they were taking her back, according to her wish, to bury her there (she had said it to me a hundred times). Of how I had asked if I should go with them, and they had looked into my wild and bloody eyes, at my swollen nose, seamed head, and gouged face, and shook their heads slowly. Then of how I knew I must leave this place which had given me so much—as much as I could hold at the time—and taken so much. My lungs were already raw with cold, I was coughing and full of fever—I felt a strange fatality in the place, as if I too must die if I stayed longer.

So that afternoon I took the train for Salzburg, drawing my breath in peace again only when I got over the Austrian border. Then four days in bed in Salzburg and on to Vienna. The first days in Vienna, still in a sort of stupor from all I had seen or felt—full of weariness and horror. Then slowly I began to read, study, and observe again. Then, just before I went to Budapest, Mrs. Boyd's first warning letter about the book I had forgotten—Scribners was interested; I should write at once. Forgot about it— believed in promises and the book no more—went to Hungary, went out among the wild and savage people of the plains, Asiatics now as they were when they came twelve hundred years ago under Attila. Then back to Vienna again and there a letter from Scribners—at last, it seemed, something really hopeful. This whole story—strange, wild, ugly and beautiful, I don't know what it means—but the drama and the struggle within me at this time was much more interesting than the purely physical things outside. What it means, I don't know, but to me it is strange and wonderful, and my next book, a short one, will probably be made from it.[6] I have never written home or to you about this before—telling the bare facts—because it takes too long and tires me out to tell it. You must say

[5] In an unpublished letter to Mrs. Bernstein, Wolfe says that his story about the death of the old lady was invented.

[6] Wolfe planned to use the story of his wanderings in Europe as part of *The River People*.

nothing of this to anyone. I will put it all down some day in a book, together with much more strange and marvelous, so that who can read may see.

Getting to present matters, the letter in Vienna six or seven weeks ago was the first indication I had of what has happened. . . . The Scribners letter was signed by one Maxwell Perkins, whom I have since come to know as a fine and gentle person, full of wisdom. Mrs. Boyd tells me to listen to him carefully—he is one of those quiet and powerful persons in the background, the sole and only excuse, she says, for Scott Fitzgerald having been successful as he is. In his letter he said he had read my book, and while interested he did not know whether any publisher could risk it as it is; he did know it was a very remarkable thing and no editor could fail to be excited by it (I didn't tell him one or two had failed). What he wanted to know, he said, was when Scribners could talk with me. I was excited and eager, and as usual too enthusiastic. I wrote him at once, saying briefly my nose was broken and my head scarred (which was beginning early with a stranger, of course) but that his words of praise filled me with hope and eagerness. Said I'd be home Christmas or New Year's. Followed two more weeks in Vienna, three in Italy, then home from Naples. Called him up morning after New Year's. He asked me if I had the letter sent to the Harvard Club [7] and I said no—it had probably been sent abroad. He asked me to come to Scribners at once. I went up—in a few minutes I was taken to his office, where I found Mr. Charles Scribner (simply there, I think, to take a look at me, for he withdrew immediately, saying he would leave us alone).

Mr. Perkins is not at all "Perkinsy"—name sounds Midwestern, but he is a Harvard man, probably New England family, early forties, but looks younger, very elegant and gentle in dress and manner. He saw I was nervous and excited, spoke to me quietly, told me to take my coat off and sit down. He began by asking certain general questions about the book and people (these weren't important—he was simply feeling his way around, sizing me up, I suppose). Then he mentioned a certain short scene in the book,[8] and in my eagerness and excitement I burst out, "I know you can't print that! I'll take it out at once, Mr. Perkins." "Take it out?" he said. "It's one of the greatest short stories I have ever read." He said he had been reading it to Hemingway week before. Then he asked me

[7] A letter from Perkins dated December 7, 1928, saying merely: "Thanks very much indeed for your letter of November nineteenth. I look forward impatiently to seeing you, and I hope you will call up as soon as you conveniently can after reading this. Then we can have a talk."

[8] "An Angel on the Porch" which was published in the August, 1929, issue of *Scribner's Magazine,* and which appears on pages 99–100 and 262–269 of *Look Homeward, Angel.*

if I could write a short introduction for it to explain the people—he was sure Scribner's Magazine would take it; if they didn't someone else would. I said I would. I was at once elated and depressed—I thought now that this little bit was all they wanted of it.

Then he began cautiously on the book. Of course, he said, he didn't know about its present form—somewhat incoherent and very long. When I saw now that he was really interested, I burst out wildly saying that I would throw out this, that, and the other—at every point he stopped me quickly saying, "No, no—you must let that stay word for word—that scene's simply magnificent." It became apparent at once that these people were willing to go far farther than I had dared hope—that, in fact, they were afraid I would injure the book by doing too much to it. I saw now that Perkins had a great batch of notes in his hand and that on the desk was a great stack of handwritten paper—a complete summary of my whole enormous book. I was so moved and touched to think that someone at length had thought enough of my work to sweat over it in this way that I almost wept. When I spoke to him of this, he smiled and said everyone in the place had read it. Then he went over the book scene by scene—I found he was more familiar with the scenes and the names of characters than I was—I had not looked at the thing in over six months. For the first time in my life I was getting criticism I could really use. The scenes he wanted cut or changed were invariably the least essential and the least interesting; all the scenes that I had thought too coarse, vulgar, profane, or obscene for publication he forbade me to touch save for a word or two. There was one as rough as anything in Elizabethan drama— when I spoke of this he said it was a masterpiece, and that he had been reading it to Hemingway. He told me I must change a few words. He said the book was new and original, and because of its form could have no formal and orthodox unity, but that what unity it did have came from the strange wild people—the family—it wrote about, as seen through the eyes of a strange wild boy. These people, with relatives, friends, townspeople, he said were "magnificent"—as real as any people he had ever read of. He wanted me to keep these people and the boy at all times foremost— other business, such as courses at state university, etc., to be shortened and subordinated. Said finally if I was hard up he thought Scribners would advance money.

By this time I was wild with excitement—this really seemed something at last—in spite of his caution and restrained manner, I saw now that Perkins really was excited about my book, and had said some tremendous things about it. He saw how wild I was—I told him I had to go out and think—he told me to take two or three days—but before I left he went out and brought in another member of the firm, John Hall Wheelock, who spoke gently and quietly—he is a poet—and said my book was one of the most interesting he had read for years. I then went out and tried to pull myself together. A few days later, the second meeting—I brought notes along as to how I proposed to set to work, and so on. I agreed to deliver one hundred pages of corrected manuscript, if possible, every week. He listened, and then when I asked him if I could say something definite to a dear friend, smiled and said he thought so; that their minds were practically made up; that I should get to work immediately; and that I should have a letter from him in a few days. As I went prancing out I met Mr. Wheelock, who took me by the hand and said: "I hope you have a good place to work in—you have a big job ahead." I knew then that it was all magnificently true. I rushed out drunk with glory. In two days came the formal letter (I wired home then), and yesterday Mrs. Boyd got the check and contract which I am now carrying in my pocket. God knows this letter has been long enough—but I can't tell you half or a tenth of it, or of what they said.

Mr. Perkins said cautiously he did not know how the book would sell— he said it was something unknown and original to the readers, that he thought it would be a sensation with the critics, but that the rest is a gamble. But Mrs. Boyd says that to print such a gigantic manuscript from a young unknown person is so unusual that Scribners would not do it unless they thought they had a good chance of getting their money back. . . . I should love it, of course, if the book were a howling success, but my idea of happiness would be to retire to my apartment and gloat . . . and to let no more than a dozen people witness my gloating. But I think if I ever see man or woman in subway, elevated, or taxicab reading it, I will track that person home to see who he is or what he does, even if it leads me to Yonkers. And Mr. Perkins and Mr. Wheelock warned me not to go too much with "that Algonquin Crowd"—the Hotel Algonquin here is where most of the celebrities waste their time and admire one another's cleverness. This also makes me laugh. I am several million miles away from these mighty people, and at the present time want to get no closer. All the Theatre Guild people, whom I know through my dear friend,[9] have called her up and sent congratulations.

But now is the time for sanity. My debauch of happiness is over. I have made promises: I must get to work. I am only one of the thousands of people who write books every year. No one knows how this one will turn out. You must therefore say nothing to the Asheville people about it yet. In course of time, I suppose, Scribners will announce it in their advertisements. As for the Civic Cup business,[10] I am afraid that's out of

---

[9] Mrs. Bernstein.

[10] In her letter to him, Mrs. Roberts had asked if he would consent to being

the question. For one thing, no one knows anything about my book at home—whether it's good, bad, or indifferent. If anything is said about it, it must be later, after its publication. For another thing—and this troubles me now that my joy is wearing down—this book dredges up from the inwards of people pain, terror, cruelty, lust, ugliness, as well, I think, as beauty, tenderness, mercy. There are places in it which make me writhe when I read them; there are others that seem to me to be fine and moving. I wrote this book in a white heat, simply and passionately, with no idea of being either ugly, obscene, tender, cruel, beautiful, or anything else—only of saying what I had to say because I had to. The only morality I had was in me; the only master I had was in me and stronger than me. I went into myself more mercilessly than into anyone else—but I am afraid there is much in this book which will wound and anger people deeply, particularly those at home. Yet terrible as parts are, there is little bitterness in it. Scribners told me people would cry out against this, because people are unable to realize that that spirit which is sensitive to beauty is also sensitive to pain and ugliness. Yet all of this goes into the making of the book, and because of this Scribners have believed in it and are publishing it. I will soften all I can but I cannot take out all the sting— without lying to myself and destroying the book. For this reason we must wait and see. If the people of Asheville some day want to heap coals of fire on my head by giving me a cup, perhaps I shall fill it with my tears of penitence—but I doubt that this will come for a long time. The people of Asheville, I fear, may not understand me after this book and may speak of me only with a curse—but some day, if I write other books, they will. And my God! What books I feel within me and what despair, since my hand and strength cannot keep up with all my heart has felt, my brain dreamed and thought!

I have spent an entire afternoon writing this to you—it is a volume, but now I have worked off my wild buoyancy and must get to work. Please keep silence about the cup business. You understand why, don't you?

God bless you for your letter, and forgive the great length of this one, so filled with my own affairs that I have not yet sent my love to Mr. Roberts. Give it to him with all my heart and tell him I want no better news from home than that he is up and hale again. I have told you about my own business at such length because I believed you really wanted to hear it all, and because I am so happy to share it with you. But God bless you all and bring you all health and happiness. If you see Scribners' advertisement you can speak, of course, but please use your excellent discretion.

---

nominated for the civic award cup which was being presented by the *Asheville Times* to the citizen who had rendered the finest service to Asheville in the past year.

I shall write you a short letter when I am calmer, telling you about N.Y.U. plans, and how my work on the book is coming. Love to all.

P.S. Whatever of this you think may interest my family pass on, but tell them also, for God's sake, to be discreet. It made me so happy to be able to wire them good news the other day. Now, let's all hope something comes of it. Again, God bless you all.

Note: I can hardly read parts of this myself, but you have had to puzzle my hen-scratching out before, and perhaps you can do it again. I wrote it in a great hurry and I was very excited—but I hope you make it out.

It's not a letter—it's a pamphlet. Maybe I'll ask you to give it back some day in order to see how foolish I felt.

To MABEL WOLFE WHEATON

[27 West 15th Street]
[New York City]
Wednesday, Feb 13 [1929]

Dear Mabel:

Thanks for your letter—and thanks again for the box of cake and candy. Everything arrived in good shape, including the jar of peaches which I have not yet eaten. I had a letter from Mrs. Roberts a day or two after I got yours: you are certainly right in saying they are "walking on air" about my book. She is soaring so high, in fact, that she has me worried—to read it you would think that I had already "arrived," that my book is already a crashing success, and so on. To think, she says, that it should come to you so soon, when you are only a kid (a 28 year old kid is getting about ready to put on long pants, don't you think?)—I had not expected you to get it (she says) for another ten years. And so on.

Now, of course, the effect of all this is to make me very nervous. That is why I wanted to be as quiet as possible about the book until it is published. I am still happy about it, I am still very hopeful about it, but, let me repeat, no one knows what kind of success it will have, or whether it will have any. And no one will know this until it is published. Of course, I was terribly stirred up about it myself when I wrote her that long letter, but I warned her again and again not to take it for granted that success and glory, and all the rest of it, is already gained. We *hope*—both publishers and myself—that the book will go well; but I ought to be satisfied if it goes just well enough to pay me enough money to live on while I write another, to pay Scribners for their expense and trouble, and to make them willing to publish my next one. You know that I hope, naturally, that it will do much better than this, but remember, there is always the chance that it will do much worse. I am a young unknown writer, this is my first book, it may perish in oblivion. So the best policy is to work, wait, and pray for the best.

I have found that your good friends—your best friends—have a bad habit of announcing your election before you have even begun to run. I certainly am grateful for their good wishes, but I shall also probably be the scapegoat later if things do not pan out as well as they want them to. For the rest of the world is not so friendly and generous—if it is talked about now that my book is a tremendous success, and then if my book turns out a failure—I shall get credit for having done a lot of premature boasting. That, unhappily, is the way things are (as you probably have found out.)

I have already had a letter of congratulation from my friend, ——— ——— of ———, —. ——— ——— opens with a rush of enthusiasm and congratulates me on the "tremendous royalties" which the publishers are already paying me. His mother, he says, has written him all about it. Now of course, I am very fond of Mrs. ——, but I know very well that she is not burdened by silence, and I am wondering just how many hundred thousand people she has told it to thus far, and how much each of them has added to her fairy tale. Since I wanted the thing—for the reasons I have mentioned—kept reasonably quiet, and since ——— is only about 1200 miles from Asheville, I am wondering just how long it will take for my little secret to reach Siberia. If Mrs. —— is in good form, the news ought to get there about Good Friday. So, if you see the lady, please try very tactfully to muzzle her.

I know you understand that I am not ungrateful for the generous good wishes of all these people. I value their friendship highly, and I have been touched and moved by all they have said. Only, I really think that too much talk at present may do more harm than good.

Scribners have also bought a story from me to print in their magazine.[1] They asked me if $150 would be satisfactory and I almost fell off the chair —it is a very short scene which they are taking from the book, and I had not expected over fifty or seventy-five dollars. N.Y.U.—that is, my good friend, Dean Munn—dug up a couple of courses to help me buy bacon and beans—they take only about half the regular teaching time, and will pay me $150 or $200 a month between now and June. So I shall manage very well at present. If I need money in the summer I can get work in the summer school, and they have already offered me a job for next September, if I need it.

[1] "An Angel on the Porch."

But I really do not need much money. My tastes seem to get simpler instead of more expensive, outside of food and books. When I was a child I dreamed of at least a million: now my imagination can not go beyond six or seven thousand a year. I hope that some day I shall have that much, but honestly I would not know how to do my work and spend much more. Yet such a sum would hardly be cigarette money for most of the people I know in New York, and I know there are dozens of people in Asheville who have more than this, although money goes twice as far there. I am simply bewildered at the amount of money in America. I have just come back from poverty-stricken Europe—from Vienna, where many a man thinks himself lucky to work for $20 a month. I have never seen anything like the wealth here, and I am sure there has never been anything like it in the world's history. . . . There are literally thousands of apartments along Park Avenue which rent . . . for twenty-five and fifty thousand. I find it very interesting to see all this wealth and power, but I certainly do not envy it. Most of these people have made it recently—they are ignorant and dull and unhappy: they don't know what to do with it. Only a few of them—(*none* that I know of)—have either the intelligence or talent of Mrs. B.[2] who saw long ago that there's no joy in life unless we can find work we love and are fitted for. She therefore works like a Trojan in the theatre, and has made a fine reputation for herself, solely through her own ability.

Another interesting thing is that money has come to mean so little that it can no longer buy people into cultivated society. On Sunday night I was lucky enough to be invited to the Dress Rehearsal of "Dynamo," O'Neill's new play, at the Theatre Guild. I was invited by Miss Helburn,[3] the head of the Guild, and I sat in the first row between Mrs. B. and a very beautiful and celebrated woman named Lynn Fontanne, who is now the Guild's star actress. Otto Kahn was three rows behind, and the place was filled with celebrities and beauties, all dazzling in evening clothes. The funny part is that people simply fight to get invited to the Guild Dress Rehearsal—but I am sure many of the people there that night were almost as poor as I am. Nevertheless, *they* are invited, while millionaire pork packers and their wives tear their hair in an effort to get in. (Of course, I got invited not through any merit of my own, but because the Guild will lay themselves out for Mrs. B. But they have certainly been friendly and kind to me and they all seemed glad my book was being published.)

I don't think I have any more news for you at present. I have done some work on the book, but not enough—must work much harder. The pub-

[2] Mrs. Bernstein.
[3] Theresa Helburn.

lisher wants the manuscript by first of May—I think they intend to publish about August. . . . Sorry to hear real estate is so dead. I think the
business here—all the buying, selling, and making of fortunes—is a kind
of boom, and that the bottom will drop out on a lot of people just as it did
in Florida and Asheville. I'll try to write other members of family as soon
as I get time.

*The following letter to Madeleine Boyd was written in reply to a note
from her enclosing a check for the sale of "An Angel on the Porch" to
Scribner's Magazine, also a letter from H. L. Mencken. Mrs. Boyd had submitted several short sections from* Look Homeward, Angel *to Mencken in
hopes that he would publish some of them as short stories in* The American
Mercury. *He had declined them, and she had suggested trying them with*
The Bookman *and* The Dial. *They were never accepted by any magazine.*

To MADELEINE BOYD

Harvard Club
New York
Friday, Feb. 15 [1929]

Dear Mrs. Boyd:

Thanks for the note from Mr. Mencken, and for the short story cheque
and receipt from Scribners. I am very much pleased by Mr. Mencken's
note—his praise was moderate, but I take it at its literal value: I do not
believe he writes such notes as a matter of form. And of course his belief in
one's work would be of tremendous value to a writer.

I should certainly be glad to have you send the scenes from the book
to *The Bookman* and *The Dial*—although *The Dial* terrifies me. I deliberately chose for Mr. Mencken scenes that are simply and clearly written,
because I thought he would like these better, but they may seem too
elementary to the subtle moderns who edit *The Dial*. If so, I could produce
other scenes that would be practically unintelligible, even to the author.
Seriously, what do you think of this?

I am at work on the book, but it is a stiff perplexing job. I stare for
hours at the manuscript before cutting out a few sentences: sometimes
I want to rip in blindly and slash, but unless I know *where* the result
would be disastrous. Also my new book [1] fills my mind—I keep making

---

[1] *The Fast Express* which finally became the first part of *Of Time and the River.*
Wolfe had stopped working on *The River People* when he returned to New York in
January, 1929.

notes for it. But I shall finish this one first. I keep digging out old manuscripts [2] as I unpack and I shall probably give you a too-long short story
for reading. Wrote it several years ago. Took Mr. Perkins another 100
pages Monday. Thanks for the check again. If you want more manuscript,
let me know. Good luck to us both.

*The following letter was found in various versions in Wolfe's pocket note-
books and on the back of pages of his manuscripts, and was evidently never
mailed. That it was written long before publication of* Look Homeward,
Angel *is indicated by its chronological position in his notebooks; also by the
fact that the title,* O, Lost, *which he uses in it for* Look Homeward, Angel
*was discarded five or six months before publication of the book. Evidently,
in his anxiety about the reception that his book would have in Asheville,
Wolfe imagined that he might be asked to write a defense of it for the*
Citizen, *and began composing the various versions of this letter for the sake
of his own peace of mind.*

To THE EDITOR OF THE ASHEVILLE *CITIZEN*

[April (?) 1929]

Thank you very much for your friendly and courteous invitation to contribute an article to your columns answering critics of my book, "O, Lost."
I must decline to do so for several reasons, the most important of which are
as follows: at the beginning of my career as a novelist I have determined,
so far as possible, to let my books speak for me. The artist is neither a
debater nor a propagandist—certainly I have no skill as either—any defense of his works should be undertaken not by himself but by critics who
are competent for such work. If the Asheville critics of my work infer from
this that I am anxious to avoid controversy, they are certainly right. But if,
as I gather from several letters in your columns, they believe that my book
is a "bitter attack" against the town, the state, the South, they are certainly wrong. One does not attack life any more than he curses the wind;
shakes his fist at the storm; spits angrily at the ocean.

That there is bitterness in my book as well as pain and ugliness, I can
not deny. But I believe there is beauty in it as well, and I leave its defense
to those of my readers who found it there.

As to the implied criticisms of my personal life, I again have nothing to
say. I honestly do not care very much what these people think. None of

[2] Probably some of the sketches he had written in 1924–25, such as the story of
Eugene and the Countess in Orléans, which were later rewritten and published in
Of Time and the River.

them knows me, a few have seen me and talked to me: their efforts to pry and intrude into a life they can never know are ugly and revolting. But they are not surprising. One who has lived in New York a few years, hears too much of the sewage of a million mean lives—people who, unable to touch the sacred garments of the celebrities, feast on the familiarity of smut, contrive spurious nastiness, transfer the glittering vices they have themselves desired and have not had courage for, to the figures they honor with their venom and malice.

If the indignant Methodist ladies and gentlemen suspect me of fleshy carnalities, let them suspect no more. I am enthusiastically guilty. I have eaten and drunk with sensual ecstacy in ten countries. I have performed the male function with the assistance of several attractive females, a few of whom were devout members of the Methodist Church.

[THE LETTER BREAKS OFF HERE]

To MABEL WOLFE WHEATON

[27 West 15th Street]
[New York]
May, 1929.

Dear Mabel:

Thanks for your letter which I got to-day. I don't suppose I have written much lately—I have very little sense of time when I am working. I am working every day with the editor of Scribners, Mr. Perkins, on the re-vision of my book. We are cutting out big chunks, and my heart bleeds to see it go, but it's die dog or eat the hatchet. Although we both hate to take so much out, we will have a shorter book and one easier to read when we finish. So, although we are losing some good stuff, we are gaining unity. This man Perkins is a fine fellow and perhaps the best publishing editor in America. I have great confidence in him and I usually yield to his judg-ment. The whole Scribner outfit think the book a remarkable thing—and Perkins told me the other day when I was in the dumps that they would all be very much surprised if the book wasn't a success. When I said that I hoped they would take another chance on me, he told me not to worry—that they expected to do my next book and the one after that, and so on indefinitely. That means a great deal to me. It means at any rate, that I no longer have to hunt for a publisher.

I've already seen the title page and a few specimen sheets of the type. They call this the "dummy." Of course, I'm excited about it. I can't say enough for the way Scribners have acted. They are fine people. They sent me to one of the most expensive photographers in town a few weeks ago, a woman who "does" the writers.[1] What it cost I can't say, but she charges $150-$200 a dozen, I understand, and she kept me half a day. What in heaven's name they're going to do with them all I don't know—they say it's for advertising. They are going to begin advertising, I believe, this month or next, and they have asked me to write something about myself. Of course, that's always an agreeable job, isn't it? When the story and the book are coming out, I don't know, but everyone has become very busy this last month—I now have to go up to see the editor every day. I think the story will be held back until just before the book is published. Scribners are good salesmen, good business people, good advertisers. They are doing a grand job for me, and they believe in me.

That's enough about the book for the present. I am very sorry to hear of Mr. Jeanneret's [2] trouble. Your letter brought back to me the memory of my childhood, and of Papa leaning on the rail talking politics, and everything else with the old man. When my short story comes out read it—you will see them again as you have seen them many times—but *don't* mention this to anyone. Jeanneret was a true friend to Papa and admired and respected him. He belongs to a world that is gone, a life and a time that is gone—the only Asheville I can remember, as it was in my childhood and boyhood. Perhaps I see the change even more clearly than you do because I have been away from it. I think the Asheville I knew died for me when Ben died. I have never forgotten him and I never shall. I think that his death affected me more than any other event in my life. I was reading some poems the other day by a woman who died very suddenly and tragically last December.[3] I met the woman once. She was very beautiful, but I suppose by most of our standards we would have to say that she was a bad person. She ruined the lives of almost everyone who loved her— and several people did. Yet this woman wrote some very fine poetry, and is spoken of everywhere now. I thought of Ben—he was one of those fine people who want the best and highest out of life, and who get nothing—who die unknown and unsuccessful.

I can certainly understand your desire to be alone. With me it's a necessity. Yet in my heart I like people and must have them. Sometimes, as you know, I have gone away for months without letting people know where I was. But I always got homesick for the familiar faces and had to come back. I think I live alone more than any person I have ever known. I know many fine people in New York—some of them I see very often, but I must spend a large part of my day alone. I hate crowds and public meet-

---

[1] Doris Ulmann. She did not charge Scribners as much as Wolfe says here.

[2] Louis William Jeanneret, the Swiss watchmaker who rented space in W. O. Wolfe's marble shop.

[3] Probably Wolfe meant Elinor Wylie. See his letter to his sister Mabel dated March 26, 1927.

ings. You could not live the way I do: you must be with people, talk to them, join with them. But this is the only life I can lead. Sometimes I love to go out and join in with the crowd, and have a good time. But not often. The truth of the matter is that most people I meet bore me until I could cry out. This ought not to be but it is. And I am not often bored with myself or with my reading or writing. I have tried a great many of the things I dreamed of when I was a child—travelling about, Paris, Vienna, theatres, ships, and so on—but about the only real satisfaction I have had has been in work, the kind of work I like to do. And I have not worked hard enough. Most people are not happy when working, simply because very few people have ever found the work they want to do. It's pretty hard to think of a cotton mill worker or a ditch-digger getting much joy out of it, isn't it? And that goes as well for most business men: "realtors," pants makers, shoe dealers.

I may take your advice and come home for a few days when school is over. I could not come for long, because of my work here at Scribners, but I should like to stay a few days or a week. . . .

I suppose you are right about most of the money being in New York: there is certainly a lot of it here, although I have seen very little of it myself. Our "Prosperity" is a very uneven thing. There are a great many rich and well-to-do people, but there are millions who just make enough to skin through on. Most of the people in New York are like this—scraping by, with nothing left over. What's your politics? I suppose you are a Democrat or Republican, since the South is the most conservative place left. I believe a Socialist is regarded down there as being the same as an Anarchist. But wait until the poor people have to endure an empty belly and you'll see a change. I think if I had any politics, I'd be a socialist—it's the only sensible thing to be (if you're not a capitalist, and I'm *not*). But you think that's "wild talk," don't you?

I don't blame you for letting some of the club work go. I buy an Asheville paper once in a while, and there seems to be a club for everything under the sun, including hog raising. Apparently the women are getting all the "culture"—what do the men do? It is probably a farce—this club business—because most of these women don't give a damn if Shakespeare wrote "Hamlet" or "The Face on the Barroom Floor": it gives them a chance to sit around on their rumps and look "literary." I am sorry Mrs. Roberts is in so much of it. She runs the business down when she talks to me and winks over my head at J. M. Of course, I see everything, but the poor woman thinks I'm fooled. She's very ambitious for Margaret, and I think has just a little bit of the snob in her. But then we all have. She's a fine woman—one of the few who have stood the test of time with me. I shall always like her.

I'm glad to know all are reasonably well—sorry to hear of Fred's automobile accident, and to know it has upset him. It upsets me just to look at them here in New York: the average taxi driver is a dangerous criminal with no respect for life. If I am ever in a taxi that runs down a child—and I have feared this a dozen times—I think I shall be tempted to kill the driver. I no longer think it's smart or daring to drive fast. I am the one remaining American who knows nothing about driving a car and who has no desire to own one. Is this another sign of my "queerness"?

Well, I sometimes feel like the only sane person on a stroll through a madhouse: all the maniacs are nudging one another, and saying: "See that guy? He's crazy."

I have written the last several pages today (Tuesday)—the weather was fine: about the first real sign of Spring. All the people were out and God knows there are plenty of them. The buildings are so big and high, and the people swarming up and down look like insects. Most of them are. I think I know pretty well what I want to do with my life—but a lot depends now on what success my book has. Pray for me.

As I say, I hate crowds and parties, but I'm being dragged out to dinner with some swells on Saturday. I hate it, but my agent has arranged the thing, and says it will be good for me. I don't believe it, but maybe they'll give me a drink.

I've written too much and said too little. Give my love to everyone and ask them to write when able. Don't be afraid of going crazy—I've been there several times and it's not at all bad. If people get too much for you take a long ride on the train.

Henry T. Volkening, to whom the following letter was written, was an instructor in the English Department at New York University from 1926 to 1928, and is now an associate of Diarmuid Russell, in the literary agency of Russell and Volkening, Inc. Excerpts from the letters he received from Wolfe were first published in his article "Thomas Wolfe: Penance No More" in the Spring, 1939, issue of The Virginia Quarterly Review.

To HENRY T. VOLKENING

Harvard Club
New York

July 4 [1929]

Dear Henry:

This is Independence Day—I just passed one of Nedick's Peerless Orange Juice Stands, and when I did I thought of you, far away in Germany and England where you are completely cut off from this and many other blessings.

Your letters and postals have given me the greatest pleasure—I cried out for joy at your rapturous letter from Vienna: I had a great personal pride in it, as if I had discovered the place. Did you go to Budapest? Long, long ago I wrote you, when I got your letter—wrote page after page, but never finished it. This can only be a little note—I'm going up the Hudson to my friend's, Olin Dows, to-morrow—he lives in a little shack of seventy rooms, and no one else is there at present. Perhaps I'll write you a nice long one from there, filled with elegant quotations from good books— they have four or five thousand beauties, Lamb, and Browning and Arnold and everything. I'm going to Maine last two weeks in July—I'll look right across the Atlantic at you. And perhaps to Canada for a few days. (But why *Canada?*)

Everything turned out beautifully for you—there was nothing here but rain, rain through April and much of June. I'm so glad you and Nat [1] love Vienna—you are like Vienna people, I think—in spite of your good Deutsch name, you are *Wiener* Deutsch. Did you go to Nurnberg? It's a grand place. And are you going to *Ambleside* and the Lake district? I hope my advice has not yet played you false—bring back an earful of adventure for me.

My other letter was filled with news—which I've forgotten! Year at N.Y.U. is over and gone (with my prayers) to oblivion. When I saw the boys last many had turned slightly green, yellow, and purple from stored-up poison and malice. It's too bad. Many of them went abroad—to Paris and everything. Gottlieb I believe went to Germany, Troy got a scholarship and is going to live—where do you suppose?—in Dear Old Paree, and Dollard's [2] epoch-making and universe-quaking quarrel with Herr Geheimrat Watt finally burst out in open battle late this Spring—he resigned, and when I said goodbye was talking of vagabonding, joining the Navy, going to Cambridge, etc. . . .

I feel splendid, and am fresh and fat. My proofs are coming in, my story [3] appears in the magazine next month (get it in England if you can— *Scribner's* for August), book's out in the Fall, and Scribners thinks it a grand thing and that it will go. I hope it makes a splash—not a flop!—but that it splashes me with a few dollars. Also writing some short stories [4] that they have asked me to write—without promises—and loaded to the decks with my new book.[5] Thank God I'm thirty pounds overweight, it's going to kill me writing it.

[1] Mrs. Volkening.
[2] Hans J. Gottlieb, William A. S. Dollard and William Troy were instructors in the English Department at New York University.
[3] "An Angel on the Porch."
[4] Nothing ever came of these. Wolfe had little or no idea of what constituted a saleable short story.
[5] At this time, Wolfe had only a rough idea of what his next book would

I am dining—or bootleg-beering—with some friends of yours next Wednesday: with Dashiell of *Scribners;* Mrs. D.; a young man named Meyer, who read my book for S. first; and your friend, the deaf young man, who is also a friend of Meyer's.[6]

This is all for the present—the free Americans have been shooting off firecrackers all day: it's about all they can do. The weather good and bad—today cool, bright, and lovely. But Hell to come. I'm naturally excited and hope something good happens to book.

I rejoice in all the joy your trip is giving you. You seem to be fortunate the whole way. Go to the Royal Oak to *drink* in Ambleside. Stay a day or two at Rosy Lewis' Cavendish Hotel in Jermyn Street—go to Bath, Lincoln, York, Fountain Abbey, Edinburgh, Trossachs—eat in Soho—Restaurant des Gourmets—Olde Cocke Tavern (Fleet St)—Simpsons: go to Trocadero bar for cocktails—Walk in old London City by moonlight (if there is a moon)—go to the bookshops, especially Foyles in Charing Cross Road. This is all for the present. Good luck and God bless you both.

The next four letters to John Hall Wheelock of Scribners were written from Boothbay Harbor, Maine, where Wolfe had gone to rest and read the galley proofs of Look Homeward, Angel. *Wheelock was the editor in charge of the final editing and proofs of all Wolfe's books published by Scribners. He is now a senior editor, occupying the office of Maxwell Perkins, who died in 1947.*

To JOHN HALL WHEELOCK

Ocean Point, Maine.

July 19, 1929.

Dear Mr. Wheelock:

Don't mind if I call you "mister" at present, but you must please not do it to me. I no longer have the slightest feeling of stiffness or diffidence

---

be. He had first thought of it as *The Fast Express,* which finally became the early part of *Of Time and the River.* Then, gradually, he began thinking of expanding *The Fast Express* and calling it *The October Fair.* He kept expanding *The October Fair* until it became so huge that it finally was cut in half, and the first half published as *Of Time and the River.*

[6] Alfred S. Dashiell, who was Managing Editor of *Scribner's Magazine* and is now Managing Editor of *The Reader's Digest;* Wallace Meyer, an editor in the book department at Scribners; and Byron Dexter, who is now Managing Editor of *Foreign Affairs.*

toward you, I have on the contrary the warmest and gratefulest feeling toward you and Mr. Perkins, but I could no more call you Wheelock than I could call him Perkins. Alone in my mind I know that I am now a man in years, and as I face my work alone I come pretty close at times to naked terror, naked nothing, I know that no one can help me or guide me or put me right—that's my job. Perhaps that is why in my personal relations with people I cling to the old child's belief—that there are older people who are wiser and stronger, and who can help me. I am far from being melancholy—I am more full of strength and power and hope than I have been in years—I have in me at the present time several books, all of which are full of life and variety, and rich detail. If I can only put down finally the great disease and distress of my spirit, which is to take in more of life than one man can hold, I can go on to do good work—because all men are certainly bound by this limit and I believe my chance to learn and experience, and my power of absorption, are as good as those of most men.

I feel packed to the lips with rich ore. In this wild and lovely place, all America stretches below me like a vast plain: the million forms that spend themselves in the city, and torture us so by their confusion and number, have been fused into a calmer temper—I am filled with a kind of tragic joy. I want to tear myself open and show my friends all that I think I have. I am so anxious to lay all my wares out on the table—when one thing that I have done is praised, to say: "You have not seen one tenth or one twentieth of what is in me. Just wait." Then I am tortured when I have talked to people that I have seemed too exuberant, too full of wild energy—I go away thinking they have this simple picture in two or three colors of me, when there are a thousand sombre and obscure shadings that have not been shown. I am full of affection and love for this first book, but when you and Mr. Perkins have praised it I have been stirred with the desire to do something far better—I will, I must show these men what is in me! Hence, again, we come to those reasons that make me say "mister" to some people—the spirit of the young man is thirsty for real praise, for admiration of his works: the creative impulse, which has such complex associations, may have roots as simple and powerful as this one.

It would be inexact to say that I feel that whatever I do is by its doing right. In my own life I am trying for greater balance, serenity, kindness to other people, but when I write at present I want to wrench the most remote and terrible things in myself and others: whatever scruples and restraints from the traditional morality I have—and I have many—vanish under the one surpassing urge to make everything blaze with light, to get intensity and denseness into everything. Thus when I write, my own lusts, fears, hatreds, jealousies—all that is base or mean—I drag up with strong joy, as well perhaps as better qualities, feeling not how bad these things may be, but what magnificent life this is, how little all else is by comparison. This is of course the most colossal egotism—but how else do people create? Not surely, by telling themselves they are dull, and their affairs petty or mean? What profit is in that, or where's the improvement? In short there are moments when I work when I feel that no one else has a quarter my power and richness—my baseness is better than their nobility, my sores more interesting than their health etc.—that, one way or another, I am a fine young fellow and a great man. I know you will not despise me for this confession. There are people all around, especially the critics, who would rail and sneer at this, but under their silly little pretenses of modesty and cynical urbanity they are nasty little mountains of egotism. I merely work in this way, by feeling when things are going well that I am something tremendous like a God; but as a person I am no longer insolent or proud at heart; I feel on the contrary a constant sense of inferiority, often to people I am in nowise inferior to. Professor Babbitt [1] at Harvard could figure all this out in 40 seconds by his patented . . . system, and have all my various romantic diseases headed with a half dozen tickets of his own manufacture—but his brand of "classicism" is so much more romantic than my wildest romanticism, that by comparison Plato might have begot me out of Lesbia.

I cannot tell you how moved I was by your letter—by its length, its patience and care: it is a symbol of my entire relation with you and Mr. Perkins. I could not a year ago have thought it possible that such good luck was in store for me—a connection with such men, and such a house, and editing and criticism as painstaking and intelligent as I have had. I should have once said that it was like a child's fantasy come true, but I know this is not exact—a child's dream is swollen with so much false magnificence that much in life seems stale and disappointing to the young man. But a slow and powerful joy is awaking in me as I come to see that life has real wonder that is more strange and marrowy than our fictions. Consider this: I was a little boy born among great mountains from obscure people, I saw strange and beautiful things when I was a child, I dreamed constantly of wonderful far off things and cities—and when I grew up I went away and saw them. I was a poor boy who grew up in anarchy, I said that one day I should go to Harvard, and I went. People who make jokes about Harvard would make a joke about this, but it was not a joke to that boy—it was magic—and the journey must first be viewed from its beginning. I read and dreamed about strange foreign cities, I grew up and went to see them, I met people in them, I wandered from place to place by myself, I had wonderful adventures in them. When I was 16 or 18 I

[1] Irving Babbitt.

hoped, I dreamed, I did not dare to speak the hope, that someday I would write a book that men would read. Now I have written a book, and a great publishing house is printing it, and men who have seen it have been moved by it and praised it. Seven months ago I came to Vienna from Budapest after months of wandering about in Europe: I had a scar on my head and a broken nose: I found there a letter from Scribners. Now I am writing this from a little cottage on the wild coast of Maine—the sky is grey and full of creaking gulls, the Atlantic sweeps in in a long grey surge. I have eaten delicious foods and drunk glorious wines in many countries: I have read thousands of noble books in several languages. I have known and enjoyed beautiful women, have loved and been loved by one or two.

Fools will sneer "How romantic!" I tell you merely what you will easily agree to—this is not romantic, this is only a bald statement of a few facts in a single ordinary life. No man can say that there is a single garnishment or distortion of fact here—whoever chooses to believe there is no wonder and no richness here is only stupidly and stubbornly hugging phantoms of sterility. No—what one comes to realize is that there is a reasonable hope that one may cherish in life, that makes it well worth living—and that the childish pessimist who denies this is as lying and dishonest a rogue as the cheap ready-made optimist—and that, indeed, of the two brands of rascals, the merchant who deals in Pollyanna optimism is a better man than he whose stock-in-trade is snivelling drivelling Pollyanna pessimism. The spirit that feels from its mother's womb the tragic under-weft of life, and never sees the End as different from what it is, is all the more certain that sunlight is not made of fog, wine of vinegar, good meat of sawdust, and a woman's lovely body of nitrogen, decaying excrement, and muddy water. To hell with such lying drivel—why do we put up with it?

I know that it is good to eat, to drink, to sleep, to fish, to swim, to run, to travel to strange cities, to ride on land, sea, and in the air upon great machines, to love a woman, to try to make a beautiful thing—all such as consider such occupations "futile," let them go bury themselves in the earth and get eaten by worms to see if that is less futile. However, these despisers of life who are so indifferent to living, are the first ones to cry out and hunt the doctor when they have bellyache.

There is an island in this lovely little harbor—I can look out on it from the porch of my cottage. It is covered by a magnificent forest of spruce trees, and a little cottage is tucked away in a clearing under the mighty trees at one end. One end of the island (where this house is) looks in on the bay and on the little cottages along the shore; the other end fronts the open Atlantic. Now I fantasy about buying this island (which has 15 or 20 acres), and so strange is possibility that one day perhaps I shall. Several weeks ago when I knew I was coming to Maine, I began to think about islands. Presently I saw myself owning one, living on one, putting off from the mainland (a decrepit old wharf) with my servant in a little motor boat stocked with provisions—to the minutest detail I saw this place even to the spring house where butter and milk and rounds of beef should be stored. This scene became a part of my dream. However blurred the actual details have become I cannot say, the picture remains vivid, only the island I dreamed about has become this one here—I am unable to distinguish one from the other, so imperceptibly have the two fused (even to the rotten old wharf from which I fish).

In a child's dream the essential thing happens—it is this that makes wonder—the long vacancies between the flare of reality are left out. He is, for example, on a great ship going to a strange country, the voyage ends, and the very next moment the ship is sailing into a harbor, he sets foot not on land, but on Paris, London, Venice. I am living in such a place—there is the harbor, with wooded islands in it, a little shore road that winds around by the water's edge, and all the little cottages, with tidy yards, bright flowers. Then immediately there is the ocean. I had ceased until recent years to believe there could be such scenes, and even now it does not seem real. I thought there would be preludes to the sea. But there are not. The other night I walked along the road. The little farm-houses slept below the moon, the gnarled apple trees full of apples getting ripe leaned over the hedges, and on the walls the wild wood lilies grew. You would not say along that road the sea was there behind the houses, behind the fir trees and the hedge, and the apples getting ripe—and yet you round a bend, and the sea is there. I thought there would be vast lengthenings into the sea, slow stoppages of land and rock, drear marshy vacancies, slow lapse and waste relinquishment of earth, but when you round the bend of the road the sea is there—he has entered at one stride into the land. This union of the vast and lonely with the little houses, the land, the little harbor, made a great music in me. I could not tell you all it meant but it was like Milton standing by a little door. And I thought that if one came into this place on a ship from open sea it would be with the suddenness of a dream.

To unspin all the meanings in these things would take too long—and my letter is much too long already.

I got the proof sent with your letter—through galley 100. I am sending off to you this afternoon the few galleys I had before—through 78 (including foul galleys for 71, 72). I am sorry the printer was upset by my one long insertion. I do not think it will happen again. I did it here to round out one detail in Leonard's life—much that showed the man in a favorable light had previously been cut, and I thought it proper to add a little here. But I shall not do this again. I note carefully all you say—I shall study the boys-going-away-from-school scene and cut where I can. I am sorry to know it is still too long. Mr. Perkins suggested a very large cut out of it, which was made. I have a much fresher mind for it now, and will perhaps find more. I shall certainly send all the proofs I now have (through 100) back to you by Tuesday of next week—they should reach you Thursday. I still have ten or eleven days in this lovely place—that is, until a good week from next Tuesday—you would therefore have time to send me more. I propose to go to Canada when I leave here, for a week, and return to New York before August 10. It would be good if I had proof to take with me.

You gave me a great start when you said 75 pages of manuscript had been lost, but on re-reading, as I understand your letter, it seems that we already have galley proofs for these pages. Even if we haven't, there is at Scribners a complete copy of the original manuscript besides the one Mr. Perkins and I cut. Of course what revisions were made in those 75 pages I don't know. It is a thrilling shock to know that you have already page proof for 70 galleys—of course I am excited and anxious to see them. I await eagerly the copies of the magazine with my story and the piece about my work [2]—what's the use of acting coy and modestly restrained when you don't feel that way!

This is another day—a glorious, blue-white, cold, sparkling day. Forgive the long letter, the personal rhapsodies—I have victimized you by making you the angel. My next letter will come with the proof and be strictly concerned with business. I fish, read, and write here.

To JOHN HALL WHEELOCK

[Ocean Point, Maine]

Monday, July 22 [1929]

Dear Mr. Wheelock:

I am sending you galleys 79–90. It was for this section (79–100) that the manuscript, you say, has been lost. Will you please urge the printer again to try to recover it? There are several places here that cause me difficulty. Naturally, without the manuscript I cannot remember word for word the original, but it seems to me that there are omissions in several places that are not covered by the cuts Mr. Perkins and I made. The most important of these is at the beginning of the boys-going-from-school scene which you say should be cut still more. Mr. Perkins and I took out a big

---

[2] The August issue of *Scribner's Magazine* in which "An Angel on the Porch" appeared, together with a short biographical sketch about Wolfe.

chunk, but there is now a confusing jump that nullifies the meaning of several speeches (you have pointed out one of these). I have tried to patch it up as well as I could. . . .

I do not remember what Mr. Perkins and I did on *galley 80*—where you have made a cut. It does not seem to me that what happens here is more likely to give offense than many other things that remain—as an alternative I have cut out parts of it, and I submit the result to your decision. If it still seems best to cut it all, please do so. (Cut).

Will you look over the titles of the German books on Galley 85 and correct mistakes in grammar—i.e. is it *Der* or *Die* Zerbrochene Krug? etc.

As I read over the proofs again, I become more worried. There is a reference, for example, by one of the boys in the coming-from-school scene to *Mrs. Van Zeck* the wife of a lung specialist—but the whole section describing her as she leaves a store has been omitted. I cannot recall making this cut with Mr. P. As to further cuts in this scene, I will do what I can—but it seems to me that conversation between the two boys, which you say is too long, has been cut down to very little—what you *do* have is the undertakers' scene, the W. J. Bryan scene, the Old Man Avery scene, the Village Idiot scene, the Old Colonel Pettingrew scene, the Men Discussing the War Scene—all of which it seems to me are good. But I'll do what I can.

In view of the gaps I have discovered, I think I shall send you by this mail only 79–90. I shall send the rest on as soon as I can do something to fill up the holes. I do hope people will not look on this section as a mere stunt—I really don't know what to do about cutting it—it is not a stunt, a great deal of the town is presented in short order. I'm going to send you galleys to 90 without further delay—I want you to go over the going-from-school scene and if you see cuts, make them. I shall cut where I can in the last part of the scene.

This is all for the present, I'm sorry to cause you all this trouble—but, as I think you know, deeply grateful. At times, getting this book in shape seems to me like putting corsets on an elephant. The next one will be no bigger than a camel at the most. I'll send more tomorrow.

To JOHN HALL WHEELOCK

(Ocean Point, Maine)

Tuesday Afternoon, July 23, 1929

Dear Mr Wheelock:

I am sending you herewith the proofs from Galley 91–100, which I have now gone over carefully. In spite of your advice to shorten this section (that part dealing with boys coming from school) I am afraid I have lengthened it a little. This was necessary because of certain omissions and gaps which it seemed to me either the printer had caused, or Mr. Perkins and I had failed to consider when we made cuts. I have written in the omitted segment on Mrs. Van Zeck somewhat shorter, I think, than it first was—I have had to pin this to the proof for want of space, and indicate the place where it is to be inserted. I have also written in various themes from poetry at places where it seemed to me there was a vacancy. This was the mood and temper with which the scene started—the inwoven poetry—and it seemed to me it should be continued.

Now Mr. Wheelock, I have not willingly run counter to your advice on this section—I am simply not able intelligently to select between what I have left. I should be troubled to think this is too long. Please consider it again as carefully as you can and, if it seems best, make cuts where you think they are needed.

Although the Van Zeck bit means extra work for the printer, I think it might take precedence over some other things in the scene for several reasons: first, it is war time, a discussion of the war, the allies, the "ancestral voices prophesying war" comes right after—the woman's German name, her position, wealth, etc. opens vistas and implication that may be interesting. Second, the boys mention her in their speeches—the whole may suggest how varied (not how uniform) may be the pattern of race, culture, background, etc. even in a small town. Please verify, if you can, my quotations. The "Nur wer *die* (?) Sehnsucht kennt" etc. is Goethe. "Drink to me only with *thine* (?) eyes," and the Keats "O for a draught of vintage" (I think its "Ode to Autumn"—not sure).[1] On Galley 93, I restored a sentence you had struck out and changed the words I thought objectionable. If you still find it too strong, cut it out. (Cut nozzles for end tips, for example.)

On galley 94, I added a sentence "Having arranged to meet her," (Mrs Pert) etc. for a scene between Ben and Mrs Pert which I cannot remember having been cut.

There was originally a burlesque of the English war books on galley 94 —was this omitted in the cuts? I have added a line here to sum up what remains.

This is all for the present. I now have left eight galleys, which I shall try to get off to you to-morrow. I am leaving here, I think, Saturday or Sunday. Do not send any more proofs after Thursday. If I get more before then, I shall return them all corrected to you before I leave. My present plan is to go to Portland and to take train or ship for Canada. I'll let you

[1] It is from "Ode to a Nightingale."

know. If I go there, I shall stay a week. I'll give you my address and also tell you when I am coming back to New York. Naturally I want to finish with the proofs now as quickly as possible.

Thanks again for your great care and patience.

To JOHN HALL WHEELOCK

[Ocean Point, Maine]
[July 25, 1929]

Dear Mr. Wheelock:

I am sending you herewith galleys 109–115. Galleys 116–125, with manuscript, and with a letter from you arrived this morning. Most of the corrections in today's batch have already been indicated by you—I think all corrections are plain. Usually when you suggest words or phrases for others that you consider of dubious meaning, I accept your revision, but once or twice I have stuck to my own. For example the other day for my "The world (or the earth) shook to the *stamp* of marching men" you suggested *to the tread*. On thinking it over I decided that *to the stamp* more nearly got my meaning. You have done glorious work on the *adverbs*—I get red in the face when I see them coming, and when they come, they come in schools and shoals. I hope my versions here are satisfactory.

Thanks for your splendid letter—the news about Mrs. Boyd is very exciting: [1] she is a shrewd and energetic woman, and knows many people. I am glad you are letting her have proofs. I wish it were possible to give her proofs for the whole book since some of the best of it, I think, comes in the closing chapters—Ben's death, etc. It would be a grand thing if a good English publisher did it.

I am very happy at the way the proofs are coming in. I shall get today's batch off to you to-morrow, and shall return all that I get hereafter in this place before I leave. I, too, am very anxious to get the galleys corrected and see it in page-proof. If I get to Canada I shall try to wire you my address. Perhaps under these circumstances I will not go, but if I do, I will not be out of touch with the book more than a week. . . . I am glad you liked my letter—it was written on impulse and I did not think until later how busy you are, and how little time you must have now for correspondence of this sort. Your own letters lift me tremendously—I hope in some way my book will deserve the labor you have put upon it.

[1] Wheelock had written Wolfe on July 24: "Mrs. Ernest Boyd sails for Ireland to-morrow on the *Westphalia*, and I am sending her all the proof we have of your book. She plans to be in London for some time, . . . and it is our hope that she may be able to find a suitable English publisher for *Look Homeward, Angel*."

I do hope there is time for the dedication. I have one that I want very much to use.[2] If you need it now let me know. I think perhaps I may have to use one of Scribners' old envelopes for to-day's proofs.

Benjamin Cone, to whom the following letter was written, was a classmate and friend of Wolfe's at the University of North Carolina, and had written to congratulate him on his "An Angel on the Porch" in the August issue of Scribner's Magazine: *also to call his attention to the biographical note written by the editors which said that Wolfe had been educated at "a small southern college." Cone is now a director of Cone Mills Corporation, cotton textile manufacturers, in Greensboro, N.C.*

To BENJAMIN CONE

Ocean Point, Maine
Saturday, July 27, 1929

Dear Ben:

I can't tell you how happy and excited I was to get your letter. It is the first (perhaps the last) I have had about the story. I read it in front of the post office here, with the Atlantic Ocean rolling in fifty feet away. I have been staying and correcting proofs at this lonely but beautiful little place on the Maine coast for a few weeks. I am going to Canada for a week Tuesday, and I shall be back in New York the rest of August, and, I suppose, for the winter too. N.Y.U. has given me another job—and, of course, I want to see what happens to my book. . . .

Now about the editor's note and the "small southern college": if you see anyone who has also read the note, for God's sake make plain what I think you understand already—that I had nothing to do with it and didn't see it until it was published. I do not deny that I may be capable of several small offenses, such as murder, arson, highway robbery, and so on—but I do deny that I have *that* sort of snob-ism in me. Whoever wrote the note probably put in "small southern college" because he did not remember where I did go, or because, for certain reasons connected with the book, he thought it advisable not to be too explicit. And after all, Ben, back in the days when you and I were beardless striplings—"forty or fifty years ago," as Eddie Greenlaw used to say—the Hill was (praise God!) "a small southern college." I think we had almost 1000 students our

[2] The dedication of *Look Homeward, Angel* to Aline Bernstein reads: "To A. B." and is followed by the fifth stanza from John Donne's "A Valediction: Of His Name in the Window."

Freshman year, and were beginning to groan about our size. So far from forgetting the blessed place, I think my picture of it grows clearer every year: it was as close to magic as I've ever been, and now I'm afraid to go back and see how it is changed. I haven't been back since our class graduated. Great God! how time has flown, but I *am* going back within a year (if they'll let me).

Your letter is the sort of kindly, spontaneous action I really associate your name with. I have the warmest and most vivid memory of you, not only at Chapel Hill, but also several years ago in Paris. Tonight, when I got your letter, I thought of our trip to Chateau Thierry, our chartered automobile, and how we rode through the battlefields clutching a six foot loaf of French bread, a four pound Camembert cheese, and six or eight bottles of good red wine which we bought at a village *epicerie*. Frank Graham [1] of course, remained steadfast and true to the ideals of Mr. Volstead, but you and I and Mark Noble,[2] I believe, did our duty like men. I remember also a magnificent meal (catch me forgetting food!) that you and your kinsman set me up to at Prunier's, the great fish place. But most of all I remember how glad I was to see you and talk to you at that time. My play and baggage had been stolen from me (you mention this) and I was not only unhappy about this; I was a great deal more miserable than you suspected because I thought I was very much in love (one of the few times the noble passion has seized me). On second thought, I believe my romance started the day after I saw you last. I left you, I believe, New Year's Eve at the Café de la Paix, but the whole thing is all mixed together in my mind now. At any rate, I pursued a respectable Boston lady, six years my senior, around Paris for several weeks, fell sobbing on my knees before her in cafés, and did various other things that no doubt upset her. I was told at the time by friends (?) that it was not the real thing—that it was my first time in Paris, I was only a young fellow, I merely *thought* I was in love, but that did very little good. It was like being told by a Christian Scientist that you only *think* you have a belly-ache, or being assured by your lawyer, after you have been put in jail, that "they can't do this to you." I wandered around Europe for about a year after this, and what mistakes I failed to make in Paris, I managed to make

[1] Frank P. Graham had been Dean of Students and Assistant Professor of History when Wolfe was at the University of North Carolina, and was in Europe on an Amherst Memorial Fellowship in 1925. He was President of the University of North Carolina from 1930 to 1949, when he was appointed to the United States Senate, filling the office made vacant by the death of Senator J. M. Broughton.

[2] Marcus C. S. Noble graduated from the University of North Carolina in 1921, and attended Harvard in 1922 to 1924 where he received his Ed. M. and Ed. D. degrees. He is now assistant professor of Education and Psychology at the University of Rhode Island.

in various other parts of the continent before I was through. I seem to have been born a Freshman—and in many ways I'm afraid I'll continue to be one. I don't suppose you remember me very well my first year at Chapel Hill, but I made history. It was I who made the speech of acceptance when elected to the Literary Society, I took the catalogue exam, went to Chapel Saturday and let a Sophomore lead me in prayer at noon. I made half the places on the Booloo Club [3] that year, and those I didn't make, I made during that first trip abroad. Even as recently as last October I got into difficulty with some nice German people in Munich which ended in a broken nose, a head laid open by a beer stein, several days in hospital and convalescence in Oberammergau, where the fellow who plays Pilate in the Passion Play bound up my wounds. It's a long story, but a good one. I'll tell you about it some time. . . .

Hope you read the book when it comes out, Ben. Even after cutting, it is still very long—it will make 600 or 700 pages—but I hope you manage to stick it to the end. I think you will like parts of it—I hope you will like it all, but some parts, I believe, will amuse and interest you. Perhaps you will regret that I have written some things in it—there may be parts of it that seem to you to be painful and ugly—but the whole effect, I hope, will not be ugly but will (excuse my solemn air!) have beauty in it. You will understand what I mean when you read it. . . . Certainly it would distress me very much to think what I had written would cause pain to any one I have known. Of course, this doesn't apply to you. You simply may not like certain things in the book. I don't know whether it will seem to be "Victorian" or "modern" to the reader: possibly it will seem "modern" to some people, and such people are very suspicious of the word. But remember I did not try to be either one or the other. I simply made a work of fiction as all fiction must be made, not out of thin air but out of the materials of human experience. Everything that could be done to make the outlines less harsh has been done—i.e. Scribners has carefully deleted all my good Anglo-Saxon words for the sexual act, urine, and human manure. I do not see how it can shock anyone, but it may.

I have written you a very long and, I'm afraid, a very dull letter, Ben but I have done it in order to explain a very simple thing which could be explained in one short sentence if I could find the words, but I can't, the simple things being the hardest. And now I'm afraid I haven't made myself clear at all. But this is perhaps the longest letter I shall write to anyone concerning my book, and I do it for this reason: you stand as a symbol of that happy and wonderful life I knew during 1916–1920 (don't think

[3] *The Carolina Magazine* satirically describes the Booloo Club as "a group of freshmen whose wit and sharply defined personalities had singled them out for special honor by the sophomores."

from this that my present life is wretched: on the contrary, now that I am really beginning to do the work I love, it is fuller and richer than it's ever been, but I shall never forget the great days at Chapel Hill and my friends there.) Such a time will come no more. I have kept silence for years. I have lived apart from most of those friends; probably most of them have forgotten me; but I think you will believe me when I tell you most earnestly that I value the respect and friendship of some of those people as much as I value anything, with two exceptions, one of which is my work. So, no matter what you think of my book, continue to remember the person who wrote it as you always have. In writing *you* this letter I somehow feel that I am speaking to all of them, although this is, of course, a personal letter, and I trust you to treat its contents with discretion.

Now please forgive me, Ben, for this long-winded letter. Excuse its solemn tone in places, and let me hear from you when you can. It is such good news to hear that you are still single, with no hope of a change. I get so depressed when I hear that another one of the boys has been folded away with the moth-balls. Look me up when you come to New York. I am thinking of wearing false whiskers and smoked glasses after the book comes out, but if I know you are coming, I will wear a red carnation in my buttonhole.

P.S. Wouldn't it be lovely if I made some money out of the book! Are you a praying man?

To HENRY T. VOLKENING

Harvard Club
New York
Aug. 9, 1929

Dear Henry:

Please forgive me for not having written you more and oftener. I've been in Maine and Canada for several weeks. When I came back the other day I found a postcard from you, written in Switzerland. . . . I am so happy to know you have had a good trip—so anxious to see you and talk to and find what things and places we know in common (but not—dear me no!—too common). . . . Maine was lovely and cool—I was at a wild little place on the coast. I fished, corrected proofs, and read John Donne and Proust all day long. . . . I also went to Canada. Montreal is four-fifths imitation American, and one-fifth imitation English—but the beer and ale were splendidly real. Quebec was more interesting: it is entirely French-Canadian, and the people speak little or no English, and no French, either, so far as I am concerned. But this place too I found disappointing—it is like Dr. Johnson's dog walking on hind legs: "the wonder is not that he walks well, but that he walks at all." People are interested in Quebec only because it is a French town in America, and that means little to me.

I envy you everything in your trip except the hordes of tourists who are, you say, beginning to swarm around you. I note you are going to Paris; when you get this I suppose you will have been. I have heard recently that prices there are terrific—they were bad last summer—but I hear they are even worse now. Whenever I think of the French since the so-called "Great" war, I control myself and mutter "Voltaire! Voltaire!" And, after all, that is how a civilization should be judged, by its best, not by its worst—but its worst is pretty damned horrible, and unfortunately it requires superhuman fortitude and vision to see through to Ronsard when one is struggling to escape the snares of ten thousand petty rascals. Nevertheless, I have thought of France recently more than of any other country: it is physically the most comfortable and civilized of nations, and its highest and best spiritually is magnificent. The greatest evil in the national temper, I think, is "glory"—what they call "la gloire" —it accounts for the flag waving, "France has been betrayed," speech-making, singing the *Marseillaise,* going to war, etc.—it represents what is cheap and melodramatic in them. I could go on like this indefinitely, but you can hear the other side from any of the 14,000 American epic poets, novelists, dramatists, composers, and painters now in Paris—they all "understand" France, and will point out my treason. We will talk of this and many other matters when I see you.

I hope you have good weather in England—it *is* possible, and there's nothing lovelier. Are you going to the Lakes? Also, did you go to old Rosie Lewis' Cavendish Hotel on Jermyn Street? . . . she—and it—are worth seeing.

My story came out in the August *Scribner's*—also a picture of the author in the back and a brief write-up of his romantic life—how he has "a trunkful of manuscript," "writes prodigiously," "forgets all about time when writing," and "goes out at 3 a.m. for his first meal of the day." I was more madly in love with myself than ever when I read it. I had expected convulsions of the earth, falling meteors, suspension of traffic, and a general strike when the story appeared—but nothing happened. I was in Maine. Nevertheless I am still excited about it. Proofs of the book will be finished in a day or two—most of the book already in page proof. Here's a final bit of news—I can send it to you because you're so far away—the Book of the Month Club heard of the book, came to Scribners and got the proofs just when S. was going to let Literary Guild have it. All I know is that the

book has been read by the first group of readers (the mechanism of this
escapes me) given the Freshman Camp grade of A, and passed on to the
judges. No decision will be made for a week or two, but Scribners are
excited, and so am I, of course. I think there's not much hope of its being
their selection—they have pure and high-minded judges like William
Allen White and Christopher Morley—and they may find some of the
stuff too strong. Besides, I am an unknown writer and they have hundreds
of manuscripts—but if! but if! but if! *Then*, of course, I should immediately
accept the Abe Shalemonitch Chair in Anglo-Saxon Philology at N.Y.U.
and devote myself to the noble profession of teaching. But I mustn't dream
on this nebulous insanity. For heaven's sake say nothing—not even to
Lady Asquith—about this. I'll tell you what happened when you come
back.[1]

Scribners have been magnificent—their best people have worked like
dogs on the thing—they believe in me and the book. To have found a firm
and association with men like this is a miracle of good luck. . . . As for
myself, I tremble now that the thing's done—I loathe the idea of giving
pain; it never occurred to me as I wrote; it is a complete piece of fiction
but made, as all fiction must be, from the stuff of human experience. . . .
This too is a complicated thing about which I shall talk to you.

I am aching with a new one [2]—it's got to come out of me. I loathe the
idea of not writing it, and I loathe the idea of writing it—I am lazy,
and doing a book is agony—60 cigarettes a day, 20 cups of coffee, miles
of walking and flinging about, nightmares, nerves, madness—there are
better ways, but this, God help me, is mine.

This is a long stupid letter—forgive me. I have talked only about myself: I think of you and Natalie often, there are so many places I want to
tell you to go to—it is hot, past midnight, and I am worn out. Naturally
I'm absorbed in my own affair at present—say a spell for my fortune and
good luck and God bless you both. Go to the lakes, look up the folks at the
Royal Oak in Ambleside, tell me about it. Please let me know when you
get back. How I wish I could be with you just for a morning walk and a
bottle of ale.

Find an Englishman and make him *walk* you through the old *City* of
London. If he has sense—and *some* have!—he'll know where to go and
what to do. It is in many ways the grandest city in the world.

[1] Neither the Book of the Month Club nor the Literary Guild adopted *Look Homeward, Angel* or any of Wolfe's books.
[2] *The October Fair* of which the first half was published as *Of Time and the River*.

The publication of "An Angel on the Porch" in the August issue of Scribner's Magazine *had given Asheville people their first inkling of what* Look Homeward, Angel *was to be about. Wolfe's letter of August 11, 1929, to Mrs. Roberts was written in reply to one from her which is now lost but which evidently expressed grave concern about what Wolfe had written and the effect it would have upon his family.*

To MARGARET ROBERTS

Harvard Club
New York

Sunday, August 11, 1929

Dear Mrs. Roberts:

I have been away in Maine and Canada on a vacation and I came back to New York only two or three days ago. . . . I found your letter here when I came back. As usual, everything you say touches and moves me deeply. I wish my work deserved half of the good things you say about it: I hope that some day it will. The knowledge that you have always believed in me is one of the grandest possessions of my life. I hope it may be some slight return for your affection and faith to know that I have always believed in you; first, as a child, with an utterly implicit faith and hope, and later, as a man, with a no less steadfast trust. Life does not offer many friendships of which one can say this. I know how few there are, and yet my own life has been full of love and loyalty for whoever understood or valued it.

In your letter you say that many facts in my life you never knew about when I was a child—that much about me you did not understand until later. This does not come from lack of understanding: it comes because you are one of the high people of the earth, with as little of the earth in you as anyone I have ever known—your understanding is for the flame, the spirit, the glory—and in this faith you are profoundly right. It is a grand quality to see only with that vision which sees the highest and rarest. All that you did not see caused me great unrest of spirit as a child when I thought of you, and perhaps more now.

I hope you may be wrong in thinking what I have written may distress members of my family, or anyone else. Certainly, I would do anything to avoid causing anyone pain—except to destroy the fundamental substance of my book. I am afraid, however, that if anyone is distressed by what seemed to me a very simple and unoffending story,[1] their feeling when the book comes out will be much stronger. And the thought of that distresses *me* more than I can tell you. Nothing, however, may now be done

[1] "An Angel on the Porch."

about this. Everything that could reasonably be done to soften impressions that might needlessly wound any reader has been done by my publishers and me. Now, the only apology I have to make for my book is that it is not better—and by "better" I mean that it does not represent by any means the best that is in me. But I hope I shall feel this way about my work for many years to come, although there is much in this first book about which I hope I shall continue to feel affection and pride.

A thousand words leap to my tongue—words of explanation, persuasion, and faith—but they had better rest unsaid. Silence is best. More and more I know that the grievous and complex web of human relationship may not be solved by words. However our motives or our acts may be judged or misjudged, our works must speak for us, and we can ultimately only trust to the belief of other men that we are of good will. I can not explain the creative act here. That has been done much better than I could hope to do it, by other people. I can only assure you that my book is a work of fiction, and that no person, act, or event has been deliberately and consciously described. The creative spirit hates pain more, perhaps, than it does anything else on earth, and it is not likely it should try to inflict on other people what it loathes itself. Certainly the artist is not a traducer or libeler of mankind—his main concern when he creates is to give his creation life, form, beauty. This dominates him, and it is doubtful if he thinks very much of the effect his work will have on given persons, although he may think of its effect on a general public. But I think you know that fiction is not spun out of the air; it is made from the solid stuff of human experience—any other way is unthinkable.

Dr. Johnson said a man would turn over half a library to make a single book; so may a novelist turn over half a town to make a single figure in his novel. This is not the only method but it illustrates, I believe, the whole method. The world a writer creates is his own world—but it is molded out of the fabric of life, what he has known and felt—in short, out of himself.[2] How in God's name can it be otherwise? This is all I can say—I think you will understand it. Having said this, I can but add that at the last ditch, the writer must say this: "I have tried only to do a good piece of work. I have not wished nor intended to hurt anyone. Now I can go no farther. I will not destroy nor mutilate my work, it represents what is best and deepest in me, and I shall stand by it and defend it even if the whole world would turn against me." That, it seems to me, is the only answer he can make. Perhaps there are two sides to this question but this, at any rate, is my side, and the one I believe in with all my heart.

And now forgive me, please, for so long and dull a letter. It is late at

[2] This passage has a marked similarity to Wolfe's note "To the Reader" at the beginning of *Look Homeward, Angel.*

night, the weather is hot and enervating, and I am tired. But I hope I
have been able to make clear what I feel about the book. . . . I hope this
finds you all well and happy. Give my love to all, and forgive me for
having again written about only my own affairs.

To GEORGE W. McCOY

Harvard Club
New York
Saturday, Aug. 17, 1929

Dear George:

Thanks very much for your note, and for your fine story about me which
you enclosed.[1] I like to think that the story was of some news-interest to
people in Asheville, but the warm and friendly temper that runs through
it was not, I know, wholly professional. For that I must thank the spontaneous and unselfish good will that I always join with your name, and I
thank you not only for writing me up, but also because you have been a
generous friend.

What you said about my Asheville friends being "numbered by the
score" touched me most of all. I think you will believe me when I tell you
I value the respect and friendship of no group of people more than that of
the people in the town where I was born, and where a large part of my
life has been passed. I earnestly hope I may always keep it. It would only
be stupid to deny that a young man is indifferent to the commendation of
people he likes: he is, on the contrary, eager for it, and one of the great
impulses of the creative act may come from a source as simple as this one.

I wish I could imitate your admirable brevity. I intended to write you
a short note, but this will probably go to five or six pages. A newspaper
would give me the sack in twenty-four hours—the murderer would be in
Canada before I finished describing where the body was found. But you
are getting off much easier than the folks at Scribners—my manuscript
when first submitted was a dainty trifle of 330,000 words (not 250,000 as
the blurb in the magazine had it). When they accepted the book the publishers told me to get busy with my little hatchet and carve off some 100,000
words. I had just come back from Italy with twenty-seven cents, but with
Scribners advance money in my pocket I was naturally full of life and
hope. I did get busy, and in a month or two had cut out twenty or thirty

[1] A piece by McCoy in the July 26, 1929 *Asheville Citizen* captioned "Asheville
Man Is New Author," and beginning: "Thomas Wolfe's Asheville friends, and they
are numbered by the score, will be much interested to learn that the August fiction
number of *Scribner's Magazine* carries his first published short story entitled 'An
Angel on the Porch.'"

thousand words, and added fifty thousand more. The editors then felt it was time to intervene: they restrained me, and helped me in every way with criticism, editing, and a vast amount of patient, careful work. They have been magnificent—I have not time or space to tell you how fine they have been—and now we have a book which can be read without demanding a six months' leave of absence.

A year ago, when I finished with the book and looked at the truck-load of typed pages, I never thought it possible that I should have such good fortune; an association with such a house and such men. But miracles *do* happen: in fact, I am coming to believe they *always* happen: no matter what success (or failure) this book has, my publishers will print the next one. I am already at work on it,[2] and hope, of course, to do a better one than the first. The publishers believe in me and in my book. I am profoundly grateful for all they have done, and hope, not only for my sake but for theirs, that we shall have some success.

Please forgive me for writing you at such length: my book is only one out of the vast number that are being printed all the time, but I can't help being happy and excited—it has happened to others, but it's the first time it has happened to me.

I finished the last set of galley proof to-day: it has been a long and tedious job, but my work on this book is practically done. All I can do now is remember all the prayers I ever heard. There are still several mechanical stages—page proofs, foundry proofs, and so on (no one who has not seen it would ever believe the amount of work that goes into printing a book)—but the people at Scribners will do most of the work now.

I think it is scheduled for release in September or October, but I can't be sure yet. I suppose the publishers send copies to reviewers (I'm still pretty green about this business): I shall ask them Monday, and have them send you one for reviewing, if this is the system. If not, I suppose they give the author a few copies, and I'll send you one of mine. I am very grateful for all the interest you have taken in my work: one of the pleasantest things I have found in the world, among a number of unpleasant ones, is that there is almost no limit to the loyal belief of old friends. The hardest thing is trying to live up to half the things they say about you, but that's a job we can work at with all our heart. So I hope you will not be disappointed in my book or in me. Of course, George, it may be a terrible flop (many or most books are) but if we can have only a modest success, that will perhaps be enough for a fellow who tries to fill a five foot shelf with his first one.

[2] *The October Fair,* of which the first half was published as *Of Time and the River.*

Thanks also for the splendid write-up of Billy Cocke.[3] I am delighted to hear of his success, but, of course, not surprised. I saw him a few years ago when I was staying at Oxford for several weeks: I knew then he would get along there and everywhere else. It is good to know he has made a connection with such a distinguished firm, and that he will be near me here in New York. There is perhaps a selfish motive in my interest —if I get put in jail for writing one of my books, I shall probably need at least an Oxford lawyer to get me out, and there is no one to whom I would trust my defense with greater confidence than Billy.

I hope to get home for a few days early in September. If I do, I want to talk to you about your plans, and mine. Thanks again for your story. Write me a few lines if you have time. My best wishes for your health and success go with this letter.

If there is any news about the book that I think you will be interested in, I'll send it on to you. Do you still work until half past three in the morning? If you do, we'll probably talk until the milk wagons come by—it's the time of day I like best for work or conversation. I used to carry *Citizens,* you know, and probably got the habit then. I've chewed many a doughnut at the Greasy Spoon at four A.M.

The following letter was written to John Hall Wheelock upon his presentation to Wolfe of a copy of his book of poems, The Bright Doom, *with the inscription: "For Thomas Wolfe—in friendship and admiration."*

To JOHN HALL WHEELOCK

[27 West 15th Street]
[New York City]
[Late August, 1929]

Dear Mr. Wheelock:

I like to write, rather than to speak, the things I feel and believe most deeply: I think I can say them more clearly that way, and keep them better.

In the last few months, when I have come to know you, I have observed again and again the seriousness with which you would deliberate even the

---

[3] William Cocke, a childhood friend of Wolfe's from Asheville, had joined the law firm of Messrs. Root, Clark, Buckner and Ballantine in New York City. He was an associate in that firm for a little more than a year before establishing his own practice in Asheville.

smallest changes in my book. As time went on, I saw that this slow and patient care came from the grand integrity of your soul. Consequently, when you presented me with a book of your poems on the day when we had finished our work together on my novel, this simple act was invested with an importance and emotion which I can not describe to you now— every one of the subtle and rich associations of your character went with that book of poems; I was profoundly moved, profoundly grateful, and I knew that I would treasure this book as long as I live.

When I got out on the street, I opened it and read your inscription to me and the magnificent lines that follow it. In this inscription you speak of me as your friend. I am filled with pride and joy that you should say so. I am honored in knowing you, I am honored in having you call me friend, I am exalted and lifted up by every word of trust and commendation you have ever spoken to me.

You are a true poet: you have looked upon the terrible face of patience, and the quality of enduring and waiting shines in every line you have written. The poets who are dead have given me life; when I have faltered I have seized upon their strength. Now I have by me living poetry and a living poet, and in his patience and in his strong soul I shall often abide.

I have now read all the poems in your book—I think I have read them all several times. But true poetry is a rich and difficult thing—we invade it slowly, and slowly it becomes a part of us. I have read few books as often as three or four times, but there are poems I have read three or four hundred times. I do not presume therefore to offer you a glib criticism of poems I shall read many times more, and I do not presume to think you would be seriously interested in my feeling. But there are some of your poems that are already communicated to me—I dare to say entirely—and that have become a part of the rich deposit of my life.

I wish to say that "Meditation" seems to me one of the finest modern poems I have ever read—*modern* only in being written by a man now living. When I read this poem, I had that moment of discovery which tells us plainly that we have gained something precious—it has now become a part of me, it is mixed with me, and some day, in some unconscious but not wholly unworthy plagiary, it will come from me again woven into my own fabric.

[THE LETTER BREAKS OFF HERE]

The following postcard was written to Maxwell Perkins from Asheville where Wolfe had gone for a two weeks' visit before the opening of the fall term at New York University.

To MAXWELL E. PERKINS

[Penny Postcard]

Asheville, N.C.
Sept 14, 1929

Dear Mr Perkins: I have had a very remarkable visit down here—the town is full of kindness and good will and rooting and boosting for the book. My family knows what it's all about, and I think is pleased about it— and also a little apprehensive. We get one another crazy—I've been here a week and I'm about ready for a padded cell. But no one's to blame. It's a strange situation, and God knows what will happen. I'll be glad when its over. Hope to see you next week in New York.

To GEORGE W. McCOY

Harvard Club
New York
Wednesday, Oct. 16, 1929.

Dear George:

Thanks for your fine letter. I am sincerely grateful for all that you have said and done. I know you understand my deep sense of obligation to you all. It is splendid to know that you and Lola will review my book,[1] and that Rodney Crowther [2] will talk about it over the radio. I can add nothing to what I have already told you, except to repeat that you have all been fine and generous, and that I know you understand and believe in the author, no matter what effect the book may have.

I have a bit of news which must not, however, be made public: they told me at Scribners yesterday that the advance sale of the book, not counting New York, is over 1600 copies, and one of the salesmen at Doubleday Doran told the advertising man that the book would be "the Fall sensation," whatever that may mean. All this is too marvelous— miraculous—the *last* I mean—to be probable. Thomas Beer, the writer, phoned Scribners last week that I was the best young writer who had emerged since Glenway Wescott wrote "The Grandmothers" (although why Wescott I don't know). Finally, my agent, Mrs. Boyd, who is abroad,

---

[1] The original plan for McCoy and his fiancée Lola Love to review *Look Homeward, Angel* together was later changed, and Miss Love reviewed it alone in the Sunday, October 20, 1929, *Asheville Citizen.*

[2] Rodney Crowther reviewed *Look Homeward, Angel* over Radio Station WWNC on October 21.

cabled Scribners that two English publishers, Cape and Heinemann, want the book for England. But for God's sake say nothing of all this!

It comes out day after to-morrow, and my nerves are ragged. Scribners are magnificent and want me to get busy at once on a new one. This I've already done, but much too excited to work at present. The new one will be better—I've many more books in me.

If I could, I should like nothing more than seeing your wedding. As it is, I shall think of you, and send you both my deepest affection. . . . Give my warmest regards to Lola. You know how I feel about you both. Thank Rodney Crowther for me and tell him I'll write him next week. Excuse this idiotic letter—I think you know how I feel at present.

To MARGARET ROBERTS

Harvard Club
New York

October 17, 1929

Dear Mrs. Roberts:

I sent you a copy of my book the other day. I hope it arrived safely. In it I wrote a few words which I ask you to accept as a sincere expression of the writer's feeling toward you.[1]

My book is published to-morrow. Nobody knows whether it will survive the avalanche of books that are being published at this season, or not: but we all hope for the best luck. Naturally I am tremendously excited about it.

I can not add anything here to what I told you when I was at home: I have tried to do a good and honest piece of work, and I hope that my friends like it. I shall be sorry if they do not like it, but I shall go on in the hope of writing something someday that may be worthy of their praise. I think I can not say more than this.

I send to you all my warmest and most affectionate regards. I shall write you a letter later, after I know more about the fate of my book.

With hope, and with love,

To GEORGE WALLACE

New York

October 25 (?), 1929.

Dear George:

Thanks for your fine letter, for your generous efforts, and simply for

[1] "To Margaret Roberts, who was the Mother of my Spirit, I present this copy of my first book, with hope and with devotion."

writing. I don't know whether I told you in my last that the book had been sold in England—Heinemann is publishing there and is sending me 100 pounds advance. The book is having a good sale in New York, although there have been no reviews yet—several booksellers, including the famous Holliday,[1] are recommending it. There will be a review in the *New York Times* on Sunday, I believe. Whether it's good or bad I can't say, but if it's good and you can do a little telling work with it, so much the better.[2] Also, there will be a review in the *Scribner's Magazine* for December, I believe, (out in November). People have told me about it—reviewer says I must be put with Whitman and Melville.[3] Hot stuff, eh? And Scribners, the publishers, insist they have nothing to do with it—that it's all straight shooting—and they've never lied yet.

Only reviews I've had are from North Carolina and, Boy! they are blowing off steam. All of them panegyrical about the writing, say it's thrilling novel, etc., but two or three say it's an insult to the state and the people, that "the worst side of people" is exposed, etc. Josephus Daniels' *Raleigh News and Observer* says the South and North Carolina "have been spat upon." [4] I am really distressed about it! In the first place, I never mentioned North Carolina, and it has never occurred to anyone up here that I was writing about either N.C. or the South—least of all to the author. Everyone thought the book was about *people*—who might have lived anywhere—and so far as their "worst side" is concerned, Scribners think them rich, magnificent and grand folks. What am I to do! I shall do nothing, say nothing. The book has many many different things and people in it, but we think its total effect is one of beauty. (Please forgive the personal bouquet!)

[1] Terence Holliday of The Holliday Book Shop.

[2] Wallace was a friend of one of the editors of the *Boston Evening Transcript*. Perhaps this was what Wolfe had in mind, or perhaps he simply thought that because Wallace was "an advertising man" he could "spread the news around" about the book.

[3] Robert Raynolds's review of *Look Homeward, Angel* in the December *Scribner's* said: "If we were to label Wolfe, we would put him with Melville and Whitman, although he has not the dramatic intensity and the perfection of epithet we find in *Moby Dick*, nor the grave purity incandescent in *Leaves of Grass*. But *Look Homeward, Angel* is a first book."

[4] *Look Homeward, Angel* was reviewed in the October 20, 1929, issue of the *Raleigh News and Observer* by Jonathan Daniels, who had known Wolfe at the University of North Carolina. The review was headlined "Wolfe's First Is Novel of Revolt. Former Asheville Writer Turns in Fury Upon North Carolina and the South," and said: "Against the Victorian morality and the Bourbon aristocracy of the South, he has turned in all his fury, and the result is not a book that will please the South in general and North Carolina in particular. Here is a young man, hurt by something that he loved, turning in his sensitive fury and spitting on that thing. In *Look Homeward, Angel*, North Carolina and the South are spat upon."

At any rate, as soon as I see what's what and get these nerves screwed down again, I'm going on with the new one.

Scribners do not want to have my book "Banned in Boston"—they are a very fine and dignified firm, and did not like the Hemingway ban,[5] although it helped the sale of the book. But—this is between *us*—if it does get banned, I hope it makes a loud noise—for God's sake try to get some publicity out of it for me.

During all this palpitating time I've got to teach school as usual and grade Freshman papers. God! the torture of it!

Give my love to Mrs. W. and the boys. Let me hear soon. Thanks for your noble efforts. In spite of my incoherence, they are deeply appreciated.

Scribners think it's a *swell* book, George—I can't tell you how much. And Thomas Beer has given it (and me) a blast that lifted my hair!

Write to me—tell me how to be *calm*.

The brief note below was written in reply to a letter from Mark Schorer praising Look Homeward, Angel *in the highest terms. Schorer is now Professor of English at the University of California, and the author of* A House Too Old, The Hermit Place, The State of Mind, William Blake: The Politics of Vision, The Wars of Love, *etc.*

To MARK SCHORER

27 West 15th Street
New York City
October 25, 1929

Dear Mr. Schorer:

Your letter about my book is the first I have had from a stranger, although I have had several from friends.

I am moved and honored by what you say about the book. It is quite a grand thing to know that what one has written has leaped across the dark, and made a light, a friend. I hope, naturally, that I shall have other letters from people who like the book, but I shall always place a particular value on yours because it was the first.

[5] The June and July, 1929, issues of *Scribner's Magazine* had been banned in Boston because of the portions of Hemingway's *Farewell to Arms* published in them.

Margaret Wallace's review of Look Homeward, Angel *in the Sunday October 27 New York Times was the first major review to be published, and one of the most favorable. Upon reading it, Wolfe immediately wrote her the following note of thanks.*

To   MARGARET WALLACE

27 West 15th Street
New York City
October 27, 1929.

Dear Miss Wallace:

I want to thank you for your splendid review of my book in to-day's *Times*. I am moved and honored by what you say—it is my first book, and it is a grand thing to know it has been valued so patiently and so highly. The people at Scribners were very happy about your review: they feel now that the book has a good chance of commercial success—which would also mean a great deal to me. If this is true, I know that you have contributed a great deal to it.

But even if the book should never sell another copy, I shall never forget what you wrote about it. I shall always feel that something I wrote made its way out into the great jungle of the world, and found a friend there. A thing like this pays for all the pain and despair of writing.

The following night letter was sent by Wolfe to his sister Mabel upon receiving a letter from her describing the furor which publication of Look Homeward, Angel *had caused in Asheville.*

To MABEL WOLFE WHEATON
[Night Letter]

New York City
October 28, 1929

Thanks for wonderful letter. Great figures in novel are Eliza, Helen, Gant and Ben. Everyone here thinks they are grand people. No book should be read as gossip nor judged in isolated passages. When the book and leading characters are judged as a whole they are seen to be fine people. Read *New York Times* review for last Sunday, also *Herald Tribune* for next Sunday or week after.[1] No matter what Asheville thinks now, they will

[1] *Look Homeward, Angel* was very favorably reviewed by Margery Latimer in the Sunday, November 3, 1929, *New York Herald Tribune*.

understand in time that I tried to write moving, honest book about great people. That is the way the world outside Asheville is taking it. Tell Mama this and say I am writing in day or so. If you doubt what I say, read over chapter on Ben's death and burial scenes that follow. Then ask if anyone dares say these are not great people. Book selling fast. Looks like success but say nothing. You are a great person. Love,

Robert Norwood, to whom the following note was written, was pastor of St. Bartholomew's Church in New York, and the author of Issa, The Steep Ascent, The Man Who Dared to be God, *etc. On October 26, 1929, he had written to John Hall Wheelock: "I am reading* Look Homeward, Angel. *It is a remarkable book, not far from* The Brothers Karamazov. *It is an epic rather than a novel, and poetry more than prose. Thus far I have the feeling of an archangel with broken wings trying to regain the heights he has lost— the anguished cry of a disappointed idealist." Wheelock had introduced Wolfe to Norwood soon afterwards.*

To ROBERT NORWOOD

27 West 15th Street
New York City
November 15, 1929

Dear Dr. Norwood:

I want to thank you for the very wonderful two or three hours I spent with you the other day. And I want also to thank you for what you said about my book. It is quite a grand thing to know that something one has written has gone out into the world and made such a friend and been so generously valued.

I am honored and moved by all you said about it. Even if the book had no further sale, it would be a great deal to know that you feel about it as you do.

I look forward to seeing you again.

To ALBERT COATES

27 West 15th St
New York City
Nov 19, 1929.

Dear Albert:

Your name on a letter gave me a tremendous thrill. Neither of us, I'm afraid, is a very steady correspondent, but if I had written to you every time I thought about you these last 6 years, you would have a trunk full of my letters now.

You will certainly not pay $3.00 for any book I write (or $2.50 either) if I can be on hand to prevent it. . . . You should receive in a few days a copy of my book from Charles Scribner's Sons, handsomely inscribed with a touching sentiment (which I have not thought out yet). If you do not get it let me know. . . .

I was glad and happy to hear from you, Albert. I think you will believe me when I tell you that you are one of my old friends that I think of very often, and whose friendship I value very highly. I am very anxious to have you read my book and to hear from you about it. The book has caused me a great deal of joy and pain—pain because some people in the South and in my home town have read it as an almanac of personal gossip, and have construed it as a cruel and merciless attack on actual persons, some now living. I have had several bitter letters and one or two pretty ugly anonymous ones (one of them beginning in a proud dignified manner as follows: "Sir: You are a son-of-a-bitch, etc.") On the other hand, I have had magnificent letters, not only from strangers, but also from old friends. And the reviewers in New York and other cities have said some very magnificent things about it and I understand that literary folks in New York are quite excited about it. . . .

For God's sake, Albert, read the book as it was meant to be read—as a book, the writer's vision of life: you will find some things in it very naked, very direct, and perhaps very terrible—but the book was written in innocence and honesty of spirit,[1] and the people here do not feel that it is terrible or ugly, but that it is perhaps grand and beautiful. Excuse me for saying all this—it sounds like boasting—but I want my old friends to understand what I have done. But I know that I can depend on your fairness and intelligence. . . .

I can not write any more now, but I will later. I still work at N.Y.U. but I hope the book may sell enough to release me from grading Freshman papers. I want to finish a new book.

This is written in great haste, but I hope you can make it out. Let me hear from you soon. With warmest regards,

The following "My Record as a Writer" and "Plans for Work" were submitted with Wolfe's application for a Guggenheim Fellowship. If there was a covering letter making definite application for the fellowship, it has been lost.

[1] Here again Wolfe is repeating almost verbatim what he said in his note "To the Reader" at the beginning of *Look Homeward, Angel*.

To THE JOHN SIMON GUGGENHEIM MEMORIAL FOUNDATION

[27 West 15th Street]
[New York]
[December 16(?), 1929]

My Record as a Writer

I have written since I was twelve or fourteen years old. In preparatory school I wrote essays, poems and stories. During my Freshman year in college I began to write more formally. I wrote for the college paper and magazine and humorous publications: [1] later I became editor of the college newspaper, *The Tar Heel,* and associate editor of the other publications. In my junior year, I met Professor Frederick H. Koch, who had come to North Carolina that year, and who was organizing the Carolina Playmakers. I wrote little one-act plays for him and had two or three of them produced by the Playmakers. [2] One of these was later published in a volume of Playmaker plays published by Henry Holt. [3] It was called "The Return of Buck Gavin." It was written when I was seventeen years old. I mention this play because it was my first work to be published in book form, although many things had been published in college publications. I was at this time young and lazy; I scribbled constantly and at random; I had not learned to work, and what I wrote did not represent the best in me.

After my graduation from North Carolina in 1920, I went to Harvard with the intention of staying one year. I stayed three years; I took courses; I read a great deal and I wrote some plays for Professor Baker and his "47 Workshop," of which I was a member. Two of these plays, a short one and a long one, were produced by the Workshop. The long one, "Welcome to Our City," caused a good deal of excitement and many people thought I had a future as a dramatist. I came to New York with these plays, believing they might be produced here. "Welcome to Our City" was seriously considered by two theatres [4]—one asked me to "cut" it since it was an hour too long. This I tried to do, but made it longer.

Two or three years had passed since I came to New York and the conviction was growing on me that I would never write plays. I had begun quite by accident at North Carolina, and continued by chance at Harvard.

[1] *The Tar Heel, The Carolina Magazine* and *The Tar Baby.*
[2] The two that were actually produced were *The Return of Buck Gavin* and *The Third Night,* but Wolfe wrote others, such as *Deferred Payment* and *Concerning Honest Bob* which were published in *The Carolina Magazine.*
[3] *Carolina Folk Plays: Second Series.*
[4] The Theatre Guild and The Neighborhood Playhouse.

I loved the theatre, but I began to see I had to find a medium where I could satisfy my desire for fullness, intensity and completeness. I could never do this in the theatre, and my creative sense was troubled further by knowing what I did would be touched and reshaped by a hundred different people—directors, actors, designers, carpenters, electricians. What I did had to be my own.

During these four or five years I had been teaching at New York University. When I had a vacation, I took what money remained from my teaching, borrowed more, if possible, and went to Europe. Once I stayed a year, and other times six or eight months. I was quite unhappy about my writing—nothing I did ever saw the light of day. I wrote at random, but all the time. When I had finished something, a powerful inertia settled upon me—I would not show what I had written to anyone; I would not send it out for publication; I did not know what to do or how to go about it. Meanwhile I was teaching in America and wandering alone, from place to place, in Europe. Three years ago I began to write my book in London. I went down to the Chelsea district, rented two rooms in a lodging house and began to work. I was alone, and my writing came as a culmination of years of wandering back and forth in Europe and America. My first book dealt with experiences observed during the first twenty years of my life, but its theme was that all men are alone and strangers and never come to know one another. I worked hard on the book in London and Oxford during the Autumn: the first of the year I came back to New York. I rented a garret in an old deserted building on Eighth Street. It had been used as a sweatshop; there was no heat and no plumbing. I worked there for seven months and did the largest part of my book there. For the first time I put all my effort and time into writing. I worked between twelve and six in the morning, and slept in the daytime. I mention these facts not to give a romantic flavor to this statement, but because they are a true and honest account of what happened, and because I am proud to know I had such devotion and loyalty to my work.

After seven months of work in this place, I was very tired. I went to Europe that summer. When I came back, I went to work at the University again. That year I finished my book, working at night. When I had finished it, all the doubt, disbelief and hopelessness that I had not been able to feel for long while working, welled up: the manuscript was over 1200 typed pages—about five times the length of an average novel. I did not believe it would ever find a publisher.

It was the end of the teaching year: I was worn out and had no further hopes for my writing. I took what money was left from teaching and went to Europe again. I wandered about for four or five months. Meanwhile a friend had given the manuscript of my book to Ernest Boyd, the critic.

Ernest Boyd turned it over to his wife, Madeleine, who now acts as my literary agent. When I was in Vienna last year, in November, I got a letter from Mrs. Boyd, and shortly thereafter one from Mr. Maxwell Perkins of Scribners. It was a very wonderful letter: when I got back from Italy the first of the year, I went to see him. He said the book was too long, but that Scribners would publish it if it was cut to a more suitable length. In the next few months we cut out over 100,000 words, and the book was published in its present form in October, 1929, under the title "Look Homeward, Angel."

The book has had, I understand, an unusual success for a first novel. People have told me it has had the best reviews of any first novel in several years. But what sale it will have, no one can at present say. I am teaching again this year at New York University. I find it increasingly difficult to grade papers and get on with my new book. I need money desperately. My publishers have been fine, courageous and generous: they believe in me and are willing to help all they can, but I have no right to impose further on their generosity. It must in honesty be said that the commercial success of my first book is still in doubt. At present, it has not earned enough to keep me going while I finish my new one. For this reason I am appealing to the Guggenheim Foundation.

Plans for Work

My new novel will be ready in the Spring or Autumn of 1931. Its title is "The October Fair." I cannot outline its plan and purpose so exactly as a scientist could his course of study: the book has a great many things in it but its dominant theme is again related to the theme of the first: it tries to find out why Americans are a nomad race (as this writer believes); why they are touched with a powerful and obscure homesickness wherever they go, both at home and abroad; why thousands of the young men, like this writer, have prowled over Europe, looking for a door, a happy land, a home, seeking for something they have lost, perhaps racial and forgotten; and why they return here; or if they do not, carry on them the mark of exile and obscure longing. This is a hasty statement, but I hope it indicates a theme, or an emotion and experience, which this writer believes in passionately, because he has felt and experienced it with all his heart. It seems to him, further, to be a very living and a very national theme.

The writer did not receive the application blanks for the Guggenheim Fellowship until the last few days: this statement has therefore been very hastily written. The writer hopes, however, he has been able to justify his application for a Fellowship.

To MAXWELL E. PERKINS

Harvard Club
New York
Dec 24, 1929

Dear Mr. Perkins:

One year ago I had little hope for my work, and I did not know you. What has happened since may seem to be only a modest success to many people; but to me it is touched with strangeness and wonder. It is a miracle.

You are now mixed with my book in such a way that I can never separate the two of you. I can no longer think clearly of the time I wrote it, but rather of the time when you first talked to me about it, and when you worked upon it. My mind has always seen people more clearly than events or things—the name "Scribners" naturally makes a warm glow in my heart, but you are chiefly "Scribners" to me: you have done what I had ceased to believe one person could do for another—you have created liberty and hope for me.

Young men sometimes believe in the existence of heroic figures, stronger and wiser than themselves, to whom they can turn for an answer to all their vexation and grief. Later, they must discover that such answers have to come out of their own hearts; but the powerful desire to believe in such figures persists. You are for me such a figure: you are one of the rocks to which my life is anchored.

I have taken the publication of my first book very hard—all the happy and successful part of it as well as the unhappy part: a great deal of the glory and joy and glamour with which in my fantasy I surrounded such an event has vanished. But, as usual, life and reality supplant the imaginary thing with another glory that is finer and more substantial than the visionary one.

I should have counted this past year a great one, if it had allowed me only to know about you. I am honored to think I may call you my friend, and I wish to send to you on Christmas Day this statement of my loyal affection.

VI

FRANCE, SWITZERLAND, AND THE BEGINNING OF OF TIME AND THE RIVER AND THE OCTOBER FAIR

1930

To MABEL WOLFE WHEATON

Harvard Club
New York
Jan. 5, 1930

Dear Mabel:

The long letter I have promised to write you never gets done. If you knew what the last two or three months have been like you'd know why. People have almost driven me mad—the telephone rings twenty times a day, and it's someone I don't know, or don't want to know, or met once, or who knows someone who knows me. In addition, I get dozens of letters— invitations to speak, dine, write. I have all my papers to grade with examinations coming on, and Scribners keep phoning me every day for a story for the magazine. The only relief is that Scribners is now going to pay me a modest sum of money each month to live on,[1] and I am stopping

---

[1] On December 18, 1929, Perkins had written Wolfe a letter saying: "We are deeply interested in your writing and have confidence in your future, and we wish to cooperate with you so far as possible toward the production of a new novel. . . . We should be glad to undertake to pay you, as an advance on the earnings of the next novel, forty-five hundred dollars in installments, at the rate of two hundred and fifty dollars a month, beginning with February 1st." Scribners accordingly made these payments for the months of February through May, 1930. By then, Wolfe had received his Guggenheim Fellowship, and *Look Homeward, Angel* had earned royalties amounting to $3,500 in excess of the $500 advance already paid on it. Therefore, the monthly payments against the new novel were discontinued until June 21, 1933, when Wolfe began drawing irregular amounts against that book.

teaching in February. I must get to work immediately on my new book, but if people don't leave me alone, I'll have to go away somewhere. All I want is a little peace and freedom to work—if they will all buy my book, well and good, but let them leave me alone. I don't want to leave America, but some people are urging me to go to Europe to live where I can at least not be disturbed. The English publisher [2] is here, and has me at work making certain cuts in the book. The English are enthusiastic—say the people are wonderful and real Anglo-Saxons that the English understand—and that the book will go well in England. It's coming out there in March.[3]

I have had two or three hundred letters from all over the country. How in God's name I'll answer them I can't say. The whole business had me so stirred up that I caved in with cold and flu a week or two ago, and am just pulling out.

I get letters and cards and phone calls from Asheville people from time to time. I want to tell you that no one has been more surprised by the effect my book has had on some people than I have. I live in my own world: I go about looking, seeing, studying, observing, but the world I create is my own. I understand that several hundred copies of the book were sold in Asheville. That is far too many. Please understand that I am not trying to be "snooty" or "highbrow"—I have the greatest respect and liking for many, many people at home—but my book is not a book that every realtor, attorney, druggist, or grocer should read. They should stick to *Collier's* and *The American* and *The S.E.P.* There are perhaps two dozen people at home who might read my book and know what it's about. And please understand this is not to say a word of criticism of many other people whom I like, but who read perhaps one or two books a year, and who try to make my book a piece of local history. If they think my book is obscene, bitter, sensational etc., let them stick to Warwick Deeping and Zane Grey.

You, at least, know what I have in my heart: to create before I die something that is as honest, grand and beautiful as I can make it. If anyone thinks my first book is ugly and filthy, and can see no beauty or good in it, I am sorry; but I shall go on with my next as well as I can, and try to make it as good as I can. One man in Asheville wrote in to Scribners saying that the rumor was Wolfe had said he had wanted to cut certain parts of the book, but that Scribners had insisted they be left in so that the book would make a lot of money. To think that any damned fool couldn't

[2] A. S. Frere-Reeves, the editor of William Heinemann Ltd. who was most closely concerned with Wolfe's books. He is now Chairman of the Board of Directors of that house, and known simply as A. S. Frere.

[3] It actually did not come out until July 14.

see that this book was not written for money—that if I'd wanted money I'd have written something one third as long, full of the soothing syrup most of them want. We are all pleased here with the success the book has had—with the wonderful reviews, and also with the sale—but nobody is going to get rich off the book: there are hundreds of hack writers who make far more than I will make, and if money is my object, I could make far more out of advertising or something else than I can ever make out of writing.

Doesn't it mean anything to people at home to know that honest and intelligent critics all over the country have thought my book a fine and moving one? Surely there are people there who are fair and generous enough to see that I am trying to be an artist, and that I am not a sensational hack. Does anyone seriously think that a man is going to sweat blood, lose flesh, go cold and dirty, work all night, and live in a sweatshop garret for almost two years as I did, if his sole purpose is to say something mean about Smith and Jones and Brown? Listen, Mabel: what my book says in the first paragraph and what it continues to say on every page to the end is that men are strangers, that they are lonely and forsaken, that they are in exile on this earth, that they are born, live, and die alone. I began to write that book in London: it is as true of people in London and Idaho as of people in Asheville. You say that women in clubs have called you up and lectured you or sympathized with you. Very well, let them. You are bigger than any of them and they cannot hurt you. I suppose the sympathy was because you had a brother like me. Very well. That's all right, too. Apparently you can rob banks, be a crooked lawyer, swill corn whiskey, commit adultery with your neighbor's wife—and be considered a fine, lovable, misunderstood fellow; but if you try to make something true and beautiful you are "viciously insane" and your "big overgrown body" ought to be dragged through the streets by a lynching mob. These phrases are from one of the letters sent to me.

Well, they can not hurt us. I do not believe one fine person, worthy of being a friend, would ever turn either on you or me because I have written a book—and anyone who would is probably not worth knowing.

I am a young man, just beginning his life's work. The sad thing about this whole thing is not that people have misunderstood my first book, but that they do not know at all what I am like or what my vision of life is. A great deal of water has gone under the bridge since I left Asheville ten years ago, but I had always hoped that when I brought my first work before the world, I would find sympathy and understanding among my old friends there. Now I feel as if I had been exiled: that they no longer know the person I have become, and that they will not recognize me in the work I shall do in the future. I say this is the sad thing about it all. It is

like death. I know now that people do not die once but many times, and
that life of which they were once a part, and which they thought they
could never lose, dies too, becomes a ghost, is lost forever. There is nothing
to be done about this. We can only love those who are lost, and grieve for
their spirits. If, then, I am dead to people who once knew me and cared
for me, there is nothing more to say or do—I must go on into a new
world and a new life, with love and sorrow for what I have lost. If you
like, remember the kid in the cherry tree, or the long-legged schoolboy, or
the kid at college—I shall always remember you all with love and
loyalty. . . .

Wolfe had met James Boyd, author of Drums, Marching On, Long Hunt,
and Roll River, *through Perkins, and had asked Boyd to recommend him for
a Guggenheim Fellowship. The following note was written in reply to one
from Boyd saying he had done so, and adding:* "Look Homeward, Angel
*has become one of our permanent possessions and though it contains things
for which I denounce you before the throne of Form and Design (no doubt
a mere certified public accountant's stool) it has the simple and undebatable
merit of containing elements of greatness, and all of the formidable vigor of
life."*

To JAMES BOYD

[27 West 15th Street]
[New York City]
[January 12(?), 1930]

Dear Jim:
    You are a swell guy even if you do have decided theories of form. It
will be a proud day in my life when you wring my hand and say "Son,
the style and structure of your last book makes Flaubert look like an
anarchist. I have done you a great wrong."
    If I buy a set of false whiskers and revisit my native state, will you
introduce me as your Irish cousin, Ernest? [1]

*The following letter to Marjorie N. Pearson was written in reply to one
from her praising* Look Homeward, Angel. *Miss Pearson is the daughter
of Mr. Richmond Pearson, whose house Wolfe describes here, and came to
know Wolfe personally when he went back to Asheville in the summer of
1937.*

[1] James and Ernest Boyd were actually no relation.

To MARJORIE N. PEARSON

27 West 15th Street
New York City
Jan. 19, 1930

Dear Miss Pearson:

I want to thank you most warmly for your letter. I am moved and honored by what you say about my book, and the fact that you are a native of Asheville gives your letter additional value.

When I was a child, my father used to take me to the little amusement park at Riverside, across the river from Bingham Heights. At night, after the movies and fireworks on the little lake, we stood by the river and watched the great trains thunder past on the other side, with the firebox glowing and throwing light. There would be a few lights on the hill above. I remember a big, rambling, magnificent Victorian house up there with spacious grounds, and I knew that Mr. Richmond Pearson and his family lived there, and I often wondered what people who lived in so great a place would look like, and talk like and *be* like. Now I think I know what they would *be* like—spacious and grand, like the old house—for I believe you belong to that family.

If I am right, what I feel more and more about the strangeness and mystery of living, which weaves our destinies out of chaos back and forth across the world, becomes deeper and stranger—for after so much water has flowed under the French Broad bridge since the child and his father stood there, and after I have put so many days and months and years and thousands of miles of wandering between that time and this, I come to know one of the people in that house through my book.

If I am wrong—that is, if you are *not* a member of that Pearson family but of another one—I still feel the deepest gratefulness to you for writing your fine letter, and I know that no matter how many Asheville people may not like my book, it has not failed in its purpose and weaving as long as it has one such friend as you.

P.S. Please forgive the solemn air of all this—but I tried to say just what I really felt, and if I have said it badly, I think you will see what I was trying to say.

The following letter was in reply to one written by Mrs. Roberts immediately upon finishing Look Homeward, Angel, *in which she protested against Wolfe's portrayal of the Gant family and of John Dorsey Leonard*

*and the Altamont Fitting School. The result of this misunderstanding was
a breach between her and Wolfe which lasted for six years.*

To MARGARET ROBERTS

Harvard Club
New York
February 2, 1930

Dear Mrs. Roberts:

. . . Two or three months ago I wrote you a very long letter in reply to
your own,[1] but that letter still remains, folded and unfinished, in my notebook. It has been almost impossible for me to write letters, or anything
else, during the last three months . . . —Now I am finishing my work at
the University. Scribners have very generously made it possible for me to
live modestly until my next book is done—I have already begun it, and it
is to be called "The October Fair." It deals with different scenes, with
different characters, and with a different theme from the first. I hope,
naturally, that it will be a better book than the first, and with all my
heart I hope that people who thought my first book ugly and painful, will
find beauty and wisdom in the second. That is a wish I shall always keep
for my work, and I hope in some measure it comes true.

I am very happy to know that most of the reviewers have found beauty
and wisdom in my first book, and many of them have found the people in
the book magnificent and heroic. I have just finished reading a review by
Carl Van Doren in which he says just that. The review is published in the
February issue of a little magazine called *Wings*: it is the journal of The
Literary Guild of America, of which Mr. Van Doren is the head. If you
can get the magazine, I hope you will read the review.[2]

I shall have time to write you the letter I want to write after next week.
Meanwhile, will you let me say again one thing in reference to your own
fine letter: I think you are mistaken in the estimate you put on some of the
characters in my book and I know you are wholly mistaken in your interpretation of one of the scenes.[3] You are certainly right in saying I would
not do such a book twenty years from now—I hope I will do one that is

[1] The letter is still among Wolfe's papers, but has been omitted here since he
rewrote the major part of it into this letter of February 2.

[2] Van Doren said: "Mr. Wolfe, with much that is heroic in his constitution, has
had the courage of his heroism. He has dared to lift his characters up above the
average meanness of mankind, to let them live by their profounder impulses, and
to tell about them the things which smooth, urbane novelists insist on leaving
untold about men and women."

[3] Probably the material on pages 232–235 in *Look Homeward, Angel,* to which
Mrs. Roberts specifically refers in one of her letters.

much better and much more beautiful, but such growth as that must come with time, and with maturity and wisdom.

But I do believe sincerely, Mrs. Roberts, that any bitterness in my book —and I would not deny that there is bitterness in it—is directed not against people or against living, but against the fundamental structure of life, which seems to me, or at least seemed to me when I wrote the book, cruel and wastefully tragic. I may be wrong in that feeling, but at any rate, it was deep-seated and real.

The other thing I want to say is longer and more difficult, and I must write you about it later at length, but here it is indicated in outline: that all creation is to me fabulous, that the world of my creation is a fabulous world, that experience comes into me from all points, is digested and absorbed into me until it becomes a part of me, and that the world I create is *always inside* me, and never *outside* me, and that what reality I can give to what I create comes only from *within*. Its relation to actual experience I have never denied, but every thinking person knows that such a relation is inevitable, and could not be avoided unless men lived in a vacuum. . . .

You said in one place of your letter that you knew I was sincere, no matter what anyone said. I thank you with all my heart; but how could you ever doubt it? Have you ever known me to be lacking in sincerity, to be evasive, dishonest, or to have my eye glued on the main chance? . . .

Finally, Mrs. Roberts, will you please believe me when I tell you sincerely and earnestly that when I began this book in London, and finished it in New York, I shaped and created its reality from within: my *own* world, my *own* figures, my *own* events shaped themselves into my *own* fable there on the page before me, and that I spent no time in thinking of actual Smiths, Jones, or Browns; nor do I see yet how such a thing is possible? If anyone thinks it is, let him take notes at street corners, and see if the result is a book.

I have written you more than I intended at present; let me, in concluding, entreat you to remember that I have written only *one* chapter of my *whole* book, and that if you do not think the first is worthy of me, I shall try to do something that will deserve your faith and affection in those that follow. Let me also say now that the saddest thing about all of this to me is not that some people have misunderstood the intention and meaning of my first book, but that some people I still love and honor have misunderstood me. I will not say a word against them—the really sad thing is that we lead a dozen lives rather than one, and that two or three of mine have gone by since I was a kid in Asheville. If people now draw back when they see the man, and say: "I do not know him. This is not the boy I knew"—I can only hope they will not think the man a bad one, and that they will be patient and wait until the boy comes back. And I think he will, after the man has made a long journey.

Good-bye for the present. I send you again my warmest, my deepest affection, and my most devoted wishes for your health and happiness. I think you are one of the grandest people I have ever known.

P.S. I hope you have seen some of the reviews of my book. They have been on the whole very wonderful—the best reviews, I understand, a first book has had in several years. I hope you have read some of the most important ones—those in the New York *Times, World, Herald Tribune, New Republic, The Bookman, Plain Talk,* and others; as well as the statements made by Hugh Walpole, Thomas Beer, F.P.A., the columnist, and many other people. I hate to speak of all this, but all of these people have found beauty and heroism in my book, both in the events and in the people; and I hope you will be interested in what they say, in what they think and feel.

If I am to be honest I must create my vision of life as I see it; but I hope that in my future work everyone I respect and like will find beauty and wonder in everything I do.

Forgive me for talking so much about the book—it is my first, and naturally close to my heart.

Again, I send you my warmest and most devoted remembrance.

In "The Conning Tower" in The New York World *for February 6, 1930, F.P.A. had published a letter from an anonymous correspondent in Asheville, saying that the townspeople were "raucous in their condemnation" of* Look Homeward, Angel *and of Wolfe, and ending with the remark which Wolfe quotes in this fragmentary letter, found in one of his notebooks, and undoubtedly never mailed. Adams himself ended the column with the remark that "all good novels—and most poor ones—the psychos [at this time the word as used here meant psychologists or psychiatrists, rather than, as at the present time, their patients] tell us, are closely related to the author's emotional life."*

To F. P. A.

[New York City]

[February 7, 1930]

Dear Mr. Adams:

I am twenty-nine years old. I have lived 10,765 days and nights. When your correspondent says "I shall be interested in a novel by Mr. Wolfe not so closely related to his own emotional life," the writer will not have it. I have only these 11,000 days to go by. "Mr. Wolfe," if he writes further, has at present eight or a dozen novels which come from his

11,000 days and nights. . . . Since your correspondent is un-interested to the extent of writing 350 words and a quarter column about my book, . . .

[THE LETTER BREAKS OFF UNFINISHED]

In an interview on January 7, 1930, with H. Allen Smith of the United Press, Hugh Walpole, who was in New York at the time, was quoted as praising Wolfe in the following words: "His novel is as nearly perfect as a novel can be. I feel it a duty as a literary man to say something in his favor. Let America awake to him, for he has the making of greatness." On January 9, Wolfe was taken by Frere-Reeves to meet Walpole and have lunch with him. In the Herald Tribune *for Sunday, March 16, an article by Walpole appeared under the title "A Londoner in New York," and said, "A few weeks ago I was interviewed by a charming young lady who asked my opinion of Mr. Wolfe's book,* Look Homeward, Angel. *I gave my opinion. I liked the book very much. I thought it a work of fine promise. In the newspaper a few days later my words were as follows: 'Awake, America! A new genius is upon you!' Well, I never begged America to awake. She seems to me awake enough as it is." Upon reading this, Wolfe wrote Walpole the following note.*

To HUGH WALPOLE

27 West 15th Street
New York City
March 16, 1930

Dear Mr. Walpole:

Almost every week I see some new evidence of your generosity toward my book: in to-day's *Herald Tribune* there was another. Please accept again my most grateful thanks. It is very fine for a man of your reputation to take such friendly interest in a young writer.

I hope you got my book. I sent it to the address you gave me, with an inscription—probably a very dull one, but at all events one that I meant. I am worn out by New York; I am going to France next month, and to England a little later.

To-day's *Tribune* said this is your last month in America. I don't know if that means you've already sailed, or not. But if you are still here, and ever have a free hour for lunch, I wonder if you could let me know? It would give me great joy to see you again. If you *have* sailed, I hope someday in England to have the pleasure of having you to dinner —a wonderful dinner with glorious food and drink.

Arthur Davison Ficke, a well known American poet, author of Sonnets of a Portrait Painter *and other books of poems, had written to congratulate Wolfe upon* Look Homeward, Angel, *saying: "You depict, with a high nobility and generosity, the mean disorder of the world we live in; and you at the same time give an equally vivid picture of the Lost Atlantis of the heart. You have unquestionably written a memorable book . . . and I can see no very good reason why you should not go on to more and more impressive novels. There has never been a great novelist in America. Are you that long-awaited white-haired boy?" The following is Wolfe's reply.*

To ARTHUR DAVISON FICKE

27 West 15th Street
New York City
March 25, 1930

Dear Mr. Ficke:

Thanks very much for your fine letter. I have known and admired your poetry for a long time, and what you say about my book fills me with pride. I agree with you entirely in your criticism, and if I were writing the book now I should cut out most of the college stuff.

Thanks also for believing I will do better work in the future. I think so, too, although the comments of some critics that "he has probably not shot the whole wad yet," "we shall see what he can do in another book" etc., do not have the effect of calming me or making me feel better. It had never occurred to me that I had made more than a beginning until I read such reviews. I am twenty-nine years old, the book was mostly written when I was twenty-six to twenty-eight; it seems to me they might allow me two or three years more before senile decay destroys me.

I hope you will read my next book, and write me about it, as you did about this. I think it's going to be a fine book, and I know it will if my vitality comes back. The last four or five months have worn me out—having a book published has happened to millions of other people, but it's the first time it ever happened to me and, thank God, I took it hard —letters, excitement, reviews good or bad, sales, invitations, telephone calls, everything.

Now I'm done with it, I'm going away to France next month, and spend several weeks looking at a cow and a hill, and drinking lots of wine. After that I'm going to write a good book. I've made this letter too long. I eat, talk, write and do everything too much, but your letter was the letter of a friend, and of a man whose work I respect. Please accept again my grateful thanks.

To MABEL WOLFE WHEATON

Harvard Club
New York.
March 29, 1930

Dear Mabel:

Thanks for your very nice letter. I have not written you in some time because the excitement and confusion of the last few months have pretty well worn me out. . . . I think I'm pretty well physically, but my mind feels like a piece of worn-out rubber. But I'll be all right with a little peace and rest.

I was very happy about getting the Guggenheim Fellowship.[1] It amounts to $2500 a year, and is given for one year, but it will be extended if the work one is doing demands more time. About the only string tied to it is that one go abroad—I do not want to go for a whole year, but I think they will let me go for six months now and six months next year or the year after. I can use this money now and keep the money Scribners might pay me as royalties or as an advance on the next book as a reserve fund for the future.

I have a new book under way—I think it will be a very beautiful book—but I need a rest and the old vitality in order to work on it hard day after day. I have done a great deal on it, but mainly scenes, notes, scraps, fragments. People know about me now, and are waiting for the next book; so I must try to do a good piece of work. I have plenty of "stuff" yet: the only thing that worries me is that I'm so damned tired at present. But getting away will fix that. New York eats up your vitality; I have been out a good deal, but I have spent even more time avoiding going out, making excuses, etc.—and all that takes it out of you. I have had enough of personal fame—modest as mine has been: now I want my books to be famous, but to be left alone myself. I want a few friends, and time to work.

By the way, the first edition of the book is now worth money. I won't get any of it, but I understand collectors are advertising for it and are already paying $7.50. It strikes me as funny as hell, but if you've got one, hold on to it.

I wish I could tell you about the last few months—but it's too long, too wild a story, and I'm too tired. . . . I wish I could see you and talk to you: I'm trying to get a story done for Scribner's before I sail,[2]

[1] Wolfe had recently been appointed a Fellow of the Guggenheim Foundation.

[2] This was evidently not completed or not accepted by *Scribner's Magazine*. No stories by Wolfe were bought by them between "An Angel on the Porch" accepted on February 4, 1929, and "A Portrait of Bascom Hawke," accepted on January 28, 1932.

and I'm having my teeth worked on. It's damned hard about your losing money on the property—I'm sure you've seen the worst of it now—that you're in the trough of the wave—and that, no matter what happens, things will get better later.

We are all going to be all right. You are still young and the best of life is before you. I think our youth is the hardest time of our lives: after that I am sure we get more wisdom and greater peace. Please have faith in me. I am still young; I have written, I hope, only the first chapter or two of my own life; and I believe I shall do some beautiful books yet, and make you all proud of me. . . .

With love,

Lenore Powell [3] called me up a few weeks ago when she was here and I went to see her. She is a fine girl, and one of my old friends. And of course my feeling for old friends is what it has always been. But there are other people who have called me up, who never knew me at home and who have never spoken or written a word to me since. When I have sidestepped their invitations, or refused to let them come to my place, some of them have been quite bitter and sarcastic— they have accused me of "forgetting my old friends," being "high hat," etc. My feeling toward such people as this is that they can go to hell. Don't you think I'm right? I am happy to think that the people who know me and care anything for me know what my value is, and that I have always been a real person.

To JAMES BOYD

27 West 15th Street
New York
April 17, 1930

Dear Jim:

I think "Long Hunt" [1] is a beautiful book, and aside from personal feeling I am proud to know the author. There was not a poor line or a shoddy page in it. The book has soaked into me and is a part of me and the other night I began a scene in my new book as follows: "In red-oak wilderness at break of day, long hunters lay for bear." [2] That was a great scene—I mean the bear fight. The book has a great deal

[3] Lenore Powell, now Mrs. Robert Whitfield, had known Wolfe for many years in Asheville.

[1] Boyd's *Long Hunt* had just been published by Scribners.

[2] This passage occurs in "The Names of the Nation" which was first published in the December, 1934, issue of *The Modern Monthly,* and appears in *Of Time and the River* on pages 861–870.

of the magnificence, the savagery, the power and the beauty that the early history of this country has. It has in it the vision of mighty rivers and of the enormous wilderness, and of the richness and glory that this country has had, and still has, and that only ignorant fools deny. I want to get that in my book. Some hundreds of my kinsmen and forefathers are buried in the earth of this country: many of them, I know, were long hunters and pioneers with Crockett's [3] blood in them. The other day I went down for the first time to the Pennsylvania Dutch country— my father came from there. One half of me is enormous red barns, immense fertile fields, and all the meaty spermy groaning plenty of nature; and one half of me is the great hills of North Carolina, the wilderness and the pioneers. I am beginning to brag like your hero did in the rum joint, but your book has done it to me: I'm a Long Hunter from Bear Creek, and a rootin', tootin', shootin' son-of-a-gun from North Carolina.

I may not get away now until after May 1, and I hope I get to see you if you come to New York by then. You have written a grand book, Jim: it has in it the sense of glory. I have been going to Atlantic City and riding in the engine cab of the fastest train in America—83 miles an hour on a steel cyclone—and I have soaked up the power and the glory until it's oozing out—and I'm going to try to get some of it in my new book. I don't think all the pioneers are dead yet. . . .

The following letter to Henry and Natalie Volkening was never mailed. Instead, Wolfe wrote and mailed a very brief note three days later.

To HENRY AND NATALIE VOLKENING

S.S. *Volendam*

Wednesday, May 14, 1930

Dear Henry and Natalie:

. . . I have had a good voyage so far—I am writing this the fifth day out which means, on this placid Dutch boat, that we are about mid-Atlantic. Most of the people, thank God, are elderly and stolid, and there are very few of those bastards who want to "get a crowd together and have a big time." The food is good and the beer is splendid. That dreadful apprehensiveness, that awful jumpy nervousness has al-

[3] Elizabeth Patton, the sister of Wolfe's great-great-grandfather, George Patton, and a cousin of his great-great-grandmother, Nancy Patton, was the second wife of David Crockett.

most left me—although I can't yet quite realize in the morning that the G.D. Telephone won't ring. My skin is bright and fresh again, and my eyes are clear as a child's. It sounds foolish but it's true.

It's all over at last—the bad part I hope forever: the ballyhoo, the gush, the trickery, the intrigue, the envy, the hatred, the horrible weariness. I remember the enormous beauty, vitality, and the horrible impermanence of New York. The sounds of the streets and subways are more real in my ears than a dream. I am haunted by our brief days: at sunset the moon comes up opposite the setting sun like a balance, and at night it makes great pools of light upon the water.

Our effort is to wreak out of chaos and the impermanent hours some lasting beauty: the effort usually fails, but it is a thing for the strong and faithful to try for. There is a Jewish family aboard who are going to visit Max Beerbohm: the wife's sister is Beerbohm's wife. They have been telling me about him. He lives quietly at Rapallo, one of the most beautiful places in the world. He sees few people; he sits on the terrace and paints a little, reads a little, walks about a little, occasionally he writes a little. He is lazy and never forces himself. Yet he has done fine work, and a considerable amount of it, too. It is a good life for an artist —but it is not my kind of life.

I like the Dutch: they are hearty, clean, calm and innocent as children—they have bright blue brittle eyes. I have a good table—a middle-aged French couple, an old Viennese and his wife, and a young German girl with straw hair. They are nice people: we all drink wine together, laugh a lot, talk about different things in Europe and America and have a big time: the various representatives of the Keokuk and Chillicothe smart sets who dress up every night for God knows what, look at us with wellbred University of Kansas snobsfaces. We have had and still have magnificent people in America, but these country club and women's club horsesbristles will ruin the place. They are all potential neo-Humanists—"genteel," the probable successors to Mencken.

Meanwhile what will the real "humanists" do—I mean myself and a few others? For God's sake, don't tell yourself lies, or let others tell them to you: if you are distressed by the savagery, the beauty, the horror and the incessant vitality of living, become a genteel fellow, but don't dress it up with fine words and reasons, or think you have found truth, or that there is any possible connection between Professor Norman Foerster and Sophocles. Anyway, I have found out that although there are millions of people who swear they are willing to live and die for what is good and beautiful, I have never known a half dozen who were willing to be out of fashion. And this is more true of the critics, the reviewers, the writers, than anyone else—most of them have the spirits of rats: they are humanists now, romantics next season, something else again. They call Dreiser a great writer in 1927 and a son of a bitch in 1930.

Enough for the present. I shall think of you often, and I want you to write me, but I shall not write anyone for some time. I am working on my book every day—I have decided that I have no one to please but myself, and I am going ahead in that way. I have decided that anyone who is either grateful or impressed by the kind of notoriety that may come to him in New York, and tries to serve it and justify it, deserves the fate that will certainly come to him. There are perhaps six people in the world whose good opinion I would like to have—I shall write the book for them and for myself, and I hope the public has good sense enough to like it.

I hope this finds you well and flourishing. I send you my best and kindest wishes for happiness.

To MAXWELL E. PERKINS

S S *Volendam*

Saturday May 17, 1930

Dear Mr. Perkins:

The ship is stopping at Plymouth tomorrow—I wanted to write you a line or two so that it would get off on an early boat. The voyage has been very quiet and uneventful—I have done little except eat and sleep and prowl all over the boat. I have had a good rest, and am now ready to get off. I am going to Paris Monday morning directly from Boulogne. I shall write you from there and let you know future plans. . . .

I feel like a man faced with a great test, who is confident of his power to meet it, and yet thinks of it with a pounding heart and with some speculation. I am impatient to get at my book: I know it will be good if I have power to put it on paper as I have thought it out. One thing is certain—I have not used up my nervous vitality: I am prowling around the decks like an animal. I am restless to get off. I have talked to all the passengers, and already I have violent likes and prejudices.

I miss Scribners and seeing you all very much—I think of you all with the warmest and most affectionate feeling. During the last year the place has become a part of my life and habit.

I wish I could tell you how magnificent a great ship at sea is, or of the glory and beauty of the sea and the sky, which are always different. We are nearing the coast of England, the days are much longer, and we have begun to pass tramps and steamers outward bound for America. All day the gulls have been sweeping over the water: I look forward with the greatest excitement to seeing land to-morrow: it has never failed to touch me very deeply.

I can't write a good letter on ship—the movement, the tremble of the engines, and the creaking of the wood destroy concentration. I'll write later from Paris. Good-bye for the present. . . .

With my best and warmest wishes,

To A. S. FRERE-REEVES

Paris

May 23, 1930

Dear Frere:

Thanks very much for your letter. I expect to come to England in June and shall look you up right away. It is very good to be away from all the jangle and noise of New York: I have seen absolutely no one I know in Paris and have not tried to find them. But it is not good to be too much alone, and you have no idea how much comfort I get from knowing you are so near at hand, and that I can go to see you. I am full of a new book and have brought some of it with me. My experience has been that Americans who come to France to work get very little done—they sit in cafés and talk about it. Perhaps one should be able to work anywhere, but England is better for me. I have about fifty pounds a month—do you know of some little village near you where I might go? My idea is as grand as renting a cottage and finding a woman to cook—do you think that is too grand for fifty pounds a month? It seems that the simple things are sometimes hardest to get, but I like to be alone when I work, and I do not like to feel I am disturbing anyone. I have a horror of those little hotels and lodging houses full of embalmed old men and women, and ugly furniture. My habits are not so bad, but I love to stay up all night if necessary, and I do a lot of walking up and down.

Perhaps you can help me with a few suggestions when I see you. I want with all my heart to do a good piece of work and I am a little terrified at the idea of complete isolation. I used to be able to do it when I came abroad, but I want someone to talk to once in a while now. Thanks again, dear Frere, for your letter: I am looking forward to seeing you next month.

To FRED W. WOLFE

Rouen

June 2, 1930.

Dear Fred:

Thanks very much for your letter and the enclosed clippings from the *Asheville Times*. I read them very carefully—I do not think that the man who interviewed me, Lee Cooper,[1] did badly. Of course he did not write the headlines, and cannot be held responsible for such flights of the poetic fancy as "Wolfe Denies Betraying Asheville." I confess that I am tired of the whole business and care very little whether the *Times* or Asheville or anyone else thinks I "betrayed" them or "portrayed" them, or whatever one pleases. But I do not think you will find, if you go back over the files of the local papers, that any of them has ever accused any of the gentlemen who had charge of the city's government several years ago and who, I am told, plunged the city several million dollars in debt—or of the gentlemen who told them that property was worth $9000 the front foot in a town of 40,000 people— or any of the other gentry who have stolen, robbed, murdered, thieved, or raped. I say I do not think you will find a single one accused of being the local Judas, or of "betraying" the town.

In all this I have no bitterness against Asheville or its people. I think some of them have acted very unintelligently, very ungenerously, and very meanly about my book, but one has to expect that from people everywhere. The dark threats that I had "better not come back to Asheville again," or that I can "never come back to this town" etc. affect me very little—apparently people who make such threats have not considered that I have lived away from the town for ten years now and may not have any overpowering desire to return. For many people in the town I feel the greatest affection and respect, but if I ever grow the least bit homesick it is not for the town of Asheville, but for the great and marvellous hills of North Carolina in which I was fortunate enough to be born, and in which Asheville had the good sense to get built. My feeling is for the land, my blood kin, and a few people— beyond that, I care very little.

What does distress me is to think that anyone I care anything about may have been caused any pain or any embarrassment because of any-

---

[1] Lee Cooper, who had been City Editor of *The Asheville Times* and was at this time a reporter on *The New York Times*, had interviewed Wolfe in New York shortly before he sailed for Europe. The interview was published in *The Asheville Times* on May 4, 1930.

thing I have ever written. I have not the least apology to make for the honest use of whatever talent I have, but I do not want nor intend to cause pain to any person. In the end those people who are capable of understanding will understand, and those who are not capable will not understand—and that will be all there is to it: those who understand and like my books will buy them and read them just as if I came from Spokane, or Topeka, or Paris, or Rouen—and those who don't understand or like them will say that "that guy Wolfe is a nut and a highbrow," and they will not buy my books but will go on very happily reading *Western Stories* and *True Confessions*. So much for that.

To talk of other things. I have been in France two weeks, and came to Rouen from Paris yesterday. This town is about 70 miles from Paris on the Seine: there are about 130,000 people here, a very old Cathedral, some old churches and wonderful old houses, and the market square where they burned Joan of Arc. She is now a saint of the church, and they had the cathedral all decorated because of her when I went there to-day.

I have seen nothing of Europe this time except France, but France is in mighty good shape: there is no unemployment at all, everyone is at work, and everyone seems to have enough to eat and drink and wear. The French are a hard-working and thrifty people: they always put by a little either in the bank or under the kitchen floor, and when it comes to haggling over a penny, the Scotch are a race of two-fisted spendthrifts by comparison. The French live for themselves, their families, and their country: they do not like foreigners and regard them with a cold and fishy eye: they endure them because they pay, but there are many other countries where I had rather go broke and trust to luck. They are in many ways a very wonderful people: they are industrious and intelligent, they have great vitality and have a great history and a great literature—but there are many people I like better. I like the country much more than the people—it is one of the most comfortable and beautiful countries in the world. . . .

I am terribly sorry to hear of the trouble Mabel and Ralph Wheaton have had with their property. You are wrong in supposing I was ever "laughing at you" for investing your money in real estate: the subject was one for tears rather than laughter. I have nothing but the deepest and sincerest regret now, and the hope that matters may turn out better than they look, and that things will come right, at least in part. Asheville is one of the saddest little cities in the country to-day—the whole place got drunk, and is now paying for it. But the place and the people will get back on their feet, I know. . . .

With my very best wishes for prosperity and health,

If the newspaper people and the newspaper readers want to believe that the angel in the photograph [2] is the angel in the book, or on the porch, or in the title, or anywhere else, let them go to it: you can't keep them from believing what they want to believe. There is not a scene or a page in the book that is not completely invention, but of course as time goes on these "old inhabitants" I read about who "remember every character" will also remember every scene, and will even remember having been present when it occurred. Such is life.

To A. S. FRERE-REEVES

Paris

June 23, 1930

Dear Frere:

Your letter came this morning. Although it probably embarrasses you to have me say so every time I write, I am so damned glad because you write me—it does me so much good, and I'm grateful beyond words for it, and for everything else you've done. You know, I'm getting soft-hearted in my senility, but I'm afraid I believe in human goodness—and in badness, too.

Frere, by God, I'm so excited I can hardly keep still, but I'm also a little *scared* it may not be true; so I go softly. I am *working* from six to ten hours a day; Paris has no more interest for me than Sauk Center. I sleep till noon, go for a walk, buy an aperitif, lunch, go to a book store and buy a book, read for an hour, then back to my room and work from four or five o'clock until ten at night. Then out to eat and walk, back at midnight or one o'clock, and at work till three or four. And by God, Frere, I mustn't talk about it, but I believe it's the real stuff this time —it's going to be a tremendous piece of work, but I hope I can do it as I plan. Perhaps when I see you I can talk to you a little about it—you and Perkins are the only people I would talk to about it—but I promise not to show you or read you the manuscript.

I have literally seen no one I know in almost two weeks—if ever anyone was a hermit, or marooned on a desert isle, I fit the bill—suppose

[2] *The Asheville Times* had published a photograph of a stone angel in Riverside Cemetery there, saying that it was the "angel on the porch" about which Wolfe had written. This was not true. As Wolfe says of this incident in *The Story of a Novel*, "The unfortunate part of this proceeding was that I had never seen or heard of this angel before, and that this angel was, in fact, erected over the grave of a well known Methodist lady who had died a few years before and that her indignant family had immediately written the paper to demand a retraction of its story, saying that their mother had been in no way connected with the infamous book or the infamous angel which had given the infamous book its name."

it's a good thing since it makes you think about your work a great deal. The French have always been to me the most *foreign* men in the world: I constantly get the sensation that they are creatures from another planet: I have never felt this with the English, Germans, or Austrians. I *do* want to get out of Paris, and think I'll go before another week. If I come to England I'll probably come like a shot—if you are not in London but at the sea, I'll wait on you.

Mr. Arlen [1] spoke to me when I was in Smith's Book Shop the other day—he pointed out one of his books just out in the Tauschnitz and I immediately bought it. I'm reading "War and Peace"—a modest affair of about 1500 closely packed pages, but a tremendous, magnificent book. There is also a grain of biography. It seems to me that all good writers draw heavily on their own experience, but I suppose most bad ones do also: not so much, though—the bad ones grind out "fiction." All good writing, I am sure, is in some measure autobiographical, but it is the right use of this with the imagination which makes a good book: there is more imaginative power in one page of *Ulysses* than in all the novels of Oppenheim together. Don't you think so?

Also, it is right to howl about living, about the scheme of existing—every good man does howl about it—but it is wrong to hate individual people in your work: I mean it is wrong to make Jones and Green out rascals, if that is your only purpose in doing it. It seems to me that *that* will cheapen a man's work as quickly as anything—a desire to "get back": but if a man is a good enough artist he rises far above that—I mean Proust and Joyce, although I suppose Joyce does pay off a few old scores.

Well, this is too much serious thinking for a sticky day. I first wrote you a long letter telling you all about my new book, but my nobler nature triumphed and I tore it (the letter) up.[2] If you go to the seaside before I see you, please soak and bask in it, but behave yourself with the mermaids: don't pinch their little tails or scales, or whatever they have. Now and then I think of London, and how great and magnificent it is, and the beer and ale, and what a good piece of meat you can get in certain places, and I kick myself for not coming. Dear Frere, I am the world's champion dawdler and proscrastinator but eventually I arrive. I think at the present time I feel that solitude and hermitage is good for my soul, because it's such bitter medicine—does that make me an old Yankee Puritan? God bless you, and please write me when you can.

[1] Michael Arlen. Frere-Reeves had come to Paris for a few days and had introduced Wolfe to him.

[2] Fragments of this letter still remain among Wolfe's papers, but are not included here since they closely resemble Wolfe's letters of June 24 to Wheelock and July 1 to Perkins.

To JOHN HALL WHEELOCK

Guaranty Trust Company
Paris

June 24, 1930

Dear Jack:

Thanks very much for your fine letter—I can't tell you how touched and grateful I was. I'm not going to write you a long one now—I'll do that later when things have settled a little more. Briefly, this has happened: I have been in Paris almost all the time since I landed, with the exception of a few days in Rouen. This not because I love Paris, but because after two weeks of casting around, moving from one hotel to the other, I suddenly decided that we spend too much of our lives looking for ideal conditions to work in, and that what we are after is an ideal condition of the soul which almost never comes. So I got tired and disgusted with myself, went to a little hotel—not very French, I'm afraid, but very touristy—and set to work. I've been doing five or six hours a day for almost two weeks now—the weather is hot and sticky, but I sweat and work—it's the only cure I've found for the bloody hurting inside me.

Dear Jack, it's been so bad I can't tell you about it: I feel all bloody inside me—but have faith in me, everything's going to be all right. What do you know about it? I am writing a book so filled with the most unspeakable desire, longing, and love for my own country and ten thousand things in it, that I have to laugh at times to think what the Mencken crowd and all the other crowds are going to say about it. But I can't help it—if I have ever written anything with utter conviction it is this. Dear Jack, I *know* that I know what some of our great woe and sickness as a people is now, because that woe is in me—it is rooted in myself; but by God, Jack, I have not written a word directly about myself yet. God knows what Maxwell Perkins will say when he sees it, but I've just finished the first section of the first part—it is called *Antæus*, and it is as if I had become a voice for the experience of a race. It begins "Of wandering forever and the earth again"—and by God, Jack, I believe I've got it—the two things that haunt and hurt us: the eternal wandering, moving, questing, loneliness, homesickness, and the desire of the soul for a home, peace, fixity, repose. In *Antæus*, in a dozen short scenes, told in their own language, we see people of all sorts *constantly in movement,* going somewhere, haunted by it—and by God, Jack, it's the *truth* about them—I saw it as a child, I've seen it ever since, I see it here in their poor damned haunted eyes.

Well there are these scenes: [1] a woman talking of the river, the ever-moving river, coming through the levee at night, and of the crippled girl clinging to the limb of the oak, and of how she feels the house break loose and go with the tide, then of living on the roof-top with Furman and the children, and of other houses and people—tragedy, pity, humor, bravery, and the great wild savagery of American nature. Then the pioneer telling of "the perty little gal" he liked, but moving on because the wilderness was getting too crowded; then the hoboes waiting quietly at evening by the water tower for the coming of the fast express; then a rich American girl moving on from husband to husband, from drink to dope to opium, from white lovers to black ones, from New York to Paris to California; then the engineer at the throttle of the fast train. Then a modest poor little couple from 123rd St—the woman earning living by painting lampshades, the man an impractical good-for-nothing temporarily employed in a filling station—cruising in their cheap little car through Virginia and Kentucky in autumn—all filled with details of motor camps, where you can get a shack for $1.00 a night, and of "lovely meals" out of cans—whole cost $0.36—etc. Then a school teacher from Ohio taking University Art Pilgrimage No. 36, writing back home "—didn't get your letter till we got to Florence . . . stayed in Prague 3 days but rained whole time we were there, so didn't get to see much, etc." Then Lee coming through Virginia in the night on his great white horse; then the skull of a pioneer in the desert, a rusted gun stock and a horse's skull; then a Harry's New York Bar American saying, "Jesus! What a country! I been back one time in seven years. That was enough. . . . Me, I'm a Frenchman. See?" But talking, talking, cursing, until he drinks himself into a stupor. Then a bum, a natural wanderer who has been everywhere; then a Boston woman and her husband who have come to France to live—"Francis always felt he wanted to do a little writing . . . we felt the atmosphere is so much better here for that kind of thing"; then a Jew named Greenberg, who made his pile in New York and who now lives in France having changed his name to Montvert, and of course feels no homesickness at all, save what is natural to 4000 years of wandering. And more, and more, and more!

Then amid all this you get the thing that does not change, the fixed principle, *the female principle*—the *earth again*—and, by God, Jack, I know *this is true* also. They want love, the earth, a home, fixity—you get the mother and the lover—as the book goes on, and you see this incessant change, movement, unrest, and the great train with the wanderers rush-

[1] This material, greatly cut, appears on pages 861–869 of *Of Time and the River*, in the section called "Kronos and Rhea: The Dream of Time," rather than in the preceding one called "Antæus: Earth Again."

ing through the night. Outside you get the eternal silent waiting earth that does not change, and the two women, going to bed upon it, working in their gardens upon it, dreaming, longing, calling for men to return upon it. And down below in the mighty earth, you get the bones of the pioneers, all of the dust now trembling to the great train's wheel, the dust that loved, suffered, died, and is now buried, pointing 80 ways across 3000 miles of earth, and deeper than all, eternal and enduring, "the elm trees thread the bones of buried lovers."

Through it all is poetry—the enormous rivers of the nation drinking the earth away at night, the vast rich stammer of night time in America, the lights, the smells, the thunder of the train—the savage summers, the fierce winters, the floods, the blizzards—all, all! And finally the great soft galloping of the horses of sleep!

Mr. Perkins may say that the first part is too much like a poem—but Jack, I've got it loaded with these stories of the wanderings of real people in their own talk, and by God, Jack, a *real unified* single story opens up almost at once and gathers and grows from then on. The chapter after "Antaeus" is called at present "Early October," [2] and begins "October is the richest of the seasons"—it tells about the great barns loaded with harvest, the mown fields, the burning leaves, a dog barking at sunset, the smell of supper cooking in the kitchen—"October is full of richness," a thousand things. Then a section begins "October is the time for all returning"—(which is true, Jack). It tells how exiles and wanderers think of home again, of how the last tourists come back on great ships, of how the old bums shiver in their ragged collars as the newspaper behind the Public Library is blown around their feet, and of how they think of going South. It tells of the summer girls who have gone back home from the resorts; of the deserted beaches; of people lying in their beds at night thinking, "Summer has come and gone—has come and gone." Then in the frosty dark and silver, they hear the thunder of the great train. Then the October of a person's life—the core, the richness, the harvest, and the richness of the end of youth.

By God, Jack, I'm just a poor bloody homesick critter, but when I think of my book sometimes I have the pride of a poet and a master of man's fate. Don't sigh and shake your head and think this is a welter of drivel— I've slapped these things down wildly in my haste, but I tell you, Jack, this book is *not* incoherent—it has a beautiful plan and a poetic logic if I am only true to it. *I have not* told you the thousandth part of it, but I hope you can see and believe in the truth and worth of it—and then if you do, please pray for me, dear Jack, to do my best and utmost, and to write the kind of book I want to write. In case you should doubt my

[2] A version of this appears in *Of Time and the River* on pages 329–332.

condition, I am perfectly sober as I write this, it is a hot day, and I am now going back to my little room to work like hell. I have really not told you *about* my book—all this has been coming in the sweat and heat of the last few days, and this letter, however crazy, has made things clearer for me.

I shall not leave Paris until I finish that first section—then I'm going like a shot to Switzerland, I think. I won't waste time moving about—I have a horror of moving now at all. Reeves,[3] the English publisher was here, took me around to see Aldington,[4] Michael Arlen, and other literary lights—I was so unhappy at the time I have not been back since, although they were very nice. Reeves wants me to come to England and stay with him, the book is coming out there next month, but I've a horror of reading more reviews—I don't want to do anything more about it. Hope and pray for me, dear Jack. Write me soon and talk to me. I've said nothing about you, forgive me, I'll write you a regular letter later.

Dear Jack—I'm sending this on a day or two later. I guess I'm really started—six hours a day, kid. . . .

To MAXWELL E. PERKINS

Guaranty Trust Co,
Paris.

July 1, 1930

Dear Mr. Perkins:

I have a long letter under way to you, but I shall probably not send it until I have left Paris. The main news is that I have been at work for several weeks, and have worked every day except last Sunday, when I met Scott Fitzgerald for the first time. He called me up at my hotel and I went out to his apartment for lunch: we spent the rest of the afternoon together talking and drinking—a good deal of both—and I finally left him at the Ritz Bar. He was getting ready to go back to Switzerland where he has been for several weeks, and had come up to close up his apartment and take his little girl back with him. He told me that Mrs. Fitzgerald has been very sick—a bad nervous breakdown—and he has her in a sanitarium at Geneva. He spoke of his new book and said he was working on it: he was very friendly and generous, and I liked him, and think he has a great deal of talent, and I hope he gets that book done soon. I think we got along very well—we had quite an argument about America: I said we were a

---

[3] A. S. Frere-Reeves of Heinemann's.
[4] Richard Aldington.

homesick people, and belonged to the earth and land we came from as much or more as any country I knew about—he said we were not, that we were not a country, that he had no feeling for the land he came from. "Nevertheless," as Galileo said, "it moves." We do, and they are all homesick or past having any feeling about anything.

I have missed America more this time than ever: maybe it's because all my conviction, the tone and conviction of my new book is filled with this feeling, which once I would have been ashamed to admit. I notice that the Americans who live here live with one another for the most part, and the French exist for them as waiters, taxi drivers, etc.—yet most of them will tell you all about the French, and their minute characteristics. I have been absolutely alone for several weeks—Fitzgerald was the first American I had talked to for some time, but yesterday I was here in the bank, and in walked Jim Boyd: I was so surprised and happy I could not speak for a moment—we went out to lunch together and spent the rest of the day together. He has been quite sick with the sinus trouble, as you know. We went to see a doctor, and I waited below: this doctor made no examination and gave no verdict, but is sending him to a specialist. I hope they do something for him—he is a fine fellow, and I like him enormously. We went to a nice café and drank beer and talked over the American soil and what we were going to do for literature, while Mrs. Boyd shopped around town. Later we all drove out to the Bois and through it to a nice little restaurant out of town on the banks of the Seine—we had a good quiet dinner there and came back. I think Jim enjoyed it, and I am going to meet them again to-night. It has done me a great deal of good to see them . . .

I am going to Switzerland—I have several places in mind but must go and see them—I would have gone long ago, but I did not want to move fast when I had started. I do not know how long I shall stay over here, but I shall stay until I have done the first part of my book, and can bring it back with me. It is going to be a very long book, I am afraid, but there is no way out of it. You can't write the book I want to write in 200 pages. It has four parts, its whole title is "The October Fair," and the names of the four parts are (1) "Antaeus"; (2) "The Fast Express"; (3) "Faust and Helen"; (4) "The October Fair."[1] I am working on the part called "Antaeus" now, which is like a symphony of many voices run through with the beginning thread of story that continues through the book. I propose to bring back to America with me the parts called "Antaeus" and "The

---

[1] *Of Time and the River,* which was only the first half of what Wolfe calls *The October Fair* here, finally had eight parts: "Orestes: Flight Before Fury"; "Young Faustus"; "Telemachus"; "Proteus: The City"; "Jason's Voyage"; "Antæus: Earth Again"; "Kronos and Rhea: The Dream of Time"; and "Faust and Helen."

Fast Express" (all these names are tentative and if you don't like them we'll get others). The book is a grand book if I have character and talent enough to do it as I have conceived it. The book has to do with what seem to me two of the profoundest impulses in man—Wordsworth, in one of his poems "To a Skylark," I think, calls it "heaven and home" and I called it in the first line of my book, "Of wandering forever and the earth again."

By "the earth again" I mean simply the everlasting earth, a home, a place for the heart to come to, and earthly mortal love, the love of a woman, who, it seems to me belongs to the earth and is a force opposed to that other great force that makes men wander, that makes them search, that makes them lonely, and that makes them both hate and love their loneliness. You may ask what all this has to do with America—it is true it has to do with the whole universe—but it is as true of the enormous and lonely land that we inhabit as any land I know of, and more so, it seems to me.

I hope this does not seem wild and idiotic to you, I have been unable to tell you much about it here, but I will in greater detail later. I ask you to remember that in the first part—"Antaeus"—the part of many voices—everything moves, everything moves across the enormous earth, except the earth itself, and except for the voices of the women crying out "Don't go! Stay! Return, return!"—the woman floating down the river in flood on her housetop with her husband and family (I finished that scene the other day and I think it is a good one). The whole scene, told in the woman's homely speech, moves to the rhythm of the great river; yet the scene has pungent and humorous talk in it, and I think does not ring false. You understand that the river is in her brain, in her thought, in her speech; and at the very end, lying in her tent at night while a new house is being built where the old one was (for *he* refuses to go up on high ground back beyond the river where nothing moves) she hears him waken beside her— he thinks she is asleep—she knows he is listening to the river, to the whistles of the boats upon the river, that he wants to be out there upon the river, that he could go floating on forever down the river. And she hates the river, but all of its sounds are in her brain, she cannot escape it . . . "All of my life is flowing like the river, all of my life is passing like the river, I think and dream and talk just like the river as it goes by me, by me, by me, to the sea." [2]

Does it sound idiotic? I don't think so if you could see the whole; it is

---

[2] This scene became very long and was finally omitted from *Of Time and the River*. However, the words "goes by me, by me, by me, to the sea" were changed to "flows by us, by us, by us, to the sea" and used as a refrain throughout the book, as on pages 333, 510, 860, etc.

full of rich detail, sounds and talk. I will not tell you any more now—this letter is too long and I have had no lunch. The river woman is only one thing . . . I'll tell you all about it later. Everything moves except the earth and the voices of the women crying out against wandering!

I miss seeing you and Scribners more than I can say. I hope I can do a good book for you and for myself and for the whole damn family. Please hope and pull for me and write me when you can. Excuse this long scrawl. I hope this finds you well and enjoying the summer, and also that you get a good vacation. Jim Boyd and I will think of you every time we drink a glass of beer and wish that you were here just for an hour or so to share it. I send everyone my best and warmest wishes.

Don't tell anyone where I am or where I'm going unless you think they have some business to find out. Tell them you don't know where I am (if anyone asks) but that mail will get to me if sent to The Guaranty Trust Co., Paris.

To MAXWELL E. PERKINS

Hotel Lorius
Montreux, Switzerland
July 17, 1930

Dear Mr. Perkins:

Your letter was sent on here from Paris, and I got it this morning. I suppose by now you have the letter I sent you from Paris several weeks ago. I have been here five or six days. . . . The other night at the Casino here I was sitting on the terrace when I saw Scott Fitzgerald and a friend of his, a young man I met in Paris. I called to them, they came over and sat with me: later we gambled at roulette and I won 15 francs, then Scott took us to a night club here. This sounds much gayer than it is: there is very little to do here, and I think I saw all the night life there is on that occasion. Later Scott and his friend drove back to Vevey, a village a mile or two from here on the lake: they are staying there. They asked me to come over to dine with them, but I am not going: I do not think I am very good company to people at present. It would be very easy for me to start swilling liquor at present but I am *not* going to do it. I am here to get work done, and in the next three months, I am going to see whether I am a bum or a man. I shall not try to conceal from you the fact that at times now I have hard sledding: my life is divided between just two things:—thought of my book, and thought of an event in my life which is now, *objectivally*,

[sic] finished. I do not write any more to anyone concerned in that event—I received several letters, but since none have come for some time I assume no more will come. I have been entirely alone since I left New York, save for these casual meetings I have told you about. Something in me hates being alone like death, and something in me cherishes it: I have always felt that somehow, out of this bitter solitude, some fruit must come. I lose faith in myself with people. When I am with someone like Scott I feel that I am morose and sullen—and violent in my speech and movement part of the time. Later, I feel that I have repelled them.

Physically my life is very good. My nerves are very steady. I drink beer and wine, mostly beer, I do not think to excess; and I have come to what is, I am sure, one of the most beautiful spots in the world. I am staying at a quiet and excellent hotel here; have a very comfortable room with a writing desk and a stone balcony that looks out on the lake of Geneva, and on a garden below filled with rich trees and grass and brilliant flowers. On all sides of the lake the mountains soar up: everything begins to climb immediately, this little town is built in three or four shelving terraces, and runs along the lake shore. Something in me wants to get up and see places, the country is full of incredibly beautiful places, but also something says "stay here and work."

That, in a way, is what my book is about. I hope in these hasty scrawls I have been able to communicate the idea of my book, and that it seems clear and good to you. I told you that the book begins with "of wandering forever, and the earth again," and that these two opposing elements seem to me to be fundamental in people. I have learned this in my own life, and I believe I am at last beginning to have a proper use of a writer's material: for it seems to me he ought to see in what has happened to him the elements of the universal experience. In my own life, my desire has fought between a hunger for isolation, for getting away, for seeking new lands—and a desire for home, for permanence, for a piece of this earth fenced in and lived on and private to oneself, and for a person or persons to love and possess. This is badly put, but I think it expresses a desire that all people have. I think the desire for wandering is more common to men, and for fixity and a piece of the earth to women, but I know these things are rooted in most people. I think you have sometimes been puzzled when I have talked to you about parts of this book—about the train as it thunders through the dark, and about the love for another person—to see how they could be reconciled or fit into the general scheme of a story; but I think you can get some idea of it now: the great train pounding at the rails is rushing across the everlasting and silent earth—here the two ideas of wandering and eternal repose—and the characters, on the train, and on the land, again illustrate this. Also, the love theme, the male and female love, represent this again: please do not think I am hammering this in in the book, I let it speak for itself—I am giving you a kind of key.

There is no doubt at all what the book is about, what course it will take, and I think the seething process, the final set of combinations, has been reached. I regret to report to you that the book will be very long, probably longer than the first one, but I think that each of its four parts makes a story in itself and, if good enough, might be printed as such. I have been reading your favorite book, "War and Peace"—it is a magnificent and gigantic work—if we are going to worship anything, let it be something like this: I notice in this book that the personal story is interwoven with the universal—you get the stories of private individuals, particularly of members of Tolstoy's own family, and you get the whole tremendous panorama of nations, and of Russia. This is the way a great writer uses his material, this is the way in which every good work is "autobiographical"— and I am not ashamed to follow this in my book.

The four parts of the book as they now stand are:

(1) "Antaeus" or "Immortal Earth" (Title to be chosen from one of these)

(2) "Antaeus" or "The Fast Express"

(3) "Faust and Helen"

(4) "The October Fair."

I do not think "Immortal Earth" or "The Immortal Earth" is a bad title; and if you are not keen upon "The Fast Express"—we might call Part I "Immortal Earth"—and Part II "Antaeus"—since in Part I the idea of eternal movement, of wandering and the earth, of flight and repose is more manifest, and in Part II, even though we have the fast train, the idea of redoubling and renewing our strength by contact with the earth (Antaeus) is more evident.

Now, the general movement of the book is from the universal to the individual: in Part I "The Immortal Earth" (?), we have a symphony of many voices (I described this briefly in my other letter) through which the thread of the particular story begins to run. I think this can be done with entire clearness and unity: we have a character called David [1] (Chapter II is called "The Song of David") but this character appears at first only as a window, an eye, a wandering seer: he performs at first exactly the same function as the epic minstrel in some old popular epic like "Beowulf," who makes us very briefly conscious of his presence from time to time by saying, "I have heard," or "it has been told me." Thus in Part I, in the chapter called "The River," the woman telling the story of the river in flood refers to him once by name. In the chapter "Pioneers, O

[1] At this time, Wolfe called his hero David Hawke instead of Eugene Gant.

Pioneers," we understand that David is a member of an American family, two or three hundred of whose members are buried in different parts of the American earth, and we get the stories and wanderings of some of these people. In the letter of the tourist from Prague he is referred to by name, in the chapter "On the Rails," we know that he is on the train, although the story is that of the engineer; in the chapter "The Bums at Sunset," we know he has seen them waiting for the train at the water-tower; in the chapter called "The Congo," the wandering negro who goes crazy and kills people and is finally killed by the posse as he crosses a creek, is known to David, the boy—etc.[2]

So much for some of the general movement: now among the twenty chapters of this first part are interspersed the first elements of the particular story—the figure of David remains almost entirely a window, but begins to emerge as an individual from what is told about him by other people, and by the way all these episodes, even the general ones—"Pioneers, O Pioneers," "The Congo," etc., give flashes of his life—but in this first part, not to tell about him, but to tell about his country, the seed that produced him, etc. It will be seen in the particular story that the desire and longing of David, is also the desire and longing of the race—"wandering forever and the earth again." These half dozen chapters, moreover, are concerned with the *female* thing: the idea of the earth, fructification, and repose—these half dozen chapters interspersed among the twenty are almost entirely about women and told in the language of women: the mother, the mistress, and the child—sometimes all included in one person, sometimes found separately in different women.

Now, if you will follow me a little farther in this, here is another development. I have said that wandering seems to me to be more of a male thing, and the fructification of the earth more a female thing—I don't think there can be much argument about this, immediately we think of the pioneers, the explorers, the Crusaders, the Elizabethan mariners, etc. I am making an extensive use of old myths in my book, although I never tell the reader this: you know already that I am using the Heracles (in my book the City is Heracles) and Antaeus myth; and you know that

[2] Most of this material was omitted from *Of Time and the River,* but parts of it were published as short stories in various magazines. The letter from the tourist in Prague became "One of the Girls in Our Party" in the January, 1935, issue of *Scribner's Magazine;* part of "On the Rails" probably became "Cottage by the Tracks" in the July, 1935, issue of *Cosmopolitan;* "The Bums at Sunset" appeared in the October, 1935, issue of *Vanity Fair;* and "The Congo" was entirely rewritten in the spring of 1937 and published as "The Child by Tiger" in the September 11, 1937, issue of *The Saturday Evening Post.* All of these stories were included in *From Death to Morning,* with the exception of "The Child by Tiger" which appears on pages 132–156 of *The Web and the Rock.*

the lords of fructification and the earth are almost always women: Maya in the Eastern legends; Demeter in the Greek; Ceres in Latin, etc.

Now I hope you don't get dizzy in all this, or think I am carrying the thing to absurdity: all intense conviction has elements of the fanatic and the absurd in it, but they are saved by our beliefs and our passion. Contained in the book like a kernel from the beginning, but unrevealed until much later, is the idea of a man's quest for his father. The idea becomes very early apparent that when a man returns he returns always to the *female* principle—he returns, (I hope this is not disgusting) to the womb of earthly creation, to the earth itself, to a woman, to fixity. But I dare go so far as to believe that the other pole—the pole of wandering—is not only a masculine thing, but that in some way it represents the quest of a man for his father. I dare mention to you the wandering of Christ upon this earth, the wanderings of Paul, the quests of the Crusaders, the wanderings of the Ancient Mariner who makes his confession to the Wedding Guest—please don't laugh:

"The moment that his face I see
I know the *man* that must hear me.
To *him* my tale I teach."

I could mention also a dozen myths, legends, or historical examples, but you can supply them quite as well for yourself. Suffice it to say that this last theme—the quest of a man for his father—does not become fully revealed until the very end of the book: under the present plan I have called the final chapter of the fourth and last part ("The October Fair"), "Telemachus."

Now, briefly, in the first part on which I am now at work (to be called "Antaeus" or "The Immortal Earth"), I want to construct my story on the model of the old folk epic: "Beowulf," for example. I want the character of David to be the epic minstrel who sings of the experience of his race, and I want to do this with eloquence, with passion and with simplicity. I want my book to be poetry—that is, I want it to be drenched in a poetic vision of life. I believe at this moment in the truth and the passion of what I have to say, and I hope, in spite of this fast scrawl, I have been able to make parts of it clear to you, and to show you it has a coherent plan and purpose.

In the first chapter of the first part (after the prelude)—the first chapter is called "The Ship"—I think I have done a good piece of writing: I tell about the sea and the earth; I tell why they are different; of the sea's eternal movement, and the earth's eternal repose. I tell why men go to sea, and why they have made harbours at the end; I tell why a ship is always called "she"; I tell of the look in the eyes of men when the last land fades out of sight, and when land comes first in view again; I tell of the earth; I describe the great ship, and the people on it—and, so help me, when I am through, I am proud of that ship and of man, who built her, who is so strong because he is so weak, who is so great because he is so small, who is so brave because he is so full of fear, who can face the horror of the ocean and see there in that unending purposeless waste the answer to his existence. I *insist*, by the way, in my book that men are wise, and that we all know we are lost, that we are damned together—and that man's greatness comes in knowing this and then making myths; like soldiers going into battle who will whore and carouse to the last minute, nor have any talk of death and slaughter.

Well, I have almost written you a book, and I hope you have stayed awake thus far. I don't know if it makes sense or not, but I think it does. Remember, although this letter is very heavy, that my book as I plan it will be full of richness, talk and humor. Please write me and tell me if all this has meant anything to you, and what you think of it. Please don't talk about it to other people. Write me as often as you can, if only a note. We like to get letters when we are in a strange land.

Please forgive me for talking so much about myself and my book. I hope I can do a good piece of work, and that any little personal distress does not get the best of me—I do not think it will.

One final thing: please understand—I think you do—that my new book will make use of experience, things I have known and felt, as the first one did—but that now I have created fables and legends and that there will be no question of identification (certainly not in the first two parts) as there was in the first. The David I have referred to is part of me, as indeed are several other characters, but nothing like, in appearance or anything else, what people think me. This is very naive and foolish, and for God's sake keep it to yourself: in making the character of David, I have made him out of the *inside* of me, of what I have always believed the inside was like: he is about five feet nine, with the long arms and the prowl of an ape,[3] and a little angel in his face. He is part beast, part spirit —a mixture of the ape and the angel. There is a touch of the monster in him. But no matter about this—at first he is the bard and, I pray God, that is what I can be. Please write me soon. I'll tell you how things come.

P.S. My book came out in England last Monday, July 14. I hope it goes well and gets good notices, but I have instructed them not to send any reviews—I can't be bothered by it now. Some *kind* friend probably will send reviews, but I hope for the best. . . .

---

[3] It is interesting to note that Wolfe thought of changing his hero's appearance as early as this date, although he did not actually resort to this device until *The Web and the Rock* and *You Can't Go Home Again*.

To MAXWELL E. PERKINS

Hotel Lorius
Montreux
July 31, 1930

Dear Mr. Perkins:

Please forgive me for flooding you with letters, but I think the news I send will interest you. I told you before that my book came out in England July 14. I wrote Frere-Reeves and told him not to send me any reviews as I am working on a new one, but this morning he sent me a great batch of clippings (twenty or more) and a long letter in which he was quite enthusiastic. He said that the book, in spite of its high price on account of its length (10/6d instead of the usual 7/6d), was selling at the rate of a thousand copies every *four* days: if this is true, it is selling faster in England than in America. He also sent one of their advertisements from *The Observer* (I am sending it to you along with one or two clippings of which I have duplicates: I'll send you the rest a little later). I've read all the clippings over briefly, and they seem to me mighty good. Four or five got in some nasty cracks about formlessness and filth, but all were favorable and some of them said things that made my head swim—as good, it seems to me, as the best we had in America. I hope he didn't handpick them to spare my feelings, but he seems to have most of the big ones: *The Times, The Sunday Times, The Times Literary Supplement, The Sunday Referee, The Morning Post, The Evening Standard, The Evening Telegraph, The Daily Mail,* etc. I want to send you Richard Aldington's review in *The Sunday Referee* [1] later (it made me dizzy), but I am sending you to-day *The Times Literary Supplement,* which Frere-Reeves says is the most important in England—it sounds pretty swell to me: please read it and tell me what you think. [2]

I suppose the book has stopped selling in America: do you think it would be a good idea to print some of these English things (in an ad, under some such heading as "What The English Are Saying")—do you think it would make some of the snobs buy the book?

I am sending you one of the Heinemann ads, together with *The Times Supplement:* later I'll send the others. Do what you think best about it, and write me. I suppose I'm jumping too fast at conclusions, but if this *thousand* every *four* days business keeps up a few weeks, I'll have nothing to complain of. I think Frere-Reeves and Heinemann have done a mighty

[1] Aldington's very favorable review of *Look Homeward, Angel* was published in the July 6, 1930, *Sunday Referee.*

[2] The very favorable unsigned review of *Look Homeward, Angel* in the *Times Literary Supplement* appeared on July 24, 1930.

fine job. I am an American but I have more English blood in me than the English royal family. They were my heroes, my mighty poets when I was a child. I was so hurt and bitter about them when I saw them after the war—but I cannot deny to you that it would make me happy if the people who invented the language I use like my work. I do not think there is one God-damned ounce of snobbishness in this!

I am very lonely here, but I work: there's nothing else to do. I think if I see it through, it will be very good—I am all alone and sometimes I doubt: do you think I'll ever amount to anything? I read Shakespeare, Racine, The English Poets—and the Bible. I have not read the Bible since I was a child—it is the most magnificent book that was ever written: when Walter Scott was dying, he called for "The Book," and they asked "What book?" and he said "There is only one"—and it is true. It is richer and grander than Shakespeare even, and everything else looks sick beside it. In the last three days I have read "Ecclesiastes" and "The Song of Solomon" several times: they belong to the mightiest poetry that was ever written—and the narrative passages in the old testament, stories like the life of King David, Ruth and Boaz, Esther and Ahasueras, etc., make the narrative style of any modern novelist look puny. I am soaking in it, and for the first part of "The October Fair," which I am calling "The Immortal Earth," I have chosen this verse from the great book of "Ecclesiastes" as a title page legend: "One generation passeth away, and another generation cometh: but the earth abideth forever." I am sorry to say that this verse comes immediately before the verse Hemingway used, "The sun also ariseth" etc., and people will say I have imitated him, but it can't be helped, it is chance, and this is the verse I want.

I am now at work on a section of "The Immortal Earth" which has the curious title of "The Good Child's River." [3] I like the title and hope you will too when you see the story: it is complete in itself, and very long—a short book—and I will send it to you when it's finished.

I'm excited about Frere-Reeves' clippings and letter, and I'm going to take a little trip this afternoon: I'm going to catch a train in a few minutes and go to the neighboring town of Lausanne and see if there are any pretty girls or women. I am very lusty: the air, the mountains, the quiet, and the very dull, very healthy food have filled me with a vitality I was afraid I'd lost.

I wish you were here and we could take a walk together—please write

[3] *The Good Child's River*, which told the story of the early life of Esther Jack, was finally omitted from *Of Time and the River*. One section of it was later published as "In the Park" in the June, 1935, issue of *Harper's Bazaar* and included in *From Death to Morning*. Other portions of it appear in *The Web and the Rock* on pages 406–433.

me when you can. I am very lonely, but I really think we must have some of it now: . . . I hope to God I can do a good piece—in "Ecclesiastes" a great passage says: "The Fool foldeth his hands and eateth his flesh," and that is what the little sneering Futility People the world over are doing—I think the Bible has very probably said everything. With their bitter, sterile thirst for failure in New York, people—some people—are waiting with bitter smiles for my ruin and wreck. I will tell you honestly I do not know if they are right or wrong. I myself am in the process of seeing, but I think the bastards are wrong, and we shall see. . . .

Write me when you can. I am glad you got a good manuscript, but I hope you won't forget me or cease to be my friend. I hope this finds you well and enjoying your vacation. I wish we could drink a big bottle of wine together.

P.S. About these people, both in England and America, who say: "This is not a great book" or "great art" or "a work of genius"—I have never said it was: but why should they be so hard and exacting on a young man's book, when they are willing to slobber over any amount of dirty trash? Even Van Doren [4] told me how lucky I was to get so much reputation out of one book, as if the vilest rubbish doesn't get ten times more, everywhere you turn. Why have things got to be made so unfair and hard for me? In addition to my personal troubles, I have to listen to eight thousand Jeremiahs yelling: "Wait and see. . . . We will be pleasantly surprised, of course, if he amounts to anything, but . . ." etc. It makes me vomit! Sometimes I think everyone in the world is that way: their idea of helping you is to kick you in the face: if you succeed, it's because you have been trampled by adversity and they've really done you a good turn. Why shouldn't people in America buy more copies of my book than they have bought? Why should I be so damned humble before them, when they will rush out and buy trash by Wilder or someone else by the million? Please write to me soon.

To A. S. FRERE-REEVES

Hotel Lorius
Montreux
Aug. 2, 1930

Dear Frere:

Thanks for your long letter and the big batch of clippings. When they came, I took them to a café, ordered a big beer, took a long breath and

[4] Carl Van Doren.

began! I am still alive, I am not cast down, I do not want to curse God and die. I don't know whether you had to hand-pick these notices carefully to spare my feelings—I hope not!—but it seems to me those you sent were pretty good, and three or four of them were pretty damned splendid. Of course, Richard Aldington is a peach—I think this is one of the most generous things I ever heard of, and I am writing him to-day to tell him so: if the rest of them had rotten-egged me, I could never forget what he's done. I thought the *Times Literary Supplement* was mighty good, too, as well as all the other *Times* notices. As for the thousand copies every four days—that sounds stupendous: I think of The Thin Red Line, and the tenacity of the Bulldog Breed, and I hope this present generation of Britons will not prove degenerate: let them stick to their guns for at least forty days (Sundays included)—and if they want to keep it up longer, they won't hurt *my* feelings.

As for [you,] Frere, I think it was a lucky day when I met you, and you became my publisher. I can never know the history of all you've done, but please don't think I accept all this complacently: I know your value, and I am filled with profound and enormous gratitude. I hope you will always be my friend and that you will find no strangeness to me because I am from another country and speak a different accent. Remember that I am an American and that I will open my heart to you on any thing that may belong to my vision of life and not to yours; but never remember me as a foreigner and a stranger—the real republic of this earth stretches from here to China, and just as you are closer to me and nearer to the color of my hand and heart and spirit than most Americans, so, I hope and believe, do I come closer to your thought and language than most Englishmen. Sometime I want to tell you how I felt that day when you took me around to see Richard Aldington and you were all old friends and talked the same language: you and Mr. Aldington and Mrs. Patmore [1] and Tom McGreevy. [2] I felt so strange and foreign, and yet I felt so close to you, as if I had only to find the knob somewhere and open the door or poke my finger through the wall. We are all four in Exile, but sometimes there are flashes of lightning and we see a way we thought we had forgotten. . . .

I suppose, Frere, that you may have spared me some rough reviews, but your letters to me seemed really cheerful about the book: I hope this is true, and that you and Heinemann are really pleased about the way it's going. Please don't be polite to me about this: speak plainly. But if some of them said I am no good, don't believe it: I will write you other books that will put this one in the shade, and we will make the Forces of Darkness eat crow before we've done. . . .

[1] Mrs. Brigit Patmore, mother of Derek Patmore.
[2] Thomas McGreevy, the Irish poet.

. . . The weather is hot but very fine here, and my pastime is to eat that good lake fish you like so well. Scott Fitzgerald telegraphed me from Paris this morning that he had just finished my first book after twenty consecutive hours, and that he was "enormously moved and grateful." I hope he repents and leads a better life hereafter. I am working on my new book every day.

P.S. And please send the author a copy of that English first edition before it becomes so damned valuable he can't afford to buy it!

The following letter to Susan Hyde (now Mrs. Joseph Tonetti) was never mailed, but was found among Wolfe's papers. He had met Miss Hyde in New York shortly before he sailed on his Guggenheim trip, and had occasionally seen her and her brother, Robert McKee Hyde, and the other members of their party in Paris in June.

To SUSAN HYDE

Geneva, Switzerland

[August, 1930]

Dear Susan:

Thanks for your nice letter, and also for the hundred French francs. I won't call it a gift, since you say you owe it to me, and I'm not going to argue with such a nice girl about a little filthy lucre. I don't honestly remember the incident at all. Anyway, I've already changed it into twenty Swiss francs, and the drinks are on you: I'm sorry you can't be here to share them with me. I will take great care not to spend a cent of this windfall on Swiss food—it's all going into French wine. Swiss cooking has easily lived up to all that has been said about it: it is not bad; it is a great deal worse than that—it is so horribly dull that when you eat it, weariness and horror rushes over your soul, you chew meditatively and black despair overwhelms you; and when you have, as you almost always have, an accompaniment of grey, soggy sky and English spinsters, you want to curse God and die. God knows what they do to it, but unquestionably food takes on the colour of one's soul, and all the grey cloudy stuff these people have in their souls gets into their cooking. Things are brought to you in magnificent style, in great silver tureens, and the waiter bends reverently over you as he serves you: when this farce is enacted I burst into insane laughter and cry out: "What a travesty! God! God! God!" He pulls off the cover of a magnificent silver dish, and there lies a piece of boiled lake fish; with pride and exulting, he puts this dead white flabby corpse, still covered with its slimy skin, upon your plate; hot boiled fumes of dreary sudsiness come up from it, and meanwhile he tells you how good it is to-day: you taste it and your mouth is full of desolation and the delicious savor of old boiled flannel—and suddenly you know the man has. . . .

[A PAGE IS MISSING HERE]

Thanks again for your letter and the hundred francs: I did not need either to make me think of you (God! Wolfe! You're turning out to be a regular Frenchman!) but I thank you and send you my warmest and kindest greetings. Write me (old address) when you get time. I do not know how long I shall be over here: it depends on whether I get my work done.

The following cablegram was evidently sent by Wolfe in reply to a letter from Mrs. Bernstein in which she expressed great anxiety about his failure to write to her and threatened to sail immediately for Europe to find him unless he cabled that he was all right.

To ALINE BERNSTEIN

[Cablegram]

[Geneva]

[August 12 (?), 1930]

Let's help each other. Be fair. Remember I'm alone. Letter follows. Hotel Bellevue, Geneva, three days. Paris address thereafter.

The following letter to Mrs. Bernstein is evidently a fragmentary rough draft of the one Wolfe actually sent, since it was found among his own papers.

To ALINE BERNSTEIN

Grand Hotel Bellevue
Geneva

[August 12 (?), 1930]

Dear Aline:

I cabled you this afternoon and said that I would write, but I am unable to say very much to you. I have tried to write you, but the letter

I started had too much bitterness in it about our life together, and about your friends, so I destroyed it. I no longer want to say these things to you because they do no good, and most of them have been said before.

We have known each other for five years, I can never forget you, and I know that nothing else to equal my feeling for you in intensity and passion will ever happen to me. But we are now at the end of the rope. My life has been smashed by this thing, but I am going to see if I can get back on my feet again. There is just one thing ahead of me:—work. It remains to be seen if I still have it in me to do it. If I have not, then I am lost.

You have your work, you have your children, you have your friends and family. If you feel the agony about me that you say you feel in your letters and cables, I can only say that you should give yourself completely to those things that you have. A letter as short as this one is bound to seem harsh and brutal, but you know what I feel and that I gave everything in me to my love for you.

[THE LETTER BREAKS OFF UNFINISHED HERE, OR THE REMAINDER
OF IT HAS BEEN . LOST]

Wolfe sent the following letter to Frere-Reeves after reading two very unfavorable English reviews of Look Homeward, Angel: *one by Frank Swinnerton in* The London Evening News *for August 8, and one by Gerald Gould in* The London Observer *for August 17.*

To A. S. FRERE-REEVES

Geneva

August 18, 1930

Dear Frere:

Please accept my sympathy for the death of your dog: I think there is a kind of sorrow over the death of a fine animal that we do not feel for a person, although people would misunderstand this and think it bad. At any rate there's not much false about how a dog feels.

I left Montreux a week ago, but returned for baggage and mail a few days later and found a letter, a note, and some clippings. I read the Swinnerton review and also one in yesterday's *Observer*. There's not much I can say to you now: I'm pretty badly hit by these reviews, and also by some personal affairs, and I had rather write you later. I have stopped writing and want a little time to think things over. Please do not think I am belly-aching when I tell you that I had hoped for a better reception from the critics of these important English papers, and that I think some of them have been unfair and prejudiced.

As for you, please understand that my feeling will always be full of warmth and gratitude because of what you have done. You have been more than my publisher, you have been my friend, and I assure you that I think of your own disappointment over the book almost as much as of my own.

I have stopped all mail from Paris, but my address will continue to be The Guaranty Trust Co. Please write me there. I still intend to come to England to see you, but I am coming later when I've forgotten about this business, and the critics have stopped writing about it.

Meanwhile, dear Frere, I send you my kindest greetings, and I hope you are getting time for a holiday and for a rest.

The following fragment was found among Wolfe's own papers and was never mailed. It undoubtedly is part of the unfinished "Answer to Critics, Point by Point" which Wolfe mentions in his letter of September 9 to Frere-Reeves.

To A. S. FRERE-REEVES

Grand Hotel Bellevue
Geneva

[August, 1930]

. . . My whole position is simply this: I was a young fellow of twenty-six or twenty-seven and I wanted to write a book, and I wrote it. I realized the book had great imperfections, and I realize them more keenly now, but I thought then, and still do, that it had good things in it, and that it might find a kindly public who would value it, and believe in it, and hope I would go on. I had a fairly comprehensive idea of the writing being done in England and America, and without comparing myself in any way to any writer, I thought that if the work of these people was valued and respected I had a right to hope for some appreciation of mine: I thought then and I still think that I have something to say, but I am rapidly coming to the point where silence seems best. I have found out during the past year that a writer is an open target for anyone in the world who wants to throw a rotten egg—and he can do nothing about it. The most personal and insulting things may be said about his work and about him, and it must all be swallowed down as "unbiased criticism." Moreover, old ladies in Akron, Ohio, in Leeds, and in Georgia, or in New York and London, open up and call a man's book dull, clumsy, incoherent, of no interest whatever and not worth reading, but they will take two columns to say this which might be said in twenty words: what they really mean is that they think your book is foul, indecent, a menace to morals and established government, etc. This kind of hypocrisy makes you want to vomit. I have had every name in the library hurled at my head from Euripides to Ruby M. Ayres. It seems that I have "imitated" all of them—I shall some day be a circulating library on my own hook if I ever finish reading all the books I am supposed to have imitated. Joyce, Dreiser, and D. H. Lawrence are pitched at me most often, and very often together (the reason, of course, these three utterly different people are lumped together, particularly Joyce and Lawrence—could two writers be *more* unlike?—is that the reviewer feels that they are very "free"—that is to say "sex, you know"—that is to say, "bordering on the salacious"—that is to say "dirty.")

Any work therefore that uses the word "*shit*" is stolen from Rabelais, and any work in which a man goes to bed with a woman, or in which the sexual act is mentioned, is obviously inspired by the good old team of "Joyce and Lawrence." Now, as to my own book, I own up to the Joyce— I read the works of that talented gentleman very assiduously and if some flavour of them has crept into my book I can not deny it: but as to Lawrence, I had read nothing of his until I finished the book except "The Captain's Doll," a short piece, and not I think sufficient to make of me the devoted disciple the reviewers would have me be. As to "Moby Dick," I read that magnificent work for the first time about six months ago in America in order to understand something about this man Melville that I had been imitating. I'm afraid these simple facts would not convince the reviewers, they would smile in a superior way and say that all this didn't matter at all, that I had soaked up "influences" from the atmosphere without knowing it, etc. God! it makes you long for the desert, Swiss cooking, lake fish—anything to bring oblivion.

Now for Dr Swinnerton: his review starts out with a long preamble about "this generation." [1] It is true the quotation marks are his own—

[1] Swinnerton's review began: "A superior-minded reviewer said last year that a certain novel by an author of the 1884 vintage 'had no interest for this generation.' As the book subsequently sold largely, I assume that the reviewer was wrong, and that all he meant was that he did not like it himself. In the circumstances, I think it needs to be stated clearly that, although the youngest writers of to-day must often feel impatient with those of their elders who are better known and more successful than themselves, they have no right to feel as they do. . . . Those novelists who are to-day big enough to be shot at could not have survived if they had not possessed exceptional talent. To sneer at that talent is to be guilty of silliness. Silliness because 'this generation' will soon be attacked in turn."

he is quoting from "a superior-minded reviewer"—but by the time he gets ready to settle my hash, the reader feels that "this generation" is my own product, or the contribution of one of my co-conspirators. Now, in the first place, dear Frere, as I have told you in other letters, I am not very much concerned with "generations" at the present. I have lately had a very thorough soaking in "Ecclesiastes" and that remarkable man had the very strange idea that one generation is very like another: "One generation passeth away, and another generation cometh: but the earth abideth forever." This talk about "generations" seems to be most common among people of Swinnerton's "generation"—I don't know what his "generation" is—(you see, he's got me to doing it, too)—I had always felt he was still a fairly young man who had written a book called "Nocturne" that I read one time and thought very good—but now, since I have been put in my place and told where I belong, I suppose I shall have to imagine Mr. Swinnerton standing at the window of the Union Club, or whatever the English equivalent is, staring out with an apoplectic face and a quivering goatee at all the young fellows who are behaving indecently in the street just to shock him.

I have observed that the "this generation" business is prevalent both in America and England, but I think it is more prevalent in England. Perhaps it is the war, but these *older* people (they have themselves insisted on that age, remember) seem to think that the young people are banded together in some deliberate movement against their traditions. For example, Swinnerton says: "As for the work of the really young, how 'new' is it." (This 'new' business of course preys upon their mind.) "Is there new technique? Are there new ideas, new feelings about life? I shall be told 'yes,' but I do not agree."—He may be told "yes," but he will never be told "yes" by me—he will probably be told "yes" by this straw dummy he has created as a sparring partner in his article, and that he knocks down so frequently with such delightful ease. Wouldn't life be wonderful, Frere, if we could settle our opponents and justify our prejudices in this way—simply by creating a little dummy that we could flatten out on every occasion, crying: "You think you are pretty smart, don't you? (Bam!) You think you have something new to offer, don't you? (Biff!) Have you any new feelings about life? (Wham!) Do you think you can shock *us?* Do you think you're the only one who has ever been young? Do you think you can sneer at your elders? *I'll* show you! (Baff! Bam! Bing! Wham! Sock!)"

As far as I am concerned, I do not think I have any "new ideas" or "any new feelings about life." Perhaps this is a discreditable confession for a member of "the new generation" to make, but I have never understood that a man is compelled to create out of the fundamental and unchanging structure of life a reality that is not there. In "Ecclesiastes," in

"Job," and in "the Song of Solomon," I have this summer found magnificently expressed what I have myself been almost thirty years in finding:
I not only have nothing to add to what I found there, I even fall far short
of the wisdom in those poems, and I fall infinitely short of their beauty
and talent. Each man weaves out bloodily his own vision of life, in each
case the combination of experience may be somewhat different, but to
demand that it be "new," to call for some phantom and impossible
"originality," is insane. Swinnerton suggests that he is past forty—I suppose he was born along in the 80's. I was born in 1900, but I imagine
he came from his mother's womb in much the same way as I came from
mine, I suppose he has drawn his breath in much the same way as the rest
of us, and that the processes attending his decay, death, and dissolution
will be the same as it is for all men.

Swinnerton uses the words "glib," "superficial" and "pretentious" [2] in
his discussion of my book, but I think he might better have applied them
to his own review. I do not put much faith in the people who rely on the
word "pretentious"—it is simply a curse-word, a term of abuse, a word
wherewith we can ease ourselves of our prejudices; and I have noticed that
it is most often used by folk who pride themselves on "the quiet note,"
"urbanity," "restraint"—and all the things that have no part of your
magnificent literature. I have loved and honored your great poetry since I
was old enough to hold a book in my hands, but my dear Frere, I thank
God it was pretentious. At the present time you have Mr. Frank Swinnerton—you have better than that, I grant you—but you *had* Dickens, you had
Donne, you had Shakespeare, you had Coleridge, you had Pope, you had
Chaucer, you had Sterne and Fielding and Sam Johnson. A nice bloody
Goddamned lot of "quiet" "restrained" "urbane" bastards, weren't they?
In the name of Jesus, where has this horrible business of "quietness,"
"restraint"—the "steady, old man" school of literature come from? You had
Smollett and Defoe and "Moll Flanders," and now you have Squire Galsworthy with his quiet manly gulps. I don't say a word against *that* man
because Perkins tells me he's a fine fellow—but Good God! Frere, where
did this great English convention of *not having any emotions* come from?
No people in the world use the word "sentimental" so often as your people
do to-day, and no people in the world are so tainted with sentimentality.

[THE LETTER BREAKS OFF HERE]

[2] Swinnerton did not actually use the words "superficial" or "pretentious" in regard
to Wolfe. He did say: "Mr. Wolfe has a very dangerous fluency. He is almost glib,
particularly in his improvisations of bar-room scenes, domestic scenes in which a
ranting father performs mechanically, and scenes of coquetry; and to my mind he
is intolerable in his passages of ecstatic apostrophe. . . . The book is a great jumble
of good and bad. It is labored with adjectives and abverbs. . . . It is emotional
without feeling, crowded with violences and blasphemies, and to one reader appears
incoherent, not from strength or intensity, but from over-excited verbosity."

To JOHN HALL WHEELOCK

Grand Hotel Bellevue
Geneva

August 18, 1930

Dear Jack:

Thanks very much for your good letter. There is very little that I can say to you now except that (1) I have stopped writing and do not want ever to write again.

The place that I had found to stay—Montreux—did not remain private very long: (2) Fitzgerald told a woman in Paris where I was, and she cabled the news to America—I have had all kinds of letters and cables speaking of death and agony, from people who are perfectly well, and leading a comfortable and luxurious life among their friends at home. In addition, one of Mrs. Boyd's "young men" descended upon me, or upon Montreux, and began to pry around. This, of course, may be an accident, but too many accidents of this sort have happened.

(3) The English edition has been a catastrophe: some of the reviews were good, but some have said things that I shall never be able to forget—dirty, unfair, distorted, and full of mockery. I asked the publisher not to send any reviews but he did all the same—he even wrote a special letter to send a very bad one, from which he said he got no satisfaction. Nevertheless the book is selling fast and they continue to advertise. All I want now is money—enough to keep me until I get things straight again. It is amusing to see the flood of letters and telegrams I began to get from "old friends" who were "simply dying to see me" when the first good reviews came out in England—but it is even more amusing to see how the silence of death has settled upon these same people recently.—I want to vomit. I should like to vomit until the thought and memory of them is gone from me forever.

There is no life in this world worth living, there is no air worth breathing, there is nothing but agony and the drawing of the breath in nausea and labor, until I get the best of this tumult and sickness inside me. I have behaved all right since I came here: I have lived by myself for almost four months now and I have made no answers: people have charged me and my work with bombast, rant and noisiness—but save for this letter to you, I have lived alone, and held my tongue, and kept my peace: how many of them can say the same? What reward in the world can compensate the man who tries to create something? My book caused hate and rancor at home, venom and malice among literary tricksters in New York, and mockery and abuse over here. I hoped that that book, with all its imperfections, would mark a beginning: instead it has marked an ending.

Life is not worth the pounding I have taken both from public and private sources these last two years. But if there is some other life—and I am sure there is—I am going to find it. I am not thirty yet, and if these things have not devoured me, I shall find a way out yet. I have loved life and hated death, and I still do.

I have cut off all mail by wiring Paris, and I am going to stay alone for some time to come. I know that that is the only way. Write me if you can. The address is the Guaranty Trust Co., Paris. I hope this finds you well and that you get a good vacation.

To MAXWELL E. PERKINS

Geneva

August 18, 1930

Dear Mr. Perkins:

Will you please have Mr. Darrow [1] send me, at his convenience, a statement of whatever money is due me? I shall not write any more books, and since I must begin to make other plans for the future, I should like to know how much money I will have. I want to thank you and Scribners very sincerely for your kindness to me, and I shall hope someday to resume and continue a friendship which has meant a great deal to me.

I hope this finds you well, and entirely recovered from the trouble that took you to Baltimore. Please get a good vacation and a rest away from the heat and confusion of New York.

The following unfinished and unmailed letter to Maxwell Perkins was evidently written during Wolfe's period of depression in August, 1930— probably soon after his letter of August 18 from Geneva.

To MAXWELL E. PERKINS

Dear Mr. Perkins:

We create the figure of our father, and we create the figure of our enemy. The figure of my enemy I created years ago: he is a person, he has a name, he is an inferior thing, he has no talent, but I made of him my Opponent: it is this person who will always appear to cheat you of what you most desire: he is nothing; he has no life save that you gave him, but

[1] Whitney Darrow was at this time head of the Trade Department at Scribners and a Director of the firm. He was a Vice President of the firm from 1931–1953.

he is there to take all you want away from you. Thus, if you love a woman, and your Opponent is millions of people, thousands of miles away, he will come to trick her from you. He is there like a fate and a destiny. He is nothing, but he is all the horror and pain on earth. This has happened to me.

Where are you? Are you crawling out of it? Send me my money or send me my ticket home. Send me your friendship or send me your final disbelief. I will tell you this very plainly: I do not think I am a good venture for Chas. Scrib. Sons. I think I may be done for utterly. I think you may now get out of it profitably. If anything's left, send it to me, and break our pub. relations.

To A. S. FRERE-REEVES

Basel, Switzerland
September 9, 1930

Dear Frere:

I have been up in the air—literally: I have made my first flight by airplane and I think there's nothing like it to ease a distressed spirit. I left Geneva several weeks ago, flew to Lyons, stayed there or in that district for a week, then flew to Marseilles. From there I went to Arles and Provence. God! it was hot: the sweat made puddles in your ears when you tried to sleep. Then I flew back from Marseilles to Geneva where I found your telegram which made me feel better. Now I am here on my way to the Black Forest, and I shall write you a long letter there. I was unwinding an immensely long letter on you when I started my travels—an answer to critics, point by point, etc.[1]—but it will never get finished now, which is a good thing. While I was flying three thousand feet above the valley of the Rhone, I looked down and saw a little moving dot in one of the fields shovelling manure: it looked so much like a critic that I have not wanted to finish my letter since. Besides, the only thing a writer can do is to keep his mouth shut: I have discovered that once his book is published he is the target for what anyone in the world wants to say about him or his work, but I think he ought to hold his tongue and his peace.

At any rate, there's much to be thankful for—I no longer have to eat lake fish. I don't know whether I told you my new theory, but here it is. I no longer believe it is boiled flannel as you say. I think it is really lake fish—only they don't tell you what lake it is from. It is from the Lake of Galilee, and it is what was left over from that great catch 2000 years ago when our Lord Jesus Christ commanded his disciples to cast in their nets.

[1] The unmailed letter of August, 1930.

What do you think of this? Don't you think there is much to be said for it?

Basel is a very German town and there are some magnificent pictures here. I have written two or three shorter pieces and done a good deal on my book but I may finally come to England and try to finish it during the winter. I am a little tired of being alone, and I am sure that there are two or three people there who would let me see them from time to time. Your secretary wrote me (enclosing clippings) that you had gone to the South of France: I hope the trip did you good, and that this letter finds you well and happy. Thanks again for the telegram and all the other marks of kindness and good cheer. I am all right now, and hope to bring something to England with me that can be typed and shown to people.

The following notes were written on a page of Wolfe's small pocket notebook, and were never mailed. "Emily" was probably Emily MacRae, now Mrs. Benjamin C. West, who had known Wolfe in Asheville and New York. "Jack" was John Hall Wheelock. "Mr. Holzknecht" was probably Professor Karl J. Holzknecht of New York University who had written Wolfe some months earlier about the possibility of his talking to the English Club there, and who may have written further about this on August 3. The initials K.M.R.A.A. in the note to Ezra Pound are evidently an American version of the following passage from James Joyce's Ulysses:

> " K. M. R. I. A.
> He can kiss my royal Irish arse, Myles
> Crawford cried loudly over his shoulder.
> Any time he likes tell him. "

NOTES WRITTEN IN THE BLACK FOREST

[Freiburg, Germany?]

[September, 1930]

Dear Mr. Perkins: I got your letter in Basel, Switzerland.

Yours,

Dear Emily: I got your note in Geneva, Switzerland.

Yours truly,

Dear Jack: I got your letter the other day. It is a fine letter. I wish I could answer it. I am all right now and will write you later.

Dear Mama: I died in Marseilles on Aug 22. I am buried in a good Christian Churchyard there and I hope you will come to see me.

Dear Mr. Holzknecht: Thanks for your letter of Aug 3.

Y'rs Tr'ly

To Mr. Ezra P'd.

Dear Mr. P'd: I r'd a p'm of y'rs once. K.M.R.A.A.

Y'rs Tr'ly

To MAXWELL E. PERKINS

[Radiogram]

Freiburg, Germany
September 13, 1930

Working again. Excuse letter. Writing you.

The following letter was never sent to Henry T. Volkening but was found among Wolfe's papers. Instead Wolfe wrote him a briefer and more restrained letter on September 22, which was less revealing and has therefore been omitted here.

To HENRY T. VOLKENING

Hotel Freiburger Hof
Freiburg, Germany
[September, 1930]

Dear Henry:

Please forgive me for having made you such a poor return for your fine letters. I haven't been too busy to write . . . I have two very long unfinished letters to you stuffed in among my junk: the reason I didn't send them was that I couldn't finish them—they would have each been ten million words long, and then I should not have been able to tell you about it. . . . The only way I'll ever be able to tell you about these last four months, Henry, is to talk to (not *with*) you, and I long to do this, although I do not know how long it will be before I have that happiness. You must prepare yourself for the ordeal in whatever far off future: clasp a bottle of your bootlegger's finest brew in your right hand and endure until the tidal wave shall have spent its force.

I am at length in the Black Forest. I arrived here a few days ago by a kind of intuition—the inside of me was like a Black Forest and I think the name kept having its unconscious effect on me. It is a very beautiful place —a landscape of rich, dark melancholy, a place with a Gothic soul, and I am glad that I have come here. These people, with all that is bestial, savage, supernatural, and also all that is rich, profound, kindly and simple, move me more deeply than I can tell you. France at the present time has completely ceased to give me anything. That is no doubt my fault, but their books, their art, their cities, their people, their conversation—nothing but their food at the present time means anything to me. The Americans in Paris would probably sneer at this—I mean these Americans who know all about it and are perfectly sure what French literature and French civilization stand for, although they read no French books, speak little of the language, and are never alone with French people.

I cannot tell you much at present about these last four months: I will tell you that I have had some of the worst moments of my life during them, and also some of the best. All told, it has been a pretty hard time, but I am going to be all right now. I don't know if you have ever stayed by yourself for so long a time (few people have and I do not recommend it) but if you are at all a thoughtful person, you are bound to come out of it with some of your basic ore—you'll sweat it out of your brain and heart and spirit. The thing I have done is one of the cruelest forms of surgery in the world, but I knew that for me it was right. I can give you some idea of the way I have cut myself off from people I knew when I tell you that only once in the past six weeks have I seen anyone I knew—that was Mr. F. Scott Fitzgerald, the master of the human heart, and I came upon him unavoidably in Geneva a week or two ago.

I can tell you briefly what my movements have been: I went to Paris from New York and, outside of a short trip to Rouen and a few places near Paris, I stayed there for almost two months. I think this was the worst time of all: I was in a kind of stupor and unfit to see anyone, but I ran into people I knew from time to time and went to dinner or the theatre with them. My publisher came over from England and was very kind—he is a very fine fellow—he took me out and I met some of the celebrities—Mr. Michael Arlen and some of the Left Bank People. This lasted little over a day: I was no good with people and I did not go back to see them. I began to work out of desperation in that noisy, sultry, uncomfortable city of Paris and I got a good deal done. Finally I got out of it and went to Switzerland. I found a very quiet, comfortable hotel in Montreux; I had a good room with a balcony over-looking the lake; and in the weeks that followed I got a great deal accomplished.

I knew no one here at all—the place was filled with itinerant English and American spinsters buying postcards of the Lake of Geneva—but one night I ran into the aforesaid Mr. Fitzgerald, your old time college pal and fellow-Princetonian.[1] I had written Mr. F. a note in Paris, because Perkins is very fond of him and told me for all his faults he's a fine fellow, and Mr. F. had had me to his sumptuous apartment near the Bois for lunch and three or four gallons of wine, cognac, whiskey, etc. I finally departed from his company at ten that night in the Ritz Bar where he was entirely surrounded by Princeton boys, all nineteen years old, all drunk, and all half-raw. He was carrying on a spirited conversation with them about why Joe Zinzendorff did not get taken into the Triple-Gazzaza Club: I heard one of the lads say "Joe's a good boy, Scotty, but you know he's a fellow that ain't got much background."—I thought it was time for Wolfe to depart, and I did.

I had not seen Mr. F. since that evening until I ran into him at the Casino at Montreux. That was the beginning of the end of my stay at that beautiful spot. I must explain to you that Mr. F. had discovered the day I saw him in Paris that I knew a very notorious young lady, now resident in Paris getting her second divorce, and by her first marriage connected with one of those famous American families who cheated drunken Indians out of their furs seventy years ago, and are thus at the top of the established aristocracy now. Mr. F. immediately broke out in a sweat on finding I knew the lady and damned near broke his neck getting around there: he insisted that I come ("Every writer," this great philosopher said, "is a social climber.") and when I told him very positively I would not go to see the lady, this poet of the passions at once began to see all the elements of a romance—the cruel and dissolute society beauty playing with the tortured heart of the sensitive young writer, etc.: he eagerly demanded my reasons for staying away. I told him the lady had cabled to America for my address, had written me a half dozen notes and sent her servants to my hotel when I first came to Paris, and that, having been told of her kind heart, I gratefully accepted her hospitality and went to her apartment for lunch, returned once or twice, and found that I was being paraded before a crowd of worthless people, palmed off as someone who was madly in love with her, and exhibited with a young French soda jerker with greased hair who was on her payroll, and who, she boasted to me, slept with her every night. ("I like his bod-dy," she hoarsely whispered, "I must have some bod-dy whose bod-dy I like to sleep with," etc.)

The end finally came when she began to call me at my hotel in the morning, saying she had had four pipes of opium the night before and was "all shot to pieces," and what in God's name would she do: she had not seen Raymond or Roland or Louis or whatever his name was for

---

[1] Volkening went to Princeton six years after Fitzgerald and did not know him, but says that Wolfe always persisted in lumping them together as Princeton men.

four hours; he had disappeared; she was sure something had happened to him; that I must do something at once; that I was such a comfort she was coming to the hotel at once; I must hold her hand, etc. It was too much. I didn't care whether Louis had been absent three or thirty hours, or whether she had smoked four or forty pipes, since nothing ever happens to these people anyhow—they make a show of recklessness but they take excellent care they don't get hurt in the end—and for a man trying very hard to save his own life, I did not think it wise to try to live for these other people and let them feed upon me.

So I told Mr. F., the great analyst of the soul, to tell the woman nothing about me, to give no information at all about me or what I was doing, or where I was. I told him this in Paris, I told him again in Switzerland, and on both occasions the man got to her as fast as he could. That ended Montreux for me. She immediately sent all the information back to America—and the heart-rending letters, cables, etc., with threats of coming to find me, going mad, dying, etc. began to come directly to my hotel. I wanted to batter the walls down. The hotel people, who had been very kind to me, charged me three francs extra because I had brought a bottle of wine from outside into the hotel. (They have a right in Switzerland to do this), but I took my rage out on them, told them I was leaving next day, went on a spree, broke windows, plumbing fixtures, etc. in the town, and came back to the hotel at 2 A.M., pounded on the door of the director and on the doors of two English spinsters, rushed howling with laughter up and down the halls, cursing and singing—and in short, *had* to leave.

I went to Geneva where I stayed a week or so. Meanwhile my book came out in England. I wrote beforehand and asked the publisher not to send reviews because I was working on the new one and did not want to be bothered: he wrote back a very jubilant letter and said the book was a big success and said "Read these reviews—you have nothing to be afraid of." I read them; they were very fine; I got in a state of great excitement. He sent me great batches of reviews then—most of them very good ones, some bad. I foolishly read them and got in a very excited condition about a book I should have left behind me months ago. On top of this, and the cables and letters from New York, I got in Geneva two very bad reviews —cruel, unfair, bitterly personal. I was fed up with everything: I wrote Perkins a brief note telling him good-bye, please send my money, I would never write again, etc; I wrote the English publisher another; I cut off all mail by telegraph to Paris; I packed up, rushed to the aviation field and took the first airplane, which happened to be going to Lyons. . . .

It was a grand trip, lasted three weeks, and did me an infinite amount of good. All the time I scrawled, wrote, scribbled. I have written a great deal—my book is one immense long book made up of four average-sized ones, each complete in itself, but each part of the whole. I stayed in Geneva one day and of course Mr. F. was on the job, although he had been at Vevey and then at Caux. His wife, he says, has been very near madness in a sanatorium at Geneva, but is now getting better. (It turned out that she was a good half hour by fast train from Geneva.) When I told him I was leaving Geneva and coming to the Black Forest, he immediately decided to return to Caux. I was with him the night before I left Geneva; he got very drunk and bitter; he wanted me to go and stay with his friends Dorothy Parker and some people named Murphy [2] in Switzerland nearby. When I made no answer to this invitation, he was quite annoyed; said that I got away from people because I was afraid of them, etc. (which is quite true, and which I think, in view of my experiences with Mr. F. et al, shows damned good sense. I wonder how long Mr. F. would last by himself, with no more Ritz Bar, no more Princeton boys, no more Mr. F.). At any rate, I came to Basel, and F. rode part way with me on his way back to Caux.

A final word about him: I am sorry I ever met him; he has caused me trouble and cost me time; but he has good stuff in him yet. His conduct to me was mixed with malice and generosity; he read my book and was very fine about it: then his bitterness began to qualify him: he is sterile and impotent and alcoholic now, and unable to finish his book, and I think he wanted to injure my own work. This is base, but the man has been up against it: he really loves his wife and I suppose helped get her into this terrible fix. I hold nothing against him now—of course he can't hurt me in the end—but I trusted him and I think he played a shabby trick by telling tales on me.

At any rate, I got over my dumps very quickly, sweated it out in Provence, and here I am, trying to finish up one section of the book before I leave here. I may go to England where Reeves, my publisher, assures me I can be quiet and work in peace: I like him immensely and there are also two or three other people there I can talk to. I have never been so full of writing in my life—if I can do the thing I want to, I believe it will be good.

I found a great batch of letters and telegrams when I got back from exile. Reeves was very upset by my letter and was wiring everywhere. He sent me a very wonderful letter: he said the book had had a magnificent reception and not to be a damned fool about a few reviews. And Perkins wrote me two wonderful letters—he is a grand man, and I believe in him with all my heart. All the others at Scribners have written me, and I am ashamed of my foolish letters and resolved not to let them down.

I know it's going to be all right now. I believe I'm out of the woods at last. Nobody is going to die on account of me; nobody is going to suffer any more than I have suffered: the force of these dire threats gets a little

[2] Mr. and Mrs. Gerald Murphy of New York.

weaker after a while, and I know now, no matter what anyone may ever say, that in one situation I have acted fairly and kept my head up. I am a little bitter at rich people at present: I am a little bitter at people who live in comfort and luxury, surrounded by friends and amusement, and yet are not willing to give an even chance to a young man living alone in a foreign country and trying to get work done. I did all that was asked of me; I came away here when I did not want to come; I have fought it out alone; and now I am done with it. I do not think it will be possible for me to live in New York for a year or two, and when I come back I may go elsewhere to live. As for the incredible passion that possessed me when I was twenty-five years old and that brought me to madness and, I think, almost to destruction—that is over: that fire can never be kindled again.

[THE LETTER BREAKS OFF HERE]

To HENRY T. VOLKENING

[POSTCARD: ST. JEAN ET LA SAINTE VIERGE: DETAIL FROM THE
CRUCIFIXION PANEL OF THE ISENTHEIMER ALTAR OF
MATHIAS GRUNEWALD]

Colmar, Alsace Lorraine
[September 23, 1930]

Dear Henry: This is one of the greatest men in the world. You've no idea how beautiful the whole thing is (it is immense—this is only a small part) until you see it.

VII

LONDON, AND WORK ON OF TIME AND THE RIVER *AND* THE OCTOBER FAIR

1930–1931

To A. S. FRERE-REEVES

Paris

September 27, 1930

Dear Frere:

Thanks for your letter. I am coming to England the first part of next week (about Tuesday, I think). Of course I shall be delighted to go down to your place in the country for a day or two: it is most kind of you to ask me, and I am looking forward to it. I think I shall go to London for a day or two in order to get the feel of England once more (it has been over three years since I was there) and to get some much-needed repairs made upon my wardrobe. If I am going to visit an English gentleman on his country estate, I ought to get patched up in the places that show.

Please forgive me for being so skittish about the book. I am prepared to talk on almost any subject under the sun—the German elections, the weather, the cathedral at Strasbourg—but I hope to God I do not hear about the book at present. I am a burden and a care to you but be patient with me a little and I shall do better.

The weather here is most dismal—where in God's name did that superstition ever come from about the beautiful weather of Paris? The London climate is universally condemned, but of the two I think it is perhaps the better.

I think I shall go to a hotel in Russell Square, and I'll phone you or send you a telegram from there. Meanwhile, good luck and God bless you.

To MAXWELL E. PERKINS

[Cablegram]

London
October 14, 1930.

Established small flat here alone in house.[1] Old woman looking after me. Seeing no one. Believe book finally coming. Excited. Too early to say. Letter follows.

The next letter to Perkins was written from London in October, but was never finished and never mailed.

To MAXWELL E. PERKINS

[London]
[October, 1930]

Dear Mr. Perkins:

I did not know how long it had been since I had written you, or sent that cable from the Black Forest, until I got your cable [1] the other day. When you are alone for a long period, Time begins to make an unreal sound, and all the events of your life, past and present, are telescoped: you wake in the morning in a foreign land thinking of home, and at night in your sleep you hear voices of people you knew years ago, or sounds of the streets in America. The changes in time also help this feeling of unreality. I am writing you this at ten o'clock at night in London, for a moment I think of what you may be doing at the same time at ten o'clock, and then I realize it is only five o'clock in New York, and that you are probably at Scribners just before going home.

I think of you a dozen times a day, and I think all of you are in my mind like a [sack (?)] of living radium deposit, whether I am consciously thinking of you or not. My longing for America amounts to a constant ache: I can feel it inside me all the time like some terrible hunger that can not be appeased. It will always be the same: the other night, after listening to miles and miles of the silliest talk by English people about America —it was not a nation but a raw mass of different peoples; Americans were incapable of real feeling, only sentimentality; the country was a matriarchy, the women ruled it; the Americans were incapable of love, with all the rest of it, including the machine age, Puritanism, Rotarians, etc.—I

[1] Frere-Reeves had found Wolfe a flat at 15 Ebury Street.
[1] A cable sent on October 8 which said: "How are you. Please write."

could listen to no more of it and I told them, I think without passion and I know with utter conviction on my part, that to anyone who had ever known America as I have known it, no life in Europe, no life anywhere, can ever seem very interesting. It surprised and angered them, for they saw I meant it, and they had never expected to hear anything like this. People here, specially Mr. Reeves at Heinemann, have been very kind to me. I have not done much going out, but I get a good many invitations.

I am resuming here after several days—it has become for some reason terribly difficult for me to write letters: the more I am away from home, the more I miss seeing a few people, the harder it seems to write to them—it has always been this way. I think the reason is that I have really got started at length, I stay alone in my place here a great deal (I will tell you about it later), I go through periods of the most horrible depression, weariness of spirit, loneliness and despair, but then I think about the book for long stretches and work on it. Only, in God's name, is there not some way to find peace and kindliness in this world, to do one's work without paying so bitterly for human relations!

I have cut almost everything away from me, and if I do not get my work done now I do not know what I shall do: there is nothing else left for me—surely to God it does not have to be made so cruelly and needlessly difficult. I must now tell you plainly certain things—much more plainly than I have ever been able to tell them to you in person, but if I can not tell them to you, who in God's name am I to talk to? I shall try never to cause you any distress or embarrassment—my great fear now is that I will cause you disappointment by failure to do the work you expect me to do. I must tell you now very plainly that you occupy an immense place in my belief and affection:—please do not think I am exaggerating, and please do not be at all embarrassed by this statement—I think it is very unfair to you for me to feel this way, I have no right to place the burden of this feeling on any man, but I think you have become for me a symbol of that outer strength. . . .

[THE LETTER BREAKS OFF UNFINISHED HERE]

To MAXWELL E. PERKINS

> The Guaranty Trust Co.
> London
>
> October 27, 1930

Dear Mr. Perkins:

I am writing you a separate letter telling you what there is to be told at present about myself: this concerns another matter. Two . . . New

York dentists are trying to extort $525 from me for two weeks unsatis-
factory work. I left instructions with Mr. Darrow to pay them, but fortunately told him not to go beyond $200 which I thought would leave a
big surplus. Now these dentists are threatening ominous things if I do not
pay in full at once. I have written them courteously telling them I have not
money enough to pay such a bill, and have never had. (One of them had
just come back from his vacation when I left, business was bad, I think he
intended me to pay for it.) In letters to Mr. Darrow they are *threatening*
to "put the matter in the hands of their Paris representative"—why Paris, I
don't know: I don't live there and have no connection there. I am
assured here in London that they can touch nothing in Europe—letter of
credit, personal belongings.

Now I have been worried enough. I am not trying to avoid payment of
my just debt, but I tell you this thing is an abomination: one man has
charged $285 for seeing me five times and doing an unsatisfactory piece
of work. If I have any money in America—i.e. at Scribners—I want it to
be protected against these people by any means possible. I do not know the
law, but I know that I have the right to dispose of my money as I see fit
and I am therefore sending you a separate statement in which I make
over to you any money that is due me. These people are trying to get
money from me that I cannot afford to lose. I left enough to pay them
amply, the thing is a cheat. Let's don't let them do it: please get my money
made over to you if that is necessary to protect it—you could let me have
it as I need it, I would not bother you, but they would not be able to
touch it. I wish to God I could have a little peace. I am writing you a long
letter. I shall finish that book, so help me God, and if agony and loneliness
can make a book, it will be good. You are the only person in the world
that I can turn to—I am a solitary and an exile. People in comfortable
homes surrounded by friends, may sneer, but it's the simple God's truth!
The weather here is like a sodden blanket of wet grey; misery is on the
faces of the poor; the King opened Parliament today; there is only one
thrilling and interesting place in the world—and that is America: but I am
not cast down, and I will do the book, only *now, now,* is the time they must
not bother me. I am writing you a long letter—I cannot begin to tell you
how I miss seeing you, it is unfair to make you the goat this way.

*On October 23, 1930, Sinclair Lewis had written to Wolfe: "Dear Thomas
Wolfe: I wish there hadn't been quite so many brisk blurb-writers these past
twenty years, using up every once respectable phrase of literary criticism,
so that I might have some fresh phrase with which to express my profound
delight in* Look Homeward, Angel! *There is, you needn't be told, authentic
greatness in it. It and* Farewell to Arms *seem to me to have more spacious*

*power in them than any books for years, American OR foreign. . . . God,
your book is good!"*

*While this letter was on its way to Wolfe in London, Lewis was awarded
the Nobel Prize for Literature for 1930, and in an interview in the* New
York Times *on November 6, again expressed his admiration for* Look Homeward, Angel, *saying: "If Mr. Wolfe keeps up the standard which he has set
in this work, he may have a chance to be the greatest American writer. In
fact, I don't see why he should not be one of the greatest world writers. His
first book is so deep and spacious that it deals with the whole of life."*

*The following fragmentary letter, found among Wolfe's own papers, is
evidently a rough draft of the one which he wrote to thank Lewis.*

To SINCLAIR LEWIS

[London]

[November, 1930]

Dear Mr. Lewis:

Thanks for your letter. I am honored and deeply grateful for what you
said about my book—it is a most generous thing and I will never forget it.
I have read your books since I was twenty: I think you are a man of
genius with the most enormous talent for writing—I am sure very few
people of my age in America have escaped your influence, and certainly I
have not. In view of some of the books I may write, you may not care to
have this crime laid upon you, but there it is.

Your letter came just a few days after we got the news here of your
winning the Nobel Prize: I was happy to hear of it, and. . . .

[THE REMAINDER OF THIS PAGE IS MISSING]

I have got a little flat here and an old woman who looks after it and
cooks for me—the whole thing for three pounds ten a week. I am really at
work every day, and think it is coming now. Sometimes I get homesick as
hell for America—this is honest God's truth, although I have spent half
my time over here for several years. I want to live at home now but I
think New York is out of it. It will be good to get home again and get a
drink of real liquor—this bootleg stuff over here is not worth a damn. I
hope you like it there in Westport—I went there once and thought it was
a beautiful place: the air has a bite and sparkle to it, it is not this wet
wooly stuff they have here at this season.

When I get back to America, I hope

[THE REMAINDER OF THE LETTER IS MISSING]

To ALFRED S. DASHIELL

The Guaranty Trust Co.
50 Pall Mall
London

[November, 1930]

Dear Fritz:

Please forgive me for not having answered your fine long letter before. I have done very little letter writing of any sort to anyone for some time: at one time I wanted to take my pen in hand and "tell you all about it," but telling you all about it seems such a long and complicated business just now that I must wait until I see you, and then I hope they are still running that German place and that I can talk eloquently until I see signs of fatigue and care on your face.

I have been here in this great cit-ee for about two months. I have a bally little digs on Ebury Street (hyah, hyah!) and for over five weeks I have been working like the son-of-a-bitch many charming but misguided bastards consider me. November—lovely London November—soft, wet, woolly, steamy, screamy, shitty November—is here: if you have ever contemplated horror and weariness, if you have ever thought of such jolly subjects as misery, damnation, and death, if you have ever wanted to curse God and die, you have really known nothing but a spirit of rollicking comedy, a child's happy prattle—you have not known London in November. You draw your breath in agony and despair, you walk the leaden air as if you were forcing your way step by step through a ponderous, resisting, and soul-destroying mush: it soaks into your skin, your legs, your bowels, it gets into your heart, it is a grey mucousy substance in which you smother in ennui and dull horror as if you are slowly drawing in some ocean of obscene and unspeakable substance. If, in addition to this, you are invited to a Sunday afternoon tea in a detached "villa" belonging to a literary architect in St. John's Wood, a gent who has written a novel that was well spoken of, and who wears grey-looking glasses on his grey-looking face, if you meet there his wife who also has glasses and a grey face, and their little child, also with glasses, if you drink the weak tea and eat the cold Sunday night lamb, if you hear Mama telling the infant the quaintest, cunningest bedtime story all about a character named Oyjee-Boyjee—Mama invented him and each night he must do the *very dullest* thing you can think of ("It's really awfully hard," Mama said, "to think of a dull thing every night!"—to which I made no reply)—if, I say, you have gone through this, and talked about art and life by the cheerful fumes of the gas burner by which London warms itself, if you have sat in the parlour reeking with its gravedamp chill, if then you go out in the steaming air into a street of villas, catch your bus, and ride home through vast areas of drab brick, lightened by an occasional pub in which you see a few sodden wretches mournfully ruminant over a glass of bitter beer— if you have gone through this, then, my boy, you will smite your brow, and rend your flesh to see the blood come, and cry, "O woe is me! O misery!" and your guts will ache with passion for the Happy Land, the beautiful glorious country with the bright Sunday evening wink of the Chop Suey signs, the roar of the elevated, the sounds of the radio, the homelike jolly glow of the delicatessen stores, and the peaceful noise of millions of Jews in the Bronx slowly turning the 237 pages of the *New York Sunday Times.* Thank God you live in the beautiful and interesting place where all these things are accessible; and also thank God for the great sounds that roar across America, the howl and sighing at the eaves, the lash and din of it at the corners, the bite and sparkle of the air, the sharp color of October, the baying of the great boats in the harbor, the thunder of the great trains in the night, the exulting and joy that grips your guts and makes you cry out—and when you see some bastard who tells you lies about Europe, and worse lies about America, when you see some fool who wants to leave the most interesting and glorious place on earth to live here—remember what I have told you: spit in his face—no, piss on him instead, for the carcass of such a lying degenerate must not be dignified by spittle from the lips of an honest man.

I have been shy and silent before these liars and fools far too long. I have eaten crow and swallowed my pride for ten years before the waste-landers, the lost generationers, the bitter-bitters, the futility people, and all other cheap literary fakes sicklied o'er with a pale coat of steer-shit— but now I will hold my tongue no longer: I know what I know, and I have learned it with blood and sweat. I have lived alone in a foreign land until I could not sleep for thinking of the sights and sounds and colors, the whole intolerable memory of America, its violence, savagery, immensity, beauty, ugliness, and glory—and I tell you I know it as if it were my child, as if it had been distilled from my blood and marrow: I know it from the look and smell of the railway ties to the thousand sounds and odours of the wilderness—and I tell you I had rather have ten years more of life there than fifty years of Continental weak tea and smothering in this woolly and lethargic air, than a hundred years of shitty ex-patriotism. You have seen them in Paris sitting on their rumps around the café tables and pretending to know France and Europe: they know nothing, and as for the superior European "culture" some of them profess their love for, how many of them do you think give one good Goddamn for it? They do not know either Europe or France, their life is a vile cardboard affair, the French hate and despise them, and they know it—but they are like pimps who will endure slaps, insults, and mockery so long as they can have their whore. I tell you this "living abroad" business is bloody balls: I know something about Europe, I have gone alone and known some of the Europeans—at least I know more of their language, literature, and ways of living than most of our Paris friends—and I have heard all their stale jargon: that we are "not a country", that we are base and mean; that there is no glory, dignity, or beauty in our life; that we are Puritans, Babbitts, Rotarians, etc., etc.—but these people know nothing of anything, they have read it all in books, and they know less than nothing of America. I tell you we have got to live in our own country and be what we are, and that no one who has ever known and felt America can find living in Europe as interesting or beautiful.

I am certainly not bitter against Europe at the present time, and in spite of my violent attack on English dullness, I have an enormous liking and sympathy for them—they have been most kind and friendly this time. I do not go out often, but there are a few people I can go to see and talk to, which is a comfort after many months of being alone. There are also other blessings: I have the top two floors of a tiny little house on Ebury Street, it is nicely furnished, and I am completely alone in it at night; also I have a charwoman who cooks for me, brings her darling tea in his little beddy, coddles and coaxes him, and is in fact a perfect priceless damned Kohinoor—all, house, woman, etc. for £3.14s a week. I stay in from 6 o'clock on, read, eat the meal she has left for me, or cook one of my own, brew vast quantities of tea and coffee, and at midnight— the present hour—when all outside is quiet save for the massive footfalls of the bobby, and a few gay dogs reeling home from the American talkies—I set to work, and work, with time off for tea, coffee, or beer, until broad daylight. Then I see life awaken in a London street, which is one of the nicest things I have seen: I see the light come on the yellow walls and the smoky brick: the milk wagon comes through with the milkman making a funny cry, and I hear the sound of a horse in the empty street— a sound that makes me think of a thousand mornings in American streets. Then the housemaids come out and scrub, the shops open, the noise be- gins. I light the "geyser," have a bottle, and go to bed, where my char- woman finds me, brings me tea and toast, all gossip to her pet about the movie she saw last night.

Farewell, dear Fritz. Someday, some far-off future day, Tommy is com- ing sailing home again, and then I will tell you all about it. There is no joy in the world comparable to the cessation of intolerable pain—some- times I think that is what joy is, the way you feel, how beautiful and glorious life is, after the tooth stops aching—and that is what it will be like when I come home again. The most exultant, the most glorious, the most incredibly magnificent experience in the modern world is the voyage to America, and I pity the poor wretches who will never know it. If you speak of me to anyone, for God's sake do not communicate any of this letter to people who would use it to mock at and injure me: I mean the futility boys and girls, the stealthy lasses, the elegant mockers, the American T. S. Elioters. They are a low but vilely cunning lot of bastards and they will not see their cheap little stock in trade—I mean the what-is-the-use-we-are-a-doomed-generation, life-here-is-a-barren-desert, we-can-do-nothing—they will not see this little business cursed without a hissing and jeering retaliation. It is all they have, and even vermin will bare their teeth and bite if their stale cheese is menaced, even bawds and pimps will fight to protect the commerce of the drab who feeds them.

You know that I am no Pollyanna now, or that I think God's in his heaven. I don't, and I agree with Ecclesiastes that the saddest day of a man's life is the day of his birth—but after that, I think the next saddest day is the day of his death. I have had some bad times recently, but I think I shall always love life and hate death, and I believe that is an article of faith. The futility people hate life, and love death, and yet they will not die; and I loathe them for it. Observe carefully: you will find that the man who kills himself is almost always the man who loves life well. The futility people do not kill themselves; they wear rubbers and are afraid of colds. The waste-lander does not waste himself: it is the lover of life who wastes himself, who loves life so dearly that he will not hoard it, whose belief in life is so great that he will not save his own: I mean Christ and Coleridge and Socrates and Dostoievsky and Jeb Stuart and David Crockett. My! how the boys would snicker if they could hear that!

Goodbye for the present, Fritz. We'll drink beer again at Weber's some happy day, and we'll be a couple of damned tourists together, and we'll stand on the bridges of Paris at midnight again, and remember the voices of men in Virginia, and the smell of the tar in the streets. . . . Tell Max Perkins that I will really write him—if I could only say in a letter all I want to say to him!—and that I am really working, and sometimes I am full of joy and hope about it, and other times depression, but that I shall finish it (when, I don't know) and that it will have to have in it the things that are bursting in my heart and mind. Forgive this long and violent letter: I did not mean to write it myself when I started. Remember me to the folks at Scribners, and love again and good wishes to you and the family. I have Scotch blood in me, and often I see spooks: there is a happy land, there is a good life, and better times are coming for all men of good will.

To MAXWELL E. PERKINS

London

Tues., Dec. 9, 1930

Dear Mr. Perkins:

I am sure this is a bad year and that all the bad news is coming at once—there is only three weeks more of it, and then things, I know, will get better. For one thing, some time next year I hope to come home again and end this sometimes ghastly pain of homesickness. I am working like hell and I hope it will be worth something when I get it down.

Before I go on with the letter I want to get something off my mind: my family have suffered the most terrible calamities—they have simply been wiped out. Mabel and Ralph (that is my sister) have been sold out in Asheville, they have lost everything they had, every piece of property, every cent of money, and he has lost his job: they are at present living in Washington where he is trying to earn a $50 a week commission salary. My other sister's big family have been for the most part out of work, and my brother Fred has been struggling to keep them up. In addition, he has had to quit his job because there is no business. Things in the South are in a horrible hell of a shape, and the last calamity I read of was that the leading bank at Asheville, where I am afraid they had some money, has smashed. Now these people are too good and too proud to ask for anything—their letters have been full of courage and cheerfulness, but they are simply wiped out. Two or three months ago from Paris, when I thought my profits on the English publication were much greater than they turned out to be, I wrote Fred and told him for God's sake to let me know if he needed money and I would let him have what I could. He wrote me the other day and assured me none of them is in actual want for food or clothing—thank God for that! Then he asked me, if I really had the money, would I let him have $500 for a year. He sent along some damned document giving me security, 8% interest, etc.—of course, I won't have the damned thing, nor a penny's interest: I tore it up.

Mr. Perkins, I know it's a bad year for everyone, but *if I've got it there* at Scribners, or even if I haven't got it, for God's sake get that money for the boy, and I will work my fingers to the bone. If it comes to a question of these damned . . . dentists and my own people, *I want my people to have the money*. Please understand my people have not asked me for a damned penny, and my brother wrote me only when I had written him and assured him that I could spare the money and would not forgive him if they needed it and would not speak. At that time I thought I would have more—but no matter: if I am able to help these people now, it is a

Godsend for me, and if I don't do it, I shall regret it bitterly as long as I live. I think you understand how much joy it gives me to think I may be of a little help now in time of trouble—we have always stood together in trouble before, and I don't want to fail them now. There is no question about Fred paying me back someday—he would do that if he had to mortgage his right arm—but even if he never did, it would be all right and I don't want his damned notes or mortgages or interest. He has never asked me nor anyone else for anything before, and he has got everybody's burden on him now. I know he would not ask unless he were hard pressed. I wrote him the other day and told him not to worry, that I could afford it and it wouldn't pinch me, and that I would get you to send him $500.— *Please* do this for me, and I will make it up to you somehow: I'm a young man and I have never failed anyone yet to whom I was indebted. . . .

Now don't get worried and think I'm going to flop on you and be a sponge—I'll make this $500 up to you in extra work and sweat: I can't promise to write a good or a great book or even one that will sell, but if that fails, I'll make it up to you in some other way. There's money in me somewhere if I'm put to it—I've always believed I could make it if I had to. I want you to know this: I believe I have acted decently and honestly to everyone—certainly I have tried to—if you hear scurrilous and slanderous stories about me, about any action of mine, about anything to do with me, spread by any of the ten million envenomed and reptilian ——— ———s who walk the streets of this earth full of hate, malice, and poison, put them down as lies. I have been in a hell of a jam this last year or so, and during the last six or eight months I have sweated out blood and agony—but *I have behaved all right:* I have done what I thought I had to do, and what people asked me to do, I have never betrayed or deserted anyone—in the end, if anyone gets betrayed or deserted it will be me. I have done the best I could, I have done some things badly, but please understand that I have behaved all right: if anyone thinks I have not, let him come forward and say so to my face—otherwise let them hold their tongues in fairness, and someday they will know I have been square. You know me much better now than any of these people, you know what a nest of lies and venom New York is, for God's sake make any judgment or opinion on me for yourself, and out of our own relation. You are my friend, and one of the two or three people that I would not let anyone in the world say a word against, so until I get back at least, don't listen to opinions and judgments from people who don't know a God-damned thing about me, whether Scott Fitzgerald, ——, or anyone else. Please don't be alarmed at all this, or think I've gone suddenly mad—there's so much I want to say to you and so little I can say in a letter that part of it comes in convulsions and bursts.

I seem to have to spend a maddening amount of time talking about dentists, and making foolish answers. I should like to tell you about the book, but I'll have to write another letter. But here is the title, at any rate, and it seems to me to be a good and beautiful title and to say what I want it to say—if anything about it puzzles you, I'll try to interpret all of it for you next time. Here it is:

"THE OCTOBER FAIR"

or

"Time and The River : A Vision:"

The Son, The Lover, and The Wanderer;
The Child, The Mistress, and The Woman;
The Sea, The City, and The Earth.

"One generation passeth away, and
another generation cometh; but the earth
abideth for ever."

For title page:

Part One

"ANTAEUS"

"Who knowth the spirit of man that goeth upward, and
the spirit of the beast that goeth downward to the earth?"—

(If this *Argument* seems bad or inadvisable we won't use it. It gives a kind of key.)

Argument: of the Libyan giant, the brother of Polyphemus, the one-eyed, and the son of Gaea and Poseidon, whom he hath never seen, and through his father, the grandson of Cronos and Rhea, whom he remembereth. He contendeth with all who seek to pass him by, he searcheth alway for his father, he crieth out: "Art thou my father? Is it thou?" And he wrestleth with that man, and he riseth from each fall with strength redoubled, for his strength cometh up out of the earth, which is his mother. Then cometh against him Heracles, who contendeth with him, who discovereth the secret of his strength, who lifteth him from the earth whence his might ariseth, and subdueth him. But from afar now, in his agony, he heareth the sound of his father's foot: he will be saved for his father cometh!

Now, don't get alarmed at all this and think I'm writing a Greek myth. All of this is never mentioned once the story gets under way, but it is a magnificent fable, and I have soaked myself in it over a year now: it says what I want to say, and it gives the most magnificent plot and unity to my book. The only other way in which the Antaeus legend is mentioned directly is in the titles to the various parts which are tentatively, at present (1) "Antaeus," (2) "Heracles," (or "Faust and Helen"), (3) "Poseidon."

To give you the key to all these symbols and people:—Antaeus of course, is a real person; he is in me but he is *not* me as the fellow in the first book was supposed to be; he is to me what Hamlet or Faust may have been to their authors. Thank God, I have begun to create in the way I want to—it is more completely *autobiographic* than anything I have ever thought of, much *more* than the first one, but it is also completely *fictitious*. Nobody can identify me with Antaeus—whose real name is David Hawke, but who is called Monkey Hawke—except to say, "He has put himself into this character." It is a magnificent story, it makes use of all the things I have seen and known about, and it is like a fable.

The other symbols are: Heracles, who is the City; Poseidon, who is the Sea, eternal wandering, eternal change, eternal movement—but who is also a real person (*never* called Poseidon) of course, the father of Monkey Hawke, whom he has never seen, and whom, I have decided he shall never see, but who is near him at the end of the book, and who saves him (the idea that hangs over the book from first to last is that every man is searching for his father). It is immensely long, I am bringing the Antaeus (which has two parts) back home with me and parts of the second—the City scenes are already written.

The woman in various forms, at different times, is Gaea, Helen, or Demeter—but these things are never told you, and the story itself is direct and simple, given shape by this legend, and by the idea I told you. But it is also tremendously varied—it gives the histories of my people and it reconstructs old time. The idea of time, the lost and forgotten moments of people's lives, the strange brown light of old time (i.e.—America, say, in 1893: photographs of people coming across Brooklyn Bridge, the ships of the Hamburg American Packet Co, baseball players with moustaches, men coming home to lunch at noon in small towns, red barns, old circus posters and many other phases of time) is over all the book.

I'd like to tell you of a chapter I'm now writing in the Second part of "Antaeus"—the chapter is called "Cronos and Rhea" (or perhaps simply "Time and the River"—that means "Memory and Change"). My conviction is that a native has the whole consciousness of his people and nation in him; that he knows everything about it, every sight sound and memory of the people. Don't get worried: I think this is going to be all right. You see, I *know* now past any denial, that *that* is what being an American or being anything means: it is not a government, or the Revolutionary War, or the Monroe Doctrine—it is the ten million seconds and moments of your life, the shapes you see, the sounds you hear, the food you eat, the colour and texture of the earth you live on. I tell you *this* is what it is, and this is what homesickness is, and by God I'm the world's champion authority on the subject at present.

"Cronos and Rhea" occurs on board an Atlantic liner—all the Americans returning home—and the whole intolerable memory of exile and nostalgia comes with it. It begins like a chant—first the smashing enormous music of the American names: [1] first the names of the States: California, Texas, Oregon, Nebraska, Idaho, and the Two Dakotas; then the names of the Indian tribes: the Pawnees, the Cherokees, the Seminoles, the Penobscots, the Tuscaroras, etc.; then the names of railways: the Pennsylvania, the Baltimore and Ohio, the Great Northwestern, the Rock Island, the Santa Fe, etc.; then the names of the railway millionaires: the Vanderbilts, the Astors, the Harrimans; then the names of the great hoboes: Oakland Red, Fargo Pete, Dixie Joe, Iron Mike, Nigger Dick, the Jersey Dutchman etc. (the names of some of the great wanderers i.e.); then the great names of the rivers (the rivers and the sea standing for movement and wandering against the fixity of the earth):—the Monongahela, the Rappahannock, the Colorado, the Tennessee, the Rio Grande, the Missouri. When I get to the Mississippi, I start the first of the stories of wandering and return— the woman floating down the river with her husband in flood time tells it. It is good—the whole thing is this pattern of memory and [neuroticism?] —don't get alarmed. I think it's all right and fits in perfectly, I have plenty of straight story anyway.

I have told you too much and too little. I have had to scrawl this down and haven't time to explain dozens of things—but please don't be worried —it's not anarchy, it's a perfectly unified but enormous plan. I want to write again and tell you some more, expecially about the last scene in "Poseidon." It is the only fabulous scene in the book. He never sees his father but he hears the sound of his foot, the thunder of horses on a beach (Poseidon and his horses); the moon [dives] out of clouds; he sees a print of a foot that can belong only to his father since it is like his own; the sea surges across the beach and erases the print; he cries out "Father" and from the sea far out, and faint upon the wind, a great voice answers "My Son!" That is briefly the end as I see it—but can't tell you anything about it now. The rest of the story is natural and wrought out of human

[1] This is a portion of "The Names of the Nation" which was published in the December, 1934, issue of *The Modern Monthly,* and appears in *Of Time and the River* on pages 861–870.

experience. Polyphemus, by the way, the one-eyed brother of Antaeus, represents the principle of sterility that hates life—i.e. waste-landerism, futility-ism, one-eyed-ism (also a character in the book).

I don't know whether you can make anything out of this or not—it is 10:30 o'clock, I have worked all night—as I finish this on the morning of Tues Dec 9, there is a fog outside that you can cut, you can't see across the street, I am dog tired. I want to come home when I know I have this thing by the well known balls. Write me if you think it's a good idea, but say nothing to anyone.

I'm a week late with this letter. I don't want my brother to suffer—*please* Mr. Perkins send him $500 at once if you can—address *Fred W. Wolfe, 48 Spruce Street, Asheville, North Carolina*—get it to him before Christmas. I'm writing you about dentists—but don't pay them if my brother has to suffer.

I'm sending this out right away to be mailed. I hope this finds you well. I'd like to be able to see and talk to you.

Address again   Fred W. Wolfe
                48 Spruce St
                Asheville
                N. C.

Don't tell anyone about this letter. If I've talked foolishness I'd rather keep it between us—at ten in the morning after being up all night you're not sane.

Wolfe never completed or mailed the following letter to Mr. Perkins, but wrote and sent him a briefer version of it on January 9, 1931. Since this first unfinished letter is more revealing, it has been included here and the one of January 9th omitted.

To MAXWELL E. PERKINS

[London]

[December, 1930]

Dear Mr. Perkins:

I suppose you have by now an enormous letter I wrote you about two weeks ago—it was filled with work and woes: I want to write you this short one to tell you my plans and intentions. First, it is only three or four days before Christmas, I have the satisfaction of feeling completely exhausted with work for the moment: my mind is tired and I can not sleep very well. I am going to keep it up until Christmas, then I am going to Paris for four or five days, and I am going to do nothing but sleep, eat and drink the best food and wine I can get. Then I propose to come back here and work till I drop for about six weeks, until I know I can bring the first part in consecutive chapters or in draft back home. Then I propose taking third class on the fastest boat I can find—the *Bremen* or *Europa*—so that I'll be in New York in five or six days after sailing. Then I should like to proceed *immediately* (this is the hard part) to a place *where I can get to work again.*

I have told you that my new book is haunted throughout by the Idea of the river—of Time and Change. Well, so am I—and the thing that is eating at my entrails at present is when can I have this formidable work ready. You have been wonderful not saying anything about *time*, but I feel you would like to see something before next Fall. I don't make any promises but I'll try like hell: I am distressed at the time I spent over personal worries, excitement over the first one, and fiddling around, but it's no good crying about that now—I think this came as fast as it could: now I've got it all inside me, and much of it down on paper, but I must work like hell. The thing that is good for me is almost *total obscurity*— I love praise and flattery for my work, but there must be no more parties, no more going out. I must live in two rooms somewhere until I hate to leave them: I want to see you and one or two people, but I want to come back without seeing anyone in New York for several weeks *except you and one or two others:* don't think I'm talking through my hat, it's the only way I can do this piece of work and I must do it in this way.

Now about the place to work. This is a hell of a lot to ask you, but I don't want you to do it if you can get someone else to do it—try to help me if you can. I don't know whether it is good to live in New York now. My present obsession is that I am going within the next few years to get married and live somewhere in America in the country or in one of the smaller cities—in Baltimore, or in Virginia, or in the Pennsylvania farm country or in the West—but I have no time to go wandering all over America now.

(My book, by the way, is filled with this kind of exuberance, exultancy and joy—I *know* if I can make people feel it, they will eat it up: I hope to God the energy is still there, this homesickness abroad has made me feel it more than ever—I mean the richness, fabulousness, exultancy and wonderful life of America—the way you feel (I mean the young fellow, the college kid, going off on his own for the first time) [1] when he is rushing through the night in a dark pullman berth and he sees the dark mys-

---

[1] This is described on pages 74 and 75 of *Of Time and the River.*

terious American landscape rolling by (Virginia, say!) and the voluptuous good-looking woman in the berth below stirring her pretty legs between the sheets, the sound of the other people snoring, and the sound of voices on the little station platforms in the night—some man and woman seeing their daughter off, then you hear her rustle down the aisle behind the nigger porter and they knock against your green curtain—it is all so strange and familiar and full of joy, it is as if some woman you loved had laid her hand on your bowels.

Then the wonderful richness and size of the country, the feeling that you can be rich and famous, that you can make money easily—the wonderful soil, sometimes desolate and lonely-looking as you found the parts of North Carolina you visited, yet that same earth, Mr. Perkins, produces enough pungent and magnificent tobacco to smoke up the world, and from that same clay come the most luscious peaches, apples, melons, all manner of juicy and wonderful things. I was thinking of it in Switzerland this summer—how incredibly beautiful Switzerland is—the story-book lakes, the unbelievable mountains, the lush velvety mountain meadows—and how desolate and ugly North Carolina would seem to a European—and yet Switzerland is a kind of fake—horribly dull food, dull stunted little fruits and vegetables, dull grapes, dull wine, dull people, and horrible dead sea fish that comes from those lovely Alpine lakes. Switzerland, for all its rich grand beauty can not produce anything one-tenth as good or pungent as North Carolina tobacco, melons, peaches, apples, or the wonderful ducks, turkeys, and marvellous fish along the lonely desolate N.C. coast—and that is America, the only country where you feel this joy, this glory, this exuberance, the thing that makes the young fellows cry out and squeal in their throats. These poor dull tired bastards with their terribly soft woolly steamy, dreary skies—do you think *they* can ever feel this way? They may sneer at us, hate us, revile and mock us, say we are base and without beauty or culture, but no matter how much they call on their dead glories, their Shakespeares, Molières, Shelleys, you know there can be no lying, no hocus-pocus about their beastly, damnable dreary air—they can't argue about that, they have to breathe it, and it will rot and decay anyone after a time, just as bad food, bad housing, will do it. I feel pity and sorrow for them—the plain truth is that the lives of most of their people are dreary compared to ours—they have to go to American movies for amusement. No, they can't have the feeling we have in Autumn when the frost comes and all the wonderful colors come out, and you hear the great winds at night and the burrs plopping to the ground and the far-off frosty barking of a dog, and the wonderful sound of an American train on the rails and its whistle.

The people of North Carolina are like that wonderful earth—they are not little, dull, dreary Babbitts: I am going to *tell the truth* about these people and, by God, it is the truth about America. I don't care what any little worn-out waste-lander, European or American, or anyone else says: I *know what I know*. The people in North Carolina have these same wonderful qualities as the tobacco, the great juicy peaches, melons, apples, the wonderful shad and oysters of the coast, the rich red clay, the haunting brooding quality of the earth. They are rich, juicy, deliberate, full of pungent and sardonic humor and honesty, conservative and cautious on top, but at bottom wild, savage, and full of the murderous innocence of the earth and the wilderness. Do you think this is far-fetched? Scott F.G.[2] did and ridiculed the idea that the earth we lived on had anything to do with us—but don't you see that 300 years upon this earth, living alone minute by minute in the wilderness, eating its food, growing its tobacco, being buried and mixed with it, gets into the blood, bone, marrow, sinew of the people—just as breathing this dreary stuff here has got into these dull, depressed, splenetic and despondent wretches who have to breathe it: how in God's name can anyone be pig-headed and stubborn enough to deny it?

You are a New Englander and quieter about it, but every American has this exultant feeling at times—the way snow comes in New England and the way it spits against your window at night and the sounds of the world get numb, you are living like a spirit in wonderful dark isolation: my bowels used to stir with it and once I got off the Fall River boat after a night of storm and snow on the dark water of the Sound, and the wind and powdery snow were blowing and howling at dawn, everything was white and smokey wonderful grey, and there was the train for Boston in the middle of it, black, warm, fast, and all around the lonely and tragic beauty of New England. (Yes! and *another* good-looking woman in the stateroom next to me coming up on the boat.)

This is glory and wonder, and I shall not be ashamed to tell all of it— what else is homesickness, loyalty, love of country than this—each one of the million moments of your life, the intolerable memory of all the sounds and sights and feelings you knew there. I shall neither try to defend or condemn anything—it is in me, all of it, I shall tell of the cruelty and horror, murder and sudden death, the Irish cop, the smell of blood and brains upon the sidewalk, along with everything else—it is all part of my story, and I *know it is time* and so do you. It is also glorious and exultant and nowhere else in the world can they feel this way: if I tell about it as it is, in all its magnificence and joy, how can it fail to be good? I do not say that I can, but we shall see.)

All this was a parenthesis: to get back to the question of lodgings—

[2] Scott Fitzgerald.

once you mentioned in conversation, also in a letter, the possibility of finding a place out in your part of the country: in a talk, you spoke of boarding-houses and said there were some good ones, but I will never get along in a boarding-house—I must have two rooms where I can be absolutely free, tramp about and work all night, and sleep all day if I want to. You can't do this with peace of mind in a house with other people. An apartment house, or rooms in a business building that's deserted at night, is more in my line. Also I must have a gas stove where I can cook bacon and eggs and make all the coffee I want. If I can get this out in the country, it would be fine: I notice they are building apartment houses out in the country now—Bronxville, etc.—the idea is not bad. I should like to be either out your way, or else I have thought of Brooklyn—somewhere I can look at the wonderful *river*. I think of Brooklyn because people will not bother you or come to see you there so much.—All I need is two rooms, one to sleep in, one to work in, a little kitchen or kitchenette, and a gas-stove—also a showerbath or bath. Don't you think I could get this in some modest place for $60 or $70 a month? I want to be quiet, and I want to see either the earth (that is, out your way) or the river. Could something be done about it? Also, in view of the present hard times, couldn't I get something without signing a year's lease—say for three or six months, or month-by-month, with a privilege of staying on if I want to. Sinclair Lewis wrote me two nice letters—he said Vermont is the most beautiful and cheapest place in the country—maybe I could go there in the hot weather.

If you don't know of anything yourself, could you speak to someone who does? There's a boy named Kizenberger (or something like that) down with Miss DeVoy in the Art Department [3]—he seemed a fine, friendly competent fellow: do you think he could help us? It is a lot to ask but it would be a Godsend if I could have a place waiting for me when I came back and not lose time. I do not want to lose at the outside over *one* month of the *nine* months that elapse between Jan 1 and next October—whether on steamers, trains, hunting rooms, or anything else. I'll stand by any arrangement you can make—just see if it's quiet and they'll let me work, eat, and sleep as I please. Will you please write me about this and tell me if it can be done?

Paris, Dec. 29, 1930. I have come to Paris for two or three days before New Year's—and I am going to finish the letter here. I was damned tired

[3] Edward Kizenberger was in the Art and Manufacturing Department of Scribners at this time. Miss S. Elizabeth DeVoy was then Associate Art Editor, and was Art Editor from 1939 until her retirement in 1951.

and had brain fag but already I am nervous and restless and feel impatient to get back to the book. I have brought the big ledgers in which I write and I keep fooling with it here, although I ought not to, I think. I have got the desperate feeling about it and think I may come through to something.

Now here is the plan: I may be here another day or two until New Year's, then I go back to London, and write like hell until the flesh can do no more, for six or eight weeks. Then America again, and a quiet place of my own to work, and I will show you something complete (a complete book and story but *not* the whole of *The October Fair*—the part called *Antaeus*) sometime during the summer. It is *bound* to be good if I can be hopeful and exultant while I write it: when I am that way I can do anything—to-night I am afraid. I am afraid of no one person, no thing, I am afraid of fear, desolation, and the nauseous sickness and horror of the guts that comes from unknown fear. Paris gives me that feeling. I can hardly bear to go to the Left Bank for fear I shall see some of these God damned life-hating, death-living bastards: but I *did* go yesterday, because one of them had been phoning me in Paris [London?] last week and I had promised to look them up here.

I refer to Mrs —— ——, . . . and my prophetic soul told me it was a frame-up of some sort—one of *three* things. Well, it turned out to be all three: one was to pry into my supposed history with someone I knew in London, another into my supposed New York history, another, how much had I written on my book, what was it about, when would it be ready? When I got there, they had the gang lined up—on one side someone who knew a friend in New York, an another side, someone who knew a person in London—they volleyed and thundered—from the right: "I believe you knew so-and-so in London—she is my cousin"—from the left: "I believe you know so-and-so in New York—she is related to me." Then the sly looks and snickers—God, it makes me vomit! Then the prize bitch, Mrs. ——, spoke of your friend, Mrs. Colum,[4] who is here. I want to see her if I can see her away from these scandal-mongering apes and baboons. This is Paris and I loathe it! They are here to *work*—Jesus Christ! none of them has ever worked here: I am here to eat and drink and sleep, and I shall stay to myself and do it.

For God's sake, don't think I am mad with suspicion and distrust—I have never hated or *in the end* suspected a good person, but I know that my exultancy is right, that the sense of joy and glory is true and just, that the richness, glory, beauty, wonder and magnificence of America—the feel of the wind, the sound of snow, the smell of a great American [steak?]. By

---

[4] Mary M. Colum, author of *From These Roots, Life and the Dream*, etc.

God, these are real things and true things, and these people are liars and cheap swindlers. But if I am going to get this glory and faith and exultancy into my book, I must feel it myself: and I *do* feel it most of the time, only when I meet these people, my heart turns rotten, and my guts are sick and nauseous.

After the book is written, I will be afraid of nothing—but now I am afraid of anything that gets in the way. That is why I want to see you and one or two others and no one else when I come back. I should like to go with you to that 49th Street speakeasy and have a few drinks of American gin and one of those immense steaks—then I should like to talk to you as we used to: these seem to me to be mighty good times, and that speakeasy was a fine place—I have remembered it and put it in my book.

Mr. Perkins, no one has ever written a book about America—no one has ever put into it the things I know and the things everyone knows. It may be grandiose and pompous for me to think I can, but for God's sake let me try. Furthermore it will be a story, and I believe a damned good story. You know what you said to me over a year ago about the book that might be written about a man looking for his father and how everything could be put into it—well, you were right: don't think that I gave up what I wanted to do, only I had this vast amount of material and what you said began to give shape to it. I have gone through the most damnable torture not merely rewriting but in re-arranging, but now I've got it, if I can get it down on paper. The advantage of your story is not only that it is immensely and profoundly true—namely, all of us are wandering and groping through life for an image outside ourselves, for a superior and external wisdom we can appeal [to] and trust—but the story also gives shape to things. Coleridge said that Ben Jonson's play, *The Alchemist*, had one of the three finest plots in the world (the other two were *Oedipus* and *Tom Jones*) and Coleridge mentions as the wonderful virtue of *The Alchemist* the fact that the action could be brought to a close at any point by the return of the master (the play, as I remember, concerns the tricks of a rascal of a servant palming himself off as the master on a world of dupes and rogues). Well, so in this story, the action could be brought to a close by the son finding his father. I have thought over the Antaeus myth a lot, and it seems to me to a true and beautiful one: it says what I want about man's jointure to the earth whence comes his strength, but Antaeus is also faithful to the memory of his father (Poseidon) to whom he builds a temple from the skulls of those he vanquishes. Poseidon, of course, represents eternal movement and wandering, and in a book where a man is looking for his father, what could be more true than this?

About Sinclair Lewis: it was a wonderful thing for him to do [5] and I wrote and told him so. He also wrote me two letters and said he would try to see me over here. I hope it sells a few copies of the book—thanks for using it and advertising it—but I am a little worried by it also: the Great American Writer business is pretty tough stuff for a man who is on his second book, and I hope they won't be gunning for me. Also, I have begun to come to a way of life—I meant what I said about *obscurity:* it's the only thing for me, otherwise I'm done for: I want to write famous books, but I want to live quietly and modestly. Also, I am determined to resist in my own heart any attempt to make or be made the great "I Am" of anything. If I tell myself that I am not anybody's "I Am," but only a fellow who is going to stick relentlessly to the things he has seen and known, to say the things he has to say as honestly and beautifully as he can, to realize that is all he has, and that if it has any value it is because other people have felt these things or will feel their truth—why, then, if I stick to this and work like hell, I don't believe they can hurt me seriously either when they praise me or turn against me. Don't you think this is the only wise and honest way to work and live?

Now, finally, about the book again. If I have been incoherent and chaotic, it has been from haste and not from lack of certainty. As well as I can tell you quickly and in this small space, this is what my book is about: First, it is a story of a man who is looking for his father—this gives it plan and direction, and it also expresses a fundamental human desire. The story of a man's love for a woman is told with the utmost passion and sincerity and sensuousness in one part of it, together with all the phenomena of lust, hunger, jealousy, madness, cruelty and tenderness—but the idea that the two sexes are from different worlds, different universes, and can never know each other, is implicit; and the father idea—the need for wisdom, strength and confession, with the kinship and companionship of one's own kind and father, hangs over the story all the time. Under this story structure are the ideas of the fixity and eternity of the earth and the beauty of man's life.

[THE LETTER BREAKS OFF UNFINISHED HERE]

[5] After praising *Look Homeward, Angel* in his interview in the November 6 *New York Times,* Lewis had gone to Stockholm to receive the Nobel Prize for Literature, and in his official speech of acceptance before the Swedish Academy, had said: "There are young Americans to-day who are doing such passionate and authentic work that it makes me sick to see that I am a little too old to be one of them. There is . . . Thomas Wolfe, a child of, I believe, thirty or younger, whose one and only novel, *Look Homeward, Angel,* is worthy to be compared with the best in our literary production, a Gargantuan creature with great gusto of life."

To MABEL WOLFE WHEATON
[Written on a Christmas card]

[London]

[December, 1930]

Dear Mabel:

I'm writing as soon as I can—I know all about things at home and how bad conditions are. Don't worry—nobody's going to starve, I will be delighted to help in any way possible and I know I can get money if I have to. We must all stick together now, and you must let me help you if I can. I think you are well out of it in Asheville for the present—later on things are going to be better everywhere. This is the real test now, if everyone keeps cheerful and courageous at this time things are bound to come all right. We will not be beaten because *we can not be beaten.* In a pinch I believe I can come back home and begin to write articles and short stories, or get a job advertising, and get more money. I wish you all a happy and cheerful Christmas. People have been kind to me here, and I get invited out but I have been terribly lonely and homesick. It will all come out right yet. Write me—

To HENRY T. VOLKENING

The Guaranty Trust Co.
London

January 14, 1931

Dear Henry:

Thanks again for another letter. I can't tell you how happy your letters make me, and with what care I read and reread them. I know I have fallen far short of doing my share—whenever I take my pen in hand, like our old friend Lord Tennyson, I would that my heart could utter the thoughts that arise in me, but it's no use: for some reason I have developed the most damnable caution in writing letters, even to the three or four people I should like to write good ones to. . . .

I am rapidly becoming a great authority on the subject of *Work* because I, my boy, have done some—"and penance more will do." By the way, that would be a good title for almost any book—"Penance More"—for that, I think, is what it takes to write one. But hearken again, lad—I have not only worked, but I have worked with metaphysical and spiritual bellyache, toothache, headache—as well as something like a virulent abscess just over my left lung,[1] and I think now that I shall probably work under almost any kind of conditions. Then, attend, and do these things at once: buy a book written by one Anthony Trollope, Esq. who wrote about ninety-seven other books in addition. It is called "An Autobiography"; it is quite short; you can . . . read it through at one sitting. The book was published after his death and, I understand, did his reputation a good deal of damage among the kind of readers who think a book gets written in two and one half hours of passionate delirium by an inspired maniac. Brother Trollope, with great good humor and some cynicism, describes his methods of work, and tells how he managed to write fifty or sixty novels while riding all over Ireland and England in the Civil Service, going hunting twice a week, entertaining many friends, and in general leading a hell of an active life. Brother Trollope was a rugged man and he let no day go by without writing for three hours—no more, no less. He worked five days a week, wrote 10,000 words, estimated the number of words and pages in a novel, wrote exactly up to that point, got it to the printer in time, and started a new one. Further, he learned to write his daily stint in railway compartments, on Channel steamers, on horseback, and in bed, and with great glee and gusto he attaches an itemized list of his books at the end, together with the exact number of pounds, shillings, and pence each one earned.

I shall never write fifty books or learn to write in railways or on boats, nor do I think it desirable, but it is certainly a damned good idea to get ideas of steady work, and I think this is a good book to read. I am able to do thirty or thirty-five hours a week—thirty-five hours is about the limit, and if I do that I am pretty tired. If a man will work—really work—for four or five hours every day, he is doing his full stint. Moreover, I find very little time for anything else—I practically spend twenty-four hours getting five hours work done: I go out very little. But it soon gets to be a habit. I wish sometimes I were less homesick, less lonely, and sometimes less heartsick: I could certainly imagine better conditions for work, and I am firmly decided (between us!) that the "going abroad to write business" is the bunk. I went to Paris Christmas: it is one of the saddest messes in the world to see all these pathetic bastards who are beginning to get ready to commence to start. Why a man should leave his own country to write—why he should write better in Spain, France, England or Czechoslovakia than at home is quite beyond me. . . . It seems to me that one of the most important things a writer can have is tenacity—without that I don't see how he'll get anything done. Someone told me a year or

---

[1] If Wolfe did have an abscess over his left lung, nothing is known about it now. The old tubercular lesion which was opened by pneumonia in 1938 and caused his death was in the right lung.

two ago that the pity about modern writers is that the people who have the greatest talent for writing never write, and an embittered and jealous Irishman told me that one of the people Joyce wrote about in "Ulysses" was a much better writer than Joyce if he wanted to write—only he didn't want to. All this, in the phrase of my innocent childhood, "makes my ass want buttermilk."

There can be no talent for writing whatever, unless a man has power to write: tenacity is one of the chief elements of talent—without it there is damned little talent, no matter what they say. Which I suppose is only another way of saying Arnold's dogma: Genius is energy. I think I would agree that the best writers are not always the people with the greatest natural ability to write. For example, I have never felt that Joyce was a man with a great natural ability: I don't believe he begins to have the natural ease, fluency, and interest of, say, H. G. Wells. But he had an integrity of spirit, a will and a power to work that far surpasses Wells. I don't mean mere manual and quantity work—Wells had plenty of that, he has written a hundred books—but I mean the thing that makes a man to do more than his best, to exhaust his ultimate resource. That is the power to work and that can not be learned—it is a talent and belongs to the spirit. At any rate, the only way out for us is work—work under all circumstances and conditions: I am sure of that! . . .

But now forgive me for being such a wiseacre: I am not nearly so easy and certain as I sound—but I am sure what I said about working is right. I do not know whether what I am doing now is good or bad—the impulse and idea are very good—but, as *always* between us, I think I have been on the verge of the deep dark pit for two years, and I am just beginning to get away from it. I am tired of madness and agony; I am willing to let the young generation have a fling of it—after all, I'm an old fellow of thirty and I deserve some peace and quiet. If work will do it, I'll come through: I'll work until my brain and the last remnant of energy go.

I suppose some people would say I have never spared others, but I should say that I never spared myself, and on the whole I think other people have done pretty well by me. I have given away what I would never sell if I had it again for diamond mines—years out of the best and most vital period of my life—and I find myself to-day where I was ten years ago, a wanderer on the face of the earth, an exile, and a stranger, and, by God, I wonder why! I can't help it if it sounds melodramatic—it is the simple truth. Frankly, I want to live in my own country. I am tired of this Europe business, I know it is all wrong—but where to live on that little strip of four thousand miles of earth is the question. I notice that people who have never been alone for five minutes in their lives cheerfully banish you to solitude, assure you there's no life like it, how they envy you, and it is all for the best, after all, etc. But I've had thirty years of it, and I confess now to a low craving for companionship, the love and affection of a few simple bastards, and evenings spent by the ingle nook with a bottle of bootleg port, a jug of imported English walnut, and a volume of the Olde Englisshe essays of —— —— on which I could wipe my arse from time to time and pretend I was back in the Olde Countrye. I have even begun fondly to meditate a loving wife (my own, this time), and a few little ones; but where to start searching for these simple joys is beyond me!

Most of the people I like, and a great many I dislike, are in New York, but I can't go back there: it would be like walking around with perpetual neuralgia at present: the place is one vast ache to me, and I've offered quite enough free entertainment to the millions of people who, having no capacity for feeling themselves, spend their lives on the rich banquet some poor buck from the sticks (like myself) has to offer. I've learned a few things and the next time the bastards want to see a good show they're going to pay up!

To-day is another *night!* and I . . . am going to see the Four Marx Brothers to-morrow with my English publishers. They are here in the flesh, and the swells have suddenly discovered they were funny, so I suppose I shall have to listen to the usual horrible gaff from the Moderns: "You know there's Something Very Grand about them—there really is, you know, I mean there's Something Sort of Epic about it, if you know what I mean, I mean that man who never says anything is really like Michael Angelo's Adam in the Sistine Chapel, He's a Very Grand Person, he really is, you know, they are really *Very* Great Clowns, they really are you know," etc. etc. etc. ad vomitatum. I took some people here to see the Marxes in a talkie, and I had to listen to it for two hours. I got so mad because the woman next to me kept saying that "There was something Very Sinister about" Harpo's face—when he began to play the harp she said: "Ah, there is something Lovely about him when he Does Things with His hands—He's doing Something he likes, you see." The dear moderns, you will find, are cut from the same cloth and pattern all over the world—unplatitudinously they utter platitudes, with complete unoriginality they are original, whenever they say something new you wonder where you heard it before, you believe you have not heard it before, you are sure you have heard it forever, you are tired of it before it is uttered, the stink of a horrible weariness is on it, it is like the smell of the subway after rush hours, the best answer to it is Groucho's famous remark: "Even if this was good I wouldn't like it," or alternatively, "The next number will be a piccolo solo which will be omitted." I am tired of these weary bastards: they hate life, but they won't die.

I had a damned good lunch at Simpson's to-day—usually I eat at home here—I had enormous portions of delicious roast beef, Yorkshire pudding, Cavendish sauce, Stilton cheese, biscuits and a bottle of Beaujolais. Simpson's is one of the best places in England: the food at most restaurants is incredibly dull and bad, and the misery and depression of millions of beaten people is constantly seeping into the dull and horrible weather —the whole thing makes a wet dreary thick compost which you breathe and eat and feel, but at Simpson's there is still joy! Do you still go to Luchows? That is a fine restaurant, Professor Wolfe the food expert speaking! Also, I remember some New York speakeasies with pleasure, one I went to just before coming here in particular: the food was most delicious. In the universal mockery and contempt of prohibish, these things and places don't always get their due—but I believe some speakeasies are very wonderful places!

In the last year I have looked at a half dozen countries and thirty or forty million people. But nowhere have I seen people walking on their hands, breathing through fins, or rolling like hoops along pavements. Today I went into a bookstore. There were millions of books. I did not find one that would teach me not to draw my breath in pain and labor, or how to cross a street, or how to find a moment's wisdom and repose. These things are in us! . . . The literary business in America has become so horrible that it is sometimes possible to write only between fits of vomiting. If you think that is extreme, I mention a few names. . . . I . . . say keep away from them: go with doctors, architects, bootleggers—but not with writers. This is not bitter advice: it is simply good advice. No one has ever written any books about America—I mean the real America. I think they bring out ten or twenty thousand books a year, but no one has ever written about America, and I do not think the "writers" will.

Good-bye for the present. I send you and Nat my love and warmest wishes for the New Year. Thanks again for all those fine letters, and for the fruit cake, and most of all for thinking of me and being my friend. Let me hear from you when you can. . . .

Just before leaving England, Wolfe wrote the following letter to Henry Allen Moe, Secretary of the John Simon Guggenheim Foundation.

To HENRY ALLEN MOE

London

February 25, 1931

Dear Mr. Moe:

This is a very belated letter, but since I hope to come in to see you very soon anyway, I shall be able to tell you myself what I have done here abroad: I am going back to New York in a day or two, and may be there as soon as this letter. I have spent about ten months here instead of the six I originally intended, and I am bringing back six enormous book-keeping ledgers with about 200,000 words of manuscript and a great many notes. I do not know if the words are good or bad ones, and a great deal remains to be done, but it is so firmly on the rails now that nothing can stop it. I am going into the woods at or about New York for about six months, and then I hope to emerge with the pelt. I have been horribly lonely and homesick at times—more, I think, than ever in my life—but for five months now, in my little flat in Ebury Street, and for months more elsewhere, I have thought and worked, and dreamed about America, and now I know what I know, which may be little or much, but it is my own. So, first of all, I want to thank you and the trustees for giving me the chance to come abroad and work, and then for the chance to achieve that meditation and solitude which, painful and difficult as both may be, are nevertheless precious things, and perhaps harder to get at home than in most places. People have been most kind and generous to me here. I have found out more about England and Europe this time than ever before—that is, I have entered doors, gone past barriers, that the stranger usually never passes, and found at least two or three friends: but I have also found out more about my own country, and I do not think I shall ever lose what I have gained.

It was most important, I think, that I went away when I did for these reasons, and for others about which I may tell you someday. I wish I could promise you, in return for your generosity, that I will write a good book or a grand book—but I can not make that promise: I hope that it will be, and I shall not let it go until I think it is worth publication, and if I work and do not falter, and say what I have to say with all the energy and ability I may have—then I think the book *will* be worth it. At any rate, I have gained something this year that I will never lose, and in the end I am a better and wiser person than when I went away.

I have just drawn the last of the letter of credit for steamer fare, clothes, some books and a little fund when I land in New York: thank you again for all of it, and for what it helped me to do. If you are interested in seeing it, I'll bring you some of the typed manuscript during the next two or three months in New York, but I hope to see you and talk to you and have lunch with you before that.

I send my best wishes for health and happiness. Please don't say anything to anyone about my coming back. Not many people would be interested anyway, and I have committed no indictable crimes, but I am coming to work, and won't be much in sight for several months. . . .

VIII

BROOKLYN AND WORK: A PORTRAIT OF BASCOM
HAWKE *AND* THE WEB OF EARTH

1931-1932

The following letter to Henry Allen Moe may be somewhat confusing to the reader since Wolfe uses in it titles for large portions of his material which were later used for smaller portions. The "book . . . in four volumes" which he says "will have the name The October Fair" *was the entire series of novels he had planned:* The October Fair *(of which the first half became* Of Time and the River), The Hills Beyond Pentland, The Death of the Enemy *and* Pacific End. *"The first of these books which . . . I hope to have completed by January" was the entire novel of* The October Fair, *for which he was considering* Time and the River *or* Of Men and Rivers *or* The River *as alternate titles. The decision to divide this novel into halves and publish the first half as* Of Time and the River *was not reached until late December 1933, after Perkins had read the rough draft manuscript of the entire novel and pointed out to Wolfe that it described two separate cycles.*

To HENRY ALLEN MOE

Harvard Club
New York
July 2, [1931]

Dear Mr. Moe:

I got your letter with its inquiry concerning the work I am doing, and I want to answer you before I go away—to Maine for a week or ten days. Since coming back from Europe in March, I have been living in Brooklyn and I rarely come over to Manhattan. I am working on the book I began in Europe when I was there on the Guggenheim Fellowship. The book, if I survive to complete it, will be in four volumes, and will have the name "The October Fair." Each of these four will be a complete novel—

the four are related more by a plan and a feeling than by a central group of characters which appear in each of the four. The first of these books, which is a very long one, I hope to have completed by January, and, if published, it will appear next year. I don't know what its name will be— I have thought of several: "Of Men and Rivers," "Time and the River"; "The River"; or simply "The October Fair," which I had thought of as a general name for all four. I am up to my neck in it and have worked like a nigger this summer. I have had it in my head for over two years, knew where I was going, but didn't get it straight until six or eight months ago. Now I think I've got it. While abroad on the Guggenheim I wrote two or three hundred thousand words, and went through hell in arranging, re-arranging, trying to get it into sequence.

I've wanted to come in to tell you about it, but I have come to New York so seldom, and I wanted to show you something more coherent than the big ledgers I had filled with writing. Anyway, when the book comes out, if it has any merit, I hope you will accept it as the work I did with the Guggenheim money, and even if coherence was long in coming, I think those first months abroad, while I stewed around in chaos plucking out separate nuts here and there, were the months I really wrote the thing, pulled it out of limbo, got it on the rails. I hope you'll like it when you see it—anyway, you'll be able to see I've worked. I will come in to see you when I come back. I'm living at 40 Verandah Place, Brooklyn—it's an alley in the Assyrian district, but it's cheap and quiet. . . . If you want to reach me, you can get me quicker there than through Scribners. . . .

Brooklyn is a fine town—a nice, big country town, a long way from New York. You couldn't find a better place to work.

Wolfe sent the following letter to a girl whom he knew, but later demanded that she return it to him, and kept it among his own papers.

To ————

[Summer, 1931]

Dear ——:

I just found your special delivery upstairs and my first impulse, on reading it, was to call you up right away. But your letter seemed so clear and fine to me that I thought I would try to answer you in the same way, before talking to you, and I wonder that I did not try it before—this is my usual means of expression—paper and pencil—and I believe I can be much more direct and less confused in this way than in conversation.

First of all, I want to say that anyone who can write such a letter as you sent me—which seemed so fine, so true, and so generous—can get anything she wants out of living: you can conquer everyone and everything by such means, and people will love you. Such a letter as that is so much more potent than the craftiest craft, the deepest and most subtle cunning that a person like myself, who is sometimes gnawed by a devil of suspiciousness and doubt, may wonder if there is not a skill and cleverness here too great for him to cope with. (Please don't think I feel this way—I am enormously touched and grateful for your letter, and so happy about getting it.) What I am trying to say is that men have been told so often, since their childhood, of the subtlety of women, and so often warned against vain-glorious assurance in their dealings with women, that even when we think we know what we know, we are checked by a fear that we are fooling ourselves—that even when we read vanity and pride into the conduct of others, however affectionately, we are really guilty of vanity and pride ourselves. Having said so much, as my only means of defense and qualification, I am now going to kick caution out of the window, and tell you exactly how I feel, and what I think went wrong.

Let us review our relation from the beginning, which was only about three months ago. That first time I met you, it seemed to me we were two young people, "alone in the world," although we had friends who were loyal and good to us, and our lives were at that time smooth enough, although both of us had had rough passages in the past. Perhaps I was still looking around for dry land. When I left you in the morning and walked toward the subway through deserted streets and among the enormous and inhuman masses of the buildings, I had a feeling of the most enormous exultancy and joy to think that there were young women like you in the world. As I have told you, I saw you in all this setting—by the great river with its bridges and its sliding lights, in the enormous city at daybreak—you were alone, strong, brave, and independent; you had been through a bad time and came through it without being warped; everything about you was sweet and lovely, and in addition to this you had a good position (which also seemed thrilling and fine to me); you were immensely capable, and probably one of the handsomest and most desirable young women on earth.

I mention the job, by the way, because I thought how much more desirable and seductive such women as you are than the Southern girls I knew as a boy: here, I thought, in New York, were wonderful girls with good jobs who had their own flats and would also stand a round of drinks. The Southern girl had become repulsive to me: her drawly voice, her coquettish airs, her apologies for working or boasts of never having worked —I thought of them now with such revulsion that I believed them to be foul, dull, stupid, nasty—with a litter of gummed combs and hair upon the dresser, and a rancid swimming chamber-pot below the bed. Everything about you was so clean, sweet, and desirable; you were as independent as I was, you asked no more of me than I of you, we were two free and decent people, and that morning as I walked home, New York seemed magnificent in the young light, and I thought discovering you was one of the best things that ever had happened to me.

I go into these particulars so fully because I want you to know something of the state of my feeling—I cannot hope to reproduce the whole state of joy that I felt, because it was touched by so many shades of things, but I think one element that was most important was this feeling of dignity and independence—I thought of us both being just and equal in our dealings, in giving and taking equally, in admitting an equal share and satisfaction. Later on, you began to say other things about our relation —how it could not be as fine or complete as it might be until there was a deeper or more fundamental relation between us. I asked you if you meant marriage, and you said that might be, but that you did not demand this— but you did want something that was complete and, however long it lasted, would be a primary experience while it did last. As I thought of this, it seemed to me that a frank and simple translation was this: you thought that the finest relation came when people loved each other with all their hearts, and lived faithfully and entirely in that love. I think so, too, and I have told you I think so; but for that very reason it is not a thing which can be planned, meditated, or determined upon deliberately. If it were, I would be a fool not to try to determine myself immediately in love with you, because you are a desirable and lovely woman. It does not come that way, however, and I told you at once what my feeling was: the joy and exultancy I had over meeting you, the deep and tender affection I had for you, the relief you brought me from the trouble I had been in, the great value I set upon you.

At one time, you accused me of using you as a stop-gap while I worked on my book and was adjusting myself after the insanity of love which obsessed me for several years and from which I was just fully emerging. What you said might be harshly and coldly true, but what seems to me more true is that I thought of you with delight and tenderness, and enormous relief, as . . . my friend, and the companion with whom I could find comfort and peace. I also hoped that you might have this same deep pleasure and comfort from me. I think I understood exactly what you hoped to get from life, and I never argued against it—I thought you were right in wanting it—but I never deceived you as to what I could give, or as to my feeling.

Now I think we come to a big difference in feeling here: I agree with you as to what is the best and most wonderful relation between people, but on that account I do not believe that all other relations are trivial or vile. There is a higher relation than the one we had, but I feel that the one we had was a good one, and I shall always be glad of it, and think I am better for having had it. I earnestly hoped you would feel the same way. I am no longer promiscuous, I do not wander from bed to bed, I have a great deal of fidelity in me: as you know, my life at the present time is very simple—I stay in Brooklyn and work, and when I went to New York I went with a feeling of delight and joy because I knew a beautiful and intelligent young woman there with whom I could talk, eat, and go to bed. As time went on you apparently got the idea that what was wrong with our relation was not the talking and eating but the going to bed. Now this is very blunt and plain, but I think it is a fair statement: you began to say a short time ago that what you valued in our relation was "friendship" and not "sexual relations." You know that the reason I have protested at this is that I do not see how you make this complete division between our friendship and our sexual relations. We began with sexual relations and our whole relation is integrated with this: I do not know how you can make a separation in your own mind, but I know that when I think of you I shall always remember that we went to bed together—you understand I am not saying this is the entire memory, but it is an integral and essential part of my picture of you. For my part, it is something I shall always remember with the deepest and most grateful tenderness.

During the last month I have not seen very much of you—it seemed to me I could no longer argue with you over what I believed was false: it seemed to me you wanted the sex relation as much as I did, but later you were always giving reasons and justifications for your action—it seemed to me everything but the real one. First you said you did it because you were trying to break the hold and memory of some former lover; then a few weeks ago, when we saw each other less frequently, you said you did it as a sort of bribe to me—you no longer cared for it with me, but it was the only way you had of holding my friendship—if you did not do it, I would not see you any more. This I felt to be intolerable and unjust. It put me in such a shabby and humiliating position. ——, I have known hundreds of women, but I have never forced myself on anyone, nor ever thought of this sort of coercion. Neither have they. I have had plenty of women as friends, and never thought of any other relation, but I have never had one tell me before that the only reason she went to bed with me was to hold my friendship. If a woman no longer wants to go to bed with you, that is her own business, but then, if that has been the relation, it is over and they can sometimes see you later and be your friend.

But I know the reason you went to bed with me was because you wanted to, and I thought it unfair and shabby for you to say later that it was because I wanted it and would not be your friend without it. You were certainly an equal partner in it all, no coercion was ever brought to bear on you, and that first night, it seemed to me you allowed it to be plainly understood that this was what you wanted. Had you not desired it, had you chosen not to, it would have showed plainly in your speech, the way you sat, in everything. . . . Now I think it is wrong for you to deny that you did it as freely and willingly as I did. If you no longer have this desire where I am concerned, I shall accept your decision, although sadly, but you ought not to say that what you did gladly and freely was done to bribe me. Also, if you now insist that this is finished, I will accept your decision, although I do not know why it has ceased to be desirable to you. and I will try to be your "friend" as you understand the term, but for me, at least, it will mean beginning anew with you and knowing you in another way. The other relation was the one in which I went to bed with you, and I will always remember it—the sound of the boats out on the river, the lights, the darkness, and you beneath me in the dark—I shall remember it with pride and delight as long as I live: I know your look, your size, your smell—the feel of your breast and belly, the swell of your hips, the taste of your mouth, the grip of your thighs. You were like the best butter and eggs and honey that was ever made, as lovely and desirable as any woman on the earth.

Finally, I think you were right in the way you felt and said you felt at first—about wanting the best and finest in human love and friendship, and I have always agreed with you. But I think what we had was, to me at least, very good and wonderful. In your letter you speak of your own "hurt and humiliation" as explaining the things you said to me:—I am giving you my own opinion without defense or explanation—I think you hoped or believed I would fall deeply and utterly in love with you and when I did not, you said you had had sexual relations with me to keep my friendship.

I want to say, ——, that no one can "hurt or humiliate" you except yourself. I have found that out in my own life. You are one of the finest and most desirable young women I have ever seen and your letter was an action of the highest order. You deserve nothing but the best and finest in life and you will get it. Do you understand from this letter of mine— this remarkable, honest, and *wholly serious* letter—that I know your value as a person, your great worth and beauty. Do you understand that I could never misprize or undervalue such a person as you—that if I could not offer you everything in me, it is because everything in me once went into something, someone, else, and if it ever returns like that, it will take time? As for myself, I think it will never come that way again but it will come in another way, and I am going to try to have a good life.

[A SECTION OF THE LETTER IS EVIDENTLY MISSING HERE]

. . . out of me as utterly as birth and death. It can never be lost now but it will never be regained. But I hope and have faith that someday I will be able to offer someone with some of your own quality something that is wise, true, and abiding, even if it is not the fiercest and most lyrical feeling we have had in us.

Meanwhile I hope this letter has made things clearer rather than obscurer, and gives us a place to start, to continue, or what you will—so long as it enables us to stand together again.

To FRED W. WOLFE

[40 Verandah Place]
[Brooklyn, N.Y.]
July 19, 1931

Dear Fred:

Thanks for your several letters. I owe you more than one answer, but will have to make this do for the present. I am plugging away at my book, and in this weather—what Papa would have called "this hellish, fearful, awful, damnable and bloodthirsty weather"—it is about all I can do to get four or five hours of writing done each day.

First of all, I got your check for $275 [1]—as you already know. Now I'm not going to talk any more about it—I believe you fully understand that I am delighted to help to the extent of my ability, and trust you to let me know if you need anything for yourself or for the family. Of one thing I am almost sure: I think I can always manage, no matter what hard times may be ahead of us yet, to get money enough to keep Mama going, and of course I think that is the first and most important consideration. There seems to be a hope and belief here that business is going to improve soon. People think Hoover's debt agreement with Europe will help. I have a feeling it's not going to be so quick or easy—the little speculators who lost their shirt last time are all ready to go again. . . . But the whole thing is wrong: how do people expect to create any real or solid prosperity by sitting on their tails in a broker's office all day long? The whole thing is cockeyed, and if they do give it a shot of dope this time, it will only bring it back temporarily. I think we may be up against

[1] In a letter to his mother dated June 8, 1931 (see page 206, *Thomas Wolfe's Letters to His Mother*), Wolfe wrote: "This morning I got a letter from Fred with a check for $275, returning almost all the money I sent to Effie."

a much more serious disaster than most of us yet realize—although how in God's name people in a town which has been wrecked and ruined as Asheville has can fail to recognize it, I don't see. I think, and other people think the same, that we may even be at the end of what is called an "era" —that the old system is shot to hell, and we will have to get busy and find a newer and better one. I went to town to see a show to-night—the weather has been hot and muggy with low-lying clouds, and when I came out and crossed Fifth Avenue, the top of the Empire State was completely hidden in mist. It's a rare sight but I've an idea it will be a hell of a time before they put up another to beat it: I understand Al Smith himself is legging it all over town in an effort to rent it, but they say he's not having much luck—it looks as if he's bitten off a mouthful this time. . . .

I note what you say about my new book. I cannot tell you much about it because I do not like to talk about anything I am writing, but I will put your mind at rest upon one score: it has nothing to do with the first book in any way—the scenes, characters, and story are all different: if the gossip-mongers in Asheville are licking their chops in anticipation of a feast, they're in for a surprise. My experience with the first book was so depressing, so far as Asheville is concerned, that I was almost sorry any-one there had ever read a line I had written. I assure you I have found out a great deal more about the world and Asheville, too, in the last year and a half than in the rest of my life put together. But if I ever return to the scenes of the first book, as someday I shall, it will be at least five years before I am ready for it. Meanwhile, I do not care, save from a business point of view, whether they read what I write or not, but if they are living in hope of scandal let them pursue their delusion to the end—I mean to the end of buying the book.

By the way, I may have made more money for them all than I ever made for myself—I don't know what ever became of all the books that were sold in Asheville, but there must have been hundreds of copies of the first edition there. I have been told that collectors will pay $10 or $15 for the first edition, and with a copy of the "dust wrapper"—that is the paper cover that came with it—and with my autograph, I have been told it brings as much as $25. At any rate I know a collector who buys them and pays this much for them, and will furnish his name on request. It's all the more a joke to me since I don't own a copy of the book myself, and have just about enough money to live on simply until I finish the new one.

Thanks for your invitation to come home. I'd like to see the family but, aside from that, I have no great interest in coming at this time. I think you understand the reason—just the thing we have been talking about. If I ever come back to Asheville I want to feel either that I can come quietly to see my family and a few friends, without having to talk to a lot of lying gossips, or that people in my own town have some respect for my work, and some understanding of me. I have heard so much slander, vituperation, gossip, and indirect and anonymous threats that I have grown weary of it, and want to forget it. Several times I have heard, indirectly as usual, that I am "afraid to come back to Asheville," and that "people there have threatened to kill me." Well, if I am afraid, it is not because of this, but for reasons they have never understood. I don't think anyone is "going to kill me": I have heard of these threats, but no one has ever made them to my face, and I assure you I lose no sleep on this account. Naturally, however, I have no great urge to go back to a place where such things are said—I might go back simply for the purpose of "showing them," but I have no desire to show them anything. Somehow a man can devote his life to the work he likes best, and, in his own way, create something that will satisfy him and hold in it his vision of life. Of this, most of them know nothing: they will never understand that I am interested neither in gossip or making money. I tried to explain this long ago, but found it useless—now I don't try. But if they do boast in Asheville that I am "afraid to come back," it seems to me a pitiful boast to make. I am not afraid of any man living, nor do I apologize for my life to anyone, but I will not walk knowingly and willingly into any place where the population has threatened to attack me, unless there was something there I had to do, something to be gained by going. That is not the case: if I ever come home I want to be treated with the consideration and respect of any ordinary citizen—I don't care either for bouquets or lynching bees.

This is all for the present . . . remember I will always help when you ask me, but I depend on you to holler when the time comes. Come up to see me if you get a chance—if you can pick up a ride, the rest of the trip will cost you nothing. Meanwhile, good luck and best wishes to every one.

To ALFRED S. DASHIELL

[Postcard: Monument Rock, Eagle Island, Me.]

Orrs Island, Maine

August 8, 1931

Dear Fritz:

I'm cooked with sunshine from head to foot—it hurts something awful. I'm taking my meals at a boarding-house and the crowd of boarders is the same as it always was—they sit on the porch and rock—they never change. . . .

On August 27, 1931, Perkins wrote Wolfe saying: "I think you ought to make every conceivable effort to have your manuscript completely finished by the end of September. I meant to speak of this when we were last together. I hope you will come in soon and tell me what you think you can do." The following was Wolfe's reply.

To MAXWELL E. PERKINS

[40 Verandah Place]
[Brooklyn]
Saturday, August 29, 1931

Dear Max:

Thanks for your note which came this morning. I am glad you wrote me, because I have some definite idea of when you expect to see my book, and I can say some things about it that I wanted to say. You say you think I ought to make every conceivable effort to have the manuscript completely finished by the end of September. I know you are not joking and that you mean *this* September, and not September four, five, or fifteen years from now. Well, there is no remote or possible chance that I will have a completed manuscript of anything that resembles a book this September, and whether I have anything that I would be willing to show anyone next September, or any succeeding one for the next 150 years, is at present a matter of the extremest and most painful doubt to me.

I realize that it has been almost two years since my first book was published and that you might reasonably hope that I have something ready by this time. But I haven't. I believe that you are my true friend and, aside from any possible business interest, are disappointed because what hope you had in me has been weakened or dispelled. I want you to know that I feel the deepest regret on this account, but I assure you the most bitter disappointment is what I feel at present in myself. I don't want you to misunderstand me, or think that, aside from you and a few other people whose friendship has meant a great deal for me, I care one good Goddamn of a drunken sailor's curse whether I have "disappointed" the world of bilge-and-hogwash-writers, . . . or any of the other literary rubbish of sniffers, whiffers and puny, poisonous apes. If what I am about to lose because of my failure to produce was, as I once believed, something beautiful and valuable—I mean a feeling of deep and fine respect in life for the talent of someone who can create a worthy thing—then my regret at the loss of something so precious would be great. But do you really think that after what I have seen during the past eighteen months, I would cling very desperately to this stinking remnant of a rotten fish, or any longer feel any sense of deference or responsibility to swine who make you sign books to their profit even while you break bread with them, who insolently command you to produce a book and "be sure you make it good or you are done for," who taunt and goad you by telling you to take care since "other writers are getting ahead of you," who try to degrade your life to a dirty, vulgar, grinning, servile, competitive little monkey's life—do you think I am losing anything so wonderful here that I can't bear the loss? You must know that I don't care a damn for all this now.

I want you to know, Max, that the only thing I do care for now is whether I have lost the faith I once had in myself, whether I have lost the power I once felt in me, whether I have anything at all left—who once had no doubt that I had a treasury—that would justify me in going on. Do you think anything else matters to me? I have been a fool and a jackass—cheapened myself by making talks at their filthy clubs and giving interviews, but my follies of that sort were done long ago. For the rest I haven't tried to do anything but live quietly by myself without fancy mysterious airs, and there is as decent stuff within me as in anyone. I have kept my head above this river of filth, some of the dirty rotten lies they have told about me have come back to me, but I have yet to find the person who uttered them to my face. I want you to know that I consider that my hands are clean and that I owe no one anything—save for the debt of friendship for a few people. I did not write the blurbs, the pieces in the paper, the foolish statements, nor did I tell lies: no one can take anything from me now that I value, they can have their cheap, nauseous, seven-day notoriety back to give to other fools, but I am perfectly content to return to the obscurity in which I passed almost thirty years of my life without great difficulty. If anyone wants to know when I will have a new book out, I can answer without apology "when I have finished writing one and found some one who wants to publish it." That is the only answer I owe to anyone (I don't mean you: you know the answer I have tried to make to you already) and please, Max, if you can tactfully and gently, without wounding anyone, suggest to whoever is responsible for these newspaper squibs about my having written 500,000 words, and more all the time, that he please for God's sake cut it out, I will be grateful. I am sure it was intended to help, but it does no good. I assure you I am not at all afraid or depressed at the thought of total obscurity again —I welcome it, and I resent any effort to present me as a cheap and sensational person. In spite of my size, appetite, appearance, staying up all night, 500,000 words, etc., I am not a cheap and sensational person: if there is going to be publicity, why can't it tell the truth—that I work hard and live decently and quietly; that no one in the world had a higher or more serious feeling about writing; that I made no boasts or promises;

that I do not know whether I will ever do the writing I want to do, or not, or whether I will be able to go on at all; that I am in doubt and distress about it, but that I work, ask nothing from anyone, and hope, for my own sake, that I have some talent and power in me. I say, I am not afraid of publicity like this, because it would be the truth, and it could not injure me save with fools.

I thank God I am in debt to no one: I have sent my family all I could, Mrs. Boyd has had her full whack, the dentists are almost paid. Now, if they will all leave me alone, they can have the rest—if anything is left. I can't find out. I wish you'd find out for me and have Darrow send it to me. I've tried for a year to find out but I can't. I appreciate this paternal attitude, but it may be wasted on me, and I want to clear the board now. Above all, I don't want to owe you money. As things stand, in my present frame of mind about my work, it is a blessing to me that I owe you no money and have no contract with you for a second book.[1] Max, won't you ask Darrow to send me whatever money is coming to me? As things stand now, it seems important to me that I should know where I stand financially, and what I am going to have to do. I have earned my living teaching and in other ways before, and I believe I can earn my living again. As I told you the only thing that matters now would be to feel that the book has value and beauty for me, and that I have the power to do it—if I felt that, I could do any work to support myself and feel good about it.

Max, I have tried to tell you how I feel about all this, and now I want to sum it up in this way: Two years ago I was full of hope and confidence: I had complete within me the plans and ideas of at least a half dozen long books. To-day I still have all this material, [but] I have not the same hope and confidence; I have, on the contrary, a feeling of strong self-doubt and mistrust—which is not to say that I feel despair. I do not. Why this has happened I do not know. I think one reason is that I cannot work in a glare; I was disturbed and lost self-confidence because of the notice I had; I think my success may have hurt me. . . . I don't know whether this means I am unable to meet the troubles of life without caving in—this may be true, and in my doubt I think of some of the old books I read: "The Damnation of Someone or Another," [2] "The Picture of Dorian

---

[1] The contract for *Of Time and the River* was not drawn until May, 1933. In his letter of December 18, 1929, in which he confirmed the agreement to pay Wolfe an advance of forty-five hundred dollars in installments, Perkins had written: "We should be glad to draw up a contract with regard to your next novel . . . which would embody this agreement. We only defer drawing this contract because it is unnecessary so far as we are concerned, since this letter is binding. . . . For the present . . . this letter may stand as a definite agreement."

[2] Probably *The Damnation of Theron Ware,* by Harold Frederic.

Grey"—in which spiritual decay, degeneration, and corruption destroys the person before he knows it. But I think that is literary nightmarishness: maybe these things happen, but I don't think they happened to me. I think I have kept my innocence, and that my feeling about living and working is better than it ever was. And I don't think I am unable to cope with the trial of life, but I think I may meet it clumsily and slowly, inexpertly, sweat blood and lose time. What I want to tell you is that I am in a state of *doubt* about all this.

Finally, the best life I can now dream of for myself, the highest hope I have is this: that I believe in my work and know it is good and that somehow, in my own way, secretly and obscurely, I have power in me to get the books inside me out of me. I dream of a quiet, modest life, but a life that is really high, secret, proud, and full of dignity for a writer in this country—I dream of a writer having work and power within him, living this fine life untouched and uncoarsened by this filth and rabble of the gossip-booster [set?]—I dream of something permanent and fine, of the highest quality, and if the power is in me to produce, this is the life I want and shall have.

Thus, at great length, I have told you what is in my mind better than I could by talking to you. Max, do you understand that this letter is not bitter and truculent, save for those things and persons I despise. I want to tell you finally that I am not in *despair* over the book I have worked on—I am in *doubt* about it—and I am not sure about anything: I think I will finish it, I think it may be valuable and fine—or it may be worthless. I would like to tell you about it, and of some of the trouble I had with it. I can only suggest it: I felt if my life and strength kept up, if my vitality moved in every page, if I followed it through to the end, it would be a wonderful book—but I doubted then that life was long enough, it seemed to me it would take ten books, that it would be the longest ever written. Then, instead of paucity, I had abundance—such abundance that my hand was palsied, my brain weary—and in addition, as I go on, I want to write about everything and say all that can be said about each particular. The vast freightage of my years of hunger, my prodigies of reading, my infinite store of memories, my hundreds of books of notes, return to drown me—sometimes I feel as if I shall compass and devour them, again be devoured by them. I had an immense book and I wanted to say it all at once: it can't be done. Now I am doing it part by part, and hope and believe the part I am doing will be a complete story, a unity, and part of the whole plan. This part itself has now become a big book: it is for the first time straight in my head to the smallest detail, and much of it is written —it is a part of my whole scheme of books as a smaller river flows into a big one.

As I understand it, I am not bound now to Scribners or to any publisher by any sort of contract: none was ever offered me—neither have I taken money that is not my own. The only bond I am conscious of is one of friendship and loyalty to your house, and in this I have been faithful—it has been a real and serious thing with me.

I know that you want to see what I have done—to see if I had it in me to do more work after the first book, or whether everything burnt out in that one candle. Well, that is what I want to see, too, and my state of doubt and uneasiness is probably at least as great as your own. It seems to me that that is the best way to leave it now: the coast is clear between us, there are no debts or entanglements—if I ever write anything else that I think worth printing, or that your house might be interested in, I will bring it to you, and you can read it, accept it or reject it with the same freedom as with the first book. I ask for no more from anyone. The life that I desire, and that I am going to try to win for myself, is going to exist in complete indifference and independence to such of the literary life as I have seen—I mean to all their threats either of glory or annihilation, to gin-party criticism or newspaper blurbs and gossip, and to all their hysterical seven-day fames. If a man sets a high value on these things he richly deserves the payment he will get. As for me, I tell you honestly it is a piece of stinking fish to me—their rewards and punishments. I see what it did to writers in what they now call "the twenties"— how foolishly and trivially they worshipped this thing, and what nasty, ginny, drunken, jealous, fake-Bohemian little lives they had, and I see now how they have kicked these men out, after tainting and corrupting them, and brought in another set which they call "the younger writers," among whom I have seen my own name mentioned. Well, I assure you I belong to neither group and I will not compete or produce in competition against any other person—no one will match me as you match a cock or a prizefighter, no one will goad me to show smartness or brilliance against another's—the only standard I will compete against now is in me: if I can't reach it, I'll quit.

It is words, words—I weary of the staleness of the words, the seas of print, the idiot repetition of trivial enthusiasms. I am weary of my own words but I have spoken the truth here. Is it possible that we are all tainted with cheapness and staleness: is this the taint that keeps us sterile, cheap, and stale in this country? When I talk to you as here and say what I know is in my heart, am I just another Brown—a cheap stale fellow who pollutes everything he talks about—justice, love, mercy—as he utters it? It isn't true—I am crammed to the lips with living. I am tired with what I've seen, I'm tired of their stale faces, the smell of concrete and taut steel, the thing that yellows, dries, or withers us—but did it mean nothing to you when I told you the beauty, exulting, joy, richness, and undying power that I had found in America, that I knew and believed to be the *real* truth, not the illusion, the thing we had never found the pattern for, the style for, the true words to express—or was it only words to you; did you just think I was trying to be Whitman again? I know what I know, it crushes the lies and staleness like a rotten shell, but whether I can ever utter what I know, whether staleness and weariness has not done for me, I don't know. Christ, I am tired of everything but what I know to be the truth, and do not utter—I have it inside me. I even know the words for it, but staleness and dullness has got into me, I look at it with grey dullness and will not say it—it's not enough to see it: you've got to feel the thick snake-wriggle in each sentence, the heavy living tug of the fish at the line.

I'm out of the game—and it is a game, a racket: what I do now must be for myself. I don't care who "gets ahead" of me—that game isn't worth a good goddam: I only care if I have disappointed you, but it's very much my own funeral, too. I don't ask you to "give me a chance," because I think you've given me one, but I don't want you to think this is a despairing letter, and that I've given up—I just say I don't know, I'm going to see: maybe it will come out right someday. By the way, I'm still working, I've been at it hard and will keep it up until I have to look for job: I may try to get work on Pacific Coast. I'll come in to see you later, Max. Please get Darrow to send me what money is coming to me.

When I was a kid we used to say of someone we thought the best and highest of that he was "a high class gentleman." That's the way I feel about you. I don't think I am one—not the way you are, by birth, by gentleness, by natural and delicate kindness. But if I have understood some of the things you have said to me, I believe you think the most living and beautiful thing on this earth is art, and that the finest and most valuable life is that of the artist. I think so, too: I don't know whether I have it in me to live that life, but if I have, then I think I would have something that would be worth your friendship. You know a good deal about me—the kind of people I came from (who seem to me, by the way, about as good as any people anywhere), and I think you know some of the things I have done, and that I was in love with a middle-aged Jewish woman old enough to be my mother—I hope you understand I am ashamed of none of these things—my family, the Jewish woman, my life —but it would be a hard thing for me to face if I thought you were repelled by these things, and did not know what I am like. I think my feeling about living and working and people is as good as you can find, and

I want you to know how I feel: it's so hard to know people and we think they feel inferior about things they really feel superior to, and the real thing that eats them we know nothing of.

I'm coming in to talk to you soon, but I can talk to you about some things better this way. Meanwhile, Max, good health and good luck and all my friendliest wishes.

P.S. I'm attaching a clipping [3] a friend sent me from a Boston paper. You see how quickly people can use an item like this injuriously. I think it has done harm, and I don't deserve it: please get them to cut it out and leave me alone.

To A. S. FRERE-REEVES

Harvard Club
New York
Saturday, September 19, 1931

Dear Frere:

I'm sorry I've been so long in answering you. I have plugged away as hard as I could during the summer—and the summer has been past all your dreams of hell. Maybe there's a law of distribution and compensation which gives England the horrible winters and America the horrible summers.

About the five shilling edition of L.H.A.—if you think it is a good move, both for Heinemann and me, go ahead and do it.[1] I'm almost stony broke—sent all I could to my family in the South and have nothing left. I'm living . . . in Brooklyn, which is a vast sprawl upon the face of the earth, which no man alive or dead has yet seen in its foul, dismal entirety. I don't know how it *looks* but I'm an authority on how it smells. . . . In the subway, where we are still using the air the subway people bountifully provided last April, all of these stinks have been mixed, melted, fused and wrought into one glamorous, nauseating whole—and *that* is the way Brooklyn smells.

Do what you think best about the five shilling edition. If it means a

[3] The clipping reads as follows: "Fiction is threatened with an epidemic of obesity. One of the latest symptoms in this country—the English situation is general and serious—is word from Thomas Wolfe who is working on a Maine coast island on a novel to be called *October Fair*. He confesses to a total of 500,000 words to date, and Charles Scribner's Sons are telegraphing their pleas for a process of selection, revision and condensation."

[1] This edition of *Look Homeward, Angel* was published by Heinemann in February, 1932.

little money for me, it will be most welcome. Whether and when I shall ever get another one finished is at present a matter of extreme and painful doubt. Whenever anyone asks me when it will be published, I tell them when I finish writing it and find a publisher who is willing to print it. Whether I find one is also a matter of doubt. For one thing, however, I am grateful—at last I am left alone—I may breathe the seventy-nine stinks of Brooklyn but I no longer breathe the unutterably fouler stink of *la vie litteraire*, as practiced in this noble city, and I suppose elsewhere. I am free, finished, deserted, left gloriously alone, by the last son of a bitch of an autograph collector and gossip writer, and the last stale whore of a literary party-giver. . . .

If you think I am talking through my hat—(I haven't got one anyway: the one I bought at Lodis is worn out)—when I say that this sweet cool gloom of obscurity again is balm and healing to my soul—then you know nothing about me; but maybe you wondered when I would find out what a piece of stinking fish the literary racket is. Well, I knew it all along, but there are some things you can't believe until they happen— the truth is so much more incredible than either *The Daily Mail* or *The Express*.

I understand Richard Aldington's book [2] has made a great stir in England, and is being denounced on the playing fields of Eton, etc., and is a big success, and I am heartily glad. It is being spoken of here a great deal, and I am going to read it as soon as possible. One doesn't have to go to war to understand bitterness. I think Renan said that the only thing which could adequately describe the idea of the infinite was the spectacle of human stupidity—and God knows he hit the nail on the head. I've just come from dear old Broadway—first visit in months—and as you look at them sweating along through this stale monotony of glare, noise and idiot illumination, you wonder at the quality of intelligence which has spent thousands of years in order to bring men to this—and yet the poor unhappy bastards try to tell themselves they are being amused!

I don't think I'd leave the country now, even if I could. I think some very interesting things may happen here, are happening, have already happened—although most of them still stand around with their mouths ajar and looking upward, as if they expected the gates of heaven to open up the next moment and piss milk and honey all over them. That really is just what they *do* expect—they think there is some law of matter or quantity which governs their crazy economic system: they talk profoundly about "the pendulum swinging backward" etc., when there's no reason to suppose it ever will, although it may. Meanwhile, Mr. Hoover ("The Great Engineer," you know) and the other noble politicians are

[2] *The Colonel's Daughter.*

giving a wonderful illustration of the blind man searching in a dark room for a black cat that isn't there. There are seven million out of work—and Mr. Hoover issues a call for $20,000,000 so that each of the unemployed will have $2.50 to squander away during the winter. It is masterly. The real Russian menace, so far as I can see, is simply that Russia does not seem to be governed by a set of Goddamned fools! Even an intelligent and purposeful lunatic would be a formidable menace against a school of feeble-minded jelly fish.

Enough, enough! Do what you can with the book and try to get me some money for it. The best I can tell you about myself is that I am well, bad-tempered, and full of work. Maybe I'll get something done some day—I don't know. . . .

The following letter was written to a mutual friend of Wolfe's and Kenneth Raisbeck's shortly after Raisbeck's body had been found in a graveyard in Connecticut. At first it was thought that he had been murdered, but an autopsy found that he had died of acute meningitis.

To ――――

[40 Verandah Place]
[Brooklyn]
[October, 1931]

Dear ――:

I have seen and talked to ―― ――, he called me up late Saturday afternoon, said he . . . would like to see me. I made an appointment with him at the Harvard Club, met him there at 7:30, went to a speakeasy for some drinks and then to a restaurant where we talked to 1:30. When I left him, he was on his way to see Emily Davies.

I think I have heard the whole story now. He showed me the remarkable letter Kenneth had written him a couple of years ago, naming a list of people whose friendship he valued—I am mentioned along with several others, including yourself. He also showed me another sensational story which he had clipped from one of the tabloid papers on Saturday. It was a mass of obscene rumours and suggestions—there was no tangible evidence, but hints of "nude cults," "fashionable artistic colonies," rendezvous with married women and vengeance by husband or lover, etc.

The cumulative horror of the story has weighed on me so heavily that at times it amounts almost to physical nausea. I understand your anxiety and desire to keep the names of innocent people whom Kenneth may have known out of this mess. But I cannot for the life of me see why any of us should cower before these slimy, scandal-mongering bastards of the yellow press. If their crooked power is so complete that they can hurl filth all over decent people whose only relation to the case is that they knew the dead man—then I think we had better not concern ourselves very much with fear of a public opinion that will swallow such muck, hook, line and sinker.

Of one thing I feel reasonably convinced now—that Kenneth came to his death by natural causes, that he was not murdered. Of these other facts which you and —— have told me, I don't know what to say or think— I have had at times a sickening sense of horror or doubt, but I think that these things must now remain forever in mystery, buried in our memory or obliterated by our faith. My final sense about the matter is this: I remember him as he was when we were students together at Harvard, as my friend—as the remarkable, fine and brilliant person I believed and believe him to have been. I believe your sentiment is the same, and I know of no reason why we should change it. . . .

[THE LETTER BREAKS OFF UNFINISHED, AND WAS EVIDENTLY NEVER MAILED.]

To FRED W. WOLFE

Harvard Club
New York
October 4, 1931

Dear Fred:

. . . I have been away for a few days, but came back Thursday night: was up in the Catskill Mountains on the estate of some friends.[1] . . . When I got back I read some news in the paper which depressed me greatly. A man I used to know at Harvard—in fact, we were the closest friends there—has just died. His body was found in a graveyard in Connecticut, and the doctor's report was that he died suddenly of acute meningitis, but the police believe he was murdered: they found bruises on his neck, and the grass round about him was torn up—the doctor says this might have happened from his own convulsions in his dying moments. He was a very brilliant young fellow who had many friends ready to help him—every one believed he had a great future; but he did nothing with it. I had a falling out with him in Paris several years ago and we have not seen each other since, although I had a chance to befriend him a year or two ago, and did it—I took his play to someone who got it put

[1] Probably the L. Effingham de Forests at Onteora Park.

on for him. But the play failed.² I have felt very depressed about it: I forget about the falling out we had and I remember the time we were both young fellows at Harvard full of hope, and what good friends we were. It seems a terrible thing that his life should end as it did.

I have not made the trip to Pennsylvania yet, but may go down later. Thanks for sending me the very full and complete information ³—it will be very useful when I make the trip. . . .

There's very little more to tell you at present, so I'll cut this short hoping it finds you and Mama well, and conditions a little improved at home. I am writing this from the Harvard Club which two years ago was full of life and bustle and laughter: to-night it's as dead as a tomb and you can cut the depression with a knife. They had their fling and they're in for a very long morning after.

Goodbye for the present and good luck and good health to everyone. . . .

If you need anything, holler: it may not do much good, but I'll always make an effort.

P.S. I think the depression's so bad they've begun to water the ink here at the club. . . .

To SINCLAIR LEWIS

[111 Columbia Heights]
[Brooklyn]

[January, 1932]

Dear Red:

I have thought of you often and I am sorry I have not written you before—anyway, I send you now my best and warmest wishes for health and happiness this New Year. I have been living in Brooklyn since I came back and working like hell—going to finish my new book this year or fall in my tracks.

Red, I want to thank you gratefully for getting your German publisher ¹ to take my book and publish it—the reason I have never written you

² Wolfe had taken the manuscript of Raisbeck's play, *Rock Me, Julie,* to Madeleine Boyd who sold it to a Broadway producer. It opened at the Royale Theatre on February 3, 1931, but ran for only seven performances.

³ Wolfe planned to go to York Springs, Pennsylvania, to look up the remaining members of his father's family there, and had written home for information about them.

¹ Rowohlt Verlag.

about it is because I never knew it was an accomplished fact until this morning. You told me in England last year that you had spoken to your German publishers and that they had accepted the book, but I heard no more about it until today. . . .

I hope you will accept this letter as a full and sufficient apology for my failure to write and thank you for your generous and kind interest in this matter: I know perfectly well that I owe the publication of my book not only in Sweden but also in Germany to your own efforts, and I want you to understand how deeply touched and grateful I am for all you have done, and how much I regret the trouble you have been put to. Whether I shall ever justify the wonderful things you said about my work I do not know, but I will try, and am trying at present with all my heart; and if I cannot do it now, maybe I will some day in the future. But I will never forget what you said or did—your praise and powerful commendation dropped on me like a bolt of beneficent lightning—it was one of the most generous and wonderful acts I ever knew or heard of, and I'll never forget it.

I'm living at 111 Columbia Heights, Brooklyn, and my phone number is Main 4–0189, and I'd like to see you and Mrs. Lewis some time. If you're too busy, it's all right, but I hope we can get together. I don't go out much: I'm working away: I've got magnificent material for a book—whether I am as good as the material is another thing. Good-bye for the present, Red, and good luck and good health always, and many many thanks for what you have done. You said something to me about Max Perkins a year ago: I'd like to say to you that he has the most genuine and whole-hearted admiration for your genius and power as a novelist—he feels, as I do, that your talent is unique and permanent, that there is no one like you, and that if they read any of our books in the future they will have to take account of you. You may think I'm laying it on with a trowel, but I'm not: I'm hurling it at you with a bucket— and what's more, I mean every damned syllable and letter of it.

I hope this finds you all well and happy, and I send you my best and warmest wishes for the New Year.

The following brief note was left on Perkins' desk with a manuscript, probably that of "A Portrait of Bascom Hawke," which was accepted by Scribner's Magazine *on January 28, 1932, and published in the April, 1932, issue. A somewhat different version of it appears in* Of Time and the River *on pages 104–111, 116–130, 132, 136–141, 141–150, 177–184, 185–186, and 192.*

To MAXWELL E. PERKINS

[January, 1932?]

Dear Max:

Part of this was written some time ago, and part very recently—and some of it quite rapidly. I've simply tried to give you a man—as for plot, there's not any, but there's this idea which I believe is pretty plain—I've always wanted to say something about *old men* and *young men,* and that's what I've tried to do here.

I hope the man seems real and living to you and that it has the unity of this feeling I spoke about. I could do a lot more to it, but I'd like you to see it. Please read all of it, Max.

To HENRY A. WESTALL

[111 Columbia Heights]
[Brooklyn, N.Y.]

[January, 1932]

Dear Uncle Henry:

Thanks very much for your letter. I was relieved to know that Mama had arrived safely,[1] and sorry to hear she has not been feeling well: I trust she is now better. . . . I thank you very sincerely for your kind invitation to come to visit you: I am afraid it is not possible for me to make such a trip at present, but I assure you nothing would delight me more if I come to Boston again. . . .

I note what you say about the advantages of seclusion and quiet for a writer. I entirely agree—but whether that is to be obtained more easily in a small town than in a great city I do not know. It seems to me that a man might find comparative peace and isolation among the swarms of people in the city, and be hounded and worried out of every attempt at privacy by the women's literary clubs, chambers of commerce, and curiosity seekers of some small town—particularly if he had reached any degree of reputation and success. I am, unfortunately, of a temperament that is easily distressed and distracted by outer disturbances, and I am constantly making an effort to control this, but my feeling is that one will get his work done wherever he is if he wants to do it hard enough. I am reminded of the saying of the poet Horace which strikes me as one of the truest and wisest things I have ever heard: "You may change your skies but not your soul"—and accordingly, I feel that it would be unwise to

---

[1] Wolfe's mother had come to visit him in Brooklyn and then gone on to see her brother, Mr. Westall, in North Reading, Mass.

move from my present home until I finish the piece of work that I am
now busy with. I feel that it would be unwise because my tendency has
been to wander and roam in search of a peace and security which I must
find inside me, and although I may some day adopt your suggestion and
move to a quieter and smaller place I shall not do that, I think, until I
have finished the job I have set myself at present.

My mother, of course, has lived a long life and seen a great many
things, but I do not think she or any of my immediate family understand
very clearly just what the difficulties of the artist are, or what pain and
labor of the spirit a man goes through in order to create something good.
My family, for example, were more concerned with the gossip and scandal of the people of Asheville about my book than with the book itself:
they still tell me what one of the Asheville butchers or grocers or lawyers
had to say about it, and I don't think they ever asked themselves whether
the book had any literary merit or not—when they read the opinions of
critics in various papers later that the book did have merit, and heard
that it was also enjoying a fair sale, they decided then that it was a success. Now please understand, Uncle Henry, that I am saying not one
word in criticism of any of my family for feeling this way about it, but
I do say that they have never understood and will never understand what
goes on inside me when I write, or why I write. My family, I think, would
like to see me succeed, but I believe their idea of my success would be
to have me write a book that would sell one hundred thousand copies and
make a lot of money. Now this would be very nice, I admit, and I should
be glad to have the money—but that is not the reason I write: I write
because I want to do the best that's in me, to create my vision of life as
I have seen and known it, and to leave something, someday, that may
have, I hope, some enduring value—and whether my book sells one hundred or one hundred thousand copies is not of primary importance to me.
Neither do I write, as many people in Asheville mistakenly thought, in
order to rake up the private lives of Brown or Jones or Smith—I was not
"writing a book about Asheville," as many of them thought—I was writing a book about people living on this earth as I had known them, and
what I said was as true of Pittsburgh or Boston or Brooklyn, as of Asheville. In doing this, of course, I used the materials I had, I made use of
life as I had seen it, of experience as I had known it, I made use of what
was my own—and, of course, this is what all men must do. I know that
you will understand this: an artist does not work in order either to praise,
wound, insult, or glorify particular people—he works in order to create
some kind of living truth which will be true for all men everywhere.

[THE LETTER BREAKS OFF HERE]

To MABEL WOLFE WHEATON

111 Columbia Heights
Brooklyn, N.Y.
Jan 27, 1932

Dear Mabel:

Your post card came this morning. I have heard nothing from Mama since she left here and I am also beginning to be a little worried. I know that she arrived safely in Boston because I wired Uncle Henry immediately after she left New York. . . . He wrote me a few days later saying that Mama had arrived and been met on time and that she had not been feeling so well since her arrival but was now better. I am sure if there were anything seriously amiss someone would have informed us. . . .

This letter is being typed for me through the kindness of a young lady friend of mine here in Brooklyn. I suffered a trifling accident last night but very fortunately, I think, escaped injuries which might have been more serious. There was some question among the doctors as to whether my left arm had been broken or not, but that was apparently all cleared up to-day when they took X-rays and assured me they were confident that there was no fracture whatever, although I must wait until tomorrow morning to get a definite decision. I also severed a vein in my arm but the doctor very neatly stitched this together and I think, I have no doubt, that I shall be perfectly all right in a few days. If you write Mama, please don't say anything to her about this. I didn't mention it in my letter, because there is no need to worry her.

The way it happened was this: I had been having dinner in town with my friend, Maxwell Perkins: he lives in New Canaan, Conn., and he made me promise to see that he made his train without fail. When he got to Grand Central Station I went into the train with him and was talking with him about a piece of manuscript I had just given him to read when the train started off. The train was gathering motion as I reached the platform and I was thrown to the concrete pavement. They took me to the Emergency Hospital in the Grand Central Station where a doctor examined my arm and stitched up the cut place. I am very fortunate indeed that the accident was no worse, and I thank God that it was my left arm rather than my right, since my whole chance of living at present depends more or less on my right hand.

I have really been awfully worried about getting my work done, but I know it is going to be all right now, if I only stick to it and let nothing come in the way until I finish. . . .

I am sending my best wishes for health and happiness. I suppose Mama will want to stay with me for a day or two when she comes back through New York, and I hope she does. I wish it were possible for me to do more for her at the present time, but if I can finish my book maybe we can all meet together for a real celebration.

Goodbye for the present, Mabel—good luck, of course, as always. Write me when you have the opportunity.

The following letter was written in answer to a list of questions asked by Julian Meade, author of I Live in Virginia, The Back Door, *etc., who was writing an article on Wolfe for publication in* The Bookman. *Evidently Wolfe's reluctance "to get any more publicity at the present time," which he expresses in the final paragraph of his letter, made him postpone mailing it. At any rate, he failed to do so until July 7, after Meade had written the rough draft of the article and sent it for him to read. The piece was then re-written and submitted to* The Bookman, *but declined by them. It finally appeared under the title "Thomas Wolfe on the Use of Fact in Fiction" in the April 14, 1935, issue of* The New York Herald Tribune Books.

To JULIAN MEADE

111 Columbia Heights
Brooklyn, N.Y.
February 1, 1932

Dear Meade:

Thanks for your latest letter. My accident fortunately did not turn out as badly as I thought it had and as I told you: it now appears it did not break my arm but that it is only strained and bruised.

I want to give you some sort of answer to the questions you asked me in your first letter but as it is still a little hard for me to sit at the table and write, I am going to have to try to answer through dictation. I should like to be a great deal more careful and detailed in considering and making these answers but what I give you at present is more or less off-hand, and I hope, therefore, you will help me by using your own discrimination and by not letting me say anything that would tend to incriminate me.

As to your first question: you ask what answer I have to those who say I did a faithful picture of one city and its people. I should like to avoid this question completely if I could, as well as the other one which asks what answer I have for those who speak of me as an autobiographical writer. I should like to avoid them, Meade, not because I am in any sense afraid of the consequences of answering them as directly as I can, but because these questions have been asked before and my answer, although it seemed perfectly clear to me, only led to fresh argument, misunderstanding, and dispute. I should like very much to say something of what I feel about the relation of the writer to what is sometimes called autobiographical material: I don't want you to misunderstand me here and I know that I could be completely coherent about this if I only had time and could make the effort of writing down a complete statement. But I will say this to you: I think the roots of all creation in writing are fastened in autobiography and that it is in no way possible to escape or deny this fact. I think that a writer must use what is his own, I know of no means by which he can use what is not his own—do you? —nor would I think it desirable that he should. I made once before what seemed to me a very clear and simple statement of this obvious fact—namely, in a short preface to the reader which I wrote at the beginning of "Look Homeward, Angel"—and I was accused by several critics, including one or two on the Asheville newspapers, of "evading the issue" and of trying to avoid a direct answer whether my book was about Asheville and its citizens by a clever twist of words. Well, I have been so exasperated by what I considered an unfair and trivial comment that I said I would never attempt to make any answer at all to such criticism, but if there are really people who still want to know whether my book is about Asheville, North Carolina, and is a faithful picture of its inhabitants, I will say here and now that it is not about Asheville, North Carolina, and that it is not a faithful picture of the inhabitants of Asheville, North Carolina, or of any other place on earth that I have ever known; and finally, that I do not believe any book ever got written in this way. Certainly I could never write anything in this way: that is not the way a writer works and feels and creates a thing—he does not write by calling Greenville Jonesville or by changing the name of Brown and Smith to Black and White: if it's that easy let's all start out for the nearest town with a trunk full of notebooks and pencils and start taking down the words and movements of the inhabitants from the most convenient corner. I could go on with this indefinitely but I get hot under the collar when the word autobiography is mentioned because the way most people use it seems to me to have no sense or meaning whatever.

And yet the whole question of a writer's use of his material and of his true and essential use of autobiography seems to me an important and a fascinating one and I really believe I could say something about it that would have value, if I only had time to set it before you here now, because it is a question I have thought about so long, so carefully and so earnestly.

But I want to repeat that nowhere can you escape autobiography when- ever you come to anything that has any real or lasting value in letters. For example as I walk around my room in the act of dictating this letter the first book my eye falls on is called "The Road to Xanadu": it was written by my old teacher, Professor John Livingston Lowes at Harvard and in it he attempts to trace the genesis, the sunken and hidden sources, of two of the most remarkable poems in the language—"The Rime of the An- cient Mariner" and "Kubla Khan." Professor Lowes has managed to track down almost all of the obscure and bewilderingly manifold elements which had gone into the making of "The Ancient Mariner." He knew, of course, that Coleridge was an enormous reader, that he literally read almost everything, and Lowes, by plowing through ten thousand for- gotten and obscure books, has managed to show where almost every line, every image, every sentence in "The Ancient Mariner" comes from. Coleridge, of course, was not even conscious of the extent to which his own reading had influenced him: he has made use of a thousand elements of apparently unrelated experience to create something that was his own and that was beautiful and real and in the highest sense of the word original. Lowes goes on to attempt to show that the thing that happened when Coleridge wrote this poem happens when the artist creates any- thing—in other words, that this use of experience which is sunken in the well of unconsciousness, or which is only half remembered, is a typical use of the creative faculty.

Now what is this, Meade, except the most direct and natural use of autobiography, and how could Coleridge have written differently from the way he did write, and how could Joyce have written differently from the way he wrote, and how could Proust have written differently from the way he wrote? Coleridge's experiences came mainly from the pages of books and Joseph Conrad's experiences came mainly from the decks of ships, but can anyone tell you that one form of experience is less real and less personal than another, or that Coleridge's books had less reality for him than Conrad's ships; and finally, could anyone tell you that Joyce and Proust are either more or less autobiographical than Coleridge or Swift, and if they do tell you so, would you think their words any longer had meaning or were worthy of serious consideration?

Well, as I told you, I could go on with this for a long time but I think I have said enough to show you anyway the trend of my thought, and I know that I can trust your understanding and intelligence not to make me seem to speak illogically or foolishly or evasively when I am really standing on very firm ground.

You ask again if I look upon writing as an escape from reality: in no sense of the word does it seem to me to be escape from reality; I should rather say that it is an attempt to approach and penetrate reality. This I think is certainly true of such a book as "Ulysses": the effort to apprehend and to make live again a moment in lost time is so tremendous that some of us feel that Joyce really did succeed, at least in places, in penetrating reality and in so doing, creating what is almost another dimension of reality. I certainly think that most writing represents a struggle with reality—that most good writing has been done because the writer was in conflict with the world about him and, of course, each writer has had his own way of expressing that conflict—Mr. Cabell has had his way which you say he calls an escape from reality, and Coleridge had his way. But I do not think "The Rime of the Ancient Mariner" was for Coleridge an escape from reality: I think it was reality, I think he was on the ship and made the voyage and felt and knew it all. Swift's terrible conflict with the world about him resulted in "Gulliver's Travels" and I should certainly not call that book an escape from reality, but one of the most savage and inspired attempts to make his comment on the real world through a fable that literature knows.

I wish I could answer your other questions as fully and clearly as I should like, but I am afraid there is not time here. You ask if I think my work will be influenced by travel or whether my most vivid impressions were formed some time ago. I can't answer this question I am afraid very satisfactorily, but I want to say this: during the last few years I have often heard from the lips of those brillant amateur psychologists who seem to be swarming all over the country now by the millions, extraordinary statements to this effect—that everything that is of any value to a man happens to him sometime before he reaches the ripe old age of three years; that all of his impressions, emotions and traits of character are defined and fixed by that time, and that, in short, everything which a writer has to write about has already happened to him by the time he quits crawling around on the floor of the nursery. To my mind this is just another of those imbecilic things people say which deserves no comment whatever. If you want to know whether the most important part of my experience was acquired during my boyhood in the South, I have no means of telling you, but I do know this: I left home for college when I was not quite sixteen years old and I have not been back for any great length of time since. Almost half my life, therefore, has been spent in wandering and in living in various places on the earth's surface. I was driven to these by an impulsion of hunger and desire about which I can say very little here, which I can never tell any one about by means of a dictated letter, and which I may never be able to tell anyone about anyway, but it represents for me as much pain, as much effort, as much loneliness, as great a struggle to find some kind of better life on earth, some sense of peace, certitude, and direction in my own life and some answer to the riddle of this whole vexed swarming and tormented world as any effort I have ever made. I gave to it all the strength and power and passion that I have in me and it represents to me as much reality as I know: perhaps I may never be able to make use of any of it in my writing, perhaps I shall have to return to the things I knew about in my childhood, but I see no reason whatever why this should be true and I certainly shall not accept without protest the silly statements of people who say that everything that is of any value to you happened before you were five years old.

As to your other questions, Meade: I will have to lump them together now and come to a hasty conclusion. You ask if I write easily or with difficulty. I think I write with the most extreme difficulty: the trouble is not so much a lack of material but an over abundance of it. Condensation and brevity are terribly difficult for me, my manuscripts are hundreds of thousands of words long and almost my whole effort at the present time is to get my book within some reasonable length. I have two lives, one which is intensely conscious of the world around me, and one which lives with an equal intensity in the past: my memory is a kind of hunger and as I go on, my memory seems to get better, or worse, depending on which way you look at it. I am haunted by a sense of time and a memory of things past and, of course, I know I have got to try somehow to get a harness on it.

You ask me if I am still interested in the stage: if you mean by this am I still interested in writing plays, or will I ever write another one, my answer is no. I haven't the slightest interest in ever making the attempt again, although I think a man who is able to write a fine play has done one of the best things in the world. I don't think I could write one and I don't believe there is any need in telling you why I lost interest in making the attempt, and why it no longer means anything to me. I suppose the real answer is that it probably never possessed as much reality for me as I thought it did. As to whether I like music: I do like it, I have always thought I liked it very much, but my interest in it cannot be of the highest kind because I really know very little about music and although I live here in New York where I could hear the best music if my desire were strong enough, I almost never attend a concert of a symphony. My real interest has been in poetry—I really know a great deal about poetry, it seems to have taken the place in my life that music takes in the lives of many people. I have known and loved it so well that I remember it and I read it constantly. I do not read a great deal of new poetry and for this I am sorry: I do not suppose I have read a dozen books as often as four times apiece, but I have read hundreds of poems hundreds of times,—that is the only kind of writing that I can return to again and again without weariness or satiety.

Finally, you ask me about my literary preferences among living and dead authors: I am afraid that's too large an order for me to deal with here. For a great many years during my childhood and later when I was at Harvard, I read everything I could lay my hands on: the amount of reading I did was incredible and I can't attempt to tell you about it here. Upon the top shelf of my bookcase, however, I have attempted to put some of the books which I use all the time and which I am able to read again and again. All I can do is to give you a few of the titles, at any rate it will tell you something of the books I like best. At the present time, reading from right to left, the books in my top shelf are as follows: my old college edition of "The Illiad" parts of which I sometimes read; the Bible which I really read a great deal—I mean a few books, "Ecclesiastes," "The Book of Job," "The Song of Solomon," "Revelations"; Webster's Collegiate Dictionary which has in it some of the best reading in the world; the plays of Shakespeare; the poems of Coleridge; the poems of John Donne; "The Anatomy of Melancholy"; "Ulysses"; "War and Peace"; "The Brothers Karamazov"; "Leaves of Grass"; "Moll Flanders"; the plays of Molière; the poems of Heinrich Heine and a book of German lyrics. I delight in all manner of anthologies: I believe some people laugh at them but I have some great fat thick ones, all of them good ones, and I go back to them again and again. I can read French and German but these are the only modern languages besides English that I know anything about. I am afraid that is all I can do for you at the present, and I hope it will be of some use to you.

If you write this piece, Meade, I wish you'd send it to me and let me see it before you show it to anyone else. If it means anything to you at all, I am, of course, glad to help as much as I can, and, of course, I am pleased and grateful to think that you should want to write a piece about me and that anyone is interested in publishing it. I don't know, however, if this is really a good time for such an article: I am quite sincere in not being very anxious to get any more publicity at the present time because I think this is the time when I should try to work and produce, and I believe your article might have greater value if you let it go until I got at least one more book finished and published. But anyway please let me know what you do about it, and if you write it, please let me see a copy in advance. . . .

The following letter was written in reply to one from Stringfellow Barr suggesting that Wolfe might have some stories suitable for publication in The Virginia Quarterly Review. *At this time, Barr was editor of the* Quarterly, *and Professor of Modern History at the University of Virginia. He is now President of The Foundation for World Government, and author of* Citizens of the World.

To STRINGFELLOW BARR

111 Columbia Heights
Brooklyn, N.Y.
February 24, 1932

Dear Mr. Barr:

Thanks for your letter and excuse this scribbled note. I've been getting the proofs ready for a piece which is coming out in *Scribner's Magazine* this spring [1]—it was 30,000 words long, and of course that meant cutting —which is agony and weariness of the soul to me. I've also finished another story which must be typed [2]—it's about 15,000 and I'm going to show it to Max Perkins at Scribners: if they can't use it, maybe you'd be interested in seeing it for the *Quarterly*. Of course, I know you probably can't afford to pay high prices and I don't expect it—I am hard up, but I don't live in a very expensive way: I must do something to earn some money now. I also had another piece of 15 or 20,000 words [3]—finished before Christmas—but knew it would not be suitable for *Scribner's*. I talk knowingly about what is "suitable" etc., but really I don't know what the magazines want—I just write and hope I can do my best once in a while— but it *does* occur to me that some pieces of writing might have merit and yet be somewhat too special even for such a liberal magazine as *Scribner's*. And of course I say this humbly—I'd like nothing better than to write something that was both very good and very popular: I should be enchanted if the editors of *Cosmopolitan* began to wave large fat checks under my nose, but I know of no way of going about this deliberately and I am sure I'd fail miserably if I tried. It seems to me all a man can do is to write what he has to write as well as he can and then hope for the best. But am I right in supposing that the *Quarterly* is even more free from these demands of popular fiction—whatever they are—than *Scribner's?* I wrote a piece about a train a year or so ago—it is called "K 19" (the name and number of a pullman car) and the action occurs while the train is crossing the state of Virginia at night. I thought it was a pretty good piece and so did Perkins—I'd always wanted to write about a train: the way it looks, smells, feels, the sounds it makes, the quiet voices on the little country

---

[1] "A Portrait of Bascom Hawke."

[2] Probably "The Web of Earth" which was accepted by *Scribner's Magazine* on May 16, 1932, published in the July, 1932, issue and later included in *From Death to Morning*. However, the final version of "The Web of Earth" was about 39,000 words long.

[3] Probably the first draft of "Death the Proud Brother." Wolfe had been working on this during the summer and fall of 1931 but temporarily abandoned it in November to write "A Portrait of Bascom Hawke."

platforms when it stops—as well as the story of the people on the train: what they say, do, and think about. It wasn't in the usual magazine sense of the word a story, although to my mind it was, and a unified story to boot. Now, one of these small private presses [4] has asked to see it and I've promised to show it to them—if they don't use it, would you like to see it? I've never been very enthusiastic about small, elegant, privately-printed books which are sold at a high price—I think a book ought to give honest value, and even though my railroad piece might be good, I don't like the idea of printing it in a book and charging four or five dollars for it: I hate the hocus-pocus of professional book collecting; there's something scavenging and stinking about it.

I've got to get back to my book. I really work hard and am able to finish things—then a kind of paralysis sets in, I won't get them typed, I won't send them out, and once a publisher gets anything I write into proofs, I become more and more reluctant, humble doubts assail me, I keep the proofs until they are taken from me—I've got to do something about this, and, no matter what happens, I'm glad I finished that piece for *Scribner's* —it's out of my hands now, I can do no more about it, and I'm going to try to forget it.

Yes, please send me the *Quarterly*. I'd be delighted to have it, and thank you gratefully for it. . . . and if you come to town, please call me: Main 4-0189. Meanwhile, with best wishes,

The following letter was evidently written in reply to letters from George McCoy and Robert McKee of The Asheville Citizen, *asking Wolfe for news about himself to be used in a piece about him in that paper. However, efforts to find such a piece have met with no success. Probably Wolfe never mailed the letter, since it was found in his own files and McCoy could find no copy of it in his.*

To GEORGE W. McCOY

111 Columbia Heights
Brooklyn, N.Y.
March 22, 1932

Dear George:

Thanks very much for your letter and please give my apologies to Mr. Robert McKee.[1] I did get a letter from him a good many months ago I

---

[4] This private press remains unidentified.

[1] McKee was at this time City Editor of the *Citizen,* and is now with *The Atlanta Journal.*

am afraid, and had all those good intentions about it which are said to be a very popular kind of paving brick. I am going to try to answer the questions you asked me in your letter, and I will try to give you the information you ask for. I don't know what kind of news is of the greatest interest to the readers, so I am just going to write you this letter, and while dictation is a new and rather awkward experience for me, I know I can trust you to weed out anything that may sound too foolish. Just use your own discretion about it, George: it will be all right.

I ought to tell you how much I appreciate any interest the people at home may have in me or what I am doing, and I have certainly not refrained from writing you because I did not value that interest. The last two years have been very busy and very exciting ones for me: at one time I was swamped under an avalanche of letters which came from everywhere: many of them were very fine ones and I was sincerely grateful for them, but I am afraid a great many of them went unanswered. I did the best I could but the job was too much for me and I had my own work which I had to get on with, but I would like to take this opportunity of thanking anyone who may have written such a letter and never got an answer. Some day I think I will write a book about what happens to a fellow who writes a book: that's one subject that I now feel like an authority about, and I think it might make strange and interesting reading. I think I was about the most surprised and excited person on earth when I saw some of the difficulties the book had and some of the meanings that were read into it.

I know I may be treading on shaky ground here—I know so well what I would like to say to you about my intention and purpose as a writer, but it is hard to do it on the spur of the moment and I don't want to say anything that might be misunderstood. I would be most grateful to you, George, if you could convey to your readers the fact that I am simply a very hard worker and, I think, a very honest man, who is trying to master a very difficult and painful art and who wants to do the best work that is in him.

I wish for your sake, and the sake of the readers who want interesting news, that I could describe to you a very gay and Bohemian life, but the plain truth of the matter is that I lead about as solitary and obscure an existence as anyone you know. I live in an old house in Brooklyn Heights. I have two big bare rooms here which at the present moment are inundated under piles of manuscript, books, and stray shirts, socks and neckties. I live on Columbia Heights, which is the last street over and commands the finest view of New York harbor that can be had: unfortunately I am on the wrong side of the street to get the harbor view, but I can hear the ships blowing out in the harbor at night, a sound which sometimes starts up in me again all of my desires to wander. Outside of this, there is really no noise over here: it is about as quiet as any street you will find in Asheville.

As to my daily schedule, I begin to work about midnight and keep at it until four or five o'clock in the morning, then I go to bed and sleep until about eleven, get up, make coffee, of which I drink a pot or two every day, and then work on my manuscript until about one or two o'clock in the afternoon when the young man who is typing my book comes. We work together until six or six-thirty when he goes, and then if I have any energy left in me, I take a bath, get shaved and dressed, and go out to eat. I have a few friends here in New York of whom I am very fond and who have been wonderfully kind and decent to me: occasionally I spend the evening with them but most often I spend it alone. Sometimes I go over to town—by town I mean Manhattan—and eat late and then go the Harvard Club and read for an hour or two before it closes at one o'clock; then I come home and, if I can, get to work again.

That is a pretty accurate picture, George, of my life at the present time. I am sorry it sounds no more exciting but it suits me a good deal better than a gayer and more social existence. I scarcely ever go to a party unless one of my friends is giving it, and I am not a success at party-going anyway. I tell you all this because it has taken me a long time and cost me a great deal of difficulty and distress to find the kind of life I am best suited to lead. I live alone a great deal of the time; I make friends slowly and I value the few I have as highly as anything on earth. It seems to me now that the only sensible and decent life for the artist is an obscure, modest and fairly solitary one. I assure you I value fame as highly as any young man and hope with all my heart that I can some day do work that will justify it, but if it comes, I want it for my work and not for myself. I assure you this is not hokum: I think you understand I am telling you the plain truth. When I was a child, of course, and I thought that some day I might write something that would be published, I had the most glittering dreams and visions of a romantic literary life in which I not only was able to do magnificent work but also to be surrounded by adoring throngs of brilliant people. This dream has long since vanished and I am really not sorry to lose it.

It seems to me the reality I have now achieved is really a far better and more satisfactory way of living. I have found out that the man who hopes to create anything in this world of any enduring value or beauty must be willing to wreak it out of his spirit at the cost of unbelievable pain and labor: I know of no other way in which it can be done; he must work in the solitude and loneliness of art; no one can do it for him, and all of his childish dreams of a various and golden life, in which he has time to do everything and to triumph in all of them, are out of the question. I have tried to tell you how I felt about this as plainly as possible because I want you to understand that the thing which happened to me two years ago when my first book was published caused me a great deal of confusion and bewilderment: I read every scrap of criticism, or near-criticism, or praise, or abuse, whether it appeared in a New York paper or in the *Podunk Daily Curse*, and I was excited, elated, depressed, confused, or full of exultant joy over all of it. I took it all with a most tremendous earnestness: I was going inside all the time like a dynamo. I don't think anyone will condemn me very much for making this confession. I was a young fellow who had got his first book published, and I would be a damn liar if I told you that I took the whole thing in a calm and matter-of-fact way, but I do want to emphasize the fact that the man who writes a book is sometimes more astonished and confused by the effect it produces than anyone else. The whole effect, not only in Asheville but also in New York, was different from anything I had ever imagined, and for several months I was like a man trying to find his way out of the labyrinth.

I was deeply distressed to know that the book had caused any misunderstanding or resentment at home, and I was grateful and happy for what success it had up here and elsewhere, for the letters I received, and for some of the reviews. Then I discovered what seemed to me to be a tendency here in New York either to leave a young man who comes here without friends or position painfully and severely alone, or if he achieves even a modest success and some public notice in the press, to overwhelm him with invitations and hospitable attention. Please understand that I am not condemning the people here in New York on this account: it simply fits in with the custom and habit of life to which they are accustomed. They like to have the latest news about everything and to see the new writer: they mean well enough by it, of course, but it does sometimes put an honest and decent person whose chief desire in life is to do the best work of which he is capable, to make his own friends in his own way and to live the kind of life he wants for himself—it sometimes puts this man, I say, in the position of a damned dressed-up monkey on a stick, and if he is young and has not had any experience before in meeting a situation of this sort, he may be swept off his feet for a time. Now please don't misunderstand me or read anything boastful into this statement—I did not get very much of this treatment, I was not being lionized all over the place and pursued and hunted by the great ones of the city, but I did have a little of it and the little was too much.

Fortunately about that time I got the Guggenheim Fellowship which enabled me to go abroad for a year. While I was over there I was able not only to do a great deal of work on my new book, but I was able to think the whole situation over and to decide what kind of life I was going to have for myself and to determine, by God, to have it. I have already described to you what that life is.

I have outlined at the present time the material and plan of eight books: [2] enough work to keep me busy for years—and all I want in addition is peace and quiet and a few friends and a very moderate income, two hundred or two hundred and fifty dollars a month. If I work hard, there is no reason why I should not achieve all of these. I assure you with complete sincerity that I do not care to make money and want no more than enough to support me modestly and with a little comfort, and, perhaps, to let me ease my hunger once in a while for making voyages. That is about as good a statement as I can make to you at the present time. . . .

When I came back from Europe about a year ago, I was really in a state of despair about my book, not because I could not write it but because I could do nothing else but write it. I had written until I had hundreds of thousands of words; it was reaching a staggering length and I did not know what I could do to cut it or get it within some reasonable reading compass. The plan and the material, every incident of it, had been clear in my mind for months and months; I saw the whole thing through to its end, down to the minutest detail, and the more I thought about it, the longer it got. Then, because I needed money and had a feeling of despair over the book, I stopped suddenly, worked furiously for a month on a short novel and completed it. *Scribner's* immediately accepted it and published a part of it, as much as they could, in the magazine: I think it came out in this April's issue.[3] I immediately got busy on another short piece which rapidly lengthened into another short novel and *Scribner's* also accepted this: it is coming out, I understand in a few months, I don't know when, and my friend, Maxwell Perkins, who is the director at Scribners and whose literary opinion means more to me than anyone's, tells me it is one of the best things I ever did.[4] Finally, I have just completed another short novel which is really a part of my long book, "The October Fair," and which Perkins has not seen as yet, but which I hope and think may be good.[5] I am getting my novel typed now at the rate of

[2] What eight books Wolfe had in mind here is difficult to tell. Perhaps he simply meant the eight "books," or sections, of *Of Time and the River*, or perhaps he meant that entire series of novels, although only six are listed for it in the Publisher's Note at the beginning of *Of Time and the River*: *Look Homeward, Angel*, *Of Time and the River*, *The October Fair*, *The Hills Beyond Pentland*, *The Death of the Enemy*, *Pacific End*.

[3] "A Portrait of Bascom Hawke." It did come out in the April issue of *Scribner's Magazine*, which was published late in March, at just about the date of this letter.

[4] "The Web of Earth."

[5] This short novel remains unidentified. According to one of Wolfe's notebooks, he wrote "The Train and the City," "Death the Proud Brother" and "No Door"

about 3,000 words a day, and I hope to have the manuscript ready within the next three months. . . .

You ask about my plans for coming back to Asheville and when I am coming back: I can't give you any definite date at present. I have got to work like hell and produce: I can think of no better or happier fate at the present moment than working myself to a frazzle in getting this book and one or two other things I have in mind completed. Then, if I can make a little money, I would like to take a short trip to Europe and then go West, where I have never been, and explore that district for a time; then I would like to find a place to settle down and live and work, and, of course, I have always had it in my heart that I would come back home some day. I think of you all a great deal, and I think you understand that it is impossible for a man ever to forget the place where he spent the first twenty years of his life and where most of his people have lived for a matter of one hundred and fifty years or so. I miss Asheville, but although I was born there and grew up there, I think that what I miss most is the country around there and the mountains.

Frankly, I don't want to come home until I have done more work and until people understand plainly, as I hope and believe they will, what it is I am trying to do and what my work is about. I know you understand, George, that I do not say this in any resentful or truculent spirit. I decided after "Look Homeward, Angel" was published that if, either through my own fault or the fault of certain readers, the intention of that book, which was simply to rig out a part of my vision of life as I had seen and known it, . . . and which certainly had in it no conscious and deliberate intention of saying a word to attack, wound or offend any living person—after the publication of that book, I say, and the experience I had with it, which I have tried to describe to you and which astounded and bewildered me more than anyone, I decided never to write a word if I could help it in answer to any criticism, whether in the form of a personal letter or in the press, which seemed to me to be unfair and unjust; and I have lived up to that decision ever since and hope that I will always be able to, although my first tendency two years ago was to take pen and paper at once and make some kind of a hot answer or impassioned defense. But I feel that a man's work itself must be his answer, and if he has not been able in his first book to reveal his intention and meaning, then I think if he is misunderstood himself, he must learn to possess his soul with patience, and stick to his job resolutely until he has revealed himself, and people know the kind of person he is.

That is what I propose to do and I want to make it very plain to you that in all that I have said, there is neither a word of truculent resentment

between March 9, 1932 and March 9, 1933. Probably he meant a version of "The Train and the City."

or of rancor toward anyone or anything in Asheville, or a word of apology and defense for myself. I have no apology and defense to make, and at the same time I want you to know, as I think you do know, that I am bound to my home and the people I knew there by the warmest and deepest ties. If I ever come home to live, I want to come neither in the role of the town villain nor as the conquering hero: I assure you I am not equipped to play either of these parts. I want to come to my own home decently and quietly and to see my old friends again, and, if necessary, to tell prying and curious people to go to hell. I think I have made my meaning clear and I don't believe that there is a word in this letter at which any sensible and decent person would take offense or disagree.

Now, George, I have tried to get it off my chest, and I hope I have been able to give you the information you asked for. I rely absolutely on your good sense and discretion not to put anything in the paper that would give people a wrong idea of how I stand. Use anything you like in this letter, whatever may be of use to you and that will not do any damage to me, but if it seems to you that it would be unwise to use part of it, or all of it, I would be grateful to you if you would chuck the whole thing. Also, if you do write a piece in the paper about me, I wish you would make it plain as gracefully as you can that I am not trying to rush into print and inform the folks at home of my doings, and say that I have written and given you this information in a personal letter in response to several requests which you and Mr. McKee made to me. I am not a publicity hound and I don't want any more of it than I can help until my new book is published. This is also the plain unvarnished truth, although it is hard to convince a good many people in this sometimes cynical world of the sincerity of such statements. I think this is all I can tell you at the present.

Thanks again for writing and for your friendly interest. I assure you once more that I am deeply grateful for any friendly interest the people at home may have in what I do. . . . With very best wishes to you and all my friends.

To A. S. FRERE-REEVES

Harvard Club
New York

April 15, 1932

Dear Frere:

Thanks very much for your letter which came a day or two ago. I have thought of you often. I wanted to write but for the past six months

I have been working harder . . . and faster than I ever did before. "The October Fair" will not be one novel, but a series of novels, and each, I hope, complete in itself but all related to a single thing. The section I am working on at present, and which I hope to have down on paper within three months, and which Scribners wants to publish in the autumn, is called "K 19," [1] which is the name of a Pullman car on an American train. I cannot tell you very much more about it now save that it will be a very long book and it will have the lives and stories of a great many people in it, and I hope it will be full of interest and movement. I am writing at the rate of three, four, and occasionally five thousand words a day, which is more work than I have ever done before. I work every day until I can literally do no more, and then I quit, get something to eat, if I still have appetite for it, take a walk across the Brooklyn Bridge and back, and then try to get some sleep if I can. This is the reason I have not had much time to write you. I get terribly tired, but I am also very happy to be getting something done at last, and I think everything is going to be all right now.

I did a terrific amount of preparation and preliminary work on that book, and I am sure my time and labor was not wasted but what I was really doing apparently was getting the cement mixed for the building. Anyway I have learned a great deal about working, and I think it will come easier in the future.

It has been a hell of a job. I think I was deluded by some fantastic notion that I could say the final and ultimate word about everyone and everything all at once in a single huge and monstrous tome. I learned bitterly that it could not be done and I will have to write my books as other men have written theirs, one at a time. At any rate, if you ever hear the sad news of my sudden and tragic extinction, which God forbid you won't, I want you to remember that I was not a man who starved to death but a man who died of gluttony, choking to death on an abundance of food, which surpassed everything but his hunger.

Spring is coming on here now. I think of you very often—also of April now that England's there, and maddening memories and visions return

---

[1] By this time, Wolfe and Perkins had decided that he could not possibly include all of his material in a single book. Wolfe accordingly went back to a variation of *The Fast Express,* which he had planned to use as part of *The October Fair* and which he now proposed to publish as a separate book under the title *K 19.* However, as he worked on it, he began writing long digressions on the lives of some of the passengers on the train, with the result that it became too long and too diffuse. Finally, in July, 1932, Perkins read the manuscript and broke the news to Wolfe that it was not good enough to be published as a separate book. Parts of it, such as many of the train scenes and the story "Boom Town," were later used in *Of Time and the River, The Web and the Rock,* and *You Can't Go Home Again.*

to me of Stone's Chop House and the ale you get there, and of Simpson's and the beef and mutton you get there, and at the present moment I could even do very nicely with an ordinary pub and half a dozen bottles of Bass Ale.

I live in Brooklyn Heights, on the last street above the harbor, and I can hear the ships blowing at night as they put out to sea for "Yurrup" and other fabulous coasts, and the desire to arise and go and fall upon your neck is very strong within me, but my purse is lean since I am only a poor American and not one of you bloated, blasted, foreign plutocrats.

I also have a publisher who has been angelic in his patience, but who is now beginning to call up from day to day and to say anxiously "when can you deliver the first 2,000,000?" So unless your employers decide suddenly and soon to hurl you across the ocean again on some mission of great and delicate trust, I must defer the pleasure of seeing you until I have freed myself of this octopus of a book with whom I am now engaged in deadly combat. Nevertheless, I am looking forward to the day when I shall reel and totter into your office, only a wisp and shell of my former self, or perhaps be borne in upon a litter, in the reclining posture which has been made so famous in recent years by all the leading British heavyweights. Anyway, Frere, if I finish that damned book and come to England will you go to Stone's with me? Will you go to Simpson's with me? If I rent an airplane, will you get in the pilot's seat and fly to Paris with me? These are only a few of the suggestions I have to make, but we might do these things right away and then settle down later to the more serious business of visiting the Scandinavian countries, Russia, Greece, India, Ireland and Japan. . . .

I think you said something about publishing "The Portrait of Bascom Hawke." I haven't thought very much about this. With the new story which *Scribner's Magazine* is going to publish and which is called "The Web of Earth" and which Perkins says is very good, and with another story which I have written, there would be enough to make a good-sized book, but I think it might be better to wait until the long book is published. I do need money and if you know of any publications in England which can print stories as long as the "Hawke" or "Web of Earth," which is also thirty or forty thousand words, and you think they might be interested in them, I should be glad if you would speak to them about it, but honestly the thing I would like most of all to do, Frere, is to get this job completed, come to England, and have a grand party with you—a barbaric and ghastly American orgy, beginning with ale, beer, port and sherry, and passing through successive nightmares of roast beef, mutton, champagne, brussels sprouts, hock and burgundy. Write and let me hear from you when you can. It will probably be some time before I am able to write to you again.

Meanwhile give my kindest and best wishes to Tom McGreevy, Richard Aldington, The Duke of York, The Prince of Wales, Mrs. Lavis, my charwoman, the Piccadilly Sirens, and any of my other friends you may happen to see. . . .

Good luck and good health, and all my best and warmest wishes, as always, Frere,

The following letter is the first in the correspondence between Wolfe and Robert Raynolds, author of Brothers in the West, *the Harper Prize Novel for 1931,* Saunders Oak, Fortune, May Bretton, Paquita, *and other novels and plays. Raynolds had reviewed* Look Homeward, Angel *very favorably in* Scribner's Magazine *(see the footnote to Wolfe's letter of October 27, 1929 to George Wallace for an excerpt from this review) but had had no personal contact with Wolfe until he had written him on March 31, 1932, to praise "A Portrait of Bascom Hawke."*

To ROBERT RAYNOLDS

111 Columbia Heights
Brooklyn, N.Y.

April 20, 1932

Dear Mr. Raynolds:

I got your letter some time ago and sat down and wrote you a very long reply which I did not finish and which stared accusingly at me for several weeks, and which has now been lost among the tottering piles of manuscript. I appreciated your letter and all you said in it tremendously, and I should be delighted and most grateful if you would send me a copy of "Brothers in the West" which I have not yet read. I have heard Fritz [1] speak of you a great deal and I knew of you as the author of "Brothers in the West" and Fritz told me something of your bold and courageous move in giving up everything and moving out into the country in order to write. Therefore, when I heard your book had won the "Harper Prize" I was genuinely delighted and felt there was justice left on earth after all, but I did not know until I got your letter that you were also the man who wrote the review of my book for *Scribner's Magazine.* I never made the connection nor completed the circuit until the

---

[1] Alfred Dashiell.

letter came. That review was the first I read about my book. Max Perkins called me up one day and read it to me over the phone, and then I went out and walked about the streets in a great many different directions. I hope that I have that feeling of jubilation and glory many times hereafter and that I shall always deserve as well and be treated as generously, but I know it will never again happen to me in just that way because that was the first time and it could not be brought back.

What you say about that circle of leering eyes which draws in about the poor wretch who is trying to write his second book, armed with tomahawks in one hand and a bouquet of roses in the other, and ready to hurl either— that also went right to the spot. It got on my nerves pretty badly for a while, but fortunately I had to forget about it the last few months out of sheer necessity. . . . The book on which I have been working for the last two or three years is not a volume but a library. I was never in the position of that fabulous creature we hear so much about who has nothing more to write about, but rather in the position of another unhappy monster who can do nothing else but write and can never come to the end of what he is writing. The book turned out to be not one volume but about four volumes, each complete in itself, and all belonging to a general thing. Goaded by desperation and necessity, I came to Brooklyn and have so far forgotten our friends of the leering eyes, but I hope to have the first folio completed in two or three months now.

I wish I could write you as good a letter as your own deserved but I cannot and I can only thank you for writing me and hope that we can get together some time when we have earned a holiday from this grievous agony of distilling out on paper your blood and marrow. . . . Meanwhile, I send you all my best and warmest wishes, for health and success in the work you are doing.

To JULIAN MEADE

Brooklyn
New York
April 21, 1932

Dear Meade:

I have just received your last letter and I want to send you some sort of answer right away. Your various notes and letters have haunted my conscience for several weeks. I have literally been too damned busy with the work which I must now complete to attend to correspondence. I really wrote you a long and detailed answer to the questions you sent me and that letter is still around the place somewhere. I think I am going to get it out and send it on to you, perhaps with this one, but I want to read it over first to see if it still seems to me to be sensible and suitable to your purpose.[1] . . .

I am going to send you that letter anyway, because you seem to want to go ahead with the article and I know you will do a good job of it. I am still so much in an experimental stage myself, I have sweated so much blood the last two or three years in a sheer agonizing effort to find out how to use my material and how to work without such tremendous expenditure of labor and energy, that I feel it might not be the best time for an article such as you propose. Everything has started to come with a great rush during the last few months. . . . Suddenly a few months ago when I was at the very bottom of a deep black pit of depression and despair, I seemed to get hold of the free end of the knot and to yank it, and since then everything has begun to come. I work now every day as long and as hard as I can and I have very little time for anything else. I have forgotten that horrible sensation of being watched with critical eyes and I have got back the self-confidence which I had almost lost.

Go ahead and write the piece if you like. I wish somehow you could tell in it plainly and simply the real truth about me which is also the best thing about me and the thing I am not ashamed of—namely, that I was a young fellow, swarming with ideas and loaded with material for books he wanted to write, who went through a period of the greatest perplexity and distress, and who has tried with all his might to learn how to work and to learn how to live decently and obscurely and like an artist.

I wish I could tell people what happens to a man when he begins to write, and how the effect his first book has on him and on his readers is entirely different from anything he ever imagined, and how even in the very element of success which he dreamed of and wanted there is something terrifying and disquieting which fills his spirit with unrest and perplexity. Well, I can't tell you about it now, but some day I want to write a piece about it and tell the story.[2] I think it would make a good one. I think what I am trying to say to you is that a man in his desire to protect his talent and his spirit from a brutal public aggression, may get a bit of a chip on his shoulder: he feels mistrustful some times and disturbed even at the praise his work may get, however generous it may be and however much his soul may thirst for it, and he resolves therefore to put himself in a position to build up a power and strength within himself that will enable him to meet triumphantly not only the clamours and shouts of

[1] The letter dated February 1, which Wolfe did not send to Meade until July 7.

[2] This piece eventually became *The Story of a Novel*, which appeared serially in the December 14, 21, and 28, 1935, issues of *The Saturday Review of Literature* and was published in book form by Scribner's in April, 1936.

success but also the contempt and scorn and sudden isolation of failure. . . .

Finally I want to make it plain that I shall go on writing, that nothing can keep me from it, that I shall not allow myself to be pushed or goaded so that I feel that my whole life and chance of fulfillment or happiness is made to depend upon a single cast of the dice, a turn of mischance or good fortune. Please don't think that I am speaking ungratefully here of the generous and liberal support which is given so freely to-day to anyone who deserves it in any degree, but I have learned to hate with all the intensity of my spirit the Goddamn pushing literary racket. I'll have no part in it and I am not going to let it touch me if I can help it in any way whatever. I will not be driven into some obscene jargon of literary competition against any man or woman living. The only man I will compete with is myself, and the only conflict I will record is the conflict of the artist with the world about him and with the elements of confusion and chaos and dissonance in his own spirit. I assure you that's a big enough job to occupy all the time and energy a man has and that's the only one I am concerned with at present. I will not say any more about this now because it is a subject I could continue with almost indefinitely, but I hope I have managed to indicate something of what I feel about the way a man has to do his work and meet the world. . . .

I wish I had more time to help you in any way I could with the piece you propose to write but I am now pressed for time and the necessity of finishing my book. Anyway, if you write the piece, won't you please send it to me before you send it to the publisher, and if you should get to New York, of course I want you to call me up and spend an evening with me if you can. . . .

P.S.—Meade, I read the piece Laurence Stallings wrote about the Bascom Hawke [story] in his column in *The Sun* [3] and I can't tell you how moved and happy and bucked up I felt about the thing. He is a grand

[3] In his column, "The Book of the Day" in *The New York Sun*, March 31, 1932, Laurence Stallings reviewed *Kamongo* by Homer W. Smith and compared it unfavorably to Wolfe's "A Portrait of Bascom Hawke" as follows: "The Scientist" (the central figure in *Kamongo*) "speaks of the eddy of energy which makes for life and throws out some pretty serious thoughts about protoplasm. . . . Has anyone failed to admire a story in the *Scribner's Magazine* (for April) by Thomas Wolfe? There's an eddy of energy for you; and a lyrical paean to life. . . . It seems to me that Thomas Wolfe has shown in this story that his *October Fair*, announced for next fall, will be even finer than . . . *Look Homeward, Angel*. . . . He seems to have all the gifts, all the talents. . . . *Kamongo* is going to cause some hoity-toity thinking among Book of the Month Club habitués. . . . But we'd still think that Thomas Wolfe's 'A Portrait of Bascom Hawke' is the book of the month."

man and really it is for this kind of reward that men work and live, and the reason they go through that agony of distilling their blood and marrow out upon a printed page which is known as writing. I wanted to tell you a while ago that we really want fame and love it as in decency we ought, but it is not the fame which is given to you by a set of driving and pushing and contriving literary racketeers who will fall upon you and rend you with gleeful howls the moment they think you have stumbled and fallen, but it is for the respect and admiration of such people as Stallings and perhaps a dozen more that we sweat and labor. Good words from people like this are sweeter than honey and it seems to me one of the best and highest rewards on earth. As for the other thing, the racketing, gossiping, hoop-de-doodle thing, it is a piece of stinking fish and the man who lets himself be seduced by its putrid fragrance deserves everything that he can and undoubtedly will get. So much for that—I forgot to tell you that in this great burst of work I have been enjoying I have written another story of about forty thousand words which *Scribner's* have taken and which they are going to publish in July or August if I can take the time off to do the proofs and revision. It is called "The Web of Earth" and Max Perkins says it's grand. It is different from anything I have ever done; it's about an old woman, who sits down to tell a little story, but then her octopal memory weaves back and forth across the whole fabric of her life until everything has gone into it. It's all told in her own language. I had the whole spring and source and fountain-head within me. I really believe, although this is a terribly boastful thing to say, that I knew this old woman better than Joyce knew that woman at the end of "Ulysses" and furthermore that my old woman is a grander, richer and more tremendous figure than his was. If I haven't been able to make her seem so, the fault is in me and not in the material I had to work with. I wish to God Max Perkins would let me write a whole long book about her. I haven't used one-tenth of the material I had, but he wants me very properly to finish the book I am doing before going on to some of these other ones, and of course he is right about it, but that story about the old woman has got everything in it, murder and cruelty, and hate and love, and greed and enormous unconscious courage, yet the whole thing is told with the stark innocence of a child. I really think it is going to be a good story if they won't make me cut out some of the things in it. Of course I know a few of the scenes can't be printed in *Scribner's Magazine* but I think that they are wrong, or rather that the world is wrong, in this attitude because the only thing that can possibly make for what is revolting and obscene is the intention, and it ought to be apparent in the very first paragraph of a good thing that the intention has nothing to do with deliberate and calculating profaneness.

P.S. I have just this minute finished an 80,000 word mss., the complete story of a man's life, part of my new book.[4] I have written it in less than a month, it is the largest completed work I have done in a long time, and I am happy because I know I'll be all right now.

Stanley Olmsted, the author of At Top of Tobin *etc., had written Wolfe inviting him to visit him at one of the Dickey House Annexes outside Murphy, North Carolina, and saying that Mrs. Dickey, the proprietress, wanted him to be her honor guest and would "kill the fatted calf" for him. The following letter was Wolfe's reply.*

To STANLEY OLMSTED

New York

June 14, 1932

Dear Mr. Olmsted:

Thanks very much for your fine long letter. Mabel has spoken of you and your sister many times and although I have not yet had the pleasure of meeting any of you personally, I no longer feel any strangeness whatever when I think of you and I am really looking forward to that happy day when I can appear suddenly before you and Mrs. Dickey and try to do justice to her fabulous table of which I have heard so much.

I suppose you know that *Scribner's Magazine* published, several months ago, a piece by a travelling salesman in which he described one of his visits to Drummer's Rest[1]—I believe that is the name of Mrs. Dickey's place. My friend, Fritz Dashiell, who is the editor of Scribner's Magazine, told me he had had several letters from subscribers after this piece was published asking if it could be true and, if it was, how to get there in the quickest way. Fritz . . . gave the people who had written him the necessary information: he told me the other night that he has since then received further letters from three or four of them and that all of them say that if the travelling salesman erred at all, it was on the side of understatement. Anyway, I wish you would thank Mrs. Dickey for me for her gracious invitation, and I assure you that I am holding before me as a reward, at the end of this desperate conflict with a book in which I am now engaged and

[4] "The Man on the Wheel" which told the story of Robert Weaver and which was written as a part of *K 19.* The greater part of it was never published, but a few sections appear in *Of Time and the River.*

[1] "Drummer's Rest" by Edward Hilts in the August, 1931, issue of *Scribner's Magazine.*

from which there can be no escape for me until it is finished, such a journey as you suggest.

I keep thinking of that travelling salesman who wrote the piece in *Scribner's* and his honeyed words. I would like to arrive there just as he did with the winds howling and night coming on and the old nigger coming out with his maddening list of delicacies. I have seen the whole thing in my mind a thousand times: I only hope the man's article didn't start such a stampede that there will be no room for me when I get there.

I am so glad you stopped off to see my mother.[2] . . . She seems to be the most completely fearless and independent person I have ever known: although she is seventy-two years old and in her old age has lost every penny she had, there are many younger people I worry about more and about whom I feel greater misgiving. Her courage is of an absolutely spontaneous and natural kind which is not even conscious of itself. She has endured the most crushing blows in life with no suggestion of ever giving in to them and with no idea that there was anything else to do expect to endure them and live through them, and, of course, with a person of this kind there is never any question of defeat or failure. Even if they lose all of their material possessions, they lose nothing of themselves because they are unconquerable. I have written a short novel which is to appear in *Scribner's Magazine* in a few days. It is called "The Web of Earth," and my friend, Maxwell Perkins, who knows you, and whose word in a matter of this sort means as much to me as anyone's, tells me it is a grand thing and as good as anything I ever did. . . . I have never yet asked anyone to read a word I had written, but if you do get the time and see a copy of the July *Scribner's,* I wish you would look at it.

There is one more thing that occurs to me: I have written and told my mother about my story. . . . I know she will understand it and see that it is all right, and I think it is obvious, as does Max Perkins, that the story has been written to the glory of man and not to his defeat. As you may know, I went through some pretty bad times two years ago because of some of the things that were said and thought about my first book in Asheville. It does not seem possible to me now that there is anything in the present story which could cause a reoccurrence of that misunderstanding, but I do not want my mother to be troubled by the attentions of prying and curious people whose only interest in a book seems to be in trying to discover whether Jim Smith is really Oscar Brown or whether such and such a thing ever happened, etc. As I say, I don't think their folly could possibly carry them to such abysmal depths this time, but if you read the story and like it, I should be grateful to you if you would write my mother and tell her so, and that if the world holds no worse

---

[2] Olmsted had written that he had spent a night at the old Kentucky home.

people than these there is a pretty good hope that it may yet be saved.

Meanwhile, with thanks again for your letter and your invitation. . . .
I am,

To JULIAN MEADE

111 Columbia Heights
Brooklyn, N.Y.

July 7, 1932

Dear Meade:

I got your letter and enclosed article yesterday. I think you have done
a good job of it and I don't believe there is much I could suggest at
present by way of change. But since you say this is a first draft, I am doing what I always intended to do—I am sending you the long letter
which I wrote you several months ago in answer to the list of questions
you sent me and which I never mailed.[1] I have read the letter over and
I think it does attempt some more detailed answer to your questions than
any I have yet given you, and therefore I am sending it along in the
hope you may still find it of use.

In your own article I have taken the liberty of making one or two slight
changes in things you quote me as saying, although you got it perfectly
right and I did say them. On page 7 the phrase "racketing, gossiping,
hoop-de-doodle thing" occurs, and I am going to change this for various
reasons, chiefly because "hoop-de-doodle" does not belong to my own
way of speech and is probably Menckenian. Likewise I am changing the
phrase "stinking fish" and the sentence which follows because it also
sounds a little awkward to me, although it does represent what I mean.

The only other thing I can qualify at the present is a very pleasant one,
my protest is only a very feeble one and if you will take the responsibility
for the statement I will say nothing whatever about it. You refer to me
in one place as a very learned man and you speak of me as reading and
speaking fluently several languages and of being a Greek and Latin
scholar. Now I wish all of this were literally true but I am afraid it does
go a little beyond the actual facts. The only thing I feel really guilty
about is the Greek and Latin. I can still read my Homer after a fashion
and I do believe I could still put up some sort of battle with Xenophon
and I can still read Caesar; I can do fairly well with Catullus; but I regret
to say that whatever modest accomplishments I may have once had with
the ancient languages I have let slip away. I do read French and German
and am in fact fairly proficient, particularly in French which I can read

[1] The letter of February 1.

about as well as my own language. And I have done an enormous amount of reading. I can make that admission without qualification. Probably all this explanation is unnecessary but although I was tremendously pleased with your soft impeachment as regards my learning, I can't quite let it go by without mumbling a few words of half-hearted protest. Having said so much, the rest is up to you.

One possible change or increase in emphasis occurs to me. You mention the fact that I have worked hard in an effort to learn how to use my material in the most effective way. I think you might even somewhat emphasize the fact that a large part of my toil and trouble at present comes from having almost too much material to deal with and the consequent effort it has cost me to find out how to shape and release the units in separate volumes of a readable and publishable length. This has really been a tremendous problem and has cost me terrific labor. Thus, out of all the writing I have done in the past two and a half years—writing which would amount quite easily, I think, to a half-million words—it is doubtful if I will be able to use over a third or a fourth of it in my next book. And yet I think that in one way or another I shall eventually use almost all of it. I suppose what I am trying to say to you is that every man has his own special problem and his own conflict with his material and it seems to me that each man has got to learn it in his own way for himself, that no one can help him very much to do it and that, for good or worse, a man's work and the way he does it is more particularly than any thing else on earth a unique possession, and his entire relation to it is a process of constant and entirely personal discovery.

This is all I have time to say to you at present. I hope that the letter which I am enclosing will be of some service to you. I thank you for the interest you have taken and for treating me so fairly and honestly and I wish you luck with the article. One thing you say I do especially agree with, in hope and aspiration at any rate, if not in actual achievement. That is that I should like my work to be of one piece with all my life, and that to me the labor of writing does seem to be united to a man's whole vision of life, and that the writer can fully appreciate, I believe, more easily than another man the whole meaning and emotion of John Keats' sonnet: "When I have fears that I may cease to be." I do think it is one of the deepest desires of the artist, or of some artists, that he will be able to give his whole and final measure before he is done.

I should greatly appreciate it if you will let me know what further progress you make in this piece and where and when it will be published. I shall also be grateful for a carbon copy if you have one. . . .

To HENRY ALLEN MOE

111 Columbia Heights
Brooklyn, N.Y.
July 12, 1932

Dear Mr. Moe:

In response to your recent inquiry asking for copies of any recent work I have published, I am instructing *Scribner's Magazine* to send you their issues for April and July, which contain two short novels of mine: "A Portrait of Bascom Hawke" and "The Web of Earth." It may be of interest to you to know that I had a great and very unexpected piece of good fortune in connection with the first of these stories, the "Bascom Hawke." *Scribner's* was holding a five thousand dollar prize contest at the time when I submitted this story, although I knew nothing of the contest at that time. Consequently I was made very happy the other day when they telephoned me and informed me that the judges had selected my story and that of another man for first prize. I shall therefore share the prize with someone else.[1] An announcement to this effect will be made in the August number of *Scribner's Magazine*, but as the editors seem to be particularly anxious that no public mention be made of it until that time, will you please say nothing about it? But I wanted to tell you about it anyway, because it was a grand and unexpected windfall and because I thought you would like to hear about it.

As for my other activity at present, I am going ahead daily with my book, or one section of it, which, no matter what publishers' announcements and statements say, will be published when I am done writing it and when I think it is fit to be published.[2] That is all I can tell you at present because that is all I know myself, but I shall certainly send you an advance copy as soon as one is available.

I have been in to see you two or three times, but have always missed you. I live in Brooklyn now, and rarely get to New York in the day time. But I do hope to find you one of these days. . . .

The following letter was written in reply to one from Elaine Westall Gould about "A Portrait of Bascom Hawke," which she had deliberately refrained from reading, but which she suspected of being an unfair and ruthless portrayal of her parents, Mr. and Mrs. Henry A. Westall.

[1] "A Portrait of Bascom Hawke" and "The Big Short Trip" by John Herrmann tied for first place in the *Scribner's Magazine* Prize Short Novel Contest. Therefore Wolfe and Hermann divided the prize of $5000 equally between them.

[2] This was written soon after Perkins had persuaded Wolfe to give up publication of *K 19*.

To ELAINE WESTALL GOULD

111 Columbia Heights
Brooklyn, N.Y.

July 15, 1932

Dear Elaine:

Your letter from the Prince George came this morning. It was sent on
to me from my old address and I am afraid I have now missed seeing you
until your return here at any rate. I have constantly intended and constantly deferred answering your last two letters and I assure you the only
reason and the only excuse I have to offer is procrastination and the
pressure of a great deal of work. I have thought all along that I would
get to Boston at least for a weekend during the summer and I still have
hopes of doing that, but I should be delighted to see you here if you have
time and the inclination when you get back. Anyway, if you don't call
me when you return I shall undoubtedly telephone you one of these days
in Boston and then, as always, hope you will be able to come into town
and chew the rag and a little lunch with me. Because in your last letter,
although you did speak to me in a very stern and straight-forward fashion, I gathered from the ending that you would not throw me out of the
window if I came knocking at your door again, and I assure you it made
me feel better than anything else could have.

I had never really intended to attempt an answer to your letter anyway, because it was too good a letter, and answering it would have been
an act of solid creation in itself and I thought I would do better if I
waited until I saw you, and then I thought I might do better if we talked
as always and I said nothing more about it. I was just going to send you a
note and to tell you I was glad you wanted to see me and that I would
call you up when I came to Boston. The only thing I will now say to you
about the letter you wrote me concerning my story which came out in
April is this: I think it was a fine letter and I think the things you said in
it about ruthlessness and the ruthless man, for example, are generally and
forcibly true, but I do not think that these things are true about me nor
about the story I wrote, nor does Maxwell Perkins at Scribners, who is
as fine a man as I know and the greatest editor in the country. The story
was not about ruthlessness nor about a ruthless man, nor was it written
to idealize those qualities. Someday I will try to tell you what I wanted
the story to be about. I should not be deeply disturbed if I thought your
objection to the story was based on the fact that you thought I had made
a heroic figure out of [the] man. . . . That, after all, is a matter of personal vision, and in that respect the writer must be true to his own—he
can do nothing else but be true to his own, whether it coincides with
that of his friends or not.

But I was seriously disturbed about another allegation in your letter. That was that in the act of making a heroic figure of your father I had made by contrast a weak and ridiculous figure of your mother, and that you and other members of your family felt so strongly about your mother's life and character that your feeling toward me could never hereafter be the same. You said your sister [1] was so furious about this that she had started to work on an "answer" to my story which would be in effect a vindication of her mother. . . . Now in reference to all this, I want to say that the business of answers and vindications or of getting revenge on anyone or "showing them up" has never yet been the motive behind anything I wrote, although I was savagely accused of doing this and threatened with anonymous letters and denounced from press and pulpit in Asheville, North Carolina, two years ago because of my first book—and now, by the way, the same people who accused me most bitterly, the same paper which attacked me in its columns, write me letters and ask for a summary of my plans and work for the future, and when am I coming home, and "your many friends here are eager to know what your plans are and what your new book is going to be about, et cetera."

I can tell you honestly that I was the most surprised and bitterly wounded person about the fate of that book in my native town. A dozen times I started to take pen in hand and write a furious answer to the local critics, but I thought the whole thing out alone and in my own mind, and I came to the conclusion then that I would never write a letter in answer to such an attack or to the public press if I could help it, and I have stuck to that ever since, and I hope I always will. The result of my conclusions is this: that the writer is creating a world of his own visioning and that in so doing he creates a new kind of reality and a new set of values, and that his work, in so far as it has living value, is not concerned in exalting or degrading a particular Jones, or Brown, or Smith, but rather in finding in any particular Jones, or Brown, or Smith the things that unite him to the whole family of the earth. I can go on and talk to you about this for a long, long time and furthermore I know that I would be standing on solid ground, but I will say nothing more about it here save that when you speak of your father and your mother, that awakens one set of memories in my mind, but when you speak of a man and a woman in one of my stories, that awakens an entirely different set of memories and a different kind of reality, and I assure you that in this statement, although I would improve it if I could and if I had the time, there is not one word of evasion or desire to deny responsibility. I also want to say this: that you may be right in saying that I have done an injustice to your mother

[1] Hilda Westall Bottomley.

in my brief picture of a woman in the story, but I hope you are not right, and I will say that if an injustice was done, it was not intended and that my fault consists not in my being too much concerned with the weaknesses and imperfections of the character but rather of being very little concerned with that particular character at all. Now in this I say an injustice may have been done, but if it was, it was not intentional and in the end you will see that it does no damage, that it can do no damage to any person, dead or living.

What I am here saying to you is that I concentrated in that story upon the portrait of a man: that I tried to show him as he looked, as he spoke, as he dressed, and as he walked along the street, and that whatever scenes or persons were introduced into the story were introduced for this purpose. The sole example of the ruthlessness of which you speak consisted in ruthlessly cutting away everything I did not find immediately useful to the purpose of this single portrait: if I had completed the story of the man's life in its connections with all the other lives about him, I should no longer have had a story, I should have had a novel of very considerable length. Now let me repeat again:—if I was unfair to your mother again, as you say I was, it came not because I was meditating her portrait, but because I was not meditating her portrait. And neither, let me say, was I meditating the portrait of your father, because that is not the way the writer works—at least that is not the way I work.

You may find this hard to believe but I do not consider the man in my story, for better or worse, to be even a close approximation of your father, although I would not deny that we both know where much of the clay that shaped that figure came from, and I could further tell you, if I had to, where a great deal of it did not come from: of sources, experiences, and actual moments of my own life and seeing of which you know nothing, but which went into the making of the story.

Finally, as an example of the confusion and perplexity that always attends this kind of argument when people try to identify by word and letter the scenes, characters, and rhythm of a piece of writing, you inform me that your sister is writing a piece in vindication of her mother; but my mother wrote me that your sister had written her about the story, expressing indignation that I should have held up to ridicule not her mother but her father, and saying that her father, for all his faults and eccentricities, was really a grand and lovable character, and so on. As I told you at the beginning, it is perhaps better not to get involved with these arguments or explanations at all because they lead to endless confusion, and in the end, a man's only explanation should be his work itself; and that explanation should cover the whole course of his life and appear in everything he does, and he should rest confident and certain in the conviction; and if his work is good or has any truth or living value in it, he has done thereby no real or lasting injury to any person, alive or dead; and this is a part of my faith and in this I shall try to live, although you say that it will leave me without friends, without love, without security, or support, in life. If that is true, then it must be true. But I hope it is not true: it seems to me that in a world which has so much affection, love, esteem, and offers so many rewards to the frauds, charlatans, thieves and criminals who betray it constantly—witness New York and its Mayor, Jimmy Walker, or Asheville and its beloved thieves and swindlers who have wrecked the town, or for that matter, the whole world for the writers who betray it constantly with lies and sugared slop—in such a liberal world, I say, there must still be a little mercy and charity left for an honest man who wants only to do the best work in him, who is out to rob, swindle, or betray no one.

You speak of me as ruthless, of being a young Freudian and a cynical intellectual who makes a virtue of ruthlessness and the gratification of what you refer to as ravening desires. I tell you that if you think these things of me, they are phantoms of your mind and have no relation to me or to my life whatever. Further, I tell you in all sincerity and with the deepest friendship that if your own life or the life of your friends or members of your family is as free from rancor and bitterness as mine is, then no one in this world can complain of any lack in charity and understanding in any of you. As to the ravening desires, if it be a ravening desire to love life fiercely and to hate death and all the living forms of sterility in death like hell, then I am a victim of these ravening desires you mention.

Well, I've got part of it off my chest now, although I did not mean to say so much. I took the liberty, which I don't think you will mind, of showing your letter to my friend, Maxwell Perkins, and he said it was a fine letter and that the person who wrote it is all right and also mistaken in some of the things she said, and with this opinion I also agree. And finally, using some of your own unvarnished speech, I think you had a nerve to write me a letter accusing me of certain crimes and misdemeanors in a story which you had not read.

I think it is grand that you and Harold are able to take this trip.[2] It sounds fascinating and also hot as hell. I wish you all kinds of happiness and good luck and good adventure on it: I hope this letter reaches you at your boat in Panama and that you will call me up and have lunch with me when you come back. But if you don't, I shall look forward to seeing you anyway in old New England later in the summer. I suppose it's too late now for the grackles—when you wrote me that letter I won-

[2] Mr. and Mrs. Gould had gone on a southern cruise.

dered what the hell a grackle was, and whether you were getting literary on me, but after consulting an authority on grackles I was assured you had used the speech of the land and that animal does exist. With love to all and best wishes for a happy vacation.

IX

BROOKLYN AND CONTINUED WORK: THE
COMPLETION OF THE FIRST ROUGH DRAFT OF
OF TIME AND THE RIVER

1932–1933

The following letter was written in answer to one from DuBose Heyward, author of Porgy, Mamba's Daughters, Peter Ashley, *etc., in inviting Wolfe to join the Conference of Southern Writers to be held in Charleston in October, 1932. He finally decided not to go, and stayed in Brooklyn and worked. Wolfe had first met Heyward through his wife, Dorothy Kuhns Heyward, who had been in the 47 Workshop and who is the author of* Porgy *(in collaboration with her husband),* South Pacific *(with Howard Rigsby),* Set My People Free, *etc.*

To DuBOSE HEYWARD

101 Columbia Heights
Brooklyn, N.Y.
September 8, 1932

Dear DuBose,

I know I am guilty as hell about not answering your last two letters. Please forgive me. I have been involved with this stinking New York heat, with having to move in the middle of summer, . . . and with this nine-headed monster of a book. I have not been away from here all summer except for a three-day trip to Montreal from which I returned last night. I hope to be able to take a vacation later on, and if I can, I will try to make it come in October during the time you are having the meeting in Charleston. . . . I assure you nothing would delight me more at present, not only for the fun I would have, but also for the good I might get out of it. God knows, I need relief, succor, help and enlightenment of some sort, but I'm afraid I will have to try to dig it out of myself—I don't believe all the writers in the world could help me now, although I suppose a good many of them have suffered from the same ailment. With me, it is now a question of eat or be eaten; of subduing the monster or being devoured by it, and above all of learning how to make an end. I think I've gone through most of the other stages. I am now an exalted master in sweating blood, beating my head against the wall, stamping across the Brooklyn Bridge in the middle of the night. I have learned almost everything, in fact, except how not to write a book in eighteen volumes, and if I thought you and our friends in Charleston could help me settle this problem, I would be down there licking my chops with greedy anticipation a week before the rest of you got there.

DuBose, I will be there if I can. I want like hell to get away from here, if only for a few days, but I really have a feeling of inescapable necessity as regards this book and a feeling of deep responsibility and obligation towards Max Perkins and the other people at Scribners who have been so decent to me. Therefore, coming to Charleston depends on what progress I make between now and the opening of the meeting. I think you will understand from this how things are. . . . Meanwhile, I send you and Dorothy my best wishes for your health and happiness and I wish you all possible success in preparing for this meeting.

Owen Francis, to whom the following letter was written, is the author of "Hunky Wedding," etc., and had written Wolfe suggesting that he come to Hollywood and work for the motion pictures.

To OWEN FRANCIS

101 Columbia Heights
Brooklyn, N.Y.
September 8, 1932

Dear Owen,
 . . . I was delighted to hear from you and jubilant about all the fine news your letter had in it. I have never known just what to say to a man when he tells me he has just been married. I suppose you know very well the feeling of the bachelor when he sees his friends slipping away from him one by one into the jaws of matrimony. He is happy about it for their sake but for his own he feels a little lonely and regretful. And the pressure on him to go and do likewise becomes a little greater all the time. Unfortunately for me, I have felt for some time that wild, growing im-

pulse but I have neither the cash to gratify it nor a willing and attractive target at which I could direct it. Owen, I am very happy about your marriage and all the other success which seems to have come along with it and I want to wish you both as much happiness and good fortune as any two people can have. You say, also, that the Hollywood sultans are giving you 200 of what it takes each Wednesday. The first thing it takes for me is my breath. Such a figure is simply appalling. I know, however, that you are worth it and ten times more, if some of their other henchmen are paid the salaries they are said to get. I hope to God you get it and also, Owen, although I am the worst person on earth to urge you to moderation in anything and particularly in the streak of lavish generosity that runs through you, I hope you manage to put a little of it aside because this coming winter looks very cold and bleak to my jaundiced eye in spite of all the hopeful prophecies and predictions of Roosevelt and Hoover.

About your warm assurance that I could make much more than you if I came out, and fatten up my lean bankroll in a few weeks, I am not so sure. I do know that you are competent and a good enough craftsman to earn every penny they would pay you but I am afraid I would be completely useless to them. I am grateful to you for your confidence, but you really have no idea how stupid and blundering I am. I swelter around and sweat blood and struggle terribly in an effort to get my own work done and by my own work I mean the work I may possibly be able to do. I swarm with lavish and sensational and gaudy ideas and stories and visions which might possibly be of some use in a moving picture but then they are no use whatever to me until I can get them woven in, somehow, into the color and vision of my own life and even then I often have to cut them out. What I am trying to say to you is that I seem to be able to write only about the things I have seen and known or imagined and which, therefore, have become a part of my own life. I swear to you that if I thought I could do such work as you suggest and earn even a portion of these fabulous salaries you mention, I would come out there like a shot, but I have not one atom of confidence in my ability to do so. I think they would give me the gate in a week's time.

I am in a maddening position as regards the movies and everything else on which I might be able to realize a profit. For two or three years I have had, from time to time, personal or written inquiries and letters from high paying publications such as the *Cosmopolitan* and *Collier's* and here, recently, for what reason I can't say, I have had a whole burst of popularity with the movie people. Owen, my mouth waters and my tongue lolls out of my mouth in my greedy lust to do something about it, but there is nothing I can do. If I could have written a *Cosmopolitan* or *Saturday Evening Post* story, I should have done so long ago with howls of triumph, and if I could write anything that might be useful to the movies, I would fall over myself in my haste to do it. But when I have had these letters from them recently asking me about my new book and when would it be ready and would I please send them proofs as soon as possible, I have usually failed to answer—not from discourtesy—but simply to avoid useless complications and trouble for us both. If some moving picture company should want to buy the rights for my new book, if and when it is completed and after reading it, I should be the happiest fellow on earth. But I don't see how this can happen; I don't see any possible chance of their being able to use it, and the only wisdom I have concerning all this is in an instinctive feeling that I may do better in the long run if I stumble and sweat in my own way and try to do some work which I may be capable of rather than work for which I have no capacity whatever. But if any of them out there are interested, even mildly, in little Tommy's moving-picture possibilities, for God's sake don't give me away to them! Because some miracle might happen, some day, where something I did might be of value to them. . . .

Owen, your invitation to come out and stay with you is the most alluring prospect I have had for a long time and your generous proposal to buy my railroad ticket is as fine as anything could be. If your letter had come during the last stinking spell of heat around Labor Day, I think I might have got in a train and come on out. As it is, it has turned now cool and fresh and delightful here, my little trip to Canada set me up, and I have decided it is best for me to stick on grimly here and to finish the thing I am trying to do or be finished by. I am exactly in the position of Macbeth when he said, in words more beautiful than I can remember, that his soul is so steeped in gore that it was easier to go on to the end of it than to attempt to go back to the place where he began. I have a little money, not much, which came to me as a result of dividing the Scribner prize. That was a wonderful windfall and so far as I was concerned it was like picking gold up in the street. . . . Now thanks to this lucky break, I can go on here for a little longer. Then, if I am as broke as I will be unless some miracle happens, I may come on out and join you, provided you are still there and you think there is any prospect of my finding anything to do.

I wish you had been with me on that little trip to Montreal. Montreal is not so much, but the beer and the ale and the Bourbon and the Scotch are as glorious as they always were and the ride back in the train, yesterday, was one of the most beautiful and magnificent journeys I have ever made. I came down the Hudson River just at sunset, it was the first brisk autumn day we have had and I doubt if even California has anything that can surpass the richness, the mystery and the beauty of that landscape at sunset on such a day. . . .

This is all for the present, Owen, and the letter has gone on too long already. But I am tremendously grateful to you for what you say and for your generous offer and if I can't accept it now, I still want to think that there is a chance of my doing so in the future. Write me when you have a chance and give me the news about yourself. I hope that every letter you send me has as good news as this last one had, and for the present, I send you both my most affectionate wishes for your good health and happiness.

To ELAINE WESTALL GOULD

101 Columbia Heights
Brooklyn, N.Y.

January 24, 1933.

Dear Elaine:

I am awfully sorry not to have acknowledged your letters and Christmas card before. . . . I have wanted for months to come to Boston and will confess to you now that I was there, or rather in Andover, for a few days at the end of October. I landed there on a ship coming from Bermuda, a place which I detested thoroughly, although many people seem to love it. I went there to spend a vacation but I spent nothing but a lot of money, and got madder and madder all the time at the island, the inhabitants and everything else they have there. Andover seemed to me ten times more beautiful and desirable in every way. I am afraid I must be a Yankee at heart. I don't believe that I could ever live in the Tropics. I was so completely shot to pieces with exhaustion and a cold on the chest that I could do nothing but emit a few feeble and incoherent bull frog croaks when I got off the ship at Boston, and that is really the reason why I did not call up. I went out to a friend's house in Andover [1] and slept for three or four days, and that fixed me up. But I am looking forward to seeing you soon, and I promise that the next time I come I will try to be fit to see and talk to you. . . . It would really be useless for me to try to put in a letter all the things I would like to talk to you about, so I am going to stop now, and hope to see or hear from you before long.

[1] George Wallace's.

To ROBERT RAYNOLDS

101 Columbia Heights
Brooklyn, N.Y.
Jan 25, 1933

Dear Bob:

The book [1] you sent me arrived safely and in good condition. I read all the stories and was deeply impressed with "Karain." . . .

I took a little trip down to Baltimore and Washington last week which set me up and made me feel good, and I am now getting some of those stories typed that I told you about. I am going to take the one I am having typed [2] at present to *Scribner's* and see if they are willing to do anything with it. If they are not, perhaps I shall make use of the addresses you gave me and consult your friend, the agent,[3] or, take it around myself to *Harper's Magazine.*

I had lunch finally today with a very elegant, highly perfumed and fancy talking Hollywood lady, an agent out there. She has sent me telegrams, written me letters, and a friend of mine who works out there among the movie people, and who sometimes allows his enthusiasm to run away with him, had already assured me that all I needed to do was to meet the lady, sign the contract, and then start raking the thousand dollar bills into an open valise. However, all I got out of it was a good lunch and an invitation to come to Hollywood. When I asked her how I was going to get there, and who was going to pay the fare, etc., and what I was going to do when I got there, she had the gall to suggest that I hitchhike, and added that she was sure she could do something wonderful and mysterious and immensely prosperous for me if I did come out. Therefore, it looks as if I will still be trying to do business at the same old address in Brooklyn for some time to come. So if you come to town call me up. . . .

[1] *Tales of Unrest* by Joseph Conrad.

[2] "The Train and the City," which contained some of the train scenes from *K 19,* and which was accepted by *Scribner's Magazine* on February 9, 1933, and published in the May issue. Portions of it appear in *Of Time and the River* on pages 407–419, in *The Web and the Rock* on pages 91–94, 441 and 447–449, and in *You Can't Go Home Again* on pages 3–4.

[3] Paul Reynolds. Raynolds had spoken to him and to Lee Hartman, editor of *Harper's Magazine,* about Wolfe's work.

To A YOUNG MAN WHO HAD ASKED FOR
ADVICE ABOUT A CAREER

[Brooklyn, N.Y.]

February 1, 1933.

Dear Mr. ——:

I have your letter of January 26th which my mother sent to me from Asheville. . . . I am sorry to have to tell you that the question you ask me is too much for me to answer. I am afraid it is a question each of us has to try to settle for himself with his own life, and that there is little we can say or do for anyone else no matter how much we want to, which will help him to conquer the confusion and distress of his own life.

I can tell you, however, that the greatest satisfaction and happiness I have had in my own life was when I was able to work hard and be proud of the work I was doing and feel that I was doing something that had some value or merit. This may not seem to you to be much of an answer to your question but it is the best one I can give you, although I know it does not apply to everyone because many people, in fact most people in the world, work hard and yet are not happy because they do not like the work they are doing and their heart and interest is not in it. I do not know how old you are but I imagine you are younger than I am, and part of your trouble at the present time may be due to the fact that you have not found the kind of work you want to do. If this is true, I can assure you that most young fellows have this same trouble. I had it when I was about eighteen in college; I was miserable and unhappy because I could not discover what I wanted to do or what I was fitted for. This may be your trouble now. What I am trying to say to you is, that if I came from the country and liked it and wanted a farm I would become a farmer and not be ashamed of it. If I liked machinery I would try to find out about machinery and become a mechanic or an engineer. If I liked business I would try to get into a business and find out about it. But I would not try to be a business man because I thought it was a higher kind of occupation, if I really liked to farm better, or I would not try to be a farmer if the thing that interested me was machinery.

I have tried to give you some kind of an honest answer to your letter and something which might be of help to you, because I think a great deal of the trouble in the world comes from this thing I have been talking about. People who are misfit do not really care for the work they do.

As you say in your letter if you are a sailor there are a great many other things in life that you know as much about as I do, and no one needs to give you any advice about what to do with food, and liquor or with girls.

I have found all these things good and I think that I have enjoyed them as much as anyone, but I know that in themselves they are not enough to complete the life of a man with any intelligence, ambition and a desire to make life better.

This is all that I can write you but I thank you again for your letter and hope that I may have said something that will be of use to you.

With best wishes for your success in everything you do,

The following hasty and undated note could have been sent to Perkins with almost any section from Of Time and the River *which Wolfe hoped to sell to* Scribner's Magazine. *It probably was sent with "No Door," which was published in the July, 1933, issue of* Scribner's. *The first part of this story appears in* From Death to Morning: *the rest appears in* Of Time and the River *on pages 2, 90–93, 327–334, 601–608, 611–613, and in* You Can't Go Home Again *on pages 37–44.*

To MAXWELL E. PERKINS

[February 1933?]

Dear Max:

Here is the manuscript. It is out of my book. Max, there are a dozen things I'd like to do to this—I have a passage about Time that I want to put in, other things I want to take out—but I want you to read it now: I believe you can see what it is about. Max, it may be no good, or it may be good—I'm too tired to know at the moment—but of one thing I'm sure: it is made from the real stuff of life, it is made out of material I know to the bottom of my heart, and I have tried to put something of my vision of life in it. I ask you to remember that my book is about Time: I hope the Time theme is evident in this story. Well, here it is, Max—it's no good explaining any more—I hope it's good and you like it.

During all this time, Wolfe had written hundreds of thousands of words for his book, but still had failed to come to grips with it by beginning at the beginning and continuing with it until he reached the end. The following letter to his sister Mabel was written just after his return from a trip to Baltimore and Washington with Perkins, during which they constantly discussed Wolfe's difficulties and found the solution to them. From this time on, Wolfe got off to a new start, which resulted in the completion of the first rough draft of Of Time and the River *and* The October Fair *in December, 1933.*

To MABEL WOLFE WHEATON

[101 Columbia Heights]
[Brooklyn, N.Y.]
February 9, 1933.

Dear Mabel:

. . . I did not come over to Washington the day after I saw you as I should have liked because I knew Fred would be here the next day and I had no way of getting him to tell him to come to Washington. Also, I had no time to call you the next morning because we [1] decided to get a morning train to New York, and managed to pack and get to the station with just a minute or two to spare but I thought you would be able to guess what had happened. Fred came up on Sunday, of course, and spent the day and suggested that I meet him in Philadelphia or Harrisburg after Mama comes up and we can drive down to Washington. Of course I plan and shall somehow arrange to get down and see her some way but just at what time I will be able to do it I do not know, that is, I do not know whether I will be there for her birthday. I will take a chance on the Inauguration. [2] I confess I would not mind seeing the Inauguration if it weren't for sweating and jamming your way through those crowds. I am so sorry it does not come down your street and under your windows. That would be fine, wouldn't it? But then I suppose you could do a rushing business yourself in renting out window space.

I have finally and at last some good news, after so much that is depressing. When I came back from my trip with Mr. Perkins I knew that it was now or never with me. My money was all gone and I really got down to my last ten dollars, with the rent to pay. Anyway during the last two or three weeks I have worked as never before in my life, wrote over 60,000 words in that period and now have, so Perkins says, the novel in the hollow of my hand. Perkins told me last night that he had been almost desperate about me, trying to figure what was wrong and how to get me out of it, but, if he was desperate you can imagine what my own state was. Now something far better than even money has happened. I seem suddenly to have found a way of getting started, which Perkins thinks was the real trouble all along, and having made the start everything has been going with a rush. Of course I have tons of stuff piled up now which I want to get in but that is the trouble, as Perkins thinks I will do too much, but I have promised to hold to the plan we have agreed on and by early Spring I feel pretty sure now that I will have the first draft of the whole book complete. This means that it will come out next fall and it also means

---

[1] Wolfe and Perkins.
[2] The inauguration of Franklin Delano Roosevelt.

that I am living again with hope and confidence for the first time in almost a year.

It has been a tough time for me and the whole trouble seemed psychological rather than anything else. I think that I got afraid after the first book. I was afraid that I could never live up to the things they said about me and furthermore tried to listen to the advice of a hundred well-meaning people, all of whom could tell you how they would do it, which after all is not what you want; you want to find out how you can do it yourself, and the only way I have found it out I have now discovered is to go ahead and do it. I do not know whether it will be as good as the first book. Perkins thinks it will and maybe better but I think it will be good, and the main thing will be to do a big piece of work once more and to get my hope and confidence back and then to go ahead to all the work I have still got in me. I feel somehow that having gotten out of this awful time, this kind of hump in my life, I will never have this same trouble again. The whole thing is almost unbelievable, because my trouble never was wondering whether I would have enough but how in God's name I would ever manage to get one-tenth of what I did, and Perkins tells me that I ought not to try to say everything in one book, but to put some of it in the others.

Anyway, when I went up to see him last night—he stayed in to talk to me—I had just $7.00 left in all the world, but he told me right away that they were going to take one short story out of the book and use it for the magazine and would pay me $200 for it,[3] so I have this for the present. Also, another long story which I think they will take and for which, of course, I will get more money.[4]

This is all the news I have to send you at present but of course it is very big news to me and I suppose you understand how things are with me at present, and that I cannot afford either the time or the money to do much travelling or to make extended visits as I would like to. I think this is really the critical time in my life and that if I can get through this I will be all right.

Of course I do not know how many copies the book will sell when it is published or how much I will make because if times continue as they have been or get worse the sale will not be one-half as great as it would have been three or four years ago; but Perkins tells me I have a big reputation which of course I know nothing about, as I stay over here in Brooklyn all the time and have no way of finding out. Anyway if it will earn me a little money I shall be glad.

[3] Probably "No Door."

[4] Probably "Death—The Proud Brother" which was accepted as of March 13, 1933 and published in the June, 1933, issue of *Scribner's Magazine*. It was later included in *From Death to Morning*.

I hope this finds you and Ralph well, Mabel, and not worrying too much over the general state of affairs which cannot be helped. I shall get down to see you if for only a day or so while Mama is there and while I am very happy to have some good news to tell you, I do not think that I shall want to talk to you about the book when I come down, lest talking spoil the charm or hoodoo it, and also since I have it on my mind all the time, [I] would like to forget it for a little.

Good bye for the present and let me know what your additional plans are, if any. Meanwhile I send you all my love and best wishes for your health and success.

Wolfe's letter of February 20, 1933 to Lora French Simmons was in answer to the first he had received from her since 1920. She had heard of his success as a writer and had written to congratulate him.

To LORA FRENCH SIMMONS

Brooklyn, N. Y.

February 20, 1933

Dear Lora:

I was delighted to get your letter and of course I knew right away who it was because I looked at the signature first to see who it was in Los Angeles that would write me such a nice fat letter. . . . I do not understand how you could think that I would have any trouble remembering you, since I have thought of you hundreds of times and have often wondered what had happened to you during these years and if you have had from life the happiness and good fortune you deserve. . . . I see that you are married and I wonder if you have a family by this time, and I can tell by your letter that you are the same nice person that you always were, just as if you were talking to me. I think we wrote each other a few letters after you left Asheville and even after you went west, but I lost your address and was unable again to find it. Therefore to hear from you again is like getting back a friend that one thinks he has lost forever, and I hope now you will not forget me but write me a few lines every year or so and let me know how it goes with you. Yes, I remember almost everything that happened during those few weeks in Asheville, although I have forgotten about jumping across the hedge and tearing my trousers, but I remember that too, now that you mention it.[1]

[1] Mrs. French says that one evening in the summer of 1921, Wolfe had talked so long on the porch of the Asheville boarding-house where she was staying that the

I cannot tell you very much here about my life since then. I had much rather hear about yours. I can tell you that after I saw you I went to Harvard for three years, wandered about the country for a while, came here to New York and got a job teaching at New York University, went abroad and wandered around Europe, living in one country after another for three or four years, meanwhile coming back here to teach again when I had no money left, and finally after a great deal of confusion, unrest, lashing about and unhappiness, such as most young men know, I suppose, I began to find myself a few years ago and started to write. My first book was an enormously long book called "Look Homeward, Angel," which came out two or three years ago and was lucky enough to have a considerable success not only here but in Europe. . . . I do not think you had better read it because a great many people at home and in the South were shocked by it, although I had no idea anyone would be, and I had no intention of shocking or offending anyone.

Since then I have written several short novels, two of which came out in *Scribner's Magazine* last year. I was lucky enough to win the Scribner prize for the best short novel for one of these which came out in the April, 1932 issue. I have two or three more of these short things coming out in *Scribner's Magazine* this year . . . and at the present time I am working night and day as hard as I can getting another of these tremendous long books done. Scribners will bring it out in the fall and its present title is "Time and the River" [2] although, of course, that may be changed. This is all that I can tell you here. I work very hard and lead a very quiet life in Brooklyn and see almost nothing of the gay literary life that I hear so much about. I understand that my books have made a reputation, that I am considered a success, but I know almost nothing about this as I go around very little and work constantly. But when this next tremendous job is done I am going off on another big trip, probably to Europe first, but then if I make any money I am coming back to see some of the parts of this country which I have not explored. That means the West and when I do go West, I shall certainly look you up.

The Hollywood people have been after me the last year or so to go out and work for the movies and even offered me more money than I believed there was in the world. I suppose that is the reason that I did not take it. I could not believe it was true and besides I do not think that I could do anything for them that would be any good anyway, since I have always

---

landlady repeatedly came out and ordered him to leave. Finally at her command, he left precipitously, jumped a hedge, stumbled and tore the knee of his trousers, swore furiously, and was embarrassed about calling there again.

[2] Wolfe was still considering *Time and the River* as an alternate title for the whole of *The October Fair*.

had to write what I want to write and what I know about, and I would not know how to begin to write a movie.

I have spent all the money I have ever made but I do not worry much about money if I can only do a good piece of work, and perhaps if what I do is good, I will make some more money. This is all that I can write you for the present, and excuse me for talking so much about myself, but your letter was so kind and friendly and you seemed so glad to hear that I had had a little success that I wanted to tell you a little more about it. Just hope and pull for me to do a fine piece of work in this book because that means more to me than anything in the world right now, and I find that a man cannot be happy unless he can love and be proud of the work he does. And now, Lora, that I have gone and unloaded all this rather uninteresting information on you, I wish you would write and tell me about yourself, because, if you want to find out about me I hope some day you will find it in my books, if they are any good, but, if I want to find out about you and I do want to very much—you will have to write it to me or tell it to me yourself.

You know, of course, that I wish you all the happiness and good fortune it is possible for anyone to have. I was so happy to hear from you again and I now send to you my warmest regards and my best wishes for your health and success.

P.S. . . . Lora—you speak of me in your letter as being a tall and proud young man, when you knew me and when I was nineteen years old. Well, I am just as tall as ever, perhaps even a little taller. I do not think that I am so proud as I used to be, and in honesty I have got to add this note which just occurred to me as I closed the letter. I am afraid my appearance has changed a great deal since you saw me and probably not for the better, although I do not think I have changed much inside, and certainly not in the way I feel about an old friend. I have got very heavy, and people who meet me I find constantly speak of my gigantic and overwhelming size. Of course, I do not feel that way about it because I do not see myself the way others do but if I ever had even a very modest claim to good looks, and I do not think that I ever had, I am afraid that I have lost them all, and therefore, when I come knocking at your door in Los Angeles you must be prepared to see a great lumbering fellow about six feet five who weighs 235 pounds. I am sure that you are going to look just the same as you always did, except that I can tell by your letter that you have got better and better all the time. . . .

The following letter was written in reply to one from Donald V. Chacey, a naval aviator, praising Look Homeward, Angel.

To DONALD V. CHACEY

February 27, 1933.

Dear Mr. Chacey:

I do not suppose I answer one letter in a dozen, and I have always felt very bad about this because procrastination and good intentions I have not followed out are the reasons I do not answer them, but I am going to answer yours even if all I can do is to bang out a short note by way of thanks.

Your letter made me feel good because if my book was as you say, meat and drink to you and you read it seven times and further are not a literary fellow, and do not know anything more about me than what you found out in the book, or whether I got any success or reputation for it—then your kind of letter is also meat and drink to me, and would make anybody proud whoever wrote a book. Your letter also touched me up a bit and got me a little hot under the collar when you asked me if I was ever going to do it again, or if the old well had gone dry.

I will tell you the plain truth to start with which is—I will be damned if I know myself. The well certainly has not gone dry, in fact, I seem to have tapped a whole subterranean river and the water is spouting up in columns and geysers more than it ever did. But whether it will be that life-giving beverage which you liked so much in the first book I do not know, but I hope and believe it will be and my publisher also thinks so. At any rate, it will be out next autumn [1] if I can hold on long enough to finish it, and I hope when it comes out people like yourself who thought well of the first one will also like this one.

I realize that a flying officer writing such a letter as you did from his ship at sea does not do so because he belongs to one of the ten thousand literary gangs who live the cute, quaint, gossiping life of the literary gangster but for some better and more substantial reason, and that is the reason I am writing you this letter. You may wonder why anything in your letter should touch me up at all or get me a little hot under the collar, but let me put in to you this way. If at one time in your life you had gone up about 30,000 feet—that is a good height isn't it?—and your colleagues congratulated you and pounded you on the back when you came down, but at the same time asked you whether you would be able to get up to that height again, you might get a little hot too. But, at the same time you

---

[1] At this time, Wolfe and Perkins hoped that he could finish the book in time for publication in the fall of 1933.

might grind your teeth together and say: "I won't eh, well by God we'll see about that. I will show these birds, and just for that I am going to hit 35,000 feet next time."

Well Chacey, that is the way it is with a writer, except that with a writer much more I guess than with a flying man, he goes through periods of doubt, despair and confusion when he does not think he is worth a damn and never will be any good again, and this is particularly true of a young fellow who is just starting out and who has not tested his strength and resources far enough to understand fully what he can do or what his limits are. Also, 10,000 well-meaning people praise him, write him letters, call him on the telephone, etc., tell him what was wrong with his first book and what was right with it, and how to do it better the next time. Finally, after lashing and batting around like a mad man, tortured by all kinds of self-doubt and loss of confidence he may have sense enough to get away from all these clever minds and forget their good advice and lose himself somewhere out in the wilds of Brooklyn and work like hell twelve or fourteen hours a day doing his job as best he can in his way, which may not be a good way, but is the only way he knows and that is what I am doing now.

The book will be out next autumn. It will not be and never would have been called *K 19,* which was only the name of a section in it which an ambitious publicity man at Scribners picked up and sent out to the press.[2] The whole final and complete book, which I hope to live long enough to write will be called *October Fair,* but this present volume which we are trying to keep to 800 or 1000 pages long will be called, according to my present intention, *Time And The River.* . . .

This is all that I can write you, and I have written you at such length because I suppose it is for the respect and belief of such persons as yourself who have no literary ax to grind and no literary style to follow that a fellow like myself is writing. Also, I would like to say this. A flying man who hits 30,000 feet on one flight can probably hit 35,000 feet on his next big effort if he sets his mind and heart on it, but it does not always go so evenly as this with a writer. I hope and believe that I am going to hit that 35 the next time, but if I do not I hope I hit 25, and still believe there is a chance left for me to break the record some day. I have myself done considerable flying in my time and spent a good part of my life up in the air, but not in the way you have, although the way you do it is the way I have always wanted to do it.

Any way, as one flying man to another, I am writing you this letter and thank you for your own, and think that it did me good.

I send you my best wishes for your success in everything you do.

[2] In the margin opposite this sentence, Wolfe wrote in longhand: "I am sorry I put this in about *K 19* because it is not just the way it happened."

To GEORGE WALLACE

101 Columbia Heights
Brooklyn

March 9, 1933

Dear George:

I got your letter this morning and want to send this answer off right away. I will be delighted to see that the manuscript of your friend, . . . gets a good reading at Scribners. No, I don't think that this is a hell of a time to submit a book, but I do think that it would be a hell of a time to publish one. The faces around Scribners have looked pretty long and gloomy during the last month or two but, of course, that simply is part of the nation's history at present. The book business has been hit and hit hard, as has everything else, and I do believe that publishers have cut down their lists in a radical fashion, but of course they are just as anxious to get something good as they ever were. . . .

I just wanted to get this letter off to you before I get to work, so I won't write much more now. I was in a horrible, ugly and furious temper when you were down here, because after all my bloody sweating in the last two years I seemed to have gotten nowhere, and in fact, the whole game seemed to be lost. But just after you left in January I took a little trip to Baltimore and Washington, came back almost completely broke—in fact I was down to my last ten dollars and had no idea where any more was coming from—and in this mood I plunged into work and in the next month wrote over 100,000 words. I seemed suddenly to get what I have been trying to get for two years, the way to begin the book, and make it flow, and now it is all coming with a rush. Perkins says I have got it in the hollow of my hand: perhaps he said in the hollow of my head—I am not sure and beyond peradventure—that's a good word, isn't it, George. *Scribner's* have taken three very long sections out of the book which they propose to publish as stories beginning with the May issue,[1] for which they are paying me a very lousy price, unless I desert *Scribner's Magazine* and take them to an agent[2] who swears he can get two or three times as much for them. Anyway I am still hanging on by my toenails but a great deal happier and more hopeful than you have seen me in a long time, and I believe everything is going to be all right with us all and with the world.

I took three days off over the weekend and carted my weary bones to Washington where my mother, brother and sister were assembled to see Franklin D. inaugurated. I saw nothing but the back of my mother's

[1] "The Train and the City," "Death—the Proud Brother" and "No Door."
[2] Probably Ray Everett of Curtis Brown Ltd. Wolfe considered having them as his literary agents at this time but never did anything definite about it.

shoulders for three hours and forty minutes, but this was good enough, for I was determined that she should miss nothing and I worked her down into the damndest jammed crowd you ever saw, sent home to my sister's house for a chair, got Mama up in it and held her there. She saw the whole show and that was what we wanted.

Well, George, I do not know whether we will be using scrip or getting rations from the Government the next time we see each other, but if it comes to that, I hope we both fare well and get enough of both. . . . It was good to see you the last time, in spite of what justifiable doubts you may have on that score, but I assure you that what you saw was Mr. Hyde and that Dr. Jekyll has now broken the evil spell and is his affectionate and benevolent self again. . . .

Wolfe had always wanted to find out all he could about his paternal ancestors, and this interest had been intensified by his visit in October, 1932, to his father's birthplace, York Springs, Pennsylvania, where he had stayed with his uncle's widow, Mrs. Gilbert Wolf and his first cousin, Edgar E. Wolf. The following letter to Dr. Hiram Shenk of the Division of Archives and History at the Pennsylvania State Library in Harrisburg is the first of many inquiries which he wrote in an effort to trace the genealogy of his father's family.

To HIRAM H. SHENK

> 101 Columbia Heights
> Brooklyn, N.Y.
> April 3, 1933.

Dear Sir:

I write to inquire if you can give me certain information about members of my father's family who lived in Pennsylvania, or if you can tell me where to go to get such information.

My father, whose name was William Oliver Wolfe, was born about 1850 a few miles from the village of York Springs, Pa., and members of his family still live in that vicinity. It is concerning the origins of my father's mother and father that I am writing you.

My father's father was a farmer or a farm laborer, named Jacob Wolf (although the name apparently was spelled both Wolf and Wolfe by members of my father's family), and his mother was a woman named Eleanor Jane Heikes Wolf, and both of them are buried in the churchyard of the church at the little settlement of Lattimer or Lattimer's

Church, Pa., which is two or three miles from York Springs. I believe that the church belongs to the United Brethren or Brothers of Christ Sect, although I am not sure of this fact. The inscription on the grave of Jacob Wolf, my grandfather, reads that he died in 1860, aged about 54 years, but without giving the exact date or year of his birth. The information for my grandmother, Eleanor Jane Heikes Wolf is a little more exact for she lived to be 96 years old and died as recently as 1912 or 1913. I judge from these inscriptions my grandfather was born about 1806 and my grandmother some ten years later.

I visited York Springs last October and found some of my relatives living there and many people in the vicinity who remembered my grandmother very well. I found no one, however, who remembered my grandfather except one old man, who said he remembered my grandfather from his own childhood and remembered that my grandfather had sometimes worked on his father's farm as a laborer. He also said that my grandfather had several brothers and that they all came from the district around York Springs but he did not remember what had become of these other members of the family. I also learned that my grandmother had been born a few miles from York Springs. These were all the facts that I could find out.

I want very much to know more about these people, to find out if possible who their parents were and where they lived and how long this branch of my family has been in America. I should be very grateful to you if you could give me some information on these facts or tell me where I could find out about them. I am writing you because I understand your department has a very complete record of the histories of the people who settled in Pennsylvania and that if anyone had such information as I desire you would be most likely to have it.

With thanks for any assistance you may be able to give me

The letter below was written to Robert Raynolds about a poem of his entitled "In Memory of a Common Man," which he had sent to Wolfe in March.

To ROBERT RAYNOLDS

101 Columbia Heights
Brooklyn, N.Y.

April 3, 1933

Dear Bob:

. . . I have wanted to write you many times but I think the responsibility of writing you about your poem probably accounts for the delay.

I am glad to think you value anything I might say to you about a poem. It is true I have read and known a great deal of poetry but to speak of it critically and academically to scan its lines has always been too much even for my own audacity. Everything I know about poetry has come to me through a terribly long process of filtration and of living until the poem has become a part of what I have known and felt about life. I can never endure to hear a poem read, which seems a favorite occupation of young poetizers, nor did I ever feel competent to express honest judgement of any poem, particularly of any poem that was any good after a first reading. To me it is and always has been the most difficult kind of reading, just as it is the most difficult of writing, and the poems that I have liked the best and that have meant the most to me are those that meant nothing at all to me when I first read them. There is in the reading of every great poem a moment of discovery, which is just exactly as if you suddenly knocked a hole through a wall and suddenly found yourself inside of places you have never been before. I had this exact experience with a poem of John Keats when I was eighteen years old, and it was suddenly like being inside a country that I had never been in before, and the first time I understood and saw what the poem was about, although I must have read it a dozen times.

I liked your poem and the story that it told and the plainness and the sincerity with which you told it. This I can say to you honestly, without committing myself to dutiful criticism which I am not competent to make at the present time. As to whether its lines scan properly I did not notice or examine it for that purpose, neither does one I think examine the monologues of Robert Browning to see if they scan as he reads them, but I should think that many of them do not, and nevertheless are powerfully moving and beautiful, and are made of the stuff which is poetry.

I would rather talk to you about it when I see you. . . . Let me hear from you when you come to town, and if you can arrange to meet me for dinner at a fairly late hour, say nine o'clock, I should like to see you and talk to you. . . .

The following brief note was clipped to a few galleys of "Death—The Proud Brother."

To ALFRED DASHIELL

[March or April, 1933]

Dear Fritz:

I have done all that I can—and maybe more than I should. There is one short passage about Death which I have written in and which may be all right.

The other *long* passage which I have inserted in the Fifth Avenue scene I want you to look at very carefully. I think the idea and purpose of it is all right, but don't let me do anything here to hurt the story—my head is not good enough to-day to know whether I have or not.

I think these proofs ought to be read again.

The following note was clipped onto the first seven galleys of "No Door" and left on Dashiell's desk after the office had closed for the day.

To ALFRED DASHIELL

[May [?] 1933]

Dear Fritz:

I am leaving you the first seven galleys and will try to get the rest to you in the morning. I have gone stale on this thing and my head won't work for me—but this is the best that I can do at present—and here is what I have done and the way I feel about it:

(1) I have rewritten about 80 lines in galleys *four* and *five* and estimate that I have saved about 350 words. Get the girl [1] to type what I have written and then judge for yourself whether I have helped or harmed that section. You can cut the rewriting down all you can, but I feel the stuff on loneliness may set the mood for the scene that follows better than the present one.

(2) I think the prologue ought to stand *as is*.

(3) Of your minor cuts, I thought the most important one was the one about the drunken woman and the men who robbed her, and since I have already softened this I don't think it should be prettified any more and would like to see it included.

(4) Finally, if you can take my revision and cut it, if necessary, so that it would balance the needed cuts elsewhere, I would be grateful to you. —And if my revision will balance up your suggested cuts in these 7

[1] Elizabeth Nowell, who at that time was secretary to the editors of *Scribner's Magazine*.

galleys, I will take my chance on the rest and try to cut so as to include the little scene I showed you.

I have taken your own galleys beyond galley 7 to work on to-night.

To MABEL WOLFE WHEATON

[101 Columbia Heights]
[Brooklyn, N.Y.]
June 5, 1933

Dear Mabel:

Thanks for your letter. I am sorry you have been having so much trouble with your lodgers and suppose this is a difficult time for everyone, particularly people in your business.

I have managed to keep going so far but have been almost broke and have the money worry hanging over me all the time now. I never worried much before but now I do want to go ahead and do the kind of work for which I seem to be best fitted and which I want to do, and I do not see much prospect at the present time of getting much money out of it. Like you, I am very tired yet must go on somehow and try to finish this huge piece of work which has taken up all my life for two or three years. I dread this summer and have got to keep going. Maybe I shall get something from it some day. . . .

I agree with you when you say that bitterness is one of the things in life that kills and there is a grim justice in the fact that [it] kills most often those who let it feed upon them. There is another thing in life that is hard to bear that fortunately you do not know much about—that is loneliness. If you have time and are interested in knowing anything about my own life for the last ten or fifteen years, you might look at a piece I have written for the next number of *Scribner's*.[1] Some of them think that it is the best piece I have ever written. I do not know about that. But, a little of my life went into it.

I think I learned about being alone when I was a child about eight years old and I think that I have known about it ever since. People, I think, mean well by children but are often cruel because of something insensitive or cruel in their own natures which they cannot help. It is not a good thing, however, for older people to tell a little child that he is selfish, unnatural and inferior to the other members of his family in qualities of generosity and nobility, because a child is small and helpless and has no defence, and although he is no worse than other children, and

[1] "No Door" in the July issue of *Scribner's*.

in fact is as full of affection, love and good-will as anyone could be, he may in time come to believe the things which are told him about himself, and that is when he begins to live alone and wants to be alone and if possible to get far, far away from the people who have told him how much better they are than he is. I can truthfully and sincerely say that I have no bitterness and nothing but pity for anyone who ever did that, but I can also say that the habit of loneliness, once formed, grows on a man from year to year and he wanders across the face of the earth and has no home and is an exile, and he is never able to break out of the prison of his own loneliness again, no matter how much he wants to.

So with all your troubles and misfortunes of the last few years you can be thankful being alone has not been one of them. I wish for you and for us all some new and wonderful happiness and success which will compensate us for all we have lost and suffered, and somehow, I believe it will yet come to us. I have led about as solitary a life as anyone could, yet I have felt much closer to people in the last two or three years than I ever did in my life before, and the misfortune and suffering everywhere around me has touched me more than it ever did before. I really think, without knowing why I think so, that better days are ahead of us and that if we go on with faith and courage we will gain a little of the security and happiness we all need. . . .

I send you all my best wishes, as always, for your health and success in everything you do, and hope we will all get together before long and at a more fortunate and happy time.

To ROBERT RAYNOLDS

101 Columbia Heights
Brooklyn, N.Y.

June 5, 1933

Dear Bob:

Thanks for your letter and for what you say about "Death the Proud Brother." It made me feel good and compensates for all the bloody sweat of writing to know that someone likes something you have done. I have another coming out next month [1] which they think may be the best of the lot, and I hope they are right, for it caused me enough anguish and groans before I was done with it. I finally got it cut down from something over fifty thousand words to about eighteen or twenty thousand, but some of the things which were left out are now painful to think about.

These pieces are only a small fraction of all the work I have done in the

---

[1] "No Door."

last two or three years and I hope some day to get most of the rest of it published. I have put myself into them and tried to do the best I can, and although I want to get better and learn more all the time, I should like to have the kind of relief, the sense of having cleared something out of my mind, that publication gives me. Today we have been tying together great bundles of manuscript which I am going to give away to someone or send away to-morrow to Scribners, I think, simply because I cannot bear to look at it any more. I have, I think, a typed copy of everything I am sending away, which is written in my own hand and which is a formidable amount of writing, enough to fill to overflowing a box four feet long by two or three feet high, but I will be relieved to get it out of the house.

I am delighted to know that you have been getting so much work done and I think to complete and get ready for publishers a manuscript of ninety thousand words in two months time is a remarkable performance. I wish you all good luck with it, and hope to hear more about it the next time you come to town. . . .

To JOHN HALL WHEELOCK

[101 Columbia Heights]
[Brooklyn, N.Y.]
June 14, 1933

Dear Jack:

I want to thank you for your kind and generous letter about my story.[1] It did me so much good to know you feel that way about it because I had worried considerably the last day or two about sections which had to come out on account of space, and I was afraid so many cuts had been made that the completeness and substance of the story had been hurt by it. In that story I was really trying to say something which comes from a deep place in my life and which I think will color almost everything I do for years to come.

It makes me so happy that I succeeded with you and Max in saying what I wanted to say, because there are no other two people in the world whose judgment and good opinion mean as much to me as yours. So thanks again for writing me as you did. I value these fine letters of yours, and particularly this last one and your belief in what I do, more than I can put down here in words.

As I have told you before, I have read some of your poems so often

_____
[1] "No Door."

in the last two or three years and have been so deeply impressed by some of them that I am sure they have passed into my own work, and if you come upon evidences of that theft I want you to believe that it was done unconsciously, and all I can hope is that it was sometimes done worthily.

I want to come in and talk to you the next time I go to the office. Meanwhile, with all my thanks again and best wishes to you,

Alfred Dashiell had sent Wolfe a letter written to Scribner's Magazine *by Donald V. Chacey in praise of the stories of Wolfe's which they were publishing. With it, Dashiell had sent a covering letter of his own, saying: "This is the way people feel about you. It is the expression of thousands who don't write. Why then should there ever come to you moments of doubt? . . . Or suspicions that people are likely to betray you? You are what you are. You can not be betrayed. . . . You have a triumph awaiting you and you should not be kept from your reward by a perturbed spirit." The following was Wolfe's reply.*

To ALFRED DASHIELL

June 28, 1933.

Dear Fritz:

Thanks for your letter and for the enclosed letter from Chacey which I am returning to you. It is certainly a heartening and splendid thing to know that anyone feels this way about one's work.

I won't say anything more about the letter now because I have just been talking to you over the telephone and said some of the things that I was going to write. Yes, I think that it would be an excellent idea to ask him, when you answer his letter, if he has ever written anything about flying or his own experiences and why he does not send it in to you. If a flying man could really put down the sensation and experience of flying in such a way as to make the rest of us feel it, I for one would be intensely interested in reading what he had to say. Of course we do not know whether he has the gift of putting such an experience into words, but it is a hunch and it could do no harm to follow it.

I cannot tell you how much good it does me to know that such a person, whose interests are so remote from a literary life and who leads, as he says, a life of action, should think so well of what I do. While I have never felt that a man could do his best work for the huge public and that all good writing is in a way limited to a special and almost indefinable public, my feeling nevertheless is very strong that the best writing is not a precious thing and not limited to a little group of adepts and professional critics. In other words, I think there is scattered throughout the world the kind of public which this man represents, which is that limited and yet hearteningly numerous group of people of fine feeling and intelligence and unprofessional appreciation. Somehow I really feel that the real mark of a writer's merit and the real measure of his success comes in the end far more from these people than from the professional literary critic, and that it is really for the respect and belief of this unseen and unknown audience that a man instinctively does his work, and that is the reason I put such a high value on a letter like this one. . . .

Last of all, Fritz, I want to thank you for your own letter which you sent along with Chacey's. I am not only deeply and sincerely grateful for what you say but I have also taken it to heart and recognize the truth of it. All I can say to you here is that the effort of writing or creating something seems to start up a strange and bewildering conflict in the man who does it, and this conflict at times almost takes on physical proportions so that he feels he is struggling not only with his own work but also with the whole world around him, and he is so beset with demons, nightmares, delusions and bewilderments that he lashes out at everyone and everything, not only people he dislikes and mistrusts, but sorrowfully enough, even against the people that he knows in his innermost heart are his true friends.

I cannot tell you how completely and deeply conscious I have been of this thing and how much bloody anguish I have sweat and suffered when I have exorcised these monstrous phantoms and seen clearly into what kind of folly and madness they have led me. But I really think that even at the worst and craziest time of conflict and delusion, we retain the saving grain of truth and judgment somewhere within us which keeps us from going completely out of our head. This is as near as I can come at present to telling you about it. But I live constantly in the hope, and I have never lost it, that a man can make his life better and cure himself of some of his grievous errors. In my good moments I do not believe any man on earth values the friendship and affection of his friends more than I, and desires more earnestly to be worthy of their belief and is more cruelly tormented when he thinks he has misused them.

At the present time, however, I have given up cursing the iniquities of mankind and am venting my curses on the weather, and even feel a great surge of brotherly love and sympathy when I think of my eight million fellow atoms who are forced to sweat, melt, and swelter their miserable way through the glutinous and interminable horror of a New

York summer. If it would only turn cool again I think I could love everyone, even Mrs. Ella Boole.[1]

I will come in to talk to you about the story in a day or two.[2]

*The following letter from Wolfe to his boyhood friend, Leroy Dock, was
evidently written during one of his intense fits of homesickness for the mountains of western North Carolina. He never did go back to stay at Balsam, but
finally rented a cabin at Oteen, N.C. in 1937.*

To LEROY DOCK

[Brooklyn, N.Y.]

June 29, 1933.

Dear Roy:

I want to write you before you go away to tell you how glad I was to
see you again and how much I enjoyed our talk and lunch together. . . .
I did not get to talk to you very much about Balsam and, as I said, it looks
at present as if I will have to be here most of the summer into the autumn,
but I am really thinking not only of a short vacation but also of a possible
future when I speak to you of Balsam. I suppose if I came for a week or
two I could put up somewhere without much difficulty, but I should also
be grateful, Roy, if you would write me after you get down there and tell
me if you know of any available shacks or cabins that would do for a
fellow who does not have much money and is not too particular about comfort and modern conveniences. Of course, I should like electric lights, if I
can have them, because I am used to working by them, and plumbing
and cooking arrangements—my cooking is confined largely to making
several pots of strong black coffee a day—would be desirable if I could
afford them. Finally, when I work I like three things very much: coolness,
quietness, and solitude.

I have been alone very much in my life that I am afraid loneliness has
become a habit with me now and it is certainly essential when I write. Yet,
I like the companionship of people as well as anyone and sometimes miss

---

[1] The late head of the W.C.T.U.

[2] Dashiell had written: "I'll talk to you about 'Exile' when I see you. I think something can be made of it." Perhaps this was an early title for "Dark in the Forest:
Strange as Time," or "Dark October." The latter was never actually published in any
magazine but appears, with changes and additions, on pages 353–404 of *Of Time and
the River.*

it desperately, and that is one reason I feel warmly about Balsam because I think my mountain blood has given me some of the same qualities as those mountain people there have—that is, we like to be alone part of the time and yet we like friendship too. I think you are that way yourself and I know you will understand it.

You spoke to me about a colony of cabins which some Daytona people had built there. I wonder if you could tell me what these cabins are like, how they are built and equipped, if any of them is for rent or sale and how much the rent or cost of such a place would be. I know that this is a hell of a lot to ask, but I am really seriously interested in this thing even if there is no immediate prospect of my doing it, but I think there is a very decided prospect of my doing it in the next year or two.

As I told you, after so many years of wandering about the world the pull towards some sort of established place and towards some sort of place where a man feels at home and among scenes and people who are familiar to him becomes very strong, and although I have seen many cities and many strange and beautiful places in the last ten years I have had that feeling of familiarity and home only in two places. One is the country where I was born, western North Carolina, and the other my father's country, among the farms and orchards of the Pennsylvania Dutch in southern Pennsylvania. I have an idea that some day I am going back to one of these two places. I have never forgotten my stay with you in Balsam, thirteen years ago,[1] and how kind and friendly the people were and what a grand and familiar place it seemed to be. It sometimes seems that it could not have been as good as I imagine it and I know I was only a kid then and full of a kid's dreams and visions about the world and maybe that is why Balsam seemed so wonderful a place. But I don't think I was mistaken about it and I am going back again to find out. Meanwhile, if you can give me any information about some of these things I have mentioned I will be sincerely grateful to you. . . .

The following letter was written in answer to one from Arthur Palmer Hudson, folklorist and Professor of English at the University of North Carolina, who was making a study of folksongs in the work of various contemporary Southern writers for his article, "The Singing South," which appeared in the July, 1936, issue of the Sewanee Review.

[1] Wolfe had visited Dock in Balsam in 1920, before he went north to enter Harvard.

To ARTHUR PALMER HUDSON

July 11, 1933.

Dear Mr. Hudson:

Thanks very much for your letter of July 8th. I have looked up your references to song-tags in *Look Homeward, Angel* and found all of them excepting the one you mention on page 288. I should be glad to help you in any way I can because your subject interests me and I recognize its value but I must admit that my knowledge of folk song, if by folk song you mean such songs as the southern mountain people have sung for generations, is very slight, or if anything I have written shows traces of such knowledge I was not conscious of it and simply absorbed it with a million other memories and sensuous impressions in childhood. I was born in Asheville and although my mother's family have lived in the hills of western North Carolina for a very long time, my own experience as a child was probably more the experience of a boy in a fair-sized American town than anything else.

The reason your subject interests me is that songs of all kinds more than almost anything else, except odors, can evoke the memory of some lost or forgotten moment of childhood with a literal and blazing intensity that makes the whole thing live again. But these songs, I am afraid are not folk songs but simply popular songs like, "Has Anybody Here seen Kelly," "Yip I addy I Aye," "Tammany," "Take Me Out To The Ball Game," "Love Me And The World Is Mine," "K-K-K-Katy," "Alexander's Rag Time Band," and so on. Many of them, I am afraid, are very trashy songs but able to make me live again some night in summer twenty or twenty-five years ago and hear the people talk on their porches, or my father's voice, and smell the earth, the honeysuckle vines, the geranium beds and live, hear, and see everything again, as nothing else on earth could do.

This is all that I can write you for the present. If I had time and it would be of any interest or value to you I should be glad to tell you about many of these songs and the memories they evoke and the meanings they have for me, not only the popular song hits of the time but also all those scraps and fragments and chants of songs that children use, such as

"I asked my mother for fifteen cents
 To see the elephant jump the fence."

and that came from God knows where. But I am afraid that none of these were folk songs, unless my understanding of a folk song is amiss. I wish I had known more of the songs you write about. What I have heard in recent years of the songs that mountain people sang makes me sorry that I missed it as a child. . . .

I am afraid that I have not been able to help you very much but I thank you again for writing and wish you the best success with your study.

Percy Mackaye, author of The Canterbury Pilgrims, Jeanne d'Arc, The Scarecrow, My Lady Dear, Arise, The Mystery of Hamlet, King of Denmark, *etc., had written Wolfe, saying: "From a quiet niche in your own mountains —your incomparable, tumultuous, earth-drinking, star-brooding peaks of the spirit—I write you this word of true gratitude that at last, in unspoiled words which are their counterparts, you have made them articulate with their own grandeur and fecundity. You have done so in 'The Train and the City,' which is for all time one of their first inspired scriptures." He had also written to John Hall Wheelock of Scribners, saying: "The work of Thomas Wolfe . . . seems to me a colossal landmark in our poetic literature, for it is all quintessential poetry, both prodigious and delicate in power." The following is Wolfe's letter of thanks to Mackaye.*

To PERCY MACKAYE

July 19, 1933.

Dear Mr. Mackaye:

. . . I cannot tell you how happy your letters have made not only me but my friends Jack Wheelock and Maxwell Perkins at Scribners. Wheelock was so pleased about your letter to him that he wrote me quoting a long excerpt from it. He is one of the kindest and most gentle people I have ever known, a man of deep feeling and I think of high poetic gift and his respect for you and the value he puts upon your judgment are immense.

I don't know if you know Mr. Perkins but I think he has met you. At any rate he has seen you and remembers you and was delighted with your letter. He is a great editor and in a quiet, devious and unobtrusive fashion, most completely his own man, I think the most extraordinary individual I have ever known. He was more delighted with your letters than if there had been a big sale for a book, and made one of his characteristic comments which never seem to get at things in the usual way and seem simple and almost irrelevant and really go right to the heart of a thing. I think he said he knew you and had talked to you, but the thing he did say was that anyone who saw your face would not forget you and would know that they were looking at *somebody* when they saw you. Knowing how to translate his reticence in my own way now, I realize this is about as great a tribute as could be paid to anyone.

It is a very fine thing for me to know that a man of your position and maturity has kept his spirit as flexible, young, and generous as it ever was and is able and happy to give the work a young man does heartening and unstinted praise. I hope that my own spirit will always be young and generous in just that way, for that, it seems to me, is the sinew, the blood, the living integument of life and passion that flows from one generation to another and that can keep the world alive.

I wish I could make the trip to Marion, Virginia with you in August.[1] I should be delighted to see a thing like that which would be new to my experience and if by any chance I come home about that time I think I would ask you if I could go along with you, but if I don't see you this summer or go home in the autumn I hope you will let me know when you are coming to New York and I will look forward with hope to seeing you then.

Meanwhile all I can do is send you again thanks for your grand letters of friendship and generous enthusiasm. I cannot hope to equal those letters in any way except with the warmth and sincerity of my grateful thanks. That I can offer and give to you, and I send it now with all my heart.

Wolfe wrote the following letter to the editors of various quality magazines in an attempt to find a wider field than Scribner's *for the sale of his short stories. However, several of the editors answered that pieces of ten to thirty thousand words were too long for short stories, although they might be publishable as novelettes or serials. This discouraged Wolfe: he did not submit any manuscripts himself but renewed his efforts to find a literary agent.*

To THE EDITORS OF *HARPER'S MAGAZINE,* THE *FORUM,* THE *AMERICAN MERCURY* AND THE *ATLANTIC MONTHLY*

[101 Columbia Heights]
[Brooklyn, N.Y.]
[August, 1933]

Dear Sir:

I am writing to inquire if your magazine ever publishes stories that are from ten to thirty thousand words in length and if you would care to

[1] Mackaye had invited Wolfe to attend with him a folk festival of fiddlers and ballad singers to be held on White Top Mountain near Marion.

consider, with a view to publication, some stories of that length which I have written.

I have published a book and have had several of these stories published in *Scribner's Magazine* during the past year but I have never yet sent a manuscript to anyone save *Scribner's Magazine,* because I did not know whether any other publication would care to publish pieces of such length. The stories I would send you have never been shown or submitted to *Scribner's Magazine,* or anyone else, and I want to send them to other publications now not only because I need money but because I think it would be a good thing for me if I could get something published in some magazine other than *Scribner's.* If I can get them published I should like to have each of them published as a unit and not in separate installments.

I now have several of these long pieces on hand and I should be grateful to you if you would let me know whether you care to see them or whether the policy of your magazine is against the publication of pieces of such length.

To MAXWELL E. PERKINS

[101 Columbia Heights]
[Brooklyn]

August 8, 1933

Dear Max:

In last Sunday's book section of *The New York Times* there was a favorable notice about the reception of "Look Homeward, Angel" in one of the Scandinavian countries—Sweden, I think. I think some sort of publicity also should be given to the fact that the book got fine reviews in Germany.[1] Jack Wheelock read me the advertisements the German publishers sent me and the excerpts which they used from some of the leading papers of Germany, Austria and Switzerland, which are as good or better than anything I ever got in this country. Why should we conceal this fact? I notice that publishers of other writers use foreign reviews which cannot touch these notices, and make full use of any favorable foreign publicity they get. The publicity I kicked about was that which seemed to me to be personal and gossipy and irrelevant and not substantiated by fact,[2] but I see no reason at all to be ashamed of the fact that my book got fine reviews in Germany and Austria, and I do not see why that is not publicity which could be honorably and creditably used.

Therefore, since we both hope that I may again come through some

[1] *Look Homeward, Angel* had been published in Sweden by Albert Bonniers Forlag, and in Germany by Rowohlt Verlag.

[2] See Wolfe's letter to Perkins of August 29, 1931.

day with a solid achievement and that you may profit from your investment in me, why not make use now of what is honestly our own and
what we might use to our advantage?

I am completing another section of my book which will be called "The
Hills Beyond Pentland," [3] and which, I think, in some ways may be as
good as anything I have done.

I will come in to see you in a few days.

To PERCY MACKAYE

[Brooklyn, N.Y.]

August 17, 1933.

Dear Mr. Mackaye:

Thanks very much for your recent letter. By now I suppose you have
returned from the song festival in Virginia which I should so much have
liked to attend.

Of course I know about George Grey Barnard and his work, although
I have never met him. I think I shall follow your suggestion and go to
see him some day, although I may not be able to demand to see him in
the same superb way he demanded to see his old friend Michelangelo,[1]
and I may, therefore, mention your own name when I go.

It is a fine thing for a young man when he meets a great old man, because I think we never lose entirely the hope that we have in childhood
and that persists strongly in the first years of our youth that we will meet
someone of such invincible strength and wisdom and experience that all
the grief and error in our own lives will be resolved by him. Perhaps this
is a deplorable weakness, but if it is it is certainly one that all humanity
shares in to some extent, and although I now know that we must find the
remedy for our own error in ourselves and get out of our own lives the
power to live by, and that there is no one on earth who can speak a word

---

[3] Only a few portions of *The Hills Beyond Pentland* were ever written, and most of
these were used in Wolfe's other novels. This book was planned to tell the history of
Mrs. Wolfe's family who had lived in the mountains of North Carolina since the Revolution.

[1] Mackaye had suggested that Wolfe call on Barnard, saying: "If this were the
Florentine era, you might just as well keep from going to see Michel Angelo in his
workshop at Florence, as keep from going to see Barnard in *his*, at New York. . . .
So, at the first opportunity, I hope you will stick this letter in your pocket (by way of
an introduction—though really needless) and . . . walk in on him there. If anyone
should intervene, just say quietly: 'You don't understand; I've come to see my friend,
Barnard; I've known him for several hundred years.' For that's exactly what *he* said to
the doorkeeper of the Sistine Chapel (substituting Michel Angelo for Barnard) when
he first called there, to commune with his old friend."

so magical as to release us from the confusion, struggle and bewilderment in our own spirit, I still feel always a great awakening of power and hope and joy when I meet a man like this, whose whole life is an act of faith and who has lived and worked with such grand fortitude.

If I do not get to see him myself this summer perhaps when you come to town you would take me out to meet him. I am going away somewhere in October and may come home, and if you are still there [2] I will come to see you. If you come to New York before that time won't you let me know? Meanwhile, I send you again my wishes for your health and happiness in all you do.

To ROBERT RAYNOLDS

101 Columbia Heights
Brooklyn, N.Y.

August 29, 1933

Dear Bob:

I haven't had my typist here in a week—hence my lazy failure in writing you. It was so nice being out there at your place—I think the place is magnificent and have never seen a finer family and such affectionate children. Can I come again and stay *two* days—and when can I come? If I come can we have some more hot cakes?—they seemed about the best I'd ever eaten.

I am doing a very exciting piece of writing—at least it's exciting to me, so much so that I'm in a delirious mental state and a horrible physical condition—a sort of cross between delirium tremens and Olympian calm. Sometimes when I'm working at it I think it's going to be so good I almost cry about it but when I'm not working at it I curse God, men, and everything. I'm calling my piece, which like everything else is a section of the fury theme,—"The Image of Fury in the Artist's Youth"—is this a good or lousy title? I just slapped it down, so it can be changed, and thought of "In the Artist's Youth" as a subtitle and not really essential to it. Anyway it's about Fury, not especially artist's fury, but the kind of fury young men have, probably more in this country than anywhere on earth —the madness, exulting, desire to eat and drink the earth, getting into the wind on lonely roads, etc.—and it starts in just about the most furious way it can, on a train smashing northwards across the State of Virginia at night with three drunken youths, as drunk with the exultant fact and fury of going to the city for the first time, out to conquer the world, do everything, see all, etc., as with the corn liquor they keep passing from

[2] Mackaye was living in Arden, North Carolina, at this time.

hand to hand.[1] The thing starts out on the end platform of the pullman car, singing, roaring, bellowing with laughter, full of the illusion of power —a wild, mad, profane and bawdy scene all mixed up with the rhythms of the wheels, the thousand sounds the train makes, the immortal pulse and eternity of the earth outside against this projectile, of fury, youth, the brevity of man's days, illusions, thoughts of power, all the tones, moods, and haunting memories the motion of the train induces in him; and finally sleep and one of the sleepers, lying in his berth not asleep but in that strange coma mixed of dreams and visions with the dark mysterious earth floating past him, finally before he sleeps a vision of two horsemen riding abreast the train over the dark earth, keeping time now to the rhythmical pounding of the wheels, with a kind of hypnotic chant about

> Lean Death and Pale Pity
> Rode out for to take
> A City a City
> Pale Death Awoke and Lean Pity
> Rode out for a City
> Rode out for a City to take—etc.

Anyway, I know it's true, the way I have felt, the way we all have felt, and I hope they publish it and the damned fools don't put it down as wild ravings, freak eccentricity, etc., I am trying to do in my limited way what the great men have done—not reality as facts literally reproduced, but reality as facts absorbed, undeniable, fused into an image—here in image of train, youth filled with all the fury of its power and joy and faith— which may not be like any one train or any group to be met on trains, but more like the basic human experience than any average of facts could be. I know it's true because I've lived it, felt it, made it part of me. Now I hope it will be good as well. This is the first time I've told anyone about anything I'm writing in years. That in itself is a youthful thing to do— the longing to display your wares before [they're built?]. So don't tell on me. The train part is only one small part. I hope to see you soon. . . .

To FREDERICK H. KOCH

[5 Montague Terrace]
[Brooklyn, N.Y.]
October 9, 1933

Dear Professor Koch:

Thanks very much for your letter of September 22nd and for the attached check for four dollars as royalty on "The Return of Buck Gavin." [1]

[1] This episode appears in *Of Time and the River* on pages 69–76.
[1] In *Carolina Folk Plays, Second Series*.

. . . I want to say something to you now about this play for which you have sent me the royalty check. If I thought for a moment there was any danger of my being misunderstood, I would not say it, but I have known you for fifteen years and I feel that I know you pretty well by now, and I know you are my friend and will understand what I want to say. And what I want to say is this:

I am very proud to call myself one of the Playmakers and to remember that I belonged to the first group you ever taught at Chapel Hill, and had a part in writing and producing some of the first plays. I want to tell you also that no one is prouder than I of the great success the Playmakers have achieved and of the distinguished work which has been done by them. The fact that I was associated with that work at its very beginning, even in an obscure and unimportant fashion, is another fact I am proud of. I am also proud to remember that two little one-act plays [2] that I wrote were among the first plays put on by the Playmakers and that I acted in them and helped produce them. I was a boy of eighteen years when I wrote those plays, and I wrote each of them in a few hours because I did not then understand what heart-breaking and agonizing work writing is, and I think those plays show this and are fair samples of the work of a boy who did not know what hard work was and who wrote them in a few hours. But I do not think they are fair samples of the best which the Playmakers can do and have done, nor of the best in me. I therefore want to ask you, as my old friend who will not misunderstand my plain and sincere feeling in this matter, that you do not allow either of these plays to be used again for production. I should like to be remembered as a Playmaker and as one who had the honor to be a member of that pioneer first group, but I do not want to be remembered for the work which a careless boy did.

Will you believe me and understand my feeling in this matter, and believe me to be as well your friend, and one who is proud to know that he was once a member of a group which has done so many fine and memorable things since? And understanding this, will you do as I ask in this matter?

Meanwhile, dear Prof, I send you, as always, my best wishes for your health and success in everything you do. Please let me know when you are coming to New York.

Ever since the expiration of his Guggenheim Fellowship in 1931, Wolfe had been living on the royalties from Look Homeward, Angel *and the money*

[2] *The Return of Buck Gavin* and *The Third Night.*

he received for stories from Scribner's Magazine. *He worried constantly about his finances, and in the following letter he approached the Guggenheim Foundation through Henry Allen Moe, its Secretary, concerning a renewal of his fellowship. However, his application was finally turned down.*

To HENRY ALLEN MOE

5 Montague Terrace
Brooklyn, N.Y.
November 15, 1933

Dear Mr. Moe:

I am writing to inquire if there would be any hope of my obtaining further help of the Guggenheim Foundation, to tell you something of the work that I have been doing and to ask if you would be interested in having me come to see you and show it to you.

During the past three and one-half years since I received the Guggenheim award, I have published in *Scribner's Magazine* two short novels, "The Web of Earth" and "A Portrait of Bascom Hawke" which divided the prize at *Scribner's Magazine* offered for the best short novel in 1932. In addition to this, there have been published in *Scribner's Magazine* this year three long pieces, "The Train and the City," "Death the Proud Brother" and "No Door." Scribner's have just taken from me two more pieces, the first of which is to be published in *Scribner's Magazine* in February, and the other in the succeeding number.[1]

All of these pieces, except the two short novels, have been taken from the book, or rather series of books, on which I have been working for the last four years, which have the inclusive title, "Time and the River." During the past four years I have written over a million words, most of which I now have in typed manuscript, and can show to you. The book, when completed, will be one of the longest books I suppose anyone ever attempted, and of course I will then have to face the problem of revision and cutting with the publishers, but the only thing I can do now, the only thing I know how to do, is to go ahead in my own way until I reach the end.

Of course, I can not judge now the merit of the book, but I do believe, and Mr. Perkins, the editor at Scribners believes, that it contains the best work I have ever done, and all my time and life and energy for several years now have been given to doing it. The only source of income

[1] These were probably "The Four Lost Men" which was published in the February, 1934, issue of *Scribner's*, and "Dark in the Forest, Strange as Time" which was published in the November, 1934, issue. Both of these stories were later included in *From Death to Morning*.

I have at the present time comes from the sale of these pieces to *Scribner's Magazine.* I have no knowledge of any other publishers or magazines besides Scribners and I have no time to try to market any of my unpublished manuscript at the present time to other magazines, even if I knew where to take them. Moreover, I do not know of any other magazine which would print pieces of such length as my stories which have been published in *Scribner's,* all of which, with one exception, were from 20,000 to 35,000 words long. Scribners tell me they propose to bring out a limited edition of one of these pieces, "No Door," which appeared in *Scribner's Magazine* in abbreviated form, and which will be published in the limited edition in its original length of 30,000 to 40,000 words some time in the spring.[2] From this they tell me I may hope to get a little money, $400.00 or $500.00.

There are also the two pieces I mentioned to you which they have taken, and which will come out in the magazine in a month or two. This is all I have to live on at present, unless I can sell something else out of the manuscript I have on hand.

Meanwhile, I am going ahead at full speed on the first part of "Time and the River." The first part is a tremendously long and complete novel in itself, and has the title "The October Fair." If I keep going at my present speed, I will finish it this winter and I already have almost a complete draft of the second part, which has at present the tentative title of "Hills beyond Pentland."

I don't believe I ever did better work than I am doing at present. I think Mr. Perkins and other people who have seen the manuscript and read some of the stories in *Scribner's* will agree to this and I am also willing to show you what I have done if you would care to see it. My difficulty of course is one of enormous length and completeness. I suppose what I should like to do would be to write a book that filled a library, but anyway, this is the only way I can do it, and if I didn't believe it was worth doing, I wouldn't live and work as I do.

I have told you the plain truth about the situation so far as I can in a letter and although I hope and we all hope that I may some day get some sort of reward and security from all this work that I have done, I am really hard up and badly in need of money at the present time and have been, in fact, badly worried about the immediate future until the other day when I sold those stories.

I should appreciate it if you would write me and let me know if you would care to talk to me and see some of this work I have been doing, and if there is any hope of my getting additional help from the Fund.

[2] The proposed limited edition of "No Door" was never published.

The following letter to Belinda Jelliffe, the wife of the psychiatrist, Dr.
Smith Ely Jelliffe, was written in reply to one from her expressing admiration
for Wolfe's work. With Wolfe's and Perkins' encouragement, Mrs. Jelliffe
later wrote an autobiographical novel, For Dear Life, *which was published*
by Scribners in 1936.

To BELINDA JELLIFFE

5 Montague Terrace
Brooklyn, N.Y.
November 21, 1933

Dear Mrs. Jelliffe:

Thanks very much for your kind letter. Anyone would be proud and
happy to know that something he has done has meant so much to any
reader. You say I may not care what you or the world thinks of me and
my work, but you would be wrong in thinking so. I assure you I am by no
means immune to what you and the world may think. In fact, I am about
as far from such an impassive and negligent assurance as anyone could
be, and have even been too much concerned about what people said and
thought, or, what was worse, with what I thought they said and thought.
But it is true that when I am at work I do not think much about anything
else and I guess it is a good thing for me that this is so.

Perhaps some people who have been unwise, furious and bewildered,
ruinously wasteful of their own and other people's lives, and tormented
and pursued by all sorts of demons, phantoms, monsters and delusions of
their own creation, may get out of the work they do the certitude and
truth that has escaped them elsewhere. This may be true of me. At any
rate, when I work I am happiest, and although I do not think of other
things and people very much when I am working, I work because the
strongest and highest wish I have ever known is to do the best work that
is in me to do, and the reason I wish to do this is to communicate it to
other people, and I want to communicate it to other people because I
want to make my life prevail, to win the fame, the high esteem, the rare
and fine success for which a young man hopes and works. If anyone says
that this desire has nothing to do with his own work, I think he speaks
falsely and with evident hypocrisy.

For these reasons, I am not indifferent to what you and the world may
think or say about my work, but am proud and happy when I get such a
letter as you wrote me, and thank you gratefully again for writing it.

Dr. Arthur C. Jacobson, to whom the following letter was written, was Wolfe's physician during the time he lived in Brooklyn, and also his personal friend. Wolfe had told him of his interest in the history of his father's people: also of his bewilderment and irritation at the rumor that they were of part-Jewish descent. Dr. Jacobson at that time was doing research in other Pennsylvania-German genealogies, and in the course of it found that a Hans Georg Wolff and Hans Bernhard Wolff had come to Philadelphia in 1727 on the ship William and Sarah. *He accordingly had written Wolfe this information and suggested that he consult the records of the Genealogical Society of Pennsylvania for further facts. However, Wolfe seems never to have got around to doing this.*

To ARTHUR C. JACOBSON

5 Montague Terrace,
Brooklyn, New York
November 25, 1933

Dear Dr. Jacobson:

Thanks very much for the references you sent me and the information contained in them. I think almost certainly you have given me the most accurate information that I have ever had about my father's people. I feel sure that with these references and other information which I have, I can now trace the origins of his family in America. Of course, the members of his family who are still living down in Adams County, Pennsylvania, have told me a good deal from what they remember and what their parents and grand-parents told them, but like most people out in the country, they have kept few records except a few letters and inscriptions in the bible, etc., and I could never go back before 1806–7, which was about the time of my grandfather's birth, although they told me where he was born, and that means there were other members of his family there before him.

Is it not a strange and wonderful thing to weave back through the past and find out where you come from? And it seems especially strange and wonderful here in America, which is such an immense and lonely country and still so like a wilderness. Most of our lives here have been so nameless and obscure and governed by blind chance. A boy grows up upon a little farm in Southern Pennsylvania. When he is fourteen or fifteen, after the Civil War, he goes to Baltimore, becomes apprenticed to a stone-cutter there, and after five years, becomes a stone-cutter himself. Four of my father's brothers followed him in this stone-cutter's trade, and that also has seemed strange to me because all of them were farming people before that.

And, still by accident, chance and the opportunity of the moment, he drifts off and after several years, he got up into the Western part of North Carolina where my mother's people came from, although where they came from before that I don't know. They were mountain people and had lived there as long as anyone. And then you send me a letter and tell me that the first of my father's family may have come over here in a ship called the William and Sarah, sailing from Rotterdam and coming to Philadelphia in September, 1727.

All these things I suppose are simple and matter-of-fact enough, but all the strangeness and mystery of time and chance and of the human destiny is in them for me and they seem wonderful. I suppose according to your theory we are what we are and have been shaped so by the past and can do nothing about it if we would.

Anyway, thanks again for so kindly sending me this information and the references. I will look them up when I can and let you know the result of my findings.

Kyle Crichton, who at this time was Associate Editor of Scribner's Magazine, had written Wolfe for biographical information to be published in the "Behind the Scenes" column of the February issue. The following was Wolfe's reply.

To KYLE S. CRICHTON

5 Montague Terrace
Brooklyn, New York
December 11, 1933

Dear Kyle:

Thanks for your note. I'd just as soon have you make up something on your own hook for the "BEHIND THE SCENES" column, as I thought what you put in before was fine and better than I could do, but I will take a chance anyway to give you something that you can use, and if you can use any of it go ahead, but please put it in your way and not as if I said it.

I have written over a million words in manuscript the past four years, which makes a box five feet long by two and one-half feet wide piled to the top. Also, I have worn a wart on my second finger, almost as large and hard, but not as valuable, as a gambler's diamond. Maybe you can say that I have come through the great depression with over a million words of manuscript and a large, hard wart on my second finger, as my tangible accumulations (but I don't think Max would want you to print such a vulgar and mercenary bit of news). Or

You can say that of the last ten years I have lived about four in Manhattan, four more in various other countries of the world, and about two and one-half in Brooklyn—and that the largest and most unknown continent of all is Brooklyn. You can say that I have gone out into the wilderness five hundred times, armed with a trusty map, now worn to tatters, and have prowled about, exploring the place in the dark hours of the night as not even Stanley explored Africa in his search for Dr. Livingston, though maybe you can say I met another white man here one time and that we recognized each other instantly, lifted our hats at once and stepped forward courteously with extended hands, saying: "Dr. Livingston, I believe?"—"Mr. Stanley, I presume?"—but maybe you'd better not put that in either.

Or perhaps you can say that I live in Brooklyn instead of Manhattan because, as my favorite Brooklyn waiter put it: "Duh difference between dese guys oveh heah and dose guys oveh dere, is dat oveh heah we have all been trained to t'ink." The Brooklyn people boast that you can live here a lifetime and never get to know their town, and they are right about it, but if I ever tell even what I know up to the present time, they would lynch me for it. If I ever do tell about it, I will not be here in Brooklyn at the time, and I shall call it "The Locusts Have No King." But maybe if you have customers out there, you'd better not put that in either.

Or finally, you might say that I'd still rather see the New York Yankees win than any other team, and go to watch them play a dozen times a year, but that I always go to see the Brooklyn Dodgers at least twice a year because they are such quaint fellows and you never know which one is going to get hit in the head next with a fly ball.

Well, this is the best I can do at present and if you can use any of it, go ahead, but please don't get me in any more trouble than I am in already.

Meanwhile, with best wishes, I am,

The following letter, found among Wolfe's own papers, is evidently a first draft of the one he sent to Mrs. Bernstein upon the publication of her book, Three Blue Suits, *in which he is portrayed as "Eugene Lyons." [1] In the final section of this book, Eugene announces to the heroine that, acting on the*

---

[1] This fictional character has no reference in any way to the well-known writer and editor, Mr. Eugene Lyons.

advice of his editor, "Mr. Watkins," he has applied for a Guggenheim Fellowship and is planning to leave her and go abroad.

To ALINE BERNSTEIN

> 5 Montague Terrace
> Brooklyn, New York
> December 11, 1933

Thanks for your letter. I have read your book and want to write you about it and congratulate you on its publication. I am sorry you did not send me a copy yourself or let me know that it was being published. Some news about its publication apparently came to Perkins some time ago, but he did not tell me about it for some reason, apparently because he thought it would worry me. I wish you or he had told me. The first news I had of it was last Sunday when I looked at the book columns of the *New York Times* and saw it listed there. I was tremendously excited about it and went out the first thing next day and bought a copy in Scribner's book-store, so you don't need to send me one now.

I can understand your feeling of happiness and achievement in having published these stories and with all my heart I want to wish you the best and finest kind of success with them—the kind of success I believe you want yourself. As you know, I had the manuscript of two of your stories, the first and the last, which you sent to me a year and one-half ago, but I had never seen the second story, the one about Herbert Wilson, until I read the book.

I think that piece about Herbert Wilson is very fine. Of course, I know where the other two stories came from and whom you had in mind, but I will talk to you about them later. I don't know if Herbert Wilson has an actual counterpart in life as has Mr. Froehlich or Eugene, or whether you got him from intuition and your observation of life, but I cannot tell you how moved I was by that story and how proud I am to know you could have done it. I am not a critic but a reader, and I believe in the reality of the character and the feeling in the story from beginning to end.

I think it is a very wonderful thing that a person who has never tried to write before can do something so true and good and full of pity. You made me live through the whole day with the man and understand all of his hope and expectancy in the morning when he saw that new and wonderful life opening up before him and then you made me feel how weariness and disappointment crept up on him as the day in the department store wore on; and finally, the cruel pity of his realization when he gets home at night and knows that his wife is dead and that there is no brave new world for him.

I thought all the other things in the story were fine: the cathedral and the shabby, dingy lives of the department store people and all the smells of food and sounds of people on the different landings of the tenement when he comes home. I think you can be proud of having written this story. As I say I am not a critic, but I do know that to get into the life of a little pavement cipher and make the reader feel and hope with him and understand him and finally feel that running pity at the loneliness and loss of life, is a rare and wonderful accomplishment and not often to be found in a piece of writing, even the writing of people with great reputations.

As you know, I was already familiar with your stories about Mr. Froehlich and Eugene, because I read them over a year ago when you sent the manuscript to me. I didn't know then what you intended to do with this manuscript and thought you were sending it to me as a kind of letter to tell me something of yourself and the way you looked at life. The other night I took your book and compared the printed version of those two stories with the manuscript you had sent to me. I found that they were practically verbatim the same, with the exception of one or two minor changes. That also seems remarkable to me—that you could on your first attempt say what you wished to say so clearly and with so little revision. I wonder if you know what agony and heartbreak it costs many people when they write.

In your story about me, you picture me as a fellow who wants to look out the window dreamily, do a dozen things at once, and escape all the sweat and labor that goes into a piece of work—just to think his books out of his head, while he looks dreamily out of the window and have them magically appear on paper with no effort of his own. Is it not a strange and sorrowful fact in life that people can live together for years and love each other, and yet find out no more about each other than this? I wonder if you've ever understood what anguish writing costs me and how hard I have worked. Didn't you ever see any of that during all the years you knew me? Well, it has been five times worse since then.

During the past four years, I have written over a million words and none of them, to my recollection appeared magically on paper while I stared dreamily out of the window, swilling down a drink of gin. Do you know how much writing a million words is? Well, it is a crate full of manuscript, six feet long and three feet deep, piled to the top, and it is more writing than most people ever do in the course of a life-time. Of those million words not over 150,000 have so far been published. A great deal more, and I hope and believe the best of it, may some day see the light of print, and there will be still more—how much I don't dare to think—which will be cut out, thrown away or destroyed.

I do not say that it is good—I only say that I have worked like hell, lived the life of a galley slave and done more hard work than anyone you know. And yet you picture me as a dreaming loafer. It seems to me that what people think and say of one another and the estimate the world puts on you and your life is usually just about as wrong as it can be—so wrong that if you stated just the opposite, you would usually come closer to the truth. You always said that you were the worker and that I had the inspiration without your capacity for work. Wouldn't it be funny if just the opposite were true?

I have never in my life been able to do a piece of writing that was so free from revision and the necessity to change, cut and rewrite as your own pages are. I don't know if you have ever seen one of my pages when I get through with it, or after I get through with the proofs—but it looks like a map of No Man's Land in Flanders. So again, you have done an extraordinary thing and shown at the beginning a clearness and certainty of purpose for which many of us would give our right eye.

But maybe, with all this talent and cleverness with which you have been so richly endowed by nature, you can still learn something from me—the final necessity of sweat and grinding effort. I think you have done some very fine writing in your stories about Mr. Froehlich and Eugene, but I think you could have done better if you had worked harder. By work in an artist's life, I do not mean eight hours a day or fourteen hours a day, or all the different things you get accomplished, but I mean an integrity of purpose, a spiritual intensity, and a final expenditure of energy that most people in the world have no conception of.

I don't believe that you really think of your husband and me as you have portrayed us in these stories. I am sorry that you said some of the things you did, and that you have been willing to give out to the world these portraits as representing your own estimates of us. Perhaps it is false for the artist to picture people as being better than they are, but I think it is even more false to picture them as being worse, and I do think that in your stories about Mr. Froehlich and Eugene, you have sometimes been uncharitable and unjust, and that you could have shown them as better people than you make them, without injuring the truth or quality of your writing.

I never got to know your husband very well and I don't suppose there was much love lost between us, but you did tell me many times that he had many fine and generous qualities—a generous devotion to his family and children and great liberality and affection for friends of the family and some of your own friends who were down on their luck, which he demonstrated time and time again by helping them. Don't you think since this is true, you could have made this element in his character plain without injuring your story? You made him a leathery-hearted broker with hardly a spark of generous human affection left in him, and I think you were unfair in doing this.[2]

I think you were also unfair in your story about me, and I want you to believe the truth of this, that I am sorry about this for your sake more than for my own. I hope and believe that through what you have done I can myself learn a valuable lesson. As you know, I have sometimes written pretty directly from my own experience—as directly as you did in your story about me—and now I admit, I want to be very careful in the future to be as fair and comprehensive in my understanding of people as I can be. I don't think that I have ever wilfully and maliciously distorted what I believed and knew to be true about people, in order to satisfy a personal grudge. I think I have generally said what was true about people I put in books, and what everyone knew to be true, and have even under-stated facts about people which were discreditable to them, but even in doing this I am now conscious that I have sometimes been thoughtless of the distress and worry that something I have written may have caused certain people.

I don't believe that anything that is good and shows the integrity of the artist's spirit can do anyone any damage in the end, and of course, as I have found out in the last four years, the trouble and confusion comes from the difference between the artist's point of view, which is concerned with the general truth drawn from his personal experience, and the point of view of people which is, particularly if they are in your book, concerned with making personal identifications from something which is intended as a general truth.

What I am trying to tell you now I tell you not to criticize or condemn you for what you have done, but simply in the hope that it may help you when you next write something. I have learned things very slowly in my life, and I think you learn them very rapidly. But what I am going to tell you now I have learned in my whole life and know that it is true: It is right to have a passionate bias in everything you create. It is right to feel the indignation, the conviction, the certitude, the sense of conflict, with which it seems to me everyone who creates something must have, but I don't think you can stack the cards against someone in order to justify yourself without being yourself the loser for it. The temptation to do this

[2] In a reply to this letter, Mrs. Bernstein vehemently denied that the character of "Mr. Froehlich" in any way resembled that of her husband.

carries with it its own punishment, and if you try to set up dummy figures of your own instead of real people just for the satisfaction it gives you to knock the dummy figures down, your work will suffer for it in the end.

I think that what you did wrong in the story you wrote about me was to identify a living person so exactly, even to giving a kind of paraphrase for my name, describing habits of disorder and confusion in my life and giving other information about me which was so unmistakable that no one who knew me could fail to identify me, and then from this basis of fact, you proceeded to create a situation and a conflict which was false. You gave some of the facts, but the other facts which were vital to an understanding of the situation you suppressed, and in doing this, I think you have been the loser.

In your story, you make the man desert the woman and all the self-sacrificing love and devotion she has given him because someone suddenly suggested to him that he could get the Guggenheim fellowship and go away to Europe for a year. As you say in the story, he sells her out for $2500. What you did not say in your story, however, and what you know to be true, is that the Guggenheim fellowship and this sudden spur-of-the-moment decision had nothing to do with the real situation. It gives you a false and easy means of justifying yourself in putting another person in a discreditable position, but of the real trouble which had already happened long before this thing you speak of, you say nothing. You say nothing of the bitter and complicated struggle which has been going on between two people for two years. You do not even mention the fact that at the time you write about, the woman in the story is almost fifty years old and the man less than thirty. Perhaps you would say that this is a trifling and unimportant fact and has nothing to do with the truth of what you want to say, but I think few impartial and fair-minded people would agree with you on this score and I doubt very much if you yourself believe it in your own heart. You do not even mention the fact that the woman in the story is a woman of wealth and fashion, a married woman and the mother of grown children, and that she has never for a moment had any intention of leaving any of these things for the sake of this man who, she says, is now basely deserting her.

You do not mention the fact that the man has no money of his own, must live on what he can earn by teaching school and that such a thing as a Guggenheim fellowship, with the chance it would give him to do the work he wants to do, would be a God-send to him. Neither do you mention countless other vital and fundamental facts about the relations between these two people, and I think so long as you were going to write the story you should have done so—that would have been a vastly more difficult thing to do, both as an artist and as a human being. It might even have been more painful for both of us, but you would have done a better, a more powerful piece of work.

I showed that story to only one person, Mr. Wheelock at Scribner's. He spoke warmly of the many fine things in it, of the skill and talent with which the appearance of the room, the meeting between the two people, etc. were presented, but in the end, he doubted the sincerity of the emotion. The situation described, the picture of self-abnegating love which the woman draws of herself, the declarations of incurable grief and intolerable suffering and the vows of eternal faithfulness, did not seem convincing to him, and I think the reason they were not convincing to him was because you shirked your task and stacked the cards against one of your two people in favor of the other one.

I have told you all this, not in the way of condemnation, but because I honestly want to give you what help I can, if it is worth anything to you and if you will take it. In all your stories you show the remarkably sharp, accurate and cynical observation of your race—a quality which I must confess I never knew you had to such a degree, but which may be a most characteristic thing about you. I think, moreover, it is a quality which you can make use of with compelling and even cruel force in writing and that it will be a great asset to you if you use it in the right way. But you cannot use it upon other people and become a romantic sentimentalist when you think about yourself, so remember that all these fine gifts, valuable as they are, carry in them an explosive and destructive power against the person who uses them if he does not use them in the right way.

I agree with you that these stories are a triumph of self-mastery on your part and I assure you I am genuinely proud of you for some of the things you have done. I doubt if your own excitement about getting them published could have been any greater than my own. You say you hope I can share in your happiness about it. I assure you that I do with all my heart and in the best way, otherwise I could not have written you as I have. I want you to have from these stories and everything you do only the best and finest kind of success, the only kind worth having, the respect of fine people for fine work.

As for the other kind of success, the ugly, cheap and rotten kind, I hope and believe you have it in you to loathe and despise it with every atom of your life. What I am trying to tell you is that if these stories get pawed over and whispered about by wretched, verminous little people who want to poke around, pick out identities and gloat over whatever scandalous morsels they think they can pick out of them, I only hope for your sake that you won't allow yourself to be touched by it, and I can't believe you would be gratified at being the center of such attention, on account of the glamour you think it might give to you. If you would, I am sorry for you.

I don't know the names of all the people who have been associated with you in this enterprise, I only know the names of two of them which were told to me the other day for the first time at Scribner's; and I can only tell you plainly that I am sorry you achieved publication with the help of such people.

In your story, you call the people at Scribners and Mr. Perkins a set of snobs. I have not found them so. I have found them thus far to be true friends of mine and among the best people I ever knew, although there are some very shabby, small people who might agree with you in your estimate. But if that kind of injury is in your mind, I don't believe it can do any real harm to any of us.

I think you will find people who would be glad to hear of any discreditable or malicious thing concerning me or of my failure, but even that does not bother me very much any more, and I still cannot believe you really had it in your heart to do me injury, even though other people that you know might want it.

I have just written you all this to hope that you will get the best from your success and happiness and not what is cheap and dirty, and I hope I have made myself plain. I think you let resentment toward me get into your story and that it made you unfair, but I cannot and will not believe you were actively malicious. Finally, after saying all this, I do want to tell you again how genuinely proud I am for all the fine and real and extraordinary writing you were able to do in this, your first piece of work. No one will hope for your success more than I do, and no one will speak more warmly about it when I have the opportunity, although, because of its personal reference to me, with the chance of misunderstanding it, I will not speak about it as often and in the way I would like to, and I know that this is also right.

But I congratulate you again with all my heart and know you will believe me when I tell you I was as happy about your fine work as you are.

The following letter to Perkins was written by Wolfe immediately after delivering to him the rough-draft manuscript of the first part of The October Fair, *which was to be published as* Of Time and the River *fifteen months later. According to* The Story of a Novel, *he then continued sorting and arranging the last part of* The October Fair, *and delivered this to Perkins on December 23.*

This completion of the rough draft of his book was one of the most impor-
tant milestones in Wolfe's life. As he says in The Story of a Novel, *"It was*
not finished in any way that was publishable or readable. It was really not a
book so much as it was the skeleton of a book, but for the first time in four
years the skeleton was all there. An enormous labor of revision, weaving to-
gether, shaping, and above all, cutting remained, but I had the book now
so that nothing, not even the despair of my own spirit, could take it from me.
He [Perkins] told me so, and suddenly I saw that he was right. I was like a
man who is drowning and who suddenly, at the last gasp of his dying effort,
feels earth beneath his feet again. My spirit was borne upward by the greatest
triumph it had ever known, and although my mind was tired, my body ex-
hausted, from that moment on I felt equal to anything on earth."

To MAXWELL E. PERKINS

> 5 Montague Terrace
> Brooklyn, N.Y.
> December 15, 1933

Dear Max:

I was pretty tired last night when I delivered that last batch of manuscript to you, and could not say very much to you about it. There is not
much to say except that to-day I feel conscious of a good many errors
both of omission and commission and wish I had had more time to arrange and sort out the material, but think it is just as well that I have
given it to you even in its present shape.

I don't envy you the job before you: I know what a tough thing it is
going to be to tackle, but I do think that even in the form in which the
material has been given to you, you ought to be able to make some kind
of estimate of its value or lack of value and tell me about it. If you do
feel on the whole I can now go ahead and complete it, I think I can go
much faster than you realize. Moreover, when all the scenes have been
completed and the narrative changed to a third person point of view,[1] I
think there will be a much greater sense of unity than now seems possible, in spite of the mutilated, hacked-up form in which you have the
manuscript; and I do feel decidedly hopeful, and hope your verdict
will be for me to go ahead and complete the first draft as soon as I
can; and in spite of all the rhythms, chants—what you call my dithyrambs
—which are all through the manuscript, I think you will find when I
get through that there is plenty of narrative—or should I say when *you*
get through, because I must shamefacedly confess that I need your help
now more than I ever did.

[1] *Of Time and the River* was originally written in the first person. Wolfe never did
get around to changing it to the third person, so Wheelock finally did this for him.

You have often said that if I ever gave you something that you could get your hands on and weigh in its entirety from beginning to end, you could pitch in and help me to get out of the woods. Well, now here is your chance. I think a very desperate piece of work is ahead for both of us, but if you think it is worth doing and tell me to go ahead, I think there is literally nothing that I cannot accomplish. But you must be honest and straightforward in your criticism when you talk about it, even though what you say may be hard for me to accept after all this work, because that is the only fair way and the only good way in the end.

I want to get back to work on it as soon as I can, and will probably go on anyway writing in the missing scenes and getting a complete manuscript as soon as I can. I wanted to write you this mainly to tell you that I am in a state of great trepidation and great hope also. Buried in that great pile of manuscript is some of the best writing I have ever done. Let's see to it that it does not go to waste.

Max, I think the total length of the manuscript I gave you is around 500,000 words.[2]

[2] Scribners' estimate of the length of the manuscript, as given in a letter written by Perkins to Frere-Reeves on January 18, 1934, was 344,000 words.

X

THE COMPLETION AND PUBLICATION OF
OF TIME AND THE RIVER

1934–1935

The following note was left on the desk of Alfred Dashiell with "Dark in the Forest, Strange as Time." This story was accepted by Scribner's Magazine *as of January, 1934, published in the November, 1934, issue, and included in* From Death to Morning.

To ALFRED DASHIELL

[New York City]

[January, 1934]

Dear Fritz:

Here's the story, with such corrections as I could now make. I think I've succeeded in changing it to *past* tense everywhere—and will you please look at the insertion which I have written in on page 9 to see if it is clear, and if I have succeeded in doing what you suggested there: namely, to leave the knowledge of whether the dying man saw or did not see his wife meeting with her lover in doubt. I've got to have another crack at this in proof, and know I can improve it.

As to the title, will you consider this one tentatively—"Dark in the Forest, Strange as Time" (or "Dark in the Forest, Dark as Time" as a variant). Don't ask me what the title means, I don't know, but think it may capture the feeling of the story, which is what I want to do.

This is all for the present—and please let me go over it again when you get proofs.

P.S. I did not make the *cuts* on pages 5 and 6 as you suggested, but rather omitted the reference to Uncle Walter's drawers to avoid arousing the natural repugnance of your readers, etc. If you think there's too much of this dialogue, go ahead and cut it out, but I wish you'd look it over again to make sure.

At Perkins' suggestion, Wolfe had given several pieces from his book to Elizabeth Nowell, who had left the editorial staff of Scribner's Magazine *to serve an apprenticeship in the literary agency of Maxim Lieber, with the understanding that she was to cut and edit them and try to sell them to magazines other than* Scribner's. *The first of these, "Boom Town," was purchased by the* American Mercury *soon after the date of the following letter, and was published in the May, 1934, issue of that magazine. It was finally omitted from* Of Time and the River, *but appears on pages 88–120 and 142–146 in* You Can't Go Home Again.

To ELIZABETH NOWELL

[5 Montague Terrace]
[Brooklyn, N.Y.]
February 2, 1934

Dear Miss Nowell:

Thanks for your letter and for the revised copy of "Boom Town." I have not been able to read your revision carefully yet, but I shall read it over the week-end. I am sorry you have had to work so hard on this and have had no better luck in placing it. Of course there's no use arguing with editors who know what they want or think they do, and I don't know of anything I can do to free them from their quaint superstitions concerning characters who stammer, etc. This was surprising news to me, and now I can no longer pretend even to guess at these prejudices or know what the next will be.

Frankly, I don't see that we can do very much more with this story, and it would seem to me to be the wiser course to let it drop. I have been very hard up and badly in need of money, but as much as I need and want it, it has never yet occurred to me that I could do honest work by carving, shaping, trimming, and finally by changing the entire structure and quality of a fundamental character. I think if I knew how to do it and understood more about the mysteries of magazine publishing, I would be tempted to go ahead and try to do it in order to get a little needed money, but I don't know how to do it, and I know nothing of these mysteries. It seems to me that it would be foolish for me to try to do something I do not understand.

One thing in your letter does surprise me, and that is that you now agree with the editors' complaint that the character of "Lee" comes as too much of a shock in the story, that he over-shadows the boom theme and takes away from the emphasis. My understanding at the beginning was that both you and Mr. Lieber liked the character of "Lee," felt definitely that he had a place in the story, and even thought that the character should be more fully developed and given a more important place which, as you remember, is exactly what we did in the revision.

I know you understand, Miss Nowell, that I am not quarreling with you about this, and that I do appreciate the pains you and Lieber have taken with this story. I am genuinely sorry not only for my sake but for yours that we are not likely now to get anything out of the work we've put into it. Moreover, I also believe that as a result of your comments and suggestions, I was able to make the piece more effective and interesting than it was in the beginning; and, of course, in the end that will always be a gain. But I do think that after we have talked and argued together about a piece we ought to come to some fairly definite agreement or conclusion about it, and that we can't go jumping around like a Jack-in-the-box changing our minds and opinions every time we come up against a new editor.

I am very grateful to you for all the extra work you've gone to on your own hook in making this new revision and shortening the piece and cutting out "Lee's" stammering; but it seems fairly evident to me now that the piece is not commercially saleable, and I doubt that we are going to have any success with it. But I will read your copy over carefully Sunday, and either call or write you about it next week.

Now about the *Esquire* proposition. I think something can be done about this, and if you can get $175 that will be swell.[1] I have been talking to Mr. Perkins about it, and he has suggested two or three short pieces which are either in the manuscript of the book or have been cut out of it. One is a piece about two boys going down to see a big circus come into town, unload, and put up the tents in the early morning. I think I will send you this piece today or tomorrow. It is out of the book and in its present form is only seven typed pages long, or about 2100 words. The thing needs an introduction which I will try to write today, but otherwise it is complete enough, although, again, I am afraid it is not what most people consider a story.[2]

I also have what Max calls one of my "dithyrambs." He and Dashiell are very kind about it, and Dashiell even suggested it might be used

---

[1] Arnold Gingrich, editor of *Esquire,* had asked to see some short pieces of Wolfe's and had agreed to pay $175 for any which he might accept.

[2] This was "Circus at Dawn" which finally appeared in the March, 1935, issue of *The Modern Monthly* and was included in *From Death to Morning.*

for the magazine, but I sold them another story the other day, which makes three they have taken recently, so I don't know whether they would care to use it. The thing is about the names of America—the names of rivers, the tramps, the railroads, the states, the Indian Tribes, etc. The only story element in it is that it begins with four episodes in dialogue of different people abroad who are thinking of home. Perkins thinks this piece goes beyond the 3,000 word limit, but I believe it could be brought within that limit without much trouble. It is to start the seventh section of my book.[3]

I also have a piece called "The Bums at Sunset" which we cut out of the book the other day, and which is about some hoboes waiting beside the track to pick up the train, but I don't know if this is any good or could be used.[4]

There are a great number of these pieces, and I think you might very probably find something among them that you could use, but I have lost confidence in my own powers of selection, and apparently have little idea which part of my writing is going to please people and what they're going to like. The piece about the names of America I wrote two or three years ago, and I'm almost positive I showed it to Mr. Perkins, but he says now he never saw it before and that it is one of the best things I ever wrote. . . . All I can do now and what I am doing in addition to revising and re-writing the book is to get all of these things typed so that he can read them. If I had time I think I'd ask you to go over my manuscript with me, but I haven't got the time because I am meeting Mr. Perkins every day now to work on the book, and all the rest of the time I spend in writing and in getting the manuscript typed. But I'll send the circus piece to you and you can see if there's any chance of doing anything with the *Esquire* people about it, and if you don't think there is, I'll send you something else.

If and when I get through with this enormous manuscript, I have a number of short pieces that I want to write, and maybe then I can really give you something that you can sell.

This is all for the present. Try to sell something to *Esquire* if you can. I do need the money badly.

---

[3] This was "The Names of the Nation" which was published in the December, 1934, issue of *The Modern Monthly* and appears on pages 861–870 of *Of Time and the River*.

[4] "The Bums at Sunset" was published in the October, 1935, issue of *Vanity Fair* and included in *From Death to Morning*.

To ROBERT RAYNOLDS

5 Montague Terrace
Brooklyn, New York
February 2, 1934

Dear Bob:

Thanks for your letter. Ever since I came back from New Year's at your place, I've wanted to write you and Marguerite and tell you how good it was to be with you New Year's and how it set me up. I am sorry that you have seen me so often just after I've been run through the sausage mill. I suppose one should want to see the people he likes best when he is sitting astride of his own world, but instinct in me seems to turn me toward the Raynolds family for succor everytime I begin to wander around in the valley of despair. I won't do it again, or not very often, anyway, and before I go away I swear I will reveal to you all the noble Jekyllesque side of my nature.

I feel fine outside of an awful crick in the back which may be cold or may be the result of my misguided efforts to shove a taxi, which I had hired the other night, out of the snow. But I really do feel grand now in every way that counts. I went into a slump of awful dejection for two or three weeks after leaving your place, was doing little work except cutting and going over the manuscript with Perkins every day. We really got a great deal accomplished, but I was not getting on with my own work at home. Then I had to hunt up typists again, and the Remington and Underwood agencies sent me several of these poor, dumb fumbling misbegotten creatures who, for the most part, inhabit the earth. One was lame and very good and willing of heart, and would come limping heavily in to my table every time she couldn't make out a word—which was every other word I wrote. I was about to go crazy with the thing, cursing her under my breath, and wanting to choke her, and feeling that awful pity and shame about it at the same time.

Now I have a young lady from Utah who has only been here ten days and doesn't know whether she's going to like New York or not, but I hope she will because she types even my most indecipherable Chinese without difficulty, and we're going like the wind, and I am very happy. It seems too good to be true that I am really out of the woods at last, but Perkins says such is really the case, and he may be right. There is a tremendous lot to be done this spring by way of cutting, revising, rewriting, and even getting new pieces typed out of my notes, but the big job, I believe, is done.

We still have to thresh out little matters such as how many of my several hundred thousand words can possibly get printed in a single volume, but these bagatelles do not disturb me after all I've suffered and endured these past four years.

I am glad you liked the last piece in *Scribner's*.[1] Perkins liked it, too, and says the time will come when every one will know what it's all about, which seems plain enough to me now, but I think some people may be puzzled by it.

I sold another story to *Scribner's*, and no longer have any confidence in my power of selection. Perkins has the most tender and paternal affection for the piece I ever saw in any editor, and swears he never saw it before, and why had I never shown it to him, which somewhat bewilders me since I wrote it seven or eight months ago as part of the manuscript that was printed as "No Door," and which we cut out of the magazine as being something which could go.[2] Now, it appears, it is a gem of purest ray serene with the same haunting strangeness as "La Belle Dame Sans Merci," but ye author goggles like an idiot now when he hears these words, grins stupidly and says, "Yes, sir." . . .

The only surprising thing about this is that I swear I showed it to him two or three years ago when I wrote it, and he swears just as positively that he never saw it until a few weeks ago. It's pretty bewildering, but, then, isn't it beautiful to think of all the buried masterpieces which I will be able to unearth out of these manuscripts and give to the world after my seventieth year.

Anyway, the young lady is going to type up everything that is untyped in my books now, and I'm going to let Max see the whole works so far as possible, since I no longer seem to be able to tell what's what myself. God knows what I would do without him. I told him the other day that when this book comes out, he could then assert it was the only book he had ever written. I think he has pulled me right out of the swamp just by main strength and serene determination. I am everlastingly grateful for what he has done. He is a grand man and a great editor, and from the bottom of my heart I know that he is hoping and praying far more for my own success and development than for any profit which may come to Scribners as a result of it—a profit which, I sometimes fear, may be very small indeed, although, of course, I hope for better luck for all of us.

If you are coming in next Wednesday, I should like to see you and have dinner with you. . . . Let me know sometime before four o'clock Wednesday because I am going into Scribner's these days at four-thirty and working with Perkins until six-thirty.

[1] "The Four Lost Men," which had appeared in the February, 1934, issue of *Scribner's*, and which was included in *From Death to Morning*.

[2] "The House of the Far and Lost" which was published in the August, 1934, issue and appears on pages 619–627 and 637–652 of *Of Time and the River*.

This is all for the present. Please give my love and best wishes to Marguerite and the children. . . .

To ROBERT RAYNOLDS

5 Montague Terrace
Brooklyn, New York
March 10, 1934

Dear Bob:

Thanks for your letter. I'm afraid we've begun to count those springtime blossoms too soon. It's snowing again in Brooklyn now. But I may yet be able to visit your establishment before the daffodils arrive.

My literary agents, of whom I am now inclined to think very highly because they finally succeeded in getting a hundred and ninety-two dollars out of the *American Mercury* for a 20,000 word story which I rewrote three times, and of the same length that *Scribner's* have paid me four hundred for,[1] were out here last night ransacking the manuscript in search of new material. Most of it was dismissed with polite regrets as "not [a] story" whatever that means—I've never been able to find out myself. But they departed at length with a half dozen pieces and seem to think they can sell something else for me.

The reason that I tell you this is because I mentioned your name to the agent and told him you had written some stories. He told me that he would like to see if he could do anything with them. I am inclined to think well of these two agents whose names are Maxim Lieber and Miss Elizabeth Nowell. Miss Nowell, in particular, I believe is a person of good judgement and ability. She worked for several years in the *Scribner's* office, and the suggestions and comments she made to me for revising the story which the *Mercury* is publishing were very concrete and definite and, I think, improved the story, although they did yield to certain assinine superstitions of various editors such as taking out the stammer from a character who stammers, and whose whole character stammers, on the ground that stammering slows up the reading, and that editors have a great prejudice against it. Anyway, we had to write my good stammering character out straight. But in other ways I think the story is improved. . . .

This is all for the present. I am doing three or four thousand words a day and by the end of the week I get pretty tired, but I think we will get there now. Scribners sold the rights to "Look Homeward, Angel" to the *Modern Library* the other day and got an advance of five hundred, which

---

[1] "Boom Town."

of course, I must split fifty-fifty with the publisher. Of course, both the royalty and the price of the book will be much lower in this edition . . . but Perkins felt it was a wise move because the chance of a considerable sale is much better now in the *Modern Library* edition. He thinks also that the kind of audience that is reached with these *Modern Library* books will be useful to us in the future.

Let me know if you want to do anything about Lieber, and write to him yourself if you do. Meanwhile, good luck and good wishes to all of you.

To JAMES BOYD

> 5 Montague Terrace
> Brooklyn
> April 23, 1934

Dear Jim:

Thanks for your letter. It made me feel good, not only because of what you said about my story [1] but also because it was you who said it. I don't think that there is any other writing man whose good opinion would mean so much to me, and your letter gives me hope that I may finally be learning something about my job. I have sweated so much blood and done so much work and I seem to learn things so slowly that often I don't think I am very bright, and for that reason I felt like cheering when I got your letter.

It seems to me that you yourself do better work constantly. I thought *Long Hunt* was the best book you had written up to that time, and although I don't know what's to come in the new one, *Roll River,* it seemed to me the first installment was as moving and exciting as anything you've ever written. [2] It is a great gift to be able to bring the past to life again and it seems to me that about the most difficult job of all is to bring the past of fifty years ago to life again, more difficult, even, I should think, than to write about three hundred years ago, yet I had constantly a feeling of complete reality and intimacy with all the people in your story. The way you evoke Pennsylvania, or the feeling that it has always given me, is quite astonishing. I know the country around Harrisburg quite well for my father came from a country village about twenty miles from there on the road to Gettysburg. I don't know if Harrisburg is the town described in your story, but at any rate it was Harrisburg and the River Street there

---

[1] "The Sun and the Rain," which was published in the May, 1934, issue of *Scribner's Magazine,* and appears in *Of Time and the River* on pages 797–802. Boyd had written Wolfe that it was "near perfection."

[2] *Roll River* was being serialized in *Scribner's Magazine.*

that I saw and felt all the time as I read it. Wherever it is, it is wonderfully real and interesting.

It was good to see you again when you were here last, and fine to see you so well and husky looking. You said something about coming back again in a month or so and if you do I hope you'll let me know and that we can get together again in those Atlantean chairs at the Plaza. Meanwhile, with best wishes, and thanks again.

To ROBERT RAYNOLDS

5 Montague Terrace
Brooklyn, New York

May 1, 1934

Dear Bob:

Thanks for your letter. I should be delighted to come up May the 14th or 19th, and unless something unfortunate happens to prevent it. . . . This will make the third time this spring that I have started out to go on a trip. The other two times I wound up by going to Brooklyn instead, but I hope this third time will break the charm.

My agent has been working me daytime and night-time, and when I had any time off I slept. I finished up another piece which we hope *The American Mercury* will take. The editor [1] saw it in its first version and practically promised to take it if I did certain definite and specific things which he enumerated. I have done them and think I've done a good job. I hope he doesn't back out on me now. It is quite a funny piece, and if it gets published it will be different from anything else I have ever written. It is all about a little man who gives up a fat job on the Hearst syndicate in order to come to Cambridge and take somebody's celebrated course in playwriting. It tells how everything he writes is about food and how his plays keep getting hungrier and hungrier as he goes on, and also of other grotesque adventures. I called the piece "The Hungry Dutchman." [2] It made the agent laugh and I hope it will have the same effect on *The American Mercury.* . . .

This is almost a red letter month with me as regards magazine publication. I have two pieces—count them, two—appearing simultaneously in two different publications, *Scribner's* and the *Mercury.* If the time ever comes when I have as many as three at the same time, I think I'll feel practically like Dumas or Edgar Wallace or one of those hydra-headed writers.

[1] Charles Angoff.

[2] Wolfe finally changed the title of this story to "Miss Potter's Party." It failed to sell to any magazine, but appears in *Of Time and the River* on pages 282–301.

The *Mercury* piece [3] is quite a long one—long, that is, for the *Mercury* —but cut so severely from its earlier forms that it hurts to think about it.

I don't know if I told you that the *Mercury* got very enthusiastic a few weeks ago and began to make all kinds of glittering proposals, none of which, unfortunately, I could accept. They first wanted, so my agent tells me, to publish the whole manuscript of my new book in three issues of their magazine, printing nothing else at the time. I have never heard of such a proposal but I am told they made it. Of course the whole thing is impossible. I don't think they could get the present manuscript in twelve issues of their magazine even if they printed nothing else, and if they could, I think it would be grossly unfair to Perkins to do such a thing after he's worked as hard as he has. The next proposal was that they should publish a series of installments out of the book which should be consecutive and about 25,000 words each. This also was not practicable because they demanded to see all the installments at once and also that they should follow each other in a kind of narrative sequence, and it would be hard to give them this because *Scribner's* has already printed so many pieces from various parts of the manuscript. However, the *Mercury* still seems to be interested in seeing my stuff and we may be able to sell them a few pieces.

I am glad to know you are coming along so well with your book. It will be good to see you again. I am looking forward to being there just when spring is at its best. Meanwhile, with best wishes for health and success to you and all the family.

To FRED W. WOLFE

[5 Montague Terrace]
[Brooklyn, N.Y.]
May 12, 1934

Dear Fred:

. . . I am sorry that I was not here your last night in Philadelphia when you tried to get me. Perkins was in Baltimore that very day and I planned to go down and meet him and Scott Fitzgerald and try to get you to meet us in Gettysburg or some other place, but I did not go, chiefly because I was pretty tired at the time and was also working at night with my agent here. . . .

I hope this new job [1] turns out better for you and that you will be able to get enough out of it to feel a little easier and a little more comfortable.

[3] "Boom Town."

[1] Fred Wolfe had taken a new job with the Bluebird Ice Cream Company, in Spartanburg, S.C.

I know you have had a hard time and have often had to figure very close, and as this is probably not according to your nature, I hope things will get better for you from now on. If you are really taking this job partly for experience and want to find out about the business, I think it may be a very good move. People seem to continue to eat ice-cream in spite of hell and high water, and perhaps it is less affected by the depression than most other businesses have been. I suppose you have sometimes thought of being your own boss and having a business of your own, and if I ever make any money, as I may possibly do some day if I have some luck and the whole system does not go to smash, I will gladly help you to get started if I can. . . .

I went over to Pennsylvania Monday on the invitation of a very nice and intelligent young lady.[2] She drove me out and we came back again on Thursday, and while I was there I did little except sleep and eat and see some very beautiful country. I was over on the banks of the Delaware River straight across New Jersey from New York, thirty or forty miles above the Delaware water gap. Coming back Thursday, we drove down through the gap and saw some very beautiful country. Spring is later this year than it was last but is just beginning to reach its peak now.

I suppose you will laugh if I tell you the kind of place I was staying at, but it is not so funny when you see it with your own eyes. The young lady who invited me was the superintendent of a private school or home for defective children. I had a good room in a studio which has been built behind the house and therefore could be as private as I pleased. The place itself was beautiful with a mountain rising right behind the house and the Delaware down below, but the first time you see and talk to the children is pretty bad. It gives you a sick feeling. They call them children, of course, because in intelligence that's all they are and some of them aren't even that. The youngest is a boy of twelve or thirteen years, and the oldest is a woman past thirty who chatters away all the time and who has no more brains than a three-year-old. Of course they all get the very best of food and care and are treated with the utmost kindness by the teachers, but it is a sad thing to see. However, you do lose somewhat that first feeling of horror, and the young lady tells me you even become very fond of them and have no feeling of revulsion at all.

One of them is a boy of twelve, as fine and healthy and handsome a child as I ever saw until he comes close to you and you look in his eyes and see that he has no more intelligence than a baby. . . . It is terribly

2 Catherine Brett, Director of the Brett School, at Dingman's Ferry. She is now Mrs. Miles Spencer.

sad for the parents of these children, too. Of course, it is something that could happen to anyone and often happens to people who are completely innocent of any wrong and who have other healthy and intelligent children. There is one girl at the place who is . . . considerably more intelligent than most of them and has a very friendly and affectionate nature, which makes it all the sadder because her mother is dying and has only about two weeks more to live. It is going to be very hard to tell her when it happens. She came in the other day laughing and excited and hugging the letter which her father had just written her, and talking about and looking forward to her next trip home when she could get to see her mother and her sister again. By the same mail, the father, who seems to be a very intelligent and high grade man, had written the young lady who is the superintendent, telling her that the mother could not live over two weeks longer and giving her instructions how to go about preparing the child for it.

I am glad that I got to see the place and had the experience. We have all been through hard times and known grief and suffering, but I think we sometimes forget how tragic and horrible life can be, and when we see a thing like this we realize that after all our own lot is fortunate. It is good to know that there are places like this in the world where these unfortunate children are treated kindly and are taken care of, but the bad part of it is that only a very few people can afford to keep their children in such a place and for the most part children like these must be sent to public institutions where they cannot receive the same care and attention and where the conditions, I understand, are sometimes very bad. The terrible thing is that there are over 2,000,000 [3] of these people in the country, which is about three times the number of people in colleges and universities.

Well, this is all on this depressing subject for the present. I thought you might be interested in hearing about it, and it has also been on my mind so since I saw it that I think about it a great deal.

If my health and energy hold up I should finish finally another big piece of work this summer, and then if I could forget about everything for two or three months I could go on and finish the next one and the next one after that. I sometimes feel that I am in the position of a tight rope walker for whom things may be very good or very bad. I have done enough work in the last four years to make three tremendous big books all of which belong to the same series. Now the first of these is almost finished. The second and third require a great deal of work, but everything

[3] This figure seems to be somewhat inaccurate. Wolfe was probably giving a rough estimate.

will be all right if I can hold out. All I can do is to keep on and see what happens.

This is all for the present. . . . Write me and give me the news when you can. Meanwhile, with all good wishes for your health and success,

To ROBERT RAYNOLDS

5 Montague Terrace
Brooklyn, New York
June 5, 1934

Dear Bob:

Thanks for your note. . . . I have written 75,000 words or more in the past three weeks, which ought to be some sort of record. Mr. Perkins and I are working at night from 8:30 to 10:30. It seems almost unbelievable that we've really got the first four chapters ready for the printer. I suffer agony over some of the cutting, but I realize it's got to be done. When something really good goes it's an awful wrench, but as you probably know, something really can be good and yet have no place in the scheme of a book. The hardest thing so far has been giving up an opening chapter which was one of the best things I ever wrote and Perkins himself said so.[1] I actually thought it had a place in the beginning of the book but we've taken it out. Mr. Perkins has done a wonderful job on the chapter that now opens the book. It was originally 25,000 or 30,000 words long and by drastic surgery we have cut it down to 10,000 words and the people he has showed it to seem to think it reads wonderfully. I have got to keep going now until we get done. I think he wants to start sending manuscript to the printer right away. . . .

I am glad to know that you have kept working on your book and that it is progressing. . . . I suppose now that you country squires are realizing dividends on the weather, you have no inclination to visit the greatest summer resort in the world—that is what one of our local patriots called New York the other day. But if you do, let me know when you are coming so that we can get together. Perkins and I, after finishing our work at night, have been going to our old haunt, the Chatham, except that we sit outdoors at their out-door café and it is really very nice, something like Paris walled in with forty-story skyscrapers on every side.

This is all for the present. Good luck and success to you in all you're doing and let me hear from you when you can.

[1] This was introductory historical material, "The Men of Old Catawba" which was published in *From Death to Morning*. One section of this appeared in the June, 1935, issue of *The North American Review* under the title "Polyphemus"; another appeared in the April, 1935, issue of *The Virginia Quarterly* under the title "Old Catawba."

To ROBERT RAYNOLDS

New York City, N.Y.

June 8, 1934

Dear Bob:

I was awfully tired when I saw you the other night and not able to talk much to you and for that I am very sorry. I know that on these rare occasions when you get into town you hope for something better than a conversation with a blank wall.

I want to tell you how much I am looking forward to getting through with this terrible job in order that I may see a few of my friends again and actually try to live among them for a while as a free man and not as a slave in a galley chained to an oar. Also I want to tell you how much faith and hope I have for you and for the book you are now doing. I think we both know what a lonely job writing is and how no one can help us very much except with their belief in what one does. That is all that I can offer you, but you have it with all my heart, and I wish for you nothing but the best and highest kind of success—the kind I know you want for yourself. . . .

P.S. The book is coming beautifully. Perkins and I did some fascinating work last night with a long pair of scissors, paste, typed manuscript and pages from *Scribner's Magazine*. The result was so good that he forgot his customary reticence so far as to say he didn't see how the book could fail. It made me feel good, and I'm in a strange mixed state of happiness and tormented doubt—sometimes regretting bitterly all that has come out and all that I can't get in, and delighted to see things falling into shape as well as they have. Someone said that writing a book is like sifting constantly with an enormous sieve, and certainly this one of mine has been done that way. I can only hope now that the customers will find the deposit to their liking.

To PERCY MACKAYE

5 Montague Terrace

Brooklyn, New York

July 1, 1934

Dear Mr. Mackaye:

Please excuse me for not having answered your letter sooner. I failed to get in touch with you when you were in New York at The Players' Club, because for several months I have been working all day at home on a manuscript and then meeting Mr. Perkins at Scribner's every night to revise and edit it. In this way time gets away from you and one loses count of the days, and I am afraid you had come and gone before I knew it. . . .

In just another month or two I expect to be finished with an enormous manuscript which has occupied most of my waking, and a good part of my sleeping time for more than four years. It is itself just one of four books, but three of them are already practically complete in manuscript; and this first one, after untold agonies of cutting, re-writing and re-weaving, is about ready for the printer. I can't tell you how long these four years seemed to me. They don't seem measurable in terms of years or days or months. They seem to stretch back over eons through fathom-less depths of memory, and they also have gone by like a dream.

I have never felt or known this great dream of time in which we live as I have felt and known it during these last four years. It has been a dream of constant wakefulness, of unceasing struggle, of naked reality. I don't think I have ever lived with such energy and with such perception of the world around me as during these four years of desperate labor. Yet the time has got by me like a dream. It is almost unbelievable now that I am really approaching the end of another piece of work. There were times in which it seemed that I was caught in an enormous web from which I can never extricate myself. I lived for nothing but the work I was doing, and I thought of the work I had yet to do. But I was too tired to work. I could not rest or get any peace or repose for thought of the work which was yet to come, and the work even invaded my sleep so that night was turned into an unending processional of blazing and incredible visions, and I would sleep and yet know that I was sleeping, and dream and know that I was dreaming. There were times when I felt sunk, lost forever, buried at some horrible sea-depth of time and memory from which I can never escape.

I don't suppose many young men attempt a work of such proportions as the one which has occupied my time these last four years; and I don't know whether I could have faced it had I known what lay before me. The sheer physical labor has been enormous. I can't use the typewriter, and have to write every word with my hand, and during these last four years, as I estimate it, I have written about two million words. The manuscript is piled up in crates and boxes and fills them to overflowing. It inundates my room.

But now I feel like a prisoner who has been given his release and comes out of a dungeon and sees the light of day for the first time in years. Perhaps I ought not to tell you this long and tedious story of my work, but you are yourself a writing man and I know you understand the intolerable amount of anguish that goes into the work of writing and you will be able to forgive an escaped prisoner who babbles drunkenly about his release.

During these four years I have had the unfailing faith, the unshaken belief and friendship of one man, and as long as any man has that, I believe he always has a chance of coming through; but if I had not had it, it is hard for me to know what I could have done. Mr. Perkins has stuck to me all this time. He has never once faltered in his belief that everything would yet turn out well—even when I had almost given up hope myself. He has stood for all the rage and desperation and the crazy fits, and, with firm and gentle fortitude, has kept after me all the time—until now, at length, it seems to be my impossible good fortune to have come through. I have never heard of another writer who had such luck. No success that this book could possibly have could ever begin to repay that man for the prodigies of patience, labor, editing and care he has lavished on it. And now I can only hope that there will be something in the book that will in some measure justify it.

I have not known such happiness in many years as I have known these last few weeks when, for the first time, it became apparent that I would have the whole thing in hand and that we were coming to the end. Perkins never lost faith that this would be so, but there was a black and bitter period when all he had to go on was faith, because I was unable to show him the whole design, and when I had the whole thing in me but for the most part still unwritten. I would bring him fifty and eighty and a hundred thousand words at a time—sometimes even as much as two hundred thousand—and although these sections would sometimes be as long as a long book, they would still be only sections and parts of a whole, and there would follow a period of exhaustion when I could not write for days or even weeks and when I would wonder if I really had the thing inside me and would some day get it out of me or was only a deluded madman being devoured by his own obsession. I know you can understand now why I feel happy no matter what happens to this book or what they say about it. I know now, and Perkins knows that I was not a madman, but that I had the whole design in me all the time and had stuck to it. Therefore, I feel like a man who has swum upward from some horrible sea-depth where he thought he was lost and buried forever and come back into the friendly and glorious light of day again.

I still have a hard summer's work ahead of me, but I am looking forward to the Autumn and toward going somewhere on a train or ship again—if I have anything to go on—and also toward seeing some people I know and renewing friendship with them. I want to see you and talk to you, and I hope that our meeting will not be deferred much longer. This letter has been all about my work, and I should not have talked so much about it. I had not intended to say anything about it when I started to write you, but I just felt a sudden desire to get it off my chest and to tell somebody else about it who had been through the mill himself.

I hope this finds you in good health and enjoying your summer holiday. It is too bad that a cranky heart forced you to leave those mountain altitudes you like so well, but I hope even that trouble has been righted now and that you will have no further recurrence of it.

I continue to meet Mr. Perkins and to work with him from 8:30 to 10:30 every night except Sunday, but if you ever come into town and have time for dinner, I wish you would let me know, and where I can meet you.

Meanwhile, with best wishes to you and your family,

P.S.—I want also to thank you for "The Faith of Poetry," and for the inscription. I shall value and keep both. Meanwhile, I have put it on the shelf beside those books to which I shall be able to return as a man comes home—soon now, when that wonderful time again comes when I shall be able to read a book instead of trying always to write one.

To ROBERT RAYNOLDS

5 Montague Terrace
Brooklyn, New York
July 8, 1934

Dear Bob:

Thanks for your note. Yes, we have all stewed in our grease here, but I have kept busy and have not minded it so much this time.

It seems unbelievable, but Perkins and I finished getting the manuscript ready for the printer last night. There are still three full scenes to be written, and parts of a few other scenes to be completed, but he wants to start getting the stuff to the printer at once. As for myself, I am fighting against an overwhelming reluctance to let it go. There are so many things I want to go back over and fill in and revise, and all my beautiful notes I long to chink in somehow, and he is doing his best to restrain me in these designs.

I had lunch with Perkins and Scott Fitzgerald yesterday, and Scott tried to console me about the cutting by saying that "you never cut anything out of a book that you regret later." I wonder if this is true. Anyway, I shall do all I can in what time is left to me, and then I suppose I will have to leave the matter on the lap of the gods and Maxwell Perkins. After all these years of bitter labor, and sometimes of despairing hope, I have come to have a strange and deep affection for this great hacked and battered creature of a manuscript as if it were my son—and now I hate to see it go.

I am glad to know you are so near the end of your own. I judge that my own idea of being near the end and yours differ radically, and you will probably see the real end sooner than I do. I think Perkins' benevolently crafty design is to start giving this thing to the printer at once so that there will no longer be any possible drawing back on my part. He has already carefully impressed it upon my mind that the thing that costs is not so much the setting up into print but keeping the setters-up waiting once they have begun.

I had a chance to sell a story to the Redbook for $750. and to my un-speakable anguish was forced to turn it down. They wanted the story for their December issue and refused to publish it any earlier and said that if the story did appear in the book, even in a completely modified form, the publication of the book would have to be deferred until November 30th.[1] Perkins refused to agree to this, so we had to turn it down, although at the present time so much money looks mountainous to me.

Max also keeps discovering wonderful new stories in the manuscript that could have been used for the magazine, but it is now too late. Any-way, it is better now to finish and to go on with finishing the next two books to follow. If it were only possible to go back some day when all these books have been published and to rewrite and work on them again and do all to them that I have always hoped to do! Perkins says he thinks it will be, but the trouble, as I well know, is that there is a kind of strange fatality to print—not only for the reader but more especially for the writer—and once a book has been printed he is inclined to turn away from it and forget it and go on to something else.

Goodbye for the present and good luck to you. I hope to take a vacation somewhere on a ship or a train in autumn, and would like nothing better than to preface it with a few days in Vermont. If you are yourself free at that time, perhaps you would go along with me. Last year's trip up there was wonderful.[2] I shall never forget some of the places we saw that awoke all of those latent and virulent passions for ownership which have been the ruination of my family, and to which I thought I was immune! So I may yet live to become a landed proprietor with forty rocky but beauti-fully green acres and an old white house set snug and low against the shoulder of a hill! Things as strange have happened.

[1] At this time, Perkins was still hoping for publication of *Of Time and the River* in the late fall of 1934. The story was called "Dark October" and appears in *Of Time and the River* on pages 334–338 and 361–401.

[2] Wolfe had gone to Vermont with Raynolds in September, 1933.

Let me know if and when you come to town and we will get together for refreshment in one of the local brasseries. Meanwhile, best wishes,

To CATHERINE BRETT

5 Montague Terrace
Brooklyn, N.Y.
July 12, 1934

Dear Catherine:

Thanks for your letter, which has just arrived. I spent three hours to-day trying to get started to work, and I hope that writing you this note will work some sort of magic spell, or bring me luck, or get me started!

. . . It seems unbelievable after all these bitter years, but Mr. Perkins sent my huge manuscript to the press yesterday. It threw me into a kind of panic for a while. I suppose I have got attached to it, as one might get attached to some great, monstrous child, and I was a little terrified when I had to give it up. It means that the proof will start coming back within a few weeks now, and it also means that all I expect, or want, or hope to get done must be done within a little more than two months.[1] After that, the die is cast.

I think Mr. Perkins is right in feeling that I ought to submit to this necessity, and that with a book which is as long as this and which has taken as much time, it is possible to get a kind of obsession, so that one can perfectly well work on it forever in an effort to perfect it and to get in everything he wants to get in, but I believe it is more important to get this one done now and to go on to other work, particularly to the next two books [2] which follow this one, which I already have in manuscript, than to spend any more time with this. But I do intend to do my damndest in the two months that are left to me, and I know that Mr. Perkins himself has lavished more care and patience and hard work on this manuscript than any other editor I ever heard of would do. . . .

This is all for the present. . . . Later on, when this job is over, I really do want to get away for an extended vacation—although I don't know how extended it can be. Mr. Perkins has already got together the material for a long book of stories,[3] made up of stories which have been published and other things which have been cut out of my manuscript. He would like to follow the big book with the book of stories next Spring, and in that case I couldn't stay away from here very long. In addition, Part II,

[1] Actually, Wolfe kept on working on *Of Time and the River* until late December 1934 or early January 1935.

[2] *The October Fair* and *The Hills Beyond Pentland*.

[3] *From Death to Morning* which was published on November 14, 1935.

or the second book in this series of long books,[4] ought to come out next year also, and that probably means I will have to be here to work on it with him. He already has most of the manuscript in his desk, but it will be another huge book and I suppose there will be another siege of cutting and revision to go through.

I hope all goes well at Dingman's, and that you succeed in getting another governess to relieve you of some of your work; also that I shall see you soon.

Elizabeth Lemmon, to whom the following letter was written, is a close friend of the Perkins'. She had telephoned from Middleburg, Virginia and had Wolfe paged at Chatham Walk to invite him to visit her at her historic farm, "Welbourne," which Perkins was anxious for him to see. He finally spent a weekend at "Welbourne," in October, 1934.

To ELIZABETH LEMMON

5 Montague Terrace
Brooklyn, N.Y.
July 27, 1934

Dear Elizabeth:

I want to thank you for your kind invitation to come down and visit you for a day or two, and to tell you a little more coherently why I can't come. I don't know what was wrong with the telephone connection last night when you called me. I heard everything you said plainly, but although I was bawling at you, apparently you couldn't make out what I said. . . .

The trouble with a holiday, as I have found, is not just that one is away for a day or two, but one has such a good time seeing someone that he likes and meeting new people, that it is hard to get back into the grind of work when he returns. This is a mortal weakness and with me, a very dangerous one. I work very hard, I think about as hard as anyone I know, but I am also a very lazy person. I don't like work, and never shall. And like all big people, the force of inertia I have to fight against constantly is horrible. I have to fight to get out of bed in the morning, and to get myself started to work. And to get myself launched into action to go anywhere. So at the present time, during this hellish weather we've been having here, I am terribly afraid to stop working, because of all the sweat and agony it would take to get started up again. I am going to be through by October, and then I should like to go somewhere by a train or a ship—

---

[4] *The October Fair.*

if I can. Perhaps I'll go south for a short time before going anywhere else. Maybe you'll let me come to see you then. Would it be all right if I were borne in on a litter? I feel now that is the way I should like to travel. I should also like to sleep for about six weeks solid, without any of these dreams, waking-sleeping visions of the night and horrible nightmares which are like being stretched out on an operating table watching yourself dream—the kind of dream I have been having for two years.

It was awfully good to hear from you. It has been a long time since I had a long distance telephone call from anyone and to get one from Virginia at the Chatham, on a hot summer's night, was one of the nicest and most exciting things that has happened to me for a long time. I was sitting there with Max and Louise and a Miss Iredell [1] (who was, I believe, a former schoolmate of yours), and I thought there was some mistake when the waiter came and said I was wanted on the long distance telephone. Everybody wanted to go to Virginia right away, when I told them it was you.

I know that no sensible person would want to stay in New York at this time of the year, if he could get out into the country. But I wish you would be delivered here by telegraph or radio, just for an hour or two some night, to join us at the Chatham. They have a big outdoor café now where people sit at night and drink. Max and I have been working together every night until half past ten or eleven, and we go there later. It seems mighty pleasant for me, maybe because I spend the day in Brooklyn and sweat at manuscripts, and then ride over in the subway to New York and meet Max and work some more. After Brooklyn and the subway in July, one's tastes become very simple. And the Chatham seems wonderful to me this summer. Most of the men there look handsome, and all of the women beautiful. The outdoor café is really a nice place. . . .

So, as I said, I wish you could be shot or cabled up here some evening and meet us there. Louise and Max and I get together and pound the table and shake our fists and argue about Communism. After the second round of drinks I make Trotsky look like a republican. Max got so alarmed about my political tendencies that he subscribed to the "Christian Science Monitor" for me. They were running a series of articles by their Russian correspondent. The total effect of which was somewhat "agin" it, but maybe I got converted in spite of them.

I think Max went to Baltimore this morning, and will be there for the rest of the week. I wish you could take him down to Virginia for a day or two. I think he is very tired, and know that a vacation would do him a lot of good. He has sweated and labored and lavished untold care and patience upon this huge manuscript of mine. There is no adequate way

[1] Mr. and Mrs. Perkins and Miss Eleanor Iredell.

in which I can ever express my gratefulness, but I can only hope the book may have something in it which will in some measure justify his patience and care.

This is all for the present. Thanks again for your kind invitation, and please give me another chance some time when I am better able to take advantage of it.

Meanwhile, with best wishes for happiness and success in all you do,

The following letter to Helen Trafford Moore, an old friend of the Wolfe family in Asheville, was written in reply to one from her praising "The House of the Far and Lost."

To HELEN T. MOORE

5 Montague Terrace
Brooklyn, N.Y.
July 30, 1934.

Dear Helen:

Thanks for your letter. I was glad you liked the last story, and as usual, were kind enough to write and tell me so.

I was sorry to have missed you on your last visits to New York. I have been trying to wind up four years' of hard work by a last desperate effort. And I have been glued to my Ms. for several months. I stay at home all day and write, and every night this summer I have been working upon the Ms. with my friend, Mr. Perkins of Scribner's. This does not leave much time for seeing one's friends, as much as I should like to. I had hoped to get away this summer, but so far I have not been out of the city even for a week-end. The weather has been hellish, particularly this horrible sticky sweltering heat which was expressly invented in Hell for the inhabitants of New York City. Nevertheless, I have kept on working, and so great is the power of Necessity, I haven't noticed or minded the heat so much as usual. Is it not strange when one is a kid in a little town, all that you think and dream about is somehow getting to the great city. And when one reaches my present doddering age, he begins to dream fondly of the green pastures again—of finding a nice cool spot on top of some fairly convenient mountain in western North Carolina.

If I ever have a little luck and make a little money, perhaps I may realize some such dream as that. And I'll also be very simple. All that I want is a comfortable cabin with a front porch—and lots of shade. Then if I can find some good strong girl who is willing to share the hardships of my lot, that is to say, who can do the chores, haul up the water from the well, cook, wash and iron, tote provisions up the mountainside, lay in the wood and cut kindling, and tidy up the place generally, while I sit on the front porch and enjoy the magnificent panorama of the smoky mountains, I will be all set. Do you know any prospects? I am not in a position to make a definite offer of employment at the present time, but if I ever am, keep me in mind when you see a likely candidate. I can promise nice easy hours—not more than eighteen a day—, a roof to shelter her, that is if she is handy at carpentering and can keep it patched —and plenty of plain substantial food—if she can cook it.

This is all for the present. Maybe these idiocies will serve the purpose of getting me started off to work. So far I have done nothing today except drink coffee. I wish you would find out why one works so much better one day than another—and let me know.

I am glad you went to see my mother and sister and found them well. At one time I had hoped that I might see them this summer, and I am afraid now that will have to wait. I am looking forward to a grand vacation in October, and have considered various parts of Europe, Asia, Africa and the North American continent, but maybe I'll just wind up by getting on a train and going somewhere. Most of all I would like to go somewhere on a ship—anywhere, so long as it's a ship that will take a long time to make the voyage, and I could spend the whole time sleeping.

Let me hear from you when you next come to New York. Meanwhile, with best wishes for health and happiness and success in all you do.

To ROBERT RAYNOLDS

5 Montague Terrace
Brooklyn, New York
August 29, 1934

Dear Bob:

Thanks for your letter written on ship-board. . . . I should very much like to be in England with you—it's a fine country. One gets fed up with it sometimes while one is there, but it comes back to haunt you later. There are a thousand things I hope you get to see, and probably you will see many of them, but if this gets to you in London while you are there, I do wish you would go up to Stone's Chop House in Panton Street— it runs off Haymarket there—and try a pint of their old ale.

Also, Sir John Soane's house, which is, I believe, in Lincoln's Inn Fields —I think you can get in for the payment of a small fee. The house has all manner of collector's junk in it, but it has some of the greatest Hogarths in the world—one room in particular, which opens out in panels, has about all "The Rake's Progress." I have always thought the National Gallery was one of the finest and best arranged art galleries in the world, and it has in it more good things and less junk, and some of the pictures that I like best are there. There is another one by Hogarth— just a small one—a canvas on which he has painted the heads of six or eight of his servants, and I think it is one of the finest and truest paintings I ever saw. But you will see it all for yourself and tell me all about it when you come home. . . .

I have already been given more than a hundred galleys of the book, which is over 150,000 words. There is still an infinitude of things to be done, but I don't think that I will get to do them. They feel, in fact, that it is almost ready and they want to publish it as soon as they can. I suppose they are right about it. When one works so long on a manuscript as I have worked on this one, it becomes very hard to stop working or willingly yield to the persuasions of the publisher that you are now ready to publish. It does read wonderfully well; they all seem to believe in it. My tendency, of course, is to want to put into one volume the huge accumulation of all I have done in the last four or five years, but that is neither a possibility nor would it be advisable, and it is good now to have such careful and wise editing to help me and restrain me.

I hope by this time you have received good news about the manuscript of your new book, and that they are getting it ready for the press. Time goes so swiftly when you are working that it is hard to realize you have been gone three weeks already, and that soon you will be coming home again. . . . I long to get out in the great world and voyage around some more myself, but since that is still impossible, the next best thing will be to talk to someone who has done so. . . .

The brief note below was left on Wheelock's desk with galleys 7 through 11 of Of Time and the River. *Wolfe read and corrected these himself, although soon afterwards he got behind on correcting the galleys as they came back from the press and gave up any attempt to read them whatever.*

To JOHN HALL WHEELOCK

[New York City]

[August, 1934?]

Dear Jack:

I am leaving you five more galleys up through galley 11. I would have had more but had to correct proofs of the stories in addition. I found little to do here although I am not wholly satisfied with the way it *flows* —I put some question marks in margins of galleys 10 and 11 for this reason: the tense changes from past to present—present when describing the look of the little town from the train window.[1] Do you find this change of tense jumpy and confusing—and if you do will you change it all to past tense? I hope to give you some more galleys tomorrow and to get on now more rapidly.

The following letter was in reply to an invitation from the L. Effingham de Forests to spend a weekend at their summer house at Onteora Park, in the Catskills. The de Forests had first known Wolfe through Alfred Dashiell, and saw him frequently at one period.

To ANNE DE FOREST

[5 Montague Terrace]
[Brooklyn, N.Y.]
September 7, 1934

Dear Anne:

. . . I have done nothing but work this summer and in fact have not gone away for a single weekend. I am pretty tired at present, completely played out, and I think that I will go away for a day or two at the end of the week when I hope to finish another big section. The proofs of my book are now coming in and although a desperate struggle is being waged between the young author and his publisher, one to put in and the other to take out, I think the publisher may soon prevail. . . .

Although only a half million of my two million words will get displayed to the public in this first installment, that is something, and it will be wonderful to get to the end of it at last, if only for a month or so.

I don't know whether or not I can accept your kind invitation to come to Onteora September twentieth. From now on until they take the manuscript away from me finally and irrevocably, I have a tremendous job of work to do, because once the thing is gone out of my hands this time, it is gone for good. There is something final and terrifying about print, even about proof, and I want to pull myself together for this big effort to keep at it if need be until I drop. My instinct prompts me to go away right now for several days and try to get myself in shape for this final struggle. . . . If I see any chance of coming to Onteora on the

[1] This probably refers to the passage which appears on page 31 of *Of Time and the River*.

twentieth I will try to let you know in sufficient time—at any rate, I wanted to explain the present situation, and to thank you for so kindly inviting me. . . .

To ELIZABETH LEMMON

Brooklyn

Thurs., Nov. 8, 1934

Dear Elizabeth:

Max showed me your letter: the reason I haven't written you before this is that I'm just a bum and haven't done a thing—not written a line or done a lick of work for six weeks now. . . .

I shall never forget my visit to your beautiful home as long as I live. Your America is not my America and for that reason I have always loved it even more. There is an enormous age and sadness in Virginia—a grand kind of death—I always felt it even when all I did was ride across the state at night in a train—it's in the way the earth looks, the fields and the woods and in the great hush and fall of evening light. I've got to find my America somehow here in Brooklyn and Manhattan, in all the fog and the swelter of the city, in subways and railway stations, on trains and in the Chicago Stock Yards. I'm so glad you let me see your wonderful place and see a little of the country and the kind of life you have down there.

I haven't done a stroke of work since I came back and I hadn't worked for almost a month when I went down there—I just led an eating sleeping drinking kind of life. All I know how to do now is work and if I don't do that I'm a bum—and I'm not going to let my life go like that— I want to live a long time and get my work done and learn how to use my talent and make my life prevail and also get something out of life besides work. . . .

I've been trying to move back to Manhattan—am fed up with Brooklyn, have lived here long enough and finished a big job here, and now it's time to go—but find it hard to get a place in Manhattan that will fit my pocketbook, which is small, and my demands, which are pretty big— i.e. air, light, space and quiet, which in N.Y. have become capitalistic luxuries. Good-bye for the present—and all good wishes and thanks to you and Mrs. Morison [1] and all of you.

Please excuse pencil—all I've got to write with.

[1] Mrs. N. H. Morison, Miss Lemmon's eldest sister.

Lura Thomas McNair, to whom the following letter was addressed, had written Wolfe to ask if she could interview him for The State, *a weekly survey of North Carolina published in Raleigh. This interview was never written.*

To LURA THOMAS McNAIR

5 Montague Terrace
Brooklyn, N.Y.
November 18, 1934

Dear Miss McNair:

Thanks for your letter, and for what you say about my work. I sincerely appreciate your interest in what I am doing and your wish to make some mention of it in "The State." At the present time I am about as busy as I can be, working on proofs and making revisions in the manuscript, and I think it would be better for both of us if the piece you want to do could be deferred until after the first of the year, either before or after publication of the book which is now in press.

I confess that I have never had much experience with interviews or personal sketches, and the two or three times I did have, it seemed to me I was not very successful. When you are conscious that someone is talking to you with a view to publishing what you say, and that every word, so to speak, will be used "agin" you, a kind of panic seizes you and you are likely either to freeze up or to blurt out something in your confusion that sounds even more foolish than usual. So I think it might be a good idea if you asked me some definite questions which you think might be of interest to your readers, and I would try to answer them if I could.

I do want you to know that I appreciate your letter and the interest you have in what I do, and if I can be of any help to you, I shall be glad to do so.

Meanwhile, with kindest regards and best wishes for your success,

The following letter was written in reply to one from a Miss Elizabeth Cattelle who had sent Wolfe some of her own stories, asking him to tell her if he thought she could write or not.

To ELIZABETH CATTELLE

5 Montague Terrace
Brooklyn, N.Y.
November 18, 1934

Dear Miss Cattelle:

I am very sorry not to have answered your letter of October second before this. I was away on a vacation when you wrote and did not have the opportunity of reading your stories until quite recently.

I want to thank you for what you say about my work, and I sincerely appreciate the faith in my judgment that led you to send the stories to me; but what talents I have are perhaps creative; they are certainly not critical, and the last thing on earth for which I have any proficiency is giving people advice on any question so delicate and grave as the one you ask me. I think the best thing I can tell you is this: that no one has a right either to tell you to keep on writing or to stop writing, and that the answer to the question is one you will have to find out for yourself. My refusal to give you any advice on this matter may seem obstinate and unreasonable to you, but it is not. I think that I myself realize, as much as anyone, the anguish and the damage that may be done to a person whose heart is set on writing by incompetent or mistaken criticism, however well-meaning it may be. Since you have been kind enough to like some of the things I have written and to believe in them, perhaps you would be interested in the following little story, which may illustrate what I am trying to say.

When I was a student at Harvard University a little more than ten years ago, I was a member of a certain celebrated course in play writing which was being given there then. At that time in my life it seemed to me that the only thing worth living for was the writing of plays, and that if I could not do that, my life would never be of any value. The first play I wrote [1] was produced there at the University, and although the play read well in class, it was a complete and dismal failure when it was put on. No one thought it was any good, and most people took pains to tell me so. It was a very desperate occasion for me. It seemed to me that my whole life and future depended upon it, and in this state of mind I went to see a man on whose judgment, honesty and critical ability I relied to the utmost. [2] I asked him what he thought of my abilities as a writer, and if he thought I would ever succeed in doing the thing

---

[1] *The Mountains.*

[2] An older member of the 47 Workshop who, at Professor Baker's request, had befriended Wolfe. However, he insists that he never advised Wolfe to give up writing, and that such advice would have been unthinkable for him.

I most wanted to do; and although he tried at first, out of the kindness of his heart, to evade the issue, he finally told me pointblank that he did not think I would ever become a writer and that he thought my abilities were critical rather than creative and therefore advised me to devote my time to graduate study in the University, leading to a Ph.D. degree and a position in the teaching profession. I know now that the man spoke honestly and according to his sincere conviction. He may also have been right in what he said, but I am not yet ready to concede that he was. I will never forget the almost inconceivable anguish and despair that his words caused me. Therefore, since that time I have never been able to give a person advice on such a matter as this one, not only because of the infinite possibilities for error, but also because of the damage that may be done either by rousing false hopes or by causing useless and unnecessary distress.

The best thing I can tell you is this: that if writing means as much to you as you say it does, I should let nothing in the world stop it. And in the end I think that that will be not only the most logical course but also the one that is inevitably the most right. In other words, I think no one in the world except yourself can find out whether you can be a writer or have the power to write within you, and I also think that no one in the world except yourself can satisfactorily find out whether you lack that power. So it seems to me that the answer to your question must be discovered by yourself.

Please do not understand by this that I am taking this method of informing you that I think your stories are without merit. I am saying no such thing, and what I have said has no reference at all to your stories, but rather to my own reasons for not wanting to give advice on such a question as you ask.

I shall be willing, however, to talk to you about your stories, with the understanding that I am talking just as an individual reader, and not as a critical expert. If you are ever in New York you can reach me by calling Triangle 5-5683, and if I am able to see you I will let you know.

Meanwhile, with thanks again for your letter, and for letting me see your stories,

To ROBERT RAYNOLDS

5 Montague Terrace
Brooklyn, New York

January 14, 1935

Dear Bob:

Thanks for your card. . . . I certainly won't go away before the first of February and since I've done absolutely nothing about it so far, I imagine it will be somewhat later than that. Perkins is going to Florida this week to visit Hemingway and I shan't go away until he gets back.

For better or for worse, everything I can now do about my book has been done and ended. It has all now been taken out of my hands and put into pages and I cannot make a change or alteration now even if I would. Of course I continue to have regrets. I feel that I have been very lazy during the last two months and think of all the additional scenes I could have written. But Perkins and Wheelock both feel that these scenes would not contribute as much as I think they would and in fact might do more harm than good. I hope they are right. At any rate, it is over, done for, ended, and in this awful fatality of print I feel now, come what may, a kind of tremendous relief. I have just finished writing out the title and dedication pages the way I want them to go and am trying my luck at an introduction which, if it is any good, I should like to see included in the book but which anyway I may be able to sell to the magazine.[1]

Did you ever try dictation, that is, for anything which you hope to get published? I am trying it in this introduction for the first time in my life, simply because I had a feeling that I should like to have the introduction sound like talking rather than like writing. We made a good start the other day and got several pages done and although a good deal of it was very clumsy, a lot of it nonessential, I had better luck than I expected, so I am going on and try to say my little piece out to the end and then get busy at it with a pencil and see what happens. Of course I suppose the idea of dictation is one that at one time or another lures every writer. Most of us are so lazy that the sheer brute labor of putting words down on paper, especially as I have to do it—a million words of writing to get perhaps a hundred thousand words of print—is something we will get out of in any way we can. Maybe it is the best way of doing it in the end because it never allows us to forget the grim nature of our occupation.

This is all the news for the present. . . . I certainly do want to see you before I go away and I hope that all goes well with you and that you can manage it. Meanwhile, with all my best wishes for you and your mother and all the family,

LeGette Blythe, to whom the following letter was written, had known Wolfe at the University of North Carolina, and was Literary Editor of The Charlotte Observer *from 1930 to 1950. He is the author of* Marshal Ney: A Dual Life; Alexandriana; Shout Freedom; Bold Galilean; William Henry

[1] This was omitted from *Of Time and the River* and published later as *The Story of a Novel*. It first appeared in the December 14, 21, and 28, 1935 issues of *The Saturday Review of Literature,* and was then brought out in book form by Scribners in April, 1936.

Belk: Merchant of the South; A Tear for Judas; Miracle in the Hills *etc.*:
also of an article, "The Thomas Wolfe I Knew," which appeared in the Au-
gust 16, 1945, issue of The Saturday Review of Literature. *At the bottom*
of a letter written to Blythe by Scribners on January 4, 1935, Wolfe had
written the following brief note: "Hello, LeGette. I'm going to Denmark in
February—as part of the freight on a freighter. Better pack up your extra
shirt and come along. How are you?" To which Blythe had answered that he
was fine and had a wife and two small sons.

To LeGETTE BLYTHE

[5 Montague Terrace]
[Brooklyn, N.Y.]
January 18, 1935

Dear LeGette:

Thanks for your nice letter. It was good to hear from you and at such
length after so long a time. No, I agree with you, if you are involved
to the extent you say, you would need a good deal more than an extra
shirt to take that trip with me. Please accept my heartiest congratulations.
I had no idea you were the head of such a thriving family and my own
lack of accomplishment in that direction makes me a little envious when
you tell me of it.

It's awfully good of you to take an interest in what I do and I want you
to know how sincerely I appreciate it and how much it means to me. I
have worked like hell these past four or five years and although I am still
in the apprentice stage I hope and believe I have learned something and
will keep on learning. It took me a long time. My idea was all right but
my calculations were a little off. In other words, I thought I was going
to write one book, a mere paragraph of two hundred thousand words or
so, and I ended up by writing three, each of which is about a half million
words long. Furthermore, I started out by writing number three first,
then number two, and at last I got back to number one [1] which is now
finished and which Scribner's are publishing in a few weeks. The end is
not yet. There are still two more to follow before the awful deed is done
and the reading public, if it manages to survive, may refer to the author
of "Anthony Adverse" as a writer of short sketches. Anyway, the story
ought to sound pretty familiar to you and I suppose it proves that the
leopard never changes its spots.

No, I don't think I have changed very much since the Chapel Hill days,

[1] Wolfe probably meant *The Hills Beyond Pentland, The October Fair,* and *Of
Time and the River,* although *The Hills Beyond Pentland* was never completed nor
anywhere near a half million words long.

not inside at any rate. Outside I regret to say I have changed heavily. The gaunt Wolfe of the mountains is no more. I weigh around two hundred and forty pounds and I am afraid I'll never get back the old greyhound model. However, if I get to Norway perhaps I can bound gaily around from crag to crag and from fjord to fjord and shake a few pounds off around the middle.

I see Bill Weber [2] at Scribner's quite often and he always tells me when he has a letter from you. Of course, I am interested in the book you are working on and I wish you the best kind of success with it. When you find a publisher I hope naturally it will be Scribners. I have the greatest reason to be grateful to them. They have not only stood behind me and believed in me in every way but the whole outfit has sweated with me in an effort to get me to deliver the goods or produce the child. And I know that the reason they have done this has been far more because they wanted to see me come through and do a good piece of work than for any commercial motive. The amount of labor, patience, and devotion which the editors put in on my huge manuscript is something that can never be reckoned in terms of money and which can never be explained or paid for except in terms of friendship and belief. I think they are the finest and most honorable group of people I have ever known, this comes right out of my heart and I can wish you therefore no better luck than to hope you find such publishers for the books you write.

This is all for the present. I was mighty glad to get your letter and to hear your voice again after so many years. I hope to see you long before another such period of time has gone by, and at any rate I hope neither of us wait so long to write another letter. I appreciate your offer to help me in any way you can.[3] I should be grateful for anything you did but the best help is the knowledge of your interest in the work I do and your good wishes. With thanks again for your letter and with best wishes for your success and happiness.

P.S. I see John Terry [4] every week or so. He lives just a few blocks away from me here on Brooklyn Heights and we get together for dinner and then discuss the strange vexed state of man until the cold, grey dawn and the last milk wagon have gone by. So you see we haven't changed much from Chapel Hill days, after all.

2 William Weber was head of the publicity department at Scribners at this time.

3 With publicity in *The Charlotte Observer*.

4 John S. Terry had graduated from the University of North Carolina in 1918 and become an Assistant Professor of English at New York University. He was the editor of *Thomas Wolfe's Letters to His Mother*, published by Scribners in 1943.

The following is probably a fragment of a letter written by Wolfe to Mrs. Bernstein from the Île de France, in answer to a letter from her congratulating him on having finished Of Time and the River. *The letter which he actually sent to her is lost. As a result of this correspondence, a reconciliation took place between them when Wolfe came back to America, but they saw each other only infrequently after that.*

Probably to ALINE BERNSTEIN

[On board the S.S. *Ile de France*]

(March 2 ? 1935.)

When I got your letter I wept with joy and pride. I have kept silence, have not spoken or written to you in over five years—but not with an ugly stubbornness, only with a stubbornness that made me want to show you something that was worthy of me—and of you. My heart is full of affection and loyalty for you—it has always been: I am devoted to the memory of everything you ever said to me, of every kind or generous thing you ever did for me. Your proud words of faith and glory make a great music in me—I know your value, know the princely ore of which you're made. You are the best, the highest

[THE FRAGMENT BREAKS OFF HERE]

To BELINDA JELLIFFE

Cie Gle Transatlantique
French Line
Wednesday, March 6, 1935

Dear Mrs. Jelliffe:

This has been a very wild and stormy day on the Atlantic, so I thought it would be appropriate to write a few lines to *you*. (I trust my delicate allusiveness is not lost on you!) The voyage has been uneventful—the ship rocked and lurched from side to side like a great cradle, until to-day when it began to heave up and down also—with the result that quite a few people seem to be feeling it. Fortunately, I have felt all right, and my appetite—I know you'll be sorry to hear this—has been too, too hearty! The food is excellent, and the accommodations about those of a good hotel—my only complaint is that the damned tremendous rocking and lurching of the boat has made sleep difficult at night—I've gone rattling about in my bunk from side to side like a pea in a pod—a delicate little 250 pound pea if you never saw one and want to know. I've done nothing yet with that beautiful little typewriter,[1] but then I can use the Atlantic Ocean as an excuse—the way tables, chairs, and other unfixed objects have gone flying across floors I'd have had to be another daring young man on the flying trapeze to use it. The ocean has been magnificently beautiful and to-day most of all—to-day a terriffic, appalling smoky welter coming immediately out of ash-grey sky, waves mountain-high exploding all around, a whistling of wind, and a hissing of water like a tornado, and spume and spray blowing by like hell, the poor little 46,000 ton *Ile de France* bounced and tossed about in it like a rotten straw— and the appalled and stricken heart of man wondering if he had ever known earth or remembered home or would ever see such things again.

I want to thank you first of all for your radiogram because it wished for me the things we all want most and would carry with us everywhere if we could. But I have had little joy or peace or love yet—still tormented, still driven on by drink, goaded by useless requests, beset by wild and foolish apprehensions—wondering what the swine will have done to me or to my book by the time this reaches you,[2] if there will still be heart and power in me to go on with my work if they damn me up and down and say that I'm no good—and knowing all the time that I'll go on!

It's no use—I think there is joy and peace and love on earth for us, but we needn't go across the sea to find it—no truer words were ever written than those of Horace—"You can change your skies but not your soul." But I'm here now and I'm glad to be here and I'm going to see something strange and new before I return. Meanwhile, thanks for all your acts of loving kindness—I'll never forget them. I don't know if I'd have got off without your help or not but I'm damned sure of one thing —I wouldn't have been on the *Ile de France*.[3] So thanks, thanks again —and *please, please*, do your home work [4]—if you don't, you'll not only bitterly disappoint me, but another friend of yours who knows more than I'll ever know and who believes in you.[5]

The Cie. Gle. Transatlantique and the U.S. Post Office apparently order their pens from the same maker—so excuse it please!

[1] Mrs. Jelliffe had given Wolfe a typewriter, knowing that if he would learn to use one his work would be much easier for him. However, he never did learn, but continued to hire various typists who either copied his longhand writing or, during the last two years of his life, typed his work from dictation.

[2] *Of Time and the River* was to be published on March 8.

[3] Mrs. Jelliffe had helped Wolfe to move out of Brooklyn, to store his manuscripts at Scribners and his furniture at her house, and to catch the *Ile de France*.

[4] The writing of her book, *For Dear Life*, published by Scribners in 1936.

[5] Maxwell E. Perkins.

On March 8, the day of publication of Of Time and the River, *Perkins cabled Wolfe as follows: "Magnificent reviews, somewhat critical in ways expected, full of greatest praise." This did not reassure Wolfe sufficiently and he wandered around Paris, drinking heavily and feeling dizzy and nauseated and mentally upset. Finally he sent Perkins the following cablegram.*

To MAXWELL E. PERKINS
[Cablegram]

Paris
March 13, 1935

Dear Max: To-day if I mistake not is Wednesday March thirteenth. I can remember almost nothing of last six days. You are the best friend I have. I can face blunt fact better than damnable incertitude. Give me the straight plain truth.

To this, Perkins cabled on March 14: "Grand excited reception in reviews. Talked of everywhere as truly great book. All comparisons with greatest writers. Enjoy yourself with light heart."

To A. S. FRERE-REEVES
[Telegram]

Paris
[Tuesday, March 19, 1935]

Dear Frere: Is England cheaper than France? Money melting fast here. Would like to come over for week or two if possible. Address Amexco Paris.

To A. S. FRERE-REEVES
[Telegram]

Paris
[Thursday, March 21, 1935]

Taking 10:30 Sunday train. Visit entirely friendly and recreational. I never read a book nor heard of one and don't want to. Best wishes,

To ROBERT RAYNOLDS

St. George's Court
26 Hanover Square
London, W.1

Friday, March 29, 1935
This is the day of the Grand National
and the talk is all of horses!

Dear Bob:

I have a heavy charge of expiation and atonement towards you and Marguerite—for not having come to see you more often when you were in the hospital, for being rude to Marguerite over the phone, for not having written you sooner. It is perhaps too much for me to expiate alone —may I ask you again to help with more forgiveness than I deserve, but with some more of the understanding and loving kindness you both have shown me. I can't go into explanations over what cannot be explained— I can only say that I hope that time of anguish, frenzy, hopelessness and madness is gone forever—and that somehow I have won through and will return restored to do better work, and to grow in wisdom, power and humanity—all that you wish for me, and I for you. May I tell you both how much I value and cherish your friendship—how much your belief has meant to me—how deeply and genuinely I want to be for you the kind of friend you have been for me?

I can't write much more here—they're closing the American Express and I am finishing this there and must get out now. As for what I've done and seen I'll have to tell you later. . . . Have had no mail from America and read no papers—Max sent me two cables and a letter—and for his sake and Scribners, and for my own, I hope and pray to God that all goes well. Love to all,

The letter below was addressed to the mother of John Hall Wheelock.

To EMILY HALL WHEELOCK

St. George's Court
26 Hanover Square
London, W.1

Sunday, March 31, 1935

Dear Mrs. Wheelock:

Will you forgive me for not having written sooner to thank you for your fine and generous steamer letter? . . . I have written no letters until the last day or two. I don't know definitely how things have gone at home about the book—I have read no American newspapers and had no mail save a letter and two cables from Mr. Perkins. These were immensely heartening and full of hope, and not only for my own sake, but for his sake and that of another dear friend of mine at Scribners— your son, Jack—who have both put into the book an incalculable labor of devotion, I hope and pray to God that all has gone well with it, and that my book is having the fortunate and happy life we all want it to have.

Dear Mrs. Wheelock, I can never adequately tell you of the great debt of gratitude I owe to Jack and Mr. Perkins, but, believe me, I am profoundly conscious of it, and hope that I may go on to do work that will in some measure justify their faith and friendship. Your own belief and words of praise are also deeply treasured by me. Let me thank you again for your wonderful generous letter and wish you all good health and happiness. . . .

To MAXWELL E. PERKINS

> St. George's Court,
> 26 Hanover Square,
> London W1.
>
> Sunday, March 31, 1935
> * This is Section *one*—am sending letter in sections.

Dear Max:

I know I should have written you before this, but until the last two or three days I have written no one at all—save for one or two letters written on the ship—and of course have saved your letter to the last, because it was probably the one which should have been written first.

Thursday, April 4th. I am picking this letter up again after three or four days intermission—I seem to have a hell of a time getting on with it, which is strange, as it is the one I most especially want to write. Charlie Scribner is in town and called me up day before yesterday and I had lunch with him and his wife at their hotel yesterday and am meeting them again for dinner tomorrow night. It was good to see him, and in spite of Mrs. Scribner's instructions that we should not talk shop, I'm afraid we did talk shop. I have stuck to my resolution not to read reviews in the American papers, but I confess that I was unable to resist the temptation to buy N.Y. papers of recent dates to see what your advertising was like, and if any mention of the book in sales-lists was made. I saw a fine big page advertisement in the *Times* for Sunday, March 24th—and also ads in other papers. Charlie had several clippings that showed the book on best seller lists, and the latest one I saw—the *N.Y. Times* for Monday, March 25, showed it leading in New York, Philadelphia, Washington and San Francisco—my own South apparently has left me flat. Of course, Max, this is good and cheering news and I hope it will continue and mean that you will sell the book—the copies that you have printed—not only in order to pay off my money-debt to Scribners,[1] but so that both Scribners and myself may get a little profit—for me, also, a little feeling of security. How unreasonable and contradictory our natures are! It would be fantastic and comical to know that I had written a "best seller," it would be wonderful to get the money that would come from it, and yet I would be troubled by it too—to know I had written a best seller, was a best-seller kind of writer: I would worry then to know what was wrong with my book, whether you and I had done something to cheapen it and make it popular.

I was in a very bad state when I got over here, but think I am much better since coming to England a week or so ago. People have been very kind to me here—Frere-Reeves, his wife, Hugh Walpole, some people I know in Hampstead and in Bloomsbury, etc.—and the English have a way of putting you into an ordered and regular way of life, which I certainly needed badly. I am living in what is called a service flat in an old square right in the heart of fashionable London, Mayfair. It is much too grand for me and much too expensive—5 guineas ($25) a week—but it is so damned comfortable and well run that I hate to leave it. There is a valet like Ruggles of Red Gap, and neat maids, and in the living room a nice coal fire. They bring up breakfast and set a morning table every morning, come in and tell me it is ready and I come out and read the morning *Times* and eat ham and eggs, kippers, sausages, marmalade and tea.

Frere-Reeves was waiting for me at Folkestone when I crossed the channel, I was in a sorry shape, but it was good to see him, and the familiar look of England again, which makes me feel at home, and as if I've always known it. He drove me up to his weekend house which was only fifteen or twenty miles from Folkestone, overlooking a beautiful tract of green country known as The Romney Marshes. His wife was waiting for us, we had tea, and went for a walk across the fields and through a wood, and I began to feel better. We came back and had a fine dinner of English roast beef, tart, cheese, wine etc., and started to drive up to London about ten o'clock that night—I was dozing off to sleep whole way up, went to a hotel for the night and got my first good night's sleep in weeks.

---

[1] As of March 8, 1935, Scribners had advanced to Wolfe a total of $2,050 against royalties on *Of Time and the River*.

In Paris I couldn't sleep at all—I walked the streets from night to morning and was in the worst shape I have ever been in in my life. All the pent-up strain and tension of the last few months seemed to explode and I will confess to *you* that there were times there when I really was horribly afraid I was going mad—all the unity and control of personality seemed to have escaped from me—it was as if I were on the back of some immense rackety engine which was running wild and over which I had no more control than a fly. I came home to my hotel one night— or rather at daybreak one morning—tried to get off to sleep—and had the horrible experience of seeming to disintegrate into at least six people —I was in bed and suddenly it seemed these other shapes of myself were moving *out* of me—all around me—one of them touched me by the arm —another was talking in my ear—others walking around the room—and suddenly I would come to with a terrific jerk and all of them would rush back into me again. I can swear to you I was not asleep—it was one of the strangest and most horrible experiences I've ever had. There were about three days of which I could give no clear accounting—and loss of memory of that sort is to me one of the worst things that can happen. That was the reason I sent you that frenzied telegram—I had found your first cable when I got to Paris, but I wanted to know the worst. Your second cable cheered me up tremendously and at last when your letter with the excerpts from the reviews came I felt enormously relieved.

I hope to God it all really is true as you said—that we have had a genuine and great success and that when I come back I will find my position enormously enhanced. If that is true I feel I can come back and accomplish almost anything. If that is true—if it is true that we have successfully surmounted the terrible, soul-shaking, heart-rending barrier of the accursed "second book"—I believe I can come back to work with the calm, the concentration, the collected force of my full power which I was unable to achieve in these frenzied, tormented, and soul-doubting last five years. More than ever before, I have come to realize during this past month when I have had time to look back on that period and take stock of it—more than ever before I have come to realize how much the making of a book becomes an affair of honor to its maker. The honor of the artist—his whole life, all his character and personal integrity, all that he hopes and wants and dreams of, everything that gives his life any value to him—is at stake each time he produces any work—and that is really what the whole business of creation amounts to in the end. I hope to God that you and I have come through this ordeal honorably—I hope that we have won a true and worthy victory. You, I think, have done so in your great labors with me as an editor and a man. As for myself, the victory, if I have really won it, while a precious one, is not entire and whole as

I would make it. If I have made my stamp come through—if through the ordeal and the agony of that book, the main outline of my full intention is revealed—that is a victory. But I can not ease my heart with the thought that I came through unshaken—I was badly shaken, time and again I was driven to the verge of utter self-doubt and despair by the sense of pressure all around me—the questions asked, the doubts expressed about my ability to write another book, the criticisms of my style, my adjectives, verbs, nouns, pronouns, etc., my length and fullness, my lack of Marxian politics and my failure to expound a set position in my writings—by all this, and countless other evidences of this pressure, I allowed myself so seriously to be disturbed and shaken that once or twice I may have been upon the very brink of total failure and submission. And now although, thanks to your great and patient efforts, I may have won through to a victory—and pray to God this may be so!—that victory, as I say, is but a partial one, the full sum and import of my purpose has not been revealed.I feel I have by no means begun to make a full and most effective use of my talent, and I hope this book will give me a position of some security, and freedom at last

This is Section Two

from the kind of perturbations that have tormented me these past five years, so that I may be able to achieve the concentration and totality I desire.

Sunday, April 7. Well, here I go again and I'm *bound* to finish this time, because it's an English Sunday and as I look out on Hanover Square there is nothing except the fronts of houses—not a person in sight, not a sound except a bird in the park—just an enormous slab of petrified time —that's England on Sunday. I saw Charlie and his wife again on Friday night—wedging into a dress suit I haven't worn for years—it is horrible how fat and heavy I've become—I've got to remedy it somehow. I told Mrs. Scribner to have a barrel ready when I got there, for I didn't know what would happen if I drew a deep breath. We had dinner together and spent the rest of the evening talking in their rooms—most of the talk being about home again, Scribners in particular: why you wore your hat in the office—Mrs. S. was particularly anxious to know about that and I volunteered my own explanation—whether Jack has had a great mysterious love—she was sure he could not have written some of his poetry if he hadn't—and the various manifestations of Whitney [2] in all his forms.

I have had several long talks with Charlie and got to know him better than I ever did before—I think he is a very fine, a very generous and sensitive man, with an almost anguished sense of his responsibility, the most earnest desire to be fair and just and generous to all his people. He told me

<hr>
2 Whitney Darrow.

that he felt that Scribners now constituted a tradition and that he felt it was somehow his duty to preserve it and pass it on. I told him that I thought he was right in feeling this way, and speaking as an "outsider" who had had some experience with the house and a chance to observe and know its people for the past five years, I was certain that dozens of people there, even people in subordinate positions, felt the same way about the place as he did; and that I had never seen another place where the spirit and feeling of the people was on the whole as good.

Charlie seemed particularly anxious to do something for Scribners while he is here in England—he told me that since Galsworthy's death there has been no one to fill his place on the list. He thought Hugh Walpole might do this, and told me that Walpole is dissatisfied with Doubleday and had approached Scribners indirectly through an agent. At any rate, I took Charlie at once up to see Frere-Reeves who, although not Walpole's English publisher, is very intimate with him, and of course had former connections with Doubleday. Charlie put the matter to him, and told him that he had heard Walpole was dissatisfied with Doubleday and would like to come to Scribners. Reeves said he thought these facts were correct and agreed it would be proper to write or speak to him— Charlie wrote a letter, but Walpole has gone away on a three weeks cruise to Greece.

That is the way the matter stands: I offered to help in any way I can— if anything I can do *will* help—and since there seems to be nothing at all improper in the circumstances. But, although I did not tell Charlie so, and have myself no knowledge of publishing, I thought he had too high an idea of Walpole's value and of his ability to take Galsworthy's place. I have not read any of his books; in recent years, of course, his reputation has been in the decline, and he has been the subject of much criticism, including a cruel portrait by Somerset Maugham in one of his books—which by the way in many respects was amazingly accurate. Walpole for example has a little book filled with names and engagements and when asking you to lunch will consult it, etc. But Charlie told Frere-Reeves jokingly that Walpole was "a good selling plater"—in contrast to a fellow like me, for instance, who was a horse who might run like hell and put up a performance that Walpole couldn't touch, but on the other hand might fall down completely. —Walpole, you see, being the kind of animal who might not touch the heights, but would always perform creditably and "never do anything bad." Now, this certainly doesn't hurt my feelings, in fact, I think human vanity is such that we are inclined to be pleased at being considered the "eccentric genius," but in the end I think such reasoning is wrong—i.e. if it were true, just for the sake of illustration, that I am a man of great talent and Walpole a mediocre one,

I think it would be much more likely that my own performance would be consistently better than his, and that the house would profit by me. This has nothing at all to do with me but simply with that rubber-stamp judgment of people that seems to me so profoundly wrong—I am going to talk to you about it in a moment in connection with these excerpts from reviews you sent me, for I think we may do something about them that is important and needs to be done.

As to Walpole again, I think it very likely that you can have him if you want him. My impression of the man is this: a very amiable, genial, robust-appearing kind of man, with much real friendliness and generous feeling in him towards other people, particularly young writers starting out. But also a man completely sold out to success, comfort, "getting on"—so much so now that, no matter what the purpose and ideal (if any) of his youth may have been, he no longer could make the sacrifice, the effort, and the risk of attempting an important work. He was apparently a little ruffled at the criticisms made of his books in recent years, and he told me never to accept the opinion of unsuccessful people about anything—this seems to have some truth in it until you reflect that it is often dangerous to accept the opinion of successful people, too. Walpole, I think, is a man for whom the work of writing has become a necessary but rather tedious adjunct to the more pleasant occupation of being a successful popular novelist. He has a magnificent apartment overlooking the Green Park, three flunkies to wait on him, and an immense treasure in original manuscripts, autographed first editions, paintings, sculpture, jade and amber ornaments etc. For three hours every morning—from ten to one—his servants have orders that he "is not to be disturbed" by anyone—it is during this time, I suppose, that he writes his novels—one a year, he told me, for the last twenty-five years. The rest of the day is all mapped out in the little black book—lunch with so-and-so, the young first-novelist at one, address Golder's Green Woman's Club at three, tea at Atheneum with Sir So-and-So at five, dinner with Lord and Lady This-and-That at seven, theatre with somebody later, read the new books and write column for *Herald Tribune* book review before going to bed. There's your "selling plater" and of course I hope you get him and that his books are profitable for the house. He has diabetes, by the way, and takes a heavy injection of insulin twice a day, almost died of arthritis Christmas, but looks the picture of ruddy, robust, English-country squire-lord.

Another bit of news that may interest you: Frere-Reeves called up the other day and told me that the Book Society (leading English book club, anyway) of which Walpole is a member [3] are apparently interested in

[3] He was Chairman.

Of Time and the River, and had indicated they might choose it, if he deferred his proposed publishing plans—I think he intended to publish in June. He said it was not a definite promise but that it looked fairly sure, and of course I agreed that it would be right to defer publication to fit in with their plans if they agree to take it—it would help the sale enormously, Frere said.[4]

As for my other plans, it looks now as if I'm going to Berlin the end of this week or beginning of next, from there to Copenhagen, and then on to Russia in time for the May Day celebrations—this because I am now planning a monumental work in three volumes on The Success of Russian Communism, and following the example of some of my American colleagues, I figure I shall need at least a week in Russia to gather the necessary material. It looks as if I've got to go to Germany—it is apparently the only way of getting any money, if there is any—I understand it can not be taken out of the country, so I might as well go there and spend it. I wired the German publisher a week ago and asked him if he wanted the new book and what his intentions were, and said I was coming to Berlin. He wired back emphatically that he did want it, was "enchanted" to welcome me to Berlin, and when would I arrive? To which I wired back, on Frere-Reeves cold business advice, that I was delighted, but was also hard up, and what sort of offer would he make. To which he answered that he was "certain" I would be satisfied with his offer, and offered to pay the expenses of my trip. That's how the matter now stands, so I suppose I'm going.

My money has melted away like snow—Europe, particularly France, is now horribly expensive for the impoverished and devaluated Americans. Of course, I bought round trip steamship's passage which was around $250 before leaving—at any rate I've got my ticket home, although it's by the French line, and if I go to Germany, there's no way of using it unless I can turn it in (as they said I could) and exchange it for passage on a German or Swedish boat. In addition to that, there have been railway fares, visas, etc. I am buying clothes—an overcoat, a hat, having shirts made, and a suit of clothes by Prince of Wales trousers-maker, and will be the damndest dude in American literature when I come back— but still owe about $65 on clothes, etc., and counting up this morning found I had only $250 left. I hope to God you really *are* selling that book. Thank heaven, I don't have to see the look on Cross's [5] face when he hears the bitter news. Having been bitten by the bug of foppishness I would

[4] In spite of Walpole's efforts on behalf of *Of Time and the River,* the Book Society finally declined it, probably chiefly because of its length.

[5] Robert Cross, head of the Accounting Department at Scribners and one of the directors of the firm.

now go the whole hog and get another suit of clothes—they make 'em so good here—but perhaps had better not until I know more about the extent of my prosperity.

Max, I have done no writing—i.e. no formal work—since coming here, but I have kept a sort of notebook, or diary, in an enormous book I carry around in my pocket. The Paris parts, because of my state at that time, are somewhat distracted, incomplete, but the whole will be fairly complete by time I finish, and in spite of my state of mind over book, etc., I have seen and noted some very amusing and interesting things, persons, events—one, for example, in Paris late one night that tells more about the French and their character than whole volumes of speculation. It was in a *bistro*—i.e. a cheap bar with a few tables, a semi-circular bar of zinc, man behind bar, avaricious dark-visaged madame at cashier's desk counting up coins with holes in them, a couple of waiters, two young, apathetic, unsuccessful-looking prostitutes at tables with a beer before them—two o'clock in the morning, Place St Michel: at the bar only two customers, one a dingy looking little man, harmless, but very drunk, pounding on zinc bar, arguing in hoarse loud voice with bar man and other customer. Bar man young, hawk-visaged Frenchman, alert and able looking, blue apron, sleeves rolled up, keeping sharp eye on situation as barmen do the world over, finally calls on drunk to pay up and get out. Little dingy drunk refuses to pay—he owes *three* francs—gets very hoarse and obstreperous, pounds on bar, and finally offers to fight. "Very well! Good!" says bar man coolly, "But if you are going to fight, why don't you take off your coat?" The little drunk considers this with drunken solemnity for a moment, then wagging his head in drunken agreement says: "Good! All right! I *will* take off my coat!", and considers the idea such a good one that he not only takes off his overcoat, which he hands to one of the waiters, but peels off his *other* coat as well, and hands it to other waiter —at which dark-visaged madame, who has been murmuring tender cajoleries to a little dog and feeding him sugar which she cleverly conceals in her hand under her shoulder and various other places, making him hunt for it, saying "Ah,

This is Section Three

you are wicked, you! You're the naughty one!" etc. (one of the grotesque things in them is this sentimentality towards animals and their hard-boiled treatment of each other)—anyway she now turns from this tender dog-baby-talk and begins to screech out harsh instructions to the waiters who have both of the poor little drunk man's coats. The bar man speaks a few curt words of instructions to them, and the waiters, grinning from ear to ear with delight, rush off triumphantly towards the back of the place bearing the little man's two coats as security for his unpaid three francs. At this, of course, he is wildly indignant, bellows with rage, and takes a drunken swing at the barman. This is just what the barman has been waiting for—he vaults over the zinc bar like a flash, the waiters rush up, and they bounce the poor little man, minus both his coats, and in his shirtsleeves, right out on his ear—on the cold and frosty pavements of the Place St. Michel. Now I submit that this is a *French* story: the little man would very probably have been bounced out on his ear in England or America, but I think it is highly improbable that we would have thought of getting his two coats away from him first.

Anyway, I have kept this sort of diary, people, events, conversations of all sorts—the great boat race between Oxford and Cambridge Saturday, which I saw, a wonderful spectacle, and the look and talk of the English poor all around me, lining the banks of the Thames as the crews came by—what it is like being back in Europe for an American after the last four years in America—how Europe seems to me now after the first abashment and bewilderment of my first visits in the twenties has worn off—why I know I could not live here—many other things. I intend to make the same sort of notes for Germany and Russia if I go there—just what I see and feel and hear—and it occurred to me that the whole thing, starting the moment I left New York on ship until I return, very much pruned and condensed, of course, might make interesting and entertaining reading under some such title as "The Busman's Holiday." What do you think?

Now, as to those excerpts from the reviews you sent me—They were splendid, wonderfully heartening, and I hope they were not too *hand-picked.*—i.e. I hope that, as you said, they were taken more or less at random, and if the reviews on the whole were, as you say, better than these excerpts would indicate, that would be wonderful. But even from these excerpts, good as they are, and from one or two indications in advance notices before I left New York, I think I can spot the trend of some of the enthusiasm. Max, Max, perhaps you think I hate all forms of criticism, but the sad truth is, how much more critical am I, who am generally supposed to be utterly lacking in the critical faculty, than most of these critics are. God knows, I could profit by a wise and penetrating criticism as much as any man alive, but as I grow older I am beginning to see how rare—how much rarer even than *Lear, Hamlet,* the greatest productions of art—such criticism is—and how wrong-headed, false, and useless almost everything that passes as criticism is. I know for example that the great length of the book will be criticized, but the real, the tragic truth is that the book is not too long, but too short. I am not talking of page-length, word-length, or anything like that—as I told you many times, I did not care whether the final length of the book was 300, 500, or a 1000 pages, so long as I had realized completely and finally my full intention—and that was not realized. I still sweat with anguish—with a sense of irremediable loss—at the thought of what another six months would have done to that book—how much more whole and perfect it would have been. Then there would have been no criticism of its episodic character—for, by God, in purpose and in spirit, that book was not episodic but a living whole and I could have made it so—the whole inwrought, inweaving sense of time and of man's past conjoined forever to each living present moment of his life could have been made manifest —the thing that I *must* and *will* get into the whole thing somehow.

Again, people will talk of the book having taken five years to write, but the real truth of the matter was that it was written practically in the whole in a year—it was written too fast, with frenzied maddened haste, under a terrible sense of pressure after I had written two other antecedent books [6] and found I had not got back to a true beginning. It is the work of frenzied, desperate, volcanic haste after too much time had slipped away, and no one will know that. Even now, I [can] not read the book, save for a page or two at a time—at every point the deficiency of my performance compared with the whole of my intent stares me in the face—the countless errors in wording and proof-reading—for which I alone am utterly to blame, but which in my frenzied state of mind I let pass by—stab me to the heart. I was not ready to read proof, I was not through *writing*—the fault is my own. I fell down on that final job, the book was written and typed and rushed in to you in such frantic haste day after day that I did not even catch the errors in wording the typist made in an effort to decipher my handwriting—there are *thousands* of them. I don't know where to begin, but for God's sake, if it should be vouchsafed us that *more* editions will be printed, try to catch these:

Page 506 "The Hudson River drinks from out *of* the inland slowly"— Cut out *of*.

Page 509 "our *craving* flesh"—for "craving" print "waning."

Page 510 "mining against the sides of ships"—for "mining" print "moving."

Page 665 "The *minute-whirring* flies buzz home to death"—for "minute-whirring"—put "minute-winning."

Page 663—"Battersea *Lodge*"—put "Battersea Bridge."

Page 678—"I can *list* to nothing else"—put "listen."

Page 678—"right across the character of my brain"—for "character" put "diameter."

Page 678—"Hummel Vee"—put "Hummel Bee."

Page 680—"I am as naked now as *sorry*"—put "sorrow."

[6] *The October Fair* and *The Hills Beyond Pentland*.

Page 517—"at this *gigantic* moment" substitute "*'propitious'*" for "*gigantic.*"

Page 519—"*ah* petty"—"so petty."

Page 545 "*envy* and departure"—"error and departure."

Page 545 "race of African *beings*"—"African *kings.*"

Page 545—"leonic"—"leonine."

Page 545 "the *bad* and almost brutal *volume*"—"the *hard* and almost brutal *violence.*"

Page 545—"*marked* his pain"—"*masked* his pain."

Page 546—"shaking his *beard*"—"shaking his *head.*"

page 549—"And nothing finally but night and dullness"—"night and darkness."

page 576 (a horrible error) a hiatus between sentences, utterly meaningless—". . . smiling his radiantly gentle and good-natured smile, 'I don't agree with you spoke with a crisp—' etc." Change to

" 'I don't agree with you.' "

She spoke with a crisp but obstinate conviction, 'Joel, I *know* I'm right!'

'All right,' he said quietly, 'Perhaps you are—about the gold—but about the pavilion—I'd like to argue with you about that' "

(Or better still, Max, since I can't remember, why not look up the manuscript and find out what I really did say!)

Page 588—"*ever-long* immortality"—put "ever-living immortality."

Page 596—"dyed hair of straw-*blade* falseness"—"straw-blonde falseness."

Page 662—"ate cinq cent mille"—"et cinq cent—"

Page 662—"a fond d'artichant *moray*"—"a fond d'artichaut mornay."

page 669—"the man who wrote *Batouale*"—"*Batouala.*"

page 671—"the great mirrors reflecting *these*"—"reflecting *them.*"

page 672—"the veteran of a million *lives*"—"a million *loves.*"

page 673—"the flat heavy *mark*"—"the flat heavy *"smack.*"

page 673—"*Light* up your heart"—"*Lift* up your heart."

page 676—"with mean and *senile* regret"—"the mean and *servile* regret."

Max, Max, I cannot go on, but I am sick at heart—we should have waited six months longer—the book, like Caesar, was from its mother's womb untimely ripped—like King Richard, brought into the world "scarce half made up."

Before I went away, you wrote me, in reference to the introduction I wanted to write, that you were trying to "save me from my enemies." Max, my enemies are so much more numerous than you expect—they include, in addition to the Henry Harts, Wassons, and others of that sort, the Benéts, the I.M.P.'s, the F.P.A.'s, the Morleys, the Nathans, the Mark Van Dorens, the Mike Golds, and others of that sort—they include also . . . the Lee Simonsons, the Theatre Guilders, the Neighborhood Playhouses, the Hound and Horners, the Kirstens, Galantières, and all that crowd with all its power and wealth—and I fear we have played directly into their hands by our carelessness and by our frenzied haste— our failure to *complete* just when completion was in our grasp. I gravely fear that by the time this reaches you the reaction will have set in—the enemy will have gathered itself together and the attack begun. I can't go through five more years like this last five—my health is gone—my youth is gone—my energy is gone—my hair is going, I have grown fat and old—and for all my agony and anguish—the loss of my youth and health—what have I got? I've got to have some security and repose— I've got to be allowed to finish what I've begun—I am no longer young enough, I have not energy or strength enough to go through it again.

For God's sake, try to kill false rumors

This is *Fourth* and Last Section

when you hear them. Before I left, I saw that they were beginning to make another rubber stamp under the name of "criticism." Apparently they had discovered that I was six and a half feet tall, and very large: therefore it follows that all my characters are seven feet tall—bellow and roar when they talk—that I can create nothing but a race of gigantic monsters. Max, for Christ's sake, I beg and plead with you, don't let this horrible god-damned lie go unanswered. I have never created a monster in my life, none of my people are seven feet tall. The *fault*, the *fault* always, as *you* should know, is not that we exceed the vital energy of life but that we fall short of it—and that a horrible misbegotten race of anaemic critics whose lives have grown underneath a barrel call out "monster" and "exaggeration" at you the moment you begin to approach the energy of life.

You yourself told me you took one of your daughters through the Grand Central Station and showed her twenty people who might have stepped out of the pages of Dickens, and not a day of my life passes— a day spent in the *anguish of intense and constant speculation* and not at *literary cocktail parties*—that I do not see a hundred—no, a thousand— who, if you put them in a book, would immediately bring down upon your head the sneers of the Patersons, the Benéts, the Van Dorens, and all their ilk, of "monsters," "seven feet tall," "untrue to life," etc.

In Christ's name, Max, what is wrong with us in America? The whole world—not myself alone—wants to know. The English ask me, everyone asks me, why do we cry out that what we want is life, and then try to destroy and kill the best people that we have? Why do our best writers,

poets, men of talent turn into drunkards, dipsomaniacs, charlatans, cock-
tail-cliquers, creators of Pop-eye horrors, pederasts, macabre distortions,
etc.? I tell you, it is not I alone who ask the question, but everyone
here—all of Europe knows it. Why is it that we are burnt out to an empty
shell by the time we are forty, that instead of growing in strength and
power we are done for—empty, burnt-out wrecks at an age when men in
other countries are just coming to their full maturity? Is it because the
seeds of destruction are *wholly* in ourselves—that there is something
in the American air, the weather of the American life that burns the lives
of men to rust as quickly as it rusts iron and steel? Or is it perhaps that
there is in us a sterile, perverse, and accursed love and lust for death
that wishes to destroy the very people that we set up—the people who
have something to give that may be of value and honor to our life? Is it
because we take a young man of talent—a young man proud of spirit,
and athirst for glory, and full with the urge to create and make his life
prevail—praise him up to the skies at first, and then press in upon him
from all sides with cynics' eyes and scornful faces, asking him if he can
ever do it again or is done for, finished, no good, through forever? Is
it because we deal this hand of death to young proud people, telling
them they are the lords of the earth one year, and the glory of their
nation's country, and the next year sneering, jeering, laughing, reviling,
scorning and mocking them with the very tongues that sang their praises
just a year before? Is this the reason why we fail—the reason that our
finest artists are destroyed? Tell me, is this the reason—men in England
also ask me; they all want to know. And then how easy for them all,
when we *are* done for—when we have been driven mad, when we are
drunkards, dipsomaniacs, perverts, charlatans, burnt out shells—how easy
it is for the whole pack to pull the face of pious regret, to sigh mournfully, to say: "What a pity!—We had hoped once —He looked so promising at one time!—What a shame he had to go and waste it all!"

I know your answer to these questions—that the strong man is as
Gibraltar, that all these assaults will fall harmlessly against his iron front,
the impregnable granite of his invincible soul—but, alas, no man is strong
as that—it is a pleasant fable—his great strength is needed, to be concentrated on the work he does, and while his brows and every sinew of
his life is bent to the giant labor of creation, what shall protect him from
these coward-hordes who come to destroy his life from every side? Why
should the artist—who is life's strongest man, earth's greatest hero—
have to endure this in America of all the countries of the earth, when
his task alone is so cruel hard there: the need for a new language,
the creation of a new form so stern and formidable? Why should he have
to do this great work, and at the same time withstand the murderous

attack of death-in-life when in every country in Europe the artist is honored, revered, and cherished as the proudest possession that a nation has?

Take this for what it is worth. If you think it extravagant, then take it so, but see the core of truth in this as well. I have given my life to try to be an artist, an honor to my country, to create beauty, and to win fame and glory, and the honor of my people, for myself, what has it got me? At the age of thirty-four I am weary, tired, dispirited, and worn out. I was a decent looking boy six years ago—now I am a bald, gross, heavy, weary-looking man. I wanted fame—and I have had for the most part shame and agony. They continue to speak of me as a "writer of promise"—and if I only do 197 impossible things—which they doubt that I *can* do—something may come of my work in the end. The Paterson woman [7] says my people are all seven feet tall and talk in bellowing voices—she says take away his adjectives, nouns, verbs, pronouns, words of violence, height, altitude, colour, size, immensity— and *where* would he be? The Mark Van Dorens [8] say take away his own experience, the events of his own life, forbid him to write about what he has seen, known, felt, experienced—and where would he be? The Fadimans say take away his apostrophes, declamations, lyrics, dreams, incantations—and where would he be? [9] The Rascoes [10] say he has no

[7] In "Turns with a Book Worm" in *The New York Herald Tribune Books* for Sunday, February 24, 1935, I.M.P. said: "Mr. Wolfe is a lavish writer. He steps up the scale of everything—all his principal characters are highly exaggerated. They are seven feet tall with megaphone voices. We don't mind; he does manage to keep up the excitement. But it might be an interesting experiment to take one of his chapters and eliminate all the superlatives, the adjectives indicating altitude, volume, and violence. Step it down again to life size and see what would remain."

[8] Mark Van Doren did not review *Of Time and the River* but in *The Nation* on April 25, 1934, he had said: "Thomas Wolfe's one novel to date, *Look Homeward, Angel*, needs to be followed by others before anybody can know whether Mr. Wolfe is an artist in anything beyond autobiography. . . . The public is justified in asking Mr. Wolfe whether he can keep himself out of the picture in books to come."

[9] Clifton Fadiman in *The New Yorker*, March 9, 1935 said: "It is open to debate whether he is a master of language or language a master of him; but for decades we have not had eloquence like his in American writing. His declamations and apostrophes . . . are astounding and even beautiful; and even when mere rhetoric, they are mere gorgeous rhetoric. . . . At their best these tempests of poetic prose . . . are overwhelming, and at their worst they are startlingly bad. . . . Thus it is impossible to say any one thing of Mr. Wolfe's style. At its best it is wondrous, Elizabethan. At its worst, it is hyperthyroid and afflicted with elephantiasis."

[10] Burton Rascoe, in *The New York Herald Tribune Books* for Sunday, March 10, 1935, said: "He has no evident sense of humor; nor any true sense of comedy. Even when he attempts to be playful or funny the effect is the disconcerting and uncomfortable one of a rictus, an attack of giggles, or the fantastic laugh of 'L'homme qui rit.' "

sense of humour—this, to the man who created old Gant, wrote the lunch room scenes in the *Angel*, Bascom Hawke in the *River*, *The Web of Earth*, Oswald Ten Eyck, the Countess, the Englishmen at the inn and all the others. The Communists say he is a romantic sentimentalist of the old worn-out romantic school, with no Marxian code; and the Saturday Reviewers [call him] a depicter of the sordid, grim, horribly unpleasant and surrealistic school—and so it goes—in Christ's name what do these people want?

Apparently, I would be a good writer if I would only correct 3,264 fundamental faults, which are absolutely, profoundly and utterly incurable and uncorrectable—so what in Christ's name am I to do?—In God's name how am I to live? What's before me? I tell you, Max, I cannot put in another five years like the last—I must have some peace, security, and good hope—I must be left alone to do my work as I have planned and conceived it, or the game is up. I am tired and ill and desperate, I can't go on like this forever. I got hurt somehow in Paris —how I don't know—during one of those three days I can't remember. I don't know whether I'm ruptured or not—I haven't the faintest idea, memory, or recollection of what happened, whether I got slugged in some joint or ran into something—but I woke up with a bruise above my groin the size of a saucer, and ever since it's felt as if something has been torn loose inside me.

Forgive these wild and whirling words—you are the friend I honor and respect more than anyone else. I hope and pray to God you may have some use and credit from my life in return for all you have done for it, just as I hope that I can make it prevail—as by God's will, I hope and trust I yet may do.

This is all for the present. If there is any great good news, for God's sake send it to me. At any rate stay with me, be my friend, and all may yet be well. Take this letter—or rather this chronicle, this history— for what it is worth—weed the good from the bad—and consider what truth is in it. I'm sending it to you in three or four instalments because I can't get it in one letter. Goodbye, good luck and good health, and love to all the family.

XI

THE SUCCESS OF OF TIME AND THE RIVER,
AND PUBLICATION OF FROM DEATH TO MORNING
1935

To MAXWELL E. PERKINS

[Postcard: *Hogarth's Servants*]

London

April 10, 1935

Dear Max:

This is the way people ought to look—and the way they always have looked—I see them around me every day. This is the only thing that *beats* time—if I could ever do it in a book I'd die happy. You didn't know I knew a lot about pictures, did you? Well, I do—about this. kind. The "old masters," Titian, Veronese, etc. mean nothing to me— only these men like Hogarth who had the sense of life that could speak to me in a language I know. This is one of the most *moving* pictures I ever saw.

To MAXWELL E. PERKINS

[Postcard: Marinus' *The Ursurers*]

London

April 10, 1935

And maybe this is the way they always *have* looked too. The real title of this picture is "Two Bankers" or "The Usurers." Does it look like anyone you ever saw? [1]

[1] There is a very slight resemblance to Robert Cross, head of the accounting department at Scribners.

451

The following letter was addressed to Mrs. Maxwell E. Perkins.

To LOUISE S. PERKINS

St. George's Court
26 Hanover Square
London W. 1.

Thursday, April 18, 1935

Dear Louise:

I was surprised and delighted to get your cable and the news that you and Elizabeth and Peggy [1] are coming over here in June. . . . Nothing would give me more pleasure than to meet you and the children and if anything I knew or could show you would be of interest to you, the occasion would give me the greatest happiness.

But as I told you in my cable I may not be in Europe when you arrive in June: my plan was to return to America sometime in May. I don't know what publishing plans Max may now have in mind concerning me, but he originally intended to publish a volume of my stories in the Fall,[2] and if he does that, I want to come back and try to make the book as good as I can before it is published. I wish you could persuade Max to take a short vacation *now*—in May—bring Elizabeth with you, if she can come, and have Peggy meet you in June when school is out. If Max felt he could not stay away for long, you could get a fast boat and he could spend three or four weeks over here and have a vacation—which he sorely needs. He could still get home by June, in ample time to make his preparations for the Fall season. I mention this, not only because the weather and the country is now getting lovely and would be beautiful in May, but also because, as I understand it, the Spring publishing season slackens up at about this time, and it seems to me, from Max's point of view, there could not be a better time to take such a vacation—particularly since I shall want his help so much a little later.

I don't think there is anyone in the world—particularly at Scribners —who would not enthusiastically approve of a holiday for Max, so I wish you'd all do it. If Elizabeth couldn't come now, or if you'd rather have her come with Peggy, you and Max could come, and the girls could meet you later. Personally, I see no reason why two grown-up girls are not perfectly capable of making a five day journey by themselves in a transatlantic liner—and that's all it would amount to. You could meet them in Paris, London, or Berlin, or at the boat—there's

---

[1] Two of the Perkins' daughters.

[2] *From Death to Morning,* which was published on November 14, 1935.

no trouble at all about it. I am urging this plan, not because I have much hope that it will happen, because frankly I do not believe Max will agree to it, but because, by one of those sudden and blinding flashes of intuition which (whether it sounds boastful or not) *have rarely played me false,* I feel profoundly that he *ought* to agree to it, that a *wise instinct* on his part would make him agree to it, that if he came now, this trip would have a good and fortunate result, which he would never regret. The one thing I have observed in Max in the last few years which worried me and which seemed wrong was a growing tenacity in the way he stuck to business—what seemed to me sometimes an unreasonable solicitude and preoccupation with affairs which might be handled by proxy or in less exhausting ways. It is surely a sort of vanity, even in so modest a man as Max, to feel that a business cannot run itself if he is absent from it for a few weeks. No one on earth —and I, as you know, have reason to know this better than anyone— no one on earth can do the kind of work Max does, no one could take his place in doing that, and if it were a question of some valuable work that *had* to be done now, there would be nothing for him to do but stay and do it. But my guess is that at just this moment, this season, there really is no such work, and that such a journey as I have proposed, brief as it is, would give him a spiritual and physical refreshment that in the end could work nothing but *the greatest good.* Max is now at the summit of his powers—the best work is still before him: it would be a tragedy if he in any way blunted or impaired his great faculties at this time simply because he failed to take advantage of a chance to recuperate and replenish his energies.

Another reason I wish you could come now is this:—I think, from certain things I have seen, that this is not only a critical and immensely interesting period in the life of Europe, but also this particular time, the month of May, has several events of extraordinary interest. Here in England, for example, they are making preparations for the King's Jubilee—if you could possibly get to London by May 6th you would be able to see a kind of stupendous pageantry that the world may never see again, and that certainly none of us are likely to see in our lifetime. It should be an immensely interesting thing. I shall not be here myself to see it unless you and Max decide to come, because I have got to go to Berlin in a day or two and from there propose to go to Russia (in time for May Day if possible) and back to Copenhagen, and so home. But if you and Max could come, I could meet you anywhere you like. . . .

Of course, in all of this, outside of my earnest conviction that such a trip could do Max nothing but good, there is also some special pleading for myself. Nothing could possibly give me greater happiness than to meet you and Max and spend some time, however brief, with you over here. The blunt truth of the matter is that none of us are chickens any more. Max is getting on to fifty and I am almost thirty-five, and this thing I have often dreamed of—of looking at some of these old societies and civilizations with him, and seeing together some of what they have to offer—this pleasant dream, I say, will probably remain forever just a dream unless it is now realized.

This is all I can say, and of course I fear my arguments are useless.[3] At any rate, I think it's grand that you and the girls are coming. If I am here I should be delighted to see you, and if I miss you, I wish you the happiest and most interesting kind of journey. . . . Meanwhile, with best wishes and love to all,

To MABEL WOLFE WHEATON

> St. George's Court
> 26 Hanover Square
> London W. 1
>
> Tuesday April 23, 1935

Dear Mabel:

I was delighted to get your letter—it was the first news I'd had from home. My mail is being held for me at Scribners until I get back, and outside of a letter and a couple of cables from Mr. Perkins, your letter, and one from Fred which came the same day yours did, is about all the mail I've had. I was sorry, however, to hear that Mama had not received my long letter at the time you wrote—I wrote her just a day or two after I got to England a month ago . . . but she must have it now. . . . The last few weeks in New York were frantic: everyone in the world, not only people I knew but people I didn't know, seemed to be on my trail. I was going crazy what with fools, freaks, bores, and the attentions of well-meaning friends, and having to pack up and sort out tons of manuscript, books, store my furniture, buy some clothes—I was in rags—etc. Our dear old pal and well-wisher Mr. ——, by the way, wrote me a letter just before I sailed and it was one of the most horrible, venomous, and dishonourable productions I ever read. He seemed about to strangle with gall and venomous hatred because I had not answered his letters, because I had not read his novel—the one he gave me and

---

[3] As Wolfe suspected, Perkins did not go abroad. For approximately the last twenty years of his association with Scribners, he never took a vacation for more than a few days, except for trips to see Hemingway or other Scribner authors.

then demanded back when I confessed I had not had time to read it—
because, in short, I had resisted in every way his efforts to make use
of me to worm his own way around here and there among places and
people he wanted to know. In particular he demanded the instant return
of a letter he sent me three or four years ago, a letter containing notes
and impressions of the mountains of western North Carolina. I haven't,
of course, the faintest idea where the damned letter is. Now, apparently,
he claims it is very precious to him and contains precious notes which
he must have—the whole truth, however, being that he wants another
outlet and excuse for his venomous hatred. He spoke of what "a pitiable
fool" he had been ever to "delude himself" with the hope that I would
read his book, or, I suppose, accept the so-called "friendship" he tried
to pour down my throat. He spoke of what a deluded fool he had been
even to "believe in Tom Wolfe's genius" and—this was the most horrible
thing he did—he then deliberately, just out of sheer malignant hatred
and a desire to hurt me in any way he could, concocted a dirty and
despicable lie to this effect:—that day, he said, he had been to the
offices of one the leading New York literary reviews, and talked to the
distinguished woman editor in charge about reviewing my book for this
paper. The woman told him, he said, that the book had already been
given to Sinclair Lewis for review (all of this information, of course,
easily identified the review as The New York *Herald Tribune* Sunday
Book Section, which along with *The Times* is one of the two most important, and *vitally* important to the success of the book)—but the
woman had told him that she didn't think he'd care to review the book
anyway, particularly after he saw what Sinclair Lewis had said about
it. She then went on with a cold and dispassionate analysis of my book,
he said, and as she did he felt his last deluded enthusiasm and belief
in "the genius of Tom Wolfe" oozing away, etc.

Mabel, I almost got sick at the stomach—not only because of the
horrible display of venom . . . but also because I thought it was really
true what he said about the *Tribune* and Sinclair Lewis and, after all
these years of work, to have my book ruined at the beginning and to
have a man like Lewis turn on me seemed about as rotten a break in
luck as I could imagine. Well, I called up Max Perkins immediately
and told him I had bad news for him, and then told him the contents
of this horrible reptile's letter. I was in a pretty excited state—in addition
to the disappointment and bad luck of it, I thought that if a high class
publication like *Herald-Tribune Books* could stoop to reveal the contents
of an unfavorable review two weeks or more before publication and to
run the book down two weeks before it was published, it was almost
as rotten and unfair a trick as I had ever heard of. Max was very quiet

and calm and told me to come in later in the day. When I got to Scribners later in the day, they had telephoned the *Herald Tribune,* explained the contents of the letter, and asked if it was true. The reply was this: That —— was known at the office as Public Nuisance and Bore Number 1; that he was constantly coming in and pestering them; that they never gave him books to review; that there was not the remotest possibility of his reviewing my book for the *Tribune;* that no one there had ever discussed my book with him; that it had *not* been given to Sinclair Lewis to review, but to Burton Rascoe, and that no one knew whether Rascoe's review was favorable or unfavorable. Incidentally, although I have read none of the reviews myself as yet, I understand indirectly—through Max Perkins' letter—that Rascoe's review was favorable.

I am sorry to take up so much space over this. . . . Perkins read the letter and said correctly: "It is the letter of a venomous old woman," but maybe you will understand a little better now the kind of price a man sometimes has to pay for public notice, and the kind of horrible slanderous lies unscrupulous and embittered people will stoop to in an effort to injure him. I am learning more about life and people all the time—I have met some wonderful and fine people these last few years but I have also met some of this sort, too. The incredible thing is that I have never injured this man in any way—was grateful and somewhat embarrassed by his letters of gushing praise, thanked him as courteously as I could, and have wronged him in no way save by my failure to read his book and to allow him to thrust his friendship forcibly upon me, make himself a part of my life, my friends, etc.—and any man alive has a right to defend himself in this way.

One amazing thing I have learned in the last few years is the number of people there are in the world who can do nothing for themselves, have no real friendship for you but who, once you achieve a little success, try forcibly to thrust themselves into your life, and when you repel them, no matter how courteously, turn on you in envenomed gall and hatred.

No, I promise you I shall try not to be too much troubled this time by what you call "rot from Asheville." I hope to God there is none—there is absolutely no reason for it from *this* book—but if there is, I went through my first baptism of fire five years ago, and should be able to stand it better now. I know that you and the family, as you say, "are with me"—and that's good enough for me. I am grateful from the bottom of my heart to all of you and I hope that I shall always live and work honorably in such a way as will bring credit to the family—and to grow better and deeper always in my work. I also hope that this book has had a creditable success, not only for myself, but for the sake of the fine man and true friend—Max Perkins—who has stood by me and believed in me and whose heart is in my work as much as my own. I know that if we have "come through" the strain and stress of the last five years, I can now go on and *far surpass*—with the confidence and experience I have gained—anything I have done before. This is all for the present. I am leaving London today, . . going to the country for a day or two, and then direct to Berlin to see my German publisher who wires he will pay expenses. Hope he does. . . . Love to all,

To ELIZABETH NOWELL

St. George's Court
26 Hanover Square
London W. 1

April 23, 1935
Easter Monday! And how! When they have
Easter here, it lasts four days—Sunday
all the time.

Dear Miss Nowell:

. . . I'm leaving London to-day after being here a month—going up to Norfolk for a few days and then to Germany via Harwich and Hook of Holland. My German publisher has wired saying he wants my book and for me to come on over and he will pay expenses, but coyly refrains from mentioning terms. I understand, however, that whatever money I get from the Germans will have to be spent there in the country—so it looks as if I'll have to go there and live riotously for a week or two or get nothing at all. I have a most humorous plan whereby I'll use Herr Hitler's currency to pay the expenses of a trip to Russia, but friends here say they think I'll strike a snag. Anyway, there's no harm trying. . . .

Have had little news from U.S.A. . . . But heard indirectly (through letter Max wrote Frere-Reeves, my English publisher) that "Tom's agent [1] has sold four stories." [2] Darling, I am torn between joy and

---

[1] Miss Nowell had left the Maxim Lieber office in September, 1934, and had started her own agency in January, 1935.

[2] "Gulliver" which appeared in the June, 1935, issue of *Scribner's Magazine*, "In the Park" which appeared in the June issue of *Harper's Bazaar*, "Arnold Pentland" which appeared in the June issue of *Esquire*, and "Cottage by the Tracks" which appeared in the July issue of *Cosmopolitan*. All four of these stories were included in *From Death to Morning*, but "Cottage by the Tracks" was retitled "The Far and the Near." These had been among the portions of manuscript cut from *Of Time and the River* which Wolfe had given to Miss Nowell when he was moving out of Brooklyn, and which she had not been able to cut and edit until after he had sailed.

trepidation. The news, if true, is swell, but I don't know where the hell you *found* the four stories. . . . Anyway, upon the strength of rumor, counting my chickens before I've seen them, and my purely hypothetical wealth, I've gone and had several suits of clothes made by the Prince of Wales' own royally-appointed pants-maker, and am now the damndest fop and triple-gazzaza dude that American literature has ever known. So for God's sake don't tell me when I get back home it ain't true! . . .

Hope this finds you well and not staying up nights writing stories for ungrateful authors. Take care of yourself, and since I'm wishing *you* good luck, why, good luck to *both* of us. Will see you, I hope, in May.

Irma Wyckoff, to whom the following letter was written, was Mr. Perkins' secretary for twenty-seven years up to the time of his death. She is now Mrs. Osmer F. Muench.

To IRMA WYCKOFF

University Arms Hotel
Cambridge, England
Wednesday, April 24, 1935

Dear Miss Wyckoff:

I've wanted to write you for a long time to say hello, and tell you again how much I appreciate all your services to me, so generously and cheerfully given even when you had other work to do, and to hope that all goes well with you and with the others at Scribners. Imagine you have quite a parcel of mail for me—hope it hasn't been too great a bother—and if not too much extra trouble will you kind of keep it in a chronological order? Also, if any beautiful women come in and ask for me, get their name, address, and telephone number and tell them I'll be back very soon and will get in touch with them immediately; but if they look and talk mean, ugly and vicious, tell them you don't know where I am, but that the last you heard I sailed from the Skaggeraks of Norway on a very slow sailing vessel for a polar expedition and that you expect me back in about five years. Good-bye and good luck and best wishes to all.

To MAXWELL E. PERKINS

The Wartburg
Germany
May 23, 1935

Dear Max:

I meant to write you before but for the last two or three weeks at any rate writing anything has been impossible. I don't know what my status quo may be in New York but in Germany I have been the white-haired boy. I don't think I could stand another two weeks of it but the last two weeks have been an extraordinary and wonderful and even enchanted period of my life because I have never known such a time before. I am so glad to have known it, so grateful, I shall never forget it. I have heard it said that Lord Byron awoke one morning at twenty-four to find himself famous. Well, I arrived in Berlin one night, when I was thirty-four, and got up the next morning and went to the American Express and for the last two weeks at least I have been famous in Berlin. I found letters, telephone messages, telegrams etc., from all kinds of people, including Rowohlt, publisher here, and the daughter of the American Ambassador, Martha Dodd.[1] For two weeks I have done nothing but meet people of all sorts, go to parties, have interviews, get photographed by the Associated Press—and I have literally lived at the Ambassador's house. I have taken most of my meals there and if I didn't have my room there—it did not matter much because I have had no time for sleeping, and since daylight now comes at three o'clock in the morning anyway in Berlin and Miss Dodd, her brother [2] and I have sat up most of the night talking, I have almost forgotten how to sleep. It did finally get a little too much for us so yesterday Miss Dodd and I and a couple of others left Berlin and all through a wonderful sunlit day drove down southwest through this magnificent, beautiful and enchanted country. We spent the night in the old town of Weimar and today we went about the town and saw first, Goethe's Gartenhaus in a wonderful green park and the rooms where he lived and worked and the saddle he sat on when he wrote, his high old writing desk and many other things that he used and lived with, that made his life and work seem real and near to us. Then we went to the fine old house in Weimar where he lived later on and where all the evidences of his great and illimitably curious intelligence—his laboratories, his workshops, his

[1] Martha Dodd, now Mrs. Alfred K. Stern, has described Wolfe's visit to Germany in her book, *Through Embassy Eyes*. She is also the author of a novel, *The Searching Light*, as well as various articles and stories.
[2] William E. Dodd, Jr.

great library, his rooms for his experiments in physics, chemistry, electricity and optics—have been exactly and truly preserved. Then we went about the town some more and visited the crypt where Goethe and Schiller are buried side by side, and finally with regret we left that wonderful and lovely old town that seems to me at least to hold in it so much of the spirit of the great Germany and the great and noble spirit of freedom, reverence and the high things of the spirit which all of us have loved. Then we came here through one of the most indescribably lovely and magical landscapes I have ever seen. And tonight we are staying here in the Wartburg, a great legendary kind of hill from which came the legend that inspired Richard Wagner to write *Tannhaüser*. We are going back to Berlin to-morrow through the wonderful Harz Mountains, and I have not space or power enough here to tell you how beautiful and fine and magical this trip has been.

I am telling you all this because you and I have often talked about Germany and the German people whom you do not like as much as I do and about what has happened here in recent years. But I want to tell you that I do not see how anyone who comes here as I have come could possibly fail to love the country, its noble Gothic beauty and its lyrical loveliness, or to like the German people who are, I think, the cleanest, the kindest, the warmest-hearted, and the most honorable people I have met in Europe. I tell you this because I think a full and generous recognition must be made of all these facts and because I have been told and felt things here which you and I can never live or stand for and which, if they are true, as by every reason of intuition and faith and belief in the people with whom I have talked I must believe, are damnable.

Now I so much want to see you and tell you what I have seen and heard, all that has been wonderful and beautiful and exciting, and about those things that are so hard to explain because one feels they are so evil and yet cannot say so justly in so many words as a hostile press and propaganda would, because this evil is so curiously and inextricably woven into a kind of wonderful hope which flourishes and inspires millions of people who are themselves, as I have told you, certainly not evil, but one of the most child-like, kindly and susceptible people in the world. I shall certainly tell you about it. Someday I should like to write something about it, but if I now wrote even what I have heard and felt in two weeks, it might bring the greatest unhappiness and suffering upon people I have known here and who have shown me the most affectionate hospitality. But more and more I feel that we are all of us bound up and tainted by whatever guilt and evil there may be in this whole world, and that we cannot accuse and condemn others without in the end coming back to an accusal of ourselves. We are all damned together, we are all tarred by the same stick, and for what has happened here we are all in some degree responsible. This nation to-day is beyond the shadow of a vestige of a doubt full of uniforms and a stamp of marching men—I saw it with my own eyes yesterday in one hundred towns and villages across two hundred miles of the most peaceful, lovely and friendly-looking country I have ever seen. A thousand groups, uncountable divisions of the people from children eight years old to men of fifty, all filled beyond a doubt with hope, enthusiasm and inspired belief in a fatal and destructive thing—and the sun was shining all day long and the fields are greenest, the woods the loveliest, the little towns the cleanest, and the faces and the voices of the people the most friendly of any I have ever seen or heard, so what is there to say?

I have felt a renewed pride and faith in America and a belief that somehow our great future still remains since I came here to Berlin and met some of the Americans here, particularly Ambassador Dodd. He is a historian, a man who was born on a farm in my own state of North Carolina and who had spent his whole life before he came here in teaching and in the contemplation of history. He is, I believe, what is known as a Jeffersonian Democrat and believes in the society of free men and the idea of democracy which he thinks has never been given a fair and practical experiment anywhere on earth. I don't know whether he is right or wrong in this . . . but their home in Berlin has been a free and fearless harbor for people of all opinions, and people who live and walk in terror have been able to draw their breath there without fear, and to speak their minds. This I know to be true, and further, the dry, plain, homely unconcern with which the Ambassador observes all the pomp and glitter and decorations and the tramp of marching men would do your heart good to see. I wish you could have been there the other night in his house when he came back from attending Hitler's two hour and forty minute speech which was delivered to that group of automatic dummies that now bears the ironical title of the "Reichstag," and which was broadcast all over Germany. It was wonderful to hear him tell his wife "the way the Jap looked and the way the Englishman looked and how the Frenchman looked pretty hot about it and how he himself shook hands with the Dutchman on the way out and said 'very interesting but not entirely historical' and how the Dutchman grinned and agreed." It was Emerson who said that if you heard the pop of a popgun not to believe it was anything else but a pop of a popgun, even if all the captains and kings of the earth told you it was the roar of a cannon—he said it better than this but that was the substance and I always felt it was an American thing to say and was glad that an American said it. I think the Ambassador here is a man like this.

I cannot tell you any more now but I will tell you all I can when I come back. This has been in many ways an extraordinary and wonderful trip. I have remembered so many vivid and exciting things about it, I have seen so many different kinds of life and people, I feel myself welling up with energy and life again and if it is really true that I have had some luck and success at home I know I can come back now and beat all hollow anything I have ever done before, and certainly I know I can surprise the critics and the public who may think they have taken my measure by this time—and I think I may even have a surprise or two in store for you. If this sounds like bragging, let me feel this way until I try to put it to the proof—in any case it can do no harm.

After leaving London I went up to the county of Norfolk in England, a somewhat remote and out of the way place but a real blunt and good England I had never seen before. I lived around the little towns in the countryside for a week or two and saw some wonderful things and people, and then I went to Holland for a week, and then came on to Germany and Berlin and am writing you to-night from the Thuringian forest. I am going on to Scandinavia next week, will stay a short time in Denmark and think I will come home from there. Anyway I hope to see you the first part of June.

Please don't go too far with the stories before I get there. There are things I can do that will make them much better, and if you will only wait on me I will do them and we will have a fine book of stories and unlike any I know of. I think "The October Fair" is going to be a grand book and we will try to meet the criticism of the critics and to show them that I am improving and learning my business all the time. The book I am living for, however, is the Pentland [3] book—it is swelling and gathering in me like a thunderstorm and I feel if there is any chance of my doing anything good before I am forty it will be this book. I feel such a swelling and exultant sense of certitude and such a feeling of gathering power and fulfillment that I tremble when I think about it and I hope to God that nothing happens to me or to my life—that I do not ruin myself with alcohol or some other craziness that can be avoided—before I get to it.

Of this I am resolved: that if there has been any stir and public interest in this book I shall become more private and withdrawn in my life than ever before when I get back home and will allow myself in no way to be drawn out of it. I will go down deeper in myself than I ever have before and you must try to help me in every way to do this. It has been a great thing for me today to go to Goethe's house in Weimar and to see the way he lived and worked. I may never be able to be a great man like

[3] *The Hills Beyond Pentland.*

this—the life of a great man always fills me with hope and strength and gives me a renewed faith and makes me despise all the cheap and low little lives and base aspirations that you see about you in the lives of so many men today.

Goodbye for the present, Max. This letter, like its author, is too long. I hope the letter will not exhaust you as the last one must have. . . . It will be good to see you again. . . .

P.S. Saturday, May 26—Dear Max—I got back to Berlin last night at midnight after a magnificent and beautiful trip. Today I went to the American Express Co., and found there a letter from one Harry Weinberger, "counsellor at law" etc. of 70 West 40th St., New York, who says he represents Mrs. Madeleine Boyd in reference to her "claim for agent's commissions on royalties on your books published by Scribners." He threatens suit, and wants to know when I will return, etc. This was the thing you said could not "happen," the thing "she would not dare to do" . . . , etc. Well, she has done it, as I told you she would, because we were foolish, benevolent, soft-hearted, weak—call it what you like. . . .

The Amended Complaint filed against Wolfe by Weinberger for Madeline Boyd with the Supreme Court of the State of New York on August 12, 1935, alleged that "on or about and prior to the month of January, 1929, defendant entered into an agreement with the plaintiff whereby defendant employed plaintiff as his literary agent and agreed to pay her ten percent of whatever royalties he may earn from the publication and sale of his literary works, in any part of the world. That pursuant to said agreement and on or about the month of January, 1929, plaintiff procured from Charles Scribner's Sons, publishers, a contract whereby said Charles Scribner's Sons agreed to publish the novel, Look Homeward, Angel, *written by defendant, and agreed to pay defendant royalties on the sale of said novel. On information and belief at the time of the making of said contract between Charles Scribner's Sons and defendant, plaintiff procured from said Charles Scribner's Sons a separate contract providing that said Charles Scribner's Sons were to have an option for publishing the next two books written by defendant." The complaint then alleged that Mrs. Boyd had secured contracts for the publication of* Look Homeward, Angel *from William Heinemann of London and Ernst Rowohlt Verlag of Berlin, and that the contract procured from Heinemann contained options "for publishing the next two works written by defendant," and the contract with Rowohlt gave Rowohlt an option on Wolfe's next work. After making allegations concerning other foreign publishers, the complaint then alleged "on information and belief, that defendant has been paid, or there has become payable to him, as royalties on the sale of* Look Homeward, Angel *and* Of Time and the River, *a sum amounting in the aggregate to at least One Hundred Thousand Dollars. On information and belief, that by reason of the aforesaid, there has become due and payable to plaintiff by defendant a sum amounting in the aggregate to at least Ten Thousand Dollars." This first part of Mrs. Boyd's Amended Complaint then concluded with the statements "that defendant has failed and refused to pay to plaintiff her commission as his literary agent although the same has been duly demanded," and "that plaintiff has duly performed all the conditions on her part to be performed."*

Next, "as and for a Second Cause of Action," Mrs. Boyd's complaint alleged "that defendant wrote Look Homeward, Angel, *the first of a trilogy of which* Of Time and the River *is the second. That pursuant to said agreement and on or about the month of January, 1929, plaintiff procured from Charles Scribner's Sons, publishers, a contract whereby said Charles Scribner's Sons agreed to publish a novel written by defendant as heretofore stated, consisting of a trilogy of which* Look Homeward, Angel *was the first and* Of Time and the River *the second, and the said Charles Scribner's Sons are proceeding with the publication of the third, and the said Charles Scribner's Sons agreed to pay defendant royalties and advances on the sale of said novels." After virtually repeating these allegations in regard to the contract made with William Heinemann, the complaint concluded by demanding "judgment against the defendant in the sum of Ten Thousand Dollars, together with the costs and disbursements of this action."*

In the answer to Mrs. Boyd's Amended Complaint which was filed for Wolfe by his attorneys, Mitchell and Van Winkle, Wolfe admitted that he employed her as his literary agent for the purpose of procuring the publication of Look Homeward, Angel, *but denied that he employed her to act any further for him. He admitted that she procured from Scribners a contract for the publication of that book, but denied that she procured from them a separate contract which gave them options on his next two books. He also admitted that Mrs. Boyd procured contracts for the publication of* Look Homeward, Angel *from Heinemann, Rowohlt, and other foreign publishers, but denied "that at present he has any knowledge or information sufficient to form a belief as to any of the other allegations" made by her concerning the existence of options in these contracts for his future works. He admitted that he had been paid or that there had become payable to him royalties on the sale of* Look Homeward, Angel *and* Of Time and the River, *but denied Mrs. Boyd's allegation that they amounted in the aggregate to at least One Hundred Thousand Dollars, and he also denied her allegations that he had refused to pay her her commission as his literary agent and that she had "duly performed all the conditions on her part to be performed." Finally, as an answer to her "Second Cause of Action," he denied that* Look Homeward, Angel *and* Of Time and the River *were the first two books of a trilogy, or were considered as such in the contracts made with Scribners and Heinemann.*

After thus replying to Mrs. Boyd's allegations, Wolfe's answer launched into "A First and Separate and Distinct Defense" which said in part that "Defendant is informed and verily believes that in or about the month of January, 1931, plaintiff, as literary agent for defendant in connection with the publication of Look Homeward, Angel, sold to Ernst Rowohlt Verlag of Berlin, Germany, the right to publish said book in the German language and at that time received from Ernst Rowohlt Verlag, as a payment on account, the sum of One Thousand Reich Marks, all of which was unknown to defendant at that time. That thereafter and in or about the month of January, 1932, defendant for the first time learned, from sources other than the plaintiff, of the said sale of the right to publish said book, Look Homeward, Angel, in the German language, and that this sale had been made by the plaintiff as his literary agent for the publication of said book and that plaintiff had received on account of said sale the sum of One Thousand Reich Marks. That the defendant thereupon immediately charged the plaintiff with breach of her obligation under her literary agency for the publication of said book, Look Homeward, Angel, in failing to disclose the making of said German contract and withholding of his portion of said One Thousand Reich Marks. Plaintiff thereupon admitted the defendant's charges and eventually, but not immediately, paid to the defendant the U.S. money equivalent of his portion of said One Thousand Reich Marks. That at some time in or about the month of January, 1932, and prior to January 28, 1932, plaintiff requested the defendant for authority to act as his literary agent in the securing of the publication of defendant's works other than the book Look Homeward, Angel, and the defendant thereupon and on or about January 28, 1932, informed the plaintiff that she would not be his literary agent for the securing of the publication of any of his works then existing or future, other than the book Look Homeward, Angel."

A settlement of this case was finally made in 1936.

To MAXWELL E. PERKINS

[Postcard: Room in Goethe's House, Weimar]

Eisenach, Germany
May 24, 1935

Dear Max: Goethe died in this little room while sitting in the chair beside the bed. His study, laboratories, work rooms and library are just outside. He made his wife and children live upstairs—out of the way.

To MAXWELL E. PERKINS

[Postcard: Statue of a Young Egyptian
Girl Carved in Wood]

Berlin

Tuesday, May 28, 1935

Dear Max: I'm just about 2500 years too late to have known this girl but she's pretty grand, isn't she? I must leave here in a few days although everyone is urging me to stay. I have never known such friendship, warmth, good will and affection as these people have shown me—hate to leave.

To MAXWELL E. PERKINS

Hotel Am Zoo
Berlin

Saturday, June 8, 1935

Dear Max:

These photographs were made by *Die Dame*—a German magazine that corresponds to *Vanity Fair*. I have written a piece [1] for them and they are using one of these pictures—the one with the fist—when they publish the piece. I thought the photos pretty good and am sending you one of each. Am leaving here for Denmark in day or two and expect to sail for New York about June 20. . . .

The gay social whirl continues. . . . When I come back to my hotel room I find it filled with magnificent flowers which beautiful women have brought here in my absence. It has been wonderful, thrilling—and very comical. There have been all sorts of stories in the papers—my name has been mentioned in connection with Sinclair Lewis and for that reason, I think, they think I'm very rich. Last week one of the papers came out with a photograph of a magnificent sailing yacht upon the Wannsee—a fashionable lake resort a few miles from town. It said the yacht belonged to "the famous American novelist Thomas Wolfe" and that I was lavishly entertaining a party of beautiful moving-picture

[1] Efforts to find this piece in *Die Dame* have met with no success, since the files of that magazine were destroyed during World War II. Probably the piece was never published there, since it concerned Ernst Rowohlt who was under Nazi trial soon after it was written. Fifteen years later, on March 19, 1950, a short humorous article by Wolfe, "Begegnung mit Rowohlt," appeared in *Der Kurier*, published in the French Zone of Berlin. This probably was the piece written for *Die Dame* but how it survived the war and turned up in *Der Kurier* is not known.

actresses aboard her. Of course I had never seen the damned yacht and someone told me I had met one beautiful moving-picture actress at a night club, but I didn't know who she was. . . . I'll tell you all about everything when I come back.

To MAXWELL E. PERKINS

[Picture Postcard: Pieter Breughel's *Die Niederlandischen Sprichworter,* with key to the proverbs illustrated]

Berlin

June 12, 1935

Dear Max: I don't know if the U.S.A. postal authorities will let me send this card to you, but if you get it, please keep it for me—this is the painter I like best.

The following postcard to Mrs. Bernstein breaks off unfinished and was never mailed. It probably refers to the suicide of Emily Davies Whitfield in Santa Fe, New Mexico, on May 25, 1935.

To ALINE BERNSTEIN

Copenhagen

[June, 1935]

Dear Aline:

I read in the paper some weeks ago that a friend of yours had shot herself through the head or heart. I always knew she would. And do you know why? Because, like poor Raisbeck, she tried everything in life but living, she knew about everything in life but life itself. I was sad for two whole days after I read it, then forgot it—did you do as well, who knew her so much better?

I think about you a great deal and all the people I met through you and your group ten years ago. . . . It was a lie of life, false, cynical, scornful, drunk with imagined power, and rotten to the core. And through that rottenness, through that huge mistaken falseness and corruption, there will run forever the memory of your loveliness—your flower face and your jolly and dynamic little figure on my steps at noon —the food, the cooking, and the love, and in the little boarded city yard the [faint?] [so?] more than forest

To MAXWELL E. PERKINS

[Picture Postcard: 21 Fredericksborg. Slot. Copenhagen]

Copenhagen

June 18, 1935

I found the girl all right, Max—not here, but in Berlin. I miss her so much it hurts. I've got to come back home and work. For God's sake keep people away from me if there are any.

To MAXWELL E. PERKINS

[Postcard: photograph of Wolfe
in front of City Hall, Copenhagen]

[Copenhagen]

[June 21, 1935]

Dear Max:

I have a letter from a New York publisher—with quoted excerpts— which informs me that *Scribners* last month carried 3 *printed attacks* on me—one from Miss Evelyn Scott, one from Mr. Ernest Hemingway —the Big Big He Man and Fighter With Words who can't take it—and one from Professor Wm Lyon Phelps.[1] He wants to know why I should still consider Scribners my friends. Can you think of an answer? This is a good picture, isn't it?

[1] In the June, 1935, issue of *Scribner's Magazine,* Evelyn Scott reviewed *Of Time and the River* under the title of "Colossal Fragment," saying: ". . . Thomas Wolfe . . . is representative of our national individualistic bent at its faulty but often splendid best. . . . In *Of Time and the River,* his concern is with the adventuring ecstasies of Eugene Gant only. . . . The sum of this turbulent writing, in which sentimentalities blend with authentic cries of agony, is an impression of young, inexhaustible vitality, by which, with the violence of his own will to beauty, the author almost convinces us of a universe made in his image. . . ." In an installment of *The Green Hills of Africa,* appearing in the same issue, Ernest Hemingway said: "Dostoevsky was made by being sent to Siberia. Writers are forged in injustice as a sword is forged. I wonder if it would make a writer of him, give him the necessary shock to cut the over-flow of words and give him a sense of proportion, if they sent Tom Wolfe to Siberia or the Dry Tortugas. Maybe it would and maybe it wouldn't. He seemed sad, really, like Carnera." William Lyon Phelps, in his selected list of 100 new books in the same issue, merely listed *Of Time and the River,* saying: "I include it because of its universally enthusiastic reception. I have not had time to read so long a book. I hope it is all 'they say' it is."

To MAXWELL E. PERKINS

[Postcard: photograph of Wolfe
in front of City Hall, Copenhagen]

Copenhagen
June 23, 1935

"Although both (Wolfe and the late D. H. Lawrence) were sprung from the socially obscure, neither shows any feeling of *class* resentment"—from a review.[1]

The following postcard from Wolfe to Mrs. Jelliffe was in reply to suggestions from her about the repairing of his furniture which he had stored at her house.

To BELINDA JELLIFFE

[Postcard]

[Copenhagen?]
[June 1935?]

Fixing the chairs etc. is fine, but I don't believe it would be worth $17 to me to have the chest of drawers fixed. It is a fine piece but I am not a furniture antiquarian and I don't much care if all the handles are on or not. What I *would* like to get fixed is my beautiful and beloved and cigarette-scarred gate-legged table! Whatever you do will be all right with me. Will write later.

No, I've got to admit that I've fallen down badly on *my* homework —the typewriter—and all I can mumble into your cynical ears is that *someday* I'll show you. But I'm beginning to eat and sleep regularly again—no cracks now about the eating—to feel more like a member of the so-called human race. The old pencil-itch has got into my fingers again—I've made fifty thousand words of notes.

[1] From the Review of *Of Time and the River* by Evelyn Scott in the June, 1935, issue of *Scribner's,* which Wolfe had been told was an "attack" on him.

To ALFRED DASHIELL

[Picture Postcard: Steckelhornflet and Nikolaikirche, Hamburg]

Hamburg, Germany
June 29, 1935

I'm crammed to the gills with kultur, küche, and antiquity, so I'm coming home again.

To ROBERT RAYNOLDS

[Picture Postcard: Nikolaiflet, Hamburg]

Hamburg
June 29, 1935

Dear Bob: This is my last night in Europe and I want to write you a word of greeting before I go, even though this card may get there after I do. I am sitting here on the terrace of a little hotel that overlooks the harbor of Hamburg. It is almost dark and I can see a great tangle of cranes and derricks against the sky—and big freighters all alight and lovely—and the rattling of a winch. Somehow it makes me think of Brooklyn and is comforting.

On returning to New York from Europe, Wolfe found waiting for him an invitation to attend the Writers' Conference at the University of Colorado as a "visiting novelist." He was asked to deliver one lecture there, to participate in round table conferences on the novel with other writers, and to confer with the students, for which he would receive a fee of two hundred and fifty dollars. In the following letter of acceptance to Edward Davison, he suggests the subject of his speech, which was based on the discarded introduction to Of Time and the River *and which finally was published as* The Story of a Novel. *Davison, a well-known poet both here and in England where his reputation was originally established, was at this time Program Director at the University of Colorado.*

To EDWARD DAVISON

New York, New York
July 8, 1935

Dear Mr. Davison:

I returned from Europe just two or three days ago and found here an enormous stack of mail which has been accumulating for the last four months, and I am hastening to answer your own letters first of all.

I am looking forward to the Colorado trip and to meeting all of you with the greatest delight. I am very proud to have been invited and I shall do the best I can. In one of your letters I think you said you were yourself going to talk on the making of a poem and suggested that I might talk on some such topic as the making of a novel. If you still feel that that is a good idea, it would suit me splendidly.

Last night I was with Fritz Dashiell, of *Scribner's Magazine*, who spoke at Boulder two or three years ago, and he said his own impression was that the people there prefer a plain, straightforward way of talking rather than a more involved and technical discussion. As you may know, among the many faults and imperfections which the critics have spoken about in my own work, is the fault of overabundance and a general too-muchness out of nature. I realize this fault, I think, more keenly than anyone and have sweated blood in an effort to correct it. How would it do if, so to speak, I "shot the works"? That is, if I just got right down into the sawdust and told the people out there the plain, straight story of what happened in the writing of this last book and of the other two books which are to follow it but which have not yet been published. Max Perkins here at Scribner's, the great editor without whose help I might have been sunk, said that the making of this book constituted the most interesting problem of his editorial experience. I believe it really might be interesting and perhaps of some value to the people at the conference if I just told about the way it happened and how the three books, over a period of five years, began finally to emerge out of the great creative chaos, and what happened to me during that time, and what mistakes I made, and what I hope I have learned from the experience, and also what a great editor can do in his relations toward a writer and an enormous manuscript.

Don't you think if I told about this in as plain and direct a way as I can, it might be interesting to the people out there? I suggest it because it is a piece of my own life, of my own direct and immediate experience; it is something I know of my own life and something I have learned with my own life; and it seems to me that for this reason it might be more interesting and valuable than a lecture of a more detached and impersonal character. But if you don't think so, won't you please write and let me know and make another suggestion?

I am so happy at the prospect of coming out there and seeing a little of the West and its people that I want to do my best, and I shall be sincerely grateful for any advice you can give me. . . .

Thanks again for your generous invitation and your letters.

Among the many letters praising Of Time and the River *which Wolfe found waiting for him on his return from Europe, was one from Sherwood Anderson which said: "Dear Thomas Wolfe: As I read it I have a hunger to write you a word about your new novel. It is such a gorgeous achievement. It makes me a little sad too. Here I've been struggling all these years, trying to write novels, and along you come and show me very simply and directly that I'm no novelist. Some things I can write but you—you are a real novelist."* [1] *The following was Wolfe's reply.*

To SHERWOOD ANDERSON

New York City

July 8, 1935

Dear Mr. Anderson:

I just got back here from Europe a few days ago and found a great stack of mail which had piled up during the past four months and in it was the letter you wrote me from Greensboro some time ago.

I want to tell you how proud and happy your letter made me. You are one of the American writers whose work I have admired most and whose work has meant a lot to me. It seemed to me ever since I first began to read your books when I was a kid of twenty that you got down below the surface of our lives and got at some of the terror and mystery and ugliness and beauty in America better than anyone else. This comes from the heart; I mean it, and for that reason I will always have the proudest and most grateful remembrance of your generous letter.

Max Perkins knows you, and he tells me he sometimes sees you when you come to New York. When you do come here next time, if you are going out to lunch with Max, I wonder if you wouldn't let me come along too? I should like to meet you. Meanwhile, with thanks again and best wishes,

[1] Copyright, 1956, by Eleanor Copenhaver Anderson.

The following letter to James Boyd was also written in reply to one praising
Of Time and the River.

To JAMES BOYD

New York City
July 8, 1935

Dear Jim:

I just came back the other day and found a great stack of mail here
with your letter of May 29 in it. I can't write you much here, nothing
that is fit to be an answer to your wonderful letter. Will you let me tell
you how much it has meant to me to have known a man as true and
straight and high grade as you are, and how proud it makes me to
have had such a letter from the artist of fine and high integrity I know
you to be. The last two or three days since I came back have been pretty
wonderful. I shall never forget them.

When I went away, I was exhausted, emptied out, and desperate, and
I did not have much hope, and now I've come back filled up, strong
and ready, and I find myself a little famous, and the whole damn thing
is wonderful, and if it makes a difference to me or my work, except to
make it better, please come up here to New York and kick me in the
pants the whole way from Scribners to the Battery.

Your letter, and a few others, fill me with such a sense of joy and
confidence and power that I'll swear to you I'm going to hit this next
book like a locomotive, and I know I can ten times surpass all that
I have done before. Jim, if this be foolish bragging, let me do it for
a day or two; the real thing is I'll never forget your friendship or your
letter, and I'll use every energy in life to live up to it. Good-bye now,
and I send my love and best wishes to all of you. It is wonderful to
hear how well "Roll River" [1] is going. I read the first part of it in
Scribner's Magazine, and I wrote you what I felt about it then. It
was, I thought, your best and highest. The second part is still before
me. I don't know what I'll find in it; I only know you'll grow and
prosper in your power forever.

---

*J. G. Stikeleather, to whom the following letter was written, was a promi-
nent Asheville real estate man, and had known the Wolfe family for many
years. He had written Wolfe a letter about his books, in which he had re-*

[1] *Roll River* had been published by Scribners in April, 1935, after being serialized in
Scribner's Magazine.

*proached him for being "too hard on your family and not just to Asheville,"
but which was friendly and fatherly in tone.*

To J. G. STIKELEATHER

New York City
July 8, 1935

Dear Mr. Stikeleather:

. . . I want to thank you for the spirit of friendship and kindness which prompted you to write me as you did, and to assure you that I am sincerely grateful for your letter. I should also like to tell you that I know I have made mistakes in the past, that I have said and written some things which I now regret, but I should like you to believe that a great many of these things were due to the inexperience, the intemperance, and the oversensitivity of youth rather than to a desire to hurt and wound people that I have known all my life. May I not tell you also that I have in my heart not one atom of bitterness or resentment towards the town and the people from which I came and which, I think, I shall always be proud and happy to acknowledge as my own.

Mr. Stikeleather, may I give you one little illustration of what I think may have happened between myself and the people in Asheville? Have you ever tried to pass a man in the street and the moment you stepped to the right to go around him he would also step the same way, when you step to the left, he would follow you, and so the thing would continue until it became funny and you both stood still and looked at each other and yet all the time all you were trying to do was to be friendly to each other and to give the other fellow a free passage? Or, better still, have you ever met some one that you knew you liked and you were pretty sure he felt the same way about you and yet, figuratively speaking, you "got off on the wrong foot" with each other? Now I think that something of this sort may have happened between Asheville and myself. When I wrote "Look Homeward, Angel" several years ago, I can honestly assure you I had no notion that the book would arouse the kind of comment and response and cause the kind of misunderstanding in my home town that it did do. I should like you to believe that I, myself, was just about the most surprised person in the world when I finally understood the kind of effect my book was having in Asheville.

I cannot go back to "Look Homeward, Angel" now nor tell you what I felt about that book or what my purpose and intentions were in writing it or how I feel about it. In fact, although this statement may surprise you, I no longer have a very clear memory or idea of what was in "Look Homeward, Angel" nor do I know exactly what I said there or what the total content of the book may be. The reason for this is pretty simple, and yet it is awfully hard to explain. It is hard to explain because the thing that makes a man write a book and the thing that makes him read a book are two such different things that it is really like the North Pole pointing toward the South. If this sounds too involved and complicated, what I am trying to say to you is that a reader reads a book in order to remember it and a writer writes a book in order to forget it. For that reason a writer, after he has got the whole thing off his chest, wants to forget it utterly, and yet he wants fame, too. He wants people to read his book, to like his book, to admire his talent as a writer. This is the thing he writes and sweats for, and yet when he meets people, and they tell him they have read his book and praise him for it or say that they have not read his book and apologize for it, he has a terrible feeling of embarrassment and constraint and wishes that they would just say nothing about it and does not know what to say himself.

It's a strange situation, isn't it? It seems very complicated and difficult, and yet it is quite simple at the bottom, and I know that a man of your experience will understand it. I suppose it boils down to this: you want to be a famous man and a great writer, and yet you want to lead an obscure, simple, and plain kind of life like other men. I have told you all these things just to indicate—I can't do anything more but indicate them because if I ever started explaining the whole thing, I could go on until tomorrow morning—but just to indicate the kind of difficulty that arises when a man tries to tell how he felt when he wrote a book, not when a man tells how he felt when he read one.

Now, having said all this, I would like plainly and frankly to admit something—something which I have already mentioned. I do think that, as you say, there may have been something of the bitterness and intolerance and hot temper of youth in "Look Homeward, Angel." And yet may I say to you—it is pretty difficult to say this because no man likes to be put in the position where he must seem to defend his own book or to point to the praise and success which it may have had—may I say to you that although the youthfulness and a certain intemperance in the book was recognized by critics elsewhere, these imperfections were on the whole considered only incidental to a book which was read, I assure you, not as a savage and vitriolic attack upon the citizens of Asheville, North Carolina, but as a young man's vision of his childhood and his youth and the world from which he came—a world which in its general humanity could have been as true of Peoria or Spokane or Berlin or any place as it was of Asheville. Anyway, Asheville and I got off on the wrong foot with each other because of that book. I think there may have been some bitterness in it but not as much bitterness as Asheville thought there was, and as for this last book, which is also finished, over, published, and out of my system as the first one was, I think I can really assure you that no matter what its many faults and imperfections may be, so far as Asheville is concerned, there is no bitterness at all.

I just ask you to believe this, and if you cannot believe it, I would hope that you have time to go back to the book and examine it for yourself. This is all I can write you at present, and I know you will understand I am writing this out of my heart because you and I come from the same town, the same people, and because I want to answer your kind and friendly letter in a way that will, I hope, bring about a better understanding between the people of my native town and myself.

I am certainly coming home to see you all some day. I don't know when that will be. I have much work to do, many things to learn and to experience, but when I do come home, I hope you will all understand that I am a man who, whatever errors he may have made, has tried to grow and learn and increase in strength and wisdom and humanity, and who would have grown beyond malice and resentment in the end. Certainly I hope the last is now true and that all of you will come, in time, to understand it and believe it.

Meanwhile with all my best and friendliest wishes, and with thanks again for your good letter, . . .

Harold Calo, who had been one of Wolfe's students at New York University, had written him, saying: "Of all my . . . friends, I am the only one who, fortunately, was a member of your first class . . . at N.Y.U. Consequently, when one of the boys charged you with intolerance and anti-semitism, inferred from a criticism of Of Time and the River, *I could not concede that. You never gave me that impression and I do not believe that to-day. . . . I cannot help wondering, however, if you have not been unduly harsh in your criticism of the students and perhaps should give them a chance to explain their reactions . . . towards the University and towards yourself." The following was Wolfe's reply.*

To HAROLD CALO

New York City

July 10, 1935

Dear Mr. Calo:

I just got back from Europe the other day. It was good to find your letter here among the stack of mail which had been accumulating during the four months which I was away. I certainly do remember very well our meeting in Europe and the pleasant talk we had together, also the days when you were a student in one of my classes at N.Y.U.

I have many, many letters to answer right away, and, therefore, I cannot give your letter the kind of answer it deserves, but I do want you to know, and I ask you to believe, as I am sure you do, that if anyone charged me with anti-semitism because of anything in the last book, that charge was absolutely groundless. I have not time to go into the matter fully here, and of course I should like to know upon just what evidence that charge is based, but I think you will believe me when I tell you that some of the best and most valued friends I have ever had here in New York have been Jews, and I believe a careful reading of the book will bear me out in that point. As for the rest of it, all I ask you to remember are the days I taught you at New York University and then to consider fairly whether you ever saw or heard me do anything that was unfair, intolerant, or unjust to any member of your faith.

This is all for the present. Yes, I should certainly like to see you again and renew our acquaintance and hear what you have been doing during the years that have passed since I last saw you. I am going West in a week or two, but shall be back here to stay later on. You can always reach me by writing me here at Scribner's.

To MARTHA DODD

New York City

July 10, 1935

Dear Martha:

. . . I have thought of you and my other friends in Berlin very often, and I have missed seeing you all. It was a wonderful trip, a wonderful crowded experience for four months, and although I did not get much rest, it did me a world of good. Copenhagen was also fine, and I met some nice people there and had a good time, but I was ready to come home.

It is wonderful to be back. Reporters met me at the boat; there were pieces in the paper; everybody here at Scribners seems excited and happy about the way the book has gone. It still keeps on, and they say it's not going to stop—not this year anyway. It's the first time in my life I've been a little famous, and the experience has been very wonderful and happy, but if it affects me or my work, please heave a brickbat at me.

Last night I stayed up until five o'clock reading hundreds and hundreds of reviews from all over the country. They took some nice, cheerful, wholehearted pokes at me, but they seemed to love me, and the total effect is overwhelming. The letters have been wonderfully moving and exciting. In addition to the regular sort of fan mail and autograph letters and flirty-girl kind of thing, there have been wonderful letters coming from people everywhere, all the way from hotel clerks to school teachers to ordinary men and women of all sorts, who said they had never written a writer before and don't want an answer and just wrote to tell me so the moment they finished the book. Among other things, I got a grand, generous letter from Sherwood Anderson who said he knew why he could never write a novel after finishing the book. The whole thing has made me pretty happy, and it also makes me feel a little guilty and ashamed. If they think this book is good, I know I am going to beat it forty ways with the next two. I failed in this book, not in the ways the critics said I did, but in another way that Max and I know about. In spite of their talk about its tremendous energy and so forth, I wrote it in less than a year before it was published, at a time when I was horribly tired and when I had exhausted myself in writing the two books which are to follow.[1] Perhaps I should have taken another year, but so much time had gone by without publication that I agreed with Max that it was more important to get it out and to go on to all the work that awaits me than to spend more time perfecting this one.

I feel grand. I am strong and happy and confident as I haven't been in several years, and if I failed last time, the time is coming when I may not fail. Anyway, I will use every energy of my life—and my life itself if need be—to justify what Max and my friends and some of the people in these letters have said and felt about what I do.

I am going to Colorado in a couple of weeks and intend to explore the West this summer, but I shall be back here in September, and I think I am ready to work this coming year as I have never worked before. We have a book of stories which are ready and which are coming in October.[2] And with six months' work on "The Fair"[3] the way I am now, I shall have far and away the best book I have written. The Pentland book comes later, and for that I am saving the best of everything I have in me.

New York these days is hot, sweaty, sticky, sweltering, and the most wonderful, terrible, gaudy and stupendous wench you ever saw. It is grand to be here. This is my air and my weather, and somehow—I don't know how or why—my kind and my people. It is good to have had

[1] *The October Fair* and parts of *The Hills Beyond Pentland.*
[2] *From Death to Morning* was actually published on November 14.
[3] *The October Fair.*

this success. I intend to use it so that it will bring me added power and wisdom and achievement. Good-bye for the present. Please give my love to your father and mother, and thank them again for all their generous kindness and hospitality which they showed me when I was in Berlin, and let me know if there is anything I can do for you ever here.

With all my best and warmest wishes to you and all the family,

The following letter was written in reply to one from Lewis Gannett of the Herald Tribune *asking Wolfe for a list of the books he had recently enjoyed reading, for publication in that paper's daily book column.*

To LEWIS GANNETT

New York City

July 10, 1935

Dear Mr. Gannett:

I have just returned from Europe and found . . . your letter of June 6 in which you ask me if I would jot down and send to you the names of six or a dozen books which I have enjoyed reading recently. If it is not too late, I should be glad to do so, but I think I ought to tell you that during the last four months that I have been traveling and seeing a great many new things, I have not had time for much reading. Consequently I am not very well informed on current books. And before this recent journey for a period of four years, I was working very hard in Brooklyn and, for the most part, read the books which belonged to me and which I had had for some time.

It is a curious fact that during my student years and for years thereafter I read prodigiously and gobbled up everything I could lay my hands on, but during these past four years when I have worked harder than any other time in my life, I must confess that I found myself more and more drawn back to find comfort and stimulation in a few books which I had read many times and to which in this period I referred again and again. For this reason I am afraid my list will not be a very contemporary one and I am afraid it may seem a little too stern and rare for some of your readers, but it is literally true that these are some of the books to which I returned again and again during that time and of which I have never grown tired and which have given me some of the best and finest moments of my life.

1. "The Book of Ecclesiastes," which it seems to me is as great a single piece of writing as I have ever read and which I must have read at least

a dozen times a year for the past four or five years. To this I should like to add the "Book of Job" and the "Songs of Solomon."

2. "King Lear," "Hamlet," second part of "King Henry IV," which I think is one of the best plays ever written, "King Richard III," "Othello," and "The Tempest."

3. A great deal of poetry, which for me, at least, is the one form of writing to which it is possible to return again and again without weariness and with a constant wonder and discovery. I cannot at the moment think of any book which I have read as often as a half dozen times, but there are scores of poems which I have read hundreds of times and which are now more wonderful than when I first read them. I cannot name them all, but some of the poets I like best and to whom I have gone back most often are Milton, Donne, Wyatt, Herrick, Herbert, Blake, Coleridge, Wordsworth, Keats, and Robert Browning, and in the last few years, Walt Whitman.

4. "The Oxford Book of English Prose."

5. Burton's "Anatomy of Melancholy," which no man, I think, could read from start to finish, but which is certainly one of the most difficult books to crack that was ever written but which, once cracked and experienced, will give the reader an unending store of pleasure, wisdom, and delight. You can read it forever. You can open it at any place and read; you will never get tired of reading it. It is certainly one of the greatest books that was ever written.

6. "War and Peace," which I have read two or three times in the last four years and which, so far as I can know or judge, is the greatest novel I have ever read.

7. I cannot leave out "The World Almanac," which, with its wonderful, hard and certain figures, its statistics concerning the population of cities, counties, towns, and states; World Series records; batting and pitching averages, etc., gave me again and again, at times when my energies were exhausted and my mind numb with fatigue, a kind of ease and comfort that no other volume on the shelves could give.

I am afraid that this is much too long, but these are honestly some of the books which I have read most often for the last four years and which have helped me most. If you care to make any use of it, please do so.

The following letter was found in Wolfe's own files, and evidently never mailed. It was addressed to an Asheville woman who had repeatedly complained that Wolfe had portrayed her in Look Homeward, Angel, *and who had now written that a friend of hers had heard a strange man in a hotel say that she was represented by a certain character in that book, and that Wolfe himself had told him so.*

To —— ——

New York City

July 18, 1935

Dear ——:

. . . I want to tell you again how terribly sorry I am to hear that you have been caused any further distress because of "Look Homeward, Angel," and I want to repeat now, as I told you before in my other letter, I had no intention of portraying you under the character of Mrs. ——, and if that character had any actual basis in fact, the basis was not only very slight but was influenced by a person I knew long after I left Asheville. As for this latest version of the story which you mention in your letter, I want to brand it here and now as an absolute and deliberate falsehood. This man, ——, who, you say, was doing the talking, is so far as I can know or recollect an utter stranger to me. I do not assert this for a positive fact because ——, as you know, is a fairly common name in western North Carolina, and it is possible that I may have met or known some one by that name. But of all the ——s that I can remember at the present moment—and I have tried hard since reading your letter to remember all of them—I can call to mind no —— ——. Further, I want to add this: if any person named —— who lives in Asheville or Hendersonville asserts that I ever discussed "Look Homeward, Angel" with him or identified any character in the book or asserted that you or any other living person are intended as the Mrs. —— in the novel, or that I ever told him or anybody else that you were a notorious woman, each and every one of these assertions is an absolute falsehood.

There is no difficulty at all in proving the truth of this. In the first place, my last visit to Asheville was in September, 1928 before "Look Homeward, Angel" was published. Although it was known at that time that the book was scheduled to appear later on that autumn, no one in Asheville knew anything about the book or what was in the book, nor could anyone have possibly known at that time what the nature of the book might be. If I talked to anyone about the book at that time, it was only in the most casual and general way because it is absolutely impossible to give a reader a clear and coherent idea of a book like "Look

Homeward, Angel" before he has read it; but I assure you that I discussed neither the plot nor the story nor any of the characters in the book with anyone while I was in Asheville. I have no recollection of meeting or talking to anyone by the name of ——, and if I did meet and talk to such a person, I certainly made no such vile and abominable statement about any person as the one you mention in your letter as having been made, and I hereby once again brand it as a complete and infamous lie.

Naturally I understand your great distress because of this outrageous story, and I not only sympathize with your distress, but I share it with you, and I want to assure you that I will do everything in my power to help you and, if need be, to denounce and expose this story for the ugly lie it is. I should also like to add this: I don't know how or by what sinister and devious ways these stories spring up and gain currency, but I suppose you know as well as I do that in addition to the many fine and honorable people one knows, there are also unfortunate people who are so warped and twisted and so full of hatred and bitterness that they will not scruple to start a malicious and slanderous story even when they know it will cause innocent people distress and pain. I say that there are unfortunately such people as this in the world and that if such a story as this has been told, it undoubtedly comes from such a source. As I said before, I cannot at the moment remember having known a person by the name of ——. I certainly know no one of that name here in New York, and if I did know anyone by that name in Asheville or Hendersonville, I certainly did not discuss my book with him or make the statement you describe in your letter, and I know that if such a person as —— does exist and I could meet him and talk to him about this, he would deny that I had ever made such a statement.

This is all for the present. I have tried to tell you just exactly how I feel and think about this whole matter, and I assure you that if such a story ever appears again, I will give you my heartiest and most energetic support in your effort to expose it.

And now with all my best and friendliest greetings to you and your family,

The following postcard was mailed by Wolfe from Greeley, Colorado, where he had stopped off to give one lecture at the Colorado State College of Education before going to the writers' conference at the University of Colorado in Boulder.

To MAXWELL E. PERKINS

> [Picture Postcard: Estes Park to Grand Lake,
> Rocky Mountain National Park, Colorado]

Greeley Colo.

July 30, 1935

Dear Max: I've seen no mountains yet but the West is wonderful—blazing hot, but crystal air, blue skies. The journey across the country was overwhelming—I've never begun to say what I ought to say about it.

To MAXWELL E. PERKINS

University of Colorado
Boulder, Colorado
Writers' Conference

August 12, 1935

Dear Max:

Thanks for your letter of August second. This is the first letter I have written since I came out here, and the first chance I have had to write you. The Writers' Conference is over, and I am leaving here to-day for Denver and expect to be on my way for Santa Fe and the Southwest in another day or two. This has been, and is going to be, an extraordinary trip. The West is like something that I always knew about. I feel good and have been immensely happy ever since I came here. The country is magnificent. I took a long trip yesterday up into the Rocky Mountain National Park and saw some of the most glorious scenery from a height of thirteen thousand feet that I have ever seen. The people here have been wonderfully kind and hospitable, and between the Writers' Conference lectures, talks, reading manuscripts, conferences, and being taken around to parties, I am pretty well tired out to-day. We're almost a mile high here. I have been constantly exhilarated and ravenously hungry ever since I came here.

Some remarkably interesting things happened out here at this Writers' Conference. It is the first one I ever attended and perhaps the last, but I have been astonished at the quality of the talks that have been made and the instruction that has been given, and I think something very interesting and important may come from here. A number of the people who attended gave me their manuscripts to read, and I have taken the liberty of suggesting to three people that they send their manuscripts to you immediately for a reading. I don't know if anything will come of it or not. Because of the pressure of time and the great amount of manuscripts to be read, I was unable to judge just what possibilities the manuscripts had, but it seemed to me that these three at any rate were interesting enough to justify a reading. . . .

Now, as briefly as possible, a few words about other things. I note what you say about the Boyd matter, and I hope you are right in believing her case has been destroyed and that we shall hear no more from her. Nevertheless, Mr. Mitchell [1] has written me by air mail and has very urgently requested me to try to find the letter she wrote in answer to my own letter dismissing her as my agent, and is further asking me to get in touch with the Czechoslovakian publishers of "Of Time and the River"—to cable them if necessary—in an effort to get a copy of their correspondence with Mrs. Boyd establishing from their side as well the fact that she wrote them saying she was no longer my agent. It is also said that Mrs. Boyd's attorney speaks of some mysterious third person who was "a mutual friend" of both of us, and who is willing to testify that, at a time subsequent to the time I wrote the letter dismissing Mrs. Boyd as my agent, he had a conversation with me in which I agreed to a reconciliation and to retain her services as my agent for future work. As you know, this is an absolute and utter falsehood, and not only have I never seen nor written to Mrs. Boyd since I wrote the letter of dismissal, but I have never had any word of communication with her through any other person in any way whatever, and of course I have no idea who this mysterious third person may be.

Upon the basis of all these things, Mr. Mitchell informs me that he has entered a notice of appearance, whatever that may be. Whatever it is, I fear it means the long, involved, and costly operation of the courts of law and of lawyers, and although I feel confident that we can eventually defeat this woman's . . . claims, I am bitterly indignant over the fact that my own honesty and pity for her, . . . my failure to secure an absolute release [from her], have now put me in a position where these people can threaten me with suit and try to take from me a portion of my earnings. It is an ugly and intolerable situation, and what is most shameful about it now is the fact that even if I defeat her claims, I can do so only at the cost of a large sum of money for legal services and of an utterly shameful waste of my time, my energy, my temper, and what is most important, of human faith in other people and in the integrity of their intentions. This business of pawing through stacks and bales of old letters, trying to find every little scrap of writing which a person once wrote to you, is a disgusting one. I worked for three days

---

[1] Cornelius Mitchell of Mitchell and Van Winkle, Wolfe's attorney in this suit.

going through great stacks of letters in an effort to find everything the woman had ever written to me and everything which seemed to me to bear on the case, till finally I had succeeded in collecting a great mass of evidence, including my letter of dismissal—everything in fact which Mr. Mitchell said he wanted. Now he wants this letter which she wrote to me, and of course I have no idea where it is and will have no opportunity to look for it until I get back to New York and have to go through the whole accumulation of years of letters again. I am not going to let my life be eaten up and consumed . . . I have my work to do, and as my friend and publisher, I ask you in the future to try to help me in every way possible to keep me from this kind of shameful and ruinous invasion.

Finally, you must not put the manuscript of a book of stories in final form until after my return to New York. If that means the book of stories will have to be deferred till next spring, then they will have to be deferred, but I will not consent this time to allow the book to be taken away from me and printed and published until I myself have had time to look at the proofs, and at any rate to talk to you about certain revisions, changes, excisions, or additions that ought to be made. I really mean this, Max. I have money enough to live on for a while now. I do not propose to trade upon the success of "Of Time and the River." I propose rather to prepare my work in every way possible to meet and refute, if I can, some of the very grave and serious criticisms that were made about the last book, and as my friend and the person whose judgment I trust most, you must help me to do this.

I am coming back to New York in September. My mind is swarming with new material and the desire to get back and finish up "The October Fair" as soon as possible, but before we do that, we must first do a thorough, honest and satisfactory job upon the book of stories, "From Death to Morning"; we must get the Boyd matter settled; we must get the deck cleared for action; otherwise another shameful and revolting waste of talent right at the time of its greatest fertility and strength is likely to occur. And if this happens, I am ready to go to Siam, Russia, Timbuctoo, or take out citizenship under the benign and democratic governance of Adolph Hitler where, by comparison, the rights of men and of freedom and integrity of the individual are respected.

This is all for the present. I will be in the Southwest next week and then on to California, the Northwest, back through Idaho, Wyoming, and St. Louis and so back east again. And if they don't kill me out here with hospitality, or in New York with . . . lawsuits and so forth, I'll have some good stories to tell you and a lot of work to do in the winter. . . .

P.S. Max, forgive my ill temper—I am *exasperated* beyond measure by this Boyd thing—and I must work now—please help me in every way. . . .

To MAXWELL E. PERKINS

[Picture Postcard: Prehistoric Cliff Dwellings,
Pueblo of Puye, near Santa Fe, N.M.]

Santa Fe, N.M.

August 26, 1935

Dear Max: This is the most magnificent country—wild and fiendish, magnificent—just the way I always knew it would be. I had a fight with Mabel Luhan the moment I walked into her house and left immediately [1] but everyone else seems to like me.

To MAXWELL E. PERKINS

Hollywood-Roosevelt Hotel
Hollywood, California
Send mail to General Delivery, San Francisco

Sunday Sept. 1 [1935]

Dear Max:

I am sending you with this letter the proposed dedication for the book of stories. Will you and Jack please read and consider it carefully and decide whether you think it should be used? I had originally intended to dedicate "The Hills Beyond Pentland" to my brother, Ben, but because of the nature of the book of stories, and the subject matter involved, it has occurred to me that the present book might be a more fitting subject for the dedication. What do you think? At any rate, here's the dedication—I will abide by your judgment.

Finally, please let me urge on you again the desirability of getting *a good order* in the arrangement of the stories. I mean . . . the arrangement really should, so far as we can make it do so, illustrate the title, "From Death to Morning"—that is, they should progress in a general way, beginning, say, with "Death—The Proud Brother," and ending perhaps, with such a piece as "The Web of Earth."

[1] Mabel Dodge Luhan had invited Wolfe to come and see her at Taos, and he had been torn between friendliness and a fear of being lionized. He finally arrived there very late at night with two society girls who had driven him there from Santa Fe. When they were not received too cordially, Wolfe became angry and left with them.

Max, I think you might be surprised to know of the interest people out here have taken in the stories. I met Miss Edna Ferber, the novelist, in Santa Fe, the other day, and had lunch with her. She spoke most generously of everything I had done, but said she thought the stories were the finest things I had yet written. In the same way, a number of these moving picture people here in Hollywood—directors and other executives—know all about my work and are *collecting* it! I have met several who have a copy of every story I ever wrote, including the college stuff of Chapel Hill days—furthermore, they've read it. I met one director yesterday who began to rave about "The Web of Earth"—others about "Death—The Proud Brother." As for myself, I feel there is as good writing as I've done in some of the stories—it represents *important* work to me, and I think we should spare no pains to present it in as important and impressive a way as possible. I think you may be a little inclined to underestimate the importance of arrangement and presentation, and may feel that the stories can go in any way, and that the order doesn't matter much. Perhaps you are right—my own feeling, however, is that in a general way the stories do have a kind of unity and should be presented with an eye to cumulative effect, as the title "From Death to Morning" indicates. There is so much more that I want to say to you—so much more I want to do, include, write—and I know I have done little. There are at least half a dozen big stories I should have written and that should be included, and all kinds of minor things: the scene in the railway station, some of the night scenes, so many things bearing upon death and night and morning that could be put in to weave the whole thing together—in particular a scene where old Bascom (in "The Hills Beyond Pentland") looks down from the mountain in the town of Altamont and tells his twelve-year-old nephew about the Pentlands.[1] This could be used wonderfully to lead right into "The Web of Earth," and by doing a few things like this I know *the whole book* could be woven together and given a tremendous feeling of unity and cumulative effect that you almost never find in a book of stories. But please consider them carefully, Max. I could say much more, but you know what I mean, and as the drunken top-sergeant in "What Price Glory" yelled after his commanding officer—"Wait on me, Captain—Baby's Coming!"

Yes, I agree with you, I've had six months vacation, and that ought to be enough for any man. And it is—I feel guilty as hell, and eager to get to work again. But Max, it has been a thrilling wonderful experience—these last six months—I am filled to bursting with the pictures and variety of it, and as for this trip to the West, I have no words here to tell

[1] This was not included in *From Death to Morning* but finally appeared in *The Web and the Rock* on pages 160–170.

you of the beauty, power and magnificence of this country. Thank God, I have seen it at last!—and I know that I did not lie about it; I know I have not yet begun to put it down on paper; my store of wonderful subject matter has been enormously enriched.

I have some amazing and fantastic stories to tell you [about] this moving picture world, as well. I have met the famous stars, directors, producers, writers etc., have seen them at work—this is simply incredible —and in the midst of all the false and unreal world, the technical, building, working world is simply amazing in its skill and knowledge. Good God! I could write a magnificent book even about this place if I lived here a year. They want me to stay, have offered me a job, and mentioned huge sums, but perhaps I shall resist.[2] Everyone has been wonderfully kind all through the West—lavish generous hospitality. I am almost worn out by it—here as well. Dorothy Parker seems to like me, swears she does, and last night told a room of people that I was built on a heroic scale and that there was no one like me. Maybe the old girl is laughing at me behind my back and making wicked jokes about me but I think she meant what she said. She and her young husband are living in a magnificent imitation Colonial house and just bought a new Packard the other day, and the liquor and hospitality flows like the Mississippi—I am going there again this afternoon.

Yes, I know I have stayed too long, but Max, Max, you *must* wait on me—I've *got* to see San Francisco—above all, I must see that wonderful town—in the end, we shall not lose by it. Then, if you like, I'll cut it short and come straight home, only I'd hope to see a little of Oregon, Salt Lake City, and stop off a day in St. Louis to see where Grover died on my way back.[3] I'll be home in two weeks. Now, Max, please wait on me— don't take the book away before I get back. I've some wonderful things to tell you. Are Louise and the girls home yet?

[2] Wolfe was approached as to the possibility of his working as a writer for Metro-Goldwyn-Mayer by Sam Marx, the Story Editor there at that time, and with the approval of Irving Thalberg, Head of Production. However, he replied quite candidly that he had "a lot of books to write" and so could not accept. Since the making and declining of the offer was only oral, there is no record of it, but according to Marx's recollection, it was either on a week-to-week basis at $1000 to $1500 a week, or on a yearly basis at $30,000 to $50,000.

[3] Wolfe described the death of his brother Grover in *Look Homeward, Angel* on pages 51–60. He also described both Grover's death and his own visit to "St. Louis to see where Grover died" in a short story, "The Lost Boy," which appeared in the November, 1937, issue of *Redbook* and is included in *The Hills Beyond*.

To MAXWELL E. PERKINS

> The Riverside,
> Reno, Nevada
> Thursday, Sept. 12, 1935

Dear Max:

I am a little worried about something, and if you see fit, won't you take steps about it right away? It is this: at various times during the last month—at Boulder and elsewhere—I have discoursed very eloquently and persuasively about my book of the night, which is beginning to interest me more and more all the time. I have told how much of my life has been lived by night, about the chemistry of darkness, the strange and magic thing it does to our lives, about America at night: the rivers, plains, mountains, rivers in the moon or darkness (last night, by the way, coming up here through the Sierra Nevadas there was blazing moonlight, the effect was incredibly beautiful)—and how the Americans are a nighttime people, which I have found out everywhere is absolutely true. Now, I'm afraid I've talked too much—please don't think I'm fool enough to think anyone is going to, or can, "steal my ideas," but people have been immensely and instantly absorbed when I told about my book, and have at once agreed to the utter truth of it. I have got hold of an immense, rich, and absolutely true thing about ourselves, at once very simple, profound, and various—and I know a great and original book, unlike any other, can be written on it—and I don't want some fool to get hold of it and write some cheap and worthless thing. The idea is so beautiful and simple that some bungler could easily mutilate it.

It will be years before I do it, but it keeps gathering in me all the time. I don't know yet exactly what form it will take, or whether it can be called a "novel" or not. I don't care—but I think it will be a great tone-symphony of night—railway yards, engines, freights, dynamos, bridges, men and women, the wilderness, plains, rivers, deserts, a clopping hoof, etc.—seen *not by a definite personality*, but haunted throughout by a consciousness *of personality*. In other words, I want to assert my divine right once and for all to be the *God Almighty* of a book—to be at once the spirit to move it, the spirit behind it, never to appear, to blast forever the charge of "autobiography" while being triumphantly and impersonally autobiographical.

Can't you do this, if you think best—and something tells me that it may be best: make an announcement to this effect: that I have for years been interested in the life of night (*not* nightclubs) and have been slowly acquiring an immense amount of material about it; that the book is slowly taking form, but will not be ready for years when these other books are out of the way; and that it is at present called "The Book of The Night." [1] You might put in something about "Saturday Night in America" (When I get back, I'll tell you about Longmont, Colorado on Saturday night. I've told you before what Saturday night does to us here in America and one part of the book has to do with this). At any rate, Max, I've talked to other people about it, and since this is one of the most precious and valuable ideas I've ever had, do what you can to protect it for me now. Why can't we do this? You could even say that I am so interested in the book that I am now at work on it, and that it *may* appear before the other books of the "Of Time and the River" series come out. This would do no harm, would arouse interest and discussion, and might serve the purpose of throwing some of my various ——s off the track for the present.

As for the Brooklyn lecture thing [2]—answer for me, as you think best. I could certainly do it, I could probably do it well, the talk at Boulder went over beautifully. But let us first consider this: do you think it is well for me to get into the lecture habit—I am getting offers now all the time— and do you think it is good for my *special* writing reputation to become known as a public lecturer? Also, what are we to work on next—"The October Fair," the Pentland book, "The Book of the Night," short stories— or what? When do you want to publish next, and when do we begin to work again? I am just mentioning these things for your consideration—I could probably do the lecture without great difficulty—and if law suits and crazy women are going to destroy my work, and take up my time again, I might as well pick up what extra money I can. But you be judge and answer the Brooklyn people as you see fit—whatever you say will be all right with me.

Other matters rest until I see you in few days. I've stopped off the day to see this town—incredible little 15,000 one-street place with gambling halls and bars and dance halls open all day and all night; gray faced faro and roulette men, silver dollars stacked up by the tons. Catching Overland Limited at 5 o'clock in morning in order to see Nevada and Utah deserts by day—then in Salt Lake for day—then St. Louis for few hours—then back home.

---

[1] Wolfe later gave this material the title of *The Hound of Darkness*. He never wrote much of it, but portions of it appear in "A Prologue to America" in the February 1, 1938, issue of *Vogue*, and are scattered through *The Web and the Rock* and *You Can't Go Home Again*, as on pages 474–475 of *The Web and the Rock*, and pages 429–431 and 506–508 of *You Can't Go Home Again*.

[2] The Brooklyn Institute of Arts and Sciences had phoned Perkins to ask if Wolfe would give the opening lecture of a series they were planning for that fall.

The following two letters were written to John Hall Wheelock about the galley proofs of From Death to Morning, *which Wolfe read and corrected with great care.*

To JOHN HALL WHEELOCK

[New York City]

[September, 1935]

Dear Jack:

Here are the remainder of the proofs for "Death the Proud Brother," which I have now read and corrected.

Now, about what is probably the most important matter first—your comment on galley 22 that my story really lacks there and that what follows is another thing. I see your point and feel a break myself, but wonder if the inclusion of a phrase at the very beginning of this passage which would refer it to the death scene that has gone before would not help? What do you think?

A much more serious question however, is this: the passage that follows to the end of the story is really one of my most ambitious apostrophes—to Loneliness, and Death and Sleep. It is the kind of thing that some of the critics have gone gunning after me for—but it is also the kind of thing that many people have liked in my writing, and that some say they hope I never lose. This passage in peroration—about Sleep and Death, etc.—has made friends. Now, what do you think? It's a pretty serious matter to me, because if it really is better that I cut out this *kind* of writing entirely, it is a fundamental thing and I must seriously change my whole method and style everywhere. *But I want you to say what you think!*

About other things: please note the changes I have made in galley 12 —taking out the word "Esther" and substituting "the woman." Do you think it is now clear, and also a change for the better?

I note your red marks on galley 14. . . . This passage now refers to "the woman" rather than to Esther. Do you want it cut? I have indicated several paragraphs on galley 20 with a line and question mark. I feel something a little stiff and inept here—it is part of a much longer part that was cut out. Will you read it, and tell me if you can find the trouble, if any?

Galley 23: you marked several phrases and sentences, as having been duplicated in "Of Time and the River." That's true, they are—this was written first. Do you think their inclusion here would be a serious error? The trouble is, I have trouble thinking of an adequate substitute for the passage "They come! Ships call!—etc."

Finally, in apostrophe to Sleep I have capitalized *Sleep* throughout save in the concluding phrase, "Sleep, sleep, sleep." I did this to avoid confusion—but do you think in the phrase "In *Sleep* we lie all naked and alone," would arouse obscene comment?

As to shorter phrases, which I had repeated in other stories, I have either modified them here, or let them stay, preferring them to go in here rather than in the other stories.

I'll try to get in before closing time to see you.

To JOHN HALL WHEELOCK

[September, 1935]

Dear Jack:

Here is the proof of the only story left (except "The Web"). Note that I have changed the title to "The Far and The Near." Also observe changes on galley 82 which have been done with a view to changing the attitude of the two women to a *timid* and *uneasy unfriendliness* rather than surly hostility. Also last sentence. If you think changes good, let them stand—if not, erase them.

Harry Woodburn Chase, to whom the following note was addressed, had been President of the University of North Carolina from 1919–1930, and had come to New York University as its Chancellor in 1933. He had sent Wolfe an anonymous poem about the University which had been published in the Year Book of the School of Architecture.

To HARRY WOODBURN CHASE

Charles Scribner's Sons
597 Fifth Avenue
New York
Oct. 30, 1935

Dear Chancellor Chase:

Thanks very much for your note and the enclosed poem. I am sorry to say that I am not working twenty-four hours a day as I feel I should be, but I hope to get started soon. I had a wonderful vacation of more than six months which took me all the way from Denmark to San Francisco, and I am back here now, ready to work and desperately eager to get at it, but somehow I find it terribly hard to break through my own inertia and get started. I wonder why people are like that. No one knows better than I that I must work, and that my life is nothing without work, and yet I do everything in the world to avoid it—that is, before I get started. . . .

Thank you for sending me the poem. Yes, I think it decidedly does say something, and is eloquent and true. As time goes on, and I have been able to get more detachment and perspective on my years at New York University, I have realized that being there is one of the most valuable and fruitful experiences of my whole life. I can think of no other way in which a young man coming to this terrific city as I came to it, could have had a more comprehensive and stimulating introduction to its swarming life, than through the corridors and classrooms of Washington Square. In April of this year I had the opportunity to revisit the great English university at Cambridge. It is gloriously beautiful, even more so than I had remembered it, but somehow it seemed remote from the life of the world around us, and my thoughts kept going back to Washington Square and to all the eager, swarming, vigorous life I knew there, and it seemed to me without making comparisons, that whatever happens to our universities in the future, Washington Square was somehow closer to reality than Cambridge. So thanks again for sending me the poem. . . .

The following note was written in a presentation copy of From Death to Morning *for Henry T. Volkening. The unfavorable review to which it refers was undoubtedly the one by Ferner Nuhn in the Sunday, November 17, 1935, issue of the* Herald Tribune Books, *which was released on Saturday, November 16. Nuhn's review was headed: "Thomas Wolfe, Six-foot-six. These Stories Reveal Again the Exuberance of an Over-sized Man in a Standard-sized World," and said in part: "The advantages of an oversized view of the world are obvious in Thomas Wolfe's work: the heightened color, mood, sweep, rush which can so easily carry lesser organisms along. But there are disadvantages too. The bulge of an excess of emotion is as flabby in the end as the slack of an insufficient one. Readers swept off their feet have a way of picking themselves up and rejecting further rides, and this would be a pity."*

To HENRY T. VOLKENING

New York City
November 13, 1935

Dear Henry:

I'm a little sad as I write you this. I've just read the first review of this book—in next Saturday's *Herald Tribune*—which pans it and sees little in it except a man six foot six creating monstrous figures in a world of five feet eight. I do not think this is true, but now I have a hunch the well-known "reaction" has set in against me, and that I will take a pounding on this book. Well, I am writing you this because I believe that as good writing as I have ever done is in this book and because my faith has always been that a good thing is indestructible and that if there is good here—as I hope and believe there is—it will somehow survive. That is a faith I want to have, and that I think we need in life, and that is why I am writing you this—not in defense against attacks I may receive but just to put this on record *in advance* with you, who are a friend of mine. So won't you put this away—what I have written—and keep it— and if someday it turns out I am right, won't you take it out and read it to me?

The following letter to Clayton Hoagland was occasioned by Hoagland's review of "From Death to Morning" in the New York Sun, *on November 14, 1935, which said: "This book of stories has in it all of Wolfe's realism, the ribaldry, the humor, the lyrical prose ascending to poetry, the gift of vitalizing a character until it stalks from the page."*

To CLAYTON HOAGLAND

865 First Avenue
New York City
[November, 1935]

Dear Clayton:

I want to tell you how moved and grateful I am about your magnificent and generous review of "From Death to Morning." I felt overwhelmed and a little guilty, too, when I read it, because in addition to being my reviewer you are also my friend; but I reflected, then, that it was because of some of these stories that we first got to know each other and become friends, and that your liking for my work really preceded your meeting with me. In spite of this, I know I am not wholly worthy of such praise as this, but perhaps a wonderful review like this will have one of the finest effects that any criticism could have—the effect of making me want to live up to it, and of making me exert every energy of my life in order to do so. I will call you up in a day or two, and hope to see you and Kitty [1] and all the family soon. Meanwhile, with love to all of you, and with all my heartfelt thanks,

[1] Mrs. Hoagland.

XII

THE BEGINNING OF THE WEB AND THE ROCK
AND YOU CAN'T GO HOME AGAIN

1936

Stark Young, author of The Three Fountains, Heaven Trees, River House,
So Red the Rose, *etc. had written Wolfe to clarify a conversation they had had
about William Faulkner, and had also congratulated him on* From Death to
Morning, *saying: "The dedication struck me almost down. I have never felt
like intruding about your brother Ben. But though people are always telling
me that time heals these things into oblivion or peace, I know better. Not
many of the living are so real as the dead that are beloved." The following
was Wolfe's reply.*

To STARK YOUNG

> 865 First Avenue
> New York City
> Saturday, March 7, 1936

Please excuse pencil and paper—
no pen or ink available.

Dear Stark:

Thanks for your letter. I don't think I misunderstood you at all in what
you said about Faulkner, and certainly no one who was present could
have failed to understand that everything you said came from a feeling
of true friendliness and admiration. And I agree utterly with your estimate in your letter—that what he writes is not like the South, but that
yet the South is *in* his books, and in the spirit that creates them.

And I think you're right in what you say about death—there's very
little in life that's as real—and I think I like to live as well as most people.
I've had a curious experience concerning this in recent years, and I

495

believe the same thing has happened to most people: I discovered a year or two ago that it was not the people one has known *least* who are hardest to remember, but the people one has known *most,* and loved the best. For example, I can remember faces seen on subway trains, a pretty girl seen for a moment on the street, a waiter in a little town in France, or the features of Wild Bill Hart, the old time movie stars, Edna Purviance, Fatty Arbuckle—thousands of faces like these. I can see them at once just the way they were, and I think the reason is that they had—for me, at least—just that one face. But a few years ago I discovered that when I tried to remember the face of someone who had died, whom I had known well, or a woman I had been in love with, it was almost impossible to remember how that person looked. There was not one person then, there were a *thousand,* and they changed and interfered with the instancy of light—and suddenly they would be there like a stroke of lightning— upon an intonation of the voice, a familiar movement of the hand, a moment's burst of laughter—but not *all* of them: just one face out of the thousand faces, one life out of their thousand lives. It is a hard thing for a novelist to solve. My own tendency, perhaps, is to try to fill books with a universe of life—hundreds of characters—making each of them as real and living as I can. And then I have the overwhelming desire to make just one person live the way he was—or anyway, the way I knew him: to restore, compare, and bring to life again all of his thousand faces and his thousand forms. And then I realize that even the pages of the largest book are far too short for such a universe as *that!*

Thanks for writing me: I hope to see you soon.

The following telegram to Perkins marks the beginning of The Vision of Spangler's Paul, *which finally became* The Web and the Rock *and* You Can't Go Home Again.

To MAXWELL E. PERKINS

[Telegram]

Boston, Mass.

March 17, 1936

Tell Calverton [1] out of town. Wrote book beginning. Goes wonderfully. Full of hope.

[1] V. F. Calverton, the editor of *The Modern Monthly.*

The following letter to V. F. Calverton, (familiarly called George) editor of the Modern Monthly, *was written as the result of one of the minor understandings which invariably arose to upset Wolfe and distract him from his work.*

To V. F. CALVERTON

865 First Avenue
New York, New York

April 3, 1936

Dear George:

I am sorry there has been a misunderstanding about my speaking at the *Modern Monthly* dinner. The first definite information I had about it came the other day when Nina [1] called me up and asked me to come to a cocktail party and then told me I was on the program to speak and that notices to that effect had been sent out to the press. If anything I said myself was responsible for this misunderstanding I regret it very much, but my own clear recollection is that when I had dinner with you and Nina a month or so ago, a *Modern Monthly* dinner was mentioned and you both told me you hoped I would be there. As I remember it, I told you that if I were in New York at the time and I had no other engagement that I had to meet I should be glad to attend. I don't remember how, or whether, the question of my speaking at the dinner came up, but if it did I am sure I expressed myself pretty vigorously as not wanting to speak at the dinner, or for that matter at any dinner, as I felt very strongly on the subject at the time because I had just been wangled into speaking at a dinner and it is my one and only such performance—I attended only on the belief and assurance that I would be present anonymously and at the most only get up and say hello to the people and then leave immediately. The off-shoot of that assurance was that I eventually found that it was being announced in large bulletins and postcards that I was going to talk to the gathering on "The Story of a Novel." [2] That experience, as I say, was my first of this kind in which I found myself involved through no fault of my own.

If I had known that there could be any possible misunderstanding on your part or on Nina's about the way I felt on the whole business of

[1] Nina Melville, Calverton's wife.

[2] *The Story of a Novel* had been published serially in the December 14, 21, and 28, 1935, issues of *The Saturday Review of Literature,* and was to be published in book form on April 21, 1936.

public speaking, or that you were going to print announcements and send them out with my name heading the list of several speakers, I should certainly have called you up and asked you not to do it. Believe me, I will cause you no embarrassment whatever, but there has been a misunderstanding here and I am compelled to tell you that I do not want to talk at the *Modern Monthly* dinner or at any other dinner. My reasons for feeling this way are many and positive but the chief of them is that I am a writer and not a public speaker and if I have anything at all to say to people I will have to say it through writing or not at all.

Perkins and I agreed upon this months ago when the question of lectures and lecture tours came up. In the last year I have repeatedly turned down offers to give lectures or to go on lecture tours which would have paid me thousands of dollars. I did this because I made the decision to stick to writing for the present at least and not to turn aside for anything else. I am telling you this simply because I wish to make wholly clear what I had hoped was clear before: I am not a public speaker. I have never in my life gone around making speeches at public gatherings and I do not intend to begin it now. I am sorry, therefore, that there has been a misunderstanding, and sincerely regretful if anything I said or didn't say was in any way responsible for the misunderstanding. But I do think that before announcements were printed and sent out I should have been informed, because I certainly had no knowledge that I was listed definitely to speak and that announcements had been sent out to the press until Nina telephoned me the other day.

I don't think Max Perkins understood this either. You said in your letter that he was glad that I had consented, but I asked him about it and he said that he had not understood that I was to speak.

If, as I told you before, I am here on Friday, April the 17th, and you want me to attend the dinner I shall be glad to come. If I have to go away, as I indicated I might have to, of course I can't attend, but the speaking is out in any event.

And now let me repeat, in conclusion, that I am genuinely sorry if I have in any way upset your plans or been the cause of any misunderstanding, but if I have done so it was because I did not myself clearly understand the nature of your plans or that you intended to put me on your printed program as one of the speakers.

Believe me I have, as you know, now as in the past, every good wish for the success of the *Modern Monthly* and I send you those good wishes now, together with all good wishes for the success of the dinner.

To V. F. CALVERTON

865 First Avenue
New York, N.Y.

April 9, 1936

Dear George:

I got your Special Delivery this morning, and am replying at once. I cannot wholly agree with you that the success of the *Modern Monthly* depends so much on my being there and speaking as you seem to think it does. But in view of what you say in your letter about the embarrassment you will be caused if I do not attend and how important you consider my attendance is to the welfare of *The Modern Monthly*, I agree to come.

I do want you to understand this, I never agreed to make a speech, I do not intend to make a speech, I have no speech at all to make, and I should heartily, earnestly, sincerely prefer to attend the dinner along with the other guests and say nothing at all. But if you really feel that you are so committed now, that it is up to me to say something to save you embarrassment, I agree to get up and say that I am glad to be there and meet the other members of the *Modern Monthly* public, or something to that effect. I am not trying to make any issue of this, or to act stubbornly and obstinately about a minor thing, but the truth of the matter is that I have been so hounded and wangled into one thing and another, ever since I came back here last October, that I have finally decided that if I am to have any peace of mind or try to find time to work in at all hereafter, I must now take a stand. As I say, I am genuinely sorry if anything I said or implied that last time I saw you and Nina, lead to this misunderstanding.

I won't go into the matter again and I will go through with this because you seem to feel so strongly that my not doing it will put you in a serious predicament. But while regretting deeply the whole misunderstanding, I feel that you did not have sufficient justification from anything I said to warrant your sending the announcements to the press and having programs printed. I am not going to harp on this any more. I hate to have to mention it all, but I am speaking about it now, simply because I want it to be understood from now on, that I am not going into the public speaking business and I have to earn my living through what I write and that I have got to be given time enough to do my own work. I wish to God that it were still possible for me not to have to speak at the dinner. If I do, I promise you that what I say will be extremely brief. I want you to understand that you can depend on my not being bad tempered about it and that the thing is settled. It may not be much of a talk and it probably will not be; but at any rate, I shall do it in good will and we will hope that the next time a thing of this sort comes up, we will both have a clearer understanding of it and so avoid this difficulty.

I will call you up before the dinner to get any other information you may care to give me about it. In the meantime, best wishes to you and Nina.

The following note was in answer to one from A. Y. C. Powers, who had written Wolfe from England to praise Of Time and the River *and* Look Homeward, Angel, *saying: "It seems to me that in your prose you are discovering something which I have always been looking for and hardly ever found except in poetry."*

To A. Y. C. POWERS

865 First Avenue
New York, N.Y.

April 9, 1936

Dear Mr. Powers:

. . . I cannot give your kind and interesting letter the thanks it deserves, but I want to thank you most sincerely for having written as you have, and for what you say about my work. I think the knowledge that a reader feels the way you say you do about something one has done, is the greatest reward a writer can have and it makes me want to exert every energy to fulfill and justify your good opinion. It is especially good to know that what one writes in one country, on one side of the ocean can waken recognition and appreciation in some one living on the other side of the ocean. I suppose it proves that no matter who you are or where you live, the fundamental material and design of human experience is everywhere the same.

I appreciate also your saying that I see life as a poet sees it: that I get the whole picture all together and that some times accounts for the super abundance of detail. I don't know whether you are right about this or not, but I hope you are right because it seems to me that what every man would like to be if he could be, is a poet. And I suppose the reason we write prose instead of poetry, is simply because the power to write poetry is not in us.

Your letter and what you say about my writing awoke many interesting and I believe, helpful speculations. Thank you again for having written as sincerely and warmly as you did.

To MABEL WOLFE WHEATON

865 First Avenue
New York, N.Y.

April 19, 1936

Dear Mabel:

I was glad to get your letter because I have been thinking about you and wondering what you were doing and even tried to get you on the telephone two or three weeks ago. I don't know what the trouble was, but the operator told me she could find no phone listed under your name, and I couldn't find your old number, which I remember was Metropolitan something. I didn't know what you were doing or whether you had temporarily or permanently gone out of the rooming-house business or not.[1] Fred and Mama had written me and said that they thought you might go back to Asheville or to Florida. I am glad to know where you are and if I could take a day or two off a little later on when the weather gets better, I will come down and see you. . . .

Several weeks ago I got a letter from one of our Westall relatives, who lives in Washington. His name is William G. Westall, he is one of the Yancey County members of the family [2] and is thirty-two years old. From what he told me, I figured out that we were second or third half cousins, if such a degree of relationship exists. His father was a half brother of Mama's father, and his grandfather was our great-grandfather. I figured that this made this young fellow and Mama first half cousins, which would mean, wouldn't it, that he is a second half cousin of ours? He wrote me an awfully interesting and intelligent letter, telling me about his own branch of the family, saying that he had read "Look Homeward, Angel" and "Of Time and the River," and he was sure I was sometimes talking about his Asheville relatives. He wanted to know if this was so and in what way we were related, and I wrote him back at considerable length and told him. I also told him that you and Ralph were living in Washington and that I wished he would go to see you. . . . He tells me he is married, and since he wrote me about what I have written in a much more friendly and understanding spirit than some of the members of the family have shown, I thought it would be a great idea to look him up if I come down. . . .

I was awfully sorry to hear about Mrs. ——. Your letter was the first news I had of her death. I always liked her and, as you say, as you get

[1] Mrs. Wheaton had been obliged to move out of her former rooming-house in Washington, the Gramercy, and was trying to get settled in another.

[2] William G. Westall is the son of John Westall who was a half-brother of Wolfe's grandfather, Thomas Casey Westall. This branch of the family lived, and still lives, in Burnsville, Yancey County, North Carolina.

a little older you begin to overlook some of a person's faults and remember more of their good and generous qualities, and I think she had lots of them. I don't know whether I ever told you that she had written me several times, two or three anyway, in the last few years and seemed to be disturbed and upset about "Look Homeward, Angel." I wrote and answered her at considerable length and tried to make it as emphatic as I could that I had the greatest liking and affection for her, as we all did, and I was sincerely sorry and regretful if anything I had written had caused her, in no matter how mistaken a way, any embarrassment or worry. She wrote me again not so long ago, within the last year or so anyway, and to this letter it seemed to me I could make no reply. It dealt with rumors, hearsay, and things she said she had heard from people I didn't know and had never heard of. And it seemed to me, after thinking it over, that the wisest course was not to become involved in a situation I knew nothing about. I know we shall always remember her, and with affection. I suppose hers was a pretty sad and difficult kind of life and I can easily see that with her great beauty of person and of character, she might have found happiness and success if circumstances had been different. . . .

This is all for the present that I have time to write. I have had almost every kind of worry, threat and annoyance this winter from suits and lawyers to . . . even blackmail letters, and I let it bother me a good deal, but I've about gotten used to the fact now that everyone who gets some public notice is likely to be the victim of this sort of thing. And I have also about come to the conclusion that if worst comes to worst, I would rather have the crooks and shysters get what little means or property I have than to let them so destroy what peace of mind or power of concentration I may have that I will be unable to work. Anyway, I am back at work—that's the main thing—and getting a good deal done, and I can only hope that no matter what happens, I will be able to go right on now day after day until I finish another big piece of work. You are dead right about work: it makes all the difference between having a happy life and an unhappy one, between taking a drink with a friend and enjoying it, or between seizing a gallon jug and trying to drown the essential horror of so much in life around you in oblivion. As long as I can work, I am all right. If I ever lose the power or capacity for work, I don't know what I would do. But I don't intend to lose it, if I can ever help it.

Write me when you feel like it, and . . . if I can get away in the next few weeks, I may come down for a day or two. Meanwhile, with love to you and Ralph and all,

P.S. I have a little book coming out to-morrow called "The Story of a Novel" and I will send you a copy. It is just a very short account of the experiences I had getting started as a writer and what happened, the mistakes I made, etc. But people seem to think it is quite interesting and, of its kind, unique. I don't think it will have much sale or get out to a very wide public, because it is a special kind of thing and likely to be of interest mainly to people who have some special interest in my own work, or who are themselves interested in writing. But it is very simply written and you can read it in an hour or so, and I thought you might want to see it, so I am sending it on to you.

The following letter to Perkins was written by Wolfe during his first serious quarrel with Scribners.

To MAXWELL E. PERKINS

865 First Avenue
New York

April 21, 1936

Dear Max:

I want to tell you that I am sorry I got angry last night and spoke as I did. The language that I used was unjustifiable and I want to tell you that I know it was, and ask you to forget it.

About the matter I was talking to you about [1] however, I feel just as strongly to-day as I did last night. I don't want to re-hash the whole thing again—we have talked and argued about it too much already—but I do want to tell you honestly and sincerely that I am not arguing about the two or three hundred dollars which would be involved if I were given my old royalty of 15%, instead of the reduced one of 10%. I admit that there can be no doubt that I agreed to this reduction of my royalty before the publication of the book and at the time when estimates of cost of publication were being prepared, I told you that I hoped the book could be published at a very moderate price of 75¢ or a dollar, not only because I thought it might be better for the success of the book itself, but also because I am not willing to make use of any past success I may have had, or take advantage of any present reputation I may have in the eyes of the public to publish so short and small a book at a high price. Now I don't want you to think that I am trying to dictate to my publishers the price for which I think my book ought to be printed. You told me an author had no right to dictate such prices and that in fact, the price the publisher put on his books was none of his business, and al-

[1] The retail price and royalty rate on *The Story of a Novel.*

though I think the subject is open to debate, I am, on the whole, inclined to agree with you and was really not trying to dictate any prices, except what I told you when the publication of the book was discussed that I hoped personally, it would be brought out at a low price of 75¢ or a dollar.

You told me that it would be impossible to bring it out for as low a price as 75¢, but we all had hoped, I believe, that it might be brought out for a dollar. Later, when estimates on the cost of publication came in, it was agreed that the price would have to be $1.25 and either then at that time or previously, I had agreed to a reduction of my customary royalty from 15% to 10% and I believe the 10% was to cover the first three thousand copies and that if the book sold more than that, I would get an increased royalty. The reason that I agreed to this reduction was because I knew the publisher was not likely to profit very much by the publication of so small a book and because I agreed with you the publication of the book was, nevertheless, probably a good thing, and finally because you told me that even at the $1.25 price, the margin was very small and you thought I ought to accept the royalty of 10%, which I agreed to do.

Now the book has been published and the other day when I got my own advance copy, I saw that the price had been still further raised from $1.25 to $1.50. This was the first knowledge that I had that the price had been raised. I agree with you that I probably have no right to argue with you about the price of a book or to have the say as to [the] price it ought to sell for. I also agree that if the book is successful and sells, I stand to profit in my share of the royalties at the increased price as well as does the publisher; but I don't think that either of these facts is the core of the matter, and they are certainly not what I am arguing about.

What I am arguing about is this: that I agreed to accept a reduced royalty upon the basis of a dollar or dollar and a quarter book, and the reason that I agreed to accept the reduction was because it was presented to me that the cost of making the book was such that it would be difficult for the publisher to give a higher royalty and have him come out clear. Then after agreeing to this reduced royalty, upon my understanding that the book would be published at a dollar and a quarter, and having signed a contract accepting the reduced royalty, I find that the price of the book, without my knowledge, has been raised to $1.50, and is being published at that price. When I discussed that fact about a week ago, when I got my own advance copy, I told you that in view of the increase in price, I thought you ought to restore my former royalty of 15%. I still think that you ought to do so and have told you so repeatedly, and you feel you ought not to do so, and have refused to do so.

You have been my friend for seven years now and one of the best friends that I ever had, I don't think anyone in the world is more conscious than I am of what you have done for me, of how you stuck to me for years when I was trying to get another book completed and when so much time elapsed that people had begun to say I might never be able to write again. I think you stuck to me not only with material aid and support that Scribners gave me during a large part of the time when I had no funds of my own, but you stuck to me also with your own friendship and belief and spiritual support, and you not only gave me these priceless things, but you also gave me unstintedly the benefits of your enormous skill and talent as an editor and a critic. I do not think a debt such as I owe you can ever sufficiently be repaid, but I have tried to do what I could through work, which I know you do value, and through public acknowledgment which I know you do not want and on which you don't put the same value as you do upon the more important fact of work. So having said all this, and feeling this way toward you, and about what you and Scribners have done, I want to repeat again that I do not think it is right or proper for you to withhold from me my full and customary royalty of 15%, the circumstances being what they are.

I do not question your legal and contractual right to do this. I agreed to the reduction at the time and for the reason I have mentioned. I signed the contract and I am, of course compelled to abide by it. But I think it is up to you now, in view of the facts I have mentioned, and since the reason of the reduction of the royalty, namely, the low price of the book, is no longer true—I think it is up to you and Scribners of your own accord to give me my 15%. It will not amount to much, even if you sell the entire three thousand copies, which the 10% royalty covers. I don't think it will amount to more than two or three hundred dollars and I am not arguing with you about that. But just because you have been generous and devoted friends, and because my feeling toward you has been one of devotion and loyalty, I do not want to see you do this thing now which may be legally and technically all right, but is to my mind a sharp business practice. I know that you yourself, personally, do not stand to profit one penny whether I get 10% or 15%. I know that you yourself, probably did not suggest the reduction in royalty or fix the price of the book, but I also know the way I expect and want you to act now as my friend. It seems to me that it is imperative that you do this just exactly for the reason that I consider you all my friends and have always lived and felt and thought about you in that way, and not as people with whom I had business dealings and who were going to use whatever business advantage they considered legitimate in their dealings with me.

You know very well that I am not a business man and have no capacity for business and that in matters of this sort, I am not able to cope with people who are skilled at it; but where it concerned you and Scribners, I have never thought for one moment, that I would have to cope with it. The thing I really feel and believe is that at the bottom of your heart, . . . you agree with me and my position in this matter and know that I am right as I know you agreed with me in the matter of almost $1,200, which I was charged for corrections in the proof of *Of Time and the River.* I'll admit that there, too, I am legally responsible and signed the contract which had a clause in it stipulating the cost to the author if the changes and corrections in the proof exceed a certain amount. But the truth of the matter is, as you know and as you said at the time when the bill was first shown to me, that a great many of these corrections came as the result of the work we were both doing on the manuscript, and as a result of the editorial help and advice and the suggestions you made which were so generous and so invaluable. For this very reason perhaps, I ought not to harp upon the subject or complain about having to pay almost $1,200 for corrections that helped the book, but you said at the time the bill was shown to me that in view of the circumstances and the way the corrections were made and done, you didn't think I ought to have to pay as much money as that, and I understood you even to say that if I felt too strongly that I ought not to pay and that the bill was unfair, I would not have to pay it. Well, I don't feel that strongly about it—I think I made a lot of corrections on the proof on my own hook and I think that if these corrections were excessive, I ought to pay for them like anyone else. But I do feel that the bill of almost $1,200 is excessive and that I am being made to pay too much for corrections which I'll admit helped me and the book, but which were partly done with your collaboration. . . .

I want to ask you this; if your refusal in this matter is final and you insist on holding me to the terms of the contract I signed for *The Story of a Novel,* don't you think that I, or anyone else on earth for that matter, would be justified henceforth and hereafter, [in] considering my relations with you and Scribners were primarily of a business and commercial nature, and if you make use of a business advantage in this way, don't you think I would be justified in making use of a business advantage too if one came my way? Or do you think it works only one way? I don't think it does and I don't think any other fair-minded person in the world would think so either. As you know, I never gave a moment's serious consideration to any offers of persuasions that were made to me by other people and I think that you know very well that such offers were made. And that in one case at least, a very large sum of money was mentioned at a time when I, myself, had nothing.[2] You not only knew of the occasion, but I telephoned you of it just as soon as the person telephoned and asked if he could talk to me. I informed you of the telephone call at once and told you I didn't know what it meant and you told me what it did mean, and furthermore told me I had a right to meet the man and listen to what he had to say and even consider what he had to offer. Well, I suppose that's business practice and everyone agrees that it is fully justified and that a man has a right not only to listen, but to take the best and most profitable offer. That's business practice, maybe, but it has not been my practice. I did meet the man, I did listen to what he had to say and I paid no attention at all to his offer. What do you think about this any way? If people are going to get hard-boiled and business-like, should it all be on one side, or doesn't the other fellow have a right to get hard-boiled and business-like too?

I understand perfectly well that even publishers are not in business for their health, even though you have said that none of them make any great amount of money out of it. And I don't expect my relations with my publisher to be a perpetual love feast, into which the vile question of money never enters, but I do say that you cannot command the loyalty and devotion of a man on the one hand and then take a business advantage on the other. I am sorry to have to say all this. I want to repeat how much I regret my language of last evening, but I also want to say that about this matter of the royalties, I feel as strongly and deeply now as I did then. I am writing this letter to you as a final appeal. You may think I am kicking up a hell of a row over nothing but I do think it is something, a great deal, not in a money way but in the matter of fair dealing, and I am writing to tell you so.

Perkins' reply to the above was written on April 22, 1936, and said in part: "I am giving directions to reckon your royalties on The Story of a Novel at 15% from the start. . . . I would rather simply agree to do this and say nothing further, but I should not have the right to do it without telling you that the terms, as proposed, on the $1.50 price are just and that if the matter were to be looked upon merely as business we should not be justified as

[2] Between 1930 and 1934, Wolfe was informally approached by several publishers, one of whom, he told Miss Nowell and others, offered him an advance of ten thousand dollars against royalties on his next novel. In 1937, after he had left Scribners, when he was first approached by Houghton Mifflin and Harper's, he again referred to this offer as a gauge of what he could expect as an advance against his new book.

business men in making this concession. You are under a misapprehension if you think that when we suggested a reduction of royalty . . . we were basing the suggestion on the question of price. . . . We could not, at that time, know what the price would have to be. We found that the price had to be higher because of the question of basic costs which come into every phase of the handling, advertising, promoting, and making of a book. . . . The terms we proposed were therefore, in my opinion, just.

"You return to the question of the excess corrections. . . . I once said to you in Charles Scribner's presence that you had a good technical argument for not paying these corrections because you did not make them . . . since you did not read your proof, but, if you had done so, is there any doubt but what these corrections would have been much larger? . . . They were rightly author's corrections, and why should the author not pay for them? I think we began wrong by making no charge in the case of excess corrections on the "Angel," which amounted to seven hundred dollars. . . .

"As to the other matter you speak of . . . I certainly would not wish you to make what you thought was a sacrifice on my account, and I would know that whatever you did would be sincerely believed to be right by you, as I know that you sincerely believe the contentions you make in this letter to me to be right. I have never doubted your sincerity, and never will. I wish you could have felt that way toward us."

For the full text of this letter, see Editor to Author, The Letters of Maxwell E. Perkins, page 110. (*Scribners, 1950.*)

To MAXWELL E. PERKINS

865 First Avenue
New York, N.Y.

April 23, 1936

Dear Max:

I got your letter this morning and I just want to write you back now to tell you that everything is settled so far as I am concerned, so let's forget about it. Now that you have told me that you would restore my old royalty of 15%, I want to tell you that I don't want it and want to stick to the contract I signed. That goes for all my other obligations as well. I really made up my mind to this yesterday, and that was the reason I called you up last night and went around to see you.

I wanted to tell you and I am afraid I didn't succeed [in] telling you very well that all the damn contracts in the world don't mean as much to me as your friendship means, and it suddenly occurred to me yesterday that life is too short to quarrel this way with a friend over something that matters so little. But I do want to tell you again just how genuinely and deeply sorry I am for boiling over the way I did the other night. We have had fireworks of this sort before and I am afraid they may occur again, but every time they do, I say something to a friend that is unjust and wrong, and sweat blood about it later. So just help me along with this by forgetting all about it, and let's look forward to the future.

I suppose it is a good thing for me to have had this experience in the last year but there is something a little grotesque and tragic in the fact that the success I wanted and looked forward to having as a child should have brought me so much trouble, worry, bewilderment and disillusion, but I am going to try to add the whole experience to the sum of things I have found out about all through my life, and I hope that I will be able to make use of it, instead of letting it make use of me. I see now what a terribly dangerous thing a little success may be because it seems to me the effort of an artist must always aim at even greater concentration and intensity and effort of the will where his work is concerned, and anything that tends to take him away from that, to distract him, to weaken his effort, is a bad thing.

I am now started on another book. I need your friendship and support more than I ever did, so please forget the worst mistakes I have made in the past and let's see if I can't do somewhat better in the future.

A bitterly critical article on Wolfe, "Genius Is Not Enough" by Bernard De Voto, had appeared in the April 25, 1936, issue of The Saturday Review of Literature, *purportedly as a review of* The Story of a Novel. *The following reaction to it was written by Wolfe to Julian Meade, who had protested against it both to Wolfe and to Henry Seidel Canby, editor of* The Saturday Review of Literature.

To JULIAN MEADE

865 First Avenue
New York, N.Y.

May 4, 1936

Dear Meade:

Thanks for your letter. It was very generous of you to feel the way you did about the *Saturday Review* piece and to register such a vigorous protest. I was over at the Canbys' for dinner last night and of course, made no reference to the article but finally Mr. Canby himself brought it up. I think your letter had made quite an impression. He didn't mention your name but said he had got a pretty vigorous letter a few days ago denouncing the article and asking why a man's book should be reviewed by his enemies and so on. So I figured it was your letter he was talking about. I told him that personally I had no hard feelings and that although I read every scrap that was written about me in the way of a review or criticism, provided I saw it, and still took the whole thing very much to heart, it didn't bother me quite as much as it once did. I added that I had my living to earn, and that the only way I have of earning it is through what I write, and that if a reviewer says I am no good, it's just too bad for me and perhaps occasionally for him, but that nevertheless, I was going to keep right on writing. This was all I said, and then got off the subject.

I think really my only objection to the *Saturday Review* piece was that it didn't review the book. It seems to me that it was hardly a review at all, but rather a kind of general denunciation of all my deficiencies as a writer, some of which, of course, I am prepared to admit and have done so already. I don't think a writer has any right to dictate to the editors of a literary review who shall review his book or what form the review should take, but I do think he has a right to expect a *review* of his book, whether hostile or favorable, rather than a mass assault on every other book he has ever done. And as I understand the remarks of our *Saturday Review* friend, he said at the beginning that the book he was reviewing was a good book. I think he called it one of the most appealing books of our generation—ahem, ahem, here he cleared his throat, low growls began to rumble from his diaphragm, smoke began to issue from his nostrils and he surged forward to the attack—an attack which by the way, an author has no chance of defending himself against unless he resorts to what seems to me the very unwise and ineffectual practice of writing a letter in reply, which of course gives the other fellow a chance to write a letter in reply to this, and so on, I suppose, ad infinitum, save that the man who has been attacked in this way and who answers in this way, is always in the undefended position, controls none of the means of publication and must yield to the attacker the privilege of delivering the final volley. Is it worth it?

And in this case at least, it seems to me that it doesn't matter enough. I do think this, and I suppose this is the most sensible way of looking at these matters in the end: I think you will find, if you have not found out already, that one of the pleasantest occupations of a great many people in this world is to shoot down a whole regiment of wooden soldiers, and then return triumphant from the wars, saying, "we have met the enemy and they are ours." This kind of warrior does exist. It is very comforting of course, to create a straw figure of your enemy and then shoot it full of holes, but it is not a very substantial victory and in the long run means nothing. . . .

As you say, there are far too many people who will seize the opportunity of making a review of a book about the introduction of plumbing into Venezuela the basis for vituperations of all the works and words and creations of any novelist, playwright, poet or historian whom they do not like. But I have been pretty well through the mill now; I guess I'll get a lot more of it before I'm done, but at any rate it doesn't come exactly as a surprise. I have found out that a man who writes anything, no matter what it is, or where he gets it published, whether in *Scribner's Magazine* or in book form or in the Oregon Fur Traders' Quarterly, lays himself open to almost any form of attack or personal abuse known. It is not only the erstwhile friends and neighbors of his native town, benevolent old ladies and Christian deacons who will threaten him with tar and feathering, lynch law or shooting at sight if he ever comes back home, but he must be prepared also to receive letters carrying tirades of abuse from young one-eyed boys from Bethlehem, Pa., expectant mothers in Wichita, Kan., the parents of pure young girls from Tulsa, Okla., who have just come back home from Miss Burkewell's finishing school, bringing with them a copy of his accursed book, to every other form of execration and abuse imaginable. Moreover, as you yourself should know by now, if the aspiring young author has any illusions concerning the temperate, reasonable and coolly impartial tone in which the matter of book-reviewing and literary criticism is carried on, it won't take him long to have this pleasant daydream kicked out of him. Under the guise of high-toned criticism and impartial literary judgment, he must be prepared to hear himself described as a manic-depressive, a pathological item of the specialist in criminal psychology, a half-wit, or the grandson of Wordsworth's idiot boy, the bird that fouls its nest, a defiler of the temple of religion, a political reactionary, or a dangerous red, or a traitor to his country.

I have lived through it all, I have known it all, I have had it all happen to me, and although, as you may infer from this letter, I am not yet exactly resigned to it, in a state of philosophic benevolence, I am at least a little prepared for it and not google-eyed with astonishment when it happens. Nevertheless, I thank you for your letter. But I suppose things like these will always happen; they seem to be baser elements of the human animal.

Only the other day in fact, I was reading a review that appeared in one of the higher toned English journals a hundred years or more ago, shortly after the publication of some of William Wordsworth's best poetry. The review begins somewhat as follows: "It is now apparent that young Mr. Wordsworth's malady is incurable. We had hoped for a while that the disease might be checked and controlled before it spread to dangerous proportions, but since it is evident that this is now impossible, we can only do what we can to prevent the malady from spreading farther, etc. etc. etc."

Don't these words have a familiar ring to you? Haven't you read them in one form or another a thousand times or more? Aren't they still being written by thousands of squirts who palm off their own hatred and venom under the guise of critical inquiry? So why worry about it too much? All we can hope for is to make things a little better. Personally, I have no panacea to use against dishonesty, injustice or hatred, masking behind a specious guise of critical utterance. These things have always been in nature and I suppose they always will be, but I do think that letters and efforts such as yours tend at all times to make things a little better, to direct things a little more in the direction of justice; and in addition, it is, of course, one of the most warming and heartening things that can happen to a man to know that anyone feels deeply enough about his work to feel indignant when he thinks that work has been unfairly dealt with. So thanks again for writing me and also for writing *them*.

Let me hear from you sometime when you are not too busy and of course, come to see me if you come to New York. I've got started on another book and have been blazing out manuscript at the rate of three thousand words a day for several weeks now. I don't know yet what will come of it, but it looks as if I may have dug in and got ahold and that I shall probably be here through the summer. Meanwhile, until I see you, with warm thanks again and all good wishes.

The following letter to Henry Seidel Canby was written in reply to a note from him which said: "If I had been on the Pulitzer Prize Committee there would have been only one question in my mind:—whether to vote for Ellen Glasgow's long established and (by then) unrecognized talent; or for your 'Of Time and the River' as the one real exhibition of new and original power of the year."

To HENRY SEIDEL CANBY

865 First Avenue
New York, N.Y.

May 7, 1936

Dear Henry:

Thanks for your letter. It is very kind and generous of you to feel the way you do and I appreciate it, but honestly, I didn't feel badly about not getting the Pulitzer award. It really didn't occur to me very seriously that I might get it and I have only the best and most cheerful good wishes in the world towards all the winners save that, like you, I should also like to see Miss Glasgow's long and impressive career fittingly recognized.

As for myself, I have been pretty fortunate during the past year. I don't need a prize and I can even see how getting one might be a very bad thing for me at the present time. The main thing is I am back at work. I did over five thousand words on Monday and I hope to get in another big day to-day. But thanks again for your kind words. I deeply value them, and send my regards to you and Marion.[1] I hope to see you again soon.

Peter Monro Jack had favorably reviewed three of Wolfe's books in the New York Times: Of Time and the River *in the March 10, 1935 issue;* From Death to Morning *in the November 24, 1935, issue; and* The Story of a Novel *in the May 3, 1936, issue. As a result of this last review he had received a letter from an unknown woman which listed, in implied protest, various episodes dealing with sex in* Look Homeward, Angel. *He therefore had forwarded it to Wolfe.*

To PETER MONRO JACK

865 First Avenue
New York, N.Y.
May 18, 1936

Dear Jack:

I came back to New York just last night after a short holiday and found your letter with the enclosed clippings from our lady friend. It is amazing, isn't it? If it were the first time this kind of thing had happened, I wouldn't believe it, but it is simply astonishing the number of people there are running around loose in this broad land who apparently spend a large part of their time in concocting this kind of thing.

There was one man in Brooklyn a few years ago, perhaps he has died a peaceful and merciful death since then, but I doubt it; anyway, I was enjoying life in Paris one fine day in May, five or six years ago after the publication of "Look Homeward Angel," when a great fat letter arrived in an envelope about eight inches long and a half inch thick. I opened it with considerable hope, thinking that some benevolent old

[1] Mrs. Canby.

gentleman or wealthy old maid had mentioned me handsomely in their will. Instead, I found twenty-eight pages of close type, which began as follows: "Dear sir: I have just finished a hasty reading of your interesting novel, 'Look Homeward, Angel.' Permit me however, to point out to you a few errors in grammar, spelling, punctuation, construction, usage, idiom, etc., which I jotted down as I was skimming through the book." There followed a staggering and appalling list of my alleged grammatical errors. I felt that I could never hold up my head again and look the world in the face, that I was ruined, done for, ditched. And in somewhat this frame of mind, I wrote the editor at Scribners who had helped me with the proof reading and asked him how in God's name, we had ever let proof go through our hands which was as full of shocking errors as apparently this one was. He wrote back and told me not to take it quite so seriously. The man, he said, who wrote the letter was noted for this kind of thing: in fact, very few authors of recent years had escaped his devilish scrutiny—even old Galsworthy was one of his victims.

This lady's interest however, seems to be somewhat more moral than grammatical. I should think that the inside of a person's mind who remembers entirely out of their context and often falsely and inadequately sentences such as those which she has quoted, would not be a very pretty thing to look at. About the other items, which she sent you, they were apparently concerning her own literary efforts, and I don't know what to say. I wish I had kept a collection of these things. All of them were astonishing, and the sum total of them perhaps indicate something appalling, I am not quite sure what, except that I doubt that any other country in the world can produce quite so many of this type of crack-pot as we can. . . .

Jack, I have tried to think of a way of thanking you without thanking you, but there seems to be none. I want to tell you how deeply I appreciated your wonderful review of my little book [1] in *The New York Times*. It set me up tremendously. I have had a great many letters from people who have read it and who all felt good about it. And all I can tell you is that I shall try to live deserving of some of the things you said. Anyway, I am back at work again.

"Of Time and the River," by the way, seems to have gone well in Germany. I found a great batch of press cuttings when I got back here last night and a letter from the publisher saying there had been a great deal of excitement about the book and that although it costs more than $5.00, in German editions, and was just out in April, they had already sold more than twelve hundred copies and that there were indications

[1] *The Story of a Novel.*

that the sale would pick up. The amount of space they gave it in their reviews was really surprising. There were two and three page articles about it and although my German limps heavily, I have read enough to judge that the reviews are extremely favorable. The publisher earnestly assures me that by some kind of international legerdemain which I can't quite follow, I will be able to get my money, and I hope he is right about it. I don't like to be too coarsely commercial about these things, but it is rather tough to have to sweat away for years at a book and then to get nothing from it. I am, of course very glad if my book has had a good reception in Germany, but there is so much hatred against the country here in New York at present that I doubt if it would do me any good if the news got out.

This is all for the present, and much too long a letter to inflict you with. I will call you up in a few days and then if you and Jane [2] have a free evening, perhaps we can all get together as we did before. Meanwhile, with all good wishes,

The following letter was written to the wife of A. S. Frere (formerly A. S. Frere-Reeves), who had sent Wolfe some photographs which she had taken of him during a visit to New York earlier that spring.

To PATRICIA FRERE

865 First Avenue
New York, N.Y.

May 19, 1936

Dear Pat:

I was delighted to get the photographs, and even though I shouldn't say so, they are awfully good, aren't they? I know now that the way to get a good photograph in America is to have friends from England come and make them.

What you say about your place at Aldington makes me very homesick. I will never forget the day I came there with Frere from the channel boat, just after two or three wretched weeks in Paris. I felt better right away and kept on feeling better from that time on.

Last year this time I was in Germany and this year I have just come back from Pennsylvania, where my father was born. It is perfectly glorious country. I wish you and Frere could come here sometime in the

[2] Mrs. Jack.

Spring or in the Autumn: there is so much I would like to show you, even within a few hours of New York. I suppose when you think of Pennsylvania, you think of places like Philadelphia or Pittsburgh, but it is really one of the most beautiful states in the Union. It has lovely mountains and a lovely rolling, undulating landscape, and in the country of the Pennsylvania Dutch, great red barns that dominate the landscape exactly as they should, like powerful and comfortable bulls. It has the most lavish and fertile farms I have ever seen. A lot of the people still believe in witches and witchcraft, and the barns have signs and symbols painted on them to scare off the devils. Perhaps you can come sometime in May or October. The young Spring wheat was just coming up. It is the greenest thing on earth, and then there were enormous sweeps of ploughed bronze earth and lovely woods just beginning to come out good. I went almost a thousand miles in five days, travelling back roads most of the way. The whole thing was simply magnificent and the variety of it is astonishing: hills, mountains, a perfect river called the Delaware that cuts through the most magnificent gap, and all the farm lands, the tiny little Pennsylvania Dutch villages.

I wish you and Frere could come here at some time of the year when you could see some of these things. Most American people, of course, never do. They get in their cars on Sundays and go out from New York on great crowded concrete highways and roar along with a million others, past filling stations and hot dog stands. But it is a nice country, if I do say so myself. And there are some wonderful things to be seen here, and some day I should like to show them to you and Frere.

I am back at work again—whenever I begin to moan and groan about working, I think of your father [1] and shut up and try to get started again—and this time I hope to do something good.

Please come back and see us again when you can. Meanwhile, with thanks again for the pictures and love to you and Frere,

On May 11, 1936, Margaret Roberts had written Wolfe for the first time since their estrangement because of Look Homeward, Angel, *saying: "I have written because I suppose that being actually in New York, the scene of your struggles and triumphs, my mind has gone back, first to the boy I loved, and next, to the eagerness with which I read your letters detailing the progress of your book—back to joy in seeing you grow; back, too, to the tide of misery caused to us by what you did to us—as you say in* Of Time and the River, *'it's all there.' I have not changed in thinking that the wounding was needless . . . I am not so dumb as not to believe that an artist has a right to get his*

[1] Edgar Wallace.

material where he pleases and twist it as he pleases, but I maintain that he has no right to twist or invent, making a pen-picture, and then write under it the name of a living person [1]. *. . . "*

The following was Wolfe's reply. Perhaps he was afraid of becoming involved in an argument about Look Homeward, Angel, *or perhaps he was simply too busy working: in any case, he did not see the Robertses until May, 1937, when he returned to Asheville.*

To MARGARET ROBERTS

865 First Avenue
New York, N.Y.

May 20, 1936

Dear Mrs. Roberts:

I had hoped to answer your letter sooner, but I was just on the point of going away for a few days' vacation when I received it and I decided to wait until I came back. I have been working hard and got pretty tired. I find that you reach a point in writing when you cannot go on farther: no matter how much the heart and soul may want to, the body and brain will not respond. So I went down to Pennsylvania for a few days. . . . I wonder if you know the state? It is one of the most beautiful places I have ever seen. It has almost every variety of landscape and the finest farms in the world. I went with a friend, we avoided main highways as much as we could and drove along back country roads. We drove a thousand miles in four days and saw some astonishing and beautiful things in the country of the Pennsylvania Dutch. . . . Everything in that part of the country has an air of thrift and of tidiness, of solid and prosperous substance. In the city here, you see such shocking contrasts of wealth and poverty, and often you hear such sad and tragic stories of human suffering and injustice and oppression. Going out to a place like the country I have just come from restores your faith, not only in nature but in man.

We got as far as York Springs, the little village a few miles from Gettysburg near which my father was born. I went out to the little country graveyard where his father and mother and a good many of his people are buried, and talked to a lot of people who remembered them all, and visited some relatives of mine who live in York Springs.[1]

Isn't the beauty of this country simply astonishing? I had never seen

[1] Copyright, 1956, by The Estate of Margaret Roberts.

[1] His first cousin Edgar E. Wolf, the son of Gilbert John Wolf, and his mother and his wife. The Pennsylvania branch of the family has always spelled their name without the final e.

the West until last summer, and I remembered that you and Mr. Roberts lived there for some time. I loved the West; I felt instantly at home the minute I got off the train in Colorado. The people were wonderful to me: there is something so spacious and free and generous in this hospitality. I had just come from Denmark. You must admit that from Denmark to New Mexico at one jump is a pretty large order. It was a wonderfully valuable and informing experience that seemed to crystallize things I have been feeling and thinking about America and Europe for years now. I wish I could see you and tell you about it.

I am back at work now. It is going to be another very long, hard pull. I am already beginning to be haunted by nightmares at night. I am probably in for several thousand hours of hell and anguish, of almost losing hope utterly, and swearing I'll never write another word and so on, but it seems to have to be done in this way and I have never found any way of avoiding it. I am both fascinated and terrified by this new book.[2] It is a thing which has been going in my mind for years and it is not one of the books that have been announced. It is a much more objective book than any I have yet written. Sometimes I am appalled by my own undertaking, and doubt that I can do it.

The best friend I have in the world, who is also the best editor this country has produced, and who has never been wrong in his judgment yet, told me at once, when I described the book to him, . . . by all means to do it at once with all my might. I think it is a good thing for several reasons. In the first place, if I succeed, it will meet the objections which some of the critics have posed about my being an autobiographical writer. In the second place, I think that one of the things that is likely to happen to the artist when he gets a little older, is that he may tend to become cautious and conservative and to stick to the thing which he has learned or is learning to do. There is a good deal to be said for this, but I do think it is a pity if a man is to lose the enthusiastic eagerness, the desire to experiment and find out new ways, the fearlessness of conception and effort which he has in his twenties. I don't want to lose it and my friend tells me I never will, and that there is no question about my being able to do this thing if I see it through. I wish you knew him, his name is Maxwell Perkins. He is not only a wonderful friend, he is also a great man and a great person with the finest qualities of character, spirit, and intelligence I have ever known. He has often asked me about you and I know he would like to meet you.

This last year has been a very extraordinary one. I have seen some wonderful things and met a great many people. I took too much time

[2] *The Vision of Spangler's Paul* which finally became *The Web and the Rock* and *You Can't Go Home Again.*

away from work, but I was desperately tired and had in fact been writing steadily for almost five years, and I have found that a man's energy and the way he uses his talent is like a reservoir: when it gets depleted, you have got to let it fill up again. Well, I think it is full again, full to overflowing. I hope and believe that I may have learned something from all the mistakes and errors of the past and that I will be able to work hereafter without quite so much useless waste and confusion and agony of spirit. I don't think by any means that I can wholly avoid these things yet, but I do think you learn something from every piece of work you do and that every piece of work you do adds something to your stature, increases the power and maturity of your experience, and helps you to use your talent with greater certainty. . . .

I am sorry you didn't see Mabel when you came through Washington, I know she will be disappointed when I tell her you couldn't find her. Yes, I think they did have their telephone taken out, but they are still living there. They have had a terribly hard time and she has suffered a great deal, but somehow, I always believe that she has it in her to pull herself together in a time of crisis or necessity and meet the situation no matter how hard or bitter. Mr. Wheaton, as you know, is a fine man in many ways. He has devotion and loyalty and great staunchness of character, but I think—and this of course is confidential—that he is a most tragic individual case of the effects of this tragic depression. I am sometimes accused by the Communist writers here in New York, of lacking what they call "social consciousness" and of not showing in my writing sufficient resentment towards the present system. Well, there are several answers to that. When I am told that I do not appreciate or understand the lot of the worker, I remember and am proud to remember that I am the son of a stonecutter, that I come from people in Pennsylvania and in the hills of Western North Carolina who have had to work hard and long for two hundred years or more by the sweat of their brow, the strength of their hands, to earn their daily bread. I am not talking of the more prosperous members of the family whom you may have known in Asheville, yet even they, my mother's brothers and my mother herself, knew poverty and want in their childhood in the years after the Civil War, and my father worked all of his life. So I think you will agree with me there is no particular reason for me to be very much impressed by the assertions of young gentlemen calling themselves Communists, whose fathers provide them with a comfortable allowance which enables them to indulge their political fancies without knowing a great deal about some of the things or people of whom they write.

What I am really telling you, and I think you agree with me in your own feeling, is that by instinct, by inheritance, by every natural sympathy and affection of my life, my whole spirit and feeling is irresistibly on the side of the working class, against the cruelty, the injustice, the corrupt and infamous privilege of great wealth, against the shocking excess and wrong of the present system, the evidences of which are horribly apparent I think, to anybody who lives here in New York and keeps his eyes open. I think that the whole thing has got to be changed, and I'll do everything within the province of my energy or talent to change it for the better, if I can, but I am not a Communist, and I believe that the artist who makes his art the vehicle for political dogma and intolerant propaganda is a lost man. I think almost every great poet and every great writer who ever wrote and whose works we all love and treasure has been on the side of the oppressed, the suffering, the confused and lost and stricken of the earth. Do you know of a single exception to this? But really isn't this just another way of saying that every great man or any good man is on the side of life, and although I am myself the son of a working man, I go so far as to say that an artist's interest, first and always, has got to be in life itself, and not in a special kind of life. His devotion, his compassion, his talent has got to be used for man and for the enrichment of man's estate and not for just one class or sect of man. Finally, I think that insofar as any artist would turn against a man because that man is rich or would have no understanding or tolerance of the lot of a man who belongs to a certain class, the artist who would feel this way is by just this much a smaller man than he should be.

To get back to Wheaton. I think he has been crushed by the catastrophe of recent years. Furthermore, although I never had much feeling one way or another about great corporations until this thing happened, I think the way he was treated by the great corporation that employed him after he had given his life, his strength, his youth and all his best energies since his fourteenth year, was simply damnable and I for one do not propose to sit around silent and acquiescent in a society where such a situation exists and where such things happen. Wheaton knows how to do nothing except to sell cash registers. His father died when he was a child and it was up to him to contribute to the support of his mother and his sister without delay. He left school at the age of thirteen or fourteen, went into the cash register factory, learned the business and finally became an agent as you knew him in Asheville. Now he is no longer a young man, he has been in poor health for many years, his reserve of physical strength and energy is very short, and he was kicked out ruthlessly, brutally, and without notice by the employers to whom he had given his life and who for thirty years or more had profited by his efforts. I suppose the cold-blooded answer to this would be that he profited too, and that he was paid well for his services, and that when the period of his usefulness waned as far as the company was concerned, they owed him nothing more, they were free to dismiss him as they chose. I say to hell with all such reasoning; it is probably in accord with the ruthless code of business procedure, but it is not in accord with human life, with human justice, with human decency, do you think so? . . .

In the face of this situation, it has been up to Mabel to keep the whole thing going, to keep body and soul together for both of them. Frankly, I think she has done amazingly well. The whole thing has been a terrible blow to her, the loss of everything they owned, the uprooting of her whole life in Asheville where, as you know, she knew everyone, and to which she was so much attached. I don't think she has ever gotten over it; for her it was really almost like being sent into exile in Siberia. She has cracked under the strain time and again, but she has always pulled herself together and kept things going. She is running, as you know, a kind of lodging house in Washington . . . Of course the strain, the anxiety of this kind of life on a person of her temperament is terrific: furthermore, as you know, in spite of her railings and tirades against this or that, she would give anyone, as the saying goes, the shirt off her back, if she thought someone needed it. As a result, she is constantly being victimized by unscrupulous and dishonest people who will stay in her place for months and then go away without paying her any of the money they owe her. So many of the other people with little gray lives and no particular color or personality of their own, will swarm about a person like Mabel as flies swarm about a sugar bowl, feed upon her vitality, use up her time and exhaust her energy. Of course, I suppose this cannot be helped: she is the kind of person who gives herself out as naturally as the sun shines, and I don't think this will ever change. But it has been a severe strain. . . . Anyway, they are still there in Washington; the address is 920 17th Street, N.W., and I know if you are in Washington she would be delighted to see you. . . .

I did not mean to write you so long a letter. But I was so glad to hear from you after all these years. I want to see you and Mr. Roberts. If you want to talk to me about some of the things you speak about in your letter, I will talk to you about them, if you think it will make for clarification and better understanding, but if it causes greater pain and confusion in the lives or hearts of anyone, I'd rather not say anything. I do believe from your letter that you want to see me again and all I can say sincerely and honestly is that that means a great deal to me. About so many other things—could I just say this: that I know I have done things that I ought not to have done, and left undone things that

I should have done, but that my hope and faith is that I grow a little in knowledge and experience and in understanding all the time, and that I shall, accordingly, do better in the future. I am digging in here for a great burst of work and may not pause for a week or two, but I shall call you up and hope you will be able to arrange a time for meeting, and perhaps you can also meet Mr. Perkins, if you feel like it.

Meanwhile, thanks again for your letter and with all good wishes to all of you,

To A. S. FRERE-REEVES

865 First Avenue
New York, N.Y.
May 28, 1936

Dear Frere:

I am glad you want to do "The Story of a Novel" in England.[1] I don't suppose the book will have any great sale over there, but I am glad you are doing it just the same. The ten percent royalty that you mention, upon the basis of a 3/7 book, is satisfactory to me and you may take this letter as confirming my agreement. I talked to Max about it over the phone a few minutes ago. He, too, was glad that you were going to do the book and I think he said he had already sent you a sheet quotation you asked for. . . .

To-day, I believe, that little ferry boat of yours, the "Queen Mary" is starting her dash across the Atlantic. There is great excitement and interest about it here, great pieces about it in the papers this morning. I suppose a goodly gathering will be at hand to cheer her as she comes in, provided New York harbor is big enough to get her in. I read the usual statements from officials of the line to the captain, etc. to the effect that they were not out to break any records, etc. which means, I suppose, they are not trying to get more than forty knots an hour out of her.

The big German zep, "the Hindenburg," has been flying back and forth over New York, star-like, recently with appalling frequency. If this kind of thing keeps up, our tired business men will be spending a weekend in London before long. I feel like a tired business man myself at present, and wish I were going back in the "Queen Mary" to pay you all a visit. I have dug into work, however, the last month or two, have done a tremendous amount of writing, and think I will keep at it until I get something accomplished.

[1] *The Story of a Novel* was published in England by Heinemann on November 9, 1936.

The Boyd matter, thank God, seems to be finished. The lawyers are still haggling over terms of the agreement, but the main argument seems to be settled. I finally gave her $500., for which she signs an agreement relinquishing all claims to everything except "Look Homeward, Angel," about which, of course, there never had been any argument . . . In addition, they told me she was hard up. I gave her $150 as a present. Of course, the whole thing was outrageous. It has caused me a year of worry, trouble, bother of consulting lawyers, digging up old letters and reading about myself in Mr. Winchell's column, and about one thousand dollars of actual expense by the time I am finished; but I suppose this is the best way out of it. At any rate, this present agreement pays her off, saves me the additional expense and worry of a court trial, and leaves me completely free for the future. Now that it is over I feel sorry for the woman and wonder why she did it. . . . As it is, there has been a year of wrangling, threats, conferences between lawyers, and I suppose from letters which she wrote Max and things I have heard elsewhere, a great deal of bitterness and bad feeling; and now that it is over, I wonder how much good it has done her. I am afraid there won't be much left after her lawyer gets through taking out his share. Anyway I am free of that particular bit of trouble. There are others, of course. It seems that once you get started on them, there always are.

Well, I am going to try to buckle down to work now and get something done. Some of the English reviews of the book of stories [2] seemed awfully good to me. I hope you managed to sell a few copies. Well, we may come through yet. I am back at work. One year of so-called success has not killed me; and if anyone has as much vitality as I, he stands a fair chance of surviving. They will be howling for my blood before long —in fact, there are blood-thirsty growlings now—but I think if I can keep on working, I will be all right.

Write me when you get a chance. Meanwhile, with all good wishes to you and Pat, and the people at Heinemann's,

The following letter was written to Heinz Ledig, now Heinz Ledig-Rowohlt, who is the son of Ernst Rowohlt and the editor at Rowohlt Verlag most closely concerned with Wolfe's books. At this time, Rowohlt was thinking of publishing The Story of a Novel *in Germany. This was finally decided against, but parts of the book were serialized in the November, 1936, issue of* Die Neue Rundschau.

[2] *From Death to Morning* had been published in England on March 16, 1936.

To HEINZ LEDIG

865 First Avenue
New York, N.Y.

June 10, 1936

Dear Heinz:

Mr. Wheelock sent me this morning a translation of your letter to
him, in which you ask for photographs, copies of "The Story of a Novel,"
and other material. I am delighted to know that you are interested in
"The Story of a Novel," and hope that you may find it possible to publish
it in Germany, although of course the demand for such a book will
probably be quite limited. . . .

I am glad to know that there will be no great difficulty in sending
me the royalties from my books. I think you understand very well that I
am not trying to make hard terms or hold you up. As you know, I am
not a business man, but an artist. It is rather hard, however, to have
to work the way I have to work and then to get no financial return whatever. I have to earn my living through what I write. There is no one
in the world who helps me and I do not want help, anyway. During
the past year I have turned down offers to go to Hollywood and write
for the movies, offers to go on lecture tours, etc., which would have
paid me a great many thousand dollars, a great deal more than I will
ever earn from writing, and I'll turn them all down, simply in order
to do the work I really want to do. I have the utmost sympathy for the
difficulties of your position, and I think I understand something of the
complicated nature of international publishing arrangements at the
present time. I certainly do not intend to add to your difficulties if I
can help it, and I am delighted to know that you want to publish a
book of stories.[1] I do want to ask you this final question and I will try
to cause you no further delay about the contract. I have never haggled
with anyone yet about royalties, but I do want to ask you if you think
it is absolutely unreasonable and impossible to restore to me the original
royalty of 10%, which you gave me for "Look Homeward, Angel." You
may remember that this royalty was cut to 7½% in the contract that
Ernst [2] gave me for "Of Time and the River." It was presented to me,
as you know, that the reason for this reduction in royalty was that
the size of the book made the cost of production very high and that [it]
would furthermore necessitate a price for the book that would make its
sale in large quantities doubtful. For these reasons, of course. I con-

[1] *From Death to Morning* was published by Rowohlt in 1937.
[2] Ernst Rowohlt.

sented, but I wonder if these reasons still apply to a book of such moderate length as the book of stories. Of course, I don't know how long my future books are going to be—some of them will certainly be quite long and others, I hope, will conform more to average proportions —but I don't think my royalty should be cut, unless there is some valid reason concerning production costs, sales, etc. What do you think? It doesn't seem to me that I am being unreasonable here and I wish you'd let me know right away how you feel about it.

I do think that, in fairness to myself, as time goes on I ought to try to be a little more business-like. I am not a money-making kind of man; I have no idea how to make a deliberate popular appeal to the writing public; I am really trying to get something out of myself as well as I can and, as time goes on, I hope to do better work, work of which I can be proud and I can feel represents the best and finest use of my talent. Feeling this way, it is not very likely that I will ever become a huge popular success. I was very fortunate with "Of Time and the River." The book had a good sale over here—over 40,000 copies—but you must remember that when I published it I had not published a book for over five years: I owed my publisher a great deal of money, which of course had to be paid back out of the profits of "Of Time and the River," and during the past year since I came back here I have been hounded, worried, and tormented . . . by almost every kind of parasite. . . .

I am learning many things about the world, dear Heinz, some of them not very pretty ones, but I have not lost faith in people. I have met many fine and honorable people as well as all those other ones—some day I shall put it all in a book. I am beginning to do so now, and really I think it may be a very extraordinary book, even though I do say so myself. I want to tell you something about it in a minute; but to finish the other matter about the contract for "From Death to Morning": I have told you some of these unhappy experiences of the past year just in order to let you understand that I am really not rolling in money, that I have very little left and that people hereabouts show an amazing talent for taking money away from me as fast as I can make it. I know that I have got to earn my living and support myself with what I write, so it has occurred to me during the last few months, as a result of all these unhappy experiences, that perhaps I have the right to be a little more businesslike in the matter of contracts and royalty arrangements than I have been in the past. You know me, we have been together, we have talked together, we have had some wonderful times together, and I think you will understand I would never take a business advantage of anyone or ask anyone to give me more than was my due; so please just try to understand the questions I have raised about the contract in the spirit in which I ask them and then don't hesitate for a moment, don't be afraid, to give me your frank and honest opinion right away.

Now, before I close, I want to tell you something about my new book. . . . Briefly—I can't tell you much about it now but the general conception of the book is this: it is not one of the books that have been announced as part of [the] "Of Time and the River" series, it is by far the most objective book I have ever written, although of course, like anything that is any good, it comes right out of my own experience, from everything I may have learned or found out during the course of my life. If I succeed in it, I want it to be a kind of tremendous fable, a kind of legend composed of all the materials of experience. The general idea, so far as I can tell you here in the limits of a letter, is the idea that so many of the great men of the past, each in his own way, has used as the fundamental idea of his book. That idea as I conceive it is the story of a good man abroad in the world—shall we say the naturally innocent man, the man who sets out in life with his own vision of what life is going to be like, what men and women are going to be like, what he is going to find, and then the story of what he really finds. It seems to me that this is the idea behind "Don Quixote," behind "The Pickwick Papers," behind "Candide," behind "Gulliver," and even it seems to me behind such works as "Faust" and "Wilhelm Meister." I am putting everything into this book of mine. Of course it has got to be the book of an American, since I am an American. Parts of it are going to be savage, parts fantastic, parts extravagant and grotesque, and some of it very coarse and very bawdy and, I think, wonderfully comical and funny; and of course I also want the book to be full of faith and poetry and loveliness and my own vision of life and of America. I know it sounds like a tremendous order, but Perkins says he knows I can do it, so I have taken the plunge. If I succeed, it ought to be a wonderfully exciting and interesting book to read. It will be another tremendously long book—God knows how long—longer perhaps even than "Of Time and the River," but I am not worrying about that at present.

I have begun to go again like a locomotive, and I am trying to get it out of me, down on paper, as fast as I can. I don't know how to write yet but I think I am learning something all the time. I think I am becoming more sure and certain of my purpose and I believe I will avoid some of the mistakes and pitfalls in this book that I fell into in the other.

Tentatively, I have called the book "The Vision of Spangler's Paul." It has a sub-title:

"The Story of His Birth, His Life,
His Going To and Fro in the Earth,

His Walking Up and Down in It:
His Vision also of the Lost, the
Never-Found, the Ever-Here America.

With an Introduction
by
A Friend."

The following quotation, which I have taken from "War and Peace" and which I intend to use as a kind of legend at the beginning of the book, may make it a little clearer:

"Prince Andrei . . . turned away . . . His heart was heavy and full of melancholy. It was all so strange, so unlike what he had anticipated."

I don't know whether you want to say anything about this in Germany or not. Scribners have not announced it here as yet. It is generally assumed, of course, that I am at work at present upon one of the remaining books of the "Of Time and the River" cycle, and we are going to surprise them. There is a tendency here among the critics to assume the kind of writing I do best is what they call "autobiographical," and we hope through this book to show them once and for all that this is not true. Perkins says I can create freely, invent and tell a story as well as anyone in the country—and I hope he is right. The "Of Time and the River" books, of course, are still waiting. I can't lose them because so much of them is already written, and really I think I am doing a very wise thing now to do this completely new kind of book at a time in my life when I am still young and full of energy and have the enthusiasm and the fire to do it.

I had not meant to write you such a long letter, and hope it has not fatigued you. Please write me at once in answer to my enquiries about the contract and give me all the news you have about "Von Zeit und Strom." Meanwhile, with all good wishes to you and Ernst, and Mrs. Rowohlt and all the other people at the Verlag,

The following letter was written in reply to one from Kent Roberts Greenfield which praised Of Time and the River *and protested against Bernard De Voto's article, "Genius Is Not Enough," in* The Saturday Review of Literature. *Greenfield was at this time Professor of Modern European History and Chairman of the Department of History at Johns Hopkins University, and is now Chief Historian of the Department of the Army and General Editor of* The U.S. Army in World War II.

Wolfe never mailed the letter but kept it in his own files. Evidently the

legal difficulties to which he refers in his postscript had made him extra-cautious.

To KENT ROBERTS GREENFIELD

865 First Avenue
New York, N.Y.

June 23, 1936

Dear Mr. Greenfield:

Your letter came this morning. It was sent over from Scribners, and before I begin my day's work I want to write a few lines to tell you that it is one of the best letters I ever got, and thank you for writing it. It makes me very proud to know that anyone feels the way you do about something I have done. I don't know whether I can yet live up to what you say in your letter, but it makes me want to try. I don't think anything else in the world—any other reward—can be as valuable and precious to the artist as the kind of reward he gets from a letter like that.

As to Mr. De Voto, I think I feel equal to all the De Votos in the world —and I guess there are a good many—after reading your letter. No, that piece of his in *The Saturday Review* didn't hurt me, and didn't worry me. My hide is by no means as tough as it should be, I still take all these things pretty hard, and so far from pretending to ignore reviews, I think I'd stay up all night to get the morning paper if I knew an old lady was going to write me up or down in the *Akron Ohio Bee:* but I have been through a good bit of it in the last seven years since I wrote my first book and the people in my home town informed me that the Vigilantes would be out with tar and feathers if I ever came back. At that time I took it pretty hard and I think I sweat as much blood in living the book backwards and forwards and every other way after I had written it as I had spent writing it, but I have been pounded on enough since to find out that these matters are not as desperate as I thought them, and what has been most valuable, I think I have really found out for myself that it is the truth that hurts. So usually when something gets in under my hide and hurts, I have found there is a measure of truth in it, and in the end have usually managed to derive some profit from it. The De Voto thing didn't hurt me—it just made me mad. I am not pretending to laugh it off, nor to dismiss utterly everything the man says as false, but I am grateful to you for thinking that the total amount of what he said was false because, even though I do say so myself, I thought so too. Truth has a thousand faces, hasn't it? For my own part, I have never been convinced that Pilate jested. It is a strange perplexing thing, isn't it, to see how a number of true things can be put together to frame a lie? I think Mr. De Voto used the subtle method of indirection in his previous remarks about me, but so far as I know, this is the first time my carcass has been delivered into his custody for a central onslaught. . . .

A year ago . . . this same man began a review of a book in *The Saturday Review of Literature* with another virulent attack upon my work.[1] This is all very well, I suppose, except that the book he was reviewing was not my book and had no possible connection with my book that I can see, except that Mr. De Voto thought that the book was a better book than mine, that the author was a better writer, all of which may be true. I think the author of the book in question, which was "Roll River" by James Boyd, is certainly a very fine artist, and the book a very fine book. The author is one of the finest people I know and a friend of mine. I told him later that if I was going to be taken for a ride, I'd rather be taken for a ride on his account than for almost anyone I know. But aside from the fact that De Voto thought that Jim Boyd's book was better than mine and that both books are for the most part about America (which, by the way, is a fairly extensive place, isn't it?) and that the word "River" occurred in both titles, it seemed to me that the reviewer exercised considerable ingenuity in getting me into the picture at all.

Well, what is there to say? . . . I still take it hard; I still get mad about it; but if there is anything true in what they say, I have got a good memory and I don't forget it; and if what they say is not true, then how can a man be hurt by it? I have had some pretty bad times when I didn't think what I did was any good, I was inclined to agree with almost anyone who felt the same way, but I have held on to this conviction, and in fact the conviction grows stronger as I go along—I genuinely believe that if a thing has something good in it, the good in it is indestructible and will be saved, no matter what anyone says or does; and if a thing has no good in it, it cannot be saved, no matter what anyone says or does, and if it is no good, the man who did it ought not to want it to be saved, anyway. Furthermore, if what a man does is good, and another man is false about it and goes on record with his falseness, then it seems to me there is no need of doing anything to him. He has done the job himself. Usually I find when our hides get nailed up to the wall, we not only supply the hide, but we also supply the hammer and the nails. It is our own job. Well, I

[1] De Voto's review of *Roll River* by James Boyd in the April 27, 1935, issue of *The Saturday Review* began as follows: "There are a number of ways to write that undefined entity, the American novel. Mr. Wolfe has recently exhibited one way: to print the word 'America' ten thousand times, to depict young Faustus as a victim of manic-depressive insanity, to fill the stage with Mardi Gras grotesques who suffer from compulsion neuroses and walk on stilts and always speak as if firing by battery, to look at everything through the lens of an infantile regression . . . and to fluff up the material of fiction, one part, with ten parts of bastard blank verse ecstasy."

am not going on record myself as saying what I do is either good or bad. I suppose if I didn't really feel there was some good in it, it would be hard to keep on working as I do, in hope of betterment, and I think that the conviction that I have just expressed to you is something more than a mere desire to believe. I believe it is a fact that the good thing can't be hurt, and that knowledge helps me a lot as I go on writing. As you can see from this letter, I don't pretend that I didn't take the De Voto thing seriously. . . . I am not trying to laugh it off, but it didn't hurt me, it doesn't rankle, I have no vengeful feelings; in the end I may even get some good from it. The main thing is I am working like a horse and I don't see how anyone, not even Mr. De Voto, is going to do anything about that.

The other thing is that I think I will learn a little, slowly, all the time; that I hope to profit by my own mistakes and errors of the past and grow in wisdom, in power, in maturity; and that whenever I get a letter like the one you wrote me, it makes me want to exert every energy of my life and talent to do so. So thanks again. Your letter meant a lot to me, and I want you to know that it did and that I am deeply and sincerely grateful. Please forgive me for writing you such a long one in return—as you may have heard, brevity is not one of my most noticeable gifts; but maybe I can do something about that too. Anyway, I'm going to try. Meanwhile, with all best wishes and thanks,

Dear Mr. Greenfield: I wrote this *ten* (10) days ago, and just failed to mail it. The letter, of course, is written to *you*—and is confidential. It does not matter about De Voto, Canby, or the rest—but I am just through with legal trouble and not through with it yet—they have got all my money, all my manuscripts—so don't give this to them.

The following letter to Hamilton Basso was called forth by Basso's article, "Thomas Wolfe," in the June 24, 1936, issue of The New Republic. *Basso is the author of* Beauregard, Courthouse Square, Days Before Lent, Wine of the Country, Sun in Capricorn, The Greenroom, Mainstream, The View from Pompey's Head, *etc., and had first known Wolfe through Scribners. His article on Wolfe ended with the following words: "In* The Story of a Novel *he . . . says, in effect, . . . that he is going to renounce his former ways and try to do better in the future. This is all very fine but I like the declaration contained in a letter I had from him much better. 'I have something I'd like you to see but it ain't wrote good yet. You wait—I'll learn 'em!' And learn 'em I think he will."*

To HAMILTON BASSO

865 First Avenue
New York, N.Y.

June 24, 1936

Dear Ham:

I want to write you a few lines just to thank you for writing that fine piece in the New Republic. People began to call me up and tell me about it last week, so I went out and got a copy at once. The whole thing has warmed me up more than I can possibly tell you, and if I was fired with the ambition to "learn 'em" before, that piece of yours has set off a bonfire. It is pretty hard for me to say everything to you I would like to say, because I am not only the recipient of the honor but in a way the subject of it; but I do think that I learned something valuable from the piece, in addition to the happiness it gave me. I think you hit the nail on the head with what you said about the railroad trains in my books and how the feeling of space is probably derived from the childhood of a man who grew up in the confinement of a mountain town. That is the truth. As I look back on it now, my whole childhood was haunted by the ringing of train bells at night, the sound of whistles fading away somewhere along the French Broad River, the sound of a train going away down the river towards Knoxville and the West. I certainly hope you are right when you say that I have been able to take materials of localized regional experience and give them communication of universal interest. That is what I should like to do. I suppose that is what every writer, with his own special material, would like to do.

I won't say any more about it, but just let me thank you again and tell you how grateful I am, and assure you that an experience of that kind can do nothing but good to a writer and his work.

"Of Time and the River," by the way, seems to be a crashing success—critically at any rate—in Germany and all through Central Europe. The reviews have been coming in by the dozens. Some of them are of immense length—six and eight-paged articles in magazines and critical reviews, column after column in newspapers. They say tremendous things. I can't believe it when I read them. The publishers write me that there has been a great deal of excitement and some of the most magnificent reviews they have ever seen. Well, I am vulgarly commercial enough to hope that some of this excitement gets translated in the sales and that the Germans find a way of getting the money out of the country to me, which they say they will be able to do.

The German Book Society, by the way, after the publication of "Of

Time and the River" have arranged with the publisher to bring out an edition of 8,000 of "Look Homeward, Angel" for their subscribers, and, although I get only a very small royalty for this, the total result ought to be good, because they may succeed in creating additional interest in "Of Time and the River." "Of Time and the River" is awfully expensive in the German edition—that's the main difficulty. They've done a grand job of printing and publishing and translating. It comes out in two volumes and costs fourteen marks, which is over five dollars at the present rate of exchange, and I understand is more than a good many working men in Germany can afford to pay for a suit of clothes. I am a little sorry it costs so much, but I suppose they did the best they could.

I am back at work again, after a year which has had everything packed into it. Everything happened to me except homicide, and I am knocking on wood. The experience of having a so-called literary success in these here parts has put some gray hairs in my head, but on the whole, I am glad I went through it and found out what it was like. Parts of it have been pleasant, parts of it grotesque, fantastical, unbelievable, and rip-roaringly, side-splittingly funny. Unfortunately, the bird who gets crowned with a brick-bat while he is smelling a rose, or is kicked in the seat of the pants when he bends over to retrieve a cigar butt is at the moment not in a favorable position for appreciating the humor of the situation, so my laughter has at times been deferred and I have got a notion that it will take years for my full enjoyment of the experience to mature. Maybe I will be like those Englishmen I have heard about whose parents told them jokes when they were young, in order that they might have a good time in their old age. I can't tell you the whole story here, it's too long and fantastic, but if we can ever get together over a jug or a bottle, I think I can give you an earful. . . . Until a year ago, I still had some lingering and naive belief that law and the courts had some connection with human justice. . . . It is, of course, not true. . . . I finally got my suit settled out of court, and I suppose you might say I won out. I simply paid a sum of money, a very trifling sum compared to the amount they were asking, in order not to be hounded, worried and tormented by the thing any more. Also I have a complete and everlasting quittance "from the beginning of the world to these presents," henceforth and forever. All in all, by the time I get through paying my lawyer, the whole miserable business will cost me a thousand dollars, to say nothing of all the other costs of time and care. . . . Well, maybe the experience has been worth a thousand dollars. It has introduced me to that fantastical never-never land of the law, and provided me with the material some day of some bawdy chapters, a half-dozen characters that most people wouldn't believe existed outside of the pages of Dickens.

I have also had innocent-looking little boys, the sons of gentle Irish families . . . with whom I was friendly, and who all solemnly assured me their friendship for me was beyond price and of undying fidelity—I have had their youngest and most holy representative walk off with my manuscripts, sell them in various parts of the country, . . . and solemnly assure himself that he had done nothing wrong in the eyes of God and of his own moral conscience, no matter what mistaken notions men might have about his conduct.[1] Some of the rest of it, the other things that have happened, is unprintable here. . . . If you give me a chance I'll confide it to you some day; but it is simply astounding to discover how many people there are in this world, and particularly in this City, who exist through some form of parasitism, who seem to have no life of their own, except as they hope to get their life from someone else—whether by taking someone's money, or his property, or his labor; or what is even more costly—trying to take his life, somehow to attach themselves to it, to stake a claim on it, chain themselves to it, somehow to get their own life from it. Well, I went through it all in less than a year. I don't suppose I am wholly out of it yet, but I am out as far as my knowledge of the situation is concerned. I was getting pretty desperate, stewing around in this huge web, trying to get myself out of this snarled tangle of dishonest scheming, insane congeries of parasites, crack-pots and hysteric neurots—most of the latter, I am afraid, being women, who write the longest, frequentest and most incredible letters.

Well, I had to get back to work, or I think I would have gone crazy myself, and I finally found, as old Daniel Webster said, that the way to resumption was to resume. Accordingly, about three months ago, I decided that if the worst came to the worst, they could take what money I had —I could probably make more money; they could steal my manuscripts— I could certainly write more manuscripts; but if they took away from me the concentration and the power of work, they had taken everything I had. In other words, I said "To Hell with it" and got busy, and since then I have

---

[1] Wolfe's legal difficulties about his manuscripts had begun in February, 1936. He had given several pieces of manuscript to a young man with the understanding that he would act as his agent in selling them in the rare book and manuscript market, but after various difficulties and misunderstandings they had quarrelled on February 10, and Wolfe had dismissed him as his agent. However, the young man claimed that his agency for Wolfe could not be terminated unless by mutual consent, had refused to return the unsold manuscripts still in his possession, and had threatened to sue Wolfe unless he paid him $1900 for services rendered and for commission on the appraised value of the unsold manuscript of *Of Time and the River*. Wolfe finally instituted suit against him on September 14, 1936, to reclaim his manuscripts and obtain an accounting of all transactions made by the young man as his agent. After many difficulties, the case was finally tried before Vice-Chancellor Kayes in Jersey City on February 8, 1939, and the judgment awarded to Wolfe.

written between 150,000 and 200,000 words. It is a new book—I can't tell you much about it here, but it is a pretty daring venture, completely different from anything I have ever attempted. . . . It came boiling to the surface all of a sudden. Of course, it had been stewing around down there for a great many years, but when I told Max about it, he snapped his fingers and said at once, "Do it, and do it now." He then told me that he had known for years that I would have to write such a book, it was unquestionably a thing I ought to do now at this period of my life. He told me to get busy on it at once. I expressed doubts to him whether I would be able to achieve such a book, and he told me there was no doubt at all, if I would go at it and keep going, that I could undoubtedly do it and that I was the only person who could.

Well, I hope the doctor is right. He has been right most of the time so far, and I hope he is right now. At any rate, we are both excited about it, and I am going to "let 'er rip." God knows how long a job it is going to be, a very long one I am afraid, but if I can do something good, if I have begun to learn to use myself, at least, it doesn't matter how long it will be.

Well, Ham, you see what happens when I set out to write a few lines. I hope you haven't sprouted whiskers while reading this letter. I just wanted to thank you for having written that fine piece and to tell you how grateful I am for it, but I managed to throw in a large part of the American continent as well. Please write me when you get a chance and tell me what you are doing. Is there any chance of your getting up here this summer? I may go away for a short vacation, but so far as I know, I will be here plugging away most of the time. I hope it won't be too long before we see each other again. Meanwhile, with love to all,

The following letter was written in answer to one from William Polk who was at this time President of the North Carolina Literary and Historical Association, and had invited Wolfe to speak at its meeting in Raleigh in December.

To WILLIAM T. POLK

865 First Avenue
New York, N.Y.

June 25, 1936

Dear Bill:

Thanks for your letter. Honestly, it is good to know that at least I have a chance of coming home without being escorted to the outskirts of the town by the local Vigilantes and told never to darken their public square again. Seriously, I am very much interested in your invitation and would like to ask for a little more information. Just how historical does a speaker have to be when he talks to the Historical Association? Knowing you as I do, I know you'll gladly give me all the rope I need to hang myself; but if I spoke, would I be tongue-tied with terror every time I looked around and found the cold and fishy eye of the experts upon me? As I mounted to my peroration, would I be checked in my full flight by the presence of J. G. de Roulhac Hamilton,[1] his face fixed on me with a very fishy look, as though to say: "If this be history, I'm a horse"?

Now you also say something about speaking for a half-hour. Think fast, Captain; as you may have heard, brevity is not one of my notable gifts, although I try to do a little better all the time. I made a speech out in Colorado last summer. It took me the first fifteen minutes to quit stuttering, hemming and hawing, and fiddling around for an opening, but after that, if I do say so as shouldn't, I did the job up pretty brown. Prepare yourself for a shock—it took one hour and forty minutes, and they were hanging on by their eyelids when I finished. Really, though, if I had to face an audience of the home folks, I'd probably be ten times as scared as I was out there, and God knows that was bad enough until I got going. If I got going in Raleigh, the Lord knows what would happen—I've got too much to tell them—in fact when I think of it, I feel like that fellow in the Leacock Nonsense Novel who jumped on his horse and went galloping off madly in all directions.

I wonder if we couldn't do this: I know you want to get your program settled as soon as possible, but couldn't you write me and tell me a little more about the thing, the kind of gathering I would have to face and the kind of talk they usually get? The real gist of the thing is simply this: I still procrastinate, I think—I try to avoid making engagements six months in advance because they weigh upon me and seem to put a sort of check and restraint upon me, to tie me down much more than I should let them. So far as I know, I'll be right here in New York in December, plugging away at a new book. If I am still here and it was still possible for me to come to Raleigh, I'd probably do it. I know this is no good to you, because you have a definite program and you've got to plan it now. There wouldn't be any chance of this, would there—it sounds pretty brazen, I know, but all this is confidential between you and me and I know you won't expose my effrontery—but could you go ahead and get another speaker, announce him and put him on your program, and if you like, say that I didn't know definitely whether I would be able to be present at the

[1] J. G. De Roulhac Hamilton had been Professor of History at the University of North Carolina when Wolfe and Polk were students there.

date of the meeting? Then, without my feeling obligated, if I was here and you wanted me to come down, perhaps I could come and without interfering with the other fellow, just attend the meeting or get up and talk for ten or fifteen minutes. I know it all sounds cockeyed, and perhaps it is against all the rules of the old noblesse. If it is, don't give me away. The main thing, really, Bill, at the present time is that I have got started working on another big piece of work. I finally got myself clear of the whole snarl of engagements and complications that were beginning to get me this last year, and am back at work, and I want to keep at it as hard as I can without feeling that I am tied down by anything outside.

I think this makes it plain, and I know you will understand. Just write me and tell me how you feel about it, and if what I suggest is in any way possible. Meanwhile, with all good wishes and regards,

P.S. Dear Bill: Rereading your letter, I notice you say there is a chance of your being in New York in July. I live at this address: 865 First Avenue, and the phone number is Plaza 3 4583. . . . I've got a fine place here, fourteen stories up, overlooking the East River, about three sticks of dilapidated furniture, but one of the coolest places and one of the most wonderful views in New York. Let's get together.

XIII

THE BEGINNING OF THE BREAK WITH SCRIBNERS

1936–1937

The reasons for Wolfe's growing conviction that he must leave Scribners were too many and too complex to describe adequately here. However, the most obvious of them was the necessity to disprove the implication made by Bernard De Voto in "Genius Is Not Enough" that Wolfe could not write his books without the help of "Mr. Perkins and the assembly-line at Scribners."

Another reason was Wolfe's realization that Perkins was opposed to his writing about Scribners and the people who worked there. The following letter was probably written because of Perkins' unfavorable reaction to Wolfe's story, "No More Rivers," which described characters similar to those of various editors at Scribners. At Wolfe's request, Miss Nowell had shown this to Perkins and one of his associates, neither of whom objected to his having written about themselves. However, Perkins told Miss Nowell that if Wolfe "wrote up" certain things which he had told him in confidence about his associates, he felt it would be his duty to resign from the firm.

This letter is the first of the many, approaching other publishers, which Wolfe wrote and never mailed, and it was accompanied by a list of firms to whom he evidently thought of sending it: "Macmillan, Harper, Viking, W. W. Norton, Little Brown, Houghton Mifflin, Longmans Green, Dodd Mead, Doubleday Doran, Harcourt Brace"—and also by a rough draft of an announcement which he may have momentarily considered sending out: "An author, Thomas Wolfe, being now without a publisher, would like to have a publisher."

"To ALL PUBLISHERS"
[Other than Scribners]

865 First Avenue
New York, N.Y.

July 15, 1936

To All Publishers:
Gentlemen:
   I am the author of four published works, of which two are novels, one

537

a volume of stories, and one a very short book about the experiences a writer has in beginning to write.

All of these books have been published by the same publishing house, with whom my relations have been satisfactory.

At the present time, I am engaged upon the composition of a long book, and since I have no obligation, whether personal, financial, contractual, moral, or of any kind soever to any firm of publishers, I am writing to inquire if you are interested in this book, and if so, upon what conditions, terms, proposals, and contractual alliances you are so interested. I am going abroad next week and should appreciate an answer now.

In all fairness, I should here state that I think my physical resources, which have been generous, are at the present moment depleted; that the kind of vital concentration which has at times in the past attended the act of creation, is diffused. But I think these things may come back, and that there is a possibility I will do better work than I have yet done. That, of course, is my hope: and despite this present depletion of my energies, I am of cheerful mood and resolute temper, and I have strong hopes that the energy and power of such talents as I have will return.

Frankly—with no disparagement of any connection I have had—I feel the need of a new beginning in my creative life.

[THE LETTER BREAKS OFF HERE]

To FRED W. WOLFE

865 First Avenue
New York, N.Y.

July 23, 1936

Dear Fred:

I am sailing in a few hours, and this letter has to be a lot shorter than I wanted it to be. Anyway I am sending you back your check.[1] I do not need any money, I won't take any money from you, so please just forget about it and make me happy. Everything is fine. This is the cheapest trip I have ever made, in fact am standing a chance to make some money out of it before I am through. The North German Lloyd has given me a credit of $150.00, or more than half my tourist class passage, on my promise to write them a piece or two for their travel magazine, and my German publishers have cabled me that they will have one thousand marks waiting for me when the boat docks at Bremerhaven. In addition to this, a couple

---

[1] During the depression, Wolfe had sent his brother Fred money to help support certain members of the family. The check was in repayment of the balance of this.

of New York magazines have promised to take travel pieces if I will write them, so you see I am sitting pretty.

I shall write you a long letter on the boat or after I get there, telling you about recent events. I have been pretty upset and wrought up by some of these things that happened in the last few months, and I was pretty badly disappointed when Mabel did not show up the other night. I had come in from the country. Mr. Perkins had driven me eight miles to make a train through the worst rain and lightning storm I have ever seen, and I guess I got a little worked up when I got home and found a telegram from her saying she was not coming after all. It is all right, of course. It is no one's fault. Everything is fine as far as the family is concerned. I was just a little excited. I had absolutely no right to call you up, but you were the first one I thought of. I wanted to get it off my chest to you, so please forget about it now. You will make me a lot happier if you do.

I hope to be back here about August 20th, and if I do, I would like to come to Asheville for a few days, but don't say anything about it. They were pretty mad at me a few years ago but I understand they feel a bit better about it now, but I do not want either one thing or the other. If I come home I would like to come as I always did without any fuss.

I have been reading about the murder [2] in the papers the last few days. It has been on the front page of all the papers here and it may amuse you to know that one of the New York papers called Mr. Perkins up and wanted to have an interview with me upon the ground that I come from Asheville. I told him to tell them that so far as this particular crime was concerned, my alibi was secure, that they did not have a thing on me. Anyway, of course I would not give such an interview. The folks back home have had hard feelings in the past. I hope most of it is over now, but I would not do anything to cause any more trouble if I could help it.

This is all for the present. Just please forget about the whole blow-up. I am sorry I bothered you. I was just tired and worried, but everything is fine with me. I am going to be better than ever when I come back. I shall try to write Mama on the boat to-night. Anyway, I shall write you all in a few days.

[2] This probably refers to the murder of a Miss Helen Clevenger, of Staten Island, in an Asheville hotel. A Negro employee of the hotel was executed for the crime the following December.

To ROBERT RAYNOLDS

[Postcard: Blick auf Rathaus und Frauen Kirche, München]

Munich

July 29, 1936

This is a wonderful city. I looked at the Durers, the Cranachs and the Grunewalds in Alte Pinothek again to-day for first time in eight years. It seems very natural to be back.

To MAXWELL E. PERKINS

[Postcard: Pariser Platz mit Blick auf Tiergarten u. Reichstag: Berlin]

Berlin

August 7, 1936

Dear Max: I've had a good trip—seen all my old friends here and lots of new people—also newspaper interviews, drawings, etc. The town is crowded with Olympic visitors, and the Germans have done their job beautifully. Wonderfully cool and clean after New York.

To MAXWELL E. PERKINS

[Postcard: Alpbach mit Galtenberg]

Alpbach
Austrian Tirol

August 26, 1936

I climbed that big mountain (the highest one) yesterday. It damned near finished me but I did it. It makes all your New England mountains look like toad-stools. This is a beautiful country and good people. On my way back to Munich and Berlin to-day. Will sail next week if I can get passage.

To ROBERT RAYNOLDS

[Postcard: Pariser Platz und Brandenburger Tor: Berlin]

Berlin

September 4, 1936

Dear Bob: All this was massed with flags and packed with people during the Olympiad but that hysteria is past now—but the Partie Tag will be here in a day or two.

To ELIZABETH NOWELL
[Postcard: München, Feldherrnhalle]

Munich

September 8, 1936

This is a wonderful city—after eight years it seems very natural and friendly. Frankly, after what happened last year, I don't very much want to come "home"—but I will.

To MAXWELL E. PERKINS
[Postcard: Die Wachtruppe am Brandenburger Tor, Berlin]

Berlin

September, 1936

We can never learn to march like these boys—and it looks as if they're about ready to go again.

To ELIZABETH NOWELL
[Postcard: La Place de l'Opera, Paris]

Paris

September 16, 1936

Dear Miss Nowell: Don't do anything about the stories until I get back. I've written a good piece [1] over here—I'm afraid it may mean that I can't come back to the place where I am liked best and have the most friends, but I've decided to publish it. So wait on me.

To FRED W. WOLFE

865 First Avenue
New York, N.Y.

October 5, 1936

Dear Fred:

Just a note to tell you I am back at this address, that I have your note saying you may be up here about the middle of October and that I am

[1] "I Have a Thing to Tell You" which was published in the March 10, 17, and 24, 1937, issues of *The New Republic*, and appears in *You Can't Go Home Again* on pages 634–640, 641–651, 655, 663–704.

delighted. I have two rooms here, with two comfortable couches in one and a good double bed in the other, so the matter of putting you up with me is easy. Will you just do this, please?—because, as you know, our family is not noted for punctuality: let me know *exactly* when you are coming, so that I can be here, and there will be no confusion or mistake in our meeting arrangements. . . . Meanwhile, until I hear from you, with love to all and best wishes,

P.S. There is a poor, desperate, unhappy man staying at the Grove Park Inn.[1] He is a man of great talent but he is throwing it away on drink and worry over his misfortunes. Perkins thought if Mama went to see him and talked to him, it might do some good—to tell him that at the age of forty he is at his prime and has nothing to worry about if he will just take hold again and begin to work. His name, I forgot to say, is Scott Fitzgerald, and a New York paper has just published a miserable interview with him— it was a lousy trick, a rotten . . . piece of journalism, going to see a man in that condition, gaining his confidence, and then betraying him. I my- self have suffered at the hands of these rats, and I know what they can do. But I don't know whether it's a good idea for Mama to see him—in his condition, he might resent it and think we were sorry for him, etc.—so better wait until I write again.

The following brief note to Irma Wyckoff was evidently written after Wolfe's renewed quarrel with Perkins about the latter's unfavorable reaction to the story "No More Rivers." When Wolfe had gone abroad in July, he had told Miss Nowell to delete some of the material which Perkins had objected to in that story, and to show it to him again. Perkins had then written her on August 26, saying: "I think this story could do no one any harm now—except perhaps Thomas Wolfe. I do not think it is up to his usual level." Wolfe had quarrelled with Perkins about this on his return to New York in October, charging him with personal bias and with attempting to censor what he wrote. From this time forth, he avoided going to Scribners almost entirely, instead of coming in every few days to talk to Perkins and pick up his mail, as he had been in the habit of doing for the past seven years. His note to Miss Wyckoff was, in effect, a notice of his determination to stay away, since he had been living at 865 First Avenue since October, 1935, and she knew his address very well.

[1] In Asheville.

To IRMA WYCKOFF

New York City
October 5, 1936

Dear Miss Wyckoff:
From now on, will you please address and send any mail that may come for me to 865 First Avenue, New York City?

The following letter was in reply to one from Elsa C. Serfling, editor of the North German Lloyd magazine, The Seven Seas, *who had written Wolfe to remind him that he owed that magazine two short articles on Germany in return for the $150 credit he had received on his passage on the* Bremen. *In accordance with Wolfe's suggestion made here, the North German Lloyd accepted his check for $150 in place of the articles.*

To ELSA C. SERFLING

865 First Avenue
New York, N.Y.
October 12, 1936

Dear Miss Serfling:
Please excuse me for my delay in answering you. I did not get your letter of September 9th, sent to the American Embassy in Berlin, until I returned home, where it was forwarded on to me. I got back about two weeks ago.

I wanted to write you while I was in Germany, telling you I'd changed my plans for sailing and would not be home as early as I had originally planned, but my whole summer, from the time I left here until I returned, was so crowded with events—seeing the Olympics, meeting old friends again, talking to my German publisher about contracts, going to the Tyrol, and becoming intensely interested in what is going on in Europe to-day—that I did not have much time for writing letters.

Now about the proposed articles for *The Seven Seas.* First of all, I want to tell you how genuinely sorry I am for any delay or inconvenience I may have caused you. Then I ought to explain my present situation to you frankly, and ask you if you would kindly agree to what I am going to propose.

This was one of the most intriguing summers, one of the most extraordinary and interesting trips I've ever made. I am boiling with ideas and with plans for work. There is no question but that I got material, not only for three articles but for thirty, during the summer. The only difficulty that I contemplate in writing such articles as you suggest for *The Seven Seas Magazine* is this: everything I do, everything I create, comes from the whole texture of my experience—from everything I have seen, thought, felt or known. As I think of these proposed articles, I find it very difficult to isolate them from this whole fabric, to separate them from lives and events and feelings which would be proper and essential in a work of the imagination but which I feel would not only be improper but decidedly unwise in a series of travel articles for a travel magazine.

May I tell you that I have the deepest and most genuine affection for Germany, where I have spent some of the happiest and most fruitful months of my life, and for the German people, among whom I have some of the best and truest friends I know. For that very reason, above all others, I want to be scrupulous now not to abuse your own generosity or to make any commitments that would not be in full accordance with certain deep and earnest convictions of my own or with anything I might write or say hereafter.

I cannot go into detailed explanation here, but I leave it to your intuition to understand what is in my mind. Briefly, what I should like to do and what I hope you will understand and agree to is to send you a check for the one hundred and fifty dollars which you advanced me upon my passage as payment for the proposed articles, and so allow me to discharge my obligation in this way.

Believe me, I am sincerely sorry for any inconvenience or delay I may have caused you, but if you can understand my desire to settle our arrangement in this way, you will greatly relieve me and I shall be sincerely grateful for your consideration. Please write me as soon as you can.

Thea Voelcker, to whom the following letter was written, had met Wolfe in Berlin in the summer of 1936, when she had made a drawing of him to illustrate an interview for the Berliner Tageblatt. *Wolfe, at first, had disliked the drawing and said that it made him look "piglike," but he and Frau Voelcker evidently fell in love, later quarrelled, and finally made up. When he first came back to America that autumn, he announced that he was going to bring her to America and marry her, but they drifted apart. She is rumored to have committed suicide some years later, after another tragic love affair.*

The letters to her which appear in this volume were dictated by Wolfe to his secretary and found in carbon copies in his own files. If he wrote her more personally in longhand, those letters are now lost.

To THEA VOELCKER

865 First Avenue
New York, N.Y.

October 13, 1936

Dear Thea:

I am writing you just a short letter this morning to let you know I'm safely at home again and to thank you for your two letters and the wonderful book you sent me for my birthday.[1] I'll write you at greater length later on and I hope you'll be able to decipher my scrawl. I am having this letter typed so you shouldn't have much trouble with it.

I was wonderfully happy to get your letters. They are fine letters and very eloquent—especially the last one, which you wrote in English. In spite of your difficulties with a foreign language, you expressed yourself beautifully and I understood and valued everything you had to say.

I am back at work again and tremendously eager to plunge into the heart of it now. I think the trip this summer, and all I saw and learned, has done me a great deal of good. For one thing it took me far enough away from my work to give me the kind of detachment I needed. And although my conscious mind was busy with all the things and places I was seeing and the people I was meeting, I think my unconscious mind must have been busy at my book, because now that I am back, the whole plan, from first to last, has become clear to me, and I think I know exactly what I want to do. It is going to be a very long and tremendous piece of work and I suppose I shall feel defeated and desperate many times before I come to the end of it. But with the knowledge that I have the belief and friendship of a few people, including yourself, I think I can accomplish it.

There's so much I should like to tell you, but I think I'd better reserve that for another letter. Your birthday book is wonderful. It has in it some of the most magnificent heads I've ever seen. This is the Germany I love and believe in—the great Germany of the mind and heart and spirit. You are very good to say that my head belongs with these. I should be only too proud if it were true. I am very happy if you think so.

After the well-kept cleanliness of Berlin, Paris stank; and the French—well, they're still the French, aren't they? And they're forever with us. Yet I am glad there is a Paris and a France, and that we have the French. If we did not have them I think it would be necessary to invent them. I have always been a stranger there. I have lived and endured some of the most bitter and lonely times of my life among those little strange dark French-

[1] She had sent him a book called *Grosse Deutsche,* an illustrated catalogue of an exhibit of portraits of great Germans, saying that his head belonged with these.

men, who are only for themselves. But I am glad I have known them, too. I have learned much from them, even though I can never be one of them. And although every time I go, the old conflict begins again—that strange mixture of like and dislike, of contempt and admiration, of disgust and affection—although I am always glad to leave them—I should be sorry if I could never come back again.

I came back on a French ship and, after the beautiful and well-run order of the *Europa,* it seemed a rather haphazard and perilous experiment. However, we got here. I am unjust, of course. I knew that we should get here. I have no doubt but that they are really good and able seamen. But I could never quite believe it. All Frenchmen on a ship look a little seasick to me and I always remember the answer of one of our wits, who, when asked why he always chose to travel on a French boat, instead of an English or a German one, replied, "Because on a French boat, if anything happens, there's none of this damn nonsense about women and children first."

I think you would have enjoyed the voyage, however. There was a terrific hurricane raging up and down the whole American coast and it caught us when we were three or four days from New York. The storm lasted for two days. It was one of the most violent and savage storms I've ever seen but if one did not get sick it was beautiful and magnificent also. Most of the people were sick but I don't think you would have been. New York also seemed very dirty, noisy and disorderly after the comparative quiet and order of Berlin, but it was good to be back here too. We are different from the French and, after all that I saw and felt this summer— the feeling of pressure and of tension, the feeling that those tragic and apparently incurable hatreds of Europe were going to explode at any minute—it is good to be here where, whatever we lack, we still have space to move in, freedom to expand.

I am still at my old apartment on First Avenue. I write you this looking out my window on the fourteenth floor—looking out upon the river, a river which is busy at almost every moment of the day with its wonderful and thrilling traffic of boats, great and small: the busy little tugs, the great barges, freighters and ships. We are now having our grand October weather. This is the best part of our autumn, one of the best times of the year. The air is clear and sharp and frosty, and out in the country the trees are burning with flaming and magnificent colors, which I think you do not have in Europe. You would like it here now.

This is all for the present. I shall write you later on and talk to you more personally about the things you speak of in your letters. Meanwhile, with all my sincerest and most affectionate greetings, with all good wishes to you for happiness and success in all you do, I am, ever sincerely,

Your friend

P.S.: I shall never forget Alpbach. No matter what happens in the world, no matter what sorrow, strife or trouble we may go through, it will always be good to know that there is in the world a place like that quiet and enchanted Alpine valley.

To HAMILTON BASSO

865 First Avenue
New York, N.Y.
October 14, 1936

Dear Ham:

I was glad to get your letter and to hear what you were doing. I've been back here two or three weeks and have been expecting a copy of "Courthouse Square," but it hasn't yet arrived. I've been too busy to read the book news, so I don't know what date the publication is scheduled for. But I suppose Bill Weber will send me a copy when the time comes.

I had a wonderfully interesting trip this summer and I am glad I went. I did a good deal of travelling, saw a great many exciting things, met a lot of people, talked to a lot more and was able to get almost completely away from things back here. As a result, I was able to think the whole situation out clearly—the whole jam of trouble, law suits, interruptions, etc., that I got into last year—and make up my mind what I was going to do about it. And what was best of all, I think I got my book straight in my head—the whole plan of it from beginning to end. At any rate I've begun to work again.

Like you, I feel pretty bad about Scott. I wish something could be done about him, but I don't know what. I had thought of asking my mother to go round and see him, and also of asking some people I know, but I don't know how much good it would do. He might resent it, especially if he thought any one was trying to help him or felt sorry for him.

I don't know whether you saw the interview which appeared here in *The New York Evening Post*. It made me sick, and I felt and still feel that some one ought to do something about him. I told Max Perkins so. His attitude, of course, and the Scribner attitude, apparently, is that any attempt at answering a thing like this, or of denouncing such journalistic practice, only adds fuel to the flames and makes the situation worse than ever. I suppose there is a lot of truth in this but I wonder just how much longer we've got to sit by meekly and submissively in the world while the scavengers, the shysters, the traducers and the filth-purveyors of every sort are allowed to go their way unchecked. It almost makes me long for dear old Adolph and his S. S. men. They at least could put a stop to a good many of our own accepted forms of thugdom. Of course, in doing so they would establish another and much more powerful one of their own, and there's the rub.

As you say, it looks as if Scott were bent on committing professional suicide, but if a man in his present condition is determined to destroy himself, I think it is a vile and cowardly act on the part of other people to help him along in his intent. From what I have heard from Max, the interviewer got in to see Scott, played him up sympathetically with conversation, gained his confidence and let him spew the whole thing out—all about being lost, done for, defeated, unable to get back and, what was worst of all, all about Zelda being in the sanitarium and all the rest of the miserable business. From the very tone of the interview it was evident what condition Scott was in at the time, and that he could not have been fully aware of what he was saying. . . .

The whole thing was smeared all over the first page of the paper and, like your pal Sherwood,[1] I want to know why. I can't see what possible news value it has—what possible public service it can achieve—why the illness, alcoholism, mental ill health of a writer, together with the mental illness of his wife, is a matter that should be aired for the instruction of the American public. It was a cheap, sensational piece of journalism, and the thing that gets me sore is that I have met the man who owns the paper, and met his wife, and had dinner in their home, and they preened themselves upon their liberalism. His paper is forever attacking Hearst for his vicious and unprincipled methods, and now this great liberal, this spokesman of decent journalism, perpetrates a thing like this. As Perkins said, one of the bitter and disheartening things in life is to find out how many of these people who set themselves up as liberals, as champions of decent living, turn out in the end to be just as filthy a flock of vultures as the worst of them.

Well, the thing is done now, and there's no use talking about it any more. Like you, I want to do something for Scott but when I think about it I come up against a blank wall and end by thinking that maybe I'll give him a good swift kick and tell him, for God's sake, to come out of it. And, of course, I know that would do no good either. I was thinking of his career the other day and, in a way, it seems to me that his greatest misfortune in life has been that he was a child of fortune. Most of us stick around and plug ahead hoping that Lady Luck may hit us with a spare horseshoe. But Scott, at the beginning, had horseshoes rained on him by the whole damn cavalry. I think that this, in a way, unfitted him for what was to follow. He not only had one of the best breaks that any one ever had, he got a very tough break too. I hope that, in a way, I got a bit prepared for it after my experience with "Look Homeward, Angel."

[1] Sherwood Anderson.

Knowing what I did about the career of the book, how the entire population of my home town wanted to draw and quarter me, how eminent reviewers, such as Mr. Harry Hansen, headed their reviews with such master strokes of sarcasm as "Ah, Life, Life," [2] etc., how everybody asked if I could ever write another book and how quickly they began to say I never would—I say I was able to smile a trifle grimly a year ago after the publication of "Of Time and the River," when I read that my career had been a bed of roses from the beginning, that "Look Homeward, Angel" had been greeted with a hurricane of applause, that my path from that time on had been as smooth as velvet. I know what happened then. I think I know what is likely to happen to me now until I get another book done. It's not going to be easy to take. But it's not going to be quite the bitter and disillusioning experience that it was five or six years ago. You know, as well as I do, how quickly they can turn, how desperately hard it is to prevail, when they make up their minds about you.

I had that happen to me a year ago, when a volume of stories came out and I am certainly not bitter about the reception of the stories. I am not sore about it. I'm only telling you that most of the criticism was as the minds made up in advance saw it. The things they'd begun to go for me for in "Of Time and the River," were carried right over and plastered on my book of stories. The stories, it appeared, were not stories at all but sections that Max Perkins and I had scissored out of the manuscript of "Of Time and The River." There was a page or two which described the movement of a regiment of negroes through a pier at Newport News during the war, and the great Mr. Chamberlain, in his critique, inquired, "We have negroes here, negroes in the mass, a regiment of negroes. But where is Booker T. Washington, where is Joe Louis, where is Father Divine, etc.?" [3] Where indeed? Where, oh where? For that matter, where is the Queen of Sheba, where is Leonardo Da Vinci, where is Tiglath Pilezar? Gone with the wind, I suppose. The thing that made me tough, however, saved me from apoplectic strangulation, and, in fact, gave me a sort of haughty indifference, was the earnest and no doubt pigheaded belief shared in by Max Perkins and a few other people that the best single

[2] This was the title of Hansen's Review of *Look Homeward, Angel* in the October 26, 1929, issue of *The New York World.*

[3] John Chamberlain's review of *From Death to Morning* was in *The New York Times* on Friday, November 15, 1935. What it actually said was this: "In 'The Face of the War,' one sees the black troops, 'powerful big men, naive and wondering as children, incorrigibly unsuited to the military discipline.' But one does not see W. E. B. DuBois, or Abram Harris or Joe Louis, strongly marked individuals, marching by in the column of black troops. Yet the column must have contained men closer to DuBois or Harris or Joe Louis than to the generalized portrait that emerges from the Wolfe pages."

piece of writing, the truest, the most carefully planned, and in the end the most unassailable that I've ever done is in that book.[4] I'm not going to tell you what it is. Apparently, most of the critics didn't take the trouble to read it, and those that did, for the most part, dismissed it as chaotic, formless, a river of incondite and meaningless energy. Well, I'll stick to the piece and I'm willing to wait. I don't believe it's gone with the wind. I think the time will come when some one will really read it. So I don't feel bad about it or about the book.

Scott, I think, had a similar experience but a much more bitter one. My own feeling is that he never got justice from the critics for "Tender Is the Night." I admit deficiencies and weaknesses in the book, but I still think that he went deeper in the book and did better writing in it than in any of his previous books. But their minds, of course, were for the most part made up in advance. For years they've been saying that he would never write anything else and accordingly he suffered.

I still feel he has it in him to do fine work. I still feel something ought to be done about him and for him. But when he himself is so set against doing anything for himself, so bent, apparently, upon announcing, publishing and consummating his own ruin, who in the name of God can help him?

I did not mean this letter to be so long or take on such a melancholy hue. I wish I could be down there for a few days, to talk to you and see the mountains at this time.[5] I know how lovely they are. I'm afraid I can't make it at present, but will you do this for me, Ham? When you write me, and I hope it will be soon, will you tell me something about New Orleans, give me the names of a few people there? I've never gone around carrying letters of introduction. I promise not to bother your friends, but there is just a chance that during the winter I might get down there for a few days, and if I should I'd deeply appreciate any advice or information you could give me. So far as I'm concerned you are the greatest living authority on New Orleansiana.[6]

This is all, now. I pray for the success of "Courthouse Square." I know you have put your heart and your life in it. I know how deeply your integrity is involved in everything you do, and I hope that now you will get your true and fitting reward. It is bound to come sooner or later but I hope you get it while you still have the mischievous twinkle in your flashing eye.

Meanwhile, with love to you and the Missus, and to them thar hills,

[4] "The Web of Earth."

[5] Basso was living at Pisgah Forest, N.C.

[6] Basso was born and grew up in New Orleans, and began his career as a newspaper reporter there.

The following letter was in reply to a note from Jonathan Daniels inviting Wolfe to dinner when he came to Raleigh for the meeting of the Literary and Historical Association. Daniels had attended the University of North Carolina with Wolfe and been a member of The Carolina Playmakers with him, appearing in the cast of two of his early plays. He is now editor and part-owner of The Raleigh News and Observer, *and the author of* A Southerner Discovers The South, A Southerner Discovers New England, Tar Heels: A Portrait of North Carolina, Frontier on the Potomac, The Man of Independence, The End of Innocence, *etc.*

To JONATHAN DANIELS

865 First Avenue
New York, N.Y.
October 23, 1936

Dear Jonathan:

Thanks for your note. Bill Polk wrote and asked me if I could speak at the meeting of the State Literary and Historical Association, and I wrote him the other day and told him not to count on me as a speaker, because the chance of my being able to go to Raleigh is so uncertain, but that I would try to come just to see and talk with some of you again if I can make it. It is certainly one of the things I'd most like to do and, of course if I do, I shall be delighted to have dinner with you and Mrs. Daniels on December 4th. . . .

I have heard everywhere of the fine work you are doing with the *News and Observer.* Jim Boyd spoke to me about it last, and he said you were producing one of the finest newspapers in the country. I'm delighted to hear it. May I also take this belated opportunity of telling you how deeply I value the fine and generous notice that was given my work in the *News and Observer* a year or more ago, after "Of Time and the River" appeared. It was not only a notice which any one would have been proud and happy to receive, but of course I valued it all the more because it came from my own state. . . .

I went abroad this summer, mainly because I had royalties awaiting me in Germany and saw small prospect, in view of their present law against letting money get out of the country, of using my royalties unless I went there and spent them. So I did this. It was a good trip—a wonderfully exciting and interesting one but not always a happy one. I like Germany. It is a wonderful country. I like the German people, who have such magnificent qualities of fortitude, of indomitable effort and devotion. But I deeply fear that these grand qualities, all this devotion and fervor and self-sacrifice, has now been given to a misdirected purpose, a false ideal. Europe this summer was a volcano of poisonous and constricted hatreds which threatened to erupt at any moment. The great engines of war are ready, are on the rails, are being constantly enlarged and magnified, and it is hard to see how, if they continue in this way, they can control these tremendous machines they have created. It is good to be back home again and to feel that, whatever we may lack, we are free of these constricting national hatreds, that we still have space and air to move in.

I think you'd be surprised if you saw how politically-minded I've become. I've become enormously interested in politics for the first time in my life, not only in Europe, but even more here at home. I think what did the trick, more than anything else, was my trip across this summer on the *Europa*.

I travelled tourist class. My room-mate, an elderly liquor salesman of kindly and generous impulses, was a delightful travelling companion until he asked me who I was going to vote for. Very innocently, presuming that such matters could still be mentioned without the instant and complete severance of diplomatic relations, I answered, "Roosevelt." At that my erstwhile friend let out a squawk you could have heard on Sandy Hook, and from that time on there was no more peace or rest for me. He began to chase me around the boat. Wherever I went I could hear him pounding after me, like the Hound of Heaven, breathing stertorously and blowing hoarse and hot upon the back of my neck, panting out all the time that such an action as I proposed was nothing short of treason to my country, that the only means of salvation was to help elect that great American, that defender of the constitution and restorer of the system of free enterprise, Governor Langdon of Kansas. Still pounding ahead in my effort to escape, I paused long enough to look over my shoulder and suggest that it might not be a bad idea if he would learn how to spell and pronounce properly, before election day, the name of his hero.

After that I began to duck when I saw him coming, hid behind life boats, tried to look like a life preserver, etc., and finally, to my enormous relief, got invited up to first class, where I felt the story of my adventures might amuse my hosts. Not so. The moment that I told my little story and announced, innocently again, my dark electoral intention, the squawk that went up made the disturbance in tourist class sound like the cooing of a dove. Their boiled shirts began to roll right up their backs like window-shades. Maidenly necks that but a moment before were white and graceful as the swan's became instantly so distended with the energies of patriotic rage that diamond dog collars and ropes of pearls were snapped and sent flying like so many pieces of rock and string. I was informed that if I voted for this vile Communist, for this sinister Fascist, for this scheming and contriving Socialist, and his gang of co-conspirators, I had no longer any right to consider myself an American citizen. I was doing my share to help destroy the country, etc.

Well, the upshot of it was that the more they talked, the less I believed them. Seriously, it was astounding. I have never, so far as my own experience and observation is concerned, seen such bitterness of feeling, such distorted prejudice, such downright hatred as I saw among these people on the *Europa,* and as I have seen among other people in this class since then. If the election of November third were to be determined by the first class passenger list of a crack trans-Atlantic liner, I have little doubt what the result would be. But fortunately, it will not be determined there. As you know yourself, there are still a lot of us truck-drivers left in the world.

Anyway, I've got all het up over politics for the first time and I agree with Mr. Dodd, whom I'm sure your father knows, and who is our ambassador in Berlin. He is a historian, and he told me that he thought this was the most important national election that had been held in this country since 1860. I want to do something about it. In spite of all the mistakes that have been made, in spite of all the formidable and disquieting expenditure of money, the grievous errors that I believe few intelligent people would deny, I nevertheless feel the worst calamity that could happen [to] this country at the present time would be the election of a reactionary government, and that this present administration, whatever its errors of commission or omission may have been, has made the only decisive movement that has been made in the direction of social progress and social justice since the administrations of Woodrow Wilson.

So I want to take the stump. I want to write letters to the newspapers. I should particularly like to riddle the editorial columns of the *New York Herald Tribune* with cannister and grape. Except, what is the use of bringing your guns up and cutting loose upon a graveyard?

In your capacity as editor of the *News and Observer,* you must have read the editorial columns of a good many newspapers. Well, honestly, have you ever known the state of journalism to sink to such an abyss of imbecilic foolishness as it has in some of these papers in recent months? I can't believe it when I read it. Such irreconcilable things and systems and ideas as Communism, Fascism and Socialism are lumped together in one indiscriminate wad and hurled wildly in the direction of the President. The other night on the radio I heard a speaker accuse Mr. Roosevelt of all three of them in the same breath. About the only thing I have not yet heard him accused of is of plotting and conspiring with the King of England and Herr Hitler to restore the ex-Crown Prince of Germany and establish an autocratic monarchy. In the name of God have these people lost their reason utterly or do they have such contempt for the public intelligence, the understanding of the ordinary man, that they think he will swallow anything regardless of the meaning or implication, so long as they shout it loud and long enough?

Herr Hitler gets up one day and makes a speech in which he attacks the idea of democracy, and the *Herald-Tribune,* by some fantastic and unfathomable editorial process, converts Herr Hitler's attack upon democracy as an evidence and a warning of what Roosevelt will do. The next day some one in Russia answers Hitler's attack and this too is translated as an overwhelming evidence that the program and ideas of the Communists and of the President are identical. This morning the *Herald-Tribune* heads its alleged account of the President's recent tour through New England with this headline: "Roosevelt Trip in Connecticut Snarls Traffic." I think, considering all its implications and all that has gone before, this is the most astoundingly funny headline I've ever read. One sees the motored cavalcade of the New Deal making its sinister way through the New England states, causing automobiles to bump each other and innocent women and children to faint in the crowds that gathered. It is all, one gathers, part of a deep, dark and sinister conspiracy to undermine American institutions, to scrap the constitution and to stamp out the spirit of rugged individualism which we inherited from our forefathers.

These are strange and disquieting symptoms for me but perhaps I shall recover my normal temperature after November third. Meanwhile I am back at work again on a new book. It's all coming with a rush and, believe it or not, for several weeks now I've done more than 5000 words a day.

I didn't mean this letter to be so long, Jonathan, but it was good to hear from you and I suppose that, remembering some of the all-night sessions we all used to have at Chapel Hill, I couldn't resist temptation to let a little of it roll out on paper.

With the hope of seeing you all soon, and with best wishes for you and Mrs. Daniels,

XIV

THE BREAK WITH SCRIBNERS

1936–1937

In November, 1936, Wolfe's conviction that he must leave Scribners was heightened by a disagreement with them concerning the suit which was brought against him and them by Marjorie Dorman, William Samuel Dorman, Louise Dorman Leonard and Mary Roberta Dorman from whom Wolfe had rented his apartment at 40 Verandah Place, Brooklyn, in 1931, and who now claimed that they had been libelled by certain passages in "No Door" in From Death to Morning. *Scribners, and the attorney whom they had retained to represent themselves and Wolfe, were in favor of settling the suit, but Wolfe was violently opposed to settlement, although he finally unwillingly consented.*

The following rough draft fragments to Perkins and the note to Charles Scribner III were found in Wolfe's own files and never mailed. They may have been written at almost any time or times during 1936 or 1937, but because they contain similarities to other letters written to Perkins in November–December, 1936, they are included as of that date.

To MAXWELL E. PERKINS

[New York City]

[November or December, 1936?]

Dear Max:

I am writing to tell you that I have at last taken the step of communicating formally to other publishers the severance of my relations with Charles Scribner's Sons. It is true that no formal relation between us existed, and that both you and Charlie have told me I was free to go. But I think the relation existed in our minds at any rate, and for me—I believe for you, as well—it existed in the heart.

If any apprehensions concerning my letter to the publishers may exist in the minds of any of you—and I know they will not exist in yours—let me assure you at once that I spoke of my former publisher in such a way as left no doubt as to my own earnestness and sincerity, or as to my own belief in the integrity and [high capacity?] of your house. No one could read that letter without understanding that the necessity for this severance is a matter of deep and poignant regret to all of us.

I am sick and tired, but I believe that I shall rise again, as I have done before—I know that for a time now the world will say that you and I have fallen out, that the great sounding-board of rumor and malicious gossip that echoes round and round the granite walls of this little universe, the city, will frame its hundred little stories and all of them, as usual, will be false. I know that they will say this and that—well, *let* them say. That is honestly the way I feel now.

The editorial relation between us, which began, it seems to me, so hopefully, and for me so wonderfully, has now lost its initial substance. It has become a myth—and what is worse than that, an untrue myth—and it seems to me that both of us are victims of that myth. You know the terms of the myth well enough—it was venomously recorded by a man named De Voto in *The Saturday Review of Literature* during this past summer—and the terms of the myth are these: that I cannot write my books without your assistance, that there exists at Scribners an "assembly line" that must fit the great dismembered portions of my manuscript together into a semblance of unity, that I am unable to perform the functions of an artist for myself. How far from the truth these suppositions are, you know yourself better than anyone on earth. There are few men —certainly no man I have ever known—who is more sure of *purpose* than myself. There are very many men, of course, who are more sure of *means* —but that assurance, with such men, is just a small one—with me it is a hard and thorny one because my means must be my own.

I know you will not be uncandid enough to deny that these differences and misunderstandings have been profound and fundamental.

Plainly may I tell you that I think that looking like a plain man, you are not a plain man; that speaking like a simple man, you are not a simple man: that speaking in words and phrases that as time went on [indicated and assured me?] by their simplicity and [————?] directness, so that they seemed to be the very [charter?] of your soul, I do not now believe that they were so.

In fact, I now believe you are not a plain man—you are an un-plain man—I do not believe you are a simple man—you are an un-simple man —I do not believe your words. . . .

I impeach your virtues and your conduct: may I tell you frankly, plainly, that I do not believe they have achieved and maintained always the quality of [unconditioned innocence?], faith, good will, and simple and direct integrity that you have always claimed for them.

The fault, I think, is here: that having so much that belonged to humankind, you lacked—or you with-held—what makes us one. And therefore I renounce you, who have already, for so long a time, renounced me and got so safely, with no guilt or wrong, so freely rid of me.

And I am writing therefore now to tell you that I am, upon the date of these words, dissolving a relationship that does not exist, renouncing a contract that was never made, severing myself and of my own accord a bond of loyalty, devotion and self-sacrifice that existed solely, simply and entirely within my own mind, and to my own past grief of doubt, my present grief of sorrow, loss, and final understanding.

With infinite regret, my dear Max, with the deepest and most genuine sorrow, with an assurance—if you will generously accept it—of my friendship for yourself,

Faithfully and sincerely yours

I understand that you have been afraid that some day I might "write about" you— Well, you need not be afraid any longer. The day has come—and I am writing about you. Your fears have been realized—I think you will find that your fears, like most fears, have been exaggerated.

This is one of the saddest and most melancholy occasions of my life. To say now that I have "thought about" this thing, or "arrived at certain conclusions" would be ludicrous. I have not thought about the thing—I have sweat blood about it: I have carried it with me like a waking nightmare in the day time, and like a sleeping torment in the night. I have not "arrived" at my conclusions: I have come to them through every anguish that the brain, heart, nerves and soul of man can know—and I am *there* at last. I can't go on in this way: it is a matter of the most desperate uncertainty whether I can go on at all. For seven years I have been increasingly aware of the seepage of my talents, the diminution of my powers, the dilution of my force—and I can not go on.

I am therefore asking you to send me at once an unqualified and unequivocal statement to this effect: that I have discharged all debts and contractual obligations to the firm of Charles Scribner's Sons, and that I am no longer under any obligation to them, whether personal, financial, or contractual on my part.

I want you to make this statement in your own language, but according to the terms I have mentioned, if you think them just.

In the name of honesty and sincerity, I can write no more than here I have written: in the name of justice and of fairness you can, and will, write no less.

I beg and request you to send me at once, without intervention of personal conversations or telephone call, this letter that I am asking you to write.

TO CHARLES SCRIBNER III

[New York City]

[November or December, 1936?]

Dear Charles:

I have upon this present date written a letter to Maxwell Perkins in which I have told him that the firm of Charles Scribner's Sons are no longer, for any publication save those which have previously been published by Charles Scribner's Sons, my publisher. It is a painful and chastising experience to renounce an agreement that does not exist, an understanding for the future that, however undefined, was mine alone, and in my mind alone; but in order that there may be no misunderstanding of my purpose, or of the meaning of this letter, I do state here and now that you are no longer my publisher, that you will never again be my publisher for anything that I may ever write; that I hereby renounce, adjure, abrogate, deny and terminate any requests, claims, offers, inducements, obligations, commitments, or persuasions which you have made formerly, shall make now, or in the future make.

The following is the letter which Wolfe actually sent to Perkins in November, 1936.

To MAXWELL E. PERKINS

865 First Avenue
New York, N.Y.
November 12, 1936

Dear Max:

I think you should now write me a letter in which you explicitly state the nature of my relations with Charles Scribner's Sons. I think you ought to say that I have faithfully and honorably discharged all obligations to Charles Scribner's Sons, whether financial, personal or contractual, and that no further agreement or obligation of any sort exists between us.

I must tell you plainly now what you must know already, that, in view of all that has happened in the last year and a half, the differences of opinion and belief, the fundamental disagreements that we have discussed so openly, so frankly, and so passionately a thousand times, and which have brought about this unmistakable and grievous severance, I think you should have written this letter that I am asking you to write long before this. I am compelled by your failure to do so to ask you, in simple justice, to write it now.

I think it is unfair to put a man in a position where he is forced to deny an obligation that does not exist, to refuse an agreement that was never offered and never made. I think it is also unfair to try to exert, at no expense to oneself, such control of a man's future and his future work as will bring one profit if that man succeeds, and that absolves one from any commitments of any kind should he fail. I also think it is unfair that a man without income, with little money, and with no economic security against the future, who has time and again in the past refused offers and proposals that would have brought him comfort and security, should now, at a time when his reputation has been obscured and when there are no offers and little market for his work, be compelled to this last and sorrowful exercise of his fruitless devotion. And finally, I do not think that life is a game of chess, and if it were, I could not be a player.

I have nothing more to say here except to tell you that I am your friend and that my feeling toward you is unchanged.

For the full text of Perkins' three answers to this letter, see Editor to Author: The Letters of Maxwell E. Perkins, *pages 115–117. The first was a personal note dated November 17, in which Perkins merely promised to answer Wolfe's letter the following day, and added: "I never knew a soul with whom I felt I was in such fundamentally complete agreement as you. . . . I don't fully understand your letter, but I'll answer it as best I can. You must surely know, though, that any publisher would leap at the chance to publish you. . . . You have with us at present a balance of over $2,000, all but about $500. of which is overdue."*

The second was also a personal note dated November 18, enclosing a more formal business letter, and saying in part: "On my part there has been no 'severance.' I can't express certain kinds of feelings very comfortably, but you must realize what my feelings are toward you. . . . Your work has been the foremost interest in my life and I have never doubted for your future on any grounds except, at times, on those of your being able to control the vast mass of material you have accumulated and have to form into books. You seem to think I have tried to control you. I only did that when you asked my help and then I did the best I could. . . ."

The third, more formal letter was also dated November 18, and said in part: "You have faithfully and honorably discharged all obligations to us, and no further agreement of any sort exists between us with respect to the future. Our relations are simply those of a publisher who profoundly admires the work of an author and takes great pride in publishing whatever he may of that author's writing . . . We do not wholly understand parts of your letter, where you speak of us as putting you in a position of denying an obligation that does not exist, for we do not know how we have done that; or where you refer to 'exerting control of a man's future,' which we have no intention of doing at all, and would not have the power or right to do. There are other phrases, in that part of your letter, that I do not understand, one of which is that which refers to us as being absolved from any commitments of any kind, 'should the author fail.' If this and other phrases signify that you think you should have a contract from us if our relations are to continue, you can certainly have one. We should be delighted to have one. You must surely know the faith this house has in you. There are, of course, limits in terms beyond which nobody can go in a contract, but we should expect to make one that would suit you if you told us what was required."

The following letter to a reader who had accused Wolfe of anti-Semitism was never mailed.

To ————

865 First Avenue
New York, N.Y.
November 18, 1936

Dear Sir:

I have read your letter of November 15th. While I agree and sympathize with your feeling about anti-Semitism, I cannot agree that my little book, "The Story of a Novel," shows any trace of that hostile and ugly feeling which, I am sure, we both abhor. Certainly, nothing of the sort was intended in that little book and if anything in it is possible of such interpretation, I, for one, would be the first to regret it and to deprecate it.

I do not have a copy of the book here at the present time but I am sending for one because I want to read it again and see if I can find out what it is that you object to. Meanwhile, may I not say this, in all kindness and in a spirit of fair reasonableness—that while I understand and sympathize with your deep feeling, it seems to me that your own remarks, about "untutored Southerners" or Gentile students whom you have encountered in various large Eastern universities where you taught and who were, you say, far more "boorish and rapacious, conceited and arrogant, more utterly repulsive culturally than any Jew that moved in the circles I frequented," are not, it seems to me, conducive to the promotion of the spirit of racial liberty and tolerance that, I am sure, we both share.

I know that you will join me in my very sincere hope that this spirit of tolerance will become universal.

To WILLIAM T. POLK

865 First Avenue
New York, N.Y.
December 2, 1936

Dear Bill:

By now you have my telegram telling you that it is impossible for me to come to the meeting. I want to follow it up with this word of explanation which I hope you will get before the meeting opens. I have been working here two months now as hard as I can go, and because I am now finishing something which I have promised to have ready for reading, and I hope for publication (not in book form) within another week or two,[1] it seems to me that I ought to keep going at this job until I finish it. In addition to that there have recently been more legal complications. Charlie Scribner and I are having to consult a lawyer on a matter of common interest to both of us.[2] I think they feel I'd better be on hand until we decide on action.

I am pretty tired. I've just stayed in and worked for two months now and I haven't even had a haircut, which of course won't be news to you. No, it wasn't the fact that I'd have to get a haircut that kept me from going to North Carolina: it was all the other things. I'm going to keep on here as hard as I can go until Christmas and then I'm coming South for a week or ten days' holiday. If you are there at that time, I hope to see you.

Bill, I am genuinely proud to know the Historical Association wanted me to appear upon their program. The only thing that distresses me is that a program arrived last night and I see that I'm really listed to appear on the same evening with you. It troubles me very much to think that my failure to come may cause you embarrassment, or to think that the Association really believed I'd given you a definite promise to be there. I did try to make it plain to you all along that it was doubtful whether I could attend the meeting and that my attendance was understood to be tentative. If there is any misunderstanding about this, won't you please explain it for me to the members of the Association and tell them how grateful I am for their invitation and how sorry I am that these present circumstances have prevented me from accepting it. Also, I hope that I get invited again.

I'm coming down to North Carolina in a few weeks for the first time in seven years to see a few of you again. It means a great deal to me— I think you understand how much. I think also the time is coming when I may have something to say to North Carolina that will interest it. But I'm not sure that I am ready yet. When I do feel ready, I hope you will give me another chance to say my piece.

Meanwhile, I send all my warmest wishes for a successful meeting, and my friendliest greetings to you and to the Literary and Historical Association.

[1] "I Have a Thing to Tell You."
[2] The libel suit brought against them by the Dorman family.

To FRED W. WOLFE

865 First Avenue
New York, N.Y.
December 7, 1936

Dear Fred:

Thanks for your letter. Yes, the pecans came in good condition and I have been devouring them with great relish for a week or so. I am glad to know that Mabel and Ralph are now at home. . . . I am very sorry to hear of all their hard luck and of Mabel's injury and, like you, I hope this new move will mark the beginning of a better time. My troubles still continue. There have even recently been additional legal complications but I hope somehow to live through all this trouble and to achieve some harbor of my own. At any rate I am faced with the stern necessity of working with all my strength and energy now, if only for the payoff of the lawyers' bills to defend myself against the crooks and try to keep my head above the water. Of course, in this hard time, so full of trouble and peril and injustice, I can only hope those who say they are my friends and who say they wish me well will stand by me, and where their own emotional or personal demands or interests are concerned, will just try to go as easy on me as they can. Few people who have never experienced the strain of creating anything, who do not know the terrible exhaustion of energy and of nervous endurance, the need for peace and concentration, and all the elements of publicity, parasitism, sensationalism, slander and treachery that strike at the very vitals of the artist's life, can understand just what it is the artist is up against and how desperately he hopes that his friends and family will try to act as thoughtfully, as humanely and as unselfishly as they can. And if they cannot help him, that they will at any rate try to refrain from doing anything that will add to the troubles he already has, or betray him into the hands of the people who would ruin and defeat him if they could.

I plan to come South Christmas for the first time in seven years. Whether I shall get to Asheville or not, I do not know. I am desperately tired and need a rest. At the present moment I do not feel that I can endure to be pawed over, talked to nineteen hours a day, pulled and tugged and yanked until every separate nerve is screaming with exasperation, and otherwise maddened or exhausted by people who are, I suppose, well-meaning, but whose total effort seems to be to try to kill you with what I suppose must be described as well-intentioned but inconsiderate and thoughtless kindness. I hope to get to Chapel Hill, and if I have time, I may go even farther South to New Orleans. As for Asheville, in my present frame of mind, my present need for peace and rest, I don't know that I can stand it.

I am neither a criminal nor an angel. I am just an honest man. I have no desire either to be sneered at or reviled by rascals, or fawned upon by fools. If I ever came back to the town in which, through accident of birth, I first saw the light of day, I could only hope that I would be met neither by a lynching mob nor by a brass band. If and when I do come back, I want to come back my own way, to be exhibited, shown about and exploited by no one. And if and when I do come back, I shall come back in that way—as my own man, my own master, and very quick and strong to resent any intrusion upon my own liberty and my private life.

This is all for the present. There is very little news to tell you except that in spite of all the sinister and exhausting troubles which have come to me during the last year, in view of what I may ironically describe as my "success," I still keep on working and shall continue so to work as long as I have strength to draw a breath or lift a hand. I hope this finds all of you well and enjoying some success. With thanks again for the pecans and with best wishes for everyone,

To THEA VOELCKER

865 First Avenue
New York, N.Y.
December 15, 1936

Dear Thea:

This will only be a very short letter because I want to get it off to you in time for Christmas and the *Bremen* sails to-night. I am going back to my home in the South for several days at Christmas and I shall try to write some better answer to the letters you have sent me. Just let me tell you now how much I value your letters and how much I thank you for having written me as you have. The reason, really, that I haven't had a chance to answer you is just that I have been working as hard as I can since I came back, and even when I stop working my mind keeps on. I have done a tremendous amount of work, over 200,000 words since October. I know you will be glad to hear it. Of course, I'm a long way off from having anything completed, but I have the whole thing shaped and working in my mind now and pouring from me in a tremendous flood. I am very tired and when my mind gets very tired it is stimulated to terrific activity, so that my sleep at night is broken by hundreds of dreams, but everything will be all right as long as I work.

I am looking forward to my trip home. You know, I was practically an exile for years in my native state, they became so angry at me because of the first book I wrote. But now, I think, they feel better and they want to see me again.

I just want to get this letter off to you in time for Christmas, to wish you a happy Christmas and all happiness and joy for the New Year. I shall probably write you from New Orleans, where I intend to spend a few days with friends during the holidays. It is a lovely old town, deep in the South, at the mouth of the Mississippi River, where the river joins the Gulf of Mexico. The population is composed largely of old French settlers. The life has been dominated by this French influence, by the negro and by the almost tropical climate. It is one of the most interesting cities in America and I hope some day you'll be able to see it.

This is all for the present as I want to take this letter out and mail it in time for the *Bremen*. And now good-bye, good luck, and may Christmas bring all happiness and good cheer to you.

Norman H. Pearson was editing The Oxford Anthology of American Literature *in conjunction with William Rose Benét, and had asked Wolfe's permission to include in that book a section of his work, preferably the portion of* Look Homeward, Angel *which describes the death of Ben. He finally used instead the section from* Of Time and the River *describing the death of Gant, in accordance with Wolfe's preference expressed in the following letter. Pearson at this time was a graduate student in American Literature at Yale, and is now a member of the Department of English there.*

To NORMAN H. PEARSON

865 First Avenue
New York, N.Y.

December 18, 1936

Dear Pearson:

I told you I would write you in a day or two after I'd had a chance to talk to Mr. Perkins about the matter we were discussing the other night. I saw Mr. Perkins last night and his own feeling, I think, is that if you had space, the best selection would be the series of scenes which deal with the death of Gant in "Of Time and the River." I have looked these up in the printed edition and they extend from page 210 to page 273 inclusive, and cover chapters XXI–XXXIV.

This, I know, is a very long selection and I don't know whether you can print it, although in a book of the dimensions you describe to me, with double columns, it would not, of course, take up as many pages as it does in mine. I think you yourself rather prefer the death of Ben scenes in "Look Homeward, Angel," and I am glad you like them because I have always liked them too. I can certainly not urge any scene upon you. It is difficult enough to recommend one's own work, particularly when one has been away from it and has not looked at it for months or years. He is likely to forget, and besides a writer's private judgment on what he has written may be valid for him without being valid for the reading public. The only reason, therefore, I should be inclined to second Mr. Perkins' selection is that I have never yet known him to err in judgment. His discriminating faculty is, I think, by all odds the most accurate I've ever known, and I would therefore accept his judgment about a piece of writing rather than my own.

I think I understand some of your own reasons for preferring the scenes about the death of Ben in "Look Homeward, Angel." I think you felt . . . that these scenes have a quality of poignant sharpness, a kind of bitterness even, which the scenes about the death of Gant in "Of Time and the River" may not have, and in this I think you are probably right. It's awfully hard to talk about one's own work, Pearson, but I would suggest this to you, relying as I do upon Mr. Perkins' judgment, that regardless of what may or may not be the better book—I, of course, am not the person to decide that—I do think "Of Time and the River" was more properly my *own* book. "Look Homeward, Angel" was a young man's book, a first book. I believe and hope I succeeded in making it completely my own book before I got through: the fact remains, however, that I was far more under the influence of writers I profoundly admired—notably, of course, Mr. James Joyce—than in the work which I was to do later. For that reason I suggest to you that "Of Time and the River" is probably more myself and more indicative of the direction in which I may go than "Look Homeward, Angel."

I suggest further—and in this I am simply following out what I believe to be Mr. Perkins' feeling as he explained it to me last night—that the sections dealing with the death of Gant in their entirety perhaps have greater sweep, include greater variety of what Perkins called "the different kinds of things you can do" than the death of Ben. . . . More briefly, I might explain it this way: the death of Ben is a tragedy; the death of Gant is not a tragedy. The death of Ben is a tragedy because Ben is a young man, little more than a boy, who has missed, has never found, has never gotten in life, any of the things he longed for and that he should have had. The death of Gant, manifestly, is not a tragedy in this way because Gant is an old man, ridden with disease and pain. His death has been awaited for years. When it comes, it comes almost as a blessed relief to everyone.

Therefore, the quality and purpose in the two scenes, although each of them deals with the death of a man, are entirely different. The important and valuable thing, I think, in the death of Ben is the personal tragedy of the death of Ben. The important thing in the death of Gant . . . is the effect of the death of the old man upon a large number of people—his friends, his children, his family, the people of the town. I would suggest to you, therefore, that although the death of Gant may lack a quality of intensity and tragedy which the death of Ben has, the death of Gant covers a wider and more varied sweep of life and character. Its implications, I believe, are greater.

I inferred from our conversation the other evening—which, by the way, I thought was a mighty good evening: I hope you enjoyed it and that we can repeat it some time—that you may have felt there was some indication in "Of Time and the River" that I had changed my position, modified my feeling, compromised my integrity with regard to some of the characters in the death of Gant scenes who also appear in the death of Ben scenes. Well, Pearson, all I can tell you is that I think I have somewhat changed my position, I have somewhat modified my feeling, but I have compromised not one atom. I do not have the same feeling of anger and bitterness about these people as I may have had in my first book, but this certainly does not mean compromise. It rather means, I think, that I may have been full of anger, of fury and of bitterness towards some of these characters, towards the whole vexed and tragic scheme of life, in my first book as I was not to the same degree in the second. But I suggest to you that is not compromise. I will not be vain enough to suggest it is growth, but at any rate I was a young man when I wrote "Look Homeward, Angel": I am approaching middle age now. I think I know more about life, more about living, more about people now than I did then. I know that I have a deeper understanding, more sympathy, more compassion, than I had ten years ago. I hope it is reflected in what I do. But I can tell you definitely that I think it would be improper and false if I attempted now to write the way I did in "Look Homeward, Angel," because I do not feel just that way now. This is a kind of integrity the artist has got to maintain: he has got to change, he has got to grow, and at the same time he has got to try to keep true.

I hope this makes my own feeling in the matter plain. Forgive me for having written at such length or for seeming to argue in this matter. I have merely tried to indicate my own feelings and what I believe is also the feeling of Mr. Perkins, who knows more about me and what I can do than anyone on earth, and whose judgment I assure you you can rely upon.

But whatever you do will be all right. I am only too proud to be represented at all in a book of the sort you described to me. I know that any selection you make would be a good one—the death of Ben, the Bascom Hawke piece—I should not be sorry to see any of these pieces included in the book. As a final suggestion, Perkins told me last night that he had been surprised that no one yet had used the death of Gant scenes. He suggested—and I recommend this to your consideration—that the reason . . . was not only one of length (the Bascom Hawke is longer, by the way) but that, being a part of the fabric of the whole book as they are, few people yet realize how complete the scenes dealing with the death of Gant are in themselves.

This is all for the present. I hope it helps you. At any rate, I've tried to indicate some of my own opinions and those of Mr. Perkins, and I hope you find them useful. Drop me a line and let me know what you are going to do and call me up when you come to town. I enjoyed the other evening and hope to see you again.

Marjorie C. Fairbanks, to whom the following note was written, had first known Wolfe in the early 1920s when he was at Harvard.

To MARJORIE C. FAIRBANKS

865 First Avenue
New York, N.Y.

December 24, 1936

Dear Marjorie:

Thanks for your Christmas card. I'm terribly sorry to hear you've been so ill. Please write and tell me what the trouble was.

I hope I'm going to survive—I've never been as tired as I am now. I've done a quarter of a million words in less than three months. I'd like to sleep solid for about a week but I want to get away from here, out of this room, away from the manuscript, try to forget it. I'm going home the day after Christmas for the first time in seven years. Yes, I think they'll let me come back now. I don't know that all is forgiven but they asked me to make a speech,[1] which is something, isn't it? Of course, I didn't make it. I'm going the whole way to New Orleans first, after a day's stop-off in Richmond, where your pal Hank Canby assured me the other day he will be guzzling egg-nogs at Miss Glasgow's house. If I can get past the egg-nogs I'll be in New Orleans for New Year's. I wish you could be there too to drink absinthe with me—if they still serve it. I

[1] The speech at the meeting of the North Carolina Literary and Historical Association in Raleigh.

haven't been there since I was nine years old. It was a lovely old town then. It ought to be a good trip.

Goodbye, Marjorie, for the present. I'll be back here after New Year's. I think I'll be fine after a few days' rest. I've a grand book coming if I live to finish it. Please write and tell me how you are and call me up when you come to town. Meanwhile, all my best for a happy Christmas and a good New Year.

Ever since the exchange of correspondence between Wolfe and Perkins of November 12, 17 and 18, Wolfe had continued to write, but never to mail, letters to complete his severance from Scribners. He had taken these letters with him when he had gone south to New Orleans, and was still brooding over them when, in early January, 1937, he became enraged at Perkins for having given his probable New Orleans address to Cornelius Mitchell, his attorney in the case over his manuscripts.

The defendant's attorney had suggested a settlement of this case whereby Wolfe would pay the sum of $500. This Wolfe had refused to do. Now the defendant, in reply to this refusal, had threatened to make public certain "salacious matter" in the Wolfe manuscripts still in his possession, to aid the Dorman family in their libel suit, and to stir up other suits in Asheville. These latest developments had been communicated to Mitchell by the lawyers acting for Wolfe against the defendant in New Jersey, and Mitchell had urged upon Perkins the necessity of communicating with Wolfe in New Orleans to ask him to return immediately to New York.

To Wolfe, in his state of exhaustion and irritation, this was the last straw. He blamed Perkins not only for divulging his address, but also for having given what he considered weak and pusillanimous advice in the matter, and this, in turn, brought to a head all his earlier complex grievances against Perkins and Scribners. The following letters and telegrams, sent and unsent, mark the climax of Wolfe's severance from Scribners, although he did not actually complete the break by approaching other publishers until eight months later.

The following letter to Perkins was written by Wolfe in New Orleans but never mailed.

To MAXWELL E. PERKINS

The Roosevelt
New Orleans, La.
[January 5(?), 1937]

Cornelius Mitchell has written me an astounding letter in answer to one I wrote him in [the] —— matter. I had supposed the evidence against —— to be complete and overwhelming, but now, instead of telling me what we are going to do, he tells me of fantastic threats that —— is making, and requests my instant return to New York. This I unconditionally refuse to do. I have come here for a rest of which I was in desperate need; this amazing letter has caused me the most intense distress; I have been hounded by this shameful business for a year and a half now—and it has got to stop! I am an honorable man and an artist—and the cursed thing now is that my work and talent are being destroyed. Mitchell says he got my address here from you. In the name of God, knowing the state of my health and the utter exhaustion I was in when I left New York, how could you do it?

Max, I have begun to lose faith in your power to stick or to help when a man is in danger. I know now that I must fight this whole horrible business out alone—the whole vicious complex of slander, blackmail, theft and parasitic infamy that . . . usually destroys the artist under this accursed and rotten system that now exists in America. You are going to get out from under when you see me threatened with calamity—but, in the name of God, in the name of all the faith and devotion and unquestioning belief I have had in you—if you cannot help me, for Christ's sake do not add your own influence to those who are now trying to destroy me. Under *no* conditions, save the death or serious illness of a member of my family, give my address hereafter to anyone. Before I come back to that black and vicious horror again, I must restore myself. I shall fight to the end, but for Christ's sake have manhood now not to aid in the attack until I can try to mend a little in energy and health.

The following fragment to Cornelius Mitchell was found in Wolfe's own files. It may or may not have been recopied into the letter which Wolfe actually sent to Mitchell from New Orleans.

Probably to CORNELIUS MITCHELL

[New Orleans, La.]

[January 7(?), 1937]

. . . heretofore—and it is gone. They may exhaust my energy and my youth—they have done so heretofore, and they are *almost* gone. But they shall not take my life from me. They shall not take my power to work from me—I shall now fight with all the strength left in me to save my talent—

my work—my creative integrity. You tell me that I must now return to New York by January 7th to discuss the ways and means of meeting the threats. . . . I tell you that in these conditions—if this is your final proposal, all you have to offer—I can not return.

I know I am alone now. You suggest that we can talk with Perkins. We can not talk with Perkins any more. The house of Scribners has now unmistakably indicated a desire for the complete severance of their publishing relations with me. As for Mr. Perkins—he is the greatest editor of this generation. I revered and honored him also as the greatest man, the greatest friend, the greatest character I had ever known. Now I can only tell you that I still think he is the greatest editor of our time. As for the rest—he is an honest but a timid man. He is not a man for danger—I expect no help from him.

The following wire sent at 6:57 A.M. on January 7, was the first communication which Wolfe actually sent to Perkins from New Orleans. Many versions of longer but similar wires which were not sent are still among Wolfe's papers, written in a hasty and almost indecipherable scrawl.

To MAXWELL E. PERKINS
[Telegram]

New Orleans, La.
January 7, 1937

How dare you give anyone my address?

Perkins did not answer this wire, but on January 9, Wolfe sent him another.

To MAXWELL E. PERKINS
[Telegram]

New Orleans, La.
January 9, 1937

What is your offer?

To this Perkins wired: "If you refer to book we shall make it verbally when you return as arrangements will depend on your requirements. Gave no one your address but suggested two possibilities to your lawyer who thought it important for you to communicate." Scribners never did make Wolfe a definite offer, probably because Perkins felt that Wolfe's desire for a severance was too deep and too complex for him to stay with Scribners anyway.

Meanwhile Wolfe had mailed the following letter of January 9, together with the letter which he had written on December 15, but postponed mailing.

To MAXWELL E. PERKINS

[The Roosevelt]
[New Orleans, La.]
Saturday, January 9, 1937

Dear Max:

I'm sorry I telegraphed you as I did. And I don't even know now exactly what I telegraphed you. But maybe you can understand a little when I tell you that all this worry, grief, and disappointment of the last two years has almost broken me, and finally this last letter of Mitchell's was almost the last straw. I was desperately in need of rest and quiet—the letter destroyed it all, ruined all the happiness and joy I had hoped to get from this trip—the horrible injustice of the whole thing has almost maddened me. I can understand none of it any more—first the Boyd thing, then Mrs. Bernstein and the [——s?] of last year, then the libel suit, then this latest . . . threat of ——'s . . . most of all your own attitude.

Max, I simply can't understand: you yourself urged—not only urged but indignantly insisted—that I take action against —— at a time when I was practically decided to let these ——s take what they could rather than let them take my life—my work—my talent. Now, you speak of paying him off—you told me only a few weeks ago that you would pay the $500 and be done with it—this after insisting at first that I take action, recover the manuscripts and that there should be no compromise. In God's name, what is your meaning? Are you—the man I trusted and reverenced above all else in the world—trying, for some mad reason I can not even guess, to destroy me? How am I going to interpret the events of the past two years? Don't you want me to go on? Don't you want me to write another book? Don't you hope for my life—my growth—the fulfillment of my talent? In Christ's name, what is it, then? My health is well-nigh wrecked —worry, grief, and disillusionment has almost destroyed my talent—is *this* what you wanted? And why?

As for Mr. Mitchell I have given up trying to fathom his motives or his reasoning. When I last saw him a few weeks ago, it seemed to me that our course was clear—that we were in entire agreement—that the evidence against —— was complete and overwhelming. At this time he gave me ——'s offer of compromise for $500. . . . My own feeling was absolutely against such a settlement, particularly since the offer was couched in such ambiguous and obscure phrases that it was impossible to know just what I was going to get in return for my money. I understood that Mr. Mitchell felt this way, too, and that it would be improper to agree to such a settlement. In addition, I wrote him a very long and very clear letter about the proposal of settlement . . . pointed out numerous ambiguities in phrasing, and said that I wanted to go ahead and compel ——, if I could, to return the manuscripts. . . . At the time of my conversation with Mr. Mitchell, he also mentioned ——'s threat to publish "salicious matter" from the manuscripts. I told Mr. Mitchell that this threat was blackmail pure and simple—and, regardless of the proposal of settlement, it would be the height of folly to yield to such a threat now. Well, the result is that this latest letter from Mitchell, instead of saying what *we* are going to do, is an apprehensive account of ——'s . . . threats from beginning to end. In addition to the publication of the alleged "salacious matter," he is going to aid and abet the libel suit of the Brooklyn woman, and "stir up" libel suits in North Carolina. As for the statement that I opened a trunkful of manuscripts and told him to help himself, this is just a lie. . . .

And you—where are you, Max? Have you, too, become terrified at these threats of libel suits? Are you going to advise me to yield . . . simply because the interests of Scribners might be involved? What are we going to do? This thing is like death to me. Have we really reached the end? I fear desperately we have—it is all so tragically sad—and as for that powerful and magnificent talent I had two years ago—in the name of God is that to be lost entirely, destroyed under the repeated assaults and criminalities of this blackmail society under which we live? *Now* I know what happens to the artist in America. *Now* I know what must be changed. *Now* truly, henceforth and forever after, I shall work with all my strength for revolution—for the abolition of this vile and rotten system under which we live—for a better world, a better life.

And you? You are in very many ways the best person I have ever known, the person for whom I have had the greatest reverence and devotion—but in some few ways, perhaps, I am a better man than you. Forgive me these wild telegrams. Even if we have now come to the end of our publishing connection—a connection for which I have sacrificed everything—a connection that is now being severed when I have nothing left, when no one wants me—for God's sake let us try to save our belief and faith in each other—a belief and faith that I still have—that I hope you have not lost. I would to God I were a better man, but I will not cease trying to be a better one—and for you, I cannot bear to see you just a good but timid man. I am in deadly peril, but right or wrong, I want you to go into battle with me—I see you as the noble captain, strong and faithful, and no matter what the cost, right to the end. I have no right to ask it, but you must be the great man that I know you are. Don't give up the ship. I am leaving here tomorrow, I think. Some friends are taking me to the country in an effort to get me some quiet and rest.[1] I hope to be in North Carolina in a few days—although now, feeling as I do, I doubt the [approval?] of my friends. But if you want to write me, you might address the letter in care of Mr. Garland Porter, *The Atlanta Georgian*, Atlanta. But whatever you do—unless it is something involving the serious sickness or death of a member of my family—don't give my address to anyone. I'm in a wretched state, and I've got to get on my feet before I come back to New York to fight. . . .

P.S. I was worn out yesterday when I wrote this. To-day I feel a little better—and I am assured now of my course. Further words, arguments, entreaties are useless. We are either at the end or we shall go on. I am sending two letters which I wrote some weeks ago and which, hoping against hope, I have withheld. These letters in a general way put the story of my relation to you and Scribners upon the record. There is nothing in either of them that can do you any harm. But, in case anything happens to me, I am sending duplicates to a friend. I think this is proper.

Wolfe actually sent only one of the two letters referred to above, the one dated December 15, 1936, which he called "the personal letter," but not the one dated December 23, 1936, which he called "the business letter" and of which the original is still in his own files. The friend to whom he sent duplicates of these letters remains unidentified in spite of queries to the most likely people. Perhaps he never actually sent duplicates to anyone at this time. However, in the fall of 1937, he gave a copy of the letter of December 15, 1936, to Hamilton Basso, after writing the following words in pencil on the bottom of the last page: "To my friend, Hamilton Basso: Dear Ham—I've gone upon the record here—this is not perhaps the whole story—but in a general way it says some of the things I felt had to be said. I am leaving this copy of the letter in your care and, if anything should happen to me, I leave it to your discretion what should be done with it."

[1] Mr. and Mrs. Allan B. Eldred had invited Wolfe to their house at Ocean Springs, Mississippi, for a few days' rest. Before her marriage, Mrs. Eldred was Margaret Folsom of Asheville: she and her brother, Theodore W. Folsom, had been childhood friends of Wolfe's.

The following is "the personal letter" which Wolfe mailed from New Orleans on January 10.

To MAXWELL E. PERKINS

865 First Avenue
New York, N.Y.
December 15, 1936

Dear Max:

I am sorry for the delay in answering your three letters of November 17th and 18th. As you know, I have been hard at work here day after day and, in addition, have recently been beset by some more of the legal difficulties, threats and worries which have hounded my life for the last year and a half. And finally, I wanted to have time to think over your letters carefully and to meditate my own reply before I answered you.

First of all, let me tell you that for what you say in your own two personal letters of November 17th and November 18th I shall be forever proud and grateful. I shall remember it with the greatest happiness as long as I live. I must tell you again, no matter what embarrassment it may cause you, what I have already publicly acknowledged and what I believe is now somewhat understood and known about in the world, namely, that your faith in me, your friendship for me, during the years of doubt, confusion and distress, was and will always be one of the great things in my life.

When I did give utterance to this fact in print [1]—when I tried to make some slight acknowledgment of a debt of friendship and of loyalty, which no mere acknowledgment could ever repay—some of my enemies, as you know, tried to seize upon the simple words I had written in an effort to twist and pervert them to their own uses, to indicate that my acknowledgment was for a technical and professional service, which it was not, to assert that I was myself incapable of projecting and accomplishing my own purpose without your own editorial help, which is untrue. But although such statements as these were made to injure me, and perhaps have done me an injury, I believe that injury to be at best only a temporary one. As for the rest, what I had really said, what I had really written about my debt to you, is plain and unmistakable, clearly and definitely understood by people of good will, who have a mind to understand. I would not retract a word of it, except to wish the words were written better. I would not withdraw a line of it, except to hope that I might write another line that would more adequately express the whole meaning and implication of what I feel and want to say.

[1] In *The Story of a Novel.*

As to those statements which were made, it seems to me, malevolently, for what purpose I do not know, by people I have never met—that I had to have your technical and critical assistance "to help me write my books," etc.—they are so contemptible, so manifestly false, I have no fear whatever of their ultimate exposure. If refutation were needed, if the artist had time enough or felt it necessary to make an answer to all the curs that snap at him, it would not take me long, I think, to brand these falsehoods for the lies they are. I would only have to point out, I think, that so far from needing any outside aid "to help me write my books," the very book which my detractors now eagerly seize on as my best one—the gauge by which the others must be measured, and itself the proof and demonstration of my subsequent decline—had been utterly finished and completed, to the final period, in utter isolation, without a word of criticism or advice from any one, before any publisher ever saw it; and that whatever changes were finally made were almost entirely changes in the form of omission and of cuts in view of bringing the book down to a more publishable and condensed form. That book, of course, was "Look Homeward, Angel," and I believe that with everything else I ever wrote, the process was much the same, although the finality of completion was not so marked, because in later books I was working in a more experimental, individual fashion and dealing with the problem of how to shape and bring into articulate form a giant mass of raw material, whose proportions almost defeated me.

The very truth of the matter is that, so far from ever having been unsure of purpose and direction, in the last five years at any rate I have been almost too sure. My sense of purpose and direction is definite and overwhelming. I think, I feel and know what I want to do: the direction in which, if I live and if I am allowed to go on working and fulfill myself, I want to go, is with me more clear and certain than with any one that I have ever known. My difficulty has never been one of purpose or direction. Nothing is more certain than this fact, that I know what I want to do and where I want to go. Nothing is more certain than the fact that I shall finish any book I set out to write, if life and health hold out. My difficulty from the outset, as you know, has never been one of direction, it has only been one of means. As I have already said and written, in language that seems to be so clear and unmistakable that no one could misunderstand it, I have been faced with the problem of discovering for myself my own language, my own pattern, my own structure, my own design, my own universe and creation. That, as I have said before, is a problem that is, I think, by no means unique, by no means special to myself. I believe it may have been the problem of every artist that ever lived. In my own case, however, I believe the difficulties of the problem may have been increased and complicated by the denseness of the fabric, the dimensions of the structure, the variety of the plan. For that reason I have, as you know, at times found myself almost hopelessly enmeshed in my own web.

In one sense, my whole effort for years might be described as an effort to fathom my own design, to explore my own channels, to discover my own ways. In these respects, in an effort to help me to discover, to better use, these means I was striving to apprehend and make my own, you gave me the most generous, the most painstaking, the most valuable help. But that kind of help might have been given to me by many other skilful people—and of course there are other skilful people in the world who could give such help, although none that I know of who could give it so skilfully as you.

But what you gave me, what in my acknowledgment I tried to give expression to, was so much more than this technical assistance—an aid of spiritual sustenance, of personal faith, of high purpose, of profound and sensitive understanding, of utter loyalty and staunch support, at a time when many people had no belief at all in me, or when what little belief they had was colored by serious doubt that I would ever be able to continue or achieve my purpose, fulfill my "promise." All of this was a help of such priceless and incalculable value, of such spiritual magnitude, that it made any other kind of help seem paltry by comparison. And for that reason mainly I have resented the contemptible insinuations of my enemies that I have to have you "to help me write my books." As you know, I don't have to have you or any other man alive to help me write my books. I do not even have to have technical help or advice, although I need it badly, and have been so immensely grateful for it. But if the worst came to the worst—and of course the worst does and will come to the worst—all this I could and will and do learn for myself, as all hard things are learned, with blood-sweat, anguish and despair.

As for another kind of help—a help that would attempt to shape my purpose or define for me my own direction—I not only do not need that sort of help but if I found that it had in any way invaded the unity of my purpose, or was trying in any fundamental way to modify or alter the direction of my creative life—the way in which it seems to me it ought and has to go—I should repulse it as an enemy, I should fight it and oppose it with every energy of my life, because I feel so strongly that it is the final and unpardonable intrusion upon the one thing in an artist's life that must be held and kept inviolable.

All this I know you understand and will agree to. As to the final kind of help, the help of friendship, the help of faith, the help and belief and understanding of a fellow creature whom you know and reverence not only as a person of individual genius but as a spirit of incorruptible integrity—that kind of help I do need, that kind of help I think I have been given, that kind of help I shall evermore hope to deserve and pray that I shall have. But if that too should fail—if that too should be taken from me, as so many rare and priceless things are taken from us in this life—that kind of dark and tragic fortitude that grows on us in life as we get older, and which tells us that in the end we can and must endure all things, might make it possible for me to bear even that final and irreparable loss, to agree with Samuel Johnson when he said: "The shepherd in Vergil grew at last acquainted with Love, and found him a native of the rocks."

You say in one of your letters that you never knew a soul with whom you felt that you were in such fundamentally complete agreement as with me. May I tell you that I shall remember these words with proud happiness and with loyal gratefulness as long as I live. For I too on my own part feel that way about you. I know that somehow, in some hard, deep, vexed and troubling way in which all the truth of life is hidden and which, at the cost of so much living, so much perplexity and anguish of the spirit, we have got to try to find and fathom, what you say is true: I believe we are somehow, in this strange, hard way, in this complete and fundamental agreement with each other.

And yet, were there ever two men since time began who were as completely different as you and I? Have you ever known two other people who were, in almost every respect of temperament, thinking, feeling and acting, as far apart? It seems to me that each of us might almost represent, typify, be the personal embodiment of, two opposite poles of life. How to put it I do not know exactly, but I might say, I think, that you in your essential self are the Conservative and I, in my essential self, am the Revolutionary.

I use these words, I hope, in what may have been their original and natural meanings. I am not using them with reference to any of the political, social, economic or religious connotations that are now so often tied up with them. When I say that you a Conservative, I am not thinking of you as some-one who voted for Governor Landon, for I can see how an action of that sort and your own considered reasons for doing it might easily have revolutionary consequences. When I say that I am a Revolutionary, I know that you will never for a moment think of me as some one who is usually referred to in America as a "radical." You know that my whole feeling toward life could not be indicated or included under such a category. I am not a party man, I am not a propaganda man, I am not a Union Square or Greenwich Village communist. I not only do not believe in these people: I do not even believe they believe in themselves. I mistrust their sincerity, I mistrust their motives, I do not believe they have any essential capacity for devotion or for belief in the very principles of Revolution, of government, of economics and of life, which they all profess.

More than that, I believe that these people themselves are parasitic excrescences of the very society which they profess to abhor, whose destruction they prophesy and whose overthrow they urge. I believe that these people would be unable to live without the society which they profess to abhor, and I know that I could live if I had to, not only under this society but under any other one, and that in the end I might probably approve no other one more than I do this.

I believe further that these very people who talk of the workers with such reverence, and who assert that they are workers and are for the worker's cause, do not reverence the workers, are not themselves workers and in the end are traitors to the worker's cause. I believe that I myself not only know the workers and am a friend of the worker's cause but that I am myself a brother to the workers, because I am myself, as every artist is, a worker, and I am myself, moreover, the son of a working man. I know furthermore that at the bottom there is no difference between the artist and the worker. They both come from the same family, they recognize and understand each other instantly. They speak the same language. They have always stood together. And I know that our enemies, the people who betray us, are these apes and monkeys of the arts, who believe in everything and who believe in nothing, and who hate the artist and who hate the living man no matter what lip service they may pay to us. These people are the enemies to life, the enemies to revolution. Nothing is more certain than that they will betray us in the end.

I have said these things simply to indicate to you a difference of which I know you must be already well aware. The difference between the revolutionary and the "radical," the difference between the artist and the ape of art, the difference between the worker and those who say they are the worker's friend. The same thing could be said, it seems to me, on your own side, about the true conservative and the person who only votes conservative and owns property and has money in the bank.

Just as in some hard, strange way there is between us probably this fundamentally complete agreement which you speak of, so too, in other hard, strange ways there is this complete and polar difference. It must be so with the South pole and the North pole. I believe that in the end they too must be in fundamentally complete agreement—but the whole earth lies between them. I don't know exactly how to define conservatism or the essential conservative spirit of which I speak here, but I think I might say it is a kind of fatalism of the spirit. Its fundaments, it seems to me, are based upon a kind of unhoping hope, an imperturbable acceptation, a determined resignation, which believes that fundamentally life will never change, but that on this account we must all of us do the best we can.

The result of all this, it seems to me, is that these differences between us have multiplied in complexity and difficulty. The plain truth of the matter now is that I hardly know where to turn. The whole natural impulse of creation—and with me, creation is a natural impulse, it has got to flow, it has got to realize itself through the process of torrential production—is checked and hampered at every place. In spite of this, I have finally and at last, during these past two months, broken through into the greatest imaginative conquest of my life—the only complete and whole one I have ever had. And now I dare not broach it to you, I dare not bring it to you, I dare not show it to you, for fear that this thing which I cannot trifle with, which may come to a man but once in his whole life, may be killed at its inception by cold caution, by indifference, by the growing apprehensiveness and dogmatism of your own conservatism. You say that you are not aware that there is any severance between us. Will you please tell me what there is in the life around us on which we both agree? We don't agree in politics, we don't agree on economics, we are in entire disagreement on the present system of life around us, the way people live, the changes that should be made.

Your own idea, evidently, is that life itself is unchangeable, that the abuses I protest against—the greed, the waste, the poverty, the filth, the suffering—are inherent in humanity, and that any other system than the one we have would be just as bad as this one. In this, I find myself in profound and passionate conflict. I hold no brief, as you know, for the present communist system as it is practiced in Russia to-day, but it seems to me to be the most absurd and hollow casuistry to argue seriously that because a good Russian worker is given a thicker slice of beef than a bad one, or because a highly trained mechanic enjoys a slightly better standard of living and is given more privileges and comforts than an inferior mechanic, the class system has been reestablished in Russia and is identical with the one existing in this country, whereby a young girl who inherits the fortune of a five-and-ten-cent-store king is allowed to live a life of useless, vicious idleness and to enjoy an income of five million dollars annually while other young girls work in the very stores that produce her fortune for ten dollars a week.

It is all very well to say that the artist should not concern himself with these things but with "life." What are these things if they are not life— one of the cruelest and most intolerable aspects of it, it is true, but as much a part of the whole human spectacle as a woman producing a child. You, better than any one, have had the chance to observe during the past year how this consciousness of society, of the social elements that govern life to-day, have sunk into my spirit; how my convictions about all these things have grown deeper, wider, more intense at every point. On your own part, it seems to me, there has been a corresponding stiffening, an increasing conservatism that has now, I fear, reached the point of dogged and unyielding inflexibility and obstinate resolve to try to maintain the status quo at any cost.

Since that is your condition, your considered judgment, I will not try to change it, or to persuade you in any way, because I know your reasons for so thinking and so feeling are honest ones. But neither must you now try to change me, or to persuade me to alter or deny convictions which are the result of no superficial or temporary influence, no Union Square, Greenwich Village cult, but the result of my own deep living, my own deep feeling, my own deep labor and my own deep thought.

Had I given full expression to these convictions in "Of Time and the River" I believe it would have been a better book. You do not think so. But I will say that these feelings, these convictions, are becoming deeper and intenser all the time, and so far from feeling that the world cannot be changed, that it cannot be made better, that the evils of life are un-remediable, that all the faults and vices at which we protest will always exist, I find myself more passionately convinced than ever of the necessity of change, more passionately confirmed than ever in the faith and the belief that the life and the condition of the whole human race can be immeasurably improved. And this is something that grows stronger with me all the time. It has been my lot to start life with an obedient faith, with a conservative tradition, only to have that faith grow weaker and fade out as I grew older. I cannot tell you all the ways in which this came about, but I think I can indicate to you one of the principal ones.

I was a child of faith. I grew up in the most conservative section of America, and as a child I put an almost unquestioning belief and confidence in the things that were told me, the precepts that were taught me. As I grew older I began to see the terrible and shocking differences between appearance and reality all around me. I was told, for example, in church, of a Sunday morning, that people should love one another as their brothers, that they should not bear false witness against their fellow-man, that they should not covet their neighbor's wife, that they should not commit adultery, that they should not cheat, trick, betray and rob their fellows. And as I grew older and my knowledge of life and of the whole community increased until there was hardly a family in town whose whole history I did not know, I began to see what a shameful travesty of good-ness these lives were. I began to see that the very people who said on Sunday that one should not bear false witness against his neighbors bore false witness all the time, until the very air was poisonous with their slanders, with their hatreds, their vicious slanderings of life and of their neighbors. I began to see how the people who talked about not coveting their neighbors' wives did covet their neighbors' wives and committed adultery with them. I saw how the minister who got up and denounced a proposal to introduce a little innocent amusement in the Sunday life of the people, a baseball game or a moving picture show—upon the grounds that it not only violated the law of God but was an imposition on our fellow-man, that we had no right to ask our fellows to do work on Sunday —had, at that very moment, two sweating negro girls in the kitchen of his own home, employed at meagre wages to cook his Sunday dinner for him. . . .

Well, it is an old, old story, but to me it was a new one. Like every other boy of sense, intelligence and imagination, who ever first discovered these things for himself, I thought I was the first one in the world to see these things. I thought that I had come upon a horrible catastrophe, a whole universe of volcanic infamy over which the good people of the earth were treading blissfully and innocently with trusting smiles. I thought I had to tell this thing to some one. I thought I had to warn the world, to tell all my friends and teachers that all the goodness and integrity and purity of their lives was menaced by this snake of unsuspected evil.

I don't need to tell you what happened. I was received either with smiles of amused and pitying tolerance or with curt reprimands, admonitions to shut up, not to talk about my betters, not to say a word against people who had won a name and who were the high and mighty ones in town. Then slowly, like some one living in a nightmare only to wake up and find out that the nightmare is really true, I began to find out that they *didn't* mean it, they *didn't* mean what they said. I began to discover that all these fine words, these splendid precepts, these noble teachings had no meaning at all, because the very people who professed them had no belief in them. I began to discover that it didn't matter at all whether you bore false witness against your neighbor, if you only said that one should not bear false witness against his neighbor. I began to see that it didn't matter at all whether you took your neighbor's ox or his ass or his wife, if only you had the cunning and the power to take them. I began to see that it did not matter at all whether you committed adultery or not, so long as it did not come out in the papers. Every one in town might know you had committed it, and with whom, and on what occasions—the whole history might be a matter for sly jesting, furtive snickerings, the lewd and common property of the whole community—and you could still be deacon of the church provided you were not sued for alienation of affection. I began to see that you could talk of chastity, of purity, of standards of morality and high conduct, of loving your neighbor as yourself, and still derive your filthy income from a horde of rotting tenements down in niggertown that were so vile and filthy they were not fit to be the habitation of pigs. You could talk to a crowd of miserable, over-worked and under-paid shop-girls about their moral life and the necessity of chastity even though your own daughter was the most promiscuous, drunken little whore in town. And it didn't matter, it didn't matter—if you had the dough. That was all that mattered.

I discovered very early that people who had the money could do pretty damn near anything they wanted to. Whoredom, drunkenness, debauchery of every sort was the privilege of the rich, the crime of the poor. And as I grew older, as my experience of life widened and increased, as I first came to know, to explore, to investigate life in this overwhelming city, with all the passion, the hope, the faith, the fervor and the poetic imagination of youth, I found that here too it was just the same. Here too, if anything, it was more overwhelming because it was so condensed, so multiplied. Here too, if anything, it was even more terrible because the privileged city classes no longer pretended to cloak themselves in the spurious affirmations of religion. The result has been, as I have grown older, as I have seen life in manifold phases all over the earth, that I have become more passionately convinced than ever before that this system that we have is evil, that it brings misery and injustice not only to the lives of the poor but to the wretched and sterile lives of the privileged classes who are supported by it, that this system of living must be changed, that men must have a new faith, a new heroism, a new belief, if life is to be made better. And that life can be made better, that life will be made better, is the heart and core of my own faith and my own conviction, the end toward which I believe I must henceforth direct every energy of my life and talent.

All this, I know, you consider elementary, and I agree with you. It is. These evidences of corruption in the life around me which I have mentioned to you, you consider almost childishly naive. Perhaps they are. But if they are, the anterior fundamental sources of corruption which have produced them are certainly neither childish nor naive. You have told me that you consider the . . . life of a young girl who, without ever having done a stroke of work herself, is privileged to enjoy an income of two million, or five million, or ten million a year, only a trifling and superficial manifestation and of no importance. With this, of course, I am in utter opposition. If these people, as you say, are only flies upon the tender of a locomotive, they are locomotive flies, and the locomotive that produced them should be scrapped.

I have gone into all this not because these bases of contention are even fundamental to you and me, but because they are indicative of all the various widening channels of difference that have come up between us in recent years. Just as my own feeling for the necessity for change, for essential revolution in this way of life, has become steadily deeper and more confirmed, so too have you, hardened by the challenge of the depression, deeply alarmed by the menace of the times to the fortune of which you are the custodian—not for yourself, I know, for you yourself I truly believe are not a man who needs material things, but alarmed by the menace of these times to the security and future of five young and tender creatures who, protected as they have been, and unprepared as they are to meet the peril of these coming times, are themselves, it seems to me, the unfortunate victims of this very system you must now try to help maintain —you have accordingly become more set and more confirmed in your own convictions. With these personal affairs, these intimate details of your fine family, I have no intention to intrude save where it seems to me to have resulted in a bias that challenges the essence of my own purpose and direction.

What I really want to say to you most earnestly now is this: there has never been a time when I've been so determined to write as I please, to say what I intend to say, to publish the books I want to publish, as I am now. I know that you have asserted time and again that you were in entire sympathy with this feeling—that, more than this, you were willing to be the eager promoter and supporter of this intention, that you were willing to publish whatever I wanted you to publish, that you were only waiting for me to give it to you. In this I think you have deceived yourself. I think you are mistaken when you say that all you have waited for was the word from me, that you would publish anything I wanted you to publish. There are many things that I have wanted you to publish which have not been published. Some of them have not been published because they were too long for magazine space, or too short for book space, or too different in their design and quality to fit under the heading of a short story, or too incomplete to be called a novel. All this is true. All this I grant. And yet, admitting all these things, without a word of criticism of you or of the technical and publishing requirements of the present time that make their publication impracticable, I will still say that I think some of them should have been published. I still think that much of the best writing that a man may do is writing that does not follow under the convenient but extremely limited forms of modern publication. It is not your fault. It is not Scribners' fault. It is just the way things are. But as I have been telling you, the way things are is not always the way, it seems to me, that things should be; and one fact that has become plain to me in recent years and is now imbedded in my conviction is that in spite of the rivers of print that inundate this broad land, the thousands of newspapers, the hundreds of magazines, the thousands of books that get printed every year, and the scores of publishers who assure you that they are sitting on the edges of their chairs and eagerly waiting, praying, that some one will come in with a piece of writing of originality and power, that all they are waiting for, all they ask for, is just for the opportunity of discovering it and printing it—the means of publication are still most limited for a life of the complexity, the variety, the richness, the fascination, the terror, the poetry, the beauty and the whole unuttered magnificence of this tremendous life around us: the means of publication are really pitifully meager, ungenerous, meanly, sterilely constricted.

Which brings me now to an essential point, a point that bears practically and dangerously on every thing that I have heretofore said to you.

About fifteen years ago, as you know, an extraordinary book was produced which startled the whole critical and publishing world. This book was the "Ulysses" of James Joyce. I know that you are well aware of the history of that book, but for the sake of the argument I am presently to make, let me review it again for you. "Ulysses" was published, if I mistake not, in 1921. I have been informed dozens of times in the last few years by reputable and well-known publishers, including yourself, that they are eagerly waiting a chance to produce a work of originality and power, that they would produce it without question, without modification, if it were given to them. What are the facts concerning "Ulysses"? Was it published by Charles Scribner's Sons? No, it was not. Was it published by Harper's, by Macmillan, by Houghton Mifflin, by one of the great English houses? It was not. Who published it then? It was published privately, obscurely, by a woman who ran a book shop in Paris. And at first, as you know, it was treated by most critics as kind of literary curiosity—either as a work of deliberate pornography or as a work of wilfully complicated obscurity, of no genuine value or importance, save to a little group of clique adepts. And as you know, the book was taken up by clique adepts everywhere and used, or rather misused, in their customary way, as a badge of their snobbish superiority. But in addition to both these groups there was also a third group, I think a very small group, composed of those people scattered throughout the world who are able to read and feel and understand and form their own judgment without prejudice of the merits of a powerful and original work. It seems to me that almost the best, the most fortunate thing in life—in a writer's life at least—is that these people do exist. A great book is not lost. It does not get done to death by fools and snobs. It may be misunderstood for years. Its writer may be ridiculed or reviled or betrayed by false idolatry, but the book does not get lost. There are always a few people who will save it. The book will make its way. That is what happened to "Ulysses." As time went on, the circle widened. Its public increased. As people overcame their own inertia, mastered the difficulty which every new and original work creates, became familiar with its whole design, they began to understand that the book was neither an obscene book nor an obscure book, certainly it was not a work of wilful dilettante caprice. It was, on the contrary, an orderly, densely constructed creation, whose greatest fault, it seems to me, so far from being a fault of caprice, was rather the fault of an almost Jesuitical logic which is essentially too dry and lifeless in its mechanics for a work of the imagination. At any rate, now, after fifteen years, "Ulysses" is no longer thought of as a book meant solely for a little group of literary adepts. The adepts of this day, in fact, speak somewhat patronizingly of the work as marking "the end of an epoch," as being "the final development of an outworn naturalism," etc., etc. But the book itself had now won an unquestioned and established place in literature. Its whole method, its style, its characters, its story and design has become so familiar to many of us that we no longer think of it as difficult or obscure. It seems no more difficult than "Tristram Shandy." For my part, I do not find "Ulysses" as difficult as "Tristram." Certainly it is nowhere near as difficult as "The Ring and the Book." Moreover, "Ulysses" can now be published openly in this country, sold over the counter as any other book is sold, without fear of arrest or action by the law. And at the present time, as you know, it is being sold that way, in what is known as "large quantities," by one of your fellow publishers. This man told me a year and a half ago that the sale up to that time, I believe, was something like 30,000 copies. "Ulysses," therefore, has made its way not only critically but commercially as well. These are the facts. I do not recall them in order to accuse you with them. I know you did not have the opportunity of publishing "Ulysses." Perhaps no other well-known publisher, either in England or America, had that opportunity. I suppose furthermore that at that time it would have been impossible for any reputable publisher to have published that book openly. But the fact remains it did get published, didn't it—not by Scribners, not by Houghton, not by any known publisher in England, but privately, by a little obscure bookseller in Paris.

And the reason your associates, the Modern Library, Inc., can now publish this book in large quantities, openly, and derive a profit from it now, is because some private, obscure person took the chance fifteen years ago—took the chance, I fear, without the profits.

What then? You say you are waiting eagerly to discover a manuscript of originality and power. You say that you are waiting eagerly to publish a manuscript of mine—that you will publish anything I want you to publish. I know you believe what you say, but I also think you deceive yourself. I am not going to write a "Ulysses" book. Like many another young man who came under the influence of that remarkable work, I wrote my "Ulysses" book and got it published too. That book, as you know, was "Look Homeward, Angel." And now, I am finished with "Ulysses" and with Mr. Joyce, save that I am not an ingrate and will always, I hope, be able to remember a work that stirred me, that opened new vistas into writing, and to pay the tribute to a man of genius that is due him.

However, I am now going to write my own "Ulysses." The first volume is now under way. The first volume will be called "The Hound of Darkness," and the whole work, when completed, will be called "The Vision of Spangler's Paul." [2] Like Mr. Joyce, I am going to write as I please, and this time, no one is going to cut me unless I want them to. Like Mr. Joyce, and like most artists, I believe, I am by nature a Puritan. At any rate, a growing devotion to work, to purpose, to fulfillment, a growing intensity of will, tends to distill one's life into a purer liquor. I shall never hereafter—I hope that I have never heretofore, but I shall never hereafter—write a word for the purpose of arousing sensational surprise, of shocking the prudish, of flaunting the outraged respectabilities of the middle-class mind. But I shall use as precisely, as truthfully, as tellingly as I can every word I have to use; every word, if need be, in my vocabulary; every word, if need be, in the vocabulary of the foulest-mouthed taxi driver, the most prurient-tongued prostitute that ever screamed an obscene epithet. Like Mr. Joyce, I have at last discovered my own America, I believe I have found my language, I think I know my way. And I shall wreak out my vision of this life, this way, this world and this America, to the top of my bent, to the height of my ability, but with an unswerving devotion, integrity and purity of purpose that shall not be menaced, altered or weakened by any one. I will go to jail because of this book if I have to. I will lose my friends because of it, if I will have to. I will be libelled, slandered, blackmailed, threatened, menaced, sneered at, derided and assailed by every parasite, every ape, every blackmailer, every scandalmonger, every little Saturday-Reviewer of the venomous and corrupt respectabilities. I will be exiled from my country because of it, if I have to. I can endure exile. I have endured it before, as you well know, on account of a book which you yourself published, although few—among them, some of the very ones who betrayed me then either by silence or evasion—now try to smile feebly when I speak of exile, but it was the truth and may be true again. But no matter what happens I am going to write this book.

You have heard me talk to you before. You have not always been disposed to take seriously what I say to you. I pray most earnestly that you will take this seriously. For seven years now, during this long and for me wonderful association with you, I have been increasingly aware of a

[2] By this time, Wolfe had decided to include the material and title of *The Hound of Darkness* in *The Vision of Spangler's Paul* (which finally became *The Web and the Rock* and *You Can't Go Home Again*). The title, *The Hound of Darkness*, is used for Book II of *The Web and the Rock*, but most of the original material was omitted or used elsewhere in that novel or in *You Can't Go Home Again*.

certain direction which our lives were taking. Looking back, I can see now that although "Look Homeward, Angel" gave you pleasure and satisfaction, you were extremely alarmed even then about its publication, and entertained the hope—the sincere and honest hope, directed, I know, to what you considered my own best interests—that the years would temper me to a greater conservatism, a milder intensity, a more decorous moderation. And I think where I have been most wrong, most unsure in these past seven years, has been where I have yielded to this benevolent pressure. Because I think that it is just there that I have allowed myself to falter in my purpose, to be diverted from the direction toward which the whole impulsion of my life and talent is now driving me, to have failed there insofar as I have yielded to the modifications of this restraint. Restraint, discipline—yes, they were needed desperately, they are needed badly still. But let us not get the issues confused, let us not again get into the old confusion between substance and technique, purpose and manner, direction and means, the spirit and the letter. Restrain my adjectives, by all means, discipline my adverbs, moderate the technical extravagances of my incondite exuberance, but don't derail the train, don't take the Pacific Limited and switch it down the siding towards Hogwart Junction. It can't be done. I'm not going to let it happen. If you expected me to grow conservative simply because I got bald and fat and for the first time in life had a few dollars in the bank, you are going to be grievously mistaken. Besides, what is there longer for me to fear? I have been through it all now, I have seen how women can betray you, how friends can sell you out for a few filthy dollars, how the whole set-up of society and of justice in its present form permits the thief, the parasite, the scavenger, the scandal-monger to rob, cheat, outrage and defame you, how even those people who swear they are your sincerest and most enduring friends, who say they value your talent and your work, can sink to the final dishonor of silence and of caution when you are attacked, will not even lift their voices in a word of protest or of indignation when they hear you lied about by scoundrels or maligned by rascals. So what am I now to lose? Even the little money that I had, the greater part of it, has now been taken from me by these thieves and parasites of life. Well, they can take it, they can have it, they have got it. They can take everything I have, but no one henceforth shall take from me my work.

I am afraid of nothing now. I have nothing more to lose except my life and health. And those I pray and hope to God will stay with me till my work is done. That, it seems to me, is the only tragedy that can now stay me.

The other day you were present when we were having an interview with a distinguished member of the legal profession. I wonder what was going on in your mind when you saw that man and when you looked at me. When you saw that man, secure in wealth, in smugness, in respectability, even though all these authorities had come to him from his accursed profession, from shuffling papers, peering around for legal crevices, seeking not for truth or justice but for technical advantages. When you heard this man ask me if I had lived in certain neighborhoods, in certain kinds of habitation, if I ever drank, etc., and when you heard him cough pompously behind his hand and say that although he of course had never led "that sort of life" he was—ahem, ahem—not narrow-minded and understood that there were those that did. Understand? Why, what could he understand of "my kind of life"? He could no more understand it than a dog could understand the books in his master's library. And I have been forced to wonder of late, after some of the sad events of this last year, how much of it you understood. What I am trying to tell you, what I am forced to say because it is the truth, is that I am a righteous man, and few people know it because there are few righteous people in the world.

But from my boyhood, from my early youth, I have lived a life of solitude, of industry, of consecration. I have cost few people anything in this world, except perhaps the pains of birth. I have given people everything I had. I think that I have taken from no one more than I have given them. Certainly, I suppose that not even my bitterest enemies have ever accused me of living or working or thinking about money. During the time that you yourself have known me you have had ample demonstrations of that fact. I know you have not forgotten them, and I hope that if anything should happen to me, if I should die, as indeed I have no wish to do, there would be some one left who had known me who would say some of these things I know to be true.

Please understand that I neither intend nor imply any criticism of you, or of your friendship when I say these things. I know you are my friend. I value your friendship more than anything else in the world: the belief that you, above all people, respected my work and found happiness in being able to help me with it has been the greatest spiritual support and comfort I've ever known. I think further that if I ever heard you slandered or defamed or lied about, I would assault the person who defamed you. But I know that that is not your way. You believe that silence is the best answer, and perhaps you are right. At any rate, I want you to know that as long as I know you are my friend to the very hilt, to the very last—if need be, and I hope it never need be, to your own peril and security—that is all that matters. And that is the way I feel about you.

I do not know if you have always been aware of how I felt about these things; of what a naked, fiercely lacerated thing my spirit was; how I have

writhed beneath the lies and injuries and at times, [been] almost maddened to insanity at the treachery, the injustice and the hatred I have had
to experience and endure; at what a frightful cost I have attained even the
little fortitude I have attained. At times, particularly during the last year
or two, the spectacle of the victim squirming beneath the lash has seemed
to amuse you. I know there is no cruelty in your nature. I do suggest to
you, however, that when one is secure in life, when one is vested with
authority, established in position, surrounded by a little world of his own
making, of his own love, he may sometimes be a little unmindful of the
lives of people less fortunate than himself. There is an unhappy tendency
in all of us to endure with fortitude the anguish of another man. There
is also a tendency among people of active and imaginative minds and
temperaments, who live themselves conventional and conservative lives,
to indulge vicariously their interest in the adventures and experiences of
other people whose lives are not so sheltered as their own. And these
people, I think, often derive what seems to be a kind of quiet, philosophic
amusement at the spectacle of what is so falsely known as the "human
comedy." But I might suggest to such people that what affords them quiet
entertainment is being paid for by another man with blood and agony,
and that while we smile at the difficulties and troubles in which an im-
pulsive and generous person gets involved, a man of genius or of talent
may be done to death.

I suppose it is very true to say that "every one has these troubles." I do
think, however, that a man in my own position, of my own temperament,
whose personality seems to penetrate his work in a peculiarly intimate
way, so that he then becomes the target for intrigues and scandals of all
sorts—such a man, I say, may have them to an exaggerated degree and
through no essential fault of his own. Certainly, I do not think he could
expect to be protected wholly from them. Certainly no one has the right
to expect that his own life will be wholly free from the griefs and troubles
that other people have. But I think a man who has not injured other
people, who has not interfered with other people's lives or solicited their
intrusion, has a right to expect a reasonable and decent amount of privacy—the reasonable and decent amount of privacy that a carpenter, a
truck driver or a railroad engineer might have.

At any rate, in spite of all these things, I shall push forward somehow
to the completion of my work. I feel that any more confusion or uncertainty might be ruinous to my purpose. There has been too much indecision
already. We postponed the completion and publication of "The October
Fair," with some intention, I suppose, of showing the critics and the public
I could create in a different vein, in a more objective manner than I had
yet done. We also deferred completion and publication of "The Hills

Beyond Pentland." I know you said you were willing to go ahead and publish these books. You have always assured me on that point. But I did feel
that your counsel and your caution were against their publication now.

I believe you may have allowed your apprehensions concerning who
and what I might now write about at the period I had now reached in
my writing to influence your judgments. I don't like to go into all this
again. The thing that happened last summer, your reaction to the manuscript Miss Nowell brought to you while I was in Europe,[3] and your own
comment as expressed to her in a note which she sent to me and which
said, after she had cut all the parts you objected to in the manuscript out
of it, that "the only person it can now possibly hurt is Thomas Wolfe,"
was to me a shocking revelation. I am not of the opinion now that the
manuscript in question was one of any great merit. I know that I've done
much better work. But the point, as I told you after my return from
Europe, the point that we discussed so frankly and so openly, was that
your action, if carried to its logical conclusions and applied to everything
I write from now on, struck a deadly blow at the very vitals of my whole
creative life. The only possible inference that could be drawn from this
matter was that from now on, if I wished to continue writing books which
Charles Scribner's Sons were going to publish, I must now submit myself
to the most rigid censorship, a censorship which would delete from all
my writings any episode, any scene, any character, any reference that
might seem to have any connection, however remote, with the house of
Charles Scribner's Sons and its sisters and its cousins and its aunts. Such
a conclusion, if I agreed to it, would result in the total enervation and
castration of my work—a work which, as I have told you in this letter, I
am now resolved must be more strong and forthright in its fidelity to
purpose than ever.

Again, in this whole situation there is a display of an almost unbelievable vanity and arrogance. It was first of all, the vanity and arrogance
that would lead certain people to suppose that I was going to "write
about them," and then the vanity and arrogance of people who said
that, although it was perfectly all right for me to write about other people
"in humble walks of life," it was an unpardonable affront to all these important high-toned personages to be "written about" freely and frankly by
a low scribbling fellow, who is good enough no doubt to supply a publisher with manuscript, to give employment to his business, to add prestige to the reputation of his firm, but who must be put in his place when
he overstepped the bounds of human sanctity.

Now, in the first place, as I told you before, whoever got the idea that

[3] "No More Rivers." This was never published, but small portions of it are scattered
through *The Web and the Rock* and *You Can't Go Home Again*.

I was going to write about him or her or them anyway? And in the second place, whoever got the idea that I was not going to go ahead and write as I damned pleased, about anything I wished to write about, with the complete freedom to which every artist is entitled, and that no one in the world was going to stand in the way of my doing this? I am certainly at the present time not interested in writing about Charles Scribner's Sons or any one connected with Charles Scribner's Sons. It has at the present time no part of my creative plan or of my writing effort. And as you know very well, I don't "write about" people: I create living characters of my own—a whole universe of my own creation. And any character that I create is so unmistakably my own that anyone familiar with my work would know instantly it was my own, even if it had no title and no name.

But, to go back to this simple, fundamental, inescapable necessity of all art, which I have patiently, laboriously, coherently, explained a thousand times, in such language that no one can misunderstand it, to all the people in this country, to all the people who, for some strange and extraordinary reason, in America and nowhere else that I have ever been on earth, keep harping forever, with a kind of idiot pertinacity, upon the word "autobiography"—you can't make something out of nothing. You can either say that there is no such thing as autobiographical writing, or you can say that all writing is autobiographical, a statement with which I should be inclined to agree. But you cannot say, you must not say, that one man is an autobiographical writer and another man is not an autobiographical writer. You cannot and must not say that one novel is an autobiographical novel and another novel is not an autobiographical novel. Because if you say these things, you are uttering falsehood and palpable nonsense. It has no meaning.

My books are neither more nor less autobiographical than "War and Peace." If anything, I should say that they are less, because a great writer like Tolstoi who achieves his purpose, achieves it because he has made a perfect utilization of all the means, all the materials at his disposal. This Tolstoi did in "War and Peace." I have never yet succeeded in doing it completely and perfectly. Accordingly, Tolstoi is a more autobiographical writer than I am, because he has succeeded better in using what he had. But make no mistake about it: both of us, and every other man who ever wrote a book, are autobiographical. You are therefore not to touch my life in this way. When you or any man tries to exert this kind of control, to modify or shape my material in an improper way because of some paltry, personal, social apprehension, you do the unpardonable thing. You try to take from the artist his personal property, to steal his substance, to defraud him of his treasure—the only treasure he has, the only property and wealth which is truly, inexorably, his own.

You can take it from him, but by so doing you commit a crime. You have stolen what does not belong to you. You have not only taken what belongs to another man, but you have taken what belongs to him in such a way that no one else can possibly claim ownership. No one owns what he has as does the artist. When you try to steal it from him he only laughs at you, because you could take it to the ends of the earth and bury it in a mountain and it would still shine straight through the mountain side like radium. You couldn't hide it. Any one on earth could find it and would know at once who the proper owner was.

That is what this final argument is about. I'm not going to be interfered with on this score. I get my material, I acquire my wealth, as every artist does, from his own living, from his own experience, from his own observation. And when any outer agency tries to interpose itself between me and any portion of my own property, however small, and says to me "hands off," [or] "you can't have that particular piece there," someone is going to get hurt.

You told me when I discussed these things with you in October, after my return from Europe, that you agreed with me, that in the last analysis you were always with the man of talent, and that if the worst comes to the worst you could resign your executive and editorial functions. Well, don't worry, you'll never have to. In the first place, your executive and editorial functions are so special and valuable that they can not be substituted by any other person on earth. They could not be done without by the business that employs them. It would be like having a house with the lights turned out. Furthermore, no one is going to resign on my account. There are still enough people in the world who value what I do, I believe, to support me freely, heartily and cheerfully, with no sense that they are enduring martyrdom on my account. So if there is ever any situation that might indicate any future necessity for any one to resign anything on my account, that situation will never arise, simply because I won't be there to be resigned about.

This business about the artist hurting people is for the most part nonsense. The artist is not here in life to hurt it but to illuminate it. He is not here to teach men hatred but to show them beauty. No one in the end ever got hurt by a great book, or if he did, the hurt was paltry and temporary in comparison to the immense good that was conferred.

Now, at a time when I am more firmly resolved than ever before to exert my full amount, to use my full stroke, to shine my purest and intensest ray, it is distressing to see the very people who published my first efforts with complete equanimity, and with no qualms whatever about the possibility of anybody getting "hurt," begin to squirm around uncomfortably and call for calf-rope and whine that their own toes are being stepped upon, even when nothing has been said, nothing written. They have no knowledge or declaration of my own intention except that I intend in my own way to finish my own book. What are you going to do about it? You say you are not aware that there have been any difficulties or any severance. If these things I have been talking about are not difficulties, if this is not a threatened severance of the gravest nature, I should like to know what you consider difficult and what severance is? We can not continue in this irresolute, temporizing "Well now, you go ahead for the present—we'll wait and see how it all turns out" manner. My life has been ravaged, my energy exhausted, my work confused and aborted long enough by this kind of miserable, time-serving procrastination. I'm not going to endure it any longer. I'm not going to pour my sweat and blood and energy and life and talent into another book now, only to be told two or three years from now that it would be inadvisable to publish it without certain formidable deletions, or that perhaps we'd better wait a few years longer and see "how everything turns out."

We stalled around this way with "October Fair," until all the intensity and passion I had put into the book was lost, until I had gone stale on it, until I was no longer interested in it—and to what purpose? Why, because you allowed your fond weakness for the female sex to get the better of your principle, because you were afraid some foolish female, who was inwardly praying for nothing better than to be a leading character in a book of mine, and who was bitterly disappointed when she was not, might get her feelings hurt—or that the pocketbook of the firm might get touched by suits for libel. Well, there would have been no suits for libel. I never libelled anybody in my life. Certainly, there was no remote danger of libel in "The October Fair," but because of our weakness and irresolution the news got around that we were afraid of publication for this reason. The rumor was spread around in the column of a . . . gossip-writer,[4] and the result now is that we have a libel suit on our hands from a person who was never libelled, who doesn't have a leg to stand on, but who is willing to take the chance and make the effort to get something because we were not firm and resolute in the beginning.

Let's make an end of all this devil's business. Let's stand to our guns

---

[4] In *The New York Daily Mirror* for Monday, September 21, 1936, Walter Winchell wrote: "Thomas Wolfe, author of *Of Time and the River* and *Look Homeward, Angel*, has held up publication of his latest novel until all the people in it die. His last two slightly autobiographical tomes brought several libel suits." This is probably what Wolfe refers to here.

like men. Let's go ahead and try to do our work without qualification, without fear, without apology. What are you willing to do? My own position is now clear. I have nothing to be afraid of. And my greatest duty, my deepest obligation now is to the completion of my own work. If that can not be done any longer upon the terms that I have stated here, then I must either stand alone or turn to other quarters for support, if I can find it. You yourself must now say plainly what the decision is to be, because the decision now rests with you. You can no longer have any doubt as to how I feel about these matters. I don't see how you can any longer have any doubt that difficulties of a grave and desperate nature do exist.

I can only repeat here what I have told you before, that the possibility of an irrevocable and permanent severance has caused me the greatest distress and anguish of the mind for months, that if it occurs it will seem to me like death, but that whatever happens, what I have said and written about the way I feel towards you will remain.

I'm going South in a few days for the first time in seven years. It is a tremendous experience for me. Those seven years to me have been a lifetime. So much has been crowded into them—exile and vituperation from my own country, modest success and recognition, then partial oblivion, years of struggling and despairing to conquer a new medium, to fashion a new world, partial success again, added recognition, partial oblivion again. It seems to move in cycles. Now I'm up against the same grim struggle, the same necessity for new discovery, new beginning, new achievement, as before. It will be strange to be back home again. I had but recently met you when I was there last. I was unknown then, but within a few weeks after my visit home a storm of calumny and abuse broke out that made me long for my former oblivion. Now that storm apparently has died down. They are willing to have me come back. So much has happened in those seven years. I've seen so many people that I know go down to ruin, others have died, others have grown up, some have lost everything, some have recovered something. People I knew well I no longer see. People who swore eternal love are now irrevocably separated. Nothing has turned out as we thought it would turn out. Nothing is the way we thought it was going to be. But Life, I now begin to see, moves in a great wheel; the wheel swings and things and people that we knew are lost, but some day they come back again. So it is a strange and wonderful event for me to be going back home. I knew so little of the world and people then, although I thought I knew so much of them. Now I really think I know a little more about the world and people than I knew then, and I think all of us understand a little more about one another.

I'm sorry this letter has had to be so long. It seemed to me there had to be some sort of final statement. I hope, now the statement has been made, the problem is more clear. I send all of you now all my best wishes for Christmas and for a New Year which I hope will bring to all of us an accomplishment and fulfillment of some of those things we most desire.

Meanwhile, with all friendship, all good wishes,

—Max, this is not a well-written letter, but it is a genuine and honest one. If you still have any interest in me, please attend to what I say here carefully!

P.S. New Orleans, Jan. 10, 1937: I have withheld this letter as long as possible. I had hoped against hope not to have to send it. But now, after the shocking events of the past two weeks since I left New York— Mitchell's letter conveying the blackmail threats of —— — the growing peril of my situation in a mesh of scoundrelism—and your own telegram—the increasing ambiguity and caution of your own statements— I have read the letter through again and decided that *it must be sent*. In spite of its great length there is much more to say—but let this stand now for a record!

For Perkins' full replies to this letter, see Editor to Author: The Letters of Maxwell E. Perkins, *pages 119-126. Perkins wrote three letters in reply. The first, dated January 13, said in part:* "My belief is that the one important, supreme object is to advance your work . . . What impedes it especially is . . . the harassment . . . of outside worries. When you spoke to me about the settlement . . . it was only because of that that I gave the advice I did. . . . As to my own self: I stand ready to help if I can, whenever you want. You asked my help on Of Time and the River. . . . No understanding person could believe that it . . . was much more than mechanical help. . . . Apart from physical or legal limitations not within the possibility of change by us, we will publish anything as you write it."

The second was a short note dated January 14, saying in part: "I've read your letter carefully. . . . I have no quarrel with any of it, except that you have greatly misunderstood some things I must explain. . . . Your position is right. I understand and agree with it."

The third letter, dated January 16, is too long and too complex to represent adequately by brief quotations, but says in part: "In the first place, I completely subscribe to what you say a writer should do. . . . But there are limitations of time, of space, and of human laws which cannot be treated as if they did not exist. I think that a writer should, of course, be the one to make his book what he wants it to be, and that if . . . it must be cut, he should be

*the one to cut it. . . . It would be better if you could fight it out alone—
better for your work, in the end, certainly. . . . I believe the writer, anyway,
should always be the final judge, and I meant you to be so. . . .*

"*I certainly do not care—nor does this House—how revolutionary your
books are. I did try to keep you from injecting . . . Marxian beliefs into
Time and the River, because they were . . . not those of Eugene in the
time of the book. . . . It seems as if you must have forgotten how we
worked and argued. You were never overruled . . . I do not want the passage of time to make you cautious or conservative, but I do want it to give
you a full control . . . over your great talent.*

"*Tom, you ought not to say . . . that I find your sufferings amusing . . .
I do try to turn your mind from them and to arouse your humor, because to
spend dreadful hours brooding over them . . . seems . . . only to aggravate
them.*

"*Then comes the question of your writing about the people here . . . I
agree that you have the same right to make use of them as of anyone else.
. . . When I spoke of resigning after we published—and the moment I inadvertently said it I told Miss Nowell she must not repeat it . . . I did not
mean I would be asked . . . to resign. But . . . it's up to you to write as
you think you should. . . .*

"*There remains the question of whether we are in fundamental agreement.
. . . I have always . . . felt that it was so. . . . But I believe in democracy
and not in dictators . . . and that violence breeds more evils than it kills.
. . . I believe that change really comes from great deep causes too complex
for contemporary men . . . fully to understand and that when even great
men like Lenin try to make over a whole society suddenly the end is almost
sure to be bad, and that the right end, the natural one, will come from the
efforts of innumerable people trying to do right, and to understand it, because
they are a part of the natural forces that are set at work by changed conditions. . . . But this is getting to be too much of a philosophy of history or
something, and I don't think it has anything to do with fundamental agreement. I had always felt it existed—and I don't feel, because you differ with
me . . . on such things . . . that it does not. . . .*

"*Anyway, I don't see why you should have hesitated to . . . send the letter. . . . There were places in it that made me angry, but it was . . . a fine
writer's statement of his beliefs . . . and . . . it gave me great pleasure
too—that which comes from hearing brave and sincere beliefs uttered with
sincerity and nobility.*"

*The following is "the business letter" which Wolfe never mailed. In it he
is quoting from his own letter of November 12 and Perkins' reply of November 18.*

To MAXWELL E. PERKINS

865 First Avenue
New York, N.Y.
December 23, 1936

Dear Max:

I have already written you a long answer to your two personal letters of November 17th and November 18th which you should have received by the time you receive this. Now, before I go away, I want to write an answer to your formal business letter of November 18th, in which you state the relations that now exist between myself and Charles Scribner's Sons.

First of all, let me thank you for acknowledging that I have faithfully and honorably discharged all obligations to you and that no further agreement of any sort exists between us with respect to the future. Then I want to tell you that I am sorry you found parts of my letter obscure and did not wholly understand them. I am sorry, because it seemed to me that the letter was clear. But if there has been any misunderstanding as to what I meant, I shall try to clarify it now.

You say you do not wholly understand the part where "you speak of us as putting you in a position of denying an obligation that does not exist, for we do not know that we have done that." Well, what I said in my letter was "I think it is unfair to put a man in a position where he is forced to deny an obligation that does not exist, to refuse an agreement that was never offered and never made." That is a little different from the way you put it, but I thought it was clear, but if further explanation be needed, I can tell you that what I meant to say by "I think it is unfair to put a man in a position where he is forced to deny an obligation that does not exist" is simply that no one has a right in my opinion to mix calculation and friendship, business caution with personal friendship, financial astuteness with personal affection. The artist cannot do that. Where his friendship, affection and devotion are involved he cannot say, "I think the world of all of you but of course business is business and I shall make such publishing arrangements as shall be most profitable to me." That is what I meant by "I think it is unfair to put a man in a position where he is forced to deny an obligation that does not exist." For, although you have acknowledged that no obligation does exist, after two years of delay since the publication of "Of Time and the River" no concrete proposal has ever been made to me concerning my novel or novels which were to follow it. I have waited in vain, with growing anxiety and bewilderment for such a proposal to be made until the matter has now reached a point of critical acuteness which compelled me to write you as I have written you and say "I think it is unfair to put a man in a position where he is forced to deny an obligation that does not exist."

As to the next phrase, "to refuse an agreement that was never offered and never made," I think the meaning of that phrase is now sufficiently clarified by what has been already said.

To proceed: You say you also do not wholly understand the part of my letter where I "refer to 'exerting control of a man's future' which we have no intention of doing at all, and would not have the power or right to do." What I said was "I think it is also unfair to try to exert, at no expense to oneself, such control of a man's future and his future work as will bring one profit if that man succeeds, and that absolves one from any commitments of any kind should he fail." I thought that sentence was clear too. But if you require additional explanation I can only say that what I meant was that I did not think it fair again to play business against friendship, to accept the loyalty and devotion of an author to the firm that has published him without saying precisely upon what terms and upon what conditions you are willing to publish him in the future. In other words, if I must be still more explicit, I am now in the undeniable position of being compelled to tell people who ask me who my publisher is, that my publisher is Charles Scribner's Sons, while Charles Scribner's Sons on their part, without risk, without involving criticism of any sort, are undeniably in the position where they are able to tell any one that they are my publishers, provided they want to be, but are not my publishers if they do not want to be.

You continue in your letter by saying "there are other phrases in that part of your letter that I do not understand, one of which is that which refers to us as being absolved from any commitments of any kind 'should the author fail.' " I do not see why you should have found this statement obscure or puzzling, but if you did I think that what I have already said in this letter precisely and exactly defines my meaning.

You continue by saying "if this and these other phrases signify that you think you should have a contract from us if our relations are to continue, you can certainly have one. We should be delighted to have one. You must surely know the faith this house has in you. There are, of course, limits in terms to which nobody can go in a contract, but we should expect to make one that would suit you if you told us what was required."

I think it is now my turn to be puzzled. I do not wholly understand what you mean when you say "we should expect to make one" (a contract) "that would suit you if you told us what was required." This really seems almost too good to be true. I have never heard of an author before being able and privileged to tell a publisher "what was required" in the terms of a contract. I cannot believe that is a practice of the publishing business. Authors do not dictate terms of a publisher's contracts. The publisher states the terms himself, and the author accepts them. For my part, so far as my relations with Scribners are concerned, I have always accepted what was offered to me instantly and without question. It seems now a delightfully unexpected, overwhelming privilege to be suddenly told that it is now up to me to state "what is required" in the way of a contract.

Well, then, if I am to be allowed this privilege, may I ask for information on these specific points? When you say in your letter that "our relations are simply those of a publisher who profoundly admires the work of an author and takes great pride in publishing whatever he may of that author's writings," in what sense and meaning am I going to understand the word "may"? I hate to quibble about words, but since you have yourself found it difficult and hard to understand phrases and sentences in my own letter which seem absolutely clear to me, it seems to me that the interpretation of even a little word like "may" may be important. Neither of us surely is so ingenuous as to believe that this statement means that Scribners is eagerly waiting my gracious permission to publish any and all manuscript that I may choose to give to them. We both know that such an interpretation as this would be ridiculous. We both know that in the past six or seven years I have written several million words of which Scribners has published approximately seven or eight hundred thousand. We both know that you have seen and read millions of words of my manuscript which have never been published, which you rejected for publication flatly, or whose publication you advised against. We both know that I not only accepted your advice gratefully but that I also accepted your decision without question, even though it sometimes caused me grievous disappointment when I found that something I had thought good and worthy of publication was not thought good or worthy of publication by the person in whose judgment and critical authority I had and still have unqualified belief. We both know that there was never a time, there has never been a moment since I first walked into your office eight years ago, when I have been in a position to hand you a piece of manuscript and arbitrarily demand that you publish it. The right of selection has always been yours. The right of rejection has always been yours. The right to say what you would or would not publish has always, and to my mind, properly, been finally and absolutely your own privilege. It seems manifest therefore that what you mean by the word "may" as used in your sentence must be interpreted as what you "may see fit" to publish. To this interpretation I have certainly never objected, but now that this misunderstanding and the danger of possible misinterpretation has arisen,

I must ask you, secondly, if you won't try to specify, insofar as you are able, what it is you may see fit to publish of mine. I understand, of course, that there are obvious limits to what a publisher may be expected to publish—limits imposed by law and custom. But within those limits, how far are you willing to go?

You say in one of your personal letters that you "have never doubted for my future on any grounds except, at times, on those of being unable to control the vast mass of material I have accumulated and have to form into books." Alas, it has now become evident that this is not the only difficulty. It is not even any longer a fundamental one. As I have explained in my long letter to you, no matter how great a man's material may be, it has its limits. He can come to the end of it. No man can exceed his own material. It is his constant effort to surpass it, it is true—but he cannot spend money when he has not got it, he can not fish coin from the empty air, he cannot plank it down across the counter when his pockets are empty. No man has more than his one life, and no man's material is greater than his one life can absorb and hold. No man, therefore, not even the artist, can become the utter spendthrift with what he has. It is spitting straight in the face of fortune, and in the end he will get paid back for his folly. You say you have been worried about my being able to control my vast masses of material. May I tell you that in the past year one of my own chief and constantly growing worries has been whether I shall have any material left that I could use if you continue to advise against my present use of it, or if these growing anxieties and perturbations in the year past as to what I should use, as to what I should write about, continued to develop to the utter enervation and castration of my work. Therefore, having as you do some approximate knowledge, a far better one than any one else at any rate, of the material at my command, can't you try, in view of all these doubts and misunderstandings, to specify what you think you may be able to publish and how much of it?

Third, at about what time would you now desire and expect to publish it, if I fulfilled my work in time? I know that I have been grievously at fault in meeting publication dates heretofore, but you know too it has not been through lack of effort or of application but rather through the difficulties imposed by my own nature and my imperfect understanding of the writer's art and the command of the tools of my profession. Nevertheless, and in spite of all these imperfections on my part, I should like to get some fairly definite notion of when it is you next expect to publish me, if ever. The reason that I am so earnestly and seriously concerned with this is that in former years, before the publication of "Of Time and the River," you did show the greatest anxiety on this score. You were constant in your efforts to spur me on, to get me to complete and finish something for publication. Now, although almost two years have gone by since the publication of my last long book, you no longer show any anxiety whatever and, so far as I can judge, no immediate interest.

Finally, if you do want to publish another book of mine, if you can try to tell me what it is you think you want to publish, what you will be able to publish, and when you would like to publish it—what, finally and specifically, are these terms of which you speak?

You say "there are, of course, limits in terms to which nobody can go in a contract, but we should expect to make one that would suit you if you told us what was required." I suppose, of course, that when you say that there are "limits in terms to which nobody can go in a contract" you mean that there are limits in terms beyond which no one can go. I understand this perfectly. But what, specifically, are these limits? What, specifically, are these terms?

Now I'm awfully sorry, Max, to have to try your patience with another long letter, and I am sorry if I seem to quibble over words and phrases, but I really do not think I quibble, since all these matters are of such vital and immediate concern to me and since we both have seemed to have trouble understanding sentences and phrases in each other's letters. I have gone to extreme lengths in this one to make everything I say as clear as possible. I shall be on my way South when you get this letter. I intend to be in New Orleans New Year's day, but since I am still uncertain whether I shall stay with friends or in a hotel, I suggest that you write me, if you have time and feel like writing, in care of General Delivery.

Meanwhile, until I hear from you, or until I see you again, with all my best and friendliest greetings to everyone at Scribners,

Max: This letter is imperative. I must have an answer—a definite one—at once.

I have deferred sending this, and accordingly am sending it from Richmond, Va. (But I deferred that too!)

P.S. I am writing you this from Richmond. Frankly, I think we are at the end. I am sending this to you now. I should have sent it to you long ago, in view of the agony, the despair, the utter desolation this thing has cost me—but I must send it to you now. As to the other letter—the enormously long letter I wrote in answer to your two personal ones [1]—I shall hold

---

[1] The "Personal Letter" dated December 15, 1936 and mailed on January 10.

on to it a day longer—reread it—perhaps make little revisions here and there. Anything! Anything!—to try to temper the sorrow and the grief of this final decision into which I—God knows—have been compelled without even the power of saying whether I wanted it or not. You must answer this *straight!*

Additional P.S. As to your statement that anyone would *want* me—that, as you must *now* know, is not true. I am almost penniless—this suit for libel has appeared with almost sinister immediacy in the last month or two—I have turned down fortunes—$10,000 *is* a fortune to me, and you knew of *that* one at once, the one that was made me two years ago when I was really penniless, and when you asked me to tell you what the offer was. I am broke—I have lost everything—I do not think we can go on. Who, then, are these eager publishers? Answer at New Orleans.

P.S. Max: You'd better send the answer air mail to New Orleans. I am afraid you did not take this thing seriously but, as I told you, it is like death to me. You'd better answer by wire. Atlanta, December 29, 1936. You'd better say *precisely* what you can offer. Atlanta December 29, 1936.

To ELIZABETH NOWELL

[Chapel Hill, N.C.]
Sunday, January 24, 1937

Dear Miss Nowell:

I have been unable to do much to this first installment [1] since coming here. People have swarmed around me—old friends I have not seen in seventeen years or so—and there has been no time for anything. I went over the first half of this installment and made—or rather indicated—a few cuts. If you and *The New Republic* think them good, make them: if not, you can leave it as it stands. This first section is something over 5,000 words but I have found it very hard to cut. I intend to be back in New York Wednesday, and will call you then.

I wish you could wait with this till Wednesday. Wouldn't *The New Republic* let you? I'm worried about a lot of things—phonetics, accents, etc. I'm not yet sure what to do about all the "zis," "zese," "zem" business.

[1] The first installment of "I Have a Thing to Tell You" which was to be published in the March 10 issue of *The New Republic*.

I want to use as little as possible and yet to be consistent. I must either do without them entirely—or use them constantly. Please go through the manuscript and, if you think best, make it consistent—that is, get all the "th" words consistent: "fazzer," "mozzer," "zis," "zat," etc. The character I had in mind really did not speak with such a marked or broken accent: yet he *did* have an accent and I had to suggest it somehow. Have I overdone it? Wait till Wednesday if you can.

Garland B. Porter, to whom the following letter was written, had known Wolfe at the University of North Carolina. They had met by accident in Atlanta when Wolfe was on his way to New Orleans, and Porter had invited Wolfe to visit him on his way back. At this time, Porter was national advertising manager of The Atlanta Georgian *and southern manager for the Hearst Advertising Service. He is now general manager of* Southern Advertising and Publishing.

To GARLAND B. PORTER

865 First Avenue
New York, N.Y.

February 1, 1937

Dear Garland:

I should have written you before this, but since I left you I haven't had much time. I got back here a week ago and had to plunge into work right away getting a long piece, which *The New Republic* is going to publish, cut down to printable proportions. It was a wonderful trip and one of the nicest things about it was seeing you again and meeting the family. Please give them all my love and tell them how much I want to see them all again.

I stayed three or four days with Jim Boyd after leaving Atlanta and had a grand time there. They are fine people. They have a beautiful place right in the pine woods. I can't tell you how good it was to be back in my own state again and just to get my number fourteens down on North Carolina clay. I went up to Chapel Hill and stayed four or five days. It was a great experience. It took me about two days to get used to the place. They've created another world since you and I were at school there, but down below I think the people are much the same as they always were. I saw Horace [1] twice and had long talks with him,

[1] Professor Horace Williams.

and also met dozens of other people I had known. Horace holds his own, I think, amazingly well. He is older, of course, and a little feebler, than when we sat in his classes, but the old man can still flash like a rapier. He can talk as he always could. I think he may be lonely now. His active connection with the University has almost ceased, and of course the greatest part of his life, for almost fifty years, was with his students. I suppose with the present student generation he is more or less of a legend, and I don't believe they'd beat a path to his door the way they used to do.

I saw Paul Green [2] and Phillips Russell,[3] Jonathan Daniels, Albert Coates and a host of other people we both know. I stayed with Shorty Spruill [4] and his wife. It was wonderful to find that so many people I had known still lived in Chapel Hill. Then I went up to Warrenton for two or three days and stayed with Bill Polk and his family. I don't know if there's any chance of you and the missus coming up here within the next few months, but if you do please let me know. . . . I'm still short on sleep, but otherwise I had a much-needed change and the wonderful stimulation of seeing old friends, home folks, home soil again. I'm getting back to work as soon and as hard as possible. I hope to do another big job this spring and to come back to North Carolina for another visit late in April. I send you all my love and best wishes. Please write me when you get a chance.

Ever since his return to New York at the end of January, Wolfe had avoided Scribners, but he still frequented Perkins' house on East 49th Street. Both men knew that his complete severance from Scribners was almost inevitable, but they continued to argue endlessly about it in some faint hope that it could be averted. The following telegram, scrawled in pencil in Wolfe's pocket notebook, was evidently written soon after his return from New Orleans but was never sent.

[2] Paul Green had attended the University of North Carolina with Wolfe and been a member of The Carolina Playmakers with him. He is the author of *Lonesome Road, In Abraham's Bosom, Tread the Green Grass, This Body the Earth, Hymn to the Rising Sun,* and other plays and novels.

[3] Phillips Russell had graduated from the University of North Carolina earlier but returned there as a teacher in 1931. He is now Professor of Journalism there, and the author of *Benjamin Franklin: First Civilized American; Emerson: The Wisest American; The Glittering Century, The Woman Who Rang the Bell,* etc.

[4] Corydon P. Spruill was in Wolfe's class at the University of North Carolina and closely associated with him. He returned to the university as Professor of Economics, and is now Dean.

To MAXWELL E. PERKINS
[Telegram]

[New York City]
[February ?, 1937]

Dear Max Perkins:
Does Scribners want my next book? Please answer immediately.

XV

THE RETURN TO ASHEVILLE AND THE FINAL
BREAK WITH SCRIBNERS

1937

To FRED W. WOLFE

865 First Avenue
New York, N.Y.
February 23, 1937

Dear Fred:

I have been wanting to write you before, but I've been down with flu
and also had to do a lot of work and spend a lot of time with the lawyers
since I returned from the South. I got a long letter from Mama this
morning in answer to one I wrote her a week or so ago. She tells me
something about her affairs in it and about the suit which the Wachovia
Bank is bringing against the family.[1] I gather that, since I am a member
of the family, I am also mentioned as one of the parties in the suit. If
this is true, I should like to have a little more specific information about
it. I've had a good deal to do with suits and lawyers in the last two years,
and, although this is one branch of human activity I never wanted to take
part in and never sought out on my own account, it is just possible I may
have learned a little and might be able to help out now with suggestions.
So why don't you write me now and try to tell me what it's all about?

---

[1] The Wachovia Bank and Trust Company of Asheville had brought suit against
Mrs. Wolfe, her heirs, itself as her trustee, and various individuals who held liens on
her property. They alleged that she had borrowed various sums of money from them
since 1927, for which she had executed certain deeds of trust and had put up various
pieces of real estate as pledges of security. They petitioned that since she owed them
various amounts of money as principal and interest on these loans, the property be
foreclosed and sold to settle her indebtedness to them. A court settlement of the case
was finally made in 1939.

I read Mama's letter carefully two or three times, and although I do understand certain things in it, I don't understand why she, or particularly the children—for certainly I knew nothing about it—are being sued. According to Mama's letter, the Wachovia, about ten years ago, persuaded her to make out what she calls a "living trust." She says she signed the trust, but that she did not fully understand what was in it, or just what it was she was signing. The gist of the letter from then on, as I understand it, is that the bank . . . sold property at prices far lower than the property was worth, etc. I can follow all this, and can understand how, if these facts are true and could be substantiated in court, we would have cause for action against the Wachovia Bank. But why has the Wachovia Bank cause for action against Mama, and, more especially, against her children? . . . I'd like to know what their side of the story is, what do they claim, upon what contention do they base their suit against Mama, you and me and all the rest of us? And the reason I ask for this information is because your side of the case and Mama's side of the case is also my side of the case. So far as possible, I should like to get the facts clear in my mind.

I now intend to come to Asheville and to go out into the mountains for a few days at the end of April or the early part of May, and perhaps I may be able to be of some assistance to you then. I hope so, because of course I am wholeheartedly on Mama's side. I think it is shameful to see them take her house away from her, and I shall do whatever I can to prevent it. Therefore, I think you ought to take me into your confidence. I know that none of you ever thought I was much of a business man and I would cheerfully agree with all of you that I am not. But I think I can also point out to you that whatever money I've lost has been lost because I have been the victim of rackets to which, my lawyers inform me, almost everyone of any public reputation here in America is exposed and against which there seems at the present time to be no defense save a defense that would cost more time and money and worry than the racket itself. There is nothing that I can do about this condition except to hope and pray that it will change, and to do whatever I can in my own individual capacity to bring it to light, to make people aware of it, and to try as a good citizen to change it. But I've never been taken in by any get-rich-quick schemes yet. I never had much belief in them. The most I have hoped for is the chance to earn a decent living, get some security against the future, and have peace and time in which to do my work. On this ground, I'm pretty sound and sure of myself, so I wish you'd try to tell me in a little more detail just what this suit against *us* is all about.

I'm just getting over flu and it's left me feeling pretty weak, but

I keep on working. I'm getting a little better every day now. The trouble with the lawyers was about to get me down, but I didn't let it happen. There's not going to be much left when I get through paying the rascals off, or what amounts to just the same thing, paying lawyers to defend me against the rascals. But I shall get through it somehow and do another big piece or work, and some day, perhaps, get a rip-snorting book out of this whole experience, which I imagine you could throw in under the general title of "Life" and not be far wrong about it.

I had a good trip through the South but didn't get much rest. People were after me all the time and, just to make things pleasant, the lawyers wrote informing me . . . that I'd better come back right away. I should have liked to come to Asheville and intended to do so, but when I called you up from Atlanta there seemed to be some excitement and confusion about my coming, or whether I wanted to come or not, so I was too tired to argue the point and decided to pass my visit up until some other time.

Yes, I got your gift of neckties, and your box of nuts and raisins. I'm sorry that I did not acknowledge them before, but let me thank you for them now.

I have tried to do the best I could towards everyone. I've had to deal with a lot of trouble. I've gone through a lot of worry and suffered a lot of disillusionment, and of course, with me as with every other man, one of the main troubles of life, one of the chief worries, is how to get a job and keep on doing it. Maybe my own experience is a little different from most people's. I have a job and a big one too—more work than I can possibly do. But the last year or two, it has sometimes seemed to me that there is a general plot abroad not to keep people like myself out of work but to keep them from doing the work they already have. Not many people realize very well what a man is up against if he has been unfortunate enough to get his name in the papers a few times, and it sometimes seems that one's old friends and acquaintance know it least of all. It sometimes seems that whenever a man gets a little public notice the very people who have known him longest show the least understanding of all the problems he has got to meet. I'll get through this somehow and, meanwhile, there's always the hope I'll get a chance to work, to get an even break, to earn enough from what I write to get rid of the lawyers and the rascals and to earn my living without getting into debt.

This is all for the present. Mama tells me she is going to Miami for a a week or so. I know the change will do her good. I am enclosing a little check for her. . . . I'd be much obliged to you if you'd send it right along to her and tell her please to try to have a little fun. . . . Write me when you can, and tell me something if you can about Mama's difficulties. With all best wishes, as ever,

On the afternoon of February 17, 1937, Wolfe and Charles Scribner had a long discussion on the telephone about the advisability of settling the libel suit, in the course of which Wolfe evidently reiterated his demand for a complete release from Scribners. Accordingly, the following day, Mr. Scribner wrote him, saying: "You can feel assured that we have no option or moral claim on any of your future books. We should like to continue as your publishers as we have every faith in your work and feel certain that you are due to write even finer books than those which we have published. On the other hand, if you find that the connection with us is not to your liking, I certainly do not wish to press you to continue. With regard to the present libel suit, we agreed at luncheon to go fifty-fifty on this, and you agreed to settle it for not over $2500. . . . The more I think of it, the more certain I am that it would be the wise thing to get this out of the way, for your own peace of mind. I fully appreciate the fact that you do not wish to be held up, but it would certainly take a lot of time and money to fight it out. If you decide, however, that you would rather not settle, I am perfectly prepared to back you in seeing it through to a finish."

A few days after this, Wolfe reluctantly agreed to settle the suit. Accordingly, his half of the settlement and lawyer's fees, which half amounted to $2745.25, were paid by Scribners from his royalty account in three separate installments on February 23, April 1, and May 3. He was horrified to see his savings thus wiped out, blamed the whole affair on Scribners, and took Charles Scribner's letter of February 18 as proof that he was "free to go." The following letter approaching publishers other than Scribners was probably written as a result of all this, in March, 1937, but was never mailed. However, in December, 1937, Wolfe handed it to Edward C. Aswell of Harper & Brothers, saying that it would explain the nature of his severance from Scribners.

To ALL PUBLISHERS

[OTHER THAN SCRIBNERS]

865 First Avenue
New York, N.Y.
[March, 1937?]

Gentlemen:

I am the author of four published books, of which two are novels, one, a book of stories, and one, a short volume about my experience as a writer. Since I am no longer under any obligation, whether financial, contractual, or personal, to any publisher, I am writing to inquire if I could talk to you about my future work.

In order that there may be nothing in this letter capable of misinterpretation, I want to state here with the utmost candor my reasons for

writing you. First of all, I want to say most earnestly that I am not approaching any publisher at the present time in an effort to secure good
terms and get a contract, but in the genuine hope that this letter will
reach some person of critical judgment and understanding who will
be interested—and disinterested—enough to listen to my story, allow me
to lay the matter before him, with all its difficulties and complexities,
and then, if he can, give me the benefit of his advice.

This would involve the discussion of unpublished manuscript that runs
into millions of words, and projects for work that will occupy me for
years. I realize that to ask for advice and guidance of this sort from
people that I do not know, when I have at the present time no completed
work to offer for examination, is a strenuous and perhaps unwarranted
demand upon the generosity of a stranger, but necessity of the gravest
kind has compelled me to this course as being the only one that is now
left open to me.

May I say here that so far as my relations with my former publishers
are concerned, they have been characterized from beginning to end on
both sides by feelings of the deepest affection and respect. I have been
fortunate in having for my publishers a firm which not only enjoys a
public and professional standing of the highest order but which, in all its
dealings with me has been eminently just and fair. Moreover, the nature
of our relationship has been so peculiarly intimate and personal that no
one can possibly know, better than myself, the gravity of the step I am
now taking, or the peril with which it is charged.

For seven years or more I have enjoyed the friendship of an editor
of extraordinary character and ability, who at a time when I needed help
desperately, when I was trying to learn how to write, when I was involved
with gigantic masses of material and struggling with a task of such magnitude that at times I almost gave up in despair, stood by me and gave
me without stint not only the benefits of his great technical and editorial
skill but also the even more priceless support of his faith and belief, a
spiritual sustenance of the grandest and most unselfish kind. To this man
I owe a debt of gratitude so deep and lasting that I feel I can never repay
it, or never sufficiently testify to it by anything I say or write. And the
prospect of this severance of our relations—professionally, at any rate—
not only with this man but with many other people in that house, is
for me not only a prospect of the utmost gravity, but it is like having to
face the prospect of making a new, and perhaps disastrous, beginning in
life.

But I can see no other course before me. For months now, perhaps
for a year, or more, there has been a steady widening of the ground
between us, a difference of opinion, of conviction, of belief, even a

spiritual severance that is so profound and grave that it touches the very heart of my life and work, and if I remain I see no prospect before me but the utter enervation of my work, my final bafflement and frustration as an artist.

I should like to say here further that the necessity which compels me to write this letter is, I believe, understood and appreciated thoroughly by my former publishers, has been examined and discussed so thoroughly in the conversation and correspondence of several months that there is now nothing more to say on either side, except that this necessity is a matter of the most genuine and profound regret to each of us.

Now I can only say, with utter candor, that I hope that I am prepared to do the best work of my life, but that, if I am to do any work at all, I can now do it only by making no compromise of artistic integrity, by making rather the most full, free, honest, and final use of my talents and of my materials that I have ever made.

Finally I should like to say that these differences, I believe, were inevitable and inescapable, that they have been honorably and honestly arrived at on both sides, and that the feeling of friendship and respect between my publishers and myself is as deep as it always was. I believe that they would confirm me in all I say.

To have to write in a formal letter, and at such length, explanations of such intimate and personal concern to myself and other people, is a painful and difficult task. But it seemed to me that, circumstances being what they are, to write less explicitly than I have might lay open to misinterpretation not only my own position but my relations to other people whose conduct has been generous and high.

As I have no wide acquaintance in the publishing profession I have taken this means, as difficult as it is, as being the only one by which I could state my problem and establish contact with someone who might help me. Accordingly, I have addressed this letter to several publishers. But, so far as possible, within these limitations, I hope that the contents of this letter will be treated as personal and confidential.

I believe that I am now engaged upon the most important book that I have ever written. But the book is far from complete: a great task is before me. Now I should like to talk to some editor of critical understanding and judgment, for the purpose of laying the matter before him, with complete frankness and with all the difficulties and perplexities it entails.

If there is such a person in your house who is willing to give me an evening's time, with no commitments on either side, I should be grateful for his courtesy in doing so. I can be reached at this address, and any evening after March twenty-fifth would be convenient.

Dixon Wecter had first met Wolfe at the University of Colorado where he was an assistant professor of English when Wolfe attended the Writers' Conference there in 1935. On Wolfe's recommendation, he had taken his book, The Saga of American Society, *to Scribners who were to publish it soon after the date of the following letter. He had therefore written Wolfe saying: "I have an impulse to write and tell you how everlastingly grateful I am for your introduction to Maxwell Perkins. As Thornton Wilder told me some time ago, he is 'the last of the great paternal editors.'" The following was Wolfe's reply.*

At the time of his death in 1950, Wecter was a professor of English at the University of California, Literary Editor of the Mark Twain Estate, and author of The Saga of American Society; Edmund Burke and His Kinsmen; The Hero in America (*with William Matthews*); Our Soldiers Speak; When Johnny Comes Marching Home; The Age of the Great Depression, *etc. His* Sam Clemens of Hannibal *was published posthumously in 1952.*

To DIXON WECTER

865 First Avenue
New York, N.Y.

March 5, 1937

Dear Dixon:

I was delighted to get your letter, and so glad to know you have at last finished your long labor on the book. I don't get around to Scribners nowadays, but I can tell you out of my own knowledge that Perkins is delighted with the book and with the job you have done, and in his reticent fashion displays as much hope of the book's success as I can remember his showing over anything. He has told me repeatedly what a fine book it is, and he told me recently that there was no doubt that it would receive a fine critical reception, but that he also hoped and believed it might have a good popular reception too. At any rate, I can assure you that you are in the hands of people on whom you can utterly rely.

I was so happy to read what you said about Perkins, because that is the way I feel too. I agree absolutely with everything you say, except your too modest estimate of your own abilities, which Perkins certainly rates very highly. But I don't believe his like is to be found anywhere in the editorial world. In fact, I think he has a faculty of intuition and understanding that amounts to genius. He has certainly done more, I think, not only to discover but to stimulate new talent than any man of his time. I called him up this morning when I got your letter and told him I'd heard from you, but I could not read him what you said because it would bring the blushes to his face. But he was awfully pleased about it, and he said again what a fine book you had written and how interested and excited they all were about it. He wanted to know if you had gone to Switzerland and I told him you were apparently just on the point of going when you wrote the letter. I suppose you're there now and I somewhat enviously wish you a most happy holiday. . . .

There's not much news that I can give you. I went South just after Christmas—my first trip back home in seven years—and was overwhelmed, in fact almost exhausted, by hospitality. I keep plugging away here and have done a lot of writing, although I have gotten pretty tired. *The New Republic,* beginning with this week's issue, is publishing three installments of a long story that I wrote about Germany.[1] They are advertising it rather lavishly as "a new short novel," but it is not a novel, long or short, and I never said it was. I think it may be pretty good. At any rate I've crossed the Rubicon as far as my relations with the Reich are concerned. It cost me a good deal of time and worry to make up my mind whether I should allow the publication of the story because I am well known in Germany, my books have had a tremendous press there, I have many friends there, and I like the country and the people enormously. But the story wrote itself. It was the truth as I could see it, and I decided that a man's own self-respect and integrity is worth more than his comfort or material advantage. . . .

I wish I could accept your invitation to spend the weekend with you at Oxford. There's nothing I'd like better. I'm sorry if anything I wrote gave you any other impression,[2] but I really love the place and thought the few weeks I spent there some of the happiest of my life. Unfortunately, I don't see much prospect of taking another long voyage until I get another big piece of work done. I sometimes wonder, when I pick up the paper and read about the vexed and tragic state of Europe as it is to-day, whether it would not be wise for all of us who have a chance to see it now, without further delay, before the big explosion comes. Of course, I hope it doesn't happen. But it sometimes seems that only a miracle could avert it now.

I had not meant to write you such a long letter, but it was good to hear from you, and I am delighted to know that your book is finished and that everyone is so hopeful about it. I shall await its publication and its reception with great eagerness. Meanwhile congratulations and all my best wishes for your success and happiness.

[1] *I Have A Thing to Tell You.*

[2] Wecter was at Merton College, Oxford, at this time and had written to Wolfe: "The only thing with which I disagreed in your last novel was the section on Oxford, and I shall undertake to convince you of a different aspect if you will spend a weekend or a week with me here next term."

P.S. On my trip South after Christmas I stopped off at Richmond and had not been there a day before I ran into Red Warren, Allen Tate, Caroline Gordon, John Crowe Ransom [3] and many others who were there for a meeting of The Modern Language Association, I think. I spent a very pleasant evening with the Warrens, the Tates, the Brooks [4] and Mr. Ransom. In fact I did almost everything except become a Southern Agrarian. I suppose I don't understand enough about that. But it was good to see Red again and to meet all the others. Red asked about you and I told him about your book and how hopeful people were about it. This is all for the present. Good-bye and good luck. Write me when you can.

To HAMILTON BASSO

Roanoke, Virginia

April 28th, 1937.

Dear Ham:

I wanted to answer your letter before but to tell the truth, this is the first letter writing or writing of any sort that I have done in a month. I have been loafing down the beautiful Shenandoah Valley all the way from Pennsylvania for the last week or ten days and have seen a great deal of flood and rain but very little of the beautiful Shenandoah Valley. The weather is fine today. I am going on to Bristol, Virginia, tomorrow, then over to Yancey County [1] for a few days, then on to Asheville and then I hope to see you and Toto either at Asheville or on your own estate.

In short, I am beginning to perk up again and I think I shall survive the wars. For a change I have begun to sleep. Every one tells me I do everything to excess and now nothing less than fourteen hours a day of slumber will suffice me. I am beginning to worry about not working again, which is also an ominous symptom.

[3] Robert Penn Warren is the author of the 1946 Pulitzer Prize novel, *All the King's Men,* and other novels, biographies and poems, and had been a "visiting novelist" at the University of Colorado Writers' Conference with Wolfe in 1935. Allen Tate, a contemporary poet and critic, is the author of *The Mediterranean and Other Poems, The Fathers, Reason in Madness, Poems, 1922–1947,* etc. Caroline Gordon (Mrs. Tate) is the author of *Penhally, The Garden of Adonis, The Women on the Porch, The Strange Children,* etc. John Crowe Ransom is the author of *God Without Thunder, The World's Body, The New Criticism, Poetics, Selected Poems,* and other books. This group of writers contributed largely to *The Southern Review,* of which Warren was an editor, and were leaders in the Southern Agrarian movement.

[4] Cleanth Brooks was then co-editor of *The Southern Review* with Warren.

[1] Burnsville, Yancey County, North Carolina, had been the home of Wolfe's maternal ancestors, the Westalls, for many years before his grandparents had moved to the mountains outside Asheville and finally to Asheville itself. John Westall, a half-brother of Wolfe's grandfather, still lived in Burnsville, and it was to see him that Wolfe was going there.

Yes, Max Perkins and I are all right. I think we always were, for that matter. Periodically I go out and indulge in a sixty-round, knock down and drag out battle with myself but I think Max understands that. I am afraid it is likely to happen again but in the end I believe I may pull through. I read somewhere that no writer has ever yet been known to hang himself as long as he had another chapter left.

Sherwood Anderson came to New York two or three weeks ago and we all had dinner together at Cherio's—Anderson, Max and I. I thought he was fine—he seems to have picked up a lot of real wisdom and real mellowness and real understanding along the way. I think there is just a shade too much of resignation in it—he told me, for example, that we writers didn't count for much anyway in the scheme of things, a statement which I am vociferously prepared to deny—but, of course, all this is probably just the effect of his age and experience and a certain sense of completion. But I liked him very much. We had a good time and I hope I shall see him again. He spoke of you with great affection.

This is all for the present. I am going to have my sleep out and mosey along in my own way until I am ready to come to town. When I get there I will let you know. Meanwhile, with love and all good wishes to you and Toto,

To CORYDON P. SPRUILL

865 First Avenue
New York, N.Y.

May 20, 1937

Dear Shorty:

I found your letter informing me that the dogwood had arrived in Chapel Hill waiting for me when I got back from Asheville the other day. I knew that you would be punctual to the dot, and my own delay in answering you is occasioned by the fact that, during all the time I was in Asheville, I did not have time to write a line to anyone.

If I can say so with any modesty, the homecoming of the prodigal was a crashing success. Everything apparently, to my enormous relief, is forgiven. At any rate, they were glad to have me back again and I do not have to tell you how glad I was to be back. I wish you would tell Julia [1] that even though I missed the Chapel Hill dogwood, I saw whole mountains full that was from North Carolina. It was one of the loveliest springs I have ever seen and I never really knew just how homesick I had been until I got back again.

[1] Mrs. Spruill.

I should have come by Chapel Hill on my way back to New York except for the fact that I so far over-stayed my visit in Asheville that I had to come back here in a hurry, but it may interest you to know that I now belong to the landed gentry. I have rented a cabin on top of a hill a few miles out of Asheville, complete isolation and fifteen or twenty acres of my own woods all around it.

I do not know where you are going this summer, or what you plan to do, but if your plans should lead you up in the direction of Asheville, I should be proud and happy to show you my estate, and to put you up. I will be here in New York until the end of June, but plan to be back in North Carolina for the beginning of July. Please let me know your own plans, and meanwhile, with best wishes and love to you all,

To FRED W. WOLFE

865 First Avenue
New York, N.Y.

May 24, 1937

Dear Fred:

Your note came this morning. I am back at work. There is little news to record except that I stopped off for a day at Washington on the way up and saw Virginia and Frederica.[1] . . .

Yes, George McCoy sent me the clippings of the piece in the *Citizen*.[2] I am glad you like it. They made a few mistakes, typographical errors in words, and left out a sentence or two, but on the whole I think it turned out all right. What worries me most at present is the row that seems to have broken out at home after my visit there had passed off so well. George McCoy and Annie Westall[3] are apparently squabbling over what shall be done with the manuscript, and my chief interest is to settle it peaceably and not be bothered about it any more. Of course, I had no idea that there would be any controversy of any sort. The whole thing came up casually. I saw Annie in the street before I left and, in the course of our conversation, she mentioned that she was a director or trustee of the Randolph Macon library and that they were making a collection of autographs and manuscripts and would I contribute something. I told her I should be glad to. This suggested to me that I had promised to write the *Citizen* a piece, and I told her I could give her this or something else if she preferred. She said this would be all right, and so the matter rested. I wrote the piece and gave it to George McCoy

[1] Wolfe's nieces, the daughters of Effie Wolfe Gambrell.
[2] "Return" in the May 16, 1937, issue of *The Asheville Citizen-Times*.
[3] Annie Westall is the daughter of Mrs. Wolfe's brother, James M. Westall.

just an hour or so before I caught the train. I told him to give it to Annie as soon as he had finished with it for the *Citizen,* and he then said that he had intended to give it to the Sondley Library and that he thought, since it was about Asheville, written on the occasion of my return, it ought to stay there. I told him I thought this was all right and to call up Annie and tell her I would send her another piece—that is, if the Randolph Macon library did not want this one. That, I thought, was the end of the whole matter. But in the last few days I have had letters from George McCoy and Miss Dickey [4] of the Sondley Library, and apparently a row has broken out in which everyone except myself is taking part. George said he called up Annie and she expressed herself at first as being perfectly satisfied, saying that as she was on the board of both libraries, it was turning out well both ways. Then Jack Westall [5] called up and, according to George, laid him out, saying that his conduct was "gratuitous." George took the manuscript to the Sondley Library and left it. Miss Dickey, the librarian, wrote me and said that Annie came around later and took it back, apparently telling her that she had promised it to Randolph Macon for commencement and was, therefore, in an embarrassing situation, all of which was news to me since I do not remember her mentioning commencement in our conversation. Then Mama apparently called up Miss Dickey and gave her version of the affair and Miss Dickey wrote me saying that she felt this particular manuscript ought to stay in Asheville at the Sondley Library and that she was sure Annie would be satisfied just as well if I gave her something else. I have written both George McCoy and Annie and tried to make peace and offered to give both of them a piece of manuscript for both libraries. I hope they get the matter adjusted to their mutual satisfaction and that it does not wind up, as these things so often do, by an innocent party, in this case myself, being heartily damned by all sides. I did not get a penny for the piece or for the manuscript, nor did I expect one. Now I just don't want to get embroiled in any petty and useless argument.

I had a letter from Max Whitson [6] this morning telling me he is fixing up the road and making repairs in the cabin and putting it in good order, and that he would be delighted to have Mama look at it when he gets it ready. He said he would take her out himself, but if you are in Asheville one Sunday soon and have time, I wish you would call him up

[4] Miss Philena A. Dickey was director of the Sondley Library.
[5] James Westall (familiarly known as Jack), the son of James M. Westall and brother of Annie Westall.
[6] Max Whitson, the cartoonist, was the owner of the cabin at Oteen which Wolfe had rented.

and get the key and drive Mama out and look the place over and let me know what you think of it. I thought it was a right nice place, and Max, who went to school with me, assured me that he was putting it in good order and that I would find it a very comfortable place to live in. . . .

Mr. Perkins has moved out to his place in the country for the summer, but of course he comes to business every day and I am seeing him this week. He called up and asked about you all, and seemed very pleased when I told him my reception at home had been such a warm, hospitable one. I was pretty tired when I left there. I certainly want to see my friends this summer, and get away from some of the troubles and worries and interruptions that have harassed me in the last year or so. I hope people will understand this and not come breaking in on me at all hours and moments of the day. Anyway, I am going to try it, and I have high hopes that it will work out well.

This is all for the present. . . . Let me know if there is any news. Meanwhile, love and best wishes to you all.

To FRED W. WOLFE

865 First Avenue
New York, N.Y.
June 26, 1937

Dear Fred:

I have wanted to answer your letter before this, but I have been driving as hard as I could go ever since I got back here five or six weeks ago in an effort to get as much work done as possible before I leave here. I am trying to wind it up to-day and to-morrow. I have been working every day, and often at night also with Miss Nowell, my agent. She is coming here again tomorrow, Sunday, for another go at it and I hope then to finish up the work I have been doing. . . .

According to my present plans I hope to leave here for Asheville some time next week, possibly around Tuesday or Wednesday. I am dogtired, just about played out, and dreading the big job of packing, getting ready, that is before me. My main concern is, of course, my manuscript. There is an immense amount of it, millions of words, and although it might not be of any use to anyone else, it is, so far as I am concerned, the most valuable thing I have got. My life is in it—years and years of work and sweating blood—and the material of about three unpublished books. I am going to bring it with me to North Carolina, but I have not fully decided yet just what means of transportation I shall use. I

hate to take the chance of letting it go out of my sight. I suppose the
Railway Express is safe enough. What I should prefer to do would be to
take it right with me in the train, but unfortunately there is so much
of it that nothing less than a good-sized packing-case would hold it.
In addition, I have to buy some clothes and supplies and take along my
bedding and towels. Mama has written me that she will need all that
she has this summer so, as you can see, I have quite a problem in moving upon my hands.

I got a letter from Max Whitson this morning in which he informs
me that he has put the cabin in good shape, waxed the floors, fixed up
the road that leads to the place, and has put in some new furniture,
and that everything is now comfortable and ready. If this is so, I think
I ought to find it a good place to live and work, if too many people
don't start coming out and paying me casual and unexpected visits.

People, of course, don't seem to be able to get this into their heads.
Most people don't realize that writing is not only hard work, but that a
writer, when he works, works several times as hard as the average business man. Moreover, when a writer is working he ought not to be interrupted, and few people are able to understand how big a difference
that makes. A great many people apparently think that they can drop
in on a man while he is writing and spend an hour or two in conversation—that it does not matter very much—that he can make it all up
later. Well, this is not the way it goes: he ought not to be interrupted:
if he is, it sometimes throws him completely off the track and he cannot
make it up.

My experience has been that most business and professional people
do not work very hard, not nearly as hard as they think they do. This
is particularly true of a town like Asheville. I have always noticed in
Asheville, even in my childhood, how much time nearly everyone has
to waste. Lawyers and bankers and business people are always coming
in and out of the drug store, fooling around and talking to one another:
apparently they have time to burn. I noticed this again when I was
home in May: a lot of the boys I know who are now lawyers would
invite me up to their offices in the Jackson Building and we would spend
an entire afternoon talking, and no one would come in. The point I am
trying to make here is that, as much as I should like to, I have not got
time to burn this way. I have got my living to earn: I have got an immense amount of work to do, and I sincerely and earnestly want to see
my friends and members of my family this summer, but I do hope they
will have understanding and consideration enough to see the problem
I am faced with and to allow me privacy and peace to get my work
accomplished.

I am appealing to you to help me in my purpose in any way you can. I know that Mama does not wholly understand how hard I have to work and how desperately serious I am when I say I have to work and must be given time and quiet in which to do it. I don't think that Mama has ever fully understood that writing is not only hard work, but harder work than she has any idea of. From what she said to me once or twice, I gathered that she may not even understand that it is work at all but rather a kind of lucky trick which the person lucky enough to possess can use when and where he chooses in his off moments and at absolutely no expense of time and trouble. Well, it is not a lucky trick. It is a desperate, back-breaking, nerve-wracking and brain-fatiguing labor. And, in addition to this, it is often a very thankless and heart-breaking labor because a man may give years of his youth and best effort to a piece of work and then get nothing for it except abuse. Of course, I am making no criticism of Mama whatever: her point of view is a familiar one among people who have had no experience with such work and who get a very romantic idea about it, but I am sure that I can explain it to you and that you will understand what I say and will help me in any way you can to get the peace and quiet that I so much want and need.

I don't think anybody quite understood when I was home just how tired I am and how much I need now a period of quiet and seclusion. But I do need it very badly, and that is the reason that I have taken the little cabin out near Asheville in the hope and belief that I can get it there. If I fail to get it there, it is going to be a bitter disappointment, but I really have high hopes that it will turn out well. I think my friends in New York all understand how much I need it now, and are earnestly hoping I shall get it this summer. Of course, you have not seen a great deal of me since the publication of "Look Homeward, Angel," almost eight years ago. But there has really been almost no rest or relaxation for me since then. First of all, as you know, there was the great stir and rumpus in Asheville about "The Angel," all of the talk and feeling of perturbation, and I got a full share of that. Then I was faced with the problem and task of getting another book done, of meeting the challenge of the critics, who praise you one month and revile you the next, and who keep pressing all the time to get another book out of you. I had very little money, and after the royalties on "Look Homeward, Angel" were exhausted I had to depend for my living on an occasional story or on money that Scribners advanced to me. Thus I was under the constant strain of knowing that I was in debt to my publisher and that I ought to try to do something to pay that off.

The book that I was writing developed into a project of such tremendous size that it turned out to be four or five books instead of one,

and five years or more went by before I was able to get the first of
these books completed and published. During most of this time I lived
in Brooklyn and worked like a dog. In addition, there were personal
troubles which I believe are all settled now, but which took from me
a heavy toll in time, worry and anxiety. When "Of Time and the River"
was published a little more than two years ago, I thought that my
troubles were over. But it seems now as if they were just beginning. I
went abroad to rest. I was as close to utter physical and nervous exhaustion as I had ever been in my life. There was a time there when I
was seriously afraid that I might not be able to pull myself back again,
but I managed to. And then, as you know, the storm broke. I returned
to America feeling sure that now, at last, I had a secure position, a very
modest income, the independence and, for the first time in my life, the
peace and comfort that would enable me to continue my work hereafter
in tranquility. I found instead that I had been thrown into a whirlpool.
I was set upon by every kind of parasite, every kind of harpy, every
kind of vulture, every kind of female egotist that had a string to pull, or
that thought they could get something out of me—whether money, manuscript, royalties, percentages, or simply a sop to their vanity. Since I
was—and this is the truth—a more or less unsuspecting and believing
person who responds very quickly to people and to apparent overtures
of friendship and good will, I was taken for quite a ride.

I am not kicking or complaining about this at all. On the whole, I
came through it all right. I think I shall always be glad I had the experience and that it taught me something. But I am merely telling you
that, instead of the peace and security I thought I should now get, I
found myself in the lions' den, and I have fought it out with the animals
for over two years now. On the whole, I do not think I have done
badly. They have taken me for quite a promenade: . . . I have learned
a good many very hard and bitter and disagreeable facts about life and
about some of the adventures and people one could meet in it, but I
have not lost my faith either in life or in people, I am more grateful
than I have ever been for my true friends and for the many fine people
I have known, and I have kept on working. So, with all humility and
deference, I think I will come out all right.

However—and this is the point of the whole matter, the reason I am
writing you this letter, the reason I am explaining all these things to
you, knowing that I can depend on your help and understanding—the
point, I say, is: I am now damn tired—and I want to get a rest. I am
not merely saying I am tired, I am not just pretending I am tired—I
am, actually, honestly and genuinely—nervously, physically and mentally. I believe a few weeks out there in the cabin will fix me up again.
I am eager—more eager than I have ever been—to work, and I believe

I will get a lot of work done out there. But I do know how I feel now; I do know what has happened to me and what I have been through these last seven or eight years; and I do know exactly what I want to do now—which is to get out to my cabin, to get some rest and relaxation, and to work—and I can only earnestly pray that all my friends and members of my family will understand this extremely normal, sensible desire, and help me every way they can. And that is why I am writing you this letter—because I know I can appeal to you and that you will understand exactly my problem when I put it before you—and that I can depend on you, tactfully and diplomatically, without hurting anyone's feelings, to get other people to understand it too.

Of course, I had a good time when I was home in May. It was wonderful to be home again after so long an absence, and it was fine to see all of you and to resume contacts with so many people that I had known. It was for me a wonderful home-coming: I am glad I got to see so many people and to talk to them, but I was pretty well fagged out when I left. My desire now, I think, is a pretty sensible one. I do not want to go out in the country and become an utter hermit; I hope that all these people who were so nice to me in May will not have forgotten they know me by the time I come back; I hope to see many of them this summer and that they will visit me at the cabin. But I also hope that they show some discretion and won't overwhelm me, and that I get a chance to rest up and to do some work. I think all of this is perfectly plain and sensible and that any intelligent person would see my point immediately and agree with me.

This is all for the present. I am sorry that the letter is so long, but I thought it would be a good idea if I wrote you and told you something of my present problems and difficulties before I come down. Of course, I should like to come to Spartanburg and meet your friends, but just at the present time, feeling as tired as I do, it seems to me it would be a better plan if I got out in the country and rested up a week or two before meeting anyone you know. At any rate, I will let you know when I arrive. Meanwhile, with all good wishes to you until I see you.

To HAMILTON BASSO

[Box 95]
[Oteen, N.C.]
July 13, 1937

Dear Ham:

I got your letter without any serious confliction with the Postal Authorities in spite of your alarming instructions to the Post Master; [1] but this

[1] On the envelope of his letter to Wolfe, Basso had written: "Postmaster: Will you

is almost my first opportunity to answer you. I have been seeing a lot of people in town including the family, and have been busy moving in out here. I wish I could see you, and very soon. If the mountain won't come here then I will have to go to the mountain, but I hope you come here because I would like you to see the place.

First of all, here are the directions; I am about 6 miles from Asheville and if you come through town the best way to get here is through the tunnel. When you get to the Recreation Park you take the road to the right that leads up around the lake at the Park. This is a gravel road but not a bad one. The entrance to my place is about two-thirds of a mile from the place where you turn off at the Recreation Park. You can recognize the place by two large wooden gates which have lanterns on top of them. If I know you are coming, the gates will be open and the lanterns lit. I am on top of the hill at the end of this road: it is a cabin completely hidden from sight by tremendous trees. It is really a good place and I hope to do a lot of work here. So far I have done little except sleep—after New York it has been a blessed relief to be out here. About the only human sound I hear out here is the wail of the train whistle going by the foot of my hill in the azalea bottoms and occasionally very faint music from the Merry-Go-Around at the Recreation Park. Of course I love the trains and I don't mind the Park a bit.

I was dog-tired when I got here but I am beginning to feel a whole lot better already. As usual I am aching to get to work again, although it might be better if I waited a bit. After I saw you in May I returned to New York and worked like fury for eight weeks in an effort to make some money. I wrote six stories [2] of which one is still in rough draft and must be worked on some more. But Miss Nowell took the other five and so far has succeeded in selling three. One to *The New Yorker*—not the Malone piece which they published some time ago but a new one—

---

be good enough to hold this until the arrival of the addressee whose presence will be made known, probably, by an earthquake or some other violent upheaval."

[2] "'E,'" which was published in the July 17, 1937, issue of *The New Yorker* and appears with some changes in *You Can't Go Home Again* on pages 513–527; "April, Late April" which was published in the September, 1937, issue of *The American Mercury* and appears with many changes and additions in *The Web and the Rock* on pages 441–452; "Katamoto" which was published in the October, 1937, issue of *Harper's Bazaar* and appears with many cuts and changes in *You Can't Go Home Again* on pages 28–36; "Chickamauga" which was published in the Winter, 1938, issue of *The Yale Review* and is included in *The Hills Beyond;* "No More Rivers" which was never published in a magazine but small portions of which are scattered through *The Web and the Rock* and *You Can't Go Home Again;* and the first rough draft of "The Party at Jack's" which was finally published in the May, 1939, issue of *Scribner's Magazine* and appears with many changes and additions in *You Can't Go Home Again* on pages 196–322.

one to *The American Mercury,* and one a few days ago to *Harper's Bazaar.* She still has the two best—and longest—and says she is sure she will sell them somewhere. But the ways of commercial editors are very strange and hard to fathom; when I was here in May, Miss Nowell sold a story to *The Saturday Evening Post.*[3] Of course we were both delighted. We had never been paid so much before and they seemed eager for more. It looked as if we had a ready market.

When I got back to New York, I wrote a story called "Chickamauga" and if I do say so, it is one of the best stories I ever wrote. I got the idea for it from an old, old man, my great-uncle, John Westall, who lives over in Yancey County and who is ninety-five years old. When I saw him this spring, he began to tell me about the Civil War and about the battle of Chickamauga, which was, he said, the bloodiest, most savage battle he was ever in. He told about it all so wonderfully and in such pungent and poetic language, such as so many of the old country people around here use, that I couldn't wait to get back to New York to begin on it. My idea was simply to tell the story of a great battle in the language of a common soldier—the kind of country mountain boy who did so much of the fighting in the war. The *Post* heard that I was writing it and they liked the story they had bought so much and were apparently so eager to get some more stories from me, that they telegraphed Miss Nowell even before I had finished and asked that they be allowed to see it before anyone else. Well, we sent it off to them and Miss Nowell and I thought it was a cinch. The story was so good, really much better than the one they had taken, and it simply crackled with action from the first line and besides that, it was so real, so true—it was all told in the old man's language and when you read it, it was just as if he was there talking to you. What do you suppose happened? In a week's time the story came back with a regretful note from *The Post* to the effect that although they appreciated its "literary merit"—I wonder by the way what the Hell people mean by "literary merit." Is there any other kind of merit where a piece of writing is concerned? I have never been able to see that there was, although so many people seem to think there is . . . that there really are two kinds of books, books that are good in a "literary sort of way," and "good" books, but of course . . . it is all nonsense— at any rate, The Post rejected "Chickamauga," apparently with the idea that it was good "in a literary sort of way," but that it did not have enough of the "story element." Nowell and I were absolutely flabbergasted. What in the name of God do these people mean by "story element"? And what is a story anyway? All this piece had was the whole

[3] "The Child by Tiger" which was published in the September 11, 1937, issue of *The Saturday Evening Post* and appears in *The Web and the Rock* on pages 132–156.

Civil War, the life of a common soldier and his account of one of the bloodiest battles that was ever fought. If it had had any more of the "story element" it would have exploded into electricity.

Of course I am not mad about it, I know we will sell it somewhere —but I am puzzled and curious to find out what they mean or what kind of standards they have. I think I have an idea: it is something that has to do with a kind of accepted and recognizable formula which is familiar to their readers, but really it does not have very much to do with story. A piece of writing might be one of the most thrilling and exciting stories ever written and still be rejected by these people if it did not fit in with one of their established patterns. Curiously enough, they are now very much interested in another piece I wrote called "No More Rivers." I would have sworn that this story was of such a quiet and unexciting kind that *The Post* would not even have considered it. But the editor wrote Miss Nowell quite a long letter and showed the most surprising interest in it: in fact he practically promised to take the story if I would condense the first twenty pages to four or five. I do not know whether or not it can be done—but there you are: the only action in this story is a telephone conversation between a man and a girl—and *there* is "story element."

Anyway, I am making enough, I hope, to pay expenses and keep going for a while and I am getting back to work immediately on my Gulliver book. I brought most of the manuscript of the last five or six years down with me—millions of words of it—and I hope to write several hundred thousand more this summer. Eventually I hope it will begin to take shape, like another monster of the deep, and I will have another tremendous book. I believe I learn a little something about writing all the time; but I am not so sure that I will be worried so much this time by apprehensions over size and length. The very nature of a book like this is that everything can go into it—to tell such a story is to try to loot the whole treasure of human experience. Well, we shall see what we shall see; there are so many things to find out. I do not even know yet whether I can work here.

It has been so long since I have really lived at home and almost all of my creative work has been done somewhere else—in New York, or in London, or in France. And already I have encountered certain learned, local psychologists, who hint darkly that I will find it impossible to work here: one even said that I would find these surroundings "allergic"—I believe that is one of the new words isn't it? At any rate the sum and substance of it is that a man like myself could write in a room in a city with a Hell of life and traffic roaring along beneath him, but that he could get no work done in the peace and quiet of the country and among people that he knows, and in the place where he was born. All of which I hold to be ridiculous: work, as you yourself know, is a desperate necessity; and if the need is desperate enough nothing will stop us—not even our own lazy bones or natural indolence of which I have so much more than a fair share—not even, by God, allergic conditions. It is going to be an interesting experience. It is the first time in almost twenty years since I left college that I have come back home with the intention of actually staying a while; and I have come back here after so many years of strife and wandering, after so much turbulence and chaos, after so much work and hope and failure and success, after such a packed and crowded life in which I have always dreamed and hoped of achieving a state of serenity and repose without ever having found it.

I have come back here as the result of a very powerful and deep-rooted instinct, which has grown slowly and steadily for years. No matter what happens or how this experience may turn out, I know the instinct was right. That is to say, this time it was inevitable; it had gathered for years and I was utterly convinced that it was right for me to come home again, to make the old connections and resume myself; and if I had done anything else at this time, this feeling in me was so strong and single I should never have been satisfied. Feeling so, of course, there was nothing else for me to do. I cannot fairly tell you that I am "through" with New York; but I have realized in recent months that I am "through" with it at this present period of my life. In other words, with the same powerful and inevitable instinct, I began to realize that I had taken all of it that I could possibly absorb at this period, and to stay there longer now would not only be foolish but barren.

I believe I must have lived through almost the whole vast kaleidoscopic range of experience that the city can give to the young man. I went there a kid from a little town, with all the fierce and passionate eagerness that such a boy could know. I had built the enchanted vision of the city in great flaming pictures in my brain from my childhood and I believe it is not too much to say that to the very end some portion of that enchantment remained—that I always saw New York, not only with all its cruelty, its ugliness, its loneliness and horror, not only with its harsh and sordid poverty and its obscene wealth; but also with all the magic of its special weather, its fierce exultant pulse, its hope, its passion and its unrecorded loveliness, seen so, pulsed so, flaming in all these hues of magic, and so built and so imagined there in the proud and flaming vision of a boy. I brought these things to it, just as you did, and just as every other boy that ever lived who came there from the little towns across America, who came burning with a fierce desire that all men know in youth, which is to be loved and to be famous.

Well, I got what I was looking for. I had both of them and none of it turned out the way I thought it would, and all of it was so different from the way we thought it would be; and yet I had it all and I would not have missed it and am glad that I have had it now. But I can have no more of it. I have got to the end of that road. I have squeezed that orange dry. It belongs there now in the province of things done—in the domain of the irrecoverable—that whole experience of youth, desire and love and fame, in the unceasing city. I knew that it was over—that no matter what may come hereafter, I shall never go along that way again; and that if I do go back, it will be now from a different point, another vision and, I hope, with a deeper purpose.

So I have come back here to "set a spell and think things over;" to rebuild here in my brain again these past fifteen years or more of youth, of conflict and of wandering. And from this substance, this accumulation of a life worn down—I pray, a little brighter, and freer, I hope, in some substantial measure, from the degrading egotisms all men know in youth —here to strike out, I hope to God, a living word: to do out of the substance of my one life, my single spirit, a better and a truer work than I have ever done.

I did not mean to load upon you all things in this way; but I did want you to understand what I believe you may have guessed already, that my coming back was not haphazard and that there was behind it a deeper sense of purpose than many people know.

Good-bye for the present, Ham. Write as soon as you can and let me know if you and Toto can come over and when you can come. Or if you prefer, I will come over and see you, if you just name a date. I got a letter from Sherwood Anderson just before I left New York. But I have had no time to answer it yet. He invited me to visit him and I believe the address is Troutdale, Virginia; but I left the letter in New York and shall not be able to accept his invitation. But I am going to ask him to let me know if he is coming here, and if he does I think it would be fine if all three of us could get together. I do not know where Scott is, but I suppose he is around here somewhere. He was in New York a month or so ago. I didn't see him, but Max told me that he seemed to be much better. He had written some stories and had plans for new work and Max believed that he was going to pull out of the hole all right. With all my heart I hope so.

I was too busy in New York to keep up with current movements which were having an especially furious career this spring and I suppose by doing so, I have lost what is called prestige. This is too bad of course; however, like you and every man, I only have what I have, I am what I am. I don't believe there is much to report, except that the boys are having meetings, congresses and demonstrations all over the place and were carrying on the Spanish war with unabated vigor, using, it seemed to me, essentially the same appeals to idealism, democracy, civilization, etc., as were current among the propagandists whose similar activities they so much abhorred twenty years ago and have so bitterly denounced since. However, let them argue and deny as they please. It is the same old business—"Plus ça change plus c'est le même chose." It's the old army game. What I say is, "it's spinach and to Hell with it." But I suppose you know all about these things and have kept informed on all these important doings. Spain and Marx have made some strange new bedfellows. . . . So runs the world away.

I hope you are getting a lot of work done and most of all, that we can wear a whole night out in talking, before long. Meanwhile I send my love to you and Toto.

The following letter was written in reply to one from Fred B. Millett asking Wolfe for biographical material for use in Millett's book, Contemporary American Authors. *Millett at this time was a member of the Department of English at the University of Chicago, and is now Professor of English at Wesleyan University and Director of the Honors College there.*

To FRED B. MILLETT

[Box 95]
[Oteen, N.C.]
July 14, 1937

Dear Professor Millett:

I am sorry for the delay in answering your letters of March and June. I was very busy in New York trying to put through a great deal of work that had to be finished by a certain time, and recently I have been moving down here and into a cabin, where I am living for the summer.

I should be glad, of course, to give you any information concerning my life and interests which might be of some use to you in the preparation of your book, and which might not be available elsewhere. But I do not know very well just what kind of information might be of value to you. May I suggest, if you are not familiar with it already, that you look at a very short book called "The Story of a Novel" which was published by Scribners last year. I think it may tell as much about some of my experiences as a writer trying to learn his job as anything else I could tell you. It contains more or less my writing experience between 1929 and 1935, after the publication of my first long book, "Look Homeward, Angel," and up to the publication of "Of Time and the

River." . . . As to the new book, the following facts about it may be of some interest to you: I have written perhaps a million words of manuscript for it in the past two years. Of course I shall use only a part of this. Furthermore the book is not one of the series that was announced with the publication of "Of Time and the River," but an entirely separate book. It is hard in a brief space to give you any comprehensive notion of it, but I think you might get some idea of it if I tell you it is a kind of modern fable or legend, and that it sets forth the chronicle of a kind of modern Gulliver—an American Gulliver—someone, let us say, that in our own special time and phrase we might call Joe Doaks. For me, the conception and creation of the book has been an exciting and, I believe important experience. I hope it has enabled me to make use of the materials of experience, of what a man is able to see, feel, hear, know and comprehend in a life-time, more wholly and fully than I have ever been able to use such experience before. But at the same time I hope and believe that through the medium of this new book and its more "fictional" quality, I have been able to gain a greater objectivity than I have known in my previous books, and to detach myself more completely from the purely personal elements of what is generally, and I believe mistakenly, referred to as "autobiographical" fiction. At any rate —and I believe this may have some special interest to you—I think this may have been happening to my work: as I have grown older and a little more experienced and, I hope, a great deal more aware of my purpose, of my materials and of the work I want to do, I think my interests have turned more and more from the person who is writing the book to the book the person is writing. I do not know whether I have said this well or plainly, but I hope that I have, because I believe that it may indicate the change of development that has occurred in my work. I am immersed in work and I hope that it goes well.

I do not know that this information will be of any use to you, but I shall be very glad if it is. With all good wishes for the success of your book . . .

To HAMILTON BASSO

(Oteen, N.C.)

July 22, 1937

Dear Ham:

I would be delighted to make the trip up to see Sherwood [1] in August, but are you sure he's going to be there? As I remember it when I had

---

[1] Basso had suggested that he and Wolfe drive up to see Sherwood Anderson in Marion, Virginia.

dinner with him in New York two or three months ago he told me he had accepted an invitation to go out to Boulder, Colorado where I was two years ago and give some lectures at the Writers Conference. If he does this I think he might be away at the time you mention. . . . Anyway I'm all for the trip if he is going to be there. But if he's not, I wish you'd come over here and spend the week-end with me anyway. My only plans for the present besides work are a trip down to South Carolina to see my older sister[2] and her family a week from this Saturday or Sunday. I could put you up here comfortably at the cabin. There is lots of room for both you and Toto if she wants to come, and I have a man here now who cooks for me and looks after the place and I believe he is going to turn out all right. There has been a lot of family, old friends and social activities so far—a good deal too much, but it was unavoidable and I believe there is going to be a lull now. I am working again on a very long, difficult and closely woven story called "The Party at Jack's." I don't know how it's going to turn out, but if I succeed with it, it ought to be good. It is one of the most curious and difficult problems I have been faced with in a long time and maybe I shall learn something from it. It is a story that in its essence and without trying or intending to be, has got to be somewhat Proustian—that is to say its life depends upon the most thorough and comprehensive investigation of character—or characters, for there are more than thirty people in it. In addition, however, there is a tremendous amount of submerged action which involves the lives of all these people and which includes not only the life of a great apartment house but also a fire and the death of two people. I suppose really a whole book could be made out of it but I am trying to do it in a story. After that, of course, I don't know what will happen. It has got to be a very long story. It is all very well to talk of classic brevity etc. but this story cannot be written that way: if it is it becomes something else. And if I do it right it is certainly worth doing. But to get it published? I don't know. All this talk about there being a market or a publisher nowadays for any good piece of writing is nonsense. A writer's market, unless he chooses to live and work and publish like James Joyce or to be one of the little magazine precious boys, is still cabin'd and confined to certain more or less conventional and restricted forms and mediums. I kick against it constantly because I know it just ain't right and because I know that the familiar answer that is made to my objection—namely that the true artist will learn to do it in the "accepted" way—is the easy and dishonest answer of people who are themselves interested in doing it in the lazy, convenient or temporarily commercial one. There is no accepted way: there are as many art forms as

[2] Effie Wolfe Gambrell.

there are forms of art, and the artist will continue to create new ones and to enrich life with new creations as long as there is either life or art. So many of these forms that so many academic people consider as masterly and final definitions derived from the primeval source of all things beautiful or handed Apollo-wise from Mount Olympus, are really worn out already, will work no more, are already dead and stale as hell.

I know—I believe I know this one thing better than most other people! The thing we have got to fight for constantly and unflaggingly in America is utterance. I don't know why but it is a curious and baffling paradox of our mind that it tends to conventionalize and harden, much more so, it seems to me than in many other countries. I don't know for certain the answer yet and the ones they tried to make me swallow ten or fifteen years ago—that is, "puritanism" "Babbittry" etc.—never meant very much to me, never gave me an essential answer. These things themselves were effects, I thought, much more than causes. And these effects are, I feel somehow powerfully sure, associated with so many other effects that we are all familiar with and which no one ever mentions in connection with these things—that is, the dry neck of the American, a kind of prognathous set and bleakness of the face and jaw, the way he moves and walks, a kind of meagerness around the hips, the nasality of the voice, a kind of dry precision in the speech—for example here in western North Carolina we say "Lee—ces—ter" and not Lester (for Leicester). At any rate the whole matter is deeper, stranger and subtler than the pedants think: it is a thorny paradox, a kind of weather of our lives conjoined of all our space and light and our immense and superhuman distances.

It has occurred to me that perhaps one fundamental reason for this conventionalizing and hardening of our thought and speech and art and life processes is that every American in a fundamental sense is a surveyor. Have you ever thought, by the way, of the great number of Americans who actually were surveyors? George Washington was one. My grandfather,[3] who was a great variety of things, a carpenter, a contractor, a hatter and a trapper, was also a surveyor. I believe you would find that millions of the pioneer Americans had some knowledge of surveying and of how to handle surveying instruments. What I am trying to say here is that America has really never yet, in any profound and essential way, been *explored*—it has rather been *surveyed*. The first problem of the people who settled in this immense and spatial continent was not to explore it but to "lay it out" —to find the shortest distance between two points, to get the best and easiest grade across the continental divide—to give, in short, a definition of the wildnerness. We have hunted always for the short cut, the practicable way, and I think the effect of this—it does not seem to me at all far-

[3] Thomas Casey Westall, Mrs. Wolfe's father.

fetched so to think—has been to hunt for the short cut, the easy and practicable way, the neat definition, everywhere: hence the neat glib finish of the O. Henry type of short story, the "punch at the end," the "gag," and many other kinds of gimcrackery.

In New York now whenever they talk of starting a new magazine, of making a new publication go—they do not talk of getting out a good magazine, of making a magazine so good, so much better than any other, that people will have to buy it. They talk of getting out one with a "new idea," of getting a new concoction that will "click" as *Life, Time, Fortune, The New Yorker* click. Well this is surveyordom—it is not exploring. In my own humble opinion they have done damn little exploring yet, and those of us who intend to do some are going to have to fight grimly and constantly from beginning to end against the conventional set in order to accomplish what we want to do.

A German—an ex-Prussian cavalry officer whom I met last summer and who had spent the last eight years trapping in Canada—told me that the most characteristic attitude of mind he had noticed in America was indicated by the phrase "that will do." He said that he had never heard this phrase used in the same way in Germany. If a reaping machine broke down, he said, he had noticed that instead of taking it apart, giving it a thorough overhauling and making new parts for those that were worn out, the tendency was to patch it up with twine, solder it together, get it to running again in the quickest possible time—do something to it, no matter what, so long as it would "do." In many respects all this is admirable, but it is surveyordom. It is the resourceful attribute of a people who are forced to meet emergencies and to meet them quickly, of people who had to fence in and house the wilderness and who could not afford to be too nice, or neat, or dainty while they were about it. In another way as well, our love of neat definitions in convenient forms, our fear of essential exploration, may be the natural response of people who had to house themselves, wall themselves, give their lives some precise and formal definition in that enormous vacancy. Anyway all of these things have seemed to me to be worth thinking of and I know that we still have to fight and fight hard to do our work the way we want to do it—not only against the accepted varieties of surveyordom—that is, book publishers, most of the critics, popular magazines, etc.—but against even deadlier and more barren forms, because they set up as friends of exploration when they are really betrayers and enemies: I mean little magazinedom, Hound and Horners, young precious boys, esthetic Marxians and all the rest of it.

Come over and talk to me sometime. I think I'm going to get some work done here and it would be good to see you and talk to you while I am doing it. I got a letter from Max praising a piece I have just written for the

New Yorker [4]—also a notice from the publishers to the effect that all of my remaining royalties have been wiped out [5] in the settlement of a suit which, if truth and justice and common honesty are at all to be defended, should never have been settled; and in the payment of lawyers' fees which were far more ruinous than both suit and settlement, and who for all they did or accomplished besides the pompous superfluity of their costly presence and the frightening eminence of their great name—an eminence which frightened Charlie Scribner but not the people who were suing us —might just as well have been supplanted by Glickstein and O'Toole, or by any little tough and combative attorney, and better so, it seems to me. At any rate, my profits on the books are not only all wiped out but I am also heavily in the red with Scribners. I suppose it's all a part of the price we have to pay for experience, but the price is a heavy and a bitter one.

As to friendship in the modern business world—well, it exists: they will bleed and die for you in conversation, but they will not lose money. In fact the principle of modern business friendship seems to be not to let the right hand know what the left hand is doing—one hand is warm and open and extended in the clasp of love, but the other is clenched grimly around a handful of accursed papers. This is the way things are, and I suppose we are fools to think it could be different. Besides, why protest? What right or justice is there in our argument? Who has defrauded me? Who has stolen my ox and my ass or committed adultery or lain with my maid servant or done any of the other things that we were brought up to believe were wrong? And since none of these things have been done, why then it follows, doesn't it, that all else that is done in life, in business and in friendship are right, and it is unfair and unjust of us to kick against the traces or to protest against the ordered scheme of things as they are.

I'm not really bitter about it. I simply know more about it than I knew or suspected two years ago. As for Max Perkins, my feeling toward him of course is the same as it always was. I used to wish the world was shaped and made more to his own measure, his high stature; but since it is not, I am glad he is here to give it the improvement of himself.

Good-bye for the present. Let me know if you can come over and when. Meanwhile, with all good wishes to you and Toto.

[4] " 'E.''

[5] As of August 1, 1937, Wolfe's royalty account at Scribners showed a deficit of $1,225.40 after payment of half the settlement and attorneys' fees in the libel suit.

To ELIZABETH NOWELL

[Oteen, N.C.]

[July 22 (?), 1937]

Dear Miss Nowell:

Thanks for your letter and for the check for "Katamoto" ($360.) which came yesterday. I am sorry "Chickamauga" got turned down by *American* but after our initial preparation it was not a great surprise. I thought this story would be the easiest to sell but it is turning out the hardest. However, go ahead and try *Harper's* if you like and let me know what happens. If Perkins really wants it for *Scribner's*, we have always got that to fall back on but it might be a good idea to try the remaining possibilities first. I've had so many pieces in *Scribner's* and I really don't think it would hurt to be spread around a little more. I am also willing, if necessary, to revise the story and perhaps to bring it back more to its original purpose—that is, the story of an old man telling about the war and the battle. I think I may have put in a little too much Jim Weaver and his love affair in an effort to make it palatable to the big magazines. I don't feel yet that all of this should be cut out, but I might reduce it and make it play a less important part than it now does.

As to the enclosed letter . . . asking for permission to translate "I Have a Thing to Tell You," [1] I am not so sure. I wouldn't mind at all having it done if it were not for the suggestion of propaganda that might attach to it. And frankly I do not think the story ought to be used in that way. It is a straight story; so far as I know, it has no propaganda in it save what the reader wishes to supply for himself by inference, and its greatest value, it seems to me, lies in that fact—that I wrote it as I wrote all my other stories about a human situation and about living characters. I think it ought to be published and read in that way, and I should be against its being read or used or published in any other way. However, I'll think about it and let you know if I change my mind. Meanwhile, you can handle the matter with your customary diplomacy.

I am working on "The Party at Jack's." I have changed and revised it a great deal with an effort to weave it together better and to get it to move more quickly. However, it is bound to be very long and the problem of finding a market for it is one I'd rather not think about now. If all goes well, it may turn out to be a very interesting piece of work; but of course there is the question of its length. However, if I get it in shape I'll send it to you and you can read it over and see what you think.

I think I may have another piece for you that from a commercial point

---

[1] Into Yiddish.

of view may be much more practicable. I put it down in rough draft the other day: it's only an outline yet but I have called it tentatively "A Great Idea For a Story"—and it might really be that. I got the idea a few days ago from a waiter in Asheville who has been hovering around my table whenever I go in and showing me a great deal of attention. The other day, after clearing his throat a good many times and looking cunningly around to make sure that he was in no danger of being overheard and that his priceless secret would be safe, he bent over and coyly whispered that he had had in his brain for years "A Great Idea for a Story." It's a little habit waiters have: all of a sudden I thought of at least a dozen of them who in exactly the same way, with the same air of hopeful secrecy, had confided to me that they had a great idea for a story which would make us both a fortune, if only a guy like me who knew all the tricks could help him out on it. Of course, as a reward for this expert supervision, yours truly will get cut in on the profits, movie rights, etc., which will be simply staggering.

Well, I composed my soul to patience, put a fixed grin on my face and murmured that I was simply dying to hear it—and you know the rest. You can imagine the kind of stories that they tell—or perhaps you can't. They make Cecil B. De Mille in his most fantastic moments look like a stern realist. This one, which he assured me had been given to him by a Greek—a fact which he evidently felt gave it at the outset a sensational value—was all about "a dame in Assyria" and her love affair. She was, the waiter assured me, the richest dame in the country, and her old man used to lock her up on the top floor of her house, which was, the waiter said, thirty stories tall. So help me God, I'm not making up a word of this: I'm even understating it. Well, "the guy" comes along then and falls for the dame and climbs up to the thirtieth floor every night to play his banjo to her and to carry on his courtship of her in other ways. The old man dies conveniently and the happy pair are married. The marriage, however, is short-lived. The guy, the waiter said, turns out to be a booze hound—these phrases are the waiter's—begins to stay out late at nights, and to run around with a bunch of hot blondes. Finally he deserts her utterly, vanishes in thin air, taking with him a lot of her dough and "joolry." She is still nuts about him, however—apparently they are gluttons for punishment in Assyria—so she hunts for him for the next two years: private detectives, rewards, advertisements in the newspapers, and all the rest of it.

And then she had "her great idea"—the waiter was really getting warm now. "The dame," he said, "opens up a swell night club, the biggest, swellest night club that anybody ever heard of in Assyria. And then she puts an ad in the paper informing the public that anyone who comes to her joint the next day will be given a ten-dollar gold piece and as much liquor as they can drink or carry away—all free for nothing." The waiter cunningly explained the cunning pyschology of this move to me. "The dame," he said, "knew that such an ad would inevitably [attract] all the booze hounds in Assyria—including her erring husband. And she was not mistaken. And when she goes downstairs the next morning she finds a line of bar-flies three blocks long, and sure enough, there is friend husband, first in line. Well, she jerks him out of line right away, tells the cashier to pay off the others but tells [friend] husband that she has her suspicions about him, that she doubts whether he is really a genuine, bonafide, high grade, number 1, 18 carat Assyrian booze hound: that he will have to come upstairs with her and convince her before she allows him to cash in. Well, he goes with her, of course, and when she gets into her boudoir, she takes off her veil." (The waiter explained to me carefully that the reason the husband didn't recognize her was because she was heavily veiled.) Well, I waited and then asked "Then what? What happens then?" and the waiter, after giving me a look of great disgust, answered: "Then nothing. That's all: she's got him back, see? And isn't it a wow?"

Well now, I got to thinking it all over and decided I might make something of it. And here is my own idea. I have talked with literary waiters of this kind before and always they have some preposterous, fantastic and utterly worthless yarn like this, which in some strange way they are all convinced will make them a fortune if only someone like me will help them put it down. Apparently the more far-fetched and preposterous the story, the less it has to do with life, the better it seems to them, simply because, I suppose, it has so little to do with the life that they have seen. And yet they all see so much; they hear so much—the material of a dozen living stories is going on around them all the time, but it never occurs to any of them that anyone would be interested in the real stuff. So that's the way I framed it. I drew upon my experience with a dozen waiters, a hundred restaurants, and let it tell itself. I told what was going on around the waiter all the time that he was talking: the people coming in and out; the other waiter who is a communist and who argues violently for revolution with any customer who will talk with him; the little waitress who has had an illegitimate child a few months before and who has put it in a Home and goes to see it every Sunday; and other human things and episodes like this—the whole weave and shift and interplay of life and comedy and tragedy that goes on in a place like this. And all the time, the waiter is earnestly telling this preposterous fable—his "Great Idea for a Story"—to the customer.

That's roughly the idea that I had in mind for it. I guess you might call it a kind of study in unconscious irony—the stuff of life, the materials for a thousand stories all around one, while someone tells a preposterous

fable of far away that never could have happened anywhere. I may revise
it and send it on to you.[2]

I hope you have some good news soon about "No More Rivers." If Redbook turns it down and you think it's worth trying, I might try to revise
and shorten it to fit the length requirements of The Saturday Evening Post.
I'd have to look at it again to find whether I could do it, or whether anything of my original story would be left if I cut the twenty pages to four
or five to meet Mr. Stout's [3] requirements. At any rate, let me know what
happens and what you think about it. I saw " 'E" in The New Yorker but
have heard nothing yet of the Post or Redbook stories. Of course I like to
get paid for them, but it is also nice to have them come out.

Goodbye for the present. I'm still hoping things will turn out well here
—that is, that I'll get some work done. I think I shall, but I'll let you know
when I am more sure about it. Meanwhile, with all the best,

To FRED W. WOLFE

Oteen, N. C.
July 22, 1937

Dear Fred:

To-morrow, Friday night is, I think, the night of the supper out at
Shope's cabin. I have written Jimmy Howell and promised to be present.[1]
I told him that I could not answer for you because you were busy and if
you came to it, it would involve coming all the way up from Spartanburg
and probably going back the same night. Of course I know that all of
them would be delighted if you came and it's for you to decide, but it
doesn't seem to me to be worth all that time and travel unless you actually
had business up here that would make it worth your while. I suppose
people will have a good time and I promised to go simply because it
would be less trouble for me to go and get it over with than have to put
it off till some other time. I appreciate all this hospitality, but I am trying
to work also, and social activity is about to get me down. After this week
I hope there is a lull.

Things at the cabin have gone pretty well. I have a new man here now
and I think it is going to turn out okay. The pests have not bothered me

[2] This appears on pages 414–423 in You Can't Go Home Again.
[3] Wesley Winans Stout at this time was editor of The Saturday Evening Post.
[1] James S. Howell had arranged for Wolfe and some of his boyhood friends to meet
for a steak supper at the cabin of William Shope in the Reems Creek section of Buncombe County. Howell had known Wolfe from early childhood and roomed with him
one year in Dr. Kemp Brattle's cottage at Chapel Hill. He is now an attorney in Asheville.

much as yet, but of course I'm still praying. Donald MacRae, who is of course my friend and always welcome, drove out last night and took me into town to see Mabel. . . . We got back out here at about eleven or eleven-thirty and as we drove up there was a loud sound of revelry in the night. One of my Yancey County cronies, the gent who was with me on the night of the shooting scrape,[2] had turned up with a gang and made himself at home. I suppose he felt a little shooting makes the whole world kin—at any rate he had some other fellow with him I had never seen and two wild looking females, all of them more or less under the influence and playing the victrola as hard as it would go. I managed to keep polite but also to plead fatigue and presently got rid of them, all of them vowing enthusiastically that they would be back soon . . . [which?] will be sweet.

This is all for the present. I am trying to get a story done and will push on in spite of hell and high water. I was tired when I got here and I probably have seen too many people and tried to get to work again too soon. But on the whole, I think I feel better, and if our friends will neither forsake me nor consume me, I believe I'll pull out all right. . . . If I can get some work done, I hope to see you . . . as planned in Spartanburg a week from Saturday or Sunday. Meanwhile, with best wishes . . .

The following letter was in reply to a note from Mrs. Roberts asking Wolfe if she could bring to call two young admirers of his work, a Mr. E. E. Miller and Miss Eula Person, who wanted to come from Nashville, Tennessee, to meet him. A reconciliation between Wolfe and Mr. and Mrs. Roberts had taken place during his first visit to Asheville in May, 1937.

To MARGARET ROBERTS

Oteen, N.C.

July 26, 1937

Dear Mrs. Roberts:

I did not get your letter until Saturday night when I was in town and went out to Mabel's house. And as it was then rather late, I did not call you but decided to write you and call you up when I am next in town. Of course I have no telephone out here and that is why I have not called you earlier. I know you must understand that I should have tried to see you or communicate with you before if I had not been so busy. I have been

[2] The shooting of James Higgins in Burnsville on May 8, which Wolfe had witnessed and about which he was to testify in the trial of Philip Ray and Otis Chase in August.

away from home so long and there have been so many connections to make, so many threads to pick up, so many people, family, relatives, friends, acquaintances and even people I had never seen before, to talk to. A great deal of it, of course, has been very pleasant and a great deal of it has been exhausting and perhaps useless but unavoidable. . . . But that is the way things have been thus far and I know you can understand it. . . .

Of course I'd be delighted to meet the two young people from Nashville, and I think the meeting could be arranged at almost any time. I don't believe this coming Saturday is a good time because I have tentatively promised my sister Effie, who was up here last week and whom I have not seen for eight years, to take the bus and come down to visit her over the week-end in Anderson, South Carolina. . . . Excepting the trip down to South Carolina this weekend, I have no definite engagements and it seems to me you might arrange the meeting with your friends at almost any other time.

The only other thing that worries me is the feeling of personal responsibility. I wish you would do what you could to ease that up a bit. It is very flattering, of course, to be the object of anyone's adoration but it is also a very hard and trying role to live up to. And I am so genuinely, so profoundly grateful for the good will and belief of people. It seems to me that the knowledge that something one has written has meant so much to anyone ought to make a writer proud and happy, and is more than anything else the reward for which he lives and works. But I was a very tired man when I left New York and I am not rested yet. . . . I don't want to disappoint your two young friends but I should like to feel relieved of the strain and pressure of having to try to live up to their image of me. I know that you can arrange the whole thing simply and without complication—get them to understand that I am no longer a wild-eyed boy or a flaming youth or anything like that, but just a man who has done a lot of work and a lot of living at high pressure, and is now trying to relax and think it over. If they will take me like this, I am sure we will all be more comfortable and have a better time. . . . I am sorry these young people are going to make the trip all the way from Nashville just to meet me. I wish they too just "happened in" so to speak—it gives me a feeling of tension and anxiety to know they are going to the expense and trouble of such a journey just to see me. But since they are, I want them to enjoy themselves; I wish they'd come out here and spend the day with me—on some Sunday if it could be arranged. Then if they like we could go in and visit Mama and Mabel or any other members of the family.

As to where they are going to stay, you will have to decide that later. Mabel and Ralph have been living in a very nice house on Kimberley Ave., but they have just rented it for the summer and they are moving to a very much smaller one, and I don't know until I see it how much extra room they have. As for Mama's house, there is certainly room there, but it is frankly in a dilapidated state—an old house in a state of disrepair, which has long since passed its palmy days. Of course it is Mama's home and she loves it and sees it with a different eye, but these are the facts and I don't know whether it would be advisable for the young people to stay there or not. However . . . all these things can be arranged. I'd keep them here if there was room. But we can easily find a place for them somewhere. . . .

I shall call you up and talk with you further about it in a day or two when I come to town. Meanwhile with all good wishes to you and Mr. Roberts,

On July 19, 1937, Scott Fitzgerald had written to Wolfe from Los Angeles, saying:
"Dear Tom:
I think I could make out a good case for your necessity to cultivate an alter ego, a more conscious artist in you. Hasn't it occurred to you that such qualities as pleasantness or grief, exuberance or cynicism can become a plague in others? That often people who live at a high pitch often don't get their way emotionally at the important moment because it doesn't stand out in relief?

Now the more the stronger man's inner tendencies are defined, the more he can be sure they will show, the more necessity to rarefy them, to use them sparingly. The novel of selected incidents has this to be said that the great writer like Flaubert has consciously left out the stuff that Bill or Joe (in his case Zola) will come along and say presently. He will say only the things that he alone sees. So Mme. Bovary becomes eternal while Zola already rocks with age. . . .

That in brief is my case against you, if it can be called that when I admire you so much and think your talent is unmatchable in this or any other country.
Ever your Friend, Scott Fitzgerald" [1]
The following was Wolfe's reply.

To SCOTT FITZGERALD

[Oteen, N.C.]
July 26, 1937

Dear Scott:

I don't know where you are living and I'll be damned if I'll believe anyone lives in a place called "The Garden of Allah" which was what the

[1] Copyright, 1956, by the Estate of Scott Fitzgerald.

address on your envelope said. I am sending this on to the old address we both know so well.[1]

The unexpected loquaciousness of your letter struck me all of a heap. I was surprised to hear from you but I don't know that I can truthfully say I was delighted. Your bouquet arrived smelling sweetly of roses but cunningly concealing several large-sized brickbats. Not that I resented them. My resenter got pretty tough years ago; like everybody else I have at times been accused of "resenting criticism" and although I have never been one of those boys who break out in a hearty and delighted laugh when someone tells them everything they write is lousy and agree enthusiastically, I think I have taken as many plain and fancy varieties as any American citizen of my age now living. I have not always smiled and murmured pleasantly "How true," but I have listened to it all, tried to profit from it where and when I could, and perhaps been helped by it a little. Certainly I don't think I have been pig-headed about it. I have not been arrogantly contemptuous of it either, because one of my besetting sins, whether you know it or not, is a lack of confidence in what I do.

So I'm not sore at you or sore about anything you said in your letter. And if there is any truth in what you say—any truth for me—you can depend upon it I shall probably get it out. It just seems to me that there is not much in what you say. You speak of your "case" against me, and frankly I don't believe you have much case. You say you write these things because you admire me so much and because you think my talent is unmatchable in this or any other country and because you are ever my friend. Well Scott I should not only be proud and happy to think that all these things are true but my own respect and admiration for your own talent and intelligence are such that I should try earnestly to live up to them and to deserve them and to pay the most serious and respectful attention to anything you say about my work.

I have tried to do so. I have read your letter several times and I've got to admit it doesn't seem to mean much. I don't know what you are driving at or understand what you hope or expect me to do about it. Now this may be pig-headed but it isn't sore. I may be wrong but all I can get out of it is that you think I'd be a good writer if I were an altogether different writer from the writer that I am.

This may be true but I don't see what I'm going to do about it, and I don't think you can show me. And I don't see what Flaubert and Zola have to do with it, or what I have to do with them. I wonder if you really think they have anything to do with it, or if it is just something you heard in college or read in a book somewhere. This either-or kind of criticism seems to me to be so meaningless. It looks so knowing and imposing but

[1] Care of Scribners.

there is nothing in it. Why does it follow that if a man writes a book that is not like "Madame Bovary" it is inevitably like Zola? I may be dumb but I can't see this. You say that "Madame Bovary" becomes eternal while Zola already rocks with age. Well this may be true—but if it is true isn't it true because "Madame Bovary" may be a great book and those that Zola wrote may not be great ones? Wouldn't it also be true to say that "Don Quixote," or "Pickwick" or "Tristram Shandy" "becomes eternal" while already Mr. Galsworthy "rocks with age."? I think it is true to say this and it doesn't leave much of your argument, does it? For your argument is based simply upon one *way*, upon one *method* instead of another. And have you ever noticed how often it turns out that what a man is really doing is simply rationalizing his own way of doing something, the way he has to do it, the way given him by his talent and his nature, into the only inevitable and right way of doing everything—a sort of classic and eternal art form handed down by Apollo from Olympus without which and beyond which there is nothing? Now you have your way of doing something and I have mine; there are a lot of ways, but you are honestly mistaken in thinking that there is a "way."

I suppose I would agree with you in what you say about "the novel of selected incidents" so far as it means anything. I say so far as it means anything because every novel, of course, is a novel of selected incidents. There are no novels of unselected incidents. You couldn't write about the inside of a telephone booth without selecting. You could fill a novel of a thousand pages with a description of a single room and yet your incidents would be selected. And I have mentioned "Don Quixote" and Pickwick and "The Brothers Karamazov" and "Tristram Shandy" to you in contrast to "The Silver Spoon" or "The White Monkey" as examples of books that have become "immortal" and that *boil* and *pour*. Just remember that although "Madame Bovary" in your opinion may be a great book, "Tristram Shandy" *is* indubitably a great book, and that it is great for quite different reasons. It is great because it *boils* and *pours*—for the *unselected* quality of its selection. You say that the great writer like Flaubert has consciously left out the stuff that Bill or Joe will come along presently and put in. Well, don't forget, Scott, that a great writer is not only a leaver-outer but also a putter-inner, and that Shakespeare and Cervantes and Dostoievsky were great putter-inners—greater putter-inners, in fact, than taker-outers—and will be remembered for what they put in—remembered, I venture to say, as long as Monsieur Flaubert will be remembered for what he left out.

As to the rest of it in your letter about cultivating an alter ego, becoming a more conscious artist, by pleasantness or grief, exuberance or cynicism, and how nothing stands out in relief because everything is keyed at the same emotional pitch—this stuff is worthy of the great minds that review books nowadays—the Fadimans and De Votos—but not of you. For you are an artist and the artist has the only true critical intelligence. You have had to work and sweat blood yourself and you know what it is like to try to write a living word or create a living thing. So don't talk this foolish stuff to me about exuberance or being a conscious artist or not bringing things into emotional relief, or any of the rest of it. Let the Fadimans and De Votos do that kind of talking but not Scott Fitzgerald. You've got too much sense and you know too much. The little fellows who don't know may picture a man as a great "exuberant" six-foot-six clod-hopper straight out of nature who bites off half a plug of apple tobacco, tilts the corn liquor jug and lets half of it gurgle down his throat, wipes off his mouth with the back of one hairy paw, jumps three feet in the air and clacks his heels together four times before he hits the floor again and yells out "Whoopee, boys, I'm a rootin, tootin, shootin son of a gun from Buncombe County—out of my way now, here I come!" —and then wads up three-hundred thousand words or so, hurls it at a blank page, puts covers on it and says "Here's my book!"

Now Scott, the boys who write book-reviews in New York may think it's done that way; but the man who wrote "Tender Is the Night" knows better. You know you never did it that way, you know I never did, you know no one else who ever wrote a line worth reading ever did. So don't give me any of your guff, young fellow. And don't think I'm sore. But I get tired of guff—I'll take it from a fool or from a book reviewer but I won't take it from a friend who knows a lot better. I want to be a better artist. I want to be a more selective artist. I want to be a more restrained artist. I want to use such talent as I have, control such forces as I may own, direct such energy as I may use more cleanly, more surely and to a better purpose. But Flaubert me no Flauberts, Bovary me no Bovarys, Zola me no Zolas, and exuberance me no exuberances. Leave this stuff for those who huckster in it and give me, I pray you, the benefits of your fine intelligence and your high creative faculties, all of which I so genuinely and profoundly admire.

I am going into the woods for another two or three years. I am going to try to do the best, the most important piece of work I have ever done. I am going to have to do it alone. I am going to lose what little bit of reputation I may have gained, to have to hear and know and endure in silence again all of the doubt, the disparagement, the ridicule, the post-mortems that they are so eager to read over you even before you are dead. I know what it means and so do you. We have both been through it before. We know it is the plain damn simple truth.

Well, I've been through it once and I believe I can get through it again. I think I know a little more now than I did before, I certainly know what to expect and I'm going to try not to let it get me down. That is the reason why this time I shall look for intelligent understanding among some of my friends. I'm not ashamed to say that I shall need it. You say in your letter that you are ever my friend. I assure you that it is very good to hear this. Go for me with the gloves off if you think I need it. But don't De Voto me. If you do I'll call your bluff.

I'm down here for the summer living in a cabin in the country and I am enjoying it. Also I'm working. I don't know how long you are going to be in Hollywood or whether you have a job out there but I hope I shall see you before long and that all is going well with you. I still think as I always thought that "Tender Is the Night" had in it the best work you have ever done. And I believe you will surpass it in the future. Anyway, I send you my best wishes as always for health and work and success. Let me hear from you sometime. The address is Oteen, North Carolina, just a few miles from Asheville. Ham Basso, as you know, is not far away at Pisgah Forest and he is coming over to see me soon and perhaps we shall make a trip together to see Sherwood Anderson. And now this is all for the present—unselective, you see, as usual. Good bye, Scott, and good luck,

Ever yours,

To HAMILTON BASSO

[Oteen, N.C.]

July 29, 1937

Dear Ham:

Pick out a week end, any one you like,[1] and I'll make it fit with my own plans which are very simple ones. I intend to keep at work, and so far as I know, except for the hordes of thirsty tourists who just happen in casually to look at the elephant, I have no definite engagements. . . . Except for casual intrusions—people driving up to demand if I've seen anything of a stray cocker spaniel, gentlemen appearing through the woods with a four-pound steak saying their name is McCracken and I met them on the train four weeks ago and they always bring their own provisions with them, and the local Police Court judge and the leading hot-dog merchant, and friends of my shooting scrape in Yancey County with bevies of wild females—all of which has and is continuing to happen —I have practically no company at all out here. At any rate it's all been very interesting and instructing and in spite of Hell and hilarity I am pushing on with my work. You come on over anyway: I can't promise you

[1] Basso had written that he would come and spend a weekend at Wolfe's cabin.

long twenty-four hour periods of restful seclusion while we meditate upon the problems of life and art, but you may have an instructive and amusing time, and of course I'd love to see you and talk it over with you.

I had a letter from Scott, and the surprise of hearing from him was so great you could have knocked me over with a brick bat. It was, for him, an amazingly long letter and a very earnest one. It was all about Art— and more especially my own lack of it. He passed out some very graceful compliments about my "unmatchable talents" and so on, and how he wouldn't be doing all this if he wasn't my friend, etc.—and then let me have it. It was all very much like those famous lines of my favorite poem:

> "It was all very well to dissemble your love
> —But why did you kick me downstairs?"

I couldn't make out very well what he was driving at and told him so. There was a whole lot in it about Flaubert and Zola and "Madame Bovary" and how much greater Flaubert is than Zola, etc.—all of which may be true, but like the celebrated flowers that bloom in the spring, have nothing to do with the case. I let him have it with both barrels when I answered him, and I hope the experience will do him good. I know he will understand I wasn't a bit sore and enjoyed writing a letter and a chance of ribbing him a little. He has come out apparently as a classical selectionist and was telling me that Flaubert would be remembered as a great writer for the things he left out. I answered, not, I thought un-neatly that Shakespeare and Cervantes and Tolstoi and Dostoievsky would be remembered as great writers for what they put in and that a great writer was not only a great leaver-outer but a great putter-inner also. Anyway I had some fun and I know Scott won't mind it. His letter was postmarked Los Angeles and I don't know whether he has got a job at Hollywood or not. His letter sounded more stable and cheerful, and I hope that everything is going better with him.

My Chickamauga story, which I liked so well myself, has now been honored with rejection slips by most of the nation's eminent popular magazines. Harper's also turned it down the other day with a pompous note from Mr. Hartman [2] to the effect that they would like a *real* Wolfe story, but they supposed this was impossible since *Scribner's* had a stranglehold on the author's best work. Well the comical pay-off on this is that *Scribner's* have no hold at all, not even a feeble clasp. I have had only one piece in the magazine in three years, and that not one of the better ones, and Perkins has been panting to get hold of "Chickamauga" which Harper's has just rejected. I don't know whether his pants will

[2] Lee Hartman was editor of *Harper's Magazine* at this time.

cease when he has read the story, but I hope not.[3] At any rate I'm gathering experience. Mr. Stout of *The Saturday Evening Post* allows as how my "No More Rivers" is a good story after page twenty and that they'd be very seriously concerned if I'd agree to cut the first twenty pages to four. As I remember it, the beautiful girl with the husky voice makes her appearance on page twenty—so that's that.

I've just taken time out to have pictures of myself, the cabin and all three of us made by a beautiful lady and her escort, Judge Phil Cocke, who weighs 340 on the hoof and is one of Asheville's famous and eminent characters. I like the Judge and the Judge curiously seems to like me; certainly I've never had as devoted and accurate a reader—he hasn't forgotten a comma or a semicolon, he annotates my book with the names of the "real" characters, and I have heard that he was especially touched and delighted because he thinks I referred to him and a very celebrated lady in Asheville who bore the name of Queen Elizabeth and who at one time was the Empress of the Red Light District. Of course, I admit nothing, I just look coy and innocent—but if that's the way they want to have it, I suppose no one can stop them. Anyway we are having fun, you must come over. This is all for the present, write and let me know what time suits you. Meanwhile, with love to you and Toto,

To ELIZABETH NOWELL

Box 95
Oteen, N.C.
July 29, 1937

Dear Miss Nowell:

It looks as if no one's right about "Chickamauga" except thee and me—and maybe even thee is a little peculiar. Anyway, we are finding out something about those great minds that direct the editorial policies of our leading magazines, aren't we? . . .

I am going on with "The Party at Jack's," but it is turning out to be a terrifically complicated and difficult job. But it is a very interesting one and if I work and weave and rework long and hard enough I may have something very good. The market is a different matter: my plan when I get through is to have a complete section of the social order, a kind of dense, closely interwoven tapestry made up of the lives and thoughts and destinies of thirty or forty people, and all embodied in the structure of the story. It is an elaborate design; it has to be: it is, I suppose, somewhat

---

[3] The editors of *Scribner's Magazine*, which by this time was virtually independent of the publishing house of Scribners, declined "Chickamauga" soon after this.

Proustian but this also has to be and the interesting thing about it is the really great amount of action. This action is submerged and perhaps not at first apparent, but if the reader will stick with me, if I can carry him along with me, it will be apparent by the time he finishes the story. In spite of all kinds of interruptions—there have been droves of thirsty tourists out here to look at the animal, all the way from a police court judge to the leading hot-dog merchant—I have done a lot of *work* and hope to see where I stand with it in another two weeks. . . .

The weather is fine, the country is beautiful, I am sleeping at night and I think I feel better than when I left New York four weeks ago. My plans for the future are still uncertain. I don't know where I'll be next year, or where I'm going to live. All I hope for is to go on with my work and get something done and to escape somehow the ruinous calamities of the last two years. . . . I am afraid some of the old connections may be worn out: there are too many scars now, too much disillusionment and disappointment. At any rate, no matter what happens, I hope to go on working and get something done. I am sorry we have had such bad luck with the two stories, but I hope to get some good news soon. Meanwhile, with all good wishes,

> The following letter was in reply to one from Mrs. Anne W. Armstrong offering to rent to Wolfe, for a purely nominal sum, a cabin belonging to her brother-in-law and sister, Major General and Mrs. Philip Peyton, on her property near Bristol, Tennessee. Mrs. Armstrong had first met Wolfe when he had passed through Bristol on his way to Asheville in late April, 1937. She is the author of two novels, The Seas of God and This Day and Time, a play, Some Sweet Day, and various magazine articles, including "As I Saw Thomas Wolfe" in the Spring, 1946, issue of The Arizona Quarterly.

To ANNE W. ARMSTRONG

Box 95,
Oteen, N. C.,

August 4, 1937.

Dear Mrs. Armstrong:

Thanks very much for your letter. The rent you mentioned for General Peyton's cabin was not only reasonable but ridiculously cheap for the place. I pay more than that for my own modest little place, which, of course, is nowhere near as comfortable and as elaborate as the Peyton place. But I think I shall try to stick it out here, at least for the present. I have taken the cabin here for another month, and should like to stay at home until I have the satisfaction of getting some work done and finding out that I can really work here. . . .

I brought down with me from New York an enormous crate containing millions of words of manuscript, the material for half a dozen books and notes and ideas and sketches and stories and dozens of other things. Another tremendous piece of work has been shaping itself in my mind and in my writing for two or three years now, and now I think I have it fully articulated and a plan clear from beginning to end. But I lose heart sometime when I think of the magnitude of the task that lies before me. I hope that my health continues and that my will will remain firm. If only things didn't take so long! If only I didn't almost always bite off more than I can chew! It's my own fault, I suppose, but I don't know what I can do about it. It really seems that such talent as I have has to realize itself through a process of torrential production—that is, by pouring it out in a Niagara flood, millions and millions of words. After that, of course, comes the ghastly and heart-breaking labor of cutting it down, shaping and re-weaving it. It's all very well for these fellows who write forty and fifty thousand word books to talk to you about Flaubert and classical brevity: you can try honestly to mend your ways, to learn through experience and work to correct some of your most excessive faults—but what's the use of talking to a man about Flaubert if his talent—such modest talent as he has—is really more like Dickens or Rabelais? Anyway, all I can do is to learn what I can and to do my work, I pray, the best I can.

Well, this is all for the present and too much as usual. If things get too much for me in my own neighborhood, I may come over to find out if that wonderful cabin is still unoccupied. Anyway, I hope to see you before the summer is over. . . . Meanwhile, I send you my thanks again for all your generous interest and consideration. . . .

To HAMILTON BASSO

Oteen, N.C.

August 21, 1937.

Dear Ham:

Thanks for your note and for the enclosed clipping on the Hemingway-Eastman matter.[1] It was all very interesting and instructive. It is good of

[1] Probably a clipping from one of the New York newspapers of August 14, 1937, referring to the encounter between Ernest Hemingway and Max Eastman in the Scribner offices on the preceding day.

you to say that you enjoyed the weekend, but I'm afraid you found it a very hectic one. However, it was quiet compared to what has happened since.

I had to attend a murder trial in Yancey and testify. It was a fascinating and thrilling and exhausting experience. I got off fairly lightly compared to some of the witnesses, but I was denounced by one of the defense lawyers in his final plea to the jury as the author of an obscene and infamous book called "Look Homeward, Angel," who had held up his family, kin-folk, and town to public odium, and whose testimony, I therefore gathered, was not to be taken into account. Also when I returned to my cabin I found that William [2] had disappeared. He showed up finally on Thursday afternoon, confessed that he was afraid of the dark and of staying alone at night, and said he wanted to quit. I looked forward to coming back and working here, but maybe it will not work out as I had hoped. I may go over and visit some friends in Virginia in a few days and perhaps see Sherwood [3] who has written me again and asked me to come. Anyway, I'll try to think my way through it and let you know how it works out.

There is not much other news to tell you. I wish I could see you, and no matter whether I go or stay, I hope to have another talk with you before you go abroad. Meanwhile, with love to you and Toto and with all good wishes,

The following fragment of a letter, found in a carbon copy in Wolfe's own files, was almost undoubtedly written to Elizabeth Nowell about the manuscript of "The Party at Jack's." The person who had told Wolfe "that the thing is a unit in itself" was probably Hamilton Basso who read the manuscript at Wolfe's request and then sent it to Miss Nowell from Pisgah Forest. The "friend in New York" to whom Wolfe intended to send another copy would seem to have been Perkins: certainly the friend referred to in the subsequent paragraph was he. However, there is no record at Scribners of the receipt of the manuscript, and no recollection of it among Perkins' close associates. Moreover, it was at about this time that Wolfe took the final step of breaking with Scribners by putting in long distance calls to various other publishers. Perhaps worrying about Perkins' possible reaction to "The Party at Jack's" was what finally brought things to a head and impelled him to complete the severance.

---

[2] The colored house boy who was working for Wolfe.
[3] Sherwood Anderson.

Probably to ELIZABETH NOWELL

[Asheville, N.C.]
(August 22 (?), 1937.)

. . . It is still only a draft, but as you will see, in a very much more complete and finished form than what you saw in New York. I have completely rewritten it and rewoven it. It was a very difficult piece of work, but I think it is now a single thing, as much a single thing as anything I've ever written. I am not through with it yet. There is a great deal more revision to be done, but I am sending it to you anyway to let you see what I have done, and I think you will also be able to see what it may be like when I'm finished with it.

As to the final disposition of it, I do not know. Someone has told me that the thing is a unit in itself and could be, when I am finished with it, published as a unit without further addition. I have not made up my mind about this yet. The whole thing belongs, as you know, to the entire manuscript of "The October Fair," of which sections and fragments have been published for years—"Death—The Proud Brother," "April, Late April," etc.—and many other things, of course, which have not been published. "Mr. Malone," by the way, belongs in the piece that I am sending you, "The Party at Jack's," but since "Mr. Malone" has already been published, I did not think it advisable to include it here. All the other parts which you have seen: the whole long section called "Morning," that is, Mr. Jack waking up and feeling the tremor, faint and instant, in the ground beneath him; Mrs. Jack and the maid; the "April, Late April" piece which the *Mercury* is publishing; the scene in the station; the long section called "The Locusts Have No King" [1] which I do not think you ever saw; "Death—The Proud Brother"; and other matter which perhaps you never read, also belong with this piece. I, therefore, kept a copy and put it all together with some tentative idea in my mind of making a complete book of all of it—a book which would occur within the limits of a single twenty-four hours, beginning [with] midnight of one day and ending with the midnight of the next, and bearing probably the title "The October Fair." I have not made my mind up definitely about this yet, but I am sending the manuscript to a friend in New York to get his opinion.

[1] This title taken from Proverbs, 30:27, was later used by Dawn Powell for her novel published by Scribners in 1949.

As you know, the whole thing has been a very vexed and perturbed part of my writing experience and it has cost me the utmost worry and difficulty because it seemed to me that so much labor, so much effort, and so much that I really think is valuable and good and needs to be saved was in danger of dying the death, of being in so many various and complicated ways—all of which apparently sprang out of a friend's [2] desire to help and perhaps some instinctive timidity and caution—suppressed and killed. I cannot say definitely as to all this, but I do know that a man must not be thwarted in the process of his creation, and I feel very strongly that this has happened to me with this piece of work.

As to this piece I'm sending you, "The Party at Jack's," I feel that whatever else may be said about it, it escapes entirely the objections that were raised about the purpose of "The October Fair." I really think that the purpose of "The October Fair" was misunderstood, and [that] people whose judgment I respected were too quick and willing to assume that the book would be a sequel to the first two books and thus lay me open to the old charges of autobiographical literalness and romanticism, etc. and not as I intended it to be: the progression of my life, the maturing of my experience and my talent. At any rate, "The Party at Jack's," I believe, escapes these feared qualities. I don't believe the charge of "autobiography" can be brought against it, except in so far as they must be brought against the work of any man. I have simply taken the lives of thirty or forty of the people I knew during my years in New York and revealed them during an evening at a party in the city.

As to the matter of action, it seems to me that the piece is crowded, although perhaps it is not apparently so. But I don't see how any intelligent reader could read it without understanding that almost everything has happened before the piece is ended. As to the rest of it, the social implication that, I fear, would make the piece anathema to almost any of the older publishers, I simply cannot help it. It is simply the way I feel and think: I hope and believe there is not a word of conscious propaganda in it. It is certainly not at all Marxian, but it is representative of the way my life has come—after deep feeling, deep thinking, and deep living and all this experience—to take its way. And I believe and hope, also, that this piece will show the energy of life, a genuine and reverent love of life, and a spirit of understanding and compassion for all the characters. I hope and believe that it has passion in it, indignation and denunciation, and I hope also it has pity and love

---

[2] Wolfe undoubtedly meant Perkins here. See his letter to him dated December 15, 1936.

and comprehension in it. You are seeing the thing in its first blocking out: if all these qualities that I hope for it are not fully revealed now, I hope they will be when I get through working on it. It is in concept, at any rate, the most densely woven piece of writing that I have ever attempted.

There is not much more that I can tell you about it except that I wish you would read it as it is, in and for itself, without too much reference to these other portions I have mentioned, of which it is also a part. But just read it, if you can, as a story in itself and see if you think it carries the unity and direction of a single thing. Because I am not certain that I shall be here more than a day or two longer, I am sending you the piece in its present unrevised and uncorrected form. Travelling around with great bags of manuscript—and I've written sixty or eighty thousand words since I came down here—is a precarious business, and I would like to know that even in its present form, you have a copy in your hands. Another copy will be in the keeping of a friend in New York, and I hope to keep the final one intact for myself. . . .

It's pretty hard to tell you what I shall do about staying here in Asheville. I wanted to come back: I thought about it for years. I think I should like still to stay and work if it were possible. As you know, I have never put much stock in looking for "places to work." It seems to me that a man can work almost any place he wants to. But my stay here this summer has really resembled a three-ring circus. I think people have wanted to be and have tried to be most kind, but they wore me to a frazzle. My cabin outside of town was situated in an isolated and quite beautiful spot, but they found their way to it, and in addition I found out that it is, to say the least, terribly difficult to keep a negro servant in such a place. They are afraid of the dark: that is about what it amounts to. As a result, they were always disappearing at night and not coming back until the next morning. . . . Of course, it's not their fault, but just the way they are.

As to living in town here, I don't know whether that can work out or not. I know so many people here and the place is really very small. People know everything you do, even before you do it—it's always that way, isn't it—and they are still, in a friendly way, living over the whole vexed experience of "Look Homeward, Angel" and of having the culprit back in their midst. It is a beautiful country here. I shall always miss it, but perhaps what I had thought possible cannot happen. At any rate, the summer has not been lost. I have established the connection again and, of course, completed gathering all the materials for perhaps the most tragic incidents of our collapse—which happened to the entire nation—in the history of our country. I don't think anything else like it could be found! The whole thing, intensified and specialized, is here. And since it is my own home place, of course I have the deepest interest, the profoundest sympathy with all of it.

I may go up to Virginia for a day or two to see Sherwood Anderson. As to mailing addresses for the present, I don't know what to tell you. I still have my cabin at Oteen until September, and I am still trying to think my way through this, to find out what I am going to do. I think for the present if you would send any communication you may have to General Delivery, Asheville, N.C., that would be the quickest and safest address. Then if there is any change, I can leave word there where the mail should be forwarded. This is all for the present, and too much as usual. Please let me know if you receive the manuscript of "The Party at Jack's" safely, and what, if any, you think the prospects are. Meanwhile, with thanks and all good wishes,

To SHERWOOD ANDERSON

[New York City]
Wednesday, September 22, 1937

Dear Sherwood:

Thanks for your letter. It was not only fine to hear from you—what you said did me a lot of good. What you say is true—I do, and have all my life gone for *everything*—not only writing—hell for leather. I seem to wrestle each experience as if, in circus talk, I am "now about to engage in a hair-raising, spine-freezing, gravity-defying duel to the death with the universe." I suppose that's why that shrewd and wise and nice mother-in-law of yours told you I was [——?] pretty hard on myself. I went home this summer for the first time in almost eight years to fight it out, talk it out, live it out, with the city of Asheville as if I was a regiment of storm troops going into a decisive battle. And of course it took it out of me. I was pretty tired when I saw you—but maybe also I was coming away with a lot of tar on my heel and large fistfuls of the native earth. I hope so, anyway.

I don't think really I'm so much worried about the bulk and flood of my writing as I once was. I've got a *feeling* about some things, after long mulling and thrashing about with them, that often turns out right —and my feeling is that I shall probably always have to do essentially about as I do now—that is, pour it out, boil it out, flood it out. I realize myself through a process of torrential production. Perhaps there are better ways but that is my way—I believe essentially my way—and it would be wrong to worry about doing it Flaubert's way, or Hemingway's way, or Henry James' way. Nevertheless, I do worry, as we all do, about my improvement: I want to be a better writer, a less wasteful writer, a surer writer, a cleaner writer, a more disciplined writer—and I believe and hope that may come through work. As to the rest of it—my death-defying duel with the universe—just the business of living which I make so damned hard but out of which I do believe I have managed to get a good deal—I think it is pretty closely bound up with my work. In fact, living and working are so close together with me that it seems to me they are damned near the same thing. I do carry my work too much with me—when I'm doing it, I take it into bars, restaurants, railroad trains, parties, upon the streets, everywhere. I guess many a row or quarrel or dispute in some joint with a sanded floor began somewhere hours or days or weeks before upon a page of manuscript, but I hope some of my better moments started there as well.

I'm wrestling with a huge leviathan of work—three monstrous books, all worked upon and sweat upon and prayed about and dreamt and cursed upon for years.[1] I'm caught in the Laocoön coils of this too-muchness. I get maddened like Tantalus with the feeling of having everything almost within my grasp and of starving to death.

For one thing, I think I am starving for publication: I love to get published: it maddens me not to get published: I feel at times like getting every publisher in the world by the scruff of his neck, forcing his jaws open, and cramming the manuscript down his throat—"God damn you, here it is—I will and must be published."

You know what it means—you're a writer and you understand it. It's not "the satisfaction of being published." Great God! it's the satisfaction of getting it out; of knowing that, so far as you're concerned, you're through with it; that—for good or ill, for better or for worse—it's over, done with, finished, out of your life forever and that, come what may, you can at least as far as this thing is concerned, get the merciful damned easement of oblivion and forgetfulness.

My troubles with Scribners are deep, grievous, and, I fear, irreparable: I'll have to try to find someone else, if anyone will have me. I can't tell you the anguish this thing has cost me: these things get deep hold of me, and this has been almost like death. But I *will* be published, if I can: I've got to be—and I will have my own picture of life, my own vision of society, of the world as, thus far, I have been able to live, sweat, feel and think it through! And my disagreement with these people with

---

[1] He probably meant *The October Fair, The Hills Beyond Pentland,* and *The Vision of Spangler's Paul.* However he usually thought of these as one great mass of manuscript.

whom I have been so close, with whom my life has been so deeply knit, has become so great, so complex and so various!—I don't see how it can be patched up now!

Really, I don't think I'm either muddled or confused. I don't think I know anyone who knows—or thinks he knows—so clearly and so desperately what he wants to do. I want to do my work and to get it published. I want to find a place where I can feel at home and to which I can go back. (Incidentally, I think there are such places, but I don't think they're either Asheville or New York.) I want to get married and try to have a family.

I'll probably always go through this kind of struggle with my work, but honestly I don't see why I shouldn't get all these things I have spoken of. At any rate, I shan't give up trying yet.

May I also say that I want to be your friend—as I am—and I want you to be mine, as I believe you are. When I told you how I felt about you and your work, I was not laying it on with a trowel. I don't think of you as a father, as an elderly influence, or anything of the kind. So far as I know, your work has not "influenced" me at all, save in the ways in which it has enriched my life, and my knowledge of my country. I think you are one of the most important writers of this country, that you plowed another deep furrow in the American earth, revealed to us another beauty that we knew was there but that no one else had spoken. I think of you with Whitman and with Twain—that is, with men who have seen America with a poet's vision, and with a poetic vision of life —which to my mind is the only way actually it can be seen.

I appreciate your letter and all you say to me. I'll have to work the whole thing out for myself, but I feel there is wisdom in you, and we never perhaps give up the wonderful image of our youth—that we will find someone external to our life and superior to our need, who knows the answer.

It does not happen—"is not my strength in me?"—but it comes, I think, from the deepest need in life, and all religiousness is in it.

Good-bye for the present, Sherwood. I hope I'll be here when you come. At any rate, I'll look forward to seeing you again before too long. Meanwhile, with love to all,

XVI

THE SEARCH FOR A NEW PUBLISHER AND
FINAL CHOICE OF HARPERS

1937

In late August or early September, 1937, Wolfe had finally completed his severance from Scribners by putting in long distance calls to several other publishers to inquire whether they would like to publish him. Nothing definite came of these first queries, either because the other publishers could not clearly hear what he said and were not sure that he actually was Thomas Wolfe, or because they hesitated to take him away from Scribners, or, because he himself decided against going with them. A few weeks later, after Wolfe had returned to New York, Robert N. Linscott of Houghton Mifflin heard the rumors that he had left Scribners and wrote him to ask if this was true. The following was Wolfe's reply.

To ROBERT N. LINSCOTT

[Prince George Hotel]
[New York City]
[October 16, 1937]

Dear Mr. Linscott:

Thanks very much for your letter. By an unfortunate coincidence I was in Boston last week at the time your letter was written and might have seen you then. I did try but found a whole column of Linscotts when I looked in the telephone book, and I couldn't decide which was you. As it was then Saturday afternoon I knew there was no use trying Houghton Mifflin.

I'm sorry there have been "rumours"; as you know New York is a pretty rumourous place, but I want to assure you that I don't go around in the groups where these presumably originate, and in fact have not seen a publisher in almost four months. I am telling you this because to my great and deep regret my former publishers and I have separated. It is not true that I have "left" them; I am simply without a publisher. I want you to know that this severance is not the result of a temperamental explosion on the part of an author who is now trying to make terms with someone else, and get the best terms that he can; but that it is, for me, at any rate, one of the most grievous and sorrowful experiences of my whole life; it involves deep and complicated differences which touch, it seems to me, my whole life and work—differences that are by no means recent, but that began two and a half years ago. I know there are people at my former publishers who could tell you that this is true —chiefly, the man who has stood closest to me for eight years now and who knows more about my life and the problem of my work than anyone else, Maxwell Perkins.

I am telling you all this to let you know that I can honorably talk about these things to other people now, and other people can talk to me about these things. And honestly, Mr. Linscott, what I need most of all right now is someone I can talk to—someone who understands the problems of publishing and of a writer's work. I do feel earnestly that this ought to be done first, because the problem is really so complex, the differences that brought about this severance are so involved that I need to lay them before someone and get the opinion and perhaps the guidance of a more detached mind. I can not go into them here, I can only tell you that the whole problem is one that involves several million words of manuscript, the material of at least three big books, and a great many stories and novelettes, and what I am going to do with this material, how I am going to use it, and whether anyone is going to support me and encourage me in my use of it.

That is why I need so badly to talk to someone. It will take a long talk, a lot of talk, maybe a whole series of talks, but that is what is needed first. And I know I can make the whole thing clear: I am completely certain of my purpose. I am very happy and grateful to know that people in your office feel as you say they do about my work. I am proud to know that a house of your standing is interested in me. I don't know if you would care to assume a publishing responsibility of this nature after I have explained it to you, or whether your house is the best one for a problem of this sort. But I do think that it would help a lot if we could talk about it, and if I could say my piece to you. And please understand, Mr. Linscott, that there is nothing underhanded about this situation: it is a sad business for me and I am sick at heart because of it, but it is a trouble that has been developing for almost three years, and that my publisher and I have debated and worked on from every side until there was no more to say. Naturally, I think they are wrong about many things, and I should like to tell you about them, and then, if you like, you can talk to the publisher—to Max Perkins—yourself. But please understand that I have no intention of indulging in bitter recriminations towards people with whom for years I had the deepest and closest relations, whose intelligence and ability I so deeply respect, and for whom I shall always have a feeling of warmth and affection. As I told you, it's a sad and bitter business for me: it's damned near got me down, I'm trying to rest up a little, but I want to get back to work. I'm staying here at this hotel, probably only for a few days until I decide where I'm going to live. You can reach me by writing me, or telephoning, care of my agent, Elizabeth Nowell, 114 East 56th St., New York City—Wickersham 2-1262. If you are coming down to New York and want to see me, please let me know through her. And excuse this long letter—like everything I do it's too long—but I wanted to give you some idea of what's in my mind.

After talking with Wolfe and also with Perkins, Robert Linscott had asked Wolfe to let him read some of his manuscript, especially that of The October Fair, *which Wolfe now thought he wanted to publish first. Wolfe had some of his manuscript with him, some was still at Scribners and some in a storage warehouse, and when he explained the difficulty of sorting and assembling it all in a small hotel room, Linscott arranged for him to take it to Houghton Mifflin's New York office. On October 22, 1937, Linscott wrote him a note acknowledging receipt of "one packing case and nine packages of manuscripts," and continued: "I am a little worried by the fact that we have no fire-proof safe in which to store material of this value, and I hope you realize that, under the circumstances, it will have to be held entirely at your risk. Let me take this opportunity to tell you how much I enjoyed our evening together and how greatly I appreciate the chance to read this manuscript."*

Wolfe became upset by this disclaimer of responsibility for the manuscript and wrote Linscott the letter which appears below; then thought better of it and never mailed it, but kept it in his own files and finally handed it to Edward C. Aswell of Harper & Brothers as a partial explanation of the situation that existed between himself and Houghton Mifflin.

Shortly after writing this letter, Wolfe went to the New York office of Houghton Mifflin and took his manuscript away. At this time he talked with LeBaron Barker, who was then New York editor of Houghton Mifflin, about their disclaimer of responsibility, but as Barker now remembers it, he did not seem as much upset as amused by the whole thing. In all fairness to Linscott, it should be pointed out that the general policy of all publishers is to disclaim responsibility for manuscripts submitted to them. Perhaps Linscott was over-conscientious in making this clear, but Wolfe had no real reason

to take offence. However, he was totally ignorant of this general policy, be-
cause Scribners had stored his crates of manuscript many times without ever
mentioning the matter of responsibility for them.

To ROBERT N. LINSCOTT

[Prince George Hotel]
[Fifth Avenue and 28th Street]
[New York City]
October 23, 1937

Dear Linscott:

I did not read the letter you gave me yesterday at your office until
I returned home. You said it was an acknowledgment of the manuscript
I had left at your New York office, but when I read it I found that you
also disclaimed responsibility for the material and said that it would
have to be held at your office entirely at my risk.

It had not occurred to me that any risk was involved in view of what
you had said to me in our previous conversations, and when I brought
the manuscript to your New York office, people there assured me there
was no risk. I wish you had let me know of this before I took the manuscript out of safe-keeping in a storage warehouse because, as I told you,
it represents the work of several years and is almost all I own in the
world. In view of your letter, however, I am removing the manuscript
from your office and shall try to put it in a place where no risk is involved.

I am sorry about all this, but just to keep the record straight, you wrote
me on October 8 saying that you had heard I was looking for a publisher
and that Houghton Mifflin was interested in my work. I wrote back on
October 16 and said that I was without a publisher and would like to
talk to someone about the matter of publishing my future work. You
telephoned Miss Nowell, my agent, from Boston and made an appointment with me. When I saw you I tried to explain the situation as far
as my manuscript was concerned, and you suggested that I give you
first for reading a part of the manuscript which was called "The October
Fair." I told you that all the manuscript was packed and stored in a
storage warehouse and that I should have to go there and take it out,
and that I had no apartment here, no place to take it. You told me I
could bring it to the Houghton Mifflin office here in New York, and you
repeated this offer in a subsequent conversation on the telephone, and
told me Mr. Barker of Houghton Mifflin would go with me and help me
get it. Mr. Barker and I did go immediately and get the manuscript

from the warehouse and bring it to the Houghton Mifflin office here. This completes the record of the transaction until your letter of October 22.

In view of the fact that I had already begun to arrange the manuscript which you had asked to read, and since the necessity for moving the manuscript now from your office to a place of safe-keeping means a further delay, I must ask you to let me know right away what you want to do as far as the manuscript of "The October Fair" is concerned. Since I promised to get it out and arrange it, I am still willing to abide by that promise, but in view of your letter that the manuscript you were keeping is entirely at my risk, I want to know what responsibility, if any, you are willing to assume for the safe-keeping, the protection, and the safe-return of the manuscript you asked to see.

If you are willing, as you say in your letter, to assume no risk, our agreement concerning this manuscript is ended. It seems to me that you must assume the risk, that the entire and whole responsibility of safe-guarding an author's property, once you have requested it, is yours and yours alone. If you can not agree to this, then I do not know why I should entrust my property into your care.

I am sorry about all this, but since you have yourself raised a question of "risk" which it never occurred to me would be raised, I must request that you explicitly state to me immediately just what, if any, you conceive as your responsibility toward the property I entrust into your care. If you do not feel you have a responsibility, then I request that you write me to that effect immediately so that I can make further efforts to find people who will assume that responsibility, and will offer me a chance of obtaining the two things I lack and that I need now more than anything in the world—a good publisher and a decent living.

I want you to understand that there is not a particle of anger, misunderstanding, or ill-feeling in this letter. But I do insist now on getting things straight. It is vitally important to me at what is to me a very critical and vitally important time. I know you are a business man, and I want you to know that I respect the rules of business so far as the rules of business respect the rights of general humanity. But I am a creating man, and hence a very practical man, and therefore can not agree that there is one set of rules that apply to business and another set that apply to general humanity. In other words, you can not talk to a man over the dinner table and a drink about your belief and interest and enthusiasm for his work, and how your organization supports and upholds such people in failure or success, and then talk about who is to take the risk, or whose responsibility is whose when he brings his property into your office and entrusts it to your care. I do not say that either set of chips is wrong, but you've got to play one or the other. You can't play both against the same man, when he has got only one set of chips and intends to use only one. I am telling you this because I've been through this whole thing before, and so far as I am [able] I shall avoid hereafter dealing with people who have two sets of chips.

I know that this, together with my previous long letter and my conversations with you, makes my own position plain.

Please let me know what you want to do about the manuscript I was to give to you. Meanwhile, with all good wishes,

To CORNELIUS MITCHELL

[New York City]
November 15, 1937

Dear Cornelius:

I have your letter of October 26th, and also a recent communication from Miss Nowell, my agent, to the effect that the New Jersey lawyers, Lum, Tamblyn & Fairlie,[1] have been trying to communicate with me through Scribners. I should like to inform you that my forwarding address is no longer Charles Scribner's Sons, as they have severed their relations with me, and are no longer my publishers. My present address for mail and for telephone calls, if it can be possibly kept this way, is in care of

> Miss Elizabeth Nowell,
> 114 East 56th Street,
> New York City

If there is really any urgent need to communicate with me in a hurry, I can be reached by a telephone call to Miss Nowell, which will be relayed to me within five minutes. All I can finally tell you with the utmost earnestness is that unless there is a real and urgent need for me and the prospect of something being done in my own behalf, I hope that I may be left to do my work, because my livelihood depends on it.

My funds are almost exhausted, and after two years of constant, nerve-racking interruptions of all sorts, I am faced now with the necessity of getting on with my work without further delay, if I am going to support

[1] Because of Wolfe's dissatisfaction with the handling of his case against ——, Mitchell had retained new counsel in New Jersey, where the case was to be tried. Lum, Tamblyn and Fairlie were the new counsel retained, and brought the case to a very successful conclusion in February, 1938.

myself at all. And if I don't support myself no one else is going to do it for me, because I have no income other than what I can earn by my own hands. I have at present an understanding with a publisher [2] to the effect that he is interested in my work and if I will push on now as hard as I can and try to get another big book finished this winter, he is willing to consider the manuscript with a view to publication. If I don't do this, the time is very soon coming when there will not be any money left for anything—to pay lawyer's bills or, what is certainly more to my own immediate purpose, to pay the rent. For that reason I am living here in New York in a rented room, and have so far as possible cut myself away from all contacts and all interruptions just in order to get my work done. I have wanted to explain all of this to you to let you know why I am doing this, that I am not hiding from any one or anything save for the one end and purpose in mind: to be allowed to work and earn my living. . . .

Economically and in every other way, I am right up against the wall. My eyes went back on me this summer and I've got to wear glasses now when I work, but I'm working as hard as I can here, day and night, and I'll get through somehow if I can only be spared the costly experience of these past two years. I have been loyal to my friends and tried to stick with the representatives I started out with. But I think you know where that led in one case: we both agreed we thought the representatives were in error in their judgment of the case, failed to take . . . decisive action, and we were compelled to seek counsel elsewhere. . . . I simply can't afford to go on like this. . . .

I have to work desperately hard for every dollar that I earn and that is why I am now putting this situation to you as I have, and I am putting it to you not as to a lawyer but as to a man who has told me that he has my interest and my welfare at heart. And that is why, Cornelius, I have not minced words here and have spoken bluntly to you about the whole situation. I know that, with the facts and circumstances being what they are, that is the way you would want me to speak. I know also that you can be depended upon to answer the same way. Meanwhile, until I hear from you, with best regards and with all good wishes,

The following letters to Fred W. Wolfe and to Maxwell E. Perkins, were written after reading the correspondence between Fred Wolfe, Mrs. Wolfe and Perkins concerning the severance with Scribners. Fred Wolfe had first

[2] Houghton Mifflin.

written to Perkins on October 28, 1937, saying: "Inasmuch as Mama seems a little perturbed because she has not heard from Tom . . . I thought it best to learn from you if he is O. K." To this, Perkins had answered on November 1: "I can tell you at any rate that Tom is all right. He has left his apartment on First Avenue, and has been living in different hotels until he finds a place to settle, I understand. He has also turned his back on me, and Scribners, so I have not seen him at all, though I would very much like to. I never could understand about all the trouble, but I hope in the end it will smooth out, at least so far as personal relations are concerned." Mrs. Wolfe herself had also written Perkins on November 3, saying: "Will you kindly give me Tom's address? . . . For his sake, I'm ashamed to let anyone know that we have not heard from him since he left September 5. I have worried, thought he might be sick . . ." To this Perkins answered that the quickest way to reach Wolfe would be in care of Miss Nowell, and referred Mrs. Wolfe to his letter of November 1 to Fred Wolfe. Meanwhile, Fred Wolfe had replied to Perkins on November 3, saying: "It is . . . a relief to know that Tom is all right. I am sorry he is having to live around in hotels and I hope he will soon make up his mind and settle and also make up his mind who his friends are. It is regrettable to be told he has turned his back on you and Scribners although I can't help but feel that there is a mistaken idea here on perhaps your part and your company's. Tom's warm statements of his affection to you personally at all times and while he was at home at Asheville are in direct . . . contradiction to your apprehensions in this direction. I rather think he is lost in a spell of worry or indecision. . . . When he gets back down to earth and realization, he will be around. If there is any trouble, I likewise fail to understand what it is all about. I can not see any reason why he should have any chip on his shoulder towards you or any members of his family, unless he is suffering from mental hallucinations. There is no normal reason for anything at all."

Upon receiving these letters from his brother, Wolfe evidently became very angry and upset and wrote him the following letter, but never mailed it. Probably when he had calmed down somewhat, he realized that it was inadvisable to involve his family in his difficulties with Scribners. Perhaps he also realized that his long metaphorical description of Scribners as an ice-cream company and himself as one of its salesmen had distorted the actual facts too far from truth and justice. It would be difficult to define just where and how he did this. However, the reader is referred to the actual correspondence between Wolfe and Perkins of November, 1936, and January, 1937, quoted in this volume as of those dates.

At any rate, after a two-day period of reflection, he wrote the letter below to Perkins and sent a copy of it to Fred Wolfe with a brief note simply saying: "I hope [this] clarifies the situation somewhat in your own mind. I think he's a fine man and that everything is bound to work out all right in the end."

To FRED W. WOLFE

[New York City]
November 17, 1937

Dear Fred:

I got your letter last night with the two enclosed letters from Mr. Perkins and the letter you wrote him on November 3rd. I am glad, at any rate, you told Mr. Perkins that you had never heard me say anything but good about him, for this is true, not only in your case but in the case of everyone that I have ever talked to. Miss Nowell, who has been, I believe, a true friend to me through all this trouble and is also a friend of Mr. Perkins', informed me the other day that he had told her I was going around "talking about him." This is so far from the truth that nothing could possibly be more wrong. The truth apparently is that of all the people in New York, I am the only one who has done no talking whatever about this whole situation—whatever talking has been done by me has been done within the past few days to publishers who have heard the rumors, and then whenever Mr. Perkins' name was mentioned, [it] was always mentioned by me in such a way as to do him nothing but honor. Moreover, in these conversations with other publishers I have been scrupulous to avoid making any statement that could be interpreted as showing bad feeling toward Scribners. All I have said was that I am no longer with a publisher, that the cause of this separation was not a recent one but a matter that had its beginnings at least two years ago, and that the situation finally reached such a state that it was understood on both sides months ago that I could not continue. Mr. Perkins' statement in his letter to you that I have "turned my back" on him and Scribners could not be further from the truth. The truth of the matter is that it was not my back that was turned, or if it was, it was because I looked for my friend and found that he had already walked away from me. Eight months ago at least, Charles Scribner Jr., [Charles Scribner III] the head of the firm, wrote me a letter in which he told me that I was now free to go if I wanted to, that they would be sorry to lose me, but if I felt that the time had come when we could no longer continue, I was free to go anywhere I liked. And about the same time, Mr. Perkins came to see me at my apartment on First Avenue, and with what I thought was deepest sincerity, told me that if I felt I had to leave Scribners, to leave, but that what was really important to him was that he and I continue to be friends. And that is what I have tried to do. Whatever talk has been done—and God knows, I suppose from what I have heard, there has been plenty, for when they start in this town they are just as bad as they are in a smaller town—has been done by others, and not by myself.

For two months after my return here in September, I stayed absolutely to myself, trying to think things out. It has been one of the saddest and most painful experiences of my whole life. To remember the devotion and loyalty and friendship that I had for all of these people for eight years, all the work I did for them, all the years of my life I gave to them, [and to have it] come to this, has been like death, like the death of a friend you can never forget. But there was simply no other way out. It had got to the point where it seemed I could no longer get them to publish the work I had done—the great mass of unpublished work on which I have expended years of effort in planning—but also it was becoming more and more a question of whether I could get them to publish anything in the future. When Perkins speaks about my "leaving" them, I can only ask you to remember that I had absolutely no contract of any sort with Scribners for any future work, nor had they offered me one.[1] I resent, therefore, the idea that I have left something that I did not even have.

I don't think you would consider an employer of yours justified in accusing you of leaving him, if he had quit paying you two years ago, had never spoken of a renewal of his employment, and had even taken away from you the work you had to do. Also, if someone had bumped into you at a cross-section, if no one in either car had been hurt and you had not even scraped any paint off anyone's fender, what would be your own feeling if the people in the other car thought they saw the chance of a little easy money and [got a] lawyer and brought suit against you and your employer for $125,000, saying that you had completely demolished their car, almost killed all the people in it, ruined the health of their sisters, their cousins and their aunts so that they will never be able to walk again, and so on. How would you feel about all of this if your own employer, not only for himself but for you, sought out not some good competent hard-boiled lawyer who would take a $50 fee and then deal with a shyster as he ought to be dealt with, but instead engaged the most expensive firm of attorneys in the South and paid them a retainer of $2,000 before they even lifted a finger. Suppose, also, that these attorneys laughed at the notion of there being any case, assured you that it was nothing but a nuisance suit and would be thrown out of court, and that you would on no account settle for anything. Then suppose within ten days or two weeks, your employer called you

[1] See Wolfe's letter to Perkins of November 12, 1936, and Perkins' formal answer of November 18, 1936; also Wolfe's wire of January 9, 1937, and the appended commentary.

into his office and the great attorneys are there and they tell you that they have now got the other people down so that they are willing to "compromise" for $2500 or $3000. Suppose you say you don't believe there ought to be any compromise whatever, even for a penny, and your employer calls you aside and tells you that he thinks a compromise is the best way out because the lawyers have already cost so much money that it will be cheaper to accept the compromise than to go on and fight the crooks and see it through. Suppose you tell the man that for your own part, although you have only a few hundred dollars in the bank, you are willing to put every penny that you have into fighting the case rather than yield to an outrageous holdup, and suppose he asks you to yield on his account.

Then suppose that the next time you ask for your salary, and for some back money which he has been keeping for you, the cashier tells you that you haven't got any salary or any back money, that you've been charged $3,000 as your share of the legal expense and compromise, and that you are in debt to them. If all of these things happened to you, wouldn't you feel that the people you worked for had let you down, had sold you out at a time when plainly the only right thing to do was stand up and fight against injustice?

Suppose, at about this time your employer wrote you a letter, saying that although he was sorry to lose you, you were now free to go. Suppose you hung on like grim death, out of your loyalty to the man and your long association with him, tried not to break off relations, did everything in your power, begged and entreated to be allowed to keep on working. Suppose he said that of course he would be glad for you to keep on working, but when you went down to the plant on Monday morning you found that they had taken your car away from you and locked it up in the garage and told you that maybe you'd better forget about all of that business in Greenville or Anderson on which you had been working for the last three years, and which gave promise, you thought, of developing into the best business you had ever done, and why didn't you instead just take a walk around the corner and see the fellow who has just opened up a little hole in the wall up there, and see if you can't persuade him to buy a few gallons of ice cream.

Suppose you were getting no more salary, no more pay, but that everyone still thought that you were, and that when another rival employer said to you one day: "I think you are the best salesman in the business, and if you'll just name the figure Jones pays you, I'll top it in a minute, but I know it's no use, because you two are such good friends and you are getting along so well there." Suppose you kept your mouth shut out of loyalty, even in the face of this—don't you think the time would come when you would have to give up, when your money was almost gone—when you were faced with the actual problem of paying the rent and keeping a shelter over your head—and you realized finally that you were left dangling in the air, and that although everybody assumed you were still working for Jones, the fact was that you were no longer being paid a cent of wages, had no understanding or contract of any sort with Jones, or [were] not even allowed to do your work any more, since he had taken away from you the equipment you had to work with—the machine you had to have to make calls fifty miles away? Do you think you could go on like that forever? Don't you think the time would come when you would be forced to realize that so far as Jones is concerned, you were through?

Suppose when that time came the knowledge was so hard to face, the memory of your past friendship with Jones and other members of his firm meant so much to you, that for four long and bitter months you did nothing except try to think your way through the thing, ached your heart out about it, were too decent and loyal and honorable to talk to anyone about it, although the time had long since passed when you were bound by any obligation of any sort. Suppose that during all that time Jones and all the members of his firm know the truth, know they do not employ you any more and yet never breathe a word to anyone to the effect that now you have no job, although they know there are many other firms which would be glad to offer you a job if you were free.

Suppose finally the news got out that you no longer work for Jones, and that then some of the other firms begin to seek you out. Wouldn't you be a bit surprised in view of all of these things to hear that Jones was pulling a long face, pretending to be terribly surprised, and going around saying that you had "turned your back on him" and the other members of his firm?

Well, this may seem to you to be some kind of devilish nightmare, or some wild invention of the fancy, but I can assure you that it is the simple truth. It is not part of the truth; it is not half of the truth; it is the whole truth. It was not something that I imagined in my mind; it was something that happened; that was done to me by Jones and his associates; that cannot be denied. The only thing that I have left out is additional evidence tending to the same end and all piling up to a staggering total. Furthermore, even in view of all that has happened, I want you to know that I have no bitterness in my heart either for Jones or his associates—that I have spoken of them all with friendship and respect.

I want you to understand also that I do not think that Jones and his associates are as bad as their conduct—their callous and indifferent treatment to [the] loyalty and devotion of a man—would indicate. I think rather that some of them may be a little hurt now, wounded to know that at last it has happened. I think also that Jones and his associates were a little bit inclined to think that they had been given special privileges by God Almighty—that to question the essential rectitude and finality of their opinions on any matter smacked of sacrilege—that there was nothing else on earth so infallibly right as everything they did as Jones and Company. I think that Jones and Company may have got to a very dangerous point where it believed that there was no other company in the world that could touch it: that it not only made good ice cream but that the ice cream that it made was so good that no one who had ever tasted it could possibly be persuaded to try another brand. I think they find it pretty hard to believe now that the old hand is really going to work for another concern: perhaps he cried "wolf, wolf" too often, and they opened the gate too many times and told him to take a walk, and at last he did. That's the story.

As for Jones's old hand, I think he was considerable of a fool—and did a lot of things he should not have done. But I know that in his heart he has nothing to be ashamed of, except the words spoken in haste and anger now and then. And I think Jones and Company know this too, and they realize at last that loyalty and devotion doesn't come a dime a dozen, and maybe next time there won't be so good to get at the gate. And so far as the old hand is concerned, I know he hopes for the time when he can see Jones again, and when he and Jones can again come together as friends. I know he is still Jones's friend and I hope and believe Jones is also his friend, and is man enough when this thing is over to forget his temporary hurt pride, and to give his friend his hand again and tell him that everything is all right as long as they are still friends. If Jones is the man I think he is, he'll do this. If he thinks he's got a [Holy?] life and that an unpardonable sin has been committed against the Holy Ghost, he won't. Whatever happens, I've got a notion that Jones's old hand will probably continue to feel about his old boss as he has always felt as long as he lives. And that's the story.

Now, I would just like to be left alone for a while. I don't think I'm going to be helped much by any of you, and I no longer expect it, but if you can't help, for God's sake when I am fighting for a living, don't rush in and shoot off your mouth about matters you know nothing of. And also, why assume, because a man happens to be your brother, he is bound to be wrong? I assure you there are many people who don't think so, and by and large, I think, my reputation among people who know me and also through the country, is a good one.

I understand that Mama wrote Perkins that because she couldn't tell people who called up my address, she felt "ashamed for me." It seems to me that's getting ashamed too easily and in the wrong direction: there are so many other more important things that I have nothing whatever to do with, that people could get ashamed about if they want to. And if my keeping my address a secret is a cause for shame, that's just too bad. It's going to stay a secret, if I can keep it so, and people will just have to keep on being ashamed. I've been through hell enough the past two years, and all I ask now is a chance to do my work and earn my living. Meanwhile, if there is any real occasion to communicate with me, I can always be reached through Miss Nowell. And that is the way things are going to stand.

About the summer I spent at home, my first return in seven years or more, the less said the better. I'd like to forget about it if I could. I went home a very tired man, not only with all of this trouble of Scribners gnawing, but the pressure and accumulation of everything that has happened in the past two years. And when I left home I was as near to a breakdown as I have ever been. My eyes began to go this summer in Asheville and I am now compelled to wear glasses. Nevertheless, if I can be left alone now to do my work, I believe I'll pull through somehow. All I ask now is to be left alone to work without letter hindrance.

It's too bad things had to turn out the way they did this summer: I had hoped that things would have changed: I had been away so long that I thought maybe they would be different. But I found out that they were just the same, only worse: so I guess that's the end of me in Asheville. I'm sorry that you felt that I did not go around to the house enough this summer. I went all I could, but the situation there was such that I could not have gone more often than I did. I am sorry for afflicted and unfortunate people and I tried to do what I could to help: I was willing to go to the wall to use what money I have, or to borrow money to help when I was appealed to. But it all turned out as it always has. I've certainly not tried to save myself: on the contrary [I] allowed my time, strength and health to be used up by all kinds of worthless people. But now I am up against it, economically, physically and in every other way, and I don't see why a good life should be thrown away for a bad one. I have something in me that people value, that has given some people happiness and pleasure, and that people think is worth saving. I think so too, and that is why I'm going to try to save it.

I'm willing to do anything I can to help any one of my own kin in any way I can, but I'm not willing to waste my life and talent in an atmosphere of ruin and defeat, among people who can't be helped and who have been so defeated that they hate anything in life that has not been, and want to drag it down. I'm sorry to have to talk this way, but I have been driven to it. I've felt pretty sick and sore at heart when I left home, as it has all been so sad and so different from what I had hoped it would be. But I'm getting better now, and I know that it will all slip into its true proportion as time goes on. And of course, I have no ill feeling toward anyone. I've just found out a man must stand alone.

If there is anything I can do for anyone, let me know. I think I'm going to get through this present trouble. I hope soon [to] find another publisher, and begin to earn some money again. Meanwhile, all I can do is keep on working.

It has been a hard thing having my eyes go bad on me, because they are just about the most important asset that I have. But if I watch my health, perhaps they will get better. The doctor told me that a good deal of it was probably nervous strain. At any rate, I hope the worst is over now, and that things will look brighter in the future. Also, I hope this finds all of you well, and that you will let me know if all goes well and if there is anything I can do. Meanwhile, with all good wishes to everyone,

To MAXWELL E. PERKINS

[New York City]
November 19, 1937

Dear Max:

My brother Fred has just written me enclosing two letters that you wrote to him and to my mother, and a copy of a letter he wrote to you. I want to go upon the record right now about several things. You told Fred that I had turned my back on you and Scribners. You told Miss Nowell that I had been going around town talking about you. And you told Basso that you were afraid now I was going to "write about" you and Scribners, and that if I did this, you would resign and move to the country. I think that if you have said or felt these things, you have been unjust and misleading. But what is a whole lot more important to me, I think they may have had an effect upon our friendship, which is the thing that matters to me most, and which I am willing to do anything I can to preserve.

Now, I am going to answer these specific things at once. In the first place, I did not "turn my back" on you and Scribners, and I think it is misleading and disingenuous for anyone to say this was the case. The facts of the matter are that the misunderstanding and disagreement between us had grown in complexity and difficulty for the past two years and perhaps longer, and you and everybody else there at Scribners have known the situation as well as I. Furthermore, you have known for at least a year, and I think longer, that the possibility of this severance in our relations was a very real and imminent one, and we have talked about the situation many times. More than this, Charlie Scribner wrote me a letter last spring, at the time of the libel suit, and told me that although he would be sorry to lose me he would not try to hold me, if I wanted to go, and that I was free to go. Further, you told me once last winter to go, if I wanted to, but not to talk about it any more. Later you came to see me in my apartment on First Avenue and told me to go if I wanted to, but that the important thing was that you and I be friends. That is exactly my own position now. Finally, you have known for at least three months, since August, that my going was no longer a possibility but an actual fact. You told Miss Nowell that I had communicated with various publishers and you asked her if it was true that I had signed up with Little Brown and Company. It was not true.

Now that's the record. It is absurd for anyone now to pretend that he is surprised, and that it has all come suddenly and is news to him.

You said in your letter to Fred that you could never understand about all this trouble, and that is the way I feel, too. But I do know that we both understood very definitely, and over a long period of time, that there was trouble, and I think it would be misleading and untruthful for either of us to say that he had absolutely no conception of what it was all about. We did have a conception, and a very clear conception, too. There are so many things about it that are still puzzling and confusing to me, although I've spent a good part of the last year, and the better part of the last four months, trying to think it out. But there are certain things that you knew and that I knew very clearly, and without going into the whole painful and agonizing business all over again, which we threshed out so many hundred times, beginning with "Of Time and the River" and continuing on with "The October Fair" and what I was going to do with it, and on to the book of stories and "The Story of a Novel," and the lawsuits and the lawyers, culminating in our final disagreement about the libel suit, the proper course to be taken, and the possible implications of the whole thing concerning my whole future life and work and the use of my material—there has been one thing after another, which we talked about and argued about a thousand times, so how can either of us truthfully say now that he has absolutely no idea what the misunderstanding is about?

You know that as a man and as a writer, I had finally reached a state of such baffled perplexity that I no longer knew what to do, what to try to accomplish and finish next, or whether, if I did finish and accomplish something, I could ever have any hope under existing circumstances, of getting it published. You know and I know that beginning with "Look Homeward, Angel," and mounting steadily, there has been a constantly increasing objection and opposition to what I wanted to do, which phrased itself in various forms, but which had the total effect of dampening my hope, cooling my enthusiasm, and almost nullifying my creative capacity—to the work that I had projected, to the use I should make of my material, and even in some cases going so far as to oppose my possible use of material on personal rather than on artistic grounds. I am not trying to put all the blame for this on someone else, either. I know that I have often been unfair and unjust, and difficult to handle, but I do think that all this difficulty came out of these troubles I have mentioned. I felt baffled and exasperated because it really seemed to me I had a great creative energy which was being bottled up, not used, and not given an outlet. And if energy of this kind is not used, if it keeps boiling over and is given no way of getting out, then it will eventually destroy and smother the person who has it.

So that is why I think you are wrong when you tell my brother Fred and other people that I have turned my back on you and Scribners, and you don't know why. I am not going to do anything to carry on the debate of who left whom or whose back was turned, but I do know that there was no agreement of any sort between us concerning future work, no contract, and no assurance except perhaps that if I did something that satisfied you and that avoided the things you were afraid of, you would publish me. But, at the very least, under those same conditions any other publisher in the land would publish me, and I can't see that a connection is much of a connection when all the risk and obligation is on one side and there is none whatever on the other. This condition has persisted and developed for at least two years and I have said nothing to anyone about it outside of Scribners until very recently. If you are going to tell people that I turned my back and walked out on you, why don't you also tell them that three years ago when I didn't have a penny and was working on "Of Time and the River" I was approached by another publisher [1] and offered what seemed to me a fortune. You know that I not only called you up and informed you of the matter instantly just as soon as it happened, but even asked you if I should even meet and talk to the people, and that with great fairness you told me that it was certainly my right to meet and talk with them and listen to what they had to offer and then submit the offer to you and Scribners and give you a chance to meet it or to say you couldn't. You know when I did meet

[1] See the footnote on page 507.

and talk with these people and heard their offer and rejected it on my own accord, and told you all about it, I never once asked you or Scribners to meet the offer, although most writers apparently, and even publishers, would have considered that entirely fair and businesslike. So if you are going to say now that I walked out on you, why not tell some of the rest of the story too, and admit that I not only never tried to hold you up about anything, but never made approaches to anybody else, and rejected all that were made to me, even when I didn't have a cent. That is just the simple truth and I think in justice to me you ought to say so. But there is no use trying to go through all of this again: we have talked about it so many times, and both of us may be partly right and partly wrong, but how can either of us deny now that a situation has existed for months which had got into such a hopeless complex snarl that at the end there was absolutely no way out of the mesh except by cutting it. That is the truth, and you know that is the truth. You have understood for a long time that it is the truth and that it existed, and I think you are now unjust to me if you pretend to anyone that you did not know it was the truth.

About your statement to Miss Nowell that I was going around "talking about you" in an injurious sense, I want to assure you that there is not an atom of truth in it. In the first place, I do not "go around": I am not a gossip monger: I have no stories about anyone to trade around. I am afraid that most of the gossip has come from the other side of the fence. You know better than I do that the profession in which you are employed and the circles in which you have to move are productive of rumor and much false report. I would injure myself before I injured you, but grim justice here compels me to remind you that those who live by the sword shall perish by the sword, and those who contemplate too often the play of the serpent's fangs and find the spectacle missing must run the risk some day of having those swift fangs buried in their own flesh.

I want to tell you now, if there were any further need of my going on the record, that if I have ever spoken about you to any man or woman, no one could have possibly construed my speech and meaning in any other way except in such a way as did you honor. And that was not only true when you were my publisher, but it is even more true now, when you are my publisher no longer.

Fred told you in his letter that he had never heard me speak of you in any way except in such a way as to plainly indicate the affection and respect I felt for you. And I can assure you that has been true not only with Fred but with everybody else, and not only in Asheville this summer but in New York since I returned to it in September; and if anyone has really given you any different idea, he has either deliberately lied, or wickedly, wilfully and maliciously twisted or perverted something I said out of its context and its plain meaning for some bad purpose of his own.

You owe me nothing, and I consider that I owe you a great deal. I don't want any acknowledgment for seeing and understanding that you were a great editor even when I first met you, but I did see and understand it, and later I acknowledged it in words which have been printed by your own house,[2] and of which now there is a public record. The world would have found out anyway that you were a great editor, but now, when people solemnly remind me that you are, with an air of patiently enlightening me on a matter about which I have hitherto been unaware, I find it ironically amusing to reflect that I myself was the first one publicly to point out the fact in such a way that it could not be forgotten—that I, as much as any man alive, was responsible for pulling the light out from underneath the bushel basket, and that it is now a part of my privilege to hear myself quoted on every hand, as who should say to me: "Have you read Wolfe?"

About the rest of it, I came up here in September and for two full months I saw no one and communicated with no one except Miss Nowell. During all this time, I stayed alone and tried to think this whole thing out. And I want to tell you that one reason I now resent these trivialities and this gossip is that this may be a matter which is only important enough to some people to be productive of false and empty rumor or nonsensical statements, but to me it has been a matter of life and death. I can only tell you straight from the heart that I have not had anything affect me as deeply as this in ten years, and I have not been so bereaved and grief-stricken by anything since my brother's death. To hear, therefore, that at a time when I have eaten my heart out thinking of the full and tragic consequences of this severance with people with whom I have been associated for eight years, who printed my first work, and for whom I felt such personal devotion, the thing that chiefly was worrying you was the tremendous question of whether I am going to "write about you" and whether you could endure such a calamity is enough to make me groan with anguish.

I cannot believe you were very serious about this when there were

[2] In *The Story of a Novel*, and in the dedication of *Of Time and the River:* "To Maxwell Evarts Perkins, a great editor and a brave and honest man, who stuck to the writer of this book through times of bitter hopelessness and doubt and would not let him give in to his own despair, a work to be known as *Of Time And The River* is dedicated with the hope that all of it may be in some way worthy of the loyal devotion and the patient care which a dauntless and unshaken friend has given to each part of it, and without which none of it could have been written."

so many more important and serious things to think about. But, if it will relieve your mind at all, I can tell you "writing about you" is certainly no part of my present intention. But what if it was, or ever should be? What possible concern, either as friend or editor, ought you to have, except to hope that if I ever "wrote about" you, I would write about you as an artist should, add something to my own accomplishment, and to the amount of truth, reality and beauty that exists. This I thought was your only concern when you considered "Look Homeward, Angel," and not whether it was about possible persons living in a specific little town. This I thought was also, with one or two reservations, your chief concern with "Of Time and the River." This, I think, has been less and less your concern ever since—with "The October Fair," with perturbations about other work that I have projected since, and finally with the crowning nothingness of this. I don't know how or why this thing has come about, or what has happened to you—but I know my grief and bewilderment have grown for two years and are immense.

Like you, I am puzzled and bewildered about what has happened, but in conclusion can offer this: that maybe for me the editor and the friend got too close together and perhaps I got the two relations mixed. I don't know how it was with you, but maybe something like this happened to you too, I don't know. If this is true, it is a fault in both of us, but it is a fault that I would consider more on the side of the angels than the devil's side.

I think, however, that what is even more likely to be a fault in modern life is when the elements of friendship and of business get confused, and when there is likely to be a misapprehension on the part of one or both of the parties as to which is which. I won't pretend to be naive about business, or to tell you that the artist is a child where business matters are concerned. The artist is not a child where business is concerned but he may seem to be so to business men, because he is playing the game with only one set of chips, and the other people are sometimes playing the game with two sets of chips. I don't want you to understand by this that I think playing the game with two sets of chips is always wrong and wicked, and playing the game with one set of chips is always right. I do not think so. But I do think that when the players sit down to play, each of them ought to know what kind of game is being played—with one set of chips or two. I think this is important, because I think most of the misunderstanding comes from this.

To give you a simple hypothetical example, which, let us say, I invented for purposes of illustration, and which I assure you certainly does not dig into the past or concern my relations with my former publishers: a publisher, let us say, hears an author is without a publisher and writes him. It is a very nice and charming letter and says that the publisher has heard that the writer no longer has a publisher and tells him, if that is the case, he would like to see him and to talk to him. He goes on further to say that everybody in his office feels as he does personally about the work that he has done and about the work that he is going to do, and that it would be a privilege and an honor to publish him.

Do I suppose that this letter is hokum and that it is only a part of a publisher's formula when approaching an author? By no means: I think the publisher is sincere and honest and means what he says.

But to proceed with this hypothetical case. The author replies to the publisher that it is true he is without a publisher, but that he is in a great state of perplexity and puzzlement about his work, about a great amount of manuscript involving the material of several books and the labor of several years, and about what he is going to do next. He tells the publisher that what he needs most of all first is someone of editorial experience and judgment he can talk to. He tells him further that he is not at all sure that the work he has in mind would be the kind of work the publisher of this house would care to publish. But he asks the man if he wants to talk it over and find out what the situation is.

The upshot of it is the publisher telephones and comes to see him right away. They go out to dinner together, they have a good meal and some good drinks, and they talk the situation over. The publisher tells the author again how he and his house feel about the author's work, and repeats and emphasizes his warm interest. The author then lays the matter before the publisher, tells him so far as he can the problems and perplexities that have been bothering him about his work and his manuscript. The publisher then asks which part of this manuscript the author thinks is nearest to completion. The author tells him that the manuscript is packed up and in storage, and the publisher asks the author to get it out and show it to him. The author replies that he would like to, but that he is living in a small rented room and that the bulk and magnitude of the manuscript is such that it would be impossible to get it out and work on it in his own place. The publisher replies that in the offices of his company there is loads of space and that he would be delighted if the author would make use of it: he can move his manuscript here and be free to work without disturbing anyone. The author agrees to this proposal, and before they part, the publisher addresses the author by his first name.

Now, so far so good. This hypothetical story must have a very familiar sound to you, and you must agree as I do that so far everything is fine. Both parties are not only sincere and mean everything they say, but both sides are also playing with one set of chips.

Now to proceed: in a day or two, the publisher calls up again and tells the author that a young man in his publishing house is free and would be very glad to help the author move the manuscript that very afternoon. The author agrees to this, meets the young man, and together they go to the storage warehouse, get the manuscript, and bring it back to the publisher's office, where it is left. The next day, the author goes to the publisher's office, the crates and boxes of manuscript have been opened up, everything is ready, and the author sets to work. The publisher comes in, jokes about the size and bulk of the manuscript, and repeats again his eagerness to see it and his desire to get at it as quickly as possible, and asks the author if he may call him by his first name, Jim. The author replies that this is his name and that he would be delighted if the publisher called him Jim. The publisher is catching a train in a few minutes; the two men shake hands very warmly; just before he leaves, the publisher says: "Oh, by the way," and hands the author an envelope. When the author asks him what the envelope is, the publisher says it is nothing, just an acknowledgment that he has received the manuscript, and to put it away among his papers. The author sticks the envelope into his pocket without looking at it. That night, however, in his room, he sees the envelope upon his table and opens it. It reads as follows:

"Dear Smith:—This is to acknowledge that we have received one large packing case of manuscript, nine pasteboard cartons, and two valises, which are now stored in our offices. In view of the possible value of this material, we wish to inform you that this house can assume no responsibility for it, and that you leave it here entirely at your own risk."

Now, what is the truth about this situation? Is the publisher wrong? By no means. Apparently, he is justified in writing such a letter by all standards of good business practice, and it would be hard to find a business person who would say that he was anything except exactly right. Furthermore, the publisher may have acted as he did out of scrupulous observance of what seemed to him the rules of business fairness and honesty. Nevertheless, the author cannot help remembering that the publisher asked if he could call him Jim when they were having drinks together over the dinner table, but calls him Smith when he writes a business letter. The author also cannot help remembering when the publisher talked to him over the dinner table, he told him it was not the money he hoped to make out of the author's books or the sales he hoped the books would have that concerned him principally, but rather the pride he would have in publishing the author's works, the privilege and the honor it would be to publish them, regardless of any commercial advantages that might accrue. He has told the author also that he can rest assured that if he comes to his house, he need not worry about the economic future—that no matter whether his next book sold or not, the house was a house which would stand by its authors through disappointments and vicissitudes and was willing to back its faith with its support. Furthermore, I believe that the publisher was sincere and meant what he said.

But the author is puzzled, and I think he has a right to be puzzled. Any business man would tell you the publisher was right, not only about what he said over the dinner table, but right also when he wrote the letter about who should assume the risk and responsibility for the manuscript. The author can understand both conversations, but what he cannot understand is both conversations together. What he objects to is "Jim" over the dinner table and in editorial relations, but "Smith" where business is concerned. From my own point of view, the author is right. The publisher did not tell him that it was going to be Jim in friendship and in editing, but Smith in business. He led the author to believe, with his talk of faith and belief and support and the privilege and the honor of publishing the author, that it was going to be Jim all the time.

Now from my own point of view, Max, I think the publisher was wrong. I know that many people will not agree with me and will say that the publisher was right, that it was business, and that he was justified in everything that he did. I do not think so, and I think that much of the misunderstanding between publishers and authors comes from just this fact. I think the trouble comes when one side is playing with one set of chips, and the other side with two. Please understand that I am not accusing the side that plays the two of dishonesty or of unscrupulous practices. But I do think they are wrong in not making it clear at the beginning—the kind of game they are playing. And I have used deliberately a trifling and relatively unimportant example to illustrate my meaning. When you multiply this example by scores of much more important and vital examples, and when Jim finds that it is always Smith when a question of business advantage, of profit or loss, is concerned —when Jim finds that friendship and business are not equal and [do not] balance each other, but that business always gets the upper hand when a question of advantage is concerned—then there is likely to be trouble.

I want to say also that I think Jim was wrong in the very beginning when he allowed his personal feelings to get so involved that he lost his perspective. I think Jim was wrong in that he based his publishing relationship too much on friendship—on feelings of personal loyalty and devotion, no matter at what cost to himself. I think in doing this, Jim was unfair to himself and unfair to his publishers. I think that perhaps the best publishing relation would be one in which Jim felt friendship and respect and belief for his publishers, and they for him, but in which neither side got too personally involved. In the end, it is likely to involve too great a cost of disillusionment and grief and disappointment for someone, perhaps upon both sides. Please believe that I have offered this not by way of criticism of anyone, but just as possibly throwing some light upon a confused and troubled problem.

Now I am faced with one of the greatest decisions of my life and I am about to take a momentous and decisive step. You are no longer my publisher, but with a full consciousness of the peril of my position and the responsibility of the obligation I am now about to assume, I want to feel that you are still my friend, and I do feel that, in spite of all that has happened. I feel that you want me to go on and grow in merit and accomplishment and do my work; and I believe that you would sincerely wish for my success and high achievement, and be sorry for my failure, no matter who became my publisher. I believe other people there at Scribners feel the same way. You said a year ago that the important thing, regardless of who published me, is that we remain friends. That expresses my own feeling now, and I am writing to tell you so, and to tell you that I hope it is the same with you. This letter is a sad farewell, but I hope also it is for both of us a new beginning, a renewal and a growth of all the good that has been.

You told Fred that I had not been to see you but that you would like to see me. I want to see you, but I do not think that now is the right time. I think you ought to see by now that I am not "sore" at anybody, but I am sore inside, and I want to wait until things heal. And my whole desire now is to preserve and save, without reservation, without any ranking doubt or bitterness, the friendship that we had, and that I hope we shall forever have. This is about all that I can say. I have felt pretty bad, and for a time my eyes went back on me but I am wearing glasses when I work now, and am now back at work again. If I can keep on working, without interruptions and the costly experiences of the last two years, I think everything may yet turn out all right.

You don't need to answer this letter. I wrote it to you just to go upon the record, to tell you how things really were, and let you know what was in my mind and heart. I hope that I have done so.

With all good wishes to you, to Louise and the children, and to Scribners,

I am your friend, Max, and that is why I wrote this letter—to tell you so. If I wrote so much else here that the main thing was obscured—the only damn one that matters—that I am your friend and want you to be mine—please take this last line as being what I wanted to say the whole way through.

For Perkins' answer of November 20, 1937, see Editor to Author: The Letters of Maxwell E. Perkins, *page 133. He said in part: "I am your friend and always will be, I think. . . . Of course I had to tell Fred and others, when they asked me about you, what the situation was. . . . I could not properly, even by silence, let it be assumed that things were as they had been. I told Fred truly too when I said I did not understand about it. I don't, but that need make no difference between us, and I won't let it on my side. Miss Nowell should never have told you of my concern as to your writing about us—it was not [about] me. . . . I know the difficulty of your problem and I never meant this point to come up to confuse you. But don't you see that serious injury to this House and to my longtime associates here, for which I was responsible, would make me wish to be elsewhere? I've missed you and felt badly about it. . . . Anyhow, I'm glad to have seen your handwriting again."*

To ROBERT N. LINSCOTT

[Hotel Chelsea]
[222 West 23rd Street]
[New York City]
November 17, 1937

Dear Mr. Linscott:

I had lunch with Mr. Barker yesterday and last night had dinner with Mr. Aswell and Mr. Saxton of Harpers. Also, I talked with Mr. Canfield.[1] Apparently some word has gotten around that I am no longer at Scribners and in the last week or two members of two publishing houses, Harpers and Doubleday, have spoken to me. Both of them made specific proposals: I cannot state definitely, as yet, with what authority the Doubleday proposal was made, but people from that house are coming to see me again on Thursday. The Harper proposal was specific, and was made with the authority of the whole house.[2]

[1] Cass Canfield was President of Harper & Brothers, and Eugene F. Saxton was Editor-in-Chief. Edward C. Aswell was Assistant Editor to Saxton and succeeded him as Editor-in-Chief on his death in 1943. He is now editor and vice-president of McGraw-Hill and administrator of the estate of Thomas Wolfe.

[2] The Harper proposal was for an advance of $10,000 against a straight royalty of 15%, to be paid immediately on signing of a contract for Wolfe's next novel. Harper's did not ask to see any of the manuscript before signing of the contract. Linscott, for Houghton Mifflin, had tentatively suggested an advance of $10,000 against a 15% royalty, to be paid in monthly installments of $500 for twenty months, but the contract was not to be drawn until Houghton Mifflin had read at least a portion of the manuscript. James W. Poling, who was Managing Editor at Doubleday and Company at that time, conferred with Wolfe several times and told him they would equal any offer from another publisher, but Wolfe was so intent on trying to choose between Houghton Mifflin and Harpers that he did not enter into any definite negotiations with Doubleday.

It has been a very puzzling and troubling situation, because I have been getting on with my work very rapidly and these developments, of course, mean that I may have to think a great deal about all the questions that have been raised. So far, I have not decided anything except that the best course is for me to get on with my work, and to think about the matter until I reach some clear conclusion. Of course, I told both the Harpers and Doubleday people about my conversations with you, and the outcome of them. I told them also that no commitments had been made on either side, and that after talking the situation over we had agreed that I should give you a piece of manuscript to read without commitment on either side. Barker suggested yesterday at lunch that I try to send you the manuscript now and then talk to you when you come down to New York in about two weeks. I told him that I should like to do this, but that I still think that it would be better if I kept on working as I have been working until I get the manuscript in some more definite shape, and that if it is satisfactory to everybody, it is what I propose to do.

I wanted to inform you of these events, and of what I have myself been doing. It is a puzzling and perplexing situation but I think it is better to think about it very carefully now rather than come to a hasty decision.

[IF THERE WAS A SECOND PAGE TO THIS LETTER, IT HAS BEEN LOST]

In answer to Wolfe's letter of November 17, Linscott wrote him on November 19: "Don't you think the common sense of the situation is to concentrate on one thing at a time and cross each bridge as you come to it? If, as I gather, you're in the writing mood now, I'd go full speed ahead until you reach a place where it will be helpful to have it professionally read. Then, and not till then, I'd cast about for the perfect publisher, giving us first shot at it, in accordance with our understanding, but with complete freedom to turn later to any other publisher if our reaction or proposal is not entirely to your liking. I'm still hoping you'll be able to send me a sizable chunk of manuscript and an outline soon enough so that I will have something tangible to say about it when I next see you. . . ." The following letter of November 29 was Wolfe's reply.

To ROBERT N. LINSCOTT

[Hotel Chelsea]
[New York]
November 29, 1937

Dear Mr. Linscott:

Thanks very much for your letter of November 19th, which I had intended to answer before this. Matters still stand very much as they did when I wrote you on November 18th. I have had some additional conversations with various people, but have come to no definite decision yet. However, I agree entirely with your suggestion that the sensible course for me at present would be to continue with my writing at full speed. I have thought about this a great deal and have had several conversations with Mr. Barker.

Mr. Barker wants me to send you a portion or portions of the manuscript before you come down here from Boston. I tentatively agreed to this when I saw him the other day and suggested that I might even try to select a few scenes or episodes, which, although they might not give any coherent idea of what the book is about, would perhaps serve to indicate what I hope the final texture will be. Mr. Barker seemed to think this was a good idea. But thinking it over I have more and more my doubts, and I will tell you what they are.

I have been writing pretty steadily ever since I saw you, and it was really not until just the other day that my secretary and I opened up the big case and bundles of manuscript and began seriously to set about the task of sorting it out, disposing of that which has already been printed, or for which I shall have no need in this book, and taking the material that I may need and arranging it in an orderly fashion. As you can imagine, it has been a big job and we are not yet done with it.

I am also aware, as I re-examine this material with a fresh eye after having been away from most of it for three or four years, that what I have is material for an enormous book, a great deal of which is not even yet in rough draft form, and a good deal more that really approaches final completion. At any rate, the stuff of the book is there and the book will also be there if I continue at the present pace and with the whole purpose that I have in mind. For that reason also I am less and less inclined to monkey with it now: I not only do not want to impede my own progress, but I should also like anyone who might be interested in reading it to see it in some form that would more nearly, as I think, do it justice. As I have said, there are parts which I am ready to have read now, but taking all of these various things into consideration, I do not really believe that is the way it ought to be read, do you?

The other thing is this: I am deeply and sincerely grateful to you for your helpful interest and your desire to read and estimate this manuscript. But, after thinking this question over from every possible angle and taking into consideration everything that has happened in these past few weeks, it doesn't seem to me that it would be fair either to myself or to the other people who have committed themselves to the extent of making specific proposals concerning the publication of this manuscript, to tie this manuscript up in any way that might imperil its chances with people who have already signified their interest to the extent of making a concrete offer, or in any way that might impede me or other people from coming to a final decision. I really think that the justice of the whole matter, with a view to the rights of everyone, is just there.

I am going to suggest to you, therefore, that instead of sending you portions of the manuscript in fragmentary form I'll wait until you come to New York when I hope we can talk together and perhaps come to a clearer decision. This seems to me to be the best course now and I believe it will seem so with you, also. Meanwhile, of course, I propose to go on working.

With all good wishes and with hopes of seeing you soon.

On December 3, 1937, Mrs. Bernstein had returned some photographs to Wolfe through Miss Nowell, with a note saying that she did not want him to write to her about them. Wolfe therefore dictated the following letter and asked Miss Nowell to send it over her signature. It was so obviously his that she rewrote it in her own words.

To ALINE BERNSTEIN

[New York City]
[December 5(?), 1937]

Thanks very much for your note and for the photographs which you are returning to Mr. Wolfe. I know he will appreciate them and will be glad to get your message. I have heard him speak of you many times with affection and respect, and I know that it will cheer him up now to hear that you too have heard of his trouble and are shocked by it. It is a matter of which I do not care to speak except to say that it has caused him the greatest distress and anguish.

He has very little money, but he is hard at work again and I know that you, like all his other friends, will be glad to hear this and will hope, as we all do, that he will succeed in finding a publisher who believes in him and who will encourage him to fulfill himself and do the work of which he is capable. He has gone through a hard time the past two years, but I believe he has been through the worst of it and that things will go better now. At any rate, I want to assure you that he has learned, as a result of these experiences, to know true friends from false ones, and to distinguish between those who have sought to exploit him for their own purposes and those who value him and believe him for his own sake.

I know he counts you among this latter group, and for that reason I know he is going to be happy to hear that you have inquired about him with such affectionate concern. I shall give him your message and photographs when I next see him.

To ANNE W. ARMSTRONG

[Hotel Chelsea]
[New York]
December 6, 1937

Dear Mrs. Armstrong:

I was so glad to get your letter. I was really just on the point of writing you and finding out if you had received my letter of several weeks ago, or if anything had happened to it. I am glad to get your new address in care of General Peyton, at Fort Sheridan. Of course if I am out that way, I'll come to see you pronto. I don't really see much prospect of it at present, because I am back at work again on the big book [1] and I am going to try to keep at it if I can until I finish.

My new address, by the way, is

> Hotel Chelsea,
> 222 West 23rd Street,
> New York City.

It is an old old place with great big rooms, and I have two of them: and all my manuscript is out and again I am on the job. It's been a pretty nerve-racking experience and in so many ways a sad one too. Breaking off relations with people one has known so well, for so many years, is never

---

[1] *The Vision of Spangler's Paul* which finally became *The Web and the Rock* and *You Can't Go Home Again*. By this time Wolfe had given up his earlier idea of working on *The October Fair*, realizing that *The Vision of Spangler's Paul* was always foremost in his mind.

an easy thing, and I think they are particularly hard for me because things get rooted in me so. However, it's over now and I believe things are going to be better. I think from what I heard there was at first a good deal of wounded feeling, but now that seems to have gone away, and I have just heard the man I know best in all the world wants to see me, and is my friend. I knew it was going to be that way, I never had any doubts about it, but it was pretty tough at first.

About definite publishing connections, I have made no new one yet. I wanted to take plenty of time thinking the whole thing over, so I didn't go around soliciting people, and on the whole, I think it is just as well that I did not. At any rate, at least three publishing houses have heard that I am without a publisher, and have signified their interest. Two of them have actually gone so far as to make specific offers, mentioning terms, and the firm of Harper and Brothers has made what seems to me a very generous and fine one. At any rate, the amount of the advance they offered was so large that I was rather overwhelmed by it. And what I think is a whole lot more important than this is that they actually seem to be intensely and deeply interested in me as a man and as a writer, which, in a publishing connection, I think is a pretty important thing.

What you said in your letter about my not going back to Asheville also shoots straight to the mark, because it is exactly what I have been thinking myself, and of course at first the knowledge of it was pretty hard to face. But you are right: *You can't go home again.* I found this out this summer, of course I had to go home to find it out, it was hard to face, but I have faced it now and I feel better. But don't be surprised some day if you see a piece, *You Can't Go Home Again.* I guess we all find this out as we go along, but it's a pretty tremendous fact and revelation in the life of any man, isn't it? But as long as I know that there are people like you, and that one meets a few of them in the course of a life time, it doesn't make things too bad. Maybe it's just there that eventually a man comes to look for home.

Dear Mrs. Armstrong, please take care of yourself and have a good winter at Fort Sheridan. And please tell General Peyton and his wife for me how much I appreciate the use of their magnificent cabin down by the Holston River in September. I think those few days there gave me more peace and quiet and rest than I had had in years, and to you, of course, I shall be everlastingly grateful. And now goodbye for the present. I hope this finds you well, and, as usual, enjoying life.

On December 19, Wolfe informed Linscott on the telephone that he had decided to accept the offer of Harper & Brothers. The next day he wrote the following letter to express his genuine regret at having disappointed him.

To ROBERT N. LINSCOTT

[Hotel Chelsea]
[New York]
December 20, 1937

Dear Bob:

I would just like to write and add this to what I said yesterday. It was one of the hardest decisions I have ever had to make, and I think last week was one of the hardest weeks I have ever been through. Now it is all settled, and I am relieved to know it is over. However, the only thing I have to regret is that in making the decision, I perhaps had to disappoint someone I like and admire very much.

I want to tell you again how sincerely I appreciate the interest you have shown in me and my work from the beginning, and I am happy to think now that although I may not have you as a publisher, I do have you as a friend—that, at any rate, is a big gain.

It may not be possible for me to go to Boston for Christmas, but I am hopeful that the next month will see me there. If I do come, of course I want to see you and shall look you up. Meanwhile, with all best wishes to you and your family for this and many future Christmases.

The following letter, of which a carbon copy was found among Wolfe's own papers, was written as the result of the quarrel which Wolfe had with Sherwood Anderson at the Hotel Brevoort on December 17, 1937. On December 1, Wolfe had gone to a dinner party given by the Andersons at the New York apartment of Mrs. Mary Emmett whom they were visiting. As Mrs. Anderson remembers, everyone was talking about the South, saying that if a person was a liberal, people in the South never attacked him for his liberalism but on some entirely different and often spurious grounds. Simply as an example of this, she said to Wolfe that she had been in North Carolina the week before, and had heard it said that he was Jewish. She says that Wolfe took violent offence; said he was going to get on a train and go right down to see his mother; that the Wolfe family was as good as Mrs. Anderson's (which came from the same part of Pennsylvania) etc. After a general discussion of anti-Semitism, Wolfe calmed down, but the incident evidently rankled in his mind. On December 17, Anderson wrote Wolfe saying: "I do hope you didn't take seriously the queer row we seemed to have got into that night at Mary's house," [1] and asking him to come to a cocktail party for the benefit of the Spanish Loyalists and to have dinner with him afterward. Meanwhile, however, Wolfe was drinking heavily and brooding over his severance from Scrib-

[1] Copyright, 1956, by Eleanor Copenhaver Anderson.

ners and the necessity of choosing between Houghton Mifflin and Harpers for
his future publishers. Before he received Anderson's note, he happened to
go into the Brevoort and found Anderson lunching there. According to what
Wolfe told Miss Nowell later, he called Anderson out into the lobby and "told
old Sherwood off," saying that Winesburg, Ohio *had meant something im-*
portant to him and his entire generation of writers, but that Anderson had
"failed them," that he was "washed up," and that "this business of sitting
around and talking, naked, on parlor sofas was no good." (This was probably
a reference to Anderson's Many Marriages *and his similar later writings which*
showed the influence of D. H. Lawrence.)

The following day, Anderson wrote Wolfe a second note, saying: "When
I wrote you yesterday, suggesting that you have dinner with me Tuesday
evening, I had no notion how you felt. As you have expressed such a hearty
desire to chuck our acquaintance—why not." ² In answer to this, Wolfe evi-
dently wrote the following letter, which he may or may not have actually
mailed.

To SHERWOOD ANDERSON

December 20, 1937.

Dear Sherwood:

I am sorry that you felt you had to write that last note. I was pretty
rough the other day, but my clear impression was that at the end we shook
hands and meant it, and not only that, but also said that we were going
to stick together, and not let anything come between us. I should have
written you anyhow, but I thought that I would wait until it was a little
closer to Christmas, but since you wrote this note I want to tell you that
if this is the way it stands, it's got to stand this way—only I don't feel
"Why not?"

I guess you thought it over—about what I said the other day—and
changed your mind. If you did, I am not blaming you and I am not trying
to get away from the point—but I would like to say that a good deal of
what happened and what was said was just accidental. I wasn't thinking
about it or you so much when it happened, as about something else—a
matter to the conclusion of which I have been working slowly for the
past two years, and which involved one of the most grievous and painful
decisions of my life.¹ I have decided it now, and ought to be happy, but I
am not. I think I am going to be happy later on, but I am worrying for
the dead this Christmas and for a lot of things that can't be helped. You
must have felt that way some time in your life, and you must know what

² Copyright, 1956, by Eleanor Copenhaver Anderson.
¹ The break with Scribners which was made irrevocable by Wolfe's agreement to
sign with Harpers.

I am talking about. Anyway, I'm trying to tell you that the immediate thing that happened—the flare-up, explosion, or whatever it was—was really not about you at all, but about something else. You just happened to be present when it happened.

About the other thing, the more immediate personal thing,[2] I'd like to tell you that I am willing to forget about it. As you said the other day, it was an ugly party, there was somehow a pretty ugly feeling there which you felt. I did too, I don't know where it came from, I only know it didn't come from me, and I would be willing to bet it didn't come from you. I have my streaks of violence and passion, but I never took ugliness to a party in my life: I always went with faith and hope as I went to that one, and all I can tell you is that nobody ever had a bad time or felt anything ugly at a party that I gave. I believe it must have been the same with you, too.

About the other thing [3]—the thing that seems to have caused so much pain and misunderstanding, I would like to forget about it too, and I certainly don't want to labor a thing that is probably trifling and that has made too much trouble already. I do have to tell you this, however, and then I hope I am done with it: I just can't agree that it is something that should not be taken seriously, because it seems to me the implications not only to myself, but to a lot of obscure decent people are pretty serious, and whether you will agree with my point of view or not, you must have understanding enough to see that such a thing would affect them pretty tragically in so many of the fundamental relations of life and their marital relations, their social and business relations, and so on. And I think also it would affect me pretty seriously too. I have been mighty fortunate as a writer, people have said some mighty fine things about me. I don't know whether they were right or not, or whether it means anything, but apparently a lot of people have thought I was a pretty American sort of writer, and what I did was indigenous to this country. I hope this is true. At any rate, I am pretty proud of it, and I would like to live up to it, and I say this honestly without a word or thought of prejudice toward any people, any race, or any creed.

So I don't think, Sherwood, it's shooting straight to the mark to say these [things] don't matter: I think I found out a lot about life in the last two years that I never knew about before, and I've seen in our own country, which we both love and believe in so much, forces that seem to me to be ugly and vicious, that I never knew about before. At any rate, I am now prepared to fight them to the death, if I need to, and the only

[2] The mentioning of the current rumor that Wolfe was part Jewish and the subsequent argument at the Andersons' party on December 1st.

[3] Wolfe is still talking about the mention of the rumor that he was part Jewish.

thing that I expect of any man who is a friend of mine is that he is prepared to fight them too. If they attack me, and [tell] other vicious lies about me or mine, with a purpose to discredit us or destroy us, I expect a friend of mine to stand his ground and to brand the lies for what they are, not only for me or mine, but for the human race as well, and I promise any friend I'll do the same for him. Maybe that's asking too much for friendship, but I don't think so, and I don't think I am taking anything too seriously now: there are some things you don't laugh off, or flash your celebrated sense of humor over and a dirty sell-out in the human race is one of them. You know where I stand now, and if you are the man I think you are, you'll stand there too.

About the rest of it the other day ⁴—put it down to a lot of things which I hope this letter will help make clear, but don't put it between you and me. I said some things which were out of order—the business of going to parties, female companionship, your own aesthetical leanings is all your own affair, no business of mine, and something I don't know much about anyway. The main thing is I always strung with you as a writer, and since I met you a year ago I also strung with you as a man. I not only do not think that you are washed-up as a writer—but if I said so the other day you can put that down as another of those things. I told you when we shook hands and parted that I thought you had done the best writing that had been done in this country in this century. I still stick to that and honestly, as far as you are concerned, I have no other idea except that the best is yet to be.

This is going on the record as well as I can just now. If as your note indicates, you feel, as a result of what happened the other day, [that] you want to "chuck our acquaintanceship" that's up to you, and I'll do nothing else to try to persuade you differently, but I shall be sorry about it. At any rate, you've got the story now as far as I am concerned. I have been wrong about many things, but I think I had a point to make, and no matter how you feel, I wouldn't let this Christmas go by without telling you that I wish you and all your family nothing but the happiest and best for Christmas and for years to come.

I think you will also remember that even when I spoke the hottest the other day I also told you that whatever I had to say to you I'd say to you man to man. You spoke of other people, here in New York or elsewhere, trying to come in and poison our minds and turn us against each other. Well, as far as I am concerned, that will never happen. Nobody's going to do that. Nobody has a chance to: I am a hard working and a serious person and I lead as hard working and as quiet a life right here in New York as you do down in Marion, Virginia. So whatever you have heard,

---

⁴ Wolfe's outburst at the Brevoort.

for good or bad, you have heard straight from me, and that's all there is. I hope you will want to see me again, but if you don't, you don't need to bother to answer this letter. Meanwhile, I would like to wish you a happy Christmas with all my heart.

To FRED W. WOLFE

December 20, 1937.

Dear Fred:

I got your letter this morning and the two enclosed post cards from Mamma. Also by the same mail a long letter from Mamma from Florida. I just want to shoot the immediate news to you now, so will not pause to give you the contents of her letter except to tell you that she seems to be well and in good health, and of course the details of the case you know all about anyway. She seemed anxious to get home, but I hope she stays for awhile—I'm writing her right away and sending her some money and I shall see that she gets it before Christmas, if I have to send it airmail.

The other news is that after two or three agonizing months in making up my mind, I have gone to the old publishing house of Harper and Brothers. The news has not been announced yet, so don't say anything about it until there is some kind of an announcement. I haven't signed a contract either, but they have offered me a tremendous advance. It's funny, but the thing that worries me now is that I don't know whether I should take it all or not, the income tax will probably be so high, etc.

I wish I could tell you that I'm happy. I believe I'm going to be because they seem to be fine people—it was not only the money that they offered but the fact that they seemed to want me with all their heart. The fellow I have had the most to do with, although I have met them all, is a young fellow named Aswell, who is exactly my own age, and who comes from Nashville, Tennessee. The rest of the story about him is that he is married and has a kid one year old, and lives out in the country. When I called up the other day to tell him that I had made up my mind, he was not at home, but his wife cried and told me he was on the way to town and to get him at Harpers. He told Miss Nowell that if necessary he was willing to change his whole life if he had to, and if he became my publisher. Of course he won't have to: the only point is the man thinks I am the best writer in the country—which he is wrong about—and he thinks I am going to get better, which I think he is right about. At any rate, I feel I am leaving the greatest editor in America, and a man of genius to boot, and maybe this young man Aswell is none of these, but I am playing a hunch—I feel he is a good man, and an able man, and if anybody's got this much faith in me I'll kill myself if I have to to live up to it.

I wish I could tell you I felt happy, but I don't. I am worn out, have been torn up about this thing coming to a point for over two months now, and of course there were two or three people interested in me, [and] all of them I liked. I had to make up my mind between them. If you've ever had to do this, you'll know how hard it is, and I'm still mourning for the dead. I mean for the people that I knew, with whom I worked so many years. I will see them again some day, but it is a pretty sad business just now. Maybe this will really be a new year. Harper's think it is going to be, both for them and for myself, and I believe they may be right. Anyway, it is a new beginning.

This is all for the present, Fred. I'll get a letter off to Mamma by airmail tomorrow morning and I will try to write to everybody before Christmas. I think you will understand the way things have been, but let's all hope it will be smoother sailing now. Please let me know right away if anything is needed, or in what way I can be of help about anything. Meanwhile, until I hear from you, with love to all and best wishes for a happy Christmas,

To MAXWELL E. PERKINS

[Hotel Chelsea]
[New York]
December 27, 1937

Dear Max:

I have had a talk at last with Mr. Ralph Lum, who is now representing me in that —— manuscript case over in New Jersey, and I am glad to say that at last it looks as if something is going to get done, and that I have a man on the job who knows how to do it. He told me the present state of affairs, outlined the situation very clearly, and asked me if I would get in touch with you to see if there was any help you could give us. I told him that I knew you would be glad to, if there was anything you could do, so to put the whole thing briefly, here is the way things stand now: the case comes up in the Court of Chancery in Jersey City early in February, and Mr. Lum seems to think it will go right through in an hour or two. He told me that I would recover my manuscripts—those that are left—and that disposes of this end of it. About the other end, Mr. Lum did not seem to be worried very much, and apparently does not believe —— has much of a case. In fact, he said that —— had gone so far with his contentions and allegations that he might find himself in a precarious and dangerous situation if he attempts to press them. He is suing me for the sum, I believe, of $2600—which Mr. Lum said might just as well be $26,000—basing his suit apparently on the contention that I owe him the money for his services as a "manuscript appraiser"—whatever that may mean—and for his services as a manuscript agent.

—— contends that a verbal agreement or contract existed between us, that there were no witnesses present to the agreement and that it is what is known as "an unlimited agreement"—which means that I gave him complete and absolute authority over all of my manuscript without reservation of any sort, to do with as he saw fit, from now on, henceforth and forever after. This, of course, as you know, is preposterous—and Mr. Lum believes it will seem to be preposterous to the Chancellor when the case comes up before him. If —— really contends this, I suppose it will simply come down to the question of his word against mine, but Mr. Lum feels that if I can now enlist the aid of some other people—yourself, Chester Arthur,[1] Ruder, the manuscript man,[2] or anyone else who might have dealt with —— or been present at conversations that I had with him—it would help.

I told Mr. Lum that the only part you had in the matter was that of a friend and adviser, but that you had been present on several occasions when I talked to ——, and I thought you would be able and willing to say that from your own observation and what you yourself saw and heard, there was no suggestion of "manuscript appraising," unlimited agreements, etc., but that rather my whole connection with —— was entirely provisional and tentative, and that I was simply letting him "try the market" with certain pieces of manuscript to see what luck he had and what came of it. This, of course, as you know, is just exactly what happened, but I do think, Max, if you could say so—that is, tell Mr. Lum that that was your understanding of the situation from what you saw of it—it would help us.

I am just as sorry as I can be to have to trouble you again about this thing, or about anything else. But I do believe we are beginning to see light at last, and I know you have always wanted me to get this thing settled and thought I ought to see it through. I agree with you absolutely, and Mr. Lum not only agrees but he says that it is imperative now that I see this through, and I think you will feel so more strongly than ever when I tell you the kind of answer —— has made. You remember he wrote some threatening letters to my former lawyers in New Jersey, revealing to them certain alleged obscene phrases and expressions which he threatened to make public if we continued with the suit. . . . As you and I both

---

[1] Chester Arthur had lived at 865 First Avenue and had been in Wolfe's apartment on one occasion when Wolfe and —— were discussing what manuscripts might or might not be sold.

[2] Barnet B. Ruder, the rare book and manuscript dealer, had bought some of Wolfe's manuscripts from ——, the defendant.

know, the threat is ridiculous: I have now seen the alleged words and phrases, and I think it may perhaps make you smile that most of them have already been printed in "Look Homeward, Angel" anyway. Nevertheless, it was intended to be an ugly threat, and Mr. Lum thinks on that account that I must go through with this thing now. . . . What —— has done in his answer is this: he apparently tried to get around the legal responsibility in which he may be involved by saying in his "Answer" that he cannot exactly describe the following manuscripts except by these phrases which he *happens* to remember. . . . : then follows, of course, a list of the alleged obscene phrases. As Mr. Lum says, he is skating on pretty thin ice. Beyond that, it's pretty ugly, isn't it?

Anyway, I wanted to describe the situation to you because I thought you would be interested to know how matters now stand, and also to ask you if you won't call Mr. Lum up or write him, and contribute anything you can by way of additional information that might help us. I think you understand the whole situation now, and will see what Mr. Lum is driving at. And honestly, Max, I hate like hell to bother you, but I do think this is one of those cases where people ought to stand together if they can, not only for personal or friendly reasons, but just because it's taking a stand in favor of the human race. But anyway, I am your friend as I told you in my letter, and I know that whatever you do will be all right.

I hope you have had a good Christmas, and I send you all my best wishes for this coming year. By the way, Martha Dodd just called up, and in behalf of all of us I gave her the hearty welcome of the American nation. I told her that old man Dodd from a diplomatic point of view might not be a good ambassador, but he was something a whole lot better than that—a good man and a good American, and that we were proud of him. She told me to go out and get to-day's *World-Telegram* because she had written a piece about the Nazis. If she can write, she certainly ought to have material for a tremendous book.

Goodbye for the present, Max. I hope that I shall see you soon. And forgive me for troubling you this time. With all good wishes,

To ANNE W. ARMSTRONG

[Hotel Chelsea]
[New York]
December 27, 1937

Dear Mrs. Armstrong:

Thanks for your letter which came last night. I am so glad you spoke as you did about Harper's, because I gave them my answer a week ago. I am going to be with them, and I believe somehow it is going to be one of the most fortunate and happy experiences of my life. They are giving me a great advance, if I want it. But really I was playing a personal hunch. They want me so much, they believe in me so utterly, and there is no doubt they meant everything they said. Moreover I will be associated with a young man just exactly my own age, who is second in command.[1] I am playing this hunch, too: I think it is going to turn out to be a wonderful experience—I feel that the man is quiet, but very deep and true: and he thinks that I am the best writer there is. I know he is wrong about this, but if anyone feels that way, you are going to do your utmost to try to live up to it, aren't you?

I spent Christmas with him, his wife and child out in the country. A lot of other people were there too—a young professor from the Harvard Law School, and his wife and sister, who has just won a great case for Roosevelt in the gold business.[2] I have never seen a higher group of people and I know if I'm going to live up to this, I've got to go some. And I believe you will be happy with me. However, I am still a little sad thinking about the past—Scribners, all of that—but you can't go home again, can you?

Now I am facing toward a New Year and a new, I hope, and greater piece of work. If you ever, of all things, see *Vogue*, please look at the, I believe, February issue, because that is where I have, of all places, written a piece about America.[3] I think it is good.

Now all the best to you and yours for this coming year.

To ELIZABETH NOWELL

[Hotel Chelsea]
[New York]
December 29, 1937

Dear Miss Nowell:

Thanks for your letter. There is nothing much to report except that Aswell brought me the contract and I took it up to the Authors' League which I joined, yesterday afternoon, and I am going back to the Authors' League to-day. . . .

[1] Edward C. Aswell.

[2] Professor and Mrs. Henry M. Hart, Jr. of Cambridge, Mass., and Mrs. Hart's sister, Miss Louise White, now Mrs. John William Willis. Professor Hart was on leave of absence from the Harvard Law School in the academic year 1937–1938, working as head attorney in the Office of the Solicitor General in Washington. He had been responsible for the briefs in the case of Smyth v. United States, 302 U.S. 329 (1937) which were argued and won by Solicitor General (now Mr. Justice) Reed.

[3] "A Prologue to America" in the February 1, 1938, issue of *Vogue*.

There were one or two . . . things in the contract that bothered me in any reference they might have to you [1]. . . In other words, no one is going to take one little red penny of the ill-gotten gains which have enabled you thus far to wallow in luxury at my expense—no sir, by gum, not if I can help it. . . .

Ed suggested to me that it would be a good idea for me to get it settled up as quickly as possible before the first of the year, because of the income tax. That is, he suggested that I might get half the advance this week before the year is out, and half next month or at some later time, so that the tax would be divided in two years. What do you think? The trouble is, I always want to talk to you, and the little problem that is bothering me now is whether it will be cheaper to get it divided or have it all paid next year.[2] I think practically all of my so-called income this year has passed through your own fair hands, but I believe it amounts to considerable, so I am not sure whether it would be cheaper to tack half the advance on to it now, or let the advance go until next year. On the other hand, it will not hurt my feelings a bit if you succeed in selling the *Redbook* and *The Saturday Evening Post* a dozen stories next year, in which case—well, you get the point.

I think on the whole this describes the situation, and if anything does occur to you, I wish you would call me up to-morrow morning (Thursday) just as soon as you get this letter. And I guess this is all for the present—I've got to hike it now to The Authors' League—except to say I know I've been a pain in your neck for the last two or three weeks, but that I think a better day is dawning for us both. Anyway, "that is no agent, that is my friend" is the way I really feel, and in one way or another I'll try to live up to it.

We really did have a swell Christmas out at Ed Aswell's—I think it was the best one I have had since I was a kid. There were a lot of nice people and everyone was really very happy and very moved, and as we finished dinner Mary Lou whispered to me and asked me if it was "all right to tell them" [3] and I said "yes" so we got out your bottle of champagne and Mary Lou told them, and I tried to say something and Ed tried to say something, and neither could very well, and everyone had tears in their eyes, and I think they meant it, too. That's why it is a little

[1] Miss Nowell was never agent for Wolfe's books: only for his short stories and for some foreign rights, subsidiary rights, etc. which he could not conveniently handle for himself.

[2] Wolfe finally decided to divide his advance between the two years, and accordingly received $2,500 of it on December 31, 1937. The balance was paid in three installments of $2,500 each on February 1, March 1, and April 1, 1938.

[3] Mrs. Aswell was asking if it was all right to announce that Harpers were to be Wolfe's publishers.

tough to have to wrangle about contracts now, but I guess that's life, isn't it? And we were right both times. Anyway, dear Agent, I send you my love and with all my heart my wishes for nothing but the best for both of us next year. . . .

Wolfe had sent Charles Scribner a Christmas card and had received from him a short personal note thanking him for it and saying that he hoped they could have a drink together sometime. The following note was Wolfe's reply.

To CHARLES SCRIBNER

[Hotel Chelsea]
[New York]
December 29, 1937

Dear Charlie:

I can't tell you how happy I was to get your letter. Believe me, nothing was further from my intention in not writing or seeing any of you before than hurting the feelings of people who mean so much to me. As I told Max in the letter I wrote him, the reason I didn't come around was for no other reason except to think things out for myself, and to try to spare everybody pain, including myself.

Whatever happiness I had this Christmas was mixed in with a lot of sadness, too. Without going into the past, hashing it all up again, trying to thread back through the whole tangled snarl—like Max, I am still confused about so many things—just let me tell you that I think you are not only the finest publishers, but among the finest people I have ever known. Whatever comes of all of this, I know we will be friends; and now that I am committed to a new and, for me, very lonely and formidable course, that knowledge gives me the deepest comfort.

Some time soon, I look forward to seeing you again. Meanwhile, with affectionate greetings to you and all of your family, and with all good wishes for the coming year,

Mary Louise Aswell was the wife of Edward Aswell and at this time a member of the editorial staff of The Reader's Digest. *She had sent Wolfe an article from the December, 1937, issue of the* Digest *entitled "One Small Unwilling Captain," a very moving letter written by a captain in the Japanese Army deploring the necessity of war. The following was Wolfe's reply to her.*

To MARY LOUISE ASWELL

Hotel Chelsea,
222 West 23rd Street,
New York, N.Y.

December 31, 1937.

Dear Mary Lou:

Ed has just left, and I am winding up the old year with a touch of grippe, and am not much to look at, but very hopeful.

The final grim technical details of business and contract signing have been attended to, and now I am committed utterly, in every way. It gives me a strangely empty and hollow feeling, and I know the importance of the moment, and feel more than ever the responsibility of the obligation I have assumed. But I guess it is good for a man to get that hollow empty feeling, the sense of absolute loneliness and new beginning at different times throughout his life. It's not the hollowness of death, but a living kind of hollowness: a new world is before me now; it's good to know I have your prayers.

Thanks so much for your letter and for the enclosed story about the small Japanese Captain. It was moving and beautiful, and the pity is, it's all so true. It's so wrong to hate people, isn't it? And yet I feel that there are times when we have got to hate *things*. Everywhere you look and listen nowadays there is so much hatred. I hear it on every side every day. I even hear that the Germans are organically different from other members of the human race; the Trotskyites hate the Stalinites, and tell you they are not as other men: the Stalinites reply with equal hatred.

I've been reading Huxley's book which you gave me for Christmas. He's a brilliant writer, isn't he? His mind is so clear and penetrating, and sees so many things, and yet I got the impression he was puzzled and confused, too. To be partisan about anything almost implies hatred. Apparently Huxley's ideal is a kind of non-partisan man—or rather, a man who is partisan only in his belief in life. And yet, I wonder if in this world of ours to-day we can be non-partisan. Of one thing I am sure: the artist can't live in his ivory tower any more, if he is, he is cutting himself off from all the sources of life. Tremendous pressure is brought to bear from all sides upon people like myself: we are told that we must be partisan even in the work we do. Here I think the partisans are wrong; and yet a man does feel to-day a tremendous pressure from within—a kind of pressure of the conscience. There are so many things that are damnable, and which must be fought—we all ask ourselves the question: can we be free and be effective at the same time? I think nearly all of us have a pretty strong and clear feeling in our hearts about the larger humanity we would like to achieve. But when we see such wrong and cruelty and injustice all around us we ask ourselves if we have any right to refrain from taking sides and joining parties, because taking sides and joining parties are likely to limit and distort us so. I wish it were also possible for me to feel like Candide that the best thing in the end is to tend one's garden. A tremendous lot can be said for that, a tremendous lot of good, but somehow garden tending doesn't seem to be the answer either, the way things are to-day.

I wish it were possible for people to hate the thing that has the small Japanese Captain in its power without hating the small Japanese Captain, but you know what happens. Men start off by hating things and wind up by hating people. Well, I don't know the answers, but I'm looking for them and I think I am learning a little all the time. At any rate, there is friendship and love and faith and work. They are not just words: I have known and had them all.—Now, in a new and thrilling way, I feel that I know and have them all again. That is why I send you all my love, and all my deep and heartfelt wishes for your happiness and success this coming year.

The following letter is included in a longhand draft of "A Statement" which Wolfe wrote for Harpers to use in announcing his signing of a contract for his new book with them. The "Statement" was too long for Harpers' purposes, so they rewrote it, quoting only brief excerpts from it.

To EDWARD C. ASWELL

[Hotel Chelsea]
[New York]
[Late December, 1937]

This is a time of year that has some sadness in it for us all. But we can feel happy too, in the knowledge that nothing gets lost, and that the people we have known will still be our friends, no matter where we are, and that although we can't go home again, the home of every one of us is in the future. And that is why I am looking forward to next year.

It has been my fortunate lot always to have as publishers in this country people of the finest ability and the highest integrity. For that reason, I am glad to know that with the New Year I shall be associated with a house like yours.

As you know, like many other young men, I began life as a lyrical writer. I am no longer a very young man—I am thirty-seven years old—and I must tell you that my vision of life has changed since I began to write about ten years ago, and that I shall never again write the kind of book that I wrote then. Like other men, I began to write with an intense and passionate concern with the designs and purposes of my own youth; and like many other men, that preoccupation has now changed to an intense and passionate concern with the designs and purposes of life.

For two years now, since I began to work on my new book, I have felt as if I was standing on the shore of a new land. About the book that I am doing, I can only tell you that it is a kind of fable, constructed out of the materials of experience and reality, and permitting me, I hope, a more whole and thorough use of them than I have had before. The book belongs in kind with those books which have described the adventures of the average man—by this I mean the naturally innocent man, every mother's son of us—through life.

Anyway, for better or for worse, my life, my talent, and my spirit is now committed to it utterly. Like Martin Luther, I can't do otherwise—"Ich kann nicht anders"—I have no other choice.

Now I can only hope the end for both of us will be well.

XVII

THE COMPLETION OF THE FIRST ROUGH DRAFT
OF THE WEB AND THE ROCK AND
YOU CAN'T GO HOME AGAIN

1938

To NORMAN H. PEARSON

> c/o Miss Elizabeth Nowell
> 114 East 56th Street
> New York, N.Y.
>
> January 21, 1938

Dear Norman:

This is a letter of thanks and also of contrition. Just to get it off my chest, let me confess the whole sordid and humiliating business to you at once: I got your fine Modern Library Hawthorne [1] just as I was setting off to Virginia for a little trip, and I took it with me. [2] On the way down to Washington, I read your fine introduction. And that was as far as I got. Because when I got to Washington, I stopped over the night at a small hotel near the station. And there your book vanished. I had it under my arm when I entered the hotel, they showed me a room that had not been made up, and then they put me in another one. I am pretty sure that I left your book on the dresser of the first room. At any rate, the next morning when I discovered my loss and inquired about it, they could not find the book. So a genuine first edition Pearson with an autographed inscription from the author is floating around somewhere, or possibly has

---

[1] *The Complete Novels and Selected Tales of Nathaniel Hawthorne,* edited and with an introduction by Pearson.

[2] Wolfe had gone to Virginia for the weekend of January 9, then come up to Baltimore for a few days.

already found its way into the greedy clutches of a collector. Whoever has it, I hope he chokes.

Now I am going to propose this to you: if I go out and buy a Giant Hawthorne, will you put your scrawl in it when you come to New York? It may interest you to know that I have a large new supply of South Carolina paper shell pecans, [and] much more floor space than I had a year ago, so the possibilities of cracking nuts and strewing the shells all over the floor are practically unlimited. If this does not seduce you, what may? I think I have told you that I am staying at the old Hotel Chelsea, which is on 23rd Street between 7th and 8th Avenues. Also I am trying to get on with my big Doaks book.[3] There is still one more bout with the lawyers, one more session of the almost endless litigation which has made my life a nightmare for the past two years—this comes up in February— but after that I hope what is left of me may be left in peace. . . .

I've written a piece which is coming out, by gum, in *Vogue,* the ladies' corset and hosiery encyclopedia.[4] But I think it's a good piece even so, and I hope you get a chance to look at it. They told me to write five thousand words about America and that's what it's about. It comes from a book, or a section of a book I hope to write some day called *The Hound of Darkness,* but the ladies at *Vogue* thought this was not sunny enough, so we called it "A Prologue to America." I also had a piece in the *New Masses* —my initiation.[5] It's been published but I've never seen the copy it appeared in. There's one thing to be said about getting published in the *New Masses:* you never have to bother about an income tax.

This is about all the news I can think of at the present. Oh yes, I attended the annual meeting of the National Institute of Arts and Letters on Wednesday night. I got elected to it a year ago, but this was the first time I had been around. Walter Damrosch was presented with a gold medal and Jonas Lie was the toastmaster and Arthur Train was the treasurer and got up and read an account of the year's finances, and Henry Seidel Canby was the secretary and got up and read the annual report and a list of the members who had died during the year and the new members who had been elected, and there were four proposed amendments to the constitution which people got up and talked about and finally it was decided to reject them because the constitution said the same thing anyway, and Robert Nathan was there and Van Wyck Brooks and Stephen Vincent Benét and many other older ones whose names I did

[3] By this time Wolfe was considering discarding the title "The Vision of Spangler's Paul" and calling his book "The Lives of the Bondsman Doaks," or "The Ordeal of the Bondsman Doaks," or "You Can't Go Home Again."

[4] "A Prologue to America."

[5] "The Company" was published in the January 11, 1938, issue of the *New Masses,* and appears with many changes in *You Can't Go Home Again* on pages 129–140.

not know, and it was very sad. I went away and drank, and wished some-one like yourself had been with me that I could talk to. And yet, what is there to say? Walter Damrosch, who, Mr. Robert Nathan whispered to me, was "a grand old lion" was full of years and honors and gold medals, and Jonas Lie read a long very touching letter from Deems Taylor regretting he could not be there in person to present the gold medal to the grand old lion, and recounting all the things the lion had done. And Mr. Jonas Lie was very smooth and cold and polished and he had a little tufted goatee that stuck out of the hollow of his underlip and he, too, was full of years and honors and I believe he referred to Walter Damrosch as "our beloved master." And there were a lot of others there who were also full of years and honors, and, it seemed to me, of straw. Didn't Eliot write a poem beginning "We are the hollow men"? Maybe I'm being unfair and un-just—I know that I ought to be grateful to be a member of such a famous body—but I'm just telling you what ensued, and it was a sad, depressing evening.

It was a little terrifying too: I think there's nothing in life quite so tragic and desolate as the artist who has gone dead. I haven't seen this recent moving picture, "Zola," that people say is very fine, but I know something of Zola's life; and in the picture, I am told, it is shown how Zola, after the stern integrity of his earlier years, gets fat and prosperous and turns away from life, but then in his last years, when the Dreyfus Case finally breaks through his consciousness, becomes an artist and a liv-ing man again and gives his life, his talent and his courage for freedom and for truth. It seems to me that is the way an artist's life should be com-pleted, but the other night I looked at them and—well, Dr. Canby read the annual report and Mr. Damrosch got a gold medal.

Hendrik Willem Van Loon was one of the new members to be elected: he came in late and made a funny speech. He is a practical, diligent, hard-working Dutchman: I think he will do well among them. Mr. Robert Nathan is also, I feel, slated for great things. He is still young and yet, as the saying goes, "he has the wisdom of one twice his years." In these strident times, it is good to know that a writer of such delicate, whimsical talents is still true to the canons of pure art: as one cultivated lady is reported to have said recently, "I can't waste my time reading the dull and gloomy works of Hebrew writers like Thomas Mann and Theodore Dreiser. I want to read someone who knows how to write beautiful Eng-lish prose like Robert Nathan, for example."

Well, this is all for the present. And really, I assure you, with charity to all. I send you all good wishes for the coming year. I hope it will be a good year for me too, and that I'll be a better writer, which also means a better man. Come to see me soon.

To FRED W. WOLFE

January 22, 1938
114 E. 56th Street
New York, New York

c/o Miss Eliz. Nowell

Dear Fred:

. . . I was unfortunately unable to write Mama in time before she made her deposition,[1] but I am glad to know that she came through all right. I was away in Virginia when your letter came—anyway, it was too late to do anything about it. Let me know how it all turns out. Of course, I have known for years that things were in a bad way and that there would not be much left, but I do hope the lawyers can save her house for her. As I found out in the last two years, litigation is a costly and gruelling process, and I am not sure that anyone wins out in the end except the lawyers. . . .

. . . I don't know much about this suit the family is bringing against the Wachovia Bank, or they against us, because no one told me very much about it when I was home this summer, but I suppose you have thought everything over carefully and know where you stand. I understand that you and Mabel have named me as one of the parties to the suit, and therefore I wish you'd keep me informed about it and let me know what happens, and just exactly what it is we are suing for. Just to get the matter straight for the record here and now about what happened, so far as I was concerned, in its connection to Papa's estate, the facts are these:

When I was graduated from Chapel Hill in 1920, I was nineteen years old. As you know, I decided then to go to Harvard and do graduate work. It was my intention to go to Harvard for a year, but as it eventually turned out I stayed three. Papa, of course, was still alive in 1920, but very feeble and very ill, and no longer able to take an active interest in what was going on around him. When I decided to go to Harvard I went to Mama and talked to her about it. We all knew, even at that time, that Papa had made a will, and that according to the terms of the will each of the children was to receive the sum of five thousand dollars, and that the remainder of the estate would go to Mama. I proposed to her, as I remember it, that I be allowed to go to Harvard for a year, and that the expenses of this year at Harvard should be deducted from my share in the estate. At the time, I believe that the matter rested there, but, as you know, I remained at Harvard for three years instead of one. Papa died

---

[1] Her deposition in the case brought against her by the Wachovia Bank and Trust Co.

in 1922: When the question of settlement finally came up, somewhere around 1923, which was my last year at Harvard, or shortly after that, it was proposed to me that I cancel any claim I had in the estate in recognition of the expenses of my three years. To this I readily agreed, and for that matter, have never made any objection to that arrangement since. But Mama did object. She said, as I recall it, that it was fair to deduct the expenses of one year from my share, but that she had herself agreed to bear the expense of the additional two years, and that she did not think it was fair to charge me the whole amount.

I certainly do remember signing a document at about this period which you and Ralph [2] gave me your capacity as executors to the estate and that document, as I remember it, was a release to the estate of my share in the inheritance.[3] And I also remember clearly within recent years, within the last three or four, I believe, receiving letters and another document from you, which was also in the form of a release. You asked me to sign it, saying that it ought to be filed as a matter of record at the Court House, as one of the final things to be done in settling up the estate. I was perfectly willing to sign this paper, as I had the first, but my recollection is I mislaid it, and never returned it to you, and I believe later on you wrote me about the matter again.

Now, Fred, I've gone in to all this just to go upon the record, and to make my own part in the whole business as clear as I can. I know you understand that I make absolutely no claim to anything besides what I have received. But this is what happened. From a technical point of view, I suppose I really did not receive a full share in the estate. But I always consider that I actually did, since the help I received at Harvard during the three years I was there was approximately equivalent to what a full share would have been. I don't know whatever became of the paper I signed, but you may have it somewhere. Of course, as far as this present litigation is concerned, I am absolutely with the family and with Mama

[2] Ralph Wheaton.

[3] This was done because, although Mr. Wolfe had willed $5000 to each of his five children, his estate at the time of his death had shrunk to less than half of its original amount. In reply to this letter, Fred Wolfe wrote on January 26, 1937: "Your statements are all correct about the papers signed, etc. with the exception that you are wrong that the signing of said paper signed away your right in your supposed inheritance. Your paper was merely an acknowledgment of having received $5000 cash on account, by terms of will, but not "all your inheritance." At that time I also signed one for $5000. . . . It all was merely the juggling of two inexperienced people, Ralph and I, to attempt to make $11,000 in cash and Liberty Bonds cover the ground in terms of $25,000 (5 x $5000) as set forth by the will."

Shortly after this exchange of letters between himself and Fred, Wolfe signed a waiver to any claim upon his inheritance from his mother, which excluded him from being named in the suit of the Wachovia Bank and Trust against her and her heirs.

where their interests are involved. But I thought it better at this time just to make it clear to you personally what actually happened as far as my own part in it was concerned. It is better to have a clear understanding of all these things.

Now, I can only hope that everything turns out in favor of our own best interests, and above all, that the bank does not succeed in taking away from Mama her house, and what remaining property she may have. If they do, I consider it an outrageous injustice, and I am willing to do what I can to help you prevent its happening.

This is all for the present. I am getting back to work again, and hope to be able to work uninterruptedly now on my new book. It certainly seems that I deserve that measure of quiet and security after the past two years. Please write and tell me the news when you get a chance. And let me know if there is anything I can do. . . .

When Wolfe's New Jersey attorney, Ralph E. Lum, had asked him to obtain witnesses for the —— case, he had written to Mrs. Jelliffe, asking if she could testify for him since she had been present at one interview between him and ——. She had replied that on that occasion she had heard Wolfe and —— arguing about what manuscripts —— could or could not take and try to sell, and that she would be glad to testify as much in denial of ——'s claim that he and Wolfe had had "an unlimited agreement." After consultation with Mr. Lum, Wolfe wrote her the following letter.

To BELINDA JELLIFFE

> 114 East 56th Street
> New York, New York
> c/o Miss Elizabeth Nowell
> February 1, 1938

Dear Mrs. Jelliffe:

I heard from Mr. Lum to-day and he told me he was writing you and telling you he would like you to come over and be present in Jersey City when the case comes up. He is not sure that he will actually need you to take the stand as a witness at all, but he thinks your very presence there would be helpful "psychologically"—I suppose just by way of showing the court what nice people I know—you and Mr. Perkins, etc. Personally, I hope he puts you on because I think you would be a swell witness: anyway, I want you to know how much I appreciate your willingness to help.

I am seeing Mr. Perkins to-night in order to talk the whole thing over with him, and let him know how matters stand. He too, is going to be present; but what moves me most of all is that to-night will be my first meeting with Mr. Perkins in seven months. A whole lot has happened since then, a kind of definition and articulation of belief and conviction in my life. I have burned some great bridges behind me: I have been grieving for the dead a lot this past year, and I have found out something which is, I think, the most important discovery of my whole life, and that is this: you can't go home again, back to your childhood, back to your town, your people, back to the father you have lost, and back to the solacements of time and memory. I found that out through exile, through storm and stress, perplexity and dark confusion. I found it out with blood and sweat and agony, and for a long time I grieved as a man grieves for a brother who is dead.

But I think I am through the jungle now, and I feel naked and alone, and maybe a little scared too, and with a kind of dryness in the throat and in the mouth, and like a man that is standing all alone upon the shore of a new land, and knows that a whole new world is there before him, and that he has to face it for himself, and that his only help is in him now.

But I am grieving for the dead no longer: I know now that you can't go home again, but I know also that our home, yours and mine, and every mother's son's of us, is in the future, and I believe in it and trust in it as I believe and trust in life, and think that it is valuable, as life is valuable, and must be won and saved, and to that end I am now willing to devote all the energy, talent, faith and hope that in me are.

And I have also found out that although you can't go home again, there are certain things you do not lose, but that grow and flourish as the years go on, and one of them is the love and belief of a friend. And that is why it means so much more to me than I can ever utter here to know that in another hour I shall meet again and hear the voice again of the wonderful and noble man who has been, I think, the greatest, best, and most devoted friend that I have ever had; of whose friendship and belief I hope I may be forever worthy. Great bridges may be burned, and there is a path which we can never take, a road down which we never shall go back again; but there is also a fire that once lighted will always burn, and that never while life lasts can be put out.

And now—here is to good citizens like you and me, and a plague to all conspirators, here or abroad, or in the Jersey swamps, who plot the ruin of honest folk like you and me. As the British national anthem has it, "Frustrate their politics, confound their knavish tricks"—or hasn't it? Anyway, you get the idea, and I am sincerely grateful to you for the help you offer to that end.

Mr. Lum informs me that the hearing will be held in Chancery

Chambers, 1 Exchange Place, top floor, Jersey City, New Jersey, before Vice-Chancellor Kays on Tuesday, February 8, 1938. He does not say at what hour of the day it is to be held, but from what he told me before, I believe we should be there by ten o'clock in the morning, and he also hoped the whole matter would not take up more than an hour or two of time. Anyway, I will find out the time exactly and let you know, and maybe all three of us, you and Mr. Perkins, can go over together. There will also be one or two others who have agreed to go, but with two such as you and Mr. P. I do not feel I lack for comfort or for strength.

Meanwhile, until you hear from me, with thanks and all good wishes,

To MARGARET ROBERTS

114 East 56th Street
New York, New York
c/o Miss Elizabeth Nowell
February 14, 1938

Dear Mrs. Roberts:

I have wanted to write you for a long time, but many things have happened to keep me busy, including courts and lawyers, and a long and ugly business of trying to recover manuscripts which a man had taken, and which he had not returned. I won the thing the other day, completely and overwhelmingly—that is, if one ever does win anything when the lawyers have taken out their pound of flesh. Anyway, for the first time in three years I am out of the woods—out of the legal woods, at any rate —the long, exhausting and complicated series of legal difficulties with which I shall not weary you here. . . .

. . . Now I want you to help me if you can, and I know that I can depend on you to keep this confidential. I am also writing to my cousin, Jack Westall, with a similar request for information and help. . . . What I want is this: I am writing a long book, and I want to put everything that I have in it: and this time the book is not about a town, nor about any certain group of people, but it is about America and what happened here between 1929 and 1937. I think you will agree with me and see what I am driving at when I tell you that what happened in Asheville in that period seems pretty important and significant in the light it throws on what happened to the whole country. So, to get down to brass tacks: first of all, do you know what is the best and completest newspaper account of the events—the bank trials, the affairs of the city, etc.—which occurred between 1930 and 1932? And do you know where I can get a copy of them? I would be willing to buy them, if I could do so at a fair price: or if you know anyone who has kept such a record and would be willing to let me have it for several weeks, I would make every guarantee to preserve it and to see that it is returned to its owner safely. And if anything else occurs to you—if there are any people you think I could write or any other information that might be useful—I should be grateful if you would let me know about this too.

There is so much that I would like to tell you now of what has been happening to me, and so much that I would like to tell you about this book. But if I ever got started here, I would never finish. . . . Please help me if you can. And please write soon. Meanwhile, with all good wishes to you and Mr. Roberts for your health and happiness,

On January 19, 1938, Charles Scribner III had written Wolfe saying: "I have been having quite a time with our cashier's department straightening out the report that they are obliged to make to the United States Government . . . regarding the money that you received from us in the year 1937. . . . I have regarded the payments on the libel suit charged against your account as a loan. . . . The royalties earned . . . subtracted from the deficit on your account leave a debit balance of $826.38. In the course of a year and a half this amount will probably be met by the royalties on the books we published and I do not wish to embarrass you by pressing you to pay the debit balance owing to us, at this time, if you cannot conveniently do so. On the other hand if you have the money that you can spare, it would seem just as well to wind this up, and as I understand you will probably receive during the year a considerable payment on your new book, it might work out better for you from the income tax point of view. . . . I hope you agree with me now that you did the sensible thing in settling this suit, as you are now free to go ahead with your work without interruption, whereas you would otherwise be tied up with us for an indefinite time in fighting the thing out at probably a considerably larger cost and all of the payment would have fallen on your shoulders."

The following was Wolfe's reply.

To CHARLES SCRIBNER III

114 East 56th Street
New York, New York
c/o Miss Elizabeth Nowell
February 14, 1938

Dear Charlie:

I am sorry to have delayed answering your letter of January 19th so long, but, as you know, I have been wrestling with a law suit—the last I pray I may ever have—and doing my level best to help the lawyer and protect myself against a series of legal outrages that included practically everything except arson. As you know, I won the case, or at least it will seem as if I won it until I begin paying the lawyer bills.

Now about your own letter and your suggestion that I pay you now the deficit which stands against my account in your books: I have thought this over very carefully, and I want to ask you to let the deficit remain unpaid for the present, and to allow it to be absorbed, as you suggest it can be, by future sales of my books which you publish.

Yes, it is true that I did receive a considerable advance from Harpers, but it was money which I hope to keep, so far as possible, for my own use, to support me until I get another piece of work done. The lawyers are already swarming around, flapping their wings and emitting blood-thirsty caws, and if I am going to begin the new year in the same way as the two or three before it, paying out large sums of money in suits and settlements and lawyers' fees, the advance is not going to stretch too far. So, if you understand my position, I should prefer it if you will agree to let the deficit be paid off by further, and, I hope, continued sales.

I hope you are right when you say that settlement of the libel suit has left me free to do my work in peace. At any rate, I shall now find out. The experience of the past three years has been a very costly one, in time, in energy, and in money: I can only hope now that I may derive some future profit from it. Please let me know if my proposal here about the deficit is agreeable to you. Meanwhile, with all good wishes,

The following letter to Edward C. Aswell was begun in the first person, then given the title "A Statement of Purpose" and changed to the third person, using the words "the author" and "the editor" instead of "I" and "you." For the sake of consistency and directness, it has all been changed back to the first person here. It was never finished and was not sent to Aswell until Perkins and Miss Nowell found it among Wolfe's papers after his death.

To EDWARD C. ASWELL

> 114 East 56th Street
> New York, N.Y.
> c/o Miss Elizabeth Nowell
> February 14, 1938

Dear Ed:

I am doing the synopsis of the book which I told you I would make out for you, and I hope to give it to you in a day or two. First of all, so far as I can now make out—and the reason for any dubiety that may be apparent here is not due to any doubt on my own part, or any lack of conviction as to purpose or direction, but rather to the enormous masses of material with which I am working, and the tides and planes and forces which shift and vary constantly while still holding the same general direction—here is my latest stage of definition as clearly as I can put it to you, and what I think the book is about:

It is about one man's discovery of life and of the world, and in this sense it is a book of apprenticeship. As I told you before, I had in mind the doing of a kind of American "Gulliver's Travels." I used this comparison deliberately, but I also likened the book to those books that had to do with the adventures of what I call "the innocent man" through life —and mentioned, in addition to "Gulliver," such books as "Don Quixote," "Pickwick," "Candide," "The Idiot," and "Wilhelm Meister." As you know, I am using these names not as examples of literary models which I intend to follow, but merely as indications of the direction I am taking. And I now think that the illustration that comes closer to the kind of book I want to do is "Wilhelm Meister's Apprenticeship" rather than "Gulliver." And the reason for this is that I now believe, as the definition of the book grows clearer, that the illustration I made to you about "Gulliver" might mislead you in that, as the name "Gulliver" implies, it might indicate to you that I was contemplating a book about a man who was "gulled," who was expecting one thing from life and found another, etc.

Well, all of this element is certainly in the book, but it does not define as directly as it should my position and direction at this time about the book. The book will have satire in it, I hope swingeing and scalding satire, but it is not essentially a satiric book. It is a book, as I have said, about discovery—about discovery not in a sudden and explosive sense as when "some new planet breaks upon his ken," but of discovery as through a process of finding out, and of finding out as a man has to find out, through error and through trial, and through fantasy and illusion, through falsehood and his own damn foolishness, through being mistaken and wrong and an idiot and egotistical and aspiring and hopeful and believing and confused, and pretty much, I think, what every damned one of us is and goes through and finds out about and becomes.

And, in order that there may be no doubt as to what this process of discovery involves, the whole book might almost be called "You Can't Go Home Again"—which means back home to one's family, back home to one's childhood, back home to the father one has lost, back home to romantic love, to a young man's dreams of glory and of fame, back home to exile, to escape to "Europe" and some foreign land, back home to lyricism, singing just for singing's sake, back home to aestheticism, to

one's youthful ideas of the "artist," and the all-sufficiency of "art and
beauty and love," back home to the ivory tower, back home to places in
the country, the cottage in Bermuda away from all the strife and conflict
of the world, back home to the father one is looking for—to someone
who can help one, save one, ease the burden for one, back home to the
old forms and systems of things that once seemed everlasting, but that are
changing all the time—back home to the escapes of Time and Memory.
Each of these discoveries, sad and hard as they are to make and accept,
are described in the book almost in the order in which they are named
here. But the conclusion is not sad: this is a hopeful book—the conclusion
is that although you can't go home again, the home of every one of us is
in the future: there is no other way.

I hope you will keep this description of the purpose of the book in
mind and read it pretty carefully, and think about it a lot, because I am
depending on you now so much. I want you to be thoroughly convinced
at the outset that I know what I am doing and where I am going; and
although there are many, many doubts in my mind, there is no doubt; and
although there are many, many confusions, there is no confusion. To get
right down to cases now, even, as it has to be here, in the most broad and
general way, here is what I have in mind:

I intend to use my own experience absolutely—to pour it in, to squeeze
it, to get every damn thing out of it that it is worth. I intend for this to be
the most objective book that I have ever written, and I also intend by the
same token, for it to be the most autobiographical. I have constructed a
fable, I have invented a story and a legend: out of my experience I have
derived some new characters who are now compacted not so much from
specific recollection as from the whole amalgam and consonance of seeing,
feeling, thinking, living, and knowing many people. I have two important
ones, for example, named Alsop and Joyner—who, each in his own way,
is pretty much what the name of each signifies—but each, I believe, are
as convincing and living people as I have ever created. I now think I may
be wrong in calling the central figure, the protagonist, Joe Doaks, but
Alsop and Joyner can probably stand as they are—that is, both are real
names, both are fairly familiar and common names. The objection to Joe
Doaks, of course, is that it may carry with it too much a connotation of
newspaper cartooning, slap-stick, the fellow in the bleachers, and so on.
The way I feel now, I have got to get more of a Wilhelm Meister kind of
name—an *American* Wilhelm Meister kind of name.

To get still further down to cases, as you will remember, when I first
met you and we talked together about what I had to do, I spoke to you of
the book which I had called "The October Fair," and told you something
of the conflict in my mind between this book and the other book which I

have been describing here. I told you, for example, of the time several years ago when all my heart and life and energy were absorbed by "The October Fair" and how, at that time, I thought this was the book I had to do and had framed it in a sequence to follow "Look Homeward, Angel" and "Of Time and the River." I told you how I had written and striven on this book for two or three years, how "Of Time and the River" finally grew out of it and preceded it, and of how finally I had gone cold on "The October Fair": that is, it was no longer the burning, all-absorbing thing I had to do.

But I described also the feeling of incompletion and discontent in my mind because of this book which had been projected and never published —the feeling that it had in it some of the best and truest work I had ever done, and the feeling that this work ought to receive the consummation and release of print. I still feel that way except—and that is what I am trying to explain about my whole position here as concerns my book—my position has changed: I no longer wish to write a whole book about a woman and a man in love, and about youth and the city, because it now seems to me that these things, while important, are subordinate to the whole plan of the book I have in mind. In other words, being young and in love and in the city now seem to me to be only a part of the whole experience of apprenticeship and discovery of which I am talking. They are also a part of the knowledge that you can't go home again.

That plan, as I now see it in my mind, as I am shaping it in the enormous masses of manuscript which I have already written, and as I am trying to clarify it for you in the synopsis, is as follows:

The protagonist, the central character, the Wilhelm Meister kind of figure—really the most autobiographical character I have ever written because I want to put everything I have or know into him—is important now because, I hope, he will be or illustrate, in his own experience every one of us—not merely the sensitive young fellow in conflict with his town, his family, the little world around him—not merely the sensitive young fellow in love, and so concerned with his little universe of love that he thinks it is the whole universe—but all of these things and much more insofar as they illustrate essential elements of any man's progress and discovery of life, and as they illustrate the world itself, not in terms of personal and self-centered conflict with the world, but in terms of ever-increasing discovery of life and the world, with a consequent diminution of the more personal and self-centered vision of the world which a young man has.

In other words, I have sometimes thought of the book as a series of concentric circles—that is, you drop the pebble in the pool—the Wilhelm Meister pebble or whatever we shall ultimately call him—but instead of pebble and pool simply in personal terms of pebble and pool, you get a widening ever-enlarging picture of the whole thing—the pebble becomes important, if important at all, only in terms of this general and constant pattern of which it is the temporary and accidental stimulus. In other words, any other pebble would produce the same effect. The important thing is to tell about the thing itself, the thing that happens. The pebble, if you like, is only a means to this end.

THE PROTAGONIST.

I feel that the figure of the protagonist may be, technically and in other ways, the most important and decisive element in this book. As I have told you, this book marks not only a turning away from the books I have written in the past, but a genuine spiritual and artistic change. In other words, I feel that I am done with lyrical and identifiable personal autobiography; I am also seeking, and hope now to obtain, through free creation, a release of my inventive power which the more shackling limitations of identifiable autobiography do not permit.

In other words, the value of the Eugene Gant type of character is his personal and romantic uniqueness, causing conflict with the world around him: in this sense, the Eugene Gant type of character becomes a kind of romantic self-justification, and the greatest weakness of the Eugene Gant type of character lies in this fact.

Therefore, it is first of all vitally important to the success of this book that there be no trace of Eugene Gant-i-ness in the character of the protagonist; and since there is no longer a trace of Eugene Gant-i-ness in the mind and spirit of the creator, the problem should be a technical one rather than a spiritual or emotional one. In other words, this is a book about discovery, and not about self-justification; it hopes to describe the pattern that the life of Everyman must, in general, take in its process of discovery; and although the protagonist should be, in his own right, an interesting person, his significance lies not in his personal uniqueness and differences, but in his personal identity to the life of every man. The book is a book of discovery, hence union with life; not a book of personal revolt, hence separation from life. The protagonist becomes significant not as the tragic victim of circumstances, the romantic hero in conflict and revolt against his environment, but as a kind of polar instrument round which the events of life are grouped, by means of which they are touched, explained, and apprehended, by means of which they are seen and ordered.

Autobiographically, therefore, he should bear perhaps about the same relation to the life of the author as Wilhelm Meister bears to the life of Goethe, or as Copperfield bears to the life of Dickens. As to the story itself—the legend—it should bear about the same relation to the life of the author as the story of Wilhelm Meister bears to Goethe's life; even perhaps as Don Quixote bears to the life of Cervantes, although this book is perhaps more in the vein of satiric legendry than the book I have in mind.

But the book certainly should have in it, from first to last, a strong element of the satiric exaggeration of Don Quixote, not only because it belongs to the nature of the legend—"the innocent man" discovering life—but because satiric exaggeration also belongs to the nature of life, and particularly American life. No man, for example, who wants to write a book about America on a grand scale can hardly escape feeling again and again the emotion of the man when he first saw a giraffe: "I don't believe it!"

So, the book certainly must have this element, and it seems to me the figure of the protagonist must have it too. He must have it because the very process of discovery, of finding out, will be intensified and helped by it.

For example—and this may serve to illustrate the *special* way I hope to use autobiography in this book—one of the facts which has played an important part in my own life, which has been of immeasurable value to me in my own voyage of discovery, has been my great height. And it has been valuable to me for none of the reasons people usually assign: that height gives a man a commanding appearance, attracts attention to him, gives him a psychological advantage in the affairs of life over other men. This is not true: any marked variation from the type of average humanity is unfortunate—the midget, or the man of dwarfed figure, the excessively fat man, or the extremely tall man must encounter every moment of the day all kinds of sizes, patterns, shapes and measures of Things as They Are, which cause him discomfort and inconvenience. The value of his own variation, if any, is psychological—in the kind of increased awareness it gives him of the structure of life, and the pattern of the world. Again, in his discovery of life, he is so strongly and passionately drawn to life because, in a sense, life rebuffs him: in his youth, he is often in passionate and angry conflict with the world and people because of these rebuffs, usually unintentional, or the result of type customs and type prejudice—(maybe a girl, for example, hesitates to dance with a man of great height because she is afraid the comparison will excite laughter and ridicule)—but later on, a man learns tolerance and wisdom and understanding out of the very discomfort and pain his own variation has caused him. He comes to realize that he is in no fundamental sense different from other people: he is compacted of the same clay, filled with the same blood, breathes the same air, has the same passions, appetites, joys, fears, hopes and aspirations as the rest of humanity. He sees that people are not often intentionally cruel, but merely myopic in their understanding of him—that they think he is different simply because his physical dimensions are not quite the same as theirs. And when he understands this, a man's vision and knowledge of life is increased immeasurably: the very handicap that once caused him so much pain and conflict now becomes an asset: instead of being driven away from life by it, he is drawn ever closer to it: now that he understands the reasons why people act as they do, he responds to them naturally, accepts all the jokes and gestures, as banal as they often are, good-naturedly, and instead of being an outcast from the fold, he now draws people to him. Once they see he is one of them, and really not one whit different from themselves, they cluster around him: they reveal themselves to him, talk to him, even when they have just met him, as they would rarely do to another stranger. The very handicap that caused him so much pain in youth has now become one of the most valuable possessions that he has.

This fact—this tremendous discovery in my own life—has been such an important part of my own experience that several years ago when the outlines of this legend began first to shape themselves in my mind, I was convinced that I ought to use this fact somehow—for it is a veritable gold-mine—in the figure of my protagonist.

But how? Obviously, to create in the character of the protagonist, a figure which is six feet and six inches tall—my own height—would be to incur the very danger of personal autobiography and personal identity I am so anxious to avoid. The danger would be not merely that the reader and the critic would tend to identify such a character literally with me, but that I myself might tend to identify myself too personally with such a figure. Certainly, in the tremendously important fact of physical experience I could not help more or less duplicating my own experience—of being six feet six—with that of my protagonist.

It seemed then, as it does now, that the really important thing—the *truly* autobiographical thing—was the fact of physical variation: to create a figure who would illustrate that variation and all the great human experience that attends it.

Thus, as the legend of the book began to shape, as I began to create and invent the boyhood friends, the family, the town, the events and characters, the whole geography of the legend, around the character of the protagonist, the appearance of the figure, from his childhood on, began to shape itself until it is now more indelibly written in my mind than the face and figure of anyone I have ever known.

The figure may seem at first a little grotesque—it will quickly become apparent he is not so at all, he is only a little off the usual scale. These differences sometimes awake laughter in those who see him for the first time. As the book opens, he is still somewhat in the ugly duckling stage of his career, a little truculently resentful of remarks on his appearance, still over-sensitive, not yet at the stage where he is able to forget himself, accept jokes and badinage good-naturedly, and welcome his body for the loyal, if ugly, friend that it is.

And his appearance, as the author has conceived it in his imagination, is as follows:

He is somewhat above the middle height, say five feet nine or ten, but he gives the impression of being somewhat shorter than that, because of the way he has been shaped and molded, and the way in which he carries himself. He walks with a slight stoop, and his head, which is carried somewhat forward, with a thrusting movement, is set down solidly upon a short neck between shoulders which, in comparison with the lower part of his figure, and his thighs and legs, are extremely large and heavy. He is barrel-chested, and perhaps the most extraordinary feature of his makeup which accounts for the nickname he has had since childhood—the boys, of course, call him "Monk"—are the arms and hands: the arms are unusually long, and the hands, as well as the feet, are very big with long spatulate fingers which curve naturally and deeply in like paws. The effect of this inordinate length of arms and hands, which dangle almost to the knees, together with the stooped and heavy shoulders, and the out-thrust head, is to give the whole figure a somewhat prowling and half-crouching posture.

Finally, the features, the face, are small, compact, and somewhat pug-nosed, the eyes set very deep in beneath heavy brows, the forehead is rather low, and the hair begins not far above the brows. The total effect of this, particularly when he is listening or talking to someone, the body prowling downward, the head thrust forward and turned upward with a kind of packed attentiveness, made the Simian analogy inevitable in his childhood; therefore the name of "Monk" has stuck.

In addition to this, it has never occurred to him, apparently, to get his figure clothed in garments suited to his real proportions: he apparently has walked into a store somewhere and picked up and worn out the first thing he could get on. In this way, a way of which he is not wholly conscious, the element of the grotesque is exaggerated.

The truth of the matter is, he is not really grotesque at all: that is to say, his dimensions, while unusual and a little startling at first sight, are in no sense of the word abnormal. He is not in any way a freak of nature, although some people might think so: he is simply a creature with big hands and feet, extremely long arms, a trunk somewhat too large

and heavy, the legs and features perhaps somewhat too small and compact for the big shoulders that support them. Since he has added to this
rather awkward but not distorted figure, certain unconscious tricks and
mannerisms of his own, such as his habit of carrying his head thrust
forward, and peering upward when he is listening or talking, it is not
surprising if the impression he first makes should sometimes arouse
laughter and surprise. Certainly he knows of this, and he has sometimes
furiously and bitterly resented it; but he has never inquired sufficiently
or objectively enough into the reasons for it.

The truth of the matter is that although he has a very intense and
apprehensive eye for the appearance of things, he does not have an intense and apprehensive eye for his own appearance: in fact, the absorption of his interest and attention in the world around him is so passionate and eager that it rarely occurs to him what kind of figure and
appearance he is himself making. In other words, he does not realize
the kind of effect he has on people, and when, as sometimes happens,
it is rudely and brutally forced upon his attention, it throws him into a
state of furious anger. He is young: and he has not learned the wisdom
and tolerant understanding of experience and maturity. In short, he does
not see that these things are accidental and of no great consequence—
that personal beauty is probably no very great virtue in a man anyway;
and that this envelope of flesh and blood in which a spirit happens to
be sheathed, has been a very loyal and enduring, even though an ugly,
friend.

THE STORY
The Story Begins With a Prologue
Prologue

The prologue as the author now sees it is to be called "The Hound of
Darkness"—and states [1] the setting. The setting is America. This is followed with "Old Catawba," a description of the place from which the
protagonist comes.

This was followed originally by The Doaksology: a satiric genealogy
of the great Doaks family since the earliest times.[2] If the name Doaks
is changed, perhaps the genealogy could still be used. Then follows

[1] This was the first chapter, now entitled "The Quick and the Dead" of "The Hills
Beyond," which appears on pages 201–210 in the book of that name.
[2] Wolfe first wrote "The Doaksology" in 1936–37, and was rewriting it and changing
the name Doaks to Joyner just before he started on his trip west in May, 1938. It is
not included in *The Web and the Rock* but appears as chapters 2–6 of "The Hills
Beyond" in the book of that title.

an account of the town of Libya Hill: how it got its name from the first Joyner who settled there, the connection of the Joyners with the family of the protagonist: a description of Libya Hill and the people there. All of this save the part about Libya Hill has been completely written. The Libya parts are incomplete.

THE DIRECT NARRATIVE

To Be Called
The Station or
The one and The Many or
The Pebble and The Pool.

The direct narrative begins with the pebble (the protagonist) rolling home. The chapter bears the title of "The Station." Perhaps a better name for it would be "The Pebble and The Pool." Another, and perhaps the best of all, would be "The One and The Many." For the purpose of this beginning—this setting—is to show the tremendous and nameless Allness of The Station—ten thousand men and women constantly arriving and departing, each unknown to the other, but sparked with the special fire of his own destination, the unknown town, the small hand's breadth of earth somewhere out upon the vast body of the continent— all caught together for a moment, interfused and weaving, not lives but life, caught up, subsumed beneath the great roof of the mighty Station, the vast murmur of these voices drowsily caught up there like the murmurous and incessant sound of time and of eternity, which is and is forever, no matter what men come and go through the portals of the great Station, no matter what men live or die.[3]

And our protagonist is introduced: he is here among them, the one and the many, the pebble and the pool.

From here on, Wolfe began writing not only the synopsis of his book but portions of the book itself: the scenes in car K 19 which appear in Chapter V of You Can't Go Home Again. *Since this portion of the letter is really not a letter at all, but an already-published section of his book, it is omitted here.*

Arthur Mann, the sports writer, had taken Wolfe to the 15th Annual Dinner of the New York Chapter of the Baseball Writers Association of America at the Commodore Hotel on January 30, 1938, and had now invited him to spend Washington's Birthday at his home in Cherry Plain, N.Y. The following was Wolfe's reply.

[3] This material appears on pages 48–51 of *You Can't Go Home Again*, in Chapter V which is entitled "The Hidden Terror."

To ARTHUR MANN

114 East 56th Street
New York, New York
c/o Miss Elizabeth Nowell
February 16, 1938

Dear Arthur:

I really have been intending to write you day by day, but now your long letter has arrived to make my protestations look a little phoney. But I have been wrestling with the law, with law courts, and with another guy who is trying to indulge in the grand old national pastime of shaking-down—in my own case of being shook—and I just got through with it a few days ago. At least I hope to God I am through with it. My lawyers assured me it was a famous victory, and the newspapers said I had won: I do not know how I will feel about it when I see the lawyer's bill.

Some people tell me that life is too short to waste one's time and energy in bickering with the courts, and my own experience of the last three years has certainly been a very costly one in both time and money. But there are times when you simply have to fight, just to protect yourself, this was one of them: the case involving a little fellow who had walked off with some of my manuscripts a year ago, sold some of them and pocketed the money, and refused to return the rest: in addition, he had mixed the whole thing up charmingly with blackmail, threatening my first set of lawyers—for be it known by all these present, I have lawyers in sets, squadrons and platoons representing me in all the American states—that if I carried the case to court he would make public certain vile and obscene and unmentionable words with the avowed object of—or—ruining me.

All of this made me yawn long and loudly when I heard it, but my first set of lawyers, whose reading experience apparently ended with the works of the late Bulwer-Lytton, and who had never heard of such word-users as Joyce, Hemingway, Faulkner, etc.—were undone: they paled at the news, and sent me a hurry-up call to New Orleans to return at once, that our affairs were teetering on the brink of ruin, etc. The result was that I had to pay them off for their own ineptitude—and I find that misrepresentation in the law costs just as much as being represented. I managed to get another lawyer who is not intimidated by the threats of a naughty little boy, and the other day we went to town.

The court instructed him to return all the manuscript which he still had, to pay me in full, without commission, the money he had received for all the manuscripts he had sold unlawfully—you can figure for yourself what a fat chance I have of getting this—and further denied all of his claims for being an agent and of being due the huge sum—two thousand dollars or so—which he said was coming to him in agent's commissions.

It was a fine proceeding: the fellow cut his own throat every time he opened his mouth—and what he did not do for himself, his lawyer completed for him. When the Judge asked him for an accounting of the manuscript, for example, he testified that he had burned some of it because of its "filthy and obscene character." When the Judge asked him if he had my letter dismissing him as agent, he said he had, but that he had not brought it to court because he was holding it in order to sell the autograph. It was an astounding proceeding. . . .

When people ask me how I got into a mess like this, I confess I do not clearly know the answer. I suppose I should have been more careful, but it is so easy to point out one's mistakes after the mistake is evident. All these experiences of the last three years, for this has only been one of a whole Pandora's box of troubles, have made me think of a lot of things concerning a man's relation with the world and of people he knows in a way I never thought about them before.

The lawyer will tell you to let this be a lesson to you, not to enter into casual and genial conversations with people you meet in elevators, barrooms, observation cars, etc., and never to have anything to do even with your own blood brother in a business way unless you have the whole thing drawn up in a contract and gone over by a lawyer in advance. And the cynic will tell you that it ought to be a lesson to you because it ought to teach you that everyone is out to do you, that life is really just a vast and complicated system of Gyp, that the sooner you place this hardboiled information in your hat, the better it will be for you.

I think that both of them are wrong: of the two evils I think it is better to be gypped than to go through life with your fangs bared in a snarl; and I would rather remain the present incomplete work of nature that I am than go to dinner at my friend's house with a dictaphone concealed in my vest pocket, my attorney in the right hand, and a court stenographer in the left. Maybe everything that happened would then be according to Hoyle, but somehow I believe I would fail to meet a lot of interesting people.

This whole experience of the last three years—ever since "Of Time and the River" came out . . . has been a painful but an interesting one. I do not know what the hell it has to do with writing, but something tells me it might have a great deal to do with it: I now see that the late

Charles Dickens by no means exhausted the subject in his observations on the law and on the courts—I think we could teach him a few new tricks nowadays that would make him rub his eyes—down below, of course, the old, old business of delay, technicality, charge and counter charge, the weaving of that unreal spider's web that is the law, goes on as it has gone on since the beginning of history.

You learn some pretty sad things about people—one is, how many people there are who say they are your friends cannot be depended on when a question of profit is involved. . . . It makes you wonder about people—maybe there is something in what the Communists say about the profit motive corrupting life. Anyway, I am out of the woods—of this kind of woods—for the first time in three years—and I am knocking on wood as I make this proud boast.

I cannot tell you how much I enjoyed the Baseball Writers' Dinner, and how much I think I got out of it. Not that I learned so much, but I think there was a big value in verification—in seeing the animal at first hand, and in communication with his fellows. The point is, one of the characters in this immense long book that I am writing is a baseball player,[1] and I realize from past observation how easy it is for a writer to go wrong when writing about a professional athlete: the sporting writer, or the writer of baseball fiction, does it best of all, I think, because they put him in a certain limited setting—on the field, or on the bench, or at the training camp. My problem is a different one: I think I may have told you that one reason I have always loved baseball so much is that it has been not merely "the great national game," but really a part of the whole weather of our lives, of the thing that is our own, of the whole fabric, the million memories of America. For example, in the memory of almost every one of us, is there anything that can evoke spring—the first fine days of April—better than the sound of the ball smacking into the pocket of the big mitt, the sound of the bat as it hits the horse hide: for me, at any rate, and I am being literal and not rhetorical—almost everything I know about spring is in it—the first leaf, the jonquil, the maple tree, the smell of grass upon your hands and knees, the coming into flower of April. And is there anything that can tell more about an American summer than, say, the smell of the wooden bleachers in a small town baseball park, that resinous, sultry and exciting smell of old dry wood.

Well, I could go on indefinitely: the point is that one of the characters is out of this weather, from this setting: he becomes a Big League player, but it is of this kind of man—strong, simple, full of earth and sun, and his life in relation to other lives that I want to write: I have got the man,

[1] Nebraska Crane.

I knew him as a child—he never made the Big League, but he could have. I mean, he would have looked real in a Big League uniform because, as I saw at the dinner, it was from just such fellows that the Big League players come. And I am not making the mistake of trying to write about him too professionally—too technically in relation to his merits as a player—I am simply trying to write about him as a living man.

Now after this unexpected deluge, about your invitation. Your description of the mad abundance has me hanging on the ropes. I would take up your invitation like a shot, here and now, if it were not for this overwhelming necessity of work. I not only feel that I ought to work now, but after all these thwarting delays of law and lawsuits, I want to work: at the present time I am trying to get done a long and very detailed synopsis of the book; and I have also been working on a piece telling what I have seen of Fascism not only in Germany, but in this country, which I think may be good, and which I want to try and get published somewhere.

At any rate, my plan for the immediate future is just to keep at it. I do not believe I can get up there for Washington's Birthday, but if you will give me a raincheck I would certainly like to know that I can come up later. Anyway, that is the way I am going to feel about it until you tell me differently.

I probably would not get much work done if I came up, nor would I try to. I suppose you are one of those fortunate people who have found out that you can work anywhere. I think I can too, except with me it takes time; that is, I like to settle into a place of my own, get used to the idea of staying there and working there. And right now for the present, while the spirit is willing, I think I had better go to it with all my might. Maybe, after getting rid of the weary burden of all these lawsuits I feel like the fellow with the toothache who said to the man who stepped on his corns in the subway train: "Do it again, it feels good."

It was grand meeting you and getting to know you, Arthur, and I guess the reason you are now the victim of this torrential deluge is that I hope to continue and proceed from where we left off. I certainly do hope to see you soon, either here or on your own acres. Meanwhile, with thanks and best wishes to you and all the family,

On February 15, Charles Scribner had written to Wolfe: "I am willing to allow your obligation on the suit we had to run along for the time being, although it is not customary to carry such accounts for an author for whom you are no longer acting as publisher, and our contract which is similar to that of other publishers and agents, calls for a settlement on the part of the author for any suits of this kind which may be brought." Wolfe's reply was as follows.

To CHARLES SCRIBNER

114 East 56th Street
New York, New York
c/o Miss Elizabeth Nowell
February 18, 1938

Dear Charlie:

I don't want to inconvenience you a bit, and if you say the deficit has got to be paid now I will pay it. My only point was that since my books made almost twenty-three hundred dollars last year, according to the royalty statement you sent along with the letter, I therefore felt they would naturally be expected to make good the eight hundred dollar deficit within a reasonable time.

I notice that you refer in your last letter to the deficit as an "obligation on the suit." Well, I am not going to argue with you about the suit. I never have. I told you last year how I felt, and I still feel the same way. I am sorry as hell that you got involved in it through something I had written which you published. But as you know and I know, and as the lawyers knew, I did not libel anyone.

You say in your letter you hope I do not have any more libel suits, and I second the motion with all my might. But I do not know what you or I or any man can do about people suing you. It is a racket, a part of a great organized national industry of shaking-down—in my case, of being shook—and you and I and every other decent citizen ought to do everything we can to stop it. And the only way to stop it is to fight it, because it lives by threat and flourishes on submission. As long as we submit it will continue to flourish.

I think that when a writer willfully, deliberately and maliciously writes something for the purpose of insulting and injuring a living person, or a dead one for that matter, he ought to be punished for it. But I do not think he ought to be punished for being honest and decent and doing his work, and having been unfortunate enough, maybe, to attract some public notice and get his name in the press. And you know that is what happened. You are yourself an honest and a decent man, and you know as well as I do that it was a shake-down. I am not going to harp upon it any more, but you have mentioned the thing several times in your letters, and I have got to tell you what I told you a year ago. I think we should have fought it out.

I want you to know, and I am sure you do know, that there is not an ounce of resentment in my heart, and that particular thing is all over now. But we should have fought it out. I do not think it is sticking to the real point to talk about publishers' contracts, and what the clause of the contract says concerning libel suits, and who is to be responsible for them. The point is, it seems to me, that a publisher ought to stick to a writer and fight with him when he knows that that writer is loyal and honest, has injured no one in his writing, and is being unfairly taken advantage of, and, believe me, Charlie, I am not saying this because I have any rankling memory of the past. I just hope that I will profit by the experience, and I also hope that in the future publishers and writers will stick together and fight for each other in matters of this sort. For, as any decent person knows, that is the only thing to do. When you publish a man, when you put the imprint of your name upon a man's book, you are for him, and not against him. I think you have always been for me, and what is more, I think you always will be, no matter who is my publisher. But I think that in that particular matter we were wrong in not fighting it, and furthermore I think we were licked before we started, because our lawyers cost so much that we were practically forced to settle to protect ourselves against our own lawyers' bill if we went on. Frankly, so far as I can see we would have done as well if we had had Abie Glickstein and paid him fifty bucks. In the end, the three floors of office space . . . the magnificent private offices, regiments of slick-looking assistants, etchings of Abraham Lincoln, etc., did not mean a damn thing except trouble and money: it was a sorry job.

I know you took it on the chin on account of something that I wrote, but Charlie, all that suit proved to me was that a man might write "The cat has whiskers" and then get sued for libel by an old maid in Keokuk. I am sorry as all hell you had to be involved, but I still think we should have fought it out. You took it on the chin to the extent of about three thousand bucks, but so did I—and maybe you have got some idea of how much three thousand bucks is in my young life. It is just about ten per cent of all the money I ever earned from the beginning out of writing. Those facts are correct, and people tell me I am a well-known writer.

So the only reason I am harping on it is not because I have got an atom of soreness or resentment in me: you did what you thought was right, but I am only saying that if guys like you and me do not stick together and fight it out sometimes when people try to shake us down, it is not only going to be too bad for writers, but too bad for publishers too. And that is that. I have spoken my little piece and I know you will take my word for it, I am not sore: I am your friend.

And now about the eight hundred dollar deficit: if you say I have got to pay it now, I will pay it. But honestly I do not think you are running much of a risk in letting it run on, in view of the fact that the work of mine which you publish earned almost three times that much last year. But if you do feel that it ought to be paid now, it seems to me that a simple and decent arrangement of the matter would be one in which we square the whole account, and you relinquish to me the rights of my books which you publish.

Frankly, I think you ought to do it. They are my books, they belong to me because I created them and because they mean something to me they cannot mean to anyone else. I would like to see you and talk to you about this, and I think we could reach an agreement that would be satisfactory to both of us, and which would clear the whole situation up in such a way that the deficit would not only be wiped out, but you would also be relieved of all the risks and responsibilities attendant on suits, publication, and keeping the books in print.

And now that is all in a business way, but I am sorry to have to protract the discussion of a matter which must already have grown tedious to you. For my own part I can only repeat what you said to me in your fine letter of Christmas, when you heard that I had definitely gone with another house—it has always seemed to me that there has been something more between us than a business connection, and, as you say, friendship is considerably more important.

I know that you will always hope for my success, and that if my next book is a good one there will be no one in the world more genuinely pleased about it than you. For that reason, I am grateful for the kind inquiry you make in your last letter about the progress I am making. I see no reason, now that the legal difficulties which have beset my life for the last three years have been settled, [why] I should not get ahead with my work very rapidly. I have collected an immense amount of material and done an immense amount of writing, and the scheme and pattern of the book is all clear. An immense labor still remains to be done, but I believe it is worth doing, and naturally I hope that the result will be one that all of us can be proud of.

I know there may be some pretty dark times ahead, times when I may almost lose hope, but when I do I shall always remember the letter you wrote a year ago, when you told me that I was free to go if I liked, but that whatever happened you would be my friend, and you expected me to go and grow and prosper in my work, as time went on. Naturally, I can only hope that you are right, and the knowledge that you feel that way will always be a source of comfort and inspiration to me. I still have that letter and shall always treasure it as a token that no matter who publishes me, or what business connections I form, I shall always have your friendship. And I still hope that some night when you have nothing else to do, and feel like having a drink, you will call me up. Meanwhile, with all good wishes to you all,

In his reply of February 24, 1938, to this letter, Charles Scribner said: "I told you not once but several times that I was perfectly prepared to go ahead with you in fighting out the libel suit, if that was what you wished to do. The lawyer advised that the cheapest and safest way was to settle, and personally I was inclined to agree with him, . . . but I distinctly left the final decision to you. . . .

"I would also like to say a word on the other point you raise with regard to our giving up to you the publishing rights on your books. I do not believe that you have thought through the whole of the partnership relationship which you say should exist between author and publisher. . . . When the libel suit came up, we waived at once our contract rights as publishers to dump the entire cost of the suit and any damages that might result on you as the author, and agreed to go into it fifty-fifty, as we felt we had entered a more or less permanent relationship. . . . With regard to the books published, it is true that they are your creation, but we made a mutual agreement to invest our money as publishers in making the plates, printing them and selling them, your share being the royalty we agreed to pay on sales, and our share being any profit we might realize after our investment was met. . . . We like your books and are proud to have them on our list, and . . . we have a right to . . . make our share of the profit from their sale. We do not wish to sell our rights, but if this should come about, it would then be up to any publisher who might take them over to buy out our rights, and they would have to pay a damn high price, as I have every faith that they will go on selling for years. . . ."

To WALTER WINCHELL

114 East 56th Street
New York, New York
c/o Miss Elizabeth Nowell

February 21, 1938.

Dear Mr. Winchell:

In your column "On Broadway" in *The Daily Mirror* for Monday, February 21, you state: "Thomas Wolfe, the novelist, is at war with

Scribners and Harcourt, Brace—both of whom rejected his new book."

This statement is wholly incorrect: my new book is not finished, Scribners did not reject it, Harcourt, Brace did not reject it, and no publisher has ever seen the manuscript. Your statement is injurious and I ask you to correct it.

In his column in The Daily Mirror *for February 25, 1938, Winchell said:* ". . . *Thomas Wolfe, the book writer, called. Said his manuscript isn't finished so how could it be rejected?"*

To MARGARET ROBERTS

> 114 East 56th Street
> New York, New York
> c/o Miss Elizabeth Nowell
>
> March 7, 1938

Dear Mrs. Roberts:

Your letter is full of good news, except, of course, poor —— ——.[1] I felt, of course, last summer that there was something wrong; and yet, I liked him. He seemed to have a genuinely good heart and good feeling. I do hope he can be cured. I wonder what is wrong with the set-up, anyhow. I suppose Asheville is no worse than other communities in this respect, and that the average of catastrophe is no higher there than anywhere else. And yet, that was one of the most disturbing revelations that I got last summer, going back as I did after an absence of eight years and with the sharp and fresh impressions that such absence gives to one. It seemed as if the whole landscape was strewn with the shipwrecks of people I had known: I inquired about person after person only to be told that they were at Dix Hill, or had just returned; or at Morganton,[2] or that they had gone completely to pieces through drugs or drink, or a combination of both. And looking back over my childhood and early youth in Asheville, it often seems to me now that the people who went down, who became these shipwrecks, were not the worthless litter of humanity, but often the best, the brightest, and the most intelligent we had.

It occurred to me that if such things happen to such people there must be something wrong with the background that produced them, something in the life around them that did not give them enough to employ their talents or waken the deepest interest in their lives. Am I wrong about this? I want to keep a clear perspective, and I think the answer

[1] An Asheville man who had gone insane.

[2] Dix Hill and Morganton are North Carolina state hospitals for the insane.

may be that my own life in so many special and intimate ways is bound up with the life of Asheville. I know so many people there—in a sense, when I go home, I inherit the life of the whole community.

Here, in this vast city, it is, of course, different: the number of people that one knows or can know is relatively small. I know that one can find every kind of human wreckage here, because I have seen it myself, but it does seem to me, among most of the people that I know best, such catastrophe does not happen with the appalling frequency it does at home. The big wicked city that one hears so much about is also a very busy and hard-working place. It would be ironic, wouldn't it, if one eventually discovered that he had come here to keep out of mischief?

Anyway, the whole problem to my mind is a pretty serious one: if there is anything in it, I would like to find out why—it seems to me that that, too, is a legitimate subject for fiction. For example, often when I have heard the learned economists talk about the boom—how and when it began, how it got going, why it collapsed, what was fundamentally wrong about it—I have kept silent, because there were so many human and spiritual things about it as well that never get mentioned. I think that one of these things—remembering my own childhood—is a deep and intense hunger in people for "something to happen"—waiting for something, they are not sure what, but something that is full of excitement, movement, color, sudden wealth.

Whatever use I make of anything you or Mr. Roberts or Jack Westall give me, I assure you it will be the best and most serious use. It is going to be a tremendous labor, but when I am done with it—at any rate, when I have set it down—I shall not only be delighted but I shall appreciate it if you will look it over to find out if I have done the job. I've bitten off a tremendous hunk to chew on this time—maybe more than I can—but as you say, we shall see. . . . The book covers a tremendous panoramic sweep of places, people, events, and times—I may be a doddering old man before I am done with it, but meanwhile I am giving it everything I have. So everything you do, together with all the trouble and labor I know this entails, is deeply and genuinely appreciated.

I don't know whether I shall come home this summer. If I do it will only be for a short visit. I have to work now at the top of my bent, and last summer I found out that one's home town is not always the best place to do it. But I can't tell you what a tremendous experience that was. I'd like to tell you all about it some day, for in a way I think it may have been one of the great turning points in my life. It crystallized a feeling, a conviction, a discovery that I had been slowly coming to for years. And I suppose that discovery and conviction might be best summarized by these words: "You can't go home again". . . .

That trip to Asheville crystallized that discovery, and I believe was one of the most important things that ever happened to me. For years, I had thought about my long absence from Asheville; I felt a sense of exile until it began to eat on me, haunt me in dreams. It became so oppressive and overwhelming that that return was inevitable—and it was a cleansing flood. I know you won't misunderstand me: I was more deeply touched and moved than I can tell you over the overwhelming reception I received, the great kindness and friendliness and interest of almost everyone I saw. And it is comforting to know that whenever I want to I can go back to my own town, and find friends there who will be glad to see me.

But my discovery that "you can't go home again" went a whole lot deeper than this: it went down to the very roots of my life and spirit— it has been a hard and at times terrifying discovery because it amounts to an entire revision almost of belief and of knowledge; it was like death almost, because it meant saying farewell to so many things, to so many ideas and images and hopes and illusions that we think we can't live without. But the point is, I have come through it now, and I am not desolate or lost. On the contrary, I am more full of faith and hope and courage than I have been in years. I suppose what I am trying to tell you here is a spiritual conviction that will inform the whole book—you could almost call that book, "You Can't Go Home Again," although I don't think I shall call it that. But I do want you to understand that it is not a *hopeless* book, but a triumphantly *hopeful* one. I've tried to tell you a little about it now, and I hope you see something of what I have in mind. Like you, like Mr. Roberts, like the late Mr. Shakespeare, I, too, believe in the brave new world, and I hope now that I am on the way to find it.

Meanwhile, until I hear from you again, with all good wishes to you and Mr. Roberts,

P.S. . . . I live here in a very old Victorian style hotel with enormous rooms and lots of other strange critters like myself. Mr. Edgar Lee Masters also lives here and has for years. I see him from time to time; in fact, he set me up to a glass of beer yesterday afternoon—but for the most part I just work.

I wish you'd tell me how to sleep as you used to. It is not a question of health, it is just a plain damn question of writing—and that is a plain damn question. I work every day from about ten in the morning until about six at night, but after that I can't stop thinking about it: it goes rumbling and roaring around in my head, or what serves me for a head. The result is there is usually no sleep until long after midnight. I don't know what to do about all this, it has always been the same—at least every time I start to work. The only satisfaction I get from it is the rather gloomy one that I must be really at work again. I don't think, otherwise, it means an early catastrophe. As "The Tempest" says, "His complexion is perfect for hanging." I may be wrong, but something tells me my time is not yet. And now good-bye.

To MABEL WOLFE WHEATON

114 East 56th Street
New York, New York.
c/o Miss Elizabeth Nowell.

March 19, 1938

Dear Mabel:

I was glad to get your letter and very interested in all the news it contained. I am very sorry to hear Ralph has not been well and that you have not been up to scratch yourself. I think the worry and the nervous strain attendant on this trial [1] and in having to do with lawyers and the courts may have something to do with it. I speak as one who has also been through the mill again and again during the past three years. Lawyers and court rooms are bad business: they take it out of you like nothing else, and in the end I do not know who wins. . . .

I was very much interested to hear what you had to say about the trial. I hope you succeed in keeping the bank from confiscating what remains of Mama's property, and in compelling them to make some restitution to the heirs. I want you to know also that I am with you heart and soul in your effort and desire to save something for the family, and if I am able to help I want to.

But now, since the family is involved in this legal dispute and certain things are going on record in the courts, I want to go on record personally with you and the family. That means that I am going to have to say some things that we all know about pretty bluntly. It may not be pleasant while it lasts, but there has been too much self-deception and evasion and rationalizing which makes for misunderstanding in the end. So believe me, it is better to get the whole thing straight now, once and for all, so that there can be no misunderstanding in the future. And I believe there is no need telling you that there is not an ounce of resentment in me over anything that ever happened, nothing but genuine good will and a desire to help and stand by all of you.

As far as I am concerned, what is past is past: if I ever had any grievance, real or imagined, at any time, or ever thought that in any way I had a tough time as a kid, that is all over now. It is all washed up, I got

---

[1] The case brought by the Asheville Wachovia Bank and Trust against Mrs. Wolfe and her heirs.

it off my chest, and whatever things I may ever have said about it in anger or in hurt that were unfair, I am sorry for. I am sorry for some things I may have said in my first book: they were written in the heat of creation and of youth, and some of them may have been exaggerated and unfair. And I am sorry for some of the things that were said at home and that came back to me, and that I heard last summer. But that is all over, too. I think the intention of everyone was at the bottom good: as far as I am concerned, it has been wiped off the slate. Now, I want to get off to a fresh clean start with everyone, and it seems to me that the best way to do it is to start off by us all being straight with one another, and not by continuing to tell a lot of old fairy tales.

When I was a kid, I was forever having it hammered into my head and pounded into my ears about how good and great and noble and self-sacrificing somebody was and what a selfish little brute I was myself. That kind of bunk used to get me down as a kid, and I guess it got me sore later on. But I am not down and I am not sore any more. I do not think I was a selfish little brute, I think I was a decent little kid, and I have tried to be decent ever since. And I do not think there was anything particularly great or noble or self-sacrificing or unselfish about anyone except insofar as we were all members of the human race, and in the bottom of my heart I have always thought we were, on the whole, pretty decent ones and pretty good ones. I think that now just as much as I ever did.

But let us not go on with the old blarney. Nobody stayed at home and made sacrifices because of some great self-sacrificing loyalty and devotion to the family, or to Mama, or to someone else. They stayed home because they wanted to stay home and could not be happy anywhere else. And I am also tired of being told that I was the "lucky one" because I "got away." I did no such thing. I got away because I had to get away, there was no place for me at home, which is the simple brutal truth. As for being lucky, I have lived alone and fought my way alone for fifteen years, and if anyone thinks that is being lucky they are invited with my permission to try it, and see how it fits.

As to the present situation, it is a little surprising now to be assured that I got nothing when I used to have it pounded into me all the time that I was getting everything—God knows why—when everyone else was getting nothing. The truth of the matter seems to be that I got about as much as everyone else, and I have no complaint to make. I do not like to dig into an old sore which is certainly as painful to me as it could be to anyone, but I have a good memory and I remember what happened right after Papa's death in 1922, and almost, it seems to me, before he was buried—the bitterness and the suspicions and the recriminations and who had had the most and who should have it.

It is all over now, and I for one want to forget it, and I hope to God it is over forever, and never comes to life again, for of all the forms of human ugliness, money-ugliness is the most hateful and most damnable, and when it gets into families, there is hell to pay. The way I feel now, I would sooner have someone I thought was my friend betray me because of envy, jealousy, hatred, a desire to get revenge, or because he was in love with my girl, than sell me out for a few dirty dollars. You can get over the other things and still retain your faith in life, because at least what was done was done in human passion—but when they do a job on you because of money you feel like turning your face to the wall and admitting you have seen enough.

And that is the reason that I do not like it when the question of money comes up, and I want to go on record now about the future. I did not get more than my share in 1922, neither did I ever consider that I got less: I was not a martyr then and I am not a martyr now. I always considered that I got the equivalent of my five thousand dollars in the three years I went to Harvard: I signed a paper to that effect and gave it to Fred and Ralph right after Papa's death, I believe. So let us keep that straight. As to anything that may come out of this trial, or that you may recover, I do not expect anything, and if there is anything, I would like to see it applied first of all to Mama's support, then to helping you and Ralph, then to helping Effie and her children.

As to my own presence and testimony being of any help to you now, as you suggest, I am certainly willing to help you if I can, but I do not see what there is that I can do. I was never asked to take any part in the matter fifteen years or more ago. As far as Papa's will is concerned, I never saw it, I do not know what is in it. Fred and Ralph were appointed executors of the estate, which it seems to me was bad, for I think in a matter where emotion and personal feeling are involved, as they were in this case, members of the family should not be given such authority; and furthermore, I think it should never be given to members of a family like ours where, so far as I have been able to see, there is not a grain of business ability, except an almost unfailing instinct for doing the wrong thing. These are stern words, but you have got to admit that in view of everything that has happened, they are deserved: and I am saying them now because I wish for nothing but your success and the family's success in this trial, and because I hope to God that if anything comes of it and you recover anything, you will salt it down somewhere where the first plausible crook who comes along with a get-rich-quick scheme, or a project for making all of you fabulously rich by selling you Florida real estate, will not get it away from you. . . .

I am back at work again—this is the first time in almost three years when I have been left uninterrupted to do my work. I got no rest at home last summer, I have had none since then, in fact, I cannot remember when I did have any rest to amount to anything in the last six or eight years. But if I can go on and get my work done, all will be well. I had to pay my income tax the other day which is a joke—the income, not the tax. Scribners returned a report to the government that they had paid out to me in royalties, etc., something over three thousand dollars last year. They did not mention the fact, however, that I never saw a penny of this sum—that all of it was used up in the form of lawyer fees and payments in a suit which we should have fought, but which they were eager to settle. I suppose our lawyers in the bank case are working on a contingent basis: if they are, I hope you find out in advance how great the contingency is, and how big a portion they propose to take.

This is all now. I hope this finds you and Ralph feeling better, and the rest of the family well. Aside from being tired, I think I am all right. My new book is all clear in my mind, I know what it is all about from beginning to end, and in the last two years I have done a lot of writing on it. I work like hell, drive myself to the point of exhaustion, but of course I am a long-winded cuss and I write hundreds of thousands of words that I never use, and go through hell before I get through. But I will get through somehow, never fear. I do not think my time has come yet, maybe I'm being saved for cannon fodder when the Fascists try to take America, which is where I'll grab a musket and go to town; but I believe I will be able to hang on until this job is done. . . .

I hope this finds Mama well, and I send love and best wishes for success to all of you. Please let me know if there is anything you want me to do.

Frieda Kirchwey, editor of The Nation, *had written to Wolfe and various other authors, asking for statements as to "How to Keep Out of War." The following is Wolfe's reply which was published in the April 2, 1938, issue of* The Nation. *The covering letter, if there ever was one, has been lost.*

To THE EDITOR OF *THE NATION*

[New York City]

[March 20(?), 1938]

Aside from the question whether even peace can be worth any price that we can pay or that can be demanded of us—a view which was seriously maintained by many people until a year or two ago—I do not think that peace can ever be won and kept in such a way. I further think that "isolation" is a rhetorical concept, useful to politicians for the purpose of strengthening the majorities at home and of reassuring their constituencies, and perhaps useful to other people who project the metaphysical idea that it is possible for a nation of one hundred and thirty million people to live sealed up hermetically in peace in a world that is ravaged by war. Beyond this, I do not believe "isolation" has any real meaning in fact, because it has no existence in reality. It is a King Canute–Christian Science kind of word, which says, there is no sickness, there is no death; or if there is, let us ignore them. The peace of the whole means the peace of every one of its parts; and the sickness of the whole means the sickness of its parts.

Because I believe in individual security, I believe in collective security, and do not think it is possible to have one without the other. And, in view of the events of the past two years, it seems manifest that the only way to get security is through collective action. And, although I hope, together with most other people, that the necessity for force may be avoided, it cannot be avoided by denying that such a necessity may exist. It becomes increasingly apparent that the only effective way to meet armed aggression may be armed resistance: the wheels of a great war machine, such as that which Germany has today, are not going to be stopped, once they have begun to roll, by a handful of reproving phrases, or by a batch of diplomatic protests. Just as the foundations of Fascism are rooted in the hopelessness and despair of a bankrupt and defeated people who, having nothing more to lose, submit to any promises of gain —this would have been apparent to anyone who visited Germany as I did in 1928 and 1930—so does the success and growth of Fascism depend upon submission, and flourish upon compromise and vacillation.

All these facts have been apparent for years, and should have surprised no one: the only thing that is surprising now is that anyone should be surprised. Where have these surprised people been living for the past ten years? If anyone ever furnished the world with a blueprint of his intentions in advance, it was Adolf Hitler. Now, since he has checked his announced objectives off the list one by one with the precision of a riveting machine, it seems reasonable to suppose that he will continue to do so as long as he is unimpeded and as long as he realizes that there is no formidable and united force that will, if necessary, resist him.

I do not know any more than any man what form that force will take, or what will be the composition and alignment of its elements, because at the present moment it does not exist; but it is evident that if Fascism is to be checked, such a force will have to exist. The failure of the major democratic powers thus far effectively to oppose the aggressions of Germany, Italy and Japan has not weakened my belief in the possibility of collective action and has not destroyed my faith in the power of the major democratic powers to act effectively. Sooner or later, it seems to me, they will have to. They will have to when they decide that democracy is valuable enough to be saved, and is worth fighting for, if need be, by those who believe in it. In the end, I think we may all have to make that decision. For Fascism is a creature that thrives but is not appeased by compromise.

To MARGARET ROBERTS

> 114 East 56th Street
> New York, New York
> c/o Miss Elizabeth Nowell
> April 6, 1938

Dear Mrs. Roberts:

I was mighty glad to get your letter and sorry to know that you had been put to so much trouble and bother to get the material I asked for. I shall appreciate it all the more on account of the labor you have expended, and I can repeat my assurances that I shall take the greatest care of anything that is entrusted to me and see that it gets returned in good condition to its owner when I am done with it.

It is an immense undertaking that I have embarked on. A week or so ago I was so tired that I simply could not force myself another foot; so I went out in the country for several days, all of which did me a lot of good, but I have about reached the conclusion that when a man gives himself completely to a tremendous piece of work, there is just no such thing as rest, and he had better reconcile himself to it.

I saw an extraordinary Russian film the other night called "Lenin in October" which brought out that point very compellingly. In a scene where Lenin is in hiding in the furious days just preceding the Revolution, Lenin is pictured as saying to one of his associates who had been appointed to guard him and who had been on the job day and night without rest: "You ought to get some sleep." The man says that he will get some sleep after the Revolution. "After the Revolution," says Lenin, "we won't sleep at all." And maybe that is the way it has got to be.

It is curious how many hard and thorny things we find out about life, and how strangely palatable they become to us. It is all so different from what we imagined it was going to be when we were children, and curiously in so many ways it is so much better. I suppose like so many other boys, I pictured a future life of brilliant works crowned by success and fame and ease, and surcease from labor; but it does not work out that way at all. Work gets harder all the time because as one digs deeper one goes into the rock. And there is no rest—those periods of delightful relaxation as a kind of reward for work accomplished that I used to look forward to with such eagerness simply do not exist. Now I would say that almost the worst time in a writer's life are those periods between work— periods when he is too exhausted and feels too empty to attempt a new piece of work, or when a new piece of work is still cloudily formulating itself in his mind. It is really hell, or worse than hell, because writing itself is hell, and this period of waiting is limbo—floating around in the cloudy upper geographies of hell trying to get attached to something.

It just boils down to the fact that there is no rest, once the worm gets in and begins to feed upon the heart—there can never after that be rest, forgetfulness, or quiet sleep again. Somewhere long ago—God knows when, or at what fated moment in my childhood—the worm got in and has been feeding ever since and will be feeding till I die. After this happens, a man becomes a prisoner; there are times when he almost breaks free, but there is one link in the chain that always holds; there are times when he almost forgets, when he is with his friends, when he is reading a great book or a great poem, when he is at the theatre, or on a ship, or with a girl—but there is one tiny cell that still keeps working, working; even when he is asleep, one lamp that will not go out, that is forever lit.

It sounds pretty grim, but like so many other grim discoveries, it is not so grim once you recognize it, accept it, make up your mind to it. In fact, when I think of all the dreams I had as a boy—my idea of "happiness," "fame," and so on—I do not know that I would have them back again, even if I could recapture them; and as for this thing I used to call happiness, I am not so sure but that it, too, is a very hard and thorny thing, and not the smooth and palatable thing I thought it was. And I am perfectly sure that whatever it is, if it exists at all, it cannot exist without work—which would have been a strange doctrine indeed when I was twelve years old. As far as I am concerned, there is no life without work —at least, looking back over my own, everything I can remember of any value is somehow tied up with work.

What to do? Like you, I have become in the last few years tremendously involved with the state of the world—as my consciousness of life has enlarged, my consciousness of self has dwindled; there are things now that so afflict me in the state of man that I think I would take up arms against them, or give my life to stop them—but what to do? There is hardly a day goes by now but what people—for the most part, I think, sincere and genuine people—call me up or write me, and ask me to sign my name to a petition or proclamation of some sort, to go to Washington with a group to protest to the President about the state of things in Spain; to appear with a group at the French Consulate and protest to the French Consul about the state of things in Spain; to serve on committees of protest about the condition of the sharecroppers in the South— about the imprisonment of Tom Mooney—about the violation of civil liberties in various places—about the Scottsboro boys—about the Moscow trials—for or against the Stalinites or Trotskyites—but what to do, what to do?

To reject these pleas for help and demonstration often seems callously indifferent and self-centered, particularly when so many of them are about things with which my mind and conscience are now seriously involved; but in the name of God, what is a man like myself to do? The observation of Voltaire in *Candide* that at the end of all the best thing is for a man to tend his garden used to seem cynically and selfishly callous to me, but I am not so sure now that it does not contain much deep wisdom, and much humanity as well. Perhaps the best thing that a man can do is just to do the work he is able to do, and for which he is best fitted, as well as he can. And perhaps his greatest service to other men can be rendered in such a way as this.

I am solicited and persuaded on all sides now by worthy people to take sides and to make proclamations on all manner of things—there are so many writers and leagues of writers who are involved in all of this, but although I admire their energy and do not question their sincerity, I do not know when these writers write—or how they can possibly find time to write: one does not write books by carrying placards in front of the French Consulate, or having interviews with President Roosevelt. It is hard enough for me to get anything done anyway, because everything comes out with such a tremendous superflux, and calls for such infinite boiling down and rearrangement—but it seems to me the best course for me is to stick at it somehow, somehow by the grace of God to get it done, somehow to get it all wrought into a single and coherent vision of life, not just as a series of explosive and isolated protests.

I think I have ploughed to the bottom now as far as this present work is concerned. It has been going on for years and it has been hell because it involved, perhaps for the first time in my life, the creation of a whole universe of the imagination into which I could pour all the materials I had gathered. Now I think I have accomplished it, I have the whole thing launched and floated in my mind, and I believe I am the master of it: an enormous labor of completion and fulfillment is before me, but if I stick to it I shall get there. . . .

Just do the best you can for me about getting the material I asked you for, and I will try to deserve it by the use I make of it. . . . I suppose it is wise, as you say, to go about the business as discreetly as possible; but I do want to assure you again, and everyone else, that I have no intention of doing a job on Asheville. God knows, after what I have known and seen and lived through myself in the last few years, I am in no mood to exult and mock at the afflicted and tormented soul of man, particularly when it comes as close to home as this does. Time and again last summer I could have groaned in anguish at the things I saw: most pitiful and moving of all, perhaps, was the pretense—people with naked terror in their eyes still whistling to keep up their courage, still speaking the old words, the old spurious phrases that had lost whatever meaning they may once have had because they referred to something that was gone forever. And I think the people knew it. I could give you an account of a meeting of the Associated Civic Clubs at which I was present —a concerted effort or "drive," as it is called, to raise funds for a Convention Hall—it would be howlingly funny if it were not for the underlying tragedy and pathos of the situation.

There has been a good deal of talk about "the lost generation," meaning the young men who came up during and after the last war, but I wonder if the real lost generation is not these men of middle or advanced middle age, who keep saying the old phrases, trying to whoop it up in the old way over something that is gone forever. It made me think of a pep meeting in a morgue, a kind of cheering squad of ghosts. And, in the name of God, what are these men going to do? They have only one language, only one set of values: the language and the values were false to begin with, but now that they know that they were false, they have not even the conviction of their previous delusion to give them hope.

I am not lost because I accept and am ready to meet the future that is before us; but what are people to do when they cannot accept it, cannot face it, are looking forever backward at the image of a world that is gone? Do not think that I could be happy at the tragic spectacle, or take pleasure in flaying the hide off something that is already quivering and raw.

I wish I could come home quietly, as you suggest, and talk to some of the people you mention, but you know what happened last summer.

A prophet may be without honor in his own country, but he is also without privacy. I shall get out of town during the hot weather and go somewhere to work; but I simply cannot go through another summer like the last one, as interesting and overwhelming as it was, particularly now that I have plunged into this thing and must go on. . . .

Let me hear from you as soon as you are conveniently able. Meanwhile, I send you and Mr. Roberts all my good wishes and best regards.

P.S. There is a popular song called "Roses in December"—well, someone ought to write one now called "Snow in April." It is the sixth day of the month, and as I look out my window at the present moment the whole world—the roofs and buildings of New York—are white and blind with snow. It looks like a blizzard, the first we have had in this nothing-of-a-winter. April, April, laugh thy girlish laughter!

To BELINDA JELLIFFE

114 East 56th Street
New York, New York
c/o Miss Elizabeth Nowell

April 11, 1938

Dear Mrs. Jelliffe:

I was delighted to read the wonderful review you sent me of your book [1] from *The London Observer*. You should be very proud of it, and since I feel I had some share in making possible the publication of your book, I feel proud of this fine recognition, too.

I believe you are prone to overestimate the importance of those people who, you say, are eagerly waiting to see what I shall do without Mr. Perkins. I hope, indeed, that I shall never be without him; for I believe he is genuinely my friend, and will continue to be, and certainly he would himself, I think, be the first to regret such small and irresponsible talk. He is not a man who would allow vanity or wounded pride to obscure his sense of justice and fair play.

I do not know where such talk comes from, and do not believe there can be very much of it. As you may know, I have been through the mill for almost ten years now, and I am as familiar as anyone with all these manifestations, and am not inclined to let them affect me as deeply as they once did. Besides, the thing to which they refer is so completely and sorrowfully over that it can never be brought to life again; and now, since I have finally won through to a strength and repose that I have

[1] *For Dear Life.*

never had before, it can surely serve no good purpose on the part of those who count themselves my friends—and I know you are one of these—to attempt to revive them.

Therefore, since you yourself are so sure in your faith in me—a faith which I value—I hope you will not allow yourself to be troubled by such a report. As for myself, I should prefer not to listen to it, since I have so much else of deep importance to me now, and I know that you yourself wish only to join with my other friends in the hope that I will be allowed to proceed now to my accomplishment without further, and too often, ignoble interference.

For you, of course, and for your own work and accomplishment, I wish you now what I have wished you from the beginning, when I brought you and your manuscript to your present fine publisher [2]—only the highest and the best that you yourself could wish.

With all good wishes,

[2] Scribners.

XVIII

THE TRIP WEST AND FINAL ILLNESS

1938

On March 31, 1938, Professor S. A. Cummings of the Department of English at Purdue University had wired Wolfe, asking him to speak at the Literary Banquet to be held at that university on May 19. Wolfe had accepted, and had then received a letter from Professor Herbert J. Muller, also of the Department of English at Purdue, inviting him to stay at his house while he was there. The following was his reply.

Professor Muller is still in the English Department at Purdue and is the author of Thomas Wolfe *in the* Makers of Modern Literature *series; also of* Modern Fiction: A Study in Values; Science and Criticism; *and other books.*

To HERBERT J. MULLER

> Hotel Chelsea
> 222 West 23rd Street
> New York, New York
>
> April 11, 1938

Dear Professor Muller:

Thanks very much for your letter and kind invitation to stay with you and your wife while I am at Purdue.

I have had a telegram from Mr. S. A. Cummings confirming our agreement, and he said also that he was writing me. Thus far I have not had his letter, but I suppose when he writes he will explain to me more fully just what the nature of the University occasion is, and what I should prepare for. I sent him quite a long telegram expressing my interest and my appreciation in his invitation, and I also asked him if he would not let me know more fully what he had in mind. I explained to him that I was hard at work on a new book and that I would not, therefore, be able to take time off now for the preparation of a formal speech. But I also tried to explain that I thought what I had to say might be more interesting if I talked informally, and out of my own working and writing experience. That is really what I have in mind. Since my present life is largely writing—for even when I am not actually engaged on it, I am thinking about it—it seems to me that anything I had to say might be more interesting if I drew it out of my own experience, and from the work I do. I should deeply appreciate it if you could write me and let me know your own opinion on this, and give me what advice you can, and tell me what I can expect when I get there.

It is most kind and generous of you to offer me the hospitality of your home while I am at Lafayette, and I hope you can hold the offer open; but I should prefer not to answer definitely now until I hear from Mr. Cummings, or until I find out how long I shall be there. I am looking forward to my trip with great interest and expectation. I have been pretty steadily at work, and shall continue to be until I leave for Lafayette, and the break in routine will not only be a most welcome one, but I think will be a most refreshing one, too. Please write me if it is convenient, and give me what advice you can on the questions I have raised. Meanwhile, with renewed thanks for your kind invitation, and with all good wishes,

To HERBERT J. MULLER

> Hotel Chelsea
> 222 West 23rd Street
> New York, New York
>
> April 15, 1938

Dear Professor Muller:

Thanks very much for writing me so promptly and giving me an idea of what is ahead of me. I feel much easier about the whole thing now, and believe I can swing it well enough. Of course, I am no sort of public speaker, but I did speak to a gathering similar to this at the University of Colorado two or three years ago and, after the first few minutes of fumbling and stumbling around, I got hold of what I wanted to say and did very well. The only trouble was that after I did get wound up it was hard to stop: I offered to at the end of three-quarters of an hour, but they very generously told me to go on. But I know what a bore a long-winded speaker can be on an occasion like this, at a banquet; so I will try to hold myself down within reasonable limits.

I hate to bother you again, but since you have so kindly given me such useful and reassuring information already, perhaps you would enlighten me on one or two other details. My wardrobe at the present time is decidedly threadbare and scanty, but I do have one pretty good blue suit and a tuxedo. I thought I would bring both along, and hope these will meet the sartorial requirements of the occasion acceptably.

Yes, I certainly would like to get together with you before the dinner and have a cocktail or two, not only for convivial reasons but because of the moral fortification they may supply. And after it is over, I am looking forward to relaxing and enjoying myself, and it would be a great pleasure to meet and talk to some of you.

I have mislaid the first telegram that Professor Cummings sent me, but I am sure that he said the date of the meeting is May 19. At any rate, I am making plans to be in Lafayette on that date, and shall arrange to leave here in sufficient time. Thank you again for all your kind assistance. With all good wishes,

Because of his new conviction that "You Can't Go Home Again," Wolfe had begun looking for a place in which to spend the summer in New York State, New Jersey, Pennsylvania or New England. Marjorie Fairbanks had suggested that he rent the Shaker House at Harvard, Massachusetts, and the following was his reply.

To MARJORIE C. FAIRBANKS

Hotel Chelsea
222 West 23rd Street
New York City

April 23, 1938

Dear Marjorie:

By all means find out about the Shaker house. I do not know what I would do with twenty rooms, unless I wrote a chapter in each of them, and some of the things I may write would give even the Shakers the Shakes, but the big meeting room as a place to work sounds wonderful, and, in fact, the idea of the whole thing sounds good if there are not too many complications and if it does not cost too much. I certainly appreciate your finding out about things so promptly, because now is the time, if ever, I should be getting things settled.

Ed Aswell, my friend at Harper's, and his wife are starting out with me next weekend in our jaunt around the countryside to look the terrain over. He is himself a Harvard University man, and he also has been to

Harvard, Mass., which he says is beautiful. But I do not know whether he is going to be able to swing it into his circle next week, for he has several things in mind, and we will only have two days to do it in. But if you find anything that looks good, let me know and I will come up some Saturday or Sunday between now and the time I go out to Purdue and look it over.

And again, thanks for all the trouble you are taking. It really means a lot to me to find a good place now, because last summer was a disappointment as far as work is concerned and now that I have got going again on a tremendous job—by far the biggest I have ever undertaken—a good place to work is mighty important. I think you understand pretty well what I want and need, and certainly I do not want to be pampered —but I have not time now to learn cooking, striking a fire between two flints, or other boy-scout tricks. Aside from the time I am taking off in May for my jaunt to the Middle West, I hope to keep going right through the summer, and anything anyone can do to further me in that design will be deeply and sincerely appreciated.

Thanks for writing the people at Olivet.[1] I am pretty tired and I do not know how much speaking I am going to be up to, but anything that would help out on expenses would be worth considering. And let me know also if you are going to be out there at about the same time as I am. You should not miss the Chicago stockyards. I have been through twice, and so far from being shocked, I found it a very wholesome and edifying spectacle, as a good many forceful and natural physical things are apt to be.

This is all for the present. It is a beautiful day here, and I envy you Single Tax plutocrats of Harvard, Mass. But I have got to work now, and so good-bye.

P.S. And by the way, if the Shaker house is available, what kind of complications are there—if any? That is, would I have it to myself, or do they still hold meetings there on Sunday etc.?

Over the weekend of May 1st, the Aswells had driven Wolfe through upper New York state and had taken him to stay at the house of their friends, Dr. and Mrs. A. P. Saunders, of Clinton. The following is his bread-and-butter letter, written the day after he returned. Dr. Saunders was Professor of Chemistry and formerly Dean at Hamilton College, and a horticulturalist specializing in the propagation of rare peonies.

[1] Mrs. Fairbanks had written to Joseph Brewer, who was President of Olivet College, to suggest that Wolfe might speak there after his talk at Purdue.

To DR. AND MRS. A. P. SAUNDERS

Hotel Chelsea
222 West 23rd Street
New York, New York
May 3, 1938

Dear Dr. and Mrs. Saunders:

We all got back in good condition yesterday afternoon, and I am writing to tell you both what a delightful and extraordinary trip it was, and that I shall never forget it.

Your house is amazing and beautiful—and I think of the whole place, the country, the campus, the trees, the flowers, and the people, as if I had just returned from a visit to the Elysian fields. Was it not Wordsworth who said: "A primrose by the river's brim, a simple primrose was to him," etc.—well, if it was, I have been telling people since I got back that one cannot even take primroses for granted at Hamilton—if he does, he will find that a primrose by the river's brim is really a rare and precious plant on which a whole encyclopaedia of knowledge, culture, love and tender care has been expended. It did me an amazing amount of good to be there and to see it all—no matter how often I come back (and I hope I have the opportunity again), I shall never forget the magic of this first trip.

Our ride down was also beautiful—the weather was glorious, everything turned out beautifully, we even found the fish place in Catskill and had Hudson River shad. We made good time, and Ed delivered me to the Harmon train yards four minutes after five o'clock. I was home shortly after six, and the Aswells, I am sure, got home before that time.

I am now about to be guilty of the supreme immodesty of sending you a photograph of the undersigned in his most recent state of dilapidation. You said you wanted it, so henceforth the consequences are on your own head. If it wilts the flowers, darkens the cheerful atmosphere of your household with its all-pervasive gloom, or causes the other photographs to shudder and withdraw and turn their faces to the wall, I accept no further responsibility. I am sending it to you in a separate envelope, and I hope this does not put me under the penalties of the acts for using the mails to defraud.

I am back at work again, it is past twelve o'clock, and I have not even been out to get my breakfast yet. Even breakfast is something that they only have at Hamilton.

With love and all good wishes to you both,

P.S. I did not sign the photograph, because I did not know if you wanted it that way. If you do, I will sign it the next time I see you.

The following letter was written in answer to one from Mrs. Roberts saying that a prominent citizen of Asheville would lend Wolfe the complete files of The Asheville Advocate, *the publication of the Asheville Taxpayers' League, if he would put up a thousand dollar bond to ensure their safe return.*

To MARGARET ROBERTS

114 East 56th Street
New York, New York
c/o Miss Elizabeth Nowell

May 3, 1938

Dear Mrs. Roberts:

Thanks very much for your letter and for the information in it. I am deeply sorry to think that you have been put to so much trouble in this matter, but I want you to know how much I appreciate it.

Now about Mr. T——'s proposal. Frankly, I am afraid what he suggests is out of the question. It may be possible, as he says, to secure a thousand dollar bond at no greater expense than five dollars to myself. But that is not the point. The point, it seems to me, lies in the responsibility he asks me to assume, and the value he attaches to his papers. It may be perfectly true that he "would not take a thousand dollars for them." But it is also true that probably no one else would give a thousand dollars for them. Certainly I would not, and I would not, therefore, care in any way, however hypothetical, to involve myself for any such amount. What he has may be very rare and precious. Not having seen it, I cannot judge. But I have also learned, from past experience, that there are many people who put an utterly unreasonable value on something that may be of very little worth.

For example, after "Of Time and the River" appeared, I received a long and rambling letter from an apparently illiterate man in Florida, who announced that he was a "doctor" who would like to build a new house and office, and take some graduate work in medicine, and would, therefore, very generously sell me his life story (which would make me fabulously rich and famous, of course) at the knock-down price of twenty-five thousand dollars. I was also besieged, tormented, interrupted, and interfered with last summer by hordes of people who could obviously do very little more than write their own names, if their literary talents went so far, but who were generously trying to cram down my throat wads of manuscript, life stories, "great ideas" and so on, that would make me immensely wealthy—and would result in "a greater book" than "Gone With the Wind." God knows why that immortal piece of bilge was invariably selected as the almost ne plus ultra in literary achievement, but invariably it was. There is also the kind of person—seven million, two hundred and sixty-seven thousand, by the most recent and conserva-tive count—who, unsolicited, send manuscripts of poems, plays and novels, and what-not to a defenseless author, and offer to split the stag-gering royalties, fifty-fifty, if he will only "write it up good" for them— I presume, in his off moments from carousing around with the Bohemian literary gang, on a quiet weekend.

All this is pretty brutal, but I have suffered from it for years. There was one painted hag last summer who wormed the location of my cabin from my sometimes too garrulous mother, hunted me out, and then de-manded that I read a manuscript of one thousand, four hundred and sixty-two handwritten pages, rewrite and revise it for her, tell her "what to do with it," find a publisher for her—all within two weeks' time. The plain truth is, the more worthless the material, the more deluded is its possessor in his estimate of its priceless value.

I had thought perhaps that I might be willing to pay as much, say, as twenty-five dollars for the loan of the papers for a few weeks—which certainly strikes me as being munificently and extravagantly generous for a file of newspapers in an obscure weekly sheet, in a small town. Mr. T—— has other notions, apparently, and while not disputing his own personal sense of their value, I simply cannot agree with him. Moreover, his frantic haste for their return is decidedly perplexing: if they had any value, to get them back within ten days or two weeks, or thirty days, would be absurd. I am a serious and hard-working man, I am engaged upon a tremendous piece of work—whatever value such information as this might be, it would only be a portion of the whole, and I cannot agree to such unreasonable demands. So we will have to call this portion of it off.

As to —— ——. I am perfectly willing to write him, and should be grateful for any information that he might give, but if he has as many sore toes to be stepped on as you say he has, perhaps I had better not try. Frankly, I am a little tired of taking it on the chin from these small-town liberals, these leaders of enlightened thought, these Buncombe County . . . Socialists who are all for social reform, world revolution, and what-not, but who are all undone when you mention casually some good old Anglo-Saxon four-letter word that can be found repeatedly in Shakespeare or in the King James version of the Bible.

When I was a child, the poet, the artist, the creative man was held up to me as an ideal of the highest and the best in human life—the man who bravely and truthfully wrought out his vision of the world, at no matter what the cost to him, according to the dictates of his conscience and his talent. In later years, when I tried to do the same thing myself, it was shocking and bewildering to find out that I was most bitterly denounced and execrated by some of the very people who had held this ideal before me—to find out that it is noble to tell the truth, so long as the truth is not too close at home, and does not refer to the wart upon Aunt Nellie's chin.

I am not bitter, but I am through with apology. The only apology I have now to make is to my conscience, to the knowledge wherein I may have failed, to the things to which I may have been unfair, to the things in which I did not fulfill myself and my work as completely as I should. I lived out my exile for more than seven years and then went back, and I saw what I saw, I know what I know. I know now that you can't go back—there is no turning back; with that knowledge also came a deeper feeling of compassion and of understanding for stricken people. But no apologies—they are not needed, they are not due. I was a citizen of Asheville, and I am now a citizen of mankind—there is my loyalty, and that is where it must go.

I know you can help me in this thing more than anyone I know at home, for I believe you understand better than anyone else what I am after. There is nothing very complex or mysterious about it; I know some other people who, I think, may help out, too, and who may have kept the records that I want, and I shall write them. When I was home last summer, I was given to understand that it would be very simple to provide them, but of course, as so often happens, results are harder to achieve than promises. If I cannot get them, I shall have to do without; but I have done without before, and I shall get along.

I do not want to harass you or Mr. Roberts with a matter that has already, I know, cost you so much of your generous time and care. But if you will keep trying and let me know what you find, I shall be grateful, and, as I said before, I think the result may be worth it in the end. Do not offend T——, simply tell him that I appreciate his position, but did not feel that I could obligate myself in so large a sum; and that I appreciate his interest and his offer.

This is all now. I have been pretty tired, for I have gone through a long, hard winter here with publishers, law suits, and finally, with the thing I want to do—work. . . . I am going out to Purdue University in about two weeks to talk to a student gathering there, and then I am going to take a short vacation. When I get back here in June, I am going somewhere out of town, and get back to work again. If I do not hear from you before then, I hope to hear from you when I come back. Meanwhile, with all good wishes to you and Mr. Roberts,

To ELIZABETH NOWELL

Hotel Chelsea
222 West 23rd Street
New York, New York
May 3, 1938

Dear Miss Nowell:

I came back last night and got your note with the letter from *The New Yorker*.[1] I think you are handling it just right—and we undoubtedly will have something sooner or later that we want to send them—perhaps even good "Dr. Turner" [2] if I get around to giving him another go. But there will be many others as well.

Anyway, I want to see you very soon now before I go West and go over the whole business with you. I have only got an even two weeks from today, and I think it would be a good idea if we could get together sometime this week—say, Saturday or Sunday. The most immediate thing of interest I want to talk to you about is this: I finally wrote *The Nation* and rejected the proposal for the "Living Philosophies" piece,[3] on the ground that it would take too much time, and would take me away from my work. At the same time I made another suggestion to them. I told them about the Purdue engagement, and told them that I proposed to go out and talk to the students right out of the workshop, so to speak —to tell them what I thought and felt about writing, what I think I have learned about it, what change and development has come about in me, and what convictions and beliefs I now have, not only about writing, but about the life around me from which I draw the sources of my material, and the writer's place in the whole world today.

As you know, this has been the principal thing that has interested me for at least a year now, it is at the bottom of everything that has happened—beginning with the *New Republic* piece,[4] leading up through all the Scribner trouble to the place where I now am, and the work I am now doing. I believe the time has come when I am ready to say it, and if the time has come and I can say it, it will knock the *New Republic* piece into a cocked hat because it will shoot the works.

---

[1] A letter from the editors of *The New Yorker* saying they would be glad to see more stories by Wolfe.

[2] The piece about "Dr. Turner" was published under the title "Portrait of a Literary Critic" in the April, 1939, issue of *The American Mercury*, and is included in *The Hills Beyond*.

[3] Frieda Kirchwey of *The Nation* had written Wolfe asking him to write a 3,000 word essay on his philosophy of life for publication in *The Nation* and later inclusion in a book to be published by Simon and Schuster under the title of *Living Philosophies*.

[4] "I Have a Thing to Tell You."

What I did, therefore, first of all, was simply to dictate a very plain and simple account of things to use at the Purdue gathering. Of course, it is immensely too long, and besides towards the end there are many, many things in it of too personal and complex a nature for an occasion of that sort. However, it did serve the purpose of getting certain things on record, and as for the Purdue thing, I do not think I shall have any difficulty with that at all, nor even to refer to a typed sheet, because I know pretty clearly in my mind now what I am going to say to them, and what will probably be most appropriate for an occasion like that.

The Nation suggested that I show them the Purdue thing pretty much as I have it for the students, but I do not want to do this, because I think the final outcome may be so much better. Briefly, what I am trying to do, as with everything in which I am most deeply interested, is to give the piece at the end the depth and permanence of imaginative truth. I hope this does not make you smile—for that is the idea.

For months now, it has occurred to me that I would conclude the tremendously long book on which I am working with a kind of epilogue that takes the form of personal address—to be called, "You Can't Go Home Again" or "A Farewell to the Fox," or perhaps by still another title.[5] That epilogue, as I have conceived it, would be a kind of impassioned summing up of the whole book, of everything that has gone before, and a final statement of what is now. The book will certainly close in some such way as this, although it may turn out at the end that the method of personal address, even in high poetic terms, is not the best way to conclude a book in which the whole narrative, hundreds of characters, and the events of more than a hundred years are stated objectively. However that may be, it is not important here, for if I succeed in doing "You Can't Go Home Again," or "A Farewell to the Fox," as I want to do it, it will stand most tremendously on its own legs. Anyway, that is what I am doing now: transforming the material for the simple Purdue statement into the terms of poetic and imaginative fact—into the truth of fiction—because it seems to me that is really my essential job. What do you think of it?

I have written *The Nation* and more or less committed myself to letting them see it, but of course, three thousand words is nonsense— thirty thousand probably will be likelier, if I can hold it down to that —they realize, although I have not explained to them what it is as I have to you—that the thing is probably out of the question for them—unless they want to pull a big one, and match their distinguished rival [6] of a

[5] This appears as the seventh and final portion of *You Can't Go Home Again* under the title of "A Wind Is Rising, and the Rivers Flow."

[6] *The New Republic.*

year ago. This, of course, in case it is good. Sooner or later, it will be good, it must be, because it is so deep in me—but I hope it is good now. I have only two weeks more to work on it—and if I was fresh, I believe I could almost put it through, because usually the length of time a piece of writing takes—the best writing, that is—can never be reckoned except in terms of the days and months and years it has been coming to a head. That certainly has happened with this one—and I know that I am ready; but it may be I have to take another breather before I put it through. I suppose I may take the Purdue trip as the chance to get one—the chance to get away by myself on a streamlined train for a week or two—before I come back and settle in for the summer. . . .

This is all now, and I hope this finds you well. With best wishes,

To FRIEDA KIRCHWEY

Hotel Chelsea
222 West 23rd Street
New York, New York
May 4, 1938

Dear Miss Kirchwey:

The attached letter was "wrote sarcastical," and if you have space for it and think it good enough, you can print it.[1] If you do, I wish you would check up on one or two details of fact. I have been unable to find the newspaper which contained an account of Franco's efforts to encourage the tourist trade this summer, but I am quite sure it was in *The New York Times* within the past two weeks, in a dispatch written by a man named Carney. If you use the letter, I would like to check up on this detail in advance, and since you probably have a file of *The Times* for the past two or three weeks, someone in your office could check up on it without much difficulty.

To the Editor of *The Nation*

Sir:

A recent dispatch in *The New York Times* announces that General Francisco Franco is making arrangements for the reception of the tourist trade in Spain this summer, and I am writing to inquire if someone in your Travel Department could inform me if there are going to be any personally conducted tours.

I have never been to Spain, but like many other Americans, its ro-

---

[1] This letter was published in "Letters to the Editor" in the May 21, 1938, issue of *The Nation*.

mantic charm has always exerted a strong influence upon my imagination, and since I have read with great interest the recent remarks of
Mr. Ellery Sedgwick, and his account of what General Franco is doing
in the interests of his people, my desire to visit Spain has naturally
been increased.

For what could be more delightful than the charm of the old Spain,
so to speak, now so happily combined, as Mr. Sedgwick describes it to us,
with the progressive and liberalizing leadership of the new. It is certainly
a proposition that should excite the imagination of every good American
because to the prospect of ancient customs and historical relics—a
prospect always fascinating to citizens of our own young country—is
added the healthy and invigorating assurance that Spain, under General
Franco's leadership, has not allowed herself to lag behind in the pit of
medievalism, but is going forward. Indeed, what could be a better indication of this new progressive spirit in modern Spain than General
Franco's efforts to stimulate and encourage, in a businesslike and yet attractive manner, the healthful and peaceful propagation of the tourist
industry.

According to the account I read in the reliable *Times,* no effort or
expense has been spared to make Spain an agreeable resort this summer
for the hordes of tourists from across the Atlantic who will flock there.
General Franco, for example, has ordered sixty new and brightly painted
charabancs, which will swiftly and comfortably transport the tourists from
one end of his beautiful country to the other. In addition, it is understood that he has not only taken considerable pains in the work of restoring and preserving the most notable of the ancient ruins, but he
has also shown extraordinary ingenuity in the creation of new ones, all
of which will now be within easy and delightful access of the inquiring
tourist, through the avenues and agencies that General Franco has so
thoughtfully opened.

For my part, although I by no means share the too general lack of
interest and veneration for the monuments of antiquity, I must confess
that on the whole the evidences of the modern spirit are more exciting
to me. In other words, if I had to choose between two sets of ruins, I
should be inclined to visit the new ones rather than the old.

To mention but a few that have already suggested themselves to my
awakened curiosity—I should like, if opportunity presents itself, to visit
the various craters and ruined masonries throughout the town of Bar-
celona, paying particular attention to the subway entrance where a bomb
exploded, and where one hundred and twenty-six men, women and children were killed in one economical gesture. I should like to visit the
ruins of Madrid, the ruined villages around Teruel; and being of a re-

ligious turn of mind, I should like to pay a visit of devotion and respect to the Chapel, a photograph of which was recently reproduced in the press, where General Franco's wife and daughter go to offer prayers for the success of the Defender of the Faith. There are many other places of historic and memorable interest which I should also like to visit, but I will not try your patience with a further record of them.

Anyway, if someone in your own Travel Department could inform me what arrangements have been made for the conduct of these tours, I should be grateful to him.

To MARJORIE C. FAIRBANKS

Hotel Chelsea
222 West 23rd Street
New York, New York

May 4, 1938

Dear Marjorie:

Thanks for all the additional trouble you have gone to in my behalf.[1] I do not know whether I will be able to get up to explore your findings before I go West, because I have only two weeks more, and I have just come back from the luxury of a long weekend. But I will be grateful if you just keep plugging, and if you find anything you could tell me about it if you come West.

I had a very nice letter from Mr. Brewer,[2] inviting me to come to Olivet, and even suggesting a fee, although he did not say how much. I have just written him and thanked him for his invitation, but decided it was best not to make any more commitments as far as speaking engagements are concerned. I suppose I might do it and get several of them, and make some money, but I am fagged out, and am really using this Purdue thing as a kind of springboard to a holiday. Since I have to come back here later on, move out of town somewhere and get to work again, I think I had better make the most of the short vacation time I have. But I do hope to see you if you go out to Olivet, it would be nice to see the others, too.

Brewer tells me Ford Madox Ford is staying with him and is "most anxious" to see me again, and although our acquaintanceship was very brief—a cocktail party, I believe, in Paris years ago—I might be able to do something to relieve an anxiety that has extended over all these years.

---

[1] Mrs. Fairbanks had written him further about places which he could rent for the summer.

[2] Joseph Brewer, who at that time was President of Olivet College.

I certainly have read some of Ford's books, and deeply respected the craftmanship and skill that was in them, because they contained so much that I myself could wish to attain; but otherwise, I imagine we are at different ends of the writing stick. I am awfully tired, it will all come out all right with a few days' rest and a complete break-away, but I am simply not up to the higher reaches of Left Bank or Left Wing dialectics at the present time; something simple and corn-fed with large open spaces in it is more in my present line.

From what Brewer says, Olivet cannot be very far from Purdue. He did not know where Purdue is, but you might tell him it is a sizeable institution of ten or twelve thousand students, located at Lafayette, Indiana, which is sixty miles northwest of Indianapolis, and I judge no more than a hundred and fifty from Olivet.

Please write and let me know what you are going to do, Marjorie. That invitation to take you on a personally conducted tour through the stockyards of Chicago still holds. After that, I know a place where you can really get a wonderful thick and juicy sirloin. . . .

With best wishes,

To S. A. CUMMINGS

Hotel Chelsea
222 West 23rd Street
New York, New York

May 5, 1938

Dear Professor Cummings:

Thanks very much for your letter. I am glad you got the photograph and biographical material from Harper's, and hope you found the material useful.

I think that everything, thanks to you and Professor Muller, is now perfectly clear in my mind, about the nature of the occasion, and what I am to do. I shall probably come out a day in advance, and spend the night in Indianapolis, and although I am pretty tired just now, having put in a long stretch of work, I think I will be in good shape for the talk, for I am really approaching it in a kind of holiday spirit, and with a sense of anticipation. In fact, I think it is going to give me the stimulus and relief of a much needed change.

I am pretty clear in my mind about what I am going to say. I am delighted to know that I shall have as much as fifty minutes or an hour to speak in and I shall try neither to misuse or over-use my time. About the talk itself: I have already written down in very simple form what I want to say—just for the sake of getting it objectively stated. But I do not think I will even refer to a typed page, when I get up to talk, because I think I may do better without it. Now this is what I have in mind:

As I told you in a previous letter, I want to make this a kind of "workshop talk"—that is, a very simple account of a writer's work and his beliefs and convictions about writing, drawn directly from his own experience. I am glad to know you have read "The Story of a Novel," and that it interested you—and that you would not object if I drew on it for material. That will be very helpful—I also had this in mind: "The Story of a Novel" was written almost three years ago, and was a kind of summary or record of my writing experience up to that time. I think there has been another development since then, and with your permission I should like to try to tell about it in my talk. It is this:

In the past three years, in particular, I have thought more and more of the writer's relation to the world around him, and what effect it has, or ought to have, on his own work. Briefly, my own experience, which I think is fairly typical of the experience of many writers, has been this: I began life, as many young men do, as a lyrical writer. That is, I wanted to express my vision of life and of the world largely in terms of my own youth and my own personality. At college and later on, when I first began to write, I went through one of the usual periods of aesthetics—that is, seeing the life of the artist and his work in aesthetic terms: perhaps you could call it a somewhat "ivory tower" view of things. As I grew older, and as I continued to work, my view began to change, and I think this, too, was natural and inevitable. That is to say, as I grew older, I think I was not so much preoccupied with the concerns and purposes of my own youth. The field of my objectivity widened—with greater maturity and experience, I believe I began to look at the life around me more objectively—to see things and people and the world in a more objective way.

This, briefly, is what I should like to tell the students. I believe I may be able to do it in very clear and simple terms. I may have something to say about the "ivory tower" view of things in terms of a writer's work and whether it now seems to me that a creative writer's work ought or ought not to reflect an interest in the political and economic life of his time, but I assure you that my talk will be in no sense of the word political, nor do I have any axe to grind for propaganda.

I might describe the talk I have in mind as a series of concentric circles, tracing briefly and simply the stages of my own development. I suppose the root of the thing is that I want to tell the students about the writer and his life not merely in terms of writing, but in terms of living also. In other words, humorously we might call the talk, "Are Writers Human?" (please do not use that one, though). But I do want to show them if I can that the writer is not a strange and mysterious creature, but very definitely a citizen of mankind, a living, breathing, acting member of the human race, with work to do, a place to fill, a function to perform like everyone. What do you think of this for a title: Writing and Living [1] —or does that seem too general and diffuse to you? That is really what the talk is about, if it meets your approval, and I can put it over clearly—and if you think the title is all right, you can use it.

I think this clears up everything. You have all been very kind and helpful, and I think it is very generous of Professor Muller to offer to drive me over from Indianapolis. I will let him know by telegram when I am arriving, and I am looking forward to meeting all of you in about two weeks' time. And if my outline of what I want to say does not satisfy you, please do not hesitate to write and let me know what you think.

With all good wishes,

To EDWARD C. ASWELL

Hotel Chelsea
222 West 23rd Street
New York, New York

May 6, 1938

Dear Ed:

. . . I have only about ten days more here before I go out to Purdue, and I hope to see you again before I go. I shall certainly call you up and talk to you. I think we [1] are going to be pretty busy for several days next week assembling the manuscript and packing away the other manuscript I shall not use. I wonder if it would be possible for you to take the assembled manuscript and put it in a place of safekeeping there at Harpers until I come back from the West. It is going to make a very large and bulky package, or possibly a series of them, but we will try to devise some means for getting it together in its present form in the most logical and accurate sequence.

Although I have not begun this work yet and cannot say for sure, I have a very strong conviction that I have now reached about the same state of articulation as I had reached with "Of Time and the River"

[1] This was the title finally used.

[1] Wolfe and his secretary at that time, Miss Gwen Jassinoff, now Mrs. Peter Campbell.

in the month of December, 1933. It was at this time that Mr. Perkins saw that manuscript in its entirety for the first time. What he saw, of course, was only a kind of enormous skeleton, but at any rate, he was able to get some kind of articulate idea of the whole. It was at that time that we went over the whole thing together, decided in general terms on the cycle of the book and on the immediate labor that remained to be done. From that point on, I moved very rapidly to completion. The whole book was written and finished within the course of the following year: although it did not appear until March, 1935, we were getting the proofs of it in November and December, 1934, within a year after we had gone over the first skeleton carefully together.

I mention all of this to you not because I think we established any kind of historic precedent that has to be invariably followed, but as indicating to you the state of things as they now stand. From the first, I have been very careful not to commit myself to any promises as to when the manuscript will be finished and ready for publication, and you have been very fair and generous in understanding this and in not asking me to make such commitments. I shall not do so now, but I can tell you that I hope with a good year of steady uninterrupted work, to complete the job. Please do not take this as a promise, but only as an expression of a reasonable hope.

The book will be a much bigger book—at least, in its first completed form—than "Of Time and the River." It will deal with a much greater sweep of time—over one hundred years, in fact. It will deal with a much greater variety of scenes, of characters, of events than "Of Time and the River," and it will present a narrative that is much more continuous and closely-woven, and that has, therefore, made a much more exacting demand upon my powers of invention and creation than anything I have done before.

I ask you to bear this in mind, because I want you to be aware of the magnitude of the task before us. I know, and deeply appreciate, your patience and your desire to help in any way you can. It would perhaps be a good idea if you could familiarize yourself, so far as possible, with this first great batch of manuscript when I give it to you, but I am not sure about that yet until I have seen it all together myself. However, we shall see what we shall see.

My own very strong conviction at present is this: I have never been so clear in my mind before as to what I am after, and what I want to do. The analogy to "Of Time and the River" is a physical one rather than an artistic one. In other words, my very strong hunch at present is that it may be best to allow me to proceed with my work without any great assistance until I have brought it to a further state of development and completion. At the same time, it might be a good idea if the editor did get a general idea of the whole thing now.

I do not believe that I am in need of just the same kind of editorial help at this moment as Mr. Perkins so generously and unselfishly gave me in 1933, 1934. At any rate, since the whole process [is that] of trying to learn, like little Duncan,[2] to stand erect, to toddle, and then to walk by myself, it might be better for me to go on by myself for awhile, and see what happens. It is, of course, comforting and of immense value to me to know that when I do need help it will be generously and patiently given. At any rate, I hope that is the program for the present, and that you can take care of the manuscript for me until I get back.

I really do feel it is pretty important for me to get some rest now, because such a tremendous job is before me—and for the past three years at least, what with law suits, publishing troubles, and an effort to get my work accomplished, there has been no let-up. I am due at Purdue on May 19, and where I shall go from there I shall try to keep my little secret. But I will not be gone for long and will see you early in June, at any rate. . . .

With best wishes,

To MABEL WOLFE WHEATON

> 114 East 56th Street
> New York, New York
> c/o Miss Elizabeth Nowell
> May 10, 1938

Dear Mabel:

I was glad to get your letter and to have the news. I certainly hope that the bank case turns out favorably and that if the lawyers make a compromise it will be a worthwhile one. I am glad you went to see Carter and tried to get some definite idea from him what he would charge, or how big a cut he expects to take. You will find that is pretty important. It is not just mere bitterness, but actual experience, that makes me say that lawyers are out, first and foremost, for themselves. This is the truth. I have found that it is a kind of great closed corporation that exists primarily for the benefit and profit of those who are engaged in it as against the rest of the world.

From my own point of view, in its present form, the profession of law as it exists in this country ought to be abolished. But it can't because the system we have produced and under which we live has created the

[2] Aswell's son, Edward Duncan Aswell, who at this time was 20 months old.

lawyer. He is a kind of parasite with a recognized established position. Our system makes it possible for a great many unscrupulous and dishonest people to take advantage of other people—to sue them, or to threaten them, or to try to worry and harass them in such a way they will pay out money to be left alone. For this reason we have the lawyer.

The lawyer works both ways, either as a representative of dishonest and unscrupulous people who say "here is a chance to get some money," or as a representative of honest people who have to defend themselves. In both cases, obviously, it is the lawyer who wins out: the so-called good lawyer gets in touch with a so-called shyster, they put their heads together and try to work out a compromise—a compromise for everybody but the lawyer. The reputable lawyer will tell you that it is all a great pity and that he himself, of course, is a very honest, noble, upright citizen, there to protect your interests against the practices of the shyster. But I am afraid that most of them—even the so-called good and upright ones—have a good deal of the shyster in them—for they are always trading and bargaining with shysters, and it is their fault, more or less, that shysters exist—that is, they all play in together: the good lawyer gets a large part of his living from the fact that the crooked lawyer is allowed to exist and menace people. He can, therefore, hold himself up as a model of righteousness and a guardian of one's interest against the forces that prey on one. But he, too, is a member of the whole bad system.

You and I were never taught this when we were children, and we were never taught a whole lot of things we should have known, and that might have been a great deal more useful to us than a great many things we were taught. We were never taught, for example, to question the life around us, which was the little world of Asheville, which in its turn is the whole world of America. If we questioned the essential and beautiful rightness of anything, we were labeled a "radical," "queer," a "freak," and all the rest of it. As a result, you are to-day in middle age a baffled person, and I am having to begin my education all over again. But I am not baffled and I am not defeated, and I think it would be a great pity if anyone with as much intelligence and energy as you have continue to allow yourself to be baffled and defeated. You and I are not going to change the world, but we can both work for a better one, and in that direction lies hope and new life, and not defeat.

Just to reassure you, and to let you know where I stand, I would like to say that I like people everywhere and my own country, America, much more than I ever did before. But I think that people everywhere have been generally misused and exploited, and I think that America, which is such a beautiful and wonderful country, has been taken away from the people to whom it should belong and given largely into the hands of a few of the exploiters.

I am afraid you will consider this "queer talk" or "radical talk" or "communistic talk," and for that reason I have felt very sorry about you all. You have been chewed up by the existing order and system of things —I will just mention the Asheville boom, the way the —— —— —— Company treated Ralph, etc.—and it never occurred to you to question or resent the thing that was chewing you up. It was right because it happened to exist, and you accepted it. Well, that's no reason for accepting anything—and you are not a radical or queer because you question and resent it and want to change it. Unless you do, I don't think you can have much hope in the future. You will go on feeling more and more defeated, vainly pining for what is gone and will never come back again—Asheville during the boom, insane speculation, Grove Park, Biltmore Forest, and all the rest of it—which was never much good in the beginning.

I think you are wise in wanting to get out of Asheville. I have known what happened to it for years, but I had a good chance to sum it all up when I went back last summer. It is a ruined and defeated town, and it is full of ruined and defeated people. If you think that I am happy about this, you do me an injustice. After all, it was my town, I was born there, and some of the people I care for most on earth still live there. But I found out last summer that you can't go home again, and now I know why.

You say that you hope I am as happy as any of our family ever get to be. Well, I think I am as happy as I have been in years, and a great deal happier than most people ever get to be, because I believe in something. And let's not get to believe about ourselves [that] there is something in us so special and different that we can't be as happy as ordinary people are. In that way also lies nothing but defeat. We are not different from other people, we are all members of the same human race, and we can hope for as much and achieve as much as other people can.

I don't know what you mean by the scandal you referred to in your letter, but I am afraid you allow yourself to be worried too much by what you think people around you are saying about you, or in what kind of estimation you are held by people in your own town. I assure you that doesn't matter very much, and if you really want to be "happy" you'll never be as long as you allow it to worry you. You will only be when you learn to feel the courage and self-respect and dignity that comes from the strength you have in you. I am sure you have it in you. Why not rely on it and be true to your own self? And for God's sake, don't let defeat get you. . . . It's not going to happen to you, it's not going to happen to me, and it's not going to happen to Fred; so let's not even mention the possibility of its going to happen. We won't be defeated, because nothing can defeat people who refuse to acknowledge defeat.

You told me one time that it almost killed you to think that people were "talking about" you. For God's sake, get over it. Get over worrying about what people say. I have been through the whole mill a lot more than any of you ever have, I have read and heard and had brought back to me every kind of lie, myth, fairy tale and legend—some vicious and malicious, some just stupid—it used to burn me up, but it doesn't any more. Why should you care or worry about such lies, as long as you know in yourself what the truth is. Love life and love people, but don't be afraid of foolish little tongues. To be afraid is also defeat.

And don't apologize for yourself, or for me, or for any of us. We don't need it. I think you're going to be all right, and that Ralph is going to be all right, and that we're going to pull out of the swamp. But we're not going to pull out of the swamp by staying in it and brooding about it and thinking of the good old days when we thought it wasn't a swamp. Keep your head up, and have faith and courage and belief in yourself and in people and in life, and don't worry about Bingville and what the Women's Club is saying about you, and you're going to be all right.

Don't worry about Papa. Don't forget him, but don't brood over him. He lived seventy-one years, he made his own life, he died sixteen years ago, and in general he got about as much as most men ever get. Don't live in the past in a sad defeated way. We've got our own home to find or make, and our home is in the future. Don't forget it. Believe in this, live for it, work for it—and you will achieve the happiness you speak of.

The old world that you knew is largely gone—I mean Grove Park, stucco houses, boom-town speculation, Wall Street, 1929—and all the rest of it. It's not coming back, Mabel. Most of those poor defeated devils in Asheville hope that it is coming back. But it's not. And most of them have nothing else to cling to, no other language to talk, because it is the only language they ever knew. I saw that last summer, and from the bottom of my heart I feel sincerely and compassionately sorry for them all.

But I don't want you to be one of them: you've still got plenty of stuff in you, and enough to face the future. It's always harder to go through the woods, remember, than to take the beaten path, but you sometimes get places going through the woods that you never see or know about if you stick to the beaten path. And the old beaten path, I am afraid, is no good any more: it doesn't lead to anywhere: it's like that great glittering tunnel through Beaucatcher Mountain that cost a million dollars. You get through, and there you are, just where you always were—in Chunn's Cove. Except you find that Chunn's Cove isn't even there—it's just something you used to think was there when you were a kid. I am going places—better places than Chunn's Cove—and I invite you to come along. And let me know if I can help you. I am your friend.

I'm dog-tired, got no rest last summer, and have had none since. But I feel good. Did you ever read a story of mine that came out about a year ago called "I Have a Thing to Tell You"? Well, I have a thing to tell you now: that is you can't go home again, but there are other places you can go. So why not try to find them?

I'm going West in a few days on a speaking engagement, and after that, I'm going to hit for the wide open spaces—probably northwest—and look at geysers and big trees and mountains and such like. I'll only have two or three weeks for it, but it's going to be a swell trip and do me a lot of good.

This is a grand country. I wish you could see it all, and could be along with me. We'd have a swell time. But meanwhile, until I come back, I send you all my love and best wishes for success and for the future.

To ELIZABETH NOWELL

> Hotel Chelsea
> 222 West 23rd Street
> New York, New York
> May 12, 1938

Dear Miss Nowell:

. . . It was awfully good of you to write me as you did. Naturally, it makes me feel good, and somehow, although I am appalled at the job I have cut out for myself, I think it is going to be all right. I am tired, but otherwise I have not felt such hope and confidence in many years. It may be that I have come through a kind of transition period in my life—I believe this is the truth—and have now, after a lot of blood-sweat and anguish, found a kind of belief and hope and faith I never had before.

At any rate, I am going to try to put it all into the book, and if you stand by and put in an occasional comforting word to people who may be getting restive,[1] that would be swell. I am sorry that you didn't see more of it the other night, but nowadays I am a little too fagged to do the whole thing at once. There has not been much let-up since I went to Germany two years ago, and there wasn't much then, because I found out that I couldn't go back to Europe again as if I were taking a trip on a Coney Island pleasure boat. Anyway, it's all gone into the mill, and I hope it comes out the right way.

This is packing-up day—I approach with considerable fear and trembling the job of assembling a good part of the manuscript I have done in the last three or four years. We are trying to arrange and audit it, so to speak, in some convenient form. Aswell is going to keep it for me until I get back, but I don't know whether it would be a good idea to let him read it now or not. I know where I stand, but it is like presenting someone with the bones of some great prehistoric animal he has never seen before—he might be bewildered. Anyway, I will know in a few days when I get it together. . . . I have written and explained the situation to him, and I think he understands it. I have a very strong hunch that I know where I am going a lot more clearly than I ever did before, and for that reason, I am not sure that it would be the best thing to have editorial advice and revision at this present time.

I hope also that he is able or will consent to take care of the rest of my stuff at Harpers until I get back. This business of being a vagabond writer with two tons of manuscript is not an easy one, particularly when one is going off somewhere, and does not want and cannot afford to keep on paying rent for an establishment he is no longer using. I had a letter from an autograph and manuscript dealer this morning, and I suppose he would gladly volunteer to keep it *but*——

This is all now. I will call you up if I have time before I leave on Tuesday night. If not, I'll see you when I return. . . . Meanwhile good luck and all good wishes,

To HERBERT J. MULLER

Hotel Chelsea
222 West 23rd Street
New York, New York

May 16, 1938

Dear Professor Muller:

Thanks again for letting me know that you will meet me. I have made

---

[1] Wolfe probably meant Harpers, though they had showed no signs of "getting restive."

reservations on the Southwestern Limited, which leaves here tomorrow night (Tuesday) at 8 o'clock EST, and arrives in Indianapolis, I understand, at noon on Wednesday. I gratefully accept your generous offer of hospitality and am looking forward to staying with you and Mrs. Muller while I am at Purdue.

Because you have been so kind, I am going to be completely frank and tell you what the situation is. I have driven myself without limit steadily for seven months now, and with only a brief interval for a long time before that. For the past week, my secretary and I have been engaged on the labor of assembling, putting in sequence, typing and binding the manuscript of my new book. It has been an enormous task, for it involved sorting and going over piece by piece a large portion of the manuscript I have written in the past four years—I should judge several million words.

I was up until five o'clock this morning working on it, and although there is still a tremendous quantity of manuscript left, I begin to see light, and feel a tremendous amount of comfort and satisfaction as the thing begins to shape up. Of course, the book is not finished yet—a tremendous labor of writing and revision is before me—but for the first time since I began it, I begin to feel a sense of wholeness: I have at least articulated a tremendous structure. All of this will be bound and minutely titled, section by section, and given to the editors at Harpers tomorrow to read and to hold for me until I come back and go at it again, and the remainder will be boxed up and kept in storage.

I have been thus tedious in telling you about all of this because I wanted to explain to you that I am not only very tired, but very happy, also. This trip is really a kind of momentous celebration for me, and that is why I am looking forward to it with so much pleasure. But just because I am looking forward to it with so much pleasure, I would like to spend the night in Indianapolis after I get there, and then, if it is convenient, meet you Thursday and drive over to Lafayette with you. That will give me a chance to rest and relax a bit, and get the memory of these millions of words out of my head, also to get a haircut, which I much need, and such like. I think you will find me fit and ready Thursday, after a night's sleep. I shall wire or telephone you from Indianapolis and let you know where I am, and you can tell me then where and when to meet you.

And I do want to thank you again for your patience and kindness in this whole matter. With all good wishes,

To ELIZABETH NOWELL

Auditorium Hotel
Chicago, Ill.
Monday, May 23, 1938

Dear Miss Nowell:

. . . Everything went off beautifully at Purdue—I talked and I talked, there was great applause, and everyone seemed very satisfied. Also met some very nice young people, teachers and instructors and their wives who took care of me. We all drove up to Chicago together Friday night,[1] and we spent two very pleasant days together, eating, drinking, driving all over Chicago, visiting the *stupendous* University, exploring the magnificent Lake Front and the not so magnificent slums. I really got it to a T in the *Vogue* piece: all of the grandeur and the misery of America is here—and yesterday we spent the whole day at the Brookfield Zoo, which is superb! I fed packages of crackerjack to the polar bears who wave their paws at you coyly and beat anything for charm you ever saw.

My friends left last night, and I am on my way West this afternoon —don't quite know where yet, but probably to Colorado first by one of the streamlined Zephyrs (it's only overnight this way—1100 miles across the continent and the plains in 15 hours—how's that?)—and later on perhaps to the North West. I hope nothing comes up that I have to be bothered about. Everything's going to be O.K. now if I get a little uninterrupted rest.

The Middle-western thing—Indianapolis, Purdue, and all of it—was swell! People say you'd get tired of it, but it was fat as a hog and so fertile you felt that if you stuck a fork in the earth the juice would spurt —one thousand miles of fat, flat, green, hog-fat fertility—barns, houses, silos, towns—the whole repeating in the recessions of a gigantic scroll —very restful, somehow, after the torment of New York and four million words of manuscript. (Aswell got the manuscript before I left— I finished completely and was completely finished! He wanted very much to read it. I had misgivings but he swore I could trust him to understand the unfinished state of things and to *feel* what I am about—and I hope to God he does, and that it is all right for him to read it now. It would be a crime if I were interrupted or discouraged now!)

Goodbye for the present, and try to take care of anything that comes up. I'll let you know where I am.

[1] The Herbert Mullers, the Kendall Tafts, Albert Fulton, William Hastings and William Braswell. Braswell later described this trip in "Thomas Wolfe Lectures and Takes a Holiday," in the October, 1939, issue of *College English*.

P.S. I'm staying here in an old hotel—not unlike the Chelsea—which I've always wanted to stay at because we had a book when I was a child called "Wonders of Science" or "The Marvels of the Modern Age" with a picture of the hotel. Have a good big room overlooking the Lake Front with the whole great system of parks, esplanades, drives, museums and freight trains right before me. Weather has been in and out—mostly good—but today awful. Sick of rain and fog from the Lake. Hope it changes before I go west. . . .

To ELIZABETH NOWELL

The Brown Palace Hotel
Denver, Colo.

Thursday, May 26, 1938

Dear Miss Nowell:—

Got here yesterday after an all night ride at eighty miles per hour across the continent in the Burlington Zephyr. No sleep, but couldn't quiet down at this altitude of one even mile. Looked up my Denver friends, they gave a swell party for me last night, and I'm afraid I talked and ate and drank them all into a state of exhaustion. Both newspapers were on my trail thirty minutes after I hit town, and I am sending you a sample of their arts.[1] I'm heading Northwest from here towards Oregon—may miss the Yellowstone because I understand it doesn't open until June 20th. Can't give you any forwarding address, because I don't know any myself at present. Am driving over to Boulder tomorrow to see my friends there—and am leaving here, I think, day after tomorrow (Saturday). Sending this air mail to you—if anything important turns up, wire me here. Meanwhile good luck and best wishes,

To HERBERT J. MULLER

Denver, Colorado

May 31, 1938

Dear Herb:

I'm late in writing you to say hello and thanks again, and to let you all know that I think about you and the good time we had together, and hope that we will do it again. I've been here almost a week—I came for just a *day!* The whole town has been swell to me—so swell that for the first few days we just eliminated sleep as a despicable

---

[1] These were probably an interview with Frances Wayne in the May 25, 1938, *Denver Post* and one with Miriam Wise in the May 26 *Rocky Mountain News.*

luxury. But I'm beginning to feel ironed out again, and if I can only keep my fingers off the cursed quill for another week or two—which I doubt!—I should be in fairly good shape for the struggle when I go back East. Am still resolute in my intention to push on to the Northwest, although my friends here now lift their eyebrows and smile sceptically when I speak of it! And I'm still hoping to stop over in Chicago long enough to see you all again. Meanwhile, I send love and best wishes to you all.

P.S. Take care of the polar bears!

To ELIZABETH NOWELL

> Hotel Boise
> Boise, Idaho
> Monday, June 7, 1938

Dear Miss Nowell:
    Just a line to tell you I'll be in Portland to-morrow night. Stopped off here to-day in order to see country to-morrow by daylight. To-morrow should be wonderful because I get the Columbia River and Oregon, but to-day—Idaho. What I saw of it to-day is the abomination of desolation: an enormous desert bounded by infinitely-far-away mountains that you never get to, and little pitiful blistered towns huddled down in the most abject loneliness underneath the huge light and scale and weather and the astounding brightness and dimensions of every-thing—all given a kind of tremendousness and terror and majesty by the dimension. And this?—their pride and joy, I guess, set in a cup of utterly naked hills, a clean little town but with a sparseness, a lack of the color, open-ness, richness of Cheyenne. I've tried to find Fisher: [1] people know him here but he's not in the telephone book. Anyway, what I've seen to-day explains a lot about him.

---

[1] Vardis Fisher, the author of the Vridar Hunter tetralogy, *Children of God, The Testament of Man,* etc., had first known Wolfe in 1928 when they had both been assistant professors in the English Department at New York University. Fisher's articles, "My Experiences with Thomas Wolfe" and "Thomas Wolfe and Maxwell Perkins" appeared in the April and July, 1951, issues of *Tomorrow.*

To ELIZABETH NOWELL

University Club
Portland, Oregon
Wednesday, June 15, 1938

Dear Miss Nowell:

I'm on my way to Seattle in a few minutes after a most wonderful week here. I'll be back here Saturday but am leaving again Sunday morning on what promises to be one of the most remarkable trips of my life. It means I'll be away about two weeks longer than I intended, but it is the chance of a lifetime and after long battlings with my conscience, I have decided I'd be foolish not to take it. Here's the program: a young fellow I know on one of the local papers [1] is starting out Sunday morning in his car on a tour of the entire West, and he has asked me to come with him. We leave here Sunday and head south for California stopping at Crater Lake on the way down; we go down the whole length of California taking in Yosemite, the Sequoias and any other national parks they have; then we swing east across the desert into Arizona to the Grand Canyon, etc., north through Utah, Zion and Bryce Canyons, Salt Lake, etc., then to the Yellowstone, then North to the Canadian Border, Montana, Glacier Park, etc., then west again across Montana, Idaho, Washington, then Ranier Park, etc.—in other words a complete swing around the West from the Rocky Mountains on, and every big national park in the West. The cost will be very little as we are stopping at roadside cabins, etc. He's writing a series of articles to show the little fellow how inexpensively he can see the West. [2] The whole thing will take two weeks to the day—perhaps a day or two less for me, because I intend to leave him at Spokane, and head straight for N.Y.

I've seen wonderful things and met every kind of person—doctors, lawyers, lumberjacks, etc.—and when I get through with this I'll have a whole wad of glorious material. My conscience hurts me about this extra two weeks, but I believe I'd always regret it if I passed it up. When I get through I shall really have seen America (except Texas).

Why didn't you write? I'm worried. I'll be back here at the University Club for a day Saturday, and if you want to reach me, use this address. Wish I could tell you more about this wonderful country, but that will come later. Meanwhile, best wishes.

[1] Edward M. Miller, who was at this time the Sunday Editor of *The Oregonian* and is now Assistant Managing Editor, and Ray Conway, Manager of the Oregon State Motor Association, had invited Wolfe to go on this tour of the Western national parks.

[2] Miller's articles, "Gulping the Great West," appeared in the July 31 and August 7, 1938 issues of *The Oregonian Magazine*.

The following letter to Elizabeth Nowell was written in answer to a letter from her which is now lost. In it, she said that she had had lunch with Maxwell Perkins at Cherio's; that he had asked about Wolfe; that he had seemed old, tired, tragic, and terribly depressed about the spread of Fascism in Europe; and that they had had a long and very enjoyable argument about the world in general. Evidently her letter reached Wolfe when he also was tired and depressed and had been brooding over certain literary gossip concerning his leaving Scribners which he had heard out West. Certainly Perkins never "instructed" anyone to "pass around" derogatory stories about Wolfe, and certainly Wolfe didn't seriously think he had, as is shown by his final letter to Perkins of August 12, 1938.

When, in 1945, Perkins began collecting Wolfe's letters for this present volume, he asked Miss Nowell to send him all the letters she had received from Wolfe. She did so, including the following letter of June 19, 1938, explaining to Perkins that she knew it would hurt him but that she had no right to suppress it or any letter of Wolfe's. Perkins answered her on August 7, 1945, saying: "Were you capable of believing—I know Tom could believe anything when his imagination got working—that we would instruct our salesmen to damage him? Besides, we should betray our profession, and everything we believe in, if we tried to injure a great talent. It's incredible that even Tom could believe that. It is possible that some of the men were so aggrieved at Tom's leaving us, that they expressed derogatory opinions of him as a man. Very likely they did, because many salesmen haven't the faintest understanding of literature, or of writers, and they might have interpreted Tom's decision in the most obvious way. But you must know that I never said much of anything about the whole matter, and that when pressed, I spoke in Tom's defence. Anyhow, a man who has spent his life as an editor, and insisted that the function of a publisher was to help bring out the truth by publishing whatever pertained to it, could never for an instant approve the suppression of a letter just because it ran against him."

To ELIZABETH NOWELL

University Club
Portland, Oregon
Sunday, June 19 (1938)

Dear Miss Nowell:

I got back here from Seattle last night and was delighted to find your letter. Our trip has been postponed until tomorrow morning—the little girl of one of the men was sick, but she's O.K. now, and by cutting a few corners we'll be back on schedule in a day or two. It ought to be a grand trip.

Washington and Seattle were wonderful, and I discovered all of my

Westall kin, the progeny of old Bacchus[1] who came out here in the '90s. There are thirty-seven of them now—I have the whole family tree and talked to three of them and have the record—I'd like to go back again and get the whole story. To me, it's mighty interesting.

This part of the country is almost fabulous. The streams and creeks and rivers swarm with fish—not 6 inch, 12 ounce ones—but great salmon, steelheads, etc., that weigh from 10 to 30 pounds. The forests are dense with enormous fir trees four and six feet through; the lumberjacks cut them down; the great lumber mills—I visited one of them—tear and slash and plane them into boards; and the enormous forests keep producing them—they keep growing everlastingly in spite of everything. The people are wonderfully good and open—I think a little too simple, maybe, and uncomplicated and *away* from the rest of the world—but it's a swell place and you're willing to believe that almost anything can happen here.

I was glad to get your letter and to know you'd seen Ed Aswell. I'll see him when I get back. I'm looking forward to the trip as a great thing in every way and shall try to put work out of my head till I get back.

I'm sorry about M. P. Everything you tell me about him touches and grieves and hurts me like hell. Please—*please* don't tell him about me, or anything about me, if you can avoid it. For six years he was my friend—I thought the best one I ever had—and then, a little over two years ago he turned against me. Everything I have done since was bad, he had no good word for it or for me, it's almost as if he were praying for my failure. I can't understand or fathom it, but it is a sad strange thing. Max still tells people that he is my friend, and then he runs me down; and out here in the West I have run on one or two stories that the Scribner salesmen apparently have been instructed to pass around that sicken me. It's like a nightmare, but I won't let it get me down. What is this thing in life anyway that causes people to do things like this? The hell of it is, the people who say they love you are often the ones who do the most to injure you. . . . I can't make it out, and now Perkins, under this mask of friendship, is doing the same thing. I don't think I'll ever change in the way I feel about him—the funny thing is I'm always supposed to be the one who changes, but at the bottom I'm the most solid of the lot.

I don't think he *consciously* wants me to fail or come to grief, but it's almost as if *unconsciously,* by some kind of *wishful* desire, he wants me

---

[1] Bacchus Westall was a half-brother of Wolfe's grandfather, Thomas Casey Westall. The three Westall descendants whom Wolfe had looked up were Albert Westall and his sister Marjorie, the grandchildren of Bacchus Westall, and Lonnie Harris, a nephew of Wolfe's grandmother, Martha (Penland) Westall.

to come to grief, as a kind of sop to his pride and his unyielding conviction that he is right in everything—the tragic flaw in his character
that keeps him from admitting that he has wronged anybody or made
a mistake. That is really his great weakness, and I believe it is at the root
of his failure—his growing reaction, his sense of defeat. . . . I shall
always remember him as one of the most wonderful people I ever knew
—but I have neither time nor energy to cope with this thing in him now;
all that I know is that it is against me, and against my work and I
can't give it any sort of break. As much as I can, I want to sever the
connection entirely. Some day, perhaps, if he is willing, I'll take it
up again—but meanwhile, let's not play with fire. Tell him nothing
about me or what I'm doing: that's the only way, believe me, to avoid
trouble. Anyway, it's not a matter of personalities any more: if I'm wrong
it will show in my work: if he's wrong it's going to show in his life. . . .

To end on a more cheerful note, I know a lot of swell people, and I
think you are one of them, and I am proud to know you are my friend.
I won't be back in Portland, and soon from now on I'll be travelling
all the time. I don't know at present what to tell you about mail or
how to reach me. Anyway, I'll write you later and I hope to see you in
about three weeks.

To ELIZABETH NOWELL

[Postcard: Crater Lake from Rim Drive, Crater Lake National Park, Oregon]

Fort Klamath, Oregon
Monday, June 20, 1938

We're off! Stop No 1, and no postcard can ever do justice to the color
and magnificence. 7500 feet up and ten feet of snow, but on to California
to-night.

To ELIZABETH NOWELL

[Postcard: The Three Brothers, Yosemite Valley]

Camp Curry, Cal
June 22, 1938

The one on the left is Canby, the middle one De Voto, with Whitney
Darrow on the right. (I'm getting a swell story out of this.)

To ELIZABETH NOWELL

Hotel Baxter
Bozeman, Mont.

Wednesday morning [June 29, 1938]

Dear Miss Nowell:

We're on the last leg of our trip.—We've gone over 3300 miles in eight days and "seen" nine national parks. We'll do 4500 in all and two more parks by the time I leave my two companions Friday night at Rainier and head in to Seattle. It has been furious, hectic, crowded and wildly comical, but I've seen a whole lot of the country and a lot of people and things. Furthermore I've got it all down—in a huge notebook—the whole thing smacked down with the blinding speed and variety of the trip.[1]

I'm going into Seattle to sleep a day or two—and perhaps to get the whole thing more or less in its present form (the whole trip from the beginning six weeks ago, I mean) typed down. Also, I've got to get some sleep before I start East. I'm ready and able to sleep now, but no time for it.

Am sending this to you air mail and want you to write or wire me Hotel New Washington, Seattle, to let me know if everything is O.K. and if it's all right if I stay a little longer to get the whole thing written and typed up. This is all now. We're on our way today to Glacier Park 400 miles away on the Canadian border—it's 6:45 A.M. and I can't dawdle, dearie, any longer.

To HAMILTON BASSO

[Postcard: Old Faithful Geyser, Yellowstone Park]

Yellowstone, Wyo.

June 30, 1938

Portrait of the author at the two million word point.

---

[1] This journal, considerably cut, appeared under the title of "A Western Journey" in the summer, 1939, issue of *The Virginia Quarterly Review*, and was published in book form under the title of *A Western Journal* in 1951 by the University of Pittsburgh Press. Wolfe used both titles for it, evidently not having decided which was better.

To EDWARD C. ASWELL

[Postcard: Two Medicine Lake, Glacier National Park]

June 30, 1938

Dear Ed: It has been a wonderful trip and at last I feel I know something about my country.

To ELIZABETH NOWELL

New Washington Hotel
Seattle, Wash.

Sunday, July 3, [1938]

Dear Miss Nowell:

I got here late yesterday afternoon and found telegrams from you and Ed,[1] and your air mail was delivered this morning: all of which relieves me and boosts me up no end. The trip was wonderful and terrific—in the last two weeks I have travelled five thousand miles, gone the whole length of the coast from Seattle almost to the Mexican border, inland a thousand miles and northward to the Canadian border. The national parks, of course, are stupendous, but what was to me far more valuable were the towns, the things, the people I saw—the whole West and all its history unrolling at kaleidoscopic speed. I have written it all down in just this way—with great speed—because I had to do most of it at night before going to bed, usually when we had driven four or five hundred miles and I was ready to drop with sleep. I've filled a big fat notebook with thirty thousand words of it [2] and looking some of it over, it occurs to me that in this way I may have got the whole thing —the whole impression—its speed, variety, etc.—pretty well.

At any rate, I've got a pretty clear record of the whole thing since I left New York six weeks or so ago, and after two or three days rest out on Puget Sound somewhere—(this is a country fit for Gods—you've never seen anything like it for scale and magnificence and abundance: the trees are as tall as the Flatiron Building and yet so much in scale that you simply cannot believe, until you measure them, they are as

---

[1] Aswell's wire of July 1, 1938, said: "Dear Tom: Your new book is magnificent in scope and design, with some of the best writing you have ever done. I am still absorbing it, confident that when you finish you will have written your greatest novel so far. Hope you come back full of health and new visions." Miss Nowell's wire and airmail letter merely told Wolfe of Aswell's enthusiasm, as repeated in a conversation with her.

[2] Wolfe always over-estimated the length of things he'd written. The actual length of the notes found in his suitcase after his death was only about 11,400 words.

big; and you throw a hook into some ordinary looking creek and pull out a twelve pound salmon. I assure you these things are literally true: you feel there's no limit, no end to anything. The East seems small and starved and meagre by comparison, and yet I'm glad there is the East, too—we've got to have the East: there's something in the East they don't have here.)

Anyway, I'd like to loaf and rest for a few days, and then get it typed, revising as much as I can but not taking too much time, and putting it down from the beginning like a spool unwinding at great speed. Perhaps it's not ready to use yet or won't be for a year or two, but I'll have it *down*—and you know what that means to me, and I thought I'd call it "A Western Journal."

Anyway, if that's O.K. by you and Ed, that's my present idea. I really feel ready to *go* again. I've had no rest, but this movement—the sense of life and discovery, the variety—has renewed and stimulated me. Writing thirty thousand words under the circumstances of the past two weeks was an accomplishment and proved to me that I am getting ready again, because I *wanted* to write them—couldn't keep from it.

Anyway, use this hotel as an address for the present. If I go to Puget Sound I'll leave an address here, and anyway I'll keep you posted. Now get some rest yourself—and thanks for everything.

P.S. I'm thinking of buying some firecrackers and spending to-morrow in H.M.'s Canadian town of Victoria, B.C.

To MARGARET ROBERTS

New Washington Hotel
Seattle, Washington

[July 4, 1938]

Dear Mrs. Roberts:

Your letter was forwarded on to me here. I think you are grand to go to so much trouble for me, and if I blow off clouds of volcanic steam, don't think I don't appreciate all you have done and are doing. I was ready to drop when I left New York six weeks ago, but I've seen a whole new continent, the entire West, and now I'm writing thousands of words a day again. I'll be back in N.Y. some time this month: meanwhile I'm trying to rewrite and put the fifty thousand words or more I've written on this trip in a typed manuscript. When I arrived here last night, after 25,000 miles around the whole West in the past 14 days, . . . I found a telegram from my editor at Harper's telling me he had read the 2,000,000 word rough draft I had left with him of the new book, that it was "magnificent in scope and design"—and far and away the best thing I'd ever done. With this wonderful assurance I'm going back and try to live up to it until it's finished as I want it. All your help is gratefully appreciated. Best wishes to you and Mr. R.,

To ELIZABETH NOWELL
[Postcard: C.P.R.S.S. *Princess Kathleen*]

Postmarked Vancouver, B.C.

July 6, 1938

I've just left Victoria B.C. on this ship on my way to Vancouver. Will be back in Seattle tomorrow or day after, and then to work.

It was on this boat trip to Victoria and Vancouver that Wolfe shared a pint of whiskey which he had bought with "a poor, shivering wretch," who probably had influenza, and from whom Wolfe is believed to have contracted the respiratory infection which finally resulted in his death. By the afternoon of July 6, Wolfe was seriously ill with high fever, pains in his lungs, and protracted chills. However, instead of going to a hospital in Vancouver, he took a train back to Seattle and remained, still desperately ill, in the New Washington Hotel there for five more days. Finally, on July 11, he was examined by Dr. E. C. Ruge, who found him to have pneumonia and hospitalized him at Firlawns Sanitarium at Bothell, Washington. By July 15th, Wolfe seemed to have passed the crisis of his pneumonia, and was able to send the following wire to Edward Aswell.

To EDWARD C. ASWELL
[Telegram]

Seattle, Wash.

July 15 (?) [1938]

Doctors say I'm out of danger now. Will write when I feel stronger.

However, during the period of his convalescence, Wolfe began to have recurrent fever and other disquieting symptoms. By the first week of August, Dr. Ruge had him taken to Providence Hospital in Seattle so that X-rays

of his lungs could be made. These revealed an unresolved condition of the upper lobe of the right lung, which the X-ray specialist and Dr. Ruge diagnosed as an old tubercular lesion, but which other doctors considered to be only the result of his pneumonia.

Wolfe remained at Providence Hospital until September 4th, by which time he was suffering from violent headaches and moments of slight irrationality. On the recommendation of the physicians who had succeeded Dr. Ruge when Wolfe entered Providence Hospital, Mabel Wolfe Wheaton, who had come to Seattle to be with Wolfe during his illness, took him by train to Johns Hopkins Hospital in Baltimore. There, on September 12, Dr. Walter E. Dandy performed an exploratory operation on his brain. It was found that germs of tuberculosis, released from an old lesion on Wolfe's lung by his recent pneumonia, had entered his blood stream and been carried to his brain. He died of this cerebral infection three days later, on September 15, 1938.

The following note, written to Maxwell Perkins on August 12, 1938, when Wolfe first had intimations of death, was the last letter which he was ever to write.

To MAXWELL E. PERKINS

Providence Hospital
Seattle, Washington
August 12, 1938.

Dear Max:

I'm sneaking this against orders, but "I've got a hunch"—and I wanted to write these words to you.

I've made a long voyage and been to a strange country, and I've seen the dark man very close; and I don't think I was too much afraid of him, but so much of mortality still clings to me—I wanted most desperately to live and still do, and I thought about you all a thousand times, and wanted to see you all again, and there was the impossible anguish and regret of all the work I had not done, of all the work I had to do—and I know now I'm just a grain of dust, and I feel as if a great window has been opened on life I did not know about before—and if I come through this, I hope to God I am a better man, and in some strange way I can't explain, I know I am a deeper and a wiser one. If I get on my feet and out of here, it will be months before I head back, but if I get on my feet, I'll come back.

Whatever happens—I had this "hunch" and wanted to write you and tell you, no matter what happens or has happened, I shall always think of you and feel about you the way it was that Fourth of July day three years [1] ago when you met me at the boat, and we went out on the café on the river and had a drink and later went on top of the tall building, and all the strangeness and the glory and the power of life and of the city was below.

Yours always,

Tom

[1] The fourth of July, 1935, was the day on which Wolfe had returned to America to find *Of Time and the River* a great success.

INDEX